TAIKO

TAIKO

AN EPIC NOVEL
OF WAR AND GLORY
IN FEUDAL JAPAN

Eiji Yoshikawa

Translated by William Scott Wilson

KODANSHA INTERNATIONAL
Tokyo • London • New York

Translator's Dedication: To Lourdes Oroza

Title page illustration by Noriyoshi Orai

This translation is an abridged version of the original Japanese work. All revisions have been made with the authorization and cooperation of the author's estate.

Distributed in the United States of America by Kodansha America, Inc., 114 Fifth Avenue, New York, NY 10011, and in the United Kingdom and continental Europe by Kodansha Europe, Ltd., Gillingham House, 38-44 Gillingham Street, London SW1 1HU.

Published by Kodansha Publishers, Ltd., 12-21 Otowa 2-chome, Bunkyo-ku, Tokyo 112, and Kodansha International, Ltd., 17-14 Otowa 1-chome, Bunkyo-ku, Tokyo 112, and Kodansha America, Inc.

Library of Congress Cataloging-in-Publication Data
Yoshikawa, Eiji, 1892-1962.
   [Shinsho Taikoki.   English]
   Taiko : an epic novel of war and glory in feudal Japan. -- 1st ed.
        p.   cm.
   Translation of: Shinsho Taikoki
   1. Toyotomi, Hideyoshi, 1536?-1598--Fiction.   I. Title
PL842.075S4313   1992
895.6'344--dc20

                            92-6194
                            CIP

CONTENTS

BOOK THREE

BOOK FOUR

BOOK FIVE

BOOK SIX

BOOK SEVEN

BOOK EIGHT

BOOK NINE

BOOK TEN

HERALDRY

FAMILY CRESTS OF THE SAMURAI LORDS IN TAIKO

 TOYOTOMI HIDEYOSHI
The Taiko

 SAITO DOSAN
Lord of the Province of Mino

 ODA NOBUNAGA
Lord of the Province of Owari

 TAKEDA SHINGEN
Lord of the Province of Kai

 TOKUGAWA IEYASU
Lord of the Province of Mikawa

 IMAGAWA YOSHIMOTO
Lord of the Province of Suruga

 AKECHI MITSUHIDE
Lord of the Province of Tamba

 ASAI NAGAMASA
Lord of the Province of Omi

 SHIBATA KATSUIE
Lord of the Province of Echizen

 MORI TERUMOTO
Lord of the western provinces

MEASUREMENT OF TIME IN MEDIEVAL JAPAN

TRADITIONAL JAPANESE TWELVE-HOUR CLOCK

DATES

Lunar Date: FIRST DAY OF THE FIRST MONTH OF THE FIFTH YEAR OF TEMMON
Solar Date: SECOND DAY OF THE MONTH OF FEBRUARY, A.D. 1536

The dates in *Taiko* follow the traditional Japanese lunar calendar. The twelve lunar months of twenty-nine or thirty days were not named but numbered from one to twelve. Because the lunar year was 353 days long—twelve days shorter than the solar year—a thirteenth month was added in some years. There is no simple way to convert a date from the lunar calendar into its solar equivalent, but a rough guide is to take the lunar First Month as the solar calendar's month of February.

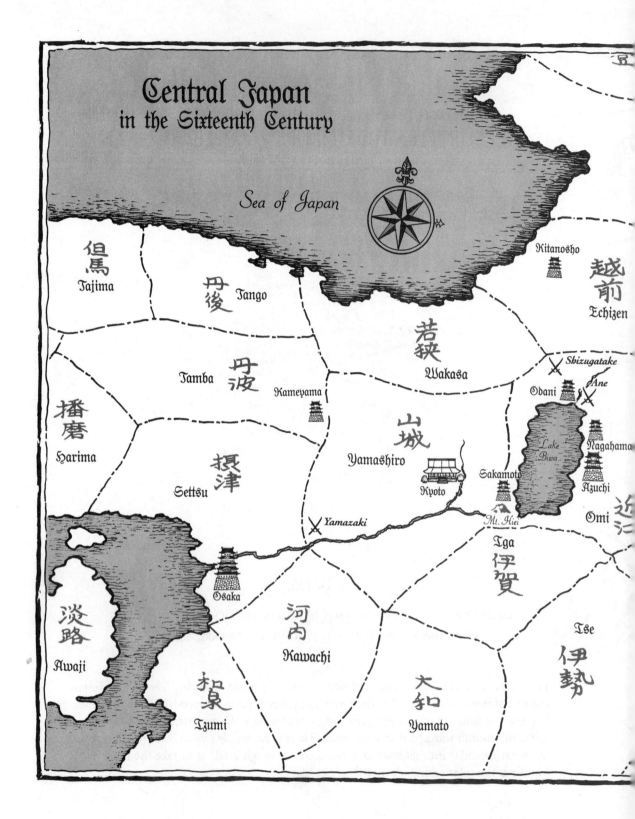

Central Japan
in the Sixteenth Century

Sea of Japan

但馬
Tajima

丹後 Tango

越前
Echizen

Kitanosho

若狭
Wakasa

丹波
Tamba

Tamba

播磨
Harima

Kameyama

山城
Yamashiro

Shizugatake

Ane

Odani

Lake
Biwa

Nagahama

摂津
Settsu

Kyoto

Sakamoto

Azuchi

近江
Omi

Yamazaki

Mt. Hiei

伊賀
Iga

淡路
Awaji

Osaka

河内
Kawachi

Tse

和泉
Izumi

大和
Yamato

伊勢
Ise

豆

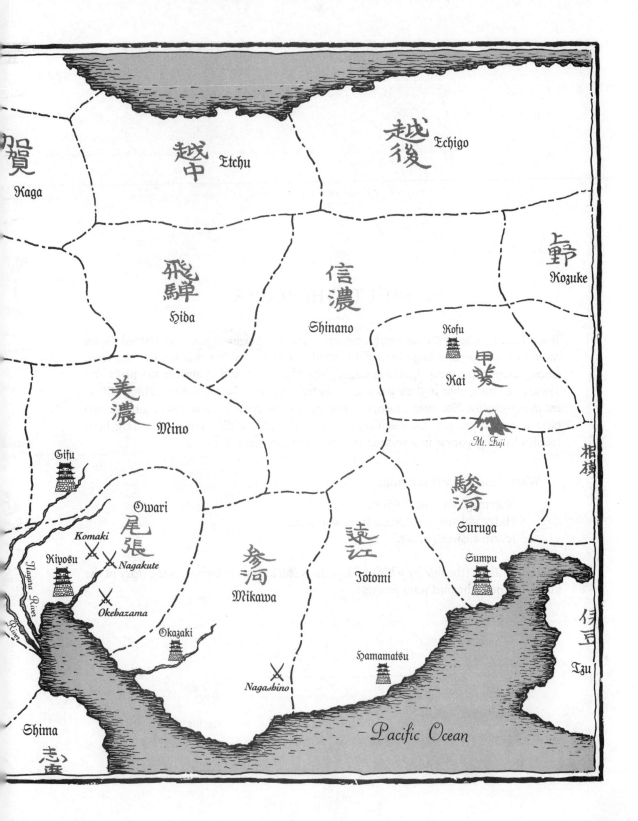

NOTE TO THE READER

Toward the middle of the sixteenth century, as the Ashikaga shogunate crumbled, Japan came to resemble one huge battlefield. Rival warlords vied for dominance, but from among them three great figures emerged, like meteors streaking against the night sky. These three men, alike in their passion to control and unify Japan, were strikingly different in personality: Nobunaga, rash, decisive, brutal; Hideyoshi, unassuming, subtle, complex; Ieyasu, calm, patient, calculating. Their divergent philosophies have long been recalled by the Japanese in a verse known to every schoolchild:

What if the bird will not sing?

Nobunaga answers, "Kill it!"
Hideyoshi answers, "Make it *want* to sing."
Ieyasu answers, "Wait."

This book, *Taiko* (the title by which Hideyoshi is still known in Japan), is the story of the man who made the bird want to sing.

BOOK ONE

FIFTH YEAR OF TEMMON
1536

CHARACTERS AND PLACES

HIYOSHI, childhood name of
Toyotomi Hideyoshi, the Taiko
OFUKU, adopted son of Sutejiro
ONAKA, Hiyoshi's mother
OTSUMI, Hiyoshi's sister
KINOSHITA YAEMON, Hiyoshi's father
CHIKUAMI, Hiyoshi's stepfather
KATO DANJO, Hiyoshi's uncle
WATANABE TENZO, leader of a band
of masterless samurai
SUTEJIRO, pottery merchant
HACHISUKA KOROKU, head of the Hachisuka clan
SAITO DOSAN, lord of Mino
SAITO YOSHITATSU, Dosan's son
AKECHI MITSUHIDE, retainer of the Saito clan
MATSUSHITA KAHEI, retainer of the Imagawa clan
ODA NOBUNAGA, lord of Owari
KINOSHITA TOKICHIRO, name given to
Hiyoshi when he became a samurai
SHIBATA KATSUIE, head of the Shibata clan
and senior Oda retainer
HAYASHI SADO, senior Oda retainer

OWARI, birthplace of Toyotomi Hideyoshi
and province of the Oda clan
KIYOSU, capital of Owari
MINO, province of the Saito clan
INABAYAMA, capital of Mino
SURUGA, province of the Imagawa clan

"Monkey! Monkey!"

"It's my bee!"

"It's mine!"

"Liar!"

Seven or eight young boys swept across the fields like a whirlwind, swinging sticks back and forth through the yellow mustard blossoms and pure-white radish flowers, looking for the bees with honey sacs, called Korean bees. Yaemon's son, Hiyoshi, was six years old, but his wrinkled face looked like a pickled plum. He was smaller than the other boys, but second to none among the village children when it came to pranks and wild behavior.

"Fool!" he yelled as he was knocked down by a bigger boy while fighting over a bee. Before he could get to his feet, another boy stepped on him. Hiyoshi tripped him.

"The bee belongs to the one who caught it! If you catch it, it's your bee!" he said, nimbly jumping up and snatching a bee out of the air. "Yow! This one's mine!"

Clutching the bee, Hiyoshi took another ten steps before opening his hand. Breaking off the head and the wings, he popped it into his mouth. The bee's stomach was a sac of sweet honey. To these children, who had never known the taste of sugar, it was a marvel that anything could taste so sweet. Squinting, Hiyoshi let the honey run down his throat and smacked his lips. The other children looked on, their mouths watering.

"Monkey!" shouted a large boy nicknamed Ni'o, the only one for whom Hiyoshi was no match. Knowing this, the others joined in.

"Baboon!"

"Monkey!"

"Monkey, monkey, monkey!" they chorused. Even Ofuku, the smallest boy, joined in. He was said to be eight years old, but he was not much bigger than the six-year-old

Hiyoshi. He was much better looking, however; his complexion was fair, and his eyes and nose were nicely set in his face. As the child of a wealthy villager, Ofuku was the only one who wore a silk kimono. His real name was probably something like Fukutaro or Fukumatsu, but it had been shortened and prefaced with the letter *o* in imitation of a practice common among the sons of wealthy families.

"You had to say it too, didn't you!" Hiyoshi said, glaring at Ofuku. He did not care when the other boys called him monkey, but Ofuku was different. "Have you forgotten that I'm the one who always sticks up for you, you spineless jellyfish!"

Thus chastened, Ofuku could say nothing. He lost courage and bit his nails. Although he was only a child, being called an ingrate made him feel much worse than being called a spineless jellyfish. The others looked away, their attention shifting from honey bees to a cloud of yellow dust rising at the far end of the fields.

"Look, an army!" cried one of the boys.

"Samurai!" said another. "They've come back from battle."

The children waved and cheered.

The lord of Owari, Oda Nobuhide, and his neighbor, Imagawa Yoshimoto, were bitter enemies, a situation that led to constant skirmishing along their common border. One year, Imagawa troops crossed the border, set fire to the villages, and trampled the crops. The Oda troops rushed out of the castles of Nagoya and Kiyosu and routed the enemy, cutting them down to the last man. When the following winter came, both food and shelter were lacking, but the people did not reproach their lord. If they starved, they starved; if they were cold, they were cold. In fact, contrary to Yoshimoto's expectations, their hardships only served to harden their hostility toward him.

The children had seen and heard about such things from the time they were born. When they saw their lord's troops, it was as if they were seeing themselves. It was in their blood, and nothing excited them more than the sight of men-at-arms.

"Let's go see!"

The boys headed toward the soldiers, breaking into a run, except for Ofuku and Hiyoshi, who were still glaring at one another. The weak-spirited Ofuku wanted to run off with the others, but he was held by Hiyoshi's stare.

"I'm sorry." Ofuku nervously approached Hiyoshi's side and put his hand on his shoulder. "I'm sorry, all right?"

Hiyoshi flushed angrily and jerked away his shoulder, but seeing Ofuku on the brink of tears, he softened. "It's just because you ganged up with the others and said bad things about me," he reproached him. "When they tease you, they always call you names, like 'the Chinese kid.' But have I ever made fun of you?"

"No."

"Even a Chinese kid, when he becomes a member of our gang, is one of us. That's what I always say, right?"

"Yeah." Ofuku rubbed his eyes. Mud dissolved in his tears, making little splotches around his eyes.

"Dummy! It's because you cry that they call you 'the Chinese kid.' Come on, let's go see the warriors. If we don't hurry, they'll be gone." Taking Ofuku by the hand, Hiyoshi ran after the others.

War-horses and banners loomed out of the dust. There were some twenty mounted samurai and two hundred foot soldiers. Trailing behind was a motley group of bearers: pike, spear, and bow carriers. Cutting across the Inaba Plain from the Atsuta Road, they began to climb the embankment of the Shonai River. The children outstripped the horses and scampered up the embankment. Eyes gleaming, Hiyoshi, Ofuku, Ni'o, and the other snotty-nosed kids picked roses and violets and other wildflowers and threw them in the air, all the time yelling at the top of their voices, "Hachiman! Hachiman!" invoking the god of war, and, "Victory for our valiant, glorious warriors!" Whether in the villages or on the roads, the children were quick to yell this whenever they saw warriors.

The general, the mounted samurai, and the common soldiers dragging their feet were all silent, their strong faces set like masks. They did not warn the children about getting too close to the horses, nor did they favor them with so much as a grin. These troops seemed to be part of the army that had withdrawn from Mikawa, and it was clear that the battle had been bitterly fought. Both horses and men were exhausted. Blood-smeared wounded leaned heavily on the shoulders of their comrades. Dried blood glistened, as black as lacquer, on armor and spear shafts. Their sweaty faces were so caked with dust that only their eyes shone through.

"Give the horses water," ordered an officer. The samurai on horseback passed the order along in loud voices. Another order went out to take a rest. The horsemen dismounted, and the foot soldiers stopped dead in their tracks. Breathing sighs of relief, they dropped wordlessly onto the grass.

Across the river, Kiyosu Castle looked tiny. One of the samurai was Oda Nobuhide's younger brother, Yosaburo. He sat on a stool, gazing up at the sky, surrounded by half a dozen silent retainers.

Men bound up arm and leg wounds. From the pallor of their faces it was clear they had suffered a great defeat. This did not matter to the children. When they saw blood, they themselves became heroes bathed in blood; when they saw the glitter of spears and pikes, they were convinced that the enemy had been annihilated, and they were filled with pride and excitement.

"Hachiman! Hachiman! Victory!"

When the horses had drunk their fill of water, the children threw flowers at them, too, cheering them on.

A samurai standing beside his horse spotted Hiyoshi and called, "Yaemon's son! How is your mother?"

"Who, me?"

Hiyoshi walked up to the man and looked straight up at him with his grimy face. With a nod, the man put his hand on Hiyoshi's sweaty head. The samurai was no more than twenty years old. Thinking this man had just come from battle, and feeling the weight of the hand in its chain-mail gauntlet on his head, Hiyoshi was overwhelmed by a feeling of glory.

Does my family really know such a samurai? he wondered. His friends, who were lined up nearby, watching him, could see how proud he was.

"You're Hiyoshi, aren't you?"

"Yes."

"A good name. Yes, a good name."

The young samurai gave Hiyoshi's head a final pat, then struck the waistband of his leather armor and straightened up a bit, studying Hiyoshi's face all the while. Something made him laugh.

Hiyoshi was quick to make friends, even with adults. To have his head touched by a stranger—and a warrior at that—made his big eyes shine with pride. He quickly became his usual talkative self.

"But you know, nobody calls me Hiyoshi. The only ones who do are my mother and father."

"Because of what you look like, I suppose."

"A monkey?"

"Well, it's good that you know it."

"That's what everyone calls me."

"Ha, ha!" The samurai had a loud voice and a laugh to match. The other men joined in the laughter, while Hiyoshi, trying to look bored, took a millet stalk from his jacket and began chewing on it. The grassy-smelling juice in the stalk tasted sweet.

He carelessly spat out the chewed-up stalk.

"How old are you?"

"Six."

"Is that so?"

"Sir, where are you from?"

"I know your mother well."

"Huh?"

"Your mother's younger sister often comes to my house. When you go home, give my regards to your mother. Tell her Kato Danjo wishes her good health."

When the rest break was over, the soldiers and horses got back in line and crossed the shallows of the Shonai River. With a backward glance, Danjo quickly mounted his horse. Wearing his sword and armor, he radiated an air of nobility and power.

"Tell her that when the fighting's over, I'll be stopping by Yaemon's." Danjo gave a yell, spurred his horse, and entered the river's shallows to catch up with the line. White water lapped at his horse's legs.

Hiyoshi, remnants of the millet juice still in his mouth, gazed after him as if in a trance.

* * *

Every trip she made to the storage shed left Hiyoshi's mother sorely depressed. She went there to fetch pickles, grain, or firewood, and was always reminded that supplies often ran out. Thinking of the future brought a lump to her throat. There were only the two children, Hiyoshi, six, and his nine-year-old sister, Otsumi—neither, of course, old enough to do any real work. Her husband, wounded in battle, was capable of nothing but sitting by the hearth and staring into the space beneath the hanging teakettle, even in summer when there was no fire.

Those things...I'd feel better if they were burned, she thought.

Leaning against a wall of the shed was a spear with a black oak shaft, above which hung a foot-soldier's helmet and what seemed to be part of an old suit of armor. In the days when her husband had gone off to battle, this equipment had been the best he had. It was now covered with soot and, like her husband, useless. Every time she looked at it, she felt nothing but disgust. The thought of war made her shudder.

No matter what my husband says, Hiyoshi is not going to become a samurai, she resolved.

At the time of her marriage to Kinoshita Yaemon, she had thought it best to pick a samurai for a husband. The house in Gokiso where she was born, while small, was that of a samurai family, and although Yaemon was just a foot soldier, he was a retainer of Oda Nobuhide. When they had become husband and wife, vowing that "in the future, we'll earn a thousand bushels of rice," the armor had been a symbol of their hopes and had taken precedence over the household goods she had wanted. There was no denying that it brought back happy memories of their marriage. But the contrast between their youthful dreams and the present was not worth a moment's thought. It was a curse eating away at her heart. Her husband had been crippled before he could distinguish himself in battle. Because he was no more than a foot soldier, he had been forced to leave his lord's service. Making a living had been difficult in the first six months, and he had ended up becoming a farmer. Now he was not even capable of that.

Help had come from a woman's hand. Taking the two children with her, Yaemon's wife had picked mulberry leaves, plowed fields, threshed millet, and warded off poverty all these years. But what of the future? Wondering if the strength of her slender arms would hold out, her heart felt as cold and gloomy as the storage shed. Finally she put the food for the evening meal—millet, a few strips of dried radish—into a bamboo basket and left the storage shed. She was not yet thirty years old, but Hiyoshi's birth had not been an easy one, and ever since, her skin had been the pale color of an unripe peach.

"Mother." It was Hiyoshi's voice. He came around the side of the house, looking for her. His mother laughed softly. She had one bright hope: to bring up Hiyoshi and make him the kind of son and heir who would grow up quickly and be able to present her husband with at least a bit of *sake* every day. The thought made her feel better.

"Hiyoshi, I'm over here."

Hiyoshi ran toward his mother's voice, then took hold of the arm that held the basket.

"Today, at the riverbank, I met someone who knows you."

"Who?"

"A samurai! Kato something. He said he knew you, and he sent you his regards. He patted my head and asked me questions!"

"Well, that must be Kato Danjo."

"He was with a big group of warriors just coming back from a battle. He was riding a good horse, too! Who is he?"

"Well, Danjo lives near the Komyoji Temple."

"Yes?"

"He is engaged to my little sister."

"Engaged?"

"My, you're persistent!"

"But I don't understand."

"They're going to be married."

"What? You mean he's going to be my mother's little sister's husband?" Hiyoshi seemed satisfied, and laughed.

His mother, when she looked at his toothy, impudent grin, even though he was her own child, could only think of him as a precocious little brat.

"Mother, there's a sword about this big in the storage shed, isn't there?"

"There is. What do you want with it?"

"Won't you let me have it? It's all beat up, and Father doesn't use it anymore."

"Playing war games again?"

"It's all right, isn't it?"

"Absolutely not!"

"Why not?"

"What's going to happen if a farmer's son gets used to wearing a sword?"

"Well, one day I'm going to be a samurai." He stamped his foot like a spoiled child, thinking the matter closed. His mother glared at him, and her eyes filled with tears.

"Fool!" she scolded him, and, clumsily wiping away her tears, she pulled him along by the hand. "Just for a bit, try to be a help to your sister and draw some water." Dragging him along by force, she went back to the house.

"No! No!" Hiyoshi fought her, yelling and digging his heels into the dirt. "No! I hate you! You're stupid! No!"

His mother pulled him along, imposing her will. Just then the sound of a cough, mixed with smoke from the hearth, came through the bamboo-screened window. When he heard his father's voice, Hiyoshi's shoulders shrank and he became silent. Yaemon was only about forty, but, condemned to spend his days as a cripple, he had the raspy, coughing voice of a man past fifty.

"I'll tell your father you're giving me too much trouble," his mother said, loosening her grip. He covered his face with his hands and wiped his eyes as he cried softly.

Looking at this little boy who was too hard to handle, his mother wondered what was to become of him?

"Onaka! Why are you shouting at Hiyoshi again? It's unbecoming. What business do you have fighting with your own child and crying like that?" asked Yaemon through the window, in the shrill voice of a sick man.

"You should scold him then," Onaka said reproachfully.

Yaemon laughed. "Why? Because he wants to play with my old sword?"

"Yes."

"He was just playing."

"Yes, and he shouldn't be doing that."

"He's a boy, and my son, too. Is it really so bad? Give him the sword!"

Onaka looked toward the window in amazement and bit her lip in frustration.

I won! Hiyoshi exulted, enjoying his victory, but only for a moment. As soon as he saw the tears streaming down his mother's pale cheeks, his victory felt hollow.

"Oh, stop crying! I don't want the sword anymore. I'll go help my sister." He ran off to the kitchen, where his sister was bent over, blowing into the clay oven through a bamboo stalk to bring the firewood to life.

Hiyoshi bounded in, saying, "Hey, shall I fetch the water?"

"No, thank you," Otsumi answered, timidly looking up in surprise. Wondering what he was up to, she shook her head.

Hiyoshi lifted the lid off the water jar and peered inside. "It's already full. Shall I mash up the bean paste?"

"No! Don't be a bother!"

"A bother? All I want to do is help. Let me do something for you. Shall I fetch the pickles?"

"Didn't Mother go and get them just now?"

"Well, what can I do?"

"If you only behaved yourself, that'd make Mother happy."

"Why, aren't I behaving now? Is there a fire in the oven? I'll start it for you. Move over."

"I'm doing fine!"

"If you'd just move…"

"Look what you did! You put it out!"

"Liar! You're the one who put it out!"

"That's not so."

"Loudmouth!"

Hiyoshi, impatient with the firewood that wouldn't ignite, slapped his sister on the cheek. Otsumi cried loudly and complained to her father. Since they were next to the living room, very soon their father's voice thundered in Hiyoshi's ears.

"Don't hit your sister! It doesn't do for a man to hit women! Hiyoshi, come in here this minute!"

On the other side of the partition, Hiyoshi swallowed hard and glared accusingly at Otsumi. His mother came in and stood by the entrance, dismayed that this was happening yet again.

Yaemon was frightening, the most frightening father in the world. Hiyoshi did as he was told. He sat straight and looked up at his father.

Kinoshita Yaemon was sitting in front of the hearth. Behind him was the staff that he needed to use to walk. Without it he was unable to go anywhere, even to the toilet. His elbow rested on a wooden box that he used for spinning and collecting hemp, a sideline he worked at when he felt so inclined. Disabled though he was, he could help a little with the family finances.

"Hiyoshi!"

"Yes, sir?"

"Don't be a nuisance to your mother."

"Yes."

"And don't argue with your sister. Think of the impression you make. What should your conduct as a man be, and how should you behave toward women, who are to be protected?"

"Well, I–I didn't—"

"Quiet! I have ears. I know where you are and what you're doing, even though I never leave this room."

Hiyoshi shuddered. He believed what his father was saying.

However, Yaemon could not repress the affection he felt for his only son. His own leg and arm could never be as they were before, but he believed that through this child his blood would go on for a hundred years. Then he looked at Hiyoshi again, and his mood changed. A father was supposed to be the best judge of his son, but even at his most optimistic, Yaemon could not see how this strange-looking, snotty-nosed little brat was going to rise above his parents and wash away the disgrace from their name. Still, Hiyoshi was his only son, and Yaemon rested impossible hopes in him.

"The sword in the storage shed—do you want it, Hiyoshi?"

"Well…" Hiyoshi shook his head.

"You don't want it?"

"I want it, but…"

"Why don't you say so, then?"

"Mother said absolutely not."

"That's because women hate swords. Wait here."

Taking his staff, he limped into the other room. Unlike the house of a poor farmer, this one had several rooms. Hiyoshi's mother's relatives had once lived here. Yaemon had few relatives, but his wife had family in the neighborhood.

Hiyoshi had not been scolded, but he still felt uneasy. Yaemon returned, carrying a short sword wrapped in cloth. It was not the one rusting away in the storage shed.

"Hiyoshi, this is yours. Wear it whenever you like."

"Mine? Really?"

"But considering your age, I'd rather you didn't wear it in public. If you do, people will laugh at you. Hurry and grow old enough so you can wear it and not make people laugh. Will you do that for me? Your grandfather had this sword made.…" After a pause, Yaemon went on. His eyes were heavy, and he spoke slowly. "Your grandfather was a farmer. When he tried to raise his station in life and make something of himself, he had a swordsmith make this for him. We Kinoshita had a record of our family tree once, but it was destroyed in a fire. And long before your grandfather could accomplish anything, he was killed. Those were turbulent times, and many people suffered the same fate."

A lamp was lit in the next room, but the room they were in was brightened by the flame of the hearth. Hiyoshi listened to his father while staring at the red flames. Whether Hiyoshi understood or not, Yaemon felt that he could not speak of such things to his wife or daughter.

"If the Kinoshita family tree still existed, I could tell you about your ancestors, but it was burned to ashes. There's a living family tree, though, and it's been transmitted to you. It is this." Yaemon stroked the blue veins in his wrist. Blood.

This was his teaching. Hiyoshi nodded, then grasped his own wrist. He had such blood vessels in his own body, too. There could be no doubt! No family tree was more alive than this.

"I don't know who our ancestors were before your grandfather's time, but I'm sure that some of them were great men. I suppose there were samurai, maybe scholars. The blood of such men continues to flow, and it's been transmitted from me to you."

"Yes." Hiyoshi nodded again.

"However, I'm not great. In the end I'm just a cripple. Therefore, Hiyoshi, you must become a great man!"

"Father," Hiyoshi said, opening his eyes wide, "to become great, what kind of man should I become?"

"Well, there's no limit to what you can achieve. If, at the very least, you become a courageous warrior and wear this keepsake from your grandfather, I'll have no regrets when I die."

Hiyoshi said nothing, looking confused. He lacked self-confidence, and he avoided his father's stare.

After all, it's only natural—he's a child, Yaemon thought, noticing his son's unworthy reaction. Maybe it's not in the blood after all, but in the surroundings. And his heart flooded over with grief.

Hiyoshi's mother had prepared their evening meal and was waiting silently in the corner for her husband to finish his talk. Her thoughts and her husband's were completely at odds. That her husband would push the child to become a samurai was hateful to her. She prayed silently for Hiyoshi's future. This is such an unreasonable thing to say to a child. Hiyoshi, your father speaks such words out of bitterness, she wanted to say. It would be wrong for you to follow in his footsteps. If you are a fool, then be a fool, but please become a farmer, even if you only have one small plot of land. Aloud she said, "Well, let's eat. Hiyoshi and Otsumi, come a little closer to the hearth." Starting with the children's father, she passed around the chopsticks and bowls.

Even though it was their usual meal—a bowl of thin millet soup—every time Yaemon looked at it, he felt a bit sadder, because he was a father who could not satisfy the needs of wife and children. Hiyoshi and Otsumi took up their bowls, their cheeks and noses turning red, and they sucked up the food with gusto, hardly thinking of it as poor at all. For them, there was no wealth beyond this.

"There's the bean paste we got from the master of the pottery shop at Shinkawa, and there are dried vegetables and dried chestnuts in the storage shed, so both Otsumi and Hiyoshi should eat a lot," Onaka said, wanting to reassure her husband about money matters. She herself did not pick up her chopsticks until her children had full stomachs and her husband had finished eating. Once the evening meal was over, they went to bed. It was pretty much the same in every other house. No lights shone in Nakamura after nightfall.

When darkness fell, footsteps could be heard scurrying across the fields and along the roads—the sounds of nearby battles. *Ronin*, fugitives, and messengers on secret missions all liked to travel at night.

Hiyoshi often had nightmares. Was it that he heard footsteps in the dead of night, or did the struggle for mastery over the land fill his dreams? That night he kicked Otsumi, who lay next to him on the sleeping mat, and when she cried out in surprise, he yelled, "Hachiman! Hachiman! Hachiman!"

Jumping up from the mat, he was instantly alert, and even though he was calmed by his mother, he remained half-awake and elated for a long time.

"It's a fever. Burn some *moxa* powder on his neck," Yaemon advised.

Hiyoshi's mother answered, "You shouldn't have shown him that sword, or told him stories about his ancestors."

* * *

The following year, the house was visited by a great change: Yaemon fell sick and died. Looking upon his dead father's face, Hiyoshi did not cry. At the funeral, he hopped and jumped around playfully.

In the autumn of Hiyoshi's eighth year, crowds of guests came to the house again. They spent the night making rice cakes, drinking *sake*, and singing. One of his relatives told Hiyoshi, "The groom is going to become your new father. He was once a friend of Yaemon's and also served the Oda clan. His name is Chikuami. You must be a good son to him, too."

Eating his rice cake, Hiyoshi went and peeked inside. His mother had made up her face and looked unusually pretty. She was with an older man he did not know, her eyes cast down. When he saw this, he became happy. "Hachiman! Hachiman! Throw flowers!" shouted Hiyoshi, who enjoyed himself more than anyone else that night.

Summer came around again. The corn grew high. Every day Hiyoshi and the other village children would swim naked in the river, and catch and eat the little red frogs in the fields. The meat of the red frog was even tastier than the honey sac of the Korean bee. Hiyoshi's mother had taught him about eating the frogs. She said they were a medicine for children's disorders, and ever since then they had become his favorite food.

It seemed that every time he was playing, Chikuami would come looking for him. "Monkey! Monkey!" called his stepfather.

Chikuami was a hard worker. In less than a year he had put the family finances in order, and the days of hunger had gone. If Hiyoshi was in the house, he was always given chores to do from morning till night. If he was lazy or naughty, Chikuami's huge hand soon landed on his head. Hiyoshi hated this beyond endurance. He did not mind the work, but he tried to avoid attracting his stepfather's eye, even for a moment. Every day, without fail, Chikuami would take an afternoon nap. As soon as he could, Hiyoshi slipped out of the house. But before long Chikuami would go to fetch him back, shouting, "Monkey! Where's our monkey gone?"

When his stepfather came looking for him, Hiyoshi dropped whatever he was doing and slipped in between the rows of millet. Chikuami would get tired of looking for him and start back. Hiyoshi would then jump out and let out a victorious shout. He never considered that when he returned home that night he would be given no dinner and punished. Carried away with his game, he couldn't help himself.

On this particular day, Chikuami was walking nervously through the millet, his eyes darting this way and that. "Where is the little devil?"

Hiyoshi ran up the embankment toward the river.

When Chikuami got to the embankment, Ofuku was standing there alone. He was the only one who wore clothes in the summertime, and he neither swam nor ate red frogs.

"Ah, aren't you the boy from the pottery shop? Do you know where our monkey is hiding?" Chikuami asked.

"I don't," Ofuku said, shaking his head a number of times. Chikuami intimidated him.

"If you lie to me, I'll go to your house and tell your father."

The cowardly Ofuku turned pale. "He's hiding in that boat." He pointed to a small river craft pulled up onto the bank. When his stepfather ran up to it, Hiyoshi leaped out like a river imp.

Chikuami sprang forward and knocked him down. As Hiyoshi fell forward, he hit his mouth against a stone. Blood ran between his teeth.

"Ow! That hurt!"

"Serves you right!"

"I'm sorry!"

After slapping Hiyoshi two or three times, Chikuami hoisted him up at arm's length and hurried back home. Although Chikuami called Hiyoshi "monkey," he did not dislike him. Because he was in a hurry to do away with their poverty, he felt he had to be strict with everyone, and he also wanted to improve Hiyoshi's character—by force if necessary.

"You're already nine years old, you little good-for-nothing," Chikuami scolded.

Once back home, he grabbed the boy by the arm and hit him several times more with his fist. Hiyoshi's mother tried to stop him. "You shouldn't be so easy on him," he barked at her.

When she started to cry, he gave the boy another beating.

"What are you crying about? I'm beating this twisted little monkey because I think it'll do him some good. He's nothing but trouble!"

At first, every time he was beaten, Hiyoshi would bury his head in his hands and beg for forgiveness. Now he just cried and cried—almost in delirium—and used abusive language.

"Why? Tell me why? You appear out of nowhere and pretend to be my father and swagger around. But my...my real father...."

"How can you say such a thing!" His mother turned pale, gasped, and put her hand over her mouth. Chikuami redoubled his rage.

"Smartass little good-for-nothing!" He threw Hiyoshi into the storage shed and ordered Onaka not to give him any dinner. From then until it got dark, Hiyoshi's shrieking could be heard coming from the shed.

"Let me out! You fool! Stonehead! Is everybody deaf? If you don't let me out, I'll burn the place down!"

He went on crying, sounding like a howling dog, but around midnight he finally cried himself to sleep. Then he heard a voice calling his name from somewhere near his head. "Hiyoshi, Hiyoshi."

He was dreaming of his dead father. Half-awake, he called out, "Father!" Then he realized that the form standing in front of him was that of his mother. She had slipped out of the house and brought him some food.

"Eat this and calm down. Come morning, I'll apologize to your father for you."

He shook his head and clung to his mother's clothes. "It's a lie. He's not my father. Didn't my father die?"

"Now, now, why do you say such things? Why be unreasonable? I'm always telling you to be a good son to your father."

To his mother, it was like being cut by a knife. But Hiyoshi could not understand why she cried until her body shook.

The next day, Chikuami started yelling at Onaka from the time the sun came up. "You went behind my back and gave him food in the middle of the night, didn't you? Because you're so soft, his character will never improve. Otsumi is not to go anywhere near the storage shed today either."

The trouble between husband and wife lasted almost half a day, until finally Hiyoshi's mother went off alone, crying again. When the sun was about to set, she returned, accompanied by a priest from the Komyoji Temple. Chikuami did not ask his wife where she'd been. Sitting outside with Otsumi and working on a straw mat, he frowned.

"Chikuami," the priest said, "your wife came to the temple to ask us if we'd take your son in as an acolyte. Do I have your consent?"

Chikuami looked silently at Onaka, who stood outside the back gate, sobbing.

"Hm, I suppose it might be all right. But doesn't he need a sponsor?"

"Happily, the wife of Kato Danjo, who lives at the foot of Yabuyama Hill, has agreed. She and your wife are sisters, I believe."

"Ah, so she went to Kato's?" Chikuami's expression was bitter, although he did not object to Hiyoshi entering the temple. He tacitly agreed to the proposal, answering questions in monosyllables.

Giving an order to Otsumi, Chikuami went to put away his farm equipment, and worked for the rest of the day with a preoccupied air.

After he was let out of the storage shed, Hiyoshi received repeated warnings from his mother. All night long he'd been eaten up by mosquitoes, and his face was swollen. When told he was going to serve at a temple, he burst into tears. But he quickly recovered.

"The temple'll be better," he declared.

While it was still light, the priest made the necessary preparations for Hiyoshi, and as the time for departure drew near, even Chikuami seemed a little sad.

"Monkey, when you enter the temple, you must have a change of heart and discipline yourself," he told the boy. "Learn to read and write a bit, and let us see you become a full-fledged priest soon."

Hiyoshi mumbled a short word of assent and bowed. Once on the other side of the fence, he looked back time after time at the figure of his mother, who watched him disappear into the distance.

The small temple was on the top of a rise called Yabuyama, a bit removed from the village. A Buddhist temple of the Nichiren sect, its head priest was of advanced years and bedridden. Two young priests maintained the buildings and grounds. Because of the many years of civil war, the village was impoverished, and the temple had few parishioners. Hiyoshi, responding quickly to his new surroundings, worked hard, as if he were a different person. He was quick-witted and energetic, and the priests treated him with affection, avowing that they would train him well. Every night they made him practice calligraphy and gave him elementary schooling, during which he displayed an unusual talent for memorization.

One day a priest told him, "I met your mother on the road yesterday. I told her you're doing fine."

Hiyoshi did not understand his mother's sorrow very well, but whatever made her happy made him happy.

But when the autumn of his tenth year came around, he began to find the temple too confining. The two younger priests had gone to neighboring villages to beg for alms. In their absence, Hiyoshi got out a wooden sword he had hidden away, and a handmade staff. Then he stood at the top of the hill, yelling down to his friends, who were getting ready to play war games.

"You enemy troops, you're stupid. Come on, attack me from any direction you like!"

Although it was not at all the usual time, the huge bell suddenly rang out from the bell tower. People at the foot of the hill were taken by surprise and wondered what was going on. A stone went flying down the hill, then a tile, which hit and injured a girl working in a vegetable patch.

"It's that kid up at the temple. He's rounded up the village boys and they're playing at war again."

Three or four people climbed the hill and stood before the main hall of the temple. The doors were wide open and the interior was covered with ashes. Both the transept and the sanctum were in a shambles. The incense burner had been broken. It looked as though the banners had been put to some questionable use, the gold brocade curtain had been ripped and tossed aside, and the drumhead was ripped.

"Shobo!" "Yosaku!" called parents looking for the children. Hiyoshi was nowhere to be seen; the other youngsters, too, had suddenly disappeared.

By the time the parents got back to the foot of the hill, there was some sort of tremor in the temple. The thickets rustled, stones flew, and the bell rang again. The sun went down, and the children, bruised and bloodied, limped down the hill.

Every night when the priests came back from begging for alms, the villagers would go to the temple and complain. But when the priests returned that evening, they could only stare at each other in shock. The incense burner in front of the altar had been split perfectly in two. The donor of this precious vessel was a man by the name of Sutejiro, who was a pottery merchant from the village of Shinkawa and one of the temple's few remaining parishioners. At the time he had made the gift to the temple, three or four years earlier, he had said, "This incense burner was fired by my master, the late Gorodayu. I have cherished it as a keepsake. He decorated it from memory, and he took particular care in applying the blue pigment. In offering it to this temple, I assume it will be treated as a treasured article until the end of time."

Ordinarily it was kept in a box, but just a week earlier Sutejiro's wife had visited the temple. The incense burner had been taken out and used, but had not been put away again.

The color drained from the priests' faces. Added to their worries was the possibility that if they reported this to the old head priest, his illness would worsen.

"It was probably Monkey," said one.

"Right," another agreed. "None of those other little devils could do this kind of evil."

"What can we do?"

They dragged Hiyoshi in and thrust the pieces of the broken vessel in his face. Hiyoshi could not remember breaking the incense burner, but said, "I'm sorry."

The apology made the priests even angrier, because the boy spoke calmly and seemed to be without a trace of remorse. "Heathen!" they called him, and tied his hands behind his back and bound him to one of the large pillars of the temple.

"We're going to leave you here for a few days. Maybe you'll get eaten by rats," the priests said.

This sort of thing happened to Hiyoshi all the time. When his friends came the next day, he thought bitterly, he would not be able to play with them. And when they did come, they saw he was being punished and ran off.

"Untie me," he called out after them. "If you don't, I'm going to beat you up."

Elderly pilgrims and the village women who made their way up to the temple made fun of him. "Say, isn't that a monkey?"

At one point he was calm enough to mutter to himself, "I'll show you." His small body, pressed against the great temple pillar, was suddenly filled with a feeling of great power. He kept his lips shut about such things and, well aware of his predicament, put on a defiant face, cursing his fate.

He fell into a deep sleep, only to be awakened by his own drooling. The day was frightfully long. Thoroughly bored, he gazed at the broken incense burner. The potter had written an inscription in small characters on the bottom of the vessel: "Made with good omen, Gorodayu."

The nearby village of Seto and, in fact, the entire province was famous for pottery. This had never interested him before, but looking at the painted landscape on the incense burner, his imagination took off.

Where is that, I wonder?

Mountains and stone bridges, towers and people, clothing and boats, the like of which he had never seen before, were painted in indigo on the white porcelain. It all left him deeply puzzled.

What country is that? he wondered.

He could not guess. He had a young boy's cleverness and thirst for knowledge and, desperate for an answer, he strained his imagination for an answer that would fill this emptiness.

Could there really be such a country?

While he was thinking hard about this, something flashed in his head—something he had been taught or had heard, but had forgotten. He racked his brains.

China! That's it! It's a picture of China!

He was pleased with himself. As he looked at the glazed porcelain, he flew to China in his imagination.

At long last the day came to an end. The priests returned from their begging. Instead of finding Hiyoshi in tears, as they had expected, they saw that he was grinning.

"Even punishment is useless. He's beyond our help. We'd better send him back to his parents."

That evening, one of the priests gave Hiyoshi some supper and took him down the hill to the house of Kato Danjo.

B O O K   O N E

Kato Danjo lay down next to the lamp. He was a samurai, used to being exposed to battle morning and night. On those rare days when he could relax, he found staying at home much too peaceful. Tranquillity and relaxation were things to be feared—he might become used to them.

"Oetsu!"

"Yes?" Her voice came from the direction of the kitchen.

"Somebody's knocking at the gate."

"It's not the squirrels again?"

"No, somebody's out there."

Wiping her hands, she went to the gate and came back right away, saying, "It's a priest from the Komyoji. He's brought Hiyoshi." A look of distress swept over her young face.

"Aha!" Danjo, who had expected this, said, laughing, "It seems that Monkey has gotten a leave of absence." Danjo listened to the priest's recital of recent events. Having sponsored Hiyoshi's entrance into the temple, he now apologized to all concerned and took charge of Hiyoshi.

"If he is unfit to be a priest, there's nothing to be done. We'll send him back home to Nakamura. You should no longer feel under any obligation to keep him. I'm sorry he's been nothing but trouble."

"Please explain the matter to his parents," the priest said, and as he turned to go, his step became lighter, as if a heavy load had been lifted from his shoulders. Hiyoshi cut a lonely figure. He looked around curiously, wondering whose house he had come to. He had not stopped here on his way to the temple, nor had he been told that relatives lived close by.

"Well, little boy, have you had anything to eat?" Danjo asked with a smile. Hiyoshi shook his head.

"Have some cakes, then."

While he was munching on the cakes, Hiyoshi eyed the spear suspended over the door, and the crest on the armor chest, then looked hard at Danjo.

Is there really something wrong with this boy? Danjo asked himself. He had his doubts. He stared back, but Hiyoshi neither turned his eyes away nor looked down. There was no trace of the imbecile in him. He smiled rather charmingly at Danjo.

Danjo laughed as he gave in. "You've gotten quite big, haven't you? Hiyoshi, do you remember me?"

This focused a hazy memory in Hiyoshi's mind of a man who had patted him on the head when he was six.

As was the custom with samurai, Danjo almost always slept at the castle at Kiyosu, or on the battlefield. The days he was able to stay at home with his wife had been few. He had returned unexpectedly the day before, and would go back to Kiyosu the next day. Oetsu wondered how many months would pass before they spent another day together.

A troublesome child! Oetsu thought. Hiyoshi's arrival was inopportune. She looked up, embarrassed. What would her in-laws think? Could this really be her sister's child?

She could hear Hiyoshi's screechy voice from her husband's sitting room: "It was you with all those samurai on the riverbank that day, riding a horse."

17

"You remember, do you?"

"Sure." He went on in a familiar tone of voice, "If that's the case, you're a relative of mine. You and my mother's younger sister are engaged."

Oetsu and the maid went to the living room to get out serving trays. Oetsu felt uncomfortably cold, listening to Hiyoshi's language and his loud country boy's voice. Opening the sliding door, she called to her husband.

"Dinner's ready."

She saw that her husband was arm-wrestling with Hiyoshi, whose face was bright red, his buttocks raised like a hornet's tail. Danjo, too, was acting like a child.

"Dinner?" he said absently.

"The soup is going to get cold."

"Go ahead and eat by yourself. This kid is playing for keeps. We're having a good time. Ha, ha! He's a strange one."

Danjo, totally absorbed, seemed to be taken in completely by Hiyoshi's artlessness. The boy, always quick to make friends, was almost leading his uncle by the nose. From arm-wrestling they went to finger puppets, then mimicry, playing children's games until Danjo was holding his sides with laughter.

The next day, as he was about to leave, Danjo said to his wife, who seemed depressed, "If his parents allow it, how about keeping him here? I doubt he'd be much use, but I suppose it'd be better than keeping a real monkey."

Oetsu was less than pleased with the idea. Going with her husband as far as the garden gate, she said, "No. He would annoy your mother. That would never do."

"Whatever you say."

Oetsu knew that whenever Danjo was away from home, his mind dwelt on his lord and on battles. Would he come back alive? she wondered. Was it such a big thing for a man to make a name for himself? Oetsu watched his retreating figure and thought of the many months of loneliness ahead. Then she finished her housework and set off with Hiyoshi for Nakamura.

"Good morning, madam," said a man coming from the opposite direction. He seemed to be a merchant, probably the master of a large establishment. He wore a resplendent half coat, a short sword, and, on his feet, leather socks with a design of small cherry blossoms. He was about forty and genial-looking.

"Aren't you Master Kato's wife? Where are you off to?"

"To my sister's house in Nakamura, to take this child home." She held Hiyoshi's hand a little tighter.

"Ah, this little gentleman. This is the lad expelled from the Komyoji."

"You've heard already?"

"Oh, yes. As a matter of fact, I've just come from the temple."

Hiyoshi looked around restlessly. Never before had he been called a "little gentleman." Ashamed, he felt himself blush.

"Oh, my, you've been to the temple because of him?"

"Yes, the priests came to my house to apologize. I was told that an incense burner I had donated to the temple was broken in two."

"This little devil did that!" said Oetsu.

"Come now, you shouldn't say such things. These things happen."

"I heard it was a very rare, famous piece."

"Most regrettably, it was the work of Gorodayu, whom I served during his travels to the country of the Ming."

"Doesn't he also use the name Shonzui?"

"Yes, but he fell ill and passed away some time ago. In recent years, many pieces of blue-and-white porcelain bearing the seal 'Made by Shonzui Gorodayu' have been made, but they are fakes. The only man who has ever been to the country of the Ming and brought back their pottery-making techniques is now in the next world."

"I've heard that you've adopted Master Shonzui's son, Ofuku."

"That's right. Children tease him by calling him 'the Chinese kid.' Lately he's been refusing to go outside at all." The merchant gazed down at Hiyoshi. The boy, unexpectedly hearing Ofuku's name, wondered about the man's business.

"You know," the merchant continued, "it turns out that Hiyoshi here is the only one who ever defended Ofuku. So when Ofuku heard about this latest incident, he asked me to intercede. Many other things are supposed to have happened. The priests told me about his bad behavior, and I couldn't persuade them to take him back again." His chest puffed up with laughter.

"His parents must have ideas about what to do with him," the man said, "but when he's to be placed somewhere else again, if his parents think an establishment like mine would be appropriate, I'd like to be of assistance. Somehow, he seems to hold promise."

With a polite farewell, he took his leave. Holding on to Oetsu's sleeve, Hiyoshi looked back at him several times.

"Tell me, Auntie, who was that man?"

"His name is Sutejiro. He's a wholesaler who handles pottery from many countries."

Hiyoshi was silent for a while as they trudged along.

"The country of the Ming, where is that?" he asked suddenly, thinking of what he had just heard.

"That means China."

"Where is it? How big is it? Are there castles and samurai and battles there, too?"

"Don't be such a nuisance. Be quiet, won't you?" Oetsu shook her sleeve irritably, but a scolding by his aunt had no more effect on Hiyoshi than a gentle breeze. He craned his neck upward and gazed fixedly at the blue sky. It was so wondrous he could hardly stand it. Why was it so incredibly blue? Why were human beings earthbound? If people were able to fly like birds, he himself could probably travel to the country of the Ming. Indeed, the birds depicted on the incense burner were the same as those in Owari. The people's clothes were different, he remembered, as were the shapes of the ships, but the birds were the same. It must be that birds had no countries; heaven and earth were all one country to them.

I'd like to visit different countries, he mused.

Hiyoshi had never noticed how small and poor a house he was returning to. But when he and Oetsu peered inside, he realized for the first time that even at midday it was as dark as a cellar. Chikuami was nowhere to be seen; maybe he was out attending to some business.

"Nothing but trouble," Onaka said, after hearing of Hiyoshi's latest escapades. She let out a deep sigh. His expression was nonchalant. As she looked at him, there was no blame in her eyes. Rather, she was impressed by how much he had grown in two years. Suspiciously, Hiyoshi eyed the infant sucking at his mother's breast. At some point his family had increased by one member. Without warning, he took the child's head, wresting it from the nipple, and peered at it.

"When was this baby born?" he asked.

Instead of answering, his mother said, "You've become a big brother. You'll have to behave."

"What's his name?"

"Kochiku."

"That's a strange name," he said excitedly, at the same time experiencing a feeling of power over the small child: the will of an older brother could be imposed on a younger brother.

"Starting tomorrow, I'll carry you on my back, Kochiku," he promised. But he was handling the baby clumsily, and Kochiku began to cry.

His stepfather appeared just as Oetsu was leaving. Onaka had told her sister that Chikuami had grown tired of trying to wipe out their poverty. He sat around drinking *sake*, and his face was flushed now as he entered the house. Spying Hiyoshi, he let out a yell.

"You scoundrel! You were expelled from the temple and you come back here?"

TENZO THE BANDIT

Hiyoshi had been back home for more than a year. He was eleven. Whenever Chikuami lost sight of him, even for a moment, he'd charge around looking for him and roar at the top of his voice, "Monkey? Have you chopped the firewood yet? Why not? Why did you leave the pail in the field?" If Hiyoshi so much as started to talk back, the rough, hard hollow of his stepfather's hand would quickly ring against the side of the boy's head. At such times his mother, the baby strapped to her back while she trod barley or cooked, would force herself to look away and remain silent. Still, her face looked pained, as if she herself had been slapped.

"It's natural for any eleven-year-old brat to help with the work. If you think you can slip away and play all the time, I'll break your ass!"

The foulmouthed Chikuami drove Hiyoshi hard. But after being sent home from the temple, he worked hard, as if he had come back a different person. On those occasions when his mother unwisely tried to shield him, Chikuami's rough hands and voice lashed out with severity. It was better, she decided, to pretend to ignore her son. Now Chikuami rarely went into the fields, but he was often away from the house. He would go into town, return drunk, and yell at his wife and children.

"No matter how much I work, the poverty of this house won't ever be eased," he complained. "There are too many parasites, and the land tax keeps going up. If it weren't for these kids, I'd become a masterless samurai—a *ronin*! And I'd drink delicious *sake*. Ah, these chains on my hands and feet!"

After one of these fits of abusiveness, he would make his wife count out what little money they had, then send Otsumi or Hiyoshi out to buy *sake*, even in the middle of the night.

If his stepfather wasn't around, Hiyoshi would sometimes give vent to his feelings.

Onaka hugged him close and comforted him.

"Mother, I want to go out and work again," he said one day.

"Please stay here. If it weren't for your being around…" The rest of what she said was unintelligible through her tears. As each tear appeared, she turned her head to the side and wiped her eyes. Seeing his mother's tears, Hiyoshi couldn't say anything. He wanted to run away, but he knew he would have to stay where he was and bear the unhappiness and bitterness. When he felt sorry for his mother, the natural desires of youth—to play, to eat, to learn, to run away—would grow within him like so many weeds. All these were pitted against the angry words Chikuami hurled at his mother and the fists that rained down on his own head.

"Eat shit!" he muttered, his defiant soul a flame within his small body. Finally he pushed himself to the point of confronting his fearsome stepfather.

"Send me out to work again," he said. "I'd rather be in service than stay in this house."

Chikuami didn't argue. "Fine," he said. "Go wherever you like, and eat someone else's rice. But the next time you get driven away, don't come back to this house." He meant what he said, and although he realized Hiyoshi was only an eleven-year-old boy, he found himself arguing with him as an equal, which made him even madder.

Hiyoshi's next job was at the village dyer's shop.

"He's all mouth, and sassy to boot. Just looking for a sunny place to pick the dirt from his navel," said one of the workmen operating the dye press.

Soon after that, word came from the go-between: "I'm afraid he's of no use." And back home he went.

Chikuami glared at him. "Well, how about it, Monkey? Is society going to feed an idler like you? Don't you yet understand the value of parents?"

He wanted to say, I'm not bad! but instead he said, "You're the one who no longer farms, and it'd be better if you didn't just gamble and drink at the horse market. Everybody's sorry for my mother."

"How dare you talk that way to your father!" Chikuami's thundering roar shut the boy up, but now he was beginning to see Hiyoshi in a different light. He thought, Bit by bit, he's growing up. Each time Hiyoshi went out into the world and came back again, he was noticeably bigger. The eyes that judged his parents and his home were maturing quickly. And the fact that Hiyoshi was looking at him with the eyes of an adult deeply annoyed, frightened, and displeased the errant stepfather.

"Go on, hurry and find work," he ordered.

The following day, Hiyoshi went to his next employer, the village cooper. He was back home within a month, the mistress of the shop having complained, "I can't have a disturbing child like this in my house."

Hiyoshi's mother could not understand what she meant by "disturbing." Other places where Hiyoshi began apprenticeships were the plasterer's shop, the lunch counter at the horse market, and the blacksmith's. Each time he stayed no longer than three to six months. His comings and goings gradually became known, and his reputation got so bad that no one would act as his go-between.

"Ah, that boy at Chikuami's house. He's a foulmouthed good-for-nothing."

Naturally, Hiyoshi's mother felt embarrassed around people. She felt awkward about her son, and in response to the gossip she would quickly deprecate him, as if his growing delinquency were incurable. "I don't know what can be done with him," she'd say. "He hates farming, and he just won't settle down at home."

In the spring of his fourteenth year, Hiyoshi's mother told him, "This time you absolutely must stick with it. If the same thing happens one more time, my sister isn't going to be able to look Master Kato in the face, and everybody's going to laugh and say, 'Again?' Mind you, if you fail this time, I won't forgive you."

The next day his aunt took him to Shinkawa for an interview. The large, imposing mansion they went to belonged to Sutejiro, the pottery merchant. Ofuku was now a pale youth of sixteen; from helping his adoptive father, the boy had learned the pottery business himself.

In the pottery store, the distinction between superior and subordinate was rigidly applied. During his first interview, Hiyoshi knelt respectfully on the wooden veranda while Ofuku sat inside, eating cakes, chatting happily with his parents.

"Well, it's Yaemon's little monkey. Your father died, and Chikuami from the village became your stepfather. And now you want to serve in this house? You'll have to work hard." This was said in such a grown-up tone of voice that no one who had known the younger Ofuku would have believed it was the same person speaking.

"Yes, sir," Hiyoshi replied.

He was taken to the servants' quarters, from which he could hear the laughter of the master's family in the living room. That his friend had not shown him the least bit of friendliness made him feel even lonelier.

"Hey, Monkey!" Ofuku did not mince his words. "Tomorrow, get up early and go to Kiyosu. Since you'll be taking goods to an official, load the packages onto the regular handcart. On your way back, stop in at the shipping agent's and check whether the pottery has arrived from Hizen. If you loiter along the way or get back too late, as you did the other day, you won't be let into the house."

Hiyoshi's answer was not a simple "yes" or "yes, sir." Like the clerks who had served much longer in the shop, he said, "Most certainly, sir, and with the greatest respect, sir."

Hiyoshi was often sent on errands to Nagoya and Kiyosu. That day he took note of the white walls and high stone ramparts of Kiyosu Castle and mused, What kind of people live inside? How can I get to live there myself?

Feeling as small and wretched as a worm, he was frustrated. As he made his way through town, pushing the heavy handcart piled high with pottery wrapped in straw, he heard the familiar words:

"Well, well, there goes a monkey!"

"A monkey pushing a handcart!"

Veiled courtesans, fashionably dressed townswomen, and the pretty young wives of good families all whispered, pointed, and stared at him as he went by. He himself had already become proficient at spotting the pretty ones. What annoyed him most was the staring, as though he were some kind of freak.

The governor of Kiyosu Castle was Shiba Yoshimune, and one of his principal retainers was Oda Nobutomo. At the spot where the castle moat and the Gojo River met, one still sensed the presence of the declining grandeur of the old Ashikaga shogunate, and the prosperity that lingered here, even in the midst of the many disturbances going on in the world, upheld Kiyosu's reputation as the most glamorous town in any of the provinces.

For *sake*, go to the *sake* shop.
For good tea, go to the tea shop.
But for courtesans, it's Sugaguchi in Kiyosu.

In the pleasure quarter of Sugaguchi, the eaves of brothels and teahouses lined the streets. In the daytime, the young girls who served in the brothels sang as they played catch. Hiyoshi pushed his handcart through their game, dreaming, How can I become great? Unable to come up with an answer, he kept thinking, Someday…someday…He spun out one fantasy after another as he walked along. The town was full of all the things that were denied to him: delicious food, opulent houses, gaudy military gear and saddlery, rich clothing and precious stones.

Thinking of his skinny sister with her pale face in Nakamura, he watched the steam rising from dumpling steamers in the sweet shops and wished he could buy some for her. Or passing an old apothecary, he would gaze in ecstasy at the bags of medicinal herbs and say to himself, Mother, if I could give you medicine like that, I bet you'd soon get much better. Ever present in his dreams was the wish to improve the wretched lives of his mother and Otsumi. The one person he gave no thought to at all was Chikuami.

As he approached the castle town, his mind was dazzled by his usual daydreams. Someday…someday…but how? was his only thought as he walked along.

"Fool!"

On his way across a busy crossroads, he abruptly found himself in the center of a noisy mob. He had run his cart into a mounted samurai, followed by ten retainers carrying spears and leading a horse. Straw-wrapped bowls and plates fell all over the road, breaking into pieces. Hiyoshi tottered uncertainly among the wreckage.

"Are you blind?"

"You idiot!"

While scolding Hiyoshi, the attendants trampled on the broken dishes. Not a single passerby drew near to offer him help. He collected the broken pieces, tossed them into the handcart, and began pushing again, his blood boiling in indignation for having been treated this way in public. And within his childish fantasies, he struck a serious note: How will I ever be able to make people like that prostrate themselves in front of me?

A little later, he thought of the scolding he would get when he got back to his master's house, and the cold look on Ofuku's face loomed large in his imagination. His great fantasy, like a soaring phoenix, vanished in a host of worries, as if he had been swallowed up in a cloud of poppy seeds.

Night had fallen. Hiyoshi had put the handcart away in the shed and was washing his feet by the well. Sutejiro's establishment, which was called the Pottery Mansion, was like the residence of a great provincial warrior clan. The imposing main house was linked to many outbuildings, and rows of warehouses stood nearby.

"Little Monkey! Little Monkey!"

As Ofuku drew near, Hiyoshi got up.

"Yeah?"

Ofuku struck Hiyoshi's shoulder with the thin bamboo cane he always carried when looking around the employees' quarters or giving orders to the warehouse workers. This was not the first time he had struck Hiyoshi. Hiyoshi stumbled, and was immediately covered with mud again.

"When addressing the master, do you say 'yeah'? No matter how many times I tell you, your manners don't improve. This is not a farmer's house!"

Hiyoshi made no reply.

"Why don't you say something? Don't you understand? Say 'yes, sir.'"

Afraid of being hit again, Hiyoshi said, "Yes, sir."

"When did you get back from Kiyosu?"

"Just now."

"You're lying. I asked the people in the kitchen, and they told me you'd already eaten."

"I felt dizzy. I was afraid I was going to faint."

"Why?"

"Because I was hungry after walking all that way."

"Hungry! When you got back, why didn't you go to the master to make your report right away?"

"I was going to, after washing my feet."

"Excuses, excuses! From what the kitchen workers told me, a lot of the pottery you were supposed to deliver in Kiyosu was broken on the way. Is it true?"

"Yes."

"I suppose you felt it was all right not to apologize to me directly. You thought you'd make up some kind of lie, make a joke of it, or ask the kitchen workers to cover for you. This time I'm not going to put up with it." Ofuku grabbed Hiyoshi's ear and pulled. "Well, come on. Speak up."

"I'm sorry."

"This is getting to be a habit. We're going to get to the bottom of this. Come along, we'll talk to my father."

"Please forgive me." Hiyoshi's voice sounded just like the cry of a monkey.

Ofuku did not loosen his grip. He started to go around the house. The path that led from the warehouse to the garden entrance of the house was screened by a thicket of tall Chinese bamboos.

Suddenly, Hiyoshi stopped in his tracks. "Listen," he said, glaring at Ofuku and knocking away his hand, "I've got something to tell you."

"What are you up to now? I'm the master here, remember?" Ofuku said, turning pale and beginning to tremble.

"That's why I'm always obedient, but there's something I want to say to you. Ofuku, have you forgotten our childhood days? You and I were friends, weren't we?"

"That belongs to the past."

"All right, it belongs to the past, but you shouldn't forget it. When they teased you and called you 'the Chinese kid,' do you remember who always stuck up for you?"

"I remember."

"Don't you think you owe me something?" Hiyoshi asked, scowling. He was much smaller than Ofuku, but he had such an air of dignity about him that it was impossible to tell who was the elder. "The other workers are all talking, too," Hiyoshi went on. "They say the master is good, but the young master is conceited and hasn't got a heart. A boy like you, who's never known poverty or hardship, should try working in someone else's house. If you bully me and the other employees again, I don't know what I'll do. But remember that I have a relative who's a *ronin* in Mikuriya. He has over a thousand men under his command. If he came here on my account, he could wipe out a house like this in a single night." Hiyoshi's threatening stream of nonsense, combined with the fire in his eyes, terrified the hapless Ofuku.

"Master Ofuku!"

"Master Ofuku! Where's Master Ofuku?"

The servants from the main house had been searching for Ofuku for some time. Ofuku, held prisoner by Hiyoshi's stare, had lost the courage to answer them.

"They're calling you," Hiyoshi muttered. And he added, making it sound like an order, "You can go now, but don't forget what I told you." With this parting remark, he turned away and walked toward the back entrance to the house. Later, his heart beating wildly, he wondered if they were going to punish him. But nothing happened. The incident was forgotten.

* * *

The year drew to a close. Among farmers and townspeople, a boy turning fifteen usually had a coming-of-age ceremony. In Hiyoshi's case, there was no one to give him a single ceremonial fan, much less a feast. Since it was New Year's, he sat on the corner of a wooden platform with the other servants, sniffling and eating millet cakes cooked with vegetables—a rare treat.

He wondered grimly, Are my mother and Otsumi eating millet cakes this New Year's? Although they were millet farmers, he could recall many a New Year's when there had been no cakes to eat. The other men around him were grumbling.

"Tonight the master will have visitors, so we'll have to sit up straight and listen to his stories again."

"I'll have to pretend to have a stomachache and stay in bed."

"I hate that. Especially at New Year's."

There were similar occasions two or three times a year, at the New Year and at the festival of the god of wealth. Whatever the pretext, Sutejiro invited a great many guests: the potters of Seto, the families of favored customers in Nagoya and Kiyosu, members of samurai clans, even the acquaintances of relatives. From that evening on, there would be a horrendous crush of people.

Today, Sutejiro was in an especially good mood. Bowing low, he welcomed his guests in person, apologizing for having neglected them that past year. In the tearoom, which was decorated with one exquisite, carefully chosen flower, Sutejiro's beautiful wife served tea to her guests. The utensils she used were all rare and precious.

It was Shogun Ashikaga Yoshimasa who, late in the previous century, had first practiced the tea ceremony as an aesthetic exercise. It had spread to the common people, and before long, without anyone consciously realizing it, tea had become a central part of people's daily lives. Within the confines of the narrow little tearoom with its single flower and single cup of tea, the turbulence of the world and human suffering could be forgotten. Even in the midst of a corrupt world, the tea ceremony could teach one the cultivation of the spirit.

"Do I have the honor of addressing the lady of the house?" The speaker was a big-boned warrior, who had come in with the other guests. "My name is Watanabe Tenzo. I am a friend of your kinsman Shichirobei. He promised to bring me tonight, but unfortunately he's been taken ill, so I came alone." He bowed politely. He was gentle in demeanor, and although he had the rustic appearance of a country samurai, he asked for a bowl of tea. Sutejiro's wife served it in a yellow Seto bowl.

"I am not acquainted with the etiquette of the tea ceremony," he said. Tenzo looked around him while contentedly sipping the tea. "As might be expected of such a famous, wealthy man, the tea implements here are certainly well crafted. While it is rude of me to ask, isn't the porcelain pitcher you are using a piece of *akae* ware?"

"Did you notice that?"

"Yes." Tenzo looked at the pitcher, deeply impressed. "If this were to fall into the hands of a Sakai merchant, I daresay it would fetch about a thousand gold pieces. Quite apart from its value, it's a beautiful piece."

As they were chatting, they were called inside for dinner. Sutejiro's wife led the way, and together they went into the hall. The place settings had been arranged in a circle around the room. As host, Sutejiro sat in the very center, greeting his guests. When his wife and the maids had finished serving the *sake,* he took his own seat at one of the tables. He picked up his cup and started to tell stories about the Ming, among whom he had spent many years. It was so that he might talk about his adventures in China, a country he knew well, but one that was still relatively unknown in Japan, that he would invite his guests and treat them to such lavish entertainments.

"Well, this was a real feast. And again tonight I've heard a number of rather interesting stories," said one guest.

"I've certainly had my fill. But it's getting late. I'd better be on my way," said another.

"Me too. I really should be taking my leave."

The guests departed one by one, and the evening came to a close.

"Ah, it's over!" said a servant. "The stories may be a great treat for the guests, but we hear about the Chinese all year round."

Not hiding their yawns, the servants, Hiyoshi among them, worked frantically to clean up. The lamps in the large kitchen, in the hall, and in Sutejiro's and Ofuku's rooms were finally blown out, and the stout bar on the gate in the earthen wall was set in place. As a matter of course, samurai mansions, and also the homes of merchants—if they were at all substantial—were enclosed by an earthen wall or surrounded by a moat, which would be backed up by two or three tiers of fortifications. When night fell, people in the cities and the countryside felt uneasy. This had been the case ever since the civil wars of the previous century, and nobody thought it strange anymore.

As soon as the sun went down, people slept. When the workers, whose only pleasure was sleeping, crawled into their beds, they slumbered like cattle. Covered by a thin straw mat, Hiyoshi lay in a corner of the male servants' room, his head on a wooden pillow. Along with the other servants, he had listened to his master's stories about the great country of the Ming. But unlike them, he had listened avidly. And he was so prone to fantasizing that he was too excited to sleep, almost as though he had a fever.

What's that? he wondered, sitting up. He strained his ears, sure he had just heard a sound like a tree branch breaking and, just before that, the sound of muffled footsteps. He got up, went through the kitchen, and stealthily peeked outdoors. On this cold, clear night, the water in the large barrel was frozen, and icicles hung like swords from the wooden eaves. Looking up, he saw a man climbing the huge tree at the back. Hiyoshi guessed that the sound he had heard earlier was the cracking of a branch the man had stepped on. He observed the strange behavior of the figure in the tree. The man was swinging a light no bigger than a firefly around and around. A fuse cord? Hiyoshi wondered. The red swirl threw faint, smoky sparks into the wind. It seemed likely that the man was sending a signal to someone outside the walls.

He's coming down, Hiyoshi thought, as he hid like a weasel in the shadows. The man slid down the tree and set off with long strides toward the back of the grounds. Hiyoshi let him pass and then trailed after him.

"Ah! He was one of the guests this evening," he muttered in disbelief. It was the one who had introduced himself as Watanabe Tenzo, the man who had been served tea by the master's wife, and who had listened raptly to Sutejiro's stories from beginning to end. All the other guests had gone home, so where had Tenzo been until now? And why? He was dressed differently from before. He wore straw sandals, the hems of his baggy trousers were rolled up and tied back, and a large sword was belted at his side. His eyes took in the surroundings with a fierce, hawklike expression. Anyone seeing him would instantly realize that he was out for someone's blood.

Tenzo approached the gate, and just at that moment, the men waiting outside crashed against it.

"Wait! I'll loosen the bar. Be quiet!"

It must be a raid by bandits! Their leader had indeed been signaling to his followers, come to pillage the house like a swarm of locusts. Hidden in the shadows, Hiyoshi thought, Robbers! Instantly his blood surged, and he forgot all about himself. Although he did not think it through, he no longer cared about his own safety because he was concerned solely about his master's house. Even so, what he did next could only be described as foolhardy.

"Hey, you!" he called out, walking brazenly out of the shadows with who knew what in mind. He stood behind Tenzo just as he was about to open the gate. A shudder of fear ran up Tenzo's spine. How could he have guessed that he was being challenged by a fifteen-year-old boy who worked for the pottery shop? When he looked around, he was puzzled by what he saw: an odd-looking youth with the face of a monkey, eyeing him with a strange expression. Tenzo stared very hard at him for a moment.

"Who are you?" he demanded, perplexed.

Hiyoshi had completely forgotten the danger of the situation. His expression was unsmiling and blank. "All right, you, what's going on here?" he asked.

"What?" said Tenzo, now thoroughly confused. Is he crazy? he wondered. Hiyoshi's unforgiving expression, so unlike a child's, overwhelmed him. He felt he had to stare the boy down.

"We are the *ronin* of Mikuriya. Raise a cry and I'll cut you down. We didn't come here to take the lives of children. Get out of here. Go lose yourself in the woodshed." Supposing the gesture would intimidate the boy, he tapped the hilt of his long sword. Hiyoshi grinned, showing his white teeth.

"So you are a robber, eh? If you're a robber, you want to leave with what you came here for, right?"

"Don't be a nuisance. Get lost!"

"I'm going. But if you open that gate, not one of you will leave here alive."

"What do you mean by that?"

"You don't know, do you? Nobody knows but me."

"You're a bit crazy, aren't you?"

"Speak for yourself. You're the one whose head isn't right—coming to rob a house like this."

Tenzo's men, tired of waiting, knocked on the gate and called out, "What's going on?"

"Hold on a minute," said Tenzo. Then he said to Hiyoshi, "You said if we go into this mansion, we won't go home alive. Why should I believe you?"

"It's true."

"If I find out you're playing games, I'll cut off your head."

"You aren't going to find out for nothing. You'll have to give me something in return."

"Huh?" Grumbling to himself, Tenzo was suspicious of this boy. Overhead, the starry sky was getting brighter, but the mansion, surrounded by its earthen wall, was still sunk in total darkness.

"What do you want?" Tenzo asked tentatively.

"I don't want a thing, only that you let me become a member of your gang."

"You want to become one of us?"

"Yes, that's right."

"You want to become a thief?"

"Yes."

"How old are you?"

"Fifteen."

"Why do you want to become a thief?"

"The master drives me like a horse. The people here bully me, they call me 'monkey' all the time, so I'd like to become a bandit like you and get even with them."

"All right, I'll let you join us, but only after you prove yourself. Now explain what you said before."

"About you all being killed?"

"Yes."

"Well, your plan's no good. This evening you disguised yourself as a guest and mixed with a large group of people."

"Yes."

"Someone recognized you."

"That's impossible."

"Think what you like, but the master clearly knew who you were. So, earlier this evening, on his instructions, I ran to the house of Kato of Yabuyama and let him know we would surely be attacked in the middle of the night and would appreciate his help."

"Kato of Yabuyama...that would be the Oda retainer Kato Danjo."

"Because Danjo and my master are relatives, he got hold of a dozen samurai who live around here, and they all came in during the evening, dressed as guests. They're on watch for you at the house right now, and that's no lie."

Hiyoshi could see from the pallor of his face that Tenzo believed him.

"Is that so?" he said. "Where are they? What are they doing?"

"They were sitting in a circle, drinking *sake* and waiting. Then they decided you probably wouldn't attack this late, so they went to sleep. They made me stand watch out in the cold."

Tenzo grabbed Hiyoshi, saying, "It's your life if you cry out." With the huge palm of his hand, he covered Hiyoshi's mouth.

Struggling, Hiyoshi managed to say, "Mister, this isn't what you promised. I won't make any noise. Take your hand away." He sank his fingernails into the robber's hand.

Tenzo shook his head.

"Nothing doing. I am, after all, Watanabe Tenzo of Mikuriya. You want me to believe this house is prepared. Even if that's true, if I left empty-handed I wouldn't be able to face my men."

"But..."

"What can you do?"

"I'll bring out anything you want."

"You'll bring it out?"

"Yeah. That's the way to do it. That way you can finish this thing without the danger of cutting people down or being cut down yourself."

"Without fail?" He tightened his grip on Hiyoshi's throat.

The gate was still closed. Afraid and suspicious, his men kept calling out in loud whispers and rattling the gate.

"Hey, boss, are you in there?"

"What's going on?"

"What's the matter with the gate?"

Tenzo loosened the bar halfway and whispered through the gap, "Something's wrong here, so keep quiet. And don't stay in a group. Split up and hide."

Going for what Tenzo had asked for, Hiyoshi crawled quietly from the entrance of the male servants' quarters into the main house. Once there, he saw that a lamp was lit in Sutejiro's room.

"Master?" Hiyoshi called out as he seated himself respectfully on the veranda. There was no answer, but he sensed that both Sutejiro and his wife were awake.

"Madam?"

"Who is it?" asked Sutejiro's wife, her voice trembling. Either she or her husband had awakened and shaken the other awake because just a moment ago there had been a vague rustling and the sound of voices. Thinking it might be an attack by bandits, both had shut their eyes in fear. Hiyoshi opened the sliding door and moved forward on his knees. Both Sutejiro and his wife opened their eyes wide.

"There are bandits outside. A lot of them," Hiyoshi said.

Husband and wife swallowed hard, but said nothing. They looked incapable of speech.

"It'd be terrible if they came rushing in. They'd tie you two up and leave five or six dead or injured. I've thought of a plan, and I've got their leader waiting for your answer."

Hiyoshi told them of his conversation with Tenzo, and ended by saying, "Master, please let the robbers have what they want. I'll take it to Tenzo, and he'll go away."

There was a slight pause before the merchant asked, "Hiyoshi, what in the world does he want?"

"He said he came for the *akae* water pitcher."

"What?"

"He said that if I handed it over, he'd go away. Since it's not worth anything, won't you let him have it? It was all my idea," Hiyoshi explained proudly. "I'll pretend I'm stealing it for him." But the despair and fear hovering around the faces of Sutejiro and his wife were almost palpable. "The *akae* pitcher was taken out of storage for the tea ceremony earlier today, wasn't it? The man must be a fool to tell me to bring that worthless thing to him!" Hiyoshi said, looking as if he found the whole matter hilarious.

Sutejiro's wife was extremely quiet, as though she had been turned to stone. With a deep sigh, Sutejiro said, "This is awful." Lost in thought, he too became quiet.

"Master, why look at it that way? One piece of pottery can finish all this without bloodshed."

"It's not just any piece of pottery. Even in the country of the Ming there are few pieces like it. I brought it back from China after considerable hardship. What's more, it is a keepsake from Master Shonzui."

"In the pottery shops of Sakai," said his wife, "it would fetch over a thousand gold pieces."

But the robbers were more to be feared. If they resisted them, there would be a massacre, and there had been cases of mansions being burned to the ground. Neither event was unusual in these unsettled times.

In such a situation, a man did not have much time to make up his mind. For a moment, Sutejiro seemed to be unable to break free from his past attachment to the pitcher. But finally he said, "It can't be helped." He felt a little better after that. He took the key to the storehouse from a small drawer of a lacquer cabinet.

"Take it to him." He threw the key down in front of Hiyoshi. Vexed at the loss of the precious water pitcher, Sutejiro could not bring himself to praise Hiyoshi at all, even though he thought the scheme was well devised for a boy of his age.

Hiyoshi went alone to the storehouse. He came out holding a wooden box and returned the key to the hand of his master, saying, "It would be best if you put out the light and quietly went back to bed. You needn't worry."

When he brought the box to Tenzo, the bandit, only half believing what was happening, opened it and examined the contents carefully. "Hm, this is it," he said. The lines on his face softened.

"You and your men should get out of here fast. When I was searching for this in the storehouse just now, I lit a candle. Kato and his samurai are probably waking up at this very moment, and will soon start to make their rounds."

Tenzo made hastily for the gate. "You come and call on me in Mikuriya anytime. I'll take you on." With these words he disappeared into the darkness.

The fearful night was over.

It was about noon of the following day. Because it was the first week of the New Year, an endless procession of guests, coming in twos and threes, made their way to the main house. Yet the atmosphere in the pottery shop was strangely uneasy. Sutejiro was moody and sullen, and his usually cheerful wife was nowhere to be seen.

Ofuku quietly went to his mother's room and sat down. She had not fully recovered from the nightmare of the previous night and lay in bed, her face a sickly white.

"Mother, I've just now come from talking with Father. It's going to be all right."

"Really? What did he say?"

"At first he was skeptical, but when I told him about Hiyoshi's behavior and the time when he grabbed me behind the house and threatened me, saying he'd call in the bandits of Mikuriya, he was surprised and seemed to think again."

"Did he say he'd dismiss him soon?"

"No. He said he still considered him to be a promising little monkey, so I asked him if he was of a mind to raise a thief's tool."

"From the very first, I disliked the look in that boy's eyes."

"I mentioned that too, and finally he said that if no one got on with him, there was no other recourse but to dismiss him. He said that because he'd taken charge of him from Kato of Yabuyama, it would be difficult for him to do it. He thought it would be better if we dealt with the matter and found some inoffensive pretext to dismiss him."

"Good. It's gotten to the point where I can't bear to have that monkey-faced boy working here for even half a day more. What's he doing now?"

"He's packing goods in the warehouse. Can I tell him you want to see him?"

"No, please don't. I can't stand the sight of him. Now that your father's agreed, wouldn't it be just as well if you told him that he's being dismissed as of today and sent him home?"

"All right," said Ofuku, but he was a little frightened. "What shall I do about his pay?"

"From the beginning, we haven't been held by any promise to put aside wages for him. And although he's not much of a worker, we've fed and clothed him. Even that is more than he deserves. Oh well, let him keep the clothes he's wearing, and give him two measures of salt."

Ofuku was too afraid to say this to Hiyoshi all by himself, so he took another man with him to the warehouse. He peered inside and saw that Hiyoshi, working alone, was covered with pieces of straw from head to toe.

"Yes? what do you want?" Hiyoshi answered in an unusually energetic voice, bounding up to Ofuku. Thinking that talking about the events of the previous night wasn't a good idea, he had not told anyone about it, but he was very proud of himself—so much so that he secretly expected his master's praise.

Ofuku, accompanied by the brawniest of the shop's clerks, the one who most intimidated Hiyoshi, said, "Monkey, you can go today."

"Go where?" Hiyoshi asked in surprise.

"Home. You still have one, don't you?"

"I do, but—"

"You're dismissed as of today. You can keep your clothes."

"We're giving you this because of the mistress's kindness," said the clerk, holding out the salt and the bundle of Hiyoshi's clothes. "Since you don't have to pay your respects, you can leave right away."

Stunned, Hiyoshi felt the blood rush to his face. The anger in his eyes seemed to leap out at Ofuku. Stepping back, Ofuku took the bundle of clothes and the bag of salt from the clerk, put them on the ground, and hurriedly walked away. From the look in Hiyoshi's eyes, it seemed that he might chase after the retreating Ofuku, but actually he couldn't see a thing; he was blinded by his tears. He remembered his mother's tear-stained face when she had warned him that if he was dismissed once more, she wouldn't be able to face anyone, and that it would be a disgrace for her brother-in-law. The memory of her face and body, so haggard from poverty and childbearing, made him sniff back his tears. His nose stopped running, but he stood there motionless for a moment, not knowing what to do next. His blood seethed with anger.

"Monkey," called one of the workers, "what's the matter? You messed up again, huh? He told you to leave, didn't he? You're fifteen, and wherever you go they'll give you your meals at least. Be a man and stop blubbering."

Without stopping their work, the other workers made fun of him. Their laughter and jeers filled his ears, and he resolved not to cry in front of them. Instead, he swung around to face them, baring his white teeth.

"Who's blubbering? I'm sick and tired of this boring old shop. This time I'm going to serve a samurai!" Fixing the bundle of clothes on his back, he tied the bag of salt to a piece of bamboo and shouldered it jauntily.

"Going to serve a samurai!" jeered one of the workers. "What a way to say good-bye!" They all laughed.

Nobody hated Hiyoshi, but no one felt sorry for him either. For his part, once he had taken his first step beyond the earthen wall, his heart filled with the clear blue of the sky. He felt he had been set free.

* * *

Kato Danjo had fought at the battle of Azukizaka in the autumn of the preceding year. Impatient to distinguish himself, he had dashed into the midst of the Imagawa forces and had been so badly injured that he had been forced to come home for good. Nowadays he slept all the time in the house at Yabuyama. As the days became colder toward the end of the year, the spear wound in his stomach gave him constant trouble. He was always groaning with pain.

Oetsu took good care of her husband, and that day she was washing his pus-stained undergarments in a stream that ran through their compound. She heard a carefree voice singing, and wondered who it might be. Annoyed, she stood up and looked around. Although the house was only halfway up Komyoji Hill, from inside the earthen wall it was possible to see the road at the foot of the hill, and beyond it the farmland of Nakamura, the Shonai River, and the wide Owari Plain.

It was bitterly cold. The New Year's sun was sinking hazily toward the horizon, bringing an end to another day. The singer's voice was loud, as if he had experienced neither the harshness of the world nor any human suffering. The song was a popular tune from the end of the last century, but here in Owari, farmers' daughters had corrupted it into a spinning song.

Well, can that be Hiyoshi? she asked herself as the figure reached the foot of the hill. He carried a dirty cloth bundle on his back, and a bag hung from the end of a bamboo rod over his shoulder. She was surprised at how big he had gotten in such a short time, and that, although he had grown so much, he was still as happy-go-lucky as ever.

"Auntie! What are you doing standing out here?" Hiyoshi bobbed his head in salutation. His song gave a certain cadence to his step, and his voice, so totally unaffected, gave his greeting a certain humorous tone. His aunt's expression was clouded; she looked like someone who had forgotten how to laugh.

"What are you doing here? Have you come with a message for the priests at the Komyoji?"

Hard put to answer, Hiyoshi scratched his head.

"The pottery shop let me go. I came here thinking I'd better let my uncle know."

"What? Again?" Oetsu said, frowning. "You came here after being sent away again?"

Hiyoshi thought about telling her the reason, but somehow it did not seem to be worth the trouble. In a sweeter tone he said, "Is my uncle at home? If he is, would you let me talk with him, please?"

"Absolutely not! My husband was badly wounded in battle. We don't know whether today or tomorrow will be his last day. You're not to go near him." She spoke bluntly, her tone severe. "I really feel sorry for my sister, having a child like you."

When he heard his aunt's news, he was dispirited. "Well, I wanted to ask my uncle a favor, but I guess it's useless, isn't it?"

"What kind of favor?"

"Since he's a samurai, I thought he could find me a place in a samurai household."

"What in the world! How old are you now?"

"Fifteen."

"At fifteen, you should know a bit about the world."

"That's why I don't want to work in any old boring place. Auntie, do you suppose there's an opening somewhere?"

"How should I know?" Oetsu glared at him, her eyes full of reproach. "A samurai household doesn't accept a man if he doesn't fit in with the family traditions. What are they going to do with a wild, carefree boy like you?"

Just then, a maidservant approached and said, "Madam, please come quickly. Your husband's pain is worse again."

Without another word, Oetsu ran to the house. Abandoned, Hiyoshi gazed at the darkening clouds over Owari and Mino. After a while he went through the gate in the earthen wall and hung around outside the kitchen. What he wanted most was to go home to Nakamura and see his mother, but he was held back by the thought of his stepfather, who made him feel that the fence around his own house was made of thorns. He decided that his first priority was to find an employer. He had come to Yabuyama out of prudence, thinking it proper to inform his benefactor, but with Danjo in so serious a condition, he was at a loss as to what to do next—and he was hungry.

While he was wondering where he would sleep from that night on, something soft wrapped itself around his cold leg. He looked down to see a little kitten. Hiyoshi picked it up and sat next to the kitchen door. The waning sun cast a cold light over them.

"Is your stomach empty too?" he asked. The cat shivered as he held it to his chest. Feeling the warmth of Hiyoshi's body, it began to lick his face.

"There, there," he said, turning his head away. He did not particularly like cats, but on that day the kitten was the only living creature to show him any affection.

Suddenly Hiyoshi pricked up his ears. The cat's eyes, too, widened with surprise. From a room next to the veranda had come the shrill cry of a man in pain. Presently, Oetsu came into the kitchen. Her eyes were swollen with tears, which she dried on her sleeve while stirring a medicinal concoction on the stove.

"Auntie," Hiyoshi began cautiously while petting the cat, "this kitten's stomach is empty and it's shivering. If you don't give it some food, it'll die." He avoided mentioning his own stomach. Oetsu ignored the remark.

"Are you still here?" she asked. "It'll soon be night, but I'm not letting you stay in this house."

She hid her tears with her sleeve. The beauty of the samurai's young wife, who had been so happy just two or three years before, had faded like a flower beaten by the rain. Hiyoshi, still holding the kitten, thought about his hunger and the bed that was beyond his reach. As he looked at his aunt, he suddenly noticed there was something different in her appearance.

"Auntie! Your belly is big. Are you pregnant?"

Oetsu raised her head with a start as though her cheek had been slapped. The sudden question was completely out of place.

"Just like a little boy!" she said. "You shouldn't ask such forward questions. You're disgusting!" Exasperated, she added, "Go home quickly while there's still some light. Go to Nakamura or anywhere! Right now I don't care what you do." Swallowing her own choked voice, she disappeared into the house.

"I'll go," Hiyoshi muttered, and stood up to go, but the cat was not willing to surrender the warmth of his chest. At that moment a maidservant brought out a little bowl of cold rice in bean paste soup, showed it to the cat, and called it outside. It promptly abandoned Hiyoshi to follow after the food. Hiyoshi watched the cat and its food with his mouth watering, but it seemed no one was going to offer him anything to eat. He made up his mind to go home. But when he got to the entrance of the garden, he was challenged by someone with a keen sense of hearing.

"Who's out there?" asked a voice from the sickroom.

Rooted to the spot, Hiyoshi knew it was Danjo and promptly answered. Then, thinking the time had come, he told Danjo that he had been dismissed from the pottery shop.

"Oetsu, open the door!"

Oetsu tried to change his mind, arguing that the evening wind would make him cold and that his wounds would ache. She made no move to open the sliding door, until Danjo lost his temper.

"Fool!" he shouted. "What difference does it make if I live another ten or twenty days? Open it!"

Weeping, Oetsu did as she was told and said to Hiyoshi, "You'll only make him worse. Pay your respects and then leave."

Hiyoshi stood facing the sickroom and bowed. Danjo was leaning against some piled-up bedding.

"Hiyoshi, you've been dismissed from the pottery shop?"

"Yes, sir."

"Hm. That's all right."

"What?" Hiyoshi said, puzzled.

"There isn't the least bit of shame in being dismissed, as long as you haven't been disloyal or unjust."

"I see."

"Your house, too, was formerly a samurai house. Samurai, Hiyoshi."

"Yes, sir."

"A samurai does not work just for the sake of a meal. He is not a slave to food. He lives for his calling, for duty and service. Food is something extra, a blessing from heaven. Don't become the kind of man who, in pursuit of his next meal, spends his life in confusion."

*　*　*

It was already close to midnight.

Kochiku, who was a sickly baby, was suffering from some childhood illness and had been crying almost incessantly. He was lying on bed of straw and had finally stopped nursing.

"If you get up, you'll freeze, it's so cold," Otsumi said to her mother. "Go to sleep."

"How can I, when your father isn't home yet?"

Onaka got up, and she and Otsumi sat by the hearth, working diligently on handiwork left unfinished that evening.

"What's he doing? Isn't he coming back again tonight?"

"Well, it is New Year's."

"But no one in this house—and especially you—has celebrated it with so much as a single millet cake. And all the time we have to work in the cold like this."

"Well, men have their own pastimes."

"Although we go on calling him master, he doesn't work. He only drinks *sake*. When he does come home, he abuses you all the time. It makes me mad."

Otsumi was of an age when a woman would ordinarily go off to get married, but she would not leave her mother's side. She knew about their money problems, and not even in her dreams did she think of rouge and powder, much less of a New Year's dress.

"Please don't talk like that," Onaka said in tears. "Your father isn't reliable, but Hiyoshi will become respectable someday. We'll get you married to a good man, although you can't say your mother has picked her own husbands well."

"Mother, I don't want to get married. I want to stay with you forever."

"A woman shouldn't have to live like that. Chikuami doesn't know it, but when Yaemon was crippled, we put aside a string of coins from the money we received from his lord, thinking that it would be enough for your marriage. And I've collected more than seven bales of waste silk to weave a kimono for you."

"Mother, I think someone's coming."

"Your father?"

Otsumi stretched her neck to see who it was. "No."

"Who then?"

"I don't know. Be quiet." Otsumi swallowed hard, suddenly feeling uneasy.

"Mother, are you there?" Hiyoshi called out of the darkness. He stood stock-still, making no move to step up into the other room.

"Hiyoshi?"

"Uh-huh."

"At this time of night?"

"I was dismissed from the pottery shop."

"Dismissed?"

"Forgive me. Please, Mother, forgive me," he sobbed.

Onaka and Otsumi nearly tripped over their feet in their haste to greet him.

"What will you do now?" Onaka asked. "Don't just stand there like that, come inside." She took Hiyoshi's hand, but he shook his head.

"No, I have to go soon. If I spend even a single night in this house, I won't want to leave you again."

Although Onaka did not want Hiyoshi to come back to this poverty-stricken house, she could not bear to think of him going right back out into the night. Her eyes opened wide. "Where are you going?" she asked.

"I don't know, but this time I'll serve a samurai. Then I'll be able to set both of your minds at rest."

"Serve a samurai?" Onaka whispered.

"You said you didn't want me to become a samurai, but that's what I really want to do. My uncle at Yabuyama said the same thing. He said now's the time."

"Well, you should talk this over with your stepfather too."

"I don't want to see him," Hiyoshi said, shaking his head. "You should forget about me for the next ten years. Sis, it's no good for you not to get married. But be patient, all right? When I become a great man, I'll clothe our mother in silk, and buy you a sash of patterned satin for your wedding."

Both women were weeping because Hiyoshi had grown up enough to say such things. Their hearts were like lakes of tears in which their bodies would drown.

"Mother, here are the two measures of salt the pottery shop paid me. I earned it by working for two years. Sis, put it in the kitchen." Hiyoshi put down the bag of salt.

"Thank you," said his mother, bowing to the bag. "This is salt you've earned by going out into the world for the first time."

Hiyoshi was satisfied. Looking at the happy face of his mother, he was so happy himself that he felt as if he were floating. He swore he would make her even happier in the future. So that's it! This is my family's salt, Hiyoshi thought. No, not just my family's, but the village's. No, better yet, it's the salt of the realm.

"I guess it'll be quite a while before I'm back," Hiyoshi said, backing toward the outer door, but his eyes did not move from Onaka and Otsumi. He already had one foot out the door when Otsumi suddenly leaned forward and said, "Wait, Hiyoshi! Wait." She then turned to her mother. "The string of money you just told me about. I don't need it. I don't want to get married, so please give it to Hiyoshi."

Stifling a sob in her sleeve, Onaka fetched the string of coins and handed them to Hiyoshi, who looked at them and said, "No, I don't need them." He held the coins out to his mother.

Otsumi, speaking with the compassion of an older sister, asked, "What are you going to do out in the world without money?"

"Mother, rather than this, won't you give me the sword Father carried, the one grandfather had made?"

His mother reacted as though she had been struck in the chest. She said, "Money will keep you alive. Please don't ask for that sword."

"Don't you have it anymore?" Hiyoshi asked.

"Ah…no." His mother admitted bitterly that it had long since been sold to pay for Chikuami's *sake*.

"Well, it doesn't matter. There's still that rusty sword in the storage shed, isn't there?"

"Well…if you want that one."

"It's all right if I take it?" Though he cared about his mother's feelings, Hiyoshi persisted. He remembered how badly he had wanted the shabby old sword at the age of six, and how he had made his mother cry. Now she was resigned to the idea of his growing up into what she had prayed he would never become—a samurai.

"Oh, well, take it. But Hiyoshi, never face another man and draw it from its scabbard. Otsumi, please go get it."

"That's all right. I'll go."

Hiyoshi ran into the storage shed. He took down the sword from the beam where it hung. As he tied it to his side, he remembered that six-year-old boy in tears, long years past. In that instant, he felt that he had grown up.

"Hiyoshi, Mother wants you," said Otsumi, looking into the shed.

Onaka had set a candle in the small shrine on the shelf. In a small wooden dish she had put a few grains of millet and a small pile of the salt Hiyoshi had brought. She joined her hands in prayer. Hiyoshi came in, and she told him to sit down. She took down a razor from the shrine. Hiyoshi's eyes opened wide. "What are you going to do?" he asked.

"I'm giving you your coming-of-age ceremony. Though we can't do it formally, we'll celebrate your departure into the world."

She shaved the front of Hiyoshi's head. She then soaked some new straw in water and tied his hair back with it. Hiyoshi was never to forget this experience. And while the roughness of his mother's hands as they brushed his cheeks and ears saddened him, he was conscious of another feeling. Now I'm like everybody else, he thought. An adult.

He could hear a stray dog barking. In the darkness of a country at war with itself, it seemed that the only thing that grew greater was the barking of dogs. Hiyoshi went outside.

"Well, I'm off." He could say nothing else, not even "take care of yourselves"—it stuck in his throat.

His mother bowed low in front of the shrine. Otsumi, holding the crying Kochiku, came running out after him.

"Good-bye," Hiyoshi said. He did not look back. His figure got smaller and smaller until it disappeared from sight. Perhaps because of the frost, the night was very bright.

KOROKU'S GUN

A few miles from Kiyosu, less than ten miles west of Nagoya, was the village of Hachisuka. Upon entering the village, a hat-shaped hill was visible from almost any direction. In the thick summer groves at noon, only the song of the cicadas could be heard; at night the silhouettes of large bats on the wing swept across the face of the moon.

"Yo!"

"Yo!" came the reply, like an echo, from within the grove.

The moat that took its waters from the Kanie River passed around the cliffs and large trees on the hill. If you didn't look closely, you probably wouldn't notice that the water was full of the dark blue-green algae found in old natural ponds. The algae clung to the weathered stone ramparts and earthen walls that had protected the land for a hundred years, and, along with it, the descendants of the lords of the area, and their power and livelihood.

From the outside, it was almost impossible to guess how many thousands or even tens of thousands of acres of residential land were on the hill. The mansion belonged to a powerful provincial clan of the village of Hachisuka, and its lords had gone under the childhood name of Koroku for many generations. The incumbent lord was called Hachisuka Koroku.

"Yooo! Open the gate!" The voices of four or five men came from beyond the moat. One of them was Koroku.

If the truth were known, neither Koroku nor his forebears possessed the pedigree they boasted of, nor had they held rights to the land and its administration. They were a powerful provincial clan, but nothing more. Though Koroku was known as a lord, and these men as his retainers, there was, in fact, something rough and ready about this household. A certain intimacy was natural between the head of a household and his retainers, but Koroku's relationship with his men was more like that which existed between a gang boss and his henchmen.

"What's he doing?" Koroku muttered.

"Gatekeeper, what's keeping you?" yelled a retainer, not for the first time.

"Yooo!"

This time, they heard the gatekeeper's response, and the wooden gate opened with a thud.

"Who is it?" They were challenged from the left and right by men carrying metal lamps shaped like bells on stalks, which could be carried on the battlefield or in the rain.

"It's Koroku," he answered, bathed in the lamplight.

"Welcome home."

The men identified themselves as they passed through the gate.

"Inada Oinosuke."

"Aoyama Shinshichi."

"Nagai Hannojo."

"Matsubara Takumi."

They proceeded with heavy footsteps down a wide, dark corridor and into the interior of the house. All along the corridor, the faces of servants, the women of the household, wives and children—the many individuals who made up this extended family— greeted the chief of the clan, come back from the outside world. Koroku returned the greetings, giving each at least a glance, and arriving at the main hall, he sat down heavily on a round straw mat. The light from a small lamp clearly showed the lines on his face. Was he in a bad mood? wondered the women anxiously, while they brought water, tea, and black bean cakes.

"Oinosuke?" Koroku said after a while, turning to the retainer sitting farthest away from him. "We were well shamed this evening, were we not?"

"We were," Oinosuke agreed.

The four men sitting with Koroku looked bitter. Koroku seemed to have no outlet for his bad mood. "Takumi, Hannojo. What do you think?"

"About what?"

"This evening's embarrassment! Wasn't the name of the Hachisuka clan shamefully blackened?"

The four men withdrew into a deep silence. The night was sultry, with no hint of a breeze. The smoke from the mosquito-repellent incense drifted into their eyes.

Earlier that day, Koroku had received an invitation from an important Oda retainer to attend a tea ceremony. He had never had a taste for such things, but the guests would all be prominent people in Owari, and it would be a good chance to meet them. If he had turned down the invitation, he would have been ridiculed. People would have said, "How pretentious they are, putting on airs. Why, he's nothing more than the leader of a gang of *ronin*. He was probably afraid to show his ignorance of the tea ceremony."

Koroku and four of his followers had gone to the affair in a very dignified manner. During the tea ceremony, an *akae* water pitcher had caught the eye of one of the guests, and in the course of the conversation, a comment had slipped carelessly from his lips.

"How odd," he said. "I'm sure I've seen this pitcher at the house of Sutejiro, the pottery merchant. Isn't it the famous piece of *akae* ware that was stolen by bandits?"

The host, who was inordinately fond of the pitcher, was naturally shocked. "That's absurd! I only recently bought this from a shop in Sakai for nearly one thousand pieces of gold!" He even went so far as to show a receipt.

"Well," the guest persisted, "the thieves must have sold it to a Sakai dealer, and through one transaction after another it finally came to your honored house. The man who broke into the pottery merchant's house was Watanabe Tenzo of Mikuriya. There is no doubt about that."

A chill went through the assembled guests. Clearly the man who spoke so freely knew nothing about the family tree of his fellow guest, Hachisuka Koroku. But the master of the house and quite a number of the other guests were well aware that Watanabe Tenzo was Koroku's nephew and one of his chief allies. Before he left that day, Koroku swore to investigate the matter fully. Koroku had felt himself dishonored, and had returned home angry and ashamed. None of his dejected kinsmen could come up with a plan. If it had been a matter involving their own families or retainers, they could have dealt with it, but the incident revolved around Tenzo, who was Koroku's nephew. Tenzo's household in Mikuriya was an offshoot of this one in Hachisuka, and he always had twenty to thirty *ronin* in residence.

Koroku was even angrier because he was related to Tenzo. "This is outrageous," he growled, feeling contempt for Tenzo's evil ways. "I've been stupid, ignoring Tenzo's recent behavior. He's taken to dressing up in fine clothes and keeping a number of women. He's brought the family name into disrepute. We'll have to get rid of him. As it is, the Hachisuka clan will be seen to be no different from a band of thieves or a bunch of shameless *ronin*. A sad state of affairs for a family that is usually regarded as one of the leading provincial clans. Even I, Hachisuka Koroku, hear in public that I am the leader of bandits."

Hannojo and Oinosuke looked down at the ground, embarrassed at suddenly seeing tears of grief in Koroku's eyes.

"Listen, all of you!" Koroku looked directly at his men. "The roof tiles of this mansion bear the crest of the *manji* cross. Although it is now covered with moss, the crest has been passed down from the time of my distant ancestor, Lord Minamoto Yorimasa, to whom it was awarded by Prince Takakura for raising an army loyal to him. Our family once served the shoguns, but from the time of Hachisuka Taro, we lost our influence. So now we are merely another provincial clan. Surely we're not going to rot away in the country and do nothing about it. No, I, Hachisuka Koroku, have vowed that the time has come! I have been waiting for the day when I might restore our family name and show the world a thing or two."

"This is what you've always said."

"I have told you before that you must think before you act, and protect the weak. My nephew's character has not improved. He has broken into the house of a merchant and done the work of a thief in the night." Chewing his lip, Koroku realized that the matter had to be settled. "Oinosuke, Shinshichi. The two of you will go to Mikuriya, tonight. Bring Tenzo here but don't tell him the reason. He has a number of armed men with him. He's not a man, as they say, to let himself be captured with a single length of rope."

The following dawn came amid the chirping of birds in the forested hills. One house among the fortifications caught the morning sun early.

"Matsu, Matsu!"

Matsunami, Koroku's wife, peeked into the bedroom. Koroku was awake, lying on his side under the mosquito netting.

"Have the men I sent to Mikuriya last night returned yet?"

"No, not yet."

"Hm," Koroku grunted, a concerned look on his face. Although his nephew was a villain who did nothing but evil, he had a sharp mind. If this turned ugly, would he sense it and try to escape? They're rather late, he thought again.

His wife untied the mosquito netting. Their son, Kameichi, who was playing at the edge of the net, was not quite two years old.

"Hey! Come here." Koroku embraced the child and held him at arm's length. As plump as the children in Chinese paintings, the boy felt heavy, even in his father's arms.

"What's the matter? Your eyelids are red and swollen." Koroku licked at Kameichi's eyes. The boy, turning restive, pulled and scratched at his father's face.

"He must have been eaten up by the mosquitoes," his mother replied.

"If it's just mosquitoes, it's nothing to worry about."

"He frets so, even when he's asleep. He keeps slipping out from under the net."

"Don't let him get cold when he's asleep."

"Of course I won't."

"And be careful of smallpox."

"Don't even talk about it."

"He's our first child. You might say he's the prize of our first campaign."

Koroku was young and sturdy. He shook off the pleasure of the moment and strode out of the room, like a man who had some great purpose to achieve. He was not one to sit indoors and peacefully sip his morning tea. When he had changed his clothes and washed his face, he went into the garden, walking with great strides toward the sound of hammering.

Along one side of the narrow path were two small smithies that had been built in an area where huge trees had been fairly recently cut down. This was the middle of a forest where no ax, until now, had touched a tree since the days of Koroku's forefathers.

The gunsmith, Kuniyoshi, whom Koroku had secretly summoned from the city of Sakai, was at work with his apprentices.

"How's it going?" he asked. Kuniyoshi and his men prostrated themselves on the dirt floor. "No luck yet, eh? Are you still unable to copy the firearm you're using as a model?"

"We've tried this and we've tried that. We've gone without sleep and food, but…"

Koroku nodded. Just then a low-ranking retainer came up to him and said, "My lord, the two men you sent to Mikuriya have just come back."

"Have they, now?"

"Yes, my lord."

"Did they bring Tenzo back with them?"

"Yes, my lord."

"Good!" Koroku nodded approvingly. "Have him wait."

"Inside?"

"Yes. I'll be there soon."

Koroku was an able strategist—the clan depended on him for it—but there was another side to his character: a tendency to be softhearted. He could be stern, but he could
be moved by tears, especially where his own flesh and blood were concerned. He had
made up his mind, though: he must do away with his nephew this morning. But he
seemed to hesitate, and stayed for quite some time watching Kuniyoshi work.

"It's only natural," he said. "After all, firearms just arrived here seven or eight years
ago. Since then, samurai clans in all the provinces have vied with each other to produce
guns or buy them from the ships of the European barbarians. Here in Owari we have a
tactical advantage. There must be many country samurai in the north and east who have
never even seen firearms. You haven't made one before, either, so take your time and
work carefully by trial and error. If you can make one, you can make a hundred, and we'll
have them on hand for later."

"My lord!" The retainer came back and knelt on the dew-covered ground. "They're
waiting for you."

Koroku turned to him. "I'll be there soon. They can wait a bit longer."

While Koroku was determined to make the costly sacrifice of punishing his nephew
for justice' sake, he was torn by a conflict between his sense of what was right and his
own feelings. As he was about to leave, he spoke to Kuniyoshi again, "Within the year
you'll be able to make ten or twenty serviceable firearms, won't you?"

"Yes," said the smith, who, conscious of his responsibility, had a serious expression on
his sooty face. "If I can make one that I feel is right, I can make forty or even a hundred."

"It's the first one that's difficult, eh?"

"You spend so much money on me."

"Don't worry about it."

"Thank you, my lord."

"I don't suppose the fighting will let up next year, the year after that, or in the years
following.... When the grasses on this earth all wither, and the buds begin to sprout
again—well, do the best you can to finish it quickly."

"I'll put everything I have into it."

"Remember, it's to be done in secret."

"Yes, my lord."

"The sound of the hammer is a little too loud. Can you work so it won't be heard
outside the moat?"

"I'll be careful about that, too."

On his way out of the smithy, Koroku saw a gun propped next to the bellows. "And
that?" he asked, pointing to it. "Is it the model, or one that you've made?"

"It's brand-new."

"Well, let me see it."

"I'm afraid it's not quite ready for your inspection yet."

"Never mind. I have a good target for it. Will it fire?"

"The ball flies out, but no matter what I do, I can't make the mechanism engage as it
does in the original. I'll try harder to make something that will work."

"Testing is also an important job. Let me have it."

Taking it from Kuniyoshi's hands, Koroku rested the barrel of the gun on his crooked elbow and made as if aiming it at a target. Just then, Inada Oinosuke appeared at the door of the smithy.

"Oh, you haven't finished yet."

Koroku turned toward Oinosuke with the butt of the gun pressed against his ribs. "Well?"

"I think you should come quickly. We were able to talk Tenzo into coming along with us, but he seems to think it strange and acts nervous. If things go wrong, he may turn into the tiger breaking out of his cage, as the proverb goes."

"Very well, I'm coming."

Handing the gun to Oinosuke, Koroku walked with long strides down the path through the forest.

Watanabe Tenzo sat just outside the study wondering what was going on. What kind of emergency had caused him to be summoned here? Aoyama Shinshichi, Nagai Hannojo, Matsubara Takumi, and Inada Oinosuke—the trusted retainers of the Hachisuka clan—all sat next to him, carefully observing his every movement. Tenzo had begun to feel uneasy as soon as he had arrived. He was thinking of making up some excuse and leaving when he caught sight of Koroku in the garden.

"Ah, Uncle." Tenzo's greeting was accompanied by a forced smile.

Koroku looked impassively at his nephew. Oinosuke rested the butt of the gun on the ground.

"Tenzo, come out into the garden, won't you?" he said. His appearance was no different from normal. Tenzo was a little reassured.

"They told me to come quickly, said there was some urgent business to take care of."

"That's right."

"What sort of business?"

"Well, come over here."

Tenzo put on a pair of straw sandals and went out into the garden. Hannojo and Takumi went with him.

"Stand there," Koroku commanded, sitting down on a large rock and raising the gun. Tenzo realized in an instant that his uncle was going to take aim at him, but there was nothing he could do. The other men stood around him, as inert as stones on a *go* board. The leader of the bandits of Mikuriya had been placed in check. His face went livid. Invisible flames of anger radiated from Koroku. The look on his face told Tenzo that words would be useless.

"Tenzo!"

"Yes?"

"Surely you haven't forgotten the things I've told you over and over again?"

"I keep them firmly in my mind."

"You were born a human being in a world in chaos. The most shameful things are vanity in clothing, vanity in eating, and oppressing ordinary, peaceable people. The so-called great provincial clans do these things, and so do the *ronin*. The family of Hachisuka Koroku is not like them, and I believe I've already cautioned you about this."

"Yes, you have."

"Our family alone has pledged to harbor great hopes and fulfill them. We have vowed not to oppress the farmers, not to act like thieves, and if we become the rulers of a province, to see to it that prosperity is shared by all."

"Yes, we have."

"Who has broken this pledge?" Koroku asked. Tenzo was mute. "Tenzo! You have abused the military strength I have entrusted to you. You have put it to evil use, doing the work of a thief in the night. It was you who broke into the pottery shop in Shinkawa and stole the *akae* pitcher, wasn't it?"

Tenzo looked as if he was about to make a break for it.

Koroku stood up and thundered, "You swine! Sit down! Do you want to run away?"

"I...I won't run." His voice quavered. He slumped down on the grass and sat as though fastened to the ground.

"Tie him up!" Koroku barked to his retainers. Matsubara Takumi and Aoyama Shinshichi were instantly on Tenzo. They twisted his hands behind his back and tied them with his sword knot. When Tenzo clearly understood that his crime had been exposed and that he was in danger, his pale face became a little more resolute and defiant.

"U-u-uncle, what are you going to do with me? I know you're my uncle, but this is beyond reason."

"Shut up!"

"I swear, I don't remember doing what you're talking about."

"Shut up!"

"Who told you such a thing?"

"Are you going to be quiet or not?"

"Uncle...you are my uncle, aren't you? If there was such a rumor going around, couldn't you have asked me about it?"

"Never mind the cowardly excuses."

"But for the head of a large clan to act on rumors without investigating them..."

Needless to say, this whining was repugnant to Koroku. He raised the gun and rested it in the crook of his elbow.

"You scum. You're just the living target I need to try out this new weapon that Kuni-yoshi's just made for me. You two, take him over to the fence and tie him to a tree."

Shinshichi and Takumi gave Tenzo a shove and grabbed him by the scruff of the neck. They marched him all the way to the far end of the garden, which was far enough away that a poor archer would not be able to shoot an arrow the entire distance.

"Uncle! I have something to say. Hear me out, just once!" Tenzo yelled. His voice, and the despair in it, were plain for all to hear. Koroku ignored him. Oinosuke had brought a fuse. Koroku took it and, after loading a ball into the musket, took aim at his frantically screaming nephew.

"I did wrong! I confess! Please hear me out!"

As unimpressed as their lord, the men stood silently, braced themselves, and watched. After several minutes, Tenzo fell silent. His head hung down. Perhaps he was contemplating death. Or maybe he was a broken man.

"It's no good!" Koroku murmured. He took his eyes from the target. "Even when I pull the trigger, the ball does not come out. Oinosuke, run over to the smithy and get Kuniyoshi."

When the smith came, Koroku held out the gun to him, saying, "I tried to fire just now, but it doesn't work. Fix it."

Kuniyoshi examined the musket. "It cannot be repaired easily, my lord," he said.

"How long will it take?"

"Maybe I can do it by this evening."

"Can't you do it sooner than that? The living target I'm going to try it out on is waiting."

Only then did the blacksmith realize that Tenzo was meant to be the target. "Your... your nephew?" he stammered.

Koroku ignored the remark. "You're a gunsmith now. It would be good if you put your energy into making a gun. If you could finish it even one day earlier than planned, that would be good. Tenzo's an evil man, but he is a relative, and instead of dying a dog's death, he'll have made a contribution if he's put to some use in trying out a gun. Now get on with your job."

"Yes, my lord."

"What are you waiting for?" Koroku's eyes were like signal fires. Even without looking up, Kuniyoshi felt their heat. He took the gun and scurried off to the smithy.

"Takumi, give some water to our living target," Koroku ordered. "Have at least three men stand guard over him until the gun is repaired." Then he went back to the main house to have breakfast.

Takumi, Oinosuke, and Shinshichi also left the garden. Nagai Hannojo was to return to his own home that day, and he soon announced his departure. At about the same time, Matsubara Takumi left on an errand, so only Inada Oinosuke and Aoyama Shinshichi remained in the residence on the hill.

The sun climbed higher. It got hotter. The cicadas droned, and the only living creatures moving in the broiling heat were ants crawling over the baked paving stones in the garden. The furious sound of hammering erupted spasmodically from the smithy. How must it have sounded to Tenzo's ears?

"Isn't the gun ready yet?" Each time the stern voice came from Koroku's room, Aoyama Shinshichi ran to the smithy through the scorching heat. He would come back to the veranda each time, saying, "It'll take a little longer," and then report on how the work was progressing.

Koroku napped fitfully, his arms and legs outstretched. Shinshichi, too, tired from the previous day's excitement, finally dozed off.

They were roused by the voice of one of the guards shouting, "He's escaped!"

"Master Shinshichi! He's escaped! Come quickly!"

Shinshichi ran out into the garden barefoot.

"The master's nephew has killed two guards and run away!" The man's face was exactly the color of clay.

Shinshichi ran along with the guard, shouting back over his shoulder, "Tenzo's killed two guards and escaped!"

"What?" shouted Koroku, suddenly awakened from his nap. The chirping of the cicadas went on uninterrupted. Almost in a single motion, he jumped to his feet and put on the sword that was always by his side when he slept. Bounding off the veranda, he soon caught up with Shinshichi and the guard.

When they got to the tree, Tenzo was nowhere to be seen. At the base of the tree lay a single piece of unknotted hemp rope. About ten paces away, a corpse lay facedown. They found the other guard propped against the foot of the wall, his head split open like a ripe pomegranate. The two bodies were drenched with blood, looking as though someone had splashed it all over them. The heat of the day had soon dried the blood on the grass, blackening it to the color of lacquer; the smell had attracted swarms of flies.

"Guard!"

"Yes, my lord." The man threw himself at Koroku's feet.

"Tenzo had both hands tied with his sword knot and was bound to the tree with a hemp rope. How did he manage to slip out of the rope? As far as I can see, it hasn't been cut."

"Yes, well…we untied it."

"Who?"

"One of the dead guards."

"Why was he untied? And with whose permission?"

"At first we didn't listen to him, but your nephew said he had to relieve himself. He said he couldn't stand it, and—"

"You fool!" Koroku roared at the guard, barely able to keep himself from stamping on the ground. "How could you fall for an old trick like that? You oaf!"

"Master, please forgive me. Your nephew told us you were a kind man at heart, and asked if we really believed you were going to kill your own nephew. He said he was being punished just to make an impression, and because you were conducting a full investigation, he would be forgiven by nightfall. Then he said that if we didn't listen to him, we were going to suffer for making him suffer so. Finally, one of them untied him and went with him and the other guard, so that he might relieve himself in the shade of those trees over there."

"Well?"

"Then I heard a scream. He killed both of them, and I ran to the house to tell you what happened."

"Which way did he go?"

"The last time I saw him, he had his hands on top of the wall, so I suppose he went over it. I think I heard something hitting the water in the moat."

"Shinshichi, run him down. Get men onto the road to the village right away." After giving these orders, he himself dashed off in the direction of the front gate with frightening energy.

Kuniyoshi, covered in sweat, was unaware of what had happened and heedless of the passage of time. Only the gun existed for him, nothing else. Sparks from the forge flew about him. At long last he had fashioned the part he needed from iron filings. Relieved at having done his job, he cradled the musket in his arms. Still, he was not fully confident that the ball would come flying out of the barrel. He pointed the empty gun at the wall and tested it. As he pulled the trigger, it gave a satisfying click.

Ah, it seems to be all right, he thought. But it would be a great embarrassment to hand it over to Koroku and have him find yet another defect. He rammed gunpowder and a ball into the barrel, filled the primer pan, pointed the muzzle at the ground, and fired. With a loud report, the ball dug a small crater into the ground.

I've done it!

Thinking of Koroku, he reloaded the gun and hurried from the hut and along the path through the dense trees that led to the garden.

"Hey, there!" cried a man barely visible in the shadow of a tree.

Kuniyoshi stopped. "Who is it?" he asked.

"It's me."

"Who?"

"Watanabe Tenzo."

"Eh? The master's nephew!"

"Don't look so surprised. Though I can understand why. This morning I was tied up to a tree, ready to be used to try out a gun. And now here I am."

"What happened?"

"That doesn't concern you. It's a matter between uncle and nephew. He gave me a good dressing down."

"He did, did he?"

"Listen, just now at Shirahata pond in the village, the farmers and some samurai from the neighborhood have gotten into a fight. My uncle, Oinosuke, Shinshichi, and their men went over there. I'm supposed to follow them right away. Were you able to finish the gun?"

"I was."

"Let me have it."

"Are those Lord Koroku's orders?"

"Yes. Give it to me. If the enemy escapes, we won't be able to try it out."

Tenzo snatched the gun from Kuniyoshi's hand and disappeared into the forest.

"This is odd," thought the blacksmith. He started after Tenzo, who was making his way through the trees along the outer wall. He saw him climb the wall and jump, landing just short of the other side of the moat. Up to his chest in the fetid water, he lost no time in splashing the rest of the way across like a wild animal.

"Ah! He's escaping! Help! Over here!" Kuniyoshi yelled as loud as he could from the top of the wall.

Tenzo crawled out of the water looking like a muddy rat and turned toward Kuniyoshi. He aimed the gun and fired.

The gun made a ghastly noise. Kuniyoshi's body tumbled from the earthen wall. Tenzo ran across the fields, bounding like a leopard in flight.

* * *

"Assemble!"

The notice was issued under the signature of the head of the clan, Hachisuka Koroku. By evening, the mansion was filled with samurai, both inside and outside the gate.

"A battle?"

"What do you suppose has happened?" they asked, excited by the prospect of fighting. Although they usually plowed their fields, sold silk cocoons, raised horses, and went to market just like ordinary farmers and merchants, fundamentally they were quite different from them. They gloried in their martial bloodlines and were discontented with their lot. If the opportunity presented itself, they would not hesitate to take up arms to challenge fate and create a storm. Men like these had been stalwarts of the clan for generations.

Oinosuke and Shinshichi stood outside the walls, giving directions.

"Go around to the garden."

"Don't make so much noise."

"Go through the main gate." The men were all armed with long battle swords; as members of a provincial clan, however, they were not in full armor, but wore only gauntlets and shin guards.

"We're going into battle," one man guessed.

The borders of the Hachisuka domain were not clearly defined. These men belonged to no castle, nor had they sworn allegiance to any lord. They had neither clear allies nor enemies. But now and again they would go to war when the clan's lands were invaded, or when it entered into alliances with the local lord; or when it hired its men out as mercenaries and agitators to the lords of distant provinces. Some clan leaders called their troops out for money, but Koroku had never been tempted by personal gain. The neighboring Oda recognized this, as did the Tokugawa of Mikawa and the Imagawa of Suruga. The Hachisuka was only one among several powerful provincial families, but it had prestige enough that no other clan threatened its lands.

Notice having been given, the entire clan appeared at once. Gathered together in the spacious garden, they looked up at their leader. He stood on a man-made hill, as silent as a stone statue, under the moon hanging in the twilight sky. His armor was of black leather, and he wore a long sword at his side. Although his equipment seemed light, there was no mistaking the dignity of the head of a warrior clan.

To the hushed assembly of almost two hundred men, Koroku announced that as of that day Watanabe Tenzo was no longer a member of their clan. After clearly setting forth the circumstances, he apologized for his own unworthiness. "Our current predicament comes from my own negligence. For running away, Tenzo must be punished with death. We will leave no stone unturned, no blade of grass unparted. If we allow him to live, the Hachisuka will bear the mark of thieves for a hundred years. For the sake of our honor, for our ancestors and for our descendants, we must hunt Tenzo down. Do not think of him as my nephew. He is a traitor!"

As he finished his speech, a scout returned at a dead run. "Tenzo and his men are in Mikuriya," he reported. "They expect an attack and are fortifying the village."

When they learned that their enemy was Watanabe Tenzo, the men seemed a little dispirited, but on hearing the circumstances, they rallied to restore the honor of the clan. With resolute step they descended on the armory, where there was an astonishing array of weapons. In the past, weapons and armor had often been abandoned in the field after every battle. Now, with no end in sight to the civil war, and the country plunged into darkness and instability, weapons had become highly prized possessions. They could be found in the house of any farmer, and, second only to foodstuffs, a spear or a sword could be sold for ready cash.

A considerable number of the weapons in the armory had been there almost since the clan was founded, and the store had increased rapidly in Koroku's time, but there were no firearms in it. The fact that Tenzo had run off with their only gun had made Koroku so furious that only action could quell his anger. He considered his nephew an animal—cutting him to pieces was too good for him. He vowed he would not take off his armor or sleep until he had Tenzo's head.

Koroku set out for Mikuriya at the head of his troops.

As they got close to the village the column halted. A scout was sent forward and came back to report that the redness in the night sky was caused by fires set by Tenzo and his men, who were plundering the village. When they moved on, they were met on the road by fleeing villagers carrying their children, the sick, and household goods, and leading their livestock. On meeting the men of Hachisuka, they became even more frightened.

Aoyama Shinshichi reassured them. "We have not come to plunder," he said. "We have come to punish of Watanabe Tenzo and his ruffians."

The villagers quieted down and gave vent to their resentment over Tenzo's atrocities. His crimes did not stop at stealing a pitcher from Sutejiro. Besides collecting the annual land tax for the lord of the province, he had made his own rules and collected a second tax, calling it "protection money" for the rice paddies and fields. He had taken over the dams in the lakes and rivers, and had charged what he called "water money." If anyone dared voice discontent, Tenzo sent men to ravage his fields and paddies. Also, by threatening to massacre entire households, he put a damper on any ideas about secretly informing the lord of the province. In any event, the lord was too preoccupied with military matters to be concerned about such details as law and order.

Tenzo and his confederates did what they liked: they gambled, they slaughtered and ate cows and chickens on the shrine grounds, they kept women, and they turned the shrine into an armory.

"What has Tenzo's gang been up to tonight?" Shinshichi asked.

The villagers all spoke at once. It turned out that the rogues had started by taking spears and halberds from the shrine. They were drinking *sake* and screaming about fighting to the death, when suddenly they began looting the houses and setting them on fire. Finally they regrouped and ran away with their weapons, food, and anything of value. It seemed that by making a lot of noise about fighting to the death, they hoped to put off any would-be pursuers.

Have I been outmaneuvered? Koroku wondered. He stamped on the ground and ordered the villagers to return to their homes. His men followed, and together they tried to get the fires under control. Koroku restored the desecrated shrine and, at dawn, bowed low in prayer.

"Although Tenzo represents only a branch of our family, his evil deeds have become the crimes of the entire Hachisuka clan. I ask forgiveness, and I swear that he will be punished by death, that these villagers will be put at ease, and that I will make rich offerings to the gods of this shrine."

While he prayed, his troops stood quietly on either side.

"Can this be the leader of a gang of bandits?" the villagers asked one another. They were confused and suspicious, as well they might be, for in the name of the Hachisuka, Watanabe Tenzo had committed many crimes. Since he was Koroku's nephew, they gave a collective shudder, assuming that because this man was Tenzo's chief, he was like him. Koroku, for his part, knew that if he did not have the gods and the people on his side, he was bound to fail.

At last the men sent after Tenzo came back. "Tenzo has a force of about seventy men," they reported. "Their tracks show that they went into the mountains at Higashi Kasugai and are fleeing toward the Mino road."

Koroku issued commands: "Half of you will return to guard Hachisuka. Half of the remainder will stay here to help the villagers and maintain public order. The rest will go with me."

Having divided his forces, he had no more than forty or fifty men to go after Tenzo. After going through Komaki and Kuboshiki, they caught up with a part of the band. Tenzo had put lookouts along various roads, and when they saw they were being followed, his men began taking a roundabout route. There were reports that they were going down from the Seto peak to the village of Asuke.

It was around noon of the fourth day after the burning of Mikuriya. It was hot. The roads were steep, and Tenzo's men had to keep their armor on. The band was obviously tired of running. Along the roads they had abandoned packs and horses, gradually lightening their load, and by the time they got to the ravine of the Dozuki River, they were famished, exhausted, and drenched with sweat. As they drank, Koroku's small force slid down both sides of the ravine in a pincer attack. Stones and boulders rained down on the fugitives, and the waters of the river soon ran red with blood. Some were run through; some were beaten to death; some were thrown into the river. These were men who ordinarily were on good terms, and the blood ties—uncle and nephew, cousin and cousin—cut across factional lines. It was an attack of the clan against itself, but it was unavoidable. They really were one body of men, and for that very reason the roots of evil had to be cut out.

Koroku, with his peerless courage, was covered with the fresh blood of his kinsmen. He called out to Tenzo to show himself, but with no success. Ten of his men had fallen, but for the other side it was almost a massacre. But Tenzo was not found among the dead. It seemed he had deserted his men and, traveling along mountain paths, had managed his escape.

The swine! thought Koroku, grinding his teeth. He's heading for Kai.

Koroku himself was standing on one of the peaks when out of nowhere came the report of a single shot, which echoed through the mountains. The sound of the gun seemed to mock him. Tears coursed down his cheeks. At that moment he reflected that he and his nephew—who was nothing more than evil incarnate—were, after all, of the same blood. His tears were tears of regret for his own unworthiness. Bitterly discouraged, he tried to think the problem through and realized the day was far off when he could rise from the status of the head of a clan and become the ruler of a province. He had to admit he was incapable of that. *If I don't even know how to control one of my own relatives....* Strength alone isn't enough, if one doesn't have a governing policy, or household discipline. Quite unexpectedly, a bitter smile shone through his tears. *That bastard has taught me something after all*, he realized. And he gave the order to withdraw.

The force, now numbering little more than thirty men, reformed and descended from the Dozuki ravine to Koromo. They bivouacked just outside the town and, the following day, sent a messenger to the castle town of Okazaki. They received permission to pass through, but because it was already late when they started off, it was close to midnight before they reached Okazaki. Along the highways leading toward home were branch and main castles and stockades closely crowded together. There were also strategic checkpoints where a group of armed men could not pass. The journey by road would take many days, so they decided to take a boat down the Yahagi River, and then from Ohama to Handa. From Tokoname, once again they would travel by boat across the open water and then up the Kanie River to Hachisuka.

When they got to the Yahagi River it was midnight, and there was not a boat to be seen. The current was swift and the river wide. Frustrated, Koroku and his men came to a halt under some trees. Various men gave their opinions:

"If there's no boat to go downriver, we could take a ferry across and go along the other bank."

"It's too late. Let's wait until morning."

What bothered Koroku most was that in order to camp here, they would have to go to Okazaki Castle to ask permission again.

"Look for a ferryboat," Koroku ordered. "If we can find just one and cross over to the other side, by dawn we'll have covered the distance a boat might have taken us downriver."

"But, sir, we haven't seen a ferryboat anywhere."

"Idiot! There's bound to be at least one boat around here. How else are people going to cross a river this size during the day? What's more, there should be scouting boats hidden among the reeds or in the high grass along the bank. Or boats to use if fighting disrupts the ferry service. Open your eyes and look!"

The men split into two groups, one going upstream, the other downstream.

"Ah. Here's one!" one man shouted from upstream, stopping in his tracks.

At a spot on the bank where the earth had been washed away during a flood, large purple willows with exposed roots stooped and bowed their branches over the water. The water was calm and dark, like a deep pool. A boat was tied up in the shadows under the trees.

"And it's usable."

The man jumped down and, planning to take the boat downstream, reached down to loosen the mooring rope wound around the roots of a willow. His hand stopped and he gazed fixedly into the boat, a small craft with a shallow draft, used for carrying baggage. It was close to falling apart, dank with slime, and listing dangerously. Nevertheless, it could be used for the crossing. What held the soldier's attention was a man fast asleep under a rotting rush mat, snoring soundly. He wore strange clothes. Both his sleeves and hem were short, and under his dirty white shirting he wore leggings and coverings for the backs of his hands. He had straw sandals on his bare feet. His age was somewhere between childhood and adulthood. He lay on his back under the open sky, the night dew on his eyebrows and eyelashes. He seemed to be at absolute peace with the world.

"Hey, you!" The soldier tried to awaken him, but when the man did not respond at all, he called to him again and tapped him lightly on the chest with the butt of his spear.

"Hey, you, wake up!"

Hiyoshi opened his eyes, grabbed the shaft of the spear with a shout, and stared back at the soldier.

The swirling water around the boat might almost have been a reflection of the state of Hiyoshi's life. On that frosty night in the first month of the previous year when he had taken leave of his mother and sister, he had told them he would be back when he became a great man. He had no desire to go from one job to another, apprenticing himself to merchants and artisans as he had done so far. What he wanted most was to serve a samurai. But his appearance was against him, and he had no evidence of his birth or lineage.

Kiyosu, Nagoya, Sumpu, Odawara—he had walked through all of them. He would sometimes screw up his courage and stand before the gate of a samurai residence, but all of his pleas were met with laughter and ridicule. Once he had even been chased away with a broom. His money was quickly running out, and he realized that the world was just as his aunt in Yabuyama had told him. Still, he refused to let go of his dream, believing his aspirations were reasonable. He was not ashamed to tell anyone of his ambitions, even if he had to sleep out in the open, on the grass, or, like tonight, with water for his bed. How to make his mother, whom he imagined to be the unhappiest person in the world, the happiest, was what drove him on. And how could he do something for his poor sister, who thought she could never marry?

He had his own desires as well. His stomach never felt full, no matter how much he ate. Seeing large mansions, he wanted to live in such places, and the sight of elegant samurai made him reflect on his own appearance; looking at beautiful women, he was overwhelmed by their perfume. Not that his priorities had changed. First came his mother's happiness. His own wants could be taken care of later. For the time being he took pleasure in wandering from place to place, ignoring his hunger, and learning new things—about the workings of the world, human passions, the customs of different areas. He tried to understand current events, compared the military strength of the different provinces, and studied the ways of farmers and townsfolk.

From the beginning of the civil wars to the end of the last century, many men had trained in the martial arts. It meant a life of hardship, and for a year and a half Hiyoshi had followed the Way of the Warrior. But he had not gone about with a long sword at his side, aiming to perfect his martial skills. In fact, with his little bit of money he had bought needles from a wholesaler and had become an itinerant peddler. He had walked as far as Kai and Hokuetsu, his sales pitch always on the tip of his tongue. "Need any needles? Here we have sewing needles from Kyoto. Won't you buy them? Needles for cotton, needles for silk. Sewing needles from Kyoto." His earnings were meager, barely enough to live on. He did not, however, become small-minded, as merchants are prone to do, seeing the world only in terms of their wares.

The Hojo clan of Odawara, the Takeda of Kai, the Imagawa of Suruga. Visiting the castle towns of the north, he sensed that the world was stirring, going through a great change. He came to the conclusion that the coming events would be different from the small battles that had, until now, been symptomatic of internal discord. There would be a great war and it would heal all the country's ills. And if it does, he thought as he walked around selling his wares, then even I....The world is getting tired of the decrepit Ashikaga regime. There's chaos all around and the world is waiting for those of us who are young.

Having traveled from the northern provinces to Kyoto and Omi, he had learned a little about life. He had crossed into Owari and arrived at Okazaki, hearing that a relative of his father lived in this castle town. He was not about to go to relatives or acquaintances to ask for food and clothing, but early that summer he had become weak and was suffering from a bad case of food poisoning. He also wanted to hear news of home.

He had walked for two days under the bright, scorching sun, but had been unable to find the man he was looking for. After eating a raw cucumber and drinking water from a well, he had felt a sharp pain in his gut. In the evening he had followed the bank of the Yahagi River until he found a boat. His stomach felt sore and rumbled. Perhaps because he had a slight fever, his mouth was dry and felt as though it was full of thorns. Even now, he thought of his mother, and she came to him in his dreams. Later he fell into a deeper sleep, and nothing—neither his mother nor the pain in his stomach nor heaven and earth—existed any longer. Until, that is, the soldier began rapping on his chest with the spear.

Hiyoshi's waking shout was disproportionate to the size of his body. He instinctively grabbed hold of the spear. In those days the chest was believed to be the location of the soul, like a shrine within the body.

"Hey, runt, get up!"

The soldier tried to pull back his spear. Hiyoshi held on to it and sat up.

"Get up? I *am* up."

The man, feeling the strength of Hiyoshi's grip on the spear, scowled and said, "Get out of the boat!"

"Get out?"

"Yes, now! We need the boat, so clear out. Get lost!"

Hiyoshi angrily sat down again. "What if I don't want to?"

"What?"

"What if I don't want to?"

"What do you mean?"

"I don't want to get out of the boat."

"You little bastard!"

"Who's the bastard? Waking a man from a deep sleep by tapping him with a spear, then telling him to get out and get lost?"

"Shit! You'd better watch how you talk. Who do you think I am?"

"A man."

"That's obvious."

"You're the one who asked."

"Your mouth works pretty well, doesn't it, for a little runt? In a second it may wrinkle up and shrink. We are men of the Hachisuka clan. Our leader is Hachisuka Koroku. We got here in the middle of the night, and we need a boat to cross the river."

"You can see the boat but not the man. Anyway, I'm using it!"

"I saw you and woke you up. Now get out of there and get lost."

"Annoying, aren't you?"

"Say that again?"

"As many times as you like. I don't want to get out. I'm not giving up this boat."

The man yanked on the shaft of the spear in an effort to pull Hiyoshi onto the bank. Choosing his moment, Hiyoshi let go. The spear sheared through the leaves of the willows, and the soldier tumbled over backwards. Reversing the spear, he thrust it point-first at Hiyoshi. Rotting planks, a bilge bucket, and the reed mat came flying out of the boat.

"Fool!" Hiyoshi mocked.

Other soldiers came running up.

"Stop! What's going on here?" one said.

"Who's this?" asked another.

They crowded together, making a lot of noise, and before long Koroku and the rest of his men were there.

"Did you find a boat?" Koroku asked.

"There's a boat here, but—"

Koroku quietly came to the front of the group. Hiyoshi, thinking that this must be the leader, sat up a little straighter, and looked Koroku straight in the face. Koroku's eyes were riveted on Hiyoshi. Neither spoke. Koroku did not notice Hiyoshi's strange appearance. He was too surprised by the way Hiyoshi looked straight into his eyes. He's bolder than he looks, Koroku thought. The longer they stared at each other, the more Hiyoshi's eyes were like those of a nocturnal animal, shining out of the darkness. Finally, Koroku looked away.

"A child," he said calmly.

Hiyoshi did not respond. His eyes, like an archer's arrows, were still aimed straight at Koroku's face.

"He's a child," Koroku repeated.

"You talking about me?" Hiyoshi asked sullenly.

"Of course. Is there anyone else besides you down there?"

Hiyoshi squared his shoulders a little. "I'm not a child. I've had my coming-of-age ceremony."

"Is that so?" Koroku's shoulders shook with laughter. "If you're an adult, I'll treat you like one."

"Now that you've got me—one man—surrounded by a large group, what are you going to do with me? I suppose you're *ronin*."

"You're very funny."

"Not funny at all. I was soundly asleep. Besides, I've got a stomachache. Anyway, I don't care who you are. I don't want to move."

"Hm, your stomach hurts?"

"Yes."

"What's seems to be the matter?"

"Food poisoning, maybe, or heatstroke."

"Where are you from?"

"Nakamura in Owari."

"Nakamura? Well, well. What's your family name?"

"I won't tell you my family name, but my given name is Hiyoshi. But wait a minute, what is this, waking a person from his sleep and asking about his parentage? Where are you from and what is your lineage?"

"Like you, I'm from Owari, the village of Hachisuka in Kaito district. My name is Hachisuka Koroku. I didn't know there were people like you so close to our village. What sort of work do you do?"

Instead of answering, Hiyoshi said, "Ah, you're from Kaito district? That's not far from my village." He suddenly became more friendly. Here was his chance to ask for news about Nakamura. "Well, seeing we're from the same district, I'll change my mind. You can have the boat."

He took the bundle of merchandise he'd been using as a pillow, slung it over his shoulder, and climbed up onto the bank. Koroku silently watched his every movement. He noticed first the air of a street vendor and the offhand retorts of an adolescent who had traveled here and there all by himself. Hiyoshi resigned himself, sighed, and started to leave with a heavy heart.

"Wait, Hiyoshi. Where are you going from here?"

"My boat's been taken, so I have no place to sleep. If I sleep in the grass, I'll get damp from the dew, and my stomach will hurt more. There's nothing else I can do. I'll walk around until dawn."

"If you like, come with me."

"Where to?"

"Hachisuka. Stay at my place. We'll feed you and look after you until you're cured."

"Thank you." Hiyoshi made a meek little bow. Looking at his own feet, he seemed to be thinking of what to do next. "Does that mean you'll let me live there and work for you?" he asked.

"I like your manner. You've got promise. If you want to serve me, I'll employ you."

"I don't." He said this very clearly, his head held high. "Because my aim is to serve a samurai, I've gone around comparing the samurai and provincial lords of various provinces. I've decided that the most important thing in serving a samurai is choosing the right one. One does not choose one's master lightly."

"Ha, ha! This is getting more and more interesting. Am I, Koroku, not good enough to be your master?"

"I wouldn't know about that until you hired me, but the Hachisuka clan is not well spoken of in my village. And the master of the house I served in before was robbed by a man said to be a member of the Hachisuka clan. It would pain my mother if I worked for a thief, so I can't go to the house of such a person and serve him."

"Well, I guess you worked for the pottery merchant Sutejiro."

"How did you know?"

"Watanabe Tenzo was a member of the Hachisuka clan. But I myself have disowned the scoundrel. He escaped, but we have defeated his band and are now on our way back home. Has the name of the Hachisuka been slandered even as far as your ears?"

"Hm. You don't seem to be like him," Hiyoshi said this very frankly, looking right at Koroku. Then, as though he had suddenly remembered something, he said, "Well, sir, without any sort of obligation, will you take me as far as Hachisuka? I'd like to go to my relative's house in Futatsudera."

"Futatsudera is right next to Hachisuka. Who do you know there?"

"The cooper Shinzaemon is related to my mother's side of the family."

"Shinzaemon is of samurai stock. Well then, your mother too must be a descendant of samurai."

"I may be a peddler now, but my father was a samurai."

The men had boarded the boat and fixed the pole in place, and were waiting for Koroku to get on board. Koroku put his arm around Hiyoshi's shoulders and they got on the boat.

"Hiyoshi, if you want to go to Futatsudera, go to Futatsudera. If you want to stay in Hachisuka, that'll be all right too."

Being small, Hiyoshi was hidden among the men and their spears, which stood like a forest of trees. The boat cut across the wide river, but the current was swift, and the crossing took time. Hiyoshi got bored. Suddenly he saw a firefly on the back of one of Koroku's soldiers. Cupping his hands, he caught it and watched its light flash on and off.

THE MOUNTAIN OF THE GOLDEN FLOWER

Even when he had returned to Hachisuka, Koroku was not about to let Tenzo get away unpunished. He had sent assassins after him and had written to clans in distant provinces to ask his whereabouts. Autumn came, and he still had nothing to show for his efforts. Rumor had it that Tenzo had found refuge with the Takeda clan of Kai. He had presented them with the stolen gun and had entered their service as one of the army of spies and agitators working for the province.

"If he's reached Kai…" Koroku muttered bitterly, but for the time being he could do nothing but resign himself to waiting.

Soon after, he was visited by a messenger from the retainer of the Oda clan who had invited him to the tea ceremony. The man brought with him the *akae* water pitcher.

"We know that this has been the cause of considerable trouble in your family. Although we bought this famous piece in good faith, we feel that we can no longer keep it. We believe that if you return it to the pottery shop, you will restore the honor of your name."

Koroku took the pitcher, promising he would pay a return visit. In the end he did not go in person, but sent a messenger with gifts: a splendid saddle and gold worth twice as much as the pitcher. That same day he summoned Matsubara Takumi and told him to get ready to go on a short trip. Then he went out onto the veranda.

"Monkey!" he called.

Hiyoshi came skipping out from the trees and knelt before Koroku. He had first gone to Futatsudera, but he had come back directly to Hachisuka and settled into his new life. He was quick-witted and would do anything. People made jokes at his expense, but he refrained from doing the same. He was talkative but never insincere. Koroku put him to work in the garden and became quite fond of him. Although Hiyoshi was a servant, he did more than just sweep the grounds. His work kept him close to Koroku, so he was under his master's eye day and night. After sunset he became a guard. Naturally, this kind of assignment was only given to the most trusted men.

"You're to go with Takumi and show him the way to the pottery shop in Shinkawa."

"To Shinkawa?"

"What are you making such a long face for?"

"But—"

"I can see you don't want to go, but Takumi is to return the water pitcher to its rightful owner. I thought it would be a good idea if you went along too."

Hiyoshi prostrated himself and touched his forehead to the ground.

Since he had come along as an attendant, when they arrived at Sutejiro's Hiyoshi waited outside. Not knowing what to make of this, his former co-workers came up and stared. He himself seemed to have completely forgotten that some of them had laughed at him and beaten him before he had been sent home. Smiling at everyone, he squatted in the sunshine, waiting for Takumi. Presently, Takumi came out of the house.

The unexpected return of the stolen pitcher made Sutejiro and his wife so happy they were not sure they weren't dreaming. They hastened to arrange their visitor's sandals so he could slip them on easily, then hurried on ahead of him to the gate, where they bowed repeatedly. Ofuku, too, was there, and he was startled to see Hiyoshi.

"We'll try to find the time to come to Hachisuka and pay our respects in person," said Sutejiro. "Please give His Lordship our very best regards. Thank you again for taking the trouble to come all this way." Husband, wife, Ofuku, and all the employees bowed low. Hiyoshi followed Takumi out and waved to them as he left.

As they walked past the Komyo hills, he wondered sadly, How's my aunt in Yabuyama? And my poor sick uncle? He may be dead already. They were close to Nakamura, and naturally he thought of his mother and sister. He would have liked nothing better than to run over for a moment and see them, but the vow he had made on that frosty night stopped him. He still had done nothing to make his mother happy. As he turned reluctantly away from Nakamura, he met a man in the uniform of a foot soldier.

"Say, aren't you Yaemon's son?"

"And who are you, may I ask?"

"You're Hiyoshi, aren't you?"

"Yes."

"My, you've gotten big! My name is Otowaka. I was a friend of your father. We served in the same regiment under Lord Oda Nobuhide."

"I remember you now! Have I really gotten that big?"

"Ah, I wish your poor dead father could see you now."

Tears came to Hiyoshi's eyes. "Have you seen my mother lately?" he asked.

"I haven't been to the house, but I go to Nakamura from time to time and hear news. She seems to be working as hard as usual."

"She's not sick, is she?"

"Why don't you go see for yourself?"

"I can't go home until I become a great man."

"Just go and show your face. She's your mother, after all."

Hiyoshi wanted to cry. He looked away. When he felt all right again, Otowaka was already walking away in the opposite direction. Takumi had moved on, and was some distance ahead.

* * *

The lingering summer heat had finally faded; the mornings and evenings felt like autumn, and the leaves of the taro plants were lush and full-grown.

"This moat hasn't been dredged for five years at least," Hiyoshi muttered. "We're forever practicing horsemanship and learning spear techniques, and we let mud pile up at our very feet! That's no good." Having returned from the bamboo cutter's house, he was inspecting the mansion's old moat. "What's a moat for, anyway? I'll have to bring this the master's attention."

Hiyoshi tested the depth of the water with a bamboo pole. The surface of the water was covered by water plants, so no one took much notice; but because fallen leaves and mud had accumulated over the years, the moat was not really very deep anymore. After testing the depth in two or three places, he threw away the pole. He was about to cross the bridge to the side gate when someone called out, "Master Half-pint." This was not a reference to his height, but the customary way to address a servant of a provincial clan.

"Who are you?" Hiyoshi asked of a hungry-looking man sitting under an oak tree, hugging his knees. He wore a dirty gray kimono with a bamboo flute stuck in the sash.

"Come here a moment." The man waved him over. He was a *komuso*, one of the mendicant flute-playing monks who came to the village now and then. Like the rest, this one was dirty and unshaven, and carried a bamboo flute in a reed mat slung over his shoulder. Some of them went from village to village like Zen monks, attracting people's attention by ringing a hand bell.

"Alms for a monk? Or are you too busy thinking of your next meal?"

"No." Hiyoshi was about to make fun of him, but knowing how tough the life of a traveler could be, he offered instead to bring him food if he was hungry and medicine if he was sick.

Shaking his head, the man looked up at Hiyoshi and laughed. "Well, won't you sit down?"

"I prefer to stand, thanks. What's on your mind?"

"Are you in service here?"

"Not really." Hiyoshi shook his head. "I get my meals but I'm not a member of the household."

"Hm … Do you work in the back, or in the main house?"

"I sweep the garden."

"A guard of the inner garden, eh? You must be one of Master Koroku's favorites?"

"I wouldn't know."

"Is he at home now?"

"He's out."

"That's a shame," the monk mumbled. He looked disappointed. "Will he be back today?"

Hiyoshi thought there was something suspicious about the man and he hesitated, thinking it best to choose his answers carefully.

"Is he coming back?" the man asked again.

Hiyoshi said, "I'll bet you're a samurai. If you're nothing but a monk, you must be a real novice."

Startled, the man stared intently at Hiyoshi. At length he asked, "Why do you think I'm either a samurai or a novice?"

Hiyoshi answered casually, "It's obvious. Although your skin is tanned, the underside of your fingers are white, and your ears are fairly clean. As for proof that you're a samurai, you're sitting cross-legged on the mat, warrior-style, as if you were still wearing armor. A beggar or monk would bend his back and slump forward. Simple, isn't it?"

"Hm . . . you're right." The man got up off the mat without taking his eyes off Hiyoshi for even a second. "You have very keen eyes. I've gone through many border posts and checkpoints in enemy territory, and no one's caught on to me yet."

"There are as many fools as wise men in the world, wouldn't you say? Anyway, what do you want with my master?"

The man lowered his voice. "The truth is, I've come from Mino."

"Mino?"

"If you were to mention Namba Naiki, a retainer to Saito Dosan, Master Koroku would understand. I wanted to see him and leave quickly without anyone knowing, but if he's not here, there's nothing to be done. I'd better keep to the village during the day and come back this evening. If he returns, tell him what I said privately."

Naiki started to walk away. But Hiyoshi called him back, saying, "It was a lie."

"Huh?"

"That he's away. I said that because I didn't know who you were. He's at the riding grounds."

"Ah, so he *is* here."

"Yes. I'll take you to him."

"You're pretty sharp, aren't you?"

"In a military household, it's only natural to be cautious. Should I assume that the men in Mino are impressed by this sort of thing?"

"No, you should not!" Naiki said, annoyed.

Following the moat, they crossed the vegetable patch, and taking the path that went behind the wood, they came to the wide riding grounds.

The earth was dry, and dust rose into the sky. The men of Hachisuka were training hard. They were not just practicing riding. In one maneuver, they drew up stirrup-to-stir-rup and exchanged blows with staves just as if they were fighting in a real battle.

"Wait here," Hiyoshi instructed Naiki.

Having observed the training session, Koroku wiped the sweat from his brow and went to the rest hut for a drink.

"Some hot water, sir?" Hiyoshi ladled out some hot water and diluted it a bit to cool it. He took the cup and, kneeling, placed it before Koroku's camp stool. Hiyoshi drew nearer and whispered, "A messenger has come from Mino in secret. Shall I bring him here? Or will you go to him?"

"From Mino?" Koroku immediately got up. "Monkey, lead the way. Just where did you leave him?"

"On the other side of the forest."

There was no official treaty between the Saito of Mino and the Hachisuka, but for many years they had been bound by a secret alliance to help one another in emergencies. In return, the Hachisuka received a handsome annual stipend from Mino.

Koroku was surrounded by powerful neighbors—the Oda of Owari, the Tokugawa of Mikawa, and the Imagawa of Suruga—but he had never sworn allegiance to any of them. He owed his independence to the watchful eyes of the lord of Inabayama Castle, Saito Dosan. Their territories being separated by some distance, the reason the Hachisuka and the Saito had entered into such an alliance was not clear.

One story was that Masatoshi, Koroku's predecessor, had rescued a man close to death in front of the Hachisuka mansion. He seemed to be a wandering swordsman following the rigorous discipline of the martial arts. Feeling sorry for him, Masatoshi had taken him in and given him the best medical care. After the man had recovered, Masatoshi had even given him some traveling money.

"I won't forget this," the man swore. On the day of his departure he pledged, "When I've made my fortune, I will send you word and repay you for your kindness." The name that he left with them was Matsunami Sokuro.

Several years later a letter had arrived, bearing the signature Lord Saito Dosan. To their surprise, it was from the man whom they had known as Sokuro. The alliance was an old one, passed on from one generation to the next. So, as soon as Koroku knew that the secret messenger was from Saito Dosan, he hurried out to meet him.

There in the shadows of the forest, the two men exchanged greetings, then, looking each other in the eye, each man raised his open palm to his chest, as if in prayer.

"I am Hachisuka Koroku."

"I am Namba Naiki of Inabayama."

As a young man, Dosan had studied Buddhism at Myokakuji Temple. This experience had led him to use the secret Buddhist terms and signs he had learned in temples and monasteries as passwords among his men.

Once they had finished these formalities and authenticated their identities, the two men felt more at their ease and talked freely. Koroku ordered Hiyoshi to stand guard and to let absolutely no one pass, and he and Naiki walked deeper into the forest. Whatever the two men talked about, or whatever secret documents Naiki might have brought with him, were, of course, not revealed to Hiyoshi, nor did he want to know. He stood faithfully at the edge of the forest, keeping watch. When he had a task to perform, he did it: if he was to sweep the garden, he swept it; if he was to stand guard, he stood guard. He did a thorough job, whatever it was. Unlike other men, he was able to find pleasure in any job that he was given, but this was not simply because he was born poor. Rather, he saw the work at hand as a preparation for the next task. He was convinced that this was the way he would one day realize his ambitions.

What do I have to do to become somebody in the world? This was a question he often asked himself. Some had pedigree and lineage, but not he. Others had money and power, but Hiyoshi did not have these, either. Well, how am I going to make my fortune?

The question depressed him because he was so short, and no healthier than the next man. He had no learning to speak of, and his intelligence was only average. What in the world did he have going for him? Faithfulness—that was all he could come up with. He wasn't going to be faithful in some things and not in others, he was determined to be faithful in all things. He would hold on to his faithfulness because he had nothing else to give.

All or nothing! That was how far he had to go. He would pursue any job to the end, just as though the gods themselves had given him a mission. Whether it was sweeping the garden, being a sandal bearer, or cleaning out the stables, he would put everything he had into it. For the sake of his ambitions, he resolved not to be idle now. To try to separate himself from the present was nonsense in terms of the future.

The small birds of the forest chirped and twittered above Hiyoshi's head. But he did not see the fruit in the trees at which the birds were pecking. When Koroku finally emerged from the forest, he was in high spirits. His eyes were fired by ambition. And his face, which would become strained when he heard about problems, was still flushed by some important news.

"Where is the monk?" asked Hiyoshi.

"He took another path out of the forest." Koroku looked hard at Hiyoshi and said, "Keep this to yourself."

"Of course, sir."

"By the way, Namba Naiki praised you to the skies."

"Really?"

"Someday I'm going to promote you. I hope you decide to stay with us forever!"

Night fell, and the principal members of the clan met in Koroku's residence. The secret council lasted into the small hours. That night, too, Hiyoshi stood beneath the stars in the role of faithful guard.

The strictest secrecy was maintained about the contents of the message from Saito Dosan, the substance being revealed only to the key men. But in the days following the nighttime council, several of Koroku's retainers began to disappear from Hachisuka. They were a select group, the ablest and shrewdest, and they left the village in disguise—bound for Inabayama, it was whispered.

Koroku's younger brother, Shichinai, was one of those chosen to go undercover in Inabayama. Hiyoshi was ordered to accompany him.

"Are we going on a scouting mission? Is there going to be a battle?" he asked.

"Never mind," was the curt reply. "Just keep quiet and come along with me." Shichinai would say nothing more. Lower-ranking members of the household, even the kitchen workers, called him "Master Pockmark," but only behind his back. He made them feel ill at ease, and they detested him. He drank heavily, was arrogant, and had none of the warmheartedness of his elder brother. Hiyoshi quite frankly felt the man was disgusting, but he did not complain about the assignment. He had been chosen because Koroku trusted him. Hiyoshi had not yet asked to become a member of the clan, but he had agreed to follow orders faithfully. He was ready and willing to serve Shichinai—even this Master Pockmark—to the end, if need be.

On the day of their departure, Shichinai changed his appearance right down to the way he tied his hair. He would be traveling incognito, disguised as an oil merchant from

Kiyosu. Hiyoshi changed back into the itinerant needle peddler of the previous summer. The two of them were going to be chance traveling companions on the road to Mino.

"Monkey, when we come to the checkpoints, we'd better go through separately."

"All right."

"You're a blabbermouth, so try to keep your mouth shut, whatever they ask you."

"Yes, sir."

"If you give yourself away, I'll pretend I don't know you and leave you there."

There were many checkpoints along the road. Despite the close ties of kinship that should have made the Oda and the Saito allies, in reality they were exactly the opposite. As a result, both sides were particularly vigilant at their common border. But even when they had crossed into Mino proper, the atmosphere of suspicion did not dissipate, and Hiyoshi asked Shichinai why.

"You're always asking the obvious! Lord Saito Dosan and his son Yoshitatsu have been at odds for years." Shichinai did not seem to be surprised by the enmity between two factions within a single family. Hiyoshi was tempted to question Shichinai's intelligence. It was not as though examples were lacking, even in ancient times, of fathers and sons in the warrior class taking up arms against one another, but there had to be good reasons.

"Why is there a bad relationship between Lord Dosan and Lord Yoshitatsu?" Hiyoshi asked again.

"Don't be a nuisance! If you want to know, ask somebody else." Shichinai clucked his tongue and refused to say anything more. Before arriving in Mino, Hiyoshi had worried that he would be forced to do something against his better judgment.

Inabayama was a picturesque castle town nestling among small mountains. The autumn tints of Mount Inabayama were misty under a fine rain, but there was a hint of sunlight shining through. Autumn was deepening, and one could look at the mountain from morning till night and never tire of it. It looked as if the cliff had been covered with a golden brocade, a phenomenon that had given Inabayama its second name: the Mountain of the Golden Flower. It soared up from the Nagara River, a splendid backdrop for the town and fields, and Hiyoshi's eyes grew wide when he saw on its peak the white walls of the castle, small in the distance, crouching like a solitary white bird.

The only way up from the town below was by a tortuous path, and the castle had a plentiful supply of water. Hiyoshi was impressed. It was the kind of stronghold that was difficult to attack and unlikely to fall. Then he reminded himself that a province was not held by castles alone.

Shichinai took a room in a merchants' inn on a street in the prosperous part of town. He gave Hiyoshi only a little money and told him to stay at one of the cheap lodging houses in the back streets.

"After a while I'll give you your orders," he said. "People are going to be suspicious if you're idle, so until I'm ready for you, go out every day with your needles."

Hiyoshi gave a respectful bow, took the money, and did as he was told. The lodging house was not very clean, but he was more at ease being on his own. He still could not imagine what he was going to be ordered to do. There were many different kinds of travelers staying at the lodging house: actors, mirror polishers, and loggers. He was familiar with their unique smell and with the fleas and lice they boarded with.

Hiyoshi went out every day to sell needles, and on his return he brought back salted vegetables and rice, for everyone did his own cooking. The stoves were available to those who paid for the firewood. Seven days passed. Still no word from Shichinai. And wasn't Shichinai himself idle every day? Hiyoshi felt as though he had been abandoned.

Then one day, while Hiyoshi was walking down a side street in a residential area, plying his trade, a man with a leather quiver at his side and a couple of old bows on his shoulder came walking toward him, calling out in a voice far louder than Hiyoshi's, "Old bows repaired! Old bows repaired!"

When he got up close, the bow mender stopped, his eyes widening with surprise. "Why, it's Monkey, isn't it? When did you get here, and who are you with?"

Hiyoshi was no less surprised. The bow mender was Nitta Hikoju, another of Koroku's men.

"Master Hikoju, what are you doing mending bows in Inabayama?"

"Hm, I'm not the only one. There are at least thirty or forty of us. But I didn't expect to find you here."

"I came seven days ago with Master Shichinai, but all he told me to do was go out and sell my needles, so that's what I've been doing. What's it all about, anyway?"

"Don't you know yet?"

"He wouldn't tell me a thing. And there's nothing worse for a man than to have to do something without knowing why."

"Yes, I can imagine."

"Surely you know what's going on."

"If I didn't, would I be walking around mending bows?"

"Please, can't you tell me anything?"

"Hm, Shichinai's unkind. You go around without knowing why your life is at risk. But we can't stand and talk in the middle of the street."

"Our lives are in danger?"

"If you were caught, there'd be a risk of the plan being exposed, but for all our sakes, maybe I should explain so you'll have some idea of what it's all about."

"I'd appreciate that very much."

"But we're too conspicuous standing out here."

"How about behind that shrine?"

"Yeah, and I'm hungry. Why don't we have lunch?"

Hikoju walked ahead, and Hiyoshi followed. The shrine was surrounded by woods, and very quiet. They opened their lunches wrapped in bamboo leaves, and started to eat. The ginkgo leaves above them danced in the sunlight. As they looked through the bright yellow foliage, they saw Mount Inabayama clad in the flaming red leaves of departing autumn. The castle on the peak soared into the blue sky above: the pride of the Saito clan and the symbol of its power.

"That is our objective." Hikoju pointed at Inabayama Castle with his chopsticks, their tips sticky with rice. They were both looking at the same castle, but each saw it quite differently. Hiyoshi's mouth fell open as he stared blankly at the tips of the chopsticks.

"Are the Hachisuka going to storm the castle?"

"Don't be stupid!" Hikoju snapped his chopsticks in two and threw them on the ground. "Lord Dosan's son, Yoshitatsu, holds the castle, and from there he controls the neighborhood and the roads to Kyoto and the east. Within its walls he drills his troops and stores new weapons. The Oda, Imagawa, and Hojo are no match for him. So what could the Hachisuka do? Don't ask such stupid questions. I was going to let you in on our plans, but now I don't know whether I should."

"I'm sorry. I won't say anything else." Scolded, Hiyoshi fell meekly silent.

"There isn't anybody around here, is there?" The bow mender looked around and then licked his lips. "I suppose you've heard about the alliance between our clan and Lord Dosan." Hiyoshi limited his reply to a nod. "Father and son have been at odds for years." Hikoju told Hiyoshi about the feud and the resulting chaos in Mino.

Dosan had once traveled under other names, one of which was Matsunami Sokuro. He was an experienced man: he had been an oil merchant, a wandering swordsman, and even a novice in a temple. Eventually he had risen from the lowly position of oil merchant and seized the province of Mino with his bare hands. To do this, he had killed his lord, Toki Masayori, and driven his heir, Yorinari, into exile. He had later taken one of Toki's concubines. There were countless stories about his brutality and the atrocities he had committed. If more proof were needed of his astuteness, once he had become master of Mino, he had not ceded a single inch of land to his enemies.

But the workings of fate are terrifying. Could it be that what happened next was divine retribution? He adopted Yoshitatsu, the son of his former lord's concubine. But he worried about whether the child was his own or Lord Toki's. As Yoshitatsu grew up, Dosan's doubts became stronger with each passing day.

Yoshitatsu was an imposing man, who stood over six feet tall. When he was made lord of Inabayama, his father moved into Sagiyama Castle, on the other side of the Nagara River. On opposite banks of the river, the destinies of father and son were in the lap of the gods. Yoshitatsu was in his prime and he ignored the man he assumed to be his father. The aging Dosan, ever more suspicious, cursed Yoshitatsu and finally disinherited him, with the idea of putting his second son, Magoshiro, in Yoshitatsu's place. Yoshitatsu, however, was quick to catch on to the plan.

But then Yoshitatsu contracted leprosy and became known as "the Leper Lord." He was a child of fate and eccentric, but also resourceful and brave. Yoshitatsu set up forts to guard against attack from Sagiyama, and never turned down an opportunity to fight. Determined to rid himself of this despicable "Leper Lord"—his own son—Dosan resigned himself to spill blood. Hikoju took a deep breath. "Dosan's retainers are, of course, well known hereabouts. We were asked to set fire to the castle town."

"Fire the town!"

"It wouldn't do any good just to suddenly set fires. Before doing that, we're to spread rumors, and when Yoshitatsu and his retainers at Inabayama are unsettled, we pick a windy night and turn the castle town into a sea of flame. Then Dosan's forces will cross the river and attack."

"I see." Hiyoshi nodded with a grown-up look. He showed neither admiration nor disapproval. "So we've been sent here to spread rumors and commit arson."

"Correct."

"So in the end, we're just agitators, aren't we? We're here to stir up the people."

"Well, yes, you could put it that way."

"Isn't being an agitator the work of the lowest outcasts?"

"There's nothing we can do about it. We Hachisuka have been dependent on Lord Dosan for many years now." Hikoju saw things very simply. Hiyoshi looked at him. A *ronin* was always a *ronin*, but he had trouble getting used to the idea. Although he got his rice from the table of a *ronin*, he considered his own life to be precious, and he did not intend to throw it away heedlessly.

"Why did Master Shichinai come?"

"He's here to direct operations. With thirty or forty men entering the area separately, you need someone to coordinate and supervise them."

"I see."

"So now you know what it's all about."

"Uh-huh. But there's one more thing I don't understand. What about me?"

"Hm. You?"

"What do you suppose I'll have to do? I've had no orders from Master Shichinai so far."

"Perhaps because you're small and agile, you'll be given the job of setting the fires on the night when there's a wind."

"I see. An arsonist."

"Since we've come to this town on secret orders, we can't afford to be careless. When we pose as bow menders and needle sellers we have to be careful and watch what we say."

"If they learn about our plan, will they start looking for us right away?"

"Of course. If Yoshitatsu's samurai get even a hint of our plans, there'll be a massacre. If we're caught, it'll be horrible, whether it's just you or all of us." At first, Hikoju had thought it too bad that Hiyoshi knew nothing; now he seemed suddenly uneasy about the possibility that the secret might leak from Monkey's mouth. Hiyoshi read this in his face. "Don't worry. I've gotten used to this sort of thing in my travels."

"You won't let anything slip?" Hikoju asked tensely. "This is enemy territory, you know."

"I know."

"Well, we should avoid looking suspicious." His back had gotten stiff, and he slapped it two or three times as he stood up. "Monkey, where are you staying?"

"In the alley just behind the inn where Master Shichinai has a room."

"Is that so? Well, I'll drop by there one of these nights. Be especially careful around the other lodgers." Shouldering his bows, Nitta Hikoju headed off in the direction of the town.

Sitting in the shrine grounds, Hiyoshi gazed at the faraway white walls of the castle above the ginkgo trees. Now that he knew more about the conflict within the Saito family and the evil it had bred, neither the ironlike walls nor the commanding position of the escarpment seemed to have any power at all in his eyes. Who will be the next lord of the castle? he wondered. Dosan won't come to a happy end, either, that's for sure. What kind of strength can there be in a land where master and retainers are enemies? How can the people have confidence when the lords of the province, father and son, distrust and plot against each other?

Mino was a fertile area backed by mountains, at a major crossroads between the capital and the provinces. It was blessed with natural resources, agriculture and industry thrived, the water was clean, and the women beautiful. But it was rotten! He did not have time to think about the worm that was wriggling at its rotten core. His mind jumped to the question of who would be the next lord of Mino.

What troubled Hiyoshi most was the part being played by Hachisuka Koroku, the man from whom he received his meals. *Ronin* did not have a good reputation, but from serving Koroku, he knew he was an upright man; he had lineage, albeit distant, and one could say his character was superior. Hiyoshi had felt there was nothing to be ashamed of in bowing to this man daily and obeying his orders, but now he had second thoughts.

Dosan had long aided the Hachisuka financially, and their friendship was a strong one. It was unthinkable that Koroku would not know of Dosan's character, or that he could be unaware of his treachery and atrocities. Nevertheless, he was an agitator in the struggle between father and son. No matter how many times he went over the matter in his mind, Hiyoshi could not agree to take part in this. There were thousands of blind men in this world. Could Koroku be one of the blindest? As his feelings of disgust grew stronger, all he wanted to do was run away.

Toward the end of the tenth month, Hiyoshi left the lodging house to go out and peddle his wares. On a corner of one of the back streets, he ran into Hikoju, whose nose was bright red from the dry wind. The bow mender drew up to him and pressed a letter into his hand. "After you read this, chew it up and spit it into the river," he warned. Then, pretending not to know him, Hikoju turned right, while Hiyoshi walked off in the opposite direction. Hiyoshi knew it was a letter from Shichinai. His anxiety hadn't left him, and his heart began to pound.

I've got to get away from these people, he realized. He had been over the problem any number of times, but running away was, in the long run, more dangerous than staying put. He was alone in the boardinghouse, but he took it for granted that his comings and goings and all his actions were continually watched. Probably the spies themselves were being observed. They were all tied to one another like links in a chain. It looks like they're really going ahead with it, he concluded, his mood darkening. Perhaps his reluctance came from timidity, but he could not convince himself he should become a brutal agitator who would confuse people, stir up trouble, and turn the town into an inferno.

He had lost all respect for Koroku. He did not want to serve Dosan, nor did he want anything to do with Yoshitatsu. If he was going to be anyone's ally, he would be the townspeople's. His sympathies lay very much with them, and especially with the parents and their children. They were always the main victims of war. He was too anxious to read the letter immediately.

As he walked along, giving his usual cry, "Needles! Needles from the capital!" he purposely wound his way toward a side street in a residential area where he would not be seen. There he stopped by a small river.

"Oh, damn, I can't get through here!" he said in a deliberately loud voice. He looked around. Luck was with him. No one was in sight. But just to be sure, he faced the small river and while relieving himself, looked around, checking out the area. Then he quietly took out the letter from the folds of his clothing and read:

Tonight, at the Hour of the Dog, if the wind is from the south or west, come to the woods behind the Jozaiji Temple. If the wind is from the north or stops altogether, stay away.

He finished reading, tore the letter into small pieces, and rolled them into a small ball, which he then chewed into a wad.

"Needle seller!"

Startled, he had no time to spit the thing into the river. He palmed the paper wad in his clenched fist.

"Who is it?"

"Over here. We'd like to buy some needles."

There was nobody in sight, and Hiyoshi couldn't tell where the voice came from.

"Needle seller, over here!"

On the other side of the road was an embankment and, atop it, double mud walls. A small wicker gate in the wall opened and a young servant stuck his head out. Hiyoshi answered hesitantly. Any samurai residence in this neighborhood must be that of a retainer of the Saito clan. But of which side? There would be nothing to worry about if this one belonged to a retainer of Dosan, but if it belonged to Yoshitatsu's faction, things could turn nasty.

"There's a person here who'd like some needles."

Hiyoshi's uneasiness intensified, but he had no choice. "Thank you," he said distractedly. Following the servant, he went in through the wicker gate and walked around an artificial hill in what seemed to be a rear garden. The mansion probably belonged to an important retainer. The main house was separated from a number of annexes. Slowing down, Hiyoshi took in the grandeur of the buildings and the neatness of the rocks and artificial streams. Who could want to buy needles from him in a place like this? The servant's words suggested that it was a member of the owner's family, but that did not make sense. In a mansion this imposing, the lady of the house or her daughter wouldn't be buying needles for herself. And, in any case, there would be no reason at all to call in a peddler who hawked his wares in the street.

"Wait here a moment," the servant said, leaving him in a corner of the garden. A two-story building with rough plaster walls, well removed from the main house, caught Hiyoshi's attention. The first floor seemed to be a study, the top floor a library. The young servant called up, "Master Mitsuhide, I brought the man in."

Mitsuhide appeared at a square window much like an opening in a battlement. He was a young man of twenty-four or twenty-five, with a fair complexion and intelligent eyes. Holding some books in his hand, he stuck his head out of the window. "I'll come down. Take him to the veranda," he said, and disappeared inside.

Hiyoshi looked up and noticed for the first time that someone could have seen him over the wall while he was standing at the river reading the letter. He was sure he must have been observed, and that this Mitsuhide had become suspicious and was about to question him. Hiyoshi thought that if he did not make up some story, he would be in trouble. Just as he was preparing an explanation, the young servant waved him over and said, "The master's nephew is coming, so wait by the veranda. And mind your manners."

Hiyoshi knelt down a little way from the veranda, his eyes downcast. After a while, when nobody came out, he looked up. The number of books inside the house amazed him. They were everywhere, on and around the desk and the bookshelves, and in the other rooms on the first and second floors. Whether it's the master or his nephew, he thought, someone seems to be quite a scholar. Books were a rare sight for Hiyoshi. Looking around, he noticed a couple of other things: between the horizontal timbers of the house frame hung a fine spear, and a musket was propped against the wall in an alcove.

Finally the man entered the room and quietly sat down in front of the desk. Resting his chin on his hands, he looked fixedly at Hiyoshi, as though he were concentrating on some Chinese characters in a book. "Hello, there."

Hiyoshi said, "I'm a needle seller. Are you interested in buying some needles, sir?"

Mitsuhide nodded. "Yes, I am. But first there's something I'd like to ask you. Are you here to sell needles or to spy?"

"To sell needles, of course."

"Well, then, what brought you into an alleyway in a residential area like this?"

"I thought it was a shortcut."

"You're lying." Mitsuhide turned his body a little to the side. "When I saw you, I could tell you were a seasoned traveler and peddler. So you should have sense enough to know whether or not you could sell needles at a samurai residence."

"I have sold them, though rarely—"

"I can imagine it's rarely."

"But it can be done."

"Well, let's put that aside for the moment. What were you reading in a deserted place like this?"

"Huh?"

"You furtively took out a piece of paper, thinking that no one was around. But anywhere there is life, there are eyes. And things, too, speak to those who have ears to hear. What were you reading?"

"I was reading a letter."

"Some sort of secret correspondence?"

"I was reading a letter from my mother," he said very matter-of-factly. Mitsuhide looked searchingly at him. "Is that so? A letter from your mother?"

"Yes."

"In that case, let me see it. According to the laws of the castle, when you come across a suspicious person, he's to be arrested and taken to the castle. As evidence, let me see the letter from your mother, or I'll have to hand you over to the authorities."

"I ate it."

"You did what?"

"Unfortunately, after I read it, I ate it, sir."

"You ate it?"

"Yes, that's what I did," Hiyoshi continued earnestly. "To me, just by my being alive, my mother is to be more respected than the gods or Buddhas. Therefore—"

Mitsuhide let out a thundering cry, "Hold your tongue! I suppose you chewed it up because it was a secret communication. That alone makes you a suspicious character!"

"No! No! You're mistaken!" Hiyoshi said, waving his hands. "To carry a letter from my mother, to whom I'm more grateful than to the gods and Buddhas, and in the end blow my nose on it and toss it away in the street, where it would be trampled under people's feet, would be impious and a crime. This is the way I think, and it's a habit of mine always to eat them. I'm not lying. It's natural for someone to miss his mother so much that he'd want to eat the letters, coming from so far away."

Mitsuhide was sure it was all a lie, but even so, here was a boy who lied much better than the common run. And he sympathized with him because he himself had left his mother behind at home.

Although it's a lie, it's not a base lie. And though it's nonsense to talk about eating a letter from one's mother, there's no mistaking that even this little monkey-faced lad must have parents, thought Mitsuhide, at the same time feeling sorry for his unpolished and uneducated adversary. Nevertheless, if this ignorant, naïve youth were the tool of an agitator, he could be as dangerous as a wild animal. He wasn't the kind of person to send off to the castle, and it would be a shame just to kill him on the spot. He thought about just letting Hiyoshi go, but he kept a sharp eye on him while trying to decide how to handle the matter.

"Mataichi!" he called. "Is Mitsuharu around?"

"I think so, sir."

"Tell him I don't want to be a bother, but please ask if he can come here for a minute."

"Yes, sir." Mataichi ran off.

Shortly after, Mitsuharu came from the house, walking with great strides. He was younger than Mitsuhide, perhaps eighteen or nineteen. He was the heir to the master of the house, the lay priest Akechi Mitsuyasu, and he and Mitsuhide were cousins. Mitsuhide's family name was also Akechi. He lived with his uncle and spent his days in study. It was not that he was financially dependent on his uncle; he had come to Inabayama because his home in provincial Ena was far removed from the centers of culture and politics. His uncle often said to his son, "Look at Mitsuhide and study a little."

Mitsuhide was a serious scholar. Even before he had come to Inabayama, he had already traveled extensively, touring the country from the capital to the western provinces. He had kept company with traveling swordsmen and sought out knowledge, studied current events, and willingly accepted life's hardships. When he got around to studying firearms, he made a special trip to the free city of Sakai and eventually made so great a contribution to the defenses and military organization of Mino that everyone, beginning with his uncle, respected him as a genius of the new learning.

"How can I be of assistance, Mitsuhide?"

"Well, it's nothing really." His tone was deferential.

"What is it?"

"I want you to do something for me, if you think it's right."

The two men went outside and, standing right next to Hiyoshi, discussed what to do with him. After hearing the details from Mitsuhide, Mitsuharu said, "You mean this nobody?" He looked Hiyoshi over casually. "If you think he's suspicious, turn him over to Mataichi. If he's tortured a bit, beaten with a broken bow, say, he'll talk soon enough. It should be easy."

"No." Mitsuhide took another look at Hiyoshi. "I don't think he's the type who'll talk with that sort of treatment. And I feel sorry for him, somehow."

"If he's taken you in and made you feel sorry for him, you're not likely to get him to talk. Give him to me for four or five days. I'll lock him up in the storage shed. He'll soon be spitting out the truth when he gets hungry."

"Sorry to trouble you with this," Mitsuhide said.

"Shall I tie him up?" Mataichi said, twisting Hiyoshi's arm.

"Wait!" said Hiyoshi, trying to free himself from Mataichi's grip. He looked up at Mitsuhide and Mitsuharu. "You just said that even if I was beaten, I wouldn't tell the truth. All you have to do is ask me and I'll tell you everything. Even if you don't ask! I can't stand being shut up in a dark place."

"You're ready to talk?"

"Yes."

"All right. I'll do the questioning," said Mitsuharu.

"Go ahead."

"What about—" But Hiyoshi's composure seemed to unnerve Mitsuharu, and he stopped in mid-sentence, muttering, "It's no good! He's a strange one. I wonder if he's quite right in the head. He must be playing a game with us." Glancing at Mitsuhide, he gave a bitter laugh. But Mitsuhide was not laughing. He was looking at Hiyoshi with an anxious look on his face. Mitsuhide and Mitsuharu took turns questioning him, as though they were humoring a spoiled child.

Hiyoshi said, "Well, then, I'll tell you what's being planned for tonight, but since I'm not part of their gang and don't have anything to do with them, can you guarantee my life?"

"Fair enough. Taking your life wouldn't be much of an accomplishment. Something's up, eh?"

"There's going to be a big fire tonight, if the wind is right."

"Where?"

"I don't know exactly, but the *ronin* staying at the lodging house discussed it in secret. Tonight, if the wind comes from the south or west, they're going to meet in the woods near the Jozaiji, split up, and set fire to the town."

"What?" Mitsuharu's mouth fell open. Mitsuhide swallowed hard, finding it difficult to believe what he had just heard.

Hiyoshi, ignoring their reaction to what he had just said, swore that he didn't know any more, just what he had heard whispered by *ronin* who happened to be his fellow lodgers. All he wanted to do was sell his stock of needles and return to his hometown of Nakamura as soon as possible, to see his mother's face.

After the color had returned to their faces, Mitsuhide and Mitsuharu stood aghast for a moment. At last, Mitsuhide gave an order.

"All right, we'll let this one go, but not before nightfall. Mataichi, take him and give him some food."

The wind that had been blowing all day began to freshen. It was coming from the southwest.

"Mitsuhide, what do you suppose they'll do? The wind's blowing from the west."

73

Mitsuharu's eyes were filled with worry as he looked up at the clouds scudding past. Mitsuhide silently sat down on the veranda of the library. Gazing off into space, he seemed to be concentrating on some complicated problem. "Mitsuharu," he said finally, "has my uncle said anything strange in the past four or five days?"

"Well, nothing that Father's said has struck me as particularly strange."

"Are you sure?"

"Now that you mention it, before he left for Sagiyama Castle this morning, he did say that because relations between Lord Dosan and Lord Yoshitatsu had worsened recently, we might be in for some trouble, though it was difficult to say when. He said that while one should always be prepared, just in case something unexpected happens, the men should prepare their armor and horses."

"He said that this morning?"

"Yes."

"That's it!" Mitsuhide slapped his knee. "He was warning you indirectly that there's going to be a battle tonight. It's common practice for military plots of this kind to be kept secret even from close kin. He must be in on it."

"Will there be a battle tonight?"

"The men meeting tonight at the Jozaiji are probably agents brought in from the outside by Lord Dosan, most likely from Hachisuka."

"So Lord Dosan's made up his mind to drive Lord Yoshitatsu from the castle."

"That's what I think." Mitsuhide, confident that he had guessed right, nodded vigorously, but then he gloomily bit his lip. "I suspect Lord Dosan's plan is not going to work. Lord Yoshitatsu is well prepared. More than that, for father and son to take up arms and spill blood runs contrary to any code of behavior. The gods will punish them! No matter who wins or loses, the blood of kinsmen will flow freely. And it won't increase the Saito clan's territory by one inch. On the contrary, the neighboring provinces will be watching for an opportunity to intervene, and the province will be on the brink of collapse." He let out a long sigh.

Mitsuharu was sunk in silence, pensively studying the dark swirling clouds in the sky. In a fight between two of one's lords, there was nothing a retainer could do. They knew that Mitsuharu's father, Mitsuyasu, a trusted retainer of Dosan, was in the vanguard of the movement to bring about Yoshitatsu's fall.

"We have to stop this unnatural battle by any means at our disposal. That is our duty as loyal retainers. Mitsuharu, you must go immediately to Sagiyama and find your father. And you two together must dissuade Lord Dosan from carrying out his plans."

"Yes, I understand."

"I'll wait until evening, go to Jozaiji, and somehow thwart their schemes. I'm going to stop them, no matter what!"

In the kitchen, three large stoves stood in a row. Huge cauldrons holding several bagfuls of rice sat on the stoves. When the lids were lifted, the starchy water boiled over in clouds of steam. Hiyoshi had worked out that for this amount of rice to be consumed in one sitting, there had to be over a hundred people in the mansion, including the master's family, and his retainers and their dependents. "With all this rice, why can't my mother and sister have enough to fill their stomachs?" He thought of his mother; he thought of rice. The rice made him think of his mother's hunger.

"It's awfully windy tonight." The old man in charge came over and checked the fires in the stoves. He said to the kitchen helpers who were cooking the rice, "The wind won't let up even after sunset. Watch the fires. And as soon as one pot of rice is ready, start making rice balls."

He was on his way out when he noticed Hiyoshi. He looked at him curiously and summoned a servant, "Who's that townsman with a face like a monkey?" he asked. "I haven't seen him around before."

"He's in Master Mitsuhide's charge. Mataichi is guarding him so he won't run away."

The old man then noticed Mataichi seated on the kindling bin.

"Good work!" he said to Mataichi, without a clue as to what was going on. "Is he under arrest for suspicious behavior?"

"No. I don't know why. Only that the orders came from Master Mitsuhide." Mataichi said as little as he could get away with.

The old man seemed to forget about Hiyoshi and said, "The truth is, Master Mitsuhide has sense and discrimination well beyond his years." The old man admired Mitsuhide and began to sing his praises. "He's much above average, don't you think? Master Mitsuhide's not one of those men who despise learning and brag about how heavy a staff they use, how well they wield a spear on horseback, or how many people they cut down on what battlefield. Whenever I peek into the library, he's lost in study. And he's a great swordsman and strategist too. He'll go far, that's for sure."

Mataichi, proud to hear his master spoken of so highly, chimed in, "It's just as you say. I've been his servant since he was a boy, and there's no kinder master than he. He's also a good son to his mother, and whether he's studying here or traveling around the provinces, he never neglects to write to her."

"It's often the case that by the age of twenty-four or twenty-five, if a man has great courage, he's also a braggart, and if he's gentle, he's a fop," the old man said. "As if he'd been born in a stable, he soon forgets what he owes to his parents and leads a selfish life."

"Well, remember he's not just a gentleman," said Mataichi. "He's got a fierce temper too, despite appearances to the contrary. Although it rarely comes to the surface, when he gets mad, there's no holding him back."

"So even though he appears to be gentle, when he gets angry..."

"Precisely. Like what happened today."

"Today?"

"In an emergency, when he's thinking over what's right or wrong, he thinks things through to the end. But when he's made his decision, it's like a dam breaking, and he immediately gives orders to his cousin, Master Mitsuharu."

"He's a leader, all right—a born general."

"Master Mitsuharu is devoted to Master Mitsuhide, and so he willingly follows his orders. Today he galloped off to Sagiyama castle."

"What do you suppose is going on?"

"I don't know."

"'Cook a lot of rice. Make some rice balls for the troops. There might be a battle in the middle of the night.' That's what Master Mitsuharu said when he left."

"Preparations for an emergency, huh?"

"I'd be happy if it stops with the preparations, because in a battle between Sagiyama and Inabayama, which side should we fight for? Whichever it is, we'll be shooting our bows at friends and relatives."

"Well, it may not come to that. It seems as though Master Mitsuhide has devised a plan to prevent a battle."

"The gods know I'll pray for his success. If the neighboring clans attack us, I'm ready to fight them right away."

Outside, night had fallen. The sky was pitch black. Gusts of wind came in, and the fire in the mouths of the huge stoves made a slight roaring noise and grew brighter. Hiyoshi, still squatting in front of the stoves, smelled burnt rice.

"Hey! The rice is burning! You're letting the rice burn!"

"Out of the way, you!" the servants said without a word of thanks. After they had dampened the fires in the stoves, one of them climbed a ladder and transferred the rice into a tub. All those who were not busy with something else began making rice balls by the score. Hiyoshi worked with them, pressing the rice into balls. He helped himself to a couple of mouthfuls, but nobody seemed to mind. Almost in a trance, they went on making rice ball after rice ball, talking as they did so.

"I guess there'll be a battle, eh?"

"Can't they end it without a fight?"

They were making provisions for the troops, but most of them hoped that the stores would not be needed.

At the Hour of the Dog, Mitsuhide called for Mataichi, who went outside but soon came back calling, "Needle seller! Where's the needle seller!"

Hiyoshi jumped up, licking rice grains off of his fingers. He only had to take one step out of the building to gauge the strength of the wind.

"Come along with me. Master Mitsuhide's waiting. And be quick about it."

Hiyoshi followed Mataichi, noticing that he had put on light armor as if he were ready to go off to battle. Hiyoshi had no idea where they were going. At length they went out the central gate and he understood. Going around the rear garden, they came to the front. Outside the gate, a mounted figure was waiting for them.

"Mataichi?" Mitsuhide had on the clothes he had worn that day. He held the reins in his hands and carried a long spear under one arm.

"Yes, sir."

"The needle seller?"

"He's right here."

"The two of you run on ahead."

Turning to Hiyoshi, Mataichi ordered, "Come on, needle seller, let's go."

The two men on foot ran into the pitch black night. Matching their pace, Mitsuhide followed on horseback. They came to a crossroads, and Mitsuhide instructed them to turn right, then left. Finally, Hiyoshi realized that they had reached the gate of the Jozaiji, the meeting place of the Hachisuka men. Mitsuhide dismounted nimbly.

"Mataichi, stay here with the horse," he said, handing him the reins. "Mitsuharu is supposed to come here from Sagiyama Castle in the last half of the Hour of the Dog. If he doesn't make it by the agreed hour, our plan is canceled." Then, with a tragic look on his face, he said, "The town has become the home of warring demons. How can a mere man guess the outcome?" The last of his words were swallowed up by the enveloping gloom.

"Needle seller! You show the way."

"The way to where?" Hiyoshi braced himself against the wind.

"The woods where the scoundrels from Hachisuka are having their meeting."

"Uh, well, I don't know where the place is either."

"Even if this is your first time here, I think they know your face well enough."

"Huh?"

"Don't play the innocent."

This is no good, thought Hiyoshi. I didn't fool him at all. Mitsuhide had seen through his lies, and he made no more excuses.

There were no lights in the wood. The wind swept through the leaves, which beat against the great temple roof like spray scouring the gunwales of a ship. The woods behind the temple were like a raging ocean—the trees groaned and the grasses roared.

"Needle seller!"

"Yes, sir."

"Are your comrades here yet?"

"How should I know?"

Mitsuhide sat down on a small stone pagoda at the rear of the temple. "It's nearing the second half of the Hour of the Dog. If you're the only person not accounted for, they'll be on the alert." His spear, caught by the full force of the wind, was right in front of Hiyoshi's feet. "Go show yourself!" Hiyoshi had to admit to himself that Mitsuhide was a step ahead of him from the very start. "Go tell them that Akechi Mitsuhide is waiting here, and that he would like to talk with the leader of the men of Hachisuka."

"Yes, sir." Hiyoshi bowed his head but did not move. "Is it all right if I say this in front of everyone?"

"Yes."

"And that's why you brought me here with you?"

"Yes. Now get going."

"I'll go, but since we may not meet again, I'd like to tell you something."

"Yes?"

"It would be a shame to leave without saying this, because you see me only as an agent of the Hachisuka."

"That's true."

"You're very clever, but your eyes are too sharp, and they go right through the thing they're looking at. When a man hits a nail, he stops where he's supposed to, because going too far is just as bad as not going far enough. Your intelligence is like that. I admit I came to Inabayama with the men from Hachisuka. But my heart's not in it—not at all. I was born in a farming family in Nakamura, and I've done things like selling needles, but I haven't reached my goal. I don't intend to spend my life eating cold rice from a *ronin*'s table. Neither am I going to work as an agitator for some worthless reward. If, by some chance, we meet again, I'll prove to you what I said about you looking too hard at things. For now, I'll go to Hachisuka Shichinai, give him your message, and leave immediately. So

77

good luck! Take good care of yourself, and study hard."

Mitsuhide listened in silence, then suddenly came out of his reverie. "Needle seller! Wait!" he called.

Hiyoshi had already vanished into the storm. He ran into the black woods without hearing Mitsuhide's call. He ran until he got to a small, level bit of land sheltered from the wind by trees. He could see men all about him, scattered like wild horses in a pasture, some sprawling, some sitting, some standing.

"Who's there?"

"It's me."

"Hiyoshi?"

"Yeah."

"Where have you been? You're the last. Everyone's been worried," scolded one man.

"I'm sorry I'm late," he said as he came up to the group. He was trembling. "Where's Master Shichinai?"

"He's over there. Go and apologize. He's real angry."

Four or five members of the gang stood talking around Shichinai.

"Is that Monkey?" Shichinai asked, looking around. Hiyoshi went over to him and made his excuses for being late.

"What were you up to?"

"During the day I was held prisoner by a retainer of the Saito clan," Hiyoshi admitted.

"What?" Shichinai and all the others stared at him nervously, afraid that their plot had been exposed. "You simpleton!" Without warning, he grabbed Hiyoshi by the collar, yanked him forward, and asked roughly, "Where and by whom were you being held? And did you say anything?"

"I talked."

"You what?"

"If I hadn't talked, I wouldn't be alive. I wouldn't be here now."

"You little bastard!" Shichinai gave Hiyoshi a good shaking. "You fool! You blabbed to save your miserable skin. For that, you're going to be the first victim of tonight's bloodbath!"

Shichinai let go and tried to kick him, but Hiyoshi jumped back agilely and Shichinai missed. The two men closest to Hiyoshi grabbed his arms and twisted them behind his back. Struggling to free his arms, Hiyoshi said in one breath, "Don't lose your heads. Hear me out, even though I was caught and talked. They're retainers of Lord Dosan."

They looked relieved, but also still a little doubtful.

"All right, who were they?"

"It was Akechi Mitsuyasu's house. I wasn't being held by him but by his nephew Mitsuhide."

"Ah, the Akechi hanger-on," someone muttered.

Hiyoshi looked at the man, then moved his eyes over the whole group. "This Master Mitsuhide wants to meet with our leader. He came here with me. He's over there. Master Shichinai, won't you go and meet him?"

"Akechi Mitsuyasu's nephew came here with you?"

"Yes."

"Did you tell Mitsuhide everything about tonight's plan?"

"Even if I hadn't, he would have guessed. He's a genius."

"Why did he come?"

"I don't know. He said only that I should guide him here."

"And so you did?"

"There was nothing else I could do."

As Hiyoshi and Shichinai talked, the men around them swallowed hard as they listened. Finally, Shichinai wound things up with a click of his tongue. He stepped forward and asked, "All right, where is he, this Akechi Mitsuhide?"

Everyone talked at once. It was dangerous for Shichinai to meet the man alone. Someone should go with him. Or they should surround the meeting place and stay hidden.

Just then a voice came from behind: "Men of Hachisuka! I have come to you. I should like to meet with Master Shichinai."

They turned toward the voice in stunned surprise. Mitsuhide had approached unnoticed and was calmly observing them.

Shichinai felt a little confused, but being the leader, he stepped forward.

"Are you Hachisuka Shichinai?" asked Mitsuhide.

"I am," Shichinai replied, his head held high. He was in front of his men, but it was common for *ronin* not to be humble before samurai who served a lord or warriors of even higher status.

Although Mitsuhide was armed with a spear, he bowed and spoke politely. "It's a pleasure to meet you. I have heard your name before, as well as the respected name of Master Koroku. I am Akechi Mitsuhide, a retainer of Lord Saito Dosan."

The politeness of the greeting left Shichinai feeling slightly paralyzed. "Well, what do you want?" he asked.

"Tonight's plan."

"What about tonight's plan?" Shichinai asked with feigned indifference.

"It has to do with the particulars I learned from the needle seller, which shocked me into coming here with great speed. Tonight's outrage—it is, perhaps, impolite to call it an outrage—but from the standpoint of military strategy it is very poorly conceived. I can't believe this is Lord Dosan's idea. I would like you to drop it immediately."

"Never!" Shichinai shouted arrogantly. "This is not being done on my orders. The orders come from Master Koroku, at Lord Dosan's request."

"That's what I assumed to be the case," Mitsuhide said in an ordinary tone of voice.

"Naturally, you wouldn't call it off on your own authority. My cousin Mitsuharu has gone to Sagiyama to remonstrate with Lord Dosan. He's to meet with us here. My request is that you all stay here until he comes."

Mitsuhide was always polite to everyone, while also being resolute and courageous. But the effect of courtesy varies with the sensibility of the person spoken to, and there are times when it may lead one party to become arrogant.

Huh! An insignificant youth. He nibbles a little bit of learning, but he's nothing more than a greenhorn, making excuses, thought Shichinai. "We're not waiting!" he shouted, and then said bluntly, "Master Mitsuhide, don't stick your nose in where it doesn't belong. You're just a useless hanger-on. Aren't you one of your uncle's dependents?"

"I don't have time to think about my duty. And this is an emergency for my lord's house."

"If you thought so, you would prepare yourself with armor and provisions, hold the torch as we do, and be at the very vanguard of the attack on Inabayama."

"No, I couldn't do that. There's a certain difficulty in being a retainer."

"How's that?"

"Isn't Lord Yoshitatsu the heir of Lord Dosan? If Lord Dosan is our master, so is Lord Yoshitatsu."

"But if he becomes an enemy?"

"That's despicable. Is it right for father and son to draw bows and shoot at each other? In this world, there are no examples even of birds and beasts doing such a dishonorable thing."

"You're a lot of trouble. Why don't you just go home and leave us alone?"

"I can't do that."

"Huh?"

"I will not leave before Mitsuharu gets here."

Shichinai perceived for the first time a resolute strength in the voice of the young man in front of him. He also saw serious intent in the spear Mitsuhide held at his side.

"Mitsuhide! Are you there?" Mitsuharu rushed up gasping for breath.

"Over here. What happened at the castle?"

"It's no good." Mitsuharu, his shoulders heaving, grasped his cousin's hand. "Lord Dosan will not hear of calling it off, no matter what. Not only he, but also my father, said this is not something that we, as dependents, should be involved in."

"Even my uncle?"

"Yes, he was furious. I was willing to stake my life on it and did the best I could. It's a desperate situation. The troops seemed to be getting ready to leave Sagiyama. I was afraid the town might already be put to the torch, so I came as fast as I could. Mitsuhide, what are we going to do?"

"Is Lord Dosan intent on burning down Inabayama, no matter what?"

"There's no way out. It seems that all we can do is our duty, and die in his service."

"I don't like it one bit! No matter if he is our lord and master, it would be too bad for a man to die in such an unworthy cause. It would be no better than a dog's death."

"Yes, but what can we do?"

"If they don't fire the town, the Sagiyama forces are not likely to move. We must take care of the source of the fire before it gets started." Mitsuhide sounded like a different person. He turned back to face Shichinai and the others, his spear at the ready. Shichinai and his men spread out into a circle.

"What do you think you're doing?" Shichinai barked at Mitsuhide. "Pointing a spear at us? And a poor one, at that?"

"That's exactly what I'm doing." Mitsuhide's voice was firm. "No one is leaving this place. But if you'll think this through, obey me and give up the idea of tonight's outrage, and if you'll go back to Hachisuka village, we'll spare your lives and I'll compensate you as best I can. What do you say?"

"Do you seriously think we can leave now?"

"This is a crisis. It could bring about the collapse of the entire Saito clan. I'm acting to prevent an incident that could bring down both Inabayama and Sagiyama."

"Fool!" a man yelled angrily. "You're still wet behind the ears. Do you think you can stop us? If you try, you'll be the first to be killed."

"I was prepared to die from the first." Mitsuhide's eyebrows were arched like those of a demon. "Mitsuharu!" called Mitsuhide, without changing his stance. "It's a fight to the death! Are you with me?"

"Of course! Don't worry about me." Mitsuharu had already unsheathed his long sword, and stood back-to-back with Mitsuhide. Keeping alive a ray of hope, Mitsuhide made one more appeal to Shichinai. "If you're concerned about losing face when you return to Hachisuka, how about taking me along as a hostage, as unworthy as I am? I'll go to Master Koroku and discuss the rights and wrongs of this affair with him. That way we can finish this business without spilling blood."

Patient and reasonable though his words were, they were heard only as whining. There were more than twenty Hachisuka men arrayed against only two.

"Shut up! Don't listen to him! It's almost past the Hour of the Dog already!"

A couple of men let out war cries, and Mitsuhide and Mitsuharu were engulfed in the fangs of a wolfpack—halberds, spears, and swords on every side. The yelling of men and the clashing of weapons mingled with the roaring of the wind, and the scene was rapidly turned into the horrible maelstrom of war.

Swords broke and the pieces went flying. Spears chased fleeing sprays of blood. Hiyoshi thought it was too dangerous to be in the midst of this carnage, so he hurriedly climbed a tree. He had seen drawn swords before, but it was the first time he had been in a real battle. Would Inabayama be transformed into a sea of flames? Would there be a battle between Dosan and Yoshitatsu? When he understood that this was life or death, he became more excited than ever in his life.

It took only two or three dead bodies to prompt the Hachisuka men to flee into the woods.

Ya! They're running away! Hiyoshi thought, and just in case they came back, he prudently stayed put in his tree. It was probably a chestnut tree, because something pricked his hands and the back of his neck. A scattering of nuts and twigs fell to the ground, for the tree was being shaken by the storm. He despised the men of Hachisuka as a bunch of loudmouthed cowards who had been routed by only two men. He listened hard. "What's that?" He became flustered. It was a rain of cinders like volcanic ash. He looked up through the branches. The men of Hachisuka had set their fires as they fled. Two or three parts of the woods were beginning to burn fiercely, and several of the buildings behind the Jozaiji had caught fire.

Hiyoshi jumped down from the tree and started to run. If he lost even a moment, he would be burned to death in the wood. In a daze, he ran to the burning town. The sky was filled with sparks of flame—birds of fire, butterflies of fire. The white walls of Inabayama Castle, now shining red, looked closer than during the day. Red clouds of war were swirling around them.

"It's war!" Hiyoshi yelled as he ran on through the streets. "It's war! It's the end!

Sagiyama and Inabayama will fall! But in the burnt ruins, the grass will grow again. This time the grass will grow straight!"

He ran into people.

A riderless horse galloped by.

At a crossroads, refugees clustered together, shuddering in terror. Hiyoshi, carried away by the excitement, ran at full speed, screaming like a prophet of doom. Where to? He had no destination. He could not go back to Hachisuka village, that was for sure. In any event, he left without regret what he disliked most: a gloomy people, a dark lord, civil war, and a tainted culture, all within the rotting earth of a single province.

He spent the winter in his thin cotton clothes, selling needles under a cold sky, wandering wherever his feet took him. The next year, the twenty-second year of Temmon, when the peach blossoms were everywhere, he was still calling out, "Won't you buy needles? Needles from the capital! Sewing needles from the capital!"

He approached the outskirts of Hamamatsu, walking along as carefree as ever.

ANOTHER MASTER

Matsushita Kahei was a native of Enshu province. The son of a country samurai, he had become a retainer of the Imagawa clan, with a domain in Suruga and a stipend of three thousand *kan*. He was governor of the fortress at Zudayama and chief administrator of the relay station at Magome Bridge. In those days the Tenryu River was divided into the Big and the Little Tenryu. The Matsushita residence was on the banks of the Big Tenryu, a few hundred yards east of Zudayama.

That day Kahei was returning from the neighboring Hikuma Castle, where he had been conferring with a fellow Imagawa retainer. The officials of the province met regularly to tighten their control over the people and to guard against invasion from the neighboring clans: Tokugawa, Oda, and Takeda.

Kahei turned in his saddle and called one of his three attendants: "Nohachiro!"

The man who answered was bearded and carried a long spear. Taga Nohachiro ran up to his master's horse. They were traveling along the road between Hikumanawata and the Magome ferry. Trees lined the road, and there was a pleasant view of fields and rice paddies.

"He's not a farmer, and he doesn't look like a pilgrim," Kahei mumbled.

Nohachiro followed Kahei's line of sight. He took in the flaming yellow of the mustard flowers, the green of the barley, and the shallow water in the paddies, but did not see anyone.

"Anything suspicious?"

"Over there, on the path next to that rice paddy, there's a man. Looks a little like a heron. What do you suppose he's up to?"

Nohachiro took another look and saw that, sure enough, there was a man stooping over on the path by the paddy.

"Find out what he's doing."

Nohachiro ran off along a narrow path. It was the rule in all the provinces that anything that looked the least bit suspicious was to be investigated immediately. Provincial officials were particularly sensitive about their borders and the appearance of strangers.

Nohachiro came back and made his report: "He says he's a needle seller from Owari. He's wearing a stained white cotton smock. That's why from here he reminds you of a heron. He's a little fellow with a face like a monkey's."

"Ha, ha! Not a heron or a crow, but a monkey, eh?"

"And a talkative one, too. Likes to spit out big words. While I was questioning him, he tried to turn things around. He asked me who my master was, and when I told him who you were, he stood up and looked over this way very boldly."

"What was he doing, stooping over like that?"

"He told me he was putting up for the night at a lodging house in Magome, and he was collecting pond snails to eat this evening."

Kahei saw that Hiyoshi had gone up onto the road and was walking on ahead of them.

He asked Nohachiro, "There was nothing suspicious about him, was there?"

"Nothing I could see."

Kahei took a fresh grip on the reins. "One shouldn't blame low-bred people for their bad manners." Then, motioning his men on with a nod of the head, he said, "Let's go." It did not take them long to catch up with Hiyoshi. Just as they passed him, Kahei looked around casually. Hiyoshi, of course, had moved off the road and was kneeling respectfully under a row of trees. Their eyes met.

"Just a minute." Kahei reined in his horse and, turning to his attendants, said, "Bring the needle seller over here." And, to no one in particular, he added with a note of wonder in his voice, "He's an unusual fellow...yes, there's something different about him."

Nohachiro decided that this was another of his master's whims and promptly ran off.

"Hey! Needle seller! My master would like a word with you. Follow me."

Kahei looked down at Hiyoshi. What was it about this short, unkempt youth in soiled clothes that he found so fascinating? It was not his resemblance to a monkey, which he had hardly taken in. He took a long, hard second look at Hiyoshi, but he could not put into words what he felt. Something that was at once complex and formless pulled at him—it was the boy's eyes! The eyes had been called the mirrors of the soul. He could see little else of value in this shriveled little creature, but the look in his eyes was so full of laughter that it was somehow fresh and seemed to contain...what? An indomitable will, or maybe a vision that knew no bounds?

He has magnetism, thought Kahei, and he decided he liked this strange-looking boy. If his assessment had been more thorough, he would have discovered, hidden beneath the traveler's black grime, ears as red as a rooster's comb. Nor did he see that, though Hiyoshi was still young, the great ability he would display in later years was already visible in the lines on his forehead, which made him look like an old man at first glance. Kahei's discernment simply did not go that far. He felt an unusual attachment toward Hiyoshi, mixed with some kind of expectation.

Unable to rid himself of the feeling but without saying a word to Hiyoshi, he turned to Nohachiro and said, "Bring him along." He tightened his reins and galloped off.

The front gate facing the river was open, and several retainers were waiting for him. A tethered horse was grazing near the gate. Apparently a visitor had arrived during his absence.

"Who is it?" he asked as he dismounted.

"A messenger from Sumpu."

Kahei acknowledged the information and went in. Sumpu was the capital of the Imagawa clan. Messengers were not especially rare, but Kahei was preoccupied with his meeting in Hikuma Castle, so he forgot all about Hiyoshi.

"Hey, you, where do you think you're going?" challenged the gatekeeper as Hiyoshi was about to follow the attendants through the gate. His hands and the straw-wrapped package he carried were spattered with mud. The splotches of mud drying on his face felt itchy. Had the gatekeeper thought that Hiyoshi was poking fun at him by twitching his nose on purpose? The gatekeeper reached out to grab Hiyoshi by the scruff of the neck.

Stepping back, Hiyoshi answered, "I'm a needle seller."

"Peddlers don't come through this gate without authorization. Off with you!"

"You better check with your master first."

"And why should I do that?"

"I followed him here because he told me to. I came with the samurai who came in just now."

"I can't imagine the master bringing the likes of you back. You look pretty shady to me."

Just then, Nohachiro remembered Hiyoshi and came back to get him. "It's all right," he told the gatekeeper.

"Well, if you say so."

"Come along, Monkey."

The gatekeeper and the other servants burst out laughing. "What is he, anyway? With his white smock and muddy straw bundle, he looks just like the Buddha's monkey messenger!"

The boisterous voices rang in Hiyoshi's ears, but during the seventeen years of his life, he had had ample opportunity to hear the taunts of others. Didn't they bother him? Had he got used to them? It seems that neither was the case. When he heard this kind of remark he blushed, just like anyone else. His ears, especially, turned bright red. This was proof that the taunts did not go unheard. But his behavior did not reflect his feelings. He was as calm as if the insults had been spoken into the ears of a horse. In fact, he could be disarmingly charming at such times. His heart was like a flower held up by a bamboo support, quietly waiting for the storm to pass. He was not going to be upset by adversity, nor would he be servile.

"Monkey, there's an empty stable over there. You can wait there, where the sight of you won't offend anyone," said Nohachiro, who then went about his business.

When evening came, the smell of cooking drifted from the kitchen window. The moon rose over the peach trees. The formal interview with the messenger from Sumpu being finished, more lamps were lit, and a banquet was prepared to send him on his way the following day. The sound of the hand drum and a flute drifted over from the

85

mansion, where a Noh play was being performed.

The Imagawa of Suruga were a proud and illustrious family. Their tastes ran not only to poetry, dance, and music but to any luxury from the capital: inlaid swords for their samurai and stylish under-kimonos for their women. Kahei himself was a man of simple tastes. Nevertheless, his opulent residence presented a quite different appearance from the mansions of the samurai of Kiyosu.

That's pretty bad Noh, Hiyoshi thought, as he lay stretched out on the straw he had spread on the floor of the empty stall. He liked music. Not that he understood it, but he liked the cheery world of dreams it created. It allowed him to forget everything. But he was distracted by his empty stomach. Oh, if I could only borrow a pot and a fire, he groaned inwardly.

Taking his dirty straw bundle with him, he stuck his head through the door of the kitchen. "Excuse me, but I wonder if you couldn't lend me a pot and a small cooking stove. I was thinking of eating my meal."

The kitchen helpers stared blankly back at him.

"Where in the world did you come from?"

"His lordship brought me back with him today. I'd like to boil the pond snails I picked from the rice paddies."

"Pond snails, eh?"

"I've been told they're good for the stomach, so I eat some every day. That's because I get stomach upset easily."

"You eat them with bean paste. Do you have any?"

"Yes."

"Rice?"

"I have rice, thank you."

"Well, there's a pot and a fire in the stove in the servants' quarters. Do it over there."

Just as he did every night in cheap lodging houses, Hiyoshi cooked up a small portion of rice, boiled his pond snails, and ate his evening meal. Then he went to sleep. The servants' quarters being an improvement over the stable, he stayed there until midnight, when the servants finished their chores and came back.

"You swine! Who told you you could sleep here?"

They kicked him, picked him up, and threw him out. He went back to the stable, only to find the messenger's horse fast asleep and seeming to say, "You don't belong here, either."

The hand drum had fallen silent, and the pale moon was waning. Hiyoshi, no longer sleepy, could not stand being idle. Work or fun, it didn't matter much to him, but if he wasn't involved in one or the other, he very quickly became bored.

Maybe the sun will come while I'm sweeping up, he thought as he started to sweep the stable, collecting the horse manure, fallen leaves, and straw into a pile, out of the master's sight.

"Who's out there?" Resting his broom, Hiyoshi looked around. "Ah, it's the needle seller."

Hiyoshi finally saw that the voice was coming from the lavatory at the corner of the main house's veranda. He could make out Kahei's face inside. "Oh, it's you, my lord."

Drinking *sake* with the messenger, who was a strong drinker, Kahei had drunk too much. Now, almost sober again, he asked in a tired voice, "Is it close to dawn?" He disappeared from the window, opened the rain shutters of the veranda, and looked up at the waning moon.

"The cock hasn't crowed yet, so it'll be a little while until dawn."

"Needle seller—no, we'll call you Monkey—why are you sweeping the garden in the middle of the night?"

"I had nothing to do."

"It would probably be a good idea to get some sleep."

"I already slept. When I've slept for a certain amount of time, for some reason I can't lie still anymore."

"Are there any sandals?"

Hiyoshi quickly found a pair of new straw sandals and arranged them so that Kahei could step into them easily.

"Here you are, my lord."

"You just got here today, and you say you've already slept enough. How is it you know the lay of the land already?"

"Please excuse me, my lord."

"What for?"

"I'm not a suspicious person at all. But in this kind of mansion, even when I'm asleep, by hearing various sounds, I can guess where things are located, the size of the grounds, the drainage system, and where the fires are."

"Hm. I see."

"I noticed where the straw sandals were earlier. It occurred to me that someone might come out and ask for sandals."

"I'm sorry. I forgot all about you."

Hiyoshi laughed but made no reply. Although he was no more than a boy, he did not seem to respect Kahei very much. Kahei then asked him about his background and whether he had hopes of serving someone. Hiyoshi assured him that he had. He had high hopes for the future and had been walking throughout the provinces from the time he was fifteen.

"You walked around the provinces for two years, wanting to serve a samurai?"

"Yes."

"Why, then, are you still a needle seller?" Kahei asked pointedly. "Looking for two years without finding a master—I wonder if there isn't something wrong with you?"

"I have good and bad points, just like any other man. At first I thought any master or any samurai household would do, but once I went out into the world, I started to feel differently."

"Differently? How?"

"Walking around and looking at the warrior class as a whole—the good generals, the bad generals, the lords of large and small provinces—led me to think that there is nothing so important as choosing a master. Therefore, I decided to go on with my needle selling, and before I knew it, two years had gone by."

Kahei thought he was clever, but there was also something of the fool about him. And though there was some truth in what he said, he sounded very pretentious and a little hard to believe. There was one thing that was beyond doubt, though: here was no ordinary young man. He decided on the spot to employ Hiyoshi as a servant.

"Will you serve me?"

"Thank you, my lord. I'll try," Hiyoshi answered with little enthusiasm in his voice.

Kahei was dissatisfied with Hiyoshi's joyless reply, but it did not occur to him, as the new master of this wandering youth clothed in nothing more than a thin cotton coat, that he himself might be deficient in some respect.

Like the samurai of the other clans, the Matsushita samurai received intensive training in the horsemanship needed for battle. At daybreak they left their dormitories with practice spears and swords, and went to the broad field in front of the rice storehouse.

"Hiyaaa!" Spear clashed against spear, sword against sword. In the morning, everyone, down to the lower-ranking samurai in the kitchen and the men who pulled guard duty, gave their all and came away from the field with faces bright red from exertion. That Hiyoshi had been taken on as a servant was soon common knowledge throughout the mansion. The stable attendants treated him as a rank beginner and ordered him about.

"Hey, Monkey! Every morning from now on, after we take the horses out to graze, clean out the stables. Bury the horse manure in that bamboo thicket." After he had finished cleaning up the horse manure, one of the older samurai told him, "Fill the big water jars." And so it went on: "Split the firewood." While he was splitting the firewood, he'd be told to do something else. In short, he was the servants' servant.

He was popular at first. People said, "Nothing makes him mad, does it? His good point is that no matter what you tell him to do, he doesn't get angry." The young samurai liked him, but in the way that children like a new toy, and sometimes they gave him presents. But it was not long before people started to complain about him.

"He's always arguing."

"He flatters the master."

"He takes people for fools."

Since the younger samurai made a lot of noise over small faults, there were times when the complaints about Hiyoshi reached Kahei's ears.

"Let's see how it goes," he told his retainers, and let the matter drop.

That Kahei's wife and children always asked for Monkey made the other young men of the household even angrier. Puzzled, Hiyoshi decided that it was difficult to live among people who did not want to devote themselves to work, as he himself preferred to do.

Living in the servants' world of petty sentiments, Hiyoshi studied human nature. With the Matsushita clan as a point of reference, he was able to understand the strengths and weaknesses of the great clans along the coastal road. And he was happy to have become a servant. He could now partly understand the true state of the country, which had been difficult to grasp when he was wandering around from place to place. An ordinary servant, who worked only to eat and survive, would hardly know what the world was really like. But Hiyoshi's mind was always on the alert. It was like watching the stones on a *go* board and catching on to the moves made by the players.

The messengers from the Imagawa of Suruga were frequent, as were those from the neighboring provinces of Mikawa and Kai. He began to see a pattern in their comings and goings, and concluded that Imagawa Yoshimoto, lord of Suruga, was making a bid to grasp supreme power in the land. The realization of his goal was probably a long way off, but he was already making the initial moves to enter the capital, Kyoto, ostensibly to protect the Shogun, but really to rule the country in his name.

To the east were the powerful Hojo of Odawara; the Takeda of Kai were on the northern flank; and barring the road to the capital was the domain of the Tokugawa of Mikawa. Thus surrounded, Yoshimoto had first aimed at subjugating Mikawa. Tokugawa Kiyoyasu, lord of Mikawa, had submitted to Yoshimoto and had resigned himself to being his retainer. Kiyoyasu's son, Hirotada, had not outlived him very long, and his successor, Ieyasu, was now living as a hostage in Sumpu.

Yoshimoto had made one of his own retainers governor of Okazaki Castle, and put him in charge of administering Mikawa and collecting taxes. The retainers of the Tokugawa were press-ganged into serving the Imagawa, and all the revenues and military supplies of the province, with the exception of its day-to-day running expenses, went to Yoshimoto's castle in Suruga. Hiyoshi thought that Mikawa's future was bleak indeed. He knew from his travels as a peddler that the men of Mikawa were stubborn and proud; they would not meekly submit forever.

But the clan he watched most closely was naturally the Oda of Owari. Although he was now far from Nakamura, Owari was his birthplace and his mother's home. Seen from the Matsushita mansion, Owari's poverty and small size compared unfavorably with other provinces, with the exception of Mikawa. The contrast with the sophisticated and prosperous Imagawa domain was especially striking. His home village of Nakamura was poor, and so was his own home. What would become of Owari? He thought that someday, something worthwhile might grow from its poor soil. He despised the effete manners of both high and low in the Imagawa domain. They aped the manners of the court, a practice that Hiyoshi had long thought dangerous.

The messengers were coming more often of late. To Hiyoshi this meant that talks were being held to tie the provinces of Suruga, Kai, and Sagami in a nonaggression pact, with the Imagawa clan as the center. The prime mover, of course, was Imagawa Yoshimoto. Before marching to the capital at the head of a great army, he would have to secure the allegiance of the Hojo and the Takeda. As a first step, Yoshimoto had decided to marry his daughter to Takeda Shingen's eldest son and have one of Shingen's daughters marry into the house of the Hojo. This, along with military and economic pacts, made Imagawa a power to be reckoned with on the eastern seaboard. This power was reflected in the bearing of the Imagawa retainers. A man like Matsushita Kahei was different from the immediate retainers of Yoshimoto, but he, too, had incomparably more wealth than did the samurai houses Hiyoshi knew in Kiyosu, Nagoya, and Okazaki. Guests were numerous, and even the servants seemed to be having the time of their lives.

"Monkey!" Nohachiro was looking for Hiyoshi in the garden.

"Up here."

Nohachiro looked up to the roof. "What are you doing up there?"

"I'm repairing the roof."

Nohachiro was amazed. "You're making it hard on yourself on such a hot day. Why are you doing it?"

"The weather has been fine so far, but it'll soon be time for the fall rains. Calling the roofers after the rains start will be too late, so I'm finding split planks and repairing them."

"That's why you're unpopular around here. At noon, everyone else has found a spot in the shade."

"If I worked near others, I'd disturb their naps. Up here, I won't bother anybody."

"You're lying. I'll bet you're up there to study the layout of the grounds."

"It's just like you, Master Nohachiro, to think like that. But if a man doesn't take note of things, when an emergency comes, he won't be ready to defend himself."

"Don't talk like that. If the master hears of it, he'll be angry. Get down from there!"

"Sure. Do you have any work for me?"

"There are guests coming this evening."

"Again?"

"What do you mean, 'again'?"

"Who's coming?"

"A student of the martial arts who's traveled throughout the country."

"How many in the group?" Hiyoshi climbed down from the roof. Nohachiro took out a parchment. "We're expecting the nephew of Lord Kamiizumi of Ogo, Hitta Shohaku. He is traveling with twelve followers. There'll be another rider and three packhorses and their attendants."

"That's a fair-sized group."

"These men have dedicated their lives to the study of martial arts. There'll be a lot of baggage and horses, so clear out the storehouse workers' quarters, and we'll put them up there for the time being. Have the place swept clean by evening, before they get here."

"Yes, sir. Will they be staying long?"

"About six months," Nohachiro said. Looking tired, he wiped the sweat off his face.

In the evening Shohaku and his men brought their horses to a halt in front of the gate and brushed the dust off their clothes. Senior and junior retainers came out to meet them, and gave them an elaborate ceremonial welcome. There were lengthy words of greeting from the hosts, and no less respectful and eloquent a reply from Shohaku, a man of about thirty. Once the formalities were over, servants took charge of the packhorses and baggage, and the guests, led by Shohaku, entered the mansion compound.

Hiyoshi had enjoyed watching the elaborate show. Its formality made him realize how much the prestige of warriors had risen with the growing importance of military matters. Lately the term "martial arts" was on everyone's lips, along with other new expressions like "sword technique" and "spear technique." Martial artists like Kamiizumi of Ogo and Tsukahara of Hitachi were household names. The travels of some of these men were far more rigorous than the pilgrimages of wandering Buddhist monks. But men like Tsukahara were always accompanied by sixty or seventy followers. Their retainers carried hawks and traveled in grand style.

The number of Shohaku's party did not surprise Hiyoshi. But since they were going to be there for six months, he suspected rightly that he was going to be ordered around until his head spun. No more than four or five days had passed before he was being worked as hard as one of their own servants.

"Hey, Monkey! My underwear is dirty. Wash it."

"Lord Matsushita's monkey! Go and buy me some ointment."

The summer nights were short, and the extra work cut into his sleeping time, so at noon one day he was fast asleep in the shade of a paulownia tree. He was leaning against the trunk, his head dangling to one side and his arms folded. On the parched earth, the only thing that moved was a procession of ants.

A couple of young samurai, who disliked him, walked past carrying practice spears.

"Well, look here. It's Monkey."

"Having a good sleep, isn't he?"

"He's just a lazy good-for-nothing. How come he's the master and mistress's pet? They wouldn't like it if they saw him like this."

"Wake him up. Let's teach him a lesson."

"What do you have in mind?"

"Isn't Monkey the only one who hasn't once gone to martial-arts practice?"

"That's probably because he knows he's not well liked. He's afraid of getting hit."

"That's not right. It's the duty of all the servants of a warrior house to train hard in the martial arts. That's what it says in the household regulations."

"You don't have to tell me. Tell Monkey."

"I say we wake him up and take him to the practice field."

"Yeah, that'd be interesting."

One of the men struck Hiyoshi's shoulder with the point of his spear.

"Hey, wake up!"

Hiyoshi's eyes stayed shut.

"Wake up!" The man lifted Hiyoshi's feet with his spear. Hiyoshi slipped down the tree trunk and awoke with a start.

"What are you doing?" he asked.

"What do you think *you're* doing, snoring away in the garden in broad daylight?"

"Me, sleeping?"

"Well, weren't you?"

"Maybe I fell asleep without meaning to. I'm awake now though."

"Impertinent little ass! I've heard that you haven't spent one single day at martial-arts practice."

"That's because I'm no good."

"If you never practice, how do you know? Even though you're a servant, the household regulations say you have to practice the martial arts. From today on, we'll see that you practice."

"No, thanks."

"Are you refusing to obey the household regulations?"

"No, but—"

"Come on, let's go!" Allowing no further protest, they dragged Hiyoshi forcibly to the field in front of the storehouse. They were going to teach him a lesson for disobeying the household regulations.

Under the burning sky, the visiting martial artists and the Matsushita retainers were training hard.

The young samurai who had brought Hiyoshi urged him forward with hard blows to the back.

"Get yourself a wooden sword or spear and fight!"

Hiyoshi tottered forward, barely able to stand, but he did not pick up a weapon.

"What are you waiting for?" One man gave him a sharp rap on the chest with his spear. "We're going to give you some practice, so get a weapon!" Hiyoshi staggered forward again but still would not fight. He just chewed his lip obstinately.

Two of Shohaku's men, Jingo Gorokuro and Sakaki Ichinojo, were having a trial of strength with real spears in response to a request from the Matsushita men. Gorokuro, who wore a headband, was spearing two-hundred-pound rice bags and flinging them in the air in a show of apparently superhuman strength.

"With that kind of skill, it must be easy to fly at a man on the battlefield. His strength is astonishing!" said one of the spectators.

Gorokuro corrected him. "If you men think this is a technique of strength, you're badly mistaken. If you put strength into this technique, the shaft of the spear will break and your arms will quickly get tired." He put his spear aside and explained, "The principles of the sword and the spear are the same. The secret of all the martial arts is in the *ch'i*, the subtle energy of the *tan t'ien*, the area two inches below the navel. This is strength without strength. One must have the mental power to transcend the need for strength and regulate the flow of *ch'i*." He lectured with enthusiasm and at length.

Deeply impressed, his audience listened attentively, until they were disturbed by a noise behind them.

"You obstinate monkey!" The young samurai swung the handle of his spear, hitting Hiyoshi in the hip.

"Ow!" yelled Hiyoshi in a tearful voice. The blow had obviously hurt. He screwed up his face and doubled over, rubbing his hip. The group broke up and re-formed around Hiyoshi.

"Lazy good-for-nothing!" yelled the man who had struck Hiyoshi. "He says he's no good and doesn't want to come to practice."

Hiyoshi found himself the center of a grumbling crowd, accused of being unrepentant and insolent.

"Well, well," said Shohaku, coming forward and calming them down. "Judging from appearances, he's still just a suckling, at an age when impertinence blooms. Flouting the household regulations while in the employ of a warrior house and having no taste for the martial arts is this fellow's misfortune. I'll do the questioning. The rest of you be quiet.

"Young man," he said to Hiyoshi.

"Yes." Hiyoshi looked straight at Shohaku as he answered. But his tone of voice had changed, for the look in his questioner's eyes said that Shohaku was the kind of man to whom he could speak freely.

"It seems you dislike the martial arts, even though you're employed in a warrior house. Is this true?"

"No." Hiyoshi shook his head.

"Then why, when these retainers kindly offer to drill you in the martial arts, do you not take them up on it?"

"Yes, well, there's a reason for that. If I were to discipline myself in the way of the spear or sword and became an expert, it would probably take up my entire life."

"Yes, you must have that kind of spirit."

"It isn't that I dislike either spear or sword, but when I consider that I won't be able to live more than one normal lifespan, I think it's probably enough to know only the spirit of these things. The reason is that there are so many other things that I would like to study and do."

"What would you like to study?"

"Learning."

"What would you like to learn?"

"About the whole world."

"What are the things you'd like to do?"

Hiyoshi smiled. "That I won't say."

"Why not?"

"I want to do things, but unless I do them, talking about them will only sound like boasting. And if I talked about them out loud, you'd all just laugh."

Shohaku stared at Hiyoshi, thinking how unusual he was. "I think I understand a little of what you say, but you're mistaken about the martial arts being the practice of small techniques."

"What are they, then?"

"According to one school of thought, when a person has learned a single skill, he will have mastered all the arts. The martial arts are not simply techniques—they are of the mind. If one cultivates the mind deeply, one is able to penetrate everything, including the arts of learning and government, see the world for what it is, and judge people."

"But I'll bet the people here consider striking and piercing their opponents as the best art of all. That should be useful for a foot soldier or the ordinary rank and file, but would it be essential for a great general who—"

"Watch your mouth!" scolded one of the samurai, landing a solid punch on Hiyoshi's cheek.

"Ow!" Hiyoshi put both hands over his mouth as though his jaw had been broken.

"These insulting remarks cannot be ignored. This is getting to be a habit. Master Shohaku, please withdraw. We'll take care of this."

The resentment was widespread. Almost all those who had heard Hiyoshi had something to say.

"He insulted us!"

"It's the same as mocking the household regulations!"

"Inexcusable ass!"

"Cut him down! The master won't blame us for it."

In their anger, it seemed they might carry out their threat, dragging him into the thicket and cutting his head off there and then. It was difficult for Shohaku to stop them. It took all his strength to calm them down and save Hiyoshi's life.

That evening, Nohachiro came to the servants' quarters and called softly to Hiyoshi,

93

who was sitting all alone in a corner, making a face as though he had a toothache.

"Yes. What is it?" His face was badly swollen.

"Does it hurt?"

"No, not much," he lied. He pressed the damp towel to his face.

"The master has asked for you. Go through the rear garden so that you won't be seen."

"Huh? The master? Well, I suppose he's heard about what happened today."

"The disrespectful things you said were bound to reach his ears. And Master Hitta came to see him a little while ago, so he must have. He may carry out the execution himself."

"Do you think so?"

"It's an iron rule of the Matsushita clan that servants should not be slack in their practice of the martial arts, day or night. When the master has to make a special effort to uphold the dignity of the household regulations, you should consider your head already lost."

"Well, then, I'll run away from here. I don't want to die over something like this."

"You're talking nonsense!" He grabbed Hiyoshi's wrists. "If you ran away, I'd have to commit *seppuku*. I've been ordered to bring you along."

"I can't even run away?" Hiyoshi asked artlessly.

"Your mouth is really too much. Think a little bit before you open it. Hearing what you said today, even I thought you nothing but a boastful monkey."

Nohachiro made Hiyoshi walk ahead of him, and he kept a firm grip on the hilt of the sword. White gnats swarmed in the gathering darkness. The light from lamps inside spilled out onto the veranda of the library, which had just been sprinkled with water.

"I've brought Monkey." Nohachiro knelt as he spoke.

Kahei appeared on the veranda. "He's here, is he?"

Hearing the voice above his head, Hiyoshi bowed so low that his forehead touched the garden moss.

"Monkey."

"Yes, my lord."

"It seems that a new type of armor is being made in Owari. It's called *domaru*. Go buy a set. It's your home province, so I presume you'll have no trouble moving around freely."

"My lord?"

"Leave tonight."

"Where to?"

"To where you can buy *domaru* armor." Kahei took some money from a box, wrapped it, and tossed it in front of Hiyoshi. Hiyoshi looked back and forth between Kahei and the money. His eyes filled with tears that rolled off his cheeks and onto the backs of his hands.

"It would be best if you left without delay, but you don't have to be in a hurry to bring back the armor. Even if it takes several years, find me the best possible set." Then he said to Nohachiro, "Let him out by the rear gate quietly, and before the night is over."

What an abrupt turnabout! Hiyoshi felt a chill creep over him. Here he had expected to be killed for running afoul of the household regulations, and now...the chill came from his reaction to Kahei's sympathy—his sense of gratitude—and it penetrated to the very marrow of his bones.

"Thank you very much." While Kahei had not spelled out what he had in mind, Hiyoshi already understood.

His quickness bewilders the people around him, Kahei thought. It's only natural that this breeds resentment and jealousy. He smiled bitterly and asked aloud, "Why are you thanking me?"

"For letting me go."

"That's right. But, Monkey..."

"Yes, my lord?"

"If you don't hide that intelligence of yours, you'll never succeed."

"I know."

"If you knew, why did you speak abusively like today, making everybody angry?"

"I'm inexperienced....I hit my head with my own fist after I said it."

"I'm not going to say any more. Because your intelligence is valuable, I'm going to help you. I can tell you now that those who resented you and were jealous of you accused you of theft on the slightest pretext. If a pin was lost, or a dirk or a pillbox was misplaced, they'd point their fingers at you and say, 'It was Monkey.' There was no end to their spiteful talk. You easily provoke the resentment of others. You should understand that about yourself."

"Yes, my lord."

"There was no reason for me to help you today. My retainers' point was well taken. As I was informed about this matter in private by Master Shohaku, it's as if I hadn't heard about it yet and were sending you off on a mission. Do you understand?"

"I understand very well. I have engraved it on my heart."

Hiyoshi's nose was stopped up. He bowed to Kahei again and again.

That night he left the Matsushita house.

Turning to look back, he vowed, I won't forget. I won't forget.

Wrapped up in this man's great kindness, Hiyoshi wondered how he could best repay him. Only one who was always surrounded by brutality and ridicule could feel another's sympathy so intensely.

Someday...someday. Whenever impressed by something or overwhelmed by events, he repeated this word like a pilgrim's prayer.

Once again he was wandering like a homeless dog, without aim and without work. The Tenryu was in flood, and when he was far away from human habitation, he felt like crying out at his loneliness, at the unknown fate that awaited him. Neither the universe nor the stars nor the waters could give him any kind of sign.

The Idiot Lord

"Excuse me!" A voice called a second time.

Otowaka, off duty that day, was in his regiment's dormitory, taking a nap. He woke up, raised his head, and looked around.

"Who is it?"

"It's me," a voice said from beyond the hedge, where the tendrils of bindweed entwined themselves around the leaves and thorns of Chinese orange. From the balcony, Otowaka could see someone on the other side of the dust-covered hedge. He went out on the veranda.

"Who is it? If you have some business, come in by the front gate."

"It's locked."

Otowaka stretched to get a good look and exclaimed, "Why, it's Yaemon's son Monkey, isn't it?"

"Yes."

"Why didn't you say who you were, instead of groaning out there like a ghost?"

"Well, the front gate wasn't open, and when I peeped through the back, you were asleep," he said deferentially. "Then you got a little restless, and I thought I'd try calling you again."

"You needn't be so reserved. I guess my wife locked the gate when she went out shopping. I'll open it for you."

After Hiyoshi had washed his feet and come into the house, Otowaka stared at him for a long time before saying, "What have you been up to? It's been two years since we met on the road. There's been no news of whether you were alive or dead, and your mother's been terribly worried. Did you let her know you were all right?"

"Not yet."

"Aren't you going home?"

"I went home just for a bit before coming here."

"And you still didn't show your face to your mother?"

"Actually, I went secretly to the house last night, but after one look at my mother and sister, I turned around and came here."

"You're a strange one. It's the house where you were born, isn't it? Why didn't you let them know you were safe, and put them at ease?"

"Well, I wanted to see them very much, but when I left home, I swore I wouldn't return until I'd made something of myself. The way I am now, I couldn't face my stepfather."

Otowaka took a second look at him. Hiyoshi's white cotton smock had been turned gray by dust, rain, and dew. His greasy hair and his thin, sunburned cheeks somehow completed the picture of exhaustion. He was the image of a man who had failed to reach his goal.

"What do you do to eat?"

"I sell needles."

"You're not working for anyone?"

"I worked at two or three places, not very high-class samurai households, but—"

"As usual, you soon got tired of them, I suppose. How old are you now?"

"Seventeen."

"There's nothing a man can do if he's born stupid, but don't overdo it in acting the simpleton. There's a limit. Fools have the patience to be treated like fools, but that doesn't hold for you and your mistakes. Look, it's natural that your mother is grieving and your stepfather's embarrassed. Monkey! What in the world are you going to do now?"

Although Otowaka scolded Hiyoshi for his lack of perseverance, he also felt sorry for him. He had been a close friend of Yaemon's, and he was well aware that Chikuami had treated his stepchildren harshly. He prayed that Hiyoshi might make something of himself for his dead father's sake.

Otowaka's wife came back just then, and she spoke up for Hiyoshi: "He's Onaka's son, not yours, isn't he? Who do you think you're scolding? You're just wasting your breath. I feel sorry for the boy." She fetched a watermelon that had been cooling in the well, cut it up, and served it to Hiyoshi.

"He's still just seventeen? Why, he doesn't know anything," she said. "Think back to when you were his age. Even though you're past forty, you're still a foot soldier. That makes you pretty ordinary, doesn't it?"

"Be quiet," Otowaka said, looking hurt. "Since I don't think young men should have to spend their lives like me, I have something to say to them. After the coming-of-age ceremony, they're considered adults, but when they're seventeen, they have to be men already. It's a bit irreverent, maybe, but look at our master, Lord Nobunaga. How old do you think he is?" He started to tell her but then quickly changed the subject, perhaps for fear of getting into an argument with his wife. "Oh, yes, we'll probably go hunting with His Lordship again tomorrow. Then, on the way back, we'll practice fording the Shonai River on horseback and by swimming. Have my things ready—a cord for my armor, and my straw sandals."

Hiyoshi, who had his head down, listening, raised it and said, "Excuse me, sir."

"Being formal again?"

"I don't mean to be. Does Lord Nobunaga go hunting and swimming that much?"

"It's not my place to say it, but he's an awfully mischievous lad."

"He's wild, is he?"

"You'd think so, but then there are times he can be very well mannered."

"He's got a bad reputation from one end of the country to the other."

"Is that so? Well, I guess he's not very popular with his enemies."

Hiyoshi suddenly stood up and said, "I'm really sorry to have bothered you on your day off."

"You don't have to leave so soon, do you? Why don't you stay the night, at least? Did I hurt your feelings?"

"No, not at all."

"I won't stop you if you insist, but why don't you go and show yourself to your mother?"

"Yes, I'll do that. I'll go to Nakamura tonight."

"That would be good." Otowaka went out as far as the gate and saw Hiyoshi off, but he felt that something was not quite right.

Hiyoshi did not go home that night. Where did he sleep? Perhaps he camped out at a roadside shrine or under the eaves of a temple. He had received money from Matsushita Kahei, but in Nakamura the night before, after peeking through the hedge to see that his mother was all right, he had tossed it into the yard. So he did not have any money left, but because the summer night was short, he did not have to wait long for the dawn.

Early the next morning he left the village of Kasugai and went in the direction of Biwajima, walking at a leisurely pace, eating as he walked. He had some rice balls wrapped in lotus leaves tied to his belt. But how did he eat without money?

Food can be found anywhere. That's because it's heaven's gift to mankind. This was an article of faith with Hiyoshi. The birds and the beasts receive heaven's bounty. But man has been ordered to work for the world, and those who don't work can't eat. Human beings who live only to eat are a disgrace. If they work, they will receive heaven's gift naturally. In other words, Hiyoshi put work before hunger.

Whenever Hiyoshi wanted to work, he would stop at a building site and offer his services to the carpenters or laborers; if he saw a person pulling a heavy cart, he would push from behind; if he saw a dirty doorway, he would ask if he could borrow a broom to sweep it. Even if he wasn't asked, he would work or make work, and because he did it conscientiously, he was always repaid by people with a bowl of food or a little traveling money. He was not ashamed of his way of life, because he did not humble himself like an animal. He worked for the world, and believed that heaven would give him what he needed.

That morning in Kasugai he had come across a blacksmith's shop that had opened early. The wife had children to take care of, so after helping to clean up the smithy, putting the two cows out to pasture, and going around to the well to fill the water jars, he was rewarded with breakfast and rice balls for the afternoon.

It looks like it's going to be hot again today, he thought, looking up at the morning sky. His meal sustained his life, transient as dew, for another day, but his thoughts were not attuned to the thoughts of others. With the weather like this, Lord Nobunaga was sure to come to the river today. And Otowaka had said he'd be there too.

In the distance he could see the Shonai River. Wet with morning dew, he got up from the grass and went to the riverbank, gazing idly at the beauty of the water.

Every year from spring to fall, Lord Nobunaga does not miss a chance to practice fording the river. But where, I wonder? I should've asked Otowaka. The stones on the riverbank were drying in the sun, which shone brightly on the grass and berries and on Hiyoshi's dirty clothes. Anyway I'll wait here, Hiyoshi said to himself and sat down near a clump of bushes. Lord Nobunaga...Lord Nobunaga. The mischievous master of the Oda. What kind of man could he be? Like a pasted-on talisman, the man's name would not leave his head, whether he was sleeping or awake.

Hiyoshi wanted to meet him. This was what brought him to the riverbank early that morning. Although Nobunaga had succeeded Oda Nobuhide, would he be able to survive very long, spoiled and violent as he was? Common opinion had it that he was stupid as well as short-tempered.

For years Hiyoshi had believed the gossip, and it made him sad that his home province should be so poor and be ruled by so worthless a lord. But after seeing the true circumstances in other provinces, he began to think differently. No, one didn't really know. A war wasn't won on the day of the battle. Each and every province had its own character, and in each one there was both appearance and reality. Even a province that seemed weak on the surface could have hidden strengths. Conversely, provinces that looked strong—like Mino and Suruga—might be rotten from within.

Surrounded by large, strong provinces, the domains of the Oda and the Tokugawa appeared small and poor. Within these small provinces, however, were concealed strengths that the larger provinces did not have, without which they would not have been able to survive.

If Nobunaga was the fool he was said to be, how had he managed to hold on to Nagoya Castle? Nobunaga was now nineteen. It was three years since his father had died. In those three years, this young, violent, empty-headed general, with neither talent nor intelligence, had not only held on to his inheritance, but had gained a firm grip on the province. How was he able to do this? Some claimed it wasn't the work of Nobunaga himself but of his able retainers, in whose charge a worried father had entrusted his son: Hirate Nakatsukasa, Hayashi Sado, Aoyama Yosaemon, and Naito Katsusuke. The collective power of these men was the pillar of the Oda, and the young lord was nothing more than a figurehead. As long as the previous lord's retainers survived, everything would be fine, but when one or two died and the pillar crumbled, the downfall of the Oda was going to be plain for everyone to see. Among those most eager to see this happen were, of course, Saito Dosan of Mino and Imagawa Yoshimoto of Suruga. No one dissented from this view.

"Hiyaa!"

At the sound of a war cry, Hiyoshi looked around over the grass. Yellow dust rose near the upper reaches of the river. Standing up, he strained his ears. I can't see anything, but there's something going on, he thought excitedly. Is it a battle? He raced through the grass, and after running about a hundred yards, he saw what was happening. The Oda troops he had been waiting for since morning had come to the river and were already carrying out their maneuvers.

Whether euphemistically referred to as "river fishing" or "hawking" or "military swimming drills," for the warlords the sole object of these exercises was military preparedness. Disregard military preparations, and your life would be over very quickly.

Hidden in the tall grass, Hiyoshi let out a sigh. On the other bank of the river, a makeshift camp lay between the embankment and the grassy plain above. Curtains, bearing the Oda family crest, hung between several small rest huts and fluttered in the wind. There were soldiers, but Nobunaga was nowhere to be seen. There was a similar camp on this bank as well. Horses were whinnying and stamping, and the excited voices of the warriors roared from both banks loudly enough to raise waves on the water. A lone riderless horse splashed around crazily in the middle of the river and finally leaped up to the dry land downstream.

They pass this off as swimming practice! Hiyoshi thought, astonished.

Popular opinion was, for the most part, wrong. Nobunaga was said to be weak-minded and violent, but if you asked for proof, it seemed that no one had really bothered to check whether or not it was true. Everyone saw Nobunaga leaving the castle during the spring and fall, to go fishing or swimming, and that was all. Seeing it with his own eyes, Hiyoshi finally realized that these outings had nothing to do with a frivolous lord taking a swim in the summer heat. This was no-holds-barred military training.

At first the samurai rode in small groups, clad in the lightweight clothes they might wear on an outing. But at the sound of the conch, and with the drums beating, they formed into regiments that clashed in the middle of the river. The waters roiled, and in the pure white spray it was samurai against samurai, one contingent of foot soldiers against another. The bamboo spears became a whirlwind, but their bearers beat rather than thrust at each other. The spears that missed their mark skimmed the water and threw up rainbows. Seven or eight mounted generals showed their colors, brandishing their spears.

"Daisuke! I'm here!" shouted a young mounted samurai, who stood out from the ranks. He wore armor over a white hemp tunic and carried a gorgeous vermilion sword. He galloped up next to the horse of Ichikawa Daisuke, the archery and spear master, and without warning struck the man's side with his bamboo spear.

"What insolence!" Yelling out and wresting the spear from his attacker, Daisuke adjusted his grip and thrust back at his opponent's chest. The young warrior was a graceful man. His face flushed, he grabbed Daisuke's spear with one hand and held his vermilion sword in the other and glowered. Unable to resist Daisuke's strength, however, he fell backward off his horse into the river.

"That's Nobunaga!" Hiyoshi yelled out involuntarily. Were there retainers who could do such a horrible thing to their master? Wasn't the servant being even more violent than the master was said to be? Hiyoshi thought so, but from that distance he could not be absolutely sure that the man was Nobunaga. Forgetting himself, Hiyoshi stood on tiptoe. The mock battle at the ford continued apace. If Nobunaga had been pushed off his horse, his retainers should be rushing over to help him, but no one paid the slightest attention.

Before long, a warrior splashed out onto the opposite bank downstream from the battle. It was the same man who had been knocked off his horse, and he looked a lot like Nobunaga. Raising himself up like a water-soaked rat, he immediately stamped his foot, shouting, "I will never be beaten!"

Daisuke caught sight of him and pointed. "The general of the eastern army is over there! Surround him and take him alive!"

Kicking up a spray, foot soldiers made straight for Nobunaga. Using a bamboo spear, Nobunaga landed a blow on one soldier's helmet and knocked him down; then he hurled the spear at the next man.

"Don't let them get close!"

A group of his men arrived to screen him from the opposing forces. Nobunaga ran up the embankment, yelling in a sharp voice, "Give me a bow!" Two pages ran from behind the curtain of his hut carrying short bows and, almost pitching over, flew to where he was. "Don't let them cross the river!" While giving orders to his troops, he notched an arrow, let it go with a snap, and rapidly notched another. They were practice arrows, without heads, but, shot square in the forehead, several "enemy" soldiers were felled. He shot off so many arrows that it was hard to believe that he alone was shooting. As he fired, his bowstring broke twice. Each time, Nobunaga changed weapons with no delay at all and went on shooting. While he was desperately holding his ground, the upstream defense gave in. The western army overran the embankment, surrounded Nobunaga's headquarters, and let out shouts of victory.

"Lost!" Nobunaga tossed his bow aside, already laughing. He turned, smiling through gritted teeth, and faced the enemy and their victory song. Daisuke and the master of strategy, Hirata Sammi, dismounted and ran toward Nobunaga.

"My lord is not injured?"

"Nothing could happen to me in the water."

Nobunaga was mortified. He said to Daisuke, "Tomorrow I'll win. Tomorrow you're going to have a hard time of it." He raised his brow slightly as he spoke.

Sammi said, "After we get back to the castle, would you care for me to offer a critique of your strategy today?"

Nobunaga was hardly listening. He had already thrown off his armor and plunged into the river to cool off.

* * *

Nobunaga's handsome features and fair complexion suggested that his forebears had been exceptionally goodlooking men and women. Turning to face someone, he would shoot them through with the unwavering light in his eyes. When he eventually became aware of this trait, he would wrap the light in laughter, leaving the onlooker baffled. And not only he, but his twelve brothers and seven sisters also, either in their refinement of manners or in their fine good looks, had the sophistication of aristocrats.

"You may find this annoying, and you may ask, 'What? Again?' But, like a prayer that you must say day and night—even while you eat—you must remember your ancestry. The founder of the Oda clan was a priest of the Tsurugi Shrine. In the distant past, one of your ancestors was a member of the Taira clan, which claimed descent from Emperor Kammu. So remember that the blood of the Imperial House has been transmitted to you. Old man that I am, I cannot say more."

Nobunaga heard this constantly from Hirate Nakatsukasa, one of the four men his father had appointed as his guardians when he had moved from his birthplace, Furuwatari Castle, to Nagoya. Nakatsukasa was a remarkably loyal retainer, but to Nobunaga he was awkward and tiresome. He would murmur, "Ah, I understand, old man. I understand," and turn away. He would not listen to him, but the old man went on, as if repeating a litany:

"Remember your honored father. To defend Owari, he fought on his northern borders in the morning and faced invasion from the east at night. The days in one month when he could take off his armor and spend time with his children were few and far between. Despite the continuous warfare, he had a deep sense of loyalty to the Throne, and he sent me to the capital to repair the mud walls of the Imperial Palace and gave four thousand *kan* to the Court. Besides that, he spared no effort in constructing the Grand Shrine at Ise. Your father was such a man. And among your ancestors—"

"Old man! That's enough! I don't know how many times I've heard this!" When Nobunaga was displeased, his beautiful earlobes became bright red, but from the time he was a child, that was the extent to which he could show his displeasure. Nakatsukasa understood his disposition well. He also knew it was more efficacious to appeal to his feelings than to try to reason with him. When his ward got restless, he would quickly change tactics.

"Shall we get a bridle?"

"Horseback riding?"

"If you like."

"You ride too, old man."

Riding was his favorite pastime. He was not content with staying on the riding grounds. He would ride three or four leagues from the castle and then gallop back.

At thirteen, Nobunaga had taken part in his first battle, and at fifteen he had lost his father. As he grew older he became more and more arrogant. On the day of his father's funeral Nobunaga was improperly dressed for the formality of the occasion.

As the guests watched in disbelief, Nobunaga walked up to the altar, grabbed a handful of powdered incense, and threw it at his father's mortuary tablet. Then, to everybody's surprise, he returned to the castle.

"What a disgrace! Is this really the heir of the province?"

"A hopelessly empty-headed lord."

"You wouldn't have thought it would come to this."

This was the view of those who had only a superficial understanding of things. But those who considered the situation more deeply shed tears of gloom for the Oda clan.

"His younger brother, Kanjuro, is well mannered, and has acted respectfully from beginning to end," one mourner pointed out. They regretted that the estate had not gone to him. But a monk who sat at the back of the room said softly, "No, no … this is a man with a future. He's frightening." This comment was later reported to the senior retainers, but not one of them took it seriously. Shortly before he died, at forty-six, Nobuhide had arranged Nobunaga's engagement to the daughter of Saito Dosan of Mino, through the good offices of Nakatsukasa. For a number of years Mino and Owari had been enemies, so the marriage was a political one. Such arrangements were almost the rule in a country at war.

Dosan had no trouble seeing through this strategy, and yet he had given his favorite daughter to the heir of the Oda clan, whose reputation for being a fool was well known from the neighboring provinces to the capital. He gave his consent to the match, with his eyes firmly fixed on Owari.

Nobunaga's foolishness, violence, and disgraceful conduct appeared to grow worse. But that was exactly what he wanted others to see. In the Fourth Month of the twenty-second year of Temmon, Nobunaga turned nineteen years old.

Anxious to meet his son-in-law, Saito Dosan proposed holding their first meeting at the Shotokuji Temple in Tonda, on the border between their two provinces. Tonda was an estate of the Ikko Buddhist sect. The temple stood a little apart from the village's seven hundred or so houses.

Leading a large body of men, Nobunaga left Nagoya Castle, crossed the Kiso and Hida rivers, and pushed on to Tonda. About five hundred of his men carried longbows or firearms; another four hundred had crimson spears eighteen feet long; and they were followed by three hundred foot soldiers. They marched in solemn silence. A corps of horsemen in the middle of the procession surrounded Nobunaga. They were prepared for any emergency.

It was early summer. The ears of the barley were a pale yellow. A gentle breeze from the Hida River refreshed the line of men. It was a peaceful noontime, and shrubs drooped over the roughly woven fences. The houses of Tonda were well built and many had rice granaries.

"There they are." Two low-ranking samurai of the Saito clan had been posted at the edge of the village as lookouts. They sped off to report. In the row of zelkova trees that cut through the village, the sparrows twittered peacefully. The samurai knelt in front of a small commoner's hut and said in a low voice, "The procession has been sighted. It will soon be passing by here."

Incongruously, the dark, sooty walls of the dirt-floored hut concealed men with gaudy swords, dressed in formal kimono.

"Good. You two go hide in the thicket in back."

The two samurai were personal attendants to Lord Saito Dosan of Mino, who was leaning against the windowsill in a small room, keeping an eye on what was going on.

There were many stories about Nobunaga. What is he really like? Dosan wondered. What kind of man is he? Before meeting him formally, I'd like to get a look at him. This was typical of Dosan's way of thinking, and it was why he was here, spying from a roadside hut.

"The men from Owari are here, my lord." So informed, Dosan grunted, and gave his attention to the road outside the window. Locking the entrance, his retainers pressed their faces against the crevices and holes in the wooden doors. They maintained strict silence.

The voices of the little birds in the row of trees fell quiet, too. Except for the sound of their wings as they suddenly took flight, the silence was pervasive. Even the soft breeze made no noise. The feet of the orderly troop of soldiers approached steadily. The musketeers, carrying their polished firearms, walked ten abreast, in detachments of forty men; the red shafts of the spears looked like a forest as they made their way past the men from Mino. With bated breath, Dosan studied the gait of the soldiers and the arrangement of their ranks. Following the wave of marching feet came the sound of horses' hooves and loud voices. Dosan could not let his eyes stray from the scene.

In the midst of the horsemen was a remarkably fine horse with a glittering muzzle. Atop the rich saddle, inlaid with mother-of-pearl, sat Nobunaga, holding reins of purple interwoven with white. He was chatting gaily with his retainers.

"What's this?" were the words that slipped slowly from Dosan's mouth. He looked astounded. Nobunaga's appearance dazzled the eye. He had heard that the lord of the Oda went about in bizarre clothing, but this far exceeded anything he had heard.

Nobunaga sat swaying in the saddle of the thoroughbred horse, his hair arranged in a general's topknot tied with pale green braid. He was dressed in a brightly patterned cotton coat with one sleeve removed. Both his long and short swords were inlaid with abalone shell and bound in sacred rice straw, twisted into the shape of a good-luck charm. Hanging from his belt were seven or eight items: a tinder bag, a small gourd, a medicine case, a string-bound folding fan, a small carving of a horse, and several jewels. Beneath his half-length skirt of tiger and leopard skin was a garment made of shiny gold brocade.

Nobunaga turned in the saddle and called out, "Daisuke, is this the place? Is this Tonda?" He shouted so loudly that Dosan heard him clearly from his hiding place.

Daisuke, who was acting as guard, rode up to his master. "Yes, and the Shotokuji Temple, where you're to meet your esteemed father-in-law, is right over there. We should be on our best behavior from now on."

"The temple belongs to the Ikko sect, doesn't it? Hm, it's quiet, isn't it. No war here, I suppose." Nobunaga gazed up through the zelkova trees, perhaps catching sight of silhouettes of hawks in the blue sky overhead. The swords at his waist clanked softly against each other and against the objects hanging from his belt.

After Nobunaga had gone by, Dosan's retainers fought back the desire to burst out laughing. Their faces showed how much they had struggled not to laugh at the ludicrousness of the display.

"Is that it?" Dosan asked. Then, "Is that the last of the procession?"

"Yes, all of it."

"Did you get a good look at him?"

"From a distance."

"Well, his appearance doesn't run counter to the rumors. His features are good and his physique is passable, but there's something missing up here," Dosan said, raising his finger to his head, smiling with apparent satisfaction.

Several retainers came hurriedly through the back door. "Please hurry, my lord. It's one thing if Nobunaga becomes suspicious, but what if his retainers do, too? Shouldn't we be at the temple first?"

They spilled out of the back door of the house and took a concealed path to the temple. Just as the vanguard of the Owari samurai stopped at the front gate of the Shotokuji, they hurried in through the back gate, acting as though nothing had happened. They

changed quickly and went out to the main entrance. The temple gate was filled with people. As all of the men from Mino had been summoned for the formalities, the main temple, the great hall, and the guest's reception room were deserted, left to the wind.

Kasuga Tango, one of Dosan's senior retainers, turned to his seated master and quietly
asked how he proposed to conduct the meeting.

Dosan shook his head. "There's no reason for me to go." To his way of thinking, Nobunaga was only his son-in-law.

It would have been fine if that was all there was to it. But Nobunaga was the lord of a
province, just as Dosan was, and his retainers had assumed that the etiquette would be
that of men meeting on an equal footing. Although Dosan was also Nobunaga's father-in-
law, wouldn't it be more appropriate to follow the form of a first meeting between two
provincial lords? That is what Tango thought, and he asked about it tentatively. Dosan
replied that it would not be necessary.

"Well then, how would it be if I went out alone?"

"No. That's not necessary either. It will be sufficient if Hotta Doku greets him."

"If my lord thinks so."

"You will attend the meeting. See that all seven hundred men in the corridor that
leads up to the room are lined up in a dignified way."

"They should be there already."

"Keep the real veterans concealed, and have them clear their throats as my son-in-law
passes by. Have the archers and musketeers stand in the garden. As for the others, tell
them they should look overbearing."

"That goes without saying. There'll never be a better opportunity to show the
strength of Mino and to crush the spirits of your son-in-law and his men. We're all
ready."

Dosan returned to the problem of the front entrance. "This son-in-law of mine is
more of a fool than I thought. Any sort of meal and any sort of etiquette will do. I'll be
waiting in the reception room." Dosan looked as though he wanted to yawn, and
stretched as he got up to leave.

Tango thought he might have to improve on his orders. He went into the corridor
and inspected the guards, then called aside a subordinate and whispered something in his
ear.

Nobunaga was coming up the steps of the main entrance. There were more than a
hundred Saito retainers, from clan elders down to young samurai still on probation. They
knelt shoulder-to-shoulder, and prostrated themselves in greeting.

Nobunaga suddenly stopped dead in his tracks and said, "How about a room to rest
in?" He spoke without a trace of reserve, and got a very hushed reaction.

"Yes, my lord!"

All the bowed heads looked up simultaneously. Hotta Doku inched forward and
prostrated himself at the feet of the lord of Owari. "This way, please. Please rest here
awhile, my lord." He stooped low as he led the way to the right of the great entrance and
along a raised corridor. Nobunaga looked to the right, then to the left. "I say, this is a nice
temple. Why, the wisteria is in full bloom. What a pleasant smell!" Fanning himself, he
entered the room with his attendants. After resting for about an hour, Nobunaga rose

from behind a folding screen, saying, "Ho, there! I need someone to show me the way. I suppose my father-in-law wants an interview, does he not? Where is the lord of Mino?"

His hair had been redone, turned down and bound. In place of his half-sleeved garment of leopard and tiger skins, he wore a split skirt and tunic of white silk embroidered with his family crest in gold thread, under a formal sleeveless coat with a paulownia pattern on a deep purple background. His short sword was tucked into his sash and he carried his long sword in his hand. He had been transformed into the very picture of an elegant young courtier.

The eyes of the retainers from Mino opened wide, and even his own retainers, who were used to seeing him in outlandish outfits, were surprised. Nobunaga strode without hesitation along the corridor on his own. He looked in both directions and said in a loud voice, "I'm not comfortable being accompanied like this. I prefer to meet with my father-in-law alone!"

Doku winked at Kasuga Tango, who had just joined them. Positioned on either side of the main hall, they introduced themselves solemnly: "I am Hotta Doku, senior retainer to Lord Dosan of Saito."

"I am also a senior retainer. My name is Kasuga Tango. You have had a long journey, and I am happy to see that you have arrived without mishap. It is felicitous, indeed, that the day of this meeting should be so splendid."

While the two men were still greeting him, Nobunaga walked briskly down the polished floor of the corridor, whose walls were lined with men. "Ah, this is well carved," he said, looking at the transom. He ignored the warriors as if they were mere grass by the roadside. Arriving at the reception room, he asked Doku and Tango, "Is it in here?"

"Yes, my lord," Doku answered, still breathless from having chased Nobunaga.

He nodded casually and stepped from the corridor into the room proper. Completely at ease, he sat down, leaning back against the pillar at the edge of the room. He looked up, as if to admire the paintings on the fretwork ceiling. His eyes were cool and his features composed. Even courtiers probably had less well-ordered features. But someone paying attention only to his looks would miss the defiance in his eyes. In one corner of the room, there was a slight rustling as a man got to his feet. Dosan stepped out from the shadows. He sat down in a dignified manner, in a position superior to Nobunaga's.

Nobunaga pretended not to notice. Or rather, he feigned indifference while toying with his fan. Dosan glanced to the side. There was no rule governing how a father-in-law should speak to his son-in-law. He held his own and was silent. The atmosphere was tense. Needles seemed to prick at Dosan's brow. Doku, finding the strain unbearable, drew near Nobunaga's side and bowed his head all the way to the tatami.

"The gentleman seated over there is Lord Saito Dosan. Would you care to greet him, my lord?"

Nobunaga said, "Is that so?" and moved his back from the pillar and straightened up. He bowed once and said, "I am Oda Nobunaga. It's a pleasure to meet you."

With Nobunaga's change of posture and salutation, Dosan's manner softened as well. "I've long hoped that we could meet. I'm happy that I could realize this long-cherished desire today."

"This is something that gladdens my heart, as well. My father-in-law is getting old, but he is making his way through life in good health."

"What are you talking about, getting old? I've just reached sixty this year, but I don't feel at all old. You're still a chick just out of the egg! Ha, ha! The prime of manhood begins at sixty."

"I'm happy to have a father-in-law I can rely on."

"In any case, this is a blessed day. I hope the next time we meet, you will show me the face of a grandchild."

"With pleasure."

"My son-in-law is openhearted! Tango!"

"Yes, my lord."

"Let's eat." Dosan gave a second order with his eyes.

"Certainly." Tango was not sure he had read the meaning in his master's eyes correctly, but the sour look on his face had cleared in the course of the meeting. He took it to mean a changed attitude: the old man would now try to please his son-in-law. Instead of the plain fare he had ordered originally, more elaborate dishes were called for.

Dosan looked satisfied with Tango's arrangements. He let out a sigh of relief. Father-in-law and son-in-law were exchanging toasts. The conversation took an amiable turn.

"Ah, I remember!" Nobunaga blurted out suddenly, as though something had just come to mind. "Lord Dosan—father-in-law—on my way here today, I came across a really odd fellow."

"How might that be?"

"Well, he was a funny old man who looked just like you, and he was peeking out at my procession from the broken window of a commoner's house. Though this is my first meeting with my father-in-law, when I first saw you, well...you looked exactly like him. Now isn't that strange?" As he laughed, Nobunaga hid his mouth behind his half-opened fan.

Dosan was quiet, as though he had drunk bitter soup. Both Hotta Doku and Kasuga Tango were sweating profusely. When the meal was over, Nobunaga said, "Well, I've overstayed my welcome. I'd like to cross the Hida River and get to tonight's lodging before sunset. I beg your leave."

"You're leaving now?" Dosan stood up with him. "I'm reluctant to see you go, but I'll go with you that far." He, too, had to get back to his castle before nightfall.

The forest of eighteen-foot spears put their backs to the evening sun and marched off to the east. Compared with them, the spearmen of Mino looked short and lacking in spirit.

"Ah, I don't want to live much longer. The day will come when my children go begging for life from that fool! Yet it can't be helped," Dosan tearfully told his retainers as he jostled along in his palanquin.

* * *

The war drum boomed, and the eerie call of the conch drifted over the fields. Some of Nobunaga's men were swimming in the Shonai River; others were riding in the fields, or training with bamboo spears. When they heard the conch, they stopped whatever they

107

were doing and lined up in rows in front of the hut, waiting for Nobunaga to mount his horse.

"It's time to go back to the castle."

Nobunaga had swum for more than an hour, sunbathed on the riverbank, then jumped into the river again, frolicking like a river imp. Finally he said, "Let's go back," and walked briskly to his makeshift hut. He took off the white bellyband he wore when swimming, wiped himself dry, and put on hunting clothes and light armor.

"My horse," he ordered impatiently. His commands always put his retainers on edge. They tried to be understanding but were often confused, for their young lord was playful and prone to act in unexpected ways. The counterbalance was Ichikawa Daisuke. When Nobunaga's impetuosity threw his orderlies into confusion, one word from Daisuke and the soldiers and horses were soon lined up like rows of rice seedlings.

A look of satisfaction spread across Nobunaga's face. He turned his men toward Nagoya Castle, and they withdrew from the river, with Nobunaga in the middle of the procession. Today's drill had lasted about four hours. The burning midsummer sun was directly overhead. The soaked horses and troops marched on. Foul-smelling fumes rose from the marshes; green grasshoppers jumped out of the way with shrill cries. Sweat poured from the men's pallid faces. Nobunaga used his elbow to wipe the sweat off his face. Gradually his color returned, along with his wild and capricious nature.

"Who's that funny-looking creature running over there?"

Nobunaga's eyes seemed to be everywhere. Half a dozen soldiers, who had seen the man before Nobunaga, ran through the shoulder-high grass to where Hiyoshi was hiding. Hiyoshi had been waiting since the morning for an opportunity to get close to Nobunaga. He had secretly observed Nobunaga at the river. Earlier he had been run off by the guards, so he had set his mind to finding Nobunaga's route back to the castle, and had crept into the tall grasses by the roadside.

It's now or never! he thought. His body and soul were one, and all he could see was the lord of Owari on horseback. Hiyoshi yelled at the top of his voice, not knowing himself what he was saying. He knew his life was on the line. Before he was able to get close to his idol and be heard, there was a distinct possibility that he would be killed by the long spears of the guards. But he was not afraid. He would either advance on the tide of his ambition or disappear in the undertow.

Jumping to his feet, he saw Nobunaga, shut his eyes, and dashed toward him.

"I have a request! Please take me into your service! I want to serve you and lay down my life for you!" At least this was what he had meant to say, but he was too excited, and when the guards blocked his way with their spears, his voice broke and what actually came out was a meaningless garble.

He looked poorer than the poorest commoner. His hair was filthy, full of dust and burrs. Sweat and grime streaked his face black and red, and it seemed that only his eyes were alive, but they failed to see the spears that blocked his way. The guards swept his legs from under him with the shafts of their spears, but he somersaulted to within ten paces of Nobunaga's horse and jumped to his feet.

"I have a request, my lord!" he yelled, lunging toward the stirrups of Nobunaga's

horse.

"Filthy swine!" Nobunaga thundered.

A soldier behind Hiyoshi grabbed him by the collar and threw him to the ground. He would have been run through, but Nobunaga shouted, "No!"

The approach of this filthy stranger intrigued him. The reason may have been that he sensed the ardent hope burning in Hiyoshi's body.

"Speak up!"

Hearing that voice made Hiyoshi almost forget his pain and the guards. "My father served your father as a foot soldier. His name was Kinoshita Yaemon. I am his son, Hiyoshi. After my father died, I lived with my mother in Nakamura. I hoped to find an opportunity to serve you, and looked for a go-between, but in the end there was no way except direct appeal. I'm staking my life on this. I'm resigned to being struck down and killed here. If you take me into your service, I won't hesitate to lay my life down for you. If you will, please accept the only life I have. In this way, both my father, who is under leaves and grass, and I, who was born in this province, will have realized our true desires." He spoke quickly, half in a trance. But his singleminded passion got through to Nobunaga's heart. More than by his words, Nobunaga was swayed by Hiyoshi's sincerity.

He let out a strained laugh. "What an odd fellow," he said to one of his attendants. Then, turning back to Hiyoshi, "So you'd like to serve me?"

"Yes, my lord."

"What abilities do you have?"

"I have none, my lord."

"You have no abilities, and yet you want me to take you into my service?"

"Other than my willingness to die for you, I don't have any special talents."

His interest piqued, he stared at Hiyoshi, the edges of Nobunaga's mouth forming into a grin. "You have several times addressed me as 'my lord,' although no permission has been granted for you to be my retainer. What business do you have addressing me like that when you are not in my service?"

"As a native of Owari, I have always thought that if I were able to serve anyone, it would have to be you. I guess it slipped out."

Nobunaga nodded with approval and turned to Daisuke. "This man interests me," he said.

"Indeed." Daisuke put on a forced smile.

"Your wish is granted. I'll take you on. From today you are in my service."

Hiyoshi, choked with tears, could not express his happiness. A good many retainers were surprised, but also thought their lord was running true to form, acting capriciously as ever. As Hiyoshi brazenly entered their ranks, they frowned and said, "Back to the end of line, you. You can hold on to the tail of a packhorse."

"Yes, yes." Hiyoshi willingly took his place at the end of the procession, as happy as he would be in the land of dreams.

As the procession moved on to Nagoya, the roads cleared as though swept with a broom. Men and women prostrated themselves, their heads on the ground, in front of their houses and by the roadside.

Nobunaga did not practice self-restraint even in public. He would clear his throat while speaking to his retainers and laugh at the same time. Saying he was thirsty, he would eat melons while in the saddle and spit out the seeds.

Hiyoshi was walking in the middle of these roads for the first time. He kept an eye on his master's back, thinking, At last, this is the road. This is the way.

Nagoya Castle appeared before them. The water in the moat was turning green. Crossing the Karabashi Bridge, the procession meandered through the outer grounds and disappeared through the castle gate. It was the first time of many that Hiyoshi would cross this bridge and pass through this gate.

* * *

It was fall. Looking at the reapers in the rice paddies as he passed, a rather short samurai hurried along on foot toward Nakamura. Arriving at the house of Chikuami, he called out in an uncommonly loud voice, "Mother!"

"Oh, my! Hiyoshi!"

His mother had given birth to yet another child. Sitting among red beans spread out to dry, she cradled the child in her arms, exposing its pale skin to the rays of the sun. Turning around and seeing the transformation in her son, a strong emotion broke across her face. Was she happy or sad? Her eyes filled with tears and her lip quivered.

"It's me, Mother. Is everybody well?"

With a little jump, Hiyoshi sat down on a straw mat next to her. The smell of milk lingered on her breast. She embraced him in the same way as the child she was nursing.

"What's happened?" she asked.

"Nothing. This is my day off. It's the first time I've been outside the castle since I went there."

"Ah, good. Your showing up so suddenly made me think that things had gone wrong again." She heaved a sigh of relief, and for the first time since his arrival, showed him a smiling face. She took a good look at her grown-up son, noting his clean silk clothes, the way his hair was tied, his long and short swords. Tears brimmed from her eyes and rolled down her cheeks.

"Mother, you should be happy. At last I'm one of Lord Nobunaga's retainers. Oh, I'm only in the servants' group, but I really am a samurai in service."

"Good for you. You've done well." She held her tattered sleeves to her face, unable to look up.

Hiyoshi put his arm around her. "Just to please you, this morning I tied my hair up and put on clean clothes. But still better things are to come after this. I'm going to show you what I can do, make you really happy. Mother, I hope you have a long life!"

"When I heard what happened last summer...I never imagined I'd see you like this."

"I suppose you heard from Otowaka."

"Yes, he came and told me you'd caught His Lordship's eye and had been taken on as a servant up at the castle. I was so happy I could have died."

"If such a little thing makes you so happy, what about the future? The first thing I want you to know is that I have been permitted to have a surname."

"And what might that be?"

"Kinoshita, like my father. But my first name has been changed to Tokichiro."

"Kinoshita Tokichiro."

"That's right. It's a good name, don't you think? You'll have to put up with this dilapidated house and these rags for a while longer, but cheer up. You're the mother of Kinoshita Tokichiro!"

"I've never been so happy." She repeated this several times, the tears freshening with each word Tokichiro spoke. He was very pleased to see how happy she was for him. Who else in the world could be so truly happy for him over such a trivial matter? He even imagined that his years of wandering, hunger, and hardship contributed to the happiness of this moment.

"By the way, how's Otsumi?"

"She's helping with the harvest."

"Is she all right? She's not sick, is she?"

"She's the same as ever," Onaka said, reminded of Otsumi's miserable adolescence.

"When she comes back. please tell her she won't have to suffer forever. Before long, when I become somebody, she'll have a sash of figured satin, a chest of drawers with a gold crest, and everything she needs for her wedding. Ha, ha! You think I'm just rambling on, as usual?"

"Are you leaving already?"

"Service at the castle is strict. So, Mother," he lowered his voice, "it's disrespectful to repeat what people say about His Lordship not being able to rule the province, but the truth is, the Lord Nobunaga seen by the public and the Lord Nobunaga in Nagoya Castle are very different."

"That's probably true."

"It's a sorry situation. He has very few real allies. Both his retainers and his own relatives are for the most part against him. At nineteen he's all alone. If you think the suffering of starving farmers is the most pitiful thing, you're far from correct. If you see the point, you can be more patient. We shouldn't give in just because we're human. We're on the road to happiness, my master and me."

"That makes me happy, but don't be too hasty. No matter how much you rise in the world, my happiness can't be any greater than it is right now."

"Well, then, look after yourself."

"Won't you stay and talk a little more?"

"I have to get back to my duties."

He silently stood up and placed some money on his mother's straw mat. Then he looked around fondly at the persimmon tree, the chrysanthemums by the fence, and the storage shed in back.

He did not come again that year, but at the end of the year Otowaka visited his mother, bringing her a little money, medicine, and cloth to make a kimono. "He's still a household servant," he reported. "When he reaches eighteen and his stipend increases a little, if he can get a house in town, he says he'll bring his mother to live with him. He's a little crazy, but he's fairly sociable too, and he's well liked. The reckless incident at the Shonai River was like an escape from death. He does have to have the devil's own luck."

That New Year Otsumi wore new clothes for the first time. "My little brother sent them to me. Tokichiro at the castle!" she told one and all, and wherever she went, she was unable to keep from repeating "my little brother did this" and "my little brother did that."

* * *

At times Nobunaga's mood changed; he became quiet and spent the entire day moping. This extraordinary silence and melancholy seemed to be natural attempts to control his extremely quick temper.

"Bring Uzuki!" he suddenly yelled one day, and ran off to the riding grounds. His father, Nobuhide, had spent his whole life in warfare, with virtually no time to relax in the castle. During more than half of each year he campaigned in the west and east. He did manage on most mornings to hold a memorial service for his ancestors, receive the salutations of his retainers, listen to lectures on ancient texts, and practice the martial arts and attend to the government of his province until evening. When the day was over, he would study treatises on military strategy or hold council meetings, or try to be a good father to his family. When Nobunaga succeeded his father, this order came to an end. It was not in his character to follow a strict daily routine. He was impulsive in the extreme, his mind like the clouds of an evening squall, ideas suddenly arising and just as suddenly discarded. It seemed that his body and spirit were beyond all regulation.

Needless to say, this kept his attendants very much on their toes. That day he had sat down with a book, and later had gone meekly to the Buddhist chapel to offer a prayer to his ancestors. In the quiet of the chapel, his call for his horse was as startling as a thunderbolt. The attendants could not find him where they had heard his voice. They rushed to the stables and followed him to the riding grounds. He said nothing, but the look on his face plainly reproached them for their slowness.

Uzuki, his favorite horse, was white. When he was dissatisfied and plied the whip, the old horse reacted languidly. Nobunaga was in the habit of leading Uzuki around by the muzzle, complaining about his slowness. Then he'd say, "Give him some water." Taking a ladle, a groom would open the horse's mouth and pour the water in, and Nobunaga would thrust his hand into the horse's mouth and grab his tongue. Today he said, "Uzuki! You've got an evil tongue, haven't you? That's why your legs are heavy."

"He seems to have a bit of a cold."

"Has age caught up with Uzuki too?"

"He was here at the time of the last lord, so he must be pretty old."

"I imagine Uzuki's only one of many in Nagoya Castle who is getting old and feeble. Ten generations have passed since the days of the first shogun, and the world is given over to ritual and deception. Everything is old and decrepit!"

He was talking half to himself; perhaps he was angry at heaven. Nobunaga jumped into the saddle and took a turn around the riding grounds. He was a born rider. His teacher was Ichikawa Daisuke, but recently he had taken to riding alone.

Suddenly horse and rider were overtaken by a dark bay, galloping at a furious pace. Left behind, an enraged Nobunaga raced after the other horse, shouting, "Goroza!"

Goroza, a spirited youth of about twenty-four and the eldest son of Hirate Nakatsukasa, was the castle's chief gunner. His full name was Gorozaemon and he had two brothers, Kemmotsu and Jinzaemon.

Nobunaga's temper rose. He had been beaten! Eating someone's dust! It was beyond endurance! He whipped his own horse furiously. The hooves rang on the earth. Uzuki ran so swiftly that you could hardly see the hooves strike the ground, and his silver tail trailed straight out behind him. He jumped into the lead.

Goroza shouted, "Watch out, my lord, his hooves are going to split!"

"What's the matter? Can't you keep up?" Nobunaga shouted back. Mortified, Goroza struck out in pursuit, digging into the bay's flanks with his stirrups. Nobunaga's horse was known far and wide as "Uzuki of the Oda," even among the clan's enemies. The bay could not compare with him in either value or character. But the bay was young and Goroza's horsemanship was better than Nobunaga's. From a lead of about twenty lengths, the distance shrank to ten, then five, then one, and then to a nose. Nobunaga was trying his hardest not to be passed, but he himself began to run out of breath. Goroza sped past, leaving his master in a cloud of dust. Annoyed, Nobunaga jumped to the ground, looking mortified. "That bay has good legs," he grumbled. There was no way he could admit any fault on his own part. To his attendants it seemed their lord had dismounted instead of going the distance.

"Being beaten by Goroza isn't going to brighten his mood," observed an attendant. Dreading his inevitable ill humor, they ran up to him in confusion. One man reached the dazed Nobunaga ahead of the others and, kneeling before him, offered him a lacquered drinking ladle.

"A drink of water, my lord?" It was Tokichiro, recently elevated to sandal bearer. Although "sandal bearer" did not sound like much, being taken from the ranks of the servants to be a personal attendant was a mark of exceptional favor. Tokichiro had come a long way in a short time, by working hard and immersing himself in his duties.

Still, his master did not see him. He neither looked at him nor grunted so much as a single syllable. He took the ladle without a word, finished it off in one gulp, and handed it back.

"Call Goroza," he ordered.

Goroza was tethering his horse to a willow at the edge of the riding grounds. He responded instantly to the summons, saying, "I was just thinking of going to him." He calmly wiped the sweat off his face, rearranged his collar and smoothed his disordered hair. Goroza had made a resolution.

"My lord," said Goroza, "I'm afraid I was rather rude just now." He knelt and spoke in a decidedly cool manner.

The contours of Nobunaga's face softened. "You gave me a good chase. When did you get such a splendid horse? What do you call him?"

The attendants relaxed.

Goroza looked up with a little smile. "You noticed? He's my pride and joy. A horse trader from the north was on his way to the capital to sell it to a nobleman. The price was high and I didn't have the kind of money he was asking for it, so I had to sell a family heirloom, a tea bowl I was given by my father. The bowl was called Nowake, and that's the name I gave the bay."

"Well, well, it's no wonder then that I've seen an excellent horse today. I'd like to have that horse."

"My lord?"

"I'll take it at any price you ask, but let me have it."

"I'm afraid I can't do that."

"Did I hear you correctly?"

"I must refuse."

"Why? You could get yourself another good horse."

"A good horse is as difficult to find as a good friend."

"That's exactly why you should turn him over to me. I'm at the point of wanting a fast horse that hasn't been ridden to death."

"I really must refuse. I love that horse, and not just for my own pride and amusement, but because on the battlefield he enables me to do my best in the service of my lord, which should be the chief concern of a samurai. My lord expressly desires this horse, but there is absolutely no reason for a samurai to give up a thing so important to him."

Reminded of a samurai's duty to serve his master, even Nobunaga could not flatly demand the horse, but neither was he able to overcome his own selfishness. "Goroza, do you seriously refuse my request?"

"Well, in this case, yes."

"I suspect the bay is above your social position. If you were to become a man like your father, you could ride a horse like Nowake. But while you're still young, it's not fitting for someone of your rank."

"Most respectfully, I must say this. Is it not a waste to have such a fine horse and then ride around the town eating melons and persimmons in the saddle? Wouldn't it be better for Nowake to be ridden by a warrior like me?" He had finally come out with it. The words that had spilled from his mouth did not come so much from concern about the horse as from the anger he experienced every day.

Hirate Nakatsukasa locked the gate and stayed by himself in his mansion for over twenty days. He had served the Oda clan without a rest for over forty years, and had served Nobunaga since the day Nobuhide, on his deathbed, had said, "I entrust him to you," and made him Nobunaga's guardian and chief retainer of the province.

One day, toward evening, he looked into the mirror and was surprised at how white his hair had become. It had reason to turn white. He was well over sixty, but he had had no time to think about his age. He closed the lid on the mirror and called for his steward, Amemiya Kageyu.

"Kageyu, has the messenger left?"

"Yes, I sent him off some time ago."

"They'll probably come, don't you think?"

"I think they'll come together."

"Is the *sake* ready?"

"Yes, sir. I'll have a meal prepared, too."

It was late winter, but the plum blossoms were still closed. It had been terribly cold that year, and the thick ice on the pond had not melted for even a day. The men he had summoned were his three sons, each of whom had his own residence. It was customary for the eldest son and his younger brothers to live with their father as one large family, but Nakatsukasa had them maintain separate residences. Saying that if he had to worry about his own children and grandchildren he might neglect his duties, he lived alone. He had brought Nobunaga up as if he were his own child, but of late his ward had treated him coldly and seemed to resent him. Nakatsukasa had questioned some of Nobunaga's attendants about the incident at the riding grounds. Ever since then Nakatsukasa had looked embarrassed.

Goroza, having incurred the displeasure of Nobunaga, had stopped going to the castle and kept to himself. Shibata Katsuie and Hayashi Mimasaka, retainers who always sided against Nakatsukasa, saw their chance, and by flattering Nobunaga they were able to deepen the rift between them. Their strength lay in the fact that they were younger, and their power and influence were definitely on the rise.

Twenty days of seclusion had brought home to Nakatsukasa an awareness of his age. Tired now, he no longer had the spirit to fight with these men. He was also aware of his lord's isolation and was worried about the future of the clan. He was making a clear copy of a long document composed the previous day.

It was almost cold enough to freeze the water in the inkstone.

Kageyu entered the room and announced, "Gorozaemon and Kemmotsu are here." Not yet knowing the purpose of the summons, they were sitting by a brazier, waiting.

"I was shocked, it was so unexpected. I was afraid he might have taken sick," said Kemmotsu.

"Yes, well, I suspect he heard what happened. I suppose I'm in for a good scolding."

"If it were that, he would have acted sooner. I think he has something else in mind."

They were grown up now, but they still found their father a bit frightening. They waited anxiously. The third son, Jinzaemon, was on a trip to another province.

"It's cold, isn't it?" their father remarked as he slid the door open. Both brothers noticed how white his hair had become, and his thinness.

"Are you all right?"

"Yes, I'm fine. I just wanted to see you. It's my age, I suppose, but there are times when I feel very lonely."

"There's nothing special on your mind, no urgent business?"

"No, no. It's been so long since we had dinner together and talked away the night. Ha, ha! Make yourselves comfortable." He was the same as always. Outside, there was a racketing on the eaves, perhaps hail falling, and the cold seemed to intensify. Being with their father made his sons forget the cold. Nakatsukasa was in such a good mood that Gorozaemon was unable to find an opportunity to apologize for his behavior. After the dishes were cleared away, Nakatsukasa ordered a bowl of the powdered green tea he was so fond of.

Quite abruptly, as though reminded of something by the tea bowl in his hand, he said, "Goroza, I hear you have let the tea bowl, Nowake, which I entrusted to you, fall into another man's hands. Is that correct?"

Goroza responded candidly. "Yes. I know it was a family heirloom, but there was a horse that I wanted, so I sold it to get the horse."

"Is that so? Well, that's good. If you have that attitude, there should be no trouble

115

about your service to His Lordship even after I'm gone." His tone changed sharply. "In selling the tea bowl and buying the horse, your attitude was admirable. But if I heard correctly, you beat Uzuki in a race, and when His Lordship asked for your bay, you refused. Is that correct?"

"That's why he's displeased with me. I'm afraid it's caused you a lot of trouble."

"Hold on a minute."

"Sir?"

"Don't think about me. Why did you refuse? It was niggardly of you." Gorozaemon was at a loss for words. "Ignoble!"

"Do you really see it that way? I feel terrible."

"Then why did you not give Lord Nobunaga what he asked for?"

"I am a samurai resolved to give up my very life if my lord so desires, so why should I be stingy about anything else? But I did not buy the bay for my own amusement. It's so I can serve my lord on the battlefield."

"I understand that."

"If I gave up the horse, the master would probably be pleased. But I cannot overlook his selfishness. He sees a horse that is faster than Uzuki and ignores the feelings of his retainers. Is that right? I am not the only one who says the Oda clan is in dangerous straits. I imagine that you, my father, understand this better than I do. While there are times when he may be a genius, his selfish and indulgent nature, no matter how old he gets, is regrettable, even if it is simply his nature. We retainers are exceedingly nervous about his character. To let him have his way might resemble loyalty, but in fact it is not a good thing to do. For this reason I have purposely been obstinate."

"That was wrong."

"Was it?"

"You may see it as loyalty but in fact it makes his bad disposition worse. From the time he was an infant I held him in my arms, much more often than I did my own children. I know his disposition. Genius he may be, but he has more than his share of faults, too. That you offended him doesn't even amount to dust."

"That may be so. It's disrespectful to say this, but Kemmotsu, and I, and most of the retainers, regret serving this fool. It's only people like Shibata Katsuie and Hayashi Mimasaka who rejoice in having such a master."

"That's not so. No matter what people say, I can't believe that. All of you must follow His Lordship to the bitter end, just as he is, whether I am alive or not."

"Don't worry about that. I do not plan to waver from my principles even if I am out of favor with my master."

"I can be at peace, then. But I've fast become an old tree. Like grafted branches, you will have to serve in my place."

Upon thinking about it later, Gorozaemon and Kemmotsu realized that there were any number of clues in Nakatsukasa's conversation that night, but they returned to their homes without realizing their father was determined to die.

Hirate Nakatsukasa's suicide was discovered the next morning. He had cut his belly open in splendid fashion. The brothers could discern no trace of regret or bitterness in his dead face. He left no last will or testament to his family—just a letter addressed to Nobunaga. Every word was charged with Nakatsukasa's deep and abiding loyalty to his master.

When he heard about his chief retainer's death, a look of great shock spread across Nobunaga's face. By his death, Nakatsukasa admonished his lord. He had known Nobunaga's natural genius and his faults, and as Nobunaga read through the document, even before his eyes filled with tears, his chest was pierced with a pain as sharp as a whiplash.

"Old man! Forgive me!" he sobbed. He had pained Nakatsukasa, who was his retainer, but who was also closer to him than his own father. And with the incident over the horse, he had imposed his will on Nakatsukasa, as usual.

"Call Goroza."

When the chief gunner prostrated himself before him, Nobunaga sat on the floor facing him.

"The message your father left me has pierced my heart. I will never forget it. I have no apology other than that." He was about to prostrate himself in front of Goroza, but the youth confusedly took his hands in veneration. Lord and retainer embraced each other in tears.

That year the lord of the Oda built a temple in the castle town, dedicated to his old guardian's salvation. The magistrate asked him, "What name are we to give the temple? As the founder, you'll have to give guidance to the head priest on the selection of a name."

"The old man would be happier with a name chosen by me." Taking up a brush, he wrote "Seishu Temple." After that, he would often set off suddenly for the temple, although he rarely held memorial services or sat with the priests reading the sutras.

"Old man! Old man!" Walking around the temple, he would mutter to himself and then just as abruptly return to the castle. These excursions appeared to be the whim of a madman. Once, when he was hawking, he suddenly tore flesh off a small bird and threw it into the air, saying "Old man! Take what I've caught!" Another time, while fishing, he splashed his foot in the water and said, "Old man! Become a Buddha!" The violence in his voice and eyes alarmed his attendants.

* * *

Nobunaga turned twenty-one in the first year of Koji. In May he found a pretext to make war on Oda Hikogoro, the nominal head of the Oda clan. He attacked his castle in Kiyosu and, after taking it, moved there from Nagoya.

Tokichiro observed his master's progress with satisfaction. The isolated Nobunaga was surrounded by hostile kinsmen—uncles and brothers among them—and the task of clearing them from his path was far more pressing than dealing with other enemies.

"He has to be watched," Hikogoro had warned. Putting pressure on him wherever he could, he planned Nobunaga's destruction. The governor of Kiyosu Castle, Shiba Yoshimune, and his son, Yoshikane, were supporters of Nobunaga. When Higokoro discovered this, he exclaimed angrily, "What a lesson in ingratitude!" and he ordered the governor's execution. Yoshikane fled to Nobunaga, who hid him in Nagoya Castle. On that same day Nobunaga led his troops in an attack on Kiyosu Castle, rallying his men with the battle cry, "To avenge the Provincial Governor!"

To attack the head of the clan, Nobunaga had to have right on his side. But it was also an opportunity to clear away some of the obstacles in his path. He put his uncle, Nobumitsu, in charge of Nagoya Castle, but he soon fell victim to an assassin.

"You go, Sado. You're the only one who can govern Nagoya Castle in my place." When Hayashi Sado took up his appointment, some of Nobunaga's retainers sighed, "He's a fool after all. Just when you think he's shown a spark of talent, he goes and does something stupid, like trusting Hayashi!"

There was good cause to be suspicious of Hayashi Sado. While Nobunaga's father lived, there had been no more loyal retainer. And for that reason, Nobuhide had appointed him and Hirate Nakatsukasa as his son's guardians after his death. But because Nobunaga had shown himself to be spoiled and unmanageable, Hayashi had given up on him. Thus he conspired with Nobunaga's younger brother, Nobuyuki, and his mother, in Suemori Castle, to overthrow Nobunaga.

"Lord Nobunaga must not know of Hayashi's treason," Tokichiro overheard troubled retainers whisper on more than one occasion. "If he did, he wouldn't have made him governor of Nagoya." But Tokichiro himself had no worries for his master. He asked himself how his master would deal with the problem. It seemed that the only ones with happy faces at Kiyosu were Nobunaga and one of his young sandal bearers.

One group among Nobunaga's senior retainers, including Hayashi Sado, his younger brother Mimasaka, and Shibata Katsuie, continued to see their lord as a hopeless fool.

"I'll admit the way Lord Nobunaga handled his first meeting with his father-in-law was different from his usual vacuous behavior. But that's what I call fool's luck. And during their formal interview, he behaved so disgracefully and shamelessly that even his father-in-law was appalled. As the saying goes, 'There's no cure for fools.' And there's no excusing his later conduct, no matter how you look at it." Shibata Katsuie and the others had convinced themselves that there was no hope for the future, and their views gradually became public knowledge. When Hayashi Sado became governor of Nagoya, he was often visited by Shibata Katsuie, and the castle soon became the seedbed of a treasonous plot.

"The rain is pleasant, is it not?"

"Yes, I find it adds to the charm of the tea." Sado and Katsuie were sitting face to face in a small teahouse, sheltered by a grove of trees, in the grounds of the castle. The rainy season had passed, but the rain still fell from a cloudy sky, and green plums plopped to the ground.

"It'll probably clear up tomorrow," Sado's brother, Mimasaka, said to himself as he sheltered under the branches of the plum trees. He had gone out to light the garden lantern. After lighting it, he lingered a bit and looked around. Finally, when he returned to the teahouse, he said in a low voice, "Nothing unusual to report. There's nobody around, so we can talk freely." Katsuie nodded.

"Well, let's get down to business. Yesterday I went secretly to Suemori Castle. I was received by Lord Nobunaga's mother and Lord Nobuyuki, and I discussed our plans with them. The decision is yours now."

"What did his mother say?"

"She is of the same opinion, and made no objections. She favors Nobuyuki over Nobunaga no matter what."

"Good. What about Nobuyuki?"

"He said that if Hayashi Sado and Shibata Katsuie rose against Nobunaga, naturally
he would join them for the good of the clan."

"You persuaded them, I suppose."

"Well, his mother is involved, and Nobuyuki is weak-willed. If I didn't egg them on,
there would be no reason for them to join us."

"We have plenty of justification to overthrow Nobunaga, as long as we have their
agreement. We're not the only retainers worried about Nobunaga's foolishness and concerned for the safety of the clan."

"'For Owari and one hundred more years for the Oda clan!' will be our rallying cry,
but what about military preparations?"

"We have a good opportunity now. I can move quickly from Nagoya. When the war
drum sounds, I'll be ready."

"Good. Well, then—" Katsuie leaned forward conspiratorially.

At that moment something fell noisily to the ground in the garden. It was just a few
unripe plums. There was a lull in the rain, but drops of water carried by gusts of wind hit
the eaves. Doglike, a human figure crawled out from the space under the floor. The plums
had not fallen by themselves a few moments before; the black-garbed man, who had
stuck his head out from under the house, had thrown them. When all eyes in the room
turned, the man took advantage of the distraction and disappeared into the wind and
darkness.

Ninja were the eyes and ears of the lord of the castle. Anyone who ruled a castle, living within its walls and constantly surrounded by retainers, had to depend on spies. Nobunaga employed a master ninja. But even his closest retainers did not know the man's
identity.

Nobunaga had three sandal bearers: Matasuke, Ganmaku, and Tokichiro. Though
they were servants, they had their own separate quarters and took turns on duty near the
garden.

"Ganmaku, what's the matter?"

Tokichiro and Ganmaku were close friends. Ganmaku was lying under the futon,
asleep. He loved nothing better than to sleep and did so at every opportunity.

"My stomach hurts," Ganmaku said from under the futon.

Tokichiro tugged at the edge of the bedding. "You're lying. Get up. I just got back
from town, and I bought something tasty on the way."

"What?" Ganmaku stuck his head out, but, realizing that he had been tricked, went
back under the bedding again.

"Fool! Don't tease a sick man. Get out of here. You're bothering me."

"Please get up. Matasuke's not here, and there's something I have to ask you."

Ganmaku got out from under the covers reluctantly. "Just when a person's sleeping…"

119

Cursing, he got up and went to rinse his mouth with water that flowed from a spring in the garden. Tokichiro followed him out.

The cottage was gloomy, but it was hidden in the innermost part of the castle grounds, giving it a commanding view of the castle town, which made the heart feel expansive.

"What is it? What do you want to ask me?"

"It's about last night."

"Last night?"

"You can pretend not to understand, but I know. I think you went to Nagoya."

"Oh, yeah?"

"I think you went to spy in the castle, and listened in on a secret conversation between the governor and Shibata Katsuie."

"Shush, Monkey! Watch what you say!"

"Well, then, tell me the truth. Don't hold back from a friend. I've known it for a long time, but said nothing and watched you. You're Lord Nobunaga's ninja, aren't you?"

"Tokichiro, I'm no match for your eyes. How did you find out?"

"Well, we share the same quarters, don't we? Lord Nobunaga is a very important master to me, too. People like me worry about Lord Nobunaga, though we keep it to ourselves."

"Is that what you wanted to ask me about?"

"Ganmaku, I swear by the gods that I won't tell anyone else."

Ganmaku stared at Tokichiro. "Okay, I'll tell you. But it's daytime and we'll be seen. Wait for the right time."

Later, Ganmaku told him what was going on in the clan. And, having both understanding and sympathy for his master's predicament, Tokichiro could serve him all the better. But he did not have the slightest misgiving for the future of his young, isolated lord, who was surrounded by such scheming retainers. Nobuhide's retainers were about to desert Nobunaga, and only Tokichiro, who had been with him for a short time, had any confidence in him.

I wonder how my master is going to get out of this one, Tokichiro thought. Still only a servant, he could only look from afar with devotion.

It was toward the end of the month. Nobunaga, who usually went out with only a few retainers, unexpectedly called for a horse and rode out of the castle. It was about three leagues from Kiyosu to Moriyama, and he would always gallop there and return before breakfast. But that day, Nobunaga turned his horse east at the crossroads and headed away from Moriyama.

"My lord!"

"Where is he going now?" Surprised and confused, his five or six mounted attendants chased after him. The foot soldiers and sandal bearers were naturally left behind, straggling along the road. Only two of his servants, Ganmaku and Tokichiro, while falling behind, ran on desperately, determined not to lose sight of their master's horse.

"By the gods! We're in for trouble!" Tokichiro said. They looked at one another, knowing that they had to keep their wits about them. This was because Nobunaga was riding straight for Nagoya Castle—which Ganmaku had told Tokichiro was the center of the plot to replace Nobunaga with his younger brother!

Nobunaga, unpredictable as ever, spurred his horse toward a place fraught with danger, where no one knew what might happen. There was no more dangerous course of action, and Ganmaku and Tokichiro were frightened that something might happen to their master.

But it was Hayashi Sado, governor of Nagoya Castle, and his younger brother who were the most surprised by the unexpected visit. A panicked retainer ran into the room in the keep. "My lord! My lord! Come quickly! Lord Nobunaga is here!"

"What? What are you talking about?" Doubting his own ears, he did not make a move to get up. It just was not possible.

"He came here with no more than four or five attendants. They suddenly rode in through the main gate. He was laughing out loud about something with his attendants."

"Is this true?"

"I swear it! Yes!"

"Lord Nobunaga, here? What does it mean?" Sado was losing his head unnecessarily. The color had drained from his face. "Mimasaka, what do you think he wants?"

"Whatever it is, we'd better go and greet him."

"Yes. Let's hurry!"

As they ran down the main corridor, they could already hear the sound of Nobunaga's vigorous footsteps coming from the entrance. The brothers stepped to the side and threw themselves to the floor.

"Ah! Sado and Mimasaka. Are you both well? I was thinking of riding as far as Moriyama, but decided to come to Nagoya for some tea first. All this bowing and scraping is far too serious. Let's forget formality. Quickly, bring me some tea." Saying this as he walked past them, he sat down on the platform in the main room of the castle that he knew so well. Then he turned to the retainers who were chasing after him, trying to catch their breath. "It's hot, eh? Really hot," he said, fanning himself through his open collar.

The tea was brought in, then the cakes, and then the cushions—all out of order because everyone was thrown into such confusion by the unexpected visit. The brothers hastily presented themselves and made their obeisance, unable to ignore the confusion of the maids and retainers, and left their master's presence.

"It's noon. He must be hungry from his ride. He'll probably order lunch soon. Go to the kitchens and have them prepare a meal." While Sado gave orders, Mimasaka tugged at his sleeve and whispered, "Katsuie wants to see you."

Hayashi nodded and replied softly, "I'll come soon. Go on ahead."

Shibata Katsuie had come to Nagoya Castle earlier that day. He was about to leave after a secret meeting, but the confusion caused by Nobunaga's sudden arrival made it awkward for him to leave. Trapped, he had crawled, shaking, into a secret room. Both men joined him there and breathed a sigh of relief.

"That was unexpected! What a surprise!" said Sado.

"It's typical of him," Mimasaka replied. "You'd go crazy trying to figure out the rules. You never know what he's going to do next! There's nothing worse than the whims of a fool!"

Glancing toward the room in which Nobunaga was sitting, Shibata Katsuie said,

"That's probably why he got the better of that old fox Saito Dosan."

"Maybe so," said Sado.

"Sado," Mimasaka had a grim expression on his face. Looking around, he lowered his voice and said, "Wouldn't it be best to do it now?"

"What do you mean?"

"He has come with only five or six attendants, so isn't this what you might call an opportunity sent by the gods?"

"To kill him?"

"Precisely. While he's eating, we sneak in some good fighters, and when I come out to serve him, I give the signal, and we kill him."

"And if we fail?" Sado asked.

"How can we? We'll put men in the garden and the corridors. We might have a few casualties, but if we attack him with all our might…"

"What do you think, Sado?" Mimasaka asked anxiously.

Hayashi Sado had his eyes cast straight down, under the intense stares of Katsuie and Mimasaka. "Well. This may be the opportunity we've been waiting for."

"Are we agreed?"

Looking each other in the eye, the three men had just drawn up their knees. Just at that moment they heard the sound of energetic footsteps walking along the corridor, and the lacquered door slid open.

"Oh, you're in here. Hayashi! Mimasaka! I drank the tea and ate the cakes. I'm going back to Kiyosu now!"

The men's knees drooped, and the three of them cowered. Suddenly, Nobunaga spotted Shibata Katsuie. "Hey! Is that you, Katsuie?" Nobunaga said with a smile over the prostrate form of Katsuie. "When I arrived, I saw a bay that looked just like the one you ride. So it was yours after all?"

"Yes…I happened to come by, but as you can see, I'm in my everyday clothes. So I thought that it would be rude of me to appear before you, my lord, and I stayed back here."

"Very good, that's very funny. Look at me. Look how shabby I am."

"Please forgive me, my lord."

Nobunaga lightly tickled Katsuie's neck with his lacquered fan. "In the relationship between lord and retainer, it's too standoffish to be so concerned with appearances or to be a slave to etiquette! Formality is for the courtiers in the capital. It's good enough for the Oda clan to be country samurai."

"Yes, my lord."

"What's the matter, Katsuie? You're trembling."

"I feel even worse, thinking I may have offended you, my lord."

"Ha, ha, ha, ha! I forgive you. Get up. No, wait, wait. The strings of my leather socks are untied. Katsuie, while you're down there, would you tie them?"

"Of course, my lord."

"Sado."

"My lord?"

"I disturbed you, didn't I?"

"Of course not, my lord."

"It's not just me who might drop in unexpectedly, but also guests from enemy provinces. Be on the alert, you're in charge!"

"I'm always on duty, from morning till night."

"Good. I'm glad to have such reliable retainers. But it's not just for me. If you made a mistake, these men would also lose their heads. Katsuie, have you finished?"

"I've tied them, my lord."

"Thank you."

Nobunaga walked away from the three still-prostrate men, went from the central corridor to the entrance by a circuitous route, and left. Katsuie, Sado, and Mimasaka looked at each other's pale faces, momentarily dazed. But when they came to themselves, they ran frantically after Nobunaga and once again prostrated themselves at the entrance. But Nobunaga could no longer be seen. Only the sound of clattering hooves could be heard on the slope that led to the main gate. The retainers, who were always being left behind, kept close to Nobunaga, trying not to lose him again. But of the servants, only Ganmaku and Tokichiro, though they could not keep up, came up behind.

"Ganmaku?"

"Yeah?"

"It went well, didn't it?"

"It did." They hurried along behind him, happy to see the figure of their master in front of them. If something had happened, they had agreed to inform Kiyosu Castle by sending a smoke signal from the fire tower, and kill the local guards if they had to.

Nazuka Castle was a vital point in Nobunaga's defenses, held by one of his kinsmen, Sakuma Daigaku. It was a day in early fall, before dawn, when the men in the castle were awakened by the unexpected arrival of soldiers. They jumped up. Was it the enemy? No, the men were their allies.

In the mist, a scout yelled out from the watchtower, "The men of Nagoya are in revolt! Shibata Katsuie has a thousand men, Hayashi Mimasaka over seven hundred!"

Nazuka Castle was shorthanded. Riders rode into the mist to report to Kiyosu. Nobunaga was still asleep. But when he heard the news, he quickly put on his armor, grabbed a spear, and ran out without a single attendant. And then, ahead of Nobunaga stood a single ordinary soldier waiting with a horse by the Karabashi Gate.

"Your horse, my lord," he said, offering the reins to Nobunaga.

Nobunaga's face wore an unusual expression, as though he were surprised that someone had been faster than he. "Who are you?" he asked.

Removing his helmet, the soldier was about to kneel. Nobunaga was already in the saddle. "That's not necessary. Who are you?"

"Your sandal bearer, Tokichiro."

"Monkey?" Nobunaga was amazed again. Why was his sandal bearer, whose duties were in the garden, the first to appear ready for battle? His equipment was simple, but he did have a breastplate, shin guards, and a helmet. Nobunaga was delighted by Tokichiro's fighting figure.

"Are you ready to fight?"

"Give me the word to follow you, my lord."

"Good! Come along!"

Nobunaga and Tokichiro had gone two or three hundred yards through the thinning morning mist when they heard the roar of twenty, thirty, then fifty mounted men, followed by four or five hundred foot soldiers, turning the mist black. The men at Nazuka had fought desperately. Nobunaga, a single horseman, dashed into the enemy ranks.

"Who dares raise his hand against me? Here I am, Sado, Mimasaka, Katsuie! How many men do you have? Why did you rebel against me? Come out and fight, man to man!" The booming of his angry voice silenced the war cries of the rebels. "Traitors! I've come to punish you! Running away is disloyal too!"

Mimasaka was so frightened that he fled. Nobunaga's voice pursued him like thunder. Even for these men, on whom Mimasaka counted, Nobunaga was their natural lord. When Nobunaga in person rode among them and spoke to them, they were incapable of turning their spears against him.

"Wait! Traitor!" Nobunaga caught up with the fleeing Mimasaka and ran him through with his spear. Shaking off the blood, he turned to Mimasaka's men and proclaimed, "Even though he struck at his lord, he will never become the ruler of a province. Rather than be the tools of traitors and leave a dishonored name to your children's children, apologize now! Repent!"

When he heard that the left flank of the rebel forces had collapsed and that Mimasaka was dead, Katsuie sought refuge with Nobunaga's mother and brother in Suemori Castle.

Nobunaga's mother cried and trembled when she heard of the defeat of their army; Nobuyuki shuddered. Katsuie, the defeated general of the rebel forces, said, "It would be best if I renounced the world." He shaved his head, took off his armor, and put on the robes of a Buddhist priest. The next day, in the company of Hayashi Sado, and Nobuyuki and his mother, he went to Kiyosu to beg forgiveness for his crimes.

Nobunaga's mother's apology was especially effective. Rehearsed by Sado and Katsuie, she begged him to spare the three men. Contrary to their expectations, Nobunaga was not angry. "I forgive them," he said simply to his mother, and turning to Katsuie, whose back was soaked with sweat, he continued, "Priest, why have you shaved your head? What a confused wretch you are!" He gave a forced smile and then spoke sharply to Hayashi Sado. "You too. This is unbecoming for a man of your age. After Hirate Nakatsukasa died, I relied on you as my righthand man. I regret causing Nakatsukasa's death." Tears came to Nobunaga's eyes and he was silent for a moment. "No, no. It was because of my unworthiness that Nakatsukasa committed suicide and you turned traitor. From now on, I am going to reflect on things more deeply. And you will serve me, giving me your hearts fully. Otherwise there is no point in being a warrior. Should a samurai follow one lord or be a masterless *ronin*?"

Hayashi Sado's eyes were opened. He saw what Nobunaga was really like, and finally understood his natural genius. He firmly pledged his loyalty and withdrew without lifting his head.

But it seemed as though Nobunaga's own brother did not understand this. Nobuyuki had rather a low opinion of Nobunaga's magnanimity and thought, My violent older brother can't do anything to me because my mother's here."

Blind, and protected by a mother's love, Nobuyuki continued his plotting. Nobunaga deplored this, thinking, I would gladly overlook Nobuyuki's behavior. But because of him, many of my retainers may rebel and err in their duty as samurai. Although he is my brother, he must die for the good of the clan. Finding a pretext, Nobunaga arrested Nobuyuki and ran him through.

Nobody considered Nobunaga a fool any longer. On the contrary, everyone crouched in fear of his intelligence and the keenness of his eye.

"The medicine was a little too effective," Nobunaga occasionally remarked with a sardonic grin. But Nobunaga had made his preparations. It had not been his intention to play the fool to deceive his retainers and relatives. With the death of his father, it had become his responsibility to defend the province from enemies on all sides. He had adopted this camouflage for safety's sake, even to the point of appearing to be a fool. He had convinced his relatives and retainers in order to deceive his enemies and their many spies. But all the while, Nobunaga studied human nature and the inner workings of society. Because he was still young, if he had shown himself to be an able ruler, his enemies would have taken countermeasures.

* * *

The head of the servants, Fujii Mataemon, came running in and called Tokichiro, who was resting inside the hut. "Monkey, come quickly."

"What is it?"

"You've been summoned!"

"Huh?"

"The master suddenly asked about you and ordered me to call you. Have you done anything wrong?"

"Nothing."

"Well, anyway, come quickly," Fujii urged him, and ran off in an unexpected direction. Something had set Nobunaga thinking that day as he inspected the storehouses, kitchens, and the firewood and charcoal warehouses.

"I've brought him along." Fujii prostrated himself as his lord walked by. Nobunaga stopped.

"Ah, you've brought him?" His eyes stopped on the figure of Tokichiro waiting behind him.

"Monkey, come forward."

"My lord?"

"From today I'm appointing you to the kitchens."

"Thank you very much, my lord."

"The kitchens aren't a place where you can distinguish yourself with a spear, but rather than a glorious place on the battlefield, it is an especially important part of our defenses. I know I don't have to tell you, but work hard."

His rank and stipend were immediately raised. As a kitchen official, he was no longer a servant. Being transferred to the kitchens, however, was then considered shameful for a samurai and was thought of as a downward slide in one's fortunes: "He has finally wound up in the kitchens." Kitchen duty was held in contempt by fighting men, as a sort of refuse heap for men of little ability. Even the other household servants and the attendants of the samurai looked down upon an appointment to the kitchen, and to the younger samurai it was a place of no opportunity or prospect for advancement. Mataemon sympathized with him and comforted him.

"Monkey, you've been transferred to a duty of little account, and I imagine that you're not satisfied. But since your stipend has been increased, instead shouldn't you consider that you've advanced in the world a bit? As a sandal bearer, though the position is a low one, there are times when you work before the master's horse, and there is some hope of promotion. On the other hand, you might have to give up your life. If you're in the kitchens, you don't have to worry about that. You can't sell the cow and keep the milk too."

Tokichiro nodded and answered, "Yes, yes." But privately he was not in the least bit disappointed. On the contrary, he was very pleased that he had received an unhoped-for promotion from Nobunaga. When he started work in the kitchens, the first things that struck him were the gloom, damp, and filth. The down-at-heel men who prepared the meals, who never saw the sun even at noon, and the old head cook had worked without a break for years in the smell of seaweed broth.

This won't do at all, Tokichiro told himself gloomily. He could not stand to be in depressing places. How about cutting a large window in that wall over there, to let in air and light? he thought. But there was a way of doing things in the kitchen, and since the man in charge was an old-timer, everything was a problem. Tokichiro quietly checked how much of the dried fish was bad, and examined the supplies that the merchants brought in daily. After he was put in charge, the suppliers retained by the castle were soon much happier.

"Somehow, when I'm not shouted at all the time, I can't help but bring in better goods and lower my prices," said one merchant.

"Up against you, Master Kinoshita, a merchant is put to shame. Why, you know the going rate for dried vegetables, dried fish, and grains! You've got a sharp eye with the goods, too. It makes us happy that you're so clever at laying up a stock of goods so cheaply," said another.

Tokichiro laughed and said, "Nonsense, I'm not a merchant, so where's the skill or the lack of it? This is not a matter of my making a profit. It's simply that the goods you supply go to feed my master's men. Life comes from what one eats. So how much, then, does the survival of this castle depend on the food prepared in the kitchen? It's the object of our service to give them the best we can." From time to time he gave tea to his suppliers, and as they relaxed, he would explain things during the conversation.

"You're merchants, so every time you deliver a cartload of goods for the castle, you immediately think how much profit you're going to make. And while it's not likely that you'll lose out, what do you suppose would happen if our castle fell into the hands of an enemy province? Wouldn't long years of billing be lost in both principal and interest? And if a general from another province took the castle, the merchants that came along with him would take over your business. So if you think of the master's clan as the root, we, as the branches, will continue to prosper. Isn't this the way we should think of profit? Therefore, short-term profit on the supplies you bring to the castle is not in your long-term interest."

Tokichiro was also considerate to the old head cook. He asked for the old man's opinions even when matters were clear-cut. He obeyed him, even if it went against his own judgment. But there were those among his colleagues who spread malicious gossip and wished to be rid of him.

"He's such a busybody."

"He sticks his nose into everything."

"He's a make-work little monkey."

When someone makes waves, he's bound to attract the resentment of others, so Tokichiro generally treated such gossip with indifference. His scheme for remodeling the kitchens was approved by both the head cook and Nobunaga. He had a carpenter open a vent in the ceiling and cut a large window into the wall. The sewage system was also rebuilt following his plans. Morning and evening, the sun shone brightly into the kitchens of Kiyosu Castle, which for decades had been so dark that food was cooked by candlelight even at noon. A refreshing breeze also blew through.

He expected the grumbling:

"Food spoils easily."

"You can see the dust."

Tokichiro ignored these complaints. After that, the place became clean; if people saw waste, they reduced it. A year later, the kitchens had become a bright and airy place with a lively atmosphere, just like his own character.

That winter, Murai Nagato, who had until then been overseer of charcoal and firewood, was relieved of his post, and Tokichiro was appointed to succeed him. Why had Nagato been sacked? And why had he himself been promoted to the post of overseer of charcoal and firewood? Tokichiro considered both of these questions when he received his posting from Nobunaga. Aha! Lord Nobunaga wanted to save more on charcoal and firewood. Yes, those were his orders last year, but it seems that Murai Nagato's style of economy did not please him.

His new duties took him all over the large castle compound, to all the places charcoal and firewood were used: in the offices, the rest huts, the side rooms, inside and out, wherever fires were built in the winter in the large hearths cut into the floors. Especially in the servants' quarters and the barracks of the young samurai, charcoal was piled high in the grates, as evidence of unnecessary expense.

"It's Master Kinoshita! Master Kinoshita's here!"

"Who's this Kinoshita?"

"Master Kinoshita Tokichiro, who's been appointed overseer of charcoal and firewood. He's making the rounds with a grim look on his face."

"Ah, that monkey?"

"Do something with the ashes!"

The young samurai hurriedly covered up the red coals with ashes, put what was black into the coal scuttle, and looked very pleased with themselves.

"Are you all here?" When Tokichiro came in, he squeezed his way in through the group and warmed his own hands over the hearth. "My unworthy self has been commanded to oversee charcoal and firewood supplies. I'd be grateful for your help."

The young samurai glanced at each other nervously. Tokichiro took up the large metal tongs that had been placed in the hearth.

"Isn't it cold this year? Covering up the live coals like this…you can't keep warm by just heating your fingers." He dug up some red coals. "Shouldn't you be more generous with the charcoal? I understand that until now the amount of charcoal to be used in each room daily was fixed, but it's dreary to be economical with heat. Use it fully, please. Come to the storehouse and take as much as you need."

He went to the barracks of the foot soldiers and the attendants of the samurai, encouraging the use of plenty of charcoal and firewood by the people who, until then, had shrunk before the exhortations to economize!

"He's being awfully generous in his position this time, isn't he? Perhaps Master Monkey has let his sudden promotion go to his head. But if we follow him too much, we may get a scolding the like of which we've never had until now."

No matter how liberal he was, the retainers set their own limits.

The expenses for one year's firewood and charcoal at Kiyosu Castle exceeded one thousand bushels of rice. Huge amounts of timber were cut and turned into ashes every year. For the two years of Murai Nagato's tenure, there had been no savings at all. On the contrary, expenses had increased. Worst of all, his calls to economize only depressed and annoyed the retainers. The first thing Tokichiro did was to release the retainers from this oppression. He then went before Nobunaga and made the following proposal: "In the winter, the younger samurai, foot soldiers, and servants spend their days indoors eating, drinking, and idly chatting. Before economizing on charcoal and firewood, I would humbly suggest that Your Lordship take steps to correct these bad habits."

Nobunaga quickly gave orders to his senior retainers. They called together the head of the servants and the commander of the foot soldiers and discussed the peacetime duties of retainers: the repair of armor, lectures, the practice of Zen meditation, and inspection tours around the province. Then, most important, training in firearm and spear techniques, engineering projects in the castle and for the servants, when they had time, the shoeing of horses. The reason? Not to give them leisure. To a military commander, his samurai retainers were as dear as his own children. The bond between lord and retainers, who had pledged themselves absolutely, was as strong as that between blood relatives.

On the day of battle, these were the people who would give up their lives before his very eyes. If he did not hold them dear, or if that affection and benevolence were not felt, there would be no brave soldiers dying for him. Therefore, during peacetime it was very easy for a lord to be too generous—against the day of battle.

Nobunaga had the daily routine strictly enforced, leaving his retainers no leisure time. At the same time, he made the serving women who looked after the housekeeping go through training and even practice being confined in a castle under siege, so that he established a daily regimen of no leisure from morning till night. This, of course, went for himself as well.

When Tokichiro was there, he would cheer up.

"Monkey, how have things been recently?"

"Good! I've seen the effect of your orders, but you have a way to go."

"It's still not enough?"

"There's still much more."

"Is something still lacking?"

"The way things are done in the castle has yet to be introduced among the townspeople."

"Hm. I see." Nobunaga listened to Tokichiro. His retainers always made bitter faces and looked askance at this. There were few examples of someone like Tokichiro, who, in such a short space of time, had risen from the servants' barracks to sitting in his lord's presence, and even fewer cases of someone going before the lord and speaking his own recommendations. Naturally, they frowned as though this were the same as some outrageous act. Nevertheless, the yearly consumption of charcoal and firewood, which had been over a thousand bushels, was significantly reduced by midwinter.

Since the retainers had no spare time, they no longer idled around the hearth, wasting charcoal. Even when there was some leisure time, because the men were moving their bodies and continually exercising their muscles, fires naturally became unnecessary and fuel was only used in cooking. The fuel formerly used in one month was now enough to last for three months.

Nevertheless, Tokichiro was not satisfied that he had carried out his duties to the fullest. The contracts for charcoal and firewood were awarded in the summer for the following year. At the head of a group of castle suppliers, he set out to make the annual survey, which until then had been a mere formality. The officials in charge had never gone beyond asking how many of this kind of oak were on this mountain, and how many of that kind on that mountain. With the suppliers acting as his guides, Tokichiro conscientiously took note of everything he saw. He believed he could understand the conditions on the farms and in the towns, but, lacking experience, he could not even guess how much fuel could be got from a single mountain. And he had to admit that the finer points of buying charcoal and firewood were beyond him.

Like other officials before him, he went through the motions of the survey, mumbling, "Hm, hm. Is that so? I see, I see." Following custom, the day ended with the suppliers inviting the official to a banquet at the house of a local magnate. Much of the time was spent exchanging small talk.

"Thank you for coming out all this way."

"We haven't got very much, but please make yourself at home."

"We hope you'll favor us with your custom in the future."

One after another, they flattered Tokichiro. Naturally, attractive young women served the *sake*. They were constantly beside him, rinsing his cup, refilling it, and offering him one delicacy after another. He only had to express a wish and it was fulfilled.

"This is good *sake*," he said. He was in a good mood; there was no reason not to be. The perfume of the serving girls charmed his senses. "They're all beautiful," he said. "Each and every one."

"Does your honor like women?" one of the suppliers asked lightheartedly.

Tokichiro replied very seriously, "I like both women and *sake*. Everything in the world is good. But if you're not careful, even good things can turn against you."

"Please feel free to enjoy the *sake* and the young flowers, too."

"I'll do just that. By the way, you seem hesitant to talk business, so I'll break the ice. Would you show me the tree ledger for the mountain we were on today?" They brought it in for his inspection. "Ah, it's very detailed," he observed. "Are there no discrepancies in the number of trees?"

"None whatsoever," they assured him.

"It says here that eight hundred bushels were delivered to the castle. Can that much charcoal and firewood come from such a small mountain?"

"That's because demand was less than the year before. Yes, that's the amount from the mountain we surveyed today."

The next morning, when the merchants presented themselves to pay their respects, they were told that Tokichiro had gone off to the mountain before daybreak. They set off after him. When they caught up with him, he was supervising a group of foot soldiers and local farmers and woodsmen. Each man had a bundle of ropes cut to about a meter in length. They tied one length of rope to every tree. Knowing that they had started out with a given number of ropes, when they finished and did their calculations, they could count the total number of trees. Checking the number of trees against the figures in the ledger, Tokichiro suspected there had been an overcharge of almost one-third.

He seated himself on a tree stump. "Call the suppliers over here," he told one of his men.

The fuel dealers prostrated themselves before him, their hearts racing at the prospect of what was to come. No matter how many surveys of the mountains were conducted, the number of standing trees was not a fact that could be easily determined by an amateur, and, in fact, the overseers of fuel supplies had always taken the amount recorded in the ledger at face value—swallowed it whole, so to speak. Now the suppliers were faced with an official who was not going to be taken in.

"Isn't there a large discrepancy between the number in this ledger and the actual number of trees?"

They answered yes, but hesitantly and full of apprehension.

"What do you mean, 'yes'? What's the reason for this? You're forgetting the many years you've reaped His Lordship's patronage. Aren't you being ungrateful, deceitful, and complacent, and isn't your sole interest in making a profit? It seems you've put your lies in writing and you've been greedy."

"Isn't that a bit too strong, your honor?"

"The numbers are different. I'm asking why. Judging from the records, only sixty or seventy bushels out of a hundred ordered—that's only six or seven hundred out of a thousand— are actually delivered to the warehouses."

"No, well, er, with that sort of reasoning—"

"Silence! There's no excuse for men who've been supplying fuel from these mountains to have engaged in this kind of huge deception year after year. If I am right, you're guilty of deceiving officials and defrauding the provincial treasury."

"We—we hardly know what to say."

"You could be convicted for what you've done and have all your possessions confiscated. However, former officials have also been guilty of neglect. I'll let it pass just this once...but on the following condition: you must correctly state the number of trees. The figures you submit in writing had better correspond exactly with the facts. Is that clear?"

"Yes, Your Excellency."

"There's one other condition."

"Your Excellency?"

"There is an old saying, 'if you cut one tree, you should plant ten.' From what I have seen on these mountains since yesterday, trees are felled every year, but virtually none are being planted. If this continues, there'll be floods and the paddies and other fields at the foot of the mountains will be devastated. The province will be weakened, and when the province declines, you will be the ones to suffer. If you want to make real profits, if you hope for true wealth for your families and desire happiness for your descendants, shouldn't you first make your province strong?"

"Yes," they agreed.

"As a tax and a punishment for your greed, from this time forth, every time you cut down a thousand trees, you are, without fail, to plant five thousand seedlings. This is a strict order. Do you agree?"

"We're very grateful. If you will let us off on those terms, we swear the seedlings will be planted."

"I suppose, then, I should increase the delivery fee by five percent."

Later in the day, he informed the farmers who had helped him that he had ordered the reforestation. How much they would be paid for planting a hundred seedlings was yet to be decided, but he told them the expenses would most likely be borne by the castle. With that, he said, "Well, let's go back now."

Encouraged by Tokichiro's attitude, the suppliers were relieved. As they descended the mountain, they whispered among themselves, "What a shock! With this fellow around, you can't leave a moment unguarded."

"He's smart."

"It's not going to be easy income like before, but we won't lose out, either. We'll make up for it, slowly but surely."

Once back in the foothills, the suppliers were eager to be on their way, but Tokichiro wanted to repay them for the previous night's entertainment. "We've finished our business. Join me for the evening, relax and enjoy yourselves," he insisted.

At a local inn, he treated them to a banquet, he himself getting pleasantly tipsy.

* * *

Tokichiro was happy. All alone, but happy.

"Monkey!" Nobunaga said—he still sometimes called him that—"you've been economical in the kitchen ever since you were put in charge of it. But sticking a man like you there is a waste. I'm promoting you to the stables."

Along with the new assignment came a stipend of thirty *kan* and a house in the quarter of the castle town set aside for samurai. This new favor brought a lingering grin to

Tokichiro's face. Almost the first thing he did was visit his former workmate Ganmaku.

"Are you free now?" he said.

"Why?"

"I want to go into town and treat you to some *sake*."

"Well, I don't know."

"What's the matter?"

"You're a kitchen official now. I'm still nothing but a sandal bearer. You don't want to be seen out drinking with me."

"Don't take such a warped view. If I thought that way, I would never have come to ask you. Being in charge of the kitchen was above my status, but the fact is, I've been ordered to the stables at a stipend of thirty *kan*."

"Well!"

"I came here because you're a true and loyal servant of His Lordship, even though you're only a sandal bearer. I want you to share this happiness with me."

"This is a matter for congratulations, surely. But, Tokichiro, you're more honest than I am."

"Huh?"

"You're open with me, concealing nothing, while I've kept a good bit hidden from you. To tell the truth, I sometimes do special services, like that time you know about. For these I receive large bonuses directly from the hand of His Lordship. I send the money secretly to my house."

"You have a house?"

"If you go to Tsugemura in Omi, you'll see I have a family and about twenty servants."

"Ah, you do?"

"So it's not an honorable thing for me to be entertained by you. Anyway, if we both rise in the world, one with the other, we'll both treat and be treated."

"I didn't know."

"Our fates lie ahead of us—that's the way I look at it."

"You're right, our fates are still ahead of us."

"Let's commit ourselves to the future."

Tokichiro felt even happier. The world was bright. Nothing before his eyes lay in darkness or shadows.

Tokichiro took pleasure in realizing that his new position involved a mere thirty *kan*, but this modest amount bespoke recognition of his two years as an official. The annual fuel expenditure had been reduced by more than half, but it was more than the reward that made him feel good. He had been praised: "You've done good work. A man like you in a place like that is a waste." To be spoken to like this by Nobunaga was a joy he would not forget. Nobunaga was a general, and he knew how to speak to his men. Filled with admiration for his master, Tokichiro's elation was almost more than he could bear. Others might have mistaken him for a halfwit as, alone and grinning, his face now and again showing his dimples, he left the castle and roamed around Kiyosu. He was in a good mood when he was walking around town.

The day his duties changed, he was given five days' leave. He was going to have to arrange for household goods, a housekeeper, and maybe a servant, although he assumed the house he had received was on a back street, had a nondescript gate, a hedge rather than a wall and no more than five rooms. It was the first time he had been the master of a house. He changed direction to go take a look at it. The neighborhood was inhabited solely by men who worked in the stables. He found the group leader's house and went to pay his respects. He was out, so he spoke with the man's wife.

"Are you still single?" she asked.

He admitted that he was.

"Well, that's a little inconvenient for you," she said. "I have servants here and extra furniture. Why don't you take what you need?"

She is kind, Tokichiro thought as he went out the gate, saying he would probably, one way or another, be relying on her fully. She herself came outside the gate and called to two of her servants.

"This is Master Kinoshita Tokichiro, who's just been given duties in the stables. He'll soon be moving into that vacant house with the stand of paulownia. Show him around, and when you have a moment, clean the place up."

Led by the servants, Tokichiro went off to see his official residence. It was bigger than he had imagined. Standing in front of the gate, he mumbled, "Well, this is a fine house."

On making inquiries, he found the previous tenant had been a man by the name of Komori Shikibu. A while had passed, it seemed, and the house was rather in disrepair, but in his eyes it was nothing less than a mansion.

"That stand of paulownia in back is auspicious, because the Kinoshita family crest has been a paulownia since the time of our ancestors," Hiyoshi said to the servant. He wasn't sure this was true, but it sounded right. He thought he had seen such a crest on his father's old armor chest or sword scabbard.

In the mellow mood he was in now, he would warm up to those around him, and if there was nothing of overriding importance, no necessity to have cool nerves, he would give in to his elation and his tendency to be talkative. Still, after the words were out of his mouth, he admonished himself for not being more judicious, not because his words came from ill will or fear, but because he himself did not attach any importance to the matter. Beyond that, he assumed it would spawn criticism that Monkey was a braggart. He might admit to himself, It's true; I am a bit of a braggart. Nevertheless, small-hearted, fastidious people who, because of his loquaciousness, harbored misconceptions about him or were prejudiced against him, were never to be his allies during his illustrious career.

Later he was seen in the bustling center of Kiyosu, where he bought furnishings. Then, at a secondhand clothing shop, he saw a coat, meant to be worn over armor, that bore a white paulownia crest. Tokichiro went straight in to ask the price. It was cheap. He quickly paid for it and just as quickly tried it on. It was a little large, but not unbecomingly so, so he kept it on as he continued on his way. The blue cotton was thin and rippled in the breeze as he walked and some rich-looking material, like gold brocade, was stitched only into the collar. He wondered who the wearer had been, the man who had the paulownia crest dyed in white on the back of the garment.

How I'd like to show this to my mother! he thought joyfully.

Right there, in the prosperous part of town, he was assailed by an almost unbearable emotion. It went back to the pottery shop in Shinkawa. He was forced to recall what a miserable figure he had made, barefoot, pushing the handcart piled high with pottery past the staring men, the beautiful inhabitants of the town. He stopped by a dry goods store where high-quality woven goods from Kyoto lined the shelves.

"Please deliver this without fail," he admonished, putting down the money for his purchases.

Outside again, he noted it was always like this: after half a day of leisure, his purse was empty.

"Steamed Buns" proclaimed the magnificent sign with mother-of-pearl letters that hung from the roof at a street corner. These buns were a specialty of Kiyosu, in whose crowded shops travelers mingled with the locals.

"Welcome!" said a servant girl in a red apron. "Come in. Will you have some here, or buy some tot take home?"

Tokichiro sat down on a stool and said, "Both. First I'll have one to eat here. Then I'd like you to deliver a box—and make it a big one—to my house in Nakamura. Ask the packhorse driver when he'll be making a trip up that way. I'll leave a tip to cover that."

A man with his back to Tokichiro was hard at work, but he seemed to be the owner of the shop. "Many thanks for your patronage, sir," he said.

"You seem to be doing good business. I was just now asking to have some buns sent to my home."

"Certainly, sir."

"It doesn't matter when, but I'll entrust this to you. Would you please put this letter in the box with the buns?" He handed the shopkeeper a letter from his sleeve. On the envelope was written, "To Mother, Tokichiro."

The shopkeeper took it and asked if it really wasn't urgent.

"No, as I said, it's not. Anytime is all right. Your buns have always been my mother's favorites."

While he was talking, he took a mouthful, and the taste of the bun brought a flood of memories and, very quickly, tears to his eyes. These were the buns his mother loved so much. He recalled the days of his youth, when he had passed by this place, yearning to buy some for her, and craving one for himself so keenly that a hand seemed to be coming out of his throat. In those days he could only push his handcart on with abject patience.

A samurai who had been looking in his direction finished off his plate of buns, stood up, and called, "Isn't it Master Kinoshita?" He had a young girl with him.

Tokichiro bowed deeply and with great courtesy. It was the archer Asano Mataemon. He had been kind to Tokichiro from the time he had been a servant and he was inclined to be especially polite to him. As the shop was far away from the castle grounds, Mataemon was relaxed and in high spirits.

"You're alone, eh?" he asked.

"Yes."

"Won't you join us? I'm with my daughter."

"Oh, your daughter?" Tokichiro looked toward where, a bench away, a girl of sixteen or seventeen rearranged herself to have her back to him, leaving exposed only the white nape of her neck, in the midst of this boisterous crowd. She was lovely. It wasn't that she only appeared this way to Tokichiro, who was equipped with a sharply appreciative eye for beauty. Anyone would say the same; she was beautiful, no two ways about it, a woman far above the ordinary.

At Mataemon's beckoning, Tokichiro sat down before the possessor of those bright eyes.

"Nene," said Mataemon. It was a pretty name, which suited her character well. Wise eyes shone serenely in the midst of her finely formed features. "This is Kinoshita Tokichiro. He's recently been promoted from kitchen staff to duties in the stables. You should meet him."

"Yes, well…" Nene blushed. "I'm already acquainted with Master Kinoshita."

"Eh? What do you mean, acquainted? When and where did you meet?"

"Master Tokichiro's sent me letters and presents."

Mataemon looked taken aback. "I'm shocked. Did you reply to his letters?"

"I've sent nothing at all in reply."

"That's all well and good, but not to show them to me, your father, is inexcusable!"

"I told my mother each time, and she had the gifts returned, except those for special occasions."

Mataemon looked at his daughter, then at Tokichiro. "As a father, I'm always worried, but I was really careless. I didn't know. I had heard that Monkey was a shrewd man, but I never imagined he would be interested in my daughter!"

Tokichiro scratched his head. He was very embarrassed, blushing a deep red. When Mataemon began to laugh, he was relieved, but still flushed. Even though he could not tell how Nene felt about him, he was in love with her.

BOOK TWO

SECOND YEAR OF KOJI
1556

CHARACTERS AND PLACES

ASANO MATAEMON, Oda retainer
NENE, Mataemon's daughter
OKOI, Mataemon's wife
MAEDA INUCHIYO, Oda Nobunaga's page
YAMABUCHI UKON, Oda retainer
TOKUGAWA IEYASU, lord of Mikawa
SESSAI, Zen Monk and military
adviser to the Imagawa clan
IMAGAWA YOSHIMOTO, lord of Suruga
IMAGAWA UJIZANE, Yoshimoto's eldest son
YOSHITERU, thirteenth Ashikaga shogun
LORD NAGOYA, Nobunaga's cousin
IKEDA SHONYU, Oda retainer
and friend of Tokichiro
TAKIGAWA KAZUMASU, senior Oda retainer

SUMPU, capital of Suruga
OKAZAKI, capital of Mikawa
KYOTO, imperial capital of Japan

A HANDSOME MAN

"Okoi!" Mataemon called out as soon as he got home. His wife hurried out to greet him. "Prepare some *sake*. I've brought home a guest," he said abruptly.

"Well, who is it?"

"A friend of our daughter's."

Tokichiro came in behind him.

"Master Kinoshita?"

"Okoi, you've kept me in the dark until today. This is inexcusable behavior for the wife of a samurai. It seems that Master Kinoshita and Nene have known each other for some time. You knew, so why didn't you tell me?"

"I deserve to be scolded. I'm very sorry."

"That's all well and good, but what kind of father does Tokichiro think I am now?"

"She got letters, but she never hid them from me."

"I should hope not."

"Besides, Nene's a bright girl. As her mother, I believe she's never done wrong. So I didn't think it was worth bothering you with each and every letter she received from the men in this town."

"There you're overestimating our daughter. I really don't understand young people nowadays—young men or young women!" He turned to Tokichiro, who stood scratching his head in embarrassment, blocked from coming in, and he burst out laughing.

Tokichiro was overjoyed to have been invited to his sweetheart's home by her father, and his heart was racing.

"Well, don't just stand there!" Mataemon led the way to the guest parlor, which, though it was the best room in the house, was nonetheless rather small.

The archers' tenement houses were no more comfortable than Tokichiro's own home.

All the retainers of the Oda, regardless of rank, lived plainly. And in this house, too, the only thing that caught the eye was a suit of armor.

"Where did Nene go?"

"She's in her room." His wife offered Tokichiro some water.

"Why doesn't she come out and greet our guest? When I'm here, she always runs away and hides."

"She's probably changing and combing her hair."

"That won't be necessary. Tell her to come and help with the *sake*. It'll be just fine to put some plain home cooking in front of Tokichiro."

"Goodness! Don't say such things."

Tokichiro stiffened in embarrassment. With the crusty retainers in the castle he was audacious and pushy, but here he was nothing more than a shy young man.

Nene finally came out to greet him formally. She had put on some light makeup. "We haven't much but please make yourself at home." She then brought out a tray of food and a flask of *sake*.

Tokichiro answered Mataemon's questions as though in a trance, all the while admiring Nene's figure and demeanor. She has a lovely profile, he thought. He was particularly taken by her unaffected grace, as plain as cotton cloth. She had none of the coquettishness of other women, who were either unpleasantly coy or put on airs. Some might have found her a little on the skinny side, but wrapped within her was the fragrance of wildflowers on a moonlit night. Tokichiro's keen senses were overcome; he was in ecstasy.

"How about another cup?" Mataemon offered.

"Thanks."

"You did say you liked *sake*."

"I did."

"Are you all right? You haven't drunk too much, have you?"

"I'll have it bit by bit, thank you." On the edge of his seat, with the lacquered *sake* flask in front of him, Tokichiro stared fixedly at Nene's face, so white in the flickering lamplight. When her eyes moved suddenly in his direction, he passed his hand over his face and said, confused, "Well, I've had quite a bit this evening." He blushed when he realized that he himself was far more aware of his behavior than Nene was.

Once again he thought that, when the time came, even he would have to get married. And if he had to take a wife, she would have to be beautiful. He wondered whether Nene could stand poverty and hardship and bear him healthy children. In his present circumstances, he was bound to have money problems after setting up a home. And he knew that in the future he would not be satisfied with mere wealth, and that there would be a mountain of troubles waiting for him.

Looking at a woman from the point of view of taking her as a wife, there were naturally considerations such as her virtue and appearance. But it was more important to find a woman who could love his mother, an almost illiterate farmer, and one who could also cheerfully encourage her husband's work from behind the scenes. Besides possessing these two qualities, she must be a woman with the kind of spirit that could endure their poverty. If Nene were such a woman…he thought again and again.

Tokichiro's interest in Nene had not begun that evening. He had long before considered Mataemon's daughter to be the right woman for him. He had noticed her before knowing who she was, and he had secretly sent her letters and presents. But that night he was sure for the first time.

"Nene, I have a private matter to discuss with Tokichiro, so would you leave us for a little while?" When Mataemon said this, Tokichiro imagined that he was already Mataemon's son-in-law, and he began to blush again.

Nene left the room, and Mataemon sat a little straighter. "Kinoshita, I want this to be a frank talk. I know you to be an honest man."

"Please say anything you like." Tokichiro was pleased that Nene's father was treating him with such familiarity, even if this was not going to be the talk that he hoped for. He, too, sat straighter, ready to be of service, no matter what Mataemon asked him.

"What I want to say is . . . well, Nene's about the right age to be married."

"To be sure." Tokichiro's throat was dry and strangely choked. Even though it would have been enough to nod, he felt that he had to make some kind of comment. He often said things when he did not have to.

"The fact is, I've received a number of offers for Nene that are well above our family's status," Mataemon continued. "And as her father, I just don't know which one to pick."

"It must be difficult."

"And yet . . ."

"Yes?"

"Someone who may look right to a father may not be to a young girl's liking."

"I understand that. A woman has only one life to live, and her happiness depends on the man she marries."

"There's a page who is always at our master's side—a young man by the name of Maeda Inuchiyo. You must know him."

"Master Maeda?" Tokichiro blinked. The conversation had taken an unexpected turn.

"That's right. Master Inuchiyo is from a good family, and he has repeatedly asked for Nene's hand in marriage."

Tokichiro let out something that sounded more like a sigh than an answer. A formidable rival had suddenly appeared on the scene. Inuchiyo's handsome face, his clear voice, and the good manners he had been taught as one of Nobunaga's pages all made Tokichiro, who had no confidence in his own looks, envious. After all, he could not stop people from calling him Monkey. So there was nothing more hateful to him than to hear someone called "a handsome man." And Inuchiyo was certainly a handsome man.

"Do you plan to give Nene to him?" Without meaning to, they had somehow gone beyond the point of mere talk.

"What? No," Mataemon said, shaking his head. He brought the cup to his lips as though roused from a deep reverie. "As a father, I would be happy to have such a well-mannered gentleman as Inuchiyo for a son-in-law, and I've already accepted. Recently, however, my daughter doesn't bow so meekly to her parents' judgment, though only in this matter."

"Do you mean that these engagement talks are not to her liking?"

"She hasn't said so in so many words, but she's never said she approved of them either. Well, I suspect she doesn't like the idea."

"I see."

"You know, these marriage talks really are a bother." As Mataemon talked, a worried look spread across his face.

In the end, it was a question of honor. Mataemon admired Inuchiyo. He considered him to be a young man with a bright future. And when Inuchiyo had asked for Nene as his wife, Mataemon had agreed, and had even rejoiced before asking his daughter. But when he had proudly told her, "I think he'd make a peerless husband," she didn't appear to be happy at all. Instead she had looked upset. Although they were father and daughter, he now understood that there was a big difference of opinion between them when it came to choosing a lifetime partner. As a result, Mataemon did not know what to do. Both as a father and as a samurai, he was ashamed to confront Inuchiyo.

Inuchiyo, on the other hand, pursued the affair openly. He told his friends that he was going to marry Master Asano's daughter, and asked them to intercede for him.

Mataemon explained his predicament to Tokichiro. The day of the engagement was approaching. He had managed to hold him off so far with such excuses as "Her mother's been in poor health lately" and "My wife says this is an unlucky year." But he was running out of excuses and was at his wits' end as to what to do next.

"People say you're a man of great ability. Don't you have any ideas?" Mataemon drained his cup and put it down.

If Tokichiro was drunk, it did not show on his face. Until then he had been enjoying his own idle fantasies, but as he listened to Mataemon's problem, he suddenly became very serious.

I have a tough rival, he thought. Inuchiyo was the "handsome man" that Tokichiro disliked so much, but he was hardly what might be called a model one. Raised in a country at war, he was brave but suffered from a stubborn and self-indulgent streak.

Inuchiyo had fought his first campaign with Nobunaga's army at the age of thirteen, and had been man enough to return with an enemy's head. In a recent battle, when a retainer of Nobunaga's brother had rebelled, Inuchiyo had fought savagely in Nobunaga's vanguard. When an enemy warrior shot an arrow into Inuchiyo's right eye, Inuchiyo had leaped from his horse, cut off the man's head, and presented it to Nobunaga. All without removing the arrow.

He was a daring, handsome man, although his right eye was now closed to a narrow slit; it looked as though a single needle had been laid on his beautiful, fair skin. Even Nobunaga could not control Inuchiyo's impetuosity.

"So what should I do about Inuchiyo?" Mataemon asked.

They sat in despair together; even Tokichiro, as resourceful as he normally was, didn't know what to suggest. Finally he said, "Well, don't worry. I'll think of something."

Tokichiro returned to the castle. He had done nothing to further his own cause and had only shared Mataemon's problems. But he considered it an honor that his sweetheart's father had relied on him and confided in him, even if those troubles became a burden to him.

Tokichiro realized he was deeply in love with Nene.

Is that what love is all about? he asked himself, trying to understand the mysterious workings of his own heart. Saying the word "love" gave him an unpleasant feeling. He disliked the word, which seemed to be on everyone's lips. Hadn't he given up on love since his youth? Certainly his looks and bearing—the weapons with which he fought against the world—had been derided by the beautiful women he had met. But he, too, was moved by beauty and romance. And he had a deep store of patience that frivolous beauties and aristocrats could never imagine.

Although he had received nothing but contempt, he was not the kind of man who gave up. Someday I will show them, he vowed. The women of the world would fight for the attentions of this ugly little man. This thought was the goad that drove him on. It was this feeling that had formed his outlook on women and love before he even knew it. Tokichiro had nothing but contempt for men who worshiped the beauty of women. He despised those who turned love into a fantasy and a mystery, thinking it the highest good in human life, amusing themselves with their own melancholy.

Nevertheless, he thought, it's all right in Nene's case—even to say that I've fallen in love. Love and hate are matters entirely up to the individual, and when he got used to the idea, Tokichiro compromised too. Just before going to sleep, he shut his eyes and imagined Nene's profile.

Tokichiro was off duty the following day as well. His new house in the paulownia stand, which he had visited the day before, was in need of some repairs, and he had to arrange for furniture. But he lingered inside the castle in order to call on Inuchiyo, who was always at Nobunaga's side. Inuchiyo looked down on Nobunaga's retainers from the raised wooden platform with a gaze more arrogant than his master's. When people like Tokichiro came to petition Nobunaga, Inuchiyo listened with a grin, the little dimples showing at the side of his mouth.

Monkey, again? Inuchiyo did not even have to say it. Somehow his single eye looked right through you. Tokichiro thought he was arrogant and did not mix with him much.

While Tokichiro was talking with the guard at the central gate, someone walked by and said, "Master Tokichiro, are you off duty today?"

Casually looking around, Tokichiro saw that it was Inuchiyo. Running after him, he said, "Master Inuchiyo. There is a delicate matter I would like to speak with you about."

Inuchiyo gave him his usual superior look. "Is this business or personal?"

"As I said, it's a delicate matter, so it's personal."

"If that's the case, right now is inappropriate. I'm just back from an errand for His Lordship, and I don't have time for a chat. Later." With this flat refusal, he left abruptly.

An unlikable fellow, but he does have some good points, Tokichiro had to admit. Left alone, he stared vacantly after Inuchiyo. Then he too went off, walking with long strides. He was headed for the castle town. Arriving at his new house, he found a man washing the gate and another man carrying in baggage.

Have I got the wrong house? Tokichiro asked himself.

As he looked around, a man's voice rang out from the kitchen. "Hey! Master Kinoshita. Over here."

"Oh, it's you."

"What do you mean, 'Oh, it's you'? Where have you been? Letting people furnish and

143

clean your house!" The man was one of his former colleagues in the kitchen. "Well, well. You've done rather well for yourself in no time at all."

Tokichiro went in as if he were a guest in his own house. There was a new lacquered chest of drawers and a shelf. These were all gifts from friends who had heard of his promotion, but who, upon finding that the happy-go-lucky master of the house was out, had cleaned the place, moved in the furniture, and finally gotten around to washing the gate.

"Thank you. You're too kind." Embarrassed, Tokichiro quickly set about to help them with whatever he could do on his own. All that was left was to fill up the *sake* flasks and put them on the trays.

"Master Kinoshita," said one of the castle suppliers, who felt indebted to him from the time Tokichiro had worked as overseer for charcoal and firewood. Peeking into the kitchen, Tokichiro found a chubby maidservant washing and scrubbing. "This is a girl from our village. You must be busy these days, so why don't you employ her for the time being?"

Tokichiro took advantage of the offer and said, "I'd also like a manservant and a handyman, so if you know of anyone, I'd be most grateful."

Then they sat down in a circle, and the housewarming party began.

It's a good thing I came here today. Imagine if I, the householder, had not shown up. Tokichiro was ashamed of himself. He had not considered himself to be easygoing, but now he could see that he must be at least a bit.

As they drank, the wives of his new colleagues in the neighborhood dropped by to congratulate Tokichiro on his promotion.

"Hey, Master Kinoshita! Master of the house!" one of the visitors called.

"What's up?"

"What do you mean, 'What's up?' Have you gone around to the other houses in the neighborhood to pay your respects?"

"No, not yet."

"What? Not yet? Are you the kind of person who dances and sings, waiting for people to come and pay their respects to you? Well, you'd better put on your best clothes and go on one round right away. You can take care of two problems at once by bowing to each house and telling them that you've moved to the neighborhood and that you've been appointed to the stables."

A few days later he had his help. A man from the same village as the maidservant came asking for work. And he employed another man. Somehow or another he had acquired a small residence and three servants, and was the master of his own house, despite his modest stipend. Now when Tokichiro left home—wearing, of course, his secondhand blue cotton coat with the white paulownia crest on the back—he was seen off by the maid and servants.

That morning, thinking that everything would be perfect if only Nene became his wife, he skirted the outer moat of the castle. As he walked along, Tokichiro failed to see the grinning man coming from the other direction. And although one might have imagined that he was still thinking of Nene, his head was really filled with thoughts of castle siege and defense: This is a moat in name only. It's so shallow that in ten days without rain you could see the bottom. In wartime, if you threw in a thousand sandbags, you could open up an avenue of attack. There isn't very much drinking water in the castle, either. The weak point of this castle, then, is water supply. There isn't enough for a good defense in case of a siege.…As he was mumbling to himself, a giant of a man approached and tapped him on the shoulder.

"Master Monkey. Are you on duty now?"

Tokichiro looked up at the face of the speaker, and in that instant hit upon a solution to his problem.

"No, this is a good time," he answered truthfully.

The man, of course, was Maeda Inuchiyo. That there had been no opportunity to talk since their former meeting, and that he now met him here by chance, outside the castle, was a good omen. But before he was able to say anything, he was cut off by Inuchiyo.

"Master Monkey, in the castle you said something about a delicate matter you wanted to talk to me about. Since I'm not on duty, I'll hear you out."

"Well, what I want to say is…" Tokichiro looked around, and brushed the dust off a rock at the edge of the moat. "This is not a matter to chat about standing. Why don't you sit down?"

"What is this all about?"

Tokichiro spoke frankly, and his eagerness and sense of the subject's importance showed in his face. "Master Inuchiyo. Do you love Nene?"

"Nene?"

"Master Asano's daughter."

"Ah, her."

"You love her, I suppose."

"What's it to you?"

"Because if you do, I would like to warn you. It seems that, being ignorant of the situation, you've gone through a go-between and have asked the girl's father for permission to marry her."

"Is there something wrong with that?"

"There is."

"What is that?"

"Well, the fact is that Nene and I have been in love for many years now."

Inuchiyo stared fixedly at Tokichiro, and suddenly his whole body shook with laughter. Tokichiro could see by the man's expression that he was not going to take him seriously, and he looked even more serious.

"No, this is not a laughing matter. Nene is not the kind of woman who would betray me and give herself to another man, regardless of the cause."

"Is that so?"

"We've made firm promises to each other."

"Well, if that's the way it is, that's fine with me."

"There is one person, however, with whom it's not so fine, and that is Nene's father. If you don't withdraw your request, Master Mataemon is going to be caught between two sides and will be forced to commit ritual suicide."

"*Seppuku?*"

"It seems that Master Mataemon had no idea of the agreement between us, so he agreed to your proposal. But because of the situation I've just explained to you, Nene is refusing to go through with it."

"Well then, whose wife will she be?"

With this challenge, Tokichiro pointed to himself and said, "Mine."

Inuchiyo laughed again, but not as loudly as before. "Put a limit on your jokes, Master Monkey. Have you ever looked in a mirror?"

"Are you calling me a liar?"

"Why should Nene be engaged to someone like you?"

"If it's true, what are you going to do?"

"If it is, I'll congratulate you."

"You mean you wouldn't object if Nene and I got married?"

"Master Monkey…"

"Yes?"

"People are going to laugh."

"There's nothing that can be done to a relationship based on love, even if we are laughed at."

"You're really serious, aren't you?"

"I am. When a woman dislikes the man who is courting her, she parries him cleverly, like a willow in the wind. When that happens, you're better off not thinking of yourself as a fool, or that you've been deceived. That aside, please don't bear a grudge against Master Mataemon if Nene and I do get married. That will just add insult to injury."

"Is this what you wanted to talk to me about?"

"Yes, and I'm very grateful for what you've said. I beg you not to forget the promise you made just now." Tokichiro bowed, but when he raised his head, Inuchiyo was gone.

A few days later, Tokichiro dropped in on Mataemon's house.

"Regarding what we talked about the other day," Tokichiro said formally. "I met with Master Inuchiyo and carefully explained your distress to him. He said that if your daughter had no intention of becoming his wife, and if there was already a promise between the two of us, there was really nothing to be done. He seemed to be resigned to the situation."

As Tokichiro told his story matter-of-factly, Mataemon's face showed that he didn't know quite what to make of it. Tokichiro continued, "Which is to say that Master Inuchiyo did have some regrets, so it would be unacceptable to him if she were given in marriage to anyone else. If she and I were engaged to be married, he would be disappointed but would resign himself. He would take it like a man and congratulate me. Still, he would be highly displeased if you were to give Nene to someone else."

"Hold on, Kinoshita. If I heard you right, Master Inuchiyo says it's all right if Nene marries you, but no one else?"

"That's correct."

"Incredible! Who told you that you could marry Nene? And when?"

"No one, I'm ashamed to say."

"What is this? Did you think that I asked you to lie to Master Inuchiyo?"

"Well…"

"But what kind of nonsense have you told Master Inuchiyo? And to say that you and Nene are engaged is nothing more than a joke. This is outrageous!" Mataemon, who was ordinarily a gentle man, was getting upset. "Because it was you who came up with this, people will think that it's probably a joke. But even as a joke, it's terribly embarrassing for an unmarried girl. Do you find it funny?"

"Of course not." Tokichiro hung his head. "I'm the one who made this mistake. I never meant for it to come to this. I'm sorry."

Mataemon looked disgusted. "I don't want you saying how sorry you are. It was my mistake, opening up to someone I thought had a little more common sense."

"Really, I—"

"Well, go home. What are you waiting for? Having said what you have, you're no longer welcome in this house."

"All right, I'll be discreet until the day the wedding is announced."

"Fool!" Mataemon's store of geniality was finally exhausted. He yelled at Tokichiro, "Do you think that someone is going to give Nene to a man like you? She wouldn't give her consent even if I ordered her to."

"Well, that's the issue, isn't it?"

"What do you mean?"

"There's nothing as mysterious as love. Nene probably conceals it in her heart that she won't have anyone else for a husband but me. It's rude of me to say so, but I haven't proposed to you; I've proposed to your daughter. Nene is the one who is hoping that I'd ask her to become my wife."

Mataemon looked at him dumbstruck. This had to be the pushiest man he had ever met! No matter what kind of man he was, maybe Tokichiro would go home if he made a sour face and remained silent and sullen. But Tokichiro sat there without a hint of getting up to leave.

To make matters worse, Tokichiro spoke up coolly, "I'm not lying. I'd like you to ask Nene once what is really in her heart."

Mataemon had had enough. Turning around as though he was unable to take any more, he yelled out to his wife in the next room, "Okoi! Okoi!" Okoi looked anxiously at her husband through the open doorway but didn't get up. "Why don't you call Nene?" he asked her.

"But—"

When she tried to calm him down, Mataemon yelled past his wife: "Nene! Nene!"

Nene, afraid that something had happened, came and knelt behind her mother.

"Come here!" Mataemon said severely, "Surely, you have not made some promise to Master Kinoshita here without your parents' consent."

This came as an unmistakable shock for Nene. Wide-eyed, she looked back and forth at her father and Tokichiro, who was sitting with his head hung low.

"Well, Nene? Our family honor is at stake. It's also for the sake of your own honor when you do get married. You had better speak up clearly. Surely nothing like that has happened."

Nene was silent for a moment, but finally she spoke clearly and modestly: "It has not, Father."

"Nothing, right?" With a look of victory combined with a sigh of relief, Mataemon stuck out his chest.

"But, Father—"

"What?"

"There's something I'd like to say while Mother is here, too."

"Go ahead."

"I have a request. If Master Kinoshita will have an unworthy person like myself as his wife, please give your consent."

"Wha–what?" Mataemon stuttered.

"Yes."

"Have you lost your senses?"

"One doesn't speak lightly of such an important subject. I feel very embarrassed to speak of such things, even to my parents, but this is so important for all of us that I must speak about it openly."

Mataemon let out a groan and stared openmouthed at his daughter.

Extraordinary! Tokichiro silently praised Nene's splendid speech, and his entire body thrilled with excitement. But more than this, he could not understand why this carefree, unaffected girl had given him her confidence.

It was evening. Tokichiro was walking along absentmindedly. Having left Mataemon's house, he was on his way to his own home in the paulownia grove.

If her parents would give their permission, she would like to become Master Kinoshita's wife, Nene had said. Even though he was putting one foot in front of another, he was so wrapped up in his happiness that he was barely conscious. Nene had spoken seriously, but he still had some doubts. Does she really love me? If she loves me that much, why didn't she tell me sooner? he wondered. He had secretly sent her letters and gifts, but until now Nene had not sent him a single answer that might be interpreted as favorable. From this he had naturally thought that Nene did not like him. And what about the way he had dealt with Inuchiyo and Mataemon? He was just being his normal pushy self. Win or lose, he had persisted in his own hopes without asking himself what Nene really felt. He should marry her. He *had* to marry her.

Nevertheless, for her to say in front of her father and mother that she wanted to marry him—and when he himself was present—required a great deal of courage. Her admission astonished Tokichiro more than it surprised her father.

Until Tokichiro left, Mataemon had sat with a sour and disappointed look on his face, without consenting to his daughter's request. Rather, he had sat silently sighing, confused, pitying and disdaining his daughter's frame of mind, saying, "There's no accounting for taste."

Tokichiro was also uneasy. "I'll come back another day and ask again," he had said as he prepared to leave.

Mataemon replied, "I'll try to think about it. I'll think about it." Which was an implicit refusal.

But Tokichiro found some hope in these words. Until then, he had not understood Nene's feelings at all. But if Nene's heart was set, he was confident that he would be able to change Mataemon's mind somehow. "I'll think about it" was not an outright no. So

Tokichiro felt that he had already made Nene his wife.

Tokichiro was still lost in thought as he entered his house and sat down in the main room. He was thinking about his own self-confidence, Nene's feelings, and the right time for their marriage.

"There's a letter for you from Nakamura."

As soon as Tokichiro had sat down, the servant put the letter and a package of millet flour in front of him. A feeling of homesickness told him that the letter was from his mother.

There are no words to express our gratitude for the gifts you always send: the dumplings and the clothes for Otsumi. We only have tears to thank you.

He had written to her several times, telling her about his house, and asking her to come and live with him. Although his stipend of thirty *kan* would not allow him to discharge his filial duties fully, she would not lack food or clothing. He also had several servants, so that her hands, which had become rough from years of work on the soil, would not have to scrub and clean again. He would also find a husband for Otsumi. And he would buy some good *sake* for his stepfather. He himself enjoyed a drink, and nothing would please him more than if the whole family could live together, talking about their former poverty over their evening meal.

Onaka's letter went on:

Although we would be happy to live with you, I am sure that this would get in the way of your work. Certainly, your mother understands that a samurai's duty is to be ready to die at any time. It is still too early to think of my happiness. When I think about former times and your present position, I thank the gods, the Buddhas, and His Lordship for their favors. Do not worry about me. Rather, work harder. There is nothing that will make your mother happier. I have not forgotten what you said at the gate that frosty night, and think of it often.

Tokichiro cried and read the letter over and over. The master of the house was not supposed to let his servants see him cry. Moreover, it was the upbringing of a samurai not to let anyone see his tears. But Tokichiro was not like that. And there were so many tears that the servant felt awkward and fidgety.

"Ah, I was wrong. What she said is perfectly correct. My mother is so smart. It's still not the time to think about myself and my family," he said aloud to himself as he folded the letter. His tears would not stop, and he rubbed his eyes with his sleeve like a small child.

That's right! he realized. There haven't been any wars here for a while, but there's no telling when war might erupt in a castle town. The people who live in Nakamura are safe. No, she's saying that that kind of selfish thinking is wrong to begin with. Service to one's lord should come first. Raising the letter to his forehead reverently, Tokichiro addressed his mother as though she were in the room with him, "No, I understand what you've said, and I'll abide by it absolutely. When my position is secure, and I have the confidence of my lord and others, I'll visit you again, so please come to live with me then." He then took the package of millet flour and gave it to the servant. "Take this to the kitchen. What are you looking at? Is there something strange about crying when you're supposed to? This is millet flour my mother ground at night with her own hands. Give it to the maid-servant. Tell her not to waste it, but to make it into dumplings for me from time to time. I've liked them since I was a child. I guess my mother remembered that."

He completely forgot about Nene, and continued thinking about his mother while he ate his solitary evening meal. What does Mother eat? Even if I sent her money, she'd use it to buy sweets for her child or *sake* for her husband and eat unseasoned vegetables herself. If my mother does not live a long life, I don't know how I'll carry on.

When he went to bed, he was still lost in thought. How can I get married before my mother comes to live with me? It's too soon, much too soon. It would be better to marry Nene later.

THE WALLS OF KIYOSU

Every year in the fall there were violent storms. But other, far more ominous winds were blowing around Owari. From the Saito of Mino to the west, from the Tokugawa of Mikawa to the south, and from Imagawa Yoshimoto of Suruga to the east—all the signs pointed to the growing isolation of Owari.

The storms that year had damaged more than two hundred yards of the outer castle wall. A great many carpenters, plasterers, coolies, and stonemasons came to the castle to take part in the reconstruction. Lumber and masonry were brought in through the Karabashi Gate, and construction materials were piled up here and there so that the pathways in the castle and around the moat were highly congested. The people who passed by every day complained openly about the inconvenience:

"You can't walk anywhere!"

"If they don't finish quickly, the stone walls are going to be in danger when the next storm comes."

But then a sign was clearly posted at the roped-off construction site: "This area is under repair. Unauthorized entry prohibited."

The work was carried out with the semblance of a military operation under the authority of Yamabuchi Ukon, the overseer of building works, so that the people who passed through the area did so in single file, with great deference and constraint.

The construction was nearing its twentieth day, but there was still no sign of progress. Certainly it was an inconvenience, but now no one complained. Everyone understood that it was going to take a long time and a good bit of construction to repair two hundred yards of the castle wall.

"Who is that man over there?" Ukon asked one of his subordinates, who turned and looked over to where he was pointing.

"I think it's Master Kinoshita from the stables."

"What? Kinoshita? Ah, yes. He's the one everyone calls Monkey. Next time he passes by, call him over," Ukon ordered.

The subordinate knew that his master was angry because every day, when Tokichiro went to work, he passed the site and never made any salutations. Not only that, but he also walked over the piles of lumber. Of course, there was nothing else to be done where lumber had been put in the paths, but this was to be used for the castle construction, and if anyone was going to step on it, he should have asked the permission of the people in charge.

"He doesn't know his manners," the subordinate said later. "At any rate, he's been promoted from servant to samurai and has just been granted a residence in the castle town. He's new, so it's not that surprising."

"No, there's nothing worse than the pride of an upstart. They're all prone to conceit. Getting his nose put out of joint once would do him some good."

Ukon's subordinate waited eagerly for Tokichiro. He finally appeared in the evening, about the time people were going off duty. He was wearing his blue coat, as he did all year round. As almost all the duties of the men who worked in the stables were outside, it served his needs, but his position was such that he could have been properly dressed if he had wanted. Nevertheless, it seemed that Tokichiro never had money to spend on himself.

"He's coming!" Ukon's men winked at one another. Tokichiro walked by slowly, the paulownia crest showing on his back.

"Wait! Master Kinoshita! Wait!"

"Who, me?" Tokichiro turned around. "What can I do for you?"

The man asked him to wait, and went over to Ukon. The workmen and coolies had been called out and were starting to go home in large groups. Ukon had called the foremen of the plasterers and carpenters and was discussing the next day's work. But when he heard his subordinate, he stood up. "It's Monkey? You stopped him? Bring him here. If I don't admonish him now, he's going to develop bad habits."

Tokichiro came over without a word of greeting, without a bow. And now he seemed to be saying arrogantly, You stopped me. What do you want?

This made Ukon all the angrier. From the standpoint of status, there was an incomparable difference between the two. Ukon was the son of Yamabuchi Samanosuke, the governor of Narumi Castle, and thus the son of a senior Oda retainer. He was far superior to this man who stood there in an old blue coat.

"What presumption!" Ukon's face was flushed.

"Monkey. Hey! Monkey!" he called, but Tokichiro did not answer. This was not like him at all. Tokichiro was called Monkey by everyone from Nobunaga down to his friends, and the nickname didn't usually bother him. But today was different.

"Are you deaf, Monkey?"

"That's nonsense!"

"What?"

"Calling someone over and then speaking nonsense to him. What's this about a monkey?"

"Everyone calls you that, so I did too. I'm often away at Narumi Castle, so I don't remember your name. Is it so bad to call you as others do?"

"Yes, it is. There are people who are permitted to call you in a certain way, and others who aren't."

"Well then, am I one of those without permission?"

"That's right."

"Hold your tongue! It's your insolence that is at issue! Why do you trample over the lumber every morning on the way to your post? And why don't you greet us properly?"

"Is that a crime?"

"Don't you have any sense of courtesy? I tell you this because you may yet become a samurai. Proper manners are very important for a warrior. When you pass by here, you look at the construction with a smug expression on your face and mumble complaints to yourself. But a castle construction site is under the same discipline as a battlefield. You insolent fool! If you act this way again I'm not going to let you off so easily. When a sandal bearer rises to the position of samurai, something like this is bound to happen." Ukon laughed and looked around at the foremen and his subordinates, and then, to show off his own exalted position, laughed again and turned his back on Tokichiro.

The foremen, thinking that the matter had been settled, crowded around Ukon and went back to discussing the plans. But Tokichiro, glaring at Ukon's back, made no move to leave.

One of Ukon's subordinates said, "We're through with you, Kinoshita."

"You've been reprimanded. Now keep it in mind," said another.

"Well, go on home," said a third.

They made as if to calm him down and send him on his way, but Tokichiro ignored them. He continued to glare at Ukon's back. As he did this, his youthful pride rose to the surface like an unchecked bubble, and he exploded into uncontrollable laughter.

The foremen and Ukon's subordinates were startled and looked up. Even Ukon looked around sternly from his seat and shouted, "What are you laughing at?"

Tokichiro laughed all the more. "I'm laughing because you're ridiculous."

"You impertinent—" Ukon leaped up from his seat in a rage. "Because I forgave this miserable wretch, he's full of himself. This is outrageous! Military rules apply in the workplace just as they do on the battlefield. You wretch! I'm going to cut you down. Come over here!" He put his hand on the hilt of his long sword. His adversary, however, stood as still as though he had swallowed a stick.

Ukon became all the angrier. "Grab him! I'm going to punish him! Hold him so he won't run away!"

Ukon's retainers quickly drew up to Tokichiro's side. But Tokichiro was silent, and looked around at the approaching men as though he were sniffing at them. They had all thought there was something strange about him before, but this was almost eerie, and although they surrounded him, not one of them put a hand on him.

"Master Ukon, you're good at spouting out big words, but not so good at doing other things."

"What! What did you say?"

"Why do you think that construction work on the castle is under battlefield regulations? You yourself have said it, but I'll bet you don't understand what it means at all.

You're not a very good overseer. And you think I'm wrong to laugh at you."

"That is unpardonably abusive language! You miserable wretch! To someone of my rank—"

"Listen!" Tokichiro stuck out his chest and, looking at the faces around him, said, "Are these times of peace or of war? The man who doesn't understand this is a fool. Kiyosu Castle is surrounded by enemies: Imagawa Yoshimoto and Takeda Shingen to the east, Asakura Yoshikage and Saito Yoshitatsu to the north, the Sasaki and the Asai to the west, and the Tokugawa of Mikawa to the south." They were overpowered. His voice was full of self-confidence, and because he was not simply speaking his own private feelings, they all listened raptly, carried away by his voice. "The retainers think these walls are impregnable, but if a storm were to blow, they would crumble. It's outrageous negligence that this little bit of construction has taken over twenty days, and is still taking day after tedious day. What would happen if an enemy took advantage of this weak point and stormed the castle one night?

"There are three rules governing castle construction. The first is to build with speed and secrecy. The second is to build with unadorned strength. This means that ornament and beauty are fine, but only in peacetime. The third is constant preparedness, which means to be ready for attack despite the confusion of construction. The most frightening thing about construction is the possibility of creating a breach. The province might fall because of one small breach in a mud wall."

His intensity was overpowering. Ukon was about to say something two or three times, but he was checked by Tokichiro's eloquence, and his lips could only quiver. The foremen, too, gaped, overawed by Tokichiro's speech. Hearing the sense in what he said, no one could interrupt him with either abusive language or force. It was now unclear who was the overseer. When Tokichiro thought that what he was saying had sunk in, he continued.

"So while it's impolite to ask, just how exactly is Master Ukon conducting this enterprise? Where is the speed, the secrecy? Where the preparedness? After almost twenty days, has even one yard of the wall been rebuilt? It takes time to replace the collapsed stones beneath the mud walls. But to state that castle construction is subject to the same military regulations as a battlefield—this is nothing more than the boast of someone who does not know his true station. If I were a spy from an enemy province, I would see that an attack could be made where the wall is weakest. It's folly to think that this won't happen, and to carry on in a leisurely fashion as though you were a retired gentleman building a teahouse!

"It's extremely inconvenient for those of us who work within the castle grounds. Rather than blame those passing through, why not discuss the matter and speed up the progress of the construction? Do you understand? Not just the overseer but you, too, his subordinates and the foremen."

When he had finished, he laughed cheerfully. "Well, excuse me. I've been rude, just speaking what's on my mind, but we all think of this as an important official matter, night and day. Well, it's gotten dark. Now, if you'll excuse me, I'll go home."

While Ukon and his men stood dumbfounded, Tokichiro quickly left the castle grounds.

The following day Tokichiro was in the stables. In his new post, his diligence was second to none.

"Nobody loves horses as much as he does," his colleagues said. To an extent that amazed even the other stable workers, he completely immersed himself in the rounds of the stables and in the grooming of the horses, and his daily life was totally taken up with these animals.

The group leader came to the stables and called to him, "Kinoshita, you've been summoned."

Tokichiro looked out from beneath the belly of Nobunaga's favorite horse, Sangetsu, and asked, "By whom?" Sangetsu had developed an abscess on his leg, so Tokichiro was washing his fetlocks with hot water.

"If it's a summons, it means by Lord Nobunaga. Hurry up." The group leader turned and shouted in the direction of the samurais' room, "Hey! Somebody take Kinoshita's place and take Sangetsu to the stable."

"No, no. I'll do it." Tokichiro did not emerge until he had finished washing Sangetsu's leg. He applied an ointment and bandaged the wound, stroked the animal's neck, and then took it back to its stall himself.

"Where is Lord Nobunaga?"

"In the garden. If you don't hurry, you're going to put His Lordship in a bad mood."

Tokichiro went into the office and pulled on his blue coat with the paulownia crest. With Nobunaga in the garden were four or five retainers, including Shibata Katsuie and Maeda Inuchiyo.

Tokichiro, dressed in his blue coat, hurried over, stopped more than twenty yards from Nobunaga, and prostrated himself.

"Monkey, come here," Nobunaga ordered. Inuchiyo immediately put up a stool for him. "Come closer."

"Yes, my lord."

"Monkey? I've heard that you shot out some pretty big words at the construction site on the outer walls last night."

"You've already heard, my lord?"

Nobunaga forced a smile. Tokichiro did not seem to be a person who would have let out those big words; he was now bowing before him, looking shamefaced.

"From now on, restrain yourself," Nobunaga reprimanded him. "Yamabuchi Ukon came to me this morning with loud complaints about your bad manners. I calmed him down because, according to others, there seemed to be a lot of sense in your words."

"I'm extremely sorry."

"Go to the construction site and apologize to Ukon."

"Me, my lord?"

"Of course."

"If it's an order, I'll go and apologize."

"Do you disapprove?"

"I hesitate to say this, but won't it encourage his vice? What I said was correct, and his work, in terms of service to you, can hardly be called conscientious. Even that little bit of repair has taken close to more than twenty days, and furthermore—"

"Monkey, are you going to spit out those big words even to me? I've heard your lecture already."

"I thought I spoke what was obvious, certainly not just big words."

"If that's so, how many days should it take to finish the job?"

"Well…" Tokichiro became a bit more cautious and thoughtful, but he answered promptly, "Well, since the work has already been started, I think I could finish it without difficulty in three days."

"Three days!" Nobunaga exclaimed involuntarily.

Shibata Katsuie looked exasperated and sneered at Nobunaga's credulity in believing Tokichiro. But Inuchiyo had absolutely no doubt that he could do exactly as he claimed.

Nobunaga promoted Tokichiro to the post of overseer of building works on the spot. He would replace Yamabuchi Ukon, and in just three days, he would be expected to repair two hundred yards of the castle walls.

He accepted the commission and prepared to withdraw, but Nobunaga asked him again, "Wait. Are you sure you can do it?" From the sympathetic tone of Nobunaga's voice, it was clear that he did not want Tokichiro to be forced to commit *seppuku* if he was to fail. Tokichiro sat a little straighter and said with certainty, "I will do it without fail."

Nevertheless, Nobunaga asked him to think about it a little more. "Monkey, the mouth is the cause of most disasters. Don't be obstinate over such a trivial matter."

"I'll have the walls ready for your inspection after three days," Tokichiro repeated, and withdrew.

That day he returned home earlier than usual. "Gonzo! Gonzo!" he called out. When his young servant peeked into the back garden at his master's call, there was Tokichiro, stripped naked and sitting cross-legged.

"Do you have an errand for me?"

"Yes, indeed!" he answered heartily. "You have some money on hand, don't you?"

"Money?"

"That's what I said."

"Well…"

"What about that little bit I gave you some time ago for the various household expenses?"

"That's been gone for a long time."

"Well, what about the money for the kitchen expenses?"

"There hasn't been any money for the kitchen for a long time, either. When I told you—it must have been a couple of months ago—you said we would have to do our best, so we've just been getting along as best we could."

"So there's no money?"

"And no reason for there to be any."

"Well then, what am I going to do?"

"Do you need something?"

"I'd like to invite some men over tonight."

"If it's just a matter of *sake* and food, I'll run around to the shops and buy some on credit."

Tokichiro slapped his thigh. "Gonzo, I'm relying on you." He picked up a fan and fanned himself with wide strokes. An autumn breeze was blowing, and paulownia leaves were falling in profusion; there were also a lot of mosquitoes.

"Who are the guests?"

"The construction foremen. They'll probably all come in a group."

Tokichiro took a bath in the tub in the garden. Just then, someone called from the entrance.

"Who is it?" asked the maidservant.

The guest removed his hat and introduced himself, "Maeda Inuchiyo."

The master of the little residence got out of the tub, put on a summer kimono on the veranda, and peered out toward the front.

"Well, well, Master Inuchiyo. I was wondering who it could be. Come on in and take a seat," Tokichiro called out in a casual manner, putting down some cushions himself. Inuchiyo sat down.

"I've come rather unexpectedly."

"Is it anything urgent?"

"No, it's not for myself. It's about you."

"Huh?"

"You act as if you don't have a care in the world. You've committed yourself to an impossible task, and I can't help feeling worried for you. It was your choice, so you must be confident of success."

"Ah, you mean the castle wall."

"Of course! You spoke out without thinking. Even Lord Nobunaga acted as if he didn't want you to commit *seppuku* over this."

"I did say three days, didn't I?"

"Do you have any chance of success?"

"None at all."

"None?"

"Of course not. I know nothing about building walls."

"What are you going to do, then?"

"If I can make the laborers on the construction site work hard, I think I should be able to do this just by using their strength to the full."

Inuchiyo lowered his voice. "Well, that's the question."

They were strange rivals in love. Even though the two men loved the same girl, they had become friends. They did not display friendship in either word or deed but rather in a somewhat uneasy relationship; each knew the other well, and they had entered into a respectful fellowship. Today in particular, it seemed that the nature of Inuchiyo's visit was one of genuine concern for Tokichiro.

"Have you thought about Yamabuchi Ukon's feelings?" Inuchiyo asked.

"He probably bears a grudge against me."

"Well, do you know what Ukon is thinking and doing?"

"I do."

"Is that so?" Inuchiyo cut his words short. "If you can discern that much, then my mind will be at ease."

Tokichiro stared intently at Inuchiyo. Then he bowed his head in a way that seemed to indicate assent. "You're something, Inuchiyo. Whatever you set your sights on, you set them well, don't you?"

"No, you're the quick one. You're clever to notice about Yamabuchi Ukon, and there's—"

"No, don't say any more." When Tokichiro made as if to put his hand over his mouth, Inuchiyo cheerfully clapped his hands and laughed.

"Let's leave it to the imagination. It's better left unsaid." Of course, he was about to mention Nene.

Gonzo returned, and the *sake* and food were delivered. Inuchiyo was about to go home, but Tokichiro stopped him.

"The *sake's* just come. Drink a cup with me before you go."

"Well, if you insist." Inuchiyo drank freely. However, not one of the guests for whom the *sake* and food had been provided showed up.

"Well, nobody's coming," Tokichiro said at last. "Gonzo, what do you suppose happened?"

When Tokichiro turned to Gonzo, Inuchiyo said, "Tokichiro, did you invite the construction foremen here tonight?"

"That's right. We have to get through some preliminaries. To finish the construction work in three days, we'll have to raise the morale of the men."

"I really overestimated you."

"Why do you say that?"

"I respected you as being twice as quick-witted as other men, but you were the only one who didn't guess that this was going to happen."

Tokichiro stared at the laughing Inuchiyo.

"If you'd think about it, you'd see," Inuchiyo said. "Your opponent is a man of little character. He is, after all, Yamabuchi Ukon, a man with limited abilities, even among those ordinarily judged not to have them. There's no reason for him to be praying that you'll successfully outwit him."

"Of course, but— "

"So is he going to just sit there sucking his thumb? I think not."

"I see."

"No doubt he's planning some obstruction so that you'll fail. So we might be right in thinking that the foremen you invited here tonight won't be coming. Both the workmen and the foremen are thinking that Yamabuchi Ukon is a good bit more important than you are."

"Right. I understand." Tokichiro hung his head. "If that's so, then this *sake* is for the two of us to drink. Shouldn't we leave it to the gods and finish it off?"

"That's fine, but your promise to do this in three days starts from tomorrow."

"I say let's drink, come what may."

"If you're decided, sit down and let's drink."

They did not drink much, but talked at length. Inuchiyo was a ready conversationalist, and Tokichiro somehow became the listener. Unlike Inuchiyo, Tokichiro had no formal education. As a boy he had not had a single day to spend, as the sons of samurai did, devoted to book learning and manners. He did not think of this as unfortunate, but he knew that it was a hindrance to his advancement in the world, and when he thought about those who had more education than he or sat in conversation with them, he was determined to make their knowledge his own. Thus he listened eagerly to the talk of others.

"Ah, I feel a little drunk, Tokichiro. Let's go to sleep. You've got to get up early, and I'm relying on you completely." So saying, Inuchiyo finally pushed his cup away, rose, and went home. When Inuchiyo had gone, Tokichiro lay down on his side, crooked his elbow beneath his head, and went to sleep. He did not notice when the maidservant came and slipped a pillow beneath his head.

He had never known a sleepless night. When he slept, there was no distinction between heaven and earth and himself. However, when he awoke, as he did early the next morning, he was himself immediately.

"Gonzo! Gonzo!"

"Yes, yes. Are you already awake, sir?"

"Bring me a horse!"

"Sir?"

"A horse!"

"A horse, sir?"

"Yes! I'll be going to work early today. I won't be returning home either tonight or tomorrow night."

"Unfortunately, we have neither horse nor stable yet."

"Dimwit! Borrow one from somewhere in the neighborhood. I'm not going out on a picnic. I need it for official business. Don't hesitate, go out and bring one back."

"It may be morning, but it's still dark outside."

"If they're sleeping, bang on the gate. If you think it's for my personal use, you'll probably hesitate. But it's for official business, so it's justifiable."

Gonzo put on a coat and hurried out in confusion. He came back leading a horse. Impatient to leave, the artless new rider galloped into the dawn without even asking where his mount had come from. Tokichiro rode round to six or seven houses of the construction foremen. They received stipends from the clan and belonged to the artisans' corps. Their houses were all built with a good bit of luxury, had maidservants and concubines, and were extraordinarily stately compared with Tokichiro's own house.

He went from house to house, beating on the gates and calling out to those still sleeping inside.

"Come to the meeting! Come to the meeting! Everyone who's working on the construction, be at the site by the Hour of the Tiger. Anyone who is late will be dismissed. By order of Lord Nobunaga!"

He gave out this message at one house after another. White steam rose from the sweat-soaked coat of his horse. Just as he reached the castle moat, light began to appear in the eastern sky. He tethered his horse outside the castle gate, took a deep breath, and stood blocking the Karabashi Gate. He held his long sword in his hand, and his eyes were shining brightly.

The foremen who had been awakened while it was still dark all wondered what had happened, and arrived one by one, leading their men.

"Wait!" Tokichiro ordered, stopping them at the entrance. After they had given their names, the location of their work, and the number of their workers and coolies, he gave them permission to pass. Then he ordered them to wait silently at their work stations. As far as he could see, almost everyone was there. The workmen were standing in order, but murmuring among themselves uneasily.

Tokichiro stood in front of them, still carrying his unsheathed sword. "Quiet!" He spoke as though he were giving a command with the tip of his raised sword. "Fall in!"

The workmen obeyed, but smiled scornfully. It was obvious from the looks in their eyes that they regarded him as a greenhorn, and that they were laughing at the way he stood in front of them with his chest stuck out. To them, his sword waving was nothing more than impertinent posturing, and it did nothing but invite their scorn.

"This is an order for all of you," Tokichiro said in a loud voice, with what seemed to be complete nonchalance. "By the order of Lord Nobunaga, I, as unworthy as I am, will be in charge of the construction from now on. Yamabuchi Ukon was in charge until yesterday, but I will take his place from today." As he spoke, he looked over the ranks of the workmen from right to left. "Until a short while ago, I was in the lowest rank of the servants. But with the favor of His Lordship, I was moved to the kitchens and am now in the stables. I have spent only a short time on the castle grounds, and I know nothing about construction work, but I plan on being second to none when it comes to serving our master. Under an overseer like myself, then, I wonder if any of you will consider working as my subordinates. I can imagine that, among artisans, there is an artisan's temperament. If any of you dislike working under these conditions, please feel free to say so, and I will promptly dismiss you."

Everyone was silent. Even the foremen, who had hidden their scorn, kept their mouths shut.

"No one? Is there no one who is dissatisfied with me as overseer?" he asked again. "If not, then let's get to work immediately. As I've said before, in wartime it is unforgivable for this work to take twenty days. I plan to finish the work by dawn three days from now. I want to say this clearly so that you'll understand and work hard."

The foremen looked at each other. It was natural that this sort of speech would elicit derisive smiles from those men with receding hairlines, who had been doing their jobs since childhood. Tokichiro noticed their reaction but chose to ignore it.

"Foremen of the masons! Head carpenters and plasterers! Come forward!"

They stepped forward, but as they looked up, scorn floated across their faces. Tokichiro suddenly struck the head plasterer with the flat of his long sword.

"What insolence! Do you stand there in front of an overseer with your arms folded? Get out!"

Thinking that he had been cut, the man fell down screaming. The others turned pale, their knees shaking.

Tokichiro went on severely, "I'm going to assign you your posts and duties. Listen carefully." Their attitude had improved. No one looked as if he was only half listening. They were quiet, though not reconciled. And even though they were not really cooperating, they looked scared.

"I've divided the two hundred yards of the wall into fifty sections, giving each group responsibility for four yards. Each group will consist of ten men: three carpenters, two plasterers, and five masons. I'm going to leave those assignments to the foremen. You foremen will each be supervising from four to five groups, so make sure that the workmen are not idle and pay attention to the distribution of men. When any of you have men to spare, move them to a station that is shorthanded. Don't leave an instant for idling."

They nodded but looked restive. They were irritated by this sort of lecture, and unhappy at being assigned to work stations.

"Ah, I almost forgot," Tokichiro said in a louder voice. "Along with the division of ten men for every four yards, I'm assigning a reserve corps of eight coolies and two workmen to each group. When I look at the way the work has been done so far, workers and plasterers are apt to leave the scaffolding and spend the day doing work that is not their own, like carrying lumber. But a worker at the workplace is the same as a soldier on the field. He should never leave his post. And he shouldn't abandon his tools, whether he be a carpenter, a plasterer, or a mason. That would be the same as a soldier throwing away his sword or spear on the battlefield."

He allocated the posts and divided the men, and then shouted with authority enough to start a battle, "Let's begin!"

Tokichiro also found work for his new subordinates. He ordered one of them to beat a drum. When he commanded the workers to begin, the man beat the drum as though they were marching into battle, one beat to every six paces.

Two beats of the drum sounded a break.

"Rest!" Tokichiro gave the order standing on top of a boulder. If someone didn't rest, he scolded him.

The construction site had been swept clean of the indolence that had prevailed until then; it was replaced by an intensity of activity more common on the battlefield, and by the sweat of excitement. But Tokichiro looked on silently, satisfaction never showing in his face. Not yet. Not like this, he thought.

Taught by their many years of labor, the workmen knew how to use their bodies in crafty ways. They gave the impression of working hard, but in fact they were not wringing out real sweat. Their resistance was such that they took a little comfort by showing obedience on the surface, but not truly working hard. Tokichiro's past life had been drowned in sweat, and he knew the true value and beauty of that sweat.

It is untrue to state that labor is a thing of the body. If labor is not filled with the spirit, there's no difference between the sweat of men and that of cows and horses. Keeping his mouth shut, he thought about the true nature of sweat and work. These men were working in order to eat. Or they were working in order to feed parents, wives, and children. They worked for food or pleasure, and they did not rise above that. Their work was small. And it was mean. Their desires were so limited that pity welled up inside Tokichiro, and he thought, I was like that too, before. Is it reasonable to expect great works from people with little hope? If he couldn't imbue them with a greater spirit, there was no reason for them to work with greater efficiency.

For Tokichiro, standing silently on the construction site, half a day passed quickly.

Half a day was one-sixth of his allotted time. Looking at the site, however, he could see no signs that they had made any progress since morning. Both above and below the scaffolding, the men seemed to be full of eagerness, but it was nothing more than a sham. On the contrary, they anticipated Tokichiro's complete and overwhelming defeat in three days.

"It's noon. Beat the drum," Tokichiro ordered. The noise and uproar of the construction site came to a halt all at once. When Tokichiro saw that the workers had taken out their lunches, he sheathed his sword and went off.

The afternoon ended with the same atmosphere at the construction site, except that discipline had broken down and indolence was more evident than it had been during the morning. It was no different from the day before, when Yamabuchi Ukon had been in charge. Even worse, the workers and coolies had been ordered to work without rest or sleep from this evening on, and knew that they were not going to be let out of the castle grounds for three days. Thus they begrudged their labor even more and did nothing but think of more ways to cheat as they worked.

"Stop your work! Stop your work! Wash your hands and meet in the square!" It was still light, but the official suddenly made the rounds beating the drum.

"What's going on?" the workers asked each other suspiciously. When they asked the foremen, they were answered with shrugs. They all went to the square where the lumber was kept, to see what this was about. There in the open, *sake* and food had been put into piles as high as mountains. They were told to be seated, and sat on straw mats, stones, and lumber. Tokichiro sat down in the very center of the workmen and raised his cup.

"Well, this isn't much, but we have three days before us. One day has already passed quickly, but I would like you to work and try the impossible. So, just tonight, please drink and rest to your hearts' content."

His manner was completely different from what it had been that morning, and he himself set an example by drinking a cup. "Come on," he shouted, "drink up. For those of you who don't like *sake*, there's food and sweets."

The workers were amazed. Suddenly they began to worry about finishing the project by the third day.

But Tokichiro was the first to get tipsy.

"Hey! There's plenty of *sake*. And it's the castle's, so no matter how much we drink, there'll be more in the storehouse. If we drink, we can dance, sing, or just sleep until the beat of the drum."

The workers soon stopped complaining. Not only were they being released from work, but they were also unexpectedly receiving food and *sake*. More than that, the overseer himself was relaxing and mixing with them.

"This gentleman has a sense of humor, doesn't he?"

When the *sake* began to take effect, they started to tell jokes. But the foremen still looked at Tokichiro coolly.

"Huh! He's being clever, but it's transparent." And this made them even more hostile. With looks on their faces that questioned the propriety of drinking *sake* in the workplace, they didn't touch their cups.

"Foremen! What's the matter?" Tokichiro got up, cup in hand, and sat down amid their cold looks. "You aren't drinking anything at all. Maybe you're thinking that foremen have responsibilities much like generals and therefore shouldn't drink, but don't be so anxious. What can be done, can be done. What can't be done, can't be done. If I was wrong, and we can't do this in three days, the matter will be closed with my suicide." Forcing the foreman who had the bitterest look to take a cup, Tokichiro poured from the flask himself. "Well, if we're talking about anxiety, it's not so much this particular construction project or even my own life that concerns me. I worry about the fate of this province in which you all live. But taking over twenty days to do just this little bit of construction—with that kind of spirit, this province is going to perish."

His words were charged with emotion. Suddenly the workers fell quiet. Tokichiro looked up at the evening stars as though in lamentation. "I imagine that all of you have seen the rise and fall of provinces, too. And you know the misery of the people who lived in fallen provinces. Well, it's something that cannot be helped. Naturally enough, His Lordship, his generals, and those of us who are the lowest samurai do not forget about the defense of the smallest part of the province, even when we sleep.

"But the rise and fall of a province is not in its castle. It's right here, in you. The people of the province are its stone walls and moats. Working on the construction of this castle, you may feel as though you're plastering the walls of somebody else's house, but you're wrong. You're building your own defenses. What would happen if this castle was burned to the ground one day? Surely it would not be the fate of the castle alone. The castle town, too, would be engulfed in flames, and the entire province would be destroyed. It would be like a scene from hell: children ripped away from their parents, old folks looking for their children, young girls screaming in panic, the sick burnt alive. Ah, if the province were to fall, it would really be the end. You all have parents, children, wives, and sick relatives. You must always, always remember."

Even the foremen stopped sneering and looked serious. They too had property and families, and Tokichiro's words struck home.

"So why is it that we are at peace today? Fundamentally, of course, it's thanks to His Lordship. But you, the people of this province, most certainly protect us with this castle as your very center. No matter how much we samurai fight, if the heart—the people—were to waver..." Tokichiro spoke with tears in his eyes, but he was not pretending. He grieved from the heart and meant every word he spoke.

Those who were struck by the truth of his words were immediately sobered and hushed. Someone wept and blew his nose. It was the carpenters' foreman—the most influential and oldest hand—who had been more openly opposed than anyone to Tokichiro.

"Ah, me!...Ah, me!" He dried the tears on his pockmarked cheeks. The others looked on, amazed. When he realized they were all looking at him, he suddenly pushed through his colleagues and threw himself down in front of Tokichiro.

"I have no excuses. I understand my own foolishness and superficiality now. You should tie me up as a lesson, and hurry on with this construction for the sake of the province." Head bowed, the old man trembled as he spoke.

At first, Tokichiro looked at him with blank amazement, but then he nodded slightly and said, "Hm. You were told to do this by Yamabuchi Ukon, right?"

"You knew it all along, Master Kinoshita."

"How could I not know? And Ukon told you and the others not to come to my house when I invited you."

"That's right."

"And he told you to be as slow as possible at the construction site, to delay the work purposely, and to disobey my orders."

"Y–yes."

"It's not surprising that he would do such things. And if all of you made a mess of things, your heads would be lined up too. Well, all right, don't blubber. I'll certainly pardon you for realizing that you've done wrong."

"But there's more. Yamabuchi Ukon told us that if we worked as poorly as possible and slowed things down so that it exceeded three days, he would give us all a load of money. But listening to what you just said, I know that accepting Master Yamabuchi's money and setting ourselves against you was working toward our own destruction. Now I see things clearly. As the leader of the mutineers, I should punished, and the construction completed without delay."

Tokichiro smiled, realizing that with a single turn, a strong enemy had become a sincere ally. Rather than tying the man up, Tokichiro gave him a cup. "There's no guilt in you. At the instant you come to this realization, you become the most loyal citizen of this province. Come on, have a drink. Then, after a rest, let's get to work."

The foreman received the cup with both hands and bowed from the heart. But he did not drink. "Hey! Everybody!" he shouted, suddenly jumping up and lifting his cup high. "We will do exactly as Master Kinoshita says. After one drink, let's get to work. We should be ashamed of ourselves, and it's a wonder that we haven't been punished by heaven. I've devoured rice in vain so far, but from now on I'm going to try to make up for it. I'm going to try to be of real service. I've made up my mind. What about the rest of you?"

As soon as the foreman had finished, the others stood up all at once.

"Let's go!"

"We'll do it!" they all shouted.

"Ah, thank you!" said Tokichiro, raising his cup too. "Well, I'm going to put away this *sake* for three days. When we've finished the work, we're going to drink it to our hearts' content! Also, I don't know how much money Yamabuchi Ukon said he would give you, but after we've finished this job, I'll reward you as much as I'm able."

"We won't need anything like that." With the pockmarked foreman leading, they all downed their cups in one gulp. And, just like warriors about to fight in the vanguard of a battle, they dashed back to the construction site.

Watching their spirit, Tokichiro experienced heartfelt relief for the first time.

"I've done it!" he blurted out without thinking. He was not going to miss this chance, however; he mixed with the others, working in the mud, laboring like a madman for the next three nights and two days.

* * *

"Monkey, Monkey!" There was somebody calling him. He saw that it was Inuchiyo, looking unusually agitated.

"Inuchiyo."

"This is good-bye."

"What?"

"I've been exiled."

"Why?"

"I cut someone down in the castle, and Lord Nobunaga reprimanded me. For the present, I've been made a *ronin.*"

"Who did you cut down?"

"Yamabuchi Ukon. You'll understand my feelings better than anyone else."

"Ah, you were too quick."

"The hot blood of youth! I thought of that right after I cut him down, but it was too late. One's nature comes out unconsciously, even if it's repressed. Well then…"

"Are you going right away?"

"Monkey, take care of Nene. This shows that she and I were not meant for one another. Look after her."

About the same time, a single unruly horse pierced the darkness as it galloped from Kiyosu toward Narumi. Seriously wounded, Yamabuchi Ukon held fast to the saddle. It was eight or nine leagues to Narumi, and Ukon's horse galloped quickly.

It was already dark and no one could see, but had it been daylight, passersby would have seen the blood that fell with the galloping of the horse. Ukon's wound was deep but not fatal. Nevertheless, as he clung to the horse's mane, he wondered which would be faster: the horse's hooves or death.

If I can only make it to Narumi Castle, he thought, remembering that when he had been struck by Maeda Inuchiyo, Inuchiyo had almost flown at him, screaming, "Traitor!"

The voice that had brought down this accusation was like a nail driven right into his skull, and would not fade away. Now, between his hazy consciousness and the wind that cut through him on the galloping horse's back, his thoughts wandered. How had Inuchiyo found out? As he considered how this event was going to affect Narumi Castle and the fortunes not only of his father but of his entire clan, panic seized him and he began to bleed heavily.

Narumi Castle was one of the branch castles of the Oda clan. Ukon's father, Samanosuke, had been made Narumi's governor by Nobuhide. Nevertheless, his vision of the world was limited, and what he saw did not portend a great future. When Nobuhide had died, Nobunaga was fifteen, and his reputation was at its lowest. At that time, Samanosuke had given up on him and secretly allied himself with Imagawa Yoshimoto.

Nobunaga had discovered Narumi's treason and had attacked the castle twice, but Narumi had not fallen. There was reason for it not to fall; it was supported at the rear by the mighty Imagawa, both militarily and economically. Nobunaga could attack in any way he liked, but his own strength was always spent in vain. Nobunaga understood this and ignored the rebels for a number of years.

But the Imagawa, in their turn, started to doubt Samanosuke's loyalty. Narumi was being looked upon with suspicion by both sides, and being regarded in this way by the ruler of a large province could only advance one's own demise. So, whatever his real intentions, Samanosuke went to Nobunaga, lamented his many years of misconduct, and begged to be returned to his former position.

"The branch never outgrows the trunk. It would be good if you understood that. Try to be loyal from now on." With these words, Nobunaga forgave him.

After that, the public works of both father and son were many and impressive, and their former treachery was forgotten. But what had been well hidden was seen by two men: Maeda Inuchiyo and Kinoshita Tokichiro. Ukon had been worried about these two for some time, but then Tokichiro had taken the position of overseer of building works, and the following day Inuchiyo had attacked and wounded Ukon. Now, assuming that he had been discovered, and stumbling from his wounds, he fled from the castle and made his way to Narumi.

It was dawn by the time he saw the gate of the castle. When he was sure he had arrived, he fainted, still clinging to the horse's back. When he came to, he was surrounded by the castle guards, who were attending to his wounds. When his head cleared and he got to his feet, the men around him looked relieved.

The situation was quickly reported to Samanosuke, and several of his attendants rushed out, their eyes wide, asking anxiously:

"Where is the young master?"

"How is he?"

They were dismayed. But the most shocked of all was his father. Seeing his son helped into the garden by the guards, he ran out himself, unable to suppress a father's anguish.

"Are his wounds deep?"

"Father..." Ukon collapsed and said, "I'm sorry...," before he fainted again.

"Inside! Quickly, take him inside!" Samanosuke's face was suffused with regret for the irrevocable. He had been anxious about Ukon's serving Nobunaga from the very beginning, for Samanosuke, not having genuinely returned to the Oda clan, was not yet committed to submission. But when Ukon was opportunely appointed to the post of overseer for the rebuilding of the castle walls, Samanosuke saw it as an opportunity for which he had been waiting for years, and immediately sent off a secret message to the Imagawa:

Now is the time to strike at the Oda clan. If you strike at Kiyosu Castle with five thousand men from the province's eastern border, I will raise my forces and take the offensive. At the same time, my son will throw the castle into confusion from within, by setting it on fire.

Thus he hoped to move Imagawa Yoshimoto to a manly resolution. The Imagawa, however, did not move suddenly, despite his request. Regardless of what was said, the Yamabuchi—both father and son—had held long service with the Oda. The Imagawa were suspicious of their plan. Hearing nothing from either the first or second messengers he had sent, Samanosuke sent a third two days later, with a note saying, "Now is the time."

Meanwhile, Ukon had been wounded and had fled back alone. And it did not look like a private quarrel. It seemed as though their plot had been discovered. Samanosuke was dismayed, and called his entire clan together for a conference.

"Even though there may not be cooperation from the Imagawa, we can do nothing more than make our military preparations and be ready for the onslaught of the Oda. If word of our rebellion reaches the Imagawa, and they join the fray, then our original hopes of crushing the Oda with a single blow may yet be realized."

Nobunaga had little to say after exiling Inuchiyo. Taking his moods into account, not one of his attendants talked about Inuchiyo. But Nobunaga was not fully satisfied, and he said, "When two warriors fight in camp, or a blade is drawn on the castle grounds, it is an absolute rule that the punishment should be strict, regardless of the reasons for the argument. Inuchiyo's a valuable man, but quick-tempered by nature. And this is the second time he's wounded a retainer. Magnanimity beyond this cannot be permitted by law."

Later that night he grumbled to the senior retainer on duty, "That Inuchiyo! I wonder where he's gone, now that he's been banished. Being a *ronin* is good for the soul. Maybe a little hardship will do him some good."

And how were things going at the construction site? Nobunaga thought with bitter regret that it was the evening of the third day since Tokichiro had taken over as construction overseer. If he did not finish by dawn, he would be forced to commit *seppuku*, no matter how much Nobunaga regretted the matter. He's a stubborn man, too—Nobunaga said to himself—blurting out absurdities right in front of everybody.

Retainers like Inuchiyo and Tokichiro were in lowly positions and were young, but he knew well that among the retainers left from his father's time, there were few men with their talents. These two were rare men, he thought with some conceit, not only in his own small clan but in the world at large. What a loss! But he could not show his concern, and hid it from his pages and older retainers.

That night he crawled into the mosquito net early. But just as he was going to sleep, a retainer crouched in the entrance of his bedroom. "My lord, it's an emergency! The Yamabuchi of Narumi have unfurled the flag of revolt and are making a show of their defense preparations."

"Narumi?" Nobunaga came out from under the net and, still in his white silk night clothes, went into the adjoining room and sat down.

"Genba?"

"My lord?"

"Come in."

Sakuma Genba came to the edge of the next room and prostrated himself. Nobunaga was fanning himself. In the evening one could already feel the cool of the early fall, but there were still swarms of mosquitoes in the castle grounds with its thick stands of trees.

"This is not really so unexpected," Nobunaga said at last, almost as if he had chewed the words and spat them out. "If the Yamabuchi are rebelling, then the boil that had been healing is festering a little again. We'll wait until it bursts by itself."

"Will you be going in person, my lord?"

"That won't be necessary."

"Your troops..."

"I don't think this will require a salve." He laughed and went on, "I doubt if they have the courage to attack Kiyosu, even if they are making military preparations. Samanosuke panicked when his son got injured. It would be better to watch them stew for a while from a distance."

Shortly after that Nobunaga went to bed again, but he got up the next morning earlier than usual. Or perhaps he couldn't sleep and was waiting for the dawn. He may have been far more worried in the back of his mind about the fate of Tokichiro than about the incident at Narumi. As soon as he got up, Nobunaga went with several attendants to inspect the construction site.

The morning sun was rising. And in place of the previous day's battlefield, not one piece of lumber, not one stone, not one clod of earth or speck of sawdust had been left behind. The ground had been swept clean. With the dawn, the construction site was no longer a construction site. This exceeded Nobunaga's expectations. He rarely experienced surprise, and if he did so now just a little, he did not show it. But Tokichiro had completed the job in three days, and, beyond that, anticipating Nobunaga's inspection, had had the remaining lumber and stones hauled out of the castle and the site swept clean.

Without thinking, Nobunaga's face glowed with joy and surprise. "He did it! Look at that! Look at what Monkey did!" Turning to his attendants, he spoke as though it were his own achievement. "Where is he? Call Tokichiro here."

"That seems to be Master Kinoshita coming across the Karabashi Bridge," an attendant said.

The bridge was directly in front of them. And there was Tokichiro, running across the bridge toward them.

The logs for the scaffolding, as well as the leftover lumber and stones, the tools and the straw mats, were piled up into a mountain beside the moat. The artisans and laborers, who had spent three days and nights working without rest, were sleeping soundly, like so many cocooned caterpillars. Even the foremen, who had worked together with the workers, had lain on the ground and fallen asleep as soon as the construction was finished.

Nobunaga observed this scene from a distance. Once again he realized how he had undervalued Tokichiro's abilities. That Monkey! He knows how to make men work! If he has the ability to get laborers to work themselves to death, I should put him in charge of trained soldiers, and he might make quite a commander. It wouldn't be a mistake to send him into battle at the head of two or three hundred men. Nobunaga suddenly recalled a verse from Sun Tzu's *Art of War*:

> The most important principle
> For victory in war
> Is having your soldiers
> Die gladly.

Nobunaga repeated this over and over, but he doubted that he himself had that ability, which certainly had nothing to do with strategy, tactics, or authority.

"You're certainly up early this morning, my lord. You can see what we have done to the castle wall."

Nobunaga looked down at his feet and there was Tokichiro, already kneeling with both hands pressed to the ground.

"Monkey?" Nobunaga burst out laughing. He had just now seen Tokichiro's face, which, after three days and nights without sleep, looked as if it were covered with a half-dried, rough plaster coat. His eyes were bloodshot and his clothes were smeared with mud.

Nobunaga laughed again, but quickly felt sorry for the man and said seriously, "You've done well. You must be sleepy. You'd better sleep for an entire day."

"Thank you very much." Tokichiro basked in the praise. To be told that he could sleep all day to his heart's content, when the province itself did not have a day of rest, was the greatest praise of all, Tokichiro thought as tears soaked his drooping eyelids. Even as he felt such satisfaction, however, he added, "I have a request, my lord."

"What is it?"

"A reward," Tokichiro said clearly, startling the attendants. Wouldn't this alter Nobunaga's rare good mood? They were concerned for Tokichiro.

"What do you want?"

"Money."

"A lot?"

"No, just a little."

"Is it for you?"

"No." Tokichiro pointed in the direction of the moat. "I'm not the one who did the construction. I would like just enough to divide among the workers over there, who are so tired they've fallen asleep."

"Speak to the keeper of the accounts and take as much as you need. But I should do something to reward you, too. How much is your stipend now?"

"I receive thirty *kan*."

"Is that all?"

"It's more than I deserve, my lord."

"I'll raise it to one hundred *kan*, move you to the spearmen's regiment, and put you in charge of thirty foot soldiers."

Tokichiro remained silent. Strictly in terms of the office, the positions of overseer of charcoal and firewood and overseer of building works were reserved for high-ranking samurai. But the blood of youth ran through Tokichiro's veins, and it had naturally been his hope for a number of years to see active service with the archers' regiment or the musketeers. Being in charge of thirty foot soldiers was the lowest rank of troop leader among the commanders. But it was a job that pleased him far more than being in charge of the stables or the kitchen.

He was so happy that he forgot discretion for the moment, and spoke thoughtlessly with the same mouth that had been so courteous before. "While I was working on this construction, there was something I was constantly thinking about. The water supply in this castle is poor, no matter how you look at it. If the castle were besieged, drinking water would be lacking, and in a short while the moat would dry up. If something were to happen, the castle would only be good for making a sortie. But in the case of an attack by an army that had no chance of victory in the field ..."

Looking off to the side, Nobunaga pretended not to hear. But Tokichiro was not going to stop halfway. "I've always thought that Mount Komaki was far superior to Kiyosu both in terms of water supply and in terms of attack and defense. I would like to suggest strongly that you move from Kiyosu to Mount Komaki, my lord."

169

At this suggestion, Nobunaga glared at him and barked, "Monkey, that's enough! You're getting carried away. Go away and sleep right now!"

"Yes, my lord." Tokichiro shrugged. I've learned a lesson, he thought. Failure is easy under favorable circumstances. One should be rebuked when he's in a good mood. I'm still not experienced enough. I let my happiness get the better of me, and went too far. I have to admit I'm still inexperienced.

After he had distributed the reward to the workers, he still did not go home to sleep, but rather walked around the castle town alone. In his heart, he could see the figure of Nene, whom he had not met for some time.

I wonder what she's been doing recently? As soon as he thought of Nene, he began to worry keenly about his self-sacrificing and obstinate friend, Inuchiyo, who had left the province and turned Nene's love over to him. Since Tokichiro had served the Oda clan, the only one to whom he had opened up his heart in friendship was Inuchiyo.

I'll bet he stopped in at Nene's house. Having to leave the province as a *ronin*, he wouldn't know when he would be able to see her again. No doubt he said something to her before he left, Tokichiro thought. To tell the truth, more than love or food, Tokichiro needed sleep right now. But when he thought about Inuchiyo's friendship, courage, and loyalty, he couldn't just sleep.

One true man will recognize another. So why did Nobunaga not recognize Inuchiyo's true value? Yamabuchi Ukon's treachery was known for some time, at least by Inuchiyo and Tokichiro. He could not figure out why Nobunaga was not aware of this, and he wondered with displeasure why Inuchiyo, who had wounded Ukon, was being punished.

Well, he said to himself, maybe it was punishment, or maybe banishing him was really an expression of Nobunaga's love. When I spoke thoughtlessly, with a know-it-all face, I got a good rap from him. I have to admit that talking about the poor water supply and advocating a move to Komaki in front of the other retainers was bad manners, he thought as he walked around the town. He was not ill, but periodically he felt as though the earth were moving beneath him. In his sleepless state, the autumn sun seemed horribly bright.

When he saw Mataemon's house in the distance, it seemed as though his drowsiness had been shaken off; breaking into a laugh, he hurried his step.

"Nene! Nene!" he shouted. This was the residential quarter of the archers, and not an area of imposing roofed gates and mansions. The small, snug samurai houses with their neat front gardens and brushwood fences were lined up peacefully in rows.

It was Tokichiro's habit to speak in a loud voice, and when he unexpectedly spied the figure of his sweetheart, whom he had not seen for some time, he waved and hurried along with unfeigned emotion. So much so that every house in the neighborhood must have wondered what was happening. Nene turned around, her white face showing open surprise.

Love was supposed to be a well-kept secret. But when someone calls out so loudly that all the neighborhood windows open, and even her mother and father hear inside the house, it's only natural that a young girl would be embarrassed. Nene had been standing in front of the gate, staring vacantly at the autumn sky. But hearing Tokichiro's voice, her face turned bright red and she hid, trembling, inside the gate.

"Nene! It's me, Tokichiro!" At this point, Tokichiro raised his voice even higher and ran up to her. "I'm sorry to have neglected you. I've been very busy with my duties."

Nene was half-hidden inside the gate, but since he had already greeted her, she bowed gracefully through necessity. "Your health should come first," she said.

"Is your father at home?" he asked.

"No, he's out."

Rather than inviting him in, she stepped back a little.

"Well, if Master Mataemon is out..." Tokichiro quickly realized how she might be embarrassed. "Then I'd better leave."

Nene nodded as though this was what she wanted, too.

"I just came to ask if Inuchiyo had dropped by."

"No, he hasn't." Nene shook her head, but the blood rushed to her face.

"He came, didn't he?"

"No."

"Really?"

Watching the red dragonflies flit about, Tokichiro was lost in thought for a moment. "He didn't show up at your house at all?" Nene hung her head, her eyes filled with tears. "Inuchiyo has displeased His Lordship and left Owari. Did you hear?"

"Yes."

"Did you hear this from your father?"

"No."

"Well, whom did you hear it from? No, there's no need to hide it. He and I are sworn friends. It doesn't make any difference, whatever he might have said to you. He came here, didn't he?"

"No. I found out about it just now—by letter."

"A letter?"

"Just a moment ago, someone threw something into the garden outside my room. When I came down to see, I found a letter wrapped around a small stone. It was from Master Inuchiyo." As she spoke, her voice faltered. She began to cry, and turned her back on Tokichiro. He had thought of her only as a wise, intelligent woman, but she was, after all, a girl.

Tokichiro had discovered yet another level of beauty and appeal in what he had seen of this woman until now. "Would you let me see the letter? Or is it something that shouldn't be shown to anyone?" When he asked this, Nene took the letter from her kimono and meekly handed it to him.

Tokichiro opened it slowly. It was unmistakably Inuchiyo's hand. Its contents were simple. But to Tokichiro, the letter conveyed far more than was written in it.

I have cut down a person of consequence and must leave Lord Nobunaga's blessed province today. At one time I had dedicated both my life and my fate to love. But, talking it over honorably and man to man, we determined that you would be better off with Kinoshita, who is the better man. I leave, entrusting you to him. Please show this letter to Master Mataemon, too, and please, please put your mind at peace. I am not sure we will ever be able to meet again.

Here and there, the characters were wet with tears. Were they Nene's or Inuchiyo's? No, he realized, they were his own.

* * *

Narumi was prepared for war, and watched the movements at Kiyosu. But as the year came to an end, there was no sign of an attack by Nobunaga.

Doubt and suspicion troubled the Yamabuchi, father and son. Their distress was augmented by yet something else. Not only had they deserted Nobunaga, but they were also being viewed with hostility by their former allies, the Imagawa of Suruga.

At this juncture, a rumor was spread around Narumi to the effect that the lord of the neighboring Kasadera Castle was in collusion with Nobunaga, and was going to attack Narumi from the rear.

Kasadera was a branch castle of the Imagawa. Whether by command of the Imagawa or by collusion with Nobunaga, an attack was certainly possible.

As the day passed, the rumor grew. Among the Yamabuchi clan and their retainers signs of panic were finally becoming apparent. The prevailing opinion was that they should mount a surprise attack on Kasadera. The father and son, who had taken such precautions shutting themselves up in an empty shell, finally took the initiative. Moving their army in the middle of the night, they set out for a morning attack on Kasadera Castle.

The same kind of rumors had been circulating at Kasadera, too, however, and had caused the same kind of nervousness. The garrison was quick to take countermeasures and was now on the alert.

The Yamabuchi attacked and the tide of battle quickly turned against the defenders, who, unable to wait for reinforcements from Suruga, set fire to the castle and perished fighting desperately in the midst of the flames.

The Narumi army that rushed into the charred castle was reduced to less than half strength, owing to heavy losses. But they drove on with their gathered momentum and stormed the smoldering ruins, waving their swords, spears, and guns.

All of them joined in the loud shouts of victory. At which point, mounted men and foot soldiers arrived from Narumi, having escaped in miserable disorder.

"What happened?" asked a surprised Yamabuchi Samanosuke.

"Nobunaga's army was incredibly fast. Somehow he knew what was happening here, and suddenly swooped down on our lightly guarded castle with more than a thousand men. The attack was furious, and we never had a chance!" The wounded man somehow made his report, gasping for breath, and went on to say that not only had the castle been taken but Samanosuke's son, Ukon, who had still not recovered from his wounds, had been captured and beheaded.

Samanosuke, who had just now raised the victory song, stood in a silent stupor. The area around Kasadera Castle, which he himself had attacked and taken, was nothing more than an uninhabited, burnt-out ruin.

"This is heaven's will!" With a shout, he took his sword and disembowelled himself on the spot. It was strange, however, that he should cry about it being heaven's will, for his end surely was one made by man and fashioned by himself.

Nobunaga had subjugated Narumi and Kasadera in a single day. Tokichiro had gone off somewhere soon after the construction of the castle wall was completed, and had not been seen for some time. But as soon as he heard that Narumi and Kasadera had come into the possession of Owari, he, too, returned unnoticed.

"Was it you who spread the rumors to both sides and caused dissension among our enemies?" When asked, Tokichiro just shook his head and said nothing.

Yoshimoto's Hostage

The people of Suruga Province did not call their capital Sumpu; to them it was simply the Place of Government, and its castle was the Palace. The citizens, from Yoshimoto and the members of the Imagawa clan down to the townsfolk, believed that Sumpu was the capital of the greatest province along the eastern seaboard. The city was imbued with an aristocratic air, and even commoners followed the fashions of imperial Kyoto.

Compared to Kiyosu, Sumpu was another world. The atmosphere of its streets and the manners of its citizens, even the speed at which the people walked, and the way they looked at one another and talked; the citizens of Sumpu were relaxed and confident. One could tell their rank from the opulence of their clothes, and when they went out, they held fans over their mouths. The arts of music, dance, and poetry flourished. The serenity visible on every face hearkened back to some halcyon spring of ancient times. Sumpu was blessed. If the weather was fine, one could see Mount Fuji; if misty, the peaceful waves of the sea were visible beyond the pine grove of Kiyomidera Temple. The Imagawa soldiers were strong, and Mikawa, the domain of the Tokugawa clan, was little more than a subordinate province.

My veins run with the blood of the Tokugawa, and yet I am here. My retainers in Okazaki somehow maintain my castle; the province of Mikawa continues to exist, but its lord and its retainers are separated. . . . Tokugawa Ieyasu meditated on these things day and night, but he could never speak of them openly. He pitied his retainers. But when he reflected on his own situation, he was thankful to be alive.

Ieyasu was only seventeen, but he was already a father. Two years before, after his coming-of-age ceremony, Imagawa Yoshimoto had arranged his marriage to the daughter of one of his own kinsmen. Ieyasu's son had been born the previous spring, so he was not yet six months old, and he often heard the baby's cries from the room in which he had set up his desk. His wife had not fully recovered from the birth and was still in the delivery room.

When this seventeen-year-old father heard his baby son crying, he was listening to his own flesh and blood. But he rarely went to see his family. He did not understand the feelings of tenderness toward children that other people talked about. When he searched his own heart for this emotion, he found it not just diminished, but totally lacking. Knowing that he was this kind of man and father, he felt sorry for his wife and child. Every time he felt this way, however, his compassion was not for his own family, but rather for his impoverished, humiliated retainers in Okazaki.

When he forced himself to think about his child, he was always sad. Soon he will set out on a journey through this bitter life and suffer the same privations I have.

At the age of five, Ieyasu had been sent as a hostage to the Oda clan. When he looked back over the trials he had suffered, he could not help but sympathize with his newborn son. The sorrow and tragedy of human life were certain to be his, too. Right now, however, on the surface, people saw that he and his family lived in a mansion no less splendid than those of the Imagawa.

What was that? Ieyasu went out onto the veranda. Someone outside had pulled on the vines that grew from the trees in the garden and wound up the mud walls. Recoiling from the torn vines, the twigs trembled faintly.

"Who is it?" Ieyasu called out. If it was a mischief-maker, the man would probably run away. He could hear no footsteps, however. Putting on a pair of sandals, he went out through the back gate in the mud wall. A man had prostrated himself as though waiting for him. A large wicker basket and staff lay by the man's side.

"Jinshichi?"

"It's been a long time, my lord."

Four years before, when he had finally received Yoshimoto's permission, Ieyasu had returned to Okazaki to visit his family graves. Along the way one of his retainers, Udono Jinshichi, had disappeared. Ieyasu was moved to pity when he saw the basket and staff and the changed figure of Jinshichi.

"You've become an itinerant priest."

"Yes, it's a convenient disguise for traveling around the country."

"When did you get here?"

"Just now. I wanted to see you in secret before setting off again."

"It's been four years, hasn't it? I've received your detailed reports, but not having heard from you after you went to Mino, I feared the worse."

"I ran into the civil war in Mino, and security at the border checkpoints and relay stations was tight for a while."

"You were in Mino? It must have been a good time to be there."

"I stayed in Inabayama for a year during the civil war. As you know, Saito Dosan's castle was destroyed, and Yoshitatsu is now lord of all Mino. When the situation had settled down, I moved on to Kyoto and Echizen, passed through the northern provinces, and went on to Owari."

"Did you go to Kiyosu?"

"Yes, I spent some time there."

"Tell me about it. Even though I am in Sumpu, I can guess what will happen to Mino, but the Oda clan's situation isn't very easily surmised."

"Shall I write a report and bring it to you this evening?"

"No, not in writing." Ieyasu turned to the rear entrance of the mud wall, but he seemed to be having second thoughts about something.

Jinshichi was his eyes and ears to the outside world. From the time he was five, Ieyasu had lived first with the Oda and then with the Imagawa, a wandering exile in enemy provinces. Living as a hostage, he had never known freedom, and this had not changed even now. The eyes, ears, and mind of a hostage are closed, and if he himself made no effort, there was no one to scold or to encourage him. In spite of this, or perhaps because of the restraint that had been imposed on him since childhood, Ieyasu had become extremely ambitious.

Four years before, he had sent Jinshichi to the other provinces so that he would be able to know what was going on—an early sign of Ieyasu's burgeoning ambition. "We'll be seen here, and if we talk in the mansion, my retainers will be suspicious. Let's go over there." Ieyasu walked away from the mansion with long strides.

Ieyasu's residence was in one of the quietest quarters of Sumpu. Walking a little way from the mud wall, they came to the bank of the Abe River. When Ieyasu was a child still carried on the backs of his retainers, it was to the Abe River that he was taken when he said that he wanted to go outside to play. The water in the river seemed to flow on eternally, and the riverbank never seemed to change. It brought back memories for Ieyasu.

"Jinshichi, untie the boat," Ieyasu said as he quickly stepped into the small fishing boat. When Jinshichi got into the boat with him and pushed on the pole, the boat floated away from the shallows like a bamboo leaf in the current. Master and retainer talked, knowing that they were hidden from the eyes of others for the first time. In the space of an hour, Ieyasu absorbed the information that Jinshichi had collected by traveling around for four years. Yet, more than what he had learned from Jinshichi , there was some distant, great thing hidden in Ieyasu's heart.

"If the Oda haven't attacked other provinces so much in the past few years—unlike in Nobuhide's time—it must be to put their house in order," Ieyasu said.

"It didn't matter whether the people against him were relatives or retainers, Nobunaga resigned himself completely to the task. He struck down the people he had to strike down and ran off the people he had to run off. He's nearly swept Kiyosu clean of them."

"The Imagawa laughed at Nobunaga for a time, and it was rumored that he was just a spoiled, stupid brat."

"There is nothing of the fool about him," Jinshichi said.

"I've long thought that it was only malicious gossip. But when Lord Yoshimoto speaks of Nobunaga, he believes the gossip and doesn't see him as a threat at all."

"The martial spirit of the men of Owari is completely different from what it was a few years ago."

"Who are his good retainers?" Ieyasu asked.

"Hirate Nakatsukasa is dead, but he has a number of able men like Shibata Katsuie, Hayashi Sado, Ikeda Shonyu, Sakuma Daigaku, and Mori Yoshinari. Just recently he's been joined by an extraordinary man by the name of Kinoshita Tokichiro. He's very low-ranking, but for some reason his name is often on the lips of the townspeople."

"How do the people feel about Nobunaga?"

"That's the most extraordinary thing. It's common for the ruler of a province to devote himself to governing his people. And people obey their masters as a rule. But in Owari, it's different."

"In what way?"

Jinshichi thought about this for a moment. "How can I put it? He doesn't do anything out of the ordinary, but as long as Nobunaga's there, the people are confident of the future—and while they know that Owari is a small, poor province with a penniless lord, the strange thing is that, like the people of a powerful province, they are not afraid of war or worried about their future."

"Hm. I wonder why?"

"Maybe because of Nobunaga himself. He tells them what is going on today and what will happen tomorrow, and he sets the goals toward which they all work."

Deep down, without really meaning to, Jinshichi was comparing the twenty-five-year-old Nobunaga with the seventeen-year-old Ieyasu. In some ways, Ieyasu was far more mature than Nobunaga—there was nothing of the child in him. Both men had grown up under difficult circumstances, but there was really no comparison between them. Ieyasu had been handed over to enemies at the age of five, and the cruelty of the world had chilled him to the very marrow.

The little boat carried Jinshichi and Ieyasu down the center of the river, the time passing during their secret conversation. When their talk was over, Jinshichi guided them back to the bank.

Jinshichi quickly shouldered his basket and took up his staff. Bidding Ieyasu farewell, he said, "I will pass on your words to your retainers. Is there anything else, my lord?"

Ieyasu stood on the bank, immediately anxious about being seen. "There's nothing more. Go quickly." Motioning Jinshichi off with a nod, he suddenly said, "Tell them that I am well—I haven't been sick once." And he walked back to his mansion alone.

His wife's attendants were looking for him everywhere, and when they saw him coming back from the riverbank, one of them said, "Her ladyship is waiting anxiously, and sent us to look for you several times. She's extremely worried about you, my lord."

"Ah, is that so?" Ieyasu said. "Calm her down and tell her I'm coming right away." And he went to his own room. When he sat down, he found another retainer, Sakakibara Heishichi, waiting for him.

"Did you take a walk to the riverbank?"

"Yes...just to kill time. What is it?"

"There was a messenger."

"From whom?" Without answering, Heishichi handed him a letter. It was from Sessai. Before cutting open the envelope, Ieyasu raised it reverently to his forehead. Sessai was a monk of the Zen sect who acted as a military adviser to the Imagawa clan. To Ieyasu, he was the teacher from whom he had received instructions in both booklearning and the martial arts. His letter was concise:

The customary lecture will be given to His Lordship and his guests tonight. I will wait for you at the Northwest Gate of the Palace.

That was all. But the word "customary" was a codeword well known to Ieyasu. It meant a meeting of Yoshimoto and his generals to discuss the march on the capital.

"Where is the messenger?"

"He left already. Will you go to the Palace, my lord?"

"Yes," Ieyasu replied, preoccupied.

"I think the proclamation of Lord Yoshimoto's march on the capital is near at hand."

Heishichi had overheard the important war councils that had touched on that subject a number of times. He studied Ieyasu's face. Ieyasu mumbled a reply, seeming to be uninterested.

The Imagawa clan's evaluations of Owari's strength and of Nobunaga were very different from what Jinshichi had just reported. Yoshimoto planned to lead a huge army, made up of the forces of the provinces of Suruga, Totomi, and Mikawa, to the capital, and they expected to meet resistance in Owari.

"If we advance with a large army, Nobunaga will surrender without bloodshed." This was the superficial view expressed by some of the members of the war council, but although Yoshimoto and his advisers, including Sessai, did not have such a low estimate of Nobunaga, none of them took Owari as seriously as Ieyasu did. He had offered an opinion on this once before, but he had been laughed down. Ieyasu was, after all, a hostage and young; and among the field staff he counted for very little.

Is this something I should bring up or not? Even if I press the point…

Ieyasu was deep in thought, with Sessai's letter in front of him, when an old lady-in-waiting who served his wife spoke to him with a worried look on her face. His wife was in a terrible mood, she said, and she urged him to visit her for just a moment.

Ieyasu's wife was a woman who thought of nothing but herself. She was completely indifferent both to affairs of state and to her husband's situation. Nothing entered her head other than her own daily life and the attentions of her husband. The old lady-in-waiting understood this well, and when she saw that he was still talking with his retainer, she waited uneasily and silently, until another maid came in and whispered in her ear. There was nothing else the old lady-in-waiting could do. She interrupted them again, saying, "Excuse me, my lord….I'm terribly sorry, but Her Ladyship is very fretful." Bowing to Ieyasu, she timidly urged him once more to hurry.

Ieyasu knew that his wife's servants were troubled more than anyone else by this situation, and he himself was a patient man. "Ah, yes," he said, turning, and then, to Heishichi: "Well, make the necessary arrangements, and come and tell me when it's time." He stood up. The women ran in front of him with small steps, looking as though they had been saved.

The inner part of the house was some way off, so it was not unreasonable that his wife often longed to see him. Passing through the many turns of the central and bridged corridors, he finally got to his wife's private apartments.

On their wedding day, the clothes of the poor hostage husband from Mikawa could not compare with the luxury and brilliance of the dress of Lady Tsukiyama, an adopted daughter of Imagawa Yoshimoto. "The man from Mikawa"—known by this epithet, he

was an object of contempt for the Imagawa clan. And living with such pride in her secluded quarters, she despised the retainers from Mikawa but showered her husband with
all the devotion of her selfish, blind love. She was also older than Ieyasu. Considered
within the limits of their shallow married life, Lady Tsukiyama saw Ieyasu as little more
than a submissive youth who owed his existence to the Imagawa.

After giving birth in the spring following their wedding, she had become even more
selfish and unreasonable. His wife taught him perseverance every day.

"Oh, you're up. Are you feeling a little better?" Ieyasu looked at his wife and, as he
spoke, was about to open the sliding doors. He thought that if his sick wife could see the
beauty of the autumn colors and the autumn sky, her mood might brighten.

Lady Tsukiyama had left the sickroom and was sitting in the middle of the reception
room with a frigid look on her livid face. She narrowed her eyebrows as she spoke. "Leave
them closed."

She was not exactly a beauty, but, as might be expected of a woman brought up in
the privileged environment of a wealthy family, her complexion had a fine sheen. Beyond
that, both her face and her fingertips were almost translucently white, perhaps because of
her first delivery. She held her hands neatly folded on her lap.

"Sit down, my lord. There is something I'd like to ask you." As she spoke, her words
and eyes were as cold as ashes. But Ieyasu did not act at all as a young husband would be
expected to behave—such mellow-spirited handling of one's spouse was more appropriate for a mature man. Or perhaps he held a certain opinion of women, and he was looking objectively at the person whom he should have loved the most.

"What is it?" he asked, sitting down in front of her as she had requested. But the
more obedient her husband was, the more unreasonable she became.

"There's something I'd like to ask you. Did you go out somewhere a moment ago?
Alone, without attendants?" Her eyes filled with tears. The blood was rising to her face,
still thin from childbirth. Ieyasu knew both the state of her health and her character, and
he smiled at her as if he were humoring a baby.

"Just now? I was tired of reading, so I took a leisurely walk along the riverbank. You
should try taking a walk there. The autumn colors and the chirping of the insects—it's
pleasant at the riverbank this time of year."

Lady Tsukiyama was not listening. She was staring at her husband, rebuking him
for his lie. She sat rigidly straight, with an air of indifference, but without her usual self-
involvement. "That's strange. If you went out for a walk to listen to insects and look at
the autumn colors, why would you go out into the middle of the river in a small boat,
hiding from people for such a long time?"

"Aha . . . you knew."

"I may be confined indoors, but I know everything you do."

"Is that so?" Ieyasu forced a smile, but did not speak of his meeting with Jinshichi.

Although this woman had become his bride, Ieyasu was never able to believe that she
was really his wife. If retainers or relatives of her adoptive father called on her, she would
tell them everything, and she was always exchanging letters with Yoshimoto's household.
Ieyasu had to be far more careful of his wife's unintentional carelessness than of the eyes
of Yoshimoto's spies.

"No, I got into that boat on the riverbank without thinking much about it, and tried to ply the oar with the flow of the water. I thought I could handle the boat, but when I got out into the current, I couldn't do a thing." He laughed. "Just like a child. Where were you when you saw me?"

"You're lying. You weren't alone, were you?"

"Well, a servant ran after me later."

"No, no. There's no reason for you to have a secret meeting in a boat, with someone who appears to be a servant."

"Who in the world has told you such a thing?"

"Even though I'm stuck inside, there are loyal people who think of me. You're hiding a woman somewhere, aren't you? Or if that's not it, perhaps you've grown tired of me and are planning to run away to Mikawa. There's a rumor going around that you've taken another woman as your wife in Okazaki. Why are you hiding that from me? I know that you only married me out of fear of the Imagawa clan."

Just as her sobbing voice, driven by illness and distrust, finally found expression, Sakakibara Heishichi appeared at the door. "My lord, your horse is ready. It's almost time."

"Are you going out?" Before Ieyasu could respond, Lady Tsukiyama cut him off. "You've been absent more and more at night recently, so where in the world are you going now?"

"To the Palace." Paying her no heed, Ieyasu was beginning to stand up.

But she was not satisfied with his brief explanation. Why was he going to the Palace so late? And was it going to take until midnight, like the other night? Who was going with him? She asked innumerable questions.

Sakakibara Heishichi was waiting for his master on the other side of the door, and although he was only a retainer, he was getting a little impatient with all of this. Ieyasu, however, cheerfully comforted his wife and finally took his leave. Lady Tsukiyama, unchecked by Ieyasu's admonition that she might catch cold again, came to the entrance and saw him off.

"Come back quickly," she begged, putting all her love and fidelity into these parting words.

Ieyasu walked in silence to the main entrance. But as he started out under the stars, cooled by the evening breeze, he tousled his horse's mane, and his mood changed completely—proof that youthful, animated blood coursed through his veins.

"Heishichi, we're a little late, aren't we?" Ieyasu asked.

"No. There was no hour clearly indicated on the note, so how can we be late?"

"That's not it. Even though Sessai is old, he's never been late. It would pain me, as a young man and a hostage, to be late for an appointment when the senior retainers and Sessai were already there. Let's hurry," he said, spurring his horse.

Besides a groom and three servants, Heishichi was the only retainer escorting Ieyasu. As Heishichi hurried along to keep up with the horse, he was moved to tears for his master, whose patient endurance with his wife and his submissive loyalty to the Palace—that is, to Imagawa Yoshimoto—must clearly cause him great anguish.

As a retainer, it was his sworn duty to free his lord from his shackles. He must remove him from his subordinate position and restore him to his rightful place as lord of Mikawa. And to Heishichi, every day that went by without attaining his goal was another day of disloyalty.

He ran along, chewing his lip as he made his vow, his eyes moist with tears.

The castle moat came into view. When they crossed the bridge, there were no longer any shops or commoners' houses. Among the pines stood the white walls and imposing gates of the mansions of the Imagawa.

"Isn't that the lord of Mikawa? Lord Ieyasu!" Sessai called from the shadow of the pines.

The broad pine grove that meandered around the castle was a military assembly field during wartime, but its long, broad pathways were used as a riding ground in peacetime.

Ieyasu quickly dismounted, giving Sessai a respectful bow. "Thank you for taking the time to come here tonight, Your Reverence."

"These messages are always sudden. It certainly must be troublesome for you."

"Not at all." Sessai was alone. He walked along in old straw sandals the size of which matched the huge proportions of body. Ieyasu began to walk along with him and, as a courtesy to his teacher, one step behind him, handing the reins of his horse to Heishichi.

Listening to his teacher, Ieyasu suddenly felt a gratitude to this man that he could not express in words. No one could argue that being a hostage in another province was anything but a misfortune, but when he thought about it, he realized that receiving an education from Sessai was more good fortune than bad.

It is difficult to find a good teacher. Had he stayed in Mikawa, he would never have had the opportunity to study under Sessai. So he would not have had the classical and military education he had now—or the training in Zen, which he regarded as the most precious thing he had learned from Sessai.

Why Sessai, a Zen monk, had entered the service of the lord of the Imagawa and become his military adviser was not understood in other provinces, and they considered it rather strange. Thus there were people who called Sessai a "military monk" or a "worldly monk," but if his lineage had been investigated, they would have discovered that Sessai was Yoshimoto's kinsman. Still, Yoshimoto was only Yoshimoto of Suruga, Totomi, and Mikawa. Sessai's fame, however, knew no boundaries; he was Sessai of all the universe.

But Sessai had used his talents for the Imagawa. As soon as he had seen the signs of defeat for the Imagawa in a war against the Hojo, the monk had helped Suruga to negotiate a peace treaty without disadvantage to Yoshimoto. And when he had arranged the marriage of Hojo Ujimasa to a daughter of Takeda Shingen, lord of Kai, the powerful province on their northern border, and the marriage of Yoshimoto's daughter with Shingen's son, he had demonstrated great political skill by tying the three provinces into an alliance.

He was not the kind of monk who went about in splendid isolation with a staff and a tattered hat. He was not a "pure" Zen monk. It could be said that he was a political monk, a military monk, or even an unmonkish monk. But whatever he was called, it did not affect his greatness.

Sessai spoke sparingly, but something he had told Ieyasu on the veranda of the Rinzai Temple had stuck in Ieyasu's mind: "Hiding in a cave, roaming about alone like the wandering clouds and the flowing water—being a great monk is not in these things alone. A monk's mission changes with the times. In today's world, to think only of my own enlightenment and live like one who 'steals the tranquillity of the mountains and fields,' as if I despised the world, is a self-indulgent kind of Zen."

They crossed the Chinese Bridge and passed through the northwestern gate. It was difficult to believe that they were inside the walls of a castle. It was as though the palace of the shogun had been transported here. Toward Atago and Kiyomizu, the majestic cone of Mount Fuji was darkening in the evening. The lamps were lit in the niches along the corridors that stretched as far as the eye could see. Women so lovely they could have been mistaken for court ladies passed by, cradling *koto* or carrying flasks of *sake*.

"Who's that in the garden?" Imagawa Yoshimoto held a fan in the shape of a ginkgo leaf over his slightly reddened face. He had crossed over the garden's red half-moon bridge. Even the pages who followed him wore elaborate clothes and swords.

One of the pages went back along the bridged corridor and hurried into the garden. Someone was screaming. It sounded like a woman's voice to Yoshimoto, so, thinking it strange, he had stopped.

"What's happened to the page?" Yoshimoto asked after a few minutes. "He hasn't come back. Iyo, you go."

Iyo went down into the garden and ran off. Although the place was called a garden, it was so large that it looked as if it led to the foothills of Mount Fuji. Leaning against the pillar where the bridged corridor angled away from the main walkway, Yoshimoto beat a rhythm with his fan and sang to himself.

He was pale enough to be mistaken for a woman, because he used light makeup. He was forty years old and in the prime of manhood. Yoshimoto was enjoying the world and was at the height of his prosperity. He wore his hair in the style of the nobility, his teeth were elegantly blackened, and a mustache sprouted beneath his nose. For the last two years he had put on weight, and, being born with a long trunk and short legs, he now looked a little deformed. But his gilded sword and his richly brocaded clothes mantled him with an aura of dignity. Someone finally came back, and Yoshimoto stopped humming.

"Is it you, Iyo?"

"No, it's Ujizane."

Ujizane was Yoshimoto's son and heir, and looked like someone who had never known hardship.

"What are you doing out in the garden when it's almost dusk?"

"I was beating Chizu, and when I unsheathed my sword she ran away."

"Chizu? Who is Chizu?"

"She's the girl who looks after my birds."

"A servant?"

"Yes."

"What could she have done that you had to punish her with your own hands?"

"She's hateful. She was feeding a rare bird that had been sent to me all the way from

Kyoto, and she let it escape," Ujizane said seriously. He was inordinately fond of song-birds. It was well known among the nobility that if someone found a rare bird and sent it to him, Ujizane would be absurdly happy. Thus, without lifting a finger, he had become the owner of a collection of extravagant birds and cages. So here, it was said, a human being could be killed for the sake of a bird. Ujizane was furious, as if the matter had been an important affair of state.

An indulgent father, Yoshimoto muttered in disappointment at his son's foolish anger. And this was in front of his retainers. Even though Ujizane was his heir, having demonstrated this kind of imbecility, Yoshimoto's retainers were unlikely to think much of him.

"You fool!" Yoshimoto shouted violently, intending to show his great love. "Ujizane, how old are you? You had your coming-of-age ceremony a long time ago. You're the heir of the Imagawa clan, but you do nothing but amuse yourself by raising birds. Why don't you do a little Zen meditation, or read some military treatises?"

Being spoken to like this by a father who almost never scolded him, Ujizane turned pale and fell silent. He generally considered his father easy to deal with; however, he was already of an age when he could look at his father's behavior with a critical eye. Now, instead of arguing, he simply pouted and sulked. Yoshimoto felt that this too was a weak point. Ujizane was very dear to him, and he knew that his own conduct had never provided a good example for his son.

"That's enough. Restrain yourself from now on. All right, Ujizane?"

"Yes."

"Why are you looking so disgruntled?"

"I'm not disgruntled about anything."

"Well then, be off with you. These are not the times for raising birds."

"Well, but…"

"What do you want to say?"

"Are these times for drinking *sake* with girls from Kyoto and dancing and beating the drum all afternoon?"

"Hold your tongue, know-it-all!"

"But you—"

"Silence!" Yoshimoto said, throwing his fan at Ujizane. "Rather than criticizing your father, you should know your place. How can I proclaim you as my heir, if you take no interest in military matters and learn nothing about administration and economics? Your father studied Zen when he was a young man, went through all sorts of difficulties, and fought countless battles. Today I am the master of this small province, but I will rule the entire country one day. How could I have had a child with so little courage and so few ambitions? There's nothing I can complain of now except dissatisfaction with you."

At some point, Yoshimoto's retainers found themselves cowering in the corridor. Struck by his words, every one of them silently stared at the floor. Even Ujizane hung his head and stared at his father's fan at his feet.

Just then, a samurai came in and announced, "His Reverence Master Sessai, Lord Ie-yasu, and the senior retainers are waiting for Your Lordship in the Mandarin Orange Pavilion."

The Mandarin Orange Pavilion was built on a slope dotted with mandarin orange trees, and it was here that Yoshimoto had invited Sessai and his other advisers, ostensibly for a nighttime tea ceremony.

"Ah! Really? Is everyone there? As the host, I shouldn't be late." Yoshimoto spoke as though he had been saved from the confrontation with his son, and walked down the corridor in the opposite direction.

The tea ceremony had been nothing but a ruse from the start. Appropriately for an evening tea ceremony, though, the flickering shadows cast by the lanterns, combined with the chirping of insects, seemed to envelop the place an in air of elegance. But as soon as Yoshimoto had entered and the door was shut, soldiers patrolled the grounds so tightly that water could not have leaked in unnoticed.

"His Lordship." A retainer announced his master as though he were heralding royalty. In the large room, built in the manner of temples, a faint light flickered. Sessai and the senior retainers were all seated in a line, with Tokugawa Ieyasu at the far end. The line of men bowed to their master.

Yoshimoto's silk clothes whispered perceptibly in the silence. He took his seat, unaccompanied by either page or attendant. His only two attendants were holding back at a distance of two or three yards.

"Excuse my lateness," Yoshimoto said in reply to the bows of his field staff. Then, paying special attention to Sessai, he said, "I'm afraid this is an imposition on you, Your Reverence." It was Yoshimoto's habit of late to inquire about the monk's health whenever they met. Sessai had been prone to illness for the last five or six years, and recently he had aged perceptibly.

Sessai had instructed, protected, and inspired Yoshimoto since childhood. Yoshimoto knew that he owed his greatness to Sessai's statecraft and planning. Thus, at first, Yoshimoto could not help feeling Sessai's age very much as he felt his own. But when he realized that the strength of the Imagawa had not suffered by not relying on Sessai, and that it was, in fact, more vital than ever, he began to believe that his successes were due to his own ability.

"As I am now an adult," Yoshimoto had told Sessai, "please don't worry yourself about the administration of the province or military matters. Spend your remaining years pleasantly, and concentrate on the promulgation of the Way of the Buddha." It was clear that he had begun to keep Sessai at a respectful distance.

But from Sessai's point of view, watching Yoshimoto was like watching a stumbling child, and he felt the same kind of distress. Sessai looked at Yoshimoto exactly as Yoshimoto looked at his son, Ujizane. Sessai thought that Yoshimoto was unreliable. He knew that Yoshimoto felt uncomfortable in his presence and had kept him away, using Sessai's illness as a pretext, but he still tried to assist in both administrative and military matters. From the beginning of spring that year, he had not missed one of the more than ten conferences in the Mandarin Orange Pavilion, even when he was ill.

Would they move now, or wait a little longer? This conference was going to decide one way or the other, and the rise or fall of the Imagawa clan would depend on the decision.

Enveloped in a light shower of cricket songs, the conference that would transform the government of the nation was conducted in the strictest privacy. When the chirping of the insects stopped suddenly, the group of guards paced back and forth along the hedges outside the pavilion.

"Did you investigate what we talked about at the last conference?" Yoshimoto asked one of his generals.

The general spread out some documents on the floor and opened the conference by explaining them in outline. He had written a report on the military and economic power of the Oda clan. "It's said to be a small clan, but recently it would seem that its economy has rallied remarkably." As he spoke, he showed diagrams to Yoshimoto. "Owari is said to be a united province, but within its eastern and southern sections there are places, like Iwakura Castle, which owe their allegiance to you, my lord. Additionally, there are men who, although they are Oda retainers, are known to feel ambivalently about their loyalties. Thus, under the present circumstances, the possessions of the Oda clan are less than one-half, possibly only two-fifths, of all of Owari."

"I see," Yoshimoto said. "It seems to be a small clan, just as we've heard. How many soldiers can they muster?"

"If you look at their possessions as being only two-fifths of Owari, the area would produce about one hundred sixty to one hundred seventy thousand bushels of rice. If you figure that ten thousand bushels supports about two hundred fifty men, then even if the entire Oda force were raised, it would not exceed four thousand men. And if you subtract those garrisoning the castles, I doubt that they could call up more than about three thousand men."

Yoshimoto suddenly broke into laughter. Whenever he laughed, it was his habit to tilt his body a little and cover his blackened teeth with his fan. "Three or four thousand, you say? Well, that's hardly enough to prop up a province. Sessai says that the enemy to watch on the way to the capital would be the Oda, and all of you have repeatedly brought up the Oda, too. So I commissioned these reports. But what are three or four thousand men going to do in the face of my military forces? What kind of trouble is it going to be to kick him around and then knock him down with a single blow?"

Sessai said nothing; the other men also kept their mouths shut. They knew that Yoshimoto was not going to change his mind. The plan had existed for some years now, and the aim of all their military preparations and the administration of the Imagawa domains was Yoshimoto's march on the capital and his domination of the entire country. The time was ripe, and Yoshimoto was unable to hold himself in check a moment longer.

Yet, if several conferences had been held since the spring, aiming at decisive action, and the goal had still not been attained, it meant that within this pivotal group there was someone who argued that it was still premature. The dissenting voice was Sessai's. More than arguing that it was still premature, Sessai conservatively advocated recommendations concerning internal administration. He did not criticize Yoshimoto's ambition of unifying the country, but neither did he ever express approval.

"The Imagawa is the most illustrious clan of its generation," he had said to Yoshimoto. "If there comes a time when there is no successor to the shogun, someone from the Imagawa clan would have to take a stand. You, by all means, must have this great ambition and begin to cultivate yourself for the capacity of ruling the nation from now on." It was Sessai himself who had taught Yoshimoto to think on a broad scale: Rather than being the master of a single castle, be the ruler of an entire province; rather than being the ruler of a single district, be the governor of ten provinces; rather than being the governor of ten provinces, be the ruler of the country.

Everyone preached this. And all samurai children faced the chaotic world with this in mind. This was also the main point in Sessai's training of Yoshimoto. So, from the time Sessai had joined Yoshimoto's field staff, the armed forces of the Imagawa clan expanded precipitously. Steadily, Yoshimoto had stepped up the ladder towards hegemony. But recently Sessai had felt a great contradiction between his training of Yoshimoto and his role as an adviser: somehow he had started to feel uneasy about Yoshimoto's plans to unify the country.

He hasn't got the capacity, Sessai thought. Watching Yoshimoto's growing confidence, especially in recent years, Sessai's thoughts had become acutely more conservative. This is his peak. This is as far as his capacity as a ruler can go. I've got to get him to drop the idea. This was the source of Sessai's anguish. Yet there was little reason to believe that Yoshimoto, so proud of his worldly advancement, would suddenly drop the idea of making his bid for supremacy. Sessai's remonstrations were laughed at as symptoms of his dotage, and went unheeded. Yoshimoto considered the country to be already in his grasp.

I should put an end to this quickly. Sessai no longer admonished him. Instead, every time there was a conference, he stressed extreme prudence.

"What kind of difficulties am I going to encounter when I march on Kyoto with all my power and the great armies of Suruga, Totomi, and Mikawa?" Yoshimoto asked again.

He planned a bloodless march on the capital, ascertaining the actual conditions of all the provinces s on the way and planning a diplomatic policy ahead of time to avoid as much fighting as possible. But the first battle on the road to Kyoto was not going to be with the strong provinces of Mino or Omi. It was going to be, first and foremost, against the Oda of Owari. They were small fry. But they were not to be conciliated by diplomacy, or bought off.

They were going to be a troublesome enemy indeed. And this was not just today's or yesterday's enemy. For the last forty years the Oda and the Imagawa had been at war. If a castle was taken, another would be captured by the other side, and if a town was burned, ten villages would be set on fire in return. In fact, from the time of Nobunaga's father and Yoshimoto's grandfather, the two clans seemed fated to bury the bones of their men at the border of the two provinces.

When the rumor of the Imagawa march to the capital reached the Oda, they were quickly resolved to fight one great decisive battle. For Yoshimoto, the Oda were the ideal victims for the army advancing on the capital, and he continued to refine his schemes against them.

This was the last council of war. Sessai, Ieyasu, and his attendants left the palace. On their way home it was pitch black; not a light was burning in Sumpu.

"There's nothing we can do but pray to heaven for good luck," Sessai mumbled. With age, even an enlightened mind gets foolish again. "How cold it is," Sessai complained, but it was not a night one would think of as being cold.

When people thought about it later, it was from this time that the abbot's illness worsened. That was the last night that Sessai's feet ever trod the earth. In the loneliness of mid-autumn, Sessai died quietly, unnoticed.

* * *

In the middle of that winter, there seemed to be a lull in the skirmishes at the border, but it was actually the season of building up strength for taking even greater actions. The following year the winter barley in the fertile fields of the coastal provinces grew tall. The cherry blossoms fell, and the smell of the young leaves on the seedlings rose to the sky.

It was early summer. Yoshimoto proclaimed the order from Sumpu for his army to advance on the capital. The huge scale and the resplendent traveling attire of the army of the Imagawa made the entire world open its eyes wide in astonishment. And his proclamation made the small and weak provinces cower in fear. The message was clear and simple:

Those who obstruct the advance of my army will be struck down. Those who welcome it with civilities will be well treated.

After the Boys' Festival, Yoshimoto's heir, Ujizane, was left in charge of Sumpu, and on the twelfth day of the Fifth Month, the main army advanced in fine array amid the cheers of the people. The magnificent warriors, whose radiance rivaled the light of the sun, marched toward the capital, like the unrolling of a gaudy picture scroll—commanders' standards, banners, flags, weapons, and armor. The army probably numbered around twenty-five or twenty-six thousand men, but it was purposely proclaimed to be an army of forty thousand.

The vanguard of the advance troops entered the post town of Chiryu on the fifteenth and, approaching Narumi on the seventeenth, set fire to the villages in that part of Owari. The weather had been continually fine and warm. The furrows of the barley fields and the earth that bloomed with flowers were dried white. In the blue sky here and there rose the black smoke of burning villages. But not a single report of a gun came from the Oda province. The farmers had been commanded beforehand to evacuate, and to leave nothing for the advancing Imagawa.

"At this rate, the castle in Kiyosu will also be empty!"

The officers and men of the Imagawa felt the heaviness of their armor in the tedium of the peaceful, flat roads.

Inside Kiyosu Castle, the lamps blazed this evening in the midst of a hushed world. They seemed, however, to be lamps lit just before the impending onslaught of a violent storm. The trees that stood in unmoving silence on the castle grounds called to mind the uncanny stillness in the eye of a typhoon. And still no instructions were sent from the castle to the townsfolk. There was no command to evacuate or to prepare for a siege, and in the absence of anything else, not even a message of reassurance. The merchants opened their shops as usual. The craftsmen were doing their work as they always did. Even the farmers were cultivating their fields. But the coming and going of traffic on the roads had halted several days before.

The town was a bit lonelier and rumors abounded.

"I've heard that Imagawa Yoshimoto is marching west with an army of forty thousand men."

Wherever the uneasy citizens met, they speculated about their fate:

"I wonder how Lord Nobunaga plans to defend the town?"

"There's just no way to defend it. No matter how you look at it, our troops don't amount to even one-tenth of the Imagawa forces."

And in the midst of this, they saw the clan's generals passing through the town, one after another. Some were commanders leaving the castle and returning to their districts, but several of them appeared to have taken their stand in the castle.

"They're probably discussing whether to capitulate to the Imagawa or risk the survival of the clan and fight." Such perceptions of the common people were concerned with things they could not witness, but they usually did not miss the mark. In fact, that very controversy had been repeatedly gone over in the castle for several days. At every conference, the generals were divided into two factions.

The advocates of "the safe plan" and "the clan first" said that the best policy would be to submit to the Imagawa. But the controversy did not last long. And this was because Nobunaga had already made up his mind.

His only motive in convening a conference of the senior retainers was to let them know his decision, not to inquire about a dependable plan of self-defense or a policy to preserve Owari. When they understood Nobunaga's resolve many of the generals responded positively and, taking heart, returned to their castles.

Thereafter, Kiyosu was as peaceful as usual, and the number of soldiers in Kiyosu did not markedly increase. As might be expected, however, Nobunaga was awakened innumerable times that night to read the reports of messengers from the front.

Again, on the following night, immediately after finishing his frugal evening meal, Nobunaga went to the main hall to discuss the military situation. There, the generals who had not yet taken their leave were still in constant attendance on him. None of them had had sufficient sleep, and their pale features showed their resolve. The retainers who were not involved in the discussion were packed into the next room and the room after that. Men like Tokichiro were far off, sitting somewhere a number of rooms away. Two nights before, last night and tonight as well, they were anxious and as silent as if they were holding their breaths. And there must have been a number of men that night who looked around at the white lamps and their companions, thinking, This is just like a wake.

In the midst of this, laughter could be heard from time to time. This came from Nobunaga alone. Those seated far away did not know the object of this laughter, but it could be heard over and over again, two or three rooms away.

Suddenly a messenger could be heard running down the corridor. Shibata Katsuie, who was to read the report to Nobunaga, turned white before the words could leave his mouth.

"My lord!"

"What is it?"

"The fourth dispatch since this morning has just arrived from the fortress at Marune."

Nobunaga moved his armrest in front of him. "Well?"

"It seems that the Imagawa are marching to Kutsukake this evening."

"Is that so?" This was all Nobunaga said as his eyes stared vacantly at the carved transom in the hall.

Even he seemed confused. Though these men had recently come to rely on Nobunaga's obstinacy, they couldn't help feeling lost. Kutsukake and Marune were within the domain of the Oda clan. And if that line of scattered but essential fortresses had been broken, the Owari Plain had almost no defenses, and the road to Kiyosu Castle could be crossed with one swift effort.

"What are you going to do?" Katsuie asked as if he could not bear the silence any longer. "We've heard that the Imagawa army may number as many as forty thousand men. Our force is less than four thousand. There are only seven hundred men at Marune Castle, at most. Even if the vanguard of the Imagawa, the forces under Tokugawa Ieyasu of Mikawa, number only two thousand five hundred, Marune is a single ship driven before the high waves."

"Katsuie, Katsuie!"

"We cannot hold Marune and Washizu until dawn—"

"Katsuie! Are you deaf? What are you babbling about? There's nothing to be gained by repeating the obvious."

"But—" Just as Katsuie began to speak, he was interrupted by the clattering footsteps of yet another messenger. The man spoke ostentatiously from the entrance of the next room.

"There is urgent news from both the fortresses of Nakajima and Zenshoji."

The reports from those at the front lines who had resolved to die gloriously in battle were always pathetic, and the ones that arrived just now from the two fortresses were no different. Both began, "This is, perhaps, the last dispatch we will be able to send to Kiyosu Castle...."

The last two dispatches contained the same information about the disposition of the enemy's troops, and both predicted an attack on the following day.

"Read the part about the disposition of the troops again," Nobunaga ordered Katsuie, leaning on his armrest. He read the itemized part of the document again, not only to Nobunaga but to all of those who were sitting there in a row.

"The enemy forces approaching the fortress at Marune: about two thousand five hundred men. The enemy forces approaching the fortress at Washizu: about two thousand men. Lateral auxiliary forces: three thousand men. The main force advancing in the direction of Kiyosu: approximately six thousand men. The main Imagawa army: about five thousand men." Reading further, Katsuie went on to comment that beyond what was apparent in these numbers, it was unclear how many small groups of the enemy were traveling undercover. While Nobunaga and all the others listened to Katsuie, he rolled up the scroll and placed it in front of him.

They would fight to the very end. The course was determined. There was no more room to debate. But it was agonizing for all of them to stand idly by and do nothing. Neither Washizu, Marune, nor Zenshoji was far away. If you put the whip to a horse's ribs, you could arrive at any of these places quickly. They could almost see this great army of

189

the Imagawa's forty thousand men approach like a tide. They could almost hear them.

From one corner of the depressed group came the voice of an old man sunk in grief. "You've made a manly decision, but you shouldn't think that dying gloriously in battle is the only way open to the samurai. Shouldn't you think this over again? Why, even if I'm called a coward, I say there's still room for more deliberation, just in order to save the clan."

It was Hayashi Sado, the man with the longest service among them all. Together with Hirate Nakatsukasa, who had admonished Nobunaga with his suicide, he was one of the three senior retainers ordered by the dying Nobuhide to take care of Nobunaga. And he was the only one of those three who was still alive. Hayashi's thoughts had the sympathy of all the men there. And they all secretly prayed that Nobunaga would take the old man's words to heart.

"What time is it now?" Nobunaga asked, changing the subject.

"It's the Hour of the Rat," someone replied from the next room. As the words trailed off and the night deepened, melancholy seemed to settle on them all.

Finally Hayashi prostrated himself and spoke with his white head bowed to the floor in Nobunaga's direction. "My lord, think this over one more time. Let's negotiate. I beg you. At dawn, all of our men and fortresses are likely to be crushed before the forces of the Imagawa and will probably suffer an irreversible defeat. Rather than that, a peace conference, to bind them in a peace conference just moments before—"

Nobunaga glanced at him. "Hayashi?"

"Yes, my lord."

"You're an old man, so it must be difficult to sit for a long time. The discussion here is over, and the hour is getting late. Go home and sleep."

"That's going too far...." Hayashi said, shedding copious tears. He wept because he thought the clan had reached its final days. At the same time, he regretted being considered a useless old man. "If you're that determined, I'm not going to say anything else about your intention to fight."

"Don't!"

"You seem to be immovable in your desire to leave the castle and fight, my lord."

"I am."

"Our forces are small—less than one-tenth of the enemy's. To go out into the field and fight would give us less than one chance in a thousand. If we closed ourselves in behind the castle walls, we should be able to devise some plan."

"A plan?"

"If we could block the Imagawa for even two weeks or a month, we could send messengers to Mino or Kai and ask for reinforcements. As for other strategies, there are more than a few resourceful men at your side who know how to harass the enemy."

Nobunaga laughed loudly enough for it to echo off the ceiling. "Hayashi, those are strategies for ordinary times. Do you think these are ordinary times for the Oda clan?"

"That's hardly necessary to answer."

"Even if we could extend our lives by five or ten days, a castle that can't be held can't be held. But who was it that said, 'The direction of our fate always remains unknown'? When I think about it, it seems to me that we're at the very bottom of adversity now.

And adversity is interesting. Our adversary is huge, of course. Still, this may be the moment of a lifetime given to me by fate. Shutting ourselves up in our tiny castle in vain, should we pray for a long life without honor? Men are born to die. Dedicate your lives to me this time. Together we'll ride out under a bright blue sky and meet our deaths like true warriors." When he finished speaking, Nobunaga quickly changed his tone of voice.

"Well, nobody looks like he's had enough sleep." A forced smile appeared on his lips. "Hayashi, you sleep too. Everyone should get some sleep. I'm sure there's no one among us so cowardly that he won't be able to sleep."

This having been said, it would have been unseemly not to sleep. But in fact, there was no one among the retainers who had slept properly for the last two nights. Nobunaga was the only exception. He slept at night and even took naps during the day, not in his bedroom, but anywhere.

Mumbling almost in resignation, Hayashi bowed to both his lord and his colleagues, and withdrew.

Like teeth being pulled, every man got up and left one by one. Finally, only Nobunaga remained in the wide audience chamber. And in the end, he even looked rather carefree. When he turned around, he saw behind him two sleeping pages leaning against each other. One of them, Tohachiro, was just thirteen years old that year. He was Maeda Inuchiyo's younger brother. Nobunaga called to him.

"Tohachiro!"

"My lord?" Tohachiro sat straight up, wiping the dribble from his mouth with his hand.

"You sleep well."

"Please forgive me."

"No, no. I'm not scolding you. On the contrary, that's high praise. I'm going to sleep a little too. Give me something to use as a pillow."

"You're going to sleep just as you are?"

"Yes. The dawn comes early these days, so it's a good season for naps. Pass me that box over there. I'll use that." Nobunaga curled up as he spoke, supporting his head with his elbow until Tohachiro brought over the box. His body felt as if it were a floating boat. The lid of the box was decorated with a gold-lacquered design of pine, bamboo, and plum trees—symbols of good luck. Putting it under his head, Nobunaga said, "This pillow will give me good dreams." Then, chuckling to himself, Nobunaga closed his eyes, and finally, as the page put out the numerous lamps one by one, the faint smile on his face faded like melting snow. He fell into a deep sleep, his face at peace amid his snores.

Tohachiro crept out to inform the samurai in the guard room. The guards were feeling gloomy, thinking that it was the end. And what was absolute, of course, was that there was nothing for them other than death. The men inside the castle stared directly at death, the hours already passing midnight.

"I don't mind dying. The question is, how are we going to die?" This was the basis of their uneasiness, and it had still not been settled in anyone's breast. Therefore, there were some men among them who had not yet gathered their courage.

"He shouldn't catch cold," Sai, his lady-in-waiting, said, and put a coverlet over Nobunaga. After that, he slept for two hours.

The oil in the lamps was now almost consumed, and the dying wicks made little sputtering sounds. Nobunaga suddenly lifted his head and called out.

"Sai! Sai! Is anyone there?"

THE LORD WITH THE BLACKENED TEETH

The cedar door slid open noiselessly. Sai bowed reverently to Nobunaga and gently closed the door behind her.

"Are you awake, my lord?"

"What time is it?"

"The Hour of the Ox."

"Good."

"What are your orders?"

"Bring me my armor and have my horse saddled. And make me some breakfast."

Sai was an efficient woman, and Nobunaga always called upon her to look after his personal needs. She accepted what was to come and did not make a fuss. After shaking awake the page who was asleep in the next room, she told the samurai on guard duty to fetch Nobunaga's horse, then she took in her master's meal.

Nobunaga picked up his chopsticks. "When dawn comes, this will be the nineteenth day of the Fifth Month."

"Yes, my lord."

"This must be the earliest breakfast being eaten in the entire country. It's delicious. I'll have another bowl. What else is there?"

"Some dried kelp and chestnuts."

"Well, you've done me proud." Nobunaga cheerfully finished his gruel and ate two or three chestnuts. "That was a feast. Sai, give me my hand drum." Nobunaga treasured the drum, which he had called Narumigata. He put it to his shoulder and tried out two or three beats. "It sounds good! Maybe because it's so early in the morning, but it sounds much clearer than usual. Sai, play a section from *Atsumori* for me to dance to."

Sai obediently took the small drum from Nobunaga's hands and began to play. The sound of the drum under her lithe fingers rang clearly through the wide rooms of the castle, almost as if it were singing: Wake up! Wake up!

To think that a man
Has but fifty years to live under heaven…

Nobunaga stood up. He began to take graceful steps as smooth as water, and sang in time with the rhythm of the drum.

Surely this world
Is nothing but a vain dream.
Living but one life,
Is there anything that will not decay?

His voice was both unusually resonant and loud. And he sang as though he had reached the end of his life.

A samurai was hurrying down the corridor. His armor clanked noisily on the wooden floor as he knelt down. "Your horse is ready. We await your orders, my lord."

Nobunaga's hands and feet stopped in the middle of the dance, and he turned to the speaker. "Aren't you Iwamuro Nagato?"

"Yes, my lord."

Iwamuro Nagato was in full armor and was wearing his long sword. Yet, Nobunaga had not yet put on his armor and was dancing to the beat of a lady-in-waiting's drum. Nagato seemed dismayed and looked around doubtfully. The messenger who had brought the command to prepare the lord's horse for battle was his page. Everyone was exhausted from lack of sleep, and the page's nerves were on edge. Wasn't this some sort of mistake? Nagato had dressed in a hurry, but he was bewildered to find the leisurely figure of Nobunaga. Usually, when Nobunaga said, "Horse!" he would fly out before his retainers had time to get ready, so Nagato thought that this was more than unusual.

"Come in," said Nobunaga, his hands still in the correct posture of the dance. "Nagato, you're a lucky man. You're the only one able to observe my farewell dance to this life. That should be quite a sight."

When Nagato understood what his lord was doing, he was ashamed of his own doubts and edged over to a corner of the room.

"That I should be the only one among my lord's many retainers to witness the most important dance of his lifetime is good fortune far beyond my lowly position. Still, I would ask permission to sing my own farewell to this world."

"You can sing? Good. Sai, from the beginning." The lady-in-waiting was silent and dropped her head a little with the drum. Nagato had realized that when Nobunaga had said dance, he meant *Atsumori.*

To think that a man
Has but fifty years to live under heaven.
Surely this world

Is nothing but a vain dream.
Living but one life,
Is there anything that does not decay?

As Nagato chanted, his many years of service, dating from Nobunaga's youth, un-folded in his mind. The minds of the dancer and the singer became one. Sai's tears shone in the lamplight on her white face while she beat the hand drum. She played it with more skill and intensity than usual that morning.

Nobunaga threw down his fan and called out, "It's death!" As he donned his armor, he said, "Sai, if you hear that I've been killed, set the castle on fire immediately. Burn it until there's nothing left to see."

She put down the drum, and with her palms together on the floor, she replied, "Yes, my lord," without raising her head.

"Nagato! Blow the conch!" Nobunaga turned toward the inner citadel, where his lovely daughters lived, then to the mortuary tablets of his ancestors. "Farewell," he said with intense emotion. The he fastened the cords of his helmet and ran out.

The conch calling the troops to battle sounded in the quiet of the predawn darkness. The light of tiny stars shone brilliantly through the rifts in the clouds.

"Lord Nobunaga is going to war!" Word was carried by an attendant, surprising the samurai who ran into him in their hurry.

The men who worked in the kitchens and the warriors who were too old to fight and would stay to guard the castle rushed to the gate to see their comrades off. To count them would have been a fair estimate of the men left in Kiyosu Castle—less than forty or fifty. This was how short of men they were, both inside the castle and riding with Nobunaga.

The horse that Nobunaga rode that day was called Tsukinowa. At the gate, the rustling of the young leaves could be heard in the dark wind, and lights flickered in the lanterns. Nobunaga leaped up onto the horse, into a mother-of-pearl saddle, and galloped to the main gate, the tassels of his armor and his long sword jangling as he rode.

Those staying behind in the castle forgot themselves and shouted as they prostrated themselves. Nobunaga spoke a few words of farewell to these old men who had served him for so many years. He felt sorry for these warriors and for his daughters, who were losing both a castle and a master. Without his being aware of it, Nobunaga's eyes moist-ened with tears.

In the time it had taken Nobunaga to shut his hot eyelids, Tsukinowa had already gal-loped like a squall out of the castle, into the dawn.

"My lord!"

"My lord!"

"Wait!"

Master and attendants were no more than six mounted men. And as usual, his re-tainers strained to keep from being left behind. Nobunaga did not look back. The enemy was to the east; their allies were also on the front lines. By the time they reached the place where they would die, the sun would already be high in the sky. As he galloped along, Nobunaga thought that, from the perspective of eternity, to be born in this province and to return to its soil meant nothing.

"Ho!"

"My lord!" someone suddenly called out from a crossroads in the town.

"Yoshinari?" he shouted back.

"Yes, my lord."

"And Katsuie?"

"Here, my lord!"

"You were quick!" Nobunaga praised them and asked, standing up in his stirrups, "How many are you?"

"A hundred twenty mounted men under Mori Yoshinari, and eighty under Shibata Katsuie, so altogether about two hundred. We held back to accompany you."

Among the archers under Yoshinari was Mataemon, and Tokichiro was also there in the throng, at the head of thirty foot soldiers.

Nobunaga noticed him at once. Monkey's here, too. From horseback, he surveyed the two hundred excited soldiers. I have followers like this, he thought, and his eyes brightened. To strike at the raging waves of an enemy forty thousand strong, his own soldiers were no more than a small ship or a handful of sand. But Nobunaga was bold enough to ask himself, I wonder if Yoshimoto has followers like this. He was proud, both as a general and as a man. Even if they were defeated, his men would not have died in vain. They were going to make their mark on this earth as they dug their own graves. "It's nearly dawn. Let's go!" Nobunaga pointed ahead.

When his horse galloped down the Atsuta Road to the east, the two hundred soldiers moved on like a cloud, stirring up the morning mist that stood as high as the eaves of the houses on both sides of the road. There was neither order nor rank. It was every man for himself. Ordinarily, when the lord of a province went to war, the commoners all stopped their work, swept the fronts of the houses, and saw the troops off. The soldiers marched by, displaying their banners and standards. The commander himself showed off his authority and power. And they marched to the battlefield, six steps to the drumbeat, with all the splendor and power that the province could muster. But Nobunaga was completely indifferent to such empty posturing. They dashed ahead so quickly that they could not fall into orderly ranks.

They were going to fight to the death. With an attitude that seemed to shout, "Whoever is coming, come on!" Nobunaga took the lead. There were no stragglers. On the contrary, as they advanced, their numbers swelled. As the call to arms had been sudden, those who were not ready in time now rushed to join them from the side streets and alleys, or caught up with them from behind.

The sounds of their footsteps and voices awoke those who still slept through the early hours of the dawn. Along the road, farmers, merchants, and artisans opened their doors, and sleepy-eyed people yelled out, "A battle!"

They may have guessed later that the man who had galloped in the lead in the morning mist was their lord, Oda Nobunaga. But nobody saw now.

"Nagato! Nagato!" Nobunaga turned in the saddle, but Nagato was not there; he was about fifty yards behind in the melee. Those who were coming up behind—their horses neck-and-neck—were Katsuie and Yoshinari. More men had joined them at the entrance of Atsuta.

"Katsuie!" Nobunaga yelled. "We'll see the great gate of the shrine soon. Stop the troops out in front. Even I am not going to go without saying a prayer." Almost as he spoke, he pulled up to the great gate. He jumped nimbly to the ground, and the waiting head priest, with some twenty attendants, rushed forward and took the reins of his horse.

"Thank you for coming out to meet me. I've come to say a prayer." The head priest led the way. The approach to the shrine, lined with cryptomeria trees, was damp with little droplets of mist. The head priest stood by the sacred spring, and invited Nobunaga to purify himself. Nobunaga took the cypress-wood ladle, washed his hands, and rinsed his mouth. Then he took one more ladleful and drank it down in one gulp.

"Look! A good omen!" Nobunaga looked up and spoke loudly enough for his troops to hear him. He pointed to the sky. Dawn had finally broken. The branches of an old cryptomeria tree had taken a reddish hue from the morning sun, and a flock of crows was cawing loudly. "The sacred crows!" The samurai around Nobunaga looked up with him.

In the meantime the head priest, also in full armor, had climbed to the holy of holies. Nobunaga sat on a mat. The priest brought *sake* on a small wooden stand and served it in an unglazed earthenware cup. Nobunaga drained the cup, clapped his hands loudly, and said his prayer to the gods. His men bowed their heads low, closing their eyes as they prayed, so that their hearts could become mirrors that would reflect the images of the gods.

By the time Nobunaga left Atsuta Shrine, the soldiers who had been running up to join him had swelled the number of his army to nearly a thousand. Nobunaga left the shrine by its southern gate and remounted his horse. Nobunaga had come to Atsuta like a gale, but leaving now, he slowed to a much more leisurely pace. He swayed as he rode sidesaddle, with his hands holding the front and rear rings of the saddle.

Dawn had already broken, and the villagers of Atsuta, including women and children, stood in front of their houses and at the crossroads to look, drawn by the sound of the horses' hooves that raced one another for first place.

When they realized it was Nobunaga, they all looked amazed and whispered among themselves:

"Is he really going into battle?"

"Can this be true?"

"They haven't got one chance in ten thousand."

He had ridden from Kiyosu to Atsuta at a single stretch, so he was now saddlesore. Riding sidesaddle and leaning back a little, he hummed to himself.

When the army came to the crossroads on the outskirts of the town, it suddenly stopped. Black smoke was rising in two places from the direction of Marune and Washizu. A sad look appeared on Nobunaga's face. The two fortresses must have fallen. He took a deep breath, then spoke quickly to his retainers. "We won't follow the coastal road. The morning tide is high right now, so it will be useless to take that route. We'll take the hill road to the fortress at Tange." Dismounting, he said to a retainer, "Call the headmen of Atsuta."

The man turned to the crowd lining the roads and yelled loudly enough to be heard. Soldiers were sent to search for the headmen. Before long, two of them were brought before Nobunaga.

"You've seen me quite often, so I'm not much of a rarity. But today I'm going to treat you to a rare sight: the head with blackened teeth of the lord of Suruga. You've never seen it, but you will see it today, because you were born in my province of Owari. Just go up to some high place and watch this great battle.

"Go around Atsuta and tell the people to collect festival banners and streamers and to make them look like flags and banners to the enemy. Put red and white or any color cloth on tree branches and on the tops of hills, and fill the sky with fluttering streamers. Do you understand?"

When the horses had advanced about half a league and he turned to look, innumerable flags and banners were fluttering all over Atsuta. It looked as though a huge army from Kiyosu had set out as far as the town and was resting there.

It was oppressively hot, hotter than it had been for many years in early summer—as the old men would later recall. The sun climbed high and the horses trampled earth that had not seen rain for ten days. The army was covered with dust as it marched.

Life or death—along with his reins, Nobunaga held them in his hands as he galloped onward. To the soldiers, Nobunaga looked either like a gallant herald of death or a leader of hope for a greater life. Regardless of which view one took, or the final result, belief in its leader ran through the entire army as it followed behind this man without complaint.

To the death. To the death. To the death.

This was the only thing in Tokichiro's mind, too. Even if he hadn't wanted to go forward, since everyone around him was marching along, it was like being swallowed up in billowing waves, and there was no time for his feet to stop. Even if it wasn't of much account, he was the leader of thirty foot soldiers and so could not indulge in complaining, no matter how bad the situation.

To the death. To the death.

The stipends of the foot soldiers were so low that they were just enough to allow their families to survive. And the soundless, desperate voice that panted in their bellies echoed in Tokichiro's belly. Could people really just toss their lives away like this? Certainly, that seemed to be what was happening, and it suddenly struck Tokichiro that he was serving an absurd general. He had had such great expectations when he had first sought out Nobunaga, and now the man seemed to be sending his soldiers—Tokichiro among them—flying bravely to their deaths. He thought of all the things he still wanted to do in this world, and of his mother in Nakamura.

These things flitted across Tokichiro's mind, but they came and were gone in an instant. The sound of a thousand pairs of marching feet and the clanging of sun-scorched armor seemed to say, Die! Die!

The soldier's faces were burned by the sun, drenched in sweat, and covered with dust. And although it was possible to detect Tokichiro's carefree character, even in this desperate situation, today he was thinking along with the others, Fight! To the death!

The soldiers advanced, ready to sacrifice their lives. As they marched over one hill after another, they drew closer to the swirling clouds of smoke they had seen earlier.

The vanguard had just reached the top of a hill when a blood-smeared, wounded man stumbled toward them, screaming something they couldn't quite hear.

He was a retainer of Sakuma Daigaku who had escaped from Marune. Taken before

Nobunaga and breathing heavily because of his wounds, he pulled himself together and made his report: "Lord Sakuma met a manly death in the flames set on all sides by the enemy, and Lord Iio was struck down gloriously during the battle at Washizu. I'm ashamed to be the last one alive, but I escaped on the order of Lord Sakuma in order to inform you of what has happened. As I fled, I could hear the enemy's victory shouts, loud enough to shake heaven and earth. And nothing remains in Marune and Washizu but the enemy army."

After he had heard the report, Nobunaga called out, "Tohachiro." Maeda Tohachiro was still a boy and so was almost buried in the great crowd of warriors. When Nobunaga called him, he answered with a loud shout and approached Nobunaga with high-spirited manliness.

"Yes, my lord?"

"Tohachiro, give me my rosary."

Tohachiro had taken great care not to drop his master's rosary. He had wrapped it in a cloth and secured it tightly across his armor. Now he quickly untied it and held it up to Nobunaga. Nobunaga took the rosary and hung it from his own shoulder, across his chest. It was made of large silver-colored beads, and it set off his light green death robe even more magnificently.

"Ah, how sad. Both Iio and Sakuma have gone on to the next world. How I wish they could have seen my exploits." Nobunaga straightened himself in the saddle and put his hands together in prayer.

The black smoke from Washizu and Marune scorched the sky like the smoke of a funeral pyre. The men watched in silence. Nobunaga stared into the distance for a moment, then suddenly turned, struck the seat of his saddle, and yelled out almost in ecstasy, "Today is the nineteenth. This day will be the anniversary of my death, as well as your own. Your stipends have been low, and you're meeting your fate as warriors today without ever having known good luck. This must be the destiny of those who serve me. But those who will follow me just one more step will be giving me their lives. Those who still have some attachment to this life may leave without shame."

The commanders and soldiers responded with one voice. "Never! Should our lord die alone?"

Nobunaga went on, "Then will you all give your lives to a fool like me?"

"You don't even have to ask," replied one of the generals.

Nobunaga gave his horse one great stroke with his whip. "Forward! The Imagawa are just ahead!" He was riding at the head of his troops, but he was hidden by the dust of the entire army galloping forward. In the dust, the indistinct form of the mounted man seemed somehow divine.

The road went through a ravine and over a low pass. As it approached the provincial border, the lay of the land became uneven.

"There it is!"

"It's Tange. The fortress of Tange," the soldiers said to one another as they gasped for breath. The fortresses of Marune and Washizu had already fallen, so they had been worried about the fate of Tange, too. Now their eyes brightened. Tange was still standing, its defenders still alive.

Nobunaga rode up to the fortress and said to its commander, "The defense of this little place is already useless, so we may as well let the enemy have it. The hope of our army lies elsewhere."

The garrison of Tange joined Nobunaga's advancing army, and they hurried without rest toward the fortress at Zenshoji. As soon as the garrison realized that Nobunaga was coming, they raised a shout. But it was hardly a cheer; it was more like crying and pathetic trembling.

"He's come!"

"Lord Nobunaga!"

Nobunaga was their lord, but not all of them knew what kind of general he was. It was beyond their expectations that Nobunaga himself had suddenly come to this isolated outpost where they had all just resolved to die. Now all of them had been given new life, and they were ready to die in front of his standard. At the same time Sassa Narimasa, who had started out in the direction of Hoshizaki and had collected a force of over three hundred mounted men, fell in with Nobunaga.

Nobunaga called the soldiers together and ordered a head count. That morning, when they had ridden out of the castle, lord and followers were a mere six or seven. Now the army numbered close to three thousand. It was announced publicly that there were at least five thousand men. Nobunaga considered the fact that this was really the entire army of his domain, which covered half the province of Owari. With neither garrisons nor reserves, these men made up the entire strength of the Oda.

A satisfied smile came to his lips. The forty thousand men of the Imagawa forces were now within hailing distance, and to spy on their lineup and morale, the Oda troops concealed their flags and banners and viewed the situation from the edge of the mountain.

Asano Mataemon's corps had gathered together on the northern slope, a little apart from the main army. Although they were archers, the battle today would not call for bows and arrows, so his men carried spears. The small group of thirty foot soldiers led by Tokichiro was also with them, and when the commander ordered the men to rest, Tokichiro passed on the order to his own men.

They responded by taking deep breaths and falling onto the grass in the mountain's shade.

Tokichiro rubbed his sweaty face with a dirty towel. "Hey! Would somebody hold my spear?" His subordinates had just sat down, but one of them yelled, "Yes, sir," and got up and took the spear. Then, when Tokichiro started to walk off, the man followed from behind.

"You don't have to come."

"Where are you going, sir?"

"I don't need any help. I'm going to relieve myself, and it's not going to smell too good." With a laugh, he disappeared into some shrubbery along the narrow cliff road. Perhaps thinking that Tokichiro had been joking, his subordinate stood for a while and gazed in the direction in which he had gone.

Tokichiro went a little way down the southern slope, looking around until he found a suitable spot. He untied his bellyband and squatted down. The troops had left so fast that morning that he had barely had enough time to put on his armor, and had certainly had no time to go to relieve himself. And even while they hurried from Kiyosu to Atsuta and Tange, if they stopped somewhere to rest, his first thoughts were to relieve himself just like in everyday life. Thus it was now very satisfying to be taking care of his bodily needs under a clear blue sky.

But even here, the rules of the battlefield allowed for no negligence. Very often, when armies confronted each other, enemy patrols would travel far from their camps, and when they discovered someone emptying his bowels, they would shoot him half in fun. So Tokichiro was unable to be completely at peace while gazing up at the sky. Looking toward the foot of the mountain, he could see that the river meandered like a sash, flowing to the sea at the Chita Peninsula. He could also see the single white road that wound its way south along the river's eastern bank.

Washizu was in the mountainous area north of the road and had probably already burned to the ground. In the fields and villages he could see the many little antlike forms of men and horses. "There's certainly a lot of them."

It might have been because Tokichiro was a part of the army of a small province, but when he saw the scale of the enemy, the clichéed phrase "like the clouds and mist" naturally came to mind. And when he considered that this army was just one part of the enemy force, he was not surprised that Nobunaga had resolved to die. But no, this wasn't just another man's affair. Emptying his bowels was probably the last thing he was going to do in this world.

Men are strange. I wonder if I'll still be alive tomorrow? While he was brooding on such things, Tokichiro was suddenly aware that someone was coming up the mountain from the marsh below.

The enemy? Being close to a battlefield, this was an intuitive, almost instinctive reaction, and now he wondered if this might be an enemy scout, trying to get behind Nobunaga's headquarters. As Tokichiro quickly tied his sash and stood up, the face of the man who had scrambled up from the marsh suddenly met his own, and the two men stood staring straight at each other.

"Tokichiro!"

"Inuchiyo!"

"What are you doing here?"

"What are *you* doing?"

"I heard that Lord Nobunaga had marched out and is resolved to die, and I've come to die with him."

"I'm glad you came." With a lump in his throat, Tokichiro extended his hand to his old friend. Countless emotions were enveloped within the men's clasped hands. Inuchiyo's armor was splendid. From the lacquered feathering to the lacing, it was new and glittered brilliantly. A banner with a plum-blossom crest was attached to his back.

"You cut a fine figure," Tokichiro said with admiration. Suddenly, he thought about Nene, whom he had left behind. But he forced his thoughts to return to Inuchiyo. "Where were you until now?"

"I was waiting for the right time."

"When Lord Nobunaga banished you, didn't you think about serving another clan?"

"No, my loyalty has always been undivided. Even after I was banished, I felt that Lord

Nobunaga's punishment made me more human, and I'm thankful for it."

Tears filled Tokichiro's eyes. Inuchiyo knew that the battle today was going to be the glorious death of the entire Oda clan, and it made Tokichiro unbearably happy that his friend had come here, wanting to die with his former lord.

"I understand. Look, Inuchiyo, this is the first time Lord Nobunaga has rested today. Now's the time. Come on."

"Wait, Tokichiro. I won't go into Lord Nobunaga's presence."

"Why not?"

"It wasn't my intention to come here at a time when Lord Nobunaga might withhold his anger from any soldier, and I would hate his retainers to see me in that light."

"What are you saying? Everybody here is going to die. Didn't you come here wanting to die in front of your lord's standard?"

"That's right."

"Then don't worry. Gossip is for the living."

"No, it's better if I die without saying anything. And that is my deepest ambition, whether Lord Nobunaga forgives me or not. Tokichiro?"

"Yes?"

"Will you hide me in your group for a little while?"

"That's no trouble at all, but my command is only thirty men in the foot soldiers. You're going to stand out."

"I'll go like this." He covered his helmet with something that looked like a horse blanket, and slipped into Tokichiro's group of soldiers. If he stood on tiptoe, he could see Nobunaga clearly. And he could hear his high-pitched voice come and go with the wind.

Like a low-flying bird, a lone rider was coming toward Nobunaga from an unexpected direction. Nobunaga saw the man before anyone else did, and watched him in silence. As the entire army looked in his direction, the man rode closer and closer.

"What is it? Do you have news?"

"The main body of the Imagawa, the troops under Yoshimoto and his generals, has just now changed its direction and is headed for Okehazama!"

"What?" Nobunaga asked with glittering eyes. "Well, then, Yoshimoto has taken the road to Okehazama without turning toward Odaka?"

Before he could finish, a shout rose: "Look! There's another!"

One rider, then two—scouts for Nobunaga's forces. The men held their breaths as the riders whipped their horses toward the camp. Adding to the previous report, the scouts informed Nobunaga of the continuing turn of events.

"The main force of the Imagawa turned on the road to Okehazama, but they've just now spread out over an area slightly above Dengakuhazama, a little to the south of Okehazama. They've moved their headquarters, and it seems as though they're resting their troops with Lord Yoshimoto right in the center."

Nobunaga fell silent for an instant, his eyes as clear as the blade of a sword. Death. He had only thought of death. With intensity, in the absolute dark, in self-abandonment. His only desire had been to die in a manly way. He had ridden furiously from dawn until the sun was high in the sky. Now, suddenly, like a single ray of light breaking through the clouds, the possibility of victory flashed across his mind.

If things went well…

The truth was that, up to that point, he had not believed in victory, and victory was the only thing a warrior fought for.

Fragments of thoughts appear and disappear in the human mind, like an endless stream of tiny bubbles, so that one's life is carved out instant by instant. Right up to the point of his death, a man's words and actions are decided by this chain of fragments. Ideas that can destroy a man. A day in a man's life is constructed according to whether he accepts or rejects these flashes of inspiration.

In ordinary situations, there is time for a mature deliberation over choices, but a man's moment of destiny comes without warning. When the crisis breaks, should he go to the right or to the left? Nobunaga was now at that fork in the road and unconsciously drew the straw of fate.

Clearly his character and training played their part at the crucial moment and kept him from taking the wrong direction. His lips were tightly shut. Yet there was something he wanted to say.

Suddenly a retainer shouted, "My lord, now is the time! Yoshimoto thinks he knows our strength after capturing Washizu and Marune. He's probably filled with pride about his army's early success. He's glorying in his victory and letting his fighting spirit slide. This is the right moment. If we launch a surprise attack on Yoshimoto's headquarters, our victory is certain."

Nobunaga joined in the man's high-strung voice. "That's it!" he said, slapping his saddle. "That's exactly what we're going to do. I'm going to have Yoshimoto's head. Dengakuhazama is straight to the east."

The generals, however, were confused and filled with misgivings when they heard the scouts' reports, and they tried to check Nobunaga's instinctive dash forward.

But Nobunaga would not listen. "You decrepit old men! What are you dithering about now? All you have to do is follow me. If I walk into the fire, you walk into it too. If I'm ready to walk into the water, then you'll follow me there. If you won't, stay on the sidelines and watch me." Leaving them with a single, cold laugh, Nobunaga gracefully raised his horse's head and galloped to the front line of his army.

* * *

Noon. Not a single bird could be heard in the hushed mountains. The wind had died, and the burning sun seemed to scorch everything under the sky. The leaves were either tightly closed or withered like dried tobacco.

"Over there!" Leading a small group of men, a warrior was running up a grassy slope. "Put up the curtain."

In one area, soldiers were clearing away the undergrowth with scythes; others unfurled curtains and tied them to the branches of the nearby pines and silk trees. In moments they had put together a curtained enclosure that would serve as Yoshimoto's temporary headquarters.

"Whew! It's scorching!" said one of the men.

"They say it doesn't often get this hot!"

203

The men wiped away their sweat.

"Look, the sweat's pouring off me. Even the leather and metal of my armor are too hot to touch."

"If I took off my armor and let a little breeze in I'd feel better. But I think the general staff will be here soon."

"Well, let's take just a little rest." There were few trees on the grass-covered hill, so the soldiers sat down together under the shade of a large camphor tree. After a short rest, they felt cooler.

The hill of Dengakuhazama was lower than the surrounding mountains, no more than a knoll in the center of a circular valley. From time to time, the white undersides of the leaves all over the hill would suddenly be rustled by a cool summer breeze descending from Taishigadake.

One of the soldiers looked up to the sky while applying ointment to his blistered toes, and muttered something to himself.

"What's the matter?" asked another soldier.

"Look."

"At what?"

"Storm clouds are gathering. It'll probably rain in the evening."

"A good rain would be nice. But I tell you, for those of us who do nothing but repair roads and carry the baggage, rain can be worse than an attack by the enemy. I hope it'll just be a light shower."

The wind incessantly ruffled the curtained enclosure they had just set up.

The officer in charge looked around and told his men, "Well, let's get up. His Lordship will be staying at Odaka Castle tonight. He's deliberately led the enemy into thinking that he'll be advancing from Kutsukake to Odaka, but with this shortcut through Okehazama, he plans to arrive this evening. It's our job to go on ahead and look for problems with the bridges, cliffs, and gullies along the way. Well, let's go!"

The voices and men were gone, and the mountain returned to its former peace. The grasshoppers were making their shrill cries. But not long afterward, horses were heard in the distance. No conches were blown, no drums beaten, and they passed between the mountain peaks as quietly as possible. Yet despite their efforts, there was no way to conceal the dust and clatter of so many horses. The sound of the horses' hooves on the stones and roots quickly filled the air, and the main forces of the great Imagawa Yoshimoto soon buried the grassy knoll and the surroundings of Dengakuhazama in soldiers, horses, banners, and curtained enclosures.

Yoshimoto was sweating more than anyone else. He had grown accustomed to the good life and, after passing the age of forty, had become grotesquely fat. It was obvious that he found these maneuvers a trial. Over his corpulent body with its long torso he wore a red brocade kimono and a white breastplate. His outsized helmet had five neckplates and was crowned with eight dragons. In addition, he wore the long sword called Matsukurago that had been in the Imagawa family for generations, a short sword—also the work of a famous swordsmith—gloves, shin guards, and boots. The entire outfit probably weighed more than eighty pounds, and lacked the smallest vent where the breeze might enter.

Covered with sweat, Yoshimoto rode on through the blazing heat, as the sun scorched even the leather and the lacquered feathering on his armor. Finally he arrived at Dengakuhazama.

"What is this place called?" Yoshimoto asked as soon as he was seated behind his headquarters' curtain. All around him were the men charged with his protection: attendants, generals, senior retainers, physicians, and others.

One of the generals replied, "This is Dengakuhazama. It's about half a league from Okehazama."

Yoshimoto nodded and handed his helmet to an attendant. After a page unlaced his armor, he stepped out of his sweat-soaked undergarments and into a spotlessly clean white robe. A gentle breeze filtered in. How refreshing, Yoshimoto thought.

When the waistband of his armor had been retied, his camp stool was moved to a leopard-skin mat spread out on the grassy knoll. The extravagant camp supplies that followed him everywhere were now unpacked.

"What's that sound?" Yoshimoto took a gulp of tea, startled by something that sounded like a cannon's roar.

His attendants also pricked up their ears. One of them raised an edge of the curtain and looked around outside. He was struck by a sight of awesome beauty: the scorching sun toyed with the shredded clouds and painted a maelstrom of light in the sky.

"Distant thunder. Just the sound of distant thunder," the retainer reported.

"Thunder?" Yoshimoto forced a smile, lightly patting his lower back with his left hand. His attendants noticed this but purposely refrained from asking the reason. That morning, when they had departed from the castle at Kutsukake, Yoshimoto had fallen off his horse. To inquire about his injury yet again would only have embarrassed Yoshimoto further.

Something was stirring. Suddenly there seemed to be a clamorous rush of horses and men from the foot of the hill, coming in the direction of the enclosure. Yoshimoto immediately turned to one of his retainers, asking anxiously, "What is it?"

Without waiting for his order to go and look, two or three men dashed outside the curtain, letting in the wind. This time it was not the sound of distant thunder. The clatter of horses' hooves and men's footsteps had already reached the top of the hill. It was a corps of about two hundred men, carrying in an enormous number of enemy heads taken at Narumi—graphic demonstration of how the war was going.

The heads were now brought in for Yoshimoto's inspection.

"The heads of the Oda samurai from Narumi. Line them up! Let's take a look!" Yoshimoto was in good spirits. "Set up my camp stool!"

Adjusting his position and holding his fan over his face, he examined the seventy-odd heads being submitted to him one after another. When Yoshimoto had finished his inspection, he exclaimed, "What a bloody mess!" and turned away, ordering the curtain to be closed. Scattered rain clouds filled the clear noon sky. "Well, well. A cool breeze is coming up the ravine. It'll soon be noon, won't it?"

"No, my lord, it's already past the Hour of the Horse," answered an attendant.

"No wonder I'm hungry. Get lunch ready, and let the troops eat and rest."

An attendant went outside to transmit his orders. Inside the enclosure, his generals, pages, and cooks moved about, but the atmosphere was one of calm. Now and again, the representatives from local shrines, temples, and villages came to present *sake* and local delicacies.

Yoshimoto studied these people from afar, and decided, "We'll reward them when we return from the capital."

When the local people had gone, Yoshimoto ordered *sake* and made himself comfortable on the leopard-skin mat. The commanders outside the curtain each presented themselves, congratulating him on his victory at Narumi, which had followed the capture of Marune and Washizu.

"You're probably all unhappy with the little bit of resistance we've encountered so far," Yoshimoto said with a playful look on his face as he offered cups of *sake* to all his retainers and attendants. He was becoming progressively more and more expansive.

"It's Your Lordship's power that has brought us to this happy situation. But as Your Lordship has said, if we continue on like this, with no enemy to fight, our soldiers will complain that all our discipline and training were for nothing."

"Have patience. Tomorrow night we'll take Kiyosu Castle, and no matter how badly beaten these Oda are, I imagine they have some fight left in them yet. Each of you will have his share of daring exploits."

"Well then, Your Lordship can stay in Kiyosu for two or three days, and will be able to enjoy both moon-viewing and entertainment."

At some point the sun vanished behind the clouds, but with all the *sake*, no one noticed the darkening of the sky. As a gust of wind lifted the edge of the curtain, rain started to fall in big drops, and intermittent thunder rumbled in the distance. But Yoshimoto and his generals were laughing and talking, arguing about who would be first to reach Kiyosu Castle the next day, and making fun of Nobunaga.

While Yoshimoto was deriding his enemy in his headquarters, Nobunaga was charging up the pathless slopes of Taishigadake. He was already nearing Yoshimoto's headquarters.

Taishigadake was neither particularly high nor steep, but its slopes were covered with oaks, zelkovas, maples, and sumacs. It was ordinarily frequented only by woodcutters, so to get a number of horses and men through quickly now, they had to cut down trees, trample down the undergrowth, leap over precipices, and splash through streams.

Nobunaga shouted to his men, "If you fall off your horse, leave it! If your banners get caught in the branches, let them go! Just hurry! The essential thing is to get to Yoshimoto's headquarters and to take his head. It's best to travel light. Carry no baggage at all! Just get into the enemy ranks and run them through. Don't take the time to cut every head you've taken. Cut them down and go on to the next, while there is life in your body. You don't have to perform heroic deeds. Showy exploits have no value at all. Fight selflessly before me today, and you will be a true Oda warrior!"

The soldiers listened to these words as though they were listening to the thunder before the storm. The afternoon sky had been completely transformed, and now looked like dark swirls of ink. The wind rose up from the layers of clouds, from the valley, from the marsh, from the roots of trees, and blew into the darkness.

"We're almost there! Dengakuhazama is on the far side of that mountain and through a marsh. Are you ready to die? If you fall behind, you'll leave only shame to your descendants until the end of time!"

The main body of Nobunaga's forces did not advance in formation. Some soldiers were late in arriving, while others advanced in loose ranks. Their hearts, however, were drawn on by his voice.

Nobunaga had yelled himself hoarse, and it was difficult for the men to catch what he was saying. But that was no longer necessary. It was enough for them to know that he was leading them. Meanwhile, a driving rain had begun to fall like shining spearheads. The raindrops were big enough to hurt when they hit the men's cheeks and noses. This was accompanied by a gale that tore away the leaves, so that they hardly knew what was striking their faces.

Suddenly a thunderbolt nearly rent the mountain in half. For an instant, heaven and earth were one color—smoky white in the downpour. When the rain let up, muddy streams and waterfalls flowed all over the marshes and slopes.

"There it is!" Tokichiro yelled. He turned and pointed past his foot soldiers, who were blinking raindrops off their eyelashes, to the Imagawa camp. The enemy's curtained enclosures seemed innumerable, all of them soaked by the rain. Before them was the marsh. Beyond that, the slope of Dengakuhazama.

When they looked again, Tokichiro's men could see the helmeted and armored figures of their allies already rushing in. They brandished swords, spears, and halberds. Nobunaga had said that the advantage was in traveling light, and many of the men had discarded their helmets, and thrown away their banners.

Threading their way through the trees, slipping over the grassy ridges, they immediately set upon the enemy's enclosures. Now and again, blue-green lightning flashed in the sky, and the white rain and black wind wrapped the world in darkness.

Yelling at his men, Tokichiro dashed through the marsh and started up the hill. They slipped and fell, but kept up with him. Rather than saying that they charged and leaped into the fray, it would be truer to say that Tokichiro's little unit was swallowed whole by the battle.

Laughter reverberated around Yoshimoto's headquarters as the thunder pealed. Even when the wind freshened, the stones that held down the curtains of the enclosure stayed put.

"This should blow away the heat!" they joked, and still they drank. But they were in the field and planned to advance as far as Odaka by evening, so no one exceeded his limit.

About then, it was announced that lunch was ready. The generals ordered the food to be brought to Yoshimoto, and as they emptied their cups, rice containers and large soup pots were placed before them. At the same time, the rain started to fall in noisy drops, striking the pots, rice containers, straw mats, and armor.

Finally noticing the ominous look of the sky, they began to move their mats. In the enclosure stood a large camphor tree with a trunk so huge it would have taken three men to circle it with outstretched arms. Yoshimoto stood under the tree, sheltered from the rain. The others hurried behind him, bringing his mats and bowls.

The swaying of the huge tree shook the ground, and its branches howled in the violent wind. As both brown and green leaves flew up like dust and blew against the men's armor, the smoke from the cooking fires was blown close along the ground, blinding and half choking Yoshimoto and his generals.

"Please endure this for just a moment. We're putting up a rain cover now." One of the generals called loudly for soldiers, but there was no response. In the bleached white spray of the rain and the roar of the trees, his voice was carried off into the void, and no reply came. Only the loud snapping of firewood could be heard from the kitchen enclosure, from which smoke spewed out furiously.

"Call the commander of the foot soldiers!" As one of the generals ran out into the piercing rain, a strange sound welled up from the surrounding area. It was a moan that seemed to come from the earth itself—the violent clash of one forged weapon against another. And the storm did not content itself with the surface of Yoshimoto's skin; the confusion now blew fiercely into his mind as well.

"What is it? What's going on?" Yoshimoto and his generals seemed utterly bewildered. "Have we been betrayed? Are the men fighting among themselves?"

Still not realizing what was going on, the samurai and generals at Yoshimoto's side instantly drew around him like a protective wall.

"What is it?" they yelled. But the Oda forces had already surged into the camp like a tide, and were now running right outside the curtain.

"The enemy!"

"The Oda!"

Spears clashed, and embers of firewood flew above the confused cries of struggling men. Yoshimoto, still standing under the huge camphor tree, seemed to have lost his ability to speak. He chewed his lip with his black teeth, apparently unable to believe what was happening right before his eyes. Yoshimoto's generals stood around him with grim faces, yelling back and forth.

"Is this a rebellion?"

"Are these men rebels?"

There was no answer except for cries, and despite the alarmed shouts coming from all over the camp, they could not believe it was the enemy attacking. But they could not doubt their own ears for long. The Oda warriors appeared right in front of them, their harsh war cries in the strange Owari dialect piercing the ears of Yoshimoto's retainers. Two or three of the enemy rushed in their direction.

"Hey! Lord of Suruga!"

When they saw the Oda men coming, screaming like demons, jumping and slipping over the mud, brandishing spears and halberds, they were finally shocked into recognizing the true situation.

"The Oda!"

"A surprise attack!"

The confusion was more terrible than if they had been attacked at night. They had underestimated Nobunaga. It was lunchtime. This, in addition to the violent storm, had allowed the enemy to enter the camp completely undetected. But it was their own advance guard that had really put Yoshimoto's headquarters totally at ease.

The two generals detached to guard the headquarters were stationed less than a mile from the hill, but suddenly, and without warning from their own lookouts, the enemy was rushing in unchecked, right before the eyes of Yoshimoto and his generals.

From the very beginning, Nobunaga had avoided the camps of the vanguard. As they went through Taishigadake and straight to Dengakuhazama, Nobunaga himself brandished a spear and fought Yoshimoto's soldiers. Very likely the soldiers speared by Nobunaga had had no idea who their adversary had been. Severely wounding two or three men as he advanced, Nobunaga galloped toward the curtained enclosure.

"The camphor tree!" Nobunaga yelled out as one of his men ran past him. "Don't let the lord of Suruga escape! He's probably in the enclosure under the big camphor tree!" Nobunaga had guessed instantly where Yoshimoto would be, just by looking at the layout of the camp.

"My lord!" In the confusion of the battle, Nobunaga nearly rode over one of his soldiers kneeling in front of him, a bloody spear at his side.

"Who are you?"

"Maeda Inuchiyo, my lord."

"Inuchiyo? Well, get to work! Fight!"

The rain fell onto the muddy paths, and the wind swept along the earth. Branches of the camphor tree and surrounding pines snapped off and were sent crashing to the ground. Water dripped off the branches onto Yoshimoto's helmet.

"My lord, over here! This way." Four or five of Yoshimoto's retainers formed a protective ring around him and hurried him from one enclosure to the next, trying to avoid a disaster.

"Is the lord of Suruga in here?" The instant Yoshimoto had left, an Oda warrior brandishing a spear challenged one of the generals who had stayed behind.

"Come here, I'll give you a fight!" the general yelled, checking the soldier's spear with his own.

The intruder identified himself, breathing heavily, "I am Maeda Inuchiyo, retainer to Lord Nobunaga!" The general replied, giving his own name and rank. He lunged forward, but Inuchiyo stepped to the side, and the spear struck into the void.

Inuchiyo had his opening, but not enough time to pull back his long spear, and so he simply struck the man full on the head with the spear shaft. The bowl of the helmet rang like a gong, and the injured man crawled out into the rain on all fours. Just then, two more men yelled out their names. When Inuchiyo adjusted his stance, someone fell on his back. Inuchiyo tripped and stumbled over the corpse of a soldier.

"Kinoshita Tokichiro!" Somewhere his friend was identifying himself. Inuchiyo smiled, the wind and rain striking his cheeks. He was blinded by the mud. There was blood wherever he looked. The moment he had slipped and fallen, he had seen that there were neither enemies nor allies in the immediate vicinity. Corpses were piled on top of corpses, and the rain made little splashing sounds on their backs. His straw sandals were dyed crimson as he kicked his way through a river of blood. Where was the lord with blackened teeth? He wanted Yoshimoto's head.

The rain called. The wind called.

Inuchiyo was not alone in his quest. Kuwabara Jinnai, a *ronin* from Kai, dressed in armor from the waist down, brandishing a spear smeared with blood, ran around the camphor tree and yelled out in his hoarse voice, "I'm coming for the lord of Suruga! Where is this great General Yoshimoto?" A gust of wind lifted the edge of a curtain, lightning flashed, and he saw a man wearing a red coat over his armor, and a crested helmet with eight dragons.

The furious voice rebuking his retainers might well be Yoshimoto's: "Never mind about me! This is an emergency! I don't need a lot of men around me. Chase an enemy who's come here to give you his head. Kill Nobunaga! Instead of protecting me, fight!" He was, after all, the commander of three armies and grasped the situation faster than anyone else. Now he was angry with the worthless commanders and warriors who ran aimlessly around him, shouting unintelligibly.

Chastened, several of the soldiers went plodding up the muddy road. When they had passed Jinnai's hiding place, he lifted the soaked curtain with the tip of his spear to make sure the man was indeed Yoshimoto.

Yoshimoto was no longer there. The enclosure was empty. A large wooden bowl of rice had been overturned, and the white grains of rice were lying sodden in the rainwater. Other than that, there were only the embers of four or five sticks of smoldering firewood.

Jinnai could see that Yoshimoto had left quickly with only a few men, so now he went from enclosure to enclosure, looking for him. Most of the curtains had either been torn and had collapsed, or were stained with blood and trampled.

Yoshimoto must be trying to escape. Certainly he was not going to flee on foot. And if this was so, he must have hurried to wherever the horses were tethered. In a camp filled with so many curtains and fighting soldiers, however, it was not going to be easy to find out where the enemy kept the horses. And the horses were not just grazing quietly. Amid the rain, the clashing of swords, and the blood, the horses had panicked and several of them were galloping wildly around the camp.

Where could he be hiding? Jinnai stood holding his spear, letting the rainwater run down the bridge of his nose and into his parched throat. Suddenly a warrior who hadn't recognized him as the enemy was yanking an excited gray horse right in front of him.

Red tassels hung from a mother-of-pearl saddle with a gold-flecked lacquer border; purple and white reins were attached to a silver bit. This must be the steed of a general. Jinnai watched as the horse was led into a dark stand of pine trees. Inside the stand, a curtained enclosure had mostly collapsed, but the part that still stood flapped wildly in the wind and rain.

Jinnai leaped forward and lifted the curtain. There was Yoshimoto. A retainer had just told him that his horse was ready, and Yoshimoto was about to step outside.

"Lord of Suruga, my name is Kuwabara Jinnai. I fight for the Oda clan. I've come to take your head. Prepare to die!" Jinnai thrust at Yoshimoto's back as he called out his name, and the clash of spear and armor resounded in their ears. In a flash, Yoshimoto turned, and his sword split the shaft in half. Jinnai jumped back with a yell, only four feet of the shaft left in his hands.

Jinnai tossed the shaft away and screamed, "Coward! Would you show your back to an adversary who has identified himself?"

Unsheathing his sword, Jinnai leaped toward Yoshimoto, only to be grabbed from behind by an Imagawa warrior. Throwing the man easily to the ground, he was attacked from the side by yet another enemy warrior. He tried to dodge the blow, but the first soldier had grabbed his ankle and prevented him from moving fast enough. The second soldier's sword cut Jinnai neatly in two.

"My lord! Please leave right away! Our men are confused and unable to control the enemy. A retreat is regrettable, but it's only for the present." The soldier's face was smeared with blood. The other soldier, completely covered with mud, jumped up, and the two of them urged Yoshimoto to leave.

"Now! Quickly! My lord!"

But then...

"I have come to see the great Yoshimoto. My name is Hattori Koheita, and I am in the service of Lord Nobunaga." A huge man stood before them, an iron helmet with black braiding pulled over his eyebrows. Yoshimoto retreated a step as the man's large, red-shafted spear struck out with a whir.

The first soldier intercepted the thrust with his body and fell, pierced through, before he had time to swing his sword. The other man quickly jumped in the way, but he, too, was skewered by Koheita's spear, and crumpled onto his comrade's corpse.

"Wait! Where are you going!" The lightning-quick spear pursued Yoshimoto, who was now circling the trunk of a pine tree.

"Here I am!" His sword poised to strike, Yoshimoto glared fixedly at Koheita. Koheita's spear jabbed out and struck the side of Yoshimoto's armor. But the armor was well tempered, and the wound was not deep, leaving Yoshimoto undaunted.

"Knave!" Yoshimoto yelled and sliced through the spear.

Koheita was resolute. Tossing away the shaft, he leaped forward. But Yoshimoto dropped to his knees and swung at Koheita's leg with his sword. His blade was an excellent one. Sparks flew from the chain-mail shin guard, and Koheita's kneecap was split open like a pomegranate, his shinbone protruding from the wound. Koheita fell backwards, and Yoshimoto fell forward, his crested helmet striking the ground.

Just as Yoshimoto raised his head, a man cried out, "I am Mori Shinsuke!"

Mori grabbed Yoshimoto's head from behind and the two men tumbled to the ground. As they grappled, Yoshimoto's breastplate was pulled forward, and blood spurted from the spear wound he had just received. Pinned underneath, Yoshimoto bit through the index finger of Mori's right hand. Even after his head had been cut off, Mori's white finger was still protruding from Yoshimoto's purple lips and elegantly blackened teeth.

* * *

Had they won or lost, Tokichiro asked himself, breathing hard.

"Hey! Where are we?" he yelled to anybody who might be within earshot, but nobody knew exactly where they were. Only about half of his men were still alive, and they were all in a daze.

The rain had let up and the wind had abated. The intense rays of the sun spilled through the scattering clouds. When the storm had spent itself, the hell of Dengaku-hazama faded away with the retreating lightning, and now nothing remained but the cries of the cicadas.

"Line up!" Tokichiro ordered.

The soldiers lined up as best they could. Counting his men, Tokichiro found that his command had been reduced from thirty to seventeen, four of whom he did not recognize at all.

"Whose unit are you from?" he asked one of the men.

"Toyama Jintaro's, sir. But when we were fighting at the western edge of the hill, I slipped over the bluff and lost my unit. Then I found your men chasing the enemy, so I fell in with them."

"All right. What about you?"

"It's the same with me, sir. I thought I was fighting alongside my own comrades, but when I looked around, I was here in Your Honor's group."

Tokichiro did not bother to question the others. It was probable that some of his men had been killed in battle, while others had got mixed up with other units. But it wasn't just the individual soldiers who had lost their bearings in the middle of the battle. Toki-chiro's unit had become separated from the main body of the army and Mataemon's reg-iment, and he had no idea where he was.

"It looks like the battle is over," Tokichiro muttered as he led his men back the way they had come.

The muddy water running from the surrounding mountains into the marsh had in-creased since the sky had cleared. When he saw how many corpses were lying in the streams and piled up on the slopes, Tokichiro was filled with a sense of wonder that he was still alive.

"We must have won. Look! All the dead around here are Imagawa samurai." Toki-chiro pointed here and there. From the way the enemy corpses were sprawled along the road, he could see the route the defeated army had taken.

His men, however, just grunted in their stupefied state, and were too tired even to sing a victory song.

They were only a few and they were lost. The battlefield was suddenly very quiet, and this could mean that Nobunaga's army had been completely wiped out. The fear that they might be surrounded by the enemy and massacred at any moment was very real.

Then they heard it. From Dengakuhazama rose three victory cheers that were loud enough to shake heaven and earth. Shouts in their own Owari dialect.

"We won! We won! Let's go!" Tokichiro ran ahead. The soldiers, who up until now had been barely conscious, somehow recovered completely. Not wanting to be left behind, they stumbled and tripped after Tokichiro toward the cheering.

Magomeyama was a low, circular hill a little beyond Dengakuhazama. A black mass of soldiers stained with blood, mud, and rain now covered the area from the hill to the village. The battle was over and the men had regrouped. The rain had stopped, the sun had come out, and now a hazy white steam rose from the closely packed assembly.

"Where's Master Asano's regiment?" Threading his way through the mass of warriors, Tokichiro rejoined his original regiment. Wherever he turned, he bumped and scraped someone's bloody armor. Although he had fully intended to fight bravely, he now felt ashamed. Certainly he had done nothing to make people notice him.

When he found his regiment and stood among the press of soldiers, he finally realized that they had won. Looking out from the hill, it struck him as odd that the vanquished enemy was nowhere to be seen.

Still spattered with mud and blood, Nobunaga stood on the hillock. Just a few steps from his camp stool, a number of soldiers were digging a large hole. Each of the enemy heads was inspected and then tossed into the hole. Nobunaga looked on, his palms pressed together, while the warriors around him stood by in silence.

No one said a prayer. But this was the highest etiquette followed when warriors buried fellow warriors. The heads buried in the hole would serve as a lesson to those who were alive and would fight again. Even the head of the most insignificant enemy was treated with the utmost solemnity.

With the mysterious boundary between life and death at his very feet, a samurai could not help thinking about what it meant to live as a warrior. Everyone stood reverently, hands joined in prayer. When the hole had been filled in and a mound built over it, they looked up to a beautiful rainbow that arched across a clear sky.

As the men stood looking at this scene, a party of scouts who had been reconnoitering the area around Odaka pulled into camp.

Tokugawa Ieyasu commanded Yoshimoto's vanguard in Odaka. Considering the skill with which Ieyasu had demolished the fortresses of Washizu and Marune, Nobunaga could not afford to underestimate him.

"When the Tokugawa heard that Yoshimoto had been killed, the camp at Odaka seemed to have panicked. They sent out scouts a number of times, however, and as they learned the facts, they quickly calmed down. At this point they are preparing to retreat to Mikawa by nightfall, and they don't seem to be inclined to fight."

Nobunaga listened to the reports and, in his own way, announced their triumphal return. "Well, then," he said, "let's go home."

The sun had still not set, and now the rainbow, which had begun to fade, stood out clearly once again. A single head was fastened to the side of Nobunaga's saddle, as a memento. It was, of course, the head of the great Imagawa Yoshimoto.

When they reached the gate of Atsuta Shrine, Nobunaga swung off his horse and went into the sanctum, while his officers and men pressed in as far as the central gate and prostrated themselves. A hand bell was ringing somewhere in the distance, and bonfires filled the forest of the shrine with a red glow.

Nobunaga presented a sacred horse to the shrine stable. This done, he was once again ready to hurry on his way. His armor had become increasingly heavy, and he was exhausted. Leaving the moonlit path to his horse, however, his spirits seemed as light as if he were wearing a thin summer kimono.

Compared with Atsuta, Kiyosu was in an uproar. Every door was festooned with lanterns, bonfires burned at the crossroads, and old folks, children, and even young girls stood excitedly in the streets, looking at the triumphant soldiers and shouting their congratulations.

Dense crowds pushed together at the roadside. Women watched to see if their husbands were among the men marching solemnly toward the castle gate. Old people called out their sons' names, and girls searched for the faces of their sweethearts. But all of them raised a cheer when they caught sight of the mounted Nobunaga, silhouetted against the night sky.

"Lord Nobunaga!"

Nobunaga meant more to them than their own children, husbands, and lovers.

"Take a look at the head of the great lord of the Imagawa!" Nobunaga announced to the crowd from horseback. "This is the souvenir I have brought back for you. From tomorrow on, the troubles at the border will be over. Be diligent and work hard. Work hard and enjoy yourselves!"

Once inside the castle, Nobunaga called for his lady-in-waiting, "Sai! Sai! Before anything else, a bath! And some rice gruel."

As he emerged from his bath, he proclaimed the rewards for more than one hundred twenty men who had fought in the battle that day. Even the deeds of the lowest-ranking soldiers had not escaped Nobunaga's eyes. Last of all he said, "Inuchiyo is granted permission to return." This news was transmitted to Inuchiyo that very night, for when the entire army had entered the castle gates, he alone had stopped outside, waiting for word from Nobunaga.

Tokichiro received no praise whatsoever. And, of course, he expected none. Nevertheless, he had received something far more precious than a stipend of a thousand *kan*: for the first time in his life, he had straddled the line between life and death, he had lived through a battle, and he had seen firsthand Nobunaga's grasp of human nature and his great capacity for leadership.

I have a good master, he thought. I'm the luckiest man alive, after Lord Nobunaga. From that time on, Tokichiro did not just look up to Nobunaga as his lord and master. He became Nobunaga's apprentice, studying his master's strong points and concentrating his whole mind on the task of improving himself.

The Go-Between

For the last five or six days, Tokichiro had been truly bored. He had been ordered to accompany Nobunaga on a secret journey to a distant province and to make preparations for the trip. They were to leave within ten days, and until then he was to stay indoors. Tokichiro sat around and waited.

He sat up and thought how strange it was for Nobunaga to be setting out on a journey. Where were they going?

Gazing at the tendrils of the morning glories on the fence, he suddenly thought of Nene. He had been ordered to go out as little as possible, but when the evening breeze picked up, he passed by the front of Nene's house. For some reason he had been hesitant to visit there recently, and whenever he met her parents, they looked right through him. So he simply walked past the house like any other passerby and returned home.

The morning glories were blooming also on the fence of Nene's house. The evening before, he had gotten a glimpse of her lighting a lamp, and had returned home as though he had achieved his purpose. Now he suddenly recalled that her profile had been whiter than the flowers on the fence.

The smoke from the firewood wafted through the house from the kitchen. Tokichiro bathed, put on a light hempen kimono, and, slipping on a pair of sandals, walked out through the garden gate. Just then a young messenger hailed him, handed him an official summons. Tokichiro hurried back inside, changed quickly, and hurried to the residence of Hayashi Sado.

Sado handed him his orders in person:

Be at the residence of the farmer Doke Seijuro, on the western highway outside Kiyosu, by the Hour of the Rabbit.

That was all. Nobunaga was traveling to a distant province incognito, and Tokichiro was one of his attendants. When he thought about it, he thought he understood Nobunaga's plans, even though he knew so little about them.

He realized that he would be separated from Nene for some time, and the desire to catch just a glimpse of her under the summer moon, there and then, welled up in his chest. It was his nature that nothing could stop him once he got an idea into his head. Tokichiro was a child of passion, and the uncontrollable passions and desires that dwelt in his heart dragged him to Nene's house. Then, just like a delinquent boy who peeps into lighted windows, Tokichiro peeked in from outside the fence.

Mataemon lived in the archers' district, and almost all of the people who passed through the neighborhood knew one another. Tokichiro was conscious of the footsteps of the passersby and was terrified that he was going to be discovered by Nene's parents. This cowardly spectacle was laughable. If Tokichiro himself had seen someone acting like this, he would have despised the man. But at that moment he did not have time to reflect on a man's dignity or reputation.

He would have been satisfied with a single glimpse through the fence of her profile and of whatever she was doing that evening. I'll bet she's already taken her bath and is putting on her makeup, he thought. Or could she be with her parents eating dinner?

Three times he went back and forth, trying to look as innocent as possible. It was evening, so few people were on the street. It would have been horribly embarrassing if somebody had called out his name just as he was peeping through the fence. No, worse than that, it could ruin the slim chance he had of marrying Nene. After all, his rival Inuchiyo had withdrawn from the competition, and after that, Mataemon had started to reconsider. For now, he should let things be. It seemed as though both Nene and her mother had made up their minds, but her father would not come to a decision so easily.

The smoke from the mosquito incense wafted by. The sound of someone putting out dishes came from the kitchen. It seemed that the evening meal had not yet been served. She's working hard, Tokichiro imagined. In the dim light of the kitchen, Tokichiro finally saw the woman he had determined would become his wife. The thought occurred to him that a woman like Nene would manage her household well.

Her mother called, and Nene's answer rang in his ears, even though he was crouching outside the fence, looking in. Tokichiro stepped aside. Somebody was coming up the street.

She works hard and she's gentle. Surely my mother would be happy with her. And Nene wouldn't mistreat my mother just because she's a farm woman. His love was transformed into lofty thoughts right through his passion. We'll endure poverty. We won't be caught by vanity. She'll help me from behind the scenes, look after me with devotion, and excuse my faults.

She was absolutely lovely. No one but this woman was going to be his wife; he was convinced of this. And with these thoughts his chest swelled and his heart beat powerfully. Looking up at the stars, he let out a deep sigh. When he finally came to himself, he realized that he had walked once around the block and was standing in front of Nene's house once again. Suddenly he heard Nene's voice just inside the fence, and as he looked through the tendrils of the morning glories, he saw her white face.

She even carries water like a servant. And with those hands that play the *koto*. Tokichiro wanted to show his mother that his wife would be this kind of woman. The sooner the better. He could not get enough of looking through the fence. He could hear the sound of water being scooped up, but suddenly Nene turned in his direction without drawing up the bucket. She must have seen me, he thought, panicked. Just as this crossed his mind, Nene left the well and started to walk toward the rear gate. Tokichiro felt a heat in his chest so intense that it might have been fire.

When she opened the gate and looked around, Tokichiro was already running away without looking back. As he reached the corner at the first crossroads, he turned around. She stood outside the gate, with a puzzled look on her pale face. Tokichiro wondered if she wasn't angry with him, but at the same time he began to think about his departure the following morning. He was accompanying Lord Nobunaga, and he had been forbidden from saying anything about the trip to others. This included Nene. Having caught a glimpse of her and knowing she was well, Tokichiro was his old self again, and he went home at full speed. When he fell asleep, his dreams were free from preoccupation.

Gonzo woke his master earlier than usual. Tokichiro splashed his face with water, ate his morning meal, and prepared himself for the trip.

"I'm off!" he announced, but did not tell his servant where he was going. And, a little before the agreed time, he arrived at Doke Seijuro's house.

"Hey, Monkey! Are you going today too?" asked a country samurai standing at Seijuro's gate.

"Inuchiyo!" Tokichiro looked at his friend with surprise. It was not just that he was surprised that Inuchiyo was coming, but that his appearance had been transformed; from the way he tied his hair right down to his leggings, Inuchiyo was dressed like a samurai right out of the backwoods.

"What is it all about?" Tokichiro asked.

"Everybody's already here. Hurry on in."

"What about you?"

"Me? I've been appointed gatekeeper for a while. I'll join you later."

Tokichiro lingered in the garden just inside the gate. For a moment he didn't know which path to take. Doke Seijuro's dwelling was an unusual old house, even to Tokichiro's eyes. He couldn't tell exactly how old it was. It seemed to be left over from an earlier age, when whole families had lived together in one large enclosure. A long, multiroomed house, smaller outhouses, gates within gates, and countless paths covered the entire grounds.

"Monkey! Over here!" Another country samurai was beckoning to him from a gate near the garden. He recognized the man as Ikeda Shonyu. Entering the garden, he found twenty or so retainers dressed up as country samurai. Tokichiro had also been informed of this plan, and he looked the most countrified of all.

A group of seventeen or eighteen mountain ascetics were resting around the edges of the courtyard. They, too, were disguised Oda samurai. Nobunaga seemed to be in a small room on the far side of the courtyard. Naturally, he too was in disguise.

Tokichiro and the others were relaxed. No one asked any questions. No one knew. But they speculated.

"His Lordship is disguised as the son of a country samurai traveling with a few retainers. He's waiting for all of his attendants to arrive. He's probably going to a distant province, but I wonder if anyone knows where we're really going?"

"I haven't heard much, but when I was called to Hayashi Sado's residence, I overheard someone say something about the capital."

"The capital?" and everyone gulped.

Nothing could be more dangerous, and Nobunaga must have some secret plan in mind if he was going there. Unobserved by the others, Tokichiro nodded in agreement and went out into the vegetable garden.

A few days later, the group of country samurai that would accompany Nobunaga and the company of mountain ascetics, who would guard him at a distance, set out for the capital.

The first group posed as country samurai from the eastern provinces, who were going on a sightseeing trip to Kyoto. The men looked relaxed as they walked. They hid the fierce light that had shone in their eyes at Okehazama, and took on the rough looks and slow speech of those they pretended to be.

Their lodgings had been arranged by Doke in a house on the outskirts of the capital. When he walked around Kyoto, Nobunaga always had the brim of his hat pulled down over his eyes, and he was dressed like a simple provincial. His attendants numbered four or five men at the most. If assassins had known who he was, he would have made an easy target.

There were days when he would let himself go completely and walk all day among the crowds and dust of Kyoto. And there were evenings when he would suddenly leave at some inopportune hour to call upon the mansions of courtiers and hold secret talks.

The young samurai understood neither the motives of these actions nor why he dared to take on this venture in the dangerous tumult of a country at war with itself. Tokichiro, of course, had no reason to understand such circumstances either. But he himself used the time for observation. The capital has changed, he thought. During the time he had wandered the country selling needles, he had often come here to buy supplies. Counting on his fingers, he figured it had only been about six or seven years before, but the conditions around the Imperial Palace had changed remarkably.

The shogunate still existed, but Ashikaga Yoshiteru, the thirteenth shogun, held the office in name only. Like the water in a deep pool, the culture and morale of the people stagnated. Everything had the feel of the end of an era. The real authority rested in the hands of his vice-governor-general, Miyoshi Nagayoshi, but he in turn had abdicated control in almost all areas to one of his retainers, Matsunaga Hisahide. This resulted in unsightly dissension and in an inefficient and tyrannical administration. The gossip of the common people was that Mastunaga's rule would soon collapse of its own accord.

What was the trend of the times? Nobody knew. The lights burned brightly every night, but the people were lost in the darkness. Tomorrow is tomorrow, they thought, and a directionless, helpless current flowed through their lives like a muddy stream.

If the administration of Miyoshi and Matsunaga was considered unreliable, what about those provincial governors who had been appointed by the shogun? Men like Akamatsu, Toki, Kyogoku, Hosokawa, Uesugi, and Shiba all faced similar problems in their own provinces.

It was just at this point that Nobunaga made his secret trip to the capital. This was something that no other provincial warlord had dreamed of doing. Imagawa Yoshimoto had marched on Kyoto at the head of a great army. His ambition—to be granted an imperial mandate, and thereby control the shogun and rule the country—was cut off halfway, but he was only the first to try. Every other great lord in the country considered Imagawa's plans to be the best. But only Nobunaga was bold enough to travel to Kyoto alone and prepare for the future.

After several meetings with Miyoshi Nagayoshi, Nobunaga finally secured an interview with Shogun Yoshiteru. Naturally he went to the Miyoshi mansion in his usual disguise, changed into formal dress, and went to the shogun's palace.

The shogunal dwelling was a luxurious palace gone to ruin. The luxury and wealth that had been created and then exhausted by thirteen successive shoguns was now nothing more than a half-remembered dream. All that remained was a self-serving and self-important administration.

"So you are Nobuhide's son, Nobunaga?" Yoshiteru said. There was no strength in his voice. His manners were perfect, but there was no life in them.

Nobunaga quickly perceived that there was no longer any vigor left in the office of shogun. Prostrating himself, he asked for the favor of Yoshiteru's acquaintance. But in the voice of the bowing man, there was a strength that overwhelmed his superior.

"I came to Kyoto incognito this time. I doubt if any of these local products from Owari will please the eye of a person from the capital." Presenting Yoshiteru with a list of gifts, he started to back away.

"Perhaps you would favor me by staying for dinner," Yoshiteru said.

Sake was served. From the banquet room they could view an elegant garden. In the evening darkness, the color of hydrangeas and the dew on the damp moss glittered in the lamplight.

Nobunaga's character was not one of strict formality, regardless of the company and the situation. He behaved without reserve when the *sake* flasks were reverently brought in and when the meal was served in a fastidiously traditional manner.

Yoshiteru gazed at his guest as though his appetite were a wonderful thing. Although weary of luxury and formality, he saw it as a point of pride that every dish that was served at his table was a delicacy from the capital.

"Nobunaga, how do you find Kyoto cooking?"

"It's excellent…"

"How's the flavor?"

"Well, the flavor of the cooking of the capital is pretty subtle. Food this insipid is rare for me."

"Is that so? Do you follow the Way of Tea?"

"I've drunk tea in the same way I've drunk water ever since I was a boy, but I'm unacquainted with the way experts practice the tea ceremony."

"Did you view the garden?"

"Yes, I saw it."

"What did you think?"

"I thought it was rather small."

"Small?"

"It's very pretty, but when I compare it with the view of the hills of Kiyosu…"

"You don't seem to understand anything at all." The shogun laughed again. "But it's better to be ignorant than have only a smattering of knowledge. Well, then, what do you have a taste for?"

"Archery. Beyond that, I have no special talents. But if you would hear something extraordinary, I was able to rush here to your very gates in three days, passing through enemy territory on the Mino-Omi road from Owari. Now that the entire country is in chaos, there's always the possibility that an incident may occur in or near the palace. I would be very thankful if you would keep me in mind," he said with a smile.

Originally it had been Nobunaga who had taken advantage of the national chaos and overthrown the Shiba governor of Owari who had been appointed by the shogun.

And, even though the matter was reviewed in the High Court of the shogun as a show of the administration's outrage and authority, this was really only a matter of form. But recently the provincial governors rarely came to visit Kyoto, and the shogun felt isolated. His boredom was relieved by Nobunaga's call, and he seemed to be anxious to talk.

Yoshiteru might have expected hints of a desire for official promotion or court rank during this talk, but none came, and finally Nobunaga cheerfully took his leave.

"Let's go home," Nobunaga said, announcing their return after a thirty-day stay in the capital. "Tomorrow," he quickly added. As the attendants in disguise as country samurai and ascetics, who had lodged separately, now busily prepared to start off on the journey home, a messenger delivered a warning from Owari.

Rumors have been spread since your departure from Kiyosu. When you go back, use extreme prudence, and please be prepared against some mishap on the road.

Whichever way they went, they were going to have to go through one enemy province after another. What road could they take safely? Perhaps they should return by ship.

Nobunaga's attendants gathered that night in the house where he had been staying and discussed the matter, but were not able to come to an agreement. Suddenly, Ikeda Shonyu came out unceremoniously from the direction of Nobunaga's room and stared at them. "You gentlemen still haven't gone to bed?"

One of the men looked at him with an irritated expression. "We're discussing something important."

"I didn't know you were in the middle of a conference. What in the world are you talking about?"

"You're pretty carefree for one of His Lordship's attendants. Don't you know about the message that came by courier this evening?"

"I heard."

"It's most important that nothing happen on the way home. We're just now banging our heads together trying to figure out which road we should take."

"Your worry is all for nothing. His Lordship has already decided."

"What? He's decided?"

"When we came to the capital, there were too many people, so he felt as though we stood out. His plan for going home is that four or five people will be enough. The retainers can go home separately, taking any road they like."

Nobunaga left the capital before sunrise. And just as Shonyu had said, twenty or thirty of the men disguised as mountain ascetics, and most of the country samurai, were left behind. Only four men accompanied him. Shonyu was among them, of course, but the one who felt most honored about being chosen for this small group was Tokichiro.

"He's rather unprotected."

"Do you suppose he's all right?"

The group of retainers that had been left behind was uneasy, and followed Nobunaga as far as Otsu, but at that point Nobunaga and his men hired horses and went east over the bridge at Seta. There were a number of checkpoints, but he passed through without difficulty. Nobunaga had asked for a letter of safe conduct from Miyoshi Nagayoshi that stated he was traveling under the protection of the governor-general. At every barrier they came to, he would show the letter and pass on.

* * *

The Way of Tea had become widespread across the country. In a violent and bloody world, people sought peace and a quiet place where they might find a brief respite from the noise and confusion. Tea was the elegant boundary where peace contrasted with action, and perhaps it was not so strange that its most devoted followers were the samurai, whose daily lives were soaked in blood.

Nene had learned the Way of Tea. Her father, whom she loved dearly, also drank tea, so this made it quite different from playing the *koto*, displaying her talent just to the people who happened to pass by the house.

There was inducement for making tea in the peace of the morning, in her father's genial smile, and in the act of whisking the hot green froth in a bowl of black Seto ware. As such, this was not just a game but a part of her daily life.

"There's a rather heavy dew in the garden, isn't there? And the chrysanthemum buds are still hard." Mataemon looked out into the tiny enclosed area from his open veranda. Nene, who was busy in front of the hearth, tea ladle in hand, did not answer. The boiling water that she ladled from the kettle fell into the tea bowl as though from a spring, cheerfully infringing on the loneliness of the room. She smiled and looked away.

"No, two or three of the chrysanthemums outside are already quite fragrant."

"Really? They've already bloomed? I didn't notice when I took the broom out and swept this morning. It seems a shame that flowers should have to bloom under the roof of the house of a provincial warrior."

The bamboo whisk poised in Nene's fingers made a crisp sound as she whisked the tea. She was embarrassed by her father's words, but Mataemon did not notice. Taking the tea bowl and raising it reverently to his lips, he drank the frothy green tea. His face showed that he was enjoying the morning. But suddenly his thoughts changed: If my daughter goes to live somewhere else, I won't be drinking tea like this anymore.

"Excuse me." A voice came from behind the sliding doors.

"Okoi?" As his wife came into the room, Mataemon handed the tea bowl to Nene.

"Shall Nene prepare tea for you, too?"

"No, I'll have some later."

Okoi was carrying a letter case, and a messenger was waiting at the entrance. Mataemon put the letter case on his lap and opened the lid. A dubious look crossed his face. "His Lordship's cousin. It's from Lord Nagoya. What can it be?" Mataemon suddenly stood up, washed his hands, and then took the letter again reverently. Even though it was only a letter, it was from a member of Lord Nobunaga's family, and Mataemon behaved as if he were standing in front of the man himself.

"Is the messenger waiting?"

"Yes, but he said that a verbal response would be fine."

"No, no. That would be impolite. Bring me the inkstone."

Mataemon put brush to paper and handed his reply to the messenger. Okoi, however, felt uneasy about its contents. It was extremely unusual for a letter from Lord Nobunaga's cousin to be sent to the house of this lowly retainer. And this one had come directly by messenger.

"What can it be about?" she asked. Even Mataemon did not know because the letter contained nothing more than pleasantries. He could find nothing that might pass as a secret message or have meaning read into it beyond what it seemed to say.

Today I'm spending the entire day reading at my country retreat at Horikawazoi. I lament the fact that no one comes on such a pleasant day to enjoy the fragrance of the chrysanthemums I have raised. If you have some leisure, please come by to see me.

There was nothing more, but there must have been something more to it than this. If Mataemon had been particularly practiced at tea, an admirable reader, or a man of exceptional taste, the invitation might have been natural. But in fact he had not noticed the chrysanthemums blooming on his own fence. He was quick to notice dust on a bow, but otherwise he was the kind of man who would happily trample chrysanthemums underfoot.

"I'll go anyway. Okoi, put out my best clothes."

Standing in the bright autumn sunlight, Mataemon turned once to look at his house. Nene and Okoi had come out as far as the gate. His heart was strangely at peace, thankful that there were days like this, even in this world of chaos. He smiled at the thought and noticed that Nene and Okoi were also smiling. He turned briskly and walked away. Neighbors called to him, and he answered them as he walked by. The archers' houses were small and poor. The many children that always accompany poverty were also in abundance in the tenements, and through the fences at every house he could see diapers hung out to dry.

Now maybe we'll have a grandchild's diapers like that in our own yard. Such thoughts naturally came to him, but they were not especially comforting to Mataemon. He was not all that pleased with the idea that someday he was going to be called "grandpa." Before that happened, he planned on making a name for himself. He had striven not to be left behind at Dengakuhazama, and he had certainly not given up the hope of heading the list of meritorious warriors in future battles. While in the midst of these thoughts, he found himself before Lord Nagoya's elegant villa.

The building had formerly been a small temple, but Nagoya had had it remodeled as a country villa.

Nagoya was exceedingly pleased with his prompt visit. "Thank you for coming. This year we've had a number of military disturbances, but I did manage to plant some chrysanthemums. Perhaps later you could do me the honor of looking at them."

Mataemon was treated graciously, but because his host was one of Nobunaga's close relatives, he sat at a respectful distance and bowed low.

What was the purpose of this? Mataemon wondered a little anxiously.

"Mataemon, make yourself more comfortable. Get yourself a cushion. You can see the chrysanthemums from here as well. Looking at chrysanthemums is not just looking at flowers, you know, it's looking at a man's work. But showing them to others is not a matter of boasting, it's sharing the pleasure, and enjoying another person's appreciation. Smelling the fragrance of chrysanthemums under a beautiful sky like this is another of His Lordship's favors."

"Most certainly, my lord."

"That we are blessed with a wise lord is something we've become acutely aware of recently. I'm sure none of us will ever be able to forget the appearance of Lord Nobunaga at Okehazama."

"With respect, my lord, he did not seem to be human, but an incarnation of the god of war."

"Nevertheless, we all did well together, didn't we? You're in the archers' regiment, but that day you were among the spearmen, weren't you?"

"That's correct, my lord."

"Were you in the attack on the Imagawa headquarters?"

"When we finally rushed the hill, the action was so confused that we could hardly tell friend from foe. But in the midst of it I heard Mori Shinsuke announce that he had taken the lord of Suruga's head."

"Was a man by the name of Kinoshita Tokichiro in your regiment?"

"He was indeed, my lord."

"What about Maeda Inuchiyo?"

"He had received His Lordship's displeasure, but was given permission to join the battle. I haven't seen him since we returned from Okehazama, but hasn't he returned to his former post?"

"He has. You probably still don't know about this, but he just recently accompanied His Lordship to Kyoto. They have returned to the castle, and Inuchiyo is in service there now."

"Kyoto! Why did His Lordship go there?"

"There's no harm in talking about it now. He went with only thirty or forty men, and he himself was disguised as a country samurai on a pilgrimage. They were gone about forty days. His retainers acted as though he were here during that time. Shall we have a look at the chrysanthemum garden?"

Mataemon followed his host into the garden as though he were a servant. Nagoya spoke of the finer points of growing chrysanthemums, and how one had to use the same care and love as in raising a child.

"I've heard you have a daughter. She's called Nene, isn't she? I would like to help you find a son-in-law."

"My lord?" Mataemon bowed almost in half. Yet he hesitated momentarily. The subject recalled to him his own confusion. Nagoya ignored his vacillation, however, and went on, "I know someone who would make an excellent son-in-law. Leave it to me. I'll handle this."

"My family is really unworthy of this honor, my lord."

"You should talk it over with your wife. The man I have in mind for your son-in-law is Kinoshita Tokichiro. You know him well, I believe."

"Yes, my lord," Mataemon answered without thinking. He reproached himself for being so ill-bred as to sound surprised, but he was unable to stop himself.

"I'll wait for your answer."

"Yes...indeed..." With that, Mataemon took his leave.

He had wanted to ask more than a few questions about the reason for this interview, but could not be so openly inquisitive with a member of Lord Nobunaga's family. When he arrived home, Mataemon related what happened, and his wife seemed troubled that he had come home without giving a prompt reply.

"You should accept his request," she said. "I think this is really good news. Relationships are always a matter of timing, and the fact that Tokichiro has spoken with Nene so many times shows they had strong connections in a previous life. Tokichiro must have some merit for a relative of His Lordship to act as his go-between. Please go tomorrow and give Lord Nagoya your answer."

"But don't you think I should ask Nene how she feels?"

"Hasn't she already spoken out about that?" Okoi asked.

"Well, I wonder if she still feels the same way."

"Nene is not very talkative, but once she's made up her mind, she doesn't often change it."

Alone, Mataemon wrestled with his worries for the future, and felt the awkwardness of being tossed aside. So at a time when they thought that Tokichiro might have been forgotten, having not shown his face there at all, he once again featured largely in the thoughts of Mataemon, his wife, and Nene.

The next day Mataemon quickly went off to deliver an answer to Lord Nagoya. As soon as he returned, he spoke to his wife. "Well, there was rather unexpected news." His wife immediately saw from his expression that this was something exceptional. As her husband told her about his meeting with Nagoya, the bright light that now shone on Nene's situation was manifest in both of their smiles.

"I had made up my mind today to ask Lord Nagoya why he had offered to be a go-between, but to ask this of a member of His Lordship's family was really difficult. Just as I was trying my best to be polite, he mentioned that Inuchiyo had asked him."

"Inuchiyo asked Lord Nagoya?" exclaimed his wife. "Are you saying that he suggested that Nene and Tokichiro get married?"

"It seems as though there was some talk on the road when His Lordship made his secret trip to Kyoto. Well, I suppose His Lordship overheard it."

"My! His Lordship himself?"

"Yes, this is really quite extraordinary. It seems that during the long hours of the trip, Inuchiyo and Tokichiro were talking about Nene quite openly, right in front of His Lordship."

"Has Master Inuchiyo given his consent?"

"Inuchiyo went to Lord Nagoya and made the same request, so we won't have to worry about him anymore."

"Well then, did you give a clear answer to Lord Nagoya today?"

"Yes, I told him that I placed the matter entirely in his hands." With that, Mataemon straightened up as though his worries had been completely cleared away.

* * *

The year passed, and on an auspicious day in the fall, the wedding was celebrated at the Asano home.

Tokichiro felt restless and fidgety. His household was in confusion, with Gonzo, the servant girl, and the others who had come to help, and he had been able to do nothing more than ramble in and out of the house since early morning. Today *is* the third day of the Eighth Month, isn't it? He kept confirming the obvious over and over in his mind. From time to time he would open up his clothes chest or try to relax on a cushion, but he just couldn't settle down. I'm marrying Nene and becoming a member of her family, he reminded himself. It's finally happening tonight, but now I somehow feel ill at ease.

After the wedding had been announced, Tokichiro became uncharacteristically shy. When his neighbors and colleagues heard the news, they came with gifts, but he would turn red and speak as though he were trying to save his reputation. "Well, no, it's really just a family celebration. I had thought it was still a little early for me to get married, but the family wants the wedding to take place as soon as possible."

Nobody knew that his desire had been turned into reality by his friend, Maeda Inuchiyo. Not only had Inuchiyo given up Nene, but he had also swayed Lord Nagoya into action.

"I heard that Lord Nagoya made a recommendation in his favor. On top of that, Asano Mataemon's given him his consent, so they must see some promise in Monkey somewhere." So, first with his colleagues, and then with people of both high and low estate, Tokichiro's reputation was enhanced by this marriage, and malicious gossip was held in check.

Tokichiro, however, was unconcerned with gossip, good or bad. To him, informing his mother in Nakamura was most important. Most assuredly, he had wanted to rush there himself and tell his mother about Nene, her lineage and character, along with all the other talk. But she had told him to serve his lord with diligence, and to let her stay in

Nakamura, and not to be distracted by her until he became a person of consequence.

He suppressed his desire to see her right away, and informed her of new developments by letter. And she often wrote in reply. What especially pleased Tokichiro was that the news of his gradual promotion and of his marriage to the daughter of a samurai, through the good offices of one of Nobunaga's cousins, was known in Nakamura. And as a result, he knew, his mother and sister were looked upon quite differently now by the villagers.

"Let me do your hair, sir?" Gonzo appeared with a box of combs and knelt beside him.

"What? I have to tie up my hair, too?"

"You're the bridegroom tonight, and you should have your hair done up properly."

When Gonzo had arranged his hair, Tokichiro went out into the garden.

White stars began to appear through the branches of the paulownia trees. The bridegroom was feeling sentimental tonight. Tokichiro was surrounded by great joy. Yet every time he encountered some happiness, he thought of his mother. Thus, there was a little sadness in his happiness. There's no end to our desires. After all, he consoled himself, there are people in the world without mothers.

Tokichiro immersed himself in the bathtub. Tonight he would be especially diligent washing the nape of his neck. When he had finished bathing, put on a light cotton kimono, and gone back into the house, he found it so full of people that it was difficult to tell whether it was his house or someone else's. Wondering why everyone was so busy, he looked once around the living room and the kitchen, and was finally reduced to sharing a corner of a room with the mosquitoes, and looking on as others worked.

Shrill voices gave out orders, and shrill voices responded.

"Arrange all of the bridegroom's personal accessories on top of his wardrobe."

"I've done that. His fan and pillbox are there, too."

There were all sorts of people running about. Whose wife was that? Whose husband over there? These people were not close relatives, but they all worked together harmoniously.

The bridegroom, who was still all alone in the corner, recalled the faces of these people and felt joy in the very depths of his heart. In one room, a boisterous old man was holding forth on the ancient customs and manners of adopting a son-in-law and taking a wife. "Are the groom's sandals worn out? Old sandals just won't do. He has to wear new ones to the bride's house. Then, tonight, the bride's father will sleep holding the sandals, and the bridegroom's feet will never leave the house."

An old lady piped up, "People have to have paper lanterns. You can't just walk to the bride's house carrying torches. Then the lanterns are handed over to the bride's family, and they put them in front of the house altar for three days and three nights." She spoke in a kindly way, as though the bridegroom were her own son.

About then, a messenger came to the house, carrying the ceremonial first letter from the bride to the groom. One of the wives stepped timidly through the crowd, carrying a lacquered letter box.

Tokichiro spoke from the veranda. "I'm over here."

"This is the first letter from the bride," the woman said. "And it's the custom that the bridegroom write something in return."

"What should I write?"

The woman giggled but gave him no instructions. Paper and a writing case were set down in front of him.

Perplexed, Tokichiro picked up the brush. He had never exactly exerted himself in literary matters. He had learned to write at the Komyo Temple, and when he had worked in the pottery shop, his calligraphy had at least been average, so he felt no humiliation about writing something in front of others. He was simply troubled about what to say. Finally he wrote:

On this pleasant night, the bridegroom, too, should come to talk.

He showed it to the housewife who had brought him the writing case.

"Is this all right?"

"It will do."

"You received a letter from your husband at your wedding, didn't you? Don't you remember what he wrote?"

"No," she replied.

He laughed. "When you yourself forget, it must not have been very important."

After that, the bridegroom was outfitted in a ceremonial kimono and given a fan.

The moon shone clearly in the early autumn evening sky, and torches burned brightly at the entrance gates. At the head of the procession was a riderless horse and two spearmen. Following these were three torchbearers, then the bridegroom himself, in new sandals.

There was no gorgeous wedding furniture such as inlaid chests, folding screens, or Chinese furniture, but there was one armor chest and a wardrobe box. For a samurai of that time who commanded thirty foot soldiers, he had nothing to be ashamed of. On the contrary, Tokichiro probably felt some secret pride. For if none of the people who had helped him this evening and who accompanied him now were relatives, neither had they been employed to do so. They had come and rejoiced in this wedding as though it were their own affair.

Bright lights danced at every gate of the tenements of the archers' neighborhood that evening, and all the gates were open. Bonfires burned here and there, and there were people carrying paper lanterns, waiting with the bride's household for the arrival of the groom. Holding their children, mothers waved, and good cheer shone on their faces, brightened by the lights and fires.

Just then, some children came running from the crossroads across the way.

"He's coming! He's coming!"

"The bridegroom is coming!"

The mother of the children called them over, gently reproaching them and calling them to her side. The moon bathed the road in a pale light. The children's announcement had acted as a herald, and from that point no one crossed the hushed street.

Two torchbearers turned the corner. Behind them walked the bridegroom. Bells had been attached to the trimmings on the horse, and as they swayed back and forth, the bells made little sounds like the chirping of crickets. The chest of armor and the two spears were borne by five attendants. It was not such a bad show for the neighborhood.

The bridegroom, Tokichiro, looked particularly admirable. He was a man of small stature, but his appearance would have been appropriate even without fine clothes. He wasn't so ugly as to cause gossip, nor did he appear to be a man whose intelligence had gone to his head. If one had asked the people who stood by their fences and gates what kind of man he was, they would all probably have said that he was an ordinary fellow, and a fitting husband for Nene.

"Welcome, welcome."

"Let the bridegroom in!"

"Congratulations!"

The relatives and family waiting near the gate of Mataemon's house greeted Tokichiro, their features momentarily brightening in the flickering light.

"Please come in." The bridegroom was led by himself to a separate room. Tokichiro sat down alone. It was a small house, with no more than six or seven rooms. The helpers were just on the other side of the sliding door. The kitchen was just across the narrow garden, and he could hear the sounds of dishes being washed, and the smell of cooking wafted toward him.

Tokichiro hadn't noticed it so much as he was walking through the streets, but now that he was sitting down, he could hear the beating of his own heart, and his mouth felt dry. He sat alone in the room, almost as though he had been forgotten. Still, it would not be proper for him to breach decorum, so he resolved to sit there in a dignified manner whether anyone saw him or not.

Happily, Tokichiro was rarely bored. Certainly, as a bridegroom who was soon to meet his bride, there was no reason to be bored at all. But even so, at some point he forgot all about the wedding and diverted himself with an unrelated reverie for the while. His mind flew off to an absurd direction for the present: Okazaki Castle. What developments were going on there? Recently this had occupied his thoughts more than anything else. Rather than wondering about how his new bride would speak to him on the following morning and how she would appear when she greeted him, his mind was caught up by these things.

Would Okazaki Castle side with the Imagawa? Would it ally itself with the Oda clan? Once again, the forked road of fate. Last year, following the Imagawa clan's terrible defeat at Okehazama, the Tokugawa clan looked at three different possibilities. Should they continue to support the Imagawa? Should they remain unaligned with both the Imagawa and the Oda, and boldly affirm their independence at this time? Or should they take the path of alliance with the Oda? They would have to choose one of these three alternatives sooner or later. For many years the Tokugawa clan had been a sort of parasitic plant whose existence depended on the great tree of the Imagawa.

The very root and trunk of that relationship, however, had fallen at Okehazama. Their own strength was still insufficient, but after the death of Imagawa Yoshimoto, the Tokugawa could hardly rely on Yoshimoto's heir, Ujizane. This was all information that came either from rumors or from distantly overheard discussions among the senior retainers, but Tokichiro was very interested and concerned.

Now we're going to see what Tokugawa Ieyasu is made of, he thought. He was more interested than others in this lord of Okazaki Castle. Tokichiro considered that even though Ieyasu had been born the lord of a castle and a province, here was a man who had suffered even more misfortune in the world than himself. The more he heard about Ieyasu's life, the more his heart went out to him. Nevertheless, Ieyasu was still just a young man, nineteen years old this year. At the time of the battle of Okehazama, he had commanded Yoshimoto's vanguard, and his performance in the capture of Washizu and Marune had been admirable. His decision to retreat to Mikawa when he heard that Yoshimoto had been killed was also admirable. Ieyasu's reputation was good, both within the Oda camp and, later, at Kiyosu. Thus, he had become the subject of much talk. Tokichiro, too, was now absorbed in his own thoughts as to what position Ieyasu and Okazaki Castle would finally take.

"Master Bridegroom. Are you in here?"

The sliding door opened. Tokichiro returned to himself. Or rather, he returned to himself as a bridegroom.

Niwa Hyozo, a retainer to Lord Nagoya, entered with his wife. They would be the go-betweens. "We're going to perform the *tokoroarawashi* ceremony," Hyozo said, "so please wait here just a little while longer."

Tokichiro was confused. "*Tokoroara*—what?"

"It's an ancient ceremony in which the bride's mother and father and their relatives come to see the bridegroom for the first time."

At which point Niwa's wife told Tokichiro, "Please sit down," and, opening the sliding door, beckoned the people who had been waiting in the next room. The very first to come in and extend their greetings were the parents-in-law, Asano Mataemon and his wife. Even though they all knew each other well, they followed the form of ceremony. Upon seeing these two well-known faces, Tokichiro felt much more relaxed, and his hand fumbled as though he wanted to scratch his head.

Following Nene's parents was a lovely girl of fifteen or sixteen, who bowed and said bashfully, "I'm Nene's sister. My name is Oyaya."

Tokichiro was puzzled. This young girl was even more beautiful than Nene. More than that, until now he hadn't even known that Nene had a younger sister. In what deep part of a warrior's narrow house could this lovely flower have been kept?

"Well, ah, thank you. I am Kinoshita Tokichiro, come here by fate. I'm pleased to meet you." Wondering if this was the bridegroom that she would be calling "elder brother," Oyaya peeked back at him as a young girl might, but another relative quickly came up from behind. One by one they came in and spoke with him. Meeting them all at once, Tokichiro could hardly remember who was whose paternal uncle or niece or first cousin, and wondered how many relatives Nene had.

He thought that this might be annoying later on, but the sudden appearance of a cute sister-in-law and kindly relatives improved his mood. He had few relatives of his own, but he loved large crowds, and a boisterous, lively, laughing family was ideal.

"Master Bridegroom, please take your seat." The go-betweens invited him to a small room hardly big enough to contain them all, and, ushered to the seat provided him, the bridegroom sat down in their midst.

It was an autumn evening, but indoors it was still hot and sultry. The rattan blinds hung from the eaves as they had throughout the summer, and through them filtered the chirping of insects and the autumn breeze that fluttered the wicks of the oil lamps. The spotlessly clean room was dark and less than luxurious.

The room set aside for the ceremony itself was small, and there was a strangely refreshing quality about the complete absence of decoration. Slatted reed mats had been spread over the floor. An altar to the gods of creation, Izanagi and Izanami, had been erected at the back of the room, in front of which had been placed offerings of rice cakes and *sake*, a single candle, and a branch of a sacred tree.

Tokichiro felt himself stiffen as he sat there.

From this night forth…

This ceremony would tie him to the responsibilities of being a husband, to a new life, and to the fate of his in-laws. All of which made Tokichiro take a fresh look at himself. More than anything, he could not help being in love with Nene. If he had not insisted, she would have quickly married another, but after tonight, her fate would be tied to his.

I must make her happy. This was the first thought that came to him as he sat down in the bridegroom's seat. He felt sorry for her because, as a woman, she did not have as much control over her fate as a man.

Before long, the simple ceremony began. After the bridegroom had sat down, Nene was led in by an old lady and took the seat at his side.

Her long hair was tied loosely with red and white cord. Her outer kimono, which was of white raw silk with a brocaded diamond pattern, was wrapped around her waist into a skirt. Beneath it she wore a gown of the same white silk, and beneath that was a final layer of red glossed silk that peeked out from the edge of her sleeves. Apart from a good-luck charm around her neck, she wore no gold or silver hair ornaments, or any thick rouge or powder. Her appearance was in total harmony with the simplicity of the surroundings. The beauty of the ceremony was not the beauty of gaudy clothes, but rather that of the unadorned. The only note of ornamentation in the room was a pair of flasks held by a little boy and girl.

"May this relationship be happy and everlasting. May you be faithful to each other for a hundred thousand autumns," the old woman said to the bride and groom.

Tokichiro held out his cup, received some *sake*, and drank. The server turned to Nene. Nene in turn made her pledge with a sip from her cup.

Tokichiro felt a rush of blood to his head and a pounding in his chest, but Nene looked remarkably calm. This was something that she herself had decided. She was determined not to hold anything against her parents or the gods, no matter what she encountered from this day on. Thus there was something touching and lovely in her appearance as she put the cup to her lips.

As soon as the bride and groom had shared the wedding cup, Niwa Hyozo began a congratulatory song in a voice seasoned by many years on the battlefield. Hyozo had just gotten through the first verse of the song, when someone outside took up the chorus.

The house had fallen silent during Hyozo's song, so the sudden, mannerless singing outside was all the more shocking. Hyozo was surprised, and hesitated for a moment. Without thinking, Tokichiro looked toward the garden.

"Who is it?" a servant asked the prankster.

Just then, a man outside the gate began to sing in a deep voice, mimicking a Noh actor, and walked toward the veranda. Completely forgetting himself, Tokichiro left his seat and walked unceremoniously to the veranda.

"Is that you, Inuchiyo?"

"Master Bridegroom!" Maeda Inuchiyo threw back the hood that was hiding his face. "We've come to perform the water-pouring ceremony. May we come in?"

Tokichiro clapped his hands. "I'm really glad you came. Come in, come in!"

"I came with friends. Is that all right?"

"Sure. We've finished the wedding ceremony, and from tonight, I'm the son-in-law of this house."

"They have a good one. Perhaps I might receive a cup from Master Mataemon." Inuchiyo turned and beckoned toward the darkness.

"Hey, everybody! They're going to let us do the water-pouring ceremony!"

Several men answered Inuchiyo's call at once and pushed their way in, filling the garden with their voices. Ikeda Shonyu was there, as was Maeda Tohachiro, Kato Yasaburo, and his old friend Ganmaku. Even the pockmarked master carpenter was there.

The water-pouring ceremony was an ancient custom in which the old friends of the bridegroom went uninvited to his father-in-law's house. The bride's family was obliged to receive them cordially, and the gate-crashers would then drag the groom out into the garden and douse him with water.

Tonight's water-pouring ceremony was a little premature. As a rule, it was carried out from six months to a year after the wedding.

Mataemon's entire household and Niwa Hyozo were appalled. But the bridegroom was elated, and welcomed them.

"What? You, too?" he said, greeting men he hadn't seen for some time, and then told his white-robed wife, "Nene, quick, bring some food. And *sake*. A lot of *sake*."

"Right away." Nene looked as if she had been expecting this visit. As Tokichiro's wife, she knew that she should not be surprised by such things. She accepted the situation without the slightest complaint. She took off her snow-white kimono and wrapped an everyday thick skirt around her waist. Tying up her long sleeves with a cord, she set to work.

"What kind of wedding is this?" complained an indignant wedding guest. Calming their relatives down, Mataemon and his wife bustled through the din and confusion of the crowd. When Mataemon had heard that the gate-crashers were led by Inuchiyo, he had been alarmed. But when he saw how Inuchiyo laughed and talked with Tokichiro, he was put at ease.

"Nene! Nene!" Mataemon said, "if there's not enough *sake*, send someone out to buy some more. These men should drink as much as they want." And then, to his wife, "Okoi! Okoi! What are you doing, just standing around? The *sake* is here, but nobody has a cup. Even if it's no great feast, bring out whatever we have. I'm so happy that Inuchiyo has come here with all these people."

When Okoi returned with the cups, Mataemon served Inuchiyo personally. He had very strong feelings for this man who might have become his son-in-law. But that fate had not been theirs. Strangely, though, their friendship had survived, the straightforward comradeship of two samurai. Emotion swelled in Mataemon's breast, but he did not let it show in his face or words—they were two samurai together.

"Well, Mataemon, I'm happy too. You've got a good son-in-law. I congratulate you with all my heart," Inuchiyo said. "Listen, I know I barged in tonight. You're not put out, are you?"

"Not at all, not at all." Mataemon himself was spurred on by this. "We'll drink all night long!"

Inuchiyo laughed loudly. "If we drink and sing all night, won't we make the bride angry?"

"Why? That's not the way she was brought up," Tokichiro said. "She's a very virtuous woman."

Inuchiyo drew closer to Tokichiro and began to tease him. "Well now, could you talk a little more about such shameful things?"

"No. I apologize. I've already said too much."

"I'm not going to let you off so easily. Now here's a big *sake* cup."

"You can spare me the big one. The little one will be just fine."

"What kind of bridegroom are you? Don't you have any pride?"

They teased each other as though they were children. But even with so much *sake* around, Tokichiro did not drink to excess—not tonight or ever. Since childhood he had carried with him the vivid memory of the effects of excessive drinking, and now when he looked at the big *sake* cup being forced on him, he saw the face of his drunken stepfather, and then the face of his mother, who was made to grieve so often because of his stepfather's drinking. Tokichiro knew his own limits well. He had grown up in great poverty, and his body was not strong compared to others. Although he was still a young man, he was careful.

"A big cup is too much for me. Give me a small one, please. In return, I'll sing something for you."

"What? You'll sing?"

Instead of giving an answer, Tokichiro had already begun to beat his lap as if it were a drum, and now started to sing.

To think that a man
Has only fifty years to live...

"No, stop." Inuchiyo put his hand over Tokichiro's mouth in mid-verse. "You shouldn't sing that. It's from *Atsumori*, the one His Lordship does so well."

"Well, I have learned the dances and songs he performs by following his example. It's not a forbidden song, so is it so bad to sing it?"

"Yes, it is. It's not good at all."

"What's so bad about it?"

"It's just inappropriate to perform at a wedding."

"His Lordship danced to *Atsumori* the morning the army set out for Okehazama. From tonight, the two of us, a poverty-stricken husband and wife, are starting out in the world. So it's not altogether inappropriate."

"The resolution to go out on the battlefield is one thing, and a wedding celebration is another. True warriors set their minds on living a long life with their wives, until they're white-haired old men and women."

Tokichiro slapped his knee. "That's right. To tell the truth, that's exactly what I hope. If there's a war, it can't be helped, but I don't want to die in vain. Fifty years is not enough. I'd like to live happy and faithful to Nene for a hundred years."

"Bragging again. You'd better dance. Come on, dance."

At Inuchiyo's urging, a great number of people egged Tokichiro on.

"Wait. Wait a moment. I'll dance." Persuading his friends to let him off for a moment, Tokichiro turned toward the kitchen, clapped his hands, and called out, "Nene! We're out of *sake*."

"Coming," Nene answered. She was not at all timid with the guests. Cheerfully carrying in the flasks, she served everyone just as Tokichiro had asked. The only people who were surprised were her parents and relatives, who had always regarded her as nothing more than a child. But Nene's heart had already become one with her husband's, and Tokichiro did not seem in the least awkward with his new wife. As might be expected, Inuchiyo, who was a little drunk, could not keep from blushing when she served him.

"Well, Nene, from tonight on, you're Master Tokichiro's wife. I should congratulate you again," he said, moving the *sake* stand in front of her. "There's something that all my friends know and that I haven't hidden from them. Rather than being ashamed and keeping it to myself, I'm going to make a clean breast of it. How about it, Tokichiro?"

"What is it?"

"I'd like to borrow your wife for a moment."

Laughing, Tokichiro said, "Go ahead."

"Well, Nene. At one time it was on everyone's lips that I loved you. And there's been no change in that at all. You are the woman I love." Inuchiyo became more serious. And even if he had not been, Nene's breast was already full of the emotions of just having become someone's wife. With this night, her life as a single young woman was over, but she was unable to extinguish her feelings for Inuchiyo.

"Nene, people say that a young girl's heart is unreliable, but you did well when you chose Tokichiro. I gave up the person whom I couldn't help loving. Passion is a foolish thing, because I really love Tokichiro even more than I love you. You could say that I gave you to him as a gift of love from one man to another. Which is to say that I treated you as a piece of goods, but that's what men are like. Isn't that right, Tokichiro?"

"For the most part, I received her without reserve, thinking that might be your motive."

"Well, if you had shown reservations about this good woman, it would have been a misjudgment on my part, and I wouldn't have thought much of you. You've got a woman who's far above you."

"You're talking foolishness."

"Ah, ha, ha, ha, ha! Anyway, I'm happy. Hey, Tokichiro. We are companions for life, but did you ever think there would be a night as happy as this one?"

"No, probably not."

"Nene, is the hand drum around? If I beat the drum, somebody get up and dance something. Since Kinoshita here isn't a man of sense, I'll bet he doesn't dance so well either."

"Well, for everyone's entertainment, I'll let you see a rather incompetent rendition." The person who spoke was Nene. Inuchiyo, Ikeda Shonyu, and the other guests opened their eyes wide in surprise. Accompanied by Inuchiyo's drum, Nene opened her fan and began to dance.

"Well done! Well done!" Tokichiro clapped his hands as though he himself had danced. Quite possibly because they were drunk, the energy of their excitement showed no signs of abating. Someone must have proposed that they move on to Sugaguchi, the liveliest quarter of Kiyosu. And there was not a single sober person among them to say no.

"Great! Let's go!" The newlywed Tokichiro got up and led the way. Ignoring his outraged relatives, the party that had come for the water-pouring ceremony forgot even that and, locking arms with the bridegroom, staggered out of the house, supporting one another and waving their arms.

"The poor, poor bride." The relatives were sympathizing with Nene, who had been left behind. But when they looked around for Nene, who just moments ago had been dancing, she was nowhere to be seen. She had pushed open a side door and had gone outside. Pursuing her husband, who was surrounded by his drunken friends, she called out, "Have a good time!"and slipped her purse into the front of his kimono.

The place that the young men of the castle frequented was a drinking spot called the Nunokawa. Situated in the old quarter of Sugaguchi, it was said that this teahouse had been converted from an old shop of *sake* merchants, who had lived there long before either the Oda or their predecessors, the Shiba, had been masters of Owari. Thus, the shop was well known for the size of its ancient building.

Tokichiro was more than a regular. In fact, if his face did not appear when people gathered there, the staff and his friends felt the loss—like a smile with a missing tooth. Tokichiro's marriage was more than enough cause for all the patrons to raise their cups at their favorite drinking haunt. As the friends pushed their way through the shop's curtained entrance, somebody announced the news in the huge entrance hall.

"Ladies and gentlemen and staff of the Nunokawa! Won't you all come out to welcome a guest? We've brought in a bridegroom unparalleled in all the world! And guess who it is. A fellow by the name of Kinoshita Tokichiro. Celebrate, celebrate! This is his water-pouring ceremony."

Their feet twisted from one unsure step to the next. Tokichiro was buffeted along among them and staggered in.

The staff looked on in blank amazement, but broke out in laughter when they finally understood what was happening. They listened with amazement to the story of the bridegroom being seized and carried away during the wedding party.

"This is not a water-pouring ceremony," they said. "It's more like bridegroom snatching." And they all laughed uproariously. Tokichiro dashed into the building, looking as though he were trying to escape, but his prank-loving friends sat down, encircling him, letting him know that he was a prisoner until dawn. Impatiently they called for *sake*.

Who knows how much they drank? There was almost no one who could distinguish what songs they sang or what dances they performed.

Eventually each went to sleep where he fell, with his arms as a pillow, or with arms and legs outstretched. As the night deepened, the smells of autumn silently made their way in.

Inuchiyo suddenly raised his head and looked around with a start. Tokichiro had raised his head, too. Ikeda Shonyu opened his eyes. Looking at one another, they pricked up their ears. The clatter of passing horses that broke the silence had woken them from their sleep.

"What is it?"

"There's quite a number of men." Inuchiyo slapped his knee as though he had thought of something. "That's right! It's just the time for Takigawa Kazumasu to be coming back. Some time ago he went as an envoy to Tokugawa Ieyasu in Mikawa. Maybe that's it."

"Of course. Will they align with the Oda or rely on the Imagawa? The messenger should have Mikawa's answer."

One after another they opened their eyes, but three of the men dashed out of the Nunokawa without waiting for the others. Following the sound of the bridles and the crowd of men and horses up ahead, they ran in the direction of the castle gate.

Kazumasu had gone to Mikawa as an envoy many times since the battle at Okehazama the year before. That he was charged with the important diplomatic mission of winning Tokugawa Ieyasu's cooperation with the Oda clan was not a secret in Kiyosu.

Until just recently, Mikawa had been a weak province, dependent on the Imagawa. And while Owari was also said to be a small province, it had dealt a fatal blow to the powerful Imagawa, sending a strong reminder to the chief contenders for national leadership that there existed today a man by the name of Oda Nobunaga. The strength and morale of the Oda were on the rise. The alliance being sought was called simply a cooperative federation, and the difficult diplomatic trick would be in making the Oda the senior partners in the alliance.

Insofar as a province was small and weak, it was essential that it act without hesitation. A province like Mikawa could be swallowed up in a single military campaign. And the fact was that after the death of Yoshimoto, the province of Mikawa stood at a life-and-death turning point. Should the Tokugawa continue to be dependents of the Imagawa under Ujizane? Or go over to the Oda?

The Tokugawa were perplexed, and there had been any number of deliberations, exchanges of envoys, discussions, and recommendations. In the meantime, minor battles were being fought between Suruga and Mikawa. The skirmishes between the Oda branch castles and their opponents in Mikawa had, naturally, not ceased, and no one was able even to estimate the risk involved to the two provinces, or when the fighting might start. And there was a large number of clans besides the Oda and Tokugawa waiting for the war to start: the Saito of Mino, the Kitabatake of Ise, the Takeda of Kai, and the Imagawa of Suruga. There was no advantage to it. Tokugawa Ieyasu did not feel like fighting, and Oda Nobunaga knew very well that to brace and fight for a final victory over the Tokugawa

T A I K O

would be ridiculous. Which is to say that Nobunaga didn't want to fight, either. But it was necessary not to show it. Nobunaga knew the stubborn and patient character of the Tokugawa and thought it important to consider their reputation.

Mizuno Nobutomo was governor of Ogawa Castle. Although he was a retainer of the Oda, he was also Tokugawa Ieyasu's uncle. Nobunaga asked him to speak to his nephew on his behalf. Nobutomo met with Ieyasu and his senior retainers, and tried to entice them from the side with diplomatic efforts. Approached both frontally and laterally, the Tokugawa finally seemed to have made a decision, and an answer to that effect had arrived from Ieyasu. Thus, Takigawa Kazumasu had been sent to Mikawa as an envoy to receive the final answer concerning Nobunaga's offer of an alliance. And when he returned that night, he went to the castle even though it was past midnight. Kazumasu was a senior Oda general, knowledgeable in firearms and a fine marksman.

Nobunaga, however, valued his intelligence far above his marksmanship. He was not what would be called an orator, but his earnest speech had the virtue of sounding extremely rational. Serious and full of common sense, he was also very quick-witted. Because of this, Nobunaga saw him as the right man for this important phase of the diplomatic process.

It was late at night, but Nobunaga was already up and was waiting for Kazumasu in the audience chamber. Kazumasu prostrated himself, still in his travel clothes. To be overly concerned at a time like this about appearing while still dressed in dirty travel clothes, and thus arranging one's hair and clothes, cleaning away the sweat and smell, and only then coming into the lord's presence, was liable to elicit a remark such as, "Did you go off flower viewing?" Kazumasu had witnessed this sort of ill-humored criticism, and so was here with both hands to the floor, still breathing hard, dressed in clothes that smelled of horses. On the other hand, there were very few times when Nobunaga had let his retainers wait a long time while he leisurely took his seat.

Nobunaga questioned him, eager for a reply.

The answer was to the point. There were retainers who, upon returning and giving their official report, would talk a long time about this or that, prattling on about what happened on the way, discussing all the minor details of the problem. As a result, it was difficult to get to the essential question: Did the errand go as planned or not? Nobunaga hated that, and when messengers gave their answers in nothing but digressions, an irritated expression would darken his face that even an outsider could have understood. "Get to the point!" he would caution.

Kazumasu had been warned about this. Having been selected to perform such an important diplomatic mission, he now looked up to Nobunaga, made a single obeisance, and went straight to the point. "My lord, I have good news. The agreement with Lord Ieyasu of Mikawa is finally in order. Not only that, but almost all of the provisions are as you desired."

"You succeeded?"

"Yes, my lord, it's settled." Nobunaga's expression was matter-of-fact, but behind it he heaved a heavy sigh of relief. "Moreover, I promised to conclude the articles covering the specifics at a later date with a discussion at Narumi Castle with Ishikawa Kazumasa of the Tokugawa clan."

236

"Well then, the lord of Mikawa has promised to cooperate with us?"

"By your command."

"Good work," Nobunaga said for the first time. Only then did Kazumasu give a detailed report.

It was near dawn when Kazumasu withdrew from Nobunaga's presence. By the time the light of early morning spilled into the castle grounds, the rumor that the Oda and the lord of Mikawa had made an alliance had already been back and forth, whispered from ear to ear.

Even such secret information as that concerning the imminent meeting of the representatives of the two clans at Narumi to sign the agreement, and the proposed New Year's visit the following year of Tokugawa Ieyasu at Kiyosu Castle to meet Nobunaga for the first time, was quickly and quietly passed among the retainers.

Inuchiyo, Shonyu, Tokichiro, and the other young samurai had recognized from as far away as Sugaguchi the identity of the messenger who was returning to the castle, and had immediately chased after him. Sitting packed together in a room in the castle, they waited breathlessly to know if it would be war or peace with Mikawa.

"Rejoice!" The page, Tohachiro, had heard the news that came swiftly from the inner council, and he told them everything he had heard.

"It's been agreed?" This outcome had generally been expected, but when they knew a settlement had been reached, their faces were brighter, and their hearts looked to the future with anticipation.

"Now we can fight," said a samurai.

Nobunaga's retainers had not been praising the alliance with Mikawa as a means of avoiding war. They heartily welcomed the treaty with Mikawa, the province to their rear, so they could face a greater enemy with all their strength.

"It's His Lordship's good fortune as a warrior."

"And advantageous for Mikawa, as well."

"Now that I've heard the outcome, I can't keep my eyes open. Come to think of it, we haven't slept since last night," said one of the previous night's revelers; to which Tokichiro yelled, "Not me! I feel just the opposite. Last night was a happy event, and so is this morning. With all of these happy things one after another, I feel like going back to Sugaguchi and drinking some more."

Shonyu joked, "You're lying. The place you feel like going back to is Nene's house. Well, well, how would the bride spend the first night? Master Tokichiro! This forbearance is futile. How about asking for a full day off today and going home? Somebody's waiting for you now."

"Bah!" Tokichiro put up a bold front in the face of his friends' laughter. The burst of loud guffaws drifted down the corridors in the dawn. Finally, a huge drum sounded from the top of the castle, and each of them quickly went off to his post.

"I'm home!" The entrance to Asano Mataemon's house was not large, but when Tokichiro stood there, it seemed awfully big. His voice was clear, and his presence brightened the surroundings.

"Oh!" Nene's little sister, Oyaya, was bouncing a ball on the step and looked up at him with round eyes. She had thought that perhaps he was a visitor, but when she saw that he was her sister's husband, she giggled and ran into the house.

Tokichiro laughed too. He felt strangely amused. When he thought about it, he had left the party and gone drinking with his friends, and then had gone straight to the castle. He was finally coming home at about dusk, the same time of the wedding ceremony the night before. Tonight there were no longer bonfires burning at the gate, but for three days now there had been some sort of family celebration, with guests coming and going. Tonight the voices of guests filled the house again, and a number of pairs of sandals had been left at the entrance.

"I'm home!" the bridegroom once again yelled cheerfully. No one came out to greet him, so they must be busy in the kitchen and the guest room, Tokichiro thought. He was, after all, the son-in-law of the house since the night before. Next to his father and mother-in-law, he was the master here. Well, perhaps he should not go in before they all came out to greet him.

"Nene! I'm home!"

A surprised voice came from the direction of the kitchen, on the other side of a low fence. Mataemon, his wife, Oyaya, some relatives and servants all came out and looked at him with exasperated expressions, as though they wondered what he was doing there. When Nene arrived, she quickly took off her apron, knelt, and greeted him by pressing both hands to the floor.

"Welcome home."

"Welcome back," the others all added hurriedly, lining up and bowing, with the exceptions, of course, of Mataemon and his wife. They appeared to have come out just to look.

Tokichiro looked at Nene and then at all the others and bowed once. He walked straight in, and this time he bowed politely to his father-in-law before reporting the day's events at the castle.

Mataemon had been disgruntled since the previous evening. He had wanted to remind his son-in-law of his duty to his relatives and of Nene's position. Tokichiro had come back without a trace of remorse, and Mataemon had resolved that he wouldn't hold back, even if it was bad manners in front of guests. But Tokichiro looked so carefree that Mataemon forgot his complaint. Moreover, Tokichiro's first words had been to inform him of his day at the castle and of their lord's state of mind. Mataemon unconsciously straightened and responded, "Well, you must have had a hard day." Thus he said just the opposite of what he had intended, and praised Tokichiro instead of reprimanding him.

Tokichiro entertained the guests by staying up late that night and drinking. Even when the guests had gone, there were a number of relatives whose homes were so far away that they had to spend the night. Nene was unable to get away from the kitchen, and the servants looked tired.

Even though Tokichiro had finally come home, he and Nene hardly had enough time to smile at one another, much less to be alone together. As the night deepened, Nene put away the cups in the kitchen, gave orders for breakfast, made sure everything was well at the bedsides of each of the befuddled sleeping relatives, and finally loosened the cords that held up her sleeves. Herself again for the first time that night, she looked for the man who had become her husband.

In the room set aside for the two of them slept relatives and children. In the room where they had all been drinking, her mother and father and their close relatives were chatting.

Where is he? she wondered. When she went out to the veranda, a voice called from a dark servant's room off to the side.

"Nene?" It was her husband's voice. Nene tried to answer, but couldn't. Her heart was pounding. Although she had never felt this way until the wedding ceremony, she had not been able to see Tokichiro since the night before.

"Come in," Tokichiro said. Nene could still hear the voices of her parents. While she was standing there, wondering what to do, she suddenly spotted mosquito-repellent incense that had been left smoldering. Picking it up, she went in timidly.

"You're sleeping here? There must be a lot of mosquitoes." He had gone to sleep on the floor. Tokichiro stared at his feet.

"Ah, mosquitoes..."

"You must be exhausted."

"And you too," he sympathized. "The relatives resolutely refused, but I just couldn't make the old folks sleep in the servants' quarters while we slept in a room with a gold screen."

"But to sleep in a place like this, without any bedding..." Nene started to get up, but he stopped her.

"It's all right. I've slept on the ground—even on bare planks. My body has been tempered by poverty." He sat up. "Nene, come a little closer."

"Y–yes."

"A new wife is like a new wooden rice container. If you don't use it for a long time, it smells bad and becomes unusable. When it gets old, the hoops are apt to come off. But it's good to remember that a husband is a husband, too, from time to time. We plan on living a long life together, and have promised to be faithful to each other until we become old and white-haired, but our life is not going to be an easy one. So, while we still have the kind of feelings we do now, I think we should make a pledge to each other. How do you feel about this?"

"Of course. I'll keep this pledge absolutely, no matter what it is," Nene answered clearly.

Tokichiro was the picture of seriousness. He even looked a little grim. Nene, however, was happy at seeing this solemn expression for the first time.

"First, as a husband, I'm going to tell you what I want from you as a wife."

"Please."

"My mother is a poor farm woman and refused to come to the wedding. But the person who was happiest at my taking a wife more than anyone, anyone in the world, was my mother."

"I see."

"One day my Mother will come to live with us in the same house, and it will be fine if helping your husband takes second place. More than anything, I would like for you to

239

be devoted to my mother and make her happy."

"Yes."

"My mother was born to a samurai family, but long before my birth, she has been poor. She raised several children in great poverty; just to bring up a single child in such circumstances was to struggle through incredible hardship. She had nothing to make her happy—not even a new cotton kimono for the winter and one for the summer. She's uneducated, she speaks in a country dialect, and she's completely ignorant of manners. As my wife, will you take care of a mother like that with real love? Can you respect and cherish her?"

"I can. Your mother's happiness is your happiness. I think that's natural."

"But you also have two parents in good health. In the same way, they're very important to me. I'm not going to be any less filial to them than you are."

"That makes me happy."

"Then there's one more thing for me," Tokichiro went on. "Your father has raised you to be a virtuous woman, disciplining you with a lot of rules. But I'm not so hard to please. I'm just going to rely on you for one thing."

"Which is?"

"I just want you to be happy in your husband's service, in his work, and in all the things he must commonly do. And that's all. It sounds easy, doesn't it? But it won't be easy at all. Look at the husbands and wives who have passed years together. There are wives who have no idea what their husbands do. Such husbands lose an important incentive, and even a man who works for the sake of the nation or province is small, pitiful, and weak when he is at home. If only his wife is happy and interested in her husband's work, he can go out on the battlefield in the morning with courage. To me, this is the best way a wife can help her husband."

"I understand."

"All right. Now let's hear what hopes you have of me. Speak up and I'll promise."

Despite this request, Nene was unable to say a thing.

"Whatever a wife wishes of her husband. If you won't tell me your desires, shall I say them for you?" Nene smiled and nodded at Tokichiro's words. Then she quickly looked down.

"A husband's love?"

"No…"

"Then an unchanging love."

"Yes."

"To give birth to a healthy child?"

Nene trembled. If there had been a lamp to see it by, her face would have burned as red as the color of cinnabar.

On the morning following the three-day wedding party, Tokichiro and his wife put on formal kimonos for yet another ceremony, and visited the mansion of their go-between, Lord Nagoya. After that, they went around to two or three houses, feeling as though all the eyes of Kiyosu were on them that day. But Nene and her young husband had nothing but good intentions for the passersby who turned to look at them.

"Let's go visit Master Otowaka's house for a moment," said Tokichiro.

"Hey, Monkey!" Otowaka yelled, and then corrected himself in a fluster, "Tokichiro."

"I've brought my wife to meet you."

"What? Of course! The honored daughter of the archer, Master Asano! Tokichiro, you're a lucky fellow."

It was only seven years ago that Tokichiro had come up to this veranda selling needles, dressed in dirty, travel-stained clothes. He had felt as though he hadn't eaten in days. When they had given him some food, he had sat there eating greedily, with his chopsticks clacking.

"You're so lucky, it's scary," Otowaka said. "Well, the house is filthy, but come in." Somewhat flustered, he yelled to his wife inside the house and then showed them in himself. Just then, they heard a voice shouting in the street. It was a herald, dashing from house to house.

"Join your regiment! Join your regiment! By His Lordship's order!"

"An official order?" Otowaka said. "The call to arms."

"Master Otowaka," Tokichiro said suddenly, "I have to get to the assembly grounds as quickly as possible."

Until this morning, there had been no indication that something like this might happen, and even when Tokichiro had visited Nagoya's residence, appearances had been nothing but peaceful. Where in the world could they be going? Even Tokichiro's usual intuition had failed him this time. Whenever the word "battle" was spoken, his intuition was usually right on target as to where they were headed. But the young bridegroom's mind had been far away from the current situation for some time. He ran into a number of men dashing from the samurai neighborhoods, shouldering their armor.

A group of horsemen raced from the castle. While he didn't know what was going on, Tokichiro had a premonition that the battlefield would be far away.

Nene hurried home ahead of her husband.

"Kinoshita! Kinoshita!" As he approached the archers' tenement houses, somebody yelled from behind him. Turning to look, he saw that it was Inuchiyo. He was on horseback, in the same suit of armor he had worn at Okehazama, a banner decorated with a plum-blossom crest fluttering from a thin bamboo pole fastened to his back.

"I was just coming by to call for Master Mataemon. Get yourself ready and come immediately to the assembly grounds."

"Are we marching out?" Tokichiro asked.

Inuchiyo jumped off his horse. "How did it go...later on?" Inuchiyo asked.

"What do you mean, 'How did it go?'"

"That would be better left unsaid. I was asking if you are now man and wife."

"That's nothing you need to ask about."

Inuchiyo laughed loudly. "But anyway we're going to the front. If you're late, they'll laugh at you at the assembly grounds, because you just got married."

"I don't mind being laughed at."

"An army of two thousand infantry and cavalry is marching to the Kiso River at dusk."

"We're going into Mino, then."

"There was a secret report that Saito Yoshitatsu of Inabayama suddenly became sick and died. This call to arms and the advance toward the Kiso River is a feeler to determine whether there's any truth in the story."

"Well, now, let's see. There was a lot of excitement when we heard that Yoshitatsu had gotten sick and died earlier this summer, too."

"But this time it seems to be true. And regardless, from the clan's standpoint Yoshitatsu murdered Lord Nobunaga's father-in-law, Lord Dosan. In terms of morality, he's the enemy, and we cannot live with him under the same sky; and if the clan is to gain the center of the field, we must have a foothold in Mino."

"That day is coming soon, isn't it?"

"Soon? We're leaving for the Kiso tonight."

"No. Not yet, not yet. I doubt if His Lordship will attack yet."

"The armies are under the commands of Lord Katsuie and Lord Nobumori; His Lordship will not go out in person."

"But even if Yoshitatsu is dead, and even if his son, Tatsuoki, is a fool, the Three Men of Mino—Ando, Inaba, and Ujiie—are still alive. Plus, while there is still a man like Takenaka Hanbei, who is said to be living in seclusion on Mount Kurihara, it's not going to be done so easily."

"Takenaka Hanbei?" Inuchiyo cocked his head to one side. "The names of the Three Men have echoed for a long time even in neighboring provinces, but is this Takenaka Hanbei so formidable?"

"Most people have never heard of him; I'm his only admirer here in Owari."

"How do you know things like this?"

"I was in Mino for a long time, and..." Tokichiro stopped in midsentence. He had never told Inuchiyo of his experiences as a peddler, the time he spent with Koroku in Hachisuka, and of his spying in Inabayama.

"Well, we've lost time." Inuchiyo remounted.

"See you at the assembly grounds."

"Right. Later." The two men sped away from each other, toward opposite ends of the neighborhood.

"Hello! I'm home!" Whenever he returned home, he always yelled out loudly at the entrance before going in. This way, they would all know that the son-in-law of the house had returned—from the servant working in the storage room to the corners of the kitchen. But today Tokichiro did not wait for people to come out and greet him.

When he entered the room, Tokichiro was struck by what he saw. A new mat had been spread out on the floor, and his armor chest placed on top of it. Naturally enough, his gloves, shin guards, body armor, and waistband were there, but also some medicine for wounds, a brace, and an ammunition pouch—everything he would need to take with him was laid out in order.

"Your equipment," said Nene.

"Very good! Very good!" He praised her without thinking, but was suddenly struck with the thought that he hadn't yet judged this woman correctly. She was even more capable than he had perceived before marrying her.

When he had finished putting on his armor, Nene told him not to worry about her. She had taken out and arranged the earthenware cup for sacred *sake*.

"Take care of everything, please, while I'm away."

"Of course."

"There's no time to say good-bye to your father. Would you do it for me?"

"My mother took Oyaya to Tsushima Temple, and they still haven't returned. Father's been ordered to duty at the castle, and sent a message a while ago that he won't be coming home tonight."

"Won't you be lonely?"

She turned away but did not cry.

She looked like a flower caught by the wind with the heavy helmet on her lap. Tokichiro took it from her, and as he put it on, the fragrance of aloeswood unexpectedly filled the air. He smiled at his wife appreciatively, tightly knotting the scented cords.

BOOK THREE

FIFTH YEAR OF EIROKU
1562

Characters and Places

Saito Tatsuoki, lord of Mino
Oyaya, Nene's sister
Sakuma Nobumori, senior Oda retainer
Ekei, Buddhist monk from
the western provinces
Osawa Jirozaemon, lord of Unuma Castle
and senior Saito retainer
Hikoemon, name given to Hachisuka
Koroku when he became Hideyoshi's ward
Takenaka Hanbei, lord of Mount Bodai Castle
and senior Saito retainer
Oyu, Hanbei's sister
Kokuma, Hanbei's servant
Horio Mosuke, Hideyoshi's page
Hosokawa Fujitaka, retainer of the shogun
Yoshiaki, fourteenth Ashikaga shogun
Asakura Kageyuki, general of the Asakura clan

Inabayama, capital of Mino
Mount Kurihara, mountain retreat of Takenaka Hanbei
Sunomata, castle built by Hideyoshi
Gifu, name given to Inabayama by Nobunaga
Ichijogadani, main castle of the Asakura clan

A Castle Built on Water

In those days the streets of the castle town of Kiyosu rang with the voices of children singing a rhyme about Nobunaga's retainers:

Cotton Tokichi
Rice Goroza
Sneaky Katsuie
Out in the cold, Nobumori

"Cotton Tokichi"—Kinoshita Tokichiro—was riding out as the general of a small army. Although the soldiers should have been marching out in splendid array, their morale was low, and they lacked spirit. When Shibata Katsuie and Sakuma Nobumori had left for Sunomata, the army had marched out to the sound of drums, with a flourish of banners. In comparison, Tokichiro looked like the leader of an inspection tour of the province, or perhaps of a relief detachment for the front.

A couple of leagues from Kiyosu, a lone rider came chasing after them from the castle, calling to them to wait.

The man leading the packhorse train looked back and said, "It's Master Maeda Inuchiyo." He sent a man to the head of the column to inform Tokichiro.

The order to rest was passed along the line. They had hardly walked far enough to work up a sweat, but the officers and men were halfhearted about the whole affair. It was an army that did not believe in the possibility of victory. And if one looked at the faces of the rank and file, one could see they were uneasy and showed no trace of a will to fight.

Inuchiyo dismounted and walked through the ranks, listening to the soldiers' talk.

"Hey! We can rest."

"Already?"

"Don't say that. A rest is all right anytime."

"Inuchiyo?"

As soon as Tokichiro saw his friend, he dismounted and rushed to greet him.

"The battle you're headed for will be the turning point for the Oda clan," Inuchiyo said suddenly. "I have absolute faith in you, but the expedition is unpopular among the retainers, and the unease in the town is extraordinary. I chased after you to say good-bye. But listen, Tokichiro, becoming a general and leading an army is very different from your previous jobs. Come on, Tokichiro, are you really prepared?"

"Don't worry." Tokichiro showed his resolve with a firm nod of the head, and added, "I have a plan."

When Inuchiyo learned what that plan was, however, he frowned. "I had heard you sent Gonzo with a message to Hachisuka, right after you received His Lordship's orders."

"You know about that? It was absolutely secret."

"The truth is, I heard it from Nene."

"A woman's mouth always leaks, doesn't it? That's a little scary."

"No. Just as I was looking in through the gate to congratulate you on your appointment, I overheard Nene talking to Gonzo. She had just come back from a visit to Atsuta Shrine to pray for your success."

"In that case, you have some idea of what I'm going to do."

"Well, do you think these bandits you're asking to be your allies are reliable? What happens if you don't pull it off?"

"I will."

"Well, I don't know what you're using as bait, but did their chief give any indication that he agreed to your proposal?"

"I don't want the others to hear."

"It's a secret, is it?"

"Look at this." Tokichiro took out a letter from under his armor and handed it silently to Inuchiyo. It was the answer from Hachisuka Koroku that Gonzo had brought back the night before. Inuchiyo read it silently, but as he returned it, he looked at Tokichiro in surprise. For a while he did not know what to say.

"You understand, I guess."

"Tokichiro, isn't this a letter of refusal? It says that the Hachisuka clan has had a relationship with the Saito clan for generations, and to break with them now and support the Oda clan would be immoral. It's clearly a refusal. How do you read it?"

"Just as it is written." Tokichiro suddenly hung his head. "It troubles me to speak so bluntly after you've shown your friendship by coming after me this far. But if you have the least bit of consideration, please just do your duty at the castle while I'm gone and don't worry."

"If you can say that, you must have faith in yourself. Well then, take care."

"I'm obliged." Tokichiro ordered the samurai at his side to bring Inuchiyo's horse.

"No, don't stand on formality. Go on ahead."

As Tokichiro remounted, Inuchiyo's steed was led up as well. "Until we meet again." Once more waving from horseback, Tokichiro rode straight ahead.

Several unmarked red banners passed before Inuchiyo's eyes. Tokichiro turned and smiled at him. Red dragonflies peacefully flitted through the blue sky. Without another word, Inuchiyo turned his horse in the direction of Kiyosu Castle.

* * *

The moss was surprisingly thick. One might look into the spacious garden of the Hachisuka clan's mansion, so like the temple gardens that one is forbidden to enter, and wonder how many centuries old the green moss actually was. Thickets of bamboo stood in the shade of large rocks. It was a fall afternoon, and absolutely quiet.

It's survived, that's for sure, Hachisuka Koroku would reflect when he went into the garden. It reminded him of the link with his ancestors, who had lived in Hachisuka for generations. Is my generation, too, going to pass without establishing a respectable family name? On the other hand, he consoled himself, in such times as these, my ancestors might appreciate my holding on to what I have. But there was always one part of his character that refused to be persuaded.

On such peaceful days, when one gazed at this old house that was just like a castle, surrounded on all four sides by thick, luxuriant greenery, it was impossible to believe that the lord of this place was just the master of a band of *ronin*, leading several thousand wolflike warriors who haunted the backroads of an unsettled land. Working secretly in both Owari and Mino, Koroku had managed to secure a power base and enough influence to resist the will of Nobunaga.

Walking across the garden, Koroku suddenly turned toward the main house and called out, "Kameichi! Get ready and come out here."

Koroku's eldest son, Kameichi, was eleven years old. When he heard his father's voice, he took two practice spears and went out into the garden.

"What were you doing?"

"Reading."

"If you're addicted to reading books, you're going to neglect the martial arts, aren't you?"

Kameichi averted his eyes. The boy was different from his powerfully built father, and his character leaned toward the intellectual and gentle. As far as the world could tell, Koroku had a worthy heir, but he was actually unhappy with his son. The more than two thousand *ronin* under his command were mostly uneducated, wild country warriors. If the clan's leader was not able to control them, the Hachisuka would vanish. It is a natural principle among wild animals that the weak become meals for the strong.

Every time Koroku looked at this son, who resembled him so little, he feared that this was the end of his family line, and deplored Kameichi's gentle nature and scholarly bent. Whenever he had even a little leisure, he would call the boy into the garden and try to pour some of his own fierce fighting spirit into him through the martial arts.

"Take a spear."

"Yes, sir."

"Adopt the usual stance and strike without thinking of me as your father." Koroku leveled his own spear and charged toward his son as though he were an adult.

249

Kameichi's weak-spirited eyes shrank at his father's terrifying voice, and he retreated. Koroku's unmerciful spear struck Kameichi's shoulder hard. Kameichi screamed and dropped to the ground in a dead faint.

Running into the garden from the house, Koroku's wife, Matsunami, was beside herself. "Where did he hit you? Kameichi! Kameichi!" Obviously angered at her husband's rough treatment of her son, she called abruptly to the servants for water and medicine.

"You fool!" Koroku scolded her. "Why are you crying and consoling him? Kameichi is a weakling because you've brought him up that way. He's not going to die. Get away from him!"

The servants who had brought the water and medicine simply looked with blank expressions at Koroku's severe face, and kept their distance.

Matsunami wiped her tears. With the same handkerchief she pressed down on the blood that flowed from Kameichi's lip as she cradled him in her arms. He had either bitten his lip when his father had struck him, or it had been cut by a rock when he fell.

"It must hurt. Were you hit somewhere else?" She never quarrelled with her husband, regardless of how displeased or excited she felt. Like any woman of her day, her only weapons were her tears.

Kameichi finally regained consciousness. "I'm all right, Mother. It was nothing. Go away." Picking up his spear and gritting his teeth in pain, he got up again, for the first time demonstrating a manliness that must have delighted his father.

"Ready!" he shouted.

A smile softened his father's face. "Come at me with that kind of spirit," he encouraged him anew.

At that moment a retainer ran in through the gate. Turning to Koroku, he announced that a man claiming to be a messenger from Oda Nobunaga had just tied his horse at the main gate and said that he absolutely must speak with Koroku in private. What should be done with him, the retainer wanted to know. "And he's a little strange," he added. "He walked in casually through the gate alone, without any ceremony, looking around as though he were familiar with the place, saying things like, 'Ah, it's just like home,' 'The turtledoves are cooing as always,' and 'That persimmon tree has gotten big.' Somehow it's hard to believe he's an Oda messenger."

Koroku cocked his head to one side. After a moment he asked, "What's his name?"

"Kinoshita Tokichiro."

"Ah!" Suddenly it was as though his doubts had melted. "Is that so? Now I understand. This must be the man who sent that message earlier. There's no need for me to meet him. Send him away!"

The retainer ran off to throw Tokichiro out.

"I have a request," said Matsunami. "Please excuse Kameichi from practice just for today. He still looks a little pale. And his lip is swollen."

"Hm. Well, take him along." Koroku left both the spear and his son with his wife. "Don't spoil him too much. And don't give him a lot of books, thinking you're doing him a favor."

Koroku walked toward the house, and was about to untie his sandals on the steppingstone, when the retainer ran up again.

"Master, this man is getting stranger and stranger. He refuses to go away. Not only that, but he walked through a side gate, went right into the stables, stopped a groom and a garden sweeper, and was talking with them as though he had known them for a long time."

"Throw him out. Why are you being so easy on someone coming around from the Oda clan?"

"No, I even went beyond what you told me, but when the men spilled out of the barracks and threatened to throw him over the mud wall, he asked me to talk to you one more time. He said that if I told you he was the Hiyoshi you met ten years ago at the Yahagi River, you would certainly remember. Then he stood there looking like you couldn't budge him with a lever."

"The Yahagi River?" Koroku couldn't remember at all.

"You don't remember?"

"No."

"Well then, this fellow must be really strange. He's just rambling on in desperation. Shall I rough him up good, slap his horse, and chase him back to Kiyosu?"

It was obvious the man was getting annoyed at being a messenger again and again. With a look that said, just wait and see, he turned and had run as far as the wooden gate when Koroku, who was standing on the steps to the house, called out and stopped him.

"Wait!"

"Yes, is there something else?"

"Wait a minute. You don't think it could be Monkey?"

"You know the name? He said to tell you it was Monkey if you didn't remember Hiyoshi."

"It *is* Monkey, then," Koroku said.

"Do you know him?" the retainer asked.

"He was a quick-witted kid we kept here for a while. He swept the garden and took care of Kameichi."

"But isn't it strange that he's come here as a messenger from Oda Nobunaga?"

"That makes no sense to me either, but what does he look like?"

"Respectable."

"Oh?"

"He wears a short coat over his armor, and it looks as though he's come quite a distance. Both his saddle and stirrups are covered with mud, and he's got a wicker basket for meals and other travel supplies on his saddle."

"Well, let him in and we'll see."

"Let him in?"

"Just to make sure, let's take a look at his face." Koroku sat on the veranda and waited.

It was a distance of only a few leagues from Nobunaga's castle to Hachisuka. By rights, the village should have been part of the Oda domain, but Koroku did not recognize Nobunaga, nor did he receive a stipend from the Oda clan. His father and the Saito of Mino had supported each other, and the sense of loyalty among *ronin* was a strong one. Actually, in those troubled days, they esteemed loyalty and chivalry, along with their

251

honor, even more than did the samurai houses. Although they were fated to live as savage plunderers, these *ronin* were bound together like father and children, so that disloyalty and dishonesty were not tolerated. Koroku was like the head of a large family, and he was the very source of these iron rules of conduct.

Dosan's murder and Yoshitatsu's death the previous year had caused one problem after another in Mino. And there had been repercussions for Koroku as well. The stipend paid to the Hachisuka while Dosan was alive had been cut off after the Oda blocked all the roads from Owari into Mino. But even so, Koroku was not going to forget his sense of loyalty. On the contrary, his enmity toward the Oda intensified, and in recent years he had indirectly aided defections from Nobunaga's camp and had been one of the major plotters of agitation in the Oda domain.

"I've brought him in," the retainer said from the wooden gate. Just in case, five or six of Koroku's men surrounded Tokichiro as he came in.

Koroku glowered at him. "Come here," he said, with an imperious nod.

An ordinary-looking man stood before Koroku. His salutation was also ordinary. "Well, it's been a long time."

Koroku stared fixedly at him. "Sure enough, it's Monkey. Your face hasn't changed much."

In contrast to his face, Koroku could not help being surprised by the transformation in Tokichiro's clothes. Koroku now clearly recalled that night ten years ago near the Yahagi River, when Tokichiro, dressed in a dirty cotton tunic, his neck, hands, and feet covered with grime, had been sleeping by the riverbank. When a soldier had shaken him awake, he had responded with such big words and such fighting spirit that they had all wondered who he could be. Under the light of the soldier's lanterns, he had turned out to be nothing more than a strange-looking youth.

Tokichiro spoke humbly, seemingly without any sense of the distinction between his former and present status. "Well, I've been quite negligent since I left. It's good to see that you're in your usual good health. I'll bet Master Kameichi has grown up. And your wife is well, too? You know, coming back here for a visit, ten years seem like an instant."

Then, looking around at the trees in the garden with heartfelt emotion and staring at the roofs of the buildings, he talked on and on about his recollections of scooping water from that stone well every day, of being scolded by the master, perhaps, next to that stone, of carrying Kameichi around on his back, and of catching cicadas for him.

Koroku, however, did not seem to be moved in the least by such memories. Rather, he focused on Tokichiro's every movement and finally spoke sharply. "Monkey," he said, addressing Tokichiro as he had done long before, "have you become a samurai?" It was obvious, though, from Tokichiro's appearance, that he had. Tokichiro, however, was not in the least disconcerted.

"Yes. As you can see, I still receive only an insignificant stipend, but somehow I'm on the verge of becoming a samurai. I hope you're pleased. In fact, today I rushed all the way from my post at the camp at Sunomata, partly because I thought you might be pleased about my promotion."

Koroku displayed a forced smile. "These are good times, aren't they? There are even people who will hire men like you as samurai. Who's your master?"

"Lord Oda Nobunaga."

"That bully?"

"By the way..." Tokichiro changed the tone of his voice a little. "I've digressed a bit about my personal affairs, but today I've come as Kinoshita Tokichiro, on the orders of Lord Nobunaga."

"Is that so? You're an envoy?"

"I'm coming in. Excuse me." With that, Tokichiro took off his sandals, went up the steps of the veranda where Koroku was sitting, and sat down, taking the seat of honor in the room for himself.

"Huh!" Koroku grunted and sat unmoving, right where he was. He had not invited him to come in, and yet Tokichiro had marched up unhesitatingly and sat down. Koroku turned toward him and said, "Monkey?"

Though Tokichiro had answered to this name before, this time he refused. He simply stared fixedly at Koroku, who teased him for his childishness. "Come, come now, Monkey. You've suddenly changed your attitude, but," he said, "until now you've been talking to me like an ordinary person. Do you want to go through the formality of being addressed as Nobunaga's envoy from now on?"

"That's correct."

"Well, then, go home immediately. Get out of here, Monkey!" Koroku rose and stepped down to the garden. His voice had taken on a rough edge, and he had a dangerous look in his eye. "Your Lord Nobunaga may think that Hachisuka is within his territory, but nearly all of Kaito is run by me. I don't recall that I or any of my forebears have ever received a single grain of millet from Nobunaga. For him to look at me with the air of a lord of a province is the height of absurdity. Go home, Monkey. And if you say something rude, I'll kill you!" He glared at him and went on, "When you get back, tell this to Nobunaga: he and I are equals. If he has some business with me, he can come himself. Do you understand, Monkey?"

"No."

"What!"

"It's a shame. Are you really nothing more than the chief of a gang of ignorant bandits?"

"Wha–what! How dare you!" Koroku jumped back up into the room, facing Tokichiro with a hand on the guard of his sword. "Monkey, say that again."

"Sit down."

"Shut up!"

"No, sit down. I have something to say to you."

"Hold your tongue!"

"No, I'm going to show you your own ignorance. I have something to teach you. Sit down!"

"You—"

"Wait, Koroku. If you're going to kill me, this is the place, and you're the person to do it, so I don't suppose there's any reason to hurry. But if you cut me down, who's going to teach you anything?"

"You–you're crazy!"

"Anyway, sit down. Come on, sit down. Put away your petty selfishness. What I want to tell you is not just about Lord Nobunaga and his relationship with the Hachisuka clan. It starts with the fact that you were both born in this country of Japan. According to you, Nobunaga is not the lord of this province. Now these are quite reasonable words, and I agree with you. But what I find impertinent is your claim that Hachisuka is your own domain. You're mistaken."

"How's that?"

"Any piece of land that is said to be personal property, whether it be Hachisuka or Owari, or any bay or inlet, or even a single clod of earth, is no longer a part of the Empire. Isn't that correct, Koroku?"

"Hm."

"With all due respect, to speak this way about His Imperial Majesty—the true owner of all land—no, to be standing over me, grasping a sword in front of me as I tell you this, is an act of the grossest disrespect, is it not? Even a commoner wouldn't behave that way, and you're the leader of three thousand *ronin*, aren't you? Sit down and listen!"

Rather than arising from courage, this last shout sounded more as though it had exploded from his entire being. Just then, someone yelled from inside the house.

"Master Koroku, sit down! You can't do otherwise!"

Who was that? Koroku wondered as he turned. Surprised, Tokichiro also looked in the direction of the voice. In the green light shining from the central garden, someone could be seen lingering in the entrance to the corridor inside. Half of the man's body was hidden in the shade of the wall. They could not tell who he was, but at a glance, he seemed to be wearing the robes of a priest.

"Oh, it's Master Ekei, isn't it?" Koroku said.

"That's right. It was rude of me to yell from outside, but I was concerned about what you two were arguing about so loudly," Ekei said, still standing there with what seemed to be a half smile on his face.

Koroku spoke calmly. "I'm sure that we disturbed you terribly. Please forgive me, Your Reverence. I'm going to toss out this impudent fellow right away."

"Wait, Master Koroku." Ekei stepped into the room. "You're being rude." Ekei was a traveling monk of about forty years of age who had stopped here as a guest. He had the physique of a broad-shouldered warrior. His large mouth was especially striking. At the hint that this monk, who was staying as a guest in his own house, might be taking Tokichiro's side, Koroku looked straight at him.

"How am I being rude?"

"Well now. There's a reason not to turn your back on the words of this envoy here. Master Tokichiro has stated that neither this area nor the province of Owari belongs to Nobunaga or the Hachisuka, but rather to His Majesty the Emperor. Can you definitely state that this is not true? You can't. To express dissatisfaction with that national polity is the same as harboring treason against His Majesty, and this is what he's saying. So sit down for a moment, bend to the truth, and listen carefully to what this messenger has to say. After that, you can decide whether it's right to chase him away or to accede to his request. This is my humble opinion."

Koroku was hardly an uneducated, ignorant bandit. He had the rudiments of an education in Japanese literature and he knew Japanese traditions, and from what bloodlines his own lineage flowed.

"I beg your pardon. It makes no difference who is speaking; it's foolish of me to oppose the principle of moral obligation. I shall hear what the envoy has to say."

When he saw that Koroku had settled down and was seated, Ekei was satisfied. "Well then, it would be rude of me to stay here, so I'll withdraw. But, Master Koroku, before you give this messenger an answer, I'd like you to stop by my room for just a moment. There's something I'd like to tell you." With that, he left.

Koroku nodded to him and then turned again toward the envoy, Tokichiro, and corrected himself. "Monkey—no, I mean Lord Oda's honorable envoy—what sort of business do you have with me? Let's hear it briefly."

Tokichiro unconsciously moistened his lips and considered that this was the turning point. Would he be able to persuade this man with an eloquent tongue and a cool head? The construction of the castle at Sunomata, the rest of his life, and, in its turn, the rise or fall of his master's clan—everything hinged on whether Koroku would say yes or no. Tokichiro was tense.

"In fact, this is not a different matter. It has to do with my previous inquiry, sent through my servant, Gonzo, about to your intentions."

"Concerning that matter, I absolutely refuse, just as I wrote in my reply. Did you see my reply or didn't you?" Koroku cut him off bluntly.

"I saw it." When he saw how unbending his opponent was, Tokichiro hung his head meekly. "But Gonzo delivered a letter from *me*. Today I'm delivering the request of Lord Nobunaga."

"It doesn't make any difference who asks, I have no intention of supporting the Oda clan. I don't need to write two answers."

"Well then, are you planning on leading the family line that your ancestors left to you to its regrettable destruction in your own generation and on this very land?"

"What?"

"Don't get angry. I, myself, received the favor of lodging and meals here ten years ago. In a larger sense, it's a great pity that people like you are hidden out here in the wilds and put to no use. Thinking of this in terms of both the public interest and my own, I thought it would be a shame if the Hachisuka went down to isolated self-destruction. So I came here as a last resort, in order to return the old favor that I owe you."

"Tokichiro."

"Yes?"

"You're still young. You don't have the capacity of running errands for your master with an eloquent tongue. You're just making your opponent angry, and I really don't want to get angry at a youngster like you. Why don't you leave before you've gone too far?"

"I'm not going to leave until I've had my say."

"I appreciate your enthusiasm, but this is the forcefulness of a fool."

"Thank you. But great achievements beyond human strength generally resemble the forcefulness of fools. Nevertheless, wise men don't take the road of wisdom. For example, I imagine that you consider yourself wiser than me. But when looked at objectively, you're just like the fool who sits on the roof and watches his own house burn down. You're still stubborn, even though the fire's spreading on all four sides. And you only have three thousand *ronin*!"

"Monkey! Your slender neck is getting closer and closer to my sword!"

"What? It's *my* neck that's in danger? Even if you remain loyal to the Saito, what kind of people are they? They have committed every treachery and every atrocity. Do you think there are any other provinces with such degenerate morals? Don't you have a son? Don't you have a family? Take a look at Mikawa. Lord Ieyasu has already bound himself to the Oda clan in an unbreakable alliance. When the Saito clan collapses, if you rely on the Imagawa, you'll be intercepted by the Tokugawa; if you ask for aid from Ise, you'll be surrounded by the Oda. No matter which clan you choose as your ally, how will you protect your family? All that remain are isolation and self-destruction, isn't that right?"

Koroku was silent now, almost as though he were dumbstruck, almost as though he had been taken in by Tokichiro's eloquence. But even though Tokichiro's sincerity showed on his face as he spoke, he never glared at his opponent or became overbearing. And sincerity, even if it speaks with a stutter, will sound eloquent when inspired.

"I'm asking you once again to reconsider. There's not an intelligent person under the sun who doesn't look askance at the immorality and misrule of Mino. By allying yourself with a faithless and lawless province, you're inviting your own destruction. Once you've accomplished this, do you think anyone is going to praise you as a man who died a martyr's death in the true Way of the Samurai? It would be better to end this worthless alliance, and meet once with my master, Lord Nobunaga. Although it's said these days that the entire country is filled with warriors, there's not one in the land with Lord Nobunaga's genius. Do you think things are going to continue as they are? It's a disrespectful thing to say, but the shogunate is at the end of the road. No one obeys the shogun, and his officials are unable to rule. Every province has withdrawn into itself, each one strengthening its own territory, supporting its own warriors, sharpening its weapons, and laying up stocks of firearms. The only way to survive today is to know who among those many rival warlords is trying to establish a new order."

For the first time, Koroku gave a single reluctant nod of assent.

Tokichiro drew closer to Koroku. "That man is among us now, and he is a man of vision. Only common men cannot see it. You've taken a loyal stand with the Saito clan, but you're so concerned with minor loyalty that you're overlooking the greater loyalty. This is regrettable for both you and Lord Nobunaga. Wipe the little things away from your mind, and think about the bigger scheme. The time is right. Unworthy as I am, I've been ordered to build the castle at Sunomata, and with that as a foothold, I've been given the command of the vanguard to strike into Mino. The Oda clan is not poor in clever or brave commanders, and for Lord Nobunaga to appoint an underling like me among them is daring, and indicates that he is not an ordinary lord like the others. Contained within Lord Nobunaga's orders is the implication that the castle at Sunomata will be commanded by the man who builds it. For people like us, is there any other time to rise up but now? I say this, but there's nothing that's going to be done with one individual's strength. No, I'm not going to embellish my words. I thought that I could put this opportunity to use, and I've gambled my life in coming here to draw you out. If I've been mistaken, I'm resolved to die. But I didn't come here empty-handed. It isn't much, but for the moment I brought three horses loaded with gold and silver as compensation and for military expenses for your men. I'd be grateful if you'd accept it." As Tokichiro finished speaking, someone addressed Koroku from the garden.

"Uncle."

A samurai prostrated himself as he spoke.

"Who's calling me 'Uncle'?"

Koroku thought this was strange, and looked carefully at the warrior.

"It's been a long time," the man said, looking up.

There was no doubt that Koroku was startled. He spoke out without intending to do so. "Tenzo?"

"I'm ashamed to say that it's me."

"What are you doing here?"

"I didn't think I would ever see you again, but owing to Master Tokichiro's compassion, I was ordered to accompany him on today's mission."

"What? You came together?"

"After I turned against you and ran away from Hachisuka, I stayed with the Takeda clan in the province of Kai for many years, working as a ninja. Then, about three years ago, I was ordered to spy on the Oda, and so I went to the castle town of Kiyosu. While there, I was discovered by Lord Nobunaga's police and thrown into prison. I was released through the good offices of Master Tokichiro."

"So now you're Master Tokichiro's attendant?"

"No, after I was let out of prison—and with Master Tokichiro's help—I worked with the Oda ninja. But when Master Tokichiro set out for Sunomata, I asked to accompany him."

"Oh?" Koroku absentmindedly stared his nephew. What had changed even more than Tenzo's appearance was his character. That uncontrollable nephew, who was so brutal and barbarous even by the Hachisuka's standards, was no longer recognizable. Now he was courteous and mild-eyed, regretting and apologizing for his former crimes. Ten years ago—it was really ten years—Koroku could have torn him limb from limb!

Angered at his nephew's evil deeds, he had chased Tenzo as far as the Kai border to punish him. But now, when he looked at Tenzo's steadfast eyes, he was hardly even able to recall his anger. This was not just the sympathy of a blood relative: Tenzo's personality had definitely changed.

"Well, I didn't say anything about this because I thought we would talk about it later," Tokichiro said, "but out of consideration for me, I'd like you to forgive your nephew. Tenzo is now an irreproachable retainer of the Oda. He himself has apologized for his former crimes. He's often told me that he wanted to apologize to you in person but was too ashamed of his former deeds to come here. And, since there were other matters to take care of in Hachisuka, I thought this might be the perfect opportunity. Please let the relationship between uncle and nephew be as harmonious as it was before, and look to a prosperous future."

As Tokichiro mediated from the side, even Koroku did not feel like badgering his nephew for his crimes of ten years before. And as Koroku began to open his heart, Tokichiro did not let the moment go by.

"Tenzo, did you bring in the gold and silver?" When he spoke to Tenzo, it was naturally in the tone of command.

"Yes, sir."

"Well, let's take a look at it along with the inventory. Tenzo, have a servant bring it here."

"Yes, sir."

As Tenzo started off, Koroku called out hurriedly, "Wait, Tenzo. I can't accept this. If I did, it would mean that I was promising to serve the Oda clan. Wait a bit until I've thought the matter over." His flushed complexion showed his anguish. With these words, then, he stood up abruptly and went inside.

Having returned to his room, Ekei had been writing in his travel journal, but now he suddenly stood up.

"Master Koroku?" Ekei said, looking in at Koroku's room, but the man was not to be seen. He went to the chapel and peeked inside, and there was Koroku, seated before the mortuary tablet of his ancestors, with his arms folded.

"Did you give an answer to Lord Nobunaga's envoy?"

"He hasn't gone yet, but the more I talked to him, the more troublesome it became, so I'm just going to leave him where he is."

"He probably won't just go away." Ekei finished speaking, but Koroku remained silent. "Master Koroku," Ekei finally said.

"What?"

"I've heard that the envoy today used to be employed here as a servant."

"I only knew him as 'Monkey' and had no idea where he was from. I picked him up around the Yahagi River and gave him a job."

"That's no good."

"No good?"

"The memory of the time when he served you has become an obstacle, and you can't see the true form of the man today."

"Do you suppose that's true?"

"I've never been so surprised as I was today."

"Why?"

"Just looking at the face of that envoy. His features are what the world would call quite unusual. Studying people's features is merely a hobby, and when I judge a man's character by looking at him, I usually keep my conclusions to myself. But in this case I was shocked. Someday this man is going to do something extraordinary."

"That monkey-face?"

"Yes, indeed. That man may move the entire country someday. If he were not in this Empire of the Rising Sun, then perhaps he might become a sovereign."

"What are you saying?"

"I thought you wouldn't take his request seriously, so I'm telling you this before you decide. Put away your preconceptions. When you look at a man, look with your heart, not your eyes. If that man leaves with your refusal today, you're going to regret it for the next hundred years."

"How can you say such a thing about a man you've never even met before?"

"I'm not saying this just from looking at his face. I was surprised when I heard his explanation of the way of justice and righteousness. And his refusal to give in to your derision and threats, while refuting you with sincerity and good faith, shows him to be a passionate, upright man. I believe without a doubt that he will one day be a man of great distinction."

Koroku immediately prostrated himself in front of Ekei and said firmly, "I submit humbly to your words. Quite frankly, if I compare my own character with his, mine is clearly inferior. I'll discard my petty egotism and immediately give him a positive answer. I'm extremely grateful for your advice."

He went off, his eyes gleaming, as though he himself had witnessed the birth of a new era.

Hours after Tokichiro's arrival in Hachisuka, two riders hurried through the night toward Kiyosu. As yet, no one knew that the riders were Koroku and Tokichiro. Later that night, Nobunaga talked to the two men in a small room in the castle. Their secret conversation lasted several hours. Only a select few, including Tenzo, knew the reason for their visit.

The following day Koroku called a council of war. All those who answered the call were *ronin*. They had been under Koroku's command for many years, and they acknowledged his authority in the same way the great provincial lords obeyed the shogun's decrees. Each leader headed a pack of warriors in his own village or mountain stronghold, and waited for the day when they would be needed. Every one of them was surprised by the presence of Watanabe Tenzo of Mikuriya, who, ten years before, had rebelled against their leader.

When the men took their seats, Koroku told them of his decision to abandon his alliance with the Saito clan and switch his allegiance to the Oda. At the same time, he explained the circumstances of his nephew's return. At the end of his address he said, "I imagine some of you will disapprove, and others have close ties with the Saito. I am not going to force you. You may leave without hesitation, and I will not bear a grudge against anyone who crosses over to Mino."

No one, however, got up to leave. In fact, no one showed what he really felt. At this point, asking Koroku's permission, Tokichiro spoke to the men.

"I have received instructions from Lord Nobunaga to build a castle at Sunomata. Until now, I imagine that each of you has lived as he pleased, but have you ever occupied a castle? The world is changing. The mountains and valleys where you can live freely are disappearing. If this were not so, there would be no progress. You've been able to live as *ronin* because the shogun is powerless. But do you think the shogunate will be able to survive much longer? The nation is changing; a new era is dawning. We will no longer be living for ourselves, but rather for our children and our grandchildren. You have a chance to establish your own households, to become real warriors following the true Way of the Samurai. Do not let this moment pass you by."

When he had finished, the entire room was silent. But there were no signs of discontent. These men, who ordinarily lived without giving much thought to the future, were reflecting on his words.

One man broke the silence: "I have no objection."

He was followed by the others who made the same reply, and all the voices in the room were raised in agreement. They knew they were risking their lives by committing themselves to the Oda, and a fierce resolution burned in their eyes.

* * *

The sound of an ax cutting a tree...then a splash as the tree falls into the Kiso River. A raft is lashed together and pushed out into the current, where it flows downstream to meet the waters of the Ibi and Yabu rivers coming from the north and west, and then comes to a broad sandbar crisscrossed by waterways: Sunomata. The boundary between Mino and Owari. The site for the castle, on which Sakuma Nobumori, Shibata Katsuie, and Oda Kageyu all had met with identical failure.

"What a stupid waste of time. They might as well be sunk in a stone ship under the sea!" From the far bank, the soldiers of the Saito looked across the river, shading their eyes with their hands and joking.

"This is the fourth time."

"They still haven't learned."

"Who's the General of the Dead this time? It's kind of sad, even though he is the enemy. I'll remember his name, if nothing else."

"He's called something like Kinoshita Tokichiro. I've never heard of him."

"Kinoshita...he's the one they call Monkey. He's just a low-ranking officer. He can't be worth more than fifty or sixty *kan*."

"A low-ranking fool like that is their general? The enemy can't really be serious, then."

"Maybe it's a trick."

"Could be. They could have a plan to draw our attention here, and then cross over somewhere else."

The more the soldiers of Mino looked at the construction on the opposite bank, the less seriously they took it. About one month passed. Tokichiro led the spirited *ronin* of Hachisuka, who had begun to work as soon as they had arrived. It had rained heavily two or three times, but that made it all the easier to float timber rafts. Even when the river overflowed the sandbar one night the men rallied as though it were nothing. Would the rain clouds come before they could finish the earthen enclosure? Would nature win, or would man?

The *ronin* worked as though they had forgotten how to eat or sleep. The two thousand who had departed from Hachisuka had swelled to five or six thousand by the time they reached their destination.

Tokichiro hardly needed his general's baton. The men were alert and hardworking, and day by day the work advanced right before his eyes.

The *ronin* were used to traveling through the mountains and plains. And they understood the laws of flood regulation and earthwork construction far better than Tokichiro did.

Their aim was to make this place their own. With this work, they took a leap away from their former lives of debauchery and indolence, and felt the satisfaction and pleasure of knowing that they were doing something real.

"Well, this embankment is not going to budge, even if there's a flood or the rivers flow together," one of the *ronin* said proudly.

Before the first month had passed, they had leveled an area larger than the castle grounds, and had even built a causeway to the mainland.

On the opposite bank, the men of Mino looked over toward the site.

"It seems to be taking shape a little, doesn't it?"

"They still haven't put up any stone walls, so it doesn't look like a castle, but the foundations have come right along."

"I can't see any carpenters or plasterers."

"I'll bet they're still a hundred days away from that."

The soldiers looked lazily across the river to relieve their boredom. The river was wide. When it was sunny, a thin mist rose from the surface of the water. It was difficult to see clearly from the other side, but occasionally there were days when the sounds of stone being cut and voices yelling from the construction site were lifted on the wind and carried from the opposite bank.

"Will we make a surprise attack this time? Right in the middle of construction work?"

"It seems not. There's a strict order from General Fuwa."

"What's that?"

"Not to fire a single shot. Let the enemy work to his heart's content."

"We've been ordered just to watch until they finish the castle?"

"The first time, the plan was to crush the enemy with a single surprise attack when he began work on the castle; the second time, to attack when the castle was half-built and smash it to smithereens. But the command this time is just to stand here and watch with our arms folded until they've finished the job."

"Then what?"

"Take the castle, of course!"

"Aha! Let the enemy build it, and then take it over."

"That seems to be the plan."

"Hey, that's clever. The other Oda generals were a bit tough, but this new commander, Kinoshita, is nothing more than a foot soldier." As the man wagged his tongue and prattled on happily, one of the others gave him a rebuking look.

A third man hurried into the guardhouse. A boat that had been poled down the river landed on the Mino bank. A general with bristly whiskers stepped onto the bank, followed by several attendants. A horse was led off the boat after them.

"The Tiger is coming!" one of the guards said.

"The Tiger of Unuma, here!" Whispers and quick glances passed between them. This was the lord of Unuma Castle, upstream; known as one of the fiercest generals in Mino, his name was Osawa Jirozaemon. So frightening was this man that the mothers of Inabayama said, "The Tiger is coming!" to quiet their crying children. Now Osawa came striding up in person, with his eyes and nose thrusting out of his tiger-like whiskers.

"Is General Fuwa here?" Osawa asked.

"Yessir. At the camp."

"I wouldn't mind calling on him at his camp, but this is a better place for a talk. Call him over here immediately."

"Yessir." The soldier ran off.

Very soon, Fuwa Heishiro, followed by the soldier and five or six officers, walked briskly toward the riverbank.

"The Tiger! What does he want?" Fuwa muttered, his ill-humored strides indicating how tiresome he thought this interview was going to be.

"General Fuwa, thank you for taking the trouble to come."

"It's no trouble at all. How can I be of assistance?"

"Over there." Osawa pointed to the opposite bank.

"The enemy at Sunomata?"

"Indeed. I'm sure you're keeping watch on them day and night."

"Of course! Please rest assured that we are always on guard."

"Well, although the castle I am in charge of is upstream, I am concerned with more than just the defense of Unuma."

"Yes, of course."

"Occasionally I board a boat or walk along the shore to see what conditions are like downstream, and when I came today, I was surprised. I suppose it's too late, but when I look over this camp, it's rather carefree. What do you have in mind at this point?"

"What do you mean, 'too late'?"

"I'm saying that construction of the enemy's castle has advanced to a surprising extent. It appears that, as you've sat watching nonchalantly from this bank, the enemy has been able to build a second line of embankments, rope off a foundation, and finish about half of their stone walls."

Fuwa grunted, annoyed.

"Couldn't the carpenters already be fitting the timbers for the citadel in the mountains behind Sunomata? And couldn't they have already finished almost everything from the drawbridge to the interior fittings, not to mention the keep and walls? This is my view of the situation."

"Hm...I see."

"These days the enemy must be tired at night from the construction work they've done during the day, and they've neglected to set up defensive positions of any kind. Not only that, but the workers and craftsmen, who would only be an impediment during a fight, are living together with the soldiers. Now if we made a general attack, crossing the river under cover of darkness, and attacked from upstream, downstream, and straight across, we should be able to rip this thing out by its very roots. But if we're negligent, we're going to wake up some morning soon and find that a very solid castle has suddenly sprung up overnight. We should not be taken off guard."

"Indeed."

"Then you agree?"

Fuwa burst out laughing. "Really, General Osawa! Did you really call me all the way here because you were worried about that?"

"I was beginning to doubt that you had eyes, so I wanted to explain the situation to you right here at the riverbank."

"Now you've gone too far! As a military commander, you're remarkably shallow. I'm allowing the enemy to build his castle this time exactly as he wishes. Can't you see that?"

"That's obvious. I suppose you plan to let them finish the castle, then attack, and use it as a foothold for Mino to gain supremacy over Owari."

"That's right."

"I'm sure those were your instructions, but it's a dangerous strategy when you don't know whom you're up against. I can't just stand by and watch the destruction of our own troops."

"Why should this mean the destruction of our troops? I don't understand."

"Clean out your ears and listen carefully to the sounds coming from the far bank, and you'll realize how far the castle construction has got. There's enough activity there for all the soldiers to be working as well. This is different from Nobumori and Katsuie. This time the baton of command has spirit. It's clear that the command has fallen to a man of real character, even if he is from the Oda."

Fuwa held his belly and laughed, ridiculing Osawa for overestimating their opponents. Although they were allies and fighting on the same side, the two men were not of one mind. Osawa clicked his tongue loudly beneath his tiger's whiskers.

"It can't be helped. Well, go ahead and laugh. You'll find out." With this parting shot, he called for his horse and went off indignantly with his retainers.

It seemed that there was someone with discrimination in Mino. Osawa Jirozaemon's prediction hit the mark, before ten days had passed. The construction of the castle at Sunomata advanced rapidly within only three nights.

When the guards got up in the morning after the third night and looked across the river, the castle was nearing completion.

Fuwa rubbed his hands and said, "Shall we go and cheat them out of it?"

Fuwa's troops were skilled in night attacks and river crossings. As they had done before, they closed in on Sunomata in the dead of night, planning to take it with a surprise attack.

But the response was quite different this time. Tokichiro and his *ronin* were ready and waiting for them. They had built this castle with their blood and spirit. Did the Saito think they were going to give it up? The fighting style of the *ronin* was completely unorthodox. Unlike Nobumori's and Katsuie's soldiers, these men were wolves. During the battle, the boats of the Mino forces were soaked with oil and set on fire. When Fuwa saw that his men did not have the advantage, he gave out the order to retreat. But by the time he had cleared the words from his hoarse throat, it was already too late.

Chased from the stone walls of the castle to the riverbank, the Mino soldiers barely escaped with their lives, leaving nearly a thousand dead. A number of the soldiers whose rafts had been destroyed were forced to flee up- and downstream, but the men of Hachisuka had no intention of letting them get away. How could the Mino troops escape from *ronin* who were so at home on rough terrain?

The attack stopped for the night. Fuwa doubled his forces and once again stormed Sunomata. The sandbar and river were dyed red with blood. But as the sun rose, the castle garrison struck up a victory song.

"Breakfast this morning will be all the tastier!"

Fuwa became desperate, and waiting for the storm that evening, he planned his third all-out assault. The Saito troops attacked from both upstream and downstream.

Upstream at Unuma Castle, the soldiers of Osawa Jirozaemon were the only ones who did not respond to the call for a general offensive. The battle was so harrowing that even the *ronin* suffered heavy casualties in the surging, muddy waters of the river that night, but the Mino forces had to write off the battle as an overwhelming defeat.

Snaring the Tiger

That year saw no more surprise attacks from Mino. In the meantime, Tokichiro nearly completed the remaining construction on the interior and on the outer defenses of Sunomata Castle. Early in the first month of the following year, accompanied by Koroku, he visited Nobunaga to give him New Year's greetings while making his report.

In his absence, there had been great changes. The plan that he had once advocated had been adopted: Kiyosu Castle, poorly situated in terms of terrain and water supply, was being abandoned, and Nobunaga was moving his residence to Mount Komaki. The townspeople were also moving to be with their lord, and were building a flourishing town under Mount Komaki Castle.

When Nobunaga received Tokichiro at his new castle, he said, "I made a promise. You will take up residence at Sunomata Castle, and I am increasing your stipend to five hundred *kan*." Finally, in an extraordinarily good mood at the end of their audience, Nobunaga gave his retainer a new name: Tokichiro would henceforth be called Kinoshita Hideyoshi.

"If you can build it, the castle is yours" had been Nobunaga's original promise, but when Hideyoshi returned to report the castle's completion, Nobunaga had only said, "Take up residence there," and had mentioned nothing about its possession. It was almost the same thing, but Hideyoshi considered this as an indication that his qualifications to be the lord of a castle had not yet been proven. This he reasoned from the order given to Koroku (who had recently become a retainer of the Oda clan through Hideyoshi's own recommendation) to take up duty at Sunomata as Hideyoshi's ward. Instead of harboring a grudge against his lord for these actions, Hideyoshi simply declared, "In all humility, my lord, instead of the five hundred *kan* of land you have offered me, I would like your leave to conquer the same amount of land from Mino." After he had received Nobunaga's permission, he returned to Sunomata on the seventh day of the New Year.

"We built this castle without injury to one of His Lordship's retainers and without using a single tree or rock from His Lordship's domain. Perhaps we can take the land from the enemy as well, and live off a stipend from heaven. What do you think, Hikoemon?"

Koroku had given up his ancient name and, from the New Year, had changed his name to Hikoemon.

"That would be interesting," Hikoemon replied. He was by now completely devoted to Hideyoshi. He behaved as if he were Hideyoshi's retainer, and forgot all about their earlier relationship.

Sending out soldiers when the opportunity presented itself, Hideyoshi attacked the neighboring areas. Of course, the lands that he was taking possession of were formerly a part of Mino. The land Nobunaga had offered him was worth five hundred *kan*, but the land he conquered was worth more than a thousand.

When Nobunaga learned this, he said with a forced smile, "That one Monkey would be sufficient to take the entire province of Mino. There *are* people in this world who never complain."

Sunomata was secured. Nobunaga felt as though he had already swallowed up Mino. But even thought they had been able to encroach into Mino, the Saito heartland, which was separated from Owari by the Kiso River, was still intact.

With the new castle at Sunomata as a foothold, Nobunaga tried to break through on two occasions, but failed. He felt as though he were beating against an iron wall. But this did not surprise Hideyoshi and Hikoemon. After all, this time it was the enemy who was fighting for survival. It would have been impossible for Owari's small army to conquer Mino with normal tactics.

And there was more. After the castle was built, the enemy realized their former negligence and took a second look at Hideyoshi. This Monkey had risen out of obscurity, and although he hadn't been put to particularly good use by the Oda, he was clearly an able and resourceful warrior who knew how to employ his men well. His reputation grew in the enemy's eyes even more than in the Oda clan, and as a consequence, the enemy strengthened its defenses all the more. It knew it could no longer afford to be negligent.

With two defeats, Nobunaga retreated to Mount Komaki to wait out the end of the year. But Hideyoshi did not wait. His castle had an unbroken view of the Mino Plain to the central mountains. As he stood there with arms folded, he thought, What shall we do about Mino? The large army he was going to call up was quartered not at Mount Komaki nor at Sunomata, but within his mind. Coming down from the watchtower and returning to his quarters, Hideyoshi summoned Hikoemon.

Hikoemon appeared immediately, asking, "How can I be of service?" Without any thought of their former relationship, he paid his respects to the younger man as his master.

"Come a little closer, please."

"With your permission."

"The rest of you withdraw until I call you," Hideyoshi said to the samurai around him. He then turned to Hikoemon. "There's something I want to talk about."

"Yes. What is it?"

"But first," he said, lowering his voice, "I think you're more familiar with the internal conditions of Mino than I am. Where do you suppose Mino's fundamental strength lies? What prevents us from sleeping in peace at Sunomata?"

"In their ablest men, I think."

"Their ablest men. It's certain that it has nothing to do with Saito Tatsuoki."

"The Three Men of Mino swore an oath of loyalty in the time of Tatsuoki's father and grandfather."

"Who are the Three Men?"

"I think you've heard of them. There's Ando Noritoshi, the lord of Kagamijima Castle." Hideyoshi put his hand on his knee and put up one finger as he nodded. "Iyo Michitomo, the lord of Sone Castle."

"Uh-huh." A second finger.

"And Ujiie Hitachinosuke, the master of Ogaki Castle." A third finger.

"Anybody else?"

"Hm." Hikoemon cocked his head to one side. "In addition to them, there's Takenaka Hanbei, but for a number of years he's stopped serving the main branch of the Saito clan and is living in seclusion somewhere on Mount Kurihara. I don't think you have to take him into account."

"Well then, first we can say that the Three Men underpin Mino's strength. Is that right?"

"I believe so."

"That's what I wanted to talk about, but don't you suppose there's some way we could pull away that support?"

"I doubt it," Hikoemon asserted. "A true man is a man of his word. He's not moved by wealth or fame. For example, if you were asked to pull out three healthy teeth, you surely wouldn't, would you?"

"It's not that clear-cut. There must be some way...," Hideyoshi answered softly. "You know, the enemy made several attacks on us during the construction of the castle, but throughout, there was one enemy general who stayed put."

"Who was that?"

"Osawa, the lord of Unuma Castle."

"Ah. That's Osawa Jirozaemon, the Tiger of Unuma."

"That man...the Tiger...I wonder if we couldn't approach him through some relative?"

"Osawa has a younger brother, Mondo," Hikoemon said. "For some years both my brother, Matajuro, and I have been on friendly terms with him."

"That's welcome news." Hideyoshi was happy enough to clap his hands. "Where does this Mondo live?"

"I think he's serving in the castle town of Inabayama."

"Send your brother at once. I wonder if he'll be able to find Mondo."

"If need be, I'll go myself," Hikoemon answered. "What's the plan?"

"Using Mondo, I'd like to alienate Osawa from the Saito clan. And then use Osawa to detach the Three Men of Mino one by one, just like pulling teeth."

"I doubt that you yourself would be able to do it, but fortunately, Mondo is not like his older brother, and is very alert to his own personal gain."

"No, Mondo is not going to be enough to move the Tiger of Unuma. We'll need another player to get that tiger into our cage. And I think we can put Tenzo to work on that."

"Brilliant! But what kind of plan do you have, using those two?"

"It's like this, Hikoemon." Hideyoshi inched closer and whispered his plan into Hachisuka Hikoemon's ear.

For a moment Hikoemon stared at Hideyoshi. A head is nothing but a head, so where did these flashes of genius come from? When he compared Hideyoshi's ingenuity with his own, Hikoemon was amazed.

"Well, I'd like to get Matajuro and Tenzo moving right away," Hideyoshi said.

"I understand. They'll be going into enemy territory, so I'll have them wait until midnight to cross the river.

"I'd like you to explain the plan in detail to them and give them their orders."

"Of course, my lord."

Knowing what he had to do, Hikoemon withdrew from Hideyoshi's room. At this time, more than half the soldiers in the castle were men who had formerly been *ronin* from Hachisuka. Now they had settled down and become samurai.

Hikoemon's younger brother, Matajuro, and his nephew, Tenzo, received their orders from Hikoemon, disguised themselves as merchants, and left the castle late that night for the heart of enemy territory, the castle town of Inabayama. Both Tenzo and Matajuro were well suited for this kind of mission. A month later, their work done, they returned to Sunomata.

Across the river in Mino, rumors began to spread:

"There's something suspicious about the Tiger of Unuma."

"Osawa Jirozaemon has been in collusion with Owari for years."

"That's why he didn't obey Fuwa's command during the construction of the castle at Sunomata. It was supposed to be a combined effort, but he didn't move his troops at all."

The rumors triggered more speculation.

"Lord Tatsuoki is going to order Osawa Jirozaemon to Inabayama Castle soon and ask him about his responsibility for the defeat at Sunomata."

"Unuma Castle is going to be confiscated. Right after the Tiger goes to Inabayama."

These rumors spread around Mino as though they were the truth. The origin of these wildfires was Watanabe Tenzo, and behind him was Hideyoshi, who sat in the castle at Sunomata.

"Don't you think it's about the right time? Go to Unuma now," Hideyoshi said to Hikoemon. "I've written a letter I'd like you to give to Osawa."

"Yes, my lord."

"The central point is to entice him. Arrange the day and the place for the meeting."

Carrying Hideyoshi's letter, Hikoemon secretly visited Unuma.

When he heard that a secret envoy from Sunomata had arrived, Osawa wondered what it could be about. The fierce Tiger of Unuma had begun to look despondent and unhappy. Feigning illness, he avoided everyone. Recently he had received a summons to go to Inabayama, and his family and retainers were apprehensive about it. Osawa himself let it be known that he was too ill to travel, and seemed in no mood to leave. The rumors had reached Unuma, too, and Osawa was aware of the danger to himself. He resented this frame-up by slandering retainers. He also lamented the disorder of the Saito clan and Tatsuoki's stupidity. But there was nothing he could do, and he could see the day when he would be forced to commit *seppuku*. At this point, Hikoemon visited him secretly from Sunomata. Osawa decided to act.

"I'll meet him," Osawa said.

Hideyoshi's letter was handed to him. As soon as Osawa read it, he burned it. Then he delivered his reply orally. "I'll let you know the time and place in a few days. I hope Lord Hideyoshi will be there."

After that, about two weeks passed. A message from Unuma arrived at Sunomata, and Hideyoshi, accompanied by only ten men, including Hikoemon, proceeded to the meeting place, a simple private house exactly midway between Unuma and Sunomata. While the retainers from both sides remained on the banks to stand watch over the area, Hideyoshi and Osawa took a small boat onto the Kiso River by themselves. As they sat knee to knee, the others wondered what secret conversation they might be having. The little boat was like a leaf left to the current of the big river, and for quite some time it was kept far away from the eyes and ears of the world, floating in a lovely scene of wind and light. The talk ended without incident.

After they returned to Sunomata, Hideyoshi told Hikoemon that Osawa would probably come within a week. And so, within a few days and in extreme secrecy, Osawa went to Sunomata. Hideyoshi received him with much courtesy, and before anybody in the castle was aware of his presence, he took him on the very same day to Mount Komaki, where Hideyoshi had a preliminary audience alone with Nobunaga.

"I've come here with Osawa Jirozaemon, the Tiger of Unuma," Hideyoshi told Nobunaga. "After listening to my arguments, he's had a change of heart and is determined to abandon the Saito and join forces with the Oda. So if you would kindly speak with him directly, you will have added an outstandingly brave general and Unuma Castle to the Oda forces without having lifted a finger."

Nobunaga, with a surprised look on his face, seemed to be considering the details of what Hideyoshi had said. Hideyoshi was mildly discontented, wondering why his lord did not seem pleased. It was not a matter of being praised for his own efforts, but to have pulled the fierce Tiger of Unuma, like a tooth right from the enemy's mouth, and to have brought him to meet Nobunaga, should have been a great present.

He had assumed that Nobunaga would be happy. But when he thought about it later, this was not a scheme he had devised with Nobunaga's consent. Maybe that was the reason. Nobunaga's expression seemed to indicate that it was. As the old saying goes, the nail that sticks out too far will be hammered down. Hideyoshi understood this well, and constantly admonished himself that his own head was sticking out as much as the head of a nail. Yet he was unable to sit on his hands and not act on what he knew would be good for his own side.

Finally, Nobunaga gave what seemed to be reluctant permission. Hideyoshi brought in Osawa.

"You've grown up, my lord," Osawa said in a friendly manner. "You may think this is the first time we have met, but today is actually the second time I've had the pleasure of meeting you. The first time was fifteen years ago, at the Shotoku Temple in Tonda, when you met my former master, Lord Saito Dosan."

Nobunaga responded simply, "Is that so?" He seemed to be evaluating his guest's character.

Osawa did not presume to flatter him. Neither did he humbly humor the man. "Even though you are my enemy, I've been impressed with what you've done in recent years. When I first saw you at the Shotoku Temple, you seemed to be a mischievous young man. But from what I have seen today, I realize that the administration of your domain belies popular opinion."

Osawa was speaking as an equal, frankly and candidly. he was not simply a brave man, but he was rather good-natured, Hideyoshi thought.

"Let's meet again on another day and talk at our leisure. I have a number of things to do today," Nobunaga said, standing up and summarily terminating the interview.

Later he summoned Hideyoshi for a private audience. Whatever was said at their meeting, Hideyoshi looked terribly perplexed afterward. But, without informing Osawa of anything, he played the part of the cordial host and entertained the general at Mount Komaki Castle.

"I'll let you know in detail what His Lordship said, after we return to Sunomata."

Once they were back at Hideyoshi's castle and the two of them were alone, Hideyoshi said, "General Osawa, I have put you in an impossible position, and I think I can only atone for this with my death. Without consulting Lord Nobunaga, I believed that His Lordship would feel exactly as I do, and happily welcome you as an ally. But his opinion of you was completely different from my own," Hideyoshi let out a sigh. Then, pausing, he looked down sadly.

Osawa had realized on his own that Nobunaga's feelings were not very favorable. "You seem terribly upset, but there's really no reason why you should be. It's not as though I can't live without a stipend from Lord Nobunaga."

"The fact is I'd be happy if that were all." Hideyoshi could hardly speak, but he sat a little straighter, as though he had suddenly found his resolve. "I'd better tell you everything. General Osawa, when I was about to leave, Lord Nobunaga summoned me in secret and scolded me for not understanding the military art of the double-cross. Why, he asked, would Osawa Jirozaemon, a man of character with such a high reputation in Mino, be taken in by my glib tongue and become his ally? I didn't foresee this at all."

"Yes, I can imagine."

"He also told me that it was this very Osawa of Unuma Castle who, as a general on the provincial border, had been the tiger protecting Mino and causing so much trouble in Owari for many years. He suggested that perhaps it was I who was being deceived by your clever words and manipulated by your daring. You can see he's full of doubts."

"Indeed."

"He also felt that if you stayed any longer at Mount Komaki, we would be letting you see the defenses of the province, so I was ordered to take you back to Sunomata immediately. Take you back and..." Hideyoshi cut his words off short as though they stuck in his throat. Even Osawa was upset, but he looked Hideyoshi straight in the eye, encouraging him to say the rest of the sentence.

"This is difficult to say, but it was His Lorship's order, so I'd like you to hear it. I was ordered by him to take you back to Sunomata, lock you up in the castle, and kill you. He thought this was a grand opportunity—one not to be missed."

When Osawa looked around, he realized that he was accompanied by not one single soldier and was inside the enemy's castle. And fearless as he was, his hair stood up on the back of his neck.

Hideyoshi continued, "But as for myself, if I obey His Lordship's order, I will have broken the pledge I already made to you, and this would be trampling the honor of a samurai. I cannot do that. At the same time, however, if I presume myself not to be lacking in the loyalty of a retainer, I'll be turning my back on my lord's orders. I've reached the point where I can neither advance nor retreat. So, on the way back from Mount Komaki, I was despondent and unhappy, which, I suppose, probably made you somewhat suspicious. But please, put away your doubts. I now have the solution very clearly in mind."

"What do mean? What are you going to do?"

"By disembowelling myself, I think I can apologize to both you and Lord Nobunaga. There's no other way. General Osawa, let's drink a farewell cup. After that, I'm resigned. I guarantee that no one is going to lay a hand on you. You can get away from here under the cover of night. Don't worry about me, just put your heart at ease!"

Osawa listened silently to everything Hideyoshi said, but his eyes were filled with tears. In contrast to the ferocity that had earned him his nickname, these were tears beyond an ordinary man's; it was clear that he had a character with a strong sense of righteousness. "I'm indebted to you," he sniffed, and wiped his eyes. Could this be the general who had fought in countless battles? "But listen, Lord Hideyoshi. It would be unpardonable for you to commit *seppuku*."

"But if I don't, there are no words for an apology, either to you or His Lordship."

"No, no matter what you say, there's no righteousness in cutting open your stomach and helping me. My honor as a samurai will not allow it."

"I was the one who explained things to you and invited you here. I'm also the one who was mistaken about the way His Lordship thinks. So to apologize to both you and His Lordship, it's only proper that I'm the one who should atone for the crime by taking my own life. Please don't try to stop me."

"No matter what kind of mistake you claim to have made, I was also to blame. This is not worthy of your suicide. Instead, let me offer my head to you in appreciation of your good faith. Take my head back to Mount Komaki." Osawa began to draw his short sword.

Shaken, Hideyoshi grabbed Osawa's hand. "What are you doing?"

"Let go of my hand."

"I will not. Nothing could be more painful than to let you commit *seppuku*."

"I understand. That's why I'm offering you my head. If you had planned some cowardly trick I could have shown you a real escape, even if I would have had to build a mountain of corpses to do it. But I've been touched by your samurai spirit."

"But wait. Think for just a moment. It seems very strange that we're both fighting to die. General Osawa, if you trust me to that extent, I have a plan that will allow us both to live and maintain our honor as warriors. But do you still have the heart to assist the Oda clan one more step?"

"One more step?"

"In the end, Nobunaga's doubts are based on his high regard for you. So at this point, if you did something that would truly manifest your support of the Oda clan, his doubts would melt."

That night, Osawa left Sunomata Castle and went off to an unknown destination. What was the plan revealed to him by Hideyoshi? There was no reason for anyone to know, but later its nature was plain to see. Someone now spoke to Iyo, Ando, and Ujiie—the Three Men of Mino, the very foundation of Saito power—proposing that they all three pledge allegiance to the Oda clan. The man who spoke to them so eloquently, and through whose good offices they were introduced, was none other than Osawa Jirozaemon.

Of course, Hideyoshi did not commit *seppuku*. Osawa fared well, and Nobunaga added four famous generals of Mino to his allies without ever leaving his castle. Was this Nobunaga's wisdom or Hideyoshi's genius? A subtle interplay of minds seemed to have taken place between lord and retainer, and no one could have said for certain which mind was actually in command.

* * *

Nobunaga was impatient. He had made a large sacrifice to build the castle at Sunomata, and it had taken a good deal of time, so he naturally felt frustrated.

"To avenge the name of my late father-in-law, I will strike down this immoral clan, and release the people who gasp under its evil administration." This had been the declaration of Nobunaga's motive, so that the battle might be one the world would accept, but as time passed, these words naturally started to lose their power. There was also the possibility that his ability was being questioned by the Tokugawa of Mikawa, whom he could feel watching him from the rear.

The actual strength of the Oda was under question, and there was a real danger to the Oda-Tokugawa alliance. Nevertheless, Nobunaga felt impatient. Certainly he had brought Osawa and the Three Men of Mino over to his camp, but this alone had not won him any victories.

To conquer Mino with a single blow was what he asked for. It seemed that, ever since Okehazama, Nobunaga's faith in the concept of "the single blow" had become much stronger than before. Therefore, on a number of occasions, men like Hideyoshi had expressed some opposition.

At the conference to discuss the conquest of Mino that summer, Hideyoshi sat silently in the lowest seat throughout the proceedings. When asked for his views he responded, "I think, perhaps, the time is still not ripe."

This answer was extremely uncongenial to Nobunaga, who asked, almost as a rebuke, "Was it not you who said that if the Tiger of Unuma were to bring the Three Men over to our side, Mino would crumble on its own without our having to leave the castle?"

"Begging your pardon, my lord, but Mino has more than ten times the strength and wealth of Owari."

"First you said it was an excess of men of talent, and now you fear their wealth and strength. If that's the case, just when are we going to attack them?" Nobunaga no longer asked for Hideyoshi's opinion about anything. The council moved on. It was decided that, in the summer, a large army would start out from Mount Komaki for Mino, using Sunomata as its base camp.

The battle to cross the river into enemy territory lasted over a month. Throughout that time, a great number of wounded were sent back. There were never any reports of victory. The battle-weary army simply retreated in complete silence, soldiers and generals alike tight-lipped and morose.

When asked by the men who had remained at the castle how the battle had gone, they all looked down and silently shook their heads. Nobunaga was silent from then on, too. It was clear he had learned that not every battle is fought like Okehazama. The castle at Sunomata was quiet now, visited only by the desolate autumn winds from the river.

A call came suddenly to Hikoemon from his master. "Among your former *ronin*, I imagine there must be a number who were born in other provinces, and quite a few from Mino," Hideyoshi began.

"Yes, there are."

"Do you suppose any of them were born in Fuwa?"

"I'll find out."

"Good. If you can find one, would you call him here?" In a while, Hachisuka Hikoemon brought one of his former *ronin*, a man named Saya Kuwaju, out to the garden where Hideyoshi waited. He appeared to be a strong man of about thirty.

"You're Saya?" Hideyoshi asked.

"Yes, my lord."

"And you're from Fuwa in Mino?"

"A village called Tarui."

"Well, I imagine you're pretty familiar with the area."

"I lived there until I was twenty years old, so I know it a little."

"Do you have any relatives there?"

"My younger sister."

"What is she doing?"

"She married into a local farming family, and I imagine she has children by now."

"Wouldn't you like to go back there? Just once?"

"I've never thought about it. It's likely that if my sister heard that her brother, the *ronin*, was coming home, she'd feel very uncomfortable around her husband's relatives and the rest of the village."

"But that was before. Now you're a retainer of Sunomata Castle and a respectable samurai. There's nothing wrong with that, is there?"

"But Fuwa is a strategic district in western Mino. What would I be doing in enemy territory?"

Hideyoshi nodded repeatedly at this obvious point, and seemed to be making up his mind about something. "I'd like you to come with me. We'll disguise ourselves so that we

273

don't attract attention. Be at the garden gate by nightfall."

Hikoemon inquired dubiously, "Where are you thinking of going so suddenly?"

Hideyoshi lowered his voice and whispered into Hikoemon's ear, "To Mount Kurihara."

Hikoemon looked at him as though he doubted his sanity. He had suspected for a while that Hideyoshi had something in mind, but Mount Kurihara! Hearing his master, he could hardly hold back his surprise. A former retainer of the Saito clan, a man who was regarded as a great strategist, was living a secluded life on the mountain. This man was Takenaka Hanbei. Some time before, Hideyoshi had made a thorough inquiry into the character of this man and his relationship with the Saito clan.

Now, if we can lead this horse through the camp gate in the same way we pulled the Tiger of Unuma and the Three Men....This was Hideyoshi's general plan, but for him to consider penetrating enemy territory and going to Mount Kurihara itself was unthinkable.

"Do you really mean to go there?" Hikoemon asked incredulously.

"Of course."

"Really?" Hikoemon pressed.

"Why are you making such a point of this?" Hideyoshi appeared to think that it was no cause for danger or concern. "In the first place, you're the only one who knows my intentions, and we're going in secret. I'm going to ask you to take care of things while I'm gone for a few days."

"You're going alone?"

"No, I'll take Saya with me."

"Going with him will be the same as going unarmed. Do you really think you're going to be able to cajole Hanbei into being our ally by going alone into enemy territory?"

"That will be difficult," Hideyoshi muttered almost to himself. "But I plan to try. If I go with an open heart, it won't make any difference how firm the ties are that bind him to the Saito clan."

Hikoemon suddenly recalled Hideyoshi's eloquence when he had argued against him at Hachisuka. Still, he wondered if Hideyoshi would really be able to bring Takenaka Hanbei down from Mount Kurihara. Even with his eloquence. No, even if things went poorly, and Hanbei decided to leave his mountain retreat, it was possible that he might choose the Saito rather than the Oda.

It was rumored at the time that Hanbei, having retired to Mount Kurihara, was leading a quiet, countrified life, perfecting himself as a hermit away from the world. But one day, if his former masters, the Saito, were in danger of ruin, he would return to lead their army. Surely it was true that when they had driven away the great Oda attack before, he had not come to be at the head of their forces, but remained viewing the war clouds over the country from Mount Kurihara, sending his meditations to the Saito one by one and teaching them secret strategies of war. There were people who spread this story around as though it were the truth. It would be difficult—Hideyoshi himself had said this. Hikoemon felt the same way but even more so, and let out something like a groan.

"That will be a difficult ambition to realize, my lord." The look on his face expressed admonishment.

"Well…" Hideyoshi's troubled expression cleared. "There's really not that much to worry about. A difficult thing can be unexpectedly easy, and what appears to be easy can in fact be extremely difficult. I think what's essential is whether or not I can make Hanbei trust in my sincerity. My opponent being who he is, I don't plan on simple stratagems or tricks."

He began preparations for his secret journey. While he thought this trip might be futile, Hikoemon was unable to stop him. Day by day his respect for Hideyoshi's resourcefulness and magnanimity increased, and he believed that the man's ability was far above his own.

Nightfall. As agreed, Saya was standing by the garden gate. Hideyoshi looked every bit as shabby as Saya.

"Well, Hikoemon, take care of everything," Hideyoshi said, and started off as though he were just going to walk around the castle grounds. It was not, in fact, very far to Mount Kurihara from Sunomata—perhaps about ten leagues. On a bright day, Mount Kurihara could be seen dimly in the distance. But that single line of mountains was Mino's fortress against the enemy. Hideyoshi took a roundabout route along the mountains and entered Fuwa.

To know the nature and special characteristics of the people who lived there, it was essential to look first at the area's natural features. The district of Fuwa was in the foothills of the mountains in the western part of Mino, and was a bottleneck in the road to the capital.

The autumn colors at Sekigahara were beautiful. Innumerable rivers crisscrossed the land like veins. Ancient history and countless legends remained at the roots of the autumn vegetation as the grave markers of a bloody past. The Yoro Mountains formed the boundary with Kai, and clouds came and went constantly around Mount Ibuki.

Takenaka Hanbei was a native of the area. It was said that he was actually born at Inabayama, but he had spent most of his childhood at the foot of Mount Ibuki. Born in the fourth year of Temmon, Hanbei would now still be only twenty-eight years old, nothing more than a young student of military affairs. One year younger than Nobunaga, one year older than Hideyoshi. Nevertheless, he had already abandoned the quest for great achievement in the chaotic world, and had built himself a hermitage on Mount Kurihara. He took pleasure in nature, made friends with the books of the ancients, and wrote poetry, never meeting with the visitors who often came to his door. Was he a fake? This was also said of him, but Hanbei's name was respected in Mino, and his reputation had traveled as far as Owari.

I'd like to meet him and judge his character for myself, was the first thought in Hideyoshi's mind. It would be regrettable for him just to pass by and not meet such a rare and extraordinary man, when they had both been born into the same world. Even more, if Hanbei was driven into the enemy camp, Hideyoshi would have to kill him. He sincerely hoped this would not happen, because it would be the most regrettable event of his entire life. I'm going to meet him, whether he'll see people or not.

THE MASTER OF MOUNT KURIHARA

Mount Kurihara, situated next to Mount Nangu, was not very high, and looked almost like a child snuggling against its parent.

Ah, it's beautiful! When they approached the peak, even Hideyoshi, who was no poet, was in ecstasy, struck by the sublime beauty of the autumn sun sinking below the horizon. But now his mind turned to a single thought: How can I get Hanbei to become my ally? And this was quickly followed by another: No, to confront a master strategist by means of strategy would be the worst strategy of all. I can only meet him as a blank sheet of paper. I'll just talk to him candidly, and speak with all my power. Thus he rallied his spirits. Nevertheless, he still did not even know where Hanbei lived, and they had been unable to find his isolated residence by the time the sun went down. Hideyoshi, however, was not in a hurry. When it got dark, a lamp would naturally be lit somewhere. Rather than walking around uselessly, taking all the wrong turns, it would be more pleasant and quicker to stay where they were. At least he seemed to be thinking this way, because he sat resting until the sun had set. Finally they spotted the tiny dot of a lamp off in the distance, beyond a swampy hollow. Following a narrow, meandering path that wound its way up and down, they at last reached the place.

It was a level plot of land surrounded by red pines, halfway up the mountain. They had expected to encounter a small thatched cottage surrounded by a broken-down fence, but they now found themselves approaching a crude mud wall encircling a large compound. As they came closer, they could see three or four lanterns burning farther within. Instead of a formal gate, only a bamboo shutter flapped loosely in the wind.

This is so big, Hideyoshi thought as he entered silently. Inside was a pine wood. A narrow path led from the entrance into the pines, and except for the pine needles covering the ground, one was not aware of a single speck of dirt. Walking on, for about fifty yards, they came to the house. A cow was lowing in its stall in a nearby shed. They could hear a fire crackling in the wind, and its smoke filled the air. Hideyoshi stood still. He rubbed his sharp eyes. With a gust of wind from the mountain, however, the place was suddenly swept clear of smoke; and when he looked, he saw a child putting twigs under the stove in a cooking hut.

"Who are you?" the boy asked suspiciously.

"Are you a servant?" Hideyoshi asked.

"Me? Yes," the boy replied.

"I am a retainer of the Oda clan. My name is Kinoshita Hideyoshi. Could you pass on a message?"

"To whom?"

"To your master."

"He's not here."

"He's out?"

"I'm telling you, he's really out. Go away." Turning his back on the visitor, the child sat in front of the stove, and once again began stoking the fire. The night mist on the mountain was chill, and Hideyoshi squatted in front of the stove, next to the child.

"Let me warm myself up a bit."

The child said nothing, but gave him a quick glance out of the corner of his eye.

"It's cold at night, isn't it?"

"This is a mountain. Of course it's cold," the boy said.

"Little monk, this—"

"This is not a temple! I'm Master Hanbei's disciple, not a monk!"

"Ha, ha, ha, ha!"

"Why are you laughing?"

"I'm sorry."

"Go away! If my master finds out some stranger has crept into the cooking hut, I'll get scolded for it later."

"No. It'll be all right. I'll apologize to your master later."

"You really want to meet him?"

"That's right. Do you think I'm going to go back down the mountain without meeting him, after coming all this way?"

"People from Owari are rude, aren't they? You're from Owari, right?"

"What's wrong with that?"

"My master hates people from Owari. I hate them too. Owari's an enemy province, isn't it?"

"That's right, I guess."

"You've come looking for something in Mino, haven't you? If you're just on a journey, you'd better go right on by. Or you'll lose your head."

"I don't intend to go any farther than this. My only plan was to come to this house."

"What did you come here for?"

"I came to seek admission."

"Seek admission? You want to become a disciple of my teacher, like me?"

"Uh-huh. I guess I want to become a brother disciple with you. At any rate, we should get along well. Now go talk to the master. I'll look after stoking the oven. Don't worry, the rice won't burn."

"That's all right. I don't want to."

"Don't be bad-tempered. There, isn't that your master coughing inside?"

"My master coughs a lot at night. He's not strong."

"So you lied to me when you said he was out."

"It's all the same whether he's here or not. He won't meet with anyone who calls, no matter who they are or what province they come from."

"Well, I'll wait for the right time."

"Yeah, come again."

"No. This hut is nice and warm. Just let me stay here for a while."

"You're joking! Go away!" The boy jumped up as if to attack the intruder, but when he glared at Hideyoshi's smiling face in the flickering red light of the oven, he was unable to stay angry no matter how hard he tried. As the child stared hard at this man's face, his initial feelings of hostility gradually lessened.

"Kokuma! Kokuma!" called a voice from the house. The boy reacted instantly. Leaving Hideyoshi where he was, he dashed from the hut into the house, and he didn't come back for quite some time. In the meantime, the smell of scorched food drifted out of the large cauldron that sat on top of the stove. Unable to think of it as just someone else's meal, Hideyoshi quickly picked up the ladle on top of the lid and stirred the contents of the cauldron—brown rice gruel mixed with dried chestnuts and dried vegetables. Others might have laughed at this pauper's food, but Hideyoshi had been born on a poor farm, and when he looked at a single grain of rice, he saw his mother's tears. To him, this was no trifling matter.

"That boy! This is going to burn. What a waster."

Taking a cloth, he grabbed the handles of the pot and lifted it up.

"Oh, thank you, mister."

"Ah, Kokuma? It was just beginning to burn, so I took the cauldron off. It seems to have boiled just enough."

"You already know my name, huh?"

"That's what Master Hanbei called from inside just now. Did you talk to the master for me while you were there?"

"He called me for something else. As for interceding for you, if I talked to my teacher about some useless thing, he'd only get mad. So I didn't say anything."

"Well, well. You're strict about following your teacher's orders, aren't you? I'm really impressed."

"Huh! You're just talking for the sake of your own pride now."

"No, it's true. I'm impatient, but if I were your teacher, I'd praise you like this. That's no lie."

Just then, someone came out of the nearby kitchen, holding a paper lantern. A female voice called repeatedly for Kokuma, and as Hideyoshi turned and looked, he could dimly see a sixteen- or seventeen-year-old girl wearing a kimono with a pattern of mountain cherry blossoms and mist, tied with a plum-colored sash. Her figure was illuminated in the sooty darkness by the light of the paper lantern she held in her hand.

"What is it, Oyu?" Kokuma stepped toward her and listened to what she said. When she finished speaking with him, the cherry-blossomed sleeve glided down the dark entrance hall together with the lamp and disappeared behind the wall.

"Who was that?" Hideyoshi asked.

"My teacher's sister," Kokuma said simply and in a gentle voice, as though he were speaking of the beauty of the flowers in his master's garden.

"Listen, I'm asking you. Just to make sure, won't you please go inside just once and ask him to see me? If he says no, I'll leave."

"You'll really leave?"

"I will."

"For sure, now." Kokuma spoke emphatically, but finally he went inside. He returned right away and said abruptly, "He says no, and that he detests receiving guests...and I got scolded, sure enough. So please go away, mister. I'm going to serve my teacher his meal now."

"Well, I'll leave tonight. Then I'll call again sometime." Submitting meekly, Hideyoshi stood up and started to go.

Kokuma said, "It won't do any good to come back!"

Hideyoshi retraced his steps in silence. Unmindful of the darkness, he descended to the foot of the mountain and slept.

When he got up the following day, he made some preparations and once again climbed the mountain. Then, just as he had done the day before, he visited the mountain residence of Hanbei at sundown. The day before, he had spent too much time with the boy, so today he tried going up to the door that appeared to be the main entrance. The person who responded and came out to his call was the same Kokuma of the day before.

"What! Mister, you've come again?"

"I wondered if I could ask to meet him today. Do me the favor of asking your teacher again." Kokuma went inside, and whether he really talked to Hanbei or not, he quickly returned and gave him the same blank refusal.

"If that's the case, I'll inquire again when he's in a better mood," Hideyoshi said politely and left. Two days later he climbed the mountain again.

"Will he meet me today?" Kokuma made a round trip inside the house in his usual fashion, and once again refused him plainly. "He says it's annoying that you come so often."

That day Hideyoshi returned in silence again. He visited the house this way any number of times. In the end, whenever Kokuma saw his face, he did nothing but laugh.

"You've got a lot of patience, haven't you, mister? But coming here is useless, no matter how patient you are. These days, when I go in to tell my teacher you're here, he just laughs instead of getting mad."

Young boys will easily become friendly with people, and a familiarity had already started to develop between Kokuma and Hideyoshi.

Hideyoshi climbed the mountain again on the following day. Waiting at the foot of the mountain, Saya had no idea of his master's frame of mind, and finally starting to get angry, he said, "Who does Takenaka Hanbei think he is? This time I'm going to go up there and call his rudeness into account."

The day of Hideyoshi's tenth visit was a day of violent wind and rain, and both Saya and the people who owned the farmhouse where they stayed did their best to stop Hideyoshi from going, but he stubbornly put on a straw raincoat and hat, and made the ascent. Arriving at dusk, he stood at the entrance and called in as usual.

"Yes. Who is it, please?" That night, for the first time, the young woman, Oyu, who Kokuma had said was Hanbei's sister stepped out.

"I know I'm bothering Master Hanbei by calling, and I regret that I'm doing so against his wishes, but I've come as my own master's envoy, and it will be difficult for me to return home until I have met him. It is part of a samurai's service to deliver his master's messages, so I'm resolved to call here until Master Hanbei agrees to see me, even if it takes two or three years. And if Master Hanbei refuses to meet me, I have decided to disembowel myself. Alas, I'm sure that Master Hanbei knows the hardships of the warrior class better than any man. Please . . . if you could put in a good word for me."

Beneath the spray of the rain gushing violently from the leaking roof, Hideyoshi knelt and made his petition. It seemed that the impressionable young lady was moved by that alone.

"Please wait for a moment," she said gently, and disappeared into the house. When she appeared again, however, she told him, evidently with some pity, that Hanbei's answer had not changed. "I'm sorry that my elder brother is so stubborn, but would you kindly withdraw? He says that no matter how often you come here, he won't see you. He dislikes speaking with people and refuses to do so now."

"Is that so?" Hideyoshi looked down in apparent disappointment but did not persist. The rain from the eaves battered against his shoulders. "There's nothing else to be done. Well, I'll wait until he's in a good mood." Putting on his hat, he walked out, dejected, into the rain. Following the path through the pine forest as he always did, he had just come out on the other side of the mud wall when he heard Kokuma chasing him from behind.

"Mister! He'll meet you! He said he'll meet you! He said to come back!"

"Huh? Master Hanbei said he would meet me?" Hideyoshi hastily returned with Kokuma. But only Oyu, Hanbei's sister, was waiting for them.

"My brother was so impressed with your sincerity that he said he would be at fault if he didn't meet you. But not tonight. He's in bed today because of the rain, but he asked you to come on another day, when he sends a message to you." It suddenly occurred to Hideyoshi that perhaps this woman had felt sorry for him and that, after he had left, she had appealed to her elder brother, Hanbei, on his behalf.

"Whenever you send word, I'll be ready."

"Where are you staying?"

"I'm staying at the foot of the mountain, at Moemon's house, a farmhouse near a large zelkova tree in the village of Nangu."

"Well, when the weather clears."

"I'll be waiting."

"It must be cold, and you're getting wet in the rain. At least dry your clothes by the fire in the cooking hut and have something to eat before you go."

"No, I'll save it for another day. I'll take my leave now." Striding through the rain, Hideyoshi went down the mountain.

The rain continued to fall the next day. The day after that, Mount Kurihara remained wrapped in white clouds, and no tidings came from a messenger. Finally the weather cleared, and the colors of the mountain were entirely renewed. The early autumn leaves of the sumac and lacquer trees had turned bright red.

That morning Kokuma arrived at Moemon's gate leading a cow. "Hey, mister!" he said. "I've come to invite you up! My teacher told me to guide you to the house. And since you're a guest today, I've brought a mount for you." With that, he handed him an invitation from Hanbei. Hideyoshi opened it and read:

Curiously, you have often come to visit this weakened man who has retired to the country. Although it is difficult for me to grant your request, please come for a bowl of plain tea.

The words seemed a bit haughty. Hideyoshi could see that Hanbei was a rather unsociable man, even before he met him face to face. Hideyoshi sat astride the cow's back, saying to Kokuma, "Well, since you brought me a ride, shall we go?" Kokuma turned toward the mountain and began walking. The autumn sky around Mount Kurihara and Mount Nangu was clear. It was the first time since he had come to the foothills that Hideyoshi was able to look up and see the mountains so clearly.

When they finally approached the entrance to the mud wall, they could see a beautiful woman standing there with an expectant expression. It was Oyu, who had dressed and made herself up more carefully than usual.

"Ah, you shouldn't have taken the trouble," Hideyoshi said, hastily jumping down from the cow's back.

Having passed inside, he was left alone in a room. The babbling of water cleansed his ears. The bamboo in the wind brushed against the window. This truly seemed to be a quiet retreat in the mountains. In an alcove with rough clay walls and pine pillars was hung a scroll on which a Zen priest had written the Chinese character for the word "dream."

How can he be here without being completely bored? Hideyoshi wondered, marveling at the thoughts of the man who lived in such a place. And he thought that he himself would be unable to stay for more than three days. He didn't know what to do with himself, even for the time he was there. Even though he was being soothed by the songs of the birds and the soughing of the pines, his mind had dashed off to Sunomata and then gone on to Mount Komaki, while his blood seethed in the winds and clouds of the times. Hideyoshi was definitely a stranger to this sort of peace.

"Well, I've made you wait." The voice of a young man came from behind him. It was Hanbei. Hideyoshi had known he was young, but hearing the man's voice, he was impressed with this fact all the more. His host sat down, leaving him the seat of honor.

Hideyoshi spoke hastily, beginning with a formal greeting. "I am a retainer of the Oda clan. My name is Kinoshita Hideyoshi."

Hanbei gently stopped him. "Don't you think we can omit stiff formalities? That certainly wasn't my intention in inviting you here today."

Hideyoshi felt that he had already been put at a disadvantage by this reply. The opening gambit that he had always taken with others had already been taken by his host with him.

"I am Takenaka Hanbei, the master of this mountain cottage. I'm honored by your coming here today."

"No, I'm afraid I've rather obstinately presented myself at your gate and been quite troublesome."

Hanbei laughed. "To be honest, you've been a real annoyance. But now that I meet you, I must say it's quite a relief to have a guest from time to time. Please make yourself at home. By the way, my honored guest, what is it that you're looking for by climbing up to my mountain cottage? People say there's nothing in the mountains but the sounds of birds."

He had taken a seat lower than his guest's, but his eyes seemed to wear a smile, and he seemed amused by this man who had shown up from nowhere. At this point, Hideyoshi studied him frankly. Hanbei's frame truly did not seem very robust. His skin was flaccid, his face pale. But he was a handsome man, and the red of his mouth was especially striking.

All in all, his demeanor must have been the result of good upbringing. He was serene and spoke quietly, and with a smile. But there was some doubt as to whether the surface of this human being really manifested the underlying truth, just as, for example, the mountain today seemed peaceful enough for happy wandering, but the other day a storm had roared out of the valley, blowing enough to make the trees howl.

"Well, in fact…" For an instant Hideyoshi smiled, and he straightened his shoulders a little. "I have come to meet you at Lord Nobunaga's order. Won't you come down from this mountain? The world is not going to allow a man of your ability to live a leisurely life in the mountains from such an early age. Sooner or later you're bound to serve as a samurai. And if that's so, who are you going to serve, if not Lord Oda Nobunaga? So I've come to encourage you to serve the Oda clan. Don't you feel like standing among the clouds of war one more time?"

Hanbei only listened and grinned mysteriously. Even with his quick tongue, Hideyoshi found his zeal considerably diminished by this kind of opponent. The man was like a willow in the wind. You couldn't tell whether he was listening or not. Holding his tongue for a while, he waited meekly for Hanbei to respond, and to the very end he carried himself like a blank sheet of paper, facing this man without stratagem or affectation.

During this time, a light breeze was fluttering from a fan in Hanbei's hand. He had previously placed three chunks of charcoal into a small brazier, and putting down the tongs, he fanned the brazier just enough to ignite the fire without raising the ashes. The water in the kettle started to boil. In the meantime, he took up the napkin used for the tea ceremony and wiped the small tea bowls for both host and guest. It seemed as though he might be judging the temperature of the water by the sound of its boiling. The man was graceful and seemingly without a fault, but very deliberate.

Hideyoshi could feel his feet beginning to fall asleep, but he was unable to find an opening for his next words. And before he noticed it, the things he had talked about in such detail had flown off in the direction of the wind in the pines. It seemed that nothing remained in Hanbei's ears.

"Well now, I wonder if you have anything to say concerning the things I spoke about just now. I'm sure that making some statement about how you will be repaid in terms of stipend and rank, and trying to entice you with money, is not the way to quicken your return from retirement, so I'm not going to mention such things at all. Now, it's true that Owari is a small province, but it's going to control the nation in the future because no one other than my lord has the capacity. So it's wasteful for you to live in seclusion in the mountains in the midst of this chaotic world. You should come down for the sake of the nation." His host suddenly turned to him as he spoke, and Hideyoshi unconsciously held his breath. But Hanbei quietly offered him a tea bowl.

"Have some tea," he said. Then, taking a small tea bowl for himself, Hanbei sipped the tea almost as though he were licking the bowl. He tasted the tea a number of times, as though there were absolutely nothing else in his heart.

"Honored guest…"

"Yes?"

"Do you like orchids? In the spring they are beautiful, but they're quite nice in the fall, too."

"Orchids! What do you mean, orchids?"

"The flowers. When you go about three or four leagues deeper into the mountain, on the precipices and cliffs there are orchids that hold the dew of ancient times. I had my servant, Kokuma, pick one and then put it into a pot. Would you like to see it?"

"N-no." Hideyoshi stopped hesitantly. "I have no use for looking at orchids."

"Is that so?"

"I hope to one day, but the fact that my dreams run off to the battleground even when I'm at home shows that I'm still a hot-blooded youth. I'm nothing more than a humble servant of the Oda clan. I don't understand the feelings of such men of leisure."

"Well, that's not unreasonable. But don't you think it's a personal waste for a man like you to be so busily worn out by the search for fame and profit? There's a rather profound significance to a life lived in the mountains. Why don't you leave Sunomata and come build a hut on this mountain?"

Isn't honesty the same as foolishness? And in the end doesn't being without strategy mean being without wisdom? Perhaps sincerity alone is not sufficient to knock at the human heart. I don't understand, Hideyoshi thought as he silently went down the mountain. It had been in vain. His visit to Hanbei's house had been for nothing. Burning with indignation, he turned around and looked back. Now nothing remained but resentment. No regrets. He had been politely sent away after today's first encounter. Perhaps I'll never meet him again, Hideyoshi thought. No. The next time I'll examine his head after they place it in front of my camp stool on the battlefield. He promised this to himself as he chewed his lip. How many times had he walked this road and lowered his head, being perfectly courteous and hiding his shame? This road was now an irritation. He turned around once again.

"You worm!" he shouted impotently. Perhaps he was recalling Hanbei's pale face and worn body. In his anger, he quickened his pace. Then, taking a turn in the road that looked out over a cliff on one side, he suddenly seemed to remember something he had been suppressing ever since leaving Hanbei's house. Standing on the cliff, he relieved himself into the valley below. The arcing stream became a rustling mist halfway down. Hideyoshi became abstracted and took care of his business, but when he finished he exclaimed, "That's enough of grumbling!" With that, he quickened his pace even more, and dashed down to the foothills of the mountain.

When he got to Moemon's house he said, "Saya, this has unexpectedly turned out to be a long trip. Let's get up early tomorrow and go home." With his master wearing such an energetic look, Saya thought that the meeting with Takenaka Hanbei must have gone well, and he felt happy for his master. Hideyoshi and Saya passed the evening with Moemon and his family, and then dropped off to sleep. Hideyoshi slept with an empty mind. Saya was so surprised at his master's snoring that he opened his eyes from time to time. But when he thought about it, he realized that the worry and physical fatigue of going up Mount Kurihara every day must have been considerable. With this knowledge, even Saya became teary-eyed.

Trying to triumph, even just a little, must be something, he told himself, but he had no idea that his master's efforts had ended in failure. Hideyoshi was already finishing his travel preparations before dawn. Stepping out into the dew, they left the village. No doubt many of the families there were still sound asleep.

"Wait, Saya."

Hideyoshi suddenly stopped and stood up straight, facing the rising sun. Mount Kurihara was still black above the sea of morning mist. Behind the mountain, the glowing clouds were moving with the colors of the brilliantly ascending sun.

"No, I was wrong," Hideyoshi muttered. "I came to get a person who is hard to get. So that he is hard to get is natural. Maybe my own sincerity is still insufficient. How can I accomplish great things with such smallness of mind?"

He turned completely around. "Saya, I'm going up Mount Kurihara one more time. You go back before me." With that, he abruptly turned and went back up the road, piercing the morning mist on the slopes of the mountain, going steadily on. So today, again, he climbed the mountain, and before long he was already halfway up. When he came to the edge of a broad, grassy swamp that was close to Hanbei's house, he heard a voice addressing him in the distance.

It was Oyu, and with her was Kokuma. She had an herb basket at her elbow and was riding the cow. Kokuma was holding the reins.

"Well, I'm surprised. You're amazing, aren't you, mister? Even my teacher said you'd had enough and probably wouldn't come back today."

Dismounting from the cow's back, Oyu made her salutations as always. But Kokuma beseeched him.

"Mister, please don't go on, just for today. He said he had had a fever in the night because he talked with you for a long time. Even this morning his mood was horrible, and I got scolded."

"Don't be rude," Oyu reprimanded him, and apologized to Hideyoshi, asking him in a roundabout way not to visit. "It's not that my brother became ill from talking to you, but he seems to have a bit of a cold. He's in bed today, so I'll tell him that you wanted to come. But, please, not today."

"I suppose it would be an annoyance. I'll drop the idea and go back, but…"

He took a brush and an ink case from his kimono, and wrote a poem on a piece of paper.

There is no leisure in a life of indolence.
That should be left to the birds and beasts.
There is seclusion even in a crowd,
Tranquillity in the streets of a town.
The mountain clouds are free from worldly attachments,
They come and go of themselves.
How can the place to bury one's bones
Be limited to the green mountains?

He knew very well that it was a poor poem, but it expressed what he felt. He added one more thing:

Where is the destination of the clouds that leave the peaks?
To the west? To the east?

"I'm sure he's going to laugh at me and call me impudent and shameless, but this is the last time I'll bother him. I'll wait here for an answer. And if I see that it will be impossible to complete my lord's order, I'll commit *seppuku* right here by this swamp. So please go speak to him for me one more time." He was even more earnest today than he had been yesterday. And there was no falseness in his use of the word *seppuku*. It had slipped out almost unconsciously, from his own zeal.

Rather than despising him, Oyu felt a deep sympathy and returned to her brother's sickbed with the letter. Hanbei read the letter once and said absolutely nothing. He kept his eyes closed for almost half a day. Evening came, and the day turned into a moonlit night.

"Kokuma, fetch the cow," Hanbei said suddenly.

Since he was obviously going to go out, Oyu became alarmed and dressed her brother warmly in padded cotton clothes and a heavy kimono. Then he left, riding on the cow. With Kokuma as his guide, they went down the mountain slope toward the swamp. On a grassy knoll in the distance, he could see the figure of someone who had had neither food nor drink, sitting cross-legged like a Zen priest under the moon. Had a hunter discovered him from afar, he would have thought that Hideyoshi made a perfect target. Hanbei got down from the cow and approached him directly. Then he knelt down in front of Hideyoshi and bowed.

"Master guest, I was discourteous today. I'm not sure what promise you've set your heart on, from a person who is nothing more than a worn-out man living in the mountains, but your manners were more than I deserved. It is said that a samurai will die for someone who truly knows him. I don't want you to die in vain, and I will carve this into my heart. And yet, at one time I served the Saito clan. I'm not saying that I will serve Nobunaga. I am going to serve you, and devote this sickly body to your cause. I came here simply to say this. Please forgive my rudeness of the last several days."

* * *

There was no fighting for a long time. Both Owari and Mino strengthened their defenses and left the winter to the snow and icy winds. With the unofficial truce, the number of travelers and the packhorse trains between the two provinces increased. The New Year passed, and finally the buds of the plum trees became tinted with color. The townspeople of Inabayama thought the world would continue untroubled for another hundred years.

The spring sun struck the white walls of Inabayama Castle and enveloped them in an air of indolence and boredom. On such days, when the townspeople looked up at the castle, they wondered why they had built a fortress on the high mountain peak. They were sensitive to the moods of the castle. When the center of their lives came under stress, they felt it right away; when it was filled with lassitude, they, too, became apathetic. No matter how many official notices were posted morning and night, no one ever took them seriously.

It was midday. White cranes and water birds chattered on the pond. The peach blossoms fell thick and fast. Even though the orchard was enclosed within the castle walls, there were few windless days on the top of lofty Mount Inabayama. Tatsuoki lay in a drunken stupor in a teahouse in the peach orchard.

Saito Kuroemon and Nagai Hayato, two of Tatsuoki's senior retainers, were looking for the lord of Inabayama. Tatsuoki's consorts may not have rivaled "the harem of three thousand beauties" of Chinese legend, but beauty was certainly not lacking here. If the ladies-in-waiting were included, they would have outnumbered the peaches in the orchard. Sitting in groups, they waited, forlorn and bored, for one idle slumberer to awaken.

"Where is His Lordship?" Kuroemon asked.

"His Lordship seems to be tired. He has fallen asleep in the teahouse," the attendant replied.

"You mean he's drunk?" Kuroemon said, and he and Hayato peeked into the teahouse. They spotted Tatsuoki in the middle of a crowd of women, lying stretched out, with a hand drum for a pillow.

"Well, let's come again later," Kuroemon said. The two started to leave.

"Who is it! I can hear men's voices!" Tatsuoki lifted his flushed face, his ears a bright red. "Is that you, Kuroemon? And Hayato? What did you come here for? We're flower-viewing. And you need *sake*!"

The two seemed to have come for a private conversation, but when he spoke to them in this way, they refrained from informing him about the reports from enemy province.

"Maybe tonight." But night held only another drinking party.

"Perhaps tomorrow." They waited again, but at noon there was an extravagant concert. There was not one day in seven when Tatsuoki looked over the affairs of state. He left that to his chief retainers. Fortunately, many of them were veterans who had served the Saito clan for three generations, and they maintained the power of the clan in the midst of chaos. Leaving Tatsuoki to his own pursuits, the senior retainers never allowed themselves the luxury of sleeping on a fine spring day.

According to the information gathered by Hayato's spies, the Oda clan had learned from the bitter experience of defeat the previous summer, and had realized the futility of trying again. "He's done nothing but lose troops and money in his attacks on Mino, so maybe he's given up completely," Hayato concluded. He gradually came to believe that Nobunaga had abandoned his plans of conquest because he had run out of money.

That spring, Nobunaga had invited a tea master and a poet to the castle, and was passing the days practicing the tea ceremony and holding poetry-writing parties. On the surface, at least, Nobunaga was taking advantage of this period of peace to enjoy life, as though he had no other care in the world.

Just after the midsummer Festival of the Dead, messengers carrying urgent dispatches galloped from Mount Komaki to all the districts in Owari. The castle town was stirring. The investigation of travelers crossing the border was becoming stricter. Retainers came and went, and met in frequent late-night conferences in the castle. Horses were being requisitioned. Samurai pressed the armorers for the armor and weapons they had sent for repair.

"What of Nobunaga?" Hayato asked his spies.

They answered, though less confidently, "Nothing has changed in the castle. The lamps shine until the early hours, and the sound of flutes and drums echoes over the waters of the moat."

As summer turned to early fall, the news broke: "Nobunaga is heading west with an army of ten thousand men! They've established their base at Sunomata Castle. They're crossing the Kiso River even now!"

Tatsuoki, who normally looked upon the outside world with complete indifference, became hysterical when he was finally forced to take notice. His advisers, too, were dismayed because they had yet to come up with appropriate countermeasures.

"It may be a lie," Tatsuoki repeated to himself. "The Oda clan cannot muster an army of ten thousand men. They haven't been able to put together an army that large for any battle until now."

But when his spies told him that this time the Oda had indeed raised an army of ten thousand men, Tatsuoki was terrified to his very marrow. Now he consulted his chief retainers.

"Well, this attack is a reckless gamble. What are we going to do to repel them?"

At length, just as people call upon the gods in times of trouble, he sent urgent summonses to the Three Men of Mino, whom he ordinarily regarded as unpleasant old men to be kept at a respectful distance.

"We sent messengers as a matter of course, but not one of them has come yet," his retainers replied.

"Well, order them to come!" Tatsuoki screamed. He himself took up a brush and wrote letters to the Three Men. But even then, not one of them hurried to Inabayama Castle.

"What about the Tiger of Unuma?"

"Him? He's been feigning illness and confining himself in his castle for some time. We can't rely on him."

Tatsuoki suddenly recovered his spirits, as though he were laughing at his retainers' foolishness, or had suddenly hit upon some plan of genius. "Did you send a messenger to Mount Kurihara? Call Hanbei! What's the matter? Why don't you do as I command? Don't procrastinate at a time like this! Send a man out right now. Right now!"

"We sent a message a few days ago without waiting for your command, informing Lord Hanbei of the urgency of the situation and urging him to come down from the mountain, but—"

"He won't come?" Tatsuoki was becoming impatient. "Why is that? Why do you suppose he doesn't come rushing down at the head of his army? He's supposed to be my loyal retainer."

Tatsuoki seemed to understand the words "loyal retainer" to mean someone who generally spoke in a straightforward manner, offending him with his unpleasant looks, but who, in times of emergency, would be the first one to dash forward no matter how far away he might be.

"Let's send a messenger one more time," Tatsuoki insisted.

The chief retainers considered it useless, but sent a fourth messenger to Mount Kurihara. The man returned crestfallen.

"I was finally able to see him, but after he read your order he made no reply. He just shed tears and sighed, saying something about the unhappy rulers of this world," the messenger reported.

Tatsuoki received this news as though he had been made sport of. He turned red with anger and chided his retainers, "You shouldn't depend on sick men!"

The days passed busily with such comings and goings. The Oda army had already begun to cross the Kiso River and was beginning to engage the Saito clan's forces in violent fighting. Reports of their army's defeats came to Inabayama hourly.

Tatsuoki could not sleep, and his eyes were glazed. The castle was quickly filled with confusion and melancholy. Tatsuoki had the peach orchard enclosed within a curtain, and there he sat on his camp stool, surrounded by gaudy armor and retainers.

"If our forces are insufficient, keep making more demands on each of our districts. Are there enough troops in the castle town? We won't need to borrow troops from the Asai clan, will we? What do you think?" His voice was shrill and filled with fear, quavering with his own terror and failing spirits. The retainers had to take care that Tatsuoki's state of mind did not influence his own warriors.

By nightfall, fires could be seen from the castle. The advance of the Oda troops continued day and night, from Atsumi and the Kano Plain in the south and extending up the tributaries of the Nagara River toward Goto and Kagamijima in the west. As the Oda advanced, the fires they set became a tide of flame that scorched the sky. By the seventh day of the month, the Oda closed in on Inabayama, the enemy's main castle.

It was the first time Nobunaga had been in charge of such a large army. His determination to succeed could be understood from that fact alone. For Owari, this meant the mobilization of the entire province. If they were defeated, both Owari and the Oda would cease to exist.

Once the army had reached Inabayama, its advance halted, and for several days both sides engaged in bitter fighting. The natural stronghold and the Saito's seasoned veterans proved their worth. What was especially damaging to the Oda, however, was the inferiority of their weapons. The wealth of Mino had enabled the Saito clan to buy a considerable number of firearms.

The Saito had a gunners' regiment, which the Oda forces lacked, that fired on the attackers from the mountainside as they approached the castle town. Akechi Mitsuhide, the man who had created the regiment, had long since left Mino and become a *ronin*. Nevertheless, the young scholar had devoted himself to the study of firearms, and the foundations of the regiment were solid.

In any event, after several days of blistering heat and close fighting, the Oda troops finally began to tire. If the Saito clan had called on Omi or Ise for reinforcements at that moment, ten thousand men would never have seen Owari again.

Most ominous of all were the shapes of Mount Kurihara, Mount Nangu, and Mount Bodai, looming in the distance.

"You really don't have to worry about that direction," Hideyoshi reassured Nobunaga.

But Nobunaga was anxious. "A siege is not the right strategy, but getting impatient will only injure my own troops. I don't see how we can take the fortress, no matter what we do."

Camp councils were held over and over again, but no one seemed to have a good idea. Finally a plan of Hideyoshi's was approved, and one night soon after that he disappeared from the advance guard.

Starting from the crossroads of the Unuma and Hida roads, which was four or five leagues from the end of the mountain range on which Inabayama stood, Hideyoshi set off with only nine trusted men. Drenched in sweat, the party scrambled up Mount Zuiryuji, which was far enough from Inabayama that no one would be on watch there. Among the men accompanying Hideyoshi were Hikoemon and his younger brother, Matajuro. Acting as their guide was a man who had recently become devoted to Hideyoshi and who felt a deep sense of obligation toward him, Osawa Jirozaemon, the Tiger of Unuma.

"Go from the base of that huge crag toward the valley. Cross that little stream yonder and head for the marsh."

Just when they thought they had reached the end of the valley and of the path as well, they saw wisteria vines clinging to a cliff. Rounding a peak, they found a hidden path to the valley that passed through a low growth of striped bamboo.

"It's about two leagues along this path to the rear of the castle. If you go that distance following this map of the mountain, you should run into a water sluice that leads inside the castle. Now with your permission, I'll take my leave."

Osawa left the group and turned back alone. He was a man who had a strong sense of loyalty. Although he was devoted to Hideyoshi and completely sincere, he had once sworn allegiance to the Saito clan. It must have pained him to lead these men up the secret path that led to the back of the castle of his former lords. Hideyoshi had guessed as much and had intentionally told him to turn back before they reached their destination.

Two leagues was no great distance, but there was virtually no path. As they climbed, Hideyoshi continually referred to the map, looking for the hidden pathway. The map and the actual terrain of the mountain did not match, however, no matter how long he compared the two.

He could not find the mountain stream that was supposed to be their landmark. They were lost. Meanwhile, the sun started to set, and it turned much cooler. Hideyoshi had not given much thought to the possibility of getting lost. His mind was on the troops laying siege to Inabayama Castle. If something went wrong at sunrise the following morning, he would be doing his comrades a great disservice.

"Wait!" one of the men said, so suddenly that they all froze. "I can see a light."

There was no reason for a light to be in the middle of the mountains, especially near a secret path leading to Inabayama Castle. They had probably got quite close to the castle, and this was certain to be an enemy guardhouse.

The men quickly hid. Compared with the *ronin*, who were extremely agile whether they were scrambling up the mountains or merely walking, Hideyoshi felt at a disadvantage.

"Hold onto this," Hikoemon said, extending the shaft of his spear. Hideyoshi held on tight, and Hikoemon clambered up the precipice, pulling Hideyoshi up behind him. They came out onto a plateau. As the night grew darker, the light they had seen before flickered brightly from a cleft in the mountain to the west of them.

Assuming that the light was from a guardhouse, the path certainly would only go in one direction.

"We have no choice," they said, determined to break through.

"Wait." Hideyoshi quickly calmed them down. "There are probably only a few men in the guardhouse, not enough to worry us, but we mustn't let them signal Inabayama. If there's a fire beacon, it must be close to the hut, so let's find it and leave two men there first. Then, to stop any guard from getting away to the castle, half of you should go behind the house."

Nodding in assent, they crawled away like forest animals, crossing a hollow and entering the valley proper. The fragrance of the hemp in the fields was unexpected. And here were plots of millet, leeks, and yams.

Hideyoshi cocked his head to one side. The hut, surrounded as it was by fields, and of rough construction, did not appear to be a guardhouse. "Don't be hasty. I'm going to take a look."

Hideyoshi crawled through the hemp, trying to keep it from rustling. From what he could see inside the hut, it was clearly nothing more than a peasant's house, and terribly run-down at that. He could see two people in the dim light of a lamp. One seemed to be an old woman, sleeping stretched out on a straw mat. The other one looked to be her son, and he was massaging the old woman's back.

Hideyoshi forgot where he was for a moment, and gazed fondly at the scene. The old lady's hair was already white. Her son was quite muscular, although he didn't seem to be more than sixteen or seventeen. Hideyoshi was unable to think of this mother and child as strangers. He suddenly felt as though he were seeing his own mother in Nakamura and himself as a boy.

The young man suddenly looked up and said, "Mother, wait just a moment. Something's strange."

"What is it, Mosuke?" The old lady raised herself up a little.

"The crickets have suddenly stopped chirping."

"It's probably some animal trying to get into the storehouse again."

"No." He shook his head strongly. "If it were an animal, it wouldn't come close while the light was still shining." The young man slid out toward the porch, ready to go outside, and picked up a sword. "Who's out there, sneaking around!" he called.

Hideyoshi suddenly stood up in the hemp patch.

Startled, the young man stared at Hideyoshi. At length he murmured, "What's going on? I *thought* someone was out there. Are you a samurai from Kashihara?"

Hideyoshi did not answer, but turned around and signaled the men hiding behind him with a wave of his hand. "Surround the hut! If anyone runs out of it, cut them down!" The warriors jumped up from the hemp patch and surrounded the hut in an instant.

"Surrounding my house with all this show," Mosuke said, almost as a challenge to Hideyoshi, who had now walked up to the house. "My mother and I are the only two people here. There's nothing here worth surrounding with so many people. What's your business here anyway, samurai?"

His attitude, as he stood on the porch, was anything but confused. On the contrary, it was almost too calm. He was obviously looking down on them with contempt.

Hideyoshi sat down on the edge of the porch and said, "No, young man, we're just being careful. We didn't mean to frighten you."

"I'm not frightened at all, but my mother was startled. If you're going to apologize, you should apologize to my mother." He spoke fearlessly. This boy did not appear to be a simple peasant. Hideyoshi looked around inside the hut.

"Come, come now, Mosuke. Why are you being so rude to a samurai?" the old woman said. Then she turned and spoke to Hideyoshi. "Well, I don't know who you are, but my son never mixes with worldly society and is just a willful country boy who doesn't know his manners. Please forgive him, sir."

"Are you this young man's mother?"

"Yes, sir."

"You say he's just a country boy who doesn't know his manners, but judging from your speech and his countenance, I find it hard to believe that you're ordinary farmers."

"We scrape out a living by hunting in the winter and making charcoal and selling it in the village in the summer."

"That may be so now, but not formerly. At the very least, you certainly belong to a family of pedigree. I'm not a retainer of the Saito, but due to certain circumstances, I'm lost in these mountains. We have no intention of harming you. If you don't mind, would you please tell me who you are?"

Mosuke, who had sat down next to his mother, suddenly asked, "Master samurai, you speak with an Owari accent too. Are you from Owari?"

"Yes, I was born in Nakamura."

"Nakamura? Not far from us. I was born in Gokiso."

"Then we're from the same province."

"If you're a retainer from Owari, I'll tell you everything. My father's name was Horio Tanomo. He served Lord Oda Nobukiyo at the fortress of Koguchi."

"How strange, if your father was a retainer of Lord Nobukiyo, then you would also be a retainer of Lord Nobunaga." I've met a good person here, Hideyoshi thought happily.

After he had been made governor of Sunomata, he had searched out men of ability to serve him. His way of handling men was not to employ them first and then make his judgment. If he trusted a man, he would immediately employ him, and then gradually put him to use. He had acted in the same way when he took a wife. He had an unusual talent for distinguishing true talent from mimicry.

"Yes, I understand. But I think, as Mosuke's mother, you don't want him to live out his life as a charcoal burner and hunter. Why don't you entrust your son to me? I know it will be taking all that you have. My status isn't high, but I'm a retainer of Lord Oda Nobunaga, Kinoshita Hideyoshi by name. My stipend is low, and I think of myself as someone who is going out into the world armed with but a single spear. Will you serve me?" Hideyoshi asked, watching mother and child.

"What? Me?" Mosuke's eyes opened wide.

So happy she wondered if it was a dream, the old lady's eyes filled with tears. "If he is able to serve as a retainer to the Oda clan, my husband—who died dishonored in battle—would be so happy. Mosuke! Accept this offer and cleanse your father's name."

Mosuke, of course, made no objection, and immediately swore the oath of allegiance of a retainer.

Then Hideyoshi gave Mosuke his first order: "We are making our way to the rear of Inabayama Castle. We have a map of the mountains, but cannot find the right path. It's a rather difficult task for your first act of service, but you must guide us there. I'm counting on you."

Mosuke studied the map for a while, folded it up, and gave it back to Hideyoshi. "I understand. Does anyone need to eat? Did you bring along enough for two meals each?"

Having lost their way, they were just at the point of exhausting the rations they had carried along.

"It's only two and a half leagues to the castle, but we'd still better bring enough for two meals."

Mosuke quickly cooked rice and mixed in millet, bean paste, and salted plums, enough for ten men. Then he shouldered a single coil of hemp rope, and fixed flint and tinder and his father's sword at his side.

"Mother, I'm leaving," Mosuke said. "To go to battle is an auspicious start in serving my lord, but depending on my fate as a samurai, this may be our last farewell. If that should come to pass, please resign yourself to the loss of your son."

It was time to leave, but mother and child were naturally unwilling to part. Hideyoshi could hardly bear to watch. He walked away from the house and looked at the pitch black mountains.

Just as Mosuke was leaving, his mother called him back. She held out a gourd. "Fill this with water and take it along," she told him. "You're bound to be thirsty along the way."

Hideyoshi and the others were pleased. Until now, they had suffered from lack of water more than once. There were only a few places where springs bubbled up in the rocky crags. But the closer they came to the peak, the less water there would be.

When they reached a cliff, Mosuke tossed his rope, tied it to the base of the root of a pine, and scrambled up first, then pulled the others up behind him.

"From here on, the path becomes even more difficult to follow," he said. "There are a number of places, like the guardhouse at Akagawa Cave, where we might be caught by the guards." Hearing that, Hideyoshi understood the extent of Mosuke's prudence when, having been shown the map of the mountain, he had looked at it for a moment, not giving any quick reply. There was still something of the child about Mosuke, but he thought things out thoroughly, and Hideyoshi felt all the more affection for him.

The water in the gourd eventually became sweat on the ten men. Mosuke wiped a torrent of perspiration from his face and said, "We'll hardly be able to fight if we're this tired. Why don't we sleep here?"

"It would be good to sleep," Hideyoshi agreed, but then asked how much farther it was to the rear of the castle.

"Just down there," Mosuke said, pointing directly into the valley.

They were all excited, but Mosuke silenced them with a wave of his hand. "We can't speak out loud anymore. The wind may carry our voices in the direction of the castle."

Hideyoshi peered down into the valley. The dark trees enveloping the valley looked like an unfathomable lake. But when he looked long and hard, he could just make out the outline of a wall made of huge rocks, a stockade, and something like a storehouse between the trees.

"We're straight above the enemy here. All right, let's sleep until dawn."

The men slept on the ground, and Mosuke wrapped the now-empty gourd in a cloth, and put it under his master's head. While the others slept for about two hours, Mosuke was awake, standing guard a little way off.

"Hey!" he called out.

Hideyoshi lifted his head. "What is it, Mosuke?"

Mosuke pointed to the east. "Sunrise."

Indeed, the night sky was beginning to show a tint of white. A sea of clouds covered the peaks. The valley behind Inabayama Castle, which was immediately below them, could not be seen at all.

"Well, let's start our raid," one of the men said, and Hikoemon and the others trembled with excitement, tying the cords of their armor and adjusting their leggings.

"No, wait. Let's eat first," Hideyoshi said.

While the sun came out over the vast ocean of clouds, they finished the second of the two meals Mosuke had prepared the night before. The gourd was empty, but the rice, mixed with millet and wrapped in oak leaves, tasted so sweet they thought they would never forget it as long as they lived.

When they had finished eating, the mist in the valley below began to clear. They could see a precipice and a vine-covered suspension bridge. Beyond the bridge was a stone wall covered with thick green moss. The place was dark, and a desolate wind blew constantly.

"Where's the flare tube?" Hideyoshi asked. "Give it to Mosuke and teach him how to set it off."

Hideyoshi stood up and asked Mosuke if he understood how to use the flare, then said, "We're going down now to cut our way in. Keep your ears open. As soon as you hear shouting, set off the flare. All right? Don't slip up."

"I understand." Mosuke nodded and stood next to the signal tube. Seeing his master and the others off as they descended into the valley in high spirits, he looked a little unhappy. He would have liked to go with them. The clouds began to look like raging billows, and the plain between Mino and Owari became visible beneath them at last.

Since it was still early fall, the sun shone down harshly. Very quickly the castle town of Inabayama, the waters of the Nagara River, and even the crossroads among the houses came into sight. Yet not a soul could be seen. The sun rose higher.

What's happening? Mosuke asked himself nervously. His heart was pounding. Then, suddenly, he heard the echoing reports of firearms. The smoke of the signal he fired trailed into the blue sky, like a squid squirting ink.

Hideyoshi and his men had walked toward the rear of the castle with faces completely composed, looking here and there around the wide, empty space where the grass was growing thick.

The first soldiers of Inabayama Castle to see the party thought that it was composed of their own men. Stationed at the neighboring fuel warehouse and rice storeroom, they ate their morning rations and gossiped. Even though there had been several days of steady fighting, this was a large citadel, and all of the action had been taking place around the front gate. Here at the rear of this natural fortress, it was so quiet you could hear the chirping of birds.

When there was fighting at the front of the castle, the soldiers at the rear could hear the sound of firearms crackling from the direction of the tortuous path to the front gate. But the few soldiers who guarded the rear thought they would not take part in the battle until the very end.

"They're really having it out, up front," one of the soldiers said complacently.

Eating their rations, the soldiers watched Hideyoshi and his men, and finally began to regard them with suspicion. "Who are they?"

"You mean those men over there?"

"Uh-huh. It's sort of strange, the way they're hanging around, don't you think? They're looking into the guardhouse by the stockade."

"They've probably come from the front lines."

"But who are they?"

"It's hard to tell when they're in armor."

"Hey! One of them's come out of the kitchen with a firebrand! What do you suppose he's going to do with it?"

As they watched with chopsticks in hand, the man carrying the firebrand ran into the fuel warehouse and ignited the piles of firewood. The others followed, carrying torches and throwing them into the other buildings.

"It's the enemy!" the guards yelled.

Hideyoshi and Hikoemon turned in their direction and laughed.

How did this seemingly impregnable stronghold fall so easily? First, the interior of the castle was thrown into confusion by the outbreak of fire at the rear. Second, the shouts of Hideyoshi and his men panicked the defenders, and they started to fight among themselves, thinking there must be traitors in their midst. But the most important factor in their defeat, understood only afterward, was the result of someone's advice.

Several days before, the dimwitted Tatsuoki had brought the wives and children of the soldiers fighting outside the castle, as well as the families of wealthy townsfolk, into the castle as hostages, so that his soldiers would not submit to the enemy.

The man who devised this policy, however, was none other than Iyo, one of the Three Men of Mino, who had already allied himself with Hideyoshi. So this "strategy" was nothing more than a seditious plot. Because of this, the confusion inside the castle during the attack was terrible, and the defenders were unable to put up full resistance to the attackers. Finally, Nobunaga, who was always looking out for an opportunity, sent Tatsuoki a letter at the height of the confusion:

Today your immoral clan is engulfed in the flames of divine punishment and will soon be overwhelmed by my soldiers. The people of this province look for a sign of rain that will put out these fires, and shouts of joy are already rising from the castle town. You are the nephew of my wife. For many years I have pitied your cowardice and folly, and cannot bear putting you to the sword. Rather, I would gladly spare your life and grant you a stipend. If you wish to live, surrender and quickly send an envoy to my camp.

As soon as Tatsuoki read the letter, he ordered his men to surrender, and he and members of his family left the castle, accompanied by only thirty retainers. Attaching his own soldiers to them as an escort, Nobunaga exiled Tatsuoki to Kaisei, but he promised to give his younger brother, Shingoro, some land so that the Saito clan might not vanish.

With the unification of Owari and Mino, the value of Nobunaga's domains rose to one million two hundred thousand bushels of rice. Nobunaga moved his castle for the third time, from Mount Komaki to Inabayama, which he renamed Gifu, after the birthplace of China's Chou Dynasty.

"Be a Friendly Neighbor"

The castle town of Kiyosu was now deserted. There were few shops and samurai residences. Nevertheless, through that very desolation there shone the satisfaction of shedding a skin. It is a principle of all living things: once the womb has carried out its function, it must be content to decay and fall away. And very much in this way, it was a joy to everyone that Nobunaga was not going to be trapped forever in his hometown, even if it meant the town's decline.

And here, such a woman who had given birth was growing old. This was Hideyoshi's mother. She would be fifty this year. For the moment she was peacefully tending to her old age, living with her daughter-in-law, Nene, at their house in the samurai district of Kiyosu. But until two or three years before she had been a farmer, and the joints of her earth-chapped hands were still calloused. Having given birth to four children, she was missing many of her teeth. Her hair, however, was still not all white.

One letter that Hideyoshi wrote to her from the field was typical of many:

How is your hip? Are you still using *moxa*? When we lived on the farm you always said, "Don't waste food on me," no matter what it was. So even here I worry that you're not eating properly. You must live a long life. I'm worried that I won't have time to take care of you as I'd like, because I'm such a dunce. Happily, I have not been sick here. My fate as a warrior seems to be blessed, and His Lordship holds me in high regard.

After the invasion of Mino, it would be difficult to count the letters he sent.
"Nene, read this. He always writes like a child." Hideyoshi's mother said to Nene.
Every time, his mother would show the letters to her daughter-in-law, and Nene

would show the old lady the letters that came to her.

"The letters he sends to me aren't nearly as tender. It's always things like 'Be careful of fire,' or 'Be a dutiful wife when your husband is away,' or 'Look after my mother.'"

"That boy is clever. He sends a letter to you and one to me; one strict, the other tender. So I guess he divides his letter writing just right when you consider that he covers both sides."

"That must be it," Nene said, laughing. She looked after her husband's mother with devotion. She did her best to serve her as though she, like Otsumi, were her natural daughter. Above all other things, however, the old lady's pleasure came from Hideyoshi's letters. Just at the point when they were worrying because they hadn't received one for a long time, a letter arrived from Sunomata. For some reason, however, this letter was just for his wife, with nothing addressed to his mother.

Sometimes letters from Hideyoshi came just to his mother, with nothing for his wife. His messages to her were ordinarily just postscripts to the letters to his mother. He had never sent one strictly to his wife until today. Nene suddenly thought that something must be wrong, or that there was something he did not want to worry his mother about. Going into her own room and cutting open the envelope, she found an unusually long letter:

> For a long time it has been my hope that I could have you and my mother living here with me. Now that I have finally become the lord of a castle and have been awarded a general's standard by His Lordship, the situation is tolerable enough to invite my mother to Sunomata. I wonder, however, if it wouldn't discomfort her. She was concerned before that her presence would be a burden to me in my service to His Lordship. She has also always said that she is just an old farm woman, and that this life would be far beyond her status. For this reason, she is certain to refuse with some excuse, even if I ask her.

What should I say? Nene had no idea. She thought that her husband's implied request was grave, indeed.

Just then the old lady's voice called to her from the rear of the house. "Nene! Nene! Come here for a moment and look!"

"Coming!" Again today she was hoeing the earth around the roots of the autumn eggplants. It was afternoon and still rather hot. Even the clods of earth in the garden were hot. Sweat shone on her hands.

"My goodness! In this heat?" Nene said.

But the old lady always replied that that was what farm people liked to do, and not to worry. No matter how many times Nene heard this, however, since she did not have a farmer's upbringing and did not know the real flavor of farming, to her it had always looked like nothing more than backbreaking work. Still, she had recently felt that she was beginning to understand, at least a little, why her husband's mother was unable to stop working.

The old lady often referred to crops as "the gifts of the earth." The fact that she had been able to raise four children in great poverty and that she herself had not starved to death was one of those gifts. In the morning she clapped her hands toward the sun in prayer and said that this, too, was a habit from her time in Nakamura. She would not forget her former life.

Occasionally she said that if she suddenly became used to gorgeous clothes and sumptuous meals and forgot the blessings of the sun and earth, she would certainly be punished and become sick.

"Oh, Nene, look at this!" As soon as she saw her daughter-in-law, Hideyoshi's mother put the mattock down and pointed happily at her work. "Look at how many of the eggplants are ripe. We'll pickle them so we can eat them this winter. Bring the baskets over, and let's pick a few now."

When Nene returned, she gave one of the two baskets to her mother-in-law. As she began picking eggplants and putting them into the baskets, she said, "With all your hard work we're going to have enough vegetables for all the soup and pickles the house will need."

"I imagine the shops we patronize are going to be annoyed."

"Well, the servants say you enjoy it, and that it's good for your health. And it's certainly economical, so it must be a good thing."

"It won't be good for Hideyoshi's reputation if people think we're doing it just to be stingy. We'll just have to try to buy something else from the merchants so they won't think that way."

"Yes, let's do that. Well, Mother, I feel badly speaking about this, but a letter arrived from Sunomata just a little while ago."

"Oh? From my son?"

"Yes...but this time it wasn't addressed to you; it came just for me."

"Either way is just fine. Well, is everything as usual? Is he all right? We haven't received any news for a while, and I thought this must be due to His Lordship moving to Gifu."

"That's right. In the letter he asked me to tell you that His Lordship has made him the governor of a castle, so he thinks the time is right for us to join him. He asked me to persuade you to come, and said that you should definitely move to Sunomata Castle in a few days' time."

"Oh...that's wonderful news. That he should become the lord of a castle is like a dream, but he shouldn't go too far and overstep himself."

As she listened to happy news about her son, her mother's heart worried lest his good fortune should prove to be short-lived. The old lady and her daughter-in-law worked together in the garden, picking eggplants. Soon the baskets were full of the bright purple vegetables.

"Mother, doesn't your back hurt?"

"What? Why, to the contrary. If I work bit by bit like this all day, my body stays fit."

"I'm learning from you, too. Since you've let me help you in the garden off and on, I've learned to enjoy picking the greens for the soup in the mornings, and working with the cucumbers and eggplants. Even after we move to Sunomata Castle, there's bound to be a place somewhere on the grounds to plant a vegetable patch. We'll be able to work all we want."

The old lady covered her mouth with her earth-stained hand and chuckled. "You're just as clever as Hideyoshi. You decided to move to Sunomata even before I knew what was happening."

"Mother." Nene prostrated herself, pressing her fingertips to the earth. "Please grant my husband's wish!" The old lady hastily took Nene's hands and tried to put them to her forehead.

"Don't do that! I'm just a selfish old woman."

"No, you're not. I understand your thoughtfulness very well."

"Please don't get mad at an old lady's willfulness. It's for that boy's sake that I don't want to go to Sunomata. And so he won't be lacking in his service to His Lordship."

"My husband understands that well."

"Even if that's true, Hideyoshi will be among people jealous of his early success, and they'll call him things like 'the monkey from Nakamura,' or 'the son of a farmer,' if a shabby farm woman is working a vegetable plot in the middle of the castle grounds. Even his own retainers will laugh at him."

"No, Mother. You're worrying about the future needlessly. That might be for someone whose character it is to dress up appearances and to worry about what people say, but my husband's heart is not controlled by public censure. And as for his retainers…"

"I wonder. The mother of a castle lord who looks like me—wouldn't it harm his reputation?"

"My husband's character is not that small." Nene's words were so frank that the old lady was surprised, and finally her eyes filled with tears of joy.

"I've said unpardonable things. Nene, please forgive me."

"Well, Mother, the sun's going down. Wash your hands and feet." Nene walked ahead, carrying the two heavy baskets.

Together with the servants, Nene took a broom and swept. She was especially diligent in the old lady's room, which she cleaned herself. The lamps were lit, and the dishes for the evening meal prepared. In addition to places for the two of them, a place was set both morning and evening for Hideyoshi.

"Shall I massage your hip?" Nene asked.

The old lady had a chronic condition that troubled her from time to time. When the evening winds blew in the early fall, she often complained of the pain. As Nene massaged her legs for her, the old lady seemed to slip gently into sleep, but during that time she must have been thinking something over. Finally she sat up and spoke to Nene.

"Listen, my dear. You want to be reunited with your husband. I'm sorry to have been so selfish. Tell my son that his mother would like to move to Sunomata."

The day before Hideyoshi's mother was due to arrive, an unexpected but very welcome guest came through the gate of Sunomata. The guest was dressed in plain clothes, with a sedge hat pulled over his eyes, and was accompanied by only two attendants, a young woman and a boy.

"When he sees me, he'll understand," the man said to the guard, who relayed word to Hideyoshi.

Hideyoshi hurried out to the castle gate to greet his guests, Takenaka Hanbei, Ko-kuma, and Oyu.

"These are my only followers," Hanbei told him. "I have a fair-sized household living in my castle on Mount Bodai, but I cut my ties with them when I withdrew from the world. As for my previous promise to you, my lord, I thought that perhaps the time had come, so I left my mountain retreat and came down to be among men once again. Would you please take in these three wanderers as the lowest of your attendants?"

Hideyoshi bowed with his hands to his knees and said, "You are much too modest. If you had sent me just a note beforehand, I would have come to the mountain myself to greet you."

"What? You'd come to greet a worthless mountain *ronin* who has come to serve you?"

"Well, anyway, please come in." Leading the way, he beckoned Hanbei inside; but when Hideyoshi tried to give him the seat of honor, Hanbei absolutely refused, saying, "That would be contrary to my intention of being your retainer."

Hideyoshi responded with his innermost feelings. "No, no. I don't have the talent to place myself over you. I'm thinking of recommending you to Lord Nobunaga."

Hanbei shook his head and refused adamantly. "As I said from the very first, I haven't the least intention of serving Lord Nobunaga. And it isn't just a matter of loyalty to the Saito clan. If I were to serve Lord Nobunaga, it would not be long before I would be forced to leave his service. When I consider my own imperfect personality together with what I have heard about his character, my intuition is that a master-retainer relationship would not be mutually beneficial. But with you I don't have to temper my disposition. You can tolerate my innate selfishness and willfulness. I'd like you to consider me the low-est of your retainers."

"Well, then, will you teach strategy not just to me but to all my retainers?"

With that, the two men seemed to arrive at a compromise, and that night they shared *sake*, talking happily until a late hour, with no thought of the time. The next day was the day of Hideyoshi's mother's arrival at Sunomata. Accompanied by attendants, he traveled a little more than a league from the castle to the outskirts of the village of Masaki to greet his mother's palanquin.

There was an azure sky, the chrysanthemums at the rough-woven fences around the people's houses gave off their fragrance, and shrikes sang their shrill songs in the branches of the ginkgo trees.

"Your honored mother's procession has come into view," announced a retainer.

Hideyoshi's face shone with a pleasure he was unable to conceal. His wife's and mother's palanquins finally arrived. When the escorting samurai saw their master coming out to greet them, they immediately dismounted. Hachisuka Hikoemon quickly drew near to the side of the old lady's palanquin and informed her that Hideyoshi had come to meet her.

Inside the palanquin, the voice of the old lady could be heard asking them to let her down. The palanquins were brought to a halt and lowered to the ground. The warriors knelt at either side of the road and bowed. Nene got out first and, going over to the old lady's palanquin, took her hand. When she glanced at the face of the samurai who had quickly placed straw sandals at the old woman's feet, she saw that it was Hideyoshi.

Deeply moved and with no time to say a word, Nene greeted her husband with a quick glance.

Taking her son's hand, the old lady pressed it to her forehead reverently and said, "As the lord of a castle, you are much too gracious. Please don't be so solicitous in front of your retainers."

"I'm relieved to see that you look so healthy. You tell me not to be solicitous, but, Mother, my very own Mother, I did not come out to greet you today as a samurai. Please don't worry."

The old lady stepped out of the palanquin. The other samurai had all prostrated themselves on the ground, and she felt too dazed to walk.

"You must be tired," Hideyoshi said. "Rest here for a little while. It's no more than a league to the castle." Taking his mother by the hand, he led her to a stool under the eaves of a house. The old lady sat down and gazed at the autumn sky that spread above the solid yellow line of ginkgo trees.

"It's just like a dream," she whispered. The words made Hideyoshi reflect on the years. He was unable to feel that this moment was like a dream. He saw very clearly the steps connecting the present reality and the past. And he felt that this moment was a natural milestone in his career.

The following month, after Hideyoshi's mother and wife had moved to Sunomata, they were followed by his twenty-nine-year-old sister, Otsumi, his twenty-three-year-old half brother, Kochiku, and his twenty-year-old half sister.

Otsumi was still unmarried. Long before, Hideyoshi had promised that if she looked after their mother, when he became successful, he would find her a husband. The following year, Otsumi married a relative of Hideyoshi's wife in the castle.

"They've all grown up," Hideyoshi said to his mother, looking at the satisfaction in her face. This was his happiness, and his great incentive for the future.

It was late spring. Cherry blossoms fell in profusion from the eaves onto the armrest on which Nobunaga was napping.

"Ah...that's right." Recalling something, Nobunaga quickly jotted down a note and had a messenger take it to Sunomata. Because Hideyoshi had become the lord of a castle, he was no longer on hand to respond immediately whenever Nobunaga called, and this seemed to make his lord a little lonely.

Crossing the large Kiso River, Nobunaga's messenger delivered the note to the gate of Hideyoshi's castle. Here, too, the spring had passed peacefully, and the flowers of the mountain wisteria swayed in the shade of the artificial hill in the garden. Behind this hill, on the edge of the wide garden, were a newly built lecture hall and a small house for Takenaka Hanbei and Oyu.

The lecture hall was a *dojo* where Hideyoshi's retainers could practice the martial arts. With Takenaka Hanbei as their teacher, the retainers were lectured on the Chinese classics in the morning, and vied with one another in techniques of the spear and sword in the afternoon.

Later Hanbei would lecture on the military precepts of Sun Tzu and Wu Chi late into the night. Hanbei applied himself zealously to the education of all the young samurai in order to discipline them in the martial habits and customs of the castle; most of Hideyoshi's retainers were the wild *ronin* who had once been members of Hikoemon's band.

Hideyoshi knew that he had to work constantly to improve himself, to overcome his faults, and to increase his capacity for self-reflection, and he was determined that his samurai must be made to do the same. If he was to play an important role in future, retainers armed with brute strength alone were not going to be useful. Hideyoshi was anxious about this. Thus, along with embracing Hanbei as a retainer, he also bowed to him as his own teacher and looked up to him as his instructor in military science, and entrusted to him the education of his retainers.

Martial discipline improved greatly. When Hanbei lectured on Sun Tzu or the Chinese classics, men like Hikoemon could always be seen on the listener's platform. The only problem was that Hanbei was not very robust. Because of that, the lectures were canceled from time to time, and the retainers were disappointed. Today, too, he had exerted himself during the day and said that he was canceling the evening lectures. When evening came, he quickly had the sliding doors of the house shut.

The evening wind from the upper reaches of the Kiso River chilled Hanbei's weak constitution all the more, even though the season was late spring.

"I've laid out your bed inside. Why don't you sleep?" Oyu placed a medicinal decoction next to his desk. Hanbei was reading, his usual occupation when he had some leisure time.

"No, it's not so much that I feel bad. I canceled the lecture because I think a summons may come from Lord Hideyoshi. Rather than preparations for bed, arrange my clothing so that if there is a call, I can go out quickly."

"Is that it? Is there a meeting in the castle tonight?"

"Not at all." Hanbei sipped the hot decoction. "A little while ago when you closed the door, you yourself told me that a boat with a messenger's flag from Gifu had crossed the river, and that someone was coming toward the castle gate."

"Is that what you're talking about?"

"If it's a message from Gifu for Lord Hideyoshi, there's no limit to what or where this business may lead. Even if I'm not summoned, I can hardly loosen my sash and sleep."

"The lord of this castle respects you as his teacher, and you venerate him as your lord, so I hardly know whose respect is greater. Are you really so resolved to serve this man?"

Smiling, Hanbei shut his eyes and turned his face toward the ceiling. "I guess it's finally come to that. It's a frightening thing for a man to be trusted by another. I could never be led astray by the beauty of a woman." Just as he was saying this, a messenger arrived from the keep. He announced Hideyoshi's request that Hanbei come quickly, and left. Shortly thereafter a page came before Hideyoshi, who was alone in quiet contemplation, and made an announcement. "Master Hanbei has come."

Hideyoshi looked up from his musings and quickly left the room to welcome Hanbei. The two returned to the room and sat down.

"I'm sorry to have called you here in the middle of the night. How do you feel?"

Hanbei looked squarely at Hideyoshi, who, for his part, was apparently going to treat him as his teacher to the very end. "This consideration is uncalled for. If you, my lord, speak to me like that, how am I going to be able to respond? Why don't you say something like, 'Oh, it's you, Hanbei'? I think this kind of solicitude toward a retainer is inappropriate."

"Really? Well, do you suppose this is no good for our relationship?"

"I just didn't think my lord should respect someone like me the way you do."

"Why not?" Hideyoshi laughed. "I'm uneducated, and you're quite learned. I was born in the country, and you're the son of the lord of a castle. Anyway, I think of you as my superior."

"If that's the way it's to be, I'm going to be more careful from now on."

"All right, all right," Hideyoshi said playfully. "We'll gradually become lord and retainer. If I become an even greater man."

For the lord of a castle, he was going to extraordinary lengths not to stand on his own dignity. In fact, he was willing to stand completely naked before Hanbei in terms of his own foolishness and ignorance.

"Well, then, why did you summon me, my lord?" Hanbei asked politely.

"Oh, yes," Hideyoshi said, suddenly recalling the object of their meeting. "I've just received a letter from Lord Nobunaga. This is what it says: 'With a little leisure, I've suddenly grown bored even with the prize of Gifu. The wind and clouds are peaceful, and I would like to look at them once again. The beauties of nature have still not become my friends. What shall we do about this year's plans?' How do you suppose I should answer it?"

"Well, the meaning is clear, so you should be able to answer it with a single line."

"Hm. I understand it, but how could I answer it in a single line?"

"Be a friendly neighbor; make plans for the future."

"'Be a friendly neighbor; make plans for the future'?"

"That's it."

"Hm. I see."

"I suspect that Lord Nobunaga is thinking that, having taken Gifu, this year is the time to put his internal administration in order, rest his troops, and wait for another day," Hanbei said.

"I'm sure that's what his plans are, but with his disposition, he can't just let the days pass in idleness. That's why he sent this letter asking about policy."

"Planning for the future, allying himself with his neighbors—I think the present is probably a splendid opportunity for that."

"So?" Hideyoshi asked.

"It's just my humble opinion, because you, rather than I, are the one who is said to be capable in so many areas. First, answer with just one line: 'Be friendly with neighbors; make plans for the future.' Then, at a convenient moment, go to Gifu Castle and explain your plan in person."

"Why don't we each write down which province we think it would be best for the Oda to ally itself with, and then compare to see if we're thinking the same thing?"

Hanbei wrote something first, and then Hideyoshi put the brush to a piece of paper.

When they exchanged the papers and unfolded them, they found that they had both written "Takeda of Kai," and they broke out in laughter, delighted that they were both thinking along the same lines.

The lamps were bright in the guest room. The messenger from Gifu was given the seat of honor, and Hideyoshi's mother and wife were also in attendance. When Hideyoshi took his seat, the lamps seemed suddenly even more cheerful and the room more lively.

Nene thought that her husband seemed to be drinking a good bit more *sake* these days, at least compared with the past. She watched his easy attitude throughout the banquet as though she saw nothing at all. He was entertaining his guest, making his mother laugh, and he seemed to be enjoying himself. Even Hanbei, who never drank, put the *sake* cup to his lips and sipped a little to toast Hideyoshi.

Others joined the banquet, and it soon became quite boisterous. When his mother and Nene had retired, Hideyoshi walked outside to sober up. The blossoms of the young cherry trees had already fallen, and only the fragrance of the mountain wisteria filled the night.

"Ah! Who's that under the trees?" Hideyoshi called out.

"It's me," replied a woman's voice.

"Oyu, what are you doing here?"

"My brother is so late in coming back, and he's so weak, I was worried."

"It's a wonderful thing to see such a beautiful relationship between brother and sister."

Hideyoshi walked up to her side. She was about to prostrate herself, but he caught her hands. "Oyu, let's walk over to the teahouse over there. I'm so drunk that I'm not sure of my footing. I'd like you to make me a bowl of tea."

"My goodness! My hands! This isn't right. Please let go."

"It's all right. Don't worry."

"You—you shouldn't be doing this."

"It's really all right."

"Please!"

"Why are you being so noisy? Please whisper. You're being cruel."

"This is not right!"

At that moment Hanbei called out. He was on his way back to his house. When Hideyoshi saw him, he immediately let go of Oyu. Hanbei stared at him in amazement. "My lord, what kind of drunken craziness is this?"

Hideyoshi slapped his head with his hand. Then, either laughing at his own foolishness or at his lack of elegance, he opened his mouth wide and said, "Yes, well, what's wrong? This is 'being friendly with neighbors and planning for the future.' Don't worry about it."

Summer turned to fall. One day Hikoemon came with a message for Hanbei, requesting that Oyu become a lady-in-waiting for Hideyoshi's mother. When Oyu heard the request, she shrank in fear. She burst into tears. That was her answer to Hideyoshi's request.

A tea bowl that has no imperfections is said to be lacking in beauty, and Hideyoshi's character, too, was not without blemish. Though the elegance of a tea bowl, or even human frailty itself, may be interesting to contemplate, from a woman's point of view this flaw cannot be "interesting" at all. When his sister broke into tears just at the mention of the matter, Hanbei thought her refusal was reasonable, and conveyed it to Hikoemon.

Autumn, too, passed without incident. In Gifu, the principle of "being a friendly neighbor and planning for the future" was put into practice. For the Oda clan, the Takeda of Kai had always been a threat at the rear. Arrangements were soon made for Nobunaga's daughter to be married to Takeda Shingen's son, Katsuyori. The bride was a young girl of thirteen and an incomparable beauty. She had been adopted, however, and was not one of Nobunaga's natural daughters. Nevertheless, after the marriage ceremony, it seemed that Shingen was extraordinarily pleased with her, and the union was soon blessed with a son, Taro.

For the time being at least, the Oda clan's northern border would have seemed to be secure, but the young bride died giving birth to Taro. Nobunaga then had his eldest son, Nobutada, betrothed to Shingen's sixth daughter, to prevent the weakening of the alliance between the two provinces. He also sent a proposal of marriage ties to Tokugawa Ieyasu of Mikawa. Thus, the military alliance that already existed between the two was strengthened by family bonds. At the time of their engagement, Ieyasu's eldest son, Takechiyo, and Nobunaga's daughter were both eight years old. This policy was also used with the Sasaki clan in Omi. And so the castle at Gifu was busy with celebrations for the next two years.

* * *

The samurai's face was hidden in the shadow of a broad hat of woven sedge. He was tall, around forty years of age. Judging from his clothes and sandals, he was a wandering swordsman who had been on the road for some time. Even from behind, his body seemed to leave no opening for attack. He had just finished his midday meal, and was stepping out into a street in Gifu. He walked about, looking around, without any particular purpose. From time to time he would comment to himself how much such-and-such a place had changed.

From any spot in the town, the traveler could look up and see the towering walls of Gifu Castle. Holding the rim of his low, conical hat, he gazed at them for a while in fascination.

Suddenly a passerby, probably a merchant's wife, turned and stopped to look at him. She whispered something to the clerk accompanying her, and then hesitantly approached the swordsman. "Excuse me. It's rude of me to stop you in the street like this, but aren't you Master Akechi's nephew?"

Caught off guard, the swordsman quickly responded, "No!" and walked off in great strides. After going ten or so steps, however, he turned and looked at the woman, who was still staring at him. That's Shunsai the armorer's daughter, he thought. She must be married by now.

He wound his way through the streets. Two hours later he was near the Nagara River. He sat down on the grassy riverbank and gazed at the water. He could have stayed there forever. The reeds rustled in desolate whispers under a pale, chilly autumn sun.

"Master Swordsman?" Someone tapped him on the shoulder.

Mitsuhide turned around to see three men—most likely a patrol of Oda samurai on police duty.

"What are you doing?" one asked casually. But the faces of the three men were tense and suspicious.

"I was tired from walking, and stopped to rest a bit," the swordsman answered calmly. "Are you from the Oda clan?" he asked, standing up and brushing the grass from his clothes.

"We are," the soldier said stiffly. "Where have you come from, and where are you going?"

"I'm from Echizen. I have a relative at the castle and have been looking for some way to get in touch."

"A retainer?"

"No."

"But didn't you just say that it was someone at the castle?"

"She's not a retainer. She's a member of the household."

"What's her name?"

"I hesitate to say it here."

"What about your name?"

"That too."

"You mean you don't want to talk in the open?"

"That's right."

"Well then, you'll have to come with us to the guardhouse."

They probably suspected him of being a spy. Just in case he was going to put up a struggle, one of the men called out toward the road, where a mounted samurai, who appeared to be their leader, and another ten foot soldiers were waiting.

"This is just what I'd hoped for. Lead on." With that, the swordsman started off quickly.

In Gifu, as in every other province, security checks at the river crossings, in the castle town, and at the borders were strict. Nobunaga had only recently moved to Gifu Castle, and with the complete change of administration and laws, the duties of the magistrates were numerous. Although some complained that the patrolling was too strict, there were still many former retainers of the deposed Saito clan in the town, and the plots of enemy provinces were often at an advanced stage.

Mori Yoshinari was well suited to the post of chief magistrate, but like any warrior, he preferred the battlefield to civilian duties. When he went back home in the evening, he would heave a sigh of relief. And he would show his wife the same weary after-work expression every night.

"A letter came for you from Ranmaru."

When he heard the name Ranmaru, Yoshinari smiled. News from the castle was one of Yoshinari's few pleasures. Ranmaru was the son he had sent as a child to serve in the castle. It was clear from the very beginning that Ranmaru would be of no real service, but he was an attractive boy and had caught Nobunaga's eye, and so he had become one of his personal attendants. Recently he had been mixing with the pages and seemed to be performing some sort of duties.

"What was the news?" Yoshinari's wife asked.

"Nothing, really. Everything is peaceful, and His Lordship is in a good mood."

"He didn't write anything about being sick?"

"No, he said he was in excellent health," Yoshinari replied.

"That boy is cleverer than most. He's probably being careful not to make his parents worry."

"I suppose so," Yoshinari said. "But he's still a baby, and it must be a strain for him to be at His Lordship's side all of the time."

"I imagine he'd like to come home from time to time and be spoiled a little."

At that point a samurai appeared and announced that soon after Yoshinari had returned home something had occurred at his office, and that some of his subordinates had come to confer with him even though it was late at night. The three officers were waiting at the entrance.

"What is it?" Yoshinari asked the three men.

The leader made his report. "Toward the end of the day, one of our patrols arrested a suspicious-looking swordsman near the Nagara River."

"And?"

"He acted very obediently all the way to the guardhouse. When we questioned him, he stubbornly refused to give his name or native province, and said that he would only do so if he could speak to Master Yoshinari. He went on to say that he was not a spy, and that a relative of his—a woman—had been working in the Oda household from the time His Lordship resided in Kiyosu. But he would not say any more unless he could meet with the man in charge. He was very stubborn."

"Well, well. How old is he?"

"About forty."

"What kind of man is he?"

"He's rather impressive. It's difficult to think of him as being just one of these wandering swordsmen."

A few moments later the arrested man was brought in. He was led to a room at the back of the house by an elderly retainer. A cushion and some food were waiting for the guest.

"Master Yoshinari will be with you soon," said the old retainer, taking his leave.

Incense smoke drifted into the room. The swordsman, his clothes stained from the journey, realized that the incense was of such quality that had the visitor not been cultivated enough to have a refined sense of smell, it would have been wasted. He waited silently for some sign of the master of the house.

The face that had been obscured by the sedge hat that afternoon was now silently contemplating the flickering light of the lamp. No doubt, he was too pale for the patrol to believe that he was a wandering swordsman. Also, his eyes were peaceful and mild—not what you would expect of a man whose daily life was the sword.

The sliding door opened, and a woman, whose clothes and demeanor showed that she was not a servant, gracefully brought him a bowl of tea. She placed the bowl in front of him without a word, then withdrew, closing the sliding door behind her. Once more, if the guest had not been important, such courtesy would not have been extended.

A few moments later the host, Yoshinari, came in and, by way of greeting, excused himself for having kept his guest waiting.

The swordsman shifted from the cushion to a more formal kneeling position. "Do I have the honor of addressing Master Yoshinari? I'm afraid I created a bit of trouble for your men with my thoughtlessness. I have come on a secret mission from the Asakura clan in Echizen. My name is Akechi Mitsuhide."

"So it is you. I hope you'll excuse the rudeness of my subordinates. I was surprised myself by what I heard a little while ago, and I hurried to meet you."

"I didn't give my name or home province, so how did you know who I am?"

"You spoke of a certain lady—your niece, I believe—who has served in His Lordship's household for some time. When this was reported to me, I guessed it must be you. Your niece is the Lady Hagiji, I believe. She has served Lord Nobunaga's wife since she accompanied Her Ladyship from Mino to Owari."

"Indeed! I am impressed by your knowledge of such details."

"It's only my job. We routinely look into such things as the home province, lineage, and the relatives of everyone from the senior ladies-in-waiting to the servant girls."

"That's sensible enough."

"We looked into Lady Hagiji's family background as well. At the time of Lord Dosan's death, one of her uncles fled Mino and disappeared. She always spoke sadly with Her Ladyship about a certain Mitsuhide from Akechi Castle. This much has come to me. So when my subordinates informed me of your age and appearance, and told me that you had been walking around the castle town for half a day, I put it all together and guessed that it was you."

"I must congratulate you on your powers of deduction," Mitsuhide said with a relaxed smile.

Yoshinari glowed with satisfaction. More formally he asked, "But, Master Mitsuhide, what business brings you so far from Echizen?"

Mitsuhide's expression turned grave, and he quickly lowered his voice. "Is anyone else here?" He looked toward the sliding door.

"You don't need to worry. I've sent the servants away. The man on the other side of the door is my most trusted retainer. Other than a man keeping guard at the entrance to the corridor, there is no one else here."

"The fact is that I have been entrusted with two letters for Lord Nobunaga, one from Shogun Yoshiaki, and the other from Lord Hosokawa Fujitaka."

"From the shogun!"

"This had to be kept secret from the Asakura clan at all costs, so I'll leave you to imagine how difficult it's been to come this far."

The previous year, Shogun Yoshiteru had been assassinated by his vice-governor-general, Miyoshi Nagayoshi, and Miyoshi's retainer, Matsunaga Hisahide, who had usurped the shogun's authority. Yoshiteru had two younger brothers. The elder, the abbot of a Buddhist temple, was murdered by the rebels. The younger brother, Yoshiaki, who was then a monk in Nara, realized the danger he was in and escaped with the help of Hosokawa Fujitaka. He hid for a while in Omi, renounced the priesthood, and took the title of fourteenth shogun at the age of twenty-six.

After that, the "wandering shogun" approached the Wada, the Sasaki, and various other clans for assistance. From the very beginning, his plan was not to live on other people's charity. He planned to defeat his brother's murderers and restore his family's office and authority. He sought help, appealing to distant clans.

This was, however, a great matter involving the entire nation, because Miyoshi and Matsunaga had seized the central government. Although Yoshiaki was shogun in name, he was in fact nothing more than a penniless exile. He had no money, much less an army of his own. Nor was he particularly popular with the people.

Mitsuhide took up the story from Yoshiaki's arrival at Asakura Yoshikage's castle in Echizen. Just at that time, there was an ill-fated man in the service of the Asakura who had not been admitted as a full retainer of the clan. This was he himself, Akechi Mitsuhide. It was there that Mitsuhide had met Hosokawa Fujitaka for the first time.

Mitsuhide went on, "The story is a little long, but if you'll do me the favor of listening to me, I'll ask you to tell it in detail to Lord Nobunaga. Of course, I must hand the shogun's letter to Lord Nobunaga in person."

Then, in order to make his own situation clear, he talked about events from the time he left Akechi Castle and fled to Echizen from Mino. For over ten years, Mitsuhide tasted the hardships of the world. An intellectual by nature, he was easily drawn to books and scholarship. He was thankful for the reverses he had suffered. The time of his wandering, the period of his distress, had certainly been long. Akechi Castle had been destroyed during the civil war in Mino, and only he and his cousin, Mitsuharu, had escaped to Echizen. In the years since Mitsuhide had dropped from sight, he had lived as a *ronin* and made a scanty living by teaching farm children to read and write.

His only desire was to find the one right lord to serve, and one good opportunity. As he looked for a way to come up in the world, Mitsuhide studied the martial spirit, economics, and castles of various provinces with the eye of a military strategist, preparing for a later day.

He traveled far and wide and visited all the provinces of western Japan. There was a good reason for this. The west was always the first place to receive foreign innovations, and it was there that he was most likely to gain new knowledge on the subject he had made his specialty—guns. His knowledge of gunnery had led to several episodes in the western provinces. A retainer of the Mori clan, Katsura by name, arrested Mitsuhide in the town of Yamaguchi on suspicion of being a spy. On this occasion he spoke openly of his origins, his situation, and his hopes, and even revealed his evaluations of the neighboring provinces.

While he questioned Mitsuhide, Katsura was so impressed by the depth of his knowledge that he later recommended the traveler to his lord, Mori Motonari. "I think he is quite clearly uncommonly talented. Were he given employment here, I suspect he would accomplish something later on."

The search for talented men was the same everywhere. Certainly such men who left their homes and served other provinces would someday end up as the enemies of their former lords. As soon as Motonari heard of Mitsuhide, he wanted to see him. One day Mitsuhide was summoned to Motonari's castle. The next day Katsura visited Motonari alone, and asked him for his opinion of his guest.

"As you said, there are very few men of talent. We should give him some money and clothes, and send him courteously on his way."

"Yes, but didn't he impress you in some way?"

"Indeed. There are two kinds of great men: the truly great and the villain. Now, if a villain is also a scholar, he is liable to bring ruin upon himself and harm to his lord." Motonari went on, "There is something shifty about his appearance. When he speaks with such composure and clarity in his eyes, he has a charm that's very enticing. Yes, he's truly a captivating man, but I prefer the stolidity of our warriors of the western provinces. If I put this man in the middle of my own warriors, he'd stick out like a crane in a flock of chickens. I object to him for that reason alone." And so Mitsuhide was not taken in by the Mori clan.

He traveled through Hizen and Higo, and the domains of the Otomo clan. He crossed the Inland Sea to the island of Shikoku where he studied the martial arts of the Chosokabe clan.

When Mitsuhide returned to his home in Echizen, he found that his wife had taken ill and died, his cousin, Mitsuharu, had gone to serve another clan, and after six years his situation had not improved. He still could not see even a flicker of light on the road that lay ahead.

At this low point, Mitsuhide went to see Ena, the abbot of the Shonen Temple in Echizen. He rented a house in front of the temple and began to teach the children of the neighborhood. From the very beginning, Mitsuhide did not see schoolteaching as his life's work. Within a couple of years he had become conversant with the administration and problems of the province.

During this period the area was regularly disturbed by uprisings of the warrior-monks of the Ikko sect. One year, when the Asakura troops were wintering in the field during a campaign against the warrior-monks, Mitsuhide asked Ena, "It's just my own humble thought, but I'd like to present a strategy to the Asakura clan. Whom do you suppose it would be best to see?"

Ena immediately understood what was in Mitsuhide's mind. "The man most likely to listen to you would be Asakura Kageyuki."

Mitsuhide entrusted the temple school to Ena and went off to Asakura Kageyuki's camp. Because he had no intermediary, he simply walked into the camp, carrying his plan written down on a single piece of paper. He was arrested, not knowing whether the plan had been given to Kageyuki, and he heard nothing for two months. Although he was a prisoner, Mitsuhide inferred from the movements in the camp and the morale of the troops that Kageyuki was carrying out his plan.

At first Kageyuki had been suspicious of Mitsuhide, which was why he'd been arrested; but since there was no way to break the deadlock in the fighting, he decided to test Mitsuhide's plan. When the two men finally met, Kageyuki praised Mitsuhide as a warrior with an extensive knowledge of the classics and of the martial arts. Giving Mitsuhide the freedom of the camp, Kageyuki summoned him from time to time. It seemed, however, that Mitsuhide was not going to be so easily granted the status of retainer, and so one day he spoke out rather forcefully, even though he was not given to boasting:

"If you loan me a firearm, I'll shoot the enemy general in the middle of his camp."

"You may take one," Kageyuki said, but, still harboring some doubts, he secretly appointed a man to watch Mitsuhide.

It was an age when, even for the wealthy Asakura clan, a single firearm was extremely precious. Thanking him for the favor, Mitsuhide took the gun, mixed in among the troops, and went to the front lines. When the fighting started, he vanished deep behind enemy lines.

Hearing about the disappearance, Kageyuki later demanded to know why the man who was watching Mitsuhide had not shot him in the back. "Perhaps he was an enemy spy after all, feeling out the internal conditions here."

But a few days later it was reported that the enemy general had been shot by an unknown assailant as he inspected the battle lines. The morale of the enemy was said to have been thrown suddenly into confusion.

Soon afterward, Mitsuhide returned to camp. When he appeared before Kageyuki he was quick to ask him, "Why didn't you call out the entire army and rout the enemy? Do you call yourself a general when you let an opportunity like this slip by with your arms folded?"

Mitsuhide had done what he had promised: he had gone into enemy territory, shot the general, and returned.

When Asakura Kageyuki went back to Ichijogadani Castle, he told the story to Asakura Yoshikage. Yoshikage took one look at Mitsuhide and asked him to serve him. Later, Yoshikage had a target put up in the castle grounds and asked for a demonstration. Mitsuhide, though he was by no means a skilled marksman, demonstrated his skill by putting sixty-eight out of one hundred rounds into the target.

Mitsuhide was now given a residence in the castle town and a stipend of one thousand *kan*, one hundred sons of retainers were put under his instruction, and he again organized a gunners' regiment. Mitsuhide was so grateful to Yoshikage for rescuing him from adversity that for several years he worked tirelessly with no other intention than to repay him for his blessings and good fortune.

His devotion, however, finally brought objections from his peers. They accused him of being conceited and putting on highbrow airs. No matter what the topic of conversation or the activity, his refinement and intellect shone brilliantly for all to see.

This attitude did not sit well with the retainers of this provincial clan, who began to complain about him: "He's plainly conceited."

"He's just a snob."

Naturally, these complaints reached the ears of Yoshikage. Mitsuhide's work also began to suffer. Cold by nature, he was now the target of equally cold looks. It might have been different if Yoshikage had protected him, but he was held back by his own retainers. Winding its way even through Yoshikage's many favorite concubines, the dispute twisted through the castle. Mitsuhide himself was without connections and had just found temporary shelter. He was miserable, but there was nothing to be done.

I made a mistake, Mitsuhide thought. He had food and clothing but was now bitterly regretting his decision. Having been in such a hurry to escape adversity, the bank he had crawled out on was the wrong one. Such were his despondent thoughts after spending nothing but unhappy days. I've wasted my entire life! This depression seemed to affect his health, and he began to suffer from a scablike skin disease, which, in time, became serious. Mitsuhide asked Yoshikage for a leave of absence to go for a cure at the spa town of Yamashiro.

While he was there, travelers reported that rebels had attacked the Nijo Palace and murdered Shogun Yoshiteru. Even there, in the mountains, people were shocked and unsettled.

"If the shogun has been murdered, the country's going to fall into chaos again."

Mitsuhide immediately made preparations to return to Ichijogadani. Confusion in Kyoto meant confusion in the whole country. Quite naturally, this event would have aftereffects in the provinces. Undoubtedly, hurried preparations were being made at that very moment.

I could sulk and be depressed about trivialities, but it would be shameful for a man in his prime, Mitsuhide decided. His skin disease had cleared up at the spa and now Mitsuhide quickly presented himself before his lord. Yoshikage barely acknowledged his return, and Mitsuhide withdrew before his lord's indifference. He was not summoned after that. He had been relieved of his command of the gunners' regiment in his absence, and everywhere the atmosphere seemed to be hostile. Now that Yoshikage's former reliance on him had completely changed, Mitsuhide was once again prey to mental agony.

It was then that he received the visit from Hosokawa Fujitaka, who could only be described as a heaven-sent visitor. Mitsuhide was so surprised that he went out to greet the man himself, overawed that a person as exalted as Fujitaka had come to his house.

Fujitaka's character was exactly to Mitsuhide's liking. He certainly had the air of a noble and learned man. Mitsuhide had long lamented that he was unable to meet men of real quality, and such a guest naturally brought joy into his heart. He felt doubt, however, about the purpose of Fujitaka's visit.

Although his lineage was noble, at the time he secretly visited Mitsuhide's home, Fujitaka was really nothing more than an exile. Having been driven out of Kyoto, the refugee shogun, Yoshiaki, was fleeing through the provinces. It was Fujitaka who approached Asakura Yoshikage on the shogun's behalf. Touring the provinces preaching loyalty and trying to stir the provincial lords to action, Hosokawa Fujitaka was the only man who suffered with Yoshiaki, trying to overcome his master's pitiful reverses.

"Surely the Asakura clan will declare itself his ally. If the two provinces of Wakasa and Echizen joined us, then all the clans of the north would rush to our cause."

Yoshikage was of a mind to refuse. Regardless of what Fujitaka preached about loyalty, Yoshikage was not inclined to fight for a powerless, exiled shogun. It was not for a lack of military strength or resources, but because Yoshikage supported the status quo.

Fujitaka quickly perceived that the situation was not in their favor and, aware of the nepotism and internal struggles within the Asakura clan, abandoned his efforts there. Yoshiaki and his retainers, however, were already on their way to Echizen.

Although the Asakura clan felt greatly annoyed about having him as a dependent, they could not mistreat the shogun, and designated a temple as his temporary residence. They treated him well but also prayed for his early departure.

Then, quite suddenly, here was Mitsuhide, receiving a visit from Fujitaka. He was, however, still unable to guess the reason for the visit.

"I've heard that you have a taste for poetry. I saw one of your works when you went to Mishima," Fujitaka said by way of an opening remark. He did not look like a man whose heart was suffering. His countenance was absolutely mild and benign.

"Oh, I'm ashamed to hear it." Mitsuhide was not just being modest; he was sincerely embarrassed. Fujitaka, of course, was famous for his verses. That day their conversation began with poetry and went on to Japanese classical literature.

"Gracious, the conversation was so interesting, I forgot this was my first visit here." Apologizing for his long stay, Fujitaka took his leave.

After Fujitaka had left, Mitsuhide was even more perplexed. Gazing at the lamp, he became lost in thought. Fujitaka called on him two or three times, but the subjects of conversation never departed from poetry or the tea ceremony. But then one day—a day of drizzling rain so dark that lamps were needed inside—at a quiet moment, Fujitaka was more formal than usual.

"Today I have something very serious and secret to discuss," he began.

Mitsuhide, of course, had been waiting for him to break the ice like this, and answered, "If you trust me enough to tell me a secret, I certainly promise to keep it. Please speak freely, on any subject."

Fujitaka nodded. "I'm sure that someone as perceptive as you has already quickly guessed why I have been visiting like this. The fact is that those of us in attendance on the shogun came here depending on Lord Asakura as the only provincial lord who would be his ally, and until now we have secretly negotiated and appealed to him a number of times. His final answer, however, has been put off from day to day, and a decision does not seem to be in the offing. In the meantime we have studied the internal administration and affairs of Lord Asakura, and I know now that he does not have the will to fight for the shogun. Those of us who have appealed to him understand that it is futile. However..." Fujitaka spoke as though he were an entirely different man from the one who had visited before. "Who among all the provincial lords—besides Lord Asakura—is a man upon whom we could rely? Who is the most reliable military leader in the country today? Does such a man exist?"

"He does."

"He does?" Fujitaka's eyes shone.

Mitsuhide calmly wrote a name on the floor with his finger: Oda Nobunaga.

"The lord of Gifu?" Fujitaka caught his breath. Raising his eyes from the floor to Mitsuhide's face, he said nothing for a short while. After that, the two men discussed Nobunaga for a long time. Mitsuhide had been a retainer of the Saito clan, and in serving his former master, Lord Dosan, he had observed the character of Dosan's son-in-law. Thus there was a certain authority in what he said.

A few days later, Mitsuhide met Fujitaka in the mountains behind the temple that had become the shogun's lodging. From him he received a personal letter written by the shogun and addressed to Nobunaga. That night, Mitsuhide quickly left Ichijogadani. Naturally he abandoned both his residence and retainers, expecting never to return. The next day the Asakura clan was in an uproar.

The cry went up, "Mitsuhide has disappeared!" A punitive force was sent out to bring him back, but he could no longer be found within the boundaries of the province.

Asakura Yoshikage had heard that one of the shogun's followers, Hosokawa Fujitaka, had visited Mitsuhide, and so now Yoshikage turned on the shogun, saying, "Assuredly he's incited Mitsuhide in this matter, and has probably sent him off to another province as a envoy." And Yoshikage drove the shogun from the province.

Fujitaka had guessed this outcome beforehand. Thus, taking it rather as an opportunity, he went with his entourage from Echizen to Omi and found shelter with Asai Nagamasa in Odani Castle. There he waited for good news from Mitsuhide.

And this was why Mitsuhide had come to Gifu. Carrying the shogun's letter, he had risked his life many times along the way. Now he had finally completed half of his objective. He had found his way to Mori Yoshinari's residence, and was this very evening quietly seated across from Yoshinari himself, explaining in detail the aim of his mission and asking Yoshinari to act as an intermediary with Nobunaga.

It was the seventh day of the Tenth Month in the ninth year of Eiroku. One might, perhaps, call it a fateful day. Mori had interceded for Mitsuhide, and the details of the situation had reached Nobunaga. This was the day that Mitsuhide entered Gifu Castle and met Nobunaga for the first time. Mitsuhide was thirty-eight, six years older than Nobunaga.

"I have carefully looked over the letters from Lord Hosokawa and the shogun," Nobunaga said, "and I see that they have requested assistance from me. Unworthy as I am, I will give them whatever strength I can."

Mitsuhide bowed and responded to Nobunaga's words. "Risking my insignificant life for the nation has been a mission far exceeding my own low status." There was nothing false in Mitsuhide's words.

His sincerity impressed Nobunaga, as did his bearing and conduct, his perceptive use of words, his admirable intelligence. The more Nobunaga watched him, the more he was impressed. This man should prove to be of service, he thought. Thus Akechi Mitsuhide came under the wing of the Oda clan. Soon, he was granted a domain in Mino of four thousand *kan*. Moreover, as the shogun and his followers were now with the Asai clan, Nobunaga sent a number of men under Mitsuhide's command to escort them to Gifu Castle. Nobunaga went to the provincial border himself to greet the shogun, who had been treated as such a troublesome man in the other provinces.

At the castle gate, he took the reins of the shogun's horse and treated him as an honored guest. In truth, Nobunaga was not just holding the reins of the shogun's horse, but taking hold of the reins of the nation. From this moment on, whatever road he took, the storm clouds and winds of the times were in the fist that held those reins so tightly.

THE WANDERING SHOGUN

After the shogun and his party had found refuge with Nobunaga, they were lodged at a temple in Gifu. Vain and small-minded as they were, all that the shogun's retainers wanted to do was to display their own authority. They did not realize the extent of the changes occurring among the common people, and as soon as they had settled in, they began to behave in a highhanded, aristocratic manner, and complained to Nobunaga's retainers:

"This food doesn't taste quite right."

"The bedding is much too coarse."

"I know this cramped temple is just a temporary residence, but it reflects poorly on the shogun's dignity."

They went on, "We would like to see the treatment of the shogun improved. For the present, you might select some picturesque spot for the new shogun's palace and begin its construction."

Nobunaga, hearing of their demands, considered these men to be pitiable. Immediately summoning Yoshiaki's retainers, he told them, "I've heard that you wish to have me build a palace for the shogun because his present residence is so cramped."

"Indeed!" their spokesman replied. "His present lodgings are so inconvenient. As the shogun's residence, they lack even basic amenities."

"Well, well," Nobunaga answered with some contempt. "Aren't you gentlemen thinking rather slowly? The reason the shogun appealed to me was so that I might drive out Miyoshi and Matsunaga from Kyoto, recover his lost lands, and restore him to his rightful place."

"That's correct."

"Unworthy as I am, I consented to take on this great responsibility. More than that, I think that I should be able to realize the shogun's hopes for him in the very near future. How am I going to have the leisure to build a palace for him? And do you gentlemen really want to give up your hopes of returning to Kyoto to reestablish a national government? Would you be satisfied to spend your lives quietly in some scenic place in Gifu, and become early recluses in a large palace, with your meals provided by your host?"

Yoshiaki's attendants withdrew without saying another word. Thereafter, they did not complain so much. There was nothing false about Nobunaga's grand words. As summer turned to fall, Nobunaga ordered a general mobilization of Mino and Owari. By the fifth day of the Ninth Month, nearly thirty thousand soldiers were ready to go. By the seventh day, they were already marching out of Gifu for the capital.

At the great feast in the castle the night before the army's departure, Nobunaga had told his officers and men, "The commotion in the country, which is the result of territorial disputes among rival lords, is causing endless distress to the people. It is hardly necessary to mention that the misery of the entire nation is the anguish of the Emperor. It has been the iron rule of the Oda clan—from the time of my father, Nobuhide, to the present—that the duty of the samurai must be, first and foremost, the protection of the Imperial House. Thus, in our march on the capital at this time, you are not an army acting for me, but one that is acting in the name of the Emperor."

Every one of the commanders and men were in high spirits at the proclamation to set out.

For this great enterprise, Tokugawa Ieyasu of Mikawa, having recently bound himself in a military alliance to Nobunaga, also sent a thousand of his own troops. At the departure of the entire army, some voiced criticism.

"The Lord of Mikawa hasn't sent many men. He's sly, just as we've always heard."

Nobunaga shrugged this off with a laugh. "Mikawa is reforming its administration and economy. It has no time for other considerations. For him to send a large number of troops right now would mean great expense. He's going to be frugal even if he is criticized, but he's no common commander. I suspect that the troops he sent are his best men."

Just as Nobunaga had expected, the one thousand soldiers from Mikawa under Matsudaira Kanshiro were never outstripped in any battle. Always fighting in the vanguard, they opened the way for their allies, their courage bringing all the more fame to Ieyasu's name.

Every day the weather continued to be beautiful. The thirty thousand troops marched in black lines beneath the clear autumn sky. The column was so long that when the vanguard had reached Kashiwabara, the rear guard was still passing through Tarui and Akasaka. Their banners hid the sky. As they passed the post town of Hirao and entered Takamiya, there was some shouting from up ahead.

"Messengers! There are messengers from the capital!"

Three generals rode out to meet them.

"We wish to have an audience with Lord Nobunaga." They carried with them a letter from Miyoshi Nagayoshi and Matsunaga Hisahide.

When this was related to headquarters, Nobunaga said, "Bring them here."

The messengers were brought in immediately, but Nobunaga sneered at the message of reconciliation in the letter as a trick of the enemy. "Tell them I will give them my answer when I reach the capital."

As the sun rose on the eleventh, the vanguard crossed the Aichi River. The following morning Nobunaga moved toward the Sasaki strongholds of Kannonji and Mitsukuri. Kannonji Castle was held by Sasaki Jotei. Jotei's son, Sasaki Rokkaku, prepared Mitsukuri Castle for a siege. The Sasaki clan of Omi were allied with Miyoshi and Matsunaga, and when Yoshiaki had sought shelter with them during his flight, they had tried to murder him.

Omi was a strategic area along Lake Biwa on the road to the south. And here the Sasaki waited, boasting that he would destroy Nobunaga just as Nobunaga had annihilated Imagawa Yoshimoto, in a single blow. Sasaki Rokkaku left Mitsukuri Castle, joined forces with his father at Kannonji, and distributed his troops among the eighteen fortresses in Omi.

Shading his eyes with his hand, Nobunaga looked down from high ground and laughed. "This is a wonderful enemy line, isn't it? Just like in a classic treatise."

He ordered Sakuma Nobumori and Niwa Nagahide to take Mitsukuri Castle, placing the Mikawa troops in the vanguard. Then he said, "As I told you the night before we left, this march on the capital is not a personal vendetta; I want it understood by every soldier in the army that we are fighting for the Emperor. Do not kill those who flee. Do not burn the people's homes. And, as far as possible, do not trample over the fields where crops have not yet been harvested."

The waters of Lake Biwa were still invisible through the morning mist. Darkly piercing that mist, thirty thousand men began to move. When Nobunaga saw the flare that signaled the attack on Mitsukuri Castle by Niwa Nagahide's and Sakuma Nobumori's troops, he ordered, "Move the headquarters to Wada Castle."

Wada Castle was an enemy stronghold, so Nobunaga's order meant to attack and take the castle. He said it, though, as if he were ordering his men to move into an unoccupied position.

"Nobunaga himself is coming to attack!" the commanding general of Wada Castle shouted in response to the lookouts on the watchtower. Striking the hilt of his sword, he harangued the garrison: "This is heaven-sent! Both Kannonji and Mitsukuri Castle would have been able to hold for at least a month, and during that time the Matsunaga and Miyoshi forces and their allies to the north of the lake would have cut off Nobunaga's path of retreat. But Nobunaga has hastened his own death by attacking this castle. A wonderful opportunity indeed! Do not let this piece of martial luck escape. Take Nobunaga's head!"

The entire army screamed its assent. They were confident that the iron walls of the Sasaki clan could hold out for a month, even though Nobunaga commanded an army of thirty thousand men and had many able generals. The powerful provinces surrounding them also believed this. But Wada Castle fell in half a day. After a battle lasting a little over four hours, the defenders were routed, and fled into the mountains and to the shores of the lake.

"Do not pursue them!" Nobunaga ordered from atop Mount Wada, and the banners erected there so quickly could clearly be seen under the noonday sun. Covered with blood and mud, the men gradually collected under the banners of their own generals. Then, raising a shout of victory, they ate their noonday rations. A number of messages continued to come in from the direction of Mitsukuri. The Tokugawa forces from Mikawa, which had been positioned as the vanguard for Niwa and Nobumori, were just now fighting courageously, bathed in blood. Moment by moment, messages of success collected in Nobunaga's hand.

The report of Mitsukuri's fall reached Nobunaga before the sun had set. As evening neared, black smoke rose from the direction of the castle at Kannonji. Hideyoshi's forces were already pressing in. The command for an all-out attack was given. Nobunaga moved his camp, and the entire force of Mitsukuri and its allies were pushed back to Kannonji Castle. By the time evening fell, the first men had breached the walls of the enemy castles.

Stars and sparks filled the clear autumn night sky. The attacking forces surged in. Victory songs were raised, and to those allied with the Sasaki, they must have sounded like the heartless voice of the autumn wind. No one had expected that this stronghold would fall in but a single day. The fortress at Mount Wada and the eighteen strategic points had been no defense at all against these billowing waves of attackers.

The entire Sasaki clan—from women and children to its leaders, Rokkaku and Jotei—stumbled and fought through the darkness, fleeing from the flames of their castles to the fortress at Ishibe.

"Let the fugitives flee as they will; there will be enemies still ahead of us tomorrow." Nobunaga spared not only their lives, but also ignored the vast amount of treasure they carried with them. It was not Nobunaga's style to tarry along the way. His mind was already in Kyoto, the center of the field. The castle at Kannonji stopped burning at the keep. As soon as Nobunaga entered what was left of it, he showed his appreciation to his troops, saying, "The horses and men should be given a good rest."

He himself, however, did not rest much. That night he slept in his armor, and as morning broke, he gathered his senior retainers for a conference. Again he commanded decrees to be posted throughout the province, and immediately sent Fuwa Kawachi off with the command to bring Yoshiaki from Gifu to Moriyama.

Yesterday he had fought at the head of an army; today he was taking the reins of the administration. This was Nobunaga. Temporarily giving four of his generals responsibilities as administrators and magistrates in the port city of Otsu, two days later he crossed Lake Biwa, nearly forgetting to eat as he issued order after order.

It was the twelfth of the month when Nobunaga struck into Omi and attacked Kannonji and Mitsukuri. Then, by the twenty-fifth, Nobunaga's army had gone from the aftermath of battle to setting up notices of the new laws for the province. One road to supremacy, to the center of the field! With that, the warships from the east shore of Lake Biwa were lined up, and they sailed for Omi. Everything from the preparation of the ships to the loading of the rations for the soldiers and feed for their horses involved the cooperation of the common people. Certainly they crouched in fear of Nobunaga's military strength. But more than that, the fact that the common people of Omi united in support of him was due to their approval of his style of government, which they trusted as reliable.

Nobunaga was the only man who had rescued the hearts of the common people from the flames of war and who had committed himself to them publicly. When they asked themselves what was to become of them, he reassured them. In such situations, there is no time to establish a detailed political policy. Nobunaga's secret was nothing more than to do things swiftly and decisively. What the common people clearly wanted in this country at civil war was not a talented administrator or a great sage. The world was in chaos. If Nobunaga was able to control it, they would accept a certain amount of hardship.

The wind on the lake reminded one that it was autumn, and the water drew beautiful long patterns in the wake of the myriad boats. On the twenty-fifth, Yoshiaki's boat crossed the waters of the lake from Moriyama and landed near Mii Temple.

Nobunaga, who had already landed, expected an attack by Miyoshi and Matsunaga, but it did not come.

He greeted Yoshiaki at the temple, saying, "It's the same as if we've already entered the capital."

On the twenty-eighth, Nobunaga at last pushed his troops toward Kyoto. When they reached Awataguchi, the army stopped. Hideyoshi, who was at Nobunaga's side, galloped forward at the same time that Akechi Mitsuhide was hurrying back from the van.

"What is it?"

"Imperial messengers."

Nobunaga, too, was surprised, and hurriedly dismounted. The two messengers arrived with a letter from the Emperor.

Bowing low, Nobunaga responded reverently, "As a provincial warrior, I have no other abilities than taking up the weapons of war. Since my father's time, we have long lamented the grievous condition of the Imperial Palace and the uneasiness in the Emperor's heart. Today, however, I have come to the capital from a far corner of the country to guard His Imperial Majesty. No other responsibility would be a greater honor for a samurai, or a greater joy for my clan."

Thirty thousand soldiers silently and solemnly swore an oath with Nobunaga that they would obey the Emperor's wishes.

Nobunaga made his camp at Tofuku Temple. On the same day, proclamations were set up throughout the capital. The disposition of the police patrols came first. The day watch was given to Sugaya Kuemon, and the night watch to Hideyoshi.

One of the soldiers from the Oda army was out drinking, and a victorious soldier will easily become arrogant. Drunk and having eaten his fill, he tossed down a few coins that amounted to less than half of what he owed, and walked out, saying, "That should do."

The proprietor ran out after him, yelling, and when he tried to grab the soldier, the man struck him and then swaggered away. Midway through his rounds, Hideyoshi witnessed the incident and immediately ordered the man's arrest. When he was brought to headquarters, Nobunaga praised the police, stripped the soldier of his armor, and had him bound to a large tree in front of the temple gate. The nature of the offense was then signposted, and Nobunaga ordered the man to be exposed for seven days and then beheaded. Every day, an immense number of people traveled back and forth in front of the temple gate. Many of them were merchants and nobles, and there were also messengers from other temples and shrines, and shopkeepers transporting their goods.

The passersby stopped to read the placard and look at the man bound to the tree. Thus the common people in the capital witnessed both Nobunaga's justice and the severity of his laws. They saw that the law posted on placards all over town—that the theft of even a single coin would be punished by death—was to be strictly enforced, starting with Nobunaga's own soldiers. No one uttered any discontent.

The phrase "a one-coin cut" became common among the people for the sort of punishment meted out by Nobunaga's rule. It had been twenty-one days since the army's departure from Gifu.

After Nobunaga had settled the situation in the capital and returned to Gifu, he turned away from the matters that had preoccupied him and found that Mikawa was no longer the weak, poverty-stricken province it had once been.

He could not help marveling secretly at Ieyasu's vigilance. The lord of Mikawa had not simply been content to be a guard dog at the back gate of Owari and Mino while his ally, Nobunaga, marched off to the center of the field. Rather than let the opportunity go by, he had expelled the forces of Imagawa Yoshimoto's successor, Ujizane, from the two provinces of Suruga and Totomi. This, of course, was not through his own strength alone. Connected with the Oda clan on the one hand, he was also in collusion with Takeda Shingen of Kai, and he had a pact with the latter to divide and share the two remaining provinces of the Imagawa. Ujizane had been a fool and had given both the Tokugawa and Takeda clans a number of good excuses to attack him.

Even though the country was in chaos, every military commander understood that he could not start a war without some reason, and that if he did, the battle would be lost in the end. Ujizane was operating an administration against which the enemy could take just such a moral stand, and was weak-minded enough to be unable to see what the future held. Everyone knew he was an unworthy successor to Yoshimoto.

The province of Suruga became the possession of the Takeda clan, while Totomi became the Tokugawa clan's domain. On New Year's Day of the thirteenth year of Eiroku, Ieyasu left his son in charge of the castle at Okazaki, and he himself moved to Hamamatsu in Totomi. In the Second Month, a message of congratulations came from Nobunaga:

> Last year, I myself mentioned my long-cherished desire and had some small success, but nothing could be more felicitous than adding the fertile land of Totomi to your own domains. Collectively, we have become all the stronger.

In early spring, Ieyasu went to Kyoto in the company of Nobunaga. Of course the purpose of the trip was to enjoy the capital in the springtime and to relax beneath the cherry blossoms, or so it appeared. From a political perspective, however, the rest of the world looked at the two leaders meeting in Kyoto and wondered what it was really about.

But Nobunaga's trip this time was really just a magnificent and leisurely progress. Alone, the two of them would spend the entire day hawking in the fields. At night Nobunaga held banquets and had the popular songs and dances of the villagers performed at their inn. All in all, it looked like nothing more than an outing. On the day Nobunaga and Ieyasu were to arrive at the capital, Hideyoshi, who was in charge of the defense of Kyoto, had gone out as far as Otsu to greet them. Nobunaga had introduced him to Ieyasu.

"Yes, I've known him for a long time. The first time I met him was when I visited Kiyosu, and he was among the samurai stationed at the entrance to greet me. That was a year after the battle of Okehazama, so it was quite a while ago." Ieyasu looked directly at Hideyoshi and smiled. Hideyoshi was surprised at how good the man's memory was. Ieyasu was now twenty-eight years old. Lord Nobunaga was thirty-six. Hideyoshi was going to be thirty-four. The battle of Okehazama had taken place a good ten years before.

When they had settled down in Kyoto, Nobunaga first went to inspect the repairs being done on the Imperial Palace.

"We anticipate that the Imperial Palace will be finished by next year," the two construction overseers informed him.

"Don't be stingy with the expenses," Nobunaga replied. "The Imperial Palace has lain in ruins for years."

Ieyasu heard Nobunaga's comments and said, "I truly envy your position. You have been able to demonstrate your loyalty to the Emperor in actual fact."

"That's so," Nobunaga answered without modesty, and nodded as though he approved of himself.

Thus, Nobunaga not only rebuilt the Imperial Palace, but he also revised the finances of the court. The Emperor was pleased, of course, and Nobunaga's loyalty impressed the people. Seeing that the nobles were at ease and that the lower classes were at peace and in harmony, Nobunaga truly enjoyed the time spent with Ieyasu during the Second Month, viewing the cherry blossoms, and attending tea ceremonies and concerts.

Who would have known that, during that time, his mind was preparing to strike through the next set of difficulties? Nobunaga initiated his actions as new situations developed, and moved ahead with the outlines of his plans and their execution even as he lay sleeping. Suddenly, on the second day of the Fourth Month, all of his generals received summonses to meet at the residence of the shogun.

The large conference room was full.

"This concerns the Asakura clan of Echizen," Nobunaga began, revealing what he had been planning since the Second Month. "Lord Asakura has ignored the numerous requests of the shogun and has not offered a single piece of lumber for the construction of the Imperial Palace. Lord Asakura was appointed by the shogun and holds the position of retainer to the Emperor, but he thinks of nothing but the luxury and indolence of his own clan. I would like to investigate this crime myself, and assemble a punitive force of soldiers. What are your opinions?"

Among those under direct control of the shogunate, there were a number of men who had old friendships with the Asakura clan and who supported the clan indirectly; but no one disagreed. And as a large number of men voiced frank approval quite readily, no one spoke under the added pressure of the large group.

To attack the Asakura would mean a campaign to the northern provinces. It was a major undertaking, but the plan was approved in a very short time. On the very same day a proclamation went out that an army would be assembled, and by the twentieth day of that month it had already been mustered at Sakamoto. Added to the troops of Owari and Mino, were eight thousand Mikawa warriors under Tokugawa Ieyasu. A force of close to one hundred thousand men now stretched along the lakeshore at Niodori, in the bright Fourth Month of late spring.

Reviewing the troops, Nobunaga pointed toward the mountain range to the north. "Look! The snow covering the mountains of the northern provinces has melted. We'll have the flowering of spring!" Hideyoshi had been included in this army, and led a contingent of troops.

He nodded to himself, thinking, "Well, while Lord Nobunaga was entertaining himself in the capital with Lord Ieyasu this spring, he was also waiting for the snows to melt in the mountain passes leading to the northern provinces."

But more than that, he considered how Nobunaga's real skill had been in inviting Ieyasu to the capital. Indirectly he had displayed his own strength and achievements so that Ieyasu would not begrudge the forces he would be sending. This was Nobunaga's skill. Even with the chaos the world is in, it's going to be united by his ability. Hideyoshi believed this was true, and understood more than anyone else that the significance of this battle was in its absolute necessity.

The army advanced from Takashima, passed Kumagawa in Wakasa, and marched toward Tsuruga in Echizen. On and on it went, burning the enemy's fortresses and border posts, crossing mountain after mountain, and attacking Tsuruga within the month.

The Asakura, who had been making light of the enemy troops, were astonished that they were already there. Just half a month earlier, Nobunaga had been reveling in the spring flowers of the capital. The Asakura could not believe, even in their dreams, that they were looking at his banners here in their own province, even if he had been able to make his military preparations so quickly.

The ancient Asakura clan, descended from the imperial line, had risen to prominence for helping the first shogun, and later had been granted the entire province of Echizen.

The clan was the strongest in all the northern provinces; this was acknowledged by itself and others. The Asakura ranked as participants in the shogunate, they were rich in natural resources, and they could depend on great military strength.

When he heard that Nobunaga had already reached Tsuruga, Yoshikage almost chided the man who had informed him. "Don't lose your head. You're probably mistaken."

The Oda army that fell upon Tsuruga made its base camp there and sent out battalions to attack the castles at Kanegasaki and Tezutsugamine.

"Where's Mitsuhide?" Nobunaga asked.

"General Mitsuhide is in command of the vanguard," a retainer replied.

"Call him back!" Nobunaga ordered.

"What is it, my lord?" Mitsuhide asked, hurrying back from the front lines.

"You lived in Echizen for a long time, so you should be especially familiar with the geography between this area and the Asakura's main castle at Ichijogadani. Why are you fighting out there for some tiny achievement with the vanguard, without devising some greater strategy?" Nobunaga inquired.

"I'm sorry." Mitsuhide bowed as though Nobunaga had somehow struck him deep inside. "If you will give me your order, I will draw you a map and submit it for your observation."

"Well then, I'll give you a formal order. The maps I have at hand are rather crude, and there seem to be places where they might be totally incorrect. Check them with the maps you have, correct them, and give them back to me."

In Mitsuhide's possession were finely detailed maps with which Nobunaga's could not compare. Mitsuhide withdrew and then returned with his own maps, which he presented to Nobunaga.

"I think you should look over the lay of the land. And I think I'd better make you an officer on my field staff." After that, Nobunaga would not let Mitsuhide stray far from headquarters.

Tezutsugamine, the castle defended by Hitta Ukon, soon surrendered. But the castle at Kanegasaki was not so quick to fall. In this latter castle, Asakura Kagetsune, a twenty-six-year-old general, stood his ground. When he had been a monk in his youth, there were those who said it would be a pity for a warrior of his physique and disposition to enter holy orders. Thus he was forced back into secular life and quickly put in charge of a castle, distinguishing himself even within the Asakura clan. Surrounded by more than forty thousand troops commanded by such veteran generals as Sakuma Nobumori, Ikeda Shonyu, and Mori Yoshinari, Kagetsune looked down from the castle watchtower with an unperturbed expression, and broke into a smile.

"How ostentatious."

Yoshinari, Nobumori, and Shonyu staged a general attack, staining the walls with blood and holding fast like ants for the entire day. When they counted the bodies at the end of the day, the enemy had lost over three hundred men, but the corpses of their own forces exceeded eight hundred. That night, however, the castle at Kanegasaki stood majestic and indomitable under a huge summer moon.

"This castle is not going to fall. And even if it does, it will not be a victory for us," Hideyoshi told Nobunaga that evening.

Nobunaga looked a bit impatient. "Why won't it be a victory for us if the castle falls?" There was, on such occasions, no reason for Nobunaga to be in a good mood.

"With the fall of this one castle, Echizen will not necessarily be overthrown. With the capture of this one castle, my lord, your military power will not necessarily increase."

Nobunaga interrupted him, asking, "But how can we advance without overcoming Kanegasaki?"

Hideyoshi suddenly turned to the side. Ieyasu had come in and was just standing there. Seeing Ieyasu, Hideyoshi hurriedly withdrew with a bow. He then brought in some matting and offered the lord of Mikawa a seat next to Nobunaga.

"Am I intruding?" Ieyasu asked, and then sat down on the seat Hideyoshi had provided. To Hideyoshi, however, he gave not the slightest recognition. "It seems as though you were in the middle of some discussion."

"No." Motioning toward Hideyoshi with his chin and softening his mood a bit, Nobunaga explained to Ieyasu exactly what they had been discussing.

Ieyasu nodded and stared fixedly at Hideyoshi. Ieyasu was eight years younger than Nobunaga, but to Hideyoshi it seemed the other way around. As Ieyasu looked at him, Hideyoshi could not imagine that his manner and expression were those of a man in his twenties.

"I agree with what Hideyoshi has said. To waste further time and injure more men with this one castle is not a sound policy."

"Do you think we should call off the attack and press on to the enemy's main stronghold?"

"First let's hear what Hideyoshi has to say. It seems he has something in mind."

"Hideyoshi."

"Yes, my lord."

"Tell us your plan."

"I don't have a plan."

"What?" Nobunaga was not the only one whose eyes showed surprise. The expression on Ieyasu's face was a little perplexed, too.

"There are three thousand soldiers inside that castle, and its walls are hardened with their will to take on an army of ten thousand men and fight to the death. Even though it's small, there's no reason why the castle should fall easily. I doubt that it would be shaken even if we did have a plan. Those soldiers are men, too, so I imagine they must be susceptible to true human emotions and sincerity...."

"You're starting up again, eh?" Nobunaga said. He did not want Hideyoshi's tongue to wag any more than it had already. Ieyasu was his most powerful ally, and he treated him with extreme courtesy; but the man was, after all, lord of the two provinces of Mikawa and Totomi, and was not a member of the Oda clan's inner circle. More than that, Nobunaga was well enough attuned to Hideyoshi's mind that he didn't have to hear his thoughts in detail in order to trust him.

"Fine. That's fine," Nobunaga said. "I give you the authority for whatever you have in mind. Go ahead and carry it through."

"Thank you, my lord." Hideyoshi withdrew as though the matter were of no particular consequence. But that night he entered the enemy castle alone and met with its commander, Asakura Kagetsune. Hideyoshi opened his heart and spoke to the young master of this castle.

"You come from a samurai family, too, so you're probably looking at the end result of this battle. Further resistance will only result in the deaths of valuable soldiers. I, in particular, do not want to see you die a useless death. Rather than that, why don't you open up the castle and retreat properly, join forces with Lord Yoshikage, and meet us again, on a different battlefield? I will personally guarantee the security of all the treasures, weapons, and women and children inside the castle, and send them to you without trouble."

"Changing the field of battle and meeting you on another day would be interesting." Kagetsune replied, and went to prepare the retreat. With the full courtesy of a samurai, Hideyoshi allowed the retreating enemy all accommodations, and saw them off to a league beyond the castle.

It took a day and a half to settle the matter of Kanegasaki, but when Hideyoshi informed Nobunaga of what he had done, his lord's only response was, "Is that so?" and he added no great praise. The look on Nobunaga's face, however, indicated that he seemed to be thinking, You did too well—there is a limit to meritorious deeds. But Hideyoshi's great achievement could hardly be denied, regardless of who judged the matter.

If Nobunaga had praised him to the skies, however, it would have created a situation in which the generals Shonyu, Nobumori, and Yoshinari would have been too ashamed to face their lord again. After all, they had sent eight hundred soldiers to their deaths and had been unable to defeat the enemy even with an overwhelming number of men. Hideyoshi was even more sensitive to the feelings of these generals, and when he made his report, he did not credit his own idea as the source of his efforts. He simply said that he had been following Nobunaga's orders.

"It was my intention to carry out everything according to orders. I hope you'll overlook my unskillful performance and the suddenness and secrecy of it all." Thus apologizing, he withdrew.

Ieyasu happened to be with the other generals at Nobunaga's side at this time. Grunting to himself, he watched Hideyoshi depart. From this point on, he realized that there was a formidable man not much older than he who had been born into this period as well. Meanwhile, having abandoned Kanegasaki and now in full retreat, Asakura Kagetsune hurried along, thinking that he would join his forces with those at the main castle at Ichijogadani, and measure his strength against Nobunaga's army once again, at another place. Still on the way, he met the twenty thousand troops that Asakura Yoshikage had sent running to relieve Kanegasaki.

"Now I've done it!" Kagetsune said, regretting that he had followed the counsel of the enemy, but it was too late.

"Why did you leave the castle without a fight?" Yoshikage shouted, enraged, but he was obliged to unite the two armies and return to Ichijogadani.

Nobunaga's men pushed on as far as Kinome Pass. If he could break through that strategic position, the very headquarters of the Asakura clan would be right before him. But an urgent message shocked the invading Oda troops.

A dispatch informed them that Asai Nagamasa of Omi, whose clan had been allied with the Asakura for several generations, had taken his army from north of Lake Biwa and cut off Nobunaga's retreat. Additionally, Sasaki Rokkaku, who had already tasted defeat at the hands of Nobunaga, was acting in concert with the Asai and coming from the mountainous area of Koga. One after another, they had led their armies to strike at Nobunaga's flank.

The enemy was now before and behind the invading army. Perhaps because of this change of events, the morale of the Asakura forces was high, and they were ready to sally from Ichijogadani and mount a furious counterattack.

"We've entered the jaws of death," Nobunaga said. He realized it was as if they had been looking for their own graves in enemy territory. What he suddenly feared was not just that Sasaki Rokkaku and Asai Nagamasa obstructed his retreat; what Nobunaga feared to the very marrow of his bones was the likelihood that the warrior-monks of the Honganji, whose fortress was in this area, would raise a war cry against the invader and unfold the banner opposing him. The weather had suddenly changed, and the invading army was a boat heading into the storm.

But where was an opening large enough for the retreat of ten thousand soldiers? Strategists warn that, by nature, an advance is easy and a retreat difficult. If a general makes one mistake, he may suffer the misfortune of the annihilation of his entire army.

"Please allow me to take charge of the rear guard. Then my lord can take the shortcut through Kuchikidani, unencumbered by too many men, and under cover of night, slip out of this land of death. By dawn the rest of the troops could retreat directly toward the capital," Hideyoshi offered.

With each moment that passed, the danger became greater. That evening, accompanied by a few retainers and a force of only three hundred men, Nobunaga followed the pathless valleys and ravines and rode all night toward Kuchikidani. They were attacked countless times by the warrior-monks of the Ikko sect and local bandits, and for two days and nights they went without food, drink, or sleep. They finally reached Kyoto on the evening of the fourth day, but by that time, many of them were so tired that they were almost invalids. But they were the lucky ones. The one more to be pitied was the man who had taken responsibility for the rear guard on his own and, after the main army had made its escape, stayed behind with a tiny force in the lone fortress of Kanegasaki.

This was Hideyoshi. The other generals, who until now had envied his successes and secretly called him a quibbler and an upstart, now parted from him with heartfelt praise, calling him "the pillar of the Oda clan" and "a true warrior," and bringing firearms, gunpowder, and provisions to his camp as they left. As they laid the supplies down and left, it was as if they were leaving wreaths at a grave.

Then, from dawn until midday on the morning after Nobunaga's night escape, the nine thousand troops under Katsuie, Nobumori, and Shonyu made good their escape. When the Asakura forces saw this and pursued to attack them, Hideyoshi struck their flank and threatened them from behind. And when the Oda force had finally been able to slip away from disaster, Hideyoshi and his troops shut themselves up in the castle at Kanegasaki, vowing, "This is where we'll leave this world."

Demonstrating their will to die fighting, they barred the castle gate tightly, eating what there was to eat, sleeping whenever there was time to sleep, and said their farewells to the world. The commander of the attacking Asakura forces was the brave general Keya Shichizaemon. Rather than injure many of his own men by dashing against troops who were ready to die, he besieged the fortress, cutting off Hideyoshi's retreat.

"Night attack!" When this warning was given in the middle of the second night, all the preparations made beforehand were deployed without the least confusion. Keya's army rushed out against the enemy moving in the dark and completely routed Hideyoshi's small force, which fled quickly back into the castle.

"The enemy is resigned to die, and is shouting its own death cry! Take this opportunity, and we'll capture the castle by dawn!" Keya ordered. They rushed to the edge of the moat, assembled rafts, and crossed the water. In no time at all, thousands of soldiers took possession of the stone walls.

Then, just as Shichizaemon had vowed, Kanegasaki fell with the coming of the dawn. But what did his forces find? Not one of Hideyoshi's men was in the castle. Their banners were standing. Smoke already curled toward the sky. Horses were neighing. Hideyoshi, however, was not there. The attack the night before had not been an attack at all.

Led by Hideyoshi, his small army had only pretended to flee back into the castle, while in fact it searched like the wind for a way of escape from certain death. By dawn, Hideyoshi's men were already at the base of the mountains that wound their way along the provincial border, making good their escape.

Keya Shichizaemon and his troops did not, of course, watch them go in mute amazement. "Make ready for pursuit!" he ordered. "After them!"

Hideyoshi's troops took the path of retreat deep into the mountains, continuing their flight throughout the night without pausing to eat or drink.

"We're not out of the tiger's den yet!" Hideyoshi warned them. "Don't slacken up. Don't rest. Don't think about thirst. Just keep your will to live!" On they marched to Hideyoshi's admonishments. As expected, Keya began to catch up with them. When he heard the enemy's battle cries behind them, Hideyoshi first ordered a short rest and then spoke to his soldiers.

"Don't be alarmed. Our enemies are fools. They're raising their war cries as they climb up the valley while we're on high ground. We're all tired, but the enemy is chasing after us in anger, and many of them are going to be exhausted. When they're in range, shower them with rocks and stones, and thrust your spears at them."

His men were tired, but they regained their confidence at his reason and clarity.

"Come and get us!" they yelled as they stood ready for the attack. Keya's chastisement of Hideyoshi's troops was returned to him in a miserable defeat. Innumerable corpses piled up beneath the rocks and spears.

"Retreat!" The voices that screamed the order finally grew hoarse in the valleys into which the Asakura retreated.

"Now's our chance! Pull back! Retreat!"

Hideyoshi seemed almost to mimic the enemy, and his men turned and fled toward the southern lowlands. Leading his surviving soldiers, Keya once again went in pursuit. Keya's men were truly implacable, and though the remaining strength of the punitive force had already weakened considerably, the warrior-monks of the Honganji joined the attack, blocking the road as Hideyoshi's men tried to pass through the mountains leading down into Omi. When the men tried to turn from the road, arrows and stones flew from the swamps and forests to the right and left, accompanied by screams of "Don't let them pass!" Even Hideyoshi started to think that his time had come. But now was the moment to summon the will to live and to resist the temptation to succumb.

"Let heaven decide whether our luck is good or bad and whether we live or die! Run down through the marsh to the west. Escape along the mountain streams. Their waters flow into Lake Biwa. Run as fast as the water itself. Your escape from death is speed!" He did not tell them to fight. This was the Hideyoshi who knew so well how to employ men, but even he did not think of ordering his starving troops, who had gone two days and two nights without sleep or rest, to repel an ambush by unknown numbers of warrior-monks. All he wanted was to help every last soldier in his pitiful force to return to the capital. And there was nothing stronger than the will to live.

Under Hideyoshi's orders, the tired and hungry troops struck their way into the marsh in a downhill rush of almost uncanny force. It was a reckless move that could have been called neither strategy nor even self-abandonment, for the warrior-monks hidden in the depths of the forest were like mosquitoes. Still, on they ran, right through the enemy. And this, in fact, opened up a fissure in the enemy ranks, and they were able to rend the carefully laid ambush into pieces. As they ran, order turned to chaos, and all the men scrambled to the south, following the mountain streams.

"Lake Biwa!"

"We're saved!" They shouted for joy.

The following day they entered Kyoto.

When Nobunaga saw them, he exclaimed, "Thank heaven you've come back alive. You're like gods. You are truly like gods."

BOOK FOUR

FIRST YEAR OF GENKI
1570

CHARACTERS AND PLACES

ASAI NAGAMASA, lord of Omi
and Nobunaga's brother-in-law
ASAKURA YOSHIKAGE, lord of Echizen
AMAKASU SANPEI, ninja of the Takeda clan
TAKEDA SHINGEN, lord of Kai
KAISEN, zen monk and Shingen's adviser
SAKUMA NOBUMORI, senior Oda retainer
TAKEI SEKIAN, senior Oda retainer
MORI RANMARU, Nobunaga's page
FUJIKAGE MIKAWA, senior Asai retainer
OICHI, Asai Nagamasa's wife and Nobunaga's sister
CHACHA, Oichi and Nagamasa's eldest daughter

HONGANJI, headquarters of the
warrior-monks of the Ikko sect
MOUNT HIEI, mountain east of Kyoto
and headquarters of the Tendai sect
KAI, province of the Takeda clan
HAMAMATSU, Tokugawa Ieyasu's castle
NIJO, shogun's palace in Kyoto
OMI, province of the Asai clan
ODANI, main castle of the Asai clan
ECHIZEN, province of the Asakura clan

ENEMY OF THE BUDDHA

On the first night after their return to Kyoto, the officers and men of the rear guard, who had narrowly escaped with their lives, could only think of one thing: sleep.

After reporting to Nobunaga, Hideyoshi wandered off in a daze.

Sleep. Sleep.

The following morning he opened his eyes for just a moment, and then went straight back to sleep. Around noon he was awakened by a servant and ate some rice gruel, but in a state between waking and dreaming, he only knew that it tasted good.

"Are you going back to sleep?" the servant asked in amazement.

Hideyoshi finally woke up two days later in the evening, feeling totally disoriented. "What day is it?"

"It's the second," the samurai on duty answered.

The second, he thought as he wearily dragged himself out of the room. Then Lord Nobunaga must have recovered, too.

Nobunaga had rebuilt the Imperial Palace and constructed a new residence for the shogun, but he himself did not have a mansion in the capital. Whenever he came to Kyoto, he would stay in a temple, and his retainers would lodge in neighboring branch temples.

Hideyoshi left the temple in which he was billeted, and looked up at the stars for the first time in several days. It's almost summer, he thought. And then he realized, I'm still alive! He felt extraordinarily happy. Although it was late at night, he asked for an audience with Nobunaga. He was shown in immediately, as though Nobunaga had been waiting for him.

"Hideyoshi, you must be pleased about something," Nobunaga said. "You've got an extraordinary smile on your face."

"How could I not be pleased?" he answered. "Before this, I wasn't aware of what a blessed thing life is. But having escaped from near death, I realize that I don't need anything more than life. Just by looking at this lamp or at your face, my lord, I know that I'm alive, and that I am blessed far more than I deserve. But how are you feeling, my lord?"

"I can't help feeling disappointed. This is the first time I've ever felt the shame and bitterness of defeat."

"Has anyone ever accomplished great things without experiencing defeat?"

"Well, can you see that on my face, too? The horse's belly only has to be whipped once. Hideyoshi, get yourself ready for a trip."

"A trip?"

"We're going back to Gifu." Just when Hideyoshi was congratulating himself for being one step ahead of Nobunaga, his lord struck out into the lead. There were several good reasons for him to get back to Gifu as quickly as possible.

Although Nobunaga was reputed to be a dreamer, he was also known to be a strong-willed man of action. That night Nobunaga, Hideyoshi, and an escort of less than three hundred men left the capital with the swiftness of a sudden storm. But even with such speed, their departure could not be kept secret.

The short night had not yet dawned when the group reached Otsu. Splitting the predawn darkness, the report of a gun echoed in the mountains. The horses reared in frenzy. Retainers galloped forward, anxious for Nobunaga, while at the same time they looked for the sniper.

Nobunaga appeared not to have noticed the shot; in fact he had already galloped ahead more than fifty yards. From that distance he turned and shouted, "Let him be!"

Because Nobunaga was alone, far ahead of the others, they left the would-be assassin behind. When Hideyoshi and the other generals overtook Nobunaga and asked if he had been wounded, Nobunaga slowed his horse and held up his sleeve, showing a small hole through the loose cloth. His only comment was, "Our fate is decreed by heaven."

It was later discovered that the man who had shot at Nobunaga was a warrior-monk famous for his marksmanship.

"Our fate is decreed by heaven," Nobunaga had said, but this did not mean he waited passively for heaven's will. He knew how rival warlords envied him. The world had not thought much of him when he had spread his wings over Owari and Mino from his small domain, which covered no more than two districts of Owari. But now that he had taken center stage and was giving orders from Kyoto, the powerful provincial clans were suddenly ill at ease. Clans with whom he had no quarrel whatsoever—the Otomo and Shimazu of Kyushu, the Mori of the western provinces, the Chosokabe of Shikoku, and even the Uesugi and Date in the far north—all looked upon his successes with hostility.

But the real danger was from his own in-laws. It was clear that Takeda Shingen of Kai was no longer to be trusted; neither could he be negligent about the Hojo; and Asai Nagamasa of Odani, who had married his sister Oichi, was living proof of the weakness of political alliances based on marriage. When Nobunaga had invaded the north, his main enemy—the man who had suddenly allied himself with the Asakura and threatened his retreat—was none other than this Asai Nagamasa, proving again that the ambitions of men cannot be trammeled by a woman's hair.

Everywhere he looked, there were enemies. The remnants of the Miyoshi and Matsu-naga clans were still troublesome adversaries lying in ambush, and the warrior-monks of the Honganji were fanning the flames of rebellion against him everywhere. It seemed that, as he took power, the whole country was turning against him, so it was prudent for him to return quickly to Gifu. If he had idled in Kyoto for another month, there might have been no castle or clan to return to, but he reached Gifu Castle without incident.

"Guard! Guard!" The short night had not yet ended, but Nobunaga was calling from his bedroom. It was about the time the cuckoo's song could be heard over Inabayama, not an unusual time for Nobunaga to wake up and unexpectedly give orders. His night watch was used to it, but it seemed that whenever they relaxed their guard a little, Nobunaga would take them by surprise.

"Yes, my lord?" This time, the guard was quick.

"Call a war council. Tell Nobumori to summon the general staff immediately," Nobunaga said on his way out of his bedroom.

The pages and attendants ran after him. They were still half asleep and could hardly tell whether it was midnight or dawn. Certainly it was still dark, and the stars shone brightly in the night sky.

"I'm going to light the lamps," said an attendant. "Please wait just a moment, my lord."

But Nobunaga had already stripped. He stepped into the bathroom and began to pour water over himself and wash.

In the outer citadel, the confusion was even worse. Men like Nobumori, Tadatsugu, and Hideyoshi were in the castle, but many of the other generals had been staying in the castle town. As messengers were sent to summon them, the hall was cleaned and the lamps lit.

At length the generals were all gathered for the war council. The white lamplight shone on Nobunaga's face. He had decided to ride out at dawn against Asai Nagamasa of Odani. Although this meeting was meant to be a war council, its purpose was not the airing of different opinions or discussion. Nobunaga simply wanted to hear if anyone had any suggestions as to tactics.

When it was clear just how determined Nobunaga was, a deathly silence fell over the assembled generals. It was as though something had struck them deep in their hearts. Nobunaga's relationship with Nagamasa, they all knew, was more than that of a political ally. Nobunaga was truly fond of his brother-in-law, and he had invited him to Kyoto and personally shown him the sights.

If Nobunaga had not told Nagamasa of his attack on the Asakura clan, it was because he knew that the Asai and Asakura were bound by an alliance much older than the Asai clan's ties with the Oda. Thinking of his brother-in-law's delicate position, he tried his best to keep him neutral.

However, once Nagamasa knew that Nobunaga's army was deep in enemy territory, Nagamasa had betrayed Nobunaga, cut off his retreat, and forced him into an inevitable defeat.

Nobunaga had been thinking about his brother-in-law's punishment ever since his return to Kyoto. A secret report had been handed to Nobunaga in the dead of night. It informed him that Sasaki Rokkaku had fomented a peasant uprising with the support of Kannonji Castle and the warrior-monks. Taking advantage of the chaos and acting in concert with the Asai, Rokkaku was aiming to crush Nobunaga with a single blow.

When the war council had ended, Nobunaga went into the garden with his generals and pointed to the sky. In the distance the flames of the insurrection turned the sky a brilliant red.

On the following day, the twentieth, Nobunaga led his army into Omi. He crushed the warrior-monks and broke through the defenses of Asai Nagamasa and Sasaki Rokkaku. Nobunaga's army moved with the speed of a storm sweeping the clouds from the plain, and struck with the suddenness of lightning.

On the twenty-first, the Oda were pressing in on the main castle of the Asai at Odani. They had already laid siege to Yokoyama Castle, a branch castle of Odani. For the enemy, it was a complete rout. They had had no time to prepare themselves, and their resistance crumbled, giving them no time to set up new positions.

The Ane River was only a few feet deep, so, although it was quite broad, a man could ford it on foot. Its clear waters, which flowed from the mountains of eastern Asai, were, however, so cold that they cut into the body even in summer.

It was just before dawn. Nobunaga, leading an army of twenty-three thousand men, with a further six thousand Tokugawa troops, deployed his men along the east riverbank.

From about midnight on the previous day, the combined forces of the Asai and the Asakura—numbering about eighteen thousand—had gradually moved in from Mount Oyose. Hiding behind the houses along the west bank of the river, they waited for the right moment to attack. The night was still dark, and only the sound of the water could be heard.

"Yasumasa," Ieyasu called one of his commanders, "the enemy is approaching the riverbank thick and fast."

"It's difficult to see anything through this mist, but I can hear the horses neighing in the distance."

"Any news from downstream?"

"Nothing so far."

"Which side is heaven going to bless? Half a day should see the turning point."

"Half a day? I wonder if it will take that long."

"Don't underestimate them," Ieyasu said as he walked into the woods at the river's edge. Here were his own silent troops, the flower of Nobunaga's army. The atmosphere in the forest was one of total desolation. The soldiers had spread out into a firing line, crouching in the undergrowth. The spearmen grasped their weapons and looked out over the river, where still nothing stirred.

Would it be life or death today?

The eyes of the soldiers shone. Untouched by life or death, they silently imagined the outcome of the battle. Not one looked as if he had confidence that he would see the sky again that evening.

Accompanied by Yasumasa, Ieyasu walked along the line, his clothes making only a slight rustling noise. No light shone, except for the smoldering fuse cords of the muskets. A man sneezed—perhaps a soldier with a cold, whose nose was itchy from the smoke of the fuses. Still, it made the other soldiers tense.

The surface of the water began to turn white, and a line of red clouds silhouetted the branches of the trees on Mount Ibuki.

"The enemy!" a man shouted.

The officers around Ieyasu immediately signaled the gunners to hold their fire. On the other bank just a little downstream, a mixed corps of mounted samurai and foot soldiers, numbering perhaps twelve or thirteen hundred, was fording the river at a diagonal. Kicking up a white spray with their feet, they looked like a white gale crossing the river.

The formidable vanguard of the Asai was ignoring the Oda vanguard and even the second and third lines of defense, and was preparing to strike at the center of the Oda camp.

Ieyasu's men swallowed hard and exclaimed all at once, "Isono Tamba!"

"Tamba's regiment!"

The famous Isono Tamba, the pride of the Asai clan, was a worthy opponent. His crested banners could be seen fluttering through the splashes and spray.

Gunfire!

Was it covering fire for the enemy, or the rifles of their own troops? No, the firing had begun from both banks at the same moment. Echoing over the water, the noise was almost deafening. The clouds began to part, and the cloudless summer sky displayed its hue. Just then the second Oda line, under Sakai Tadatsugu, and Ikeda Shonyu's third line suddenly struck out into the river.

"Don't let the enemy put one foot on our side! Don't let a single one of them return to their own!" shouted the officers.

The Sakai corps attacked the enemy's flank. In an instant, hand-to-hand fighting broke out in the middle of the river. Spear clashed against spear, sword rang against sword. Men grappled and tumbled from horses, and the waters of the river ran with blood.

Tamba's regiment of crack troops pushed Sakai's second line back. Shouting, "We have been shamed!" so loudly that he could be heard on both sides of the river, Sakai's son, Kyuzo, dashed into the middle of the fight. He achieved a glorious death in battle, with more than one hundred of his men.

With unstoppable force, Tamba's soldiers broke through the third Oda line. Ikeda's spearmen readied their spears and tried to break the enemy onslaught, but they could do nothing.

Now it was Hideyoshi's turn to be amazed. He muttered to Hanbei, "Have you ever seen such intimidating men?" But even Hanbei had no tactics to deal with this attack. This was not the only reason for Hideyoshi's defeat. Within his line were a great number of men who had surrendered at enemy castles. These new "allies" had been put under Hideyoshi's command, but they had once received their stipends from the Asai and Asakura. Quite naturally, their spears were rarely accurate, and when they were ordered to charge the enemy, they were more likely to get in the way of Hideyoshi's own men.

Thus Hideyoshi's line was defeated, and the Oda's fifth and sixth lines were also

335

soundly beaten. In all, Tamba routed eleven of the thirteen Oda lines. At this point the Tokugawa forces upstream crossed the river, overrunning the enemy on the opposite bank, and gradually they made their way downstream. Looking back, however, they saw that Tamba's soldiers were already pressing close on Nobunaga's headquarters.

With the yell, "Attack their flank!" the Tokugawa soldiers leaped back into the river. Tamba's soldiers thought these men were their own allies entering the river from the west bank, even when they drew near. With Kazumasa in the lead, the Tokugawa samurai cut into Isono Tamba's regiment.

Suddenly aware of the enemy, Tamba yelled himself hoarse, ordering his men to fall back. A warrior, brandishing a dripping spear, struck him from the side. Tamba collapsed in a spray of water. Grasping the shaft of the spear that had pierced his side, he attempted to get up, but the Tokugawa warrior had no intention of letting him do so. A sword flashed over Tamba's head and crashed down on his iron helmet. The sword shattered into pieces. Tamba stood up, the water around his feet turning into a bright red pool of blood. Three men surrounded Tamba, stabbing and hacking him to pieces.

"The enemy!" the retainers around Nobunaga shouted. They ran from the headquarters to the riverbank with their spears ready.

Takenaka Kyusaku, Hanbei's younger brother, was in Hideyoshi's regiment, but in the confusion of battle he had become separated from his unit. Pursuing the enemy, he was now close to Nobunaga's headquarters.

What? he thought in amazement. The enemy's here already? As he looked around, he spotted a samurai coming around from the back of the enclosure. The man, whose armor was not that of a common foot soldier, lifted the curtain and looked stealthily inside.

Kyusaku flung himself at the man and grabbed his leg, which was covered by chain mail and armor. The warrior might be one of their own men, and Kyusaku did not want to kill an ally by mistake. The samurai turned without a hint of surprise. He looked like an officer of the Asai army.

"Friend or foe?" Kyusaku asked.

"Foe, of course!" the man yelled, working his spear through his hands and moving in to strike.

"Who are you? Do you have a name worth repeating?"

"I am Maenami Shinpachiro of the Asai. I've come to take Lord Nobunaga's head. You disgusting runt! Who are you?"

"I am Takenaka Kyusaku, a retainer of Kinoshita Hideyoshi. Come and try me!"

"Well, well. Takenaka Hanbei's little brother."

"That's right!" The instant he said this, Kyusaku yanked away Shinpachiro's spear and threw it back at his chest. But before Kyusaku could draw his sword, Shinpachiro grabbed him. Both men fell to the ground, Kyusaku on the bottom. He kicked himself free, but he was once again pinned down beneath his enemy. At that moment he bit on Shinpachiro's finger, making him loosen his grip a little.

Now was his chance! Giving Shinpachiro a shove, Kyusaku was able to free himself at last. In an instant his hand found his dagger and struck at Shinpachiro's throat. The point of the dagger missed the man's throat, but sliced across Shinpachiro's face from his chin to his nose, piercing his eye.

"An enemy of my comrade!" a voice shouted out from behind. There was no time to cut off the dead man's head. Leaping up, Kyusaku immediately exchanged blows with a new adversary.

Kyusaku knew that several of the Asai suicide corps had made their way into the area, and this man now showed his back and ran. Chasing him, Kyusaku struck at his knee with his sword.

As he fell on top of the wounded man and straddled him, Kyusaku shouted, "Do you have a name worth saying? Yes or no?"

"I'm Kobayashi Hashuken. I have nothing to say except that I regret falling into the hands of a low-class samurai like you before getting close to Lord Nobunaga."

"Where is the Asai's bravest man, Endo Kizaemon? You're an Asai, you must know."

"I have no idea."

"Speak! Spit it out!"

"I don't know!"

"Then I've no use for you!" Kyusaku cut off Hashuken's head. He ran off, his eyes blazing. He was determined not to let Endo Kizaemon's head fall to someone else's hand. Before the battle, Kyusaku had boasted that he would have Kizaemon's head. He now ran off in the direction of the riverbank where countless bodies lay among the grass and pebbles—a riverbank of death.

There, among the others, was a corpse whose bloodied face was hidden by a tangle of hair. Bluebottle flies buzzed in a swarm at Kyusaku's feet. Kyusaku turned around when he stepped on the foot of the corpse whose face was hidden by its hair. There was nothing wrong with that, but it gave him a strange sensation. He looked around suspiciously, and in that instant the corpse leaped up and dashed off in the direction of Nobunaga's headquarters.

"Protect Lord Nobunaga! The enemy is coming!" Kyusaku screamed.

Seeing Nobunaga, the enemy samurai was about to jump over a low embankment when he stepped on the cord of his sandal and tripped. Kyusaku leaped on top of the man and quickly subdued him. As he was dragged off by Kyusaku to Nobunaga's headquarters, the man roared out, "Cut off my head quickly! Right now! Don't heap shame on a warrior!"

When another prisoner who was being led away saw the screaming man, he blurted out, "Master Kizaemon! They took even you alive?"

This extraordinary man who had pretended to be dead and whom Kyusaku had captured was the very one he had been seeking—the fierce Asai warrior Endo Kizaemon.

At first the Oda army had been near collapse. But as the Tokugawa forces under Ieyasu struck the enemy flank, the acute angle of the enemy attack was deflected. However, the enemy had also had a second and third line of attack. As they pushed and then retreated, trampling through the waters of the Ane River, both the enemy and Nobunaga's troops were breaking their sword guards and shattering their spears. The battle was in such chaos that no one could tell who was going to win.

"Don't be distracted! Just strike straight into Nobunaga's camp!"

From the very beginning, this had been the objective of the second line of Asai troops. But they had driven through too far and had actually come out to the rear of the

Oda troops. The Tokugawa forces had also broken through to the opposite bank with the cry, "Don't be bested by the Oda troops!" and had advanced toward the camp of Asakura Kagetake.

Finally, however, the Tokugawa had advanced too far from their allies and were surrounded by the enemy. The battle was in total chaos. Just as a fish cannot see the river in which it swims, no one was able to grasp the entire situation. Each soldier was simply fighting for his life. As soon as a man struck down one of the enemy, he immediately looked up to see the face of another.

From above, it would have looked as though both armies, forced into the waters of the Ane River, had entered a giant vortex. And, as might be expected, Nobunaga coolly observed the situation in exactly that way. Hideyoshi also took a general view of the battle. He sensed that this very instant would decide either victory or defeat. The turning point was a very subtle moment.

Nobunaga was striking the ground with a staff, yelling, "The Tokugawa have struck in deep! Don't leave them there alone! Somebody go to the aid of Lord Ieyasu!" But the troops on both right and left did not have enough remaining strength. Nobunaga was shouting in vain. Then, from a stand of trees on the northern bank, a single corps of men dashed directly through the chaos to the opposite bank, kicking up a pure-white spray of water.

Hideyoshi, while he had not received Nobunaga's orders, had also understood the situation. Nobunaga saw the standard with Hideyoshi's golden gourd and thought, Ah, good! Hideyoshi has done it.

Wiping the sweat from his eyes with his gauntlet, Nobunaga said to his pages, "A moment like this won't come again. Go down to the river and see what you can do."

Ranmaru and the others—even the youngest—all ran at the enemy, each one vying to be first. The Tokugawa, who had pushed in so deeply, were quite definitely in trouble, but in this game of battlefield chess, the astute Ieyasu was the one piece that had been placed on the vital point.

Nobunaga is not likely to let this one piece die, Ieyasu told himself. Ittetsu's men followed Hideyoshi's. Finally, Ikeda Shonyu's men poured in. Suddenly the tide of the battle had changed, and the Oda were winning. Asakura Kagetake's forces retreated more than three leagues, and Asai Nagamasa's forces fled hurriedly toward Odani Castle.

From that point on, it was a battle of pursuit. The Asakura were chased to Mount Oyose, and Asai Nagamasa retreated behind the walls of Odani Castle. Nobunaga dealt with the aftermath of the battle in two days, and on the third day he led his army back to Gifu. He had moved with the speed of the cuckoo that nightly flew over the Ane River, which now washed the bodies of the dead on its shores.

* * *

A great man is not made simply by innate ability. Circumstances must give him the opportunity. These circumstances are often the malevolent conditions that surround a man and work on his character, almost as if they were trying to torture him. When his enemies have taken every form possible, both seen and unseen, and ally themselves to confront him with every hardship imaginable, he encounters the real test of greatness.

Directly after the battle of the Ane River, Nobunaga returned home with such speed that the generals of his various units asked themselves if something had happened in Gifu. Quite naturally, the strategies of the field staff are not understood by the rank and file. A rumor now circulated among the soldiers that Hideyoshi had strongly advocated taking the main castle of the Asai at Odani and putting an end to them once and for all, but Lord Nobunaga had not agreed. Instead, the very next day he had made Hideyoshi commander of Yokoyama Castle, a branch castle that the enemy had abandoned, while he himself withdrew to Gifu.

The soldiers were not the only ones who did not understand the reasons behind Nobunaga's sudden return to Gifu. Very likely his closest retainers did not understand their lord's real intentions, either. The only man who might have had some idea was Ieyasu, whose impartial eye never strayed for long from Nobunaga: not too close at hand, but not too distant; without excessive emotion, but not too coolly.

On the day Nobunaga left, Ieyasu returned to Hamamatsu. On the way, he said to his generals, "As soon as Lord Nobunaga takes off his bloodstained armor, he'll dress himself for the capital and whip his horse straight for Kyoto. His mind is like a restless young colt."

In the end, that is exactly what happened. By the time Ieyasu arrived at Hamamatsu, Nobunaga was already on his way to Kyoto. Which is not to say that there was anything going on in the capital at the time. What Nobunaga feared was something that he could not see—a phantom enemy.

Nobunaga had disclosed his concern to Hideyoshi. "What do you think my biggest worry is? I imagine you know, don't you?"

Hideyoshi cocked his head to one side and said, "Well, now. It isn't the Takeda of Kai, who are always lying in wait at your rear, or the Asai or Asakura clan. Lord Ieyasu is someone to be careful of, but he's an intelligent man and so shouldn't be feared altogether. The Matsunaga and Miyoshi are like flies, and there are plenty of rotting things for them to swarm around, as it's their nature to go after the dying. Your only really troublesome enemies are the warrior-monks of the Honganji, but they don't trouble my lord too much yet, I think. That only leaves one person."

"And who is he? Speak up."

"He's neither enemy nor ally. You have to show him respect, but if that's all you do, you might quickly become trapped. He's a two-faced apparition—oh, dear, I've spoken improperly. Aren't we talking about the shogun?"

"Right. But don't mention this to anyone." Nobunaga's anxiety was about this man, who was indeed truly neither friend nor foe: Yoshiaki, the shogun.

Yoshiaki had shed tears of gratitude over Nobunaga's past favors to him, and had even said that he thought of Nobunaga as his own father. So why Yoshiaki? Duplicity is always found hidden away in places where one would least imagine it to be. Yoshiaki's and Nobunaga's characters were not matched at all; their educations were different, and so were their beliefs. As long as Nobunaga had helped him, Yoshiaki treated Nobunaga as a benefactor. But once he had warmed the shogun's seat a little, his gratitude turned to loathing.

"The bumpkin is annoying," Yoshiaki was heard to say. He began to avoid Nobunaga, and even regarded him as a stumbling block, whose authority exceeded his own. He was not, however, brave enough to bring matters out into the open and fight him. Yoshiaki's nature was completely negative. And, opposed to Nobunaga's positiveness, it played itself out in secrecy to the very end.

In a secluded room deep within Nijo Palace, the shogun conversed with an emissary from the warrior-monks of the Honganji.

"Abbot Kennyo resents him too? It's not surprising that Nobunaga's unparalleled arrogance and high-handedness anger the abbot."

The messenger concluded before leaving, "Please make sure that everything I've said is kept secret. At the same time, perhaps it would be advisable to send secret messages to Kai and to the Asai and Asakura clans so as not to miss this opportunity."

On the very same day, in another part of the palace, Nobunaga was waiting for Yoshiaki in order to announce his arrival in the capital. Yoshiaki composed himself, assumed an air of complete innocence, and went into the reception room to meet with Nobunaga.

"I hear that the battle of the Ane River was a splendid victory for you. Yet another example of your military prowess. Congratulations! This is a happy event indeed."

Nobunaga was unable to suppress a bitter smile at this flattery, and he replied with some irony, "No, no. It was thanks to Your Excellency's virtue and influence that we were able to fight so bravely, knowing there would be no unhappy events in the aftermath."

Yoshiaki turned slightly red, blushing like a woman. "Put your mind at ease. The capital is at peace, as you can see. But have you heard of some untoward event? After the battle, you came here with such frightening speed."

"No, I came to pay my respects at the completion of the rebuilding of the Imperial Palace, to look after affairs of state, and, of course, to inquire after Your Excellency's health."

"Ah, is that so?" Yoshiaki felt slightly relieved. "Well, you can see that I'm healthy and that the government is moving along without any problems, so you shouldn't be so anxious and come here so often. But come, let me treat you to a banquet to congratulate you officially upon your triumphal return."

"I must refuse, Your Excellency," Nobunaga said, waving off the suggestion. "I still haven't sent words of thanks to my officers and men. I wouldn't feel quite right about accepting an invitation to an extravagant banquet on my own. Let us postpone it until the next time I'm in attendance on Your Excellency."

With this, he took his leave. When he returned to his lodgings, Akechi Mitsuhide was waiting to submit his report.

"A monk who appeared to be a messenger from Abbot Kennyo of the Honganji was seen leaving the shogun's palace. These recent comings and goings between the warrior-monks and the shogun are pretty suspicious, don't you think?"

Nobunaga had appointed Mitsuhide commander of the Kyoto garrison. In this capacity, he meticulously recorded all visitors to Nijo Palace.

Nobunaga gave the report a quick look and said only, "Very good." He was disgusted that this shogun was so difficult to save, but he also felt that Yoshiaki's behavior was really a blessing. That night he called in the officials in charge of the construction of the Imperial Palace, and as he listened to the reports on the progress of the rebuilding, his mood brightened.

The next morning he rose early and inspected the nearly completed buildings. Then, after paying his respects to the Emperor at the old palace, he returned to his lodgings as the sun was coming up, ate breakfast, and announced that he was leaving the capital.

When Nobunaga had arrived in Kyoto, he had been dressed in a kimono. On his return, however, he wore armor, because he was not returning to Gifu. Once again he made a tour of the battlefield at the Ane River, met with Hideyoshi, who was stationed at Yokoyama Castle, flew about giving orders to the units left in various places, and then laid siege to Sawayama Castle.

Having made a clean sweep of his enemies, Nobunaga returned to Gifu, but for him and his men there was still no time to rest from the fatigue of the lingering summer heat.

It was in Gifu that urgent letters reached Nobunaga from Hosokawa Fujitaka, who was at Nakanoshima Castle in Settsu, and from Akechi Mitsuhide in Kyoto. These letters informed him that in Noda, Fukushima, and Nakanoshima in Settsu, the Miyoshi had more than a thousand men building fortresses. These had been joined by the warrior-monks of the Honganji and their followers. Both Mitsuhide and Fujitaka stressed that there was no time to delay, and asked for Nobunaga's orders.

The main temple of the Honganji had been built during a period of civil disorder and confusion. It had been constructed to withstand the disturbances of the day: outside its stone walls was a deep moat, spanned by a fortified bridge. Although the Honganji was a temple, its construction was that of a castle. To be a monk here meant to be a warrior, and this place had no fewer warrior-monks than Nara and Mount Hiei. Very likely there was not a single priest living in this ancient Buddhist fortress who did not hate the upstart Nobunaga. They accused him of being an enemy of Buddhism who flouted tradition, a destroyer of culture, and a devil who knew no bounds—a beast among men.

When, instead of negotiating, Nobunaga had confronted the Honganji and forced them to cede some of their land to him, he had gone too far. The pride of the Buddhist fortress was strong, and the privileges it enjoyed were ancient. Reports from the west and other regions began to trickle in that the Honganji was arming itself. The temple had bought two thousand guns, the number of warrior-monks had increased manifold, and new defensive moats were being dug around the fortress.

Nobunaga had anticipated that they would ally themselves with the Miyoshi clan, and that the weak shogun would be seduced to their side. He had also expected that malicious propaganda would be spread among the common people, and that this would most likely set off a popular uprising against him.

When he received urgent messages from Kyoto and Osaka, he was not particularly surprised. Rather, he was more fully resolved to take the opportunity, and quickly went to Settsu himself, stopping in Kyoto on the way.

"I humbly request that Your Excellency accompany my army," he told the shogun. "Your presence will be an inspiration to my troops, and will speed the quelling of the insurrection."

Yoshiaki was naturally reluctant, but he could not refuse. And although it seemed that Nobunaga was taking along a useless hanger-on, it benefited him to have the shield of the shogun's name as one more ploy to sow dissension among his enemies.

* * *

The area between the Kanzaki and Nakatsu rivers in Naniwa was a vast marshy plain, dotted with occasional patches of farmland. Nakajima was divided into the northern and southern districts. The fortress in the north was held by the Miyoshi, and the small castle in the south by Hosokawa Fujitaka. The battle was centered in this area, and continued violently from the beginning to the middle of the Ninth Month, now with a victory, now with a defeat. It was open warfare, with the new style of both small and large firearms in use.

In the middle of the Ninth Month, the Asai and Asakura, who had remained barricaded in their mountain castles, meditating on the bitterness of defeat and watching for Nobunaga to make a mistake, took up arms, crossed Lake Biwa, and set up their camps on the beaches at Otsu and Karasaki. One unit went to the Buddhist stronghold of Mount Hiei. For the first time, all the warrior-monks of the various sects were united against Nobunaga.

Their common complaint was, "Nobunaga has arbitrarily confiscated our lands and trampled our honor and the mountain that has been inviolate since the time of Saint Dengyo!"

There were close ties between Mount Hiei and the Asai and Asakura clans. The three agreed to cut off Nobunaga's retreat. The Asakura army moved out from the mountains north of the lake, while the Asai army crossed the lake and went ashore. The disposition of their troops indicated that they intended to grip the throat of Otsu and enter Kyoto. Then, waiting at the Yodo River, they would move in concert with the Honganji and destroy Nobunaga in a single offensive.

Nobunaga had been fighting hard for several days, confronting the warrior-monks and the large Miyoshi army from the fortress at Nakajima in the swamps between the Kanzaki and Nakatsu rivers. On the twenty-second, an alarming but cryptic report that a calamity was approaching from the rear reached his ears.

The details were not yet available, but Nobunaga inferred that when they came they would not be pleasant. He ground his teeth, wondering what this calamity might be. Calling Katsuie, he ordered him to take charge of the rear guard. As for himself he said, "I'm going to pull back immediately and crush the Asai, the Asakura, and Mount Hiei."

"Shouldn't we wait one more night for the next detailed report?" Katsuie said, trying to stop him.

"Why? Now is the time when the world is going to change!" That said, nothing was going to change his mind. He rode hard to Kyoto, changing horses more than once.

"My lord!"

"What a tragedy!"

Crying bitterly, a number of retainers crowded in front of his horse. "Your younger brother, Lord Nobuharu, and Mori Yoshinari met with heroic deaths at Uji, struck down after two days and two nights of bitter fighting."

The first man could not go on, so one of his companions continued, his voice quavering, "The Asai and Asakura and their allies, the monks, had a great army of over twenty thousand, so their strength could not be withstood."

Seemingly unmoved, Nobunaga replied, "Don't just read the names of dead men who are never going to come back at a time like this—what I want to hear is what's going on now! How far has the enemy advanced? Where is the front line? I suppose none of you knows that. Is Mitsuhide here? If he's at the front, call him back immediately. Call Mitsuhide!"

A forest of banners surrounded the Mii Temple—the headquarters of the Asai and Asakura. The day before, the generals had inspected the severed head of Nobunaga's younger brother, Nobuharu, before a large crowd. After that, they had examined the heads of other famous warriors of the Oda clan, one after another, until they were almost bored.

"That avenges our defeat at the Ane River. I feel a lot better now," one man muttered.

"Not until we've seen Nobunaga's head!" another man said.

Then someone laughed in a hoarse voice, thick with the accent of the north. "We've as good as seen it already. Nobunaga's got the Honganji and the Miyoshi in front of him, and us behind. Where is he going to run? He's a fish in a net!"

They inspected the heads for well over a day, until they became sick of the smell of blood. When night fell, the *sake* jars were carried into the headquarters, helping to raise the spirits of the victors. As the liquor was ladled out and drunk, the discussion turned to strategy.

"Should we enter Kyoto, or seize the bottleneck of Otsu and take him by gradually shrinking the encirclement and drawing him in like a big fish in a net?" one general suggested.

"We should definitely advance to the capital, and annihilate Nobunaga at the Yodo River and in the fields of Kawachi!" another countered.

"That's no good."

If one man advocated one tactic, another immediately opposed him. For although the Asai and Asakura clans were united in their aims, when it came to a discussion within the upper command, each man felt that he had to demonstrate his own shallow knowledge and uphold his reputation. The result was that nothing was decided until midnight.

Tired of the fruitless discussion, one of the Asai generals went outside. Looking up at the sky, he commented, "The sky has turned awfully red, hasn't it?"

"Our men have set fire to the peasants' houses from Yamashina to Daigo," a sentry responded.

"What for? It's futile to burn that area, isn't it?"

"Not at all. We have to contain the enemy," the Asakura general who had given the order countered. "The Oda garrison in Kyoto under Akechi Mitsuhide is tearing around as if its members were eager to die. And we, too, should show our own ferocity."

Dawn had come. Otsu was the crossroads of the major routes to the capital, but there was not one traveler or packhorse to be seen. Then one mounted man rode by, followed moments later by two or three others. These were military messengers, riding from the direction of the capital, galloping to the Mii Temple as if their lives depended on it.

"Nobunaga is almost at Keage. The troops of Akechi Mitsuhide are in the vanguard, and they are smashing through with unstoppable force."

The generals could hardly believe their ears.

"Surely it's not Nobunaga in person! There's no way he could have withdrawn from the battlefield at Naniwa so quickly."

"Two or three hundred of our men in Yamashina have already been killed. The enemy is on the rampage, and, as always, Nobunaga himself is giving the orders. He's riding like a mounted demon or god, and he's coming right this way!"

Both Asai Nagamasa and Asakura Kagetake blanched. Nagamasa felt this especially keenly; Nobunaga was his wife's brother, a man who had formerly treated him kindly. The show of Nobunaga's fury made him shudder.

"Retreat! Fall back to Mount Hiei!" Nagamasa blurted out.

Asakura Kagetake picked up the urgent tone of his ally's voice. "Back to Mount Hiei!" At the same time, he screamed orders to his retainers. "Set fire to the peasants' houses along the road! No, wait until our vanguard has gone through. Then set the fires! Set the fires!"

The hot wind scorched Nobunaga's brow. Sparks had ignited his horse's mane and the tassels on his saddle. From Yamashina to Otsu, the burning beams of the peasants' houses along the road and the flames that seemed to swirl through the air could not prevent him from reaching his destination. He had become the flames of a torch himself, and his men, as they galloped on, were a horde of fire.

"This battle will be a memorial service for Lord Nobuharu."

"Did they think we wouldn't avenge the spirits of our dead comrades?"

But when they came to the Mii Temple, there was not an enemy soldier to be seen. They had climbed Mount Hiei with all the speed of flight.

Looking up at the mountain, they saw that the huge enemy army of more than twenty thousand men, in addition to the warrior-monks, stretched as far as Suzugamine, Aoyamadake, and Tsubogasadani. Their fluttering banners almost seemed to say, We haven't run away. This battle array will speak for itself from here on.

Nobunaga looked at the towering mountain and thought, It's here. It's not the mountain that is my enemy; it's the mountain's special privileges. He saw it in a new light now. From ancient times, through the reigns of successive emperors, how much had the tradition and special privileges of the mountain troubled and pained the country's rulers and the common people? Was there even the faintest glimmer of the real Buddha on the mountain?

When the Tendai sect had been introduced to Japan from China, Saint Dengyo, who had built the first temple on Mount Hiei, had chanted, "May the light of the merciful Buddha give its divine protection to the timbers that we raise up in this place." Was the lamp of the Law lit on this holy peak so that the monks could force their petitions on the Emperor in Kyoto? Was it so that they could interfere with government and grow ever more powerful with special privileges? Was it so they could ally themselves with warlords, conspire with laymen, and throw the country into confusion? Was the lamp lit so that the Law of Buddha might be accoutered with armor and helmet, and line the entire mountain with warriors' spears, guns, and war banners?

Tears of rage ran from Nobunaga's eyes. It was clear to him that this was all blasphemy. Mount Hiei had been established to protect the nation, and so had been granted special privileges. But where was the original purpose of Mount Hiei now? The main temple building, the seven shrines, the monasteries of the eastern and the western pagodas were nothing more than the barracks of armed demons in monks' robes.

All right! Nobunaga bit his lip so hard that his teeth became stained with blood. Let them call me a demon king who destroys Buddhism! The magnificent beauties of the mountain are nothing more than the false allures of an enchantress, and these armored monks are nothing more than fools. I'm going to burn them with the flames of war and let the true Buddha be called forth from these ashes!

On the same day he gave the order for the entire mountain to be surrounded. Naturally, it took several days for his army to cross the lake, pass over the mountains, and join him.

"The blood of my brother and Mori Yoshinari has not yet dried. Let their unswervingly loyal souls sleep in peace. Let their blood be like lanterns that will light up the world!"

Nobunaga knelt on the earth and folded his hands in prayer. He had made an enemy of the holy mountain and had ordered his army to surround it. Now, on a lump of earth, Nobunaga put his hands together in prayer and wept. Suddenly he saw one of his pages crying, with his hands together in the same way. It was Ranmaru, who had lost his father, Mori Yoshinari.

"Ranmaru, are you crying?"

"Please forgive me, my lord."

"I'll forgive you. But stop crying, or your father's spirit will laugh at you."

But Nobunaga's own eyes were becoming red. Ordering his camp stool moved to the top of a hill, he looked out over the disposition of the besieging troops. As far as the eye could see, the foothills of Mount Hiei were filled with the banners of his own men.

Half of the month passed by. The siege of the mountain—an unusual strategy for Nobunaga—continued. He had cut off the enemy's supply of provisions and was going to try to starve them out. His plan was in fact already working. With an army of over twenty thousand men, the granaries of the mountain had quickly been emptied. They had already started to eat the bark off the trees.

Winter set in, and the cold weather on the mountaintop caused more suffering for the defenders.

"It's about the right time, don't you think?" Hideyoshi said to Nobunaga.

Nobunaga summoned a retainer, Ittetsu. Receiving Nobunaga's instructions and accompanied by four or five attendants, he climbed up Mount Hiei and met with Abbot Sonrin of the western pagoda. They met at the main temple, the warrior-monks' headquarters.

Sonrin and Ittetsu had known each other for some time, and as a mark of that friendship, Ittetsu had come to persuade him to surrender.

"I'm not sure what your purpose was in coming here, but as a friend, I advise you not to carry this joke too far," Sonrin replied, shaking with laughter. "I agreed to meet you because I thought you had come to ask permission to surrender to us. How stupid to ask us to give up and leave! Don't you see that we are resolved to resist to the end? You must be mad to come here to talk such foolishness!"

Excitement burned in the eyes of the other warrior-monks, and they glared at Ittetsu.

Having allowed the abbot his say, Ittetsu began to speak deliberately. "Saint Dengyo established this temple for the peace and preservation of the Imperial House and the tranquillity of the nation. I suspect it is not the monks' most fervent prayer to put on armor, to marshal swords and spears, to involve themselves in political strife, to ally themselves with rebel armies, or to make the people of the Empire suffer. The monks should return to being monks! Drive the Asai and Asakura from the mountain, throw down your weapons, and return to your original roles as disciples of the Buddha!" He spoke this from the very depths of his body, not giving the priests a moment to put in a single word. "Moreover," he went on, "if you do not follow his orders, Lord Nobunaga is determined to burn down the main temple, the seven shrines, and the monasteries, and kill everyone on the mountain. Please give this careful thought, and put away your stubbornness. Will you turn this mountain into an inferno or sweep away the old evils and preserve the single lamp of this hallowed ground?"

Suddenly the monks with Sonrin began to shout.

"This is pointless!"

"He's just wasting time!"

"Silence!" Sonrin commanded them with a sardonic smile. "That was an extremely boring, worn-out sermon, but I'm going to answer it politely. Mount Hiei is an authority unto itself, and has its own principles. You are just meddling unnecessarily. Master Ittetsu, it's getting late. Leave the mountain right away."

"Sonrin, can you say this on your own authority? Why don't you meet with the men of great learning and the elders, and discuss the matter carefully?"

"The mountain is of one mind and one body. Mine is the voice of all of the temples on Mount Hiei."

"Then, no matter what—"

"You fool! We'll resist military aggression to the very end. We'll protect the freedom of our traditions with our very blood! Get out of here!"

"If that's the way you want it." Ittetsu made no move to get up. "This is such a shame. How are you going to protect the infinity of Buddha's light with your blood? Just what is this freedom you're going to protect? What are these traditions? Aren't they nothing more than deceptions, convenient for the temples' prosperity? Well, those charms have no currency in the world today. Take a good look at the times. It is inevitable that greedy men, who close their eyes and obstruct the tide of the times with their selfishness, will be burned up together with the fallen leaves." With that, Ittetsu returned to Nobunaga's camp.

The cold winter wind swirled the dry leaves around the mountain peaks. There was frost both morning and night. From time to time the cold wind was spotted with snow. About this time fires began to break out on the mountain almost every night. One night, fires broke out in the fuel storehouse of the Daijo Hall; the night before that, in the Takimido. This night again, although it was still early, there was a fire in the monks' quarters of the main temple, and the bell rang furiously. Since there were many large temples in the area, the warrior-monks worked frantically to keep the flames from spreading.

The deep valleys of Mount Hiei were dark under the bright red sky.

"What confusion!" one Oda soldier said and laughed.

"This happens every night," another added. "So they must never get a chance to sleep."

The cold winter wind whistled through the branches of the trees, and the men clapped their hands. Eating their meal of dried rice, they watched the nightly conflagrations. These fires were planned by Hideyoshi, so rumor had it, and carried out by the retainers of the old Hachisuka clan.

At night the monks were distressed by fires, and during the day they were exhausted by their preparations for defense. Also, their food and fuel were running low, and they had no protection against the cold.

Winter finally came to the mountain, and the snow flew furiously. The twenty thousand defending soldiers and the several thousand warrior-monks were now drooping like frost-blighted vegetables.

It was the middle of the Twelfth Month. Without armor and wearing only a monk's robes, a representative of the mountain approached Nobunaga's camp, accompanied by four or five warrior-monks.

"I would like to speak with Lord Nobunaga," the emissary said.

When Nobunaga appeared, he saw that it was Sonrin, the abbot who had previously met with Ittetsu. He brought the message that, because the views of the main temple had changed, he would like to plead for peace.

Nobunaga refused. "What did you say to the envoy I sent before? Don't you know what shame is?" Nobunaga drew his sword.

"This is an outrage!" the priest cried. He stood up and tottered sideways as Nobunaga's sword flashed horizontally.

"Pick up his head and go back. That's my answer!"

The monks turned pale and fled back to the mountain. The snow and sleet that blew across the lake that day also blew hard into Nobunaga's camp. Nobunaga had sent Mount Hiei an unmistakable message of his intent, but thoughts of how to deal with yet another great difficulty were taxing his mind. The enemy that appeared before him was nothing more than the reflection of a fire on a wall. Throwing water on the wall was not going to put the fire out, and in the meantime the real flames would be burning at his back. This was a common admonition in the art of war, but in Nobunaga's case, he was unable to fight against the source of the fire even though he knew what it was. Just the day before, an urgent report had come from Gifu that Takeda Shingen of Kai was mobilizing his troops and was about to attack in Nobunaga's absence. And more: there had been an uprising of tens of thousands of the Honganji's followers at Nagashima, in his own province of Owari, and one of Nobunaga's relatives, Nobuoki, had been killed and his castle taken. Finally, every possible evil rumor slandering Nobunaga had been let loose among the people.

It was understandable that Takeda Shingen had broken out. Having arranged a truce with his traditional enemy of many years, the Uesugi of Echigo, Shingen had turned his attention toward the west.

"Hideyoshi! Hideyoshi!" Nobunaga called.

"Yes! I'm here!"

"Find Mitsuhide, and the two of you take this letter to Kyoto immediately."

"To the shogun?"

"Correct. In the letter, I've asked the shogun to mediate, but it would be better if he heard it from your mouth, too."

"But then why did you just decapitate the messenger from Mount Hiei?"

"Don't you understand? If I hadn't done that, do you think we could wrap up a peace conference? Even if we had succeeded in coming to terms, it's clear that they would tear up the treaty and come chasing right after us."

"You're right, my lord. I understand now."

"No matter which side you pick, no matter where the flames are, the blaze has but a single source, and there's no mistake that this is the work of that two-faced shogun, who loves to play with fire. We need explicitly to make the shogun the mediator of peace accords and withdraw as quickly as possible."

Peace negotiations were initiated. Yoshiaki came to the Mii Temple and made an effort to mollify Nobunaga and arrange a peace settlement. Delighted at what they saw as a happy opportunity, the armies of the Asai and the Asakura left for home on that very day.

On the sixteenth, Nobunaga's entire army took the land route and, crossing the floating bridge at Seta, withdrew to Gifu.

SHINGEN THE LONG-LEGGED

Although Amakasu Sanpei was related to one of Kai's generals, he had spent the past ten years in a lowly position, because of a unique talent—his ability to run at high speed over long distances.

Sanpei was the leader of the Takeda clan's ninja—the men whose job it was to spy on enemy provinces, form clandestine alliances, and spread false rumors.

Sanpei's talent as a swift walker and runner had amazed his friends since his youth. He could climb any mountain and walk twenty to thirty leagues in a single day. But even he could not keep up this speed day after day. When hurrying back from some remote place, he rode wherever the terrain permitted, but when he encountered steep paths, he would rely on his own two strong legs. For this reason he always had horses stationed at essential points along the routes he traveled—often at the huts of hunters and woodsmen.

"Hey, charcoal maker! Old man, are you at home?" Sanpei called as he dismounted in front of a charcoal burner's hut. He was covered with sweat, but no more so than the horse he had been riding.

It was early summer. In the mountains the leaves were still a pale green, while in the lowlands the buzzing of cicadas could already be heard.

He's not here, Sanpei thought. He kicked the broken-down door, which opened immediately. Sanpei led the horse that he planned on leaving here inside the hut and, fastening it to a post, went into the kitchen and helped himself to rice, pickled vegetables, and tea.

As soon as he had filled his stomach, he found ink and a brush, wrote down a message on a scrap of paper, and stuck it to the lid of the rice tub with leftover grains of rice.

This was not the work of foxes and badgers. It was I, Sanpei, who ate these things. I am leaving you my horse to take care of while I am gone. Feed him well and keep him strong until I pass through again.

As Sanpei was leaving, his horse began to kick at the wall, unwilling for his master to leave. His heartless owner, however, did not even look back, but closed the door firmly on the sound of the hooves.

It would be an exaggeration to say that he flew off on his gifted legs, but he did hurry toward the mountainous province of Kai at a speed that made him look nimble indeed. His destination from the start had been Kai's capital city of Kofu. And the speed at which he was traveling suggested that he was carrying a very urgent report.

By the morning of the following day, he had already crossed several mountain ranges and was looking at the waters of the Fuji River right at his feet. The roofs that could be seen between the walls of the gorge were those of the village of Kajikazawa.

He wanted to reach Kofu by afternoon, but since he was making good time, he rested awhile, gazing at the summer sun beating down on the Kai Basin. No matter where I go, and regardless of the inconveniences and disadvantages of a mountain province, there's just no place like home. As he said this to himself, hugging his knees with his arms, he saw a long line of horses loaded with buckets of lacquer being led up the mountain from the foothills. Well, I wonder where they're going, he asked himself.

Amakasu Sanpei stood up and started down the mountain. Halfway down, he met the packhorse train of at least a hundred animals.

"Heyyy!"

The man on the leading horse was an old acquaintance. Sanpei quickly asked him, "That's an awful lot of lacquer, isn't it? Where are you taking it?"

"To Gifu," the man answered, and at Sanpei's dubious expression, he added an explanation. "We finally manufactured the amount of lacquer ordered by the Oda clan the year before last, so I'm just now taking it to Gifu."

"What! To the Oda?" Knitting his brow, Sanpei appeared unable even to smile and wish him a safe trip. "Be very careful. The roads are dangerous."

"I hear that the warrior-monks are fighting too. I wonder how the Oda troops are doing."

"I can't say anything about that until I report to His Lordship."

"Ah, that's right. You're just coming back from there, aren't you? Well, we shouldn't be standing here chatting. I'm off." The packhorse driver and his hundred horses crossed the pass and went off to the west.

Sanpei watched them go, thinking that a mountain province is, after all, exactly that. News of the rest of the world is always slow to arrive there, and even if our troops are strong and the generals clever, we are at a serious disadvantage. He felt the weight of his responsibilities even more, and ran down to the foothills with the speed of a swallow. Sanpei picked up another horse in the village of Kajikazawa and, with a stroke of the whip, galloped toward Kofu.

In the hot and humid Kai Basin stood Takeda Shingen's heavily fortified castle. Faces that were rarely seen except in times of weighty problems and war councils were now entering the castle gates one after another, so that even the guards at the entrance knew something was afoot. Inside the castle, which was wrapped in the green of new leaves, it was silent except for the occasional buzzing of the summer's first cicadas.

Since morning, not one of the many generals who had come to the castle had left. It was at this point that Sanpei hurried toward the gate. Dismounting beyond the moat, he ran across the bridge on foot, grasping the horse's reins in his hand.

"Who's there?" The eyes and spearheads of the guards glittered from a corner of the iron gate. Sanpei tied the horse to a tree.

"It's me," he replied, showing his face to the soldiers, and walked briskly into the castle. He often passed back and forth through the castle gate, so while there may have been those who did not know exactly who he was, there was not a soldier at the gate who did not know his face and the nature of his work.

There was a Buddhist temple inside the castle, called the Bishamondo after the guardian god of the north; it served as Shingen's meditation room, as a place to discuss governmental affairs, and from time to time as a place for war councils. Shingen was now standing on the veranda of the temple. His body seemed to flutter in the breeze that blew into the hall from the rocks and streams in the garden. Over his armor, he wore the red robe of a high priest, which looked as if it were made from the flaming flowers of the scarlet tree-peonies.

He was of average height, with a solidly built, muscular frame. There was clearly something unusual about the man, but while those who had never met him would remark on how intimidating he must be, he was not really so difficult to approach. On the contrary, he was a rather kindly man. Just looking at him, one could feel that he possessed natural composure and dignity, while his shaggy beard gave his face a certain unyielding quality. These features, however, were common to the men of the mountain province of Kai.

One after another, the generals rose from their seats and took their leave. They spoke a few parting words and bowed to their lord standing on the veranda. The war council had lasted since morning. And Shingen had worn his armor under his scarlet robe, exactly as he did on the battlefield. He seemed to be a little tired from the heat and the lengthy discussions. Moments after the council had ended, he had gone out to the veranda. The generals had departed, no one else was in attendance, and there was nothing in the Bishamondo other than the gilded walls that glittered in the wind and the peaceful buzzing of the cicadas.

This summer? Shingen seemed to be looking into the distance at the silhouette of the mountains that encircled his province. From his very first battle, when he was fifteen, his career had been filled with events that had occurred from summer through fall. In a mountain province, there was nothing else to do in the winter but confine oneself indoors and maintain one's strength. Naturally, when the spring and summer came, Shingen's blood would rise, and he would turn toward the outside world, saying, "Well, let's go out and fight." Not only Shingen, but all the samurai of Kai shared this attitude. Even the farmers and townspeople would suddenly feel that the time had come with the summer sun.

This year Shingen would turn fifty, and he felt a keen regret—an impatience with expectations of his life. I've fought too much just for the sake of fighting, he thought. I imagine that over in Echigo, Uesugi Kenshin is realizing the same thing.

When he thought about his worthy opponent of many years, Shingen could not suppress a bitter smile for the man's sake. This same bitter smile, however, gnawed bitterly in his breast when he thought of those fifty years. How much longer did he have to live?

Kai was snowed in for a third of the entire year. And although it could be argued that the center of the world was far away and the procurement of the latest weapons difficult, he felt that he had wasted the years of his prime, fighting with Kenshin in Echigo.

The sun was strong, and the shade beneath the leaves deep.

For many years Shingen had assumed he was the best warrior in eastern Japan. Certainly the efficiency of his troops and of his province's economy and administration were respected by the whole country.

Nevertheless, Kai had been placed to one side. From about the previous year, when Nobunaga had gone to Kyoto, Shingen had thought about the position of Kai and looked at himself again with a new perspective. The Takeda clan had set its sights too low.

Shingen did not want to spend his life shaving off bits of surrounding provinces. When Nobunaga and Ieyasu were sniffling children in the arms of their wet nurses, Shingen already dreamed of uniting the country under his iron rule. He felt that this mountain province was only a temporary abode, and his ambition was such that he had even let this thought slip to envoys from the capital. And certainly his never-ending battles with neighboring Echigo were really only the first of many battles to come. But most of the battles he had fought had been against Uesugi Kenshin, and had consumed a large portion of his provincial resources and taken much time.

But by the time he realized this, the Takeda clan had already been left behind by Nobunaga and Ieyasu. He had always considered Nobunaga "the little brat from Owari" and Ieyasu "the kid from Okazaki."

When I think about it now, I've committed a great blunder, he admitted bitterly. When he had only been involved in battles, he had hardly ever regretted anything; but nowadays, when he reviewed his diplomatic policies, he realized that he had bungled the job. Why hadn't he headed for the southeast when the Imagawa clan was destroyed? And, having taken a hostage from Ieyasu's clan, why had he watched silently as Ieyasu expanded his territory into Suruga and Totomi?

An even bigger error was in becoming Nobunaga's kinsman by marriage at the latter's request. Thus Nobunaga had fought with his neighbors to the west and south and, at a single stroke, stepped toward the center of the field. In the meantime, the hostage from Ieyasu had watched for his opportunity and escaped, and Ieyasu and Nobunaga were bound by an alliance. Even now it became clear to everyone how effective this had been diplomatically.

But I'm not going to be taken in by their scheming forever. I'm going to teach them that I am Takeda Shingen of Kai. The hostage from Ieyasu has escaped. This severs my connection with Ieyasu. What other excuse do I need?

He had said as much at the military council today. Having heard that Nobunaga was camped at Nagashima and apparently locked in a hard battle, this astute warrior saw his opportunity.

Amakasu Sanpei asked one of Shingen's close attendants to announce his return. As a summons was not forthcoming, however, he made his request once again.

"I wonder if His Lordship was informed of my arrival. Please tell him once more."

"A conference has just now been concluded, and he seems a little tired. Wait a little longer," the attendant replied.

Sanpei pressed further, "My business is urgent precisely because of that conference. I'm sorry, but I must insist that you inform him immediately."

It appeared that this time the message was passed on to Shingen, and Sanpei was summoned. One of the guards accompanied him as far as the central gate of the Bishamondo. From there, he was handed over to a guard of the inner citadel and led to Shingen.

Shingen was seated on a camp stool on the veranda of the Bishamondo. The young leaves of a large-trunked maple rustled speckles of light over him.

"What news do you bring, Sanpei?" Shingen asked.

"First of all, the information I sent you before has completely changed. So, thinking that something untoward might happen, I rushed here as fast as I could."

"What! The situation at Nagashima has changed? How is that?"

"The Oda had temporarily abandoned Gifu, and it seemed as though they were making a combined effort in their attack on Nagashima. But as soon as Nobunaga arrived on the battlefield, he ordered a general withdrawal. His troops paid dearly for it, but they receded like the tide."

"They retreated. And then?"

"The retreat seemed to have been unexpected, even by his own troops. His men were saying among themselves that they couldn't understand what was on his mind, and not a few of them were very confused."

This man is shrewd! Shingen thought, clicking his tongue and chewing his lip. I had a plan to bring Ieyasu out in the open and destroy him while Nobunaga was trapped by the warrior-monks in Nagashina. But it has all come to naught, and I have to be careful now, he said to himself. Then, turning toward the interior of the temple, he suddenly called out, "Nobufusa! Nobufusa!" He quickly gave the command to inform his generals that the decisions taken at the war council that day to depart for the front was being canceled forthwith.

Baba Nobufusa, his senior retainer, had no time to ask the reason why. Still more, the generals who had just now left were going to be confused, thinking there was no better opportunity than the present for smashing the Tokugawa clan. But Shingen knew, with a sudden illumination, that he had missed his opportunity, and that he was not going to be able to hold on to his former plan. Rather, he must quickly seek the next countermeasure and the next opportunity.

After taking off his armor, he met with Sanpei again. Sending his retainers away, Shingen listened carefully to the detailed reports of the situation in Gifu, Ise, Okazaki, and Hamamatsu. Later one of Sanpei's doubts was dispelled by Shingen.

"On my way here I noticed the transport of a large amount of lacquer for the Oda clan, who are allies of the Tokugawa. Why are you sending lacquer to the Oda?"

"A promise is a promise. Also, the Oda might be careless, and as the packhorses first had to pass through the Tokugawa domain, it was a good opportunity to survey routes into Mikawa, but that has turned out to be useless, too. Well, not useless. The time may come again tomorrow." Muttering self-scorn, he unburdened himself somewhere in solitude.

The departure of Kai's efficient and powerful army was postponed, and the men spent the summer in idleness. But when autumn came around, rumors could once again be heard in the western mountains and the eastern hills.

On a fine autumn day Shingen rode to the banks of the Fuefuki River. With only a few attendants accompanying him, his spirited figure, bathed in the autumn sun, seemed to be taking pride in the perfect administration of his own province. His senses were atuned to the dawning of a new age. Now is the time! he thought.

The plaque of the temple gate read "Kentokuzan." This was the temple where Kaisen lived, the man who had taught Shingen the secrets of Zen. Shingen acknowledged the greetings of the monks and went into the garden. Because he really was just dropping by for a short visit, he purposely did not enter the main temple.

Close by was a small teahouse with only two rooms. Water flowed from a spring; yellow ginkgo leaves had fallen into the water pipe running through the fragrant moss of a rock garden.

"Your Reverence, I've come to say good-bye."

Kaisen nodded at Shingen's words. "You're finally resolved, then?"

"I've been pretty patient, waiting for this opportunity to arrive, and I think this autumn the tide has somehow turned in my favor."

"I've heard that the Oda are going to make an offensive westward," Kaisen said. "Nobunaga seems to be gathering together an army even bigger than last year's, in order to destroy Mount Hiei."

"All things come to those who wait," Shingen replied. "I've even received a number of letters from the shogun saying that if I struck the Oda from the rear, the Asai and Asakura would rise up at the same time and, with the added help from Mount Hiei and Nagashima, just by kicking Ieyasu, I will advance quickly on the capital. But no matter what I do, Gifu is going to continue to be dangerous. I don't want to repeat Imagawa Yoshimoto's performance, so I've watched for the right opportunity. My intention is to catch Gifu off guard, to streak through Mikawa, Totomi, Owari, and Mino like a clap of thunder, and then go on to the capital. If I can do that, I think I will greet the New Year in Kyoto. I hope Your Reverence will remain in good health."

"If that's the way it's going to be," Kaisen said gloomily.

Shingen consulted Kaisen on almost every matter, from military to governmental matters, and trusted him implicitly. He was very alert to the expression he now perceived. "Your Reverence seems to have some misgivings about my plan."

Kaisen looked up. "There's no reason for me to disapprove of it. It is, after all, your life's ambition. What disturbs me are the petty schemes of Shogun Yoshiaki. The incessant secret letters urging you to the capital don't go to you alone. I've heard that they've also been received by Lord Kenshin. It also appears that he had called upon Lord Mori Motonari to mobilize, although he has since died."

"I'm not unaware of that. But regardless of everything else, I must go to Kyoto to realize the great plans I have for this country."

"Alas, even I have not been able to resign myself to the fact that a man of your ability should live out his life in Kai," Kaisen said. "I think you're going to have many troubles on the way, but the troops under your command have never been defeated. Just remember that your body is the only thing that is truly your own, so use your natural term of existence wisely."

Just then, the monk who had gone to scoop water from a nearby spring suddenly threw down the wooden bucket and, yelling unintelligibly, went running through the trees. Something like the sound of a running deer echoed through the garden. The monk who had been chasing after the fleeing footsteps finally dashed back to the teahouse.

"Get some men quickly! A suspicious-looking character has just escaped," he announced.

There was no reason for anyone suspicious to be inside the temple, and when Kaisen questioned the monk, the full story came out.

"I hadn't spoken to Your Reverence about it yet, but the fact is that a man knocked at the gate late last night. He was dressed in the robe of a wandering monk, so we let him stay overnight. If he had been someone we didn't know, we would not have allowed him in, of course. But we recognized him as Watanabe Tenzo, who was formerly in His Lordship's ninja corps and who used to visit this temple quite often with His Lordship's retainers. Thinking there was no problem, we let him stay."

"Wait a minute," Kaisen said. "Isn't that all the more suspicious? A member of the ninja corps disappears in an enemy province for a number of years and is never heard of again. Suddenly he's knocking at the gate in the middle of the night—dressed as a monk, mind you—and asks to stay overnight. Why didn't you question him a little more carefully?"

"Certainly we were at fault, my lord. But he told us that he had been arrested while spying on the Oda. He claimed to have spent several years in jail, but he had managed to escape, and had come back to Kai in disguise. He certainly seemed to be telling the truth. Then this morning he said that he was going to Kofu to meet with Amakasu Sanpei, the leader of his corps. We were completely taken in, but just now, when I was fetching water from the spring, I saw the bastard beneath the window of the tearoom, stuck to it like a lizard."

"What! He was listening in on my conversation with His Lordship?"

"When he heard my footsteps and turned in my direction, he looked quite surprised. Then he walked quickly toward the rear garden, so I called out to him , ordering him to stop. He ignored me and picked up his pace. Then, when I yelled out 'Spy!' he turned and glared at me."

"Has he gotten away?"

"I screamed at him at the top of my lungs, but all of His Lordship's retainers were eating their noonday meal. I couldn't find anyone around, and unfortunately he was too fast for me."

Shingen had not even glanced at the monk and had listened silently, but when his eyes met Kaisen's glance, he spoke quietly. "Amakasu Sanpei is among my attendants today. Let's have him run the man down. Call him here."

Sanpei prostrated himself in the garden and, looking up at Shingen, who was still seated in the teahouse, asked what his mission might be.

"A number of years ago, there was a man under your command by the name of Watanabe Tenzo, I believe."

Sanpei thought for a moment, then said, "I remember. He was born in Hachisuka in Owari. His uncle Koroku had had a gun made, but Tenzo stole it and fled here. He presented the gun to you and was given a stipend for a number of years."

"I recollect that business about the gun, but it seems that a man from Owari will always be just exactly that—a man from Owari—and now he's working for the Oda clan. Run the man down and cut off his head."

"Run him down?"

"Go after you've heard the details from that monk. You're going to have to chase after him quickly so he won't get away."

West from Nirasaki, a narrow path follows the foot of the mountains around Komagatake and Senjo, crossing over Takato in Ina.

"Heeyyy!"

The sound of a human voice was rare in these mountains. The lone monk stopped and turned around, but was there nothing but an echo, so he hurried on up the road over the mountain pass.

"Heeyyy! You there, monk!" The second time the voice was closer. And, as it was clearly calling him, the monk stopped for a moment, holding the brim of his hat. Very soon another man climbed up to him, breathing hard. Approaching the monk, the man shot him an ironic smile.

"This is a surprise, Tenzo. When did you come to Kai?"

The monk looked surprised, but he quickly recovered his composure and let out a snicker under his hat.

"Sanpei! I was wondering who it was. Well, it's been quite a while. You look to be in good health, as usual."

Irony was returned with irony. Both were men whose duties had taken them into enemy territory as spies. Without this kind of audacity and composure they would not have been equal to their work.

"That's quite a compliment." Sanpei seemed very relaxed, too. To have made a fuss because an enemy spy had been found on his home ground would have been the act of a heedless, common man. But looking at it through the eyes of a thief, he knew that there are thieves about even in broad daylight, and so it was hardly a surprise.

"Two nights ago you stopped at the Eirin Temple, and yesterday you eavesdropped on a secret conversation between Abbot Kaisen and Lord Shingen. When you were discovered by one of the monks, you ran away as fast as you could go. This is correct, isn't it, Tenzo?"

"Yes, were you there too?"

"Unfortunately."

"That's the only thing I didn't know."

"For you, that's a piece of bad luck."

Tenzo feigned indifference, as though this were someone else's affair. "I had thought that Amakasu Sanpei, the Takeda ninja, was still spying on the Oda in Ise or Gifu, but you had already come back. You should be praised, Sanpei, you're always so fast."

"Don't waste your breath. You can flatter me as much as you like, but now that I've found you, I can't let you return alive. Did you intend to cross the border as one of the living?"

"I don't have the least intention of dying. But, Sanpei, the shadow of death is drifting across your face. Surely you didn't come chasing after me because you wanted to die."

"I came to take your head, on orders from my lord. And upon my life, I'll have it."

"Whose head?"

"Yours!"

The instant Sanpei drew his long sword, Watanabe Tenzo stood ready with his staff. There was some distance between the two men. As they continued to glare at each other, their breathing quickened and their faces took on the pallor of people on the verge of death. Then something must have crossed Sanpei's mind, for he sheathed his sword.

"Tenzo, put down your staff."

"Why? Are you scared?"

"No, I'm not scared, but isn't it a fact that we both have the same duties? It's all right for a man to die for his mission, but to kill each other in this fight would serve no purpose at all. Why don't you take off that monk's robe and give it to me? If you will, I'll take it back and say I killed you."

Ninja had a particular faith among themselves that was not common to other warriors. It was a different view of life naturally brought about by the singularity of their duties. To the ordinary samurai, there could be no higher duty than to die for his lord. The ninja, however, thought quite differently. They held life dear. They had to return alive, regardless of the shame or hardships they had to suffer. For even if a man was able to enter into enemy territory and collect some valuable information, it did no good at all if he did not return to his home province alive. Therefore, if a ninja died in enemy territory, it was a dog's death, no matter how glorious the circumstances might have been. No matter how steeped in the samurai code the individual may have been, if his death was of no value to his lord, it was a dog's death. Thus, even though the ninja might be called a depraved samurai whose sole aim was to keep himself alive, it was his mission and responsibility to do so at all costs.

Both men held to these principles, right to the marrow of their bones. So, when Sanpei had reasoned with his opponent that killing each other would do no one any good and had sheathed his blade, Tenzo immediately drew back his weapon as well.

"I didn't like the idea of becoming your opponent and gambling with my head. If we can finish this thing with a monk's robe, let's do it." He ripped off a piece of the robe he was wearing and threw it at Sanpei's feet. Sanpei picked it up.

"This is enough. If I bring this back as proof, and announce that I've cut down Watanabe Tenzo, the matter will be over and done with. His Lordship certainly won't demand to see the head of a mere ninja."

"This works well for the both of us. Well, then, Sanpei, I'll be going. I'd like to say that I'll see you again, but I'd better pray that it'll never happen, because I know it would be the last time." With these parting words, Watanabe Tenzo walked away quickly, as though he had suddenly become afraid of his opponent and was happy to have saved his own skin.

As Tenzo began to descend the slope of the pass, Sanpei picked up the gun and fuse that he had previously hidden in a clump of grass, and followed him.

The report of the gun could be heard echoing through the mountains. Immediately, Sanpei tossed the weapon aside and leaped down the slope like a deer, intending to deal the finishing blow to his fallen enemy.

Watanabe Tenzo had fallen on his back in a clump of weeds on the road. But at the moment Sanpei stood over him and aimed the tip of his sword at his breast, Tenzo grabbed Sanpei's legs and pulled them from under him, bringing him to the ground with terrific force.

Now Tenzo's wild nature came to the fore. While Sanpei lay stunned, he jumped up like a wolf, seized a nearby rock in both hands, and smashed it down onto Sanpei's face. The impact made a sound like a splitting pomegranate.

Then Tenzo was gone.

* * *

Hideyoshi, now commander of Yokoyama Castle, had spent the summer in the cool mountains of northern Omi. Soldiers say that for a fighting man, inactivity is more trying than the battlefield. Discipline cannot be neglected for a day. Hideyoshi's troops had been at rest for one hundred days.

At the beginning of the Ninth Month, however, the command was given to depart for the front, and the gates of Yokoyama Castle were opened. From the time they left the castle until they arrived at the shore of Lake Biwa, the soldiers had no idea where they were going to fight.

There were three large ships berthed by the lake. Built over the New Year, they smelled of newly sawed timber. It was not until after the horses and men had clattered aboard that the soldiers were told that their destination would be either the Honganji or Mount Hiei.

Having crossed the autumnal face of the great lake and arriving at Sakamoto on the opposite shore, Hideyoshi's men were amazed to see that the army under Nobunaga and his generals had arrived ahead of them. In the foothills of Mount Hiei, the banners of the Oda stood as far as the eye could see.

After Nobunaga had lifted the siege of Mount Hiei and withdrawn to Gifu the previous winter, he had ordered the building of large troop ships capable of crossing the lake at a moment's notice. Now the soldiers finally understood his forethought, and the words he had spoken when he abandoned the attack on Nagashima and returned to Gifu.

The flames of rebellion that burned all over the country were merely reflections of the real fire—the root of the evil—whose source was Mount Hiei. Nobunaga was again laying siege to the mountain with a great army. His face showed new resolve, and he spoke loudly enough to be heard from the curtained enclosure of his headquarters all the way to the barracks, almost as if he were addressing the enemy.

"What! You're saying that you won't use fire because the flames might spread to the monasteries? What is war, anyway? Every one of you is a general, and you don't understand even that? How did you ever get this far?"

This much could be heard from the outside. Inside the enclosure, Nobunaga was sitting on his camp stool, surrounded by his veteran generals, all of whom were hanging their heads. Nobunaga was exactly like a father lecturing his children. Even if he was their lord, this sort of criticism was going too far. At least this was what the bitter expression on the faces of the generals indicated as they looked up, daring to look Nobunaga directly in the eye.

What were they fighting for, indeed? If they thought or worried about it, they risked their reputations by rebuking Nobunaga.

"You're being heartless, my lord. It's not that we don't understand, but when you've given us an outrageous order—to burn down Mount Hiei, a place respected for hundreds of years as holy ground dedicated to the peace and preservation of the country—as your retainers—and precisely because we *are* your retainers—there is all the more reason why we should not obey you," Sakuma Nobumori said.

A do-or-die expression showed clearly on Nobumori's face. If he had not been prepared to die on the spot, he could not have said this to Nobunaga. Especially the way Nobunaga was looking now. Although it was always rather difficult to speak frankly to their lord, today Nobunaga resembled a demon wielding a fiery sword.

"Silence! Silence!" Nobunaga roared, quieting Takei Sekian and Akechi Mitsuhide, who were about to back up Nobumori. "Have you not felt indignation when you watched the insurrections and this disgraceful state of affairs? Monks transgress the Laws of the Buddha, stir up the common people, store wealth and weapons, and spread rumors; under the guise of religion, they are nothing more than self-serving agitators."

"We do not object to punishing these excesses. But it is impossible, in a single day, to reform a religion in which all men fervently believe and which has been granted special authority," Nobumori argued.

"What good is that kind of common sense?" Nobunaga exploded. "It's because we've had eight hundred years of common sense that no one has been able to change the situation, despite people's lamenting over the church's corruption and degeneracy. Even His Majesty the Emperor Shirakawa said that there were three things over which he had no control: dice, the waters of the Kamo River, and the warrior-monks of Mount Hiei. What role in the peace and preservation of the country did this mountain play during the years of civil war? Has it given peace of mind or strength to the common people?" Nobunaga suddenly waved his right hand to the side. "For hundreds of years, when disasters have occurred, the monks have done nothing more than protect their own privileges. With the money donated by the credulous masses, they build stone walls and gates that would befit a fortress and inside they hoard guns and spears. Worse, the monks flaunt their vows openly by eating meat and indulging in sexual intercourse. Let's not even speak of the decadence of Buddhist scholarship. Where is the sin in burning down something like that?"

Nobumori replied, "Everything you say is true, but we must stop you, my lord. We're not going to leave this place until we do, even if it costs us our lives." The three

359

men simultaneously prostrated themselves and remained motionless before Nobunaga.

Mount Hiei was the headquarters of the Tendai sect; the Honganji was the principle stronghold of the Ikko sect. Each called the other "the *other* sect" in matters of doctrine, and it was only in their opposition to Nobunaga that they were united. If Nobunaga had not had a moment's rest, it was because of the schemes of the men dressed in monks' robes, living on Mount Hiei. They had plotted with the Asai and Asakura clans and the shogun, helped enemies defeated by Nobunaga, sent secret calls for assistance as far as Echigo and Kai, and even incited peasant revolts in Owari.

The three generals knew that without the destruction of this reputedly impregnable Buddhist fortress, the Oda army would be stymied at every turn, and Nobunaga would be unable to realize his dreams.

As soon as Nobunaga had set up his camp, he had given an incredible order: "Attack the mountain and burn everything to the ground, starting with the shrines, the Great Hall, the monasteries, and all the sutras and the holy relics." This was extreme enough, but he went on, "Let no one escape if they're wearing monkish robes. Make no distinction between the wise and the foolish, aristocratic or common monks. Show no mercy to women and children. Even if someone is dressed as a layman, if he's been hiding on the mountain and runs away because of the fire, you may look upon him as part of the present plague as well. Massacre the entire lot, and burn the mountain until there's not a sign of human life left in the ruins!"

Even the Rakasa, the bloodthirsty cannibal demons of the Buddhist hells, could not have done such a thing. The generals who heard his order were unnerved.

"Has he gone mad?" Takei Sekian muttered under his breath, but well within earshot of the other generals. However, only Sakuma Nobumori, Takei Sekian, and Akechi Mitsuhide dared to express their opinions in front of Nobunaga.

Before going to confront their lord, they had pledged, "We may be forced to commit *seppuku* one after another for going against His Lordship's orders, but we cannot let him carry out this reckless fire attack."

Nobunaga could simply besiege and take Mount Hiei. But where was the need for such slaughter with an attack by fire? If they dared to commit this outrage, they feared that popular sentiment would turn against the Oda. Nobunaga's enemies would rejoice, and they would use the attack as propaganda to blacken his name at every opportunity. He would only be bringing upon himself the kind of evil reputation that men had feared and avoided for hundreds of years.

"We are not going to fight a battle that will bring you to ruin," the three generals said, speaking for all the men present. Their voices quaked with their tearful devotion.

Nobunaga, however, was determined, and he gave no indication that he would even think twice about the three men's words. On the contrary, he became even more determined. "You may retire. Don't say anything more," he told them. "If you refuse to obey the order, I'll give it to someone else. And if the other generals and soldiers won't follow me, then I'll do it myself, alone!"

"Why is it necessary to commit such an atrocity? I would think that a true general could bring about the fall of Mount Hiei without shedding a single drop of blood," Nobumori asked again.

"No more 'common sense'! There speaks eight hundred years of 'common sense.' If we don't burn out the roots of the old, the buds of the new will never sprout. You keep talking about this one mountain, but I'm not concerned only with Mount Hiei; burning it down is going to save the church everywhere else. If by slaughtering all the men, women, and children on Mount Hiei, I can open the eyes of the imprudent in other provinces, then I will have done some good. The hottest and deepest hells are nothing to my eyes and ears. Who else can do this but me? I have heaven's mandate to do it."

The three men, who believed that they, more than anyone else, knew Nobunaga's genius and methods, were appalled by this statement. Was their lord possessed by demons?

Takei Sekian pleaded, "No, my lord. No matter what orders you give us, as your retainers we can do nothing but try to dissuade you. You cannot burn a place sacred since ancient times—"

"That's enough! Shut up! In my heart I've received an Imperial decree to burn the place down. I'm giving you the order for this massacre because the mercy of the Founder, Saint Dengyo, is in my heart. Don't you understand?"

"No, my lord."

"If you don't understand, leave! Just don't get in the way."

"I'm going to object until you kill me yourself."

"You're already damned! Get out!"

"Why should I leave? Rather than watch my lord's insanity and the destruction of his clan in my lifetime, I can try to obstruct this with my own death. Look back to the many examples given by antiquity. Not one man who made a hellfire of Buddhist temples and shrines, or who massacred priests, has come to a good end."

"I'm different. I'm not going into battle for my own sake. In this battle, my role will be to destroy ancient evils and build a new world. I don't know whether this is the command of the gods, the people, or the times; all I know is that I'm going to obey the orders I've received. You are all timid, and your view is limited. Your cries are the sorrows of small-minded people. The profit and loss you talk about only concerns me as an individual. If my turning Mount Hiei into an inferno protects countless provinces and saves countless lives, then it will be a great achievement."

Sekian did not desist. "The people are going to see this as the work of demons. They will rejoice if you show a little humanity. Be too severe, and they'll never accept you—even if you are motivated by great love."

"If we hold back because of popular opinion, we won't be able to act at all. The heroes of antiquity feared popular opinion and left this evil to plague future generations. But I'm going to show you how to extirpate it once and for all. If I'm going to do it, I must do it completely. If I don't, there's no point in taking up arms and marching toward the center of the field."

There are intervals even between the raging waves. Nobunaga's voice softened a little. His three retainers hung their heads, their protests almost exhausted.

Hideyoshi had just arrived, having crossed the lake at about noon. The debate was in progress when he approached headquarters, so he had waited outside. Now he stuck his head through a split in the curtain and apologized for intruding.

Abruptly they all looked in his direction. Nobunaga's expression was like a raging fire, while the faces of his three generals, who were resolved to die, were frozen, as if covered with a coating of ice.

"I've just arrived by ship," Hideyoshi said genially. "Lake Biwa in the fall is absolutely beautiful; places like Chikubu Island are covered with red leaves. Somehow it didn't feel as though I was heading for the battlefield at all, and I even made up some poor poetry on board. Maybe I'll read it to you after the battle."

Stepping inside, Hideyoshi chattered away about whatever came into his head. Nowhere on his face was there anything like the solemnity that had transfixed lord and retainers just moments ago. He seemed to have no worries at all.

"What's going on?" Hideyoshi asked, looking back and forth at Nobunaga and his retainers, who were sunk in silence. His words were like a clear spring breeze. "Ah. I heard what you were talking about when I was outside just now. Is that why you're silent? Thinking so much of their lord, the retainers have resolved to admonish him and die; knowing the innermost feelings of his retainers, the lord is not so violent that he would cut them down. Yes, I can see there's a problem. You could say there are good and bad points to both sides."

Nobunaga turned his head sharply. "Hideyoshi, you've come at a good time. If you've heard almost everything, you must understand what's in my heart and what these three men are saying as well."

"I do understand, my lord."

"Would you obey the order? Do you think it is wrong?"

"I don't think anything at all. No, wait. This order is based on the recommendation I wrote up and gave to you some time ago, I believe."

"What! When did you make such a proposal?"

"It must have slipped your mind, my lord. I believe it was sometime in spring." Then he turned to the three generals and said, "But listen, it nearly made me weep as I stood out there unseen and heard your loyal admonitions. Yours is the sincerity of true retainers. In a word, however, I think what each one of you is most worried about is that if we do attack Mount Hiei with fire, it is certain that the country will turn against His Lordship."

"That's it exactly! If we commit this atrocity," Sekian said, "both the samurai and the people will feel resentment. Our enemies will take advantage of it to blacken His Lordship's name forever."

"But it was I who recommended that when we attacked Mount Hiei, we should go all the way, so it was not His Lordship's idea. Now, if that's so, I would be the one to bear whatever curse or bad reputation that might be forthcoming."

"How presumptuous!" Nobumori cried out. "Why would the public blame someone like you? Whatever the Oda army does reflects on its commander-in-chief."

"Of course. But won't all of you help me out? Couldn't we proclaim to the world that the four of us were so eager to carry out His Lordship's orders that we went too far? It's said that the greater part of loyalty is delivering one's admonition even if one is forced to die for it. But if it were left to me, I would say that even delivering an admonition and dying is not enough proof of the loyalty of a truly devoted retainer. It's my view that while we are alive, we should answer, in our lord's place, for the bad reputation, abuse, persecution, stumbling, and anything else. Do you agree?"

Nobunaga listened silently, without signaling agreement or disagreement.

Sekian was the first to respond to Hideyoshi's suggestion. "Hideyoshi, I agree with you." He looked around at Mitsuhide and Nobumori; they also made no objections. And they swore to attack Mount Hiei with fire, and to let it be known that their actions had exceeded Nobunaga's orders.

"A masterful plan." In a voice that betrayed admiration, Sekian congratulated Hideyoshi for his resourcefulness, but Nobunaga did not look the least bit pleased. On the contrary, without saying a word, his expression clearly showed that this was something that hardly warranted so much praise.

The same opinion could be clearly seen on Mitsuhide's face. In his heart, Mitsuhide understood what Hideyoshi had suggested, but he also felt that the merit of the truth of their own loyal remonstrances had been snatched away by the newcomer's words. He was jealous. An intelligent man, however, he was quickly ashamed of his selfishness. He censured himself, reflecting that someone who was ready to die in objecting to his lord's command should avoid shallow thinking, even for a moment.

The three generals were satisfied with Hideyoshi's plan, but Nobunaga acted as though he were not committing himself to it, and certainly he did not seem to have changed his original aim. One after another, Nobunaga summoned his commanders.

"Tonight, at the sound of the conch, we will make an all-out attack on the mountain!" He himself gave the same severe orders that he had given previously to the three generals. It appeared that there were many officers there who, along with Sekian, Mitsuhide, and Nobumori, were against the attack by fire, but since those three had already accepted the order, they all did the same and left without a dissenting word.

Messengers from headquarters galloped to the outlying units and carried the orders to the front-line troops at the foot of the mountain.

The evening clouds settled in brilliant colors behind Shimeigadake as the sun set. Broad shafts of red light ran across the lake like rainbows, as waves rose on the surface.

"Look!" Nobunaga stood at the top of the hill and spoke to those around him, gazing up at the clouds around Mount Hiei. "Heaven is with us! A strong wind has come up. We'll have the best weather conditions for a fire attack!"

As he spoke, the cold evening wind rustled through their clothes and gradually freshened. There were only five or six retainers with him, and at that moment a man peeked inside the billowing curtain as though he were looking for someone.

Sekian shouted at the man, "What's your business? His Lordship is over here."

The samurai quickly approached and knelt down. "No, I have nothing to report to His Lordship. Is General Hideyoshi here?"

When Hideyoshi emerged from the group, the messenger told him, "A man dressed as a priest has just now come into camp. He says he is Watanabe Tenzo, one of your retainers, and that he has just returned from Kai. His report seemed to be extremely urgent, so I hurried here."

Although Nobunaga was a little distance from Hideyoshi, he suddenly turned toward him.

"Hideyoshi, the man who just returned from Kai is one of your retainers?"

"I think you know him, too, my lord. Watanabe Tenzo, Hikoemon's nephew."

"Tenzo? Well, let's hear if he has any news," Nobunaga said. "Call him here. I'd like to listen to his report, too."

Tenzo knelt in front of Hideyoshi and Nobunaga and told them about the conversation he had eavesdropped on at the Eirin Temple.

Nobunaga grunted. This was a dangerous threat to his rear. As with his attack on Mount Hiei the year before, the danger had not decreased in the least. On the contrary, both his position in regard to the Takeda and the conditions in the area of Nagashima had worsened. In the campaign the previous year, however, the large armies of the Asai and Asakura had joined forces and retreated to Mount Hiei. This time he had not given his enemies such an opportunity, so the forces that faced him now were not so powerful. It was just that there was always danger from the rear.

"I imagine the Takeda clan has already dispatched messages to Mount Hiei, so the monks are certain to be optimistic about our army turning tail and heading for home," Nobunaga said, dismissing Tenzo. "This is help from heaven," he said, laughing with satisfaction. "Which is going to be faster—the Takeda army as it crosses the mountains of Kai and presses in on Owari and Mino, or the Oda army when it returns after having destroyed Mount Hiei and conquered the capital and Settsu? It would seem as though they're giving us extra incentive for competition, and increasing our desperate conviction. Everybody get back to your posts."

Nobunaga disappeared into the enclosure. Smoke rose from the cooking fires of the huge camp that encircled the foothills of Mount Hiei. As night fell, the wind freshened. The temple bell that was usually heard from the Mii Temple was silent.

The sound of the conch shell reverberated on top of the hill, and the soldiers raised their battle cries in reply. The carnage lasted from that evening until dawn of the following day. The soldiers of the Oda army broke through the barricades the warrior-monks had built across the passes on the way to the summit.

Black smoke filled the valley, and flames howled through the mountain. Looking up from the foothills, one could see huge pillars of fire everywhere on Mount Hiei. Even the lake glowed a fiery red. The location of the biggest fire showed that the main temple was burning, as well as the seven shrines, the great lecture hall, the bell tower, the library, the monasteries, the treasure pagoda, the great pagoda, and all the minor temples. By dawn the following day not one temple was left standing.

The generals, who encouraged one another each time they looked up at the fearful sight, would recall Nobunaga's claim of having heaven's mandate and the blessing of Saint Dengyo, and urge themselves on. The apparent conviction of the generals inspired the troops. Making their way through the flames and black smoke, the attacking soldiers followed Nobunaga's orders to the letter. Eight thousand warrior-monks perished in an echo of the most horrible Buddhist hell. The monks who crawled through the valleys, hid in caves, or climbed trees trying to get away were hunted down and killed, like insects on rice plants.

Around midnight, Nobunaga himself climbed the mountain to see what his iron will had wrought. The monks of Mount Hiei had miscalculated. Even though they had been surrounded by Nobunaga's army, they had made light of the situation, thinking the show of force a pretentious bluff. They had vowed to wait until the Oda started to retreat, and then they had planned to pursue and destroy them. And they had sat by idly, their minds at ease because they received frequent letters of encouragement and reassurance from nearby Kyoto—which meant, of course, from the shogun.

For all the warrior-monks and their followers across the country, Mount Hiei had been the focal point of the opposition to Nobunaga. But the man who had incessantly supplied provisions and weapons to Mount Hiei and who had done his best to stir up the monks and urge them to fight was Shogun Yoshiaki.

"Shingen is coming!" So had promised a dispatch from Kai to the shogun. Yoshiaki had held on to this great expectation and had passed it on to Mount Hiei.

The warrior-monks, naturally enough, had faith that the army from Kai would attack Nobunaga's rear. When that happened, Nobunaga would have to retreat just as he had the year before at Nagashima. And there was one more thing. Because they had lived undisturbed for the past eight hundred years, the monks had underestimated the changes that had overtaken the country in recent years.

The mountain was transformed into an earthly hell in only half a night. A little too late, at about midnight, when flames were leaping everywhere, representatives of Mount Hiei, consumed with fear and panic, came to Nobunaga's camp to sue for peace.

"We'll give him whatever amount of money he wants, and we will agree to whatever conditions he sets."

Nobunaga only flashed a smile and spoke to those around him, as though he were throwing bait to a hawk. "There's no need to give them an answer. Just cut them down on the spot." Once more messengers came from the priests, and this time begged before Nobunaga himself. Nobunaga turned his head and had the monks killed.

Dawn broke. Mount Hiei was covered in the lingering smoke, ashes, and black withered trees, while everywhere corpses were frozen in the poses death had found them in.

Among these there must have been men of profound learning and wisdom, and the young monks of the future, thought Mitsuhide, who had been in the vanguard of the slaughter the night before. He stood this morning in the thin smoke, covering his face and feeling a pain in his breast.

That same morning, Mitsuhide had received Nobunaga's gracious command. "I'm putting you in charge of the district of Shiga. From now on you'll live in Sakamoto Castle, down in the foothills."

Two days later, Nobunaga descended the mountain and entered Kyoto. Black smoke still rose from Mount Hiei. Apparently quite a number of warrior-monks had fled to Kyoto to escape the carnage, and these men now spoke of him as though he were the incarnation of evil.

"The man's a living demon king!"

"A messenger from hell!"

"He's an atrocious destroyer!"

The citizens of Kyoto were given a vivid description of Mount Hiei and the pitiful situation that night. Now, when they heard that Nobunaga was withdrawing his troops and heading down the mountain, they were shaken. The rumors flew:

"It's Kyoto's turn!"

"The shogun's palace will never be able to withstand a fire attack."

People shut their doors even though it was daytime, packed their belongings, and prepared to flee. Nobunaga's soldiers, however, bivouacked on the bank of the Kamo River and were forbidden to enter the city. The man who forbade this was the demon king who had commanded the attack on Mount Hiei. Accompanied by a small number of generals, he now went inside a temple. After taking off his armor and helmet and eating a hot meal, he changed into an elegant court kimono and headdress and went out.

He rode a dappled horse with a gorgeous saddle. His generals remained in their armor and helmets. With these fourteen or fifteen men, he rode nonchalantly through the streets. The demon king was extraordinarily at peace, and smiled kindly at the people. The citizens spilled out onto the roadside and prostrated themselves as Nobunaga passed. Nothing was going to happen. They began to cheer, as relief spread across the city like a wave.

Suddenly the single report of a gun rang out from the cheering crowds. The bullet grazed Nobunaga, but he acted as though nothing had happened, and only turned to look in the direction of the report. The generals around him naturally leaped off their horses and rushed to capture the villain, but the city people, even more than the generals, were taken in a fit of anger, yelling out in a rage: "Get him!" The perpetrator, who had thought that the people of Kyoto would be on his side, had miscalculated, and now had no place to hide. He was a warrior-monk, said to be their very bravest, and he continued to pour abuse on Nobunaga even though he was pinned down.

"You're an enemy of the Buddha! The king of the demons!"

Nobunaga's expression did not change in the least. He rode to the Imperial Palace as planned, and dismounted. After washing his hands, he stepped calmly up to the gate of the palace and knelt.

"The raging fires of the night before last must have given Your Majesty some surprise. I hope you will forgive me for having caused you anxiety."

He knelt this way for a long time so that one might have thought that he felt this apology deep within his heart, but presently he looked up at the palace's new gate and walls, and then looked around in a satisfied way at the generals to his right and left.

1. It is unlawful to leave one's occupation.
2. Those who spread rumors or false reports will be put to death immediately.
3. Everything should remain as it has been.

By order of Oda Nobunaga, Chief Magistrate

When these three edicts had been posted throughout the city, Nobunaga returned to Gifu. He left without meeting with the shogun, who for some time had been busy deepening his moats, buying guns, and steeling himself for a fire attack. Heaving a sigh of relief, the residents of the shogun's palace were, however, filled with unease as they watched Nobunaga go.

THE GATELESS GATE

The smoke from the fires of war was thick not only on Mount Hiei but was rising, as if from the leaping flames of a prairie fire, from the western districts of Mikawa, to the villages on the Tenryu River, as far as the borders of Mino. The troops of Takeda Shingen had crossed the mountains of Kai and were flowing southward.

The Tokugawa, who had dubbed their enemy "the long-legged Shingen," vowed to stop his march on the capital. This was not for the sake of their Oda allies. Kai was critically close to the provinces of Mikawa and Totomi, and if the Takeda forces were to break through, it would mean the annihilation of the Tokugawa clan.

Ieyasu was thirty-one years old and in the prime of manhood. His retainers had suffered every privation and hardship for the past twenty years. But at last Ieyasu had come of age, his clan was on friendly terms with the Oda, and bit by bit he was encroaching on the territory of the Imagawa clan.

His province was filled with the hope of prosperity and the courage of expansion, so much so that the elder retainers, the samurai, the farmers, and the townspeople seemed to be aroused and inspired.

Mikawa could hardly match Kai in armaments and resources; in determination, however, it was not the least bit inferior. There was a reason why the Tokugawa warriors had given Shingen the nickname "Long-legged." This witticism had once been included in a letter to Ieyasu from Nobunaga, and when Ieyasu read it, he thought it was worth relating to his retainers.

The appellation was a clever one, for if only yesterday Shingen had been fighting at the northern border of Kai against the Uesugi clan, today he was in Kozuke and Sagami and was threatening the Hojo clan. Or, turning quickly, he would release the fires of war in Mikawa or Mino.

Moreover, Shingen himself was always in the field giving directions. Thus people said he must have had mannequins to take his place, but the fact was that whenever his men fought, he did not seem to be satisfied unless he was there on the battlefield himself. But if Shingen was long-legged, it could be said that Nobunaga was fleet-footed.

Nobunaga had written to Ieyasu:

It would be better not to face the full force of the Kai attack right now. Even if the situation becomes pressing and you have to withdraw from Hamamatsu to Okazaki, I hope you will persevere. If our time must wait for another day, I doubt it will be long in coming.

Nobunaga had sent this message to Ieyasu before burning Mount Hiei, but Ieyasu had turned to his senior retainers and declared, right in front of the Oda messenger, "Before abandoning Hamamatsu Castle, it would be better to break our bows and leave the samurai class!"

To Nobunaga, Ieyasu's province was one of his lines of defense; but to Ieyasu, Mikawa was his home. Ieyasu was going to bury his bones in no other province but this one. When he received the messenger's reply, Nobunaga mumbled something about the man being too impatient, and returned to Gifu just as soon as he had finished with Mount Hiei. Shingen must have had something to say about that speed as well. As might be expected, he too was alert in looking for his opportunity.

Shingen had stated clearly that to be one day late could mean disasters for an entire year, and now he felt the need to hurry all the more to fulfill his long-cherished desire of entering the capital. For this reason, all of his diplomatic moves were expedited. His friendship with the Hojo clan, therefore, was now brought to fruition, but his negotiations with the Uesugi clan were as unsatisfactory as before. Thus he was obliged to wait until the Tenth Month to leave Kai.

Snow would soon close off his borders with Echigo, so his concern about Uesugi Kenshin would be alleviated. His army of about thirty thousand men comprised troops conscripted from his domain, which included Kai, Shinano, Suruga, the northern part of Totomi, eastern Mikawa, western Kozuke, a part of Hida, and the southern part of Etchu —land holdings amounting to almost one million three hundred thousand bushels in all.

"The best thing we could do is put up a defense," one general argued.

"At least until reinforcements come from Lord Nobunaga."

One party of the men in Hamamatsu Castle spoke in favor of a defensive campaign. Even if all the province's samurai were mustered, the military strength of the Tokugawa clan was hardly fourteen thousand men—barely half that of the Takeda army. Still, Ieyasu chose to order a mobilization of his army.

"What! This is not a matter of waiting around for Lord Nobunaga's reinforcements."

All of his retainers expected a great number of the Oda soldiers to come to their aid out of a natural sense of duty—or even out of gratitude for the past service rendered by the Tokugawa clan at the Ane River. Ieyasu, however, did his best to appear as though he had no expectation of reinforcements at all. Now was exactly the time for him to determine whether his men were resigned to a life-and-death situation, and to make them realize they could rely on nothing but their own strength.

"If it's destruction to retreat and destruction to advance, shouldn't we strike out in an all-or-nothing effort, make our names as warriors, and die a glorious death?" he asked calmly.

While this man had known misery and hardships from the time of his youth, he had matured into an adult who did not make a fuss over trifles. Now, with this situation upon them, the castle of Hamamatsu was as full of fury as a boiling kettle, but while Ieyasu sat there and advocated a violent confrontation more than anyone else, the tone of his voice hardly changed at all. For this reason there were those among his retainers who had misgivings about the difference between his words and their intent. But Ieyasu hastened steadily to make preparations to depart for the battlefield, as he received the reports of his scouts.

One by one, like teeth being plucked from a comb, reports of each defeat were coming in. Shingen had attacked Totomi. By now, it was likely that the castles at Tadaki and Iida had had no other choice but to surrender. In the villages of Fukuroi, Kakegawa, and Kihara, there was no place that the Kai forces had not trampled underfoot. Worse, Ieyasu's three-thousand-man vanguard under Honda, Okubo, and Naito had been discovered by the Takeda forces in the neighborhood of the Tenryu River. The Tokugawa had been routed and forced to retreat to Hamamatsu.

This report made everyone in the castle turn pale. But Ieyasu continued his military preparations. He was especially careful to secure his lines of communication, and had been taking care of the defense of that area until nearly the end of the Tenth Month. And, to secure Futamata Castle at the Tenryu River, he had sent reinforcements of troops, weapons, and supplies.

The army left Hamamatsu Castle, advanced as far as Kanmashi village on the bank of the Tenryu River, and found the camp of the Kai army, each position linked to Shingen's headquarters like spokes around a hub.

"Ah, just as you'd expect." Even Ieyasu stood on the hill for a moment with his arms folded and let out a sigh of admiration. The banners in Shingen's main camp were visible even at this distance. From closer up, one could make out the inscription. They were the words of the famous Sun Tzu, familiar to enemy and ally alike.

Fast as the wind,
Quiet as a forest,
Ardent as fire,
Still as a mountain.

Still as a mountain, neither Shingen nor Ieyasu made any move for several days. With the Tenryu River between the opposing camps, winter came in with the Eleventh Month.

* * *

Two things there are
Surpassing Ieyasu:

369

Ieyasu's horned helmet
And Honda Heihachiro.

One of the Takeda men had posted this lampoon on the hill of Hitokotozaka. Ieyasu's men had been soundly defeated and routed there—or at least that was the opinion of the Takeda ranks, elated by their victory. But as the poem admitted, the Tokugawa had some fine men, and Honda Heihachiro's retreat had been admirable.

Ieyasu was certainly not unworthy as an enemy. But in this next battle the entire forces of the Takeda would be up against the entire forces of the Tokugawa. They would strike at one another in a battle that would decide the outcome of the war.

Anticipation of the fight only heightened the spirits of the men of Kai. That was the kind of composure they had. Shingen moved his main camp to Edaijima and had his son, Katsuyori, and Anayama Baisetsu move their forces against Futamata Castle, with strict orders not to delay.

In response, Ieyasu quickly sent reinforcements, saying "Futama Castle is an important line of defense. If the enemy captures it, they'll have an advantageous place from which to make their attack."

Ieyasu himself gave orders to his rear guard, but the ever-changing Takeda army quickly went through yet another transformation and began pressing in on all sides. It seemed that if he made a false move now, he would be cut off from his headquarters in Hamamatsu.

Futamata Castle's water supply—its weakest point—was cut by the enemy. On one side the castle abutted the Tenryu River, and the water that sustained the lives of the soldiers inside had to be lifted into the castle with a bucket lowered from a tower. To put an end to this, the Takeda forces launched rafts from upstream and undermined the base of the tower. From that day on, the soldiers in the castle were afflicted by a lack of water, even though the river flowed right in front of their walls.

On the evening of the nineteenth, the garrison surrendered. When Shingen learned that the castle had capitulated, he gave new orders: "Nobumori will occupy the castle. Sano, Toyoda, and Iwata will maintain communications and get ready along the enemy's road of retreat."

Like a *go* master watching each move of the stones, Shingen was cautious with his army's formation and advance. The twenty-seven thousand soldiers of Kai moved slowly but surely, like black clouds across the land, as the beat of the drums resounded up to heaven. After that, Shingen's main force crossed Iidani Plain and started to move into eastern Mikawa.

It was midday on the twenty-first, and the cold was sharp enough to slice off a man's nose and ears. A red dust rose in Mikatagahara, mocking the weak winter sun. There had been no rain for days; the air was parched.

"On to Iidani!" came the order. It caused a divergence of opinion among Shingen's generals.

"If we're going to Iidani, he must have decided to surround Hamamatsu Castle. Wouldn't that be a mistake?"

Some had misgivings because the Oda troops had been arriving at Hamamatsu, and no one knew for sure how many soldiers might be there now. Such was the secret intelligence that had been trickling in since the morning. No matter how much they pressed the enemy, his real situation could not be calculated. The reports were always the same: there was some truth to the rumors that were circulating in the villages along the road—which probably contained a good many of the enemy's own false reports—that a large Oda force was heading south to join Ieyasu's troops at Hamamatsu.

Shingen's generals offered their opinions:

"If Nobunaga arrives with a great army acting as a rear guard for Hamamatsu, you should probably give the matter careful thought right here, my lord."

"If the attack on Hamamatsu Castle takes us into the New Year, our men will have to winter in the field. With constant surprise attacks from the enemy, our supplies will run out and the troops will fall victim to disease. In any case, the men will suffer."

"On the other hand, I fear that they may cut off our retreat along the coast and elsewhere."

"When reinforcements are added to the Oda rear guard, our men will be trapped on a narrow strip of enemy territory—a situation that will not easily be reversed. If this happens, Your Lordship's dream of marching into Kyoto will be frustrated, and we will have to open up a bloody path to retreat. Since we're mobilized at this point, why not go on with your foremost objective and march on the capital instead of attacking Hamamatsu Castle?"

Shingen sat on a camp stool in the middle of his generals, his eyes narrow slits, like needles. He nodded at each of their opinions, then said deliberately, "All your opinions are extremely reasonable. But I am certain that the Oda reinforcements will amount to no more than a small force of three or four thousand men. If the greater part of the Oda army was to turn toward Hamamatsu, the Asai and Asakura, whom I have already contacted, would strike Nobunaga from the rear. Furthermore, the shogun in Kyoto would send messages to the warrior-monks and their allies, urging them on. The Oda are not a major worry for us."

He stopped for a moment and then went on calmly, "Entering Kyoto has been my fervent desire from the very beginning. But if we just bypassed Ieyasu now, when we got to Gifu, Ieyasu would come to the aid of the Oda by obstructing our rear. Isn't the best policy to smash Ieyasu at Hamamatsu Castle, before the Oda can send him sufficient reinforcements?"

There was nothing the generals could do but accept his decision, not just because he was their lord but because they had faith in him as a superior tactician.

As they returned to their regiments, however, there was one among them, Yamagata Masakage, who thought as he looked up at the cold, pale winter sun, This man lives for war, and he has an uncommon genius as a general, but this time...

It was the night of the twenty-first when the report of the sudden change in direction of the Kai army arrived at Hamamatsu Castle. Just three thousand men under Takigawa Kazumasu and Sakuma Nobumori had arrived at the castle as reinforcements from Nobunaga.

"A miserably small number," a Tokugawa retainer said, disappointed, but Ieyasu displayed neither joy nor dissatisfaction. And as the reports came in one after another, a war council began, at which many of the castle's generals and the Oda commanders prudently recommended a temporary retreat to Okazaki.

Ieyasu alone did not move from his former position of holding out for battle. "Are we going to retreat and not let one arrow fly in reprisal while the enemy insults my province?"

There was an elevated plain north of Hamamatsu, more than two leagues in breadth and three leagues in length—Mikatagahara.

In the early dawn of the twenty-second, Ieyasu's army left Hamamatsu and took a position north of an escarpment. There they waited for the approach of the Takeda forces.

The sun rose, then the sky clouded over. The silhouette of a single bird peacefully crossed the wide sky above the dry, wilted plain. From time to time the scouts of both armies, looking like the shadows of birds, crawled through the dry grass and then hurried back to their lines. That morning Shingen's army, which had previously camped on the plain, crossed the Tenryu River, continued marching, and arrived at Saigadani a little after noon.

An order went out to the entire army to halt. Oyamada Nobushige and the other generals collected at Shingen's side to ascertain the positions of the enemy that would soon be directly in front of them. After a momentary deliberation, Shingen ordered one company to be left behind as a rear guard, while the main army continued as planned across the plain of Mikatagahara.

Nearby was the village of Iwaibe. The vanguard of the army had already entered the village. The men at the head of this serpentine procession of well over twenty thousand men could not see the men at the rear of it, even if they stood in their stirrups.

Shingen turned and said to the retainers around him, "Something's going on at the rear!"

The men stared hard, trying to pierce the yellow dust rising in the distance. It seemed that the rear guard was under enemy attack.

"They must have been surrounded."

"They're only two or three thousand! If they're surrounded, they'll be wiped out."

The horses had lowered their heads and were moving off at a clatter—but the generals all sympathized with the men beneath the dust. Grasping their reins, they watched together uneasily. Shingen was silent, speaking to no one. Though it was what they had expected, their men were being struck down and falling one after another in the far-off cloud of dust, even as they looked on.

Some surely had a son, a father, or a brother in the rear guard. And not just among the retainers and generals that had gathered around Shingen. The whole army—right down to the foot soldiers—now looked to the side as they marched.

Riding up along the column, Oyamada Nobushige galloped to Shingen's side. Nobushige's voice was unusually excited and could clearly be heard by those nearby as he spoke from horseback: "My lord! We'll never have an opportunity like this again to massacre ten thousand of the enemy. I've just come from reconnoitering the enemy formation attacking our rear guard. Each company is spread out in a stork-wing formation. At a glance, it looks like a huge army, but the second and third ranks have no depth at all, and Ieyasu's center is protected by a small force hardly amounting to anything. Not only that, but the companies are in extreme disorder, and it's clear that the Oda reinforcements have no will to fight. If you'll take this opportunity and attack, my lord, you are bound to win."

As Nobushige blurted this out, Shingen looked back and then ordered some scouts to verify Nobushige's report.

Hearing the tone of Shingen's voice, Nobushige reined in his horse a little and held himself in check.

The two scouts galloped away. It was known that the enemy force was much smaller than their own, and Nobushige respected Shingen's refusal to make unconsidered movements, but he himself had the impatience of an unruly horse stamping at the ground and he was almost unable to restrain himself.

A military opportunity can disappear in the instant it takes lightning to strike!

The two scouts returned at a gallop and made their report: "Oyamada Nobushige's observations and our own reconnaissance are in complete agreement. This is an opportunity sent by heaven."

Shingen's voice boomed out. The white mane of his helmet shook back and forth as he gave out commands to the generals on his right and left. The conch rang out. When the twenty thousand men heard its sound, as it reverberated from the vanguard to the rear of the army, the marching line broke up with a pounding of the earth. And just as it appeared to be breaking up completely, it re-formed into a fish-scale formation and marched toward the Tokugawa army to the beating of drums.

Ieyasu was overawed when he saw the speed with which Shingen's army was moving, and how it responded to his every command. He said, "If I ever reach Shingen's age, just once I'd like to be able to move a large army as skillfully as he does. Having seen his style of command, I wouldn't want him killed, even if someone offered to poison him right now."

Shingen's ability to command impressed even the generals of the enemy to that extent. Battles were his art. His brave generals and intrepid warriors decorated their horses, armor, and banners to achieve a more glorious passage to the next world. It was almost as though tens of thousands of hawks had been released at once from Shingen's fist.

In a single breath, they dashed close enough to see the enemies' faces. The Tokugawa turned like a huge wheel, holding their stork-wing formation, and faced the enemy like a human dam.

The dust raised by the two armies darkened the sky. Only the spears shining in the setting sun glittered in the darkness. The spear corps of Kai and that of Mikawa had advanced to the front and now stood facing each other. When either side raised a war cry, the other side answered—almost as an echo. When the clouds of dust began to settle, the two sides could clearly see each other, but the distance that separated them was still considerable. No one would take a step out from the twin lines of spears.

At a time like this, even the bravest warriors shook with fear. One could say they were "scared," but this was completely different from ordinary fear. It was not that their wills were shaken; when they trembled, it was because they were making the change from everyday life to the life of battle. This took only seconds, but in that instant a man's skin turned to gooseflesh as purple as a rooster's comb.

For a province at war, the life of a soldier was no different from that of the farmer carrying the hoe or the weaver at his loom. Each was equally valuable, and if the province should fall, all would perish with it. Those who nevertheless ignored the rise and fall of their province and led lives of sloth were just like the dirt that clings to the human body—of less value than a single eyelash.

All of that aside, it was said that the instant of meeting the enemy face to face was terrifying. Heaven and earth were dark even at noon; You could not see what was right before your eyes, you could not go forward or retreat, and you were only jostled and shoved around on a line of readied spearheads.

And the man who was brave enough to step out from this line before all the others was granted the title of the First Spear. The man who became the First Spear won glory in front of the thousands of warriors of both armies. That first step, however, was not so easily taken.

Then one man stepped forward.

"Kato Kuroji of the Tokugawa clan is the First Spear!" a samurai shouted out. Kato's armor was plain and his name unknown; he was most likely a common samurai of the Tokugawa clan.

A second man dashed from the Tokugawa ranks.

"Kuroji's younger brother, Genjiro, is the Second Spear!"

The older brother was swallowed by the enemy and disappeared into the confusion.

"I'm the Second Spear! I'm Kato Kuroji's younger brother! Take a good look, you Takeda insects!" Genjiro brandished his spear at the mass of warriors four or five times.

A Kai soldier, turning to meet him, yelled an insult and leaped forward to strike. Genjiro fell backward, but grabbed the spear that had slipped across the breastplate of his armor and jumped to his feet with a curse.

By that time his comrades had pushed their way through, but the Takeda had also turned and now came charging toward them. The scene was like billowing waves of blood, spears, and armor crashing into one other. Trampled by his own comrades and the horses' hooves, Genjiro screamed for his brother. Crawling on his hands and knees, however, he grabbed a Kai soldier by the foot and brought him down. He immediately cut off the man's head and threw it away. After that, no one saw him again.

The battle erupted in total confusion. But the clash between the right wing of the Tokugawa and the left wing of the Takeda had not reached this pitch of violence.

The lines were spread out over a wide area. The droning of the drums and the sound of the conch shells rang within the dust clouds. Somehow, Shingen's retainers seemed to be situated to the rear. Neither army had the time to send their gunners to the front, so the Takeda sent the Mizumata—lightly armored samurai armed with stone slings—to the front line. The stones they shot fell like rain. Facing them were the forces of Sakai Tadatsugu, and behind them the reinforcements from the Oda clan. Tadatsugu was on horseback, clicking his tongue in annoyance.

The stones raining down on them from the front line of the Kai army were hitting his horse and making it go wild. And not only his horse. The horses of the mounted men who were waiting for their chance behind the spearmen reared and became so panicked that they broke formation.

The spearmen waited for orders from Tadatsugu, who had been holding them back with hoarse cries: "Not yet! Wait until I give the word!"

The slingers on the front line of the enemy had played the part of army sappers opening up an avenue of attack for the main force. Therefore, although the Mizumata corps was not particularly fearsome, the hand-picked troops behind them were waiting for their chance. Here were the banners of the Yamagata, Naito, and Oyamada corps, famed for their valor even within the Kai army.

It looks as though they're trying to provoke us by sending in the Mizumata, Tadatsugu thought. He could see through the enemy's strategy, but the left wing of the Tokugawa troops was already engaged in hand-to-hand combat, so the second line of the Oda was on its own. Furthermore, he couldn't be sure how Ieyasu was viewing this from his position in the center.

"Charge!" Tadatsugu yelled, opening his mouth almost wide enough to snap the cords of his helmet. He knew full well that he was falling into the enemy's trap, but he had been unable to gain the advantage since the beginning of the battle. The defeat of the Tokugawa and their allies began here.

The shower of rocks suddenly stopped. At the same moment the seven or eight hundred Mizumata broke off to the right and left and abruptly fell back.

"We're done for!" Tadatsugu yelled.

By the time he had seen the second line of the enemy, it was already too late. Lying concealed between the slingers and the cavalry was yet another line of men: the gunners. Each man was lying on his stomach in the tall grass, his gun at the ready.

There was a staccato clatter of musket fire as all the guns went off in a single volley, and a cloud of smoke rose from the grass. Because the angle of fire was low, many of the charging men of the Sakai corps were hit in the legs. The startled horses reared and were hit in the belly. Officers leaped from the saddle before their horses fell, and ran with their men, stepping over the corpses of their comrades.

"Fall back!" the commander of the Takeda gunners ordered.

The gunners immediately withdrew. To stay where they were would have meant being overrun by the charging Oda spearmen. With the muzzles of their horses in line, the Yamagata corps, the flower of Kai, galloped out with composure and dignity, followed immediately by the Obata corps. In minutes they had annihilated Sakai Tadatsugu's line.

Victory cries were raised proudly from the Kai army, when just as suddenly the Oyamada corps took a roundabout route and advanced on the flank of the Oda forces—second line of the Tokugawa defense—their horses raising the dust as they came. In the twinkling of an eye the Tokugawa were surrounded by the huge Kai army, as though by an iron wheel.

Ieyasu stood on a knoll and looked over at the lines of his men. We've lost, he said to himself. It was inevitable.

Gazing fixedly ahead, Torii Tadahiro, the ranking general of the Tokugawa under Ieyasu, had warned his lord not to advance, but rather to send out incendiary raids where the enemy would be bivouacking that night. But Shingen, ever the crafty enemy, had purposefully thrown out the bait with the small rear guard, and encouraged Ieyasu's attack.

"We can't just sit here. You must retreat to Hamamatsu," Tadahiro urged. "The faster you withdraw, the better."

Ieyasu said nothing.

"My lord! My lord!" Tadahiro pleaded.

Ieyasu was not looking at Tadahiro's face. As the sun set the white evening mist and the darkness were gradually becoming deeply divided at the edge of Mikatagahara. Riding the wintry wind, the banners of the messengers repeatedly brought in the sad news:

"Sakuma Nobumori of the Oda clan was crushed. Takigawa Kazumasu fell back in disorder, and Hirate Nagamasa was killed. Only Sakai Tadatsugu stands fast in hard fighting."

"Takeda Katsuyori combined his strength with the Yamagata corps and surrounded our left wing. Ishikawa Kazumasa was wounded, and Nakane Masateru and Aoki Hiro-tsugu are both dead."

"Matsudaira Yasuzumi galloped into the midst of the enemy and was cut down."

"The forces of Honda Tadamasa and Naruse Masayoshi aimed for Shingen's retainers and cut deeply into the enemy, but they were completely surrounded by several thousand men, and not one returned alive."

Suddenly, Tadahiro grabbed Ieyasu's arm and, with the help of other generals, pushed him up onto his horse.

"Get out of here!" he yelled at the horse, slapping it on the rump.

When Ieyasu was in the saddle and his horse was galloping away, Tadahiro and the other retainers mounted and went after him.

Snow began to fall. Perhaps it had been waiting for the sun to set. As the wind blew the snow thick and fast, it swept around the banners, men, and horses of the defeated army, making their way even less sure.

The men shouted out in confusion, "His Lordship...where is His Lordship?"

"Which way to headquarters?"

"Where is my regiment?"

The Kai gunners took aim at the fleeing men lost by the roadside, and fired volleys at them from the midst of the swirling snow.

"Retreat!" a Tokugawa soldier shouted. "The conch shell is sounding a withdrawal!"

"They must already have evacuated the headquarters," another rejoined.

A tidal wave of defeated men swept along in a black line toward the north, lost its way toward the west, and suffered many more casualties. Finally the men began to stampede in one direction, toward the south.

Ieyasu, who had just escaped from danger with Torii Tadahiro, looked back at the men following along behind, and suddenly stopped his horse. "Raise the banners. Raise the banners and assemble the men," he commanded.

Night was approaching fast, and the snow was steadily increasing. Ieyasu's retainers gathered around him and sounded the conch shell. Waving the commanders' standards, they called the men in. Gradually the men of the defeated army gathered around them. Every man was soaked in blood.

The corps of Baba Nobufusa and Obata Kazusa of the Kai army, however, knew that the main body of enemy troops was there, and very quickly began pressing in on them with bows and arrows from one side and guns from the other. It appeared that they would try to cut off their retreat.

"It's dangerous here, my lord. You'd better retreat as quickly as possible," Mizuno Sakon urged Ieyasu. Then, turning to the men, he announced, "Protect His Lordship. I am going to take a few men and attack the enemy. Anyone who wants to sacrifice his life for His Lordship, follow me."

Sakon galloped straight for the enemy line, without a look back to see whether anyone was following him. Thirty or forty soldiers followed after him, riding to certain death. Almost immediately, wailing, shouting, and the clash of swords and spears mingled with the moaning of the wind-borne snow and blurred into a vortex.

"Sakon must not die!" Ieyasu shouted. He was not his normal self at all. His retainers tried to stop him by grabbing the bridle of his horse, but he threw them off, and by the time they got up, he was already riding fast into the black and white vortex, looking exactly like a demon.

"My lord! My lord!" they yelled.

When Natsume Jirozaemon, the officer left in charge of Hamamatsu Castle, heard of the defeat of his comrades, he set out with a small force of thirty mounted men to ensure the safety of Ieyasu. Arriving at this point and finding his lord in the midst of a desperate fight, he jumped off his horse and ran toward the melee, shifting his spear to his left hand.

"Wha–what is this? This violence is not like you, my lord. Go back to Hamamatsu! Withdraw, my lord!" Grasping the horse's muzzle, he pulled it around with difficulty.

"Jirozaemon? Let me go! Are you fool enough to get in my way in the middle of the enemy?"

"If I'm a fool, my lord, you're an even bigger one! If you're cut down in a place like this, what good will all of our hardships have been until now? You'll be remembered as a fool of a general. If you want to distinguish yourself, then do something important for the nation on another day!" With tears in his eyes, Jirozaemon yelled at Ieyasu so loudly that his mouth almost split to his ears, and at the same time he beat Ieyasu's horse unmercifully with his spear. Of the retainers and close attendants who had been with Ieyasu the night before, there were many whose faces were no longer seen this evening. More than three hundred of Ieyasu's men had died in battle, and no one knew how many had been wounded.

Bearing the onus of belonging to a disastrously defeated army, the men filed back to the snow-covered castle town, looking as though they were disgusted with themselves. The retreat went on from evening until after midnight.

The sky had turned red, perhaps because there were bonfires at each of the castle gates. But the red color of the fallen snow was clearly from the blood of the returning warriors.

"What happened to His Lordship?" the men asked in tears. They had retreated thinking that Ieyasu had already returned to the castle, and were now told by the guards that he had not yet returned. Was he still surrounded by the enemy or had he been killed? Whichever it was, they had fled before their lord, and they were so ashamed that they refused to enter the castle. They simply stood outside, stamping their feet in the cold.

Adding to the confusion, gunfire was suddenly heard from beyond the western gate. It was the enemy. Death was pressing in on them. And if the Takeda had already come this far, Ieyasu's fate was truly in doubt.

Thinking that the end had come for the Tokugawa clan, they ran with a shout toward the sound of the guns, prepared to die in battle, their eyes devoid of any hope. As a group of them jostled through the gate, they nearly collided with several mounted men galloping in.

Beyond all expectation, the riders were their own commanders returning from battle, and the soldiers turned their pathetic cries into shouts of welcome, waving their swords and spears and leading the men inside. One rider, then another, and then yet another galloped in; the eighth was Ieyasu, one sleeve of his armor torn, and his body covered with blood and snow.

"It's Lord Ieyasu! Lord Ieyasu!"

As soon as they saw him, the word went from mouth to mouth, and the men leaped in the air, completely forgetting themselves.

Striding into the keep, Ieyasu yelled out in a loud voice, "Hisano! Hisano!" as if he were still on the battlefield.

The lady-in-waiting hurried toward him and prostrated herself. The flame on the small lamp she carried guttered in the wind, casting flickering light on Ieyasu's profile. There was blood on his cheek, and his hair was in appalling disarray.

"Bring a comb," he said, sitting down heavily. While Hisano arranged his hair, he gave her another order: "I'm hungry. Bring me something to eat."

When the food was brought in, he immediately picked up his chopsticks, but instead of eating he said, "Open up all the doors to the veranda."

Even with the lamps flickering, the room was brighter when the doors were wide open, because of the snow outside. Dark groups of warriors were resting on the veranda. As soon as Ieyasu had finished his meal, he left the keep and went around checking the castle's defenses. He ordered Amano Yasukage and Uemura Masakatsu to guard against an attack, and positioned the other commanders all the way from the main gate to the main entrance of the keep.

"Even if the entire Kai army attacks with all its strength, we're going to show them our own force of arms. They're not going to take possession of even one inch of these stone walls," they boasted.

Even if their voices were strained, their aim was to put Ieyasu at ease and to give him encouragement.

Ieyasu understood their intentions and nodded vigorously, but just as they were ready to run off to their posts, he called them back: "Don't close any of the castle gates from the main gate to the keep. Leave them all open. Do you understand?"

"What? What are you saying, my lord?" The commanders were hesitant. This order conflicted with the basic tenets of defense. The iron doors of all the gates had been shut. The enemy army was already closing in on the castle town, as it bore down to destroy them. Why would he order them to open the floodgates of the dike, just when a tidal wave was at hand?

378   Tadahiro said, "No, I don't think the situation warrants going that far. When our

retreating troops arrive, we can open the gates and let them in. Certainly we don't need to leave the castle gates wide open for them."

Ieyasu laughed and admonished him for misunderstanding. "This is not for the men who are returning late. It's in preparation for the Takeda who are coming in like an arrogant tide, sure of their victory. And I don't just want the castle gates opened; I want five or six large bonfires lit in front of the entrance. You should also build some bonfires inside the castle walls. But make sure the defense is strictly in order. Be very quiet and watch for the enemy's approach."

What sort of fearless counter-strategy was this? But without the slightest hesitation, they did as he ordered.

According to Ieyasu's wishes, the castle gates were opened wide, and blazing bonfires cast their reflections in the snow from beyond the moat to the entrance of the keep. After gazing at the scene for a moment, Ieyasu once again went inside.

It appeared that the senior generals understood, but the soldiers in the castle for the most part seemed to believe the rumor spread by Ieyasu's own officer that Shingen was dead, and that the advancing enemy had lost its foremost general.

"I'm tired, Hisano. I think I'll have a cup of *sake*. Pour one for me, please." Ieyasu returned to the main hall and, after draining a cup, lay down. He pulled up the bedding that Hisano had put over him and then went to sleep with a snore.

Not much later, the troops of Baba Nobufusa and Yamagata Masakage poured in near the moat, in readiness for a night attack.

"What's this? Wait!" When Baba and Yamagata drew up in front of the castle gate, they reined in their horses and stopped the entire army from running hastily ahead.

"General Baba, what do you think?" Yamagata asked, drawing his horse up next to his colleague. He seemed to be totally puzzled. Baba had his doubts as well and looked out toward the enemy's gate. There, burning in the distance, were the bonfires, both before and within the castle gate. And the iron doors were wide open. It was gateless, and yet there was a gate. The situation seemed to pose a disturbing question.

The water in the moat was black, the snow on the fully manned castle was white. Not a sound could be heard. If the men listened very carefully, they could hear the crackling sound of the firewood in the distance. And if they had concentrated both mind and ears, they might have heard the snores of Ieyasu, the defeated general, as he dreamed—the very heart of this gateless gate—inside the keep.

Yamagata said, "I think our pursuit was so fast and the enemy has become so confused that they've had no time to close the castle gate and are lying low. We should attack at once."

"No, wait," Baba interrupted. He had a reputation as one of the cleverest tacticians in Shingen's army. A wise man who cultivates wisdom may sometimes drown in it. He explained to Yamagata why his plan was wrong.

"To have secured the castle gates would have been the natural psychology of defeat in this case. But leaving the castle wide open and taking the time to build bonfires is proof of the man's fearlessness and composure. If you think about it, he's undoubtedly waiting for us to attack rashly. He's concentrating on this one castle and is fully confident of his victory. Our opponent is a young general, but he is Tokugawa Ieyasu. We shouldn't step in carelessly, only to bring shame on the martial reputation of the Takeda and be laughed at later."

They had pressed that far, but in the end, both generals pulled their men back.

Inside, when Ieyasu heard his attendant's voice penetrating his sleep, he leaped up with a start. "I'm not dead!" he shouted, and jumped for joy. He immediately sent troops in pursuit. As might be expected of them, Yamagata and Baba did not lose their heads in the confusion, but rather threw up a resistance, set fires in the neighborhood of Naguri, and executed several brilliant maneuvers.

The Tokugawa had suffered a grave defeat, but it might be said that they had shown their mettle. Not only that, but they had once again caused Shingen to abandon his march to the capital and left him with no other choice than to withdraw to Kai. Many men had been sacrificed. Compared with the four hundred men of the Takeda, the dead and wounded on the Tokugawa side numbered as many as eleven hundred eighty.

Funeral for the Living

Red and white petals fluttered down from Gifu Castle on its high mountain peak, and fell on the roofs in the town below.

Year by year, the people's confidence in Nobunaga increased—a confidence that grew from the security of their lives. The laws were strict, but Nobunaga's words were not empty. The things he promised concerning the people's livelihood were always put into effect, and this was reflected in their wealth.

> To think that a man
> Has but fifty years to live under heaven.
> Surely this world
> Seems but a vain dream....

The people of the province knew the verses Nobunaga loved to chant when he drank. But he understood these words quite differently from the way the monks did—that the world was nothing more than a fleeting and impermanent dream. "Is there anything that will not decay?" was his favorite line, and every time he sang it, he raised the pitch of his voice. His view of life seemed to be contained in this one line. A man would not make the most of his life if he did not think deeply about it. Nobunaga knew this about life: In the end, we die. For a man of thirty-seven, the future would not be a long one. And for such a short time, his ambition was extraordinarily large. His ideals were limitless, and facing these ideals and overcoming the obstacles fulfilled him completely. Man, however, has an allotted span of life, and he could not help his feelings of regret.

"Ranmaru, beat the drum."

He was going to dance today again. Earlier that day, he had entertained a messenger from Ise. He continued to drink through the afternoon.

Ranmaru brought the drum from the next room. Instead of playing it, however, he delivered a message: "Lord Hideyoshi has just arrived."

At one time it had seemed that the Asai and Asakura were going to make their move after Mikatagahara, as they had begun to wriggle and squirm repeatedly. But after Shingen had retreated, they cowered inside their own provinces and began to strengthen the defenses.

Anticipating peace, Hideyoshi had secretly left Yokoyama Castle and toured the area around the capital. None of the castle commanders anywhere, regardless of how chaotic the conditions of the country, remained locked up in their castles. Sometimes they would pretend to be gone but would really be there; at other times they would pretend to be there but would really be gone, for the way of a soldier lay in properly using the forms of truth and falsehood.

Of course, Hideyoshi had also traveled incognito on this trip, and quite likely that was also the reason he had arrived so suddenly at Gifu.

"Hideyoshi?" Nobunaga had him wait in another room, and soon came in and sat down. He was in an extraordinarily good mood.

Hideyoshi was dressed with extreme simplicity, looking no different from an ordinary traveler. In this attire he prostrated himself, but then looked up and laughed. "I'll bet you're surprised."

Nobunaga looked as though he didn't understand. "About what?" he asked.

"My sudden arrival."

"What kind of foolishness is this? I've known you were not in Yokoyama for the last two weeks."

"But you probably didn't expect me to show up here today."

Nobunaga laughed. "You think I'm blind, don't you? You probably got tired of playing around with the prostitutes in the capital, came down the Omi Road as far as some rich man's house in Nagahama, secretly called Oyu, and came here after a rendezvous."

Hideyoshi mumbled a reply.

"*You're* the one who's probably surprised," Nobunaga said.

"I am surprised, my lord. You see everything."

"This mountain is high enough for me to look out over ten provinces at least. But there's someone who knows your behavior in even more detail than I do. Do you have any idea who that is?"

"You must have a spy trailing me."

"Your wife."

"You're joking! Aren't you a little intoxicated today, my lord?"

"I may be drunk, but I'm hardly mistaken about what I'm saying. Your wife may be living at Sunomata, but if you think she's far away, you're making a serious mistake."

"Oh, no. Well, I've come at a bad time. With your permission, I—"

"You can't be blamed for playing around," Nobunaga said, laughing. "There's nothing at all wrong with looking at the cherry blossoms from time to time. But why don't you call Nene, and the two of you get together?"

"Of course."

"It's been a while since you've seen her, hasn't it?"

"Has my wife been bothering you with letters or the like?"

"Don't worry. There hasn't been anything like that, but I sympathize. And not just with your wife. Every wife has to look after the home while her husband is away at war, so even if he has only a little bit of time, a man should show his wife before anyone else that he's all right."

"As you wish, but…"

"Do you refuse?"

"I do. There's been nothing untoward for a number of months, but my state of mind has not moved away from the battlefield by even a hair's breadth."

"Always the clever talker! Are you going to start wagging that tongue again? It's quite unnecessary."

"I'll retire, my lord. I'm rolling up my banners here."

Lord and retainer laughed together. After a while they started drinking and even sent Ranmaru away. Then the talk turned to a topic serious enough for them to lower their voices.

Nobunaga asked expectantly, "So how are things in the capital? I have messengers constantly going back and forth, but I want to hear what you have seen."

What Hideyoshi was about to say seemed to have to do with his expectations.

"Our seats are a little far apart. Either my lord or I should move a little closer for this."

"I'll move." Nobunaga took the *sake* flask and his cup and moved down from the seat of honor. "Close the sliding doors to the next room too," he ordered.

Hideyoshi sat down directly in front of Nobunaga and said, "The conditions are the same as ever. Except that, since Shingen failed to reach the capital, the shogun seems to have become more despondent. His schemes have become openly hostile to you, my lord."

"Well, I can imagine. After all, Shingen got as far as Mikatagahara, and then the shogun heard that he had withdrawn."

"Shogun Yoshiaki is a crafty politician. He fidgets about, bestowing favors on the people, and indirectly makes them fear you. He's made good propaganda out of the burning of Mount Hiei, and seems to be inciting other religious groups to rebellion."

"Not a pleasant set of circumstances."

"But it's not worth worrying about. The warrior-monks have seen what happened to Mount Hiei, and it has cooled their courage considerably."

"Hosokawa is in the capital. Did you see him?"

"Lord Hosokawa has fallen out of favor with the shogun and has confined himself to his country estate."

"He was driven away by Yoshiaki?" Nobunaga asked.

"It seems that Lord Hosokawa thought that allying with you would be the best way to preserve the shogunate. He risked his own reputation and advised Lord Yoshiaki several times."

"It's apparent that Yoshiaki won't listen to anyone."

"More than that, he's taking a rather extravagant view of the remaining powers of the shogunate. In a period of transition, a cataclysm separates past and future. Almost all of those who perish are those who, because of their blind attachment to the past, fail to realize that the world has changed."

"Are we living through such a cataclysm?"

"In fact a very dramatic event has just occurred. Word was just sent to me, but—"

"What kind of dramatic event?"

"Well! This has still not leaked out to the world, but since it was heard by the keen ears of my agent Watanabe Tenzo, I think that it can perhaps be believed."

"What is it?"

"It's incredible, but the guiding star of Kai may have finally set."

"What! Shingen?"

"During the Second Month, he attacked Mikawa, and one night while he was laying siege to Noda Castle, he was shot. This is what Tenzo heard."

For a moment, Nobunaga's eyes widened and he looked straight at Hideyoshi's face. If it was true that Shingen was dead, the course of the nation was going to change very quickly. Nobunaga felt as though the tiger at his back had suddenly disappeared, and he was shocked. He wanted to believe this story, but at the same time he could not. As soon as he heard the news, he felt an incredible surge of relief, and an indescribable joy welled up inside of him.

"If this is true, a very gifted general has left this world," Nobunaga said. "And from now on history has been entrusted into our hands." His expression was not nearly as complex as Hideyoshi's. In fact, he looked as though he had just been served the main course at a meal.

"He was shot, but I still have no idea whether he died immediately, what were the extent of his wounds, or where he was hit. But I've heard that when they suddenly lifted the siege of Noda Castle and withdrew into Kai, they did not display the usual Takeda fighting spirit."

"I suspect not. But it doesn't matter how fierce the Kai samurai are, if they have lost Shingen."

"I received this report secretly from Tenzo on my way here, so I immediately sent him back to Kai to get confirmation."

"Has no one heard this yet in the other provinces?"

"There are no indications that anyone has. The Takeda clan will probably keep it a secret, and will make it appear that Shingen is in good health. So if some policy is promulgated in Shingen's name, the chances are nine out of ten that Shingen is dead, or at least in a serious condition."

Nobunaga nodded thoughtfully. He seemed to want to confirm this story. Suddenly he took the cup of cold *sake*, and sighed. *To think that a man has but fifty years....* But he did not feel like dancing. Reflecting on another man's death moved him far more than reflecting on his own.

"When will Tenzo return?"

"He should be back within three days."

"To Yokoyama Castle?"

"No, I told him to come straight here."

"Well then, stay here until then."

"I had planned on doing that, but if I could, I'd like to wait for your orders at an inn in the castle town."

"Why?"

"No particular reason."

"Well, how about staying in the castle? Keep me company for a while."

"Well…"

"What a dullard! Do you feel constrained to be at my side?"

"No, the truth is…"

"The truth is what?"

"I left a…companion in that inn in the castle town, and since I imagined it would be lonely there, I promised I would go back tonight."

"Is this companion a woman?" Nobunaga was dumbfounded. The emotions that the report of Shingen's death aroused in him were so far removed from Hideyoshi's worries.

"Go to the inn tonight, but come back to the castle tomorrow. You can bring your 'companion' with you." These were Nobunaga's last words to him as he turned to go.

He had hit the nail right on the head, Hideyoshi thought on his way back to the inn. He felt as though he had been reprimanded, but this was, again, Nobunaga's grace. He was wrapping the head of the nail in an artistic decoration without the nail even noticing. The following day he went up to the castle with Oyu, but it did not cause him any embarrassment.

Nobunaga had moved to a different room and, unlike the day before, was not surrounded by the smell of *sake*. Sitting in front of Hideyoshi and Oyu, he looked down at them from a dais.

"Aren't you Takenaka Hanbei's sister?" he asked familiarly.

This was the first time Oyu had met Nobunaga, and here she was with Hideyoshi. She hid her face and would have liked to have sunk through the floor, but she answered with a faint voice that was a thing of beauty.

"I am honored to make your acquaintance, my lord. You have also favored my other brother, Shigeharu."

Nobunaga gazed at her, impressed. He had felt like teasing Hideyoshi a little, but now he felt guilty and became serious.

"Has Hanbei's health improved?"

"I haven't seen my brother for some time, my lord. He's busy with his military duties, but I do receive letters from time to time."

"Where are you living now?"

"At Choteiken Castle in Fuwa, where I have a slight connection."

"I wonder if Watanabe Tenzo has returned yet," Hideyoshi said, trying to change the subject, but Nobunaga was an old fox and was not going to be taken in.

"What are you saying? You're getting confused. Didn't you yourself just tell me that Tenzo wouldn't return for another three days?"

Hideyoshi's face turned bright red. Nobunaga seemed to be satisfied with this. He had wanted to see him look self-conscious and troubled for a while.

Nobunaga invited Oyu to the evening's drinking party, and commented, "You haven't seen my dancing, although Hideyoshi has seen it on several occasions."

When Oyu asked to take her leave later that evening, Nobunaga did not insist on her staying, but he said bluntly to Hideyoshi, "Well then, you go too."

The couple left the castle. Soon, however, Hideyoshi returned alone somewhat flustered.

"Where is Lord Nobunaga?" he asked a page.

"He has just now retired to his bedroom."

Hearing this, Hideyoshi hurried to the private apartments with an unusual lack of composure and asked the samurai attendant to convey a message.

"I must have an audience with His Lordship this evening."

Nobunaga had not yet gone to sleep, and as soon as Hideyoshi was ushered into his presence, he asked for everyone to leave the room, but although the men on night watch withdrew, Hideyoshi still looked around the room nervously.

"What is it, Hideyoshi?"

"Well, it seems there's still someone in the next room."

"It's no one to be worried about. It's just Ranmaru. He should be no problem."

"He is also a problem. I'm sorry to ask, but..."

"He should go too?"

"Yes."

"Ranmaru, you leave too." Nobunaga turned and spoke toward the next room.

Ranmaru bowed silently, got up, and left.

"It should be all right now. What is this?"

"The fact is that when I took my leave and went back to town just now, I ran into Tenzo."

"What! Tenzo's back?"

"He said that he hurried across the mountains to get here, hardly knowing day from night. Shingen's death is a certainty."

"So...after all."

"I can't give you many details, but the inner circle in Kai seems to have put on a façade of normality, beneath which a melancholy air can clearly be detected."

"Their mourning is being kept a strict secret, I'll bet."

"Of course."

"And the other provinces know nothing?"

"So far."

"So, now's the time. I assume you forbade Tenzo to speak about this."

"That's not something you have to worry about."

"But there are some unscrupulous men among the ninja. Are you sure about him?"

"He's Hikoemon's nephew, and he is loyal."

"Well, we should be extremely cautious. Give him a reward, but keep him inside the castle. It would probably be better to imprison him until this is all over."

"No, my lord."

"Why not?"

"Because if we treat a man like that, the next time the opportunity comes up, he won't feel like jeopardizing his life as he did this time. And if you cannot trust a man, but give him a reward, he might be tempted with a lot of money by the enemy someday."

"Well, then, where did you leave him?"

"As luck would have it, Oyu was just about to return to Fuwa, so I ordered him to go along as a guard for her palanquin."

"The man risked his life coming back from Kai, and you immediately ordered him to accompany your mistress? Isn't Tenzo going to resent that?"

"He went along with her happily. I may be a foolish master, but he knows me very well."

"You seem to employ people a little differently than I do."

"You can be doubly at ease, my lord. She may be a woman, but if it appears that Tenzo is about to spill any secrets to anyone, she'll protect our interests, even if she has to kill him."

"Put away your self-congratulations."

"Sorry. You what I'm like."

"That's not the point," Nobunaga said. "The Tiger of Kai has died, so we can't delay. We've got to move before Shingen's death is known by the world at large. Hideyoshi, leave tonight and hurry back to Yokoyama."

"I had planned to do that immediately, so I sent Oyu back to Fuwa, and—"

"Forget the rest. I've hardly got time to sleep. We're going to mobilize at daybreak."

Nobunaga's thoughts were perfectly in line with Hideyoshi's. The opportunity they had always sought—the time to finish up a former problem—was now at hand. The problem being, of course, the liquidation of the troublesome shogun and the old order.

Needless to say, as Nobunaga was an actor in the new age that was about to replace the old, his advance was quickly realized. On the twenty-second day of the Third Month, his army thundered out of Gifu. When it arrived at the shores of Lake Biwa, the army split into two. One half of the army was under the command of Nobunaga. He boarded ship and sailed across the lake to the west. The remaining half, composed of the troops led by Katsuie, Mitsuhide, and Hachiya, took the land route and advanced along the southern edge of the lake.

The land army ousted the anti-Nobunaga forces made up of the warrior-monks in the area between Katada and Ishiyama, and destroyed the fortifications that had been erected along the road.

The shogun's advisers quickly held a conference.

"Shall we resist?"

"Shall we sue for peace?"

These men had a big problem: they had not yet given a clear answer to the seventeen-article document that Nobunaga had sent to Yoshiaki on New Year's Day. In it, Nobunaga had itemized all his grievances against Yoshiaki.

"What audacity! I am the shogun, after all!" Yoshiaki had said angrily, conveniently forgetting that it was Nobunaga who had protected him and returned him to Nijo Palace. "Why should I submit to a nonentity like Nobunaga?"

Messengers had come from Nobunaga one after another to work out peace terms, but had withdrawn without being granted audiences. Then, as a sort of response, the shogun had barricades erected on the roads that led to the capital.

The opportunity that Nobunaga had been waiting for and that Hideyoshi had been planning against was the arrival of the appropriate moment for reproving Yoshiaki for his lack of response to the Seventeen Articles. That opportunity had come sooner than either of them had imagined—hastened by Shingen's death.

In any period of history, a man on his way to ruin always holds on to the ludicrous illusion that he is not the one about to fall. Yoshiaki fell straight into that trap.

Nobunaga saw him in yet another way, saying, "We can use him, too." Thus he was handled with delicate disrespect. But the members of the worthless shogunate of this period did not know their own value, and no matter what the subject of their thoughts, intellectually speaking, their understanding did not go beyond the past. They saw only the narrow face of culture in the capital and believed that it prevailed throughout Japan. Entrusting themselves to the cramped policies of the past, they relied on the warrior-monks of the Honganji and on the many samurai warlords throughout the provinces who hated Nobunaga.

The shogun was still unaware of Shingen's death. And so he played tough. "I am the shogun, the pillar of the samurai class. I'm different from the monks on Mount Hiei. If Nobunaga were to aim his weapons at Nijo Palace, he would be branded a traitor."

His attitude indicated that he would not decline war if it was offered. Naturally, he called on the clans around the capital and sent urgent messages to the faraway Asai, the Asakura, the Uesugi, and the Takeda, setting up a showy defense.

When Nobunaga heard this, he turned toward the capital with a laugh and, without stopping his army for a single day, entered Osaka. The ones who were shocked this time were the warrior-monks of the Honganji. Suddenly face to face with Nobunaga's army, they had no idea what to do. But Nobunaga was content simply to line his men up in battle array.

"We can strike anytime we like," he said. At this point he wanted most strongly to avoid any unnecessary expenditure of military strength. And, until this time, he had repeatedly sent envoys to Kyoto asking for a response to the Seventeen Articles. So this was a sort of ultimatum. Yoshiaki took a highhanded view: he was shogun and he simply did not feel like listening to Nobunaga's opinions of his administration.

Among the Seventeen Articles, Yoshiaki was pressed quite firmly by two articles in particular. The first was concerned with the crime of disloyalty to the Emperor. The second article had to do with his disgraceful conduct. While it was his duty to maintain the peace of the Empire, he himself had incited the provinces to rebellion.

"It's useless. He'll never accept this kind of grilling—just written notes and messengers," Araki Murashige said to Nobunaga.

Hosokawa Fujitaka, who had also joined Nobunaga, added, "I suppose it's no use hoping that the shogun will wake up before his fall."

Nobunaga nodded. He seemed to understand only too well. But it would not be necessary to use the drastic violence here that he had employed at Mount Hiei; neither was he so poor in strategy that he would have to use the same method twice.

"Back to Kyoto!" Nobunaga had given this order on the fourth day of the Fourth Month, but it had seemed nothing more than an exercise to impress the masses with the size of his army.

"Look at that! He's not going to have them bivouac for very long. Just like the last time, Nobunaga's uneasy about Gifu and is hurriedly withdrawing his soldiers," Yoshiaki said, elated. With the reports that came to him one after another, however, his color began to change. For just as he was congratulating himself about the troops bypassing Kyoto, the Oda army flowed into the capital from the Osaka road. Then, without a single war cry and more peacefully than if they had been simply performing maneuvers, the soldiers surrounded Yoshiaki's residence.

"We're close to the Imperial Palace, so be careful not to disturb His Majesty. It will be enough to censure this impudent shogun's crimes," Nobunaga ordered.

There was no gunfire, and not even the hum of a single bowstring. It was uncanny, far more than if there had been a great commotion.

"Yamato, what do you think we should do? What is Nobunaga going to do to me?" Yoshiaki asked his senior adviser, Mibuchi Yamato.

"You're pitifully unprepared. At this point, do you still not understand what Nobunaga has in mind? He's clearly come to attack you."

"B-but... I'm the shogun!"

"These are troubled times. What good is a title going to do you? It appears that you have only two choices: either resolve to fight or sue for peace." As his retainer spoke these words, tears fell from his eyes. Along with Hosokawa Fujitaka, this honorable man had not left Yoshiaki's side since the days of his exile.

"I do not remain to protect my honor or to seek fame. Nor am I following a strategy for survival. I know what's going to happen tomorrow, but somehow I just can't abandon this fool of a shogun," Yamato had once said. Certainly he knew that Yoshiaki was hardly worth saving. He knew the world was changing, but he seemed resolved to stand his ground at Nijo Palace. He was already over fifty years old, a general past his prime.

"Sue for peace? Is there any good reason why I, the shogun, should beg someone like Nobunaga for peace?"

"You're so obsessed by the title of shogun that your only course is self-destruction."

"Don't you think we'll win, if we fight?"

"There's no reason why we should. It would be completely laughable if you put up a defense of this place with any thought of victory."

"Well then, w-why are you and the other generals dressed up in your armor so ostentatiously?"

"We think it would at least be a beautiful way to die. Even though the situation is hopeless, to make our final stand here will be a fitting end to fourteen generations of shoguns. That is the duty of a samurai, after all. It's really nothing more than arranging flowers at a funeral."

"Wait! Don't attack yet! Put down your guns."

Yoshiaki disappeared into the palace and consulted with Hino and Takaoka, two courtiers with whom he was on friendly terms. After noon, a messenger was secretly sent out of the palace by Hino. Following that, the governor of Kyoto came from the Oda side and, toward evening, Oda Nobuhiro appeared as a formal envoy from Nobunaga.

"Hereafter, I will carefully observe each of the articles," Yoshiaki assured the envoy. With a bitter look on his face, Yoshiaki pledged himself with words that were not in his heart. That day he begged for peace. Nobunaga's soldiers withdrew and peacefully returned to Gifu.

Only one hundred days later, however, Nobunaga's army once again surrounded Nijo Palace. And that was because, of course, Yoshiaki had fallen back on his old tricks once again after the first peace.

The great roof of the Myokaku Temple at Nijo was beaten desolately by the rains of the Seventh Month. The temple served as Nobunaga's headquarters. There had been a terrible wind and rain from the time his fleet had started across Lake Biwa. But this had only increased the determination of the troops. Soaked by the rain and covered in mud, they had surrounded the shogun's palace and were poised, waiting only for the command to attack.

No one knew if Yoshiaki was to be executed or taken prisoner, but his fate was entirely in their hands. Nobunaga's troops felt as though they were looking into the cage of a fierce, noble animal that they were about to slaughter.

The voices of Nobunaga and Hideyoshi drifted on the wind.

"What are you going to do?" Hideyoshi asked.

"At this point there are no two ways about it." Nobunaga was firm. "I'm not forgiving him this time."

"But he's the—"

"Don't belabor the obvious."

"Is there no margin for a little more deliberation?"

"None! Absolutely not!"

The room in the temple was gloomy from the darkening rain outside. The combination of the lingering summer heat and the long autumn rains had resulted in such humid weather that even the gold leaf of the Buddhas and the monochrome ink drawings on the sliding doors looked mildewed.

"I'm not criticizing you for being rash when I ask for a little more deliberation," Hideyoshi said. "But the position of shogun is granted by the Imperial Court, so we cannot treat the matter lightly. And it will give the anti-Nobunaga forces an excuse to call for justice against the man who killed his rightful lord, the shogun."

"I suppose you're right," Nobunaga replied.

"Happily, Yoshiaki is so weak that though he is trapped, he'll neither kill himself nor come out to fight. He's just going to lock up the gates of his palace and rely on the water in his moat to keep rising from all this rain."

"So, what is your plan?" Nobunaga asked.

"We purposely open one part of our encirclement and provide a way for the shogun to escape."

"Won't he become a nuisance in the future? He might be used to strengthen the ambitions of some other province."

"No," Hideyoshi said, "I think that people have gradually become disgusted with Yoshiaki's character. I suspect that they would understand even if Yoshiaki were driven from the capital, and they would be satisfied that your punishment was fitting."

That evening the besieging army created an opening and made an obvious display of a shortage of soldiers. Inside the palace, the shogun's men seemed to suspect that this was some sort of trick, and by midnight they had still made no move to leave. But during a lull in the rain near dawn, a corps of mounted men suddenly crossed the moat and fled from the capital.

When Nobunaga was told that it was certain that Yoshiaki had escaped, he addressed his troops. "The house is empty! There's not much benefit in attacking an empty house, but the shogunate that has lasted fourteen generations has brought about its own downfall. Attack and raise your victory cries! This will be the funeral service for the evil government of the Ashikaga shoguns."

The Nijo Palace was destroyed in one attack. Almost all the retainers in the palace surrendered. Even the two nobles, Hino and Takaoka, came out and apologized to Nobunaga. But one man, Mibuchi Yamato, and more than sixty of his retainers fought to the very end without submitting. Not one of them fled and not one of them yielded. All were cut down in battle and died gloriously as samurai.

Yoshiaki fled Kyoto and entrenched himself in Uji. Reckless as always, he had with him only a small defeated force. When, not long afterward, Nobunaga's troops closed in on his headquarters at the Byodoin Temple, Yoshiaki surrendered without a struggle.

"Everyone leave," Nobunaga ordered.

Nobunaga sat a little straighter and looked directly at Yoshiaki.

"I suppose you've not forgotten that you once said you thought of me as your father. It was a happy day when you were sitting in the palace I had rebuilt for you." Yoshiaki was silent. "Do you remember?"

"Lord Nobunaga, I have not forgotten. Why are you talking of those days now?"

"You're a coward, my lord. I'm not thinking of taking your life, even after things have come to this. Why are you still telling lies?"

"Forgive me. I was wrong."

"I'm happy to hear it. But you certainly are in trouble—even though you were born to the position of shogun."

"I want to die. Lord Nobunaga...I...won't you...assist me in committing *seppuku*?"

"Please stop!" Nobunaga laughed. "Excuse my rudeness, but I suspect you don't even know the proper way of cutting open your own stomach. I've never really felt inclined to hate you. It's just that you never stop playing with fire, and the sparks keep flying to other provinces."

"I understand now."

"Well, I think it might be better if you retired somewhere quietly. I'll keep your son and bring him up, so you won't need to worry about his future."

Yoshiaki was released and told that he was free to go—into exile.

Guarded by Hideyoshi, Yoshiaki's son was taken to Wakae Castle. This arrangement was really a case of malice rewarded with favor, but Yoshiaki took it with his usual jaundiced view and could only feel that his son had been politely taken hostage. Miyoshi Yoshitsugu was governor of Wakae Castle, and later Yoshiaki too found shelter with him.

391

Not wanting to play host to a bothersome, defeated aristocrat, however, Yoshitsugu soon made him feel uneasy, saying, "I think you're going to be in danger if you stay here much longer. Nobunaga could change his mind at the slightest provocation and have your head cut off."

Yoshiaki left in a hurry and went to Kii, where he tried to incite the warrior-monks of Kumano and Saiga to rebel, promising them grandiose favors in return for striking Nobunaga down. Using the name and dignity of his office, he did nothing more than bring down upon himself the derision and laughter of the people. It was rumored that he did not stay long in Kii, but soon crossed into Bizen and became a dependent of the Ukita clan.

And with this, a new era started. It could be said that the destruction of the shogunate was a sudden opening in the thick clouds that had covered the sky. Now a small portion of blue could be seen. There is nothing more frightening than a period of aimless national government administered by rulers in name only. The samurai ruled in every province, protecting their privileges; the clergy acquired wealth and strengthened its authority. The nobles were changed to mice in the Imperial Court, one day relying on the warriors, the next imploring the clergy, and then abusing the government for their own defense. Thus the Empire was sundered into four nations—the nation of priests, the nation of samurai, the nation of the court, and the nation of the shogunate—each of which fought its private wars.

The eyes of the people were opened wide at Nobunaga's actions. But even though they looked up at the deep blue sky, all the thick clouds had not yet dispersed. Nobody could guess what would happen next. During the past two or three years, several key men had passed away. Two years before both Mori Motonari, the lord of the largest domain in western Japan, and Hojo Ujiyasu, the master of eastern Japan, had died. But for Nobunaga these events did not carry nearly as great a significance as the death of Takeda Shingen and the exile of Yoshiaki. To Nobunaga, it was especially the death of Shingen—who had constantly threatened him from the north—that left him free to concentrate his strength in one direction, a direction that made more fighting and chaos almost inevitable. There was certainly no doubt that, after the demise of the shogunate, the warrior clans in every province would raise their banners and compete to be the first to enter the field.

"Nobunaga has burned down Mount Hiei and overthrown the shogun. Such lawlessness must be punished!" This would be their battle cry.

Nobunaga knew that he would have to steal the initiative and defeat his rivals before they were able to form an alliance against him. "Hideyoshi, you hurry back first. I'll probably come visit you at Yokoyama Castle soon."

"I'll be waiting for you." Hideyoshi seemed to have grasped the direction of events, and after accompanying Yoshiaki's son to Wakae, he quickly returned to his castle at Yokoyama.

It was the end of the Seventh Month when Nobunaga returned to Gifu. At the beginning of the next month, an urgent letter written in Hideyoshi's own poor hand arrived from Yokoyama: "The opportunity is ripe. Let's move!"

In the lingering heat of the Eighth Month, Nobunaga's army left Yanagase and crossed into Echizen. Opposing it was the army of Asakura Yoshikage of Ichijogadani. At the end of the Seventh Month, Yoshikage had received an urgent message from Odani, from Asai Hisamasa and his son, Nagamasa, his allies in northern Omi:

The Oda army is coming north. Send reinforcements quickly. If help is slow in coming, we will be lost.

There were those in the war councils who doubted that this could be true, but the Asai were allies, so ten thousand soldiers were hastily dispatched. And when this vanguard had marched as far as Mount Tagami, they realized that the Oda attack was a fact. Once the reality was understood, a rear guard of more than twenty thousand men was sent. Asakura Yoshikage considered the crisis grave enough to lead the army in person. Any fighting in northern Omi was obviously extremely alarming to the Asakura, because the Asai formed the first line of defense for their own province.

Both the Asai father and son were at Odani Castle; about three leagues away stood Yokoyama Castle, in which Hideyoshi had entrenched himself, keeping watch on the Asai like a hawk for Nobunaga.

By autumn, Nobunaga was already attacking the Asai. He struck Kinomoto in a surprise attack against the army of Echizen. Over two thousand eight hundred heads were taken by the Oda. They pressed on against the enemy, now fleeing from Yanagase, running them down and blackening the dry early-autumn grasses with blood.

The Echizen warriors lamented the weakness of their army. But the fierce generals and brave warriors who turned back to fight were struck down in battle. Why were they so weak? And why were they unable to strike at the Oda? In anyone's fall, there is an accumulation of factors, and natural collapse comes in an instant. But when this particular instant came, both ally and enemy wondered at its suddenness and magnitude. The rise and fall of provinces, however, are always based on natural phenomena, and here, too, there was really nothing miraculous or strange. The weakness of the Asakura could be understood simply by looking at the behavior of their commander-in-chief, Yoshikage. Caught in the stampede of his men fleeing from Yanagase, Yoshikage had already lost his head.

"It's all over! We can't even flee! Both my horse and I are exhausted. To the mountains!" he cried.

He had neither a plan for a counterattack nor any spirit left to fight. Thinking only of himself, he quickly abandoned his horse and tried to find a hiding place.

"What are you doing!" Scolding him with tears in his eyes, his chief retainer, Takuma Mimasaka, pulled him back by his sash, forced him onto his horse, and pushed him off toward Echizen. Then, standing his ground in order to give his lord time to escape, he took over a thousand soldiers and fought against the Oda army as long as he could.

It is hardly necessary to say that Takuma and all his men died, suffering a wretched and complete annihilation. While such loyal retainers were being sacrificed, Yoshikage shut himself up in his main castle at Ichijogadani. But he did not even have the spirit to put up a stubborn defense of the land of his ancestors.

Soon after his return to the castle, he took his wife and children and fled to a temple in the Ono district. He reasoned that if they had been inside the castle, when worst came to worst, he would have had no escape route. With their lord demonstrating such a lack of resolve, all of his generals and soldiers deserted.

Autumn was at its fullest. Nobunaga returned to his camp on Mount Toragoze, from which point he had already surrounded Odani. From the time he arrived, he had seemed extraordinarily composed, as though he were simply waiting for the castle to fall. With the precipitous collapse of Echizen, he had immediately returned while the ashes of Ichijogadani were still smoldering. Now he was giving out orders.

Maenami Yoshitsugu, the surrendering general of Echizen, was given Toyohara Castle. Similarly, Asakura Kageaki was commanded to defend Ino Castle, and Toda Yarokuro was ordered to the castle at Fuchu. Thus Nobunaga employed a large number of Asakura retainers who were familiar with the conditions of the province. Finally, Akechi Mitsuhide was left in charge as their overseer.

In all likelihood there could not have been anyone better suited for this responsibility than Mitsuhide. During his unsettled days as a wanderer, he had been a retainer of the Asakura clan and lived in the castle town of Ichijogadani, suffering the cold glances of his colleagues. Now, in a completely reversed situation, he was keeping watch over his former masters.

Considerable pride and a stream of other emotions must have passed through Mitsuhide's breast. Furthermore, Mitsuhide's intelligence and ability had been recognized on a number of occasions, and he was now one of Nobunaga's favorite retainers. In his observation of others, Mitsuhide was far more intelligent than most men, and after a number of years of battles and daily service, he understood Nobunaga's character quite well. He knew his master's expressions, words, and looks—even at a distance—just as well as he did his own.

Mitsuhide dispatched riders from Echizen many times a day. He did not make even the smallest decision on his own, but asked for Nobunaga's instructions in every situation. Nobunaga made his decisions while looking at these notes and letters in his camp on Mount Toragoze.

Mountains in full autumn colors lined the cloudless blue sky, which in turn was reflected in the bright blue lake below. The chattering of birds invited a yawn here and there.

Hideyoshi quickly crossed the mountains from Yokoyama. Joking with his men on the way, his teeth shone white as he laughed in the autumn sun. As he approached, he greeted everyone around him. This was the man who had built the castle at Sunomata and later had been put in charge of Yokoyama Castle. His responsibilities and position among the generals of the Oda army had very quickly become prominent, and yet he was the same as he had always been.

When other generals compared his behavior with their own solemn ways, there were some who judged him to be frivolous and indiscreet, but others saw him in a different light, saying, "He's worthy of his rank. He hasn't changed from what he was before, even though his stipend's increased. First he was a servant, then a samurai, and then suddenly he was governing a castle. But he's still the same. I imagine he's going to earn an even larger domain."

Hideyoshi had just before then leisurely shown his face in camp before luring Nobunaga away with a few simple words, and they were both climbing up toward the mountains.

"How impertinent!" Shibata Katsuie exclaimed as he and Sakuma Nobumori went out beyond the barracks.

"That is why he's so disliked, even when he doesn't have to be. There's nothing more unpleasant than listening to someone who rattles on about his own cleverness." Almost spitting out their words, they watched the figure of Hideyoshi thread his way through the far-off marsh in the company of Nobunaga.

"He doesn't tell us anything—doesn't consult with us at all."

"First of all, isn't that awfully dangerous? It may be broad daylight, but the enemy could be lurking anywhere in these mountains. What would happen if they started shooting at him?"

"Well, His Lordship is His Lordship."

"No, it's Hideyoshi who's at fault. Even if a large crowd accompanies His Lordship, Hideyoshi fawns all over him until he catches his eye."

There were other commanders besides Katsuie and Nobumori who were unhappy with the situation. Most of them assumed that Hideyoshi was off with Nobunaga in the mountains, planning some battle strategy with his usual glib tongue. This was the primary source of their discomfort.

"He's ignoring *us*—the inner circle of his generals."

Whether Hideyoshi did not understand such inner workings of human nature or simply chose to ignore them, he led Nobunaga off into the mountains, occasionally laughing with a voice that would have been more fitting for a holiday excursion. With his and Nobunaga's retainers combined, their small force was made up of no more than twenty or thirty men.

"A man really sweats when he climbs mountains. Shall I give you a hand, my lord?"

"Don't be insulting."

"It's just a little farther."

"I haven't climbed enough. Aren't there any mountains higher than this?"

"Unfortunately no, not in this area. But this is pretty high!"

Wiping the sweat from his face, Nobunaga looked down into the neighboring valleys. He saw that Hideyoshi's troops were hiding among the trees, standing guard.

"The men accompanying us should stay here. It wouldn't be good for us to go in a large group past this point." This said, Hideyoshi and Nobunaga walked thirty or forty paces the crest of the hill.

There were no longer any trees. Tender grains and grasses that would have made good fodder stretched along the surface of the mountain. Chinese balloon flowers rustled among the pampas grass. Blooms of beggar's purse clung to the scabbards of their swords. The two of them advanced in silence. It was as though they were looking out to sea, with nothing before them.

"Stoop down, my lord."

"Like this?"

"Hide yourself in the grass." As they crawled to the edge of the precipice, a castle appeared in the valley right beneath them.

"That's Odani," Hideyoshi said softly as he pointed toward the castle.

Nobunaga nodded and looked on silently. His eyes were shrouded in some deep emotion. It was not simply that he was looking at the enemy's main castle. Inside this castle that was now besieged by his own army lived his younger sister, Oichi, who had already borne four children since becoming the wife of the castle's lord.

Both lord and retainer sat down. The flowers and the ears of the autumn grasses came up to their shoulders. Nobunaga stared unblinkingly at the castle beneath them, and then turned toward Hideyoshi.

"I daresay my sister is angry with me. I was the one who married her into the Asai clan without even letting her speak her own mind. She was told to sacrifice herself for the good of the clan, and that the match was necessary to protect the province. Hideyoshi, I feel as though I can still see that scene today."

"I remember it well myself," Hideyoshi said. "She had an enormous amount of baggage and a beautiful palanquin, and she was surrounded by attendants and decorated horses. It was a splendid event, the day she went off to be married north of Lake Biwa."

"Oichi was only an innocent girl of fourteen."

"She was such a small, pretty bride."

"Hideyoshi."

"Yes?"

"You understand, don't you? How painful this is for me…"

"For that very reason, it's hard for me too."

Nobunaga motioned toward the castle with his chin. "There is no difficulty in the decision to destroy this castle, but when I think about trying to get Oichi out of there without her getting hurt…"

"When you ordered me to spy out the lay of the land around Odani Castle, I guessed that you were planning a campaign against the Asakura and the Asai. I probably sound as though I'm flattering myself again, but if you'll allow me to speak frankly, I think you're somewhat reserved about showing your natural feelings, and certainly the cause of your distress, my lord. It's rude of me to say this, but I think I've discovered one more of your better qualities."

"You're the only one." Nobunaga clicked his tongue. "Katsuie, Nobumori, and the others look at me as though I've been wasting my time for the last ten days. Their faces show that they don't understand me at all. It seems that Katsuie especially is laughing at me behind my back."

"That's because, my lord, you are still confused about which way to go."

"I can't help but be confused. If we were to pulverize the enemy bit by bit, there's no doubt that Asai Nagamasa and his father would drag Oichi down with them to the bottom of the flames."

"That's probably the way it would be."

"Hideyoshi, you say you've felt the same way I do from the very beginning, but you're listening to this with extraordinary composure. Don't you have some sort of plan?"

"I'm not without one."

"Well, why don't you hurry up and put my mind to rest?"

"I've been doing my best not to make recommendations recently."

"Why?"

"Because there are a lot of other people in the staff headquarters."

"Are you afraid of other people's jealousy? That's annoying, too. But the main thing is that I am the one who decides everything. Tell me your plan right away."

"Look over there, my lord." Hideyoshi pointed at Odani Castle. "What makes this castle special is that the three enclosures are more distinct and independent than in most other castles. Lord Hisamasa lives in the first enclosure; and his son, Nagamasa, and Lady Oichi and her children live in the third."

"Over there?"

"Yes, my lord. Now, the area you see between the first and third enclosures is called the Kyogoku enclosure, and that's where the senior retainers, Asai Genba, Mitamura Uemondayu, and Onogi Tosa are quartered. So, in order to capture Odani, rather than hitting the tail or striking the head, if we can first get our hands on the Kyogoku enclosure, the other two will be cut off."

"I see. You're saying that our next move is to attack the Kyogoku."

"No, if we storm the Kyogoku, the first and third enclosures will send reinforcements. Our men will be attacked on both flanks, and a fierce battle will ensue. In that case, would we try to break our way through or retreat? Either way, we cannot be sure of Lady Oichi's fate inside the castle."

"So what should we do?"

"Of course, it's clear that the very best strategy would be to send a messenger to the Asai, explain the advantages and disadvantages of the situation clearly, and take possession of both the castle and Oichi without incident."

"You should know that I've already tried that twice. I sent a messenger to the castle and informed them that if they surrendered, I would allow them to keep their domains. I made sure that they knew that Echizen had been conquered, but neither Nagamasa nor his father is going to budge. They're only going to show off how tough they are, just like before. Their 'toughness,' of course, is nothing more than using Oichi's life as a shield. They think that I'll never make a reckless attack as long as they have my own sister in the castle."

"But it's not just that. For the two years I've been at Yokoyama, I've been watching Nagamasa carefully, and he does have some talent and willpower. Well, I've been trying to think of a plan to capture this castle for a long time, to figure out the best strategy in case we ever had to attack it. I have captured the Kyogoku enclosure without losing a single man."

"What? What are you saying?" Nobunaga doubted his own ears.

"The second enclosure you see over there. Our men are already in control of it," Hideyoshi repeated, "so I'm saying you don't have to worry anymore."

"Is this true?"

"Would I lie to you at a time like this, my lord?"

"But...I can't believe it."

"That's understandable, but you'll be able to hear it with your own ears soon, from two men I've summoned. Would you meet with them?"

"Who are they?"

"One is a monk called Miyabe Zensho. The other is Onogi Tosa, the commander of the enclosure."

Nobunaga could not rid himself of his surprised expression. He believed Hideyoshi, but he could not help wondering how he had persuaded a senior retainer of the Asai clan to come over to their side.

Hideyoshi explained the situation as though there were nothing unusual about it at all. "Shortly after Your Lordship awarded me the castle at Yokoyama…" he started.

Nobunaga was a little startled. He was unable to look without blinking at the man who was speaking. Yokoyama Castle was situated on the front line of this strategic area, and Hideyoshi's troops were there to check the Asai and Asakura. He remembered the order posting Hideyoshi there temporarily, but he had no memory of a promise to give him the castle. But here was Hideyoshi saying that he had been given the castle. Nobunaga, however, put this in the back of his mind for the moment.

"Wasn't that the year right after the attack on Mount Hiei, when you came to Gifu to make a New Year's call?" Nobunaga asked.

"That's right. On the way back, Takenaka Hanbei fell ill and we were delayed. By the time we arrived at Yokoyama Castle, it was after dark."

"I don't feel like listening to a long story. Get to the point."

"The enemy had found out that I was away from the castle and was making a night attack. We repulsed them, of course, and at the time we captured the monk Miyabe Zensho."

"You took him alive?"

"Yes. Rather than cutting off his head we treated him kindly, and later, when I had a moment, I counseled him about the coming times and instructed him in the true significance of being a samurai. He, in turn, talked to his former master, Onogi Tosa, and persuaded him to surrender to us."

"Really?"

"The battlefield is no place for jokes," Hideyoshi said.

Lost in admiration, even Nobunaga was amazed at Hideyoshi's cunning. The battlefield is no place for jokes! And, just as he had bragged, Miyabe Zensho and Onogi Tosa were led in by Hideyoshi's retainer for an audience with Nobunaga. He questioned Tosa closely to confirm Hideyoshi's story.

The general responded clearly. "This surrender is not at my own discretion. The other two senior retainers stationed in the Kyogoku have realized that opposing you is not only foolish, but it would also hasten the fall of the clan and impose needless suffering on the people of the province."

Nagamasa was under thirty, but he already had four children by the Lady Oichi, who herself was twenty-three. He occupied the third enclosure of Odani Castle, which was really three castles in one.

Gunfire could be heard from the ravine to the south until the evening. The report of cannon sounded periodically, and each time the fretwork ceiling shook as if it were going to come loose.

Oichi looked up instinctively with frightened eyes, and held a baby more tightly against her breast. The child was as yet unweaned. There was no wind, but soot was blowing everywhere, and the light of the lamp flickered wildly.

"Mother! I'm scared!" Her second daughter, Hatsu, clung to her right sleeve while her eldest daughter, Chacha, silently held fast to her left knee. Her son, however, did not come to his mother's lap even though he was still small. He was brandishing an arrow shaft at a lady-in-waiting. This was Nagamasa's heir, Manjumaru.

"Let me see! Let me see the battle!" Manju cried petulantly, striking the lady-in-waiting with the headless arrow.

"Manju," his mother reproved him, "why are you hitting her? Your father is fighting. Have you already forgotten that he told you to behave during the fighting? If you're laughed at by the retainers, you won't become a good general even when you grow up."

Manju was old enough to understand a little of his mother's reasoning. He listened to her silently for a moment, but then suddenly began to cry out loud fretfully.

"I wanna see the battle! I wanna see!" The child's tutor did not know what to do either, and simply stood there watching. Just then there was a lull in the fighting, but gunfire could still be heard. The eldest girl, Chacha, was already seven years old, and she somehow understood the difficult circumstances her father was in, her mother's sorrow, and even the feelings of the warriors in the castle.

She said precociously, "Manju! Don't say things that upset Mother! Don't you think this is horrible for her? Father's out there fighting the enemy. Isn't that right, Mother?"

Taken to task, Manju looked at his sister and jumped on her, still brandishing the arrow shaft. "You stupid Chacha!" he shouted.

Chacha put her sleeve over her head and hid behind her mother.

"Be good now!" Trying to humor him, Oichi took the arrow shaft and talked to him quietly.

Suddenly there was the sound of violent footsteps in the entrance hall outside.

"What's that? To the likes of the Oda? They're nothing but little samurai who have pushed their way from the backwoods of Owari. Do you think I'm going to surrender to a man like Nobunaga? The Asai clan is in a different class from them!" Asai Nagamasa entered unannounced, followed by two or three generals.

When he saw that his wife was out of harm's way in this cavernous, poorly lit room, he was relieved. "I'm a little tired," he said, sitting down and loosening the cords on a section of his armor. Then he said to the generals behind him, "With the way things are going this evening, the enemy may well make an all-out attack around midnight. We'd better rest now."

When the commanders got up to leave, Nagamasa heaved a sigh of relief. Even in the midst of battle, he was able to remember that he was both a father and a husband.

"Was the sound of the guns this evening frightening, my dear?" he asked his wife.

Surrounded by her children, Oichi replied, "No, we were in here, so it was all right."

"Didn't Manju or Chacha get scared and cry?"

"You should be proud of them. They acted like adults."

"Really?" he said, forcing a smile. Then he continued, "Don't worry. The Oda made a fierce attack, but we pushed them back with a volley from the castle. Even if they continue attacking us for twenty or thirty, or even one hundred days, we'll never surrender. We are the Asai clan! We're not going to yield to someone like Nobunaga." He railed against the Oda almost as though he could spit, but then suddenly fell silent.

With the light of the lamp behind her, Oichi's face was buried in the child suckling at her breast. This was Nobunaga's little sister! Nagamasa shook with emotion. She even looked like him. She had her brothers' delicate complexion and his profile.

"Are you crying?"

"The baby sometimes gets fretful and chews my nipple when the milk doesn't come out."

"The milk isn't coming out?"

"No, not now."

"That's because you have some unseen sorrow and you're getting too thin. But you are a mother, and this is a mother's true battle."

"I know."

"I suspect you think I'm a hard husband."

She edged up to her husband's side, still holding the child to her breast. "No, I don't! Why should I bear a grudge? I look at it all as fate."

"People can't be reconciled just by saying that it's fate. The life of a samurai's wife is more painful than swallowing swords. If you are not completely resolved, it won't be a true resolution at all."

"I'm trying to come to that kind of an understanding, but all I can think of is that I'm a mother."

"My dear, even on the day I married you, I didn't think that you would be mine forever. Neither did my father give his permission for you to become a true bride of the Asai."

"What! What are you saying?"

"At a time like this, a man has to tell the truth. This moment will never come again, so I'm going to open my heart to you. When Nobunaga sent you to marry me, it was really nothing more than a political strategem. I could see through to what was in his heart from the very first." He paused. "But even while I knew that, a love grew between us that nothing could ever stop. Then we had four children. At this point you are no longer Nobunaga's sister. You're my wife and the mother of my children. I won't allow you to shed tears for our enemy. So why are you growing so thin and holding back the milk you should be giving to our child?"

Now she could see. Everything that had been a result of "fate" had been conceived as political strategem. She was a bride of political strategy: from the very first Nagamasa had seen Nobunaga as someone to watch. But Nobunaga had sincerely loved his brother-in-law.

Nobunaga believed that the heir of the Asai clan had a future, and he had trusted him. He had pushed for the marriage enthusiastically. But the match had been in doubt from the very beginning, because of the much older alliance between the Asai and the

Asakura of Echizen. Their pact was not simply one of mutual defense, but a complex relationship based on friendship and mutual favors. The Asakura and Oda had been enemies for years. When Nobunaga had attacked the Saito in Gifu, how much had they hindered him and come to the aid of the Saito?

Nobunaga overcame this obstacle to the match by sending a written pledge to the Asakura, promising not to invade their domain.

Soon after the wedding, both Nagamasa's father and the Asakura clan—to which he owed so many favors—began to pressure Nagamasa to regard his wife with suspicion. In the meantime, the Asai had joined the Asakura, the shogun, Takeda Shingen of Kai, and the warrior-monks of Mount Hiei in an anti-Nobunaga alliance.

The following year Nobunaga had invaded Echizen. Suddenly he was struck from behind. Cutting off Nobunaga's path of retreat and acting in concert with the Asakura clan, Nagamasa had plotted the man's utter annihilation. At the time, Nagamasa made it clear to Nobunaga that he was not going to let his judgment be affected by his wife, but Nobunaga would not believe it. The forces of the Asai and the martial valor of the man whom Nobunaga had trusted had become a fire at his very feet. Indeed, they had become chains. After the destruction of Echizen, however, Odani Castle was no longer either a fire or constricting chains.

Nevertheless, at this time Nobunaga was still hopeful that he would not have to kill Nagamasa. Of course, he respected Nagamasa's courage, but more than that, he was troubled with his affection for Oichi. People thought this strange, remembering that, when he had destroyed Mount Hiei with fire, this lord had thought nothing of being called "the king of the demons."

Autumn deepened day by day. At dawn, the dew on the grass around the castle was wet and cold.

"My lord, something terrible has happened." Fujikake Mikawa's voice was unusually perturbed. Nagamasa had slept that night near the mosquito netting that protected his wife and children, but he had not taken off his armor.

"What is it, Mikawa?" He quickly left the bedroom, breathing heavily. A dawn attack! That was his first thought. But the disaster that Mikawa was reporting was worse than that.

"The Kyogoku enclosure was taken by the Oda during the night."

"What!"

"There's no doubt. You can see it from the keep, my lord."

"It can't be." He climbed quickly to the watchtower, stumbling many times on the dark stairs. Although the Kyogoku was far away from the watchtower, the enclosure looked as if it were just below him. There, fluttering at the top of the castle in the distance, were a great number of banners, but not one of them belonged to the Asai. One of the commanders' standards, flying brilliantly and proudly in the wind, quite clearly evidenced the presence of Hideyoshi.

"We've been betrayed! Fine! I'll show them. I'll show Nobunaga and all the samurai in this country," he said, forcing a smile. "I'll show them how Asai Nagamasa dies!"

Nagamasa descended the darkened stairway of the watchtower. For the retainers who followed him, it was like accompanying their lord deep beneath the surface of the earth.

"What—what's going on?" lamented one of the generals, halfway down the staircase.

"Onogi Tosa, Asai Genba, and Mitamura Uemon have gone over to the enemy," one general answered.

Another man said bitterly, "Even though they were senior retainers, they betrayed the trust placed in them when they were put in charge of the Kyogoku."

"They're inhuman!"

Nagamasa turned around and said, "Stop complaining!"

They stood in the wide, wooden-floored room at the bottom of the stairs, which was brightened by a faint light. The fortified room resembled a huge cage or jail cell. Many of the wounded had been brought here, and they lay on straw mats, groaning.

When Nagamasa passed through, even the samurai who were lying down made an effort to kneel.

"I won't let them die in vain! I won't let them die in vain!" Nagamasa said with tears in his eyes as he passed through. Yet he turned again to his generals and strictly forbade them to complain.

"There is no use in insulting others. Each of you must pick your own course—whether you surrender to the enemy or die with me. There's moral duty on both sides. Nobunaga is fighting to rebuild the nation; I'm fighting for the name and honor of the samurai class. If you think you had better submit to Nobunaga, then go to him. I'm certainly not going to stop you!" So saying, he walked out to check the defenses of the castle, but he had not taken a hundred paces when something much more serious than losing the Kyogoku was reported to him.

"My lord! My lord! Terrible news!" One of his officers, drenched in blood, came running toward him and dropped to his knees.

"What is it, Kyutaro?"

A premonition that something was very wrong settled quickly in Nagamasa's breast. Wakui Kyutaro was not a samurai stationed in the third enclosure; he was a retainer of Nagamasa's father.

"Your honored father, Lord Hisamasa, has just committed *seppuku*. I cut my way here through the enemy to bring you this." Kyutaro dropped to his knees. Gasping, he took out Hisamasa's topknot and the silk kimono it was wrapped in and put them into Nagamasa's hand.

"What! The first enclosure has also fallen?"

"Just before dawn, a corps of soldiers took the secret path from Kyogoku to just outside the castle gate, flying Onogi's standard, saying that Onogi urgently needed to see Lord Hisamasa. Assuming that Onogi was leading his own men, the guards opened the castle gate. As soon as that happened, a large force of soldiers rushed in and cut their way through to the inner citadel."

"The enemy?"

"The greater part of them were Lord Hideyoshi's retainers, but the men who showed him the way were undoubtedly the retainers of that traitor Onogi."

"Well, what about my father?"

"He fought gallantly to the very end. He himself set fire to the inner citadel and then committed suicide, but the enemy put out the fire and occupied the castle."

"Ah! So that's why we didn't see any flames or smoke."

"If flames had been rising from the first enclosure, then you would have sent reinforcements, or you might have set fire to this castle and committed suicide with your wife and children when your father perished. I think this is what the enemy feared and planned against."

Suddenly, Kyutaro dug his nails into the ground and said, "My lord…I am dying…" With his palms pressed down in obeisance, his head dropped to the floor. He had fought and won a far more bitter battle than on the field.

"Another brave soul gone," someone lamented behind Nagamasa, and then softly intoned a prayer.

The sound of prayer beads clicked in the silence. When Nagamasa turned, he saw that it was the head priest, Yuzan—another refugee from the war.

"I was sorry to hear that Lord Hisamasa met his end early this morning," Yuzan said.

"Your Reverence, I have a request," Nagamasa said in a steady voice. His words were calm, but there was no concealing their plaintive tone. "It will be my turn next. I would like to gather all of my retainers together and hold a funeral service, at least in form, while I am still alive. In the valley behind Odani, there is a memorial stone carved with the Buddhist death name you yourself gave me. Would you please have the stone moved inside the castle? You're a priest, and surely the enemy would let you through."

"Of course."

Yuzan left immediately. As he did so, one of Nagamasa's generals nearly ran into him as he hurried in.

"Fuwa Mitsuharu has come to the castle gate."

"Who is he?"

"A retainer of Lord Nobunaga."

"The enemy?" Nagamasa spat. "Chase him away. I don't have any use for Nobunaga's retainers. If he won't go away, feed him some rocks from the castle gate."

The samurai obeyed Nagamasa's command and dashed off immediately, but soon another commander arrived.

"The messenger from the enemy is still standing at the castle gate. He won't leave, no matter what we say. He protests that war is war, and negotiations are negotiations, and asks why we lack the proper etiquette toward him as a representative of his province."

Nagamasa ignored these complaints, and then berated the man who had repeated them. "Why are you explaining the protests of a man I told you to chase off?"

Just then, yet another general came forward. "My lord, the rules of war dictate that you should meet with him, even for just a moment. I would not have it said that Asai Nagamasa was so distracted that he lost his composure and refused to grant an audience to an enemy envoy."

"All right, let him in. I'll see him, at least. Over there," Nagamasa said, pointing to the guard room.

More than half of the soldiers in the castle of the Asai hoped that peace was walking in through the gate. It was not that they lacked admiration or devotion for Nagamasa, but the "duty" that Nagamasa preached and the reasons for this war were entwined with his relationship with Echizen and his resentment of Nobunaga's ambitions and achievements. The soldiers understood this contrast only too well.

And there was more. Although Odani Castle had held out steadfastly until then, both the first and second enclosures had already fallen. What chance of victory did they have, entrenched in an isolated and desolate castle?

Thus, the arrival of the Oda envoy was like the clear blue sky they had been waiting for. Fuwa entered the castle, went into the room where Nagamasa awaited him, and knelt in front of him.

The men inside fixed Fuwa with hostile stares; their hair was disheveled, and they had wounds on their hands and heads. The kneeling Fuwa spoke so gently that one might have doubted that he was a general at all.

"I have the honor of being Lord Nobunaga's envoy."

"Formal greetings are not necessary on the battlefield. Let's get to the point," Nagamasa said peremptorily.

"Lord Nobunaga admires your loyalty to the Asakura clan but today, the Asakura have already fallen, and their ally, the shogun, is in exile. Both favors and grudges are now far in the past, so why should the Oda and Asai clans be fighting? Not only that, but Lord Nobunaga is your brother-in-law; you are the beloved husband of his sister."

"I've heard this all before. If you're asking for a peace treaty, I absolutely refuse. It won't make any difference how persuasive you are."

"With all due respect, there's nothing left for you to do but to capitulate. Your behavior so far has been exemplary. Why not give up the castle like a man, and work for your clan's future? If you agree, Lord Nobunaga is willing to give you the entire province of Yamato."

Nagamasa let out a scornful laugh. He waited until the envoy had finished. "Please tell Lord Nobunaga that I am not going to be fooled by such clever words. What he is really concerned about is his sister, not me."

"That's a cynical view."

"Say whatever you like," he hissed, "but go back and tell him that I'm not considering saving myself through my ties with my wife. And you had better tell Nobunaga to persuade himself of the fact that Oichi is my wife and no longer his sister."

"Well then, I take it you plan to share the fate of this castle, no matter what?"

"I'm resolved on that not only for myself but for my wife, too."

"Then there's nothing more to be said." With that Fuwa returned directly to Nobunaga's camp.

After that, hopelessness—or, more properly, emptiness—filled the castle with gloom. The soldiers who had expected peace from the Oda messenger could only assume that the talks had broken down. They were now openly despondent, because they had briefly hoped that their lives would be spared.

There was another reason for gloom to settle on the castle. Although there was a battle going on, the funeral for Nagamasa's father was taking place, and voices intoning the sutras drifted out from the interior of the keep until the following day.

Oichi and her four children wore white silk garments of mourning from that day on.

The cords that held up their hair were black. They seemed to possess a purity that was not of this world, even though they were yet alive, and even those retainers who were resolved to die in the castle quite naturally felt their fate was too pitiful for words.

Yuzan now returned to the castle, accompanied by workmen carrying the stone monument. Just before dawn, incense and flowers were placed in the main hall of the castle for the funeral service for the living.

Yuzan addressed the assembly of the Asai clan's retainers. "Valuing his name as a member of the samurai class, Lord Asai Nagamasa, the master of this castle, has passed away like a beautiful fallen flower. Therefore, as his retainers it is proper for you to pay your last respects."

Nagamasa sat behind the stone monument as though he had really died. At the beginning, the samurai looked as though they did not understand. They asked themselves if all this was necessary and fidgeted in the strange atmosphere.

But Oichi and the children and other members of the family knelt in front of the monument and put incense into the burner.

Someone began to weep, and soon everyone was affected. Filling the broad room, the armored men hung their heads and averted their eyes. Not one of them could look up.

When the ceremony was over, Yuzan took the lead, and several samurai shouldered the monument and carried it out of the castle. This time they went down to Lake Biwa, took a small boat, and at a place about one hundred yards from Chikubu Island, sunk the stone to the bottom.

Nagamasa spoke fearlessly, facing the death that pressed in on him, and he had not overlooked the laxity of the martial spirit of those soldiers who had put their hopes on peace talks. His "funeral for the living" had a salutary effect on the faltering morale of the defenders. If their lord was resolved to die in battle, they too were resolved to follow him. It was time to die. Nagamasa's pathetic determination thus inspired his retainers. But although he was a gifted general, he was not a genius. Nagamasa did not know how to make his men die gladly for him. They stood, waiting for the final assault.

THREE PRINCESSES

At about noon, the soldiers at the castle gate started to yell.

"They're coming!"

The gunners on the walls jostled one another, searching out targets. But the only enemy who was approaching was a solitary rider, and he was ambling up to the gate in a very nonchalant way. If he were an envoy, he would be arriving with an escort of mounted men. Filled with doubt, the defenders watched the man approach.

As he came closer, one of the commanders spoke to a soldier with a rifle. "He's got to be an enemy general. He doesn't look like an envoy, and he's being very audacious. Fire on him once."

The commander had meant for one man to fire a warning shot, but three or four men fired together.

As they fired, the man stopped, as if surprised. He then held up a war fan with a red sun on a gold background, waved it over his head, and shouted, "Hey, soldiers! Wait a minute! Is Kinoshita Hideyoshi a man you want to shoot? Do it after I've talked to Lord Nagamasa." He ran as he yelled, until he was almost directly under the castle gate.

"Well, it's Kinoshita Hideyoshi of the Oda, all right. I wonder what he wants." The Asai general who peered down at him was skeptical about his reason for coming, but forgot about trying to shoot him.

Hideyoshi looked up at the castle gate. "I would like you to convey a message to the citadel," he shouted again.

What was going on? Voices that seemed to be deliberating noisily could be heard. Soon a derisive laugh mixed with the voices, and a general from the Asai stuck his head out over the parapet.

"Forget it. I suppose you're one more advocate coming as an envoy from Lord

Nobunaga. You're just wasting your time once again. Go away!"

Hideyoshi raised his voice. "Silence! Where is the rule allowing a man with the status of a retainer to drive away his lord's guest without ever inquiring into his lord's intentions? This castle is as good as taken already, and I'm not so stupid as to take the time and trouble to come here playing the role of an envoy to hurry its destruction." His words were not exactly humble. "I've come here as Lord Nobunaga's representative, to offer incense in front of Lord Nagamasa's mortuary tablet. If we've heard correctly, Lord Nagamasa is resolved to die and has had his own funeral conducted while he is yet alive. They were friends during this life, so shouldn't Lord Nobunaga be allowed to offer incense too? Isn't there still grace enough here for men to exchange that kind of courtesy and friendship? Is the resolution of Lord Nagamasa and his retainers nothing but an affectation? Is it a bluff or the false courage of a coward?"

The face over the castle gate withdrew, perhaps out of embarrassment. No answer came for a little while, but finally the gate opened a little.

"General Fujikake Mikawa has agreed to speak with you for a few moments," the man said as he beckoned Hideyoshi in. But then he added, "Lord Nagamasa has refused to see you."

Hideyoshi nodded. "That's only natural. I consider Lord Nagamasa to have already passed away, and I am not going to press the point."

As he spoke, he walked in without looking to the right or left. How could this man walk into the midst of the enemy so calmly?

As Hideyoshi walked up the long sloping path from the first gate to the central gate, he paid absolutely no attention to the man who was leading him. When he approached the entrance to the citadel, Mikawa came out to meet him.

"It's been a long time," Hideyoshi said, as though it were nothing more than a normal greeting.

They had met once before, and Mikawa returned the greeting with a smile. "Yes, it certainly has been a long time. Meeting you in these circumstances is quite unexpected, Lord Hideyoshi."

The men in the castle all had bloodshot eyes, but the face of the old general did not look hard-pressed at all.

"General Mikawa, I haven't seen you since Lady Oichi's wedding day, have I? It's been quite a long time."

"That's right."

"That was a splendid day for both our clans."

"It's hard to tell what fate has in store. But when you look at the disturbances and cataclysms of the past, even this situation is not so unusual. Well, come inside. I can't give you much of a reception, but can I offer you at least a bowl of tea?"

Mikawa led him to a teahouse. Looking at the back of the old, white-haired general, it was clear that he had already transcended life and death.

It was a small, secluded teahouse, down a lane through the trees. Hideyoshi sat down and felt that he was in a different world entirely. In the quiet of the teahouse, both host and guest were temporarily cleansed of the bloodiness of the outside world.

It was the end of autumn. The leaves of the trees fluttered outside, but not a speck of dust settled on the polished wooden floor.

"I hear that Lord Nobunaga's retainers have recently taken up the art of tea." Making amiable conversation, Mikawa lifted the ladle toward the iron kettle.

Hideyoshi noted the man's decorum and hastily apologized. "Lord Nobunaga and his retainers are well versed in tea, but I'm a dullard by nature and don't know the first thing about it. I only like the taste."

Mikawa put down the bowl and stirred the tea with the whisk. His graceful movements were almost feminine in nature. The hands and body that had been hardened by armor did not seem cramped in the least. In this room furnished with nothing more than a tea bowl and a simple kettle, the gaudiness of the old general's armor looked out of place.

I've met a good man, Hideyoshi thought, and he drank in the man's character more than his tea. But how was he going to get Oichi out of the castle? Nobunaga's distress was his own. Since his plan had been employed so far, he felt responsible for solving this problem too.

The castle would probably fall on any day they wanted it to, but it would not do to bungle the job now and have to pick through the ashes for the gem. Furthermore, Nagamasa had let both parties know that he was determined to die, and that his wife was of the same mind.

Nobunaga's impossible hope was to win the battle and recover Oichi without harm.

"Please don't worry about formalities," Mikawa said, offering him the tea bowl from where he knelt in front of the hearth.

Sitting crossed-legged in the warrior style, Hideyoshi artlessly received the tea and drank it down in three gulps.

"Ah, that was good. I didn't think tea could taste this good. And I'm not trying to flatter you."

"How about another bowl?"

"No, my thirst has been quenched. The thirst in my mouth, at least. But I don't know how to quench the thirst in my heart. General Mikawa, you seem to be someone I can talk to. Would you hear me out?"

"I'm a retainer of the Asai, and you're an envoy of the Oda. I'll listen to you from that standpoint."

"I'd like you to arrange for me to meet with Lord Nagamasa."

"Such a thing was refused when you were at the castle gate. You were let in because you said that you had not come to meet Lord Nagamasa. Coming this far and then going back on your word is a dishonorable trick. I can't put myself in that position and allow you to meet him."

"No, no. I'm not talking about meeting the living Lord Nagamasa. As Nobunaga's representative, I would like to salute the soul of Lord Nagamasa."

"Stop playing with words. Even if I did convey your intentions to him, there's no reason to think that Lord Nagamasa would consent to see you. I had hoped to partake in the highest warrior etiquette by sharing a bowl of tea with you. If you have any sense of shame, leave now while you haven't dishonored yourself."

Don't move. Refuse to go. Hideyoshi had resolved not to budge until he had achieved his goal. He sat there in silence. Mere words were clearly not going to be any kind of strategy against this seasoned old general.

"Well, I'm going to take you back," Mikawa offered.

Hideyoshi looked grimly in the other direction and said nothing. Meanwhile, his host had prepared a bowl of tea for himself. After drinking it in a dignified manner, he put away the tea implements.

"I know this is selfish, but let me stay here a while longer, please," Hideyoshi said, and did not make a move. His expression indicated that he probably could not have been moved with a lever.

"You can stay there as long as you like, but it won't do you any good."

"Not necessarily."

"There are no two ways about what I said just now. What are you going to do here?"

"I'm listening to the sound of the water boiling in the kettle."

"The kettle?" he laughed. "And you said you didn't know anything about the Way of Tea!"

"No, I don't know the first thing about tea, but it is a pleasant sound, somehow. Maybe it's from hearing nothing but war cries and the whinnying of horses during this long campaign, but it's extremely pleasant. Let me sit here for a moment by myself and think things through."

"It won't make any difference what your meditations are. I'm certainly not going to let you meet Lord Nagamasa, or even step one foot closer to the keep," Mikawa said as he got up to leave.

Hideyoshi made no answer other than to say, "This kettle really has a nice sound to it." He edged a little closer to the hearth and, lost in admiration, gazed intently at the iron kettle. What had suddenly caught his attention was the pattern raised on the antique surface of the iron. It was hard to say whether it was a man or a monkey, but the tiny creature, its arms and legs supported by the branches of a tree, was standing insolently between heaven and earth.

It looks like me! Hideyoshi thought, unable to suppress a spontaneous smile. He suddenly recalled the time he had left the mansion of Matsushita Kahei and roamed the mountains and forests with nothing to eat and nowhere to stay.

Hideyoshi did not know whether Mikawa was outside, peeping in on him, or had gone away in exasperation, but in any case, he was no longer in the teahouse.

Ah, this is interesting. This is really interesting, thought Hideyoshi. He looked as if he were talking to the kettle. Alone, he shook his head. As he did so, he thought about his decision not to move, no matter what.

Somewhere in the garden, Hideyoshi heard the guileless voices of two young children, trying hard not to burst out laughing. They were looking at him through the gaps in the fence around the teahouse.

"Look how much he looks like a monkey."

"Yes! He's just like one."

"I wonder where he's come from."

"He must be the messenger from the Monkey God."

Hideyoshi turned his head and spotted the children hiding behind the fence.

While Hideyoshi had been engrossed in the design on the kettle, the two children had been secretly observing him.

Hideyoshi was struck with jubilation. He was certain that these were two of Nagamasa's four children—the boy, Manju, and the girl his elder sister, Chacha. He shot them a smile.

"Hey! He's smiling!"

"Mister Monkey smiled."

The two children immediately started whispering. Hideyoshi pretended to scowl at them. This had even more of an effect than smiling. Seeing that the monkey-faced stranger was so quick to join in their games, Manju and Chacha stuck out their tongues and made faces at him.

Hideyoshi glared at them and the two children glared back, trying to see who could last the longest.

Hideyoshi burst out laughing, conceding defeat.

Manju and Chacha laughed excitedly. Scratching his head, Hideyoshi beckoned them with a wave to come over and play another game.

The two children were intrigued by his invitation, and stealthily pushed open the brushwood gate.

"Where did you come from, mister?"

Hideyoshi came down from the veranda and began to tie the cords of his straw sandals. Half in fun, Manju tickled the back of Hideyoshi's neck with a stalk of pampas grass. Enduring this mischief, Hideyoshi finished tying the cords.

But when he stood up to his full height, and they saw the look on his face, they lost heart and tried to run away.

For his part, Hideyoshi was taken by surprise. As soon as the boy began to run away, he caught him by the collar. At the same time, he tried to grab Chacha with his other hand, but she screamed at the top of her voice and ran off crying. Manju was so shocked at being caught that he did not let out a whimper. But, falling down, he looked up underneath Hideyoshi, and seeing the man's face and the entire sky upside down, he finally screamed.

Fujikake Mikawa had left Hideyoshi alone in the teahouse and was walking along the garden path. He was the first to hear Chacha's cries as she fled and Manju's screams. Alarmed, he ran back to see what the matter was.

"What! You wretch!" He let out a horrified shout, and his hand instinctively grasped the hilt of his sword.

Standing astride Manju, Hideyoshi shouted in a commanding voice for the old man to stop. It was a difficult moment. Mikawa was about to strike Hideyoshi with his sword, but shrank back in fear when he saw what Hideyoshi was ready to do. For Hideyoshi's eyes and the sword he held in his hand both showed that he was ready to cut Manju's throat without the least hesitation.

The skin of the self-possessed old general turned to gooseflesh, and his white hair stood on end.

"Y–you wretch! What are you going to do with the boy?" Mikawa's voice was almost plaintive. He edged closer, his whole body shaking with regret and anger. When the retainers who had accompanied the general understood what was happening, they yelled for all they were worth, waving their hands, informing everyone of the situation immediately.

The guards from the central gate and the inner citadel had also heard Chacha's cries and now hurried toward the scene.

Around this bizarre enemy who glared at them while holding his sword at Manju's throat, the samurai formed a steel circle of armor. They remained at a distance, frightened perhaps at what they saw in Hideyoshi's eyes. They had no idea what to do, other than raise an uproar.

"General Mikawa!" Hideyoshi called out at one face among them. "What is your answer? This method is a bit violent, but if I don't do this, I don't see any other way of not embarrassing my lord. If you don't give me an answer, I'm going to kill Master Manju!" He looked around with big fiery eyes and went on, "General Mikawa, have these warriors withdraw! Then we'll talk. Is it so difficult to see what to do? Your understanding is slow. It would be difficult, after all, to kill me and save the boy's life without causing him injury. It's exactly the same as Lord Nobunaga taking this castle and wanting to save Oichi. How could you save Master Manju's life? Even if you shot me with a musket, this blade would be likely to pierce his throat in that very moment."

For some time it was only his tongue that was enlivened, and it had been like a rushing stream. But now his eyes were moving as well as his tongue, and along with his eloquence, all of the extremities of his body were keenly and constantly attentive to the enemy on all sides.

No one was able to do a thing. Mikawa felt the immensity of his mistake, and seemed to be listening carefully to what Hideyoshi was saying. He had recovered from his temporary shock and returned to the calm he had displayed in the teahouse. Mikawa could move at last; he waved his hand at the men around Hideyoshi. "Move away from him. Leave this to me. Even if I have to take his place, the young lord must not be harmed. Each of you return to your posts." Then he turned to Hideyoshi and said, "As you wished, the crowd has dispersed. Now, would you please hand over young Manju to me?"

"Absolutely not!" Hideyoshi shook his head forcefully, but then changed his tone of voice. "I will return the young lord, but I want to return him to Lord Nagamasa in person. Will you please see about getting me an audience with Lord Nagamasa and Lady Oichi?"

Nagamasa had been standing in the crowd that had dispersed a little before. When he heard Hideyoshi, he lost his self-control. Overcome with his love for his son, he ran forward, screaming abuse at Hideyoshi.

"What kind of foul play is this, holding an innocent child's fate in your hands, just so you can talk! If you're really the Oda general Kinoshita Hideyoshi, you should be ashamed of such a sinister scheme. All right! If you'll hand Manju over to me, we'll talk."

"Oh! Lord Nagamasa, were you here?" Hideyoshi said, politely bowing to Nagamasa despite the man's expression. But he still straddled Manju and held the point of his short sword to the boy's throat.

Fujikake Mikawa spoke from one side in a quavering voice. "Lord Hideyoshi! Please release him! Isn't His Lordship's word sufficient? Put Master Manju into my hands."

411

Hideyoshi took no notice of what he was saying, and looked in the direction of Asai Nagamasa. Staring straight at Nagamasa's pale face and desperate eyes, he finally gave a deep sigh.

"Ah. So you too know what it is to love a blood relative? You actually understand compassion toward a loved one? I didn't think you understood that at all."

"Aren't you going to give him to me, you scum? Are you going to murder this young boy?"

"I haven't the least intention of doing that. But you, who are a father, don't have any respect for family affections."

"Don't talk foolishness! Doesn't every parent love his child?"

"That's right. Even the birds and beasts," Hideyoshi agreed. "And if that's the case, I suppose you cannot ridicule as foolish the fact that Lord Nobunaga, because of his desire to save Oichi, cannot destroy this castle. And what about you? You're Oichi's husband, after all. Aren't you taking advantage of Lord Nobunaga's weakness by tying the lives of a mother and her children to the fate of your castle? That's exactly the same as the way I now hold down Lord Manju and press this sword to his throat so that I can talk with you. Before you declare my method to be cowardly, please consider whether your own strategy isn't just as cowardly and cruel."

As he spoke, Hideyoshi picked up Manju and held him in his arms. Seeing the relief spreading over Nagamasa's face, he abruptly stepped toward him, put Manju into his arms, and prostrated himself at his feet. "I fervently beg forgiveness for this violent and rude act; from the very beginning, my heart was not in it. I took such a measure first of all to try to lessen the plight of Lord Nobunaga. But also I thought it regrettable that you, a samurai who has shown such admirable resolution to the end, might hereafter be spoken of as someone who lost control of himself in his final moments. Make no mistake; this was partly for your own sake, my lord. Please grant me the release of Oichi and her children."

He did not really feel as though he were appealing to the enemy commander. He faced the man's soul and completely divulged his true emotions. His palms were folded at his breast and he was kneeling respectfully in front of Nagamasa; it was obvious that this gesture arose from complete sincerity.

Nagamasa closed his eyes and listened silently. He folded his arms, his feet planted firmly. He looked just like a statue in full armor. Hideyoshi seemed to be mouthing a prayer to the soul of Nagamasa, who seemed to have become, as Hideyoshi had declared when he entered the castle, a living corpse.

The hearts of the two men—one intent on prayer, the other intent on dying—came into contact for just a moment. The barrier between enemies was lifted, and the complex emotions that Nagamasa felt toward Nobunaga suddenly fell away from his body like flaking whitewash.

"Mikawa, take Lord Hideyoshi somewhere and entertain him for a while. I would like time to make my farewells."

"Your farewells?"

"I'm leaving this world and I want to tell my wife and children good-bye. I'm already anticipating death and have even had a funeral service for myself, but…can separation during life be worse than separation at the moment of death? I think Lord Nobunaga's envoy will agree that it is worse."

Shocked, Hideyoshi lifted up his face and looked at the man. "Are you saying that Oichi and her children can go?"

"To embrace my wife and children in the arms of death and let them perish with this castle was ignoble. I had resolved that my body was already dead, and yet my shallow prejudices and evil passions remained. What you've said has made me feel a sense of shame. I earnestly beg you to look after Oichi, who is still so young, and my children."

"With my life, my lord." Hideyoshi bowed his head to the ground. In that instant he could imagine Nobunaga's happy face.

"Well then, I'll meet with you later," Nagamasa said as he turned to leave, and he walked back toward the keep in long strides.

Mikawa led Hideyoshi to a guest room, this time as Nobunaga's formal envoy.

Relief could be seen in Hideyoshi's eyes. Then he turned and spoke to Mikawa. "I'm sorry, but would you wait a moment while I send a signal to the men outside the castle?"

"A signal?" Mikawa was suspicious, and not unreasonably so.

Hideyoshi, however, spoke as though his request were natural. "That's right. I promised to do that when I came here at Lord Nobunaga's command. In case things did not go well, I was to set a fire as a signal of Lord Nagamasa's rejection, even at the cost of my life. Lord Nobunaga would then attack the castle at once. On the other hand, if everything went well and I was able to meet Lord Nagamasa, I was to raise a banner. In any case, we agreed that the troops would simply wait until a signal was given."

Mikawa looked surprised at the man's preparations. But what surprised him even more was the signal shell that Hideyoshi had hidden near the hearth in the teahouse.

After raising the banner and returning to the guest room, Hideyoshi laughed and said, "If I had seen that the situation was not going well, I had planned to run as fast as possible to the teahouse and kick the signal-fire shell into the hearth. That would have been some tea ceremony!"

Hideyoshi was left on his own. It had been well over three hours since Mikawa had brought him to the guest room and asked him to wait for just a moment.

He certainly is taking his time, Hideyoshi thought, bored. The evening shadows were already darkening the fretwork ceiling of the empty room. It was dark enough in the room for lamps to be lit, and when he looked outside he could see the setting sun of late fall turning the mountains around the castle a deep crimson.

The plate in front of him was empty. At last he heard the sound of footsteps. A tea master walked into the room.

"As the castle is under siege, I'm afraid I have little to offer you, but His Lordship has asked me to prepare you an evening meal." The tea master cheered the guest by lighting a couple of lamps.

"Well now, under the circumstances you don't have to worry about a meal for me. Rather than that, I'd like to talk with General Mikawa. I'm sorry to trouble you, but could you call him?"

413

Mikawa appeared soon afterward. In a little under four hours he had aged ten years; he seemed to have lost all vigor, and his eyelids showed the traces of tears. "I'm sorry," he said, "I've been terribly rude."

"This is really no time to be thinking about normal etiquette," Hideyoshi replied, "but I am wondering what Lord Nagamasa is doing. Has he said his farewells to Oichi and the children? It's getting late."

"You're absolutely right. But what Lord Nagamasa said so bravely at first...well, now that he's telling his wife and children that they must leave him forever...I think you can imagine..." The old general looked down and wiped his eyes with his fingers. "Lady Oichi says that she does not want to leave her husband's side to return to her brother. She keeps pleading with him, so it's difficult to see when they'll be finished."

"Yes, well..."

"She's even pleaded with me. She said that when she was married, she resolved that this castle would be her grave. Even little Chacha seems to understand what is happening to her mother and father, and she's crying pitifully, asking why she has to leave her father and why he has to die. General Hideyoshi...forgive me, I'm being rude." He dabbed his eyes, cleared his throat, and broke down crying.

Hideyoshi sympathized with what Mikawa was going through and could understand only too well Nagamasa and Oichi's grief. Hideyoshi was more easily moved to tears than other men, and now they quickly streaked down his face. He sniffled repeatedly and looked up toward the ceiling. But he did not forget his mission and reprimanded himself —he must not be led astray by mere emotion. He wiped away his tears and pressed ahead.

"I promised to wait, but we can't wait forever. I would like to request that a time limit be put on their leave-taking. You might say until what hour, for example."

"Of course. Well...I'll make this my own responsibility, but I'd like to ask you to wait until the Hour of the Boar. I can declare that mother and children will have left the castle by then."

Hideyoshi did not refuse. Yet there was no time for such leisure: Nobunaga was determined to take Odani before sunset. The entire army was waiting expectantly. Although Hideyoshi had flown the banner signaling that the rescue attempt had been successful, too much time was passing. There was no way for Nobunaga or any of his generals to know what was going on inside the castle. During this time, Hideyoshi could imagine their perplexity, the various opinions going around headquarters, the indecision and confusion on Nobunaga's face as he listened to the voices of doubt.

"No, that's not unreasonable," Hideyoshi agreed. "So be it. Let them make their unhurried farewells until the Hour of the Boar."

Cheered by Hideyoshi's consent, Mikawa went back to the keep. By that time the colors of evening were already deepening. Servants and the tea master served Hideyoshi delicacies and *sake* that would not ordinarily have been found inside a besieged castle.

When the servants withdrew, Hideyoshi drank by himself. It seemed as though his entire body was soaking up the autumn from the thin-edged lacquer cup. It was a *sake* on which you could not get drunk—cold and slightly bitter. Well, I should drink this with gusto, too. How much difference is there between those going to their deaths and those left behind? I suppose you could say only an instant, when you take the long-term philo-sophical view, considering the flow of thousands of years. He did his best to laugh out loud. But every time he drank, the *sake* chilled his heart. Somehow, he felt as if sobbing were pressing in on him in the oppressive silence.

Oichi's sobs and sorrow; Nagamasa; the innocent faces of the children: he could imagine what was taking place in the keep. What would it be like if I were Asai Naga-masa? he asked himself. After thinking this way, his emotions took a sudden swing, and he remembered his last words to Nene:

"I am a samurai. I might die in some battle this time. If I am killed, you should marry again before you are thirty years old. After you reach thirty, your beauty is going to wane, and the possibility of a happy match is going to be dim. You are capable of discre-tion, and it is better for a human being to be prepared with discrimination in this life. So if you've passed thirty, choose a good path with your own sense of discrimination. I'm not going to order you to remarry. And again, if we have a child, plan a future for that child to be your mainstay, whether you're young or on in years. Don't give yourself up to the complaints of women. Think as a mother, and use your mother's discrimination in everything you do."

At some point Hideyoshi had fallen asleep. Which is not to say that he had lain down; he just sat there and looked as though he were practicing meditation. From time to time he nodded his head. He was good at sleeping. He had developed this ability during the unfavorable circumstances of his youth, and was so disciplined that he could nod off whenever he wanted to, regardless of time or place.

He awoke to the sound of a hand drum. The food trays and *sake* had been taken away. Only the lamps still flickered with a white light. His lightheadedness had cleared away, and the fatigue had left his body. Hideyoshi realized that he must have slept for quite a while. At the same time he somehow felt a sense of cheer wrapping his entire being. Before he had gone to sleep, the atmosphere in the castle had been one of gloom and melancholy; but now it had changed with the sounds of the drum and laughing voices, and strangely, a genial warmth seemed to be floating in from somewhere.

He couldn't help feeling as though he had been bewitched. He was clearly awake, however, and everything was real. He could hear the sound of a hand drum, and some-one was singing. The sounds were coming from the keep and were far away and indis-tinct, but he was sure someone had burst out laughing.

Hideyoshi suddenly wanted to be with people and went out onto the veranda. He could see a great number of lamps as well as people in the lord's residence on the other side of the wide central garden. A light breeze carried the smell of *sake*, and when the wind blew in his direction, he could hear the samurai beating time and singing.

The flowers are crimson,
The plums are scented.
The willows are green,
And a man's worth is decided by his heart.
Men among men,
Samurai that we are;

Flowers among flowers,
Samurai that we are.
Human life passes like this.
What is it without some pleasure?
Even if you'll never see tomorrow.

No, especially if you'll never see tomorrow. This was Hideyoshi's cherished theory.
He, who despised the dark and loved the light, had found something that was a blessing
in this world. Almost unconsciously he ambled in the direction of the gaiety, pulled along
by the singing voices. Servants went running by in a hurry. They were carrying large trays
piled high with food, and a barrel of *sake*.

They hurried with the same kind of eagerness they would probably show in the battle
for the castle. It was certainly a gay party, and the vigor of life appeared on every face. It
was enough to make Hideyoshi a little doubtful. "Hey! Isn't that Lord Hideyoshi?"

"Oh, General Mikawa."

"I wasn't able to find you in the guest room and was looking all over for you." Mikawa had the blush of *sake* on his cheeks too, and he no longer looked so haggard.

"Why all this gaiety in the keep?" Hideyoshi asked.

"Don't worry. As I promised you, it will end at the Hour of the Boar. It is said that
since we must all die, the manner of our dying should be glorious. Lord Nagamasa and
all his men are in high spirits, so he opened up all the *sake* vats in the castle and let it be
known that there would be an Assembly of the Samurai. This way they're going to drink
their farewells to each other before they leave this world."

"What about his farewell to his wife and children?"

"That's been taken care of." Through his intoxication, tears once again began to well
up in Mikawa's eyes. An Assembly of the Samurai—this was a common affair in any clan,
a time when the iron-clad divisions between classes and between lord and retainers were
relaxed, and everyone enjoyed themselves with drunken song.

The assembly served a dual purpose: it was Nagamasa's farewell to his retainers, who
were going to their deaths, and to his wife and children, who would live.

"But it's going to be boring for me just to hide away until the Hour of the Boar,"
Hideyoshi said. "With your permission, I'd like to attend the banquet."

"That's exactly why I was looking around for you. It's what His Lordship desires as
well."

"What! Lord Nagamasa wants me to come?"

"He says that if he's entrusting his wife and children to the Oda clan, you must look
after them from now on. Especially his young children."

"He shouldn't worry! And I'd like to tell him that in person. Would you take me to
him?"

Hideyoshi followed Mikawa into a large banqueting hall. Every eye in the room
turned toward him. The smell of *sake* filled the air. Naturally, everyone was in full armor,
and every man there had resolved to die. They were going to die together; like blossoms
shaking in the wind, they were ready to fall all at once. But now, as they were having the
best time they could, suddenly here was the enemy! Most of them glared at Hideyoshi

with bloodshot eyes—eyes that would make most men cower.

"Excuse me," Hideyoshi said to no one in particular. He entered, walking with small steps, and advanced right up to Nagamasa, in front of whom he prostrated himself.

"I have come, grateful that you've commanded that a cup should be extended even to me. Concerning the future of your son and three daughters, I will protect them even at the cost of my own life," Hideyoshi said in one breath. Had he paused or appeared to be in the least bit afraid, the samurai around him might have been driven to some unfortunate action through their inebriation and hatred.

"That is my request, General Hideyoshi." Nagamasa took a cup and passed it directly to him.

Hideyoshi took the cup and drank.

Nagamasa seemed satisfied. Hideyoshi had not dared to mention the name of Oichi or Nobunaga. Nagamasa's beautiful young wife was sitting with her children off to the side, hidden by a silver folding screen. They huddled together like irises blooming at the edge of a pond. Hideyoshi looked at the flickering of the silver lantern from the corner of his eye, but did not look at them directly. He returned the cup respectfully to Nagamasa.

"For the time being, we should forget that we are enemies," Hideyoshi said. "Having accepted this *sake* at your assembly, with your permission, I would like to perform a short dance."

"You want to dance?" Nagamasa said, expressing the surprise of all the men present. They were a little overawed by this little man.

Oichi drew her children to her knee, just as a mother hen might protect her chicks. "Don't be frightened. Mother is here," she whispered.

Having received Nagamasa's permission to dance, Hideyoshi got up and walked to the middle of the room. He was just about to begin when Manju cried out, "It's him!"

Manju and Chacha held fast to their mother's lap. They were looking at the man who earlier had been so frightening. Hideyoshi began to beat the time with his foot. At the same time, he slapped open a fan that showed a red circle on a golden field.

> Having so much leisure,
> I gaze at the gourd at the gate.
> Now and then, a gentle breeze
> Unexpectedly there, by chance here;
> Unexpectedly, by chance,
> The gourd vine, how amusing.

He sang in a loud voice, and danced as though he had not one other thing in his mind. But before his dance had ended, gunfire rang out from one section of the castle wall. Then came the sound of return fire from a shorter distance. It seemed that the forces both inside and outside the castle had started to fire on each other at the same moment.

"Damn it!" Hideyoshi swore, throwing down his fan. It was not yet the Hour of the Boar. The men outside the castle had known nothing about that, however. Hideyoshi had given no second signal. Thinking that they would not make an attack, he had felt more or

417

less secure. But now it seemed that the generals at headquarters had lost patience and decided to press Nobunaga to take immediate action.

Damn it! Hideyoshi's fan fell at the feet of the castle's commanding generals, who had all stood up together, and this brought their attention quite clearly to Hideyoshi, whom until now they had not thought of as an enemy.

"An attack!" shouted one man.

"The coward! He lied to us!"

The crowd of samurai split into two. The larger group dashed outside while the rest of the men surrounded Hideyoshi, ready to hack him to pieces with their swords.

"Who ordered this? Don't strike him! That man is not to be killed!" Nagamasa suddenly yelled at the top of his voice.

His men shouted back as though they were challenging him, "But the enemy has started a general attack!"

Nagamasa ignored their complaints and called, "Ogawa Denshiro, Nakajima Sakon!"

The two men were his children's tutors. When they came forward and prostrated themselves, Nagamasa also called for Fujikake Mikawa. "The three of you are to protect my wife and children and guide Hideyoshi out of the castle. Go now!" he commanded.

Then he looked sternly at Hideyoshi and, calming himself as much as possible, said, "All right, I'm entrusting them to you."

His wife and children threw themselves at his feet, but he shook them off and shouted, "Farewell." With that one word, Nagamasa grasped a halberd and ran off into the howling darkness.

One side of the castle was engulfed in mounting pillars of flame. Nagamasa instinctively shielded his face with one hand as he ran. Splinters of burning wood, like wings of flame, grazed his face. A thick black smoke was winding its way over the ground. The first and second Oda samurai to breach the castle walls had already called out their names. The flames had reached the mansion in the keep and were running up the gutters faster than the rain had ever gone down them. Nagamasa spied a corps of iron-helmeted men concealed in that area and suddenly lunged to the side.

"The enemy!"

His close retainers and family members stood around him and struck at the invading troops. Above them were the flames, all around them was black smoke. The clanging armor rang out, spear against spear, sword against sword. The ground was soon covered with the bodies of the dead and wounded. The larger part of the soldiers in the castle followed Nagamasa and fought as long as they could, each achieving a glorious death. Few of them were captured or surrendered. The fall of Odani Castle was nothing like the defeat of the Asakura in Echizen or of the shogun in Kyoto. So it could be said that Nobunaga's judgment in choosing Nagamasa as a brother-in-law had not been wrong.

The troubles of Hideyoshi, who had saved Oichi and her children from the flames, and those of Fujikake Mikawa, were not concerned with the battle. If the attacking troops had only waited another three hours, Hideyoshi and his charges could have been led out of the castle easily. But only minutes after they had left the keep, the inside of the castle was engulfed in flames and fighting soldiers, so that Hideyoshi was finding it very difficult just to protect the four children and get them out.

Fujikake Mikawa carried the youngest girl on his back, her elder sister, Hatsu, went on the back of Nakajima Sakon, and Manju was strapped on the back of his tutor, Ogawa Denshiro.

"Hop up onto my shoulders," Hideyoshi told Chacha, but the little girl refused to leave her mother's side. Oichi held the girl close as though she would not let her go. Hideyoshi wrenched them apart and scolded them. "It would not do for you to be hurt. I'm begging you, this is what Lord Nagamasa asked me to do."

This was no time to treat them sympathetically, and even though his words were polite, his tone was frightening. Oichi put Chacha on his back.

"Is everybody ready? Stay by me. My lady, please give me your hand." Shouldering Chacha, Hideyoshi pulled Oichi by the hand and started out straight ahead. Oichi stumbled along, barely able to keep from falling. Soon she pulled her hand free from Hideyoshi's grasp without saying a word. She followed as a mother would follow, half-crazed with distraction for the children who were in front of her and behind her in the midst of the fury.

Nobunaga was now watching the flames of Odani Castle, which were almost close enough to burn his face. The mountains and valleys on all three sides were red, and the burning castle roared like a huge smelting furnace.

When the flames finally turned to smoking ashes and it was all over, Nobunaga could not hold back his tears over his sister's fate. The fool! he cursed Nagamasa.

When all the temples and monasteries on Mount Hiei had been consigned to the flames along with the lives of every monk and layman on the mountain, Nobunaga had watched unmoved. Now those same eyes were filled with tears. The slaughter on Mount Hiei could not be compared with the death of his sister.

Human beings possess both intellect and instinct, and they often contradict each other. Nobunaga, however, had great faith in his destruction of Mount Hiei—that by destroying one single mountain, countless lives would be promised happiness and prosperity. The death of Nagamasa held no such great significance. Nagamasa had fought with a narrow-minded sense of duty and honor, and thus Nobunaga had been forced to do the same. Nobunaga himself had asked Nagamasa to abandon his stunted sense of duty and to share his own larger vision. Certainly he had treated Nagamasa with a large degree of consideration and generosity to the very end. But that generosity had to have a limit. He would have been lenient with the man right up to this evening, but his generals would not permit it.

Even though Takeda Shingen of Kai was dead, his generals and men were still in very good health, and his son's abilities were supposed to excel his father's. Nobunaga's enemies were only waiting for him to stumble. It would be folly to wait passively in northern Omi for a long time after he had defeated Echizen with one blow. Listening to this sort of reasoning and argument from his generals, even Nobunaga had been unable to speak up for his sister. But then Hideyoshi had requested permission to be Nobunaga's envoy for just one day. And although he had sent a signal of good news while it was still light, evening came, and then night, and he had sent no further report whatsoever.

Nobunaga's generals were indignant.

"Do you think he was tricked by the enemy?"

"He's probably been killed."

"The enemy is planning some scheme while we're off guard."

Nobunaga resigned himself and finally gave the order for an all-out attack. But after making his decision, he wondered if he had not sacrificed Hideyoshi's life, and his regret was nearly unbearable.

Suddenly a young samurai wearing black-threaded armor ran up in such a hurry that he almost hit Nobunaga with his spear.

"My lord!" he gasped.

"Kneel!" a general ordered. "Put your spear behind you!"

The young samurai fell heavily to his knees under the stares of the retainers surrounding Nobunaga.

"Lord Hideyoshi has just returned. He was able to get out of the castle without mishap."

"What! Hideyoshi is back?" Nobunaga exclaimed. "Alone?" he asked hurriedly.

The young messenger added, "He came with three men of the Asai clan, and with the Lady Oichi and her children."

Nobunaga was trembling. "Are you sure? Did you actually see them?"

"A group of us guarded them on the way back, right after they ran from the castle, which was collapsing in flames. They were exhausted, so we took them to a place of safety and gave them some water. Lord Hideyoshi commanded me to run ahead and make this report."

Nobunaga said, "You're Hideyoshi's retainer; what is your name?"

"I'm his chief page, Horio Mosuke."

"Thank you for bearing such good news. Now go and take a rest."

"Thank you, my lord, but the battle is still raging." With this, Mosuke quickly took his leave and dashed out toward the faraway clamor of warriors.

"Divine help…" someone mumbled off to the side with a sigh. It was Katsuie. The other generals also congratulated Nobunaga.

"This is an unanticipated blessing. You must be very happy."

A thread of emotion found its way wordlessly among them. These men were jealous of Hideyoshi's accomplishments, and were the very ones who had advocated abandoning him and hastening a general attack on the castle.

Nevertheless, Nobunaga's joy was overflowing, and his excellent mood immediately caused a brighter spirit to spread through his headquarters. While the others were offering their congratulations, the shrewd Katsuie said privately to Nobunaga, "Shall I greet him?"

Receiving Nobunaga's permission, he hurried off with a few retainers down the steep slope toward the castle. Finally, under the protection of Hideyoshi, the long-awaited Oichi climbed up to the headquarters on the plateau. A small corps of soldiers went in front, carrying torches. Hideyoshi panted along behind the men, still carrying Chacha on his back.

The first thing Nobunaga saw was the sweat on Hideyoshi's forehead, glistening in the light of the torches. Next came the old general, Fujikake Mikawa, and the two tutors, each carrying a child on his back. Nobunaga gazed at the children silently. No emotion showed on his face at all. Then, from about twenty paces to the rear, Shibata Katsuie came up, a white hand holding the shoulder of his armor. The hand belonged to Oichi, who was now half-dazed.

"Lady Oichi," Katsuie said, "your brother is right here." Katsuie quickly led her to Nobunaga.

When Oichi had fully regained her senses, all she could do was weep. For an instant the woman's sobbing blotted out every other sound in the camp. It wrung the hearts of even the veteran generals who were present. Nobunaga, however, looked disgusted. This was the beloved sister he had worried about so much until just a few moments before. Why wasn't he greeting his sister with wild joy? Had something ruined his mood? The generals were dismayed. The situation passed even Hideyoshi's understanding. Nobunaga's close retainers were constantly troubled by their lord's quick changes of mood. When they saw the familiar expression on his face, not one of them could do anything but stand by silently; and in the midst of the silence, Nobunaga himself found it difficult to cheer up.

There were not very many of Nobunaga's retainers who could read his inner thoughts and disentangle him from his moody and introverted self. In fact, Hideyoshi and the absent Akechi Mitsuhide were about the only ones who had this ability.

Hideyoshi watched the situation for a moment, and since no one seemed about to do anything, he said to Oichi, "Now, now, my lady. Go to his side and greet him. It won't do just to stand here crying for joy. What's the matter? You're brother and sister, aren't you?"

Oichi did not budge; she could not even look at her brother. Her mind was set on Nagamasa. To her, Nobunaga was nothing more than the enemy general who had killed her husband and had brought her here, a shamed captive in the enemy camp.

Nobunaga could tell exactly what was in his sister's heart. So, along with his satisfaction at her safety, he felt an uncontrollable revulsion for this foolish woman who could not understand her brother's great love.

"Hideyoshi, let her be. Don't waste your breath." Nobunaga stood up abruptly from his camp stool. He then lifted a section of the curtain surrounding his headquarters.

"Odani has fallen," he whispered, gazing at the flames. Both the battle cries and the fires burning the castle were dying down, and the waning moon cast a white light on the peaks and valleys as they waited for the dawn.

Just then, an officer and his men ran up the hill, yelling victory cries. When they set down the heads of Asai Nagamasa and his retainers in front of Nobunaga, Oichi screamed, and the children clinging to her started to cry.

Nobunaga shouted, "Stop that noise! Katsuie! Get the young ones out of here! I'm putting them in your care—both Oichi and the children. Hurry up and take them off someplace where no one will see them."

Then he summoned Hideyoshi and told him, "You will be in charge of the former Asai domain." He had decided to return to Gifu as soon as the castle had fallen.

Oichi was helped away. Later she would marry Katsuie. But one of Nagamasa's three young daughters who had come down the fiery mountain that night held a fate even stranger than her mother's. The eldest, Chacha, was later to become Lady Yodogimi, Hideyoshi's mistress.

It was the beginning of the Third Month of the following year. Good news had come to Nene, which, of course, was a letter from her husband.

> While some of the walls of Nagahama Castle are still a bit rough, it's been so long that I can hardly wait to see the two of you. Please tell Mother to start preparations to move here soon.

With such a short note, one could hardly have imagined what was going on, but actually a number of letters had been passing back and forth between husband and wife since the New Year. Hideyoshi had no leisure at all. He had been campaigning in the mountains of northern Omi for many months, and having to fight battles here and there, even when he did have some small respite he was soon sent running off to some other place.

Hideyoshi's services had been unsurpassed during the invasion of Odani. Nobunaga rewarded him by granting him his own castle for the first time, and a hundred eighty thousand bushels of the former Asai domain. Until then he had only been a general, but in one leap he joined the ranks of the provincial lords. At the same time, Nobunaga awarded him a new surname: Hashiba.

Hashiba Hideyoshi came into prominence that fall and now stood shoulder to shoulder with the other veteran Oda generals. He was not satisfied with his new castle at Odani, however; the castle was a defensive one, good for retreating into and withstanding a siege, but not a suitable base for an offensive. Three leagues to the south, on the shore of Lake Biwa, he found a better place to reside: a village by the name of Nagahama. Receiving Nobunaga's permission, he began construction immediately. By spring the white-walled keep, the sturdy walls, and the iron gates had been completed.

Hachisuka Hikoemon had been given the task of escorting Hideyoshi's wife and mother from Sunomata, and he arrived from Nagahama a few days after Nene had received Hideyoshi's letter. Nene and her mother-in-law were carried in lacquer palanquins, and their escort consisted of one hundred attendants.

Hideyoshi's mother had asked Nene to pass through Gifu and to ask for an audience with Lord Nobunaga to thank him for the many favors he had bestowed upon them. Nene felt this duty to be a heavy responsibility and considered it to be an ordeal. She was sure that if she went up to Gifu Castle and presented herself alone before Lord Nobunaga, she would be able to do nothing but sit and quake.

Nevertheless, the day came and, leaving her mother-in-law at the inn, she went alone to the castle, bringing gifts from Sunomata. At the castle she seemed to forget all of her anxiety. Once there, she looked up to her lord for the first time and, contrary to her expectations, found that he was completely open-minded and affable.

"You must have really exerted yourself, taking care of the castle for such a long time and looking after your mother-in-law. More than that, you must have been very lonely," Nobunaga said with such familiarity that she realized that her own family was in some way connected to Nobunaga's. She felt that she could be completely unreserved.

"I feel unworthy to be living peacefully at home while others are out on campaign. Heaven might punish me if I complained of loneliness."

Nobunaga stopped her with a laugh. "No, no. A woman's heart is a woman's heart, and you shouldn't have to conceal it. It's by thinking about the loneliness of caring for the household alone that you'll come to a deeper understanding of your husband's good points. Somebody wrote a poem about this; it goes something like, 'Off on a journey; the husband understands his wife's value at the snow-laden inn.' I can imagine that Hideyoshi too can hardly wait. Not only that, but the castle at Nagahama is new. Waiting alone during the campaign must have been difficult, but when you meet, you will be like newlyweds again."

Nene blushed all the way to her collar, and prostrated herself. She must have remembered being a new bride. Nobunaga guessed what she was thinking and smiled.

Food and lacquered vermilion *sake* cups were brought in. Receiving her cup from Nobunaga, Nene sipped her *sake* gracefully.

"Nene," he said, laughing. Finally able to look at him directly, she raised her eyes, wondering what he would say. Nobunaga spoke suddenly. "Just one thing: don't be jealous."

"Yes, my lord," she answered without really thinking, but she blushed right away. She, too, had heard a rumor about Hideyoshi visiting Gifu Castle in the company of a beautiful woman.

"That's just Hideyoshi. He's not perfect. But then a tea bowl that is too perfect has no charm. Everyone has faults. When an ordinary person has vices, he becomes a source of trouble; but very few men have Hideyoshi's abilities. I've often wondered what kind of woman would choose a man like him. Now I know after meeting you today, that Hideyoshi must love you, too. Don't be jealous. Live in harmony."

How could Nobunaga have understood a woman's heart so well? Although a little frightening, he was a man both her husband and herself could rely upon, She didn't know whether to be pleased or embarrassed.

She returned to her lodgings in the castle town. But what she spoke about most of all to her anxiously waiting mother-in-law was not Nobunaga's admonition about jealousy. "Whenever someone says the name Nobunaga, everyone shakes with fear, so I wondered what kind of person he would be. But there must be very few lords in this country who are as tender as he is. I couldn't imagine how a man who is so refined could turn into the fearsome demon they say he is on horseback. He also knew something about you, and said that you have a wonderful son and should be the happiest person in Japan. He told me that there are very few men like Hideyoshi in the whole country, and that I had chosen a good husband. Why, he even flattered me and told me I had discerning eyes."

The journey of the two women continued peacefully. They crossed through Fuwa and finally looked out from their palanquins at the springtime face of Lake Biwa.

BOOK FIVE

THIRD YEAR OF TENSHO
1575

CHARACTERS AND PLACES

TAKEDA KATSUYORI, son of Takeda Shingen and Lord of Kai
BABA NOBUFUSA, senior Takeda retainer
YAMAGATA MASAKAGE, senior Takeda retainer
KURODA KANBEI, Odera retainer
MYOKO, name taken by Ranmaru's mother
when she became a nun
UESUGI KENSHIN, lord of Echigo
YAMANAKA SHIKANOSUKE, senior Amako retainer
MORI TERUMOTO, lord of the western provinces
KIKKAWA MOTOHARU, Terumoto's uncle
KOBAYAKAWA TAKAKAGE, Terumoto's uncle
ODA NOBUTADA, Nobunaga's eldest son
UKITA NAOIE, Lord of Okayama Castle
ARAKI MURASHIGE, senior Oda retainer
NAKAGAWA SEBEI, senior Oda retainer
TAKAYAMA UKON, senior Oda retainer
SHOJUMARU, Kuroda Kanbei's son
SAKUMA NOBUMORI, senior Oda retainer

NAGAHAMA, Hideyoshi's castle
KOFU, capital of Kai
AZUCHI, Nobunaga's new castle near Kyoto
HIMEJI, Hideyoshi's base for the invasion of the west
WESTERN PROVINCES, domain of the Mori clan
ITAMI, Araki Murashige's castle

SUNSET OF KAI

Takeda Katsuyori had seen the coming of thirty springs. He was taller and broader than his father, Takeda Shingen, and it was said that he was a handsome man.

It was the third year after Shingen's death; the Fourth Month would be the end of the official period of mourning.

Shingen's final command, "Hide your mourning for three years," had been followed to the letter. But every year on the anniversary of his death, the lamps of all the temples of Kai—and particularly those of the Eirin Temple—were lit for secret memorial services. For three days Katsuyori had forsaken all military matters and stayed shut up in the Bishamon Temple, deep in meditation.

On the third day, Katsuyori had the doors of the temple opened to let out the smoke of the incense burned during Shingen's memorial service. As soon as Katsuyori had changed his clothes, Atobe Oinosuke requested an urgent, private audience.

"My lord," Oinosuke began, "please read this letter immediately and give me an answer. A spoken one will do; I'll write the reply for you."

Katsuyori quickly opened the letter. "Well, now...from Okazaki." It was clear that he had been expecting the letter for some time, and it was no ordinary expression that moved across his face as he read. For a moment he seemed unable to come to a decision.

The song of a bush warbler could be heard coming from amid the young greenery of approaching summer.

Katsuyori stared at the sky through the window. "I understand. That's my answer."

Oinosuke looked up at his master. "Will it be enough, my lord?" he asked, just to make sure.

"It will," Katsuyori replied. "We shouldn't miss this heaven-sent opportunity. The messenger has to be a trustworthy man."

"This is an extremely important matter. You need have no worries about that." Not too long after Oinosuke had left the temple, the Office of State Affairs issued a call to arms. Soldiers could be seen moving throughout the night, and there was constant activity inside and outside the castle. When dawn broke, fourteen or fifteen thousand men, wet with the morning dew, were already silently waiting on the assembly ground outside the castle. And still more soldiers were coming. The conch shell proclaiming the departure of the troops rang out over the sleeping houses of Kofu several times before the sun rose.

Katsuyori had slept only a little during the night, but now he was in full armor. He did not look like a man suffering from lack of sleep, and his extraordinary good health and his dreams of greatness shone forth from his body like the dew on the new leaves.

He had not been idle for even one day during the three years since his father's death. Mountains and swift rivers formed strong natural defenses around Kai, but he was not content with the province he had inherited. He had, after all, been given more courage and resourcefulness than his father. Katsuyori—unlike the offspring of many great samurai clans—could not be called an unworthy son. Instead, it might be said that his pride, his sense of duty, and his military prowess were excessive.

No matter how secret the clan had tried to keep it, news of Shingen's death had leaked out to the enemy provinces, and many had considered it too good an opportunity to miss. The Uesugi had made a sudden attack; the Hojo had also changed their attitude. And it was certain that if the opportunity were to arise, the Oda and the Tokugawa would make incursions from their own territories.

Katsuyori, like the son of any great man, found himself in a difficult position. Still he had never disgraced his father's name. In almost every engagement he fought, he came away with the victory. For this reason, rumors had spread that Shingen's death was just a fabrication, because he seemed to appear whenever an opportunity presented itself.

"Generals Baba and Yamagata have requested an audience before the campaign begins," a retainer announced.

The army was on the point of leaving when this message was delivered to Katsuyori. Both Baba Nobufusa and Yamagata Masakage had been senior retainers in Shingen's day.

Katsuyori asked in return, "Are they both ready to march?"

"Yes, my lord," the messenger replied.

Katsuyori nodded at the man's reply. "Show them in, then," he said.

Moments later the two generals appeared before Katsuyori. He already knew what they were going to say to him.

"As you can see," Baba began, "we hurried to the castle without a moment's delay at the call to arms last night. But this is extraordinary; there was no war council, and we were wondering what the prospects of this campaign are. Our situation these days does not allow us the luxury of frivolous troop movements." Yamagata continued, "Your late father, Lord Shingen, tasted the bitter cup of defeat too many times when he attacked the west. Mikawa is small, but its warriors are stouthearted men, and the Oda have had time to come up with a number of countermeasures by now. If we were to get in too deep, we might not be able to extricate ourselves."

Speaking in turn, the two men outlined their objections. These men were experienced veterans trained by the great Shingen himself, and they had no great regard for either Katsuyori's resourcefulness or his valor. On the contrary, they saw them as a danger. Katsuyori had felt this for some time, and his character would not let him accept their conservative advice—that the best thing to do would be to guard the borders of Kai for several years.

"You know I wouldn't start out on a rash campaign. Ask Oinosuke for the details. But this time we are sure to take Okazaki Castle and Hamamatsu Castle. I'll show them how to accomplish a long-cherished dream. We must keep our strategy a secret. I don't plan on telling our men what we're doing until we're pressing in on the enemy."

Katsuyori deftly avoided the remonstrances of his two generals, who both looked unhappy.

The advice to ask Oinosuke did not sit well with them; they were not used to being spoken to in this way. Of the same mind, the two men exchanged glances and for a moment looked at each other in blank amazement. Troops were being moved without anyone having consulted them—Shingen's veteran generals—and decisions were being made with the likes of Atobe Oinosuke.

Baba tried to speak to Katsuyori one more time. "We will listen to everything Master Oinosuke has to say later on, but if you would first tell us just a word or two about this secret plan, old generals like us will be able to make a stand with our eyes on a place to die."

"I'm not saying anything else here," Katsuyori said, looking at the men around him. Then he added severely, "I'm pleased that you're concerned, but I am not unaware of how important this present matter is. Moreover, I cannot now abandon the plan. Early this morning I swore an oath on the *Mihata Tatenashi*."

When they heard the sacred names, the two generals prostrated themselves and said a silent prayer. The *Mihata Tatenashi* were sacred relics venerated for generations by the Takeda clan. The *Mihata* was the banner of the war god Hachiman, and the *Tatenashi* was the armor of the clan's founder. It was an unbreakable rule of the Takeda clan that once an oath was sworn on these objects, it could not be broken.

Katsuyori's declaration that he was acting under this sacred oath meant that there were no further grounds upon which the two generals could continue to raise objections. At that moment the conch signaled the troops to get into formation and prepare to march out, forcing the two generals to take their leave. But, still worried about the fate of the clan, they rode to see Oinosuke at his position in the ranks.

Oinosuke cleared the area and proudly informed them of the plan. In Okazaki, which was now governed by Ieyasu's son, Nobuyasu, there was a man in charge of finances by the name of Oga Yashiro. Some time before, Oga had changed his allegiance to the Takeda clan and was now a trusted ally of Katsuyori.

The messenger who had come to Tsutsujigasaki two days before had carried a secret letter from Oga, which had informed them that the time was ripe. Nobunaga had been in the capital since the beginning of the year. Even before that, when Nobunaga had tried to destroy the warrior-monks of Nagashima, Ieyasu had sent no reinforcements, and the alliance between the two provinces had become somewhat strained.

When the Takeda army attacked Mikawa with its legendary speed, Oga would find a means to throw Okazaki Castle into confusion, open the castle gates, and let the Kai forces in. Katsuyori would then kill Nobuyasu and take the Tokugawa family hostage. Hamamatsu Castle would be forced to surrender, and its garrison would join the Takeda army, leaving Ieyasu no other choice but to flee to Ise or Mino.

"What do you think? Doesn't this sound like good news from heaven?" Oinosuke spoke proudly, as though the entire scheme had been his own. The two generals had no desire to hear any more. Leaving Oinosuke, they returned to their own regiments, looking at each other in silence.

"Baba, it's said that a province may fall, but the mountains and rivers endure. Neither of us wants to live to see the mountains and rivers of a ruined province," Yamagata said with deep feeling.

Baba nodded and said with a sad look in his eyes, "The end of our lives is swiftly approaching. All that is left for us is to find a good place to die, to follow our former lord, and to atone for the crime of being unworthy counselors."

Baba's and Yamagata's reputations as Shingen's bravest generals had traveled far beyond the borders of Kai. They were already gray when Shingen was alive, but after his death, their hair had quickly turned white.

The leaves on the mountains of Kai were a young and tender green, before the coming of that year's broiling summer, and the waters of the Fuefuki River babbled the song of eternal life. But how many soldiers wondered if they would ever see those mountains again?

The army was not what it had been when Shingen was alive. A plaintive note sounding the uncertainty of life was heard in the banners fluttering in the wind and in the sound of their marching feet. But the fifteen thousand troops beat the war drums, unfurled their banners, and marched across the border of Kai; and their majesty was reflected in the eyes of the people just as brilliantly as in Shingen's day.

Just as the crimson of the setting sun is similar to the sun at dawn, no matter where one looked—whether at the colorful standard bearers and banners of each regiment, or at the massed armored cavalry that rode tightly around Katsuyori—there was no sign of decline. Katsuyori was supremely self-confident as he imagined the enemy castle at Okazaki already in his hands. With the gold inlay of his visor reflecting on his handsome cheeks, the future of this young general seemed brilliant. And in fact he had already achieved victories that had stirred up Kai's fighting spirit, even after the death of the great Shingen.

Setting forth from Kai on the first day of the Fifth Month, they finally crossed Mount Hira from Totomi and entered into Mikawa proper, bivouacking in front of a river in the evening.

From the opposite bank, two enemy samurai came swimming toward them. The guards quickly took them captive. The two men were Tokugawa samurai who had been chased out of their own province. They asked to be taken before Katsuyori.

"What? Why have they fled here?" Katsuyori knew that it could only mean one thing: Oga's treachery had been discovered.

Katsuyori's mighty army had already entered Mikawa. Should I attack or fall back? Katsuyori asked himself over and over again. He was badly confused and discouraged. His strategy had depended on Oga's treachery and the confusion he would cause inside

Okazaki Castle. Oga's detection and arrest were a disastrous setback. But having come this far, it would not be very gallant to fall back without accomplishing anything. On the other hand, it wouldn't be right to advance carelessly. Katsuyori's manly character was distressed in earnest. And it pricked his obstinate nature to recall that, when the army had left Kai, Baba and Yamagata had warned him not to do anything rash.

"Three thousand soldiers should start off toward Nagashino," he ordered. "I myself will attack Yoshida Castle and sweep the entire area."

Katsuyori struck camp before dawn and headed toward Yoshida. Lacking any confidence of success, he set fire to a few villages in a show of force. He did not attack Yoshida Castle, possibly because Ieyasu and his son, Nobuyasu, had made a clean sweep of the traitors and had quickly moved troops as far as Hajikamigahara.

Quite different from Katsuyori's army, which now, unable either to advance or to retreat, could only move to preserve its dignity, the Tokugawa forces had massacred the rebels and dashed out with great impetus.

"Are we a dying province or a rising one?" was their war cry. Their numbers might have been small, but their morale was completely different from that of Katsuyori's troops.

The vanguards of the two armies met in small clashes two or three times at Hajikamigahara. But the Kai forces were of no common order, either, and understanding that it would be difficult to match themselves to the enemy's martial spirit, they suddenly withdrew.

The cry went up, "To Nagashino! To Nagashino!" Making a quick reversal in their march, they showed the Tokugawa forces their backs and took off as though they had important business elsewhere.

Nagashino was an ancient battleground, and its castle was said to be impregnable. In the earlier part of the century, it had been controlled by the Imagawa clan; later it had been claimed by the Takeda clan as part of Kai. But then, in the first year of Tensho, it had been taken by Ieyasu and was now commanded by Okudaira Sadamasa of the Tokugawa clan, with a garrison of five hundred men.

Because of its strategic value, Nagashino was the center of all kinds of plots, betrayals, and bloodlettings, even during peacetime.

By the evening of the eighth day of the Fifth Month, the Kai army had besieged the castle's tiny garrison of five hundred men.

Nagashino Castle stood at the confluence of the Taki and Ono rivers in the mountainous region of eastern Mikawa. Behind it to the northeast there was nothing but mountains. Its moat, which drew its water from the fast-flowing streams of the two rivers, had a width that ranged from one hundred eighty to three hundred feet. The bank was ninety feet in height at its lowest point, and at its highest was a precipice of one hundred fifty feet. The depth of the water was no more than five or six feet, but the current was swift. And indeed, there were some frighteningly deep spots where water rose in sprays or twisted into seething rapids.

"How ostentatious!" said Nagashino Castle's commander as he surveyed the meticulous disposition of Katsuyori's troops from the watchtower.

From around the tenth, Ieyasu had begun to send messengers to Nobunaga several times a day, to report on the situation at Nagashino. Any emergency for the Tokugawa was considered an emergency for the Oda, and the atmosphere in Gifu Castle was already uncommonly tense.

Nobunaga responded positively but didn't seem to be making any sudden move to mobilize his troops. The war council lasted two days.

"There's no hope for victory. Mobilizing the army would be useless," cautioned Mori Kawachi.

"No! That would be turning our backs on our duty!" someone else argued.

Others, like Nobumori, took the middle path. "As General Mori says, it's obvious that the chances of victory against Kai are slim, but if we put off mobilizing our troops, the Tokugawa may accuse us of bad faith, and if we're not careful, it's not impossible for them to change sides, make an accord with the Kai army, and turn against us. I think it best that we execute a passive deployment of the troops."

Then, from the midst of those attending the war council, a voice shouted out, "No! No!" It was Hideyoshi, who had hurried from Nagahama, bringing the troops under his command.

"I suppose the castle at Nagashino does not seem very important at this point," he went on, "but after it becomes a foothold for an invasion by Kai, the Tokugawa's defenses are going to be just like a broken dike, and if that happens, it's clear that the Tokugawa will not hold Kai for long. If we give that sort of advantage to Kai now, how will our own Gifu Castle have any security at all?" He spoke loudly, and his voice rang with emotion. Those present could do nothing other than look at him. He continued, "There is no military strategy I know of that advocates a passive deployment of troops once they are mobilized. Instead of that, shouldn't we march out immediately and confidently? Will the Oda fall? Will the Takeda win?"

All the generals thought that Nobunaga would send six or seven thousand troops— no more than ten thousand—but on the following day he gave the order to make preparations for a huge army of thirty thousand men.

Although Nobunaga had not said that he agreed with Hideyoshi during the council, he was showing it now by his actions. His decision was in earnest and he was going to lead his troops himself.

"We may be calling these men reinforcements," he said, "but it is the fate of the Oda clan that hangs in the balance."

The army left Gifu on the thirteenth and reached Okazaki the next day. Nobunaga's army rested only one day. By the morning of the sixteenth day of that month, it had reached the front.

Horses throughout the village began to neigh as the clouds of dawn became visible. Banners rustled in the breeze, and the conch sounded far and wide. The number of troops that started out from the castle town of Okazaki that morning was indeed enormous, and the people of the small province were awed. They were both relieved by and envious of the number of troops and equipment mustered by the mighty province with which they were allied. When the thirty thousand Oda soldiers marched past with their various banners, insignia, and commanders' standards, the number of corps they were divided into was difficult to determine.

"Look at all the guns they have!" the people along the roadside exclaimed with surprise. The Tokugawa soldiers were unable to hide their envy: out of Nobunaga's thirty thousand soldiers, close to ten thousand were gunners. They also pulled along huge cast-iron cannons. But what was strangest of all was that almost every foot soldier who was not carrying a gun shouldered instead a stake of the kind used to make a palisade, and a length of rope.

"What do you think the Oda are going to do with all those stakes?" the onlookers wondered.

The Tokugawa army that had set off for the front lines that morning had numbered fewer than eight thousand men. And that was the bulk of the army. The only thing they did not fall short in was morale.

To the Oda, this was foreign territory—an area they were coming to as relief troops. But to the warriors of the Tokugawa clan, this was the land of their ancestors. It was a land the enemy was not to take a single step into, and from which there was absolutely no place to retreat. Even the foot soldiers were filled with the spirit of this belief from the time they started out, and they shared a certain tragic feeling. Comparing their equipment with that of the Oda army, they could see that they were sadly inferior; in fact, there was no comparison at all. But they did not feel inferior. When they had distanced themselves several leagues from the castle town, the Tokugawa forces quickened their pace. When they approached the village of Ushikubo, they changed their direction, hurrying away from the Oda troops and toward Shidaragahara like storm clouds.

Mount Gokurakuji stood directly in front of the plain of Shidaragahara, and from its peak one could point to the Takeda positions at Tobigasu, Kiyoida, and Arumigahara.

Nobunaga set up his headquarters on Mount Gokurakuji, while Ieyasu chose Mount Danjo. The thirty-eight thousand Tokugawa and Oda forces deployed on these two mountains had already finished their preparations for the coming battle.

The sky filled with clouds, but there was no hint of lightning or wind.

On Mount Gokurakuji, the generals of both the Oda and Tokugawa clans gathered in a temple at the top of the mountain for a joint military conference. In the middle of the conference it was announced to Ieyasu that the scouts had just returned.

When Nobunaga heard this, he said, "They've come at a good time. Bring them here, and we can all listen to their reports on the enemy's movements."

The two scouts made their reports in a rather pompous way. The first began, "Lord Katsuyori has made his headquarters to the west of Arumigahara. His retainers and cavalry are, indeed, quite hale. They seemed to number close to four thousand men, and appeared to be quite composed and self-possessed."

The second went on, "Obata Nobusada and his attack corps are overlooking the battlefield from a low hill a little to the south of Kiyoida. I could see that the main army of about three thousand men under Naito Shuri is encamped from Kiyoida to Asai. The left wing, which also numbers about three thousand, is under the standards of Yamagata Masakage and Oyamada Nobushige. Finally, the right wing is under Anayama Baisetsu and Baba Nobufusa. They look extremely impressive."

"What about the troops laying siege to Nagashino Castle?" Ieyasu asked.

"About two thousand troops have remained around the castle and are keeping it tightly in check. There also seems to be a surveillance corps on a hill to the west of the castle, and it's possible that about a thousand soldiers are concealed in the fortresses around Tobigasu."

The reports of the two men were, for the most part, rather incomplete. But the generals of the units they mentioned were famous beyond measure for their ferocity and valor, and Baba and Obata were both strategists of immense reputation. As the Oda and Tokugawa generals listened to the scouts' account of the enemies' positions, the vehemence of their will to fight, and their composure and self-confidence, the color drained from their faces.

They were silent, like men consumed by dread just before a battle. Suddenly Sakai Tadatsugu spoke, in a voice so loud it surprised the men around him.

"The outcome is already clear. There is no need for further discussion. How is an enemy of such scant numbers going to be a match for our own huge army?"

"That's enough conferring!" Nobunaga agreed, and slapped his knee. "Tadatsugu has spoken admirably. To the eyes of a coward, the crane that flies across the paddies looks like an enemy banner and makes him quake with fear," he laughed. "I feel greatly relieved by the reports of these two men. Lord Ieyasu, we should celebrate!"

Having been praised, Sakai Tadatsugu got a bit carried away and said, "My own opinion is that the enemy's greatest weakness is at Tobigasu. If we took a roundabout route and struck at their weak point from the rear with some lightly armed soldiers, the morale of their entire army would be thrown into confusion, and our men—"

"Tadatsugu!" Nobunaga said sharply. "What good is such a ploy in this great battle? You're being presumptuous. I think everybody had better withdraw!" Using the reprimand as an excuse, Nobunaga adjourned the conference. Shamefaced, Tadatsugu left with the others.

When all had left, however, Nobunaga said to Ieyasu, "Forgive me for rebuking that brave Tadatsugu so severely in front of all the others. I think his plan is excellent, but I was afraid that it might leak out to the enemy. Would you console him later?"

"No, it was clearly an indiscretion on Tadatsugu's part to reveal our plans, even though he was among allies. It was a good lesson for him. And I learned something, too."

"I rebuked him so severely that I doubt that even our own men will expect us to use the plan. Call Tadatsugu, and give him permission to make a surprise attack on Tobigasu."

"I'm sure it is his fondest wish to hear just that."

Ieyasu summoned Tadatsugu and related Nobunaga's wishes.

Tadatsugu needed no further urging to go into action. Under extreme secrecy, he finished the preparations for his unit and then had a private audience with Nobunaga.

"I'll be leaving at sunset, my lord," were Tadatsugu's only words.

Nobunaga, too, said little. Nevertheless, he assigned five hundred of his gunners to Tadatsugu. The entire force comprised more than three thousand men.

They left the encampment at nightfall, in the absolute darkness of the Fifth Month. About the time they got under way, stripes of white rain were cutting diagonally through the darkness. The downpour drenched them to the skin as they marched along in silence.

Before climbing Mount Matsu, the entire company hid in a temple compound at the foot of the mountain. The soldiers took off their armor, left their horses behind, and shouldered whatever equipment they would take with them.

The slope was painfully steep and muddy from the torrential rain. Every time the men took a step forward, they would slip back. Hanging on to the shafts of the spears and grasping the hands of their comrades above them, they scaled the three hundred fifty yards to the summit.

A pale whiteness was beginning to appear in the night sky, announcing the coming dawn. The clouds began to part, and the splendor of the morning sun pierced the thick sea of mist.

"It's clearing!"

"Luck from heaven!"

"Conditions are perfect!"

At the top of the mountain the men put on their armor and divided into two groups. The first would make a dawn raid on the enemy fortress on the mountain, and the other would attack Tobigasu.

The Takeda had underestimated the danger, and now their waking shouts broke out in confusion. The fires set by Tadatsugu's forces sent black smoke rising from the mountain stronghold. The Takeda fled in a disorderly rout toward Tobigasu. But by then Tadatsugu's second division had already breached the castle walls.

The night before, after Tadatsugu's departure, Nobunaga's entire army had been given the order to advance. But this was not to be the outbreak of the battle.

The army defied the driving rain and moved on toward the neighborhood of Mount Chausu. From that time until dawn, the soldiers pounded the stakes they had carried into the ground, and bound them together with rope to create a palisade that looked like a meandering centipede.

As dawn was nearing, Nobunaga inspected the defenses on horseback. The rain had stopped, and the construction of the palisade had been completed.

Nobunaga turned to the Tokugawa generals and yelled at them with a laugh, "Wait and see! Today we're going to let the Kai army come close, and then we'll handle them like molting skylarks."

I wonder, each of them thought. They imagined that he was just trying to reassure them. But what they could clearly see was that the soldiers from Gifu—the troops who had shouldered the stakes and ropes all the way from Okazaki—were now on the battlefield. And the thirty thousand stakes had become a long, serpentine palisade.

"Let the picked troops of Kai come on!"

The construction itself, however, could not be used to attack the enemy. And to annihilate the enemy in the way Nobunaga had described, they would have to draw him toward the palisade. To lure him, one of Sakuma Nobumori's units and Okubo Tadayo's gunners were sent outside the palisade to wait for the enemy.

Suddenly a chorus of voices lifted skyward. The Takeda had been careless with their enemies, and their shouts of dismay came when they saw the black smoke rising from the direction of Tobigasu, behind them.

"The enemy is behind us, too!"

435

"They're pressing in from the rear!"

As their agitation began to turn to panic, Katsuyori gave the command to charge. "Don't delay for a moment! Waiting for the enemy will only give them the advantage!"

His own self-confidence, and the faith of his troops that was based on that self-confidence, amounted to this creed: Don't even question me! Have faith in a martial valor that has never known defeat since the time of Lord Shingen.

But civilization moves on like a horse at full gallop. The Southern Barbarians—the Portuguese—had revolutionized warfare with the introduction of firearms. How sad that Takeda Shingen had not had the wisdom to foresee this. Kai, protected by its mountains, ravines, and rivers, was cut off from the center of things and isolated from foreign influences. In addition, its samurai were consumed by an obstinacy and conceit particular to the men of a mountainous province. They had very little fear of their own shortcomings, and no desire to study the ways of other lands. The upshot was that they relied completely on their cavalry and picked troops. The forces under Yamagata fiercely attacked the troops of Sakuma Nobumori outside the palisade. In contrast, Nobunaga had planned a fully scientific strategy, using modern tactics and weapons.

The rain had just stopped; the ground was muddy.

The left wing of the Kai army—the two thousand troops under Yamagata—received their general's command not to attack the palisade. They took a roundabout route to bypass it. But the mire was horrible. The downpour of the night before had caused the brook to overflow its banks. This natural calamity was unforeseen even by Yamagata, who had fully surveyed the lay of the land beforehand. The soldiers sank into the mud up to their shins. The horses were unable to move.

To add to their troubles, the Oda gunners under Okubo began to fire at Yamagata's flank.

"Turn!" Yamagata ordered.

With this short command, the mud-covered army changed its direction once again and thrust toward Okubo's gunners. Tiny sprays of mud appeared to spatter all over the two thousand armored men. Struck by the rifle fire, they fell, yelling as red blood spurted from them. Trampled by their own horses, they cried out in pathetic confusion.

Finally the armies collided. For decades, warfare had been changing. The ancient fighting style in which each samurai called out his own name and declared that he was the descendant of so-and-so, that his master was the lord of such-and-such a province, was fast disappearing.

Thus, once hand-to-hand fighting broke out—naked blade biting against naked blade and warrior grappling with warrior—its horror was beyond words.

The best weapons were first the gun and then the spear. The spear was not used for stabbing, but rather for brandishing, flailing, and striking, and these were the methods taught for the battlefield. Advantage, therefore, was perceived in length, and there were spears with shafts anywhere from twelve to eighteen feet long.

The common soldiers were lacking both in the training and in the courage that the situation demanded, and were really only capable of striking with their spears. Thus there were many occasions when a skillful warrior would rush into their midst with a short spear, thrust in every direction, and, almost with ease, win himself the fame accorded a single warrior who had struck down dozens of men.

Attacked by swarms of these men, both the Tokugawa and the Oda forces were help-less. The Okubo corps was wiped out almost instantly. The reason the Okubo corps and the Sakuma forces were outside of the palisade, however, was to draw the enemy in, not to win. For this reason it would have been all right for them to turn and run. But as soon as they saw the faces of the Kai soldiers in front of them, they were unable to keep years of animosity from igniting in their hearts.

"Come and get us!" they cried.

Neither would they stand for the jeers and insults of the Kai warriors. Inevitably, the Oda men cast caution aside in the midst of all the blood, and thought only of their own province and reputations.

While this was going on, Katsuyori and his generals must have thought that the time was right, for the center battalions of Kai's fifteen-thousand-man army began to advance like a giant cloud. Their orderly formations broke up like a gigantic flock of birds taking flight, and as they finally approached the palisade, each corps simultaneously screamed its war cries.

To the eyes of the Takeda, the wooden palisade clearly appeared to be nothing much at all. They thought they would force their way through, breaking through with a single charge, boring right into the central Oda army like a drill.

Raising a battle cry, the Kai forces charged the palisade. They were determined—some tried to clamber over, some to beat the fence down with huge mallets and iron staffs, some to cut through it with saws, and some to douse it with oil and burn it down.

Nobunaga had left the fighting to the Sakuma and Okubo corps outside the palisade until then, and the ranks on Mount Chausu were silent. But suddenly...

"Now!"

Nobunaga's golden war fan cut through the air, and the commanders of the firearms regiments competed with each other in yelling out the order:

"Fire!"

"Fire!"

The earth shook at the volleys of gunfire. The mountain split open and the clouds were shredded. Powder smoke shrouded the palisade, and the horses and men of the Kai army fell like mosquitoes into piles of corpses.

"Don't retreat!" their commanders urged. "Follow me!"

Recklessly charging the palisade, the soldiers leaped over the dead bodies of their comrades, but they were unable to avoid the oncoming rain of bullets. Screaming pathetically, they ended up as corpses themselves.

In the end, the Kai army could no longer stand its ground.

"Retreat!" screamed four or five mounted commanders, pulling back their horses, the command somehow wrung from their throats even in their panic. One fell, covered with blood, while another was thrown from his whinnying horse as it went down under a hail of bullets.

No matter how badly they had been beaten, however, their spirit was not broken. They had lost almost one-third of their men in the first charge, but the instant they re-treated, a fresh force once again hastened toward the palisade. The blood that had spattered the thirty thousand stakes had not yet dried.

The gunfire coming from the palisade answered their charge directly, as if to say, We've been waiting.

Glaring at the palisade dyed red with the blood of their comrades, the fierce soldiers of Kai screamed as they charged, encouraging one another, vowing that they would never retreat a single yard.

"It's time to die!"

"On to our deaths!"

"Make a death shield so the others can leap over us!"

The "death shield" was a last-ditch tactic in which soldiers in the front rank sacrificed themselves to protect the advance of the next rank. Then that rank in turn acted as a shield for the troops following, and in this way the troops pressed on step by step. It was a terrible way to advance.

These were, indeed, brave men; but surely this charge was nothing more than a futile display of brute strength. And yet there were able tacticians among the generals leading the assault.

Katsuyori, of course, was at the rear, urging his men to go forward, but had his commanders known that victory was an absolute impossibility, there would have been no reason to ask for such an immense sacrifice and repeatedly to push the troops too far.

"That wall must be broken down!"

They must have believed that it could be done. Once the guns of that period were fired, reloading the ball and repacking the gunpowder took time. Thus, once a volley had been fired, the sound of gunfire would stop for a while. It was that interval that the Kai generals considered a window to be taken advantage of; thus the "death shield" was not begrudged.

Nobunaga, however, had considered that particular weak point, and for the new weapons he had devised new tactics. In this case, he divided his three thousand gunners into three groups. When the first thousand men had fired their weapons, each man would quickly step to the side and the second group would advance through their ranks, immediately firing their own volley. They, too, would then open their ranks and be quickly replaced by the third group. In this way, the interval the enemy so hoped for was never given to them throughout the entire battle.

Again, there were openings here and there in the palisade. Measuring the intervals between the tides of charges, the Oda and Tokugawa spear corps would dash out from inside the palisade and quickly strike at both wings of the Kai army.

Obstructed by the protective palisade and the gunfire, the Kai soldiers were unable to advance. When they attempted to retreat, they were harassed by the enemy's pursuit and the pincer attack. Now the Kai warriors, who took such pride in their discipline and training, did not have even a moment to exhibit their courage.

The Yamagata corps had retreated altogether, leaving behind a large number of men who had sacrificed their lives. Only Baba Nobufusa had not fallen into the trap.

Baba had clashed with the troops of Sakuma Nobumori, but as Nobumori had only been there originally as a decoy, the Oda troops feinted a retreat. The Baba corps chased after them and took possession of the encampment at Maruyama, but Baba's orders were to go no deeper, and he did not send a single soldier beyond Maruyama.

"Why don't you advance!" Baba was repeatedly asked by both Katsuyori's headquarters and his own officers.

Baba, however, would not move. "I have my own reasons to ponder over for a moment, and I'd better stop here to observe what is occurring. The rest of you should go ahead and advance. Win some glory for yourselves."

Every commander who got near enough to attack the palisade met with the same overwhelming defeat. And then Katsuie and Hideyoshi led their battalions far around the villages to the north and began to cut off the headquarters of the Kai army from the front lines.

It was almost noon, and the sun was high in a sky that promised the end of the rainy season. It now burned down on the earth with an abrupt heat and with a color that announced an intense summer.

Hostilities had begun at dawn, at the second half of the Hour of the Tiger. With the continual change of new troops, the men of the Kai army were by this time bathed in sweat and breathing hard. The blood that had been shed in the morning had dried like glue on the leather of their armor and on their hair and skin. And now there was fresh blood wherever one looked.

Behind the central army, Katsuyori was howling like a demon. Finally he had sent in every battalion, including the reserve corps usually held back for emergencies. If Katsuyori had understood the situation more quickly, he might have finished the matter with only a fraction of the damage his army incurred. But instead, moment by moment, he himself turned a small mistake into a monstrous one. In short, this was not simply a matter of martial spirit and courage. It was the same as if the forces of Nobunaga and Ieyasu had set snares at the hunting grounds and waited for wild ducks or boars to come. The Kai regiments that attacked so fiercely did nothing more than lose their valuable soldiers in a pointless "death shield."

Alas, it was said that even Yamagata Masakage, who had fought so well with the left wing since morning, had been struck down in battle. Other famous generals, men of great courage, went down one after another, until the dead and wounded numbered over half of the entire army.

"It's obvious that the enemy is going to be defeated. Isn't this the right moment?"

The general who spoke was Sassa Narimasa, who had been watching battle with Nobunaga.

Nobunaga immediately had Narimasa transmit his orders to the troops inside the palisade. He said, "Leave the palisade and attack. Destroy them all!"

Even Katsuyori's headquarters collapsed in the attack. The Tokugawa pressed in on the left. The Oda broke through the Takeda vanguard and made a fierce assault on the central army. Caught in the middle, the numerous banners, commanders' standards, signal flags, whinnying horses, shining armor, and spears and swords that sparkled like constellations around Katsuyori were now enveloped in blood and panic.

Only the forces of Baba Nobufusa, which had remained at Maruyama, were still intact. Baba sent a samurai to Katsuyori with a message advocating retreat.

Katsuyori stamped the ground with vexation. But he was unable to defy reality. Defeated, the central corps had retreated, covered with blood.

"We should retreat temporarily, my lord."

"Swallow your anger and think of what our prospects are."

Desperately leading the men of the main camp, Katsuyori's generals somehow extricated him from the trap he was in. To the enemy it was clear that the central Kai army was in a disorderly retreat.

When they had accompanied Katsuyori as far as a nearby bridge, the generals turned back, forming a rear guard to fight with the pursuing troops. They were heroically struck down in battle. Baba had also accompanied the fleeing Katsuyori and the pathetic remnants of his army as far as Miyawaki, but finally the old general turned his horse to the west, his breast filled with a thousand thoughts.

I've lived a long life. Or I could say it's been short, too. Truly long or truly short, only this one moment is eternal, I suppose. The moment of death...Can eternal life be anything more than that?

Then, just before galloping into the midst of the enemy, he swore, I'll make my excuses to Lord Shingen in the next world. I was an incompetent counselor and general. Good-bye, you mountains and rivers of Kai!

Turning around, he shed a single tear for his province, then suddenly spurred his horse. "Death! I won't dishonor the name of Lord Shingen!"

His voice sank into the sea of the great enemy army. It is hardly necessary to add that each of his retainers followed him, to be struck down gloriously.

From the very beginning, no one had been able to see through this battle as Baba had. He had doubtless perceived that, after it, the Takeda clan would fall and would even be destroyed, and that that was its fate. Nevertheless, even with his foresight and loyalty, he was unable to save the clan from disaster. The huge forces of change were simply overwhelming.

Together with a dozen or so mounted attendants, Katsuyori crossed over the shallows of Komatsugase and finally sought shelter in Busetsu Castle. Katsuyori was a courageous man, but now he was as speechless as a deaf mute.

The entire surface of Shidaragahara was red—a deep red—as the sun began to sink. The great battle this day had commenced around dawn and finished in the late afternoon. No horse neighed; not a soldier cried out. The wide plain quickly sank into darkness in complete desolation.

The dew of night settled before the dead could be carried away. The Takeda corpses alone were said to have numbered more than ten thousand.

THE TOWERS OF AZUCHI

The Emperor had appointed Nobunaga to the court rank of Councillor of State not long before, and now he had been named General of the Right. The congratulatory ceremony for this latest promotion was conducted during the Eleventh Month with a pomp that exceeded anything seen in preceding eras.

Nobunaga's lodgings in the capital were in the shogun's former palace at Nijo. Guests crowded into the palace every day: courtiers, samurai, tea masters, poets, and merchants from the nearby trading cities of Naniwa and Sakai.

Mitsuhide had planned on leaving Nobunaga and returning to his castle in Tamba, and while it was still light, he had come to the Nijo Palace from his own lodgings to take his leave.

"Mitsuhide," Hideyoshi greeted him with a broad smile.

"Hideyoshi?" Mitsuhide answered with a laugh.

"What brings you here today?" Hideyoshi asked, taking Mitsuhide by the arm.

"Oh, just that His Lordship is leaving tomorrow," Mitsuhide said with a grin.

"That's right. Where do you suppose we'll meet again?"

"Are you drunk?"

"There's not a day I don't get drunk while I'm in the capital. His Lordship drinks more when he's here, too. In fact, if you went to see him now he'd make you drink quite a bit of *sake*."

"Is he having another drinking party?" Mitsuhide asked.

Certainly Nobunaga had been drinking more recently, and an old retainer, who had served Nobunaga for many years, had remarked that Nobunaga had never drunk to the extent that he did now.

Hideyoshi always took part in these revelries, but he did not have Nobunaga's resistance.

Nobunaga seemed to have the more delicate constitution, but he was by far the stronger of the two men. If you looked carefully, you could see his spiritual strength. Hideyoshi was just the opposite. Outwardly he seemed a healthy countryman, but he did not have real stamina.

His mother still lectured him about neglecting his health: "It's fine to have a good time, but please take care of your health. You were sickly from the time you were born, and until you were four or five years old, none of the neighbors thought you would live to be an adult."

Her concern had an effect on Hideyoshi, because he knew the reason for his weakness as a youth. When his mother had been pregnant with him, their poverty had been such that they had sometimes had no food on the table, and this state of adversity had surely affected his growth in the womb.

The fact that he had been able to survive was due almost solely to his mother's devotion. Thus, while he certainly did not dislike *sake*, he would recall his mother's words every time he held a cup in his hands. And he could hardly forget the times when his mother had cried so much because of her drunkard husband.

No one, however, would have thought he took drinking so seriously. People said of him, "He doesn't drink much, but he sure loves drinking parties. And when he does drink, he drinks freely." In fact, there was no one more prudent than Hideyoshi. And speaking of drinking, it was Mitsuhide, whom he now met in the corridor, who had just been doing a good bit of it himself. Nevertheless, Mitsuhide looked disappointed, and it was clear that Nobunaga's drinking—just now confirmed by Hideyoshi—was troubling his retainers a great deal.

Hideyoshi laughed and denied what he had just said. "No, that was a joke." Amused at Mitsuhide's wavering there so seriously, he shook his red face. "The truth is, I was just having fun with you a little. The drinking party is over, and the proof is that here I am, leaving intoxicated. And that's a lie too," he laughed.

"Ah, you're a bad man." Mitsuhide forced a smile. He tolerated Hideyoshi's teasing, for he did not dislike him. Neither did Hideyoshi hold any ill feelings toward Mitsuhide. He always joked freely with his sober-minded colleague, but at the same time he respected him when respect was required.

For his part, Mitsuhide seemed to acknowledge that Hideyoshi was a useful man. Hideyoshi was just a bit ahead of Mitsuhide in seniority and was above him in the seating at field staff headquarters, but like the other veteran generals, Mitsuhide was proud of his own family status, bloodline, and education. Certainly he did not take Hideyoshi lightly, but he somehow manifested a condescending attitude toward his senior with such comments as, "You're a likable man."

This condescension was due, of course, to Mitsuhide's character. But even when Hideyoshi felt that he was being condescended to, he didn't feel unhappy. On the contrary, he considered it natural to be looked down upon by a man of superior intellect such as Mitsuhide. He was comfortable acknowledging of Mitsuhide's great superiority in terms of intellect, education, and background.

"Ah, that's right. I forgot something," Hideyoshi said, as if he had suddenly remembered. "I should congratulate you. Being awarded the province of Tamba should make you happy for a while. But I think it's natural after so many years of devoted service. I pray that this marks the beginning of better fortune for you, and that you prosper for many years to come."

"No, all of His Lordship's favors are honors beyond my station." Mitsuhide always returned courtesy for courtesy with great seriousness. But then he continued. "Even though I've been granted a province, it used to be held by the former shogun, and even now there are a good number of powerful local clans who have shut themselves in behind their walls and are refusing to submit to my authority. So congratulations are a little premature."

"No, no, you're too modest," Hideyoshi protested. "As soon as you moved into Tamba with Hosokawa Fujitaka and his son, the Kameyama clan capitulated, so you've already had results, haven't you? I observed with interest the way you took Kameyama, and even His Lordship praised you for the skill with which you subjugated the enemy and took the castle without losing a single man."

"Kameyama was just the beginning. The real difficulties are yet to come."

"Life is worth living only when we have difficulties in front of us. Otherwise there's no incentive. And nothing could be sweeter than having restored peace to a new domain given to you by His Lordship and governing it well. Why, you'll be master there yourself and able to do anything you like," Hideyoshi said.

Suddenly both men felt that this chance meeting had lasted much too long.

"Well, until we meet again," Mitsuhide said.

"Wait just a minute," Hideyoshi said, and suddenly changed the subject. "You're a learned man, so perhaps you'll know this. Among the castles in Japan right now, how many have donjons, and in which provinces are they?"

"The castle of Satomi Yoshihiro, at Tateyama in the province of Awa, has a three-story donjon that can be seen from the sea. Also, at Yamaguchi in the province of Suo, Ouchi Yoshioki built a four-story donjon at his main castle. It is probably the most imposing in all of Japan."

"Only those two?"

"As far as I know. But why are you asking about this now?"

"Well, today I was with His Lordship, talking about various castle designs, and Master Mori was eagerly explaining the advantages of donjons. He strongly advocated including one in the design of the castle that Lord Nobunaga will be building at Azuchi."

"Huh? Which Master Mori?"

"His Lordship's page, Ranmaru."

Mitsuhide's brow furrowed for a moment. "Are you a bit doubtful about this?"

"Not especially."

Mitsuhide's face quickly returned to a nonchalant expression, and he changed the subject and chatted for a few minutes. He finally excused himself and hurried off toward the interior of the palace.

"Lord Hideyoshi! Lord Hideyoshi!"

The great corridor of the Nijo Palace was busy with people coming and going to visit Lord Nobunaga. Again, someone called.

"Well, Reverend Asayama," Hideyoshi said as he turned around with a smile.

Asayama Nichijo was an uncommonly ugly man. Araki Murashige, one of Nobunaga's generals, was noted for his ugliness, but at least he had a certain charm. Asayama, on the other hand, was only an oily-looking priest. He approached Hideyoshi and quickly lowered his voice as though he were privy to some important matter.

"Lord Hideyoshi?"

"Yes, what is it?"

"You seemed to be having a confidential discussion with Lord Mitsuhide just now."

"Confidential discussion?" Hideyoshi laughed. "Is this the place for a confidential discussion?"

"When Lord Hideyoshi and Lord Mitsuhide whisper for a long time in the corridors of Nijo Palace, people are going to be startled."

"Surely not."

"No, absolutely!"

"Is Your Reverence a little drunk too?"

"Quite a bit. I drank too much. But really, you should be more careful."

"You mean with *sake*?"

"Don't be a fool. I'm cautioning you to be more discreet about being on familiar terms with Mitsuhide."

"Why?"

"He's a little too intelligent."

"Why, everybody says that you're the most intelligent man in Japan today."

"Me? No, I'm much too slow," the priest demurred.

"By no means," Hideyoshi assured him. "Your Reverence is quite knowledgeable in just about everything. The samurai's weakest points are in his dealings with the nobility or with powerful merchants, but no one surpasses you in shrewdness among the men of the Oda clan. Why, even Lord Katsuie is quite awestruck by your talents."

"But on the other hand, I've achieved no military exploits at all."

"In the construction of the Imperial Palace, in the administration of the capital, in various financial affairs, you have shown an uncanny genius."

"Are you praising or disparaging me?"

"Well now, you are both a prodigy and a good-for-nothing in the samurai class, and speaking honestly, I will both praise you and disparage you."

"I'm no match for you." Asayama laughed aloud, showing the gaps where he had lost two or three of his teeth. Though Asayama was much older than Hideyoshi—old enough to be his father—he thought of Hideyoshi as his senior.

Asayama could not accept Mitsuhide so easily. He recognized that Mitsuhide was intelligent, but he was unnerved by Mitsuhide's dry wit.

"I was thinking that it was just my own imagination," Asayama said, "but recently a person famous for discerning men's personalities from their features has expressed the same opinion."

"A physiognomist has made some sort of judgment about Mitsuhide?"

"He's not a physiognomist. Abbot Ekei is one of the most profound scholars of the age. He told me this in the utmost secrecy."

"Told you what?"

"That Mitsuhide has the look of a wise man who could drown in his own wisdom. Moreover, there are evil signs that he will supplant his own lord."

"Asayama."

"What?"

"You're not going to enjoy your old age if you let things like that out of your mouth," Hideyoshi said sharply. "I've heard that Your Reverence is a shrewd politician, but I suspect that a political hobby should not be pushed as far as spreading such talk about one of His Lordship's retainers."

* * *

The pages had spread out a large map of Omi in the wide room.

"Here's the inner section of Lake Biwa!" one said.

"There's the Sojitsu Temple! And the Joraku Temple!" another exclaimed.

The pages sat together on one side and craned their necks to look, just like baby swallows. Ranmaru separated himself from the group and sat modestly on his own. He was not yet twenty, but he had long passed the age of a man's coming-of-age ceremony. If his forelock had been shaved, he would have had the appearance of a fine young samurai.

"You just stay the way you are," Nobunaga had said. "I want you as a page, no matter how old you get."

Ranmaru could compete with other boys in terms of grace, and his topknot and silk garments were those of a child.

Nobunaga studied the map carefully. "It's well drawn." he said. "It's even more accurate than our military maps. Ranmaru, How did you come up with such a detailed map in such a short time?"

"My mother, who is now in holy orders, knew that there was a map in the secret storehouse of a certain temple."

Ranmaru's mother, who had taken the name Myoko when she had become a nun, was the widow of Mori Yoshinari. Her five sons had been taken in by Nobunaga as retainers. Ranmaru's two younger brothers, Bomaru and Rikimaru, were also pages. Everyone said that there was very little similarity among them. It wasn't that his brothers were dull children, but that Ranmaru was outstanding. And this was not just in the eyes of Nobunaga, whose affection for him was unending. It was obvious to anyone who saw him that Ranmaru's intelligence stood far above that of the others. When he frequented the generals of the field staff or the senior retainers, he was never treated like a child, regardless of his clothes.

"What? You got this from Myoko?" Nobunaga suddenly fixed an unusual stare on Ranmaru. "She's a nun, so it's natural that she should be going back and forth to a number of the temples, but she shouldn't be deceived by the spies of the warrior-monks who are still chanting curses against me. Perhaps you should look for the right time and then give her a warning."

"She's always been very careful. Even more so than I, my lord."

Nobunaga stooped down and studied the map of Azuchi intently. It was here that he would build a castle as his new residence and seat of government.

This was something of which Nobunaga had spoken only just recently, a decision he had made because the location of Gifu Castle no longer suited his purposes.

The land that Nobunaga had really wanted was in Osaka. But on it stood the Honganji, the stronghold of his bitter enemies, the warrior-monks.

After studying the foolishness of the shoguns, Nobunaga did not even consider setting up a government in Kyoto. That had been the old state of affairs. Azuchi was closer to his ideal: from there he could guard against the provinces to the west as well as check the advances of Uesugi Kenshin from the north.

"Lord Mitsuhide is in the waiting room, and says he would like to speak with you before his departure," a samurai announced from the door.

"Mitsuhide?" Nobunaga said good-humoredly. "Show him in." And he continued studying the map of Azuchi.

Mitsuhide came in with a sigh of relief. There was no smell of *sake* in the place, after all, and his first thought was, Hideyoshi got me again.

"Mitsuhide, come over here."

Nobunaga ignored the man's courteous bow and beckoned him over to the map. Mitsuhide edged forward respectfully.

"I hear that you've been thinking of nothing but plans for a new castle, my lord," he said affably.

Nobunaga may have been a dreamer, but he was a dreamer who was second to none in executive ability.

"What do you think? Isn't this mountainous region facing the lake just right for a castle?"

Nobunaga, it seemed, had already designed the structure and scale of the castle in his head. He drew a line with his finger. "It's going to stretch from here to here. We'll build a town around the castle at the bottom of the mountain, with a quarter for the merchants that will be better organized than in any other province in Japan," he said. "I'm going to devote all the resources I have to this castle. I've got to have something here imposing enough to overawe all the other lords. It won't be extravagant, but it's going to be a castle that will have no equal in the Empire. My castle will combine beauty, function, and dignity."

Mitsuhide recognized that this project was not a product of Nobunaga's vanity nor some high-flown amusement, so he expressed his feelings honestly. His overly serious answer, however, did not suffice; Nobunaga was too accustomed to showy responses in total agreement with him and to witty statements that only echoed his own.

"What do you think? No good?" Nobunaga asked uncertainly.

"I wouldn't say that at all."

"Do you think this is the right time?"

"I'd say this is very timely."

Nobunaga was trying to bolster his self-confidence. There was no one who regarded Mitsuhide's intelligence more highly than he did. Not only did Mitsuhide have a modern intelligence, but he had also faced political problems too difficult to surmount on conviction alone. Thus, Nobunaga was even more aware of Mitsuhide's genius than was Hideyoshi, who praised him so highly.

"I've heard that you're quite conversant with the science of castle construction. Could you take care of this responsibility?"

"No, no. My knowledge is not sufficient to build a castle."

"Not sufficient?"

"Building a castle is like fighting a great battle. The man in charge must be able to use both men and materials with ease. You should really assign this duty to one of your veteran generals."

"And who would that be?" Nobunaga asked.

"Lord Niwa would be most suitable because he gets along so well with others."

"Niwa? Yes…he'd be good." This opinion seemed to agree with Nobunaga's own intentions, and he nodded vigorously. "By the way, Ranmaru has suggested that I build a donjon. What do you think of the idea?"

Mitsuhide did not answer. He could see Ranmaru out of the corner of his eye. "Are you asking me about the pros and cons of building a donjon, my lord?" he asked.

"That's right. Is it better to have one or not to have one?"

"It's better to have one, of course. Even if only from the standpoint of the dignity of the structure."

"There must be various styles of donjon. I've heard that when you were young, you traveled through the country extensively and acquired a detailed knowledge of castle construction."

"My knowledge of such things is really very shallow," Mitsuhide said humbly. "On the other hand, Ranmaru over there should be quite well versed in the subject. When I toured the country, I only saw two or three castles with donjons, and even those were of extremely crude construction. If this is Ranmaru's suggestion, he certainly must have some thoughts on the subject." Mitsuhide seemed to be hesitant to speak further.

Nobunaga, however, did not even consider the delicate sensitivities of the two men, and went on artlessly, "Ranmaru, you're no less a scholar than Mitsuhide, and you've done some research in castle construction, it seems. What are your thoughts on the building of a donjon? Well, Ranmaru?" After an embarrassed silence from the page, he asked, "Why don't you answer?"

"I'm too confused, my lord."

"Why is that?"

"I'm embarrassed," he said and prostrated himself with his face over both hands as though he had been deeply shamed. "Lord Mitsuhide is unkind. Why should I have any original ideas about donjon construction? To tell the truth, my lord, everything you heard from me—even the fact that the castles of the Ouchi and Satomi both have donjons—was told me by Lord Mitsuhide one night on guard duty."

"Well then, it wasn't your idea after all."

"I thought you would be annoyed if I confessed that every bit of it was someone else's idea, so I just rambled on and suggested building a donjon."

"Is that so?" Nobunaga laughed. "That's all there is to it?"

"But Lord Mitsuhide didn't take it that way," Ranmaru went on. "His answer just now made it sound as if I had stolen someone else's ideas. Lord Mitsuhide himself told me that he had some valuable illustrations of the Ouchi and Satomi donjons and even a

447

rare sketchbook. So why should he be so reserved and shift the onus to an inexperienced person like me?"

Although Ranmaru looked like a child, it was clear that he was a man.

"Is that right, Mitsuhide?" Nobunaga asked.

With Nobunaga looking directly at him, Mitsuhide was unable to remain calm. He stammered out, "Yes." Neither was he able to control his resentment of Ranmaru. He had purposely withheld his own opinions and spoken up for Ranmaru's erudition because he knew of Nobunaga's affection for the young man and was secretly expressing his own goodwill toward him. He had not only been letting Ranmaru hand the flower to his lord but had taken pains not to embarrass him.

Mitsuhide had told Ranmaru all he knew of donjon and castle construction during the leisure hours of a night watch. It was absurd that Ranmaru had related it all to Nobunaga as though it were his own idea. If he plainly said that now, however, Ranmaru would be all the more embarrassed, and Nobunaga would really be disgusted. Thinking that avoiding such an unhappy situation would also be to his own benefit, he had given the credit to Ranmaru. But the result had been exactly the opposite of what he had planned. At this point he could not help feeling a chill move down his back at the perversity of this adult in child's clothing.

Seeing his perplexity, Nobunaga seemed to understand what was going on in Mitsuhide's mind. Suddenly he laughed out loud. "Even Mitsuhide can be unbecomingly prudent. At any rate, do you have those illustrations at hand?"

"I have a few, but I wonder if they will suffice."

"They will. Loan them to me for a little while."

"I'll get them for you right away."

Mitsuhide blamed himself for having told even the smallest lie to Nobunaga, and though the matter had ended, he was the one who had suffered. When the subject changed to the castles of the various provinces and other chitchat, however, Nobunaga's mood was still good. After dinner was served, Mitsuhide withdrew without any ill feeling.

The next morning, after Nobunaga had left Nijo, Ranmaru went to see his mother.

"Mother, I heard from both my younger brother and the other attendants that Lord Mitsuhide had told His Lordship that because you go in and out of temples, you might leak military secrets to the warrior-monks. So yesterday, when he was in attendance on His Lordship, I sent him a little arrow of retribution. At any rate, since my father passed away, our family has received far more kindness from His Lordship than others have, so I'm afraid people are jealous. Be careful and don't trust anyone."

* * *

Immediately after the New Year's celebrations of the fourth year of Tensho, the construction of the castle at Azuchi was begun, along with a project for a castle town of unprecedented size. Craftsmen gathered at Azuchi with their apprentices and workmen. They came from the capital and Osaka, from the faraway western provinces, and even from the east and north: smiths, stonemasons, plasterers, metalworkers, and even wallpaper hangers—representatives of every craft in the nation.

The famous Kano Eitoku was selected to illustrate the doors, sliding partitions, and ceilings. For this project, Kano did not simply rely on the traditions of his own school. Rather, he consulted with the masters of each school and then created the masterpieces of a lifetime, sending brilliant shafts of light into the world of the arts, which had been in decline during the many years of civil war.

The mulberry fields disappeared in a single night, becoming a well laid-out street plan, while on top of the mountain, the framework of the donjon appeared almost before people were aware of it. The main citadel, modeled after the mythical Mount Meru, had four towers—representing the Kings of the Four Directions—around the central five-story donjon. Below it stood a huge stone edifice, and leading off from this were annexes. Above and below there were more than one hundred related structures, and it was difficult to tell how many stories each structure comprised.

In the Plum Tree Room, the Room of the Eight Famous Scenes, the Pheasant Room, and the Room of Chinese Children, the painter applied his art with no time for sleep. The master lacquerer, who hated even the mention of dust, lacquered the vermilion handrails and the black walls. A Chinese-born ceramicist was appointed master tilemaker. The smoke from his lakeside kiln rose into the air day and night.

A solitary priest mumbled to himself as he gazed at the castle. He was only a traveling monk, but his heavy brow and wide mouth gave him an unusual look.

"Isn't it Ekei?" Hideyoshi asked, patting the man gently on the shoulder so as not to startle him. Hideyoshi had detached himself from a group of generals standing a little way off.

"Well, well, now! Lord Hideyoshi!"

"I wouldn't have expected to find you here," Hideyoshi said cheerfully. He patted Ekei's shoulder again, and then smiled affectionately. "It's been a long time since we last met. I believe it was at Master Koroku's house in Hachisuka."

"Yes, that's right. Not long ago—I think it was at the end of the year at Nijo Palace—I overheard Lord Mitsuhide say that you had come to the capital. I came with an envoy from Lord Mori Terumoto, and stayed in Kyoto for a while. The envoy has already returned home, but since I'm just a country priest with no urgent business, I've been stopping here and there at temples both in and out of Kyoto. I thought Lord Nobunaga's present construction project would make a good travel story back home, so I stopped to take a look. I must say I'm very impressed."

"Your Reverence is involved in some construction, too, I hear," Hideyoshi remarked abruptly. Ekei looked startled, but Hideyoshi laughed, adding, "No, no. Not a castle. I understand you're building a monastery, called Ankokuji."

"Ah, the monastery." Ekei's face relaxed, and he laughed. "Ankokuji has already been completed. I'll hope you'll find time to visit me there, though I fear that as the master of Nagahama Castle your schedule will not allow it."

"I may have become the lord of a castle, but my stipend is still low, so neither my position nor my mouth carries much weight. But I'll bet I look a little more grown up than when you last saw me in Hachisuka."

"No, you haven't changed a bit. You're young, Lord Hideyoshi, but then almost everyone on Lord Nobunaga's field staff is in the prime of life. I've been struck from the very first by the grandeur of the plan for his castle and by the spirit of his generals. He seems to have the force of the rising sun."

"Ankokuji was paid for by Lord Terumoto of the western provinces, was it not? His own province is wealthy and strong, and I suspect that even in terms of men of talent, Lord Nobunaga's clan is no match."

Ekei seemed anxious not to become involved in such a conversation, and once again he praised the construction of the donjon and the superb view of the area.

Finally, Hideyoshi said, "Nagahama is on the coast just north of here. My boat is berthed nearby, so why don't you come and stay for a night or two? I've been granted some leave, and I thought I'd go back to Nagahama."

Ekei used this invitation to make a hasty withdrawal. "No, perhaps I'll call on you at another time. Please give my regards to Master Koroku, or rather Master Hikoemon, that is, now that he's one of your retainers." And he suddenly walked off.

As Hideyoshi watched Ekei go, two monks, who seemed to be his disciples, came out from a commoner's house and chased after him.

Accompanied only by Mosuke, Hideyoshi went to the construction site, which had the look of a battlefield. As he had not been assigned important responsibilities in the building work, he did not have to stay permanently in Azuchi, nevertheless he made frequent trips from Nagahama to Azuchi by ship.

"Lord Hideyoshi! Lord Hideyoshi!" Someone was calling him. Looking around, he saw Ranmaru, displaying a beautiful line of white teeth in his smiling mouth, running toward him.

"Well now, Master Ranmaru. Where is His Lordship?"

"He was at the donjon all morning, but he's now resting at the Sojitsu Temple."

"Well, let's go over there."

"Lord Hideyoshi, that monk you were just now talking to—wasn't he Ekei, the famous physiognomist?"

"That's right. I've heard that from someone else. I wonder if a physiognomist can really see a man's true character," Hideyoshi said, pretending that he had little interest in the subject.

Whenever Ranmaru spoke with Hideyoshi, he did not guard his words as he did with Mitsuhide. This did not mean Ranmaru thought that Hideyoshi was an easy mark, but there were times when the older man played the fool, and Ranmaru found him easy to get along with.

"A physiognomist really can tell!" Ranmaru said. "My mother says that all the time. Just before my father died in battle, one of them predicted his death. And the fact is, well, I'm interested in something Ekei said."

"Have you had him look at you?"

"No, no. It's not about me." He looked up and down the street, and said confidentially, "It's about Lord Mitsuhide."

"Lord Mitsuhide?"

"Ekei said there were some evil signs: that he looked like a man who would turn against his lord."

450   "If you look for that quality, you'll find it. But not just in Lord Mitsuhide."

"No, really! Ekei said so."

Hideyoshi listened with a grin. Many people would have censured Ranmaru for being an unscrupulous rumormonger, but when he talked like this, he seemed not much more than a freshly weaned child. After Hideyoshi had humored him for a while, he asked Ranmaru more seriously, "Who in the world did you hear these things from?"

Ranmaru promptly took him into his confidence, replying, "Asayama Nichijo."

Hideyoshi nodded his head as though he could well imagine.

"Asayama didn't tell you this himself, did he? Certainly it must have gone through someone else. Let me see if I can guess."

"Go ahead."

"Was it your mother?"

"How did you know?"

Hideyoshi laughed.

"No, really. How did you know?" Ranmaru pressed.

"Myoko would believe such things from the outset," Hideyoshi said. "No, it might be better to say that she's fond of such things. And she's on familiar terms with Asayama. If it were up to me, however, I would say that Ekei is more proficient at looking into the physiognomy of a province than into that of a man."

"The physiognomy of a province?"

"If judging a man's character from observing his features can be called physiognomy, then judging a province's character by the same method could be called the same thing. I've realized that Ekei has mastered that art. You shouldn't get too close to men like him. He may look like nothing more than a monk, but he's really in the pay of Mori Terumoto, lord of the western provinces. What do you think, Ranmaru? Aren't I much better than Ekei at the study of physiognomy?" he laughed.

The gate to the Sojitsu Temple came into view. The two men were still laughing as they climbed the stone steps.

The construction of the castle was progressing visibly. By the end of the Second Month of that year, Nobunaga had already vacated Gifu and moved. Gifu Castle was given to Nobunaga's eldest son, the nineteen-year-old Nobutada.

However, while Azuchi Castle—incomparable in strength and announcing the beginning of an entirely new epoch in castle construction—towered so loftily over this strategic crossroads, there were those who were greatly concerned about its military value—among them the warrior-monks of the Honganji, Mori Terumoto of the western provinces, and Uesugi Kenshin of Echigo.

Azuchi stood on the road that ran from Echigo to Kyoto. Kenshin, of course, also had designs on the capital. If the right opportunity presented itself, he would cross the mountains, come out north of Lake Biwa, and, at a stroke, raise his banners in Kyoto.

The ousted shogun, Yoshiaki, of whom there had been no news for some time, sent letters to Kenshin, trying to incite him to action.

Only the exterior of Azuchi Castle has been finished. Realistically, the completion of its interior will take another two and a half years. Once the castle is built, you might as well say that the road between Echigo and Kyoto will have ceased to exist.

Now is the time to strike. I will tour the provinces and forge an alliance of all the anti-Nobunaga forces, which will include Lord Terumoto of the western provinces, the Hojo, the Takeda, and your own clan in Echigo. If you do not take a spirited stand as the leader of this alliance first, however, I do not anticipate any success at all.

Kenshin forced a smile, thinking, Does this little sparrow plan to dance until he's a hundred years old? Kenshin was not the kind of soft-witted leader who would fall for such a ploy.

From the New Year into the summer, Kenshin moved his men into Kaga and Noto, and began to threaten the Oda borders. A relief army was dispatched from Omi with the speed of lightning. With Shibata Katsuie in command, the forces of Takigawa, Hideyoshi, Niwa, Sassa, and Maeda chased the enemy and burned the villages they would use as protection as far as Kanatsu.

A messenger came from Kenshin's camp and shouted loudly that the letter he brought should be read only by Nobunaga.

"This is undoubtedly written in Kenshin's own hand," Nobunaga said as he broke the seal himself.

I have long heard of your fame and regret that I have not yet had the pleasure of meeting you. Now would seem the best opportunity. If we should miss each other in the fighting, we would both regret it for many years to come. The battle has been set for tomorrow morning at the Hour of the Hare. I will meet you at the Kanatsu River. Everything will be settled when we meet man to man.

It was a formal challenge to battle.

"What happened to the envoy?" Nobunaga asked.

"He left right away," the retainer replied.

Nobunaga was unable to conceal a shudder. That night he suddenly announced that he would strike camp, and his forces withdrew.

Kenshin got a big laugh out of this later on. "Isn't that just what you'd expect from Nobunaga! If he had stayed where he was, the next day he could have left everything to my horse's hooves, and along with meeting him, I could have done him the favor of cutting his head off right there at the river."

But Nobunaga quickly returned to Azuchi with a squad of his soldiers. When he thought about Kenshin's old-fashioned letter of challenge, he couldn't help grinning.

"That's probably how he lured Shingen at Kawanakajima. He certainly is a fearless man. He has great pride in that long sword of his, fashioned by Azuki Nagamitsu; I don't think I'd want to see it with my own eyes. How sad for Kenshin that he wasn't born during the colorful olden days when they wore scarlet-braided armor with gold plates. I wonder what he thinks of Azuchi, with its mixture of Japanese, Southern Barbarian, and Chinese styles? All of the changes in weaponry and strategy in the last decade have brought us into a new world. How could anyone say the art of war hasn't changed too? He's probably laughing at my retreat as cowardice, but I can't help laughing at the fact that his outdated thinking is inferior to that of my artisans and craftsmen."

Those who truly heard this learned a great deal. There were those, however, who were taught, but never learned a thing.

After Nobunaga returned to Azuchi, he was told that something had occurred during the northern campaign between the commander-in-chief, Shibata Katsuie, and Hideyoshi. The cause was unclear, but a quarrel had been brewing between the two of them over strategy. The result of it was that Hideyoshi had collected his troops and returned to Nagahama while Katsuie quickly appealed to Nobunaga, saying, "Hideyoshi felt it unnecessary to comply with your orders and returned to his own castle. His behavior is inexcusable, and he should be punished."

No word came from Hideyoshi. Thinking that Hideyoshi must have had some plausible explanation for his actions, Nobunaga planned on handling the matter by waiting until all the generals had returned from the northern campaign. Rumors, however, came in one after another.

"Lord Katsuie is extraordinarily angry."

"Lord Hideyoshi is a bit quick-tempered. Pulling out one's troops during a campaign is not something a great general can do and keep his honor."

Finally, Nobunaga had an attendant look into the matter.

"Has Hideyoshi really returned to Nagahama?" he asked.

"Yes, he seems to be quite definitely in Nagahama," the attendant replied.

Nobunaga was provoked to anger, and sent an envoy with a stern rebuke. "This is insolent behavior. Before anything else, show some penitence!"

When the messenger returned, Nobunaga asked, "What kind of expression did he have when he heard my reprimand?"

"He looked as though he were thinking, 'I see.'"

"Is that all?"

"Then he said something about resting for a while."

"He is audacious, and he's becoming presumptuous." Nobunaga's expression did not show real resentment toward Hideyoshi, even though he had censured him verbally. Nevertheless, when Katsuie and the other generals of the northern campaign had finally returned, Nobunaga became truly angry.

First of all, even though Hideyoshi had been ordered to remain under house arrest in Nagahama Castle, instead of manifesting his penitence, he was having drinking parties every day. There was no reason for Nobunaga not to be angry, and people conjectured that at worst, Hideyoshi would be ordered to commit *seppuku*, and at best he would probably be ordered to Azuchi Castle to face a court-martial. But after a while Nobunaga seemed to forget all about it and later never even mentioned the incident.

* * *

In Nagahama Castle, Hideyoshi had gotten into the habit of sleeping late. Certainly, by the time Nene saw her husband's face every morning, the sun was high in the sky.

Even his mother seemed worried and commented to Nene, "That boy just isn't himself these days, is he?"

Nene had trouble finding an answer. The reason he was sleeping late was that he was drinking every night. When he drank at home, he would quickly turn bright red after four or five small cups, and hurry through his meal. Then he would gather together his veterans and, as everyone's spirits rose, would drink late into the night, unmindful of the hour. The result was that he would fall asleep in the pages' room. One night, when his wife was walking down the main corridor with her ladies-in-waiting, she saw a man walking slowly toward her. The man looked like Hideyoshi, but she called out, "Who is that over there?" pretending not to know him.

Her surprised husband turned around and tried to hide his confusion, but succeeded only in looking as though he were practicing some sort of dance. "I'm lost." He lurched over to her and steadied himself by grabbing her shoulder. "Ah, I'm drunk. Nene, carry me! I can't walk!"

When Nene saw how he was trying to hide his predicament, she burst out laughing. She spoke to him with feigned ill temper. "Sure, sure, I'll carry you. Where are you going, by the way?"

Hideyoshi got up on her back and began to giggle.

"To your room. Take me to your room!" he implored, and kicked his heels in the air like a child.

Nene, her back bent at the weight, joked with her ladies, "Listen, everyone, where shall I put this sooty traveler I just picked up on the road?"

The ladies were so amused they were holding their sides as tears streamed down their cheeks. Then, like revelers around a festival float, they surrounded the man Nene had picked up, and amused themselves all night in Nene's room.

Such events were rare. In the mornings, it quite often seemed to Nene that her role was to look at her husband's sullen face. What was it that he was concealing inside of himself? They had been married for fifteen years. Nene was now past thirty, and her husband was forty-one. She was unable to believe that Hideyoshi's bitter expression every morning was simply a matter of mood. While she dreaded her husband's bad temper, what she earnestly prayed for was the ability to somehow understand his afflictions—even just a little—and to assuage his suffering.

In times like this, Nene considered Hideyoshi's mother to be a model of strength. One morning her mother-in-law rose early and went out into the vegetable garden in the north enclosure while the dew was still heavy on the ground.

"Nene," she said, "it'll be a while before the master gets up. Let's pick some eggplants in the garden while we have the time. Bring a basket!"

The old lady began to pick the eggplants. Nene filled one basket, and then carried over another.

"Hey, Nene! Are you and Mother both out here?"

It was the voice of her husband—the husband who so rarely got up early these days.

"I didn't realize you were up," Nene apologized.

"No, I suddenly woke up. Even the pages were flustered." Hideyoshi wore a bright smile, a sight she had not seen for some time. "Takenaka Hanbei reported that a ship with an envoy's banner is on its way from Azuchi. I got up immediately, paid my respects to the castle shrine, and then came here to apologize for neglecting you in recent days."

"Aha! You've apologized to the gods!" his mother chuckled.

"That's right. Then I have to apologize to my mother, and even to my wife, I think," he said with great seriousness.

"You came all the way here for that?"

"Yes, and if you would only understand how I feel, I wouldn't have to go through the form of doing this anymore."

"Oh, this boy is cunning." His mother laughed outright.

Although Hideyoshi's mother was probably somewhat suspicious of her son's suddenly cheerful behavior, she was soon to understand the reason.

"Master Maeda and Master Nonomura have just arrived at the castle gate as official messengers from Azuchi. Master Hikoemon went out immediately and led them to the guests' reception room," Mosuke announced.

Hideyoshi dismissed the page and began picking eggplants with his mother. "They're really ripening well, aren't they? Did you put the manure along the dirt ridges yourself, Mother?"

"Shouldn't you be hurrying off to see His Lordship's messengers?" she asked.

"No, I pretty much know why they've come, so there's no need to get flustered. I think I'll pick a few eggplants. It would be nice to show Lord Nobunaga their shiny emerald color, covered with the morning dew."

"You're going to give things like this to the envoys as presents for Lord Nobunaga?"

"No, no, I'm going to take them this morning myself."

"What!"

Hideyoshi had, after all, incurred his lord's displeasure and was supposed to be penitent. This morning his mother began to have doubts about him and soon was almost worried to distraction.

"My lord? Are you coming?" Hanbei had come to hasten Hideyoshi, who finally left the eggplant field.

When the preparations for the trip had been made, Hideyoshi asked the envoys to accompany him back to Azuchi.

Hideyoshi suddenly stopped. "Oh! I've forgotten something! His Lordship's present." He sent a retainer to fetch the basket of eggplants. The eggplants had been covered with leaves, and morning dew still clung to the purple beneath. Carrying the basket with him, Hideyoshi boarded the ship.

The castle town of Azuchi was not yet a year old, but fully a third of it had been finished and was already bustling with prosperity. All travelers who stopped here were struck by the liveliness of this dazzling new city, its road spread with silver sand leading to the castle gate; the masonry steps made of huge stone blocks; the plastered walls and the burnished metal fittings.

And while the sight was indeed dazzling, the grandeur of the five-story donjon was beyond description, whether seen from the lake, from the streets of the town below, or even from within the castle grounds themselves.

"Hideyoshi, you've come." Nobunaga's voice resounded from behind the closed sliding door. The room, set amid all the gold, red, and blue lacquer of Azuchi, was decorated with a simple ink painting.

Hideyoshi was still at some distance, prostrating himself in the next room.

"I suppose you've heard, Hideyoshi. I've set your punishment aside. Come in."

Hideyoshi edged forward from the next room with his basket of eggplants.

Nobunaga looked at him suspiciously. "What's that?"

"Well, I hope this will please you, my lord." Hideyoshi moved forward and put the eggplants in front of him. "My mother and wife grew these eggplants in the garden at the castle."

"Eggplants?"

"You may consider them a silly, strange present, but since I was traveling by fast ship, I thought you would be able to see them before the dew evaporated. I picked them from the field this morning."

"Hideyoshi, I suspect that what you wanted to show me was neither eggplants nor unevaporated dew. What exactly is it that you would like me to taste?"

"Please guess, my lord. I'm an unworthy servant and my merit is negligible, but you have elevated me from a simple farmer to a retainer who holds a domain of two hundred twenty thousand bushels. And yet my old mother never neglects taking up the hoe with her own hands, watering the vegetables, and putting manure around the gourds and eggplants. Every day I give thanks for the lessons she teaches me. Without even having to speak, she tells me, 'There's nothing more dangerous than a farmer rising up in the world, and you should get used to the fact that the envy and fault-finding of others comes from their own conceit. Don't forget your past in Nakamura, and always be mindful of the favors your lord has bestowed on you.'"

Nobunaga nodded, and Hideyoshi went on, "Do you think I could devise any strategy on a campaign that would not be to you benefit, my lord, when I have a mother like that? I consider her lessons as talismans. Even if I quarrel openly with the commander-in-chief, there is no duplicity in my breast."

At that point, a guest at Nobunaga's side slapped his thigh and said, "These eggplants are really a good present. We'll try them later on."

For the first time Hideyoshi noticed that someone else was in the room: a samurai who looked to be in his early thirties. The man's large mouth indicated the strength of his will. His brow was prominent, and the bridge of his nose was somewhat wide. It was difficult to say whether he was of peasant stock or simply robustly built, but the light in his eyes and the luster of his dark red skin showed that he possessed a strong inner vitality.

"Have Hideyoshi's mother's home-grown eggplants pleased you, too, Kanbei? I'm pretty happy with them myself," Nobunaga said, laughing, and then, growing serious, he introduced the guest to Hideyoshi.

"This is Kuroda Kanbei, the son of Kuroda Mototaka, chief retainer of Odera Masamoto in Harima."

Hearing this, Hideyoshi was unable to conceal his surprise. Kuroda Kanbei was a name he had been hearing constantly. Moreover, he had often seen his letters.

"My goodness! So you're Kuroda Kanbei."

"And you're the Lord Hideyoshi I'm always hearing about?"

"Always in letters."

"Yes, but I can't think of this as our first meeting."

"And now here I am, shamefully begging my lord for forgiveness. I'm afraid you're going to laugh at me: this is Hideyoshi, the man who's always being scolded by his lord." And he laughed with a voice that seemed to sweep everything away. Nobunaga laughed heartily, too. With Hideyoshi, he could laugh happily about things that were not actually very amusing.

The eggplants Hideyoshi had brought were quickly prepared, and very soon the three men were enjoying a drinking party. Kanbei was nine years younger than Hideyoshi, but was not the least bit inferior in his understanding of the current of the times or in his intuition of who would grasp supreme power in the land. He was nothing more than the son of a retainer of an influential clan in Harima, but he did possess a small castle in Himeji and had embraced a great ambition from early on in his life. Moreover, among all who lived in the western provinces, he was the only one who had gauged the trend of the times clearly enough to come to Nobunaga and secretly suggest the urgency of the conquest of that area.

The great power in the west was the Mori clan, whose sphere of influence extended over twenty provinces. Kanbei lived in the midst of them but was not overawed by their power. He perceived that the history of the nation was flowing in one direction. Armed with this insight, he had sought out one man: Nobunaga. From that point alone, it could hardly be said that he was a common man.

There is a saying that one great man will always recognize another. In their conversation at this one meeting, Hideyoshi and Kanbei were tied as tightly together as though they had known each other for a hundred years.

MONKEY MARCHES WEST

Not long after his meeting with Kuroda Kanbei, Hideyoshi received a special assignment from Nobunaga.

"The truth is," Nobunaga began, "I'd like to risk my entire army on this expedition, but the situation won't permit that yet. For that reason I've chosen you as the one in whom I put all of my trust. You're to take three armies, lead them into the western provinces, and persuade the Mori clan to submit to me. This is a great responsibility that I know only you could take on. Will you do it?"

Hideyoshi was silent. He was so elated and so filled with gratitude that he was unable to answer immediately.

"I accept," he said finally with deep emotion.

This was only the second time Nobunaga had raised three armies and entrusted their command to one of his retainers. The first time was when he had put Katsuie in charge of the campaign in the northern provinces. But because it was so important and so difficult, an invasion of the western provinces could not be compared with the northern campaign.

Hideyoshi felt as though an incredible weight had been put on his shoulders. Observing Hideyoshi's unusually cautious expression, Nobunaga suddenly felt uneasy, wondering if this were not too heavy a responsibility for him after all. Does Hideyoshi have the confidence to take on this responsibility? he asked himself.

"Hideyoshi, will you go back to Nagahama Castle before you mobilize the troops?" Nobunaga asked. "Or would you prefer to leave from Azuchi?"

"With your permission, my lord, I will depart from Azuchi this very day."

"You have no regrets about leaving Nagahama?"

"None. My mother, my wife, and my foster son are there. What is there for me to feel unhappy about?"

The foster son was Nobunaga's fourth son, Tsugimaru, whom Hideyoshi was bringing up.

Nobunaga laughed and then asked, "If this campaign is prolonged and your home province falls into the hands of your foster son, where are you going to make your own territory?"

"After I subjugate the west, I'll ask for it."

"And if I don't give it to you?"

"Perhaps I could conquer Kyushu and live there."

Nobunaga laughed heartily, forgetting his earlier misgivings.

Elated, Hideyoshi returned to his quarters and quickly told Hanbei of Nobunaga's orders. Hanbei immediately sent off a courier to Hikoemon, who was in charge of Nagahama in Hideyoshi's absence. Hikoemon marched through the night, leading an army to join his master. In the meantime, an urgent dispatch was circulated to all of Nobunaga's generals, informing them of Hideyoshi's appointment.

When Hikoemon arrived in the morning and looked in at Hideyoshi's quarters, he found him alone, applying *moxa* to his shins.

"That's a good precaution for a campaign," Hikoemon said.

"I still have half a dozen scars on my back from when I was treated with *moxa* as a child," Hideyoshi answered, gnashing his teeth from the intense heat. "I don't like *moxa* because it burns, but if I didn't do this, my mother would worry. When you send news to Nagahama, please write that I'm applying *moxa* every day."

As soon as he finished the *moxa* treatment, Hideyoshi departed for the front. The troops that left the castle town of Azuchi that day were truly awe-inspiring. From his donjon, Nobunaga watched them leave. The Monkey from Nakamura has come far, he thought, countless deep emotions passing through his breast as he watched Hideyoshi's standard of the golden gourd disappear into the distance.

The province of Harima was the jade pearl in this struggle between the dragon of the west and the tiger of the east. Would it ally itself with the newly arisen forces of the Oda? Would it side with the ancient power of the Mori?

Both the greater and the smaller clans of the western provinces that stretched from Harima to Hoki were now facing a difficult decision.

Some said, "The Mori are the mainstay of the west. Surely they will not fail."

Others, not so sure, countered, "No, we can't ignore the Oda's sudden rise to power."

People made up their minds by comparing the strength of the adversaries: territories on both sides, numbers of soldiers and of allies. In this case, however, given the immensity of Mori's influence and the vast possessions of the Oda, the strength of the two sides seemed about equally matched.

Which of them would make the future his own?

It was toward these western provinces lost between light and dark and unable to pick a course of action that Hideyoshi's troops marched on the twenty-third day of the Tenth Month.

To the west. To the west.

The responsibility was heavy. As Hideyoshi rode under his standard of the golden gourd, the face shaded by his visor was troubled. He was forty-one years old. His mouth was drawn into a large wordless frown as his horse trotted on stolidly. Wind-borne dust covered the entire army.

Periodically, Hideyoshi reminded himself that he was advancing on the western provinces. He would probably not have made so much of it himself, but when he had left Azuchi, Nobunaga's other generals had congratulated him.

"His Lordship has finally made up his mind and put you to use. Lord Hideyoshi, you've become second to none. You will have to repay His Lordship for his favors."

In contrast to this, Shibata Katsuie seemed extremely displeased. "What? *He* was made commander-in-chief of the western campaign!" Katsuie laughed derisively at the very idea.

It was easy to see why Katsuie thought that way. When Hideyoshi was still a servant, carrying Nobunaga's sandals and living in the stables with the horses, Katsuie had been a general of the Oda clan. Moreover, he had married Nobunaga's younger sister, and ruled a province of more than three hundred thousand bushels. Finally, when Katsuie was commander-in-chief of the northern campaign, Hideyoshi had disobeyed his orders and returned without warning to Nagahama. As a senior retainer, Katsuie now did a good bit of political maneuvering to put the invasion of the western provinces out of the limelight.

Mounted on his horse on the way to the western provinces, Hideyoshi chuckled to himself incessantly.

These things would suddenly come to mind as he lost interest in the peaceful westward road. Hideyoshi burst out laughing; Hanbei, who was riding along next to him, thought he had perhaps missed something and asked, "Did you say something thing, my lord?" just to make sure.

"No, nothing," Hideyoshi answered.

His army had traveled a good distance that day, and they were already approaching the border of Harima.

"Hanbei, a certain pleasure awaits you when we enter Harima."

"Well now, what would that be?"

"I don't think you've met Kuroda Kanbei before."

"No, I haven't, but I've been hearing his name for a long time."

"He's a man of the times. When you meet him, you'll become fast friends, I think."

"I've heard a number of stories about him."

"He's the son of a senior retainer of the Odera clan, and is still in his early thirties."

"Wasn't this campaign conceived by Lord Kanbei?"

"That's right. He's an intelligent man with a keen eye."

"Do you know him well, my lord?"

"I've known him through letters, but I met him for the first time at Azuchi Castle a little while ago. We talked completely openly for half a day. Ah, I feel confident. With Takenaka Hanbei on my left and Kuroda Kanbei on my right, I've put together a field staff."

Just then, something caused a boisterous disorder among the troops behind them. Someone in the pages' corps was laughing loudly.

Hikoemon turned around and took Mosuke, the head page, to task. In turn, Mosuke yelled at the pages in the company. "Quiet! An army advances with dignity!"

When Hideyoshi asked what had happened, Hikoemon looked embarrassed. "Since

I allowed the pages to ride, they're frolicking around in the ranks as though they were on a picnic. They're making a lot of noise and joking with each other, and even Mosuke is unable to control them. Perhaps it's better to make the pages walk, after all."

Hideyoshi forced a laugh and looked back. "They're in high spirits because they're so young, and their playfulness would probably be difficult to control. Let them be. Nobody's fallen off his horse yet, has he?"

"It seems that the youngest of them, Sakichi, is not used to riding, and someone thought it would be fun to make him fall off."

"Sakichi fell off his horse? Well, that's good training too."

The army marched on. The road entered Harima, and they finally arrived at Kasuya in the evening, just as they had planned.

Unlike Shibata Katsuie's gloomy leadership, which only respected regulations and form, or Nobunaga's severity and rigor, Hideyoshi's style of command was distinguished by one characteristic: cheerfulness. No matter what sort of hardship or desperate fighting beset his troops, they still radiated that cheerfulness and a harmonious sense that the entire army was one family.

Thus, while it was easy for this group of pages, made up of boys from eleven to sixteen, to disrupt military discipline, Hideyoshi, as the "head of the family," would just wink and say, "Let them be."

It began to grow dark as the vanguard quietly entered Harima, an allied province in the middle of enemy territory. At a loss concerning what action to take, and under heavy pressure from their neighbors, the people of this province now lit bonfires and welcomed Hideyoshi's troops.

Hideyoshi's forces had taken the first step in the invasion of the western provinces. As the long column of troops entered the castle in double file, a clacking sound filled the evening. The first corps was made up of the banners; the second of the gunners; the third of the archers; the fourth of spears and lances; the fifth, of swordsmen and halberdiers. The central corps was made up of mounted men and officers who crowded around Hideyoshi. With the drummers, the standard bearers, the military police, the inspectors, the reserve horses, the packhorses, and the scouts, there were about seven thousand five hundred men altogether, and an onlooker could only see that this must be a formidable force indeed.

Kuroda Kanbei stood at the gate of Kasuya Castle and welcomed them. When Hideyoshi saw him, he quickly dismounted and walked up to him with a smile. Kanbei came forward too, with a shout of welcome and his hands extended. Greeting each other like friends who had known each other for years, they walked into the castle, and Kanbei introduced Hideyoshi to his new retainers. Each man gave his own name and swore an oath of loyalty to Hideyoshi.

Among them was one man who seemed to be of excellent character. "I am Yamanaka Shikanosuke," he introduced himself, "one of the few surviving retainers of the Amako clan. Until now we've fought side by side, but in different regiments, so we've never met. But my heart jumped when I heard you were invading the west, and I asked Lord Kanbei to put in a good word for me."

Even though Shikanosuke was kneeling, head bowed, Hideyoshi could see from the breadth of his shoulders that he was far taller and broader than average. When he stood up, he topped six feet, and he looked to be about thirty years old. His skin was like iron, and his eyes were as piercing as a hawk's. Hideyoshi looked at him for a moment as though he could not quite recall who the man was.

Kanbei helped him out. "This is a man whose loyalty is rare these days. He formerly served Amako Yoshihisa, a lord ruined by the Mori. For many years he has shown undying devotion and faithfulness in the most adverse circumstances. For the last ten years he has taken part in various battles and wandered from place to place, harassing the Mori with small forces, in an attempt to restore his former lord to his domain."

"Even I have heard of the loyal Yamanaka Shikanosuke. But what did you mean when you said we've been in different regiments?" Hideyoshi asked.

"During the campaign against the Matsunaga clan, I fought alongside the forces of Lord Mitsuhide at Mount Shigi."

"You were at Mount Shigi?"

Kanbei once again took up the conversation. "Those years of loyalty amid such adversity were brought to nought when the Amako were defeated by the Mori. Later, he secretly asked for assistance from Lord Nobunaga through the good offices of Lord Katsuie. It was at the battle at Mount Shigi that Shikanosuke took the head of the fierce Kawai Hidetaka."

"It was you who struck down Kawai," Hideyoshi said, as though his doubts were now cleared up, and he looked again at the man, this time with a broad smile.

* * *

Hideyoshi very quickly demonstrated the might of his troops. The two castles of Sayo and Kozuki fell, and within the same month he defeated the neighboring Ukita clan, an ally of the Mori. Takenaka Hanbei and Kuroda Kanbei were always at Hideyoshi's side.

The main camp was moved to Himeji. During this time, Ukita Naoie constantly requested reinforcements from the Mori clan. At the same time Naoie gave Makabe Harutsugu, Bizen's bravest warrior, a force of eight hundred men, with which he successfully recaptured Kozuki Castle.

"This Hideyoshi isn't much, after all," Makabe bragged.

Kozuki Castle's stores of gunpowder and food were replenished, and fresh troops were sent as reinforcements.

"I suppose we couldn't just let it go," Hanbei suggested.

"I think not," Hideyoshi said deliberately. Since coming to Himeji, Hideyoshi had studied the whole situation of the western provinces. "Whom do you suppose I should send? I think this battle is going to be rough."

"Shikanosuke is the only choice."

"Shikanosuke?"

"Kanbei, what do you think?" Hideyoshi asked.

Kanbei voiced his immediate agreement.

Shikanosuke received Hideyoshi's orders, readied his forces during the night, and pressed on toward Kozuki Castle. It was the end of the year and bitterly cold.

Shikanosuke's officers and men were fired with the same zeal as their commander. Sworn to strike down the Mori and to restore Katsuhisa, the head of the Amako clan, they were men of the most loyal courage.

When the Ukita generals heard from their scouts that the enemy was the Amako clan, with Shikanosuke at its head, they were struck with dread. Just hearing the name of Shikanosuke sent them into the kind of terror a small bird might feel in front of a raging tiger.

And there was no doubt that they feared the reports of Shikanosuke's advance far more than they would have feared a direct attack from Hideyoshi himself.

From that standpoint, Shikanosuke was the best man to send against Kozuki Castle. He had, after all, with his singleminded loyalty and courage, wreaked havoc and inspired terror like an angry god. Even the bravest general of the Ukita clan, Makabe Harutsugu, abandoned Kozuki Castle without a fight, figuring he would simply lose too many soldiers if he stayed and opposed Shikanosuke.

By the time Shikanosuke's men entered the castle and reported to Hideyoshi that its capture had been executed without bloodshed, Makabe had already asked for reinforcements. Joining forces with an army led by his brother, to make a combined force of fifteen or sixteen hundred men, Makabe rode forward for a counterattack, stopping in a cloud of dust on a level plain a short distance from the castle.

Shikanosuke looked out from the watchtower. "It hasn't rained for over two weeks. Let's give them a fiery reception," he laughed.

Shikanosuke divided his soldiers into two groups. Late that night they made a sortie from the castle, one group of soldiers lighting fires upwind from the enemy and setting the dry grasses ablaze. Surrounded by the brushfires, the Ukita forces were completely routed.

Shikanosuke's second corps now went into action and moved in to annihilate them. No one knew how many of the enemy perished in this massacre, but the enemy commander, Makabe Harutsugu, and his brother were both slain.

"I guess they'll be discouraged now."

"No, they'll keep coming."

Shikanosuke's forces marched back to Kozuki, raising a victory song. However, a messenger from the main camp in Himeji arrived with an order from Hideyoshi to abandon the castle and retreat to Himeji. Not unnaturally, a cry of outrage rang out in all the ranks, from Amako Katsuhisa, the head of the clan, on down. Why should they abandon a castle they had fought so hard to take—and one in a strategically advantageous area?

"Nevertheless, if it's our commander-in-chief's order..." said Shikanosuke, obliged to console both Lord Katsuhisa and his troops, and to return to Himeji.

On his return, he immediately consulted with Hideyoshi. "If I may speak without reserve, every one of my officers and men were incredulous about your orders. I also share their feelings."

"To keep the matter secret, I didn't tell the messenger the reason for the retreat, but I'll tell you now. Kozuki Castle has been a fine bait to draw out the Ukita. If we abandon it, the Ukita are sure to reprovision it with supplies, weapons, and gunpowder. They'll probably even strengthen the garrison. And that's when we'll move!" Hideyoshi laughed.

Lowering his voice to a whisper, he leaned forward on his camp stool and pointed his war fan in the direction of Bizen. "No doubt, Ukita Naoie is anticipating that I will attack Kozuki Castle yet again. Only this time he will lead a large army himself, and we are going to outmaneuver him. Don't be angry, Shikanosuke."

The old year ended. The scouts' reports were exactly as expected: large amounts of supplies were already being transported by the Ukita to Kozuki Castle; the command of the castle had been given to Ukita Kagetoshi; and picked troops had been sent to man the castle walls.

Hideyoshi surrounded the castle and ordered Shikanosuke and his force of ten thousand men to hide in the vicinity of the Kumami River.

Meanwhile, Ukita Naoie, who had planned a pincer attack on Hideyoshi's troops, acting in concert with the castle garrison, led his army from Bizen in person.

The bait was set. When Naoie attacked Hideyoshi, Shikanosuke struck like a whirlwind, cutting his army to pieces. Naoie was barely able to escape with his life. Having dealt with the Ukita, Shikanosuke rejoined Hideyoshi for a full-scale attack on the castle.

Hideyoshi attacked the castle with fire. So many were burned to death in the castle that the place became known to later generations as "the Hell Valley of Kozuki."

"This time I won't tell you to abandon the castle," Hideyoshi told Amako Katsuhisa. "Guard it well."

Once Hideyoshi had finished mopping up Tajima and Harima, he made a triumphal return to Azuchi. He was there for less than a month before setting out again for the west in the Second Month.

During this respite, the western provinces hastily prepared themselves for war. Ukita Naoie sent an urgent message to the Mori:

The situation is grave. This is not a matter involving only the province of Harima. At present, Amako Katsuhisa and Yamanaka Shikanosuke occupy Kozuki Castle, with the support of Hideyoshi. This matter will have serious repercussions that the Mori clan cannot afford to overlook. What else can this be but a first step of the vengeful and vehement Amako—who were destroyed by the Mori clan—toward the restoration of their lost lands? You should not ignore this matter, but instead dispatch a large army quickly and annihilate them now. We, the Ukita, will take up the vanguard and repay you for your many past favors.

Mori Terumoto's most trusted generals were the sons of his grandfather, the great Mori Motonari. They were known as "the Two Uncles of the Mori." Both had inherited their fair measure of Motonari's talents. Kobayakawa Takakage was a man of broad wisdom; Kikkawa Motoharu was a man of self-possession, virtue, and talent.

While he was alive, Motonari had lectured his children in the following way: "Generally, there's no one more likely to bring disaster to the world than a man who aspires to grasp the nation's government but lacks the ability to govern. When such a man takes advantage of the times and actually tries to seize the Empire, destruction will surely follow.

You should reflect on your own status and remain in the western provinces. It will be sufficient if you are resolved not to fall behind others."

Motonari's admonition was respected to that very day. Which is why the Mori lacked the ambition of the Oda, Uesugi, Takeda, or Tokugawa. So even though they sheltered the ex-shogun, Yoshiaki, communicated with the warrior-monks of the Honganji, and even made a secret alliance with Uesugi Kenshin, it was all for the protection of the western provinces. In the face of Nobunaga's advances, the fortresses of the provinces under their control were used only as a first line of defense for their own domain.

But now the west itself was under violent attack. One corner of that line of defense had already crumbled, demonstrating that even the western provinces were unable to remain outside the whirlwind of the times.

"The main army should be made up of the combined strength of Terumoto and Takakage, and they should attack Kozuki together. I will lead the soldiers of Inaba, Hoki, Izumo, and Iwami, uniting with the soldiers of Tamba and Tajima on the way and, with one stroke, advance on the capital, act in concert with the Honganji, and strike directly at Nobunaga's headquarters at Azuchi."

This bold strategy was advanced by Kikkawa Motoharu, but neither Mori Terumoto nor Kobayakawa Takakage would approve it, their argument being that the plan was too ambitious. Instead, it was decided that they should attack Kozuki Castle first.

In the Third Month, a Mori army of thirty-five thousand men marched north. Some time before, Hideyoshi had gone to Kakogawa Castle in Harima, but his army amounted to no more than seven thousand five hundred men. Even if he included his allies in Harima, his troops were no match for the Mori.

Hideyoshi maintained an outward calm, declaring that reinforcements would come if needed. His troops and allies, however, were shaken by the smallness of their numbers compared to the Mori. The first sign of disaffection came quickly: Bessho Nagaharu, the lord of Miki Castle and Nobunaga's main ally in eastern Harima, defected to the enemy. Bessho spread false rumors about Hideyoshi to excuse his betrayal, while at the same time he invited the Mori into his castle.

Around that time, Hideyoshi received unexpected news: Uesugi Kenshin of Echigo was dead. It was common knowledge that Kenshin was a heavy drinker, and it was supposed that he might have collapsed from apoplexy. But there were some who put forward the theory that he had been assassinated. That night, Hideyoshi stood on Mount Shosha, his gaze lost in the stars, reflecting on the extraordinary character and life of Uesugi Kenshin.

Miki Castle had a number of branch castles at Ogo, Hataya, Noguchi, Shikata, and Kanki, and each had followed Miki's lead and unfurled the banner of rebellion. Their commanders derided Hideyoshi and his small army.

At this point, Kanbei suggested a new strategy to Hideyoshi.

"We may be obliged to crush these small castles one by one. But I think that taking Miki Castle by removing the surrounding small stones is the easiest strategy."

Hideyoshi first took Noguchi Castle, forced Kanki and Takasago to surrender, and burned the neighboring villages one by one. He had half-subjugated the Bessho clan when an urgent letter from Shikanosuke arrived from the beleaguered Kozuki Castle.

A large Mori army has surrounded the castle. Our situation is desperate. Please send reinforcements. Kobayakawa's soldiers number over twenty thousand; Kikkawa is leading about sixteen thousand men. In addition, the army of Ukita Naoie has joined them with about fifteen thousand men, so the entire force cannot be less than fifty thousand troops. In order to cut off communications between Kozuki and its allies, the enemy army is digging a long trench across the valley and putting up stockades and barriers. They also have about seven hundred warships sailing the seas of Harima and Settsu, and seem prepared to send reinforcements and supplies overland.

This report could not but put a halt to Hideyoshi's present course. This was, indeed, a grave problem. And an urgent one. But it was not a complete surprise, because the mobilization of the Mori had been considered in his plans beforehand.

Whenever Hideyoshi was troubled, his feelings were manifested in the shape of a large frown. Having predicted the present situation, he had already requested reinforcements from Nobunaga, but no word had yet come from the capital. He had no idea whether reinforcements had already been sent or whether none would be coming.

Kozuki Castle, now held desperately by Amako Katsuhisa and Shikanosuke, was at the juncture of three provinces: Bizen, Harima, and Mimasaka. Though it was only a small castle near a mountain village, it occupied a very important strategic position.

If one ever wanted to enter the Sanin area, Kozuki was the barrier one would first have to control. It was natural that the Mori would give this serious consideration, and Hideyoshi was impressed with the enemy's astute grasp of the situation. But he did not have enough strength to divide his army in two.

Nobunaga was not so small-minded as to be unable to delegate important tasks to the men under his command. But the general rule was that everything had to be in his own hands. His guiding principle was that if someone threatened his control, that person was not to be trusted at all. Hideyoshi had learned this lesson well. Even though he had been given the responsibility of commander-in-chief of the campaign, he never took major decisions on his own.

Thus he would send inquiries by dispatch and always ask for Nobunaga's advice, even though it may have looked as though he were asking instructions from Azuchi for every single trifling matter. He sent trusted retainers as envoys to make detailed reports on the situation, so that Nobunaga could have a clear understanding of what was going on.

Having made up his mind in his usual fashion, Nobunaga immediately ordered preparations for his departure. The other generals, however, admonished him in chorus. Nobumori, Takigawa, Hachiya, Mitsuhide—all were of the same opinion.

"Harima is a place of difficult peaks and pathways, a battlefield of mountains and hills. Shouldn't you first send reinforcements and then wait to see what the enemy does?"

Another general continued the argument, "And if His Lordship's campaign in the west drags on unexpectedly, the Honganji may cut us off from the rear and threaten our men from both land and sea."

Nobunaga was persuaded by their arguments and postponed his departure. But one must not overlook the emotions of the generals toward Hideyoshi each time a war council was called. Without actually saying so, they seemed to be asking why Hideyoshi had been made commander-in-chief, implying that the responsibility was too much for him. And as these insinuations circulated, there was one more at the bottom of them all: if Nobunaga went himself, it would still be Hideyoshi who took all the credit.

Leading reinforcements of about twenty thousand men, Nobumori, Takigawa, Niwa, and Mitsuhide left the capital and reached Harima at the beginning of the Fifth Month. Nobunaga later sent his son, Nobutada, to join them.

In the meantime, having increased his main army with the advance party of reinforcements led by Araki Murashige, Hideyoshi moved the entire force, now east of Kozuki Castle, to Mount Takakura. Reviewing the position of Kozuki Castle from this vantage point, he could see that it would be extremely difficult to establish contact with the men trapped inside.

Both the main stream and the tributaries of the Ichi River flowed around the mountain upon which the castle stood. Moreover, the castle was closed to both the northwest and southwest by the inaccessible crags of Mount Okami and Mount Taihei. There was simply no way open to approach it.

There was only a road, and it was blockaded by the Mori. Beyond that, the enemy fortifications and banners appeared at every river, valley, and mountain. A castle with such natural defenses could be held, but the very nature of its position made it extremely difficult for reinforcements to reach it.

"There's nothing we can do," Hideyoshi lamented. It was as though he were confessing that, as a general, he had not the first idea for a strategy.

Finally, when night fell, he ordered his men to make bonfires. And to make them big. Soon, huge flames could be seen from Mount Takakura to the neighborhood of Mount Mikazuki, rising over the peaks and valleys. During the day, innumerable banners and flags were hung between the trees on the high ground, which at least showed the enemy that Hideyoshi's army was present and also encouraged the tiny force inside the castle. This went on until the Fifth Month and the arrival of twenty thousand reinforcements under Nobumori, Niwa, Takigawa, and Mitsuhide.

Everyone's spirits were raised, but the actual results did not justify such elation. The reason was that there were now too many illustrious generals present in one place. With all of them shoulder to shoulder with Hideyoshi, there was not one who wanted to be put into a subordinate position. Niwa and Nobumori were both Hideyoshi's seniors, while Mitsuhide and Takigawa were his equals in terms of popularity and intelligence.

They themselves engendered an atmosphere of doubt concerning who the commander-in-chief really was. Orders cannot come down even two roads, and now they were being issued by several generals. The enemy was able to sniff out such internal difficulties. The Mori forces were awake enough to see through the inefficiency of the situation. One night the troops of Kobayakawa skirted the rear of Mount Takakura and made a surprise attack on the Oda camp.

Hideyoshi's men sustained a number of casualties. Next, the troops of Kikkawa moved quickly from the plains to the rear up to the area of Shikama and made a surprise attack on the Oda supply corps, burning its ships and generally doing their best to cause disruption.

One morning, as Hideyoshi looked in the direction of Kozuki, he saw that the castle's watchtower had been completely destroyed overnight. Inquiring into the matter, he was informed that the Mori army possessed one of the Southern Barbarians' cannons and had probably pulverized the tower by making a direct hit with a huge ball. Impressed by this show of force, Hideyoshi left for the capital.

* * *

When Hideyoshi arrived in Kyoto, he went straight to Nijo Palace, his clothes still dusty from the road, his face covered with stubble.

"Hideyoshi?" Nobunaga had to look twice at Hideyoshi just to make sure it was him. He certainly looked different from the man who had marched off at the head of his troops; his eyes had a hollow look, and a sparse, reddish beard surrounded his mouth like a scrubbing brush.

"Hideyoshi, why have you come here looking so pressed?"

"I haven't had a moment to spare, my lord."

"If that's so, why are you here?"

"I've come to ask for instructions."

"What a troublesome general you are! I made you commander-in-chief, didn't I? If you keep asking my opinion about everything, there'll be no time to put your tactics into action. Why are you so reserved on this particular occasion? Can't you act on your own?"

"Your irritation is entirely reasonable, my lord, but your orders have to come through a single channel."

"When I put the baton of command in your hand, I gave you authority in every situation. If you understand what I want, then your instructions are my instructions. What is there to be confused about?"

"With all due respect, that's exactly the point I'm having some difficulty with. I don't want to let one single soldier die in vain."

"What are you trying to say?"

"If the present situation persists, we cannot win."

"Why do you say that this is a lost battle?"

"Unworthy as I am, now that I am in command, I do not intend to lead my men into a pitiful rout. But defeat is inevitable. In terms of fighting spirit, equipment, and geographical advantage, we're hardly a match for the Mori right now."

"The first thing to remember," Nobunaga countered, "is that if the commander-in-chief anticipates defeat, there's no reason for him to win."

"But if we miscalculate, thinking that we can win, our defeat might be disastrous. If your troops are stained with one defeat in the west, the enemies who are waiting here and elsewhere, and, of course, the Honganji, will think that the lord of the Oda has stumbled, and that now is the time for his downfall. They'll beat their gongs and scream their incantations, and even the north and east will rise up against you."

"I'm aware of that."

"But shouldn't we take into consideration that the invasion of the western provinces, which is so important, might be fatal for the Oda clan?"

"I have that in mind, of course."

"Then why didn't you come to the western provinces yourself, after I had made so many requests to you? Time is of the essence. If we miss this opportunity, we'll have no chance in the real battle. It's almost foolish to mention this, but I know you are the first general ever to perceive this opportunity, and I do not understand why you did nothing when I sent request after request to you. Even though I've tried to draw the enemy out, they're not so easily provoked. Now the Mori have raised a huge army and attacked Kozuki, using Miki Castle as a base. Is this not a heaven-sent opportunity? I would be happy to be a decoy to lure them out further. Then couldn't you, my lord, come in person, and finish this game with a single stroke?"

Nobunaga was lost in thought. Because he was not the kind of man to be indecisive at a time like this, Hideyoshi understood that Nobunaga did not mean to grant his request.

Finally Nobunaga said, "No, this is no time to move rashly. First I need to ascertain exactly the Mori clan's strength." This time it was Hideyoshi who looked lost in thought. Nobunaga went on as if he were rebuking him, "Haven't you become a little overawed at the Mori's strength, expecting defeat even before you've put up a reasonable fight?"

"I don't account it as loyalty to you, my lord, to fight a battle that I know will end in defeat."

"Are the forces of the western provinces that strong? Is their morale that high?"

"It is. They're protecting the borders they've held since the time of Motonari, and are taking pains to strengthen the interior of their domain. Their wealth cannot be compared even with the Uesugi of Echigo or the Takeda of Kai."

"It's foolish to think that a wealthy province is always a strong one."

"Strength depends on the *quality* of wealth. If the Mori were extravagant and arrogant, they wouldn't be worth worrying about, and in fact their very wealth might be taken advantage of. But the two generals, Kikkawa and Kobayakawa, are of great aid to Terumoto, and they maintain the traditions of their former lord; their commanders and soldiers act virtuously, following the Way of the Samurai. The few soldiers we take alive are of an awe-inspiring mettle and burn with hostility. When I see all this, I can't help lamenting that this invasion is going to be so diff—"

"Hideyoshi, Hideyoshi," Nobunaga interrupted with a look of displeasure. "What about Miki Castle? Nobutada is headed there."

"I doubt that it will fall easily, even with your son's abilities."

"What kind of commander is Bessho Nagaharu, the governor of the castle?"

"He is a man of character."

"You're only praising the enemy, you know."

"The first rule of the military man is to know his enemy. I suppose it's not a good thing to praise both their commanders and their soldiers, but I've spoken frankly because I feel it's my duty to give you a correct evaluation."

"I suppose that's right." Nobunaga finally seemed to recognize the strength of the enemy, although he did so reluctantly. Nevertheless, the determination to win was still festering somewhere within him, and presently he said, "I suppose that's so, but it's still another thing for our troops not to be spirited, Hideyoshi."

"Absolutely!"

"The role of commander-in-chief is not an easy one. Takigawa, Nobumori, Niwa, and Mitsuhide are all senior generals. It's not that they don't follow your instructions, is it?"

"You have excellent insight, my lord." Hideyoshi hung his head, his battle-weary face turning red. "Perhaps it was too much of a responsibility for their junior, Hideyoshi."

Certainly he could see through the subtle machinations of the senior retainers, and how they had prevented Nobunaga from riding into battle himself. Even if the large army of the Mori was nothing to be worried about, he had to caution himself to be wary of the danger from his own allies.

"This is what you must do, Hideyoshi. Abandon the castle at Kozuki temporarily. Join Nobutada's forces, proceed to Miki Castle, and bring down Bessho Nagaharu. Then watch what the enemy does for a while."

The primary cause of the troops' depression was the fact that the army had been split in two, one half to attack Miki Castle and the other to relieve Kozuki. This was the result of differing opinions in the Oda military conferences up to now. And the reason for the split was clear. The small Amako force, entrenched in Kozuki Castle, was depending on the Oda clan. To abandon them for a quick strategic gain would make other western clans feel uneasy and lead them to wonder what kind of man Nobunaga was. Certainly the Oda would gain the reputation of being unreliable allies.

The man who had placed Amako Katsuhisa and Shikanosuke's troops in Kozuki Castle was Hideyoshi, and now misery, friendship, and an almost unbearable sympathy filled his heart. He knew that he was going to watch them die. Nevertheless, as soon as he received Nobunaga's new orders, he responded with an immediate "Yes, my lord," and withdrew.

Repressing his own feelings, he returned to the western provinces, deep in thought all the way. Avoid the difficult battle, and be victorious over that which is easy—this is the natural law of military strategy, he said to himself. It seems that taking this measure has little to do with good faith, but we have been fighting for a greater objective from the very beginning. So I'm going to have to bear the unbearable.

When Hideyoshi returned to his base on Mount Takakura, he called the other generals and informed them of Nobunaga's decision exactly as it had been told to him. Then he immediately gave the order to strike camp and join Nobutada's army. With Niwa and Takigawa's forces left behind as a rear guard, Hideyoshi's and Araki Murashige's main army began the retreat.

"Has Shigenori returned yet?" Hideyoshi asked a number of times before leaving Mount Takakura.

Takenaka Hanbei, who knew exactly what was on Hideyoshi's mind, looked back toward Kozuki Castle as though he were reluctant to leave.

"He's not back yet?" Hideyoshi asked again.

Shigenori was one of Hideyoshi's retainers. Two nights before, he had received Hideyoshi's instructions to go alone to Kozuki Castle as a messenger. Now Hideyoshi was anxious and kept wondering to himself if his messenger had been able to slip through the enemy lines. What would Shikanosuke do? Hideyoshi's message, carried by Shigenori, was to inform the men in the castle of the changing direction of the battle.

Can you be determined to seek life in the midst of death, and strike out from the castle and join our forces? We will wait for you until tomorrow.

Tomorrow had come, and they watched in anticipation, but the soldiers inside the castle did not move, nor did the Mori army surrounding the castle make the slightest change. Giving them up for lost, Hideyoshi and his men left Mount Takakura.

The men in Kozuki Castle were sunk in a pit of despair. To defend the castle was death; to leave the castle was death. Even the indomitable Shikanosuke was in a daze. He had no idea what to do.

"No one is at fault," Shikanosuke had told Shigenori. "We can only hold a grudge against heaven."

After discussing the matter with Amako Katsuhisa and the other retainers, Shikanosuke gave Shigenori his answer: "In spite of Lord Hideyoshi's kind offer, it is inconceivable that this small, tired force could break out and join him. We must somehow search for another plan."

When he had sent back the messenger, Shikanosuke secretly wrote a note addressed to the commander of the attacking forces, Mori Terumoto. It was a letter of surrender. He also made separate requests for intervention to Kikkawa and Kobayakawa. These were, of course, to spare the life of his lord, Katsuhisa, and to plead for the lives of the seven hundred troops in the castle. But neither Kikkawa nor Kobayakawa would listen to Shikanosuke's repeated pleas. There was only one way they would be satisfied. "Open the castle," they said, "and present us with Katsuhisa's head."

It was an extravagance to look for mercy when forced to capitulate. Swallowing tears of grief, Shikanosuke prostrated himself before Katsuhisa. "There is nothing more that your retainer can do. How pitiful that you have had the misfortune of having a worthless retainer like myself. It is inevitable, my lord, you must prepare yourself to die."

"No, Shikanosuke," Katsuhisa said, and turned away. "That the situation has come to this pass is not because my men have poor abilities. But we cannot hold a grudge against Lord Nobunaga either. Rather, it is a great, great joy to me to have earned my retainers' devotion and to have served as the leader of a samurai clan. It was you who gave me the will to restore the name of our clan, and presented the opportunity to harass our sworn enemies. What regrets have I, even if we are defeated now? I think I have done everything I could do as a man. I can rest in peace now."

At dawn on the third day of the Seventh Month, Katsuhisa committed *seppuku* in a manly fashion. The grudge between the Mori and Amako clans had lasted for a full fifty-six years.

But the greatest surprise was yet to come. Yamanaka Shikanosuke, the man who had fought on against the Mori despite the worst hardships and pains, and who had just asked his lord to commit *seppuku*, chose not to follow him in death. Instead he surrendered and went to Kikkawa Motoharu's camp like a common foot soldier, ignominiously becoming a prisoner of war.

The human heart is unfathomable. Shikanosuke was criticized by both his enemies and his allies, who said of him that no matter how he cloaked himself in loyalty, when it got to the point of no return, he couldn't help showing his true colors.

But these same critics would hear something even more unexpected several days later, news that would leave them disgusted and incredulous. Yamanaka Shikanosuke had become a retainer of the Mori and had been given a castle in Suo in exchange for his future loyalty.

"What a shallow dog!"

"This man is unfit to associate with samurai!"

The name of Yamanaka Shikanosuke was soon worth nothing but contempt. For twenty years he had been considered—by both enemy and ally alike—a warrior of undying devotion and loyalty who had remained unbending through many difficulties. But now people felt ashamed that they had been taken in so badly. Their hatred was in direct proportion to Shikanosuke's earlier fame.

In the hottest part of the Seventh Month, Shikanosuke—who appeared to be giving no ear at all to the taunts of the world—his family and his retainers were led to his new estate in Suo. They were escorted by several hundred Mori troops who were acting officially as guides but who were really nothing more than guards. Shikanosuke was like a captured tiger that could still turn violent at any time. Before he was caged and accustomed to being fed, his new allies did not feel truly comfortable with him. After a few days' march they came to the Abe River ferry at the foot of Mount Matsu.

Shikanosuke dismounted and sat down on a large rock facing the riverbank.

Amano Kii of the Mori clan dismounted and approached him. He said, "The women and children are poor walkers, so we'll let them cross the river first. Rest here for a little while."

Shikanosuke simply nodded. He had recently become quite reticent, not wanting to waste his words. Kii walked toward the ferry and yelled something to the men on the riverbank. There were only one or two boats. Shikanosuke's wife, son, and retainers piled into them one after another until the boats appeared to be filled with little mountains, and set off for the opposite shore.

Watching the boat, Shikanosuke wiped the sweat from his face and asked his attendant to dip a cloth into the icy water of the river. His only other attendant had led his horse downstream to drink.

Green-winged insects buzzed around Shikanosuke. A pale moon floated in the late afternoon sky. Flowering bindweed crept along the ground.

"Shinza! Hikoemon! Now's your chance!" Kii's eldest son, Motoaki, whispered to two men standing in the shade of a stand of trees where about ten horses were tethered. Shikanosuke did not notice them. The boat carrying his family was almost halfway across the river.

The river wind filled his breast, and the entire scene dazzled his tear-filled eyes. How pitiful, he lamented. As a husband and father, he was heartbroken to think of the fate of his vagabond family.

Even the bravest warrior has feelings, and it was said that Shikanosuke was more sentimental than most men. His courage and chivalrous spirit burned in his eyes with more intensity than the hot summer sun. He had been abandoned by Nobunaga; he had severed his ties with Hideyoshi; he had delivered Kozuki Castle; and then he had presented the head of his lord to his enemies.

And now he was still here, obstinately clinging to life. What were his hopes? What honor did he still have? The world's insults sounded like the chirping of the grasshoppers that surrounded him now. But as he listened while the cool breeze played on his breast, he did not care.

One sorrow
Heaped upon another
Will test my strength to its limits.

This was a poem he had written years before. Now he said it in his heart. He remembered what he had sworn to the mother who had encouraged him when he was young, to his former lord and to heaven, and to the new moon in the empty sky before he went into battle: Give me every obstacle!

Surmounting one after another, he had been able to overcome every obstacle until now. Shikanosuke considered this to be man's greatest pleasure and his own greatest satisfaction.

A hundred obstacles are not in themselves a cause for grief. Advancing through life with this belief, Shikanosuke had tasted great joy in the midst of all his hardships. He had maintained this attitude even when Hideyoshi's messenger told him that Nobunaga had changed strategy. It was true that he had been temporarily discouraged, but he had begrudged no one. Neither had he grieved. Never, not even now, did he sink into despair and think, This is the end. Instead, he burned with hope. I'm still alive, and I'm going to live as long as I continue to breathe! He had one great hope: to get close to his mortal enemy, Kikkawa Motoharu, and die stabbing him to death. After he had snatched away Kikkawa's life, he would rejoice to meet his former lords in the afterworld.

Even though Shikanosuke had surrendered, Kikkawa was not foolish enough to meet him face to face, but politely gave him a castle and sent him on his way. Now Shikanosuke was unhappy, wondering when he might have his chance in the future.

The boat that carried his family and retainers docked on the opposite shore. For a moment his attention was taken by the sight of his family stepping out of the boat in the middle of a large crowd.

Without a sound, a naked blade leaped out from behind Shikanosuke and struck him on the shoulder. At the same time, another blade struck the rock he was sitting on, sending sparks flying in all directions. Even a man like Shikanosuke could be taken unawares. Although the blade had cut deep, Shikanosuke jumped up and grabbed the would-be assassin by the topknot.

"Coward!" he shouted.

He had sustained a single sword wound, but his attacker had an accomplice. Seeing his companion in trouble, the second man ran at Shikanosuke, brandishing his sword and yelling, "Prepare yourself to die! It's our lord's command!"

"Bastard!" Shikanosuke spat back in anger. He pushed the first attacker away into his companion, making the second man fall. Seeing his chance, Shikanosuke ran into the river, kicking up a huge spray of foam.

"Don't let him escape!" a Mori officer shouted, breaking into a run. He flung his spear with all his might from the bank. It caught Shikanosuke in the back and knocked him face down into the river. The spear shaft stood straight up in the reddening water, like a harpoon stuck in a whale.

The two assassins waded into the river. They dragged the wounded Shikanosuke out by the legs, pinned him down on the riverbank, and cut off his head. Blood ran in rivulets through the small stones on the bank, while the waves of the Abe River almost appeared to be on fire as they rolled back and forth. At the same time, cries and bellowing came from farther up the bank.

"My lord!"

"Lord Shikanosuke!"

Shikanosuke's two attendants began to run toward him, but the Mori had planned for this as well. As soon as they yelled out, they were surrounded by a cage of steel and could go no farther. When they realized that their master had met his end, they fought with all the strength they had, until they followed Shikanosuke into death.

A man's body cannot live forever. An unswerving loyalty and sense of duty, however, will live long in the annals of war. Warriors of later times would say that whenever they looked up and saw the new moon in an indigo-blue evening sky, they would think of Yamanaka Shikanosuke's indomitability and would be struck by feelings of reverence. In their hearts Shikanosuke would live forever.

Shikanosuke's sword and the tea container "Great Ocean" were sent along with his head to Kikkawa Motoharu.

"If we had not struck you down," Kikkawa said as he looked at the head, "you would be holding my head in your hands one day. That is the Way of the Samurai. Having accomplished what you did, you should resign yourself to finding peace in the next world."

* * *

When Hideyoshi's seven thousand five hundred men left Kozuki, it looked as though they would be advancing toward Tajima, but suddenly they turned toward Kakogawa in Harima and joined forces with Nobutada's thirty thousand troops. It was already the end of summer.

Attacked by this large army, both the castles at Kanki and Shikata fell quickly. The only remaining castle was at Miki, the stronghold of the Bessho clan. The battles the Oda fought as they pressed in on Miki Castle seemed to have gone rather easily, but the reduction of fortress after fortress on the first line of Mori defenses had been at the sacrifice of a large number of men. The combined forces of the Oda numbered thirty-eight thousand men, but it was clear that the enemy was going to put up considerable resistance.

One of the reasons this campaign would require time was that, along with advances in weaponry, there had been a revolution in tactics. Generally, the weapons of the western provinces' armies were more advanced than those of the Oda's enemies in Echizen or Kai.

It was the first time the Oda forces had come into contact with such powerful gunpowder and cannon. For Hideyoshi, this was an enemy from whom he could learn many things. Kanbei probably did the buying, but Hideyoshi himself was the first to abandon the old Chinese cannons and equip himself with a cannon made by the Southern

Barbarians, which he placed on top of a reconnaissance tower. When the other Oda generals saw this, they too rushed to acquire the latest cannon.

When they heard of the fighting in the western provinces, a large number of arms merchants came up from Hirado and Hakata in Kyushu, dodging the Mori fleet at the risk of their lives while seeking the ports on the Harima coast. Hideyoshi helped these men by mediating with the other generals, whom he told to purchase the new weapons, regardless of cost.

The power of the new cannons was first tested on Kanki Castle. The Oda built a small hill facing the point of attack, and erected a wooden reconnaissance tower upon it. A large cannon was then placed at the top of the tower and fired at the castle. The castle's earthen wall and gate were destroyed easily. The real targets, however, were the towers and the inner citadel.

But the enemy also possessed artillery, as well as the newest small arms and gunpowder. The reconnaissance tower was pulverized or burned to the ground a number of times, only to be rebuilt and knocked flat again.

During this hard fighting, Hideyoshi's engineers filled in the moat and pressed in beneath the stone wall, while the sappers excavated tunnels to undermine the walls. This work continued without interruption day and night, never allowing the soldiers in the castle a moment to undo the damage. Such a strategy eventually brought about the fall of the castles. Because victory over the small castles at Shikata and Kanki had required such efforts, it looked as if the attack on the main castle at Miki might be even more difficult.

There was an elevated area called Mount Hirai, about half a league from Miki Castle. Hideyoshi set up his camp there and positioned eight thousand men in the surrounding area.

One day Nobutada visited Mount Hirai, and the two of them went out and observed the enemy's positions. To the south of the enemy were the mountains and hills connected to the mountain ranges of western Harima. To the north ran the Miki River. To the east were bamboo thickets, farmland, and scrub. Finally, a number of strongholds on the neighboring hills encircled the castle walls on three sides. These in turn centered around the main citadel, the second citadel, and yet a third enclosure.

"It makes you wonder if it can be taken quickly, Hideyoshi," said Nobutada, gazing at the castle.

"I doubt seriously that it'll be taken easily. It's like a rotten tooth with a deep root."

"A rotten tooth?" Nobutada unintentionally broke into a smile at Hideyoshi's image. Nobutada had been suffering from toothache for four or five days. Because of the swelling, his face was a little distorted. Now he held his cheek and couldn't help laughing at Hideyoshi's observation. The parallel of the unassailable Miki Castle and his rotten tooth was both amusing and painful.

"I see. Just like a rotten tooth. To pull it, you need patience."

"It may be only one tooth, but it offends the body in its entirety. Bessho Nagaharu makes our men suffer. It's not enough to say that he's like a rotten tooth. But if we give in to our irritation and try to subjugate the castle thoughtlessly, not only could the gums be damaged but it could be fatal to the patient."

"Well, what shall we do, then? What's your strategy?"

"This tooth's fate is clear. Let's just loosen the root naturally. What if we cut off the supply roads and then shake the tooth from time to time?"

"My father, Nobunaga, told me to withdraw to Gifu if the prospects were not good for a quick attack. You can take care of the delaying tactics and other arrangements; I'm returning to Gifu."

"Set your mind at ease, my lord."

The next day Nobutada withdrew from the battlefield in the company of the other generals. Hideyoshi disposed his eight thousand soldiers around Miki Castle, placing a corps commander at each position and erecting wooden palisades. He posted sentries and cut off all roads leading into the castle. Special emphasis was placed on the observation corps guarding the road to the south of the castle. If one followed the road about four leagues to the west, one would come out on the coast. The Mori navy often sent large convoys of ships to this point, and from here it transported weapons and provisions to the castle.

"The Eighth Month is so refreshing," Hideyoshi said, gazing up at the evening moon. "Ichimatsu! Hey, Ichimatsu!"

The pages came running out of the camp, each of them jockeying to arrive first. Ichimatsu was not among them. While the other pages took stances to outshine one another, Hideyoshi gave them their instructions.

"Prepare a mat at a spot on Mount Hirai with a commanding view. We're going to have a moon-viewing party tonight. Now don't fight among yourselves. This is a party, not a battle."

"Yes, my lord!"

"Toranosuke."

"My lord?"

"Ask Hanbei to join me if he feels well enough for moon viewing."

Two of the pages quickly returned and announced that they had prepared the mat. They had chosen a place near the summit of Mount Hirai, a short climb from the camp.

"A superb view, indeed," Hideyoshi commented. Then he once again turned to the pages and said, "Go ask Kanbei too. It would be a shame if he didn't see this moon." And he sent a page running to Kanbei's tent.

The moon-viewing platform had been set up under a huge pine tree. There was cold *sake* in a crane-necked flask, and food on a square cypress-wood tray. Although the setting was hardly luxurious, it was quite sufficient for a brief respite during a military campaign—especially with the shining moon overhead. The three men sat on the mat in a line, with Hideyoshi in the center and Hanbei and Kanbei on either side.

It was the same moon that the three men gazed up at, but it evoked completely different thoughts in each of them. Hideyoshi thought about the fields of Nakamura; Hanbei remembered the magical moon over Mount Bodai; and only Kanbei thought about the days ahead.

"Are you cold, Hanbei?" Kanbei asked his friend, and Hideyoshi, perhaps from sudden concern, also turned and looked at Hanbei.

"No, I'm fine." Hanbei shook his head; but just at that moment his face looked paler than the moon.

This talented man has frail health, Hideyoshi sighed without cheer. He worried about Hanbei's health far more than Hanbei himself did.

Once Hanbei had vomited blood while riding at Nagahama, and he had often been ill during the northern campaign. When they had started out this time, Hideyoshi had tried to stop his friend from coming, protesting that he was overstraining himself.

"What are you talking about?" Hanbei had replied lightly, and joined him in the field anyway.

It was reassuring to Hideyoshi to have Hanbei at his side. He was both a visible and an invisible strength—the relationship was one of lord and retainer, but in his heart Hideyoshi looked up to Hanbei as a teacher. Now, especially, he was faced with the diffi- cult task of the western campaign, the war was dragging on, and many of his fellow gen- erals were envious of him. He was approaching the steepest climb of life, and his reliance on Hanbei was all the more critical.

But Hanbei had already fallen ill twice since they had entered the western provinces. Hideyoshi had been so worried that he had ordered Hanbei to see a doctor in Kyoto. Hanbei, however, had quickly returned.

"I've been ill since my birth, so I'm used to infirmity. Medical treatment would be useless in my case. A warrior's life is on the battlefield." With that, he worked at staff headquarters as diligently as before, without the least sign of fatigue. His weak constitu- tion, however, was a grim fact, and there was no way to beat the disease, regardless of how strong his spirit might be.

Heavy rain had poured down on them when the army moved from Tajima. Possibly because of the excesses of that trip, Hanbei had pleaded ill health and did not show his face to Hideyoshi for two days after they set up camp at Mount Hirai. It was normal for Hanbei not to appear before Hideyoshi on days when he was very ill; he very likely did not want to give his lord cause for concern. But because Hanbei had looked fit during the past few days, Hideyoshi had thought they could sit together under the moon and talk as they had not been able to for a long time. But it was not just the light of the moon: as Hideyoshi had feared, there was something not quite right in Hanbei's complexion.

When he sensed Hideyoshi's and Kanbei's concern, Hanbei purposely steered the conversation in another direction.

"Kanbei, according to the news I received yesterday from a retainer in my home province, your son, Shojumaru, is quite healthy and has finally gotten used to his new surroundings."

"Because Shojumaru is in your home province, Hanbei, I have no worries. I hardly ever think about it."

The two of them spoke about Kanbei's son for a little while. Hideyoshi, who still had no children of his own, could not help feeling a little envious as he listened to this talk be- tween fathers. Shojumaru was Kanbei's heir, but when Kanbei had realized what the fu- ture held, he had entrusted his son to Nobunaga as a pledge of good faith.

The young hostage had been put into of Hanbei's care, who had sent him to his castle in Fuwa and was raising him as though he were his own son. Thus, with Hideyoshi as the

477

linchpin of their relationship, Kanbei and Hanbei were also bound by ties of friendship. And while they were rivals as generals, there was not the least bit of jealousy between them. The saying that "two great men cannot stand side by side" was hardly applicable in Hideyoshi's field headquarters.

Looking at the moon, drinking *sake*, and talking about the great men of past and present, and the rise and fall of provinces and clans, it seemed that Hanbei managed to forget his illness.

Kanbei, however, returned to the subject. "Even if a man leads a great army in the morning, he doesn't know whether he'll be alive in the evening. But if you hold some great ambition—no matter how great a man you are—you must live a long time to bring it to fruition. There have been many glorious heroes and loyal retainers who left their names to eternity and whose lives were short, but what if they had lived a long time? It's only natural to feel regret about the shortness of life. The destruction that goes with pushing aside the old and striking at evil is not the only work of a great man. His work is not accomplished until he has rebuilt the nation."

Hideyoshi nodded vigorously. He then said to the silent Hanbei, "That's why we must cherish our lives. I'd like you to take care of your health for those reasons, too, Hanbei."

"I feel the same way," Kanbei added. "Rather than push yourself to excess, why don't you retire to a temple in Kyoto, find a good doctor, and take care of yourself? I suggest this as a friend, and I think you could say that it would be an act of loyalty to give our lord peace of mind."

Hanbei listened, quite overcome by gratitude toward his two friends. "I'll do as you say, and go to Kyoto for a while. But right now we're laying our plans, so I'd like to leave after I see them completed."

Hideyoshi nodded. Thus far he had based his strategy on Hanbei's suggestions, but he still had not seen it succeed.

"Are you worried about Akashi Kagechika?" Hideyoshi asked.

"Exactly," Hanbei said, nodding. "If you'll give me five or six days before my convalescent leave, I'll go to Mount Hachiman and meet Akashi Kagechika. I'll try to persuade him to join our side. Do I have your permission?"

"Of course, it would be a great achievement. But what if something happens? You must see that the odds of running into trouble are about eight or nine out of ten. What then?"

"I will only die," Hanbei answered without blinking. From the way he spoke, it was clearly no braggart's bluff.

After Miki Castle fell, Hideyoshi's next enemy would be Akashi Kagechika. But for the time being, Hideyoshi was unable to take Miki Castle. He was not, however, obsessed with the siege. Miki Castle was only one part of the campaign to subdue the whole of the west. So he had little choice but to accept Hanbei's plan to subvert Akashi.

"Will you go, then?" Hideyoshi asked.

"I will."

Hideyoshi was still hesitating, despite Hanbei's spirited resolve. Assuming Hanbei did get past the many dangers on the road and met with Akashi, if the negotiations ended in disagreement, it could not be taken for granted that the enemy would let him return alive.

Neither could Hideyoshi be sure that Hanbei would want to return empty-handed. Was Hanbei's true motive to die? Whether he died from disease or was killed by the enemy, he could only die once.

At this point, Kanbei put forward another plan. He had several acquaintances among the retainers of Ukita Naoie. While Hanbei approached the Akashi clan, he himself could go to the senior retainers of the Ukita clan.

When he heard this idea, Hideyoshi intuitively felt reassured. It might be possible to subvert the Ukita clan. Since the invasion of the western provinces had begun, the Ukita had appeared to be somewhat lukewarm, waiting to see which side had the advantage. Ukita Naoie had appealed to the Mori for help, but if he could be persuaded that the future was Nobunaga's....More than that, the Ukita's alliance with the Mori might prove worthless if they received no military support. It could spell the demise of the Ukita clan. The Ukita had learned this after the withdrawal of the Mori army once it had recaptured Kozuki Castle.

"If the Ukita come to an agreement with us, Akashi Kagechika will have no alternative but to come to terms too," Hideyoshi observed. "And if Kagechika submitted to us, the Ukita would immediately sue for peace. To carry on both negotiations at the same time is an excellent idea."

The following day, Hanbei publicly requested leave owing to illness, and announced that he would be going to Kyoto for convalescence. Under this pretense, he left the camp at Mount Hirai, accompanied by only two or three attendants. After a few days, Kanbei also left the camp.

Hanbei first called on Kagechika's younger brother, Akashi Kanjiro. He was not a friend of Kanjiro's, but he had met him twice at the Nanzen Temple in Kyoto, where they had both practiced Zen meditation. Kanjiro was attracted to Zen. Hanbei reasoned that if he appealed to him from the standpoint of the Way, they would come to a quick understanding. Then he could go on to talk to his older brother, Kagechika.

Until they met him, both Akashi Kanjiro and his elder brother, Kagechika, had waited, wondering what kind of policy Hanbei would advocate and how eloquent he would be. He was, after all, both Hideyoshi's teacher and a renowned military tactician. But when they did speak to him, contrary to their expectations they found him to be a plainspoken man who seemed devoid of the least bit of showmanship or guile.

Hanbei's conviction and sincerity were so different from the stratagems usually employed during negotiations between samurai clans that the Akashi were convinced. They cut their ties to the Ukita clan. Only when his mission was accomplished did Hanbei finally ask for a short period of leave. This time he truly did put aside his military responsibilities and go to Kyoto to convalesce.

Hideyoshi spoke with him upon his departure and asked him to visit Nobunaga. He was to inform Nobunaga that they had successfully persuaded Akashi Kagechika to join the Oda alliance.

When he learned the news, Nobunaga was overjoyed. "What? You took Mount Hachiman without losing a drop of blood? You did well!" The Oda forces that had occupied the entirety of Harima had now entered Bizen for the first time. It was a first step of great significance.

"You look as though you've lost weight. Take good care to recuperate," Nobunaga said, sympathizing with Hanbei's ill health, and in appreciation for his meritorious deed, he rewarded him with twenty pieces of silver.

To Hideyoshi he wrote:

You have used uncommon wisdom in this situation. I'll hear the details when we meet in person, but for the present, here is a token of my gratitude.

And he sent him one hundred gold pieces. When Nobunaga was happy, he was happy to excess. Taking his vermilion seal in hand, he appointed Hideyoshi military governor of Harima.

* * *

The long campaign at Mount Hirai, with the extended siege of Miki Castle, had reached a stalemate. But with the defection of the Akashi to their side, the Oda were gradually succeeding in their maneuvers. However, as might be expected of a clan of such distinction, the Ukita were not as easily influenced by negotiations, even though Kanbei used every bit of his acumen in dealing with them. Holding the provinces of Bizen and Mimasaka, the Ukita were caught between the Oda and the Mori. Thus it was not an overstatement to say that the future of the western provinces depended entirely on their attitude.

Ukita Naoie followed the advice of four senior retainers: Osafune Kii, Togawa Higo, Oka Echizen, and Hanabusa Sukebei. Among them, Hanabusa had a slight connection with Kuroda Kanbei. And it was to Hanabusa that Kanbei first addressed himself. Kanbei talked all night, discussing the present and future of the country. He spoke of Nobunaga's aspirations and of Hideyoshi's character, and succeeded in winning over Hanabusa.

Hanabusa then persuaded Togawa Higo to join them, and having won over these two men, Kanbei was able to meet with Ukita Naoie.

After hearing their arguments, Naoie said, "We must consider the fact that a great national force is rising in the east. If we are attacked by Lord Nobunaga and Lord Hideyoshi, the entire Ukita clan will perish to defend the Mori. To save the lives of thousands of soldiers and benefit the nation, my own three sons would gladly meet their deaths as hostages in enemy territory. If I'm able to protect this domain and save thousands of lives, my prayers will be fulfilled."

These words from Naoie ended the discussion among his retainers. The conference was concluded, and a letter pledging the cooperation of the Ukita clan was given to Hikoemon, who delivered it to Mount Hirai. Thus, Hideyoshi won a victory to the rear of his army without expending a single arrow. The two provinces of Bizen and Mimasaka bloodlessly became allies of the Oda.

Hideyoshi naturally wanted to inform his lord of this happy event as quickly as he could, but a letter might be dangerous, he thought. This was a matter of the greatest secrecy: until the right opportunity presented itself, it would be necessary to conceal the alliance from the Mori clan.

He sent Kanbei to Kyoto to inform Nobunaga.

Kanbei immediately set off for the capital. When he arrived, he had an audience with Nobunaga.

As he listened to Kanbei's report, Nobunaga seemed to become extraordinarily displeased. Previously, when Takenaka Hanbei had come to Nijo Palace and had reported on the submission of the Akashi, Nobunaga had been overjoyed and had praised him. This time, however, his reaction was completely different.

"On whose orders did you do this? If it was on Hideyoshi's, he is going to get a grilling! For him to enter into an agreement with the two provinces of Bizen and Mimasaka at all is the worst form of audacity. Go back and tell that to Hideyoshi!" Then, as though this blunt rebuke were not enough, he continued, "According to Hideyoshi's letter, he'll be coming to Azuchi in a few days with Ukita Naoie. You tell him that I won't see Naoie even if he does come. In fact, I won't even see Hideyoshi!"

He was so angry that even Kanbei could not deal with him. Having come in vain, Kanbei returned to Harima nursing feelings of discontent.

Even though he felt ashamed to tell Hideyoshi exactly what had happened in view of all the hardships Hideyoshi had been through, he could hardly keep the matter secret. When Kanbei looked surreptitiously at Hideyoshi's face, he could see a forced smile appear on his haggard cheeks.

"Yes, I understand," Hideyoshi said. "He got angry because I made an unnecessary alliance on my own authority." He didn't seem to be as discouraged as Kanbei. "I imagine Lord Nobunaga wanted us to destroy the Ukita so that he could divide their lands among his retainers." Then, trying to console the downcast Kanbei, he said "It's a real battle when things don't go as planned. The plans you thought through last night change in the morning, and the schemes you have in the morning change by the afternoon."

Kanbei, for his part, was suddenly aware that his life was in this man's hands. Deep in his heart, he felt that he would not even begrudge dying for Hideyoshi.

Hideyoshi had read Nobunaga's heart. If he truly knew how to serve Nobunaga, he obviously understood his way of thinking. Nevertheless, Kanbei now fully understood that the present confidence and status that Hideyoshi enjoyed had been won through twenty years of service with Nobunaga.

"Well then, does this mean that you went ahead with the alliance with the Ukita even though you knew it would be against Lord Nobunaga's will?" Kanbei asked.

"Considering Lord Nobunaga's ambitions, there was no doubt he was going to be angry. When Takenaka Hanbei reported the submission of Akashi Kagechika, His Lordship was so happy that he rewarded both Hanbei and me excessively. Certainly he saw that the submission of the Akashi clan would ease the attack on the Ukita, and a successful attack would have allowed him to divide up the Ukita province and offer it as rewards. But now that I have made the Ukita submit to us, he cannot very well grab their lands, can he?"

"When you explain it that way, I can understand Lord Nobunaga's feelings. But he was so angry that you're not easily going to get a chance to talk frankly with him. He said that if Ukita Naoie comes to Azuchi, or even if you come to intercede for him, he won't give an audience to either one of you."

"I'll have to call on him, regardless of how angry he is. There are ways of avoiding a row when a husband and wife are angry with each other, but it's not good to avoid the anger of one's lord. Nothing is going to make him feel better than my going to apologize, even if I get a beating or he yells at me while I lie prostrate at his feet, looking foolish."

The written pledge procured from Ukita Naoie was in Hideyoshi's hands, but Hideyoshi was only the commander of an expeditionary army. If the treaty did not meet with Nobunaga's approval, it would be worthless.

Moreover, as a matter of formality, etiquette demanded that Ukita Naoie go to Azuchi, pay obeisance to Nobunaga, and ask his further orders. On the date they had prearranged, Hideyoshi accompanied Naoie to Azuchi. Nobunaga's anger, however, had not yet cooled off.

"I won't meet with them." This is all he would tell Hideyoshi through his attendant.

Hideyoshi was at a loss. He could only wait. He went back to the guest room where Naoie was waiting and reported the outcome.

"His Lordship is not in such a good mood today. Would you wait for me awhile back at your lodgings?"

"Is he indisposed?" Naoie asked unhappily. In suing for peace, he had not been seeking Nobunaga's pity. He could still count on a formidable army. What's the matter? Why this cold reception? These words never left his mouth, but he could not help indignantly thinking them.

Naoie could not bear further humiliation. He was beginning to think that he should return to his home province and once again send out the salutations that were appropriate for enemy provinces.

"No, no," Hideyoshi told him. "If there's a problem now, we can meet him later. For the time being, let's go to the castle town."

Hideyoshi had arranged for Naoie's lodgings in the Sojitsu Temple. The two hastily returned to the temple, where Naoie changed from his formal clothing and spoke to Hideyoshi.

"I'm going to leave Azuchi before nightfall and stay overnight in the capital. Then I think it would be better if I returned to Bizen."

"Now, why would you want to do that? At least why would you want to leave before we meet Lord Nobunaga again?"

"I don't feel like meeting him any longer." For the first time, Naoie manifested his feelings in both his countenance and his words. "And I think that Lord Nobunaga does not want to see me, either. Moreover, this is an enemy province with which I have no connection. It would probably be better for both of us if I left right away."

"It will compromise my honor."

"I'll come and thank you properly for the way you've treated me on another day, Lord Hideyoshi. And I shall not forget your kindness."

"Please stay one more night. I can't bear to see the two clans that I have brought together for a peace conference suddenly become enemies again. Lord Nobunaga refused to grant us an audience today, and he has his reasons. Let's meet again this evening and I'll explain them to you. Right now I'm going back to my lodgings to change out of these clothes. Wait for me before eating dinner."

There was nothing Naoie could do but wait until evening. Hideyoshi changed and returned to the temple. They talked and laughed as they ate their evening meal, and as they finished, Hideyoshi remarked, "Ah, that's right. I promised to tell you why Lord Nobunaga was so displeased with me."

And he started to talk as though he had just remembered the subject. In his desire to hear Hideyoshi's explanation, Naoie had put off his departure. Now Hideyoshi had his undivided attention.

With artless candor, Hideyoshi explained why his own arbitrary settlement had offended Nobunaga. "It's rude of me to say so, but both the provinces of Mimasaka and Bizen would sooner or later have become the possessions of the Oda clan. So to make a peace treaty now with you was not really necessary. But if Lord Nobunaga did not crush the Ukita clan, he would not be able to divide its territory among his generals as rewards for their meritorious deeds. In addition, it was unpardonable that I didn't even seek His Lordship's permission. This is why he's so angry." He laughed as he spoke, but because there was not the slightest fabrication in what he said, the truth was manifested with a clear conscience even from behind his smile.

Naoie was overwhelmed. His face, flushed by *sake*, suddenly went pale as the blood drained from it. He did not doubt, however, that Nobunaga was thinking in this way.

"So he's in a bad mood," Hideyoshi went on. "He won't give me an audience and he won't meet you either. Once he's that resolved, he's not going to bend. I'm stumped, and I feel horrible for you. The pledge that you entrusted to me is still unauthorized, and as long as it doesn't receive His Lordship's vermilion seal, there's nothing I can do. I will return it to you, so you might as well sever your connections with us, renounce the treaty, and hurry back to Bizen tomorrow morning."

With that, Hideyoshi took out Naoie's pledge and handed it back to him. Naoie, however, quietly stared at the light flickering in the tall lamps and refused even to touch the document.

Hideyoshi remained silent.

"No," Naoie said, suddenly breaking the silence. Courteously, he put his hands together. "I'm going to entreat you to do everything you can once again. Please mediate with Lord Nobunaga for me."

This time his attitude was that of a man who had surrendered from the bottom of his heart. Until now he had appeared to surrender only because of the forcible arguments of Kuroda Kanbei.

"All right. If you have that much confidence in the Oda," Hideyoshi said, nodding vigorously, and he consented to undertake the matter.

Naoie stayed at the Sojitsu Temple more than ten days waiting for the outcome. Hideyoshi hurriedly sent off a messenger to Gifu, hoping that Nobutada could mollify Nobunaga somewhat. Already having some business in the capital, Nobutada left for Kyoto soon thereafter.

Accompanied by Naoie, Hideyoshi then had an audience with Nobutada. Finally, through the latter's intercession, Nobunaga relented. Later that day the vermilion seal was affixed to the pledge, and the Ukita clan completely severed its ties to the Mori and allied itself with the Oda.

Hardly seven days later, however, whether by coincidence or for reasons of military expediencey, one of Nobunaga's generals, Araki Murashige, betrayed his lord and joined the enemy camp, raising the banner of rebellion right at the Oda's feet.

MURASHIGE'S TREACHERY

"It's a lie! It must be a lie!"

Nobunaga could not believe it at first. When the news of Murashige's revolt reached Nobunaga in Azuchi, his first reaction was denial. But the gravity of the situation was quickly confirmed when two of Murashige's senior retainers, Takayama Ukon of Takatsuki and Nakagawa Sebei of Ibaragi, cited moral obligations and followed Murashige in unfurling the banner of revolt.

The look of dismay deepened on Nobunaga's brow. The strange thing was that he showed neither anger nor his usual hot temper at this unexpected turn of events. It would be a mistake to judge Nobunaga's character as one of fire. But it would also be an error, in observing his coolness, to classify him as water. When you thought of him as fire, he was water; when you thought of him as water, he was fire. Both the heat of flames and the chill of water coexisted in his body.

"Call Hideyoshi," Nobunaga suddenly ordered.

"Lord Hideyoshi left for Harima early this morning," Takigawa replied nervously.

"He's already left?"

"He probably hasn't gotten very far. With your permission, I'll take a horse and go fetch him back." It was rare for someone to seize the moment and rescue Nobunaga from his own impatience. When the retainers who were present turned to see who this someone might be, they discovered that it was Ranmaru, Nobunaga's page.

Nobunaga granted his request and urged him to hurry.

Noon came, and Ranmaru had not yet returned. In the meantime, reports from the scouts in the areas of Itami and Takatsuki Castle were arriving frequently. The one report among them that made Nobunaga's blood run cold announced yet another new fact.

"Just this morning at dawn, a large Mori fleet approached the Hyogo coast. Soldiers disembarked and entered Murashige's castle at Hanakuma."

The coastal highway through Hyogo that ran beneath Hanakuma Castle was the only route from Azuchi to Harima.

"Hideyoshi is not going to be able to get through." At the moment Nobunaga realized this, he also understood the danger of communications being cut between the expeditionary army and Azuchi. He could almost feel the hands of the enemy at his throat.

"Is Ranmaru back yet?" Nobunaga asked.

"No, my lord."

Nobunaga was once again sunk in thought. The Hatano, the Bessho, and Araki Murashige had now suddenly revealed their links with the enemy—the Mori and the Honganji—and Nobunaga felt that he was being surrounded. Moreover, when he looked to the east, he saw that the Hojo and Takeda had recently come to terms.

Ranmaru whipped his horse through Otsu, and finally caught up with Hideyoshi near the Mii Temple. Hideyoshi was resting there, or rather, having come that far, he had heard about Araki Murashige's rebellion and sent Horio Mosuke and two or three others to verify the reports and find out the details.

Ranmaru pulled up and said, "His Lordship ordered me to come after you. He desires to talk with you again. Would you return to Azuchi as quickly as possible?"

Leaving his men at the Mii Temple, he turned back toward Azuchi, accompanied only by Ranmaru. On the way back, Hideyoshi thought through what was likely to occur. Nobunaga would be furious at Murashige's rebellion. The first time Murashige had served Nobunaga was during the attack on Nijo Palace, when they had driven out the former shogun. Nobunaga was the kind of man who would show favor toward anyone who pleased him a little, and he showed recognition of Murashige's valor especially. Nobunaga had loved Murashige more than he had loved most men. And Murashige had betrayed Nobunaga's trust. Hideyoshi could imagine what Nobunaga's feelings must be.

As Hideyoshi hurried back to Azuchi, he blamed himself as well as Murashige. The man had been his second-in-command, and their personal relationship had been a close one. And yet he had not known that Murashige was up to this kind of foolishness.

"Ranmaru, have you heard anything?" Hideyoshi asked.

"You mean about Lord Murashige's treachery?"

"What sort of dissatisfaction might have motivated him to rebel against Lord Nobunaga?" They were a long way from Azuchi, and if they had sped all the way back, their horses would have become exhausted. As Hideyoshi trotted along, he looked back at Ranmaru, whose horse was coming a few paces behind at the same pace.

"There were rumors about this sort of thing before," Ranmaru said. "The story goes that one of Lord Murashige's retainers was selling army rice to the warrior-monks of the Honganji. There's a shortage of rice in Osaka. The land road has been cut for the most part, and the sea routes have been blockaded by our fleet, so there is not even the prospect of transporting provisions with the Mori's warships. The price of rice has gone way up, and if a man sells rice there, he can make an immense profit. That's just what Lord Murashige's retainer did, and when the affair was exposed, Lord Murashige took the initiative and unfurled the flag of rebellion, fearing that he would be questioned about this crime by Lord Nobunaga anyway."

"That sounds like a seditious rumor spread by the enemy. Surely it's a baseless lie."

"I think it's a lie, too. From what I've seen, people are jealous of Lord Murashige's meritorious deeds. I think this disaster has been brought on by a certain person's slander."

"A certain person?"

"Lord Mitsuhide. Once this rumor about Lord Murashige came out, Lord Mitsuhide had nothing good to say about him to His Lordship. I'm always at His Lordship's side, listening secretly, and sure enough, I'm one of the people who feels miserable about this incident."

Ranmaru suddenly fell quiet. He seemed to realize that he had spoken a little too much, and regretted it. Ranmaru concealed his feelings about Mitsuhide as a young maiden might. At such times, Hideyoshi never seemed to pay attention to the conversation at all. In fact, he appeared to be completely indifferent.

"I can already see Azuchi. Let's hurry!" As soon as he pointed into the distance, Hideyoshi whipped his horse, completely disregarding his companion's concerns.

The main entrance of the castle was bustling with the attendants of retainers who had heard about Murashige's rebellion and were coming to the castle, and with messengers pouring in from the nearby provinces. Hideyoshi and Ranmaru shoved their way through the throng and into the inner citadel, only to be told that Lord Nobunaga was in the middle of a conference. Ranmaru went in and spoke to Nobunaga and then quickly returned, telling Hideyoshi, "He requested that you wait in the Bamboo Room." He guided Hideyoshi to a three-story tower in the inner citadel.

The Bamboo Room was part of Nobunaga's living quarters. Hideyoshi sat down alone and gazed out at the lake. Soon Nobunaga appeared, shouted happily when he saw Hideyoshi, and sat down without formality. Hideyoshi bowed politely and remained silent. The silence continued for some time. Neither man wasted his words.

"What have been your thoughts about this, Hideyoshi?" These were Nobunaga's first words, and they indicated that a resolution had not emerged out of the various confused views given at the conference.

"Araki Murashige is an extremely honest man. He is, if I may say it, a fool who excels in martial valor. I just didn't think he was *that much* of a fool," Hideyoshi replied.

"No." Nobunaga shook his head. "I don't think it was foolishness at all. He's nothing but scum. He had misgivings about my prospects and initiated contacts with the Mori, blinded by the thought of profit. This is the act of a moderately talented man. Murashige got lost in his own superficiality."

"He's really nothing but a fool. He received excessive favors and had nothing to be dissatisfied about," Hideyoshi said.

"A man who is going to rebel will do so, no matter how favorably he's treated." Nobunaga was being frank with his emotions. This was the first time Hideyoshi had ever heard him use the word "scum" to describe someone. As a rule, he would not have spoken that way from malice or anger; it was because he had not openly expressed his anger or hatred that nothing had been decided during the council. Had Hideyoshi been asked, however, even he would have been at a loss. Should they strike at Itami Castle? Should they try to mollify Murashige and get him to abandon the idea of rebellion? The problem was how to choose between these two alternatives. It would not be very difficult to capture the one castle of Itami. But the invasion of the west had just started. If they took a false step in this minor affair, they would in all likelihood have to revise their plans.

"Why don't I go as an envoy and talk with Murashige?" Hideyoshi suggested.

"So you think it would be better not to use force here, either?"

"Not if we don't have to," Hideyoshi replied.

"Mitsuhide and two or three others have advocated not using force. You're of the same opinion, but I think it would be better if someone else went as the envoy."

"No, I bear part of the responsibility for this. Murashige was my second-in-command and so was my own subordinate. If he were to do something foolish…"

"No!" Nobunaga shook his head emphatically. "There would be nothing imposing about sending an envoy with whom he's too familiar. I'll send Matsui, Mitsuhide, and Mami. Rather than appease him, they'll simply verify the rumor."

"That should be fine," Hideyoshi agreed. He spoke these few words for the sake of both Murashige and Nobunaga. "It's a common saying that the lie of a Buddhist priest is called expedient, and a revolt within a samurai clan is called strategy. You must not be pulled into fighting, for it would play into the Mori's hands."

"I know."

"I'd like to wait for the results of the envoys' meeting, but I feel uneasy about the problems in Harima. I should probably take my leave soon."

"Really?" Nobunaga sounded a little reluctant to let him go. "What about the road back? You probably won't be able to pass through Hyogo."

"Don't worry, there's also the sea route."

"Well, whatever the outcome, I'll keep you informed. Don't be negligent about sending me news."

Hideyoshi finally took his leave. Although he was exhausted, from Azuchi he crossed Lake Biwa to Otsu, spent that night in the Mii Temple, and the following day turned toward Kyoto. He sent two pages ahead with instructions to have a ship waiting at Sakai, while he and his retainers took the road to the Nanzen Temple. There he announced that they would stop for a short rest.

There was someone in the temple whom he very much wanted to see. That person, of course, was Takenaka Hanbei, who was convalescing in a hermitage on the temple grounds.

The monks were flustered by the sudden arrival of so exalted a guest, but Hideyoshi took one of them aside and requested that they omit the treatment they would ordinarily offer to a guest of his rank.

"My retainers have all brought provisions, so don't be concerned about anything other than hot water for tea. And since I've only stopped to visit Takenaka Hanbei, you won't need to entertain me with either *sake* or tea. After I have my talk with Hanbei, I'd be grateful if you'd make a light meal." Finally he asked, "Has the patient improved since he arrived?"

"It seems he has made little progress, my lord," the priest answered dolefully.

"He takes his medicine regularly?"

"Both morning and night."

"And a doctor visits him regularly?"

"Yes, a doctor comes from the capital, and Lord Nobunaga's personal physician visits him regularly."

"Is he up?"

"No, he hasn't been up for the past three days."

"Where is he?"

"In a hermitage away from the bustle."

When Hideyoshi went out into the garden, an attendant who served Hanbei ran out to meet him. "He's just changing so that he can see you, my lord," the boy said.

"He's not to get up," Hideyoshi scolded, and walked quickly toward the hermitage.

When Hanbei had heard that Hideyoshi was on his way, he had had his sickbed put away and ordered a servant to sweep the room clean, while he himself changed. Then, putting on some wooden clogs, he had stooped over the little stream that wound its way through the chrysanthemums at the bamboo gate, and washed his mouth and hands. He turned as someone tapped him on the shoulder.

"Oh, I didn't know you were here." Hanbei quickly knelt on the ground. "Over there, my lord," he said, inviting Hideyoshi into his room. Hideyoshi sat down happily on the mat. There was nothing in the room but a Zen master's ink painting hanging on the wall. Hideyoshi's clothing had been completely neutralized by the colors of Azuchi, but here in this simple hermitage, both his coat and his armor looked brilliant and imposing.

Bowing as he walked, Hanbei went around and up to the veranda, where he inserted a single white chrysanthemum into a flower container cut from a section of bamboo. He sat down meekly next to Hideyoshi and put the bamboo container in the alcove.

Hideyoshi understood: even though the sickbed had been put away, Hanbei was afraid that the smell of the medicine and the mustiness of the room would still be lingering, and instead of incense, had tried to freshen the air with the fragrance of this flower.

"I'm not bothered at all. Don't even think of it," Hideyoshi said considerately, and looked at his friend with concern. "Hanbei, isn't it difficult for you to get up like this?"

Hanbei withdrew to a short distance and once again bowed low. Even through his formality, however, his happiness at Hideyoshi's visit could be seen on his face. "Please don't worry," he began. "For the last few days it's been cold, so I've been careful to keep indoors, under quilts. But today it started to warm up, and I had just been thinking that I should get out of bed."

"It'll be winter in Kyoto soon enough, and they say it's particularly cold in the morning and at night. How about moving to a warmer place during the winter?"

"No, no. I'm beginning to get better and better every day. I'll be well before winter comes."

"If you're really getting better, that's all the more reason why you shouldn't move out of the sickroom this winter. This time you should convalesce until you're completely cured. Your body is not just your own, you know."

"You think more of me than I deserve." Hanbei's shoulders slumped, and he sat with downcast eyes. His hands slipped from his knees and—along with his tears—touched the floor as he bowed in obeisance. For a moment he was silent.

Ah, he has grown so thin, Hideyoshi thought, and sighed. The wrists of those hands that bowed at the mat were so emaciated, the flesh around his cheekbones so gaunt. Was this wasting disease really incurable? With these thoughts, Hideyoshi felt a pain in his chest. Who was it, after all, who had pulled this sick man out into the chaotic world against his will? In how many battlefields had he been soaked by the rain and chilled by the wind? And who was it who, even in times of peace, had put him through the hardships of both domestic affairs and diplomatic relations without even thinking of a day of rest? Hanbei was a man whom he should have looked up to as a teacher, but he had treated him the same as any retainer.

Hideyoshi felt that he was to blame for the seriousness of Hanbei's condition and finally, as he looked off to the side, his own tears fell heavily. In front of him, the white chrysanthemum in the bamboo container turned whiter and more fragrant as it soaked up water.

Hanbei silently blamed himself for Hideyoshi's tears. It was an inexcusable act of disloyalty as a retainer and lack of resolve as a warrior to have caused his lord to lose heart when the latter's military responsibilities were so heavy.

"I thought you would be exhausted by this long campaign, so I picked this chrysanthemum from the garden," Hanbei said.

Hideyoshi was silent, but his eyes were drawn to the flower. He seemed relieved that the subject of their conversation had changed.

"What a wonderful smell. I suppose that the chrysanthemums were blooming on Mount Hirai, but I didn't notice their smell or color. We probably trampled them with our bloodied sandals," he laughed, trying to cheer up the ailing Hanbei.

The compassion with which Hanbei attempted to sympathize with his lord was equaled by Hideyoshi's efforts to cheer his retainer.

"As I sit here now, I can really feel the difficulty of maintaining my life with body and mind acting clearly as one being," Hideyoshi said. "The battlefield keeps me busy and makes me rough. Here I feel calm and happy. Somehow it seems that that contrast has become clear, and that I have become wonderfully resolved."

"Well, people obviously value free time and a peaceful frame of mind, but there's no real benefit in becoming a so-called man of leisure; it's an empty life. You, my lord, do not have an instant of peace between one worry and the next. So I suspect that it's quite a marvelous medicine to have this sudden little moment of peace. As for me—"

Hanbei was probably going to blame himself and apologize once again, so Hideyoshi suddenly interrupted him. "By the way, have you heard the news about Araki Murashige's insurrection?"

"Yes, last night someone came here with a detailed report." Hanbei spoke without raising an eyebrow, as though it were of little importance.

"Well, I'd like to talk about it a little," Hideyoshi said, and moved forward a little on his knees. "In Lord Nobunaga's council meeting at Azuchi, it was more or less decided to listen to Murashige's grievances and then do everything possible to calm him down and come to terms with him. But I wonder if that is really a good idea. And what should we do if Murashige rebels in earnest? I would like to hear your frank opinion. That's really another reason why I came here." Hideyoshi was asking for a strategy in order to cope with the situation, but Hanbei answered him briefly.

"I think that's fine. It's a very clever measure."

"Well, if an envoy is sent from Azuchi with a soothing message, is Itami Castle going to be pacified without incident?"

"No, of course not." Hanbei shook his head. "It will not. I think that now that Itami Castle has unfurled the banner of rebellion, it is definitely not going to roll it up again and submit to Azuchi."

"If that's true, then isn't it just wasted effort to send an envoy?"

"It may seem so, but it will serve some purpose. You could say that to act first with humanity and show a retainer his mistake would let the world know of Lord Nobunaga's virtue. During that time, Lord Murashige will most likely be anguished and confused, and thus the arrow that is pulled back unjustifiably and without real conviction is going to weaken as the days go by."

"What do you think our strategy should be in our attack on him, and what is your forecast for the western provinces?"

"I think that neither the Mori nor the Honganji are likely to move precipitously. Murashige has already revolted, so they're more likely to let him get into a bloody fight of resistance. Then, if they see that our men in Harima and His Lordship's headquarters in Azuchi are weakening, they'll leap into the vacuum and attack from all sides."

"That's right, they'll take advantage of Murashige's stupidity. I don't know what kind of grievances he may have had, or what kind of bait they waved in front of him, but essentially he's being used as a shield for the Mori and the Honganji. Once that role as a shield is finished, there'll be nothing left for him but self-destruction. In terms of martial valor, he's far above others; but he's dull-witted. If there's any way of keeping him alive, I'd like to do it."

"The very best strategy would be to keep him from getting killed. It would be good if we could keep a man like that alive and also keep him as an ally."

"But if you think that an envoy from Azuchi would be useless, who could go that Murashige might submit to?"

"First try sending Kanbei. If Kanbei speaks to him, he should be able to enlighten Murashige on the matter, or at least wake him up from his bad dream."

"What if he refuses to see Kanbei?"

"Then the Oda can send their last envoy."

"Their last envoy?"

"You, my lord."

"Me?" Hideyoshi was momentarily lost in thought. "Well, if it comes to that, it will be too late."

"Teach him duty and enlighten him with friendship. If he doesn't accept what you say, you can do nothing more than strike at him firmly, citing the crime of revolt. If it does come to that, it would be foolish to attack Itami with a single stroke. Lord Murashige has not been emboldened by the strength of Itami Castle but rather by the cooperation of the two men he relies on like his right and left hands."

"You mean Nakagawa Sebei and Takayama Ukon?"

"If you can get those two men away from him, he'll be like a body with no arms. And if you win either Ukon or Sebei over, getting them away from Murashige should not be that much of a problem." Hanbei seemed to forget about his illness at some point and talked about this subject and that, until his sickly pallor almost disappeared.

"How do I win over Ukon?" Hideyoshi asked him eagerly, and Hanbei did not disappoint him.

"Takayama Ukon is an enthusiastic follower of Christianity. If you give him conditions permitting the propagation of his faith, he'll leave Murashige without a doubt."

"Yes, that's clear," Hideyoshi said in admiration. If he could get Ukon to convince Sebei, it would kill two birds with one stone. He stopped his questions. Hanbei appeared to be tired, too. Hideyoshi got up to leave.

"Wait just a moment," Hanbei requested. He got up and went from the room, possibly toward the kitchen.

Hideyoshi remembered that he was hungry. His attendants must have finished eating their lunches by this time. But before he even thought about returning to the temple's guest quarters and having some rice, a boy, who seemed to be Hanbei's attendant, brought in two trays, one bearing a *sake* container.

"What happened to Hanbei? Did he get tired after our long conversation?"

"No, my lord. He went to the kitchen a little while ago and prepared the vegetables for your meal himself. He's cooking the rice right now, so he'll be in as soon as he's done."

"What? Hanbei's cooking for me?"

"Yes, my lord."

Hideyoshi took a bite of taro—it was still hot—and the tears once again came to his eyes. The taste of the vegetable seemed to be not only on his tongue but filling his entire body. He felt that the taste was almost too good for someone like him. Although Hanbei was a retainer, he had taught Hideyoshi all of the secret principles of ancient Chinese military lore. The things that Hideyoshi had learned while sitting with him every day were not ordinary things: the governing of the people during times of peace and the necessity of self-discipline.

"He shouldn't be doing that." Suddenly, Hideyoshi put down his cup and, leaving the page who had been serving him, went to the kitchen, where Hanbei was cooking rice.

Hideyoshi took him by the hand. "Hanbei, this is too much. Won't you come sit and talk with me for a while instead?"

He led Hanbei back to the room and made him take a cup of *sake* but because of his illness, Hanbei could do no more than touch it to his lips. The two of them then ate together. It had been a long time since lord and retainer had enjoyed the pleasure of a meal in each other's company.

"It's time to go. But I've been invigorated. Now I can go fight. Hanbei, please take good care of yourself."

When Hideyoshi left the Nanzen Temple, the day had already begun to end, and the sky over the capital was turning crimson.

* * *

It was quiet, without even the report of a single firearm—so quiet that one might doubt it was a battlefield, so quiet that the sound of a praying mantis sliding through the dry grass rustled in the ear. It was mid-autumn in the western provinces. The maples had been turning red everywhere on the peaks for the last two or three days, and their redness burned in Hideyoshi's eyes.

Hideyoshi was back at the camp at Mount Hirai. He was seated across from Kanbei, underneath the pine on the hill from which they had viewed the moon some time before. Having talked over a number of things, they had come to an important conclusion.

"Well, you'll go for me, then?"

"I'll be happy to undertake this mission. Whether I succeed is up to heaven."

"I'm counting on you."

"I will do my best, and leave the rest to providence. My going there is just the last chance. If I don't come back alive, you know what follows."

"Nothing but force."

They stood up. The high-pitched cry of the bulbul could be heard from across the valley to the west. The red leaves in that direction were stunning. The two men silently descended the hill and walked toward the camp. The specter of death—and imminent parting—filled the atmosphere of the peaceful afternoon and lay quietly in the thoughts of these two good friends.

"Kanbei." Hideyoshi looked back as he went down the narrow, sloping path. The possibility that his friend would not be coming back again struck him deeply, and he thought Kanbei might have some last things to say. "Is there anything else?"

"No."

"Nothing for Himeji Castle?"

"No."

"Have you got a message for your father?"

"Just explain to him why I'm going on this mission."

"Very well."

The air had become clear, and it was possible to see the enemy castle at Miki far in the distance. The road leading to the castle had been cut off since summer, so it was easy to imagine the hunger and thirst inside. Nevertheless, as might be expected of the garrison of Harima's most spirited general and bravest soldiers, it continued throughout the siege to manifest a martial spirit as biting as the autumn frost.

The besieged enemy had been driven to make sallies against the surrounding Oda troops. Hideyoshi, however, gave his men strict orders not to give in to their provocations, and sharply cautioned them against impulsive action.

Again, minute care was taken to allow no news of the external situation to reach the castle. If the men inside the castle heard that Araki Murashige had revolted against Nobunaga, it would strengthen their morale. After all, Murashige's revolt did not simply cause dismay in Azuchi; it threatened the whole western campaign. As a matter of fact, as soon as Odera Masamoto, the lord of Gochaku Castle, became aware of Murashige's revolt, he made a clear declaration separating himself from Nobunaga and even went one night to the enemy's camp.

"The western provinces should not just be given over into the hands of the invader," Odera told them. "We should make the Mori clan our rallying point, reorganize our forces, and strike down these outsiders."

Odera Masamoto was Kanbei's father's lord and, therefore, Kanbei's as well. Kanbei, therefore, was placed in a dilemma: on the one hand were Nobunaga and Hideyoshi, on the other were his father and his overlord.

Araki Murashige was a man known for his courage, but he was also one who bragged about it. Sensitivity and a clear understanding of the times were far beyond him. He was at the age described by Confucius as "free from vacillation," that is, he was about forty, the age when a man should be mature, but it seemed that Murashige's character had not changed much from what it had been ten years before. Lacking the qualities of thought-fulness and refinement that he should naturally have possessed, even though he was the lord of a castle he had not advanced a single step from what he was formerly: a fearsome samurai warrior.

It could be said that in attaching him to Hideyoshi as second-in-command, Nobu-naga had made up for Hideyoshi's deficiencies. Murashige, however, did not think of himself in that way. He was always very free with his advice, yet neither Hideyoshi nor Nobutada ever employed his ideas.

He found Hideyoshi annoying. But his feckless thoughts aside, he never showed his antipathy when he met Hideyoshi face to face.

From time to time he would expose his resentment and even laugh out loud before his own retainers. There are some men in this world you can't offend, no matter how angry you get, and to Murashige, Hideyoshi was one of them. At the time of the attack on Kozuki Castle, Murashige had been on the front lines. Yet, when the time was right for the battle and Hideyoshi had given him the order to attack, he had sat there with folded arms and would not budge.

"Why didn't you go out and fight?" Hideyoshi had reprimanded him later.

"I don't participate in a battle I'm not interested in," Murashige had replied without flinching.

Since Hideyoshi had laughed good-naturedly at the time, Murashige had forced a smile too. The matter was closed, but the rumors that passed among the generals in camp were extremely uncomplimentary.

Mitsuhide censured Murashige's conduct heavily. Murashige held in contempt gener-als like Akechi Mitsuhide and Hosokawa Fujitaka, who had the scent of cultured men. He liked to characterize such men as effeminate. This judgment was based on his abhorrence of the poetry parties and tea ceremonies they held in camp. The only thing that did im-press Murashige was that Hideyoshi appeared not to have made a report of his behavior to either Nobunaga or Nobutada.

Murashige looked down on Hideyoshi as a warrior who was more soft-hearted than he, and yet he figured Hideyoshi a hard man to handle precisely because of this. At any rate, the people who really understood his attitude while he was in the field were his ene-mies, the Mori. To them it appeared that Murashige held some grievances, and that if they could talk to him, there was a good possibility they could get him to change sides.

The fact that the secret messengers from both the Mori and the Honganji were able to avoid detection and repeatedly slip in and out of his camp, and even Itami Castle, would indicate that they were not unwelcomed guests. The enemy had already been en-couraged by Murashige, and his actions had been a wordless invitation to them.

When a man without real substance or resourcefulness begins to play at being clever, he is playing with fire. His advisers cautioned their lord any number of times that such a plot could never succeed, but Murashige turned a deaf ear.

"Don't talk foolishness! Especially when the Mori clan has sent me a written pledge."

Having such absolute faith in a written pledge, he very quickly and clearly demonstrated his spirit of rebellion toward Nobunaga. How highly could a written pledge from the Mori—who had been enemies until yesterday—be regarded in these chaotic times, when men tossed aside a pledge between lord and retainer like a pair of worn-out sandals? Murashige neither thought that far ahead nor felt such a large contradiction to be a contradiction at all.

"He's a fool—an honest man with whom it isn't worth getting angry," Hideyoshi had said to Nobunaga to calm him down, and it was probably the best thing he could have said at the time.

Nobunaga, however, could not look at the situation lightly, and cautioned, "But he's a strong man."

Added to this were the important questions of how the revolt would affect the other generals under his command and what its psychological influence might be. For these reasons, Nobunaga had tried everything, including sending Akechi Mitsuhide to pacify Murashige.

In the end, however, Murashige responded with all the more suspicion, and in the meanwhile strengthened his preparations for war, saying, "I've already demonstrated my hostility, so if I were to fall for Nobunaga's sweet words and respond to Azuchi's summons, I have no doubt that I would be murdered or thrown into prison."

Nobunaga was outraged. Finally, the decision to fight Murashige was announced, and on the ninth day of the Eleventh Month, Nobunaga himself led a force as far as Yamazaki. The army of Azuchi was divided into three parts. The first army, composed of the forces of Takigawa Kazumasu, Akechi Mitsuhide, and Niwa Nagahide, surrounded Ibaragi Castle; the second, made up of the forces under Fuwa, Maeda, Sassa, and Kanamori, besieged Takatsuki Castle.

Nobunaga's headquarters was at Mount Amano. And, while his resplendent line-up was unfolding itself, he still had a faint hope of subjugating the rebellious army without bloodshed. That hope was tied to Hideyoshi, who had now returned to Harima and from whom a message had just arrived.

"I have one more idea," Hideyoshi had written. Behind his words was Hideyoshi's friendship for the man as well as his feeling that Murashige's valor was too valuable to waste, and he appealed earnestly to Nobunaga to wait just a little longer. Hideyoshi's right-hand man, Kuroda Kanbei, had suddenly left the camp at Mount Hirai one night.

The following day, Kanbei hurried to Gochaku Castle, where he met with Odera Masamoto.

"There is a rumor that you are supporting Lord Murashige's revolt, and that this castle has turned it back on the Oda clan." He spoke simply and directly, and first appealed to the man heart-to-heart.

A thin smile floated to Masamoto's lips as he listened. In terms of years, Kanbei was the age of his own son; and even in status, he was nothing more than the son of a senior retainer. Thus, his answer was, not surprisingly, extremely arrogant.

"Kanbei, you appear to be serious, but think for a moment. Since this clan became Nobunaga's ally, what have we gotten in return? Nothing."

"I don't think it's just a problem of profit and loss anymore."

"Well then, what is it?"

"It's a matter of loyalty. You are the head of a well-known clan, and have been an ally of the Oda in Harima. Suddenly to join Araki Murashige's revolt and betray your former allies would be a blow to the ideal of loyalty."

"What are you saying?" Masamoto asked. He treated Kanbei as an inexperienced negotiator, and the more fervent Kanbei became, the more coolly Masamoto behaved toward him.

"My reliance on Nobunaga was never a matter of loyalty," he said. "You and your father seem to think that the future of this country is in Nobunaga's hands; and when he took the capital, it was expedient to collude with him. At least that's the way the situation was presented to me, and even I was persuaded. But the truth is that there are many dangers facing Nobunaga from now on. Think of it as looking at a large ship out at sea. From the shore it looks safe; you think that if you boarded it, you would have no fear of sailing through turbulent seas. But then you actually get on board and tie your own fate to that of the ship. Now that you've put yourself into its keeping, instead of peace of mind, you find yourself without confidence. Every time you're battered by the waves, you feel uneasy and have doubts about the boat's endurance. This is human nature."

Kanbei unconsciously slapped his knee. "And once you've gotten on board, you can't disembark halfway through the trip."

"Why not? If you see that the boat's not going to make it through the crush of the waves, there may be no other way to save your life than to abandon ship and swim for shore before the ship wrecks. Sometimes you have to close your eyes to your feelings."

"That's shameful thinking, my lord. When the weather clears and the boat that seemed so much in danger raises its sails and finally arrives in port, it is exactly the man who shuddered during a gale, doubted the boat he'd entrusted himself to, betrayed his fellow travelers, and jumped overboard in confusion into the sea, who will be seen as a laughable fool."

"I'm no match for you when it comes to words," Masamoto laughed. "The truth is that you're eloquent beyond eloquence. First you said that when Nobunaga turned his hand to the west, he would quickly sweep over it. But the forces sent with Hideyoshi number a mere five or six thousand. And even though Lord Nobutada and other generals have frequently come to his aid, there's uneasiness in the capital, and it appears as though the army may not be here for very long. Then I am simply used as Hideyoshi's vanguard and am requisitioned for soldiers, horses, and provisions, but it will amount to nothing more than positioning me as a barrier between the Oda and their enemies. Consider the Oda clan's prospects judging simply by the way Araki Murashige—who was promoted to such a responsible post by Nobunaga—completely turned around the situation in the capital when he allied himself with the Mori clan! The reason I left the Oda clan with Murashige should be clear."

"What I've been listening to is a truly wretched plan. I suspect you're going to regret it soon."

"You're still young. You're strong in battle, but not in worldly affairs."

"My lord, I'm begging you to change your mind."

"That's not going to happen. I've made it clear to my retainers that I've made a promise to Murashige and taken a stand to ally myself with the Mori."

"But if you considered your decision once more…"

"Before you say any more, talk to Araki Murashige. If he rethinks his defection, I will too."

Adult and child. The difference between the two was not just sophistry. It might be said that even a man like Kanbei, who was considered unique in the west for his talents and progressive ideas, could not have held his own against an opponent like Odera Masamoto, regardless of right or wrong.

Masamoto spoke once more to emphasize his point. "At any rate, take this with you and go to Itami. Then bring me an answer quickly. When I've heard Lord Murashige's thoughts, I'll give you a definite answer."

Masamoto wrote a note to Araki Murashige. Kanbei put it in his kimono and hurried off to Itami. The situation was pressing, and his own actions could have great consequences. As he approached Itami Castle, he saw that the soldiers were digging trenches and building a palisade.

Seemingly oblivious of the fact that he was quickly surrounded by a ring of spears, he said, as if he had nothing to fear, "I'm Kuroda Kanbei from Himeji Castle. I'm an ally neither of Lord Nobunaga nor of Lord Murashige. I've come alone for an urgent private talk with Lord Murashige." And he pushed his way through.

He passed through several fortified gates, finally entered the castle, and quickly met Murashige. His first impression upon looking at Murashige's face was that the man was not as strong-willed as he had expected. Murashige's countenance was not very impressive. Kanbei perceived his opponent's lack of spirit and self-confidence and wondered why he had chosen to fight Nobunaga, who was considered the most outstanding man of his generation.

"Well, it's been a long time!" Murashige said desultorily. It sounded almost like flattery. Kanbei guessed that for a fierce general like Murashige to treat him in this way meant that he was still somewhat unsure of himself.

Kanbei responded with small talk, smiling fixedly at Murashige. For his part, Murashige was unable to conceal his innate honesty, and looked extraordinarily embarrassed under Kanbei's gaze.

Murashige felt his face turn red. "What is your business?" he asked.

"I've heard rumors."

"About my raising an army?"

"You've gotten yourself into a mess."

"What is everyone saying?"

"Some are saying good things, some bad."

"I suppose opinions are divided. But people should wait until the fighting's over to decide who was right and who was wrong. A man's reputation is never settled until after his death."

"Have you considered what will happen after you die?"

497

"Of course."

"If that's so, then I'm sure you know that the consequences of your decision are irrevocable."

"Why is that?"

"The bad name you'll get from turning against a lord from whom you've received so many favors won't die out for generations."

Murashige fell silent. The throbbing of his temples showed that he was full of emotion, but he did not have the eloquence for a refutation.

"The *sake* is ready," a retainer announced.

Murashige looked relieved. He stood up. "Kanbei, come inside. It has been a long time, everything else aside. Let's have a drink together," he suggested.

Murashige showed himself a generous host. A banquet had been prepared in the main citadel. The two men naturally avoided any argument as they drank *sake*, and Murashige's expression relaxed considerably. At some point, however, Kanbei broached the subject again.

"How about it, Murashige? Why don't you stop this thing before it goes too far?"

"Before what goes too far?"

"This petty show of strength."

"My resolution in this grave concern has nothing to do with a show of strength."

"That may be true, but the world is calling it treachery. How do you feel about that?"

"Come on, have some more *sake*."

"I'm not going to deceive myself. You've gone to a lot of trouble for me today, but your *sake* tastes just a little bitter."

"You were sent here by Hideyoshi."

"Of course. Even Lord Hideyoshi is extraordinarily worried about you. Not only that, but he defends you absolutely, regardless of what other people say about you. He calls you 'a valuable man' and 'a stalwart warrior.' He says that we should not make a mistake, and I can tell you that he'll never forget your friendship."

Murashige sobered up a little and, in some measure, spoke from his heart. "In fact, I received two or three letters from Hideyoshi admonishing me, and I'm moved by his friendship. But Akechi Mitsuhide and other Oda retainers came one after another as Lord Nobunaga's envoys and I rebuffed them all. Certainly I can't comply with Hideyoshi's request now."

"I don't think that's true. If you'll leave the matter to Lord Hideyoshi, he'll surely be able to manage some way of mediating with Lord Nobunaga."

"I don't think so," Murashige said sullenly. "They're saying that when Mitsuhide and Nobumori heard that I had rebelled, they clapped their hands and rejoiced. Mitsuhide came here to appease me. He soothed me with pretty words, but who knows what kind of report he made when he returned to Nobunaga. If I opened my castle and returned to kneel before Nobunaga, in the end he'd only order his men to grab me by the scruff of the neck and cut off my head. None of my retainers is of a mind to return to Nobunaga. They're at the point where they feel that fighting to the end would be best, so this is not just my own opinion. When you go back to Harima, please tell Hideyoshi not to think badly of me."

It seemed that Kanbei was not going to be able to persuade Murashige easily. After a few more cups of *sake*, he took out Odera Masamoto's letter and handed it to Murashige.

Kanbei had already looked over the gist of the contents. It was simple, but it censured Murashige's behavior earnestly. Murashige moved closer to the lamp and opened it, but just as he finished reading it, he excused himself and left the room.

As he went out, a group of soldiers crowded into the room. They surrounded Kanbei, forming a wall of armor and spears around him.

"Get up!" they shouted.

Kanbei put down his cup and looked at the agitated faces around him. "What happens if I do?" he asked.

"Lord Murashige's orders are to escort you to the castle jail," answered one of the soldiers.

"Jail?" he blurted out, and he wanted to laugh out loud. At the moment he thought it was all over for him, and he saw how funny he must look for having fallen into Murashige's trap.

He stood up, a smile on his face. "Let's go, then. There's nothing I can do but go meekly, if this is Lord Murashige's show of courtesy."

The warriors escorted Kanbei down the main corridor. The noisy clatter of their armor blended with their footsteps. They went down any number of dark corridors and stairways. Kanbei was made to walk in places that were so dark he could have been blindfolded, and he wondered if he might not be killed at any time. He was more or less prepared for such an event, but it did not seem to be forthcoming. At any rate, the lightless place he walked along seemed to be a complicated passageway weaving through the bowels of the castle. After a while, a heavy sliding door clattered open.

"Inside!" he was ordered, and after taking about ten paces forward, he found himself in the middle of a cell. The door slammed shut behind him. This time, Kanbei did laugh out loud into the darkness. Then he turned to the wall and spoke with self-scorn, almost as though he were reciting a poem.

"I myself have fallen into Murashige's trap. Well, well…public morals certainly have become complicated, haven't they?"

He guessed that he was beneath an armory. As far as he could tell by feeling with the soles of his feet, the floor was made of thick, knotted planks. Kanbei walked along calmly, following the four walls. He was able to judge that the area of the cell was about thirty square meters.

No, the way I see it is that Murashige is the man to be pitied. What does he think he's going to accomplish by imprisoning me?

He sat down cross-legged in what was evidently the center of the cell. His buttocks were cold, but there seemed to be nothing to sit on in the room.

He suddenly realized that he hadn't had to give up his short sword, and thought, That's something to be thankful for. If I just have this one weapon…at any time I could….

He silently told himself that even if his buttocks were numbed, his spirit would.not be. The Zen meditation that he had practiced so hard in his youth would now perhaps be of use. Such things came to mind as time went by. I'm glad I came, was his next thought.

If Hideyoshi had come himself, this small disaster would have been replaced by a great one. I'm grateful that it has turned out this way.

Soon a thin stripe of light shone in his face. Kanbei calmly looked toward the light. A window had been opened. A man's face appeared on the other side of the lattice. It was Araki Murashige.

"Is it cold in there, Kanbei?" Murashige asked. Kanbei looked in his direction and finally answered him with total calm. "No, I'm still warm from the *sake*, but it might get uncomfortable around midnight. If Lord Hideyoshi hears that Kuroda Kanbei has frozen to death, he'll probably arrive before dawn and expose your head on the gate in the frost. Murashige, you're a man with decent brains. What do you plan to accomplish by keeping me here?"

Murashige was at a loss for words. He was also aware that he was being shamed by his own actions. Eventually, however, he laughed scornfully.

"Stop your grumbling, Kanbei. You're saying that I have no brains, but aren't you the one who witlessly fell into this trap?"

"Abusive language is not going to help you. Can't you talk logically?"

Murashige said nothing, and Kanbei went on, "You're prone to admonishing me as some sort of strategist or demon of tactics, but I concern myself with fundamental policies, not petty tricks. I have never considered plotting against a friend and making a merit of it. I was simply thinking of you, and of Lord Hideyoshi's distress. That's why I came here alone. Can't you understand? What about Lord Hideyoshi's friendship? What about your loyalty?"

Murashige did not know how to answer. He fell silent for a while, but finally pulled together a rebuttal. "You talk about friendship and moral principles, but these are words that only have luster during times of peace. It's different now. The country is at war with itself, and the world is in chaos. If you don't plot, you're plotted against; if you don't inflict injury, someone will inflict injury on you. This is a world so grim that you may have to kill or be killed in the time it takes you to pick up your chopsticks. Yesterday's ally is today's enemy, and if a man is your enemy—even if he is your friend—there's nothing you can do but throw him in prison. It's all tactics. One could say that it's out of compassion that I haven't killed you yet."

"I see. Now I understand your view of the world, your everyday thoughts on warfare, and the extent of your morality. You have the pitiful blindness of the times, and I don't feel like talking things over with you anymore. Go ahead, destroy yourself!"

"What? You're saying I'm blind?"

"That's right. No, even though it's come to this, I can't seem to abandon the last little bit of friendship I have for you. I have one more thing I'll teach you."

"What? Does the Oda clan have some secret strategy?"

"It's not a matter of advantages and disadvantages. You're a pitiful individual. Although you're famous for your courage, you're ignorant of how to live in this chaotic country. Not only that, but you have no desire to save the world from this chaos. You're inhuman, lower than a townsman or a farmer. How can you call yourself a samurai?"

"What! You're saying I'm not human?"

"That's right. You're a beast."

"What did you say?"

"Go ahead! Get as angry as you can. It's all directed against yourself. Listen, Murashige. If men lose morality and loyalty, the world becomes nothing but a world of beasts. We fight and fight again, and the hellfire of human rivalry is never exhausted. If you consider only battle, intrigue, and power, and forget morality and human-heartedness, you won't stop at being an enemy of Lord Nobunaga. You'll be an enemy of all humankind and a plague to the entire earth. As far as I'm concerned, if you're that kind of person, I'd be glad to twist off your head."

Speaking his mind and then sinking into silence, Kanbei could hear a clamor going on. Outside the prison window, Murashige was surrounded by his retainers and personal attendants, and they were all yelling.

"Cut him down!"

"No, we can't kill him."

"He's insufferable."

"Calm yourselves!"

It appeared that Murashige was caught between those who wanted to pull Kanbei out and butcher him on the spot and those who declared that killing him would have adverse results. And he seemed unable to come to a decision.

In the end, however, they concluded that even if they were going to kill him, there was no particular hurry to do so. After that they seemed to settle down, and the footsteps of Murashige and the rest could be heard clattering off into the distance.

From observing this event, Kanbei quickly understood the mood of the entire castle.

Although the banner of revolt had been clearly unfurled, even now there were those who indignantly wanted to fight the Oda and others who advocated cooperating with their former allies. Under the same roof, they feuded on almost every single point, and the situation could be read easily.

Murashige, who was caught up in this dispute, had driven away Nobunaga's envoys and increased his military preparations. Now he had thrown Kanbei into prison.

It appears that he's come to his doom. Ah, how sad, Kanbei thought. Without regretting his own fate, he lamented Murashige's ignorance. After the voices had drifted away, the peephole was closed again, but Kanbei was suddenly aware of a slip of paper that had fallen through. He picked it up, but could not read it that night. It was so dark in the cell he could hardly see his own fingers.

The next day, however, when the faint light of morning filtered in, he remembered the paper right away and read it. It was a letter from Odera Masamoto in Harima, addressed to Araki Murashige.

This same bothersome character we talked about has come here, admonishing me to change my mind. I deceived him into trying to ascertain your mind first, so he'll probably arrive at your castle at the same time this letter arrives. He is a man of broad resources, so he'll be a burden as long as he's alive. When he gets to Itami Castle, I suggest that you take the opportunity and not let him loose in the world again.

Kanbei was shocked. When he looked at the date on the letter, he saw that it was indeed the same day that he himself had offered his remonstration to Masamoto and left Gochaku Castle.

"Well then, he must have sent this letter right afterward," he muttered to himself in amazement. He was struck by the realization that there are a large number of clever people in the world. And yet the world had called him—he who had taken such pains to abstain from shallow thinking and petty schemes—a tactician.

"It's interesting, isn't it? Being in the world."

Looking up at the ceiling, he spoke without being aware of it. The sound of his voice echoed as though he were in a cave. How interesting to be in the world.

As one might expect, there were lies and there were truths, there was form and there was void, there was anger and there was joy, there was faith and there was confusion. This was being in the world. But for a few weeks at least, Kanbei would be far away from the world.

* * *

The attacking forces disposed around Itami, Takatsuki, and Ibaragi castles were ready to strike at any time. Nevertheless, the order to attack had not yet come from Nobunaga's headquarters on Mount Amano. In the various camps, the days passed so quietly that the soldiers' patience was beginning to wear thin.

"Still no word?"

Nobunaga had already asked this question twice that day. What he was having difficulty waiting for, however, was just the opposite of the source of the soldiers' impatience. At this point, the Oda clan's position was extraordinarily and dangerously complex—not in regard to the western or eastern provinces, but right around the capital. If at all possible, Nobunaga did not want to fight a war here, at this time. And as the days passed, he worried over this policy of avoiding action in his home area at all costs.

Whenever he was anxious, Hideyoshi occupied his thoughts. He wanted him constantly at his side. Not long before, a report had come from this general upon whom he relied so much, telling him that Kanbei had stated his case to his former master, Odera Masamoto, and then had gone immediately to Itami Castle, where he intended to persuade Murashige to negotiate. Kanbei was even prepared to die on this mission, Hideyoshi had said, and he asked Nobunaga to wait.

"This shows a lot of self-confidence," Nobunaga said, "and Hideyoshi's not apt to be negligent."

But even though Nobunaga in this way persuaded himself to be patient, the atmosphere at his field headquarters was becoming charged with his generals' extreme annoyance. Whenever Hideyoshi made some trivial mistake, their resentment would erupt as though it had been smoldering under the ashes for a long time.

"I don't understand why Hideyoshi sent the man! Who is this Kanbei, anyway? If you look into his background, he turns out to be a retainer of Odera Masamoto. And his father is a senior retainer of Masamoto too. For his part, Masamoto is conspiring with Araki Murashige in communicating with the Mori and betraying us. He's acting in concert with Murashige while he has raised the banner of rebellion in the western provinces.

How could Hideyoshi have chosen Kanbei for such an important mission?"

Hideyoshi was criticized for his lack of foresight, and some even went so far as to suspect him of negotiating with the Mori.

The reports that began to come in all contained the same information: far from submitting to Kanbei's argument, Odera Masamoto had spoken out against Lord Nobunaga all the more. He had spread stories about the weakness of the Oda forces in the area. Moreover, his communications with the Mori had become more and more frequent.

Nobunaga had to admit that this was true.

"Kanbei's action was nothing but a deception. While we wait for good news from such an unreliable man, the enemy strengthens his connections and perfects his defenses, so that in the end our forces will achieve nothing, regardless of how fierce our attack is."

At that point, news finally came from Hideyoshi. It was, however, not good. Kanbei had still not returned, and there was no clear information. Moreover, the letter sounded hopeless. Nobunaga clicked his tongue. Suddenly he tossed aside the satchel that had contained the letter.

"It's too late!" Finally provoked, Nobunaga suddenly roared out angrily, "Secretary! Write this immediately and address it to Hideyoshi. Tell him he's to come here without a moment's delay."

Then he looked at Sakuma Nobumori and said, "I've heard that Takenaka Hanbei has confined himself in the Nanzen Temple in Kyoto to convalesce. Is he still there?"

"I believe he is."

Nobunaga's response to Nobumori's reply was as quick as an echo. "Well then, go there and tell this to Hanbei: Kuroda Kanbei's son, Shojumaru, was sent to his castle by Hideyoshi some time ago as a hostage—he is to be beheaded immediately, and his head sent to his father in Itami."

Nobumori bowed. Everyone around Nobunaga momentarily crouched in fear of his sudden anger. Not a voice was heard, and for a moment, Nobumori did not get up. Nobunaga's mood was capable of changing from one moment to the next, and his anger exploded without much difficulty. The patience he had exhibited until now was not part of his true nature. That had been strictly a matter of reasoning, into which he had had to put much effort. Therefore, when he did throw off the self-control that he so disliked and raised his voice, his earlobes began to redden, and his face suddenly took on a ferocious appearance.

"My lord, please wait a moment."

"What is it, Kazumasu? Are you admonishing me?"

"It would be presumptuous for someone like me to admonish you, my lord, but why have you so suddenly given an order to kill Kuroda Kanbei's son? Shouldn't you deliberate on this a bit longer?"

"I don't need to deliberate any more to see Kanbei's treason. He pretended to talk to Odera Masamoto, and then deceived me again into thinking that he was negotiating with Araki Murashige. That I've refrained from taking action for the last ten days is entirely because of that damned Kanbei's schemes. Hideyoshi reported that to me just now. Hideyoshi's had enough of being made a fool of by Kanbei."

"But what if you summoned Lord Hideyoshi to give you a full report of the situation, and talked with him about punishing Kanbei's son?"

"I can't make a peacetime decision at a time like this. And I'm not ordering Hide-yoshi here to listen to his opinion. I'm asking him to explain how he fomented this disaster. Hurry up and take the message, Nobumori."

"Yes, my lord. I'll convey this to Hanbei, as you wish."

Nobunaga's mood was gradually becoming darker. He turned to the scribe and asked, "Did you write my summons to Hideyoshi, secretary?"

"Would you like to read it, my lord?"

The letter was shown to Nobunaga and then immediately passed to the chief messenger, who was ordered to take it to Harima.

But before the messenger was able to leave, a retainer announced, "Lord Hideyoshi has just now arrived."

"What? Hideyoshi?" Nobunaga's expression remained the same, but for an instant it seemed that his anger had softened.

Soon Hideyoshi's voice could be heard, and it rang out as cheerfully as usual. As soon as Nobunaga heard Hideyoshi, he had to make an effort to maintain his angry expression. His anger melted in his breast the way ice melts under the sun, and there was nothing he could do about it.

With a casual greeting to the generals who were present, Hideyoshi entered the enclosure. He passed through the assembled generals and knelt courteously before Nobunaga, then looked up at his lord.

Nobunaga said nothing. He was trying hard to show his anger. There were not many commanders who could do anything other than prostrate themselves in fear when they encountered Nobunaga's silence.

In fact, there was no one even in Nobunaga's family who could withstand this treatment. If veteran generals like Katsuie and Nobumori came under Nobunaga's angry eye, they would turn absolutely pale. Seasoned men like Niwa and Takigawa would become confused and mumble excuses. With all his wisdom, Akechi Mitsuhide had no way of dealing with it, and even all of Nobunaga's affection was no help at all to Ranmaru. But Hideyoshi's handling of such situations was quite different. When Nobunaga was angry and would scowl and glare at him, Hideyoshi would manifest no reaction at all. It was not that he took his lord lightly. On the contrary, he was, more than most men, awed by Nobunaga. Generally, he would look up placidly as though gazing at a threatening sky and desist from speaking except in the most commonplace way.

His Lordship is a little angry again, Hideyoshi was now thinking. This composure seemed to be part of Hideyoshi's own special nature, and certainly no one was able to imitate him. If Katsuie or Mitsuhide had copied Hideyoshi's behavior, they would have been throwing oil on a fire, and Nobunaga would have exploded into a fit of anger. Nobunaga appeared to be losing the game of patience. Finally he spoke.

"Hideyoshi, why did you come here?"

"I came to receive your reprimand," Hideyoshi answered with deep respect.

He always has a good answer, Nobunaga thought. It was growing more and more difficult to stay angry. He was going to have to speak deliberately, as though he had chewed the words up and were spitting them out. "What do you mean, you've come to be reprimanded? Did you think this matter was going to be finished with an apology? You've made a great error that affects not only me but the entire army."

"You've already read the letter I sent to you?"

"I have!"

"Sending Kanbei as an intermediary clearly ended in failure. In this connection—"

"Is that an excuse?"

"No, but to serve as an apology, I galloped through enemy lines to offer a plan that might turn this disaster into good fortune. I would like to ask you either to order the area cleared of everyone here or to move elsewhere. After that, if there is to be some punishment for my crime, I will respectfully accept it."

Nobunaga thought for a moment, then granted his request and ordered everyone to leave. The other generals were dumbstruck by Hideyoshi's audacity, but, looking back and forth at each other, they could only withdraw. There were some who accused him of impudence even in the face of his crime. Others clicked their tongues and called him self-seeking. Hideyoshi looked as though he were paying no attention, and waited until he and Nobunaga were the only ones left in the enclosure. When everyone had gone, Nobunaga's appearance softened somewhat.

"So what kind of suggestion do you have that made you ride all the way here from Harima?"

"I have a way to attack Itami. At this point, the only thing left to do is to strike at Araki Murashige resolutely."

"That's been true from the beginning. Not that Itami is so important, but if the Honganji and Murashige act in concert with the Mori, there could be considerable trouble."

"Not that much, I think. If we move too fast, our troops could suffer considerably; and if there is even the slightest failure among our allies, the embankment you have built up so carefully until now could crumble all at once."

"So what would you do?"

"I had no plan of my own, but Takenaka Hanbei, who has been in the capital convalescing, was able to see through the present situation." Hideyoshi then related the plan to Nobunaga exactly as he had heard it from Hanbei. Essentially, the plan against Itami Castle called for allowing as little damage to their own troops as possible. Taking whatever time was required, they would first put all of their strength into isolating Murashige by clipping his wings.

Nobunaga accepted the plan without the least hesitation. It was, more or less, what he had been thinking of doing himself. The plan was set, and Nobunaga completely forgot about reprimanding Hideyoshi. There were still a number of things to ask Hideyoshi about in regard to their later strategies.

"Since we've dealt with the most urgent business, perhaps I should start off for Harima today," Hideyoshi said, looking up at the evening sky. Nobunaga, however, told him that the roads were so dangerous that he should return by ship that night. And since he was going by ship and there would be enough time, his lord was not going to let him go without a drink.

Hideyoshi sat a little straighter and asked, "Are you going to let me go without being punished?"

Nobunaga forced a smile. "Well, what should I do?" he joked.

"When you forgive me but still don't say anything, somehow the *sake* I receive from you doesn't go down my throat very well."

Nobunaga broke out laughing happily for the first time.

"That's good, that's good."

"In that case," Hideyoshi said, as though he had been waiting for the right moment, "Kanbei shares no blame either, does he? And the messenger with the command to cut off his son's head has already left, I believe."

"No, you can't be the guarantor for what is in Kanbei's mind. How can you say he's without blame? I'm not going to withdraw my order to have his son's head sent to Itami Castle. It's a matter of military discipline, and it won't do any good to intervene." Thus Nobunaga highhandedly sealed his retainer's mouth.

Hideyoshi returned to Harima that night, but upon his return, secretly had a messenger take a letter to Hanbei in the capital. What was in the letter will be understood later on, but essentially it concerned his private agony over the son of his friend and adviser, Kuroda Kanbei.

Nobunaga's messenger also hurried to Kyoto. On his way back, he stopped for a short time at the Church of the Ascension. When he returned to Nobunaga's main camp on Mount Amano, he was accompanied by the Italian Jesuit, Father Gnecchi, a missionary who had been in Japan for many years. There were many Christian missionaries in Sakai, Azuchi, and Kyoto, but among them, Father Gnecchi was the foreigner whom Nobunaga most favored. Nobunaga did not dislike Christians. And, even though he had fought the Buddhists and burned their strongholds, he did not dislike Buddhism either, for he recognized the intrinsic value of religion.

Not just Father Gnecchi, but all of the many Catholic missionaries who were invited to Azuchi from time to time went to great pains to try to convert Nobunaga to Christianity. But grasping Nobunaga's heart was the same as trying to ladle the reflection of the moon out of a bucket of water.

One of the Catholic fathers had given Nobunaga a black slave he had brought with him from across the sea, because Nobunaga had looked upon the man with considerable curiosity. Whenever Nobunaga left the castle, even when he went to Kyoto, he included the black slave in his entourage. The missionaries were a little jealous and once asked Nobunaga, "You seem so interested in your black slave, my lord. Exactly what is it that you find so pleasing in him?"

"I'm good to all of you, aren't I?" he quickly replied. This quite clearly indicated Nobunaga's feelings toward the missionaries. The way in which he liked Father Gnecchi and the other fathers was essentially equal to his affection for his black slave. Which brings up another point: when Father Gnecchi had his first audience with Nobunaga, he presented him with gifts from overseas. The list included ten guns, eight telescopes and magnifying glasses, fifty tiger skins, a mosquito net, and one hundred pieces of aloeswood. There were also such rare items as a timepiece, a world globe, textile goods, and chinaware.

Nobunaga had all of these things lined up on display, and gazed at them as a child might. He was especially taken by the globe and the guns. With the globe in front of them, he listened intently night after night as Father Gnecchi told him about his home,

Italy; the distances across the seas; the differences between northern and southern Europe; and about his travels through India, Annam, Luzon, and southern China. There was one other man present who would listen even more intently and asked any number of questions—Hideyoshi.

"Ah, I'm really glad you've come." Nobunaga happily welcomed Father Gnecchi to his camp.

"What can this be about, my lord? Your summons was so urgent."

"Well, sit down." Nobunaga pointed to a chair used by Zen abbots.

"Why, thank you," Father Gnecchi said, easing into the chair. He was like a reserve pawn on a chessboard, wondering when he might be used. And Nobunaga had invited him here for precisely that reason.

"Father, you once gave me a petition on behalf of the missionaries in Japan, in which you asked permission to build a church and to spread Christianity."

"I don't know how many years we have longed for the day when you would accept our plea."

"Somehow it seems that that day is approaching."

"What? Do we have your permission?"

"Not unconditionally. It is not a custom of the samurai simply to give out special privileges to men who have done no meritorious deeds."

"What exactly do you mean, my lord?"

"I understand that Takayama Ukon of Takatsuki was converted to Christianity when he was about fourteen years old and is even now a fervent believer. I can imagine you're on quite friendly terms with him."

"Takayama Ukon, my lord?"

"As you know, he's joined Araki Murashige's rebellion and has sent two of his children to Itami Castle as hostages."

"This is truly a sad situation, and we, his friends in religion, are much pained by it. I don't know how many prayers we have sent to God for His divine protection."

"Is that so? Well, Father Gnecchi, in times like these, the prayers you offer at the chapel in your temple do not seem to manifest any effects. If you're really that anxious about Ukon, you'll obey the command I'm giving you now. I want you to go to Takatsuki Castle and enlighten Takayama Ukon on the matter of his indiscretion."

"If that's something I can do, I'll be happy to go anytime. But I understand that his castle is already surrounded by the forces of Lord Nobutada as well as those of Lords Fuwa, Maeda, and Sassa. Perhaps they won't let me through."

"I'll provide you an escort and give you a guarantee of passage. It will be a great meritorious deed for the missionaries if you can explain this issue to the Takayama—both father and son—and convince them to enter my ranks. Then you will have my permission to have a church and the freedom to do missionary work. You have my word."

"Oh, my lord..."

"But wait," Nobunaga told Father Gnecchi. "You should understand very clearly that if, on the contrary, Ukon rejects your proposal and continues to defy me, I'm going to regard all Christians the same way that I regard the Takayama; and that I will quite naturally demolish your temple, exterminate your religion in Japan, and execute every last one of your missionaries and their followers. I want you to leave with that understanding."

The blood drained from Father Gnecchi's face, and for a moment, he cast his eyes to the ground. Not one of the men who had boarded a sailing ship and come east from faraway Europe could have possessed a faint or cowardly heart, but sitting before Nobunaga and being spoken to in this manner, Father Gnecchi felt his body shrink and his heart grow cold with fear. There was really nothing that gave the figure of Nobunaga the appearance of the devil himself, and in fact both his features and his speech were quite elegant. It had been engraved into the missionaries' minds, however, that this man said nothing he did not put into practice. Previous examples of this fact could be seen in both the destruction of Mount Hiei and the subjugation of Nagashima. In fact, this truth could be seen in every policy Nobunaga had ever conceived.

"I'll go. I'll be the envoy you're ordering me to be, and I'll go to meet with Lord Ukon," Father Gnecchi promised.

With an escort of a dozen mounted men, he headed out on the road to Takatsuki. After seeing Father Gnecchi off, Nobunaga felt that everything had gone exactly as he had desired. But Father Gnecchi, who had seemingly been led off by the nose to Takatsuki Castle, was congratulating himself as well. This foreigner was not as easy to manipulate as Nobunaga thought. It was well known among the common people of Kyoto that few people were as shrewd as the Jesuits. Before Nobunaga had even summoned him, Father Gnecchi had already exchanged letters with Takayama Ukon several times. Ukon's father had often asked his spiritual adviser what heaven's will might be in the matter at hand. Father Gnecchi had written the same response over and over again. The correct way did not lie in acting contrary to the wishes of one's lord. Lord Nobunaga was Murashige's master and Ukon's as well.

Ukon had written expressing his deepest feelings.

We've sent two of our children to the Araki as hostages, so that my wife and mother are strongly against submitting to Lord Nobunaga. If it were not for that, I would not want my name associated with rebellion, either.

So, for Father Gnecchi, the success of this mission and the rewards to follow were a foregone conclusion. He had the conviction that Ukon already agreed with what he himself was suggesting.

Soon afterward, Takayama Ukon announced that he could not just look away as his religion was destroyed, even if his wife and children hated him for defending it. One could abandon one's castle and family, he declared, but not the one true way. Secretly leaving the castle one night, he fled to the Church of the Ascension. His father, Hida, immediately sought refuge with Araki Murashige at Itami, and bitterly explained the situation, saying, "We've been betrayed by my worthless son."

There were many people in Murashige's camp who had close and friendly relations with the Takayama clan, and so he could not insist on the punishment of the Takayama hostages. So, although Murashige was a rather insensitive man, he was vaguely aware of the intricacies of the situation.

"There's nothing to be done. If Ukon has run away, the hostages are useless." Regarding the two little children as nothing more than hangers-on, he returned them to Ukon's father. When Father Gnecchi received this information, he went with Ukon to Mount Amano for an audience with Nobunaga.

"You did well." Nobunaga was delighted. He told Ukon that he would grant him a domain in Harima, and presented him with silk kimonos and a horse.

"I would like to take the tonsure and dedicate my life to God," Ukon pleaded.

But Nobunaga would not hear of it, saying, "That's ridiculous for a man so young."

So, in the end, the affair went as Nobunaga had planned and as Father Gnecchi had anticipated. However, the way in which Ukon had conducted himself, resulting in the return of his children, had all been Father Gnecchi's clever scheme.

Yesterday's conditions can hardly be thought of in terms of today's, for time works its transfigurations moment by moment. Neither is it unreasonable to change one's course of action. The reasons for which men have erred in their ambitions and lost their lives are as plentiful as mushrooms after a shower.

It was toward the end of the Eleventh Month. Nakagawa Sebei—the man upon whom Araki Murashige depended as on his own right arm—suddenly left his castle and submitted to Nobunaga.

"This is a significant time for the nation; we should not punish small mistakes," Nobunaga said, and not only did not question Sebei about his crime but also presented him with thirty gold coins. He presented gold and clothing to the three retainers who had come with him, as well. Sebei had surrendered in response to Takayama Ukon's appeal.

The Oda generals wondered why these men were being treated so kindly. While Nobunaga was aware that there was some dissatisfaction among his own men, there was nothing else he could do if he wanted to achieve his military objectives.

Conciliation, diplomacy, and patience did not conform with his nature. Violent, fierce attacks, therefore, continually rained down upon the enemy. For example, Nobunaga attacked Hanakuma Castle in Hyogo and showed no mercy in burning down the temples and surrounding villages. He did not forgive the slightest hostile action, whether it was committed by the old or the young, by men or by women. But now his maneuvering on the one hand and his intimidations on the other were coming to fruition.

Araki Murashige was isolated in Itami Castle, a stronghold that had had both of its wings clipped. His battle array no longer included Takayama Ukon or Nakagawa Sebei.

"If we strike now, he'll fall down like a scarecrow," Nobunaga said. He believed that Itami could now be taken anytime he liked. A combined attack was commenced at the beginning of the Twelfth Month. On the very first day, the attack began before evening and continued into the night. Resistance, however, was unexpectedly stiff. The commander of one corps of the attacking troops was struck down and killed, and there were hundreds of dead and wounded.

On the second day the number of casualties continued to increase, but not a single inch of the castle walls had been taken. Murashige was famous for his courage, after all, and there were a good many gallant men among his troops. More than that, when Murashige himself had been ready to fold up the flag of revolt following Nobunaga's attempts at appeasing him, it had been his family members and officers who had restrained him by saying, "To give up now would be the same as presenting him with our own heads."

509

The news of the start of these hostilities also quickly echoed throughout Harima and shook the officials in Osaka. Shock waves were spreading as far as Tamba and the Sanin.

First, in the western provinces, Hideyoshi immediately started the attack on Miki Castle, and had the auxiliary troops of Nobumori and Tsutsui push the Mori back to the borders of Bizen. He had thought that as soon as the Mori clan heard the shouts from the capital, its army would march on Kyoto. In Tamba, the Hatano clan considered that the tide was now favorable, and began to rebel. Akechi Mitsuhide and Hosokawa Fujitaka had been governing that area, and rushed to its defense in the nick of time.

The Honganji and the huge forces of the Mori communicated by ship-borne messengers, and the enemies that now faced Nobunaga, Hideyoshi, and Mitsuhide all danced to the music of these two powers.

"It's probably finished here," Nobunaga said, gazing at Itami Castle. Which was to say that he considered everything to be in order. Although Itami Castle was completely isolated, it had not surrendered. In Nobunaga's eyes, however, it had already fallen. Leaving the encircling army, he suddenly returned to Azuchi.

It was the end of the year. Nobunaga planned on spending New Year's at Azuchi. It was a year that had been filled with unexpected disturbances and campaigns, but as he looked over the streets of the castle town, he caught the scent of a rich new culture rising through the air. Shops both large and small were lined up in an orderly fashion, bringing Nobunaga's economic policies to fruition. Guests overflowed the inns and post stations, while at the lakeside, the masts of the anchored ships resembled a forest.

Both the residential area of the samurai, wound all through with small paths, and the magnificent mansions of the great generals had for the most part been completed. The temples, too, had been expanded, and Father Gnecchi had also begun to build a church.

What is called "culture" is as intangible as mist. What had begun as a simple act of destruction was suddenly taking form as an epoch-making new culture right at Nobunaga's feet. In music, theater, painting, literature, religion, the tea ceremony, clothing, cooking, and architecture, old styles and attitudes were being abandoned, and the new and fresh were being adopted. Even the new patterns for women's silk kimonos rivaled each other in this burgeoning Azuchi culture.

This is the New Year I've been waiting for, and it is a New Year for the nation. It's hardly necessary to say that to build is more pleasant than to destroy, Nobunaga thought, imagining that the new dynamic culture would move like an incoming tide, flooding the eastern provinces, the capital, and even the west and the island of Kyushu, leaving no place untouched.

Nobunaga was absorbed in such thoughts when Sakuma Nobumori, with the bright sun shining at his back, greeted him and stepped into the room. Seeing Nobumori, Nobunaga suddenly remembered.

"Ah, that's right. How did that affair go afterward?" he asked quickly, passing the cup in his hand to the page who delivered it to Nobumori.

Nobumori raised the cup reverently to his forehead, and said, "That affair?" He peered at his master's brow.

"That's right. I told you about Shojumaru, didn't I? Kanbei's son—the one who's in Takenaka Hanbei's castle as a hostage."

"Ah, you mean the matter of the hostage."

"I sent you with an order for Hanbei to cut off Shojumaru's head and send it to Itami. But afterward there was no response even though the head was supposed to have been cut off and sent. Have you heard anything?"

"No, my lord." Nobumori shook his head and, as he spoke, he appeared to be remembering his mission of the year before. He had accomplished his mission, but Shojumaru had been placed in Takenaka Hanbei's care in Mino, so the execution was unlikely to have been carried out immediately.

"If this is Lord Nobunaga's command, it will be carried out, but I will need some more time," Hanbei had said, acknowledging the request in a normal fashion and, of course, Nobumori had understood.

"Well then, I have given you His Lordship's order," Nobumori had added, and promptly returned to report to Nobunaga.

Owing possibly to his own responsibilities, Nobunaga seemed to have forgotten about the matter; but the fact was that Nobumori, too, had not really kept the fate of Shojumaru in mind. He had simply assumed that Hanbei would report the boy's execution directly to Nobunaga.

"You have heard nothing else about it from either Hideyoshi or Hanbei, my lord?"

"They haven't said a word about it."

"That's rather suspicious."

"You're sure you spoke to Hanbei?"

"That's hardly necessary to ask. But he's been extraordinarily lazy recently," Nobumori mumbled vexatiously, and then added, "To have considered this simply as a measure affecting the child of a traitor, and not yet to have taken any action on Your Lordship's important command, would be a crime of disobedience that could not be ignored. On my way back to the front, I'll stop in Kyoto and very definitely question Hanbei about it."

"Really?" Nobunaga's response did not show much interest. The strictness of the command he had given at that time and the way he was recalling the matter right now reflected two completely different frames of mind. He did not, however, tell Nobumori to forget about it. Certainly, that would have meant a complete loss of face for the man who had been sent on the mission.

How was Nobumori to take this? Perhaps he thought that Nobunaga believed he had executed his mission incompetently, for he quickly finished with his congratulations for the New Year, took his leave from the castle and, on his return to the besieged castle at Itami, purposely stopped at the Nanzen Temple.

He told the priest who greeted him, "I know Lord Hanbei is confined indoors because of his illness, but I've come on a mission from Lord Nobunaga." His request for a interview was expressed in extraordinarily severe and imperative terms. The monk left, then returned quickly, and invited to follow him.

Nobumori replied with a nod, and followed the priest. The sliding paper doors of the thatched building were closed, but incessant coughing—probably prompted by Hanbei's leaving his sickbed in order to meet his guest—could be heard coming from inside. Nobumori lingered outside for a moment. The appearance of the sky suggested snow.

Though it was still midday, it was frigid in the shadow of the mountains around the temple.

"Come in," a voice invited from within, and an attendant opened the sliding doors to a small reception room. The lean figure of his master was propped up on the floor.

"Welcome," Hanbei said in greeting.

Nobumori walked in and said without preamble, "Last year I brought you His Lordship's order to execute Kuroda Shojumaru, and I expected the matter to be dealt with without delay. There has been no positive response since then, however, and even Lord Nobunaga has become concerned. What you have to say for yourself."

"Well, well…" Hanbei began, bowing with his hands to the floor and exposing a back as thin as a board. "Have I inadvertently made His Lordship worry because of my carelessness? I am doing as much as I can to hurry and obey His Lordship's will as my illness gradually gets better."

"What! What are you saying?" Nobumori was losing his self-control. Or better said, judging by the color of his face, he was so angered by Hanbei's answer that he could not repress his exasperation or untangle his tongue. Heaving a sigh, Hanbei coolly observed his guest's agitation.

"Well then…isn't there something…?" Apart from the voice that disgorged itself from his mouth, Nobumori's agitated eyes remained entangled with the calm eyes of his host. Nobumori coughed uncontrollably, then asked, "Haven't you sent his head to Kanbei at Itami Castle?"

"It's as you say."

"It's as I say? That's a rather unusual answer. Have you deliberately disobeyed His Lordship's command?"

"Don't be absurd."

"If that's so, why haven't you killed the boy yet?"

"He was strictly entrusted to me. I thought that I could do it at any time, without too much hurry."

"That's excessive leniency. There's a limit to this leisurely pace, you know. I do not recall having ever been so inept on a mission as I was on this one."

"There was never any fault in the way you carried out your mission. It's absolutely clear that I purposely delayed the matter because of my own thoughts on the subject."

"Purposely?"

"While I knew that it was a grave errand, I've been thoughtlessly preoccupied by this illness…"

"Wouldn't it be sufficient if you sent a courier with a note?"

"No, he may be a hostage from another clan, but he's been entrusted to us for a number of years. The people around such a lovely child naturally feel sympathy toward him and would find it difficult to kill him. I'm concerned that if the worst happened and some indiscreet retainer sent someone else's head for His Lordship's inspection, I would have no excuse to offer Lord Nobunaga. So I think that I myself should go to behead him. Perhaps my condition will improve before long." As Hanbei spoke, he began coughing uncontrollably. He put a paper handkerchief over his mouth, but it seemed that he was not going to be able to stop.

An attendant nearby moved behind him and began rubbing Hanbei's back. Nobumori could do nothing but keep quiet and wait until Hanbei settled down. But just sitting in front of a man who was trying to control his violent coughing fit and who was having his sick body massaged began to be painful in itself.

"Why don't you rest in your room?" For the first time Nobumori mumbled something sympathetic, but the look on his face bore no sympathy at all. "At any rate, in the next few days there should be some action taken as a result of these words from His Lordship. I'm amazed at your negligence, but there's nothing else I can do after what I've said here now. I'll be sending a letter to Azuchi explaining the situation exactly as it is. No matter how sick you may be, any further delay will only provoke His Lordship's anger. It's tedious, but I'll definitely have to inform him about this!"

Ignoring the pained figure of Hanbei, who was still racked by coughing, Nobumori had his say, announced his leave, and departed. As he reached the veranda, he passed by a woman carrying a tray from which floated the thick smell of some medicinal decoction.

The woman hurriedly put down her tray and bowed to her guest. Nobumori inspected her at length, from the white hands that touched the wooden-floored veranda to the back of her neck, and finally said, "It seems that I've met you before. Ah, yes, that's right. The time I was invited by Lord Hideyoshi to Nagahama. I remember that you were waiting upon him at that time."

"Yes. I was given leave to take care of my brother."

"Well then, you're Hanbei's younger sister?"

"Yes, my name is Oyu."

"You're Oyu," he muttered rudely. "You are pretty." Mumbling to himself, he stepped down on the stepping stone.

Oyu simply nodded as he left. She could hear her brother still coughing, and she seemed more concerned about the medicine growing cold than about what her guest's feelings might be. Just when she thought that he had left, however, Nobumori turned again and said, "Has there been any news recently from Lord Hideyoshi in Harima?"

"No."

"Your brother was purposely negligent with Lord Nobunaga's orders, but I'm sure that couldn't have been a result of Hideyoshi's instructions, could it? I fear that our lord may have some doubts about that. If Hideyoshi is incurring Lord Nobunaga's wrath, he may be in for a great deal of trouble. I'm going to say this once again: I think it would be a good thing if Kuroda Kanbei's son were executed immediately."

Looking up into the sky, Nobumori quickly walked away. Obscuring his retreating figure and the huge roof of the Nanzen Temple, specks of snow fell obliquely, turning everything white.

"My lady!" The coughing had suddenly stopped behind the sliding doors, and the agitated voice of the retainer could now be heard in its place. Her chest pounding, Oyu opened the doors and looked inside. Hanbei lay face down on the floor. The paper handkerchief that had been over his mouth was covered with bright red blood.

BOOK SIX

SEVENTH YEAR OF TENSHO
1579

CHARACTERS AND PLACES

SHOJUMARU, Kuroda Kanbei's son
KUMATARO, retainer of Takenaka Hanbei
BESSHO NAGAHARU, lord of Miki Castle
GOTO MOTOKUNI, senior Bessho retainer
IKEDA SHONYU, senior Oda retainer
ANAYAMA BAISETSU, senior Takeda retainer
NISHINA NOBUMORI, Takeda Katsuyori's brother
SAITO TOSHIMITSU, senior Akechi retainer
YUSHO, painter

MIKI, Bessho Nagaharu's castle
NIRASAKI, new capital of Kai
TAKATO, Nishina Nobumori's castle

A RETAINER'S DUTY

Hideyoshi's campaign in the western provinces, Mitsuhide's campaign in Tamba, and the long siege of Itami Castle were Nobunaga's real work. The campaign in the western provinces and the siege of Itami were still stalemated, and only in Tamba was there some minor action. Day by day, a vast number of letters and reports arrived from these three areas. The documents were screened by staff officers and private secretaries, so that Nobunaga saw only the most important ones.

Among them was a letter from Sakuma Nobumori. Nobunaga read it and tossed it aside with an expression of extreme displeasure. The person whose job it was to pick up any discarded letters was Nobunaga's trusted page, Ranmaru. Thinking that Nobunaga's orders had been disobeyed, he surreptitiously read the letter. There was nothing in it that should have upset Nobunaga. It read:

> To my surprise, Hanbei has not yet taken any action to carry out your orders. As your messenger, I impressed upon him the error of his ways, informing him that if he disobeyed the order, I would be accused of negligence. I think your order will be carried out soon. This has been extremely trying for me, and I humbly request your magnanimity in this matter.

Behind Nobumori's words one sensed that he was, more than anything else, trying to justify his own faults. In fact, his intention really was nothing more than that. Ranmaru was not able to read more meaning into it.

Nobunaga's anger at the letter, and his perception that Nobumori had changed, would not be manifested until later on. Until then, it would have been difficult for anyone other than Nobunaga to have understood his own true feelings. The only hints presaging the future that did not go unnoticed were that Nobunaga did not seem angry about Hanbei's disobedience and negligence—even after he received such a letter from Nobumori—and that after this event, the matter was ignored. Nobunaga himself certainly did not press it. But there was no reason for Hanbei to be aware of such complicated changes in Nobunaga's thinking. It was not Hanbei, however, but Oyu and the retainers who were taking care of him, who thought that Hanbei should do something. It seemed he had not yet decided what to do about the problem.

A month went by. The plum trees were blossoming at the main gate of the Nanzen Temple and around Hanbei's retreat. As the days went by the sun became warmer, but Hanbei's condition did not improve.

He could not bear uncleanliness, so every day he would have the sickroom swept clean and then, bathing himself in the sunlight on bright mornings, he would sit on the veranda.

His sister would prepare tea for him, and his one pleasure during his illness was to watch the steam rise from the tea bowl in the bright morning sun.

"Your color has improved a little this morning, brother," Oyu said brightly.

Hanbei rubbed his cheek with a thin hand. "Spring has come to me, too, it seems. This is pleasant. For the last two or three days I've felt rather well," he answered with a smile.

Both his mood and color had indeed become much better in the past two or three days, and Oyu felt the greatest pleasure in looking at him this fine morning. But suddenly she felt a sense of desolation as she recalled the doctor's words: "There is little hope of recovery." But she was not going to give in to her feeling. How many patients had recovered after their doctors had given them up for dead? She promised herself that she would nurse Hanbei back to health—to see him healthy was a goal she shared with Hideyoshi, who the day before had written from Harima to encourage him.

"If you continue to get better at this rate, you'll be able to get out of bed by the time the cherry trees are blooming."

"Oyu, I've been nothing but trouble, haven't I?"

"What nonsense are you talking now?"

Hanbei laughed weakly. "I haven't thanked you before, because we're brother and sister, but this morning somehow I feel I should say something. I wonder if it's because I'm feeling so much better."

"It makes me happy to think it might be so."

"It's already been ten years since we left Mount Bodai."

"Time passes quickly. When you look back, you realize life goes by just like a dream."

"You've been at my side since then—and me, nothing but a mountain hermit—cooking my meals morning and night, taking care of me, even preparing my medicine."

"No, it's only been for a little while. Back then, you kept saying that you would never get better. But as soon as your health improved, you joined Lord Hideyoshi, fought at the Ane River, Nagashino, and Echizen. You were in pretty good health then, weren't you?"

"I suppose you're right. This sick body has stood up pretty well."

"So if you take care of yourself, you'll certainly get better this time, too. I'm determined that you're going to become your old self again."

"It's not that I want to die."

"You're not going to die!"

"I want to keep living. I want to live to make sure this violent world finds peace again. Ah, if only I were healthy, I'd be able to help my lord to the best of my ability." Suddenly Hanbei's voice fell. "But the length of a man's life is beyond his control. What can I do in this condition?"

Looking into his eyes, Oyu was suffused with pain. Was there something that her brother was keeping from her?

The bell of the Nanzen Temple announced the hour of noon. Although the country was still in a state of civil war, people could be seen viewing the flowering plum trees, and the song of the nightingales could be heard among the falling blossoms.

That spring was considered to be a pleasant one, but it was still only the Second Month. When night fell, and the lamps began to flicker coldly, Hanbei began to cough again. During the night, Oyu would have to get up several times to rub his back. There were other retainers nearby, but Hanbei was unwilling to let them take care of him in this way.

"They are all men who will ride out with me into battle. It wouldn't be right to ask them to rub a sick man's back," he explained.

That night, too, she got up to massage her brother's back. Going into the kitchen to prepare his medicine, she suddenly heard a noise outside the kitchen door that sounded as if someone was brushing past the old bamboo of the hedge. Oyu listened carefully. She could hear whispering outside.

"I can see a light. Wait just a moment. Somebody must be up." The voices outside gradually came closer to the house. Then someone tapped lightly on the rain shutter.

"Who is it?" Oyu asked.

"Is that you, Lady Oyu? It's Kumataro from Kurihara. I've just come back from Itami."

"It's Kumataro!" she called excitedly to Hanbei. She slid open the door to the kitchen and saw three men standing in the starlight.

Kumataro stretched out his hand took the bucket Oyu offered him. He called the other two men, and all three went to the well.

Oyu wondered who the other two men were. Kumataro was the retainer they had brought up on Mount Kurihara. At that time he had been called Kokuma, but now he was a fine young samurai. After Kumataro drew up the well bucket and poured the water into the bucket he had taken from Oyu, the other two men washed the mud from their hands and feet and the blood from their sleeves.

Hanbei instructed her to light the lamp in the small guest room, put some burning coals in the brazier, and lay out cushions for the guests, even though it was late at night.

When Hanbei told her that one of the men with Kumataro must be Kuroda Kanbei, she could not hide her surprise. Kuroda was the man about whom there had been so many rumors: either that he had been a prisoner in Itami Castle since the previous year, or that he had changed sides and was staying in the castle of his own free will. Ordinarily, Hanbei did not talk at all to his retainers about official business—much less about secrets matters of this nature—so even Oyu had no idea where Kumataro had gone before the

519

New Year, or why he had stayed away for such a long time.

"Oyu, please bring me my coat," Hanbei said.

Although she was worried about him, Oyu knew that he would insist on getting out of bed and meeting his guests, no matter how sick he was. She slipped the coat over his shoulders.

Having combed his hair and rinsed his mouth, Hanbei went to the reception room where Kumataro and the other two guests were already sitting and waiting quietly for him.

Hanbei responded to the guests' greeting with deep emotion, "Ah, you're safe!" and he sat down, grasping Kanbei's hands. "I was worried."

"Don't worry on my account; as you see, I'm quite well," Kanbei replied.

"I'm glad you made it."

"I seem to have made you worry. I apologize."

"Anyway, heaven has blessed us by bringing us together again. For me, this is a real joy."

But who was the other, older man who had been watching in silence, reluctant to disturb the emotional reunion of the two friends? At last Kanbei asked him to introduce himself.

"I think this is not the first time we have met, my lord. I am also in the service of Lord Hideyoshi and I have seen you from a distance many times. I'm a member of the ninja corps, which doesn't mix with the other samurai much, so you may not remember me. I am Hachisuka Hikoemon's nephew, Watanabe Tenzo. I'm very pleased to make your acquaintance."

Hanbei slapped his knee. "You're Watanabe Tenzo! I've heard a lot about you. And now that you mention it, it seems I have seen you once or twice before."

Just then Kumataro said, "I met Tenzo quite by accident in the prison of Itami Castle. He had the same purpose I had in penetrating the place."

"I don't know if it happened completely by chance or through divine providence, but it was only because we met each other that we were able to get Lord Kanbei out. If we had each been acting on our own, we probably would have been killed in the attempt," Tenzo said, smiling.

Tenzo had been in Itami Castle because Hideyoshi had also tried to engineer Kuroda Kanbei's rescue. Hideyoshi had first dispatched an envoy to beg Araki Murashige for Kanbei's release, and later, had sent a Buddhist priest in whom Murashige had faith to preach for the same thing. He had used every means at his disposal, but Murashige had stubbornly refused to let Kanbei go. As a last resort, Hideyoshi had ordered Tenzo to get Kanbei out of prison.

Tenzo had broken into the castle, and a chance to rescue Kanbei had presented itself. There was a celebration of some kind taking place in the castle, and all of Araki Murashige's family and retainers were in the main hall, while every last soldier had been treated to *sake*. As luck would have it, it was a dark night with neither moon nor wind. Tenzo knew that it was the moment to act decisively. Having already completed his reconnaissance of the grounds, he was investigating the area beneath the keep when he saw someone else spying into the prison, someone who did not look like a guard. In fact, the man must have broken into the castle just as he had. The other man introduced himself as Takenaka Hanbei's retainer, Kumataro.

"I am an agent of Lord Hideyoshi," Tenzo replied. With this exchange, they knew they had come on the same mission. Working together, they broke through the prison window and helped Kanbei to escape. Concealed by the darkness, they went over the castle ramparts, took a small boat from the floodgate across the moat, and fled.

After listening to the detailed circumstances of the difficulties they had been through, Hanbei turned to Kumataro and and said, "I was worried that I had sent you out on an impossible mission, and I realized that your chances of success were only one or two out of ten. This absolutely has to be the work of heaven. But what happened in the days after that? And how did you make your way here?"

Kumataro knelt respectfully, apparently without the least bit of pride in having done something worthy of praise. "We had little trouble in getting out of the castle; our real problems began afterward. The Araki forces were stationed at wooden palisades here and there, so we were surrounded several times, and sometimes we were separated from each other in the midst of the enemy's swords and spears. We were finally able to cut our way through, but in one of the fights Lord Kanbei received a sword wound to his left knee, and his injury kept us from going too far. In the end, we had to sleep in a barn. We traveled at night and slept in roadside shrines during the day. Finally we made our way to Kyoto."

Kanbei took up the story. "If we had been able to find refuge with the Oda troops that surrounded the castle, our escape would have been easier. According to what I heard in the castle, however, Araki Murashige was letting it be known that Lord Nobunaga was very suspicious of my actions. He told people that I should join their side because of the kind of person Nobunaga was, but I smiled at this chicanery."

Kanbei forced a sad smile, and Hanbei nodded silently.

By the time all the questions and stories were over, the night sky had begun to turn pale white. Oyu was preparing soup in the kitchen.

The men were tired after talking all night, and after finishing their breakfast, each took a short nap. Upon awakening, they spoke again.

"By the way," Hanbei said to Kanbei, "I know it's awfully sudden, but I was thinking that I would leave today for my home province of Mino and then go on to Azuchi to see Lord Nobunaga. As I will tell your story to His Lordship, I suggest you go directly to Harima."

"Of course, I don't want to be idle for a single day," Kanbei said, but then he looked dubiously at Hanbei's face. "You're still ill, and how is a sudden trip going to affect your health?" he asked.

"I planned on getting up today anyway. If I let my illness defeat me, there'll be no end to it, and I've been feeling much better for a while now."

"But it's important to be completely cured. I don't know what kind of pressing business you have, but couldn't you put it off just a while longer and convalesce here?" Kanbei asked.

"I prayed that I might get better quickly with the coming of the New Year, and I've been taking good care of myself. Now that I'm sure you're all right, I have no worries about that anymore. At the same time, I've committed a crime for which I have to receive punishment at Azuchi, and today's a good day to get out of the sickbed and say good-bye."

"A crime for which you have to receive punishment at Azuchi?"

Hanbei now told Kanbei for the first time about how he had disobeyed Nobunaga's orders for over a year.

Kanbei was shocked. That Nobunaga had doubted him was one thing. But that he would order the decapitation of Shojumaru was something he could not even begin to imagine.

"Is that the way it was?" Kanbei moaned. Suddenly he felt cold and hollow toward Nobunaga. He had risked so much: gone into Itami Castle alone, been imprisoned, and only narrowly avoided death—and in the end, whom was he working for? At the same time, he was unable to keep from shedding tears at Hideyoshi's inordinate show of affection and Hanbei's friendship.

"I'm very grateful, but why should you do this for my son's sake? If that's the situation, then I should go to Azuchi to explain myself."

"No, the crime of disobedience was mine. The only request I have is that you join Lord Hideyoshi in Harima. I doubt that I'm going to be in the world much longer, whether I'm found guilty or innocent. I'd like you to go to Harima as quickly as possible."

Hanbei prostrated himself in front of his friend as if to beg him. He had a sick man's determination. Even more, he was Hanbei, a man not lacking in mature deliberation; once he had spoken, he did not go back on his decisions.

That day the two friends parted company, one going east, the other west. Kanbei went on to the campaign in Harima, accompanied by Watanabe Tenzo. Hanbei set off for Mino, accompanied only by Kumataro.

As Oyu saw her brother off at the gate of the Nanzen Temple, there were tears in her eyes, for in her mind was the possibility that he might never return. The priests tried to comfort her by telling her that her grief would be as fleeting as all things, but in the end they almost had to carry her back through the main gate.

Hanbei most likely had the same thoughts as well. No, it was clear that he felt an even more intense grief. In the saddle of his horse, his body swayed as he neared a rise.

Hanbei suddenly pulled back on the reins as though he had just remembered something. "Kumataro," he said, "there's something I've forgotten to say. I'm going to write it down, and I'd like you to run back and give it to Oyu." Taking out a piece of paper, he scribbled something and handed it to Kumataro. "I'll go on ahead slowly, so you can catch up with me."

Kumataro took the letter, bowed respectfully, and ran back toward the temple.

I've made mistakes, he thought sadly, as he looked down at the Nanzen Temple one last time. I have no regrets at all about the road I have taken, but for my sister.... He let the horse walk at its own pace.

A samurai's road was a straight one; and after Hanbei had come down from Mount Kurihara, he had not deviated from it. Nor would he have had any regrets, even if his life were to end that day. But what pained him most was that Oyu had become Hideyoshi's mistress. As her brother, he constantly felt censured by his conscience. She had, after all, been at his side at the crucial time of choosing her own path, he told himself. The fault lay with him, not with his sister. He secretly worried about the many years that were ahead of Oyu after his own death.

It was a woman's misfortune that her happiness never lasted her whole life. What was especially painful to him was the feeling that he had stained the pure whiteness of the Way of the Samurai—the way that based itself on death. How many times had he grumbled to himself about this matter, thinking that he should apologize to Hideyoshi and ask to be dismissed, or that he should unburden himself of his anguish to his sister, and ask her to live in seclusion? But the appropriate course of action had never presented itself.

He was embarking on a journey from which he would never return, and naturally he felt that he should say something about the matter to Oyu. He had been unable to say anything when she stood so sweetly in front of him, but now, perhaps, he could write a few lines of verse, which his sister might appreciate more easily. After he was gone, on the pretext of mourning him, she might be able to extricate herself from the crowd of women that clustered around Hideyoshi's bedroom like flowering vines at a gate.

When he arrived at his own estate in Mino, Hanbei spent the day worshiping at the grave of his ancestors and then went briefly back to Mount Bodai. He had not been there for a long time but would not give in to his desire to stay longer.

On arising the next morning, he quickly arranged his hair and heated up water for a rare bath.

"Call Ito Hanemon," he ordered.

The song of the nightingale could be heard frequently both in the plains around Mount Bodai and in the trees inside the castle compound.

"I am at your service, my lord." With the sliding paper doors at his back, a sturdy-looking elderly samurai bowed deeply. Ito was Shojumaru's guardian.

"Hanemon? Come in. You're the only one I've ever talked to about this in detail, but the day has finally come when Shojumaru must go to Azuchi. We will leave today. I know this is sudden, but please inform the attendants and have them make travel preparations at once."

Hanemon understood his master's distress very well, and the color suddenly drained from his face.

"Then Master Shojumaru's life is ..."

Hanbei could see that the old man was shaking, and to reassure him he said, smiling, "No, he won't be beheaded. I'm going to appease Lord Nobunaga's anger, even if it's at the expense of my own life. As soon as he was freed from Itami, Shojumaru's father went to the campaign in Harima, a wordless statement of his innocence. Now the only thing remaining is my crime of ignoring my lord's orders."

Hanemon withdrew silently and went to Shojumaru's room. As he approached, he could hear the happy sounds of the child's voice as he beat upon a hand drum. Shojumaru was treated so well by the Takenaka clan that one would hardly think he had been put in its care as a hostage.

Thus, when his guardians, who knew little of the real situation concerning the child, heard that they were to make preparations for a journey, they were fearful for Shojumaru's life.

Hanemon did his best to reassure them. "You have nothing to fear. If Master Shoju-maru is going to Azuchi, have faith in Lord Hanbei's sense of justice. I think we should leave everything to him."

Shojumaru knew nothing of what was occurring and continued to play happily, beating the drum and dancing. Even though he was a hostage, he had his father's fortitude and was undergoing the robust training of a samurai. He was by no means a timid child.

"What did Hanemon say?" Shojumaru asked, putting down the drum. Seeing his guardian's face, the child seemed to realize something had happened and he looked worried.

"It's nothing to worry about," one of the guardians said. "But we have to make quick preparations for a trip to Azuchi."

"Who's going?"

"You are, Master Shojumaru."

"I'm going too? To Azuchi?"

The guardians turned away so that the boy could not see their tears. As soon as Shojumaru heard their words, he jumped up and clapped his hands.

"Really? How wonderful!" And he ran back to his room. "I'm going to Azuchi! They said I'm going on a trip with Lord Hanbei! The dancing and drumming is over. Stop, everyone!"

Then he asked loudly, "Are these clothes all right?"

Ito came in and said, "His Lordship reminds you to take a bath and arrange your hair nicely."

The guardians led Shojumaru to the bath, put him in the tub, and did his hair. But when they began to dress him for the trip, they saw that both the underclothes and the kimono provided for him were of the purest white silk—the vestments of death.

Shojumaru's attendants immediately thought that Ito had lied to console them and that the boy's head was going to be cut off in front of Nobunaga. They started to cry again, but Shojumaru paid absolutely no attention and put on the white kimono, a red brocade armor coat, and a skirt of China silk. Dressed in this finery and flanked by his two attendants, he was taken to Hanbei's room.

In high spirits, Shojumaru ignored the tear-streaked faces of his attendants. "Well then, let's go!" he urged Hanbei again.

Hanbei finally stood up and said to his retainers, "Please take care of everything afterward." When they considered this later, it seemed that all of his intent was contained in the one word, "afterward."

* * *

After the battle of the Ane River, Nobunaga had granted Hanbei an audience. On that occasion Nobunaga had said, "I've heard from Hideyoshi that he looks upon you not only as his retainer but as his teacher. Be sure to understand that I don't think lightly of you, either."

Thereafter, whether Hanbei was given an audience or simply went to Azuchi, Nobunaga always treated him as though he were one of his own direct retainers.

Hanbei now climbed to Azuchi Castle, bringing with him Kanbei's son, Shojumaru.

Because of his illness, his fatigue showed on his face, but, dressed in his best clothes, he went step by step in a dignified manner up into the tower where Nobunaga sat. Nobunaga had received notice of their arrival the night before, and was waiting.

"I so rarely see you," Nobunaga said in high spirits as soon as he saw Hanbei. "I'm glad you're here. Come closer. You have permission to take a cushion. Someone give Hanbei something to sit on." Showing exceptional sympathy, he spoke to Hanbei, who remained prostrate at a distance in deep respect. "Are you better now? I imagine you were exhausted both mentally and physically by the long campaign in Harima. According to my doctor, it would be dangerous to send you to the battlefield right now. He said you need at least one or two more years of complete rest."

For the past two or three years it had been rare for Nobunaga to use such gentle words when speaking to a retainer. Hanbei felt some disorientation in his heart that was neither happiness nor grief.

"I do not deserve such sympathy, my lord. Going to the battlefield, I become ill; returning, I do nothing more than receive your kind favors. I'm just a sick man who's done nothing of service for you at all."

"No, no! I'll be in real difficulty if you don't take care of yourself. The first thing we must think of is not to discourage Hideyoshi."

"Please don't say such things, my lord, you make me blush," Hanbei said. "Originally, the reason I dared to show my face asking for an audience was that last year Sakuma Nobumori delivered your orders concerning Shojumaru's execution. But until now—"

"Wait a minute," Nobunaga interrupted. Ignoring Hanbei for the moment, he looked at the youth kneeling by Hanbei's side. "Is that Shojumaru?"

"Yes, my lord."

"Hm, I see. He resembles his father, and he looks a little different from other children. He's a promising young man. You should be good to this boy, Hanbei."

"Well then, what about sending his head?" Hanbei tensed and gazed steadily at Nobunaga. If Nobunaga insisted on cutting off the child's head, he was resolved to risk his own life by admonishing his lord. But, from the beginning of the audience, that did not seem to be Nobunaga's intention, Hanbei now began to realize.

Feeling Hanbei's direct stare, Nobunaga suddenly burst out laughing and spoke as though he could no longer hide his own foolishness. "Forget all that. I myself regretted that order almost immediately after I gave it. Somehow, I'm just a very suspicious person. This has been awkward for both Hideyoshi and Kanbei. But the wise Hanbei resisted my orders and did not slay the child. In fact, when I heard about how you had dealt with this, I was relieved. How am I going to blame you? The blame is mine. Forgive me, I didn't act very well." Nobunaga didn't hang his head or bow to the ground, but he looked as though he wanted to change the subject quickly.

Hanbei, however, was not so easily contented with Nobunaga's forgiveness. Nobunaga had said to forget the matter, to let it flow downstream, but Hanbei's expression displayed no joy at all.

"My having disobeyed your order may reflect on your authority at a later time. If you've spared Shojumaru's head because of Kanbei's innocence and merit, allow this young man to prove himself worthy of your mercy. Also, you could do me no better favor, my lord, than to command me to do some meritorious deed to atone for the crime of having ignored your order." Hanbei spoke as though he were opening his heart, once again prostrating himself and waiting for Nobunaga's benevolence. This was what Nobunaga had wanted from the beginning.

When Hanbei had once again received his lord's pardon, he told Shojumaru in a whisper to thank Nobunaga courteously. He then turned to Nobunaga again. "This may be the last time the two of us will meet in this life. I pray that you will prosper even more in the fortunes of war."

"That's sort of a strange thing to say, isn't it? Does that mean you're going to disobey me yet again?" Nobunaga pressed Hanbei for his meaning.

"Never." Hanbei shook his head as he looked down at Shojumaru. "Please look at the way this child is dressed. He is leaving here to fight in the Harima campaign beside Kanbei; he is resolved to distinguish himself no less than his father, gallantly ready to leave everything to destiny."

"What? He wants to go to the battlefield?"

"Kanbei is a famous warrior, and Shojumaru is his son. My request is that you encourage him in his first campaign. It would be a great blessing if you would tell him to exert himself in a manly way."

"But what about you?"

"As a sick man, I doubt that I can complement the strength of our men much at all, but I think it is the right time for me to accompany Shojumaru to the campaign."

"Are you all right? What about your health?"

"I was born a samurai, and to die peacefully in my bed would be mortifying. When it's time to die, one cannot do otherwise."

"Well then, go with my blessing, and I wish Shojumaru good fortune in his first campaign, too." Nobunaga beckoned the youth with his eyes and gave him a short sword made by a famous swordsmith. Then he ordered a retainer to bring *sake*, and they drank together.

Hanbei's Legacy

No one could have predicted that Bessho Nagaharu would hold out in Miki Castle for so long. The castle had been besieged for three long years, and it had been completely blockaded by Hideyoshi's troops for more than six months. What were its occupants eating? How had they managed to survive?

Hideyoshi's troops were amazed each time they observed the activity and heard the hearty voices of those inside the castle. Was some sort of miracle taking place? Sometimes they believed the enemy's survival was almost supernatural. The battle of endurance was being lost by the attacking troops. It seemed that no matter how they beat, struck, kicked, or choked the enemy, he was still moving.

The garrison of three thousand five hundred men had had their provisions cut off and their water routes blocked. They should have been on the brink of starvation in the middle of the First Month, but at the end of the month the castle still had not fallen. It was now the beginning of the Third Month.

Hideyoshi saw the weariness of his troops but forced himself to hide his concern. The scraggly beard on his chin and the hollowness of his eyes were clear symptoms of the anxiety and fatigue caused by the long siege.

I've miscalculated, Hideyoshi realized. I knew they would hold out, but I never thought it would be this long. He had learned the lesson that war is not simply a matter of numbers and logistical advantages.

The morale of the men inside the castle had actually strengthened; there was not even a hint that they might capitulate. Of course, there could have been no food. The besieged soldiers must have eaten their cows and horses, even tree roots and grass. All of the things that Hideyoshi had thought would decide the castle's fall were only strengthening the morale and unity of the defenders.

In the Fifth Month the rainy season began. This was a mountainous region of the western provinces, so, adding to the misery of the constant rain, the roads turned into waterfalls and the empty moats overflowed with muddy water. Now, as the men slipped in the mud while going up and down the mountain, the siege—which had seemed at last to be having some effect—was once again turned into a stalemate by the power of nature.

Kuroda Kanbei, whose knee—which had been injured during his escape from Itami Castle—had never completely healed, inspected the front lines from a litter. He would force a smile at the thought that he would probably be limping for the rest of his life.

When Hanbei witnessed his friend's efforts, he forgot about his own suffering and tackled his own arduous task. Hideyoshi had a strange field staff, indeed. Neither of his two chief generals, whom he valued like a pair of bright jewels, was in perfect health. One was chronically sick; the other had to direct the fighting from a litter.

But the considerable help these two men gave Hideyoshi went beyond their resourcefulness. Every time he looked at their tragic figures, he could not help but be moved to tears by sublime emotions. At this point his field staff was absolutely of one body and mind. It was only because of this that the morale of the troops did not waver. It had taken at least half a year, but now the resistance of Miki Castle was beginning to weaken. If the field staff of the attacking troops had not had this indestructible center, Miki Castle might never have fallen. Then the Mori fleet might have broken through the encircling troops and brought in provisions, or their troops might have crossed the mountains, combined with the soldiers in the castle, and crushed the attacking troops. And the name of Hideyoshi might have met its end right there. With this kind of spirit, there were times when even Hideyoshi felt outstripped by Kanbei's quick wit and resources, and, half in jest, would express his admiration by calling Kanbei "that damned cripple." But it was clear that in his heart he felt a deep respect for this man upon whom he relied so much.

The rainy season was long over, the intense heat of the summer had passed, and the coolness of fall had come in with the beginning of the Eighth Month. Hanbei's illness suddenly took a turn for the worse, and this time it seemed as though he would never be putting armor on his sick body again.

Ah, is heaven abandoning me, too, at last? Hideyoshi lamented. Hanbei is too young and talented to die. Can't fate give him more time?

He had shut himself in the hut where Hanbei lay, sitting with his sick friend day and night, but that evening, when he was called to other important affairs, Hanbei's condition appeared to worsen hourly. The enemy fortresses at Takano and Mount Hachiman were wrapped in the evening mist. As night approached gunfire echoed through the mountains.

It must be that damned cripple again! Hideyoshi thought. He shouldn't go that far inside enemy lines.

Hideyoshi worried about Kanbei, who had pressed in on the enemy but had not yet returned. Hurried footsteps approached and stopped at his side. When he looked around, someone was tearfully prostrating himself.

"Shojumaru?"

After Shojumaru had joined the camp at Mount Hirai, he had gone into battle on several occasions. In a short time he had been transformed into a stouthearted adult. About one week before this, when Hanbei's condition had seemed to be deteriorating quickly, Hideyoshi had ordered Shojumaru to watch Hanbei.

"I'm sure the patient would be more pleased with you at his bedside than someone else. I would like to be there taking care of him myself, but I'm afraid that if he worried about troubling me, his condition would worsen."

For Shojumaru, Hanbei was both teacher and surrogate father. Now he waited upon Hanbei day and night without taking off his own armor, putting all his energy into preparing the man's medicine and caring for his needs. This was the Shojumaru who had come running in and had tearfully prostrated himself on the ground. Intuitively, Hideyoshi felt as though he had been struck in the chest.

"Why are you crying, Shojumaru?" he scolded him.

"Please forgive me," Shojumaru said, wiping his eyes. "Lord Hanbei is almost too weak to speak; he may not last until midnight. If you can take time from the battle, could you come for a moment?"

"He's on the verge of dying?"

"I–I'm afraid so."

"Is that what the doctor says?"

"Yes. Lord Hanbei strictly ordered me not to tell you or anyone else in camp of his condition, but the doctor and Lord Hanbei's retainers said that his departure from this world is imminent and that it would be better if I told you."

Hideyoshi was already resigned. "Shojumaru, would you stay here for a short while in my place? I suspect your father will be withdrawing from the battlefield at Takano soon."

"My father's fighting at Takano?"

"He's directing everything from his litter as usual."

"Well then, could I go to Takano, lead the fighting in my father's place, and tell him to go to Lord Hanbei's bedside?"

"You've spoken well! Go, if you have that kind of courage."

"As long as Lord Hanbei is still breathing, my father will want to be with him. He won't say it, but I'm sure that Lord Hanbei wants to see my father, too." Shojumaru spoke gallantly and, grasping a spear that looked much too big for him, dashed off toward the foothills.

Hideyoshi walked off in the opposite direction, gradually lengthening his stride. Lamplight spilled from one of the huts. It was the one Takenaka Hanbei slept in, and just at that moment the moon began to shine faintly over the roof. The doctor Hideyoshi had sent was at the bedside, as were Hanbei's retainers. The hut was hardly more than a wooden fence, but white coverlets had been piled on the rush mats, and in one corner stood a folding screen.

"Hanbei, can you hear me? It's me, Hideyoshi. How do you feel?" He sat quietly at his friend's side, looking at his face on the pillow. Perhaps because of the darkness, Hanbei's face was as luminescent as a jewel. One could not help shedding tears, wondering that a man could become so thin. It was a heartrending sight for Hideyoshi; just looking at the man was painful.

"Doctor, how is he?"

The doctor could say nothing. His silent answer meant that it was only a matter of time, but Hideyoshi really wanted to hear that there might be some hope.

The sick man moved his hand slightly. He seemed to have heard Hideyoshi's voice, and, barely opening his eyes, he tried to say something to one of his attendants, who replied, "His Lordship has been kind enough to come visit you...to be at your bedside...."

Hanbei nodded but seemed to be fretful about something. He appeared to be ordering the man to help him up.

"What do you think?" an attendant inquired, looking at the doctor. The doctor was hardly able to answer. Hideyoshi understood what Hanbei wanted.

"What? You want to sit up? Why not stay in bed?" he said, soothing him as though he were calming a child. Hanbei shook his head slightly and once again chided his attendants. He was unable to speak in a loud voice, but his desire could plainly be seen in his hollow eyes. They gently raised the upper half of the sick man's plank-thin body, but when they tried to help him sit up, Hanbei pushed them away. He bit his lip and gradually got out of bed. This act clearly require a huge effort on the part of a sick man who by now could hardly breathe.

Transfixed by what they were witnessing, Hideyoshi, the doctor, and Hanbei's retainers could only hold their breath and watch. Finally, when he had crawled a few paces from his bedding, Hanbei knelt properly on the reed matting. With the sharp points of his shoulders, his thin knees, and his sallow hands, Hanbei looked almost like a young girl. He closed his mouth tightly and appeared to be controlling his breath. Finally he bowed so low that it seemed he might break.

"My farewell to you is approaching this evening. Once again I must show my gratitude for the many years of your great benevolence." Then he paused for a moment. "Whether the leaves fall or bloom, live or die, when you reflect deeply on the matter, it would appear that the colors of autumn and spring fill the entire universe. I have felt that the world is an interesting place. My lord, I have been tied by karma to you and have received your kind treatment. When I look back, my only regret at parting is that I have been of no service to you at all."

There was only a thread of his voice left, but it smoothly left his lips. Everyone present adjusted his posture and sat quietly at this solemn miracle. Hideyoshi, especially, straightened his back, hung his head, and, with both hands on his lap, listened as though he could not bear to miss a single word. The lamp ready to go out will flare up brightly just before it dies. Hanbei's life now was like that, for one sublime moment. He continued to speak, desperately struggling to leave Hideyoshi his last words.

"All the events...all the events and changes the world will go through hereafter...I sympathize with truly. Japan is presently on the verge of a great change. I would like to see what will happen to the nation. This is what is in my heart, but my allotted span of life will not allow me to have my wish." His words gradually became more and more clear, and he appeared to be speaking with the last strength left to him. His body naturally gasped for air momentarily, but he controlled the heaving of his shoulders and held his breath to continue speaking.

"But...my lord...do you, yourself, not think that you were chosen to be born in a time like this? Looking carefully at you, I cannot see in you the ambition to become the ruler of the nation." Here he paused for a moment. "Until now, this had been a strong point and part of your character. It's rude of me to bring it up, but when you were Lord Nobunaga's sandal bearer, you put your whole heart into the duties of a sandal bearer; and when you had the status of a samurai, you put all of your capacities into carrying out the duties of a samurai. Never once did you have the wild fancy of looking up and trying to launch yourself higher. What I fear most now is that—true to this mentality—you will complete your duties in the western provinces, or totally satisfy your commission from Lord Nobunaga, or again, that you will simply subdue Miki Castle, and that except for the close attention you pay to these things, you will not think about current events or of ways of distinguishing yourself."

It was so quiet that it seemed as if no one else were in the room. Hideyoshi was listening so intently that it looked as if he could not lift his head or move.

"But…the great capacity that a man needs to gain control over this kind of age is given by heaven. Rival warlords fight for hegemony, each of them bragging that no one but he will be able to bring a new dawn to the chaotic world and save the people from their distress. But Kenshin, who was such an excellent man, has gone on to his death; Shingen of Kai has passed away; the great Motonari of the western provinces left the world having advised his descendants to protect their inheritance by knowing their own capacities; and beyond that, both the Asai and the Asakura brought destruction upon themselves. Who is going to bring this problem to a conclusion? Who has the force of will to be able to create the culture of the next era and be accepted by the people? Such men are fewer than the fingers on one hand."

Hideyoshi suddenly lifted his head, and a beam of light seemed to come directly at him from Hanbei's sunken eyes. Hanbei was close to death, and even Hideyoshi could not be sure of his own life span, but for a moment their eyes wrestled in silence.

"I know that in your heart you are probably confused by the things I am saying, because you now serve Lord Nobunaga. I can understand your feelings. But Providence has clearly set him on the stage to perform a difficult mission. Neither you nor Lord Ieyasu has the kind of spirit that is required to break through the present situation, nor the faith to rise above all the many difficulties that have presented themselves until now. Who, other than Lord Nobunaga, would have been capable of leading the country thus far through the chaos of the age? But that is still not to say that the world has been renewed by his actions. Just by subjugating the western provinces, attacking Kyushu, and pacifying Shikoku, the nation will not necessarily be pacified, the four classes of people will not live peace and harmony, a new culture will not be established, nor will the cornerstone of prosperity for succeeding generations be laid."

Hanbei seemed to have reflected on these things deeply, drawing insights from the wisdom of the ancient Chinese classics. He had compared the transitions of modern times with historical events and had analyzed the complex undercurrents of the present situation.

During the years he had served on Hideyoshi's field staff, his mind had been forming a general view of Japan's development. His conclusions he kept secret. Was Hideyoshi not "the next man"? Even among his retainers, who were close to him day and night, and

531

who saw him fighting periodically with his wife, rejoicing over some trivial matter, looking dispirited, and talking foolishly—or who compared him in terms of appearance with the lords of other clans and did not find him superior at all—there did not seem to be one out of ten who considered their lord to have superior natural talents. But Hanbei did not regret having served at this man's side or having spent half his life for his sake, rather, he rejoiced greatly that heaven had bound him to such a lord, and he felt that life had been absolutely worth living right up to the point of his death.

If this lord carries out the role that I believe he will, and accomplishes the great task of the future, Hanbei thought, my life will not have been in vain. My own ideals will most likely be carried out in the world in some form with his spirit and future. People may say that I died young, but I will have died well.

"Beyond that," he said, "there is really nothing more to say. Please, my lord, take good care of yourself. Believe that you yourself are irreplaceable, and strive even harder after I am gone." As Hanbei finished speaking, his chest crumpled like a piece of rotten wood. There was no longer any strength in the thin hands that should have supported him. His face fell flat against the floor; a pool of blood spread over the matting like the blooming of a red peony.

Hideyoshi jumped forward and held Hanbei's head, and the blood that was now gushing out stained his lap and chest.

"Hanbei! Hanbei! Are you leaving me alone? Are you going off by yourself? What am I going to do on the battlefield without you from now on?" he cried, weeping copiously, without regard for either his appearance or his reputation.

Hanbei's white face now lay limply, his head resting on Hideyoshi's lap. "No, from now on you won't have to worry about anything."

Those who are born the morning, die before the evening; and those who are born in the evening are dead before the dawn. Such facts do not necessarily bespeak the Buddhist view of impermanence, so one might wonder why it was specifically Hanbei's death that sent Hideyoshi into the depths of despair. He was, after all, on a battlefield, where every day men fell like autumn leaves from the branches. But the extent of his grief was such that even the people who were grieving with him were dumbfounded, and when he finally came to himself—like a child after a tantrum—he softly lifted Hanbei's cold body from his lap and, unaided, placed it on top of the white bedding, whispering to it as though Hanbei were still alive.

"Even if you had lived two or three times the normal life span, you had such great—almost unbearable—ideas that your hopes might still have been only half fulfilled. You did not want to die. If it had been me, I wouldn't have wanted to die either. Right, Hanbei? How many things you must have regretted leaving undone. Ah, when your kind of genius is born into this world, and less than a hundredth of your thoughts are brought to fruition, it's natural that you wouldn't want to die."

How much love he had for the man! Over and over he complained to Hanbei's corpse. He did not fold his hands and recite a prayer, but his pleas to the dead man were endless.

Kanbei, who had been informed of Hanbei's condition by his son, had just arrived.

"Am I too late?" Kanbei asked anxiously, limping in as fast as he could. There was

Hideyoshi, sitting with red eyes at the bedside, and there lay the cold, lifeless body of Hanbei. Kanbei sat down with a heavy groan, as though both his body and his spirit had been crushed. Kanbei and Hideyoshi sat quietly, without speaking, looking at Hanbei's body.

The room was as dark as a cave, but no lamp was lit. The white bedding beneath the corpse looked like snow at the bottom of a ravine.

"Kanbei," Hideyoshi finally said, sounding as though grief were pouring from his entire body, "it's pitiful. I had thought it would be difficult, but…"

Kanbei could not say much in response. He seemed to be in a daze, too. "Ah, I just don't understand it. He was fine six months ago. And now this." After a pause, he continued as though he had suddenly come to himself. "Well, come on. Are all of you just going to sit here crying? Someone light a lamp. We should clean his body, sweep the room, and lay him out in state. Everything must be done for a proper battlefield funeral."

While Kanbei gave orders, Hideyoshi disappeared. In the flickering light of the lamps, as people began to work stiffly, someone discovered a letter left that Hanbei had left beneath his pillow. It was addressed to Kanbei, and had been written two days before.

They buried Hanbei on Mount Hirai, the autumn wind blowing sadly through the mourning flags.

Kanbei showed Hanbei's last letter to Hideyoshi. It contained nothing about himself; he had written about Hideyoshi, and about the plans he had had in mind for future operations. In part it read:

> Even if my body should die and turn to white bones beneath the earth, if my lord will not forget my sincerity and will recall me in his heart even accidentally, my soul will breathe into my lord's present existence and never fail to serve him even from the grave.

Considering his service to have been insufficient but not begrudging his early death, Hanbei had waited for that death in the full belief that he would serve his lord even after he had become nothing but whitened bones. Now, when Hideyoshi considered Hanbei's inmost feelings, he could not help but cry. No matter how hard he tried to control his tears, he could not stop them.

Kanbei finally spoke sternly. "My lord, I don't think you should go on grieving like this. Please read the rest of the letter, and think carefully. Lord Hanbei has written down a plan to take Miki Castle."

Kanbei had always been completely devoted to Hideyoshi, but in the present situation, his voice was showing a little impatience at Hideyoshi's unreserved demonstration of the emotional side of his character.

In his letter Hanbei had predicted that Miki Castle would fall within one hundred days. But he also cautioned that a victory should not be accomplished simply by making a frontal attack and injuring their own soldiers, and he had written down a final plan:

> In Miki Castle there is no man with more discrimination than General Goto Moto-kuni. In my own view, he is not the kind of soldier who does not understand the

country's situation and demonstrates his toughness by going blindly into a battle. Before this campaign, I sat and talked with him a number of times at Himeji Castle, so you might say there is a slight friendship between us. I have written a letter to him, urging him to explain the advantages and disadvantages of the present situation to his lord, Bessho Nagaharu. If Lord Nagaharu understands everything that Goto says, he should be enlightened enough to surrender the castle and sue for peace. But to put this plan into operation, it is essential to gauge the right psychological moment. The best time of all, I think, would be late fall, when the earth is covered with dead leaves, the moon is solitary and cold in the sky, and in their hearts, the soldiers yearn for their fathers, mothers, sisters, and brothers, and have feelings of nostalgia in spite of themselves. The soldiers in the castle are already pressed by starvation, and when they feel that winter is coming, they're sure to realize that death is near and to feel all the more full of self-pity and misery. To make a strong attack at that time will do nothing more than give them a good place to die and provide them with traveling companions for their climb over the mountain of death. But if you were to postpone the attack for a while at this point and, after giving them the chance to think coolly, send a letter explaining the matter to Lord Nagaharu and his retainers, I have no doubt that you will see a conclusion within the year.

Kanbei saw that Hideyoshi had doubts about whether Hanbei's plan could succeed, and now he added a point of his own.

"The fact is that Hanbei spoke about this plan two or three times when he was alive, but it was put off because the time was still not ripe. If I may have my lord's permission, I will go at any time as an envoy and meet Goto in Miki Castle."

"No, wait," Hideyoshi said, shaking his head. "Wasn't it just last spring that we used this same plan, approaching one of the generals in the castle through the connections of Asano Yahei's relatives? There was no answer. We found out later that when our man advised Bessho Nagaharu to capitulate, the generals and soldiers got angry and cut him to pieces. The plan that Hanbei has left us sounds a little like that one, doesn't it? In fact, it's the same thing, I believe. If it's handled badly, we'll only let them know our weakness, and nothing will be gained."

"No, I think that is why Hanbei emphasized the importance of judging the correct moment. And I suspect that that moment is now."

"You think it's the right time?"

"I believe it absolutely." Just then, they heard voices outside the enclosure. Along with the voices of the generals and soldiers they were accustomed to, they could also hear a woman's voice. It was that of Hanbei's sister, Oyu. As soon as she had been informed that her brother was in a critical condition, she had left Kyoto, accompanied by only a few attendants. With the thought of seeing his face just once more while he was still in this world, she had rushed anxiously to Mount Hirai, but as she came closer to the front lines, the road had become more difficult. In the end, she was too late.

To Hideyoshi, the woman now bowing before him had completely changed. He gazed at her traveling outfit and emaciated face and then, as he started to speak, Kanbei and the pages deliberately went outside to leave them alone. Oyu could only shed tears at first, and for a long time could not look up at Hideyoshi. Throughout his absence during the long campaign she had longed to see him, but now that she was in front of him, she could hardly go to his side.

"You have heard that Hanbei is dead?"

"Yes."

"You must be resigned to it. There was nothing we could do."

Oyu's heart collapsed like melting snow, and her body was convulsed with sobs.

"Stop crying; this is unbecoming." Hideyoshi lost his composure, hardly knowing what to do. Even though there was no one else present, the attendants were immediately outside the enclosure, and he felt constrained by the thought of what they might hear.

"Let's go to Hanbei's grave together," Hideyoshi said, and he led Oyu along the mountain path behind the camp to the top of a small hill.

A chilly late-autumn wind moaned through the branches of a solitary pine. Beneath it was a mound of fresh earth, upon which a single stone had been placed as a grave marker. In former times, during leisure hours in the long siege, a reed mat had been placed at the foot of this pine, and Kanbei, Hanbei, and Hideyoshi had sat together, talking over the past and present while looking at the moon.

Oyu parted the bushes, looking for some flowers to put on the grave. Then she faced the mound of earth and bowed beside Hideyoshi. Her tears no longer fell. Here at the top of the mountain, the grasses and trees of late autumn demonstrated that such a condition was a natural principle of the universe. Autumn passes into winter, winter passes into spring—in nature there is neither grief nor tears.

"My lord, I have a request, and I'd like to ask it in front of my brother's grave."

"Yes?"

"Perhaps you understand...in your heart."

"I do understand."

"I would like you to let me go. If you'll grant me that, I know my brother will be relieved, even under the earth."

"Hanbei died saying that his spirit would serve me even from the grave. How can I turn my back on something that he worried about when he was alive? You should do as your heart tells you."

"Thank you. With your permission, I will do my best to honor his dying wish."

"Where will you go?"

"To a temple in some remote village." Once again she shed tears.

* * *

Granted a dismissal by Hideyoshi, Oyu received a lock of her brother's hair and his clothes. It was inappropriate for a woman to be in a military camp for a long time, and the next day Oyu went immediately to Hideyoshi and told him she had made her travel preparations.

"I'm here to say good-bye. Please, please take care of yourself," she told him.

"Won't you stay two or three more days in camp?" Hideyoshi asked.

For the next few days Oyu stayed alone in an isolated hut, praying for her brother's soul. The days passed without any word from Hideyoshi. Frost had descended on the mountains. Each time the early-winter rains came down, the leaves fell from the trees. Then, on the first night that the moon appeared clearly, a page came to Oyu and said, "His Lordship would like to see you. He has asked that you make preparations to leave this evening and that you go up now to Lord Hanbei's grave on the mountain."

Oyu had few preparations to make for the trip. She set off for her brother's grave with Kumataro and two other attendants. The trees had lost their leaves and the grass had withered, and the mountain had a desolate appearance. The ground looked white in the moonlight, as if there had been a frost.

One of the half-dozen retainers in attendance on Hideyoshi announced Oyu's arrival.

"Thank you for coming, Oyu," Hideyoshi began gently. "I've been so busy with military matters since we last met that I haven't been able to visit you. It's become so cold lately, you must be lonely."

"I have resigned myself to spending the rest of my life in an isolated village, so I won't be lonely."

"I hope that you'll pray for Hanbei's soul. Wherever you choose to live, I suspect we'll meet again." He turned to Hanbei's grave under the pine tree. "Oyu, I have something prepared for you over there. I doubt that I'll ever be able to hear the lovely sound of your *koto* again, after tonight. A long time ago, you were with Hanbei at the siege of the castle at Choteiken in Mino. You played the *koto* and softened the hearts of soldiers who had become like demons, and they finally surrendered. If you would play now, it would be an offering to Hanbei's soul, I think, as well as becoming a remembrance for me. Also, if the notes were carried by the wind to the castle, they might shock the enemy soldiers into thinking of their own humanity and make them aware that their deaths now would be meaningless. That would be a great achievement, and even Hanbei would rejoice."

He led her over to the pine tree, where a *koto* had been placed on top of a reed mat.

Having resisted a siege of three years with all their courage and integrity, the warriors of the western provinces, who looked down on other men as being frivolous and vain, were now reduced to shadows of their former selves.

"I don't care if I die fighting today or tomorrow, I just don't want to die of starvation," one of the defenders said.

They had fallen into such an extremity that dying in battle was their last remaining hope. The defenders still looked like men, but they were now reduced to sucking the bones of their own dead horses and eating field mice, tree bark, and roots, and they anticipated having to boil the tatami mats and eating the clay on the walls in the coming winter. As they consoled each other, sunken eye to sunken eye, they still had enough spirit to be able to plan on getting through the winter as best as they could. Indeed, even in small skirmishes, when the enemy drew near, they could suddenly forget their hunger and fatigue and go out to fight.

For more than half a month, however, the attacking troops had not approached the castle, and this neglect was more bitter to the defending troops than any desperate death. When the sun went down, the entire castle was sunk into a darkness so deep it might just as well have fallen to the bottom of a swamp. Not one lamp was lit. All of the fish oil and rapeseed oil had been consumed as food. Many of the small shrikes and sparrows that had flocked morning and night to the trees in the grounds had been caught and eaten, and recently the ones that remained had stopped coming to the castle, knowing, perhaps, what would be in store for them. The men had eaten so many crows that now they were rarely even able to catch one. In the midst of the darkness, the eyes of the sentries would quicken at the sound of something like a weasel scampering by. Instinctively, their gastric juices would begin to flow, and they would look at each other and grimace. "My stomach feels like it's being wrung out like a damp cloth."

The moon that evening was beautiful, but the soldiers only wished it could be eaten. The dead leaves fell in profusion on the roofs of the fortress and around the castle gate. A soldier munched greedily on them.

"Taste good? someone asked.

"Better than straw," he answered, and picked up another one. Suddenly looking queasy, he coughed several times and vomited the leaves he had just eaten.

"General Goto!" someone suddenly announced, and everyone stood to attention. Goto Motokuni, chief retainer of the Bessho clan, walked toward the soldiers from the darkened keep.

"Anything to report?" Goto asked.

"Nothing, sir."

"Really?" Goto showed them an arrow. "Sometime this evening, this arrow was shot into the castle by the enemy. A letter was tied to it, asking me to meet with one of Lord Hideyoshi's generals, Kuroda Kanbei, here tonight."

"Kanbei is coming here tonight! A man who betrayed his lord for the Oda. He's not fit to be a samurai. When he shows up, we'll torture him to death."

"He's Lord Hideyoshi's envoy, and it would not be right to kill someone whose arrival has been announced beforehand. It's an agreement among warriors that one does not kill messengers."

"That would be all right even for an enemy general if it were someone else. But with Kanbei, I feel like I wouldn't be content even eating the meat off his bones."

"Don't let the enemy see what's in your heart. Laugh when you greet him."

Just as Goto gazed out into the darkness, he and the men seemed to hear the intermittent sounds of a distant *koto*. At that moment Miki Castle became enveloped in a strange hush. In a night the color of India ink, it seemed as though no one could even breathe while the falling leaves swirled and danced formlessly in an uncanny sky.

"A *koto*?" one of the soldiers said, looking up into the void.

They listened almost in ecstasy to the nostalgic sound. The men in the watchtower, in the guardroom, and in every section of the fortress were caught by the same thoughts. Through storms of arrows, gunfire, and war cries—from dawn until dusk, and from dusk again until dawn—the men who had been in this castle for three years cut off from the outside world had steadfastly dug themselves in, without yielding or withdrawing. Now the sound of the *koto* suddenly called up various thoughts in their minds.

My ancestral home,

Will you wait
For a man who knows not
If tonight will be
His last?

This was the death poem that Kikuchi Taketoki, Emperor Godaigo's loyal general, had sent to his wife when he was surrounded by a rebel army.

As the men considered their own situations, there were some who unconsciously recited the poem to themselves. Surely there were soldiers, far away from their homes, who thought of their mothers, children, and brothers and sisters of whom they had had no news. Even the soldiers who had nothing to go back to did not have hearts made of stone, and were swayed by the feelings evoked by the *koto*. No one could stop his tears.

In his heart, Goto felt just the same as his men, but when he saw the expressions on the faces of the soldiers around him, he quickly pulled himself together. He spoke to his men with intentional cheer. "What? Sounds of the *koto* are coming from the enemy camp? What fools! Why would they have a *koto*? That shows how soft the enemy warriors really are. They've probably gotten tired of the long campaign, have grabbed some singing girl from a village, and are trying to amuse themselves. For minds to be so disheveled is unpardonable. The steel and rock-hard souls of true warriors are not so weak!"

As he spoke, each man awoke from his reverie.

"Instead of listening to such foolery, let each man guard his own post. These castles are just like a dike that holds back a flood of dirty water. The dike is meandering and long, but if one little bit of it crumbles, the entire structure will collapse. Each of you should stand, and linked breast to breast, not move even if you die. As for Miki Castle, if it were said that someone abandoned his post and the entire castle collapsed as a result, his ancestors would weep from beneath the earth and his descendants would bear the shame of the province and be nothing more than laughing-stocks."

Goto was urging his men on like this when he saw two or three soldiers running up to the castle. They quickly informed him that the enemy general whose visit had been announced earlier had come as far as the palisade at the bottom of the slope.

Kanbei arrived, carried in a litter. The litter was a light structure made of wood, straw, and bamboo. There was no roof, and the sides were low. He had learned to brandish his long sword from the litter when he fought with the enemy in battle. But tonight he had come as an envoy of peace.

Over a light yellow robe, Kanbei wore armor threaded with pale green, and a coat of silver embroidery on a white background. Luckily he was a small man, about five feet tall and lighter than average, so the men who carried him were not uncomfortable, and he himself did not feel cramped.

Footsteps could soon be heard inside the palisade gate. A number of soldiers from the castle had run back down the slope.

"Envoy, you may pass through!" they announced. At the same time Kanbei heard this stern shout, the palisade gate before him opened. In the darkness he thought that he could see a hundred or more soldiers jostling together. Each time the wave of men pitched and rolled, the glint of their spears pierced his eyes.

"I'm sorry to trouble you," Kanbei said to the man who had shouted at him. "I am lame, so I'll be coming through in a litter. Please excuse my lack of manners." With this apology, he turned and spoke to his son, Shojumaru, the only attendant who had accompanied him, and ordered, "Walk in front of me."

"Yes, sir." Edging around his father's litter, Shojumaru walked straight through the enemies' spears.

The four soldiers shouldering the litter followed through the palisade gate behind Shojumaru. When they saw how composed the thirteen-year-old boy and the lame warrior looked as they walked into their camp, the bloodthirsty and ravenous soldiers could hardly feel any anger, even though they were looking at the enemy. They could now understand that the enemy was fighting this battle with a determination and perseverance equal to their own and so could sympathize with the envoys as warriors. Strangely, they even felt a sort of compassion for them.

After passing through the palisade and the castle gate, Kanbei and his son quickly came to the main entrance, where Goto and his picked troops were waiting with solemn indifference.

I can see how this castle has been defended by these men, Kanbei thought as he approached the gate. The castle won't fall even though there's no food. They'll hold out, no matter what the cost. He could see that the courage of the men had not waned in the least, and he felt the weight of his own responsibility even more. This feeling immediately became transformed into a deep concern for the grave situation that Hideyoshi now faced. Kanbei silently renewed his pledge in his own heart. Somehow, he thought, this mission I've been entrusted with has got to succeed.

Goto and his men were surprised by the envoy's demeanor. Here was the general of the attacking troops, but, instead of looking at them with arrogance, he had come accompanied by only a charming young man. Not only that, but when this Kanbei greeted Goto, he hurriedly had his litter lowered to the ground and, standing on his legs, greeted him with a smile.

"General Goto, I am Kuroda Kanbei, and I am here as Lord Hideyoshi's envoy. I'm certainly obliged that everyone has come out to meet me."

Kanbei was completely unaffected. As an envoy from the enemy, he had made an exceptionally favorable impression. This was probably because he had approached them from his heart, disregarding concern for victory or defeat, and had acted with the custom and understanding that both he and his enemy were samurai. This, however, was not reason enough for the enemy to accept the point of his mission: to persuade them to capitulate. Kanbei talked with Goto in a room in the lightless castle for an hour or so and then rose from his seat, saying, "Well then, I'll wait for your answer."

"I'll give you one after conferring with Lord Nagaharu and the other generals," Goto said, also standing up. Thus the pattern of the interview that night indicated that the negotiations were to be successful beyond Kanbei's and Hideyoshi's expectations—but five days passed, then seven, then ten, and still there was no sign of an answer from the castle. The Twelfth Month came and went, and the opposing armies greeted the third New Year of the siege. In Hideyoshi's camp, the men at least had some rice cakes to eat and a little *sake* to drink, but they could hardly forget that the men in the castle, although they were the enemy, had nothing to eat and were barely holding on to their fragile lives. From the time of Kanbei's mission at the end of the Eleventh Month, Miki Castle had truly sunk into desolation and silence. It was understood that the soldiers lacked even bullets to shoot at the attackers. Hideyoshi, however, still refrained from an all-out offensive, saying, "Perhaps the castle will not hold out much longer."

If, then, the siege was simply an endurance contest, Hideyoshi's present position was hardly difficult or unfavorable. But the fact was that neither the camp at Mount Hirai nor Hideyoshi's position were matters of his own private battle. He was essentially striking against one link in the enemy alliance made up of those who opposed Nobunaga's supremacy; and he was nothing more than one of the limbs of Nobunaga's body that was trying to break open a hole to break through the encircling chain of his enemies. Little by little, therefore, Nobunaga had started to wonder about the lack of action in the protracted western campaign.

And Hideyoshi's enemies on Nobunaga's field staff were wondering about his choice of commander, saying that Hideyoshi's responsibilities had been too heavy for him from the start.

His rivals cited as proof their feelings that, either Hideyoshi was wasting military expenses in a bid for popularity among the local people, or he was not very strict about the prohibition of *sake* in camp because he was afraid of the soldiers' antipathy. But whatever his rivals wished to question, it was easy to see that, one by one, all the trifling matters that were not worth reaching Nobunaga's ears were heard in Azuchi and were considered material for slander. But Hideyoshi never paid much attention to the talk. Certainly he was a human being and had normal feelings like everyone else, and it wasn't that he didn't notice such things; he simply didn't worry about them.

"Trivial matters are nothing but that," he said. "Whenever they're investigated, they'll be cleared up." The only thing that did make him unhappy was the thought that with every passing day, the anti-Nobunaga coalition was getting stronger: the powerful Mori clan was building up its defenses, making plans with the Honganji, calling on the faraway Takeda and Hojo in the east, and inciting the clans of the Japan Sea coast. How strong these forces really were could be understood by observing the fact that Araki Murashige's castle in Itami, which the central army was presently besieging, had still not fallen.

What Murashige was depending on, and what the Bessho clan was stubbornly holding on to, was not only their own strength and their own castle walls. Soon the Mori army will come to our aid! Nobunaga will be defeated soon! That was it. Generally, the worst state of affairs was not in the enemy Nobunaga faced directly but in the enemy waiting in the shadows.

The two ancient forces of the Honganji and the Mori were quite correctly Nobunaga's enemies, but it was Araki Murashige at Itami and Bessho Nagaharu, at Miki Castle, who were grappling directly with Nobunaga's ambition.

That evening Hideyoshi suddenly decided to have a bonfire lit, and was warding off the night cold, when he turned to see the carefree young pages drawing up close to the fire. They were half naked even in the cold of the First Month, and were making a noise over something that seemed to be amusing them.

"Sakichi! Shojumaru! What in the world are you two in an uproar about?" Hideyoshi asked, almost envious of their lightheartedness.

"Nothing at all," answered Shojumaru, who had recently become a page, and he hurriedly dressed and adjusted his armor.

"My lord," Ishida Sakichi interjected. "Shojumaru's embarrassed to talk to you about it because it's disgusting. But I'm going to speak up, because if we don't tell you, you might get suspicious."

"All right. What is this disgusting thing?"

"We've been picking lice off each other."

"Lice?"

"Yes. At first someone found one crawling on my collar, then Toranosuke found one on Sengoku's sleeve. Finally, everybody was saying that everyone else was infested, and in the middle of it all, when we came here to warm ourselves by the fire, we found lice crawling all over everyone's armor. Now they've started to itch, so we're going to massacre the entire enemy army. We're going to purge our underwear just like the burning of Mount Hiei!"

"Is that so?" Hideyoshi laughed. "I guess the lice are also worn out from being besieged in this long campaign."

"But our situation is different from that of Miki Castle. The lice have plenty of provisions, so if we don't burn them out, they'll never give up."

"That's enough. I'm beginning to itch, too."

"You haven't taken a bath for over ten days, have you, my lord? I'm sure the 'enemy' must be holding out all over you in swarms!"

"That's enough, Sakichi!" To the delight of the pages, Hideyoshi rushed over and shook his body at them as further proof that the lice were not swarming over them alone. They laughed and danced around.

Just then a soldier peeked in from outside the camp enclosure at the happy, laughing voices and the billowing warm smoke.

"Is Shojumaru here?"

"Yes, I'm here," Shojumaru said. The soldier was one of his father's retainers.

"If you're not busy with some errand, your father would like to see you."

Shojumaru asked for Hideyoshi's permission. Since this request was not ordinarily made, Hideyoshi looked surprised, but quickly gave his assent. Shojumaru ran off, accompanied by his father's retainer. Fires were burning at all of the small encampments, and every one of the units was in a cheerful mood. They had already run out of rice cakes and *sake*, but some of the New Year's spirit remained. This evening marked the fifteenth day of the First Month. Shojumaru's father was not in camp. Despite the cold, he was sitting on a camp stool that had been placed at the crest of a hill far from the makeshift barracks.

There was no shelter from the wind, and it stung the flesh and almost froze the blood. But Kanbei stared out intently into the dark expanse, as though he were a wooden statue of a warrior.

"Father, it's me."

Kanbei moved slightly as Shojumaru stepped to his side and knelt.

"Did you receive your lord's permission to come?"

"Yes, and I came right over."

"Well then, sit on my camp stool for just a little."

"Yes, sir."

"Look at Miki Castle. The stars are not out, and there's not a single lamp lit in the castle, so you probably can't see a thing. But the castle will appear dimly out of that void as your eyes get accustomed to the darkness."

"Is that what you wanted me for, sir?"

"Yes," Kanbei said, as he yielded the camp stool to his son. "For the last two or three days I've been watching the castle, and somehow I get the feeling that there is movement going on inside. We haven't seen a bit of smoke for half a year, but some is rising now, and perhaps that's evidence that the grove that envelops the castle—and the only thing that screens it from the outside—is being cut down and used for firewood. If you listen very carefully late at night, it seems that you can hear voices, but it's difficult to say whether they are crying or laughing. Whichever it is, the fact is that something unusual has happened inside the castle over the New Year."

"Do you really think so?"

"There's nothing that has actually appeared in form, and if I made a mistake and talked about it carelessly, it might cause our men to become tense for no reason. That could be a serious mistake on my part and create an unguarded moment the enemy could take advantage of. No, it's simply that I sat here on this camp stool looking at the castle last night and the night before, feeling that something was going on. Not just looking with my eyes but with my mind's eye."

"This is a difficult watch."

"Yes, it is difficult, but you could also say that it's easy. All you have to do is calm your mind and get rid of delusion. That's why I can't call any of the other soldiers. I want you to sit here instead of me for just a little while."

"I understand."

"Don't doze off. You're right in the middle of a chilly wind, but once you get used to it, you'll get sleepy."

"I'll be all right."

"One other thing. Inform the other generals as soon as you get even a glimpse of something like fire in the castle. And if you see soldiers leaving the castle from any point, light the fuse of the signal flare and then run to His Lordship."

"Yes, sir."

Shojumaru nodded as he looked calmly at the flare that had been planted in the ground in front of him. It was a natural battlefield situation, but his father did not once ask him if the task was difficult or painful, nor did he ever try to soothe the boy. Shojumaru understood quite well, however, that his father was always teaching him the common sense of military science, according to the event or time. He could feel an inward warmth, even in his father's gravity, and considered himself to be extremely lucky.

Kanbei picked up his staff and limped off toward the barracks. But instead of entering the camp, he seemed to be continuing on alone down the mountain, and his attendants asked nervously where he was going.

"To the foothills," Kanbei answered simply, and even though he was supporting himself with the staff, he began to hop down the mountain path almost with a lightness in his step. The men who had been accompanying him, Mori Tahei and Kuriyama Zensuke, bounded down the mountain after him.

"My lord!" Mori called. "Please wait!"

Kanbei stood, holding his staff for a moment, and looked back toward them. "It's you two?"

"I'm surprised how fast you're going," Mori said, panting. "With that injured leg, I'm afraid you'll get hurt."

"I've gotten used to the limp," Kanbei laughed. "I'll only fall down if I think about it when I walk. Recently I've been able to get around fairly naturally. But I don't want to show off."

"Could you do that in the middle of a battle?"

"I think the litter is best on the battlefield. Even in close fighting, I'm free to hold the sword with both hands or to grab the spear from the enemy and even to thrust it back at him. The only thing I can't do as I am is to run back and forth. When I'm up on top of the litter and see the surging enemy troops, I'm filled with an irresistible feeling. I feel like the enemy's going to retreat just at the sound of my voice."

"Ah, but it's dangerous now. There's still snow in the shaded areas of the steep cliff roads around here, and you're liable to slip in the wash from the melting snow."

"There's a mountain stream right below here, isn't there?"

"Shall I carry you across?" Mori offered his back.

Kanbei was carried piggyback across the stream. Where were they going? The two retainers still had no idea. A few hours before, they had seen a warrior come down from the palisade at the foot of the mountain and hand Kanbei something that looked like a letter, and soon thereafter, they had been called abruptly to accompany Kanbei to the foothills, but they had heard nothing more.

When they had walked a good distance, Kuriyama broached the subject. "My lord, did the commander at the post in the foothills invite you this evening?"

"What? Did you think we'd been called out for a meal?" Kanbei chuckled. "How long do you think the New Year lasts? Even Lord Hideyoshi's tea ceremonies are over."

"Well then, where are we going?"

"To the palisade at the Miki River."

"The palisade near the river? That's a dangerous place!"

"Of course it's dangerous. But the enemy considers it dangerous, too. It's right where the two camps meet."

"Well, shouldn't we bring more men?"

"No, no. The enemy isn't bringing a big crowd either. I think there will be only one attendant and a child."

"A child?"

"Right."

"I don't understand."

"Well, just come along quietly. It's not that I can't tell you, but it's better to keep it a secret for the time being. After the castle falls, I will inform Lord Hideyoshi about it, too, I think."

"The castle is going to fall?"

"What are we going to do if it doesn't? First of all, the castle is probably going to fall in the next two or three days. It might even happen tomorrow."

"Tomorrow!" The two retainers stared at Kanbei. His face shone dimly white with the shimmering of the clear water. The dry reeds rustled in the shallows. Mori and Kuriyama stopped in fear. They could see a figure standing among the reeds on the far bank.

"Who is it?" Their next surprise was different from their first. The man appeared to be an important enemy general, but his only attendant was carrying a young child on his back. There was no indication the three of them had come with a hostile intent. They simply seemed to be waiting quietly for Kanbei's party to approach.

"Wait here," Kanbei ordered.

Obeying their lord's orders, the two retainers watched him closely as he walked away.

As Kanbei approached, the enemy standing in the reeds also stepped forward a pace or two. As soon as they could see each other clearly, they exchanged greetings as though they were old friends. If a secret meeting between enemies in such a place had been witnessed by others, a conspiracy would have been suspected immediately; but the two seemed completely indifferent to such concerns.

"The child whom I shamelessly requested you to aid is on the back of that man over there. When the castle falls and I meet my end tomorrow on the battlefield, I hope you won't laugh at the passion of a father's love. He's still so innocent and naïve." This was the enemy general, the commander of Miki Castle, Goto Motokuni. He and Kanbei spoke now on familiar terms, for it had only been in the late fall of the previous year that Kanbei had gone to the castle as Hideyoshi's envoy, counseling capitulation. At that time they had spoken on very friendly terms.

"You brought him along, after all? I want to meet him. Have him brought here."

As Kanbei beckoned gently, Goto's retainer stepped out hesitantly from behind his master, loosened the cords that had strapped the child to his back, and let him down.

"How old is he?"

"Just seven." The retainer must have been waiting upon the child as a guardian for some time; he answered Kanbei while wiping tears from his eyes, bowed once, and retreated again.

"His name?" Kanbei asked, and this time the boy's father answered.

"He's called Iwanosuke. His mother has already passed away and his father will too, soon. Lord Kanbei, I entreat you to look after the child's future."

"Don't worry. I am also a father. I understand your feelings very well, and will absolutely see to it that he is brought up under my own hand. After he becomes an adult, the Goto family name will not die out."

"Then I can die tomorrow morning with no regrets." Goto knelt down and held his son to the breast of his armor. "Listen well to what your father is saying now. You're already seven years old. The child of a samurai never cries. Your coming-of-age ceremony is still far away, and you're at an age when you would like to have your mother's love and be at your father's side. But now the world is full of battles like this one. We can't help it that you're being separated from me, and it's natural that I should die with my lord. But you are not really so unfortunate. You've been lucky enough to be with me until this evening, and you should give great thanks to the gods of heaven and earth for that good luck. All right? So from tonight on, you'll be by the side of that man right there, Kuroda Kanbei. He'll be your master and the parent who brings you up, so serve him well. Do you understand?"

As his father patted his head and spoke to him, Iwanosuke silently nodded again and again while tears rolled down his cheeks. Miki Castle's hours were now numbered. The several thousand people in the castle had quite naturally sworn to perish with their lord and were resolved to die bravely. Goto's will was adamantine, and he did not waver in the least now. But he did have a young son and could not bear to see an innocent child die. Iwanosuke was still much too young to carry the weight of having been born a samurai.

In the days preceding this meeting, Goto had sent a letter to Kanbei, whom—although an enemy—he viewed as a reliable man. Goto had opened his heart to Kanbei, asking him to bring up his son.

As he lectured his little son, he knew this was the end, and was unable to check an unguarded tear. Finally he stood up and strongly ordered him off in Kanbei's direction, almost as if he were thrusting the pitiful thing away.

"Iwanosuke, you too should request Lord Kanbei's favor."

"Put your mind completely at ease," Kanbei reassured the man as he took the child's hand. He ordered one of his retainers to take the child back to camp.

Now, for the first time that evening, Kanbei's retainers understood their master's intentions. Mori hoisted Iwanosuke onto his back and set off with Kuriyama at his side.

"Well then," Kanbei said.

"Yes, this is good-bye," replied Goto.

As they spoke, it was difficult to part. Kanbei did his best to harden his heart and leave quickly, but even though he thought it would be the kindest thing to do, he hesitated.

Finally Goto said with a smile. "Lord Kanbei, when I meet you on the battlefield tomorrow, if we're both pinned down by our personal feelings and the edge is taken off our spears, we'll be disgraced to the end of time. If the worst should happen, I'm prepared to take your head. Don't you be remiss either!" He blurted out his words like a parting shot, then immediately turned and walked off in the direction of the castle.

Kanbei quickly returned to Mount Hirai, went before Hideyoshi, and showed him Goto's son.

"Bring him up well," Hideyoshi said. "It will be an act of charity. He looks like a fine boy, doesn't he?" Hideyoshi loved children, and he looked at Iwanosuke's face fondly and patted his head.

Perhaps Iwanosuke did not yet understand; he was only seven. Being in a strange camp with strange man, he simply stared goggle-eyed at everything around him. Many years later he would become famous as a warrior of the Kuroda clan. But right now he was a solitary child, almost like a mountain monkey that had fallen out of its tree.

Finally the day came: it was announced that Miki Castle had fallen. It was the seventeenth day of the First Month of the eighth year of Tensho. Nagaharu, his younger brother Tomoyuki, and his senior retainers disemboweled themselves, the castle was opened, and Uno Uemon delivered a letter of surrender to Hideyoshi.

We resisted for two years and did everything we could as warriors. The only thing I would not be able to bear is the death of several thousand brave and loyal warriors and the members of my family. I plead for my retainers and hope that you will show them mercy.

Hideyoshi agreed to this manly request and accepted the surrender of Miki Castle.

MEN OF GOD

Although Hideyoshi and Nobunaga were stationed far apart, Hideyoshi considered it one of his military responsibilities to send news regularly to Azuchi. In this way Nobunaga was given a bird's-eye view of the situation in the west, and thus he felt at ease with the strategy being used in the campaign.

After seeing Hideyoshi off to the western provinces, Nobunaga greeted the New Year in Azuchi. It was the tenth year of Tensho. That New Year was even busier than the previous one, and the celebrations did not go off without mishap. The following incident is recorded in *The Chronicles of Nobunaga*:

> When the neighboring lords, relatives, and others came to Azuchi to pay their respects to His Lordship for the New Year, the crush was such that a wall collapsed and many were killed by the falling stones. The confusion was stupendous.

"Charge each guest from who comes for New Year's calls on the first day one hundred *mon*, no matter who he is," Nobunaga ordered on New Year's Eve. "A 'calling tax' is not much to ask of a visitor in return for the divine privilege of having an audience with me to express his New Year's wishes."

But that was not all. In recompense for the 'calling tax,' Nobunaga also gave permission to have parts of the castle grounds that were usually closed to the public opened up.

The inns of Azuchi had already been booked long before by eager sightseers—lords, merchants, scholars, doctors, artists, craftsmen, and samurai of every rank—who waited impatiently for the opportunity to see the Sokenji Temple, to pass through the Outer Gate and approach the Third Gate, and from there to go through the residential apartments and enter the garden of white sand, there to express their greetings.

The New Year's sightseers walked through the castle, looking at room after room. They admired the sliding doors illustrated by Kano Eitoku, stared wide-eyed at the tatami mats with their borders of Korean brocade, and gazed in awe at the polished, gilded walls.

The guards shepherded the crowd out through the stable gate, where, unexpectedly, its way was barred by Nobunaga and several attendants.

"Don't forget your contribution! One hundred *mon* each!" Nobunaga shouted. He took the money with his own hands and tossed it over his shoulder.

A mountain of coins quickly piled up behind him. Soldiers stuffed the money into bags, and it was then given to officials and distributed among the poor of Azuchi. Thus Nobunaga fondly imagined that there was not one hungry face in Azuchi that New Year's.

When Nobunaga spoke to the official in charge of collecting the tax, who at first had worried about Nobunaga getting involved with such plebeian actions, the official now had to admit, "It was truly a fine idea, my lord. The people who came to visit the castle will have a story to tell for the rest of their lives, and the poor who received the 'contributions' will spread the news. Everybody is saying that those coins are not just ordinary coins, but money that was touched by the hand of Lord Nobunaga himself, and as such, it would be a travesty to waste it. They said they would keep it as capital. Why, even the officials are pleased. I think this kind of good work would be a good precedent for next New Year's and for the years following."

To the official's surprise, Nobunaga coldly shook his head and said, "I'm not going to do it again. It would be a fault for the man who runs the government to let the poor get used to charity."

* * *

Half of the First Month had passed. After the New Year's decorations had been taken down from the doors of people's homes, the citizens of Azuchi realized that something was going on—so many ships were being loaded at the port and were sailing every day.

The ships, without exception, were sailing from the southern part of the lake northward. And thousands of bales of rice, carried along the land routes in meandering processions of horses and carts, were also going up the coast toward the north.

As always, the streets of Azuchi were filled with the traffic of travelers and the goings and comings of the various lords. Not a day went by that a messenger was not seen galloping down the road, or that an envoy from another province didn't pass by.

"Aren't you coming?" Nobunaga called out happily to Nakagawa Sebei.

"Where to, my lord?"

"Hawking!"

"That's my favorite sport! May I accompany you, my lord?"

"Sansuke, you come too."

It was on a morning in early spring that Nobunaga set out from Azuchi. His attendants had been picked the night before, but Nakagawa Sebei—who had just come to the castle—had now been invited, and Ikeda Shonyu's son, Sansuke, was added to the group as well.

Nobunaga had a liking for riding, sumo wrestling, hawking, and the tea ceremony, but the chase was certainly one of his favorite pastimes.

The beaters and archers would be exhausted by the end of the day. Such interests might be called pastimes, but Nobunaga did nothing halfheartedly. With sumo wrestling, for example, when a *basho* was arranged at Azuchi, he would gather well over fifteen hundred wrestlers from Omi, Kyoto, Naniwa, and other faraway provinces. In the end, the various lords would gather to watch in large crowds, and Nobunaga would rarely grow tired of the sight even as the hour grew late. Instead, he would pick men from among his own retainers and order them to go up into the ring for match after match.

This First Month's hawking trip to the Echi River, however, was extremely simple. It was nothing more than an outing, and the hawks were never released. After a short rest, Nobunaga ordered the party to return to Azuchi.

As the party entered the town of Azuchi, Nobunaga reined in his horse and turned toward a foreign-looking building in the middle of a stand of trees. The sound of a violin was coming from a window. He suddenly dismounted and went in through the door with a few of his attendants.

Two or three Jesuits came down hurriedly to greet him, but Nobunaga was already striding into the house.

"Your Lordship!" the fathers exclaimed in surprise.

This was the school that had been built next to the Church of the Ascension. Nobunaga had been one of the benefactors of the school, but everything from the timber to the furnishings had been contributed by provincial lords who had been converted to Christianity.

"I'd like to see how you conduct classes," Nobunaga announced. "I assume the children are all here."

Hearing what Nobunaga wanted, the fathers were nearly in ecstasy, and told each other what an honor the visit was. Ignoring their chatter, Nobunaga climbed rapidly up the stairs.

Nearly in panic, one of the priests ran ahead to the classroom and informed the students of the unforeseen inspection by a noble visitor.

The sound of the violin stopped suddenly, and the whispering was silenced. Nobunaga stood at the rostrum for a moment and looked over the room, thinking what an odd sort of school it was. The seats and desks in the classroom were all of foreign design, and a textbook had been placed on each desk. As might be expected, the pupils were the sons of provincial lords and retainers. They bowed solemnly to Nobunaga.

The children were between ten and fifteen years of age. All of them came from noble families, and the entire scene, imbued with the exoticism of European culture, was like a flower garden that no Japanese temple school in Azuchi could rival.

But the question of which kind of school—Christian or Buddhist—offered the best form of education had already been answered in Nobunaga's mind, it seemed, and so he had neither admiration nor wonder for what was in front of him. Taking a student's textbook from a nearby desk, he thumbed through the pages silently but quickly returned it to its owner.

"Who was playing the violin just now?" he asked.

Repeating Nobunaga's question, one of the fathers queried the students again.

Nobunaga quickly understood: the teachers had not been in the room until now, and the students had plainly taken advantage of their absence to play musical instruments, gossip, and frolic happily.

"It was Jerome," the priest said.

The students all looked at one boy who sat among them. Nobunaga followed the direction of their stares, and his eyes rested on a youth of fourteen or fifteen.

"Yes. There he is. It was Jerome." When the father pointed at him, the youth turned bright red and looked down. Nobunaga was not sure whether he knew the child or not.

"Who is this Jerome? Whose son is he?" he asked again.

The priest spoke to the boy sternly. "Stand up, Jerome. Answer His Lordship."

Jerome stood and bowed to Nobunaga.

"I'm the one who was playing the violin just now, my lord." His words were distinct, and there was no servility in his eyes; one could see that he was the offspring of samurai family.

Nobunaga looked rigidly into the child's eyes, but the child did not look away.

"What was that you were playing? It must have been a tune from Southern Barbarian music."

"Yes, it was. It was a Psalm of David." The child seemed elated. He spoke with such facility that it was as though he had been waiting for the day when he could answer such a question.

"Who taught it to you?"

"I learned it from Father Valignani."

"Ah, Valignani."

"Do you know him, my lord?" Jerome asked.

"Yes, I've met him," Nobunaga replied. "Where is he now?"

"He was in Japan at New Year's, but he may already have left Nagasaki and returned to India via Macao. According to a letter from my cousin, his ship was to set sail on the twentieth."

"Your cousin?"

"His name is Ito Anzio."

"I've never heard the name 'Anzio.' Doesn't he have a Japanese name?"

"He's Ito Yoshimasu's nephew. His name is Yoshikata."

"Oh, is that who he is? A relative of Ito Yoshimasu, the lord of Obi Castle. And what about you?"

"I'm Yoshimasu's son."

Nobunaga was strangely amused. As he looked at this impertinent, charming youth educated in the flower garden of Christian culture, he could only envision the reckless and bewhiskered figure of the boy's father, Ito Yoshimasu. The castle towns along the coastline of Kyushu in western Japan were ruled by lords like Otomo, Omura, Arima, and Ito. Recently they were becoming heavily influenced by European culture.

Whatever was brought in from Europe—firearms, gunpowder, telescopes, medicines and medical equipment, leather, dyed and woven goods, and everyday utensils—Nobunaga accepted with gratitude. He was especially enthusiastic about—and even desirous of—innovations connected with medicine, astronomy, and military science.

However, there were two things that his digestion absolutely rejected: Christianity and Christian education. But if these two things had not been allowed to the missionaries, they would not have come with their weapons, medicines, and other wonders.

Nobunaga was aware of the importance of fostering different cultures and had given permission for the establishment of a church and school in Azuchi. But now that the shoots he had let grow were beginning to bud, he worried about the future of these students. He realized that if the situation was recklessly ignored for a long time, it would lead to trouble.

Nobunaga left the class and was led by the priests to a well-appointed waiting room. There he rested on a colorful, glittering chair reserved for noble visitors. The fathers then brought out the tea and tobacco from their own country, which they valued so highly, and offered them to their guest, but Nobunaga did not touch a thing.

"The son of Ito Yoshimasu just now told me that Valignani was sailing from Japan this month. Has he already left?" he asked.

One of the fathers answered, "Father Valignani is accompanying a mission from Japan."

"A mission?" Nobunaga looked suspicious. Kyushu was not yet under his control, so friendship and commerce between Europe and the provincial lords of that island concerned him more than a little.

"Father Valignani believes that if the children of influential Japanese do not see the civilization of Europe at least once, true commerce and diplomatic relations will never really begin. He communicated with the various kings of Europe and His Holiness the Pope and persuaded them to invite a mission from Japan. The oldest person among those chosen for the mission is sixteen years old."

He then listed the boys' names.

Almost all of them were sons of the great clans in Kyushu.

"That's quite courageous of them." Nobunaga actually rejoiced that a mission of young men, whose oldest member was only sixteen, had journeyed to faraway Europe. Inwardly, he thought that it would have been good to meet with them and, as a parting gift, talk a little about his own spirit and faith.

Why would the kings of Europe and someone like Valignani so enthusiastically want the children of provincial lords to visit Europe? Nobunaga understood their intentions, but he also saw through their ulterior motives.

"When he departed from Kyoto for this mission, Valignani expressed his regrets... about you, sire."

"Regrets?"

"That he was returning to Europe without having baptized you."

"Is that so? He said that?" Nobunaga laughed. He stood up from the chair and turned around to his attendant. The man had a hawk perched on his fist. "We've tarried too long. Let's go."

Almost as soon as the words left his mouth, he was descending the stairs in great strides. He quickly called for his horse outside the door. Ito Jerome—the student who had been playing the violin—and all of the others were lined up in the school playground to see him off.

* * *

The castle at Nirasaki, the new capital of Kai, had been completed up to as the kitchens and the quarters of the ladies-in-waiting.

Regardless of the fact that it had been the twenty-fourth day of the Twelfth Month and at the very end of the year, Takeda Katsuyori had moved from Kofu, the old provincial capital for generations of his ancestors, to this new capital. The grandeur and beauty of the move itself was still the talk of the farmers along the roadside, even now during New Year's.

Beginning with the palanquins for Katsuyori and his wife and for the many ladies who waited upon them, and continuing with those for his aunt and her daughter, the lacquered litters for the various nobles and ladies must have numbered into the hundreds.

In the midst of this endless procession of sights—the samurai and retainers, the personal attendants, the officials with their gold and silver saddles, the mother-of-pearl inlay, the sparkle of gold lacquer, the open umbrellas, the archers with their bows and quivers, the forest of red-shafted spears—what caught everyone's eye above everything else were the banners of the Takeda. Thirteen Chinese characters sparkled in gold on a bright red cloth next to another banner. Two lines of gold characters were displayed on the long banner of deep blue:

> Swift as the wind
> Quiet as a forest
> Ardent as fire
> Still as a mountain

Everyone knew that the calligraphy for this poem had been executed by Kaisen, the head priest of the Erin Temple.

"Ah, how sad that the very soul of that banner is leaving the castle at Tsutsujigasaki and moving on today."

Everyone in the old capital seemed sad. Every time the banner with Sun Tzu's words and the one with the thirteen Chinese characters had been unfurled and taken into battle, the brave soldiers had returned with them. At those times, they and the townspeople had shouted themselves hoarse with deeply felt cries of shared victory. Such events had occurred in Shingen's time, and now everyone missed those days.

And although the banner emblazoned with Sun Tzu's words was the same physically, the people could not help feeling that it was somehow different from the one they had looked upon in former times.

But when the people of Kai watched the enormous treasure and the stores of munitions being moved to the new capital, along with the palanquins and golden saddles of the entire clan, and the meandering procession of ox-drawn carts stretching for many leagues, they were reassured that theirs was still a strong province. The same feelings of pride that had been with them since the days of Shingen still lingered in the soldiers and even in the general population.

Not long after Katsuyori moved to the castle in the new capital, the red and white plum blossoms in the garden were in bloom. Katsuyori and his uncle, Takeda Shoyo-ken—indifferent to the songs of the bush warblers—walked through the orchard.

"He didn't even come to the New Year's celebrations. He said he was sick. Hasn't he sent some news to you, Uncle?" Katsuyori asked.

He was talking about his cousin, Anayama Baisetsu, who was the governor of Ejiri Castle. Located on the border with Suruga, it was considered by the Takeda to be an important strategic area to the south. For over half a year now, Baisetsu had not come to wait upon Katsuyori, always sending the excuse that he was ill, and Katsuyori was worried.

"No, I think he's probably really sick. Baisetsu's a priest and an honest man; I don't think he would pretend to be ill."

Shoyoken was an exceptionally good-natured man, so this answer did not put Katsu-yori's mind at ease.

Shoyoken fell silent.

Nor did Katsuyori say anything more, and the two of them walked on silently.

Between the keep and the inner citadel was a narrow ravine filled with different kinds of trees. A bush warbler dropped almost as if it had fallen, fluttered its wings, and flew away in surprise. At the same time a voice came suddenly from a row of plum trees.

"Are you there, my lord? I have important news."

The retainer's face had lost its color.

"Pull yourself together. A samurai should speak with self-control about important matters," Shoyoken scolded him. Shoyoken was not just disciplining the young man but was also trying to calm his nephew. Quite unlike his ordinary resolute self, Katsuyori had turned pale in surprise.

"This is not some small matter. It's really important, my lord," Genshiro replied as he prostrated himself. "Kiso Yoshimasa of Fukushima has committed treason!"

"Kiso?" Shoyoken's voice expressed a shock that was half doubt, half refusal. As for Katsuyori, he had probably already guessed this would happen. He was just biting his lip and looking down at the retainer prostrated in front of him.

The beating in Shoyoken's breast was not going to be calmed easily, and his lack of composure was echoed in his shaking voice. "The letter! Let's see the letter!"

"The messenger told me to tell Lord Katsuyori that the matter was so urgent there was not a moment to spare," the retainer said, "and that we are to wait for a letter from the next messenger."

As he walked away in great strides, Katsuyori stepped right past the still prostrate re-tainer and yelled back to Shoyoken. "It won't be necessary to see Goro's letter. There have been plenty of suspicious signs from Yoshimasa and Baisetsu in recent years. I know it's a lot of trouble, Uncle, but I'm going to need you to lead an army again. I'll be going too."

Before two hours had passed, the sound of a great drum rang out from the tower of the new castle, and the call of the conch shell floated through the castle town, proclaiming mobilization. The plum blossoms were almost white as this peaceful spring evening came to a close in the mountain province. The army set out before the end of the day. Hastened by the setting sun, five thousand men started out on the Fukushima Road, and by night-fall almost ten thousand troops had left Nirasaki.

"Well, this is just fine! He's made his revolt quite clear to us. If it hadn't happened, the day for me to strike down the ungrateful traitor might never have come. This time we'll have to purge Fukushima of everyone with divided loyalties."

Giving vent to the resentment that was so hard to control, Katsuyori mumbled to himself as his horse took him along the road. But the voices of indignation that traveled with him—the voices of resentment over Kiso's betrayal—were few.

Katsuyori was as confident as always. When he had cut off his relations with the Hojo, he had abandoned an ally without even looking back at the strength of the clan that had been such a great support to him.

At the suggestion of those around him, Katsuyori had returned Nobunaga's son—who had been a hostage with the Takeda for many years—to Azuchi; but there was still plenty of contempt left in his heart for the lord of the Oda clan, and even more for Tokugawa Ieyasu in Hamamatsu. He had displayed this aggressive attitude since the battle of Nagashino.

There was nothing wrong with the strength of his spirit. He was extremely positive. Certainly, strength of spirit is a substance that should fill the jar of the heart to the brim. And during this period of warring provinces, the samurai class as a whole could be said to have possessed that kind of spirit. But in the situation in which Katsuyori found himself, there was an absolute need for unerring adherence to a composed strength that, at a glance, might be taken for weakness. A reckless show of strength would not intimidate an opponent. On the contrary, it only encouraged him. For a number of years, Katsuyori's manliness and courage had been looked down upon for this reason by both Nobunaga and Ieyasu.

And not only by these men, his enemies. Even in his own province of Kai there were voices expressing the wish that Shingen were still alive.

Shingen had insisted on a strong military administration of the province. And because he had given both his retainers and the people of Kai the feeling that they would be absolutely secure as long as he was there, they depended on him completely.

Even during Katsuyori's reign, military service, tax collection, and all other phases of the administration were conducted according to Shingen's laws. But something was missing.

Katsuyori did not understand what that something was; regrettably, he did not even notice that something *was* missing. But what he lacked was a reliance on harmony and the ability to inspire confidence in his administration. Thus it was Shingen's powerful government, now lacking in these two qualities, that began to cause conflict within the clan.

In Shingen's time, there was a general article of faith shared by the upper and lower classes, one of which they were very proud: no enemy had ever been permitted to take even one step inside the boundaries of Kai.

But misgivings seemed to be springing up everywhere now. It is hardly necessary to mention that it was obvious to everyone that a line had been drawn with the great defeat of Nagashino. That disaster had not been simply a matter of the failure of the Kai army's equipment and strategy. It had resulted from the shortcomings of Katsuyori's character; and those around him—even the general population, who looked to him as their mainstay—felt a horrible disappointment. Katsuyori, they realized, was not Shingen.

Although Kiso Yoshimasa was Shingen's son-in-law, he was plotting to betray Katsuyori and did not believe that he could survive. He was beginning to tally up Kai's prospects for the future. Through an intermediary in Mino, he had secretly been in touch with Nobunaga for already two years now.

The Kai army split up into a number of lines and marched to Fukushima.

As the soldiers marched they were confident, and they could often be heard to say, "We'll crush Kiso's forces right under our feet."

But as the days passed, the news relayed to headquarters did not make Takeda Katsuyori smile in satisfaction. On the contrary, the reports were all disturbing.

"Kiso is being stubborn."

"The terrain is hilly, and they have good defenses, so it will take a number of days for our vanguard to approach it."

Every time Katsuyori heard these kinds of things, he bit his lip and muttered, "If I went there myself…"

It was part of his character to become angry and exasperated when a war situation was going badly.

The month passed, and it was now the fourth day of the Second Month.

Horribly distressing news came to Katsuyori: Nobunaga had suddenly given the order for the Oda troops to mobilize in Azuchi, and he himself had already left Omi.

Another spy brought more bad news:

"The forces of Tokugawa Ieyasu have left Suruga; Hojo Ujimasa's troops have left the Kanto; and Kanamori Hida has left his castle. All of them are marching toward Kai, and it's said that Nobunaga and Nobutada have split their troops into two and are about to invade. When I climbed a high mountain and looked out, I could see columns of smoke in every direction."

Katsuyori felt as if he had been hurled to the ground. "Nobunaga! Ieyasu! And even Hojo Ujimasa?"

According to these secret reports, his own situation was about the same as that of a mouse in a trap.

Dusk was approaching. New reports came in that Shoyoken's troops had deserted during the previous night.

"That can't be true!" Katsuyori said. But it was a fact that such a thing had occurred during the night, and the urgent messages that came in one after another brought proof that could not be denied.

"Shoyoken! Isn't he my uncle, and an elder of the clan? What's the idea of leaving the battlefield and running away without permission? And all those others. It only sullies my mouth to speak about such disloyalty and ingratitude."

Railing against heaven and against humankind, Katsuyori should instead have felt such rancor against himself. Ordinarily he was not so weak-minded. But even a man with tremendous courage could not have helped being frightened by such a turn of events.

"It can't be helped. You must give the order to strike camp."

So advised by Oyamada Nobushige and the others, Katsuyori suddenly retreated. How desolate he must have felt! Although the twenty thousand soldiers he had counted on at the time of his departure had not engaged in a single battle, the retainers and men returning to Nirasaki with him now numbered no more than four thousand.

Perhaps trying to find an outlet for feelings he hardly knew how to deal with, he ordered the monk Kaisen to come to the castle. His bad luck seemed to be increasing, for even after he returned to Nirasaki, he received one depressing report after another. The worst, perhaps, was the news that his kinsman Anayama Baisetsu had deserted him and, as if that weren't enough, had not only given up his castle at Ejiri to the enemy but had been engaged to guide Tokugawa Ieyasu. He was now said to be in the vanguard of the troops invading Kai.

So his own brother-in-law had openly betrayed him and was even trying to destroy him. With this knowledge, he was now forced to reflect a little on himself in the midst of his agony. Where have I gone wrong? he asked himself. While on the one hand he had made his indomitable spirit more and more unyielding and had ordered more defenses everywhere, when he received Kaisen at his new castle he displayed a willingness to engage in self-examination that was, for him, quite a gentle attitude. The change was probably too late.

"It has been just ten years since my father passed away, and eight years have gone by since the battle of Nagashino. Why have the generals of Kai so suddenly lost fidelity to their principles?" Katsuyori asked the priest.

Kaisen, however, sat facing him in silence, and Katsuyori continued, "Ten years ago, our generals weren't like this. Each of them had a sense of shame and was careful of his own reputation. When my father was still in this world, men rarely betrayed their lord, much less left their own clan."

Kaisen sat silently with his eyes closed. In comparison with the priest, who seemed like cold ashes, Katsuyori talked on like a wildfire.

"But even the men who were poised and ready to strike down the traitors have all scattered without having engaged in a single battle or waited for their lord's command. Is this behavior worthy of the Takeda clan and its generals—who would not even allow the great Uesugi Kenshin to take one step into Kai. How can there be such deterioration of discipline? How degraded can they be? Many of the generals under my father, like Baba, Yamagata, Oyamada, and Amakasu either are old or have passed away. The ones that remain are completely different people: they're either the children of those generals or warriors who were not directly connected with my father."

Kaisen still said nothing. The monk had been more intimate with Shingen than had anyone else, and he must have been over seventy years old. From beneath his snowlike brow, he had observed Shingen's heir very carefully.

"Venerable teacher, you may think it's too late because things have already come to this pass, but if my way of administering the government has been remiss, please show me how. If my command of military discipline has not been correct, give me some strict way of enforcement. I'm anxious to correct myself. I have heard that you were taught a great deal by my father, who was your friend in the Way. Could you not teach some good strategies to his unworthy son as well? Please don't be stingy with what you have to teach. Consider me as Shingen's son. Please tell me, without reserve, what I've done wrong and how I can correct myself by doing things this way or that. Well then, let me say it. Have I offended the people after my father passed away by suddenly raising the tariffs at river crossings and barriers in order to strengthen the province's defenses?"

"No," Kaisen said, shaking his head.

Katsuyori became even more agitated.

"Then there must have been some failing in rewards and punishments."

"None at all." The old man shook his snowy brow once again.

Katsuyori prostrated himself and was on the verge of tears. In front of Kaisen, the fierce warlord who had so much self-esteem could only cry in agony.

"Don't cry, Katsuyori," Kaisen finally said. "You are certainly not unworthy, and neither are you an unworthy son. Your only error has been lack of awareness. It is a cruel age that has made you stand face to face with Oda Nobunaga. You are not his enemy, after all. The mountains of Kai are far away from the center, and Nobunaga has the advantage of geography, but that is not a great cause of your problem, either. Although Nobunaga has fought battle after battle and has administered the government, in his heart he has never forgotten the Emperor. The construction of the Imperial Palace is just a single instance of all the things he has done."

Kaisen and Shingen had had a deep understanding of the heart, and Shingen's reverence for the old abbot had been extraordinarily deep. But Kaisen had also believed strongly in Shingen—he was a dragon among men; a mythical fiery horse from the heavens. But while he praised Shingen so highly, he never compared him with his son, Katsuyori, or considered the latter to be unworthy by contrast.

On the contrary, he viewed Katsuyori with sympathy. If someone criticized Katsuyori's mistakes, Kaisen always responded that it was unreasonable to expect more; his father had simply been too great a man. Kaisen did, perhaps, feel one small dissatisfaction: certainly if Shingen had lived on until now, his influence would not have been restricted to the province of Kai; he would have put his great ability and genius to work on something of greater significance. And now Kaisen regretted that Shingen had not survived. The man who had perceived something of greater significance was Nobunaga. It was he who had broadened the provincial role of the samurai to one of national importance. And it was Nobunaga who had even showed himself to be a model retainer. Kaisen's expectations for Katsuyori, who did not have the character of his father, had absolutely disappeared. The abbot clearly perceived that the long civil war was over.

So, to help Katsuyori force the troops of the Oda to kneel to him, or to plan some safe solution was impossible. The Takeda clan had been founded centuries before, and Shingen's name had shone too brightly in the sky: Katsuyori was not going to beg for capitulation at Nobunaga's feet.

Takeda Katsuyori had a strong will and knew a sense of shame. Among the common people of the province, there were voices saying that the government had declined since the time of Shingen, and the levying of heavy taxes was perceived as a major cause of the complaints. But Kaisen knew that Katsuyori had not levied taxes for his own luxury or pride. Every tax had been directed toward military expenditure. In the last few years, military tactics and technology had been progressing in rapid strides in the capital and even in the neighboring provinces. But Katsuyori could not afford to spend as much money on new weapons as his rivals.

"Please take care of yourself," Kaisen told Katsuyori as he prepared to leave.

"Are you going back to the temple already?" There were still many questions Katsuyori wanted to ask, but he knew that the answers to whatever he asked would be the same. He pressed his palms to the floor in reverence. "This is, perhaps, the last time I will see you."

Kaisen put his hands, draped with a string of prayer beads, to the floor and left without another word.

THE FALL OF THE TAKEDA

"Let's spend this spring in the Kai mountains," Nobunaga said as he rode out of Azuchi at the head of his army. "We can view the cherry blossoms, pick flowers, and then sightsee around Mount Fuji on the coast on our way back."

The success of the expedition against Kai seemed assured this time, and the army's departure was almost leisurely. By the tenth day of the Second Month, the army had reached Shinano and had completed the disposition of men at the entrances to Ina, Kiso, and Hida. The Hojo clan would enter from the east, while the Tokugawa would attack from Suruga.

In comparison with the battles of the Ane River and Nagashino, Nobunaga was invading Kai as serenely as he might have gone out to pick vegetables from a garden. In the middle of the enemy province were forces that were no longer considered to be enemies at all. Both Naegi Kyubei of Naegi Castle and Kiso Yoshimasa of Fukushima were men who were eagerly waiting for Nobunaga's arrival, not Katsuyori's; and the troops that marched from Gifu into Iwamura did so without encountering any resistance. The various fortresses of the Takeda had been abandoned to the wind. When night turned to dawn, both Matsuo Castle and the castle at Iida were nothing but empty shells.

"We have advanced to Ina and found barely an enemy soldier to defend it."

That was the report Nobunaga received at the entrance to Kiso. There the soldiers also joked among themselves that their advance was almost too easy to be satisfying. What had made the Takeda so fragile? The cause was complicated, but the answer could be put into simple terms. This time the Takeda would not be able to preserve Kai.

Everyone associated with the Takeda clan was convinced of its inevitable defeat. Some, perhaps, had even been disposed to look forward to this day. Traditionally, however, samurai—of no matter what clan—did not display an unseemly attitude at such times, even when they knew defeat was inevitable.

"We're going to let them know that we are here," said Nishina Nobumori, commander of Takato Castle and Katsuyori's younger brother.

Nobunaga's son Nobutada, whose forces had poured into the region, estimated that his prospects were generally good. After writing a letter, he summoned a strong archer and had the man shoot the message into the castle. It was, of course, an invitation to surrender.

An answer from the castle came quickly. "I have read over your letter..." From the opening line to the ending, the letter had been written in an extremely stately style.

The men in this castle will one day compensate Lord Katsuyori's favors with their lives, and not one of them is likely to be a coward. You should have your men attack immediately. We will show you the tempered prowess and valor that has been ours since the time of Lord Shingen.

Nobumori had answered with a resolution that almost scented the ink.

Nobunaga had made his son a general, even though he was still quite young. "Well, if that's the way they want it," Nobutada said, ordering the assault.

The attacking forces were divided into two divisions, and they assaulted the castle simultaneously from the mountain at the rear and from the area leading to the front gate. It was a battle worthy of the name. The one thousand defending soldiers expected to die. As might be imagined, the valor of the Kai warriors had not yet declined. From the beginning of the Second Month to the beginning of the Third, the stone walls of Takato Castle were drenched with the blood of both the attacking and the defending armies. After breaking through the first palisades, which stood fifty yards from the moat, the attacking troops filled the moat with stones, shrubs, trees, and earth. Then they crossed over very quickly to the base of the stone walls.

"Come on!" shouted the men from the clay bulwarks and roofed mud walls as they threw spears, timbers, and rocks and poured hot oil onto the men below. The attacking soldiers that had scrambled up the stone wall went tumbling down under the rocks, timbers and sprays of oil. But no matter how far they fell, they were even more gallant. Even if they tumbled to the earth, as long as they were conscious, they would jump to their feet and start to climb again.

The soldiers who came up behind these men shouted in admiration for their comrades' resolute courage, and clambered up the walls behind them. They were not going to be outdone. As they climbed and fell, climbed once again, and grasped the stone walls, it seemed that nothing could stand before their fury. But the defenders of the castle were not the least bit inferior in their own united, desperate effort. Those who accepted the challenge, who could be glimpsed above the clay bulwarks and the roofed dirt walls, gave the illusion that the castle was filled only with the sturdy warriors of Kai. But if the attacking forces had been able to see the activity inside, they would have known that the entire castle was involved in a pathetic but wholehearted struggle. While the castle was being besieged, the many people inside—the old and young, and even pregnant women —each worked desperately along with the soldiers to help in the defense. The young women carried arrows, while the old men swept away the burnt refuse from the guns. They tended the wounded and worked at cooking the soldiers' meals. No one had given them any commands, but they worked in perfect order and without a single word of complaint.

"The castle will fall if we throw everything we've got at them." Thus spoke Kawajiri, one of the generals of the attacking troops, who had gone to see Nobutada.

"We've had too many dead and wounded," Nobutada said; he had been reflecting on the matter himself. "Do you have any good ideas?"

"It seems to me that the strength of the soldiers in the castle is dependent on their belief that Katsuyori is still in his new capital. With that in mind, we might withdraw from this field of action for the time being and attack Kofu and Nirasaki instead. That, however, would require a complete change in strategy. It would be better, perhaps, to convince the defenders of the castle that Nirasaki has fallen and that Katsuyori is dead." Nobutada nodded his agreement. On the morning of the first day of the Third Month, another message was tied to an arrow and shot into the castle.

Upon reading it, Nobumori laughed. "This letter is such a transparent deception that a child might have written it. It shows how disheartened the enemy has become with the siege."

The message read read as follows:

On the twenty-eighth day of the last month, Kai fell and Lord Katsuyori committed suicide. The other members of the clan either committed suicide with him or were taken prisoner. It is meaningless for this castle to continue to demonstrate its martial valor, for it is nothing more than a single fortress in a conquered domain. You should surrender the castle immediately and put your efforts into the relief of the province.

Oda Nobutada

"How sweet. Do they really think a transparent little trick like this is the art of war?" That night, Nobumori held a drinking party and showed the letter to his retainers. "If this moves anyone here, he can leave the castle without hesitation before dawn."

They beat the drum, intoned chants from Noh plays, and passed the evening happily. That night, the wives of all the generals were also called and offered a round of *sake*. Everyone quickly realized what Nobumori's intentions were. On the following morning, just as everyone had expected, he picked up a large halberd to use as a staff, fastened a straw sandal to his swollen left foot—injured in the battle for the castle—and hobbled over to the castle gate.

He summoned the defenders to assemble, climbed up inside the roofed gate tower, and surveyed his forces. He had less than a thousand soldiers, excluding the very young, old men, and the women, but there was not one fewer than the night before. He bowed his head for a while, as if in silent prayer. In fact, he was praying to the soul of his father, Shingen: Look! We still have such men in Kai. Finally he looked up. He could see his entire army from where he was.

He did not have his brother's full face and broad features. As he had contented himself for a long time with the simplicity of country life, he knew nothing of extravagant food or luxury. He had been endowed with looks like those of a young hawk brought up on the whistling winds that blew over the mountains and plains of Kai. At the age of thirty-three, he resembled his father, Shingen: thick hair, bushy brows, and a wide mouth.

"Well, I thought it was going to rain today, but it's cleared up nicely. With the cherry blossoms on the distant mountains, the season is giving us a beautiful day to die. We're certainly not going to throw away our reputations, hoping for the promise of material reward. As you have seen, I was wounded in the fighting two days ago. Because my mobility is so limited, I'm going to watch each of you fight your last battle as I wait here calmly for the enemy. Then I can finish it up by fighting to my heart's content. So go out! Force your way through the gates at both the front and the rear, and bravely show them how the mountain cherry blossoms fall!"

The responding shouts of the fierce warriors, proclaiming that they would do exactly as he commanded, were like a whirlwind. All of them looked up at the figure of their lord atop the entrance gate, and for a while the same proclamation was heard over and over: "This is our farewell."

It was not a question of living or dying. It was an desperate rush toward death. The front and rear gates of the castle were defiantly pushed wide open by the men inside, and a thousand warriors rushed out, war cries rising from their throats.

The besieging troops were routed. For a moment the confusion was such that even Nobutada's headquarters were threatened.

"Fall back! Regroup!" The commander of the castle forces watched for the proper moment, and called for a retreat into the castle.

"Fall back! Fall back!"

The men turned back toward the castle, each warrior displaying to Nobumori, who was still seated up in the roofed castle gate, the heads he had taken.

"I will come in and drink, then go out again," one of the warriors shouted. And so it went on. Resting for a moment at either the front or the back gate, then dashing back out and cutting through the enemy—the men repeated this pattern of violent attack and retreat six times until four hundred thirty-seven heads had been taken. As the day came to a close, the numbers of the defenders were reduced conspicuously, and those who remained were covered with wounds. Almost no one was uninjured. Flames shot up with a roar from the burning trees around the castle. The enemy had already been flowing into the fortress from every direction. Nobumori unblinkingly watched the final moments of each of his warriors from the top of the gate.

"My lord! My lord! Where are you?" a retainer called out as he ran around at the bottom of the gate.

"I'm up here," Nobumori called, letting his retainer know he was alive and well. "My final hour is near. Let me see where you are." And he looked down from his seat. The retainer looked up through the smoke at the figure of his master.

"Nearly all the men have been killed. Have you made preparations for suicide, my lord?" he asked, panting for breath.

"Come up here to assist me."

"Yes, my lord." The man staggered around to the stairway inside the gate, but he never made it up to the balcony. Thick flames lapped at the entrance to the stairway. Nobumori pushed in the shutters of another window and peered down. The only soldiers he could see beneath him belonged to the enemy. Then he saw one person fighting hard in the middle of a huge crowd of enemy soldiers. Amazingly, it was a woman, the wife of one of his retainers, and she was brandishing a halberd.

Even though Nobumori was about to die, he struggled to accept the unexpected emotion in which he was suddenly enveloped.

That woman is so shy she usually can't even speak in front of men, much less hold a halberd up to them, he thought. But now he was pressed by something he had to do, and he shouted out to the enemy from the narrow window by which he stood.

"All you men fighting for Nobunaga and Nobutada! Listen to the voice of the Void. Nobunaga is taking pride right now in his one moment of triumph, but every cherry blossom falls and every ruler's castle will burn. I'm going to show you something now that won't fall or burn for all eternity. I, Shingen's fifth son, Nobumori, am going to show you!"

When the Oda soldiers were finally able to climb up, they found a corpse with its stomach cut open in the pattern of a cross. But the head was no longer there. Then, an instant later, the spring night sky was enveloped by red and black pillars of flame and smoke.

The confusion at Nirasaki Castle in the new capital was as great as if people were proclaiming the end of the world.

"Takato Castle has fallen and everyone, including your brother, has been killed."

As he listened to his retainer, Katsuyori seemed completely unmoved. Still, his expression showed that he clearly perceived that his own strength was no longer sufficient. The next report came in.

"The soldiers of Oda Nobutada have already broken into Kai from Suwa, and our men are being killed without mercy, whether they fight or surrender. Their severed heads are exposed on the roadside, and the enemy is flowing in this direction like a tide."

Another urgent message arrived. "Shingen's kinsman, the blind priest Ryuho, was captured and butchered by the enemy."

This time Katsuyori raised his eyes and spoke abusively of the enemy.

"The Oda forces have no compassion. What fault could they find in a blind priest? How could he even have had the power to resist?" But now he was able to think more deeply about his own death. He bit steadily on his lip and repressed the waves roiling at the bottom of his heart. If I give vent to my anger like this, he thought, they may think I've become distracted, and even the retainers around me will feel disgraced. There were many people who saw nothing more than Katsuyori's manly exterior and who considered him bold and even coarse. But the truth was that he was very deliberate in his actions toward his retainers. In addition, he was extremely strict in adhering to his own principles—to his honor as a lord and to self-reflection. He had continued in his father's tradition and had been taught the principles of Zen by Kaisen. But although he had had the same teacher and had studied Zen, he was unable to bring it to life as Shingen had done.

How could Takato Castle have fallen? I was sure it could hold out for another two weeks to a month, Katsuyori thought, which showed that the situation had resulted less from a miscalculation of defensive strategy than from a lack of human maturity. Now, however, regardless of what his natural temperament might be, he had to meet this new tide of fortune.

The sliding partitions had been taken from the wide conference room and even from the outlying rooms of the main citadel; and now the entire clan lived together as though they were refugees from a great cataclysm that continued day and night. Naturally, curtains were set up even in the garden, shields were set up side by side, and soldiers went without sleep, holding large paper lanterns and policing the area at night. Messengers with reports of the situation were taken hourly directly from the entrance through the central gate to the garden, so that Katsuyori listened to the dispatches in person. Everything that had just been part of the construction the year before—the scent of new wood, the gold and silver inlay, the beauty of the furniture and utensils—now seemed only to be in the way.

Accompanied by a maid and binding up the train of her kimono, a lady-in-waiting with a message from Katsuyori's wife stepped out of the confusion of the garden and into the dark hall, and bravely looked through the crowd of men. At that time, the room was full of generals, both young and old, all noisily expressing their opinions about what to do next.

The woman finally came before Katsuyori and appealed to him with the message from his wife. "The women are all standing around crying in confusion, and won't stop no matter how we console them. Your wife has said that our last moment comes only once, and she thinks that perhaps the women would be a little more easily resolved if they could be here with the samurai. If she has your permission, she will move here immediately. What are my lord's wishes?"

"That's fine," Katsuyori answered quickly. "Bring my wife here and the young ones too."

At that moment his fifteen-year-old heir, Taro Nobukatsu, came forward and tried to dissuade him. "Father, that wouldn't be very good, would it?"

Katsuyori turned to his son, less with displeasure than with a nervous preoccupation. "Why?"

"Well, if the women come here, they'll just get in the way. And if the men see them crying, even the bravest samurai may become disheartened." Taro was still a boy, but he insisted on giving his opinion. He continued to argue that Kai had been their ancestral land since the time of Shinra Saburo, and it should be their land to the very end, even if they have to fight and die. To abandon Nirasaki and flee, as one general had just recommended, would bring the greatest shame to the Takeda clan.

A general argued the opposite position: "Nevertheless, the enemy is on all four sides, and Kofu is situated in a basin. Once the enemy invades, it will be like water rushing into a lake. Wouldn't it be better to escape to Agatsuma in Joshu? If you got to the Mikuni mountain range, there would be any number of provinces where you might find asylum.

Once you called together your allies, you could certainly reestablish yourself."

Nagasaka Chokan agreed, and Katsuyori's mind was inclined in that direction. He set his eyes on Taro and was silent for a moment. He then turned toward the lady-in-waiting and said, "We will go."

Taro's advice was thus refused by his father. Taro turned away silently and hung his head. The remaining question was whether to flee to Agatsuma or to entrench themselves in the area of Mount Iwadono. But whichever route they chose, abandoning their new capital and fleeing was the unavoidable fate to which both Katsuyori and his generals were resigned.

It was the third day of the Third Month. If it had been any other year, Katsuyori and his retinue would have been enjoying the Doll Festival in the inner citadel. But on this bright day, the entire clan was driven from behind by black smoke as they abandoned Nirasaki. Katsuyori, of course, also left the castle, as did every samurai that served him. But as he turned and looked at his entire force, his expression was one of amazement.

"Is this all?" he asked. At some point, senior retainers and even kinsmen had disappeared. He was told that they had taken advantage of the confusion during the darkness of dawn, and had fled each to his own castle with his retainers.

"Taro?"

"I'm here, Father." Taro drew his horse up to the solitary figure of his father. With all the retainers, the common samurai, and the foot soldiers combined—there were less than a thousand men. There were large numbers, however, of lacquered palanquins and litters for his wife and her court ladies, and the pathetic figures of veiled women, both walking and on horseback, filled the road.

"Oh! It's burning!"

"The flames are so high!"

The crowd of women could hardly stand to leave, and when they had traveled only about a league from Nirasaki, they turned to look even as they walked. Flames and black smoke rose high in the morning sky as the castle at the new capital burned. They had set the fires at dawn.

"I don't want to live a long life," said one of the women. "What kind of future would I see? Is this the end of Lord Shingen's clan?" The nun who was Katsuyori's aunt, the charming young girl who was Shingen's granddaughter, the wives of the clan members and their servant ladies—all of them were drowning in their tears, holding each other as they cried, or calling out the names of children. Golden hairpins and other ornaments were left on the road, and no one even bothered to pick them up. Cosmetics and jewelry were smeared with mud, but no one gazed at them with regret.

"Hurry up! Why are you crying? This is what it is to be born a human being. You're going to shame yourselves in front of the farmers!" Katsuyori rode in among the slow-moving palanquins and litters, urging them on, to escape farther and farther to the east.

Hoping to reach Oyamada Nobushige's castle, they looked at the old castle in Kofu as they passed by but could only walk on toward the mountains. As they walked on, the carriers who shouldered the palanquins gradually disappeared, the menials who carried the baggage and litters ran off one after another, and their number was reduced by half and then by half again. By the time they had entered the mountains near Katsunuma, their entire force numbered only two hundred men, and less than twenty of those were mounted, counting Katsuyori and his son. When Katsuyori and his followers had struggled along as far as the mountain village of Komagai, they found that the one man they had been relying upon had suddenly had a change of heart.

"Take refuge somewhere else!" Obstructing the summit path to Sasago, Oyamada Nobushige prevented Katsuyori's party from passing through. Katsuyori, his son, and the entire group were at a complete loss. There was nothing they could do but change their direction, and they now fled toward Tago, a village at the foot of Mount Temmoku. Spring was in full bloom, but the mountains and fields, as far as the eye could see, held neither comfort nor hope. So now the small group that remained put all their trust in Katsuyori, as they might in a staff or a pillar. Katsuyori himself was at his wits' end. Huddling together in Tago, his followers waited in a daze, swept over by the mountain wind.

The combined forces of the Oda and the Tokugawa entered Kai like raging waves. Led by Anayama, Ieyasu's army marched from Minobu to Ichikawaguchi. Oda Nobutada attacked upper Suwa and burned the Suwa Myojin Shrine and a number of Buddhist temples. The common people's homes along the road he burned to ashes as he hunted for surviving enemy soldiers and pushed on—day and night—toward Nirasaki and Kofu. Finally, the end came. It was the morning of the eleventh day of the Third Month.

One of Katsuyori's personal attendants had gone to the village the night before and returned after reconnoitering the enemy positions. That morning he gave the report to his lord as he gasped for breath.

"The vanguard of the Oda forces has entered the nearby villages and seems to have learned from the villagers that you and your family are here, my lord. It appears that the Oda have surrounded the area and cut off all the roads, finally starting their last push in this direction."

Their group now numbered only ninety-one—the forty-one remaining samurai with Katsuyori and his son, and Katsuyori's wife and her ladies-in-waiting. In the preceding days they had ensconced themselves in a place called Hirayashiki and had even erected a sort of palisade. But when they heard the report, every one of them knew that the time had come, and they hurried to prepare themselves for death. Among them, Katsuyori's wife sat as though she were still in the mansion of the inner citadel. Her face was like a white flower as she looked off in a daze. The women who surrounded her had broken into tears.

"If it was going to come to this, it would have been better to stay in the new castle at Nirasaki. How pitiful. Is this how the wife of the lord of the Takeda should look?"

Left to themselves, the women cried miserably and lamented to each other without end.

Katsuyori went to his wife and pressed her to leave. "I've just ordered my attendant to bring you a horse. Even if we could stay here for a long time, our regrets would never end, and now the enemy is closing in on the foothills. I've heard that we're close to Sagami, so you should go there as quickly as possible. Cross the mountains and go back to the Hojo clan." His wife's eyes were filled with tears, but she made no move to leave. Rather, she looked as though she resented her husband's words.

"Tsuchiya! Tsuchiya Uemon!" Katsuyori called, summoning a retainer. "Get my wife on the back of a horse."

The attendant strode up to Katsuyori's wife, but she suddenly turned to her husband and said, "It is said that a true samurai will not have two masters. In the same way, once a woman has taken a husband, she should not go back to live with her family again. Though it may seem to be compassionate of you to send me back to Odawara by myself, just those words feel so unsympathetic....I'm not moving from this place. I'll be at your side until the very end. Then, perhaps, you will let me go with you to the hereafter." Just at that moment, two retainers rushed up with the information that the enemy was closing in.

"They've reached the temple in the foothills."

Katsuyori's wife strictly scolded her attendants for their sudden wailing. "There is no time to do anything but grieve. Come here and help with the preparations."

This woman was not yet twenty years old, yet she did not lose her sense of propriety even as death pressed in. She was as serene as a pool of water, and Katsuyori himself felt reproved by her composure.

Her attendants went off but returned shortly with an unglazed cup and a *sake* flask, and set them down in front of Katsuyori and his son. It appeared that his wife had thought far enough ahead to prepare even for this moment. Silently she offered her husband the cup. Katsuyori held it in his hand, took a sip, and passed it to his son. He then shared it with his wife.

"My lord, a cup for the Tsuchiya brothers," his wife said. "Tsuchiya, you must say farewell while we are all still in this world."

Tsuchiya Sozo, Katsuyori's personal attendant, and his two younger brothers had truly been devoted to their lord. Sozo was twenty-six years old, the next oldest was twenty-one, and the youngest brother was only eighteen. Together they had protected their ill-fated lord with fidelity all along the way, from the fall of the new capital to their last stand on Mount Temmoku.

"With this, I can leave without regrets." Emptying the cup he had received, Sozo turned and smiled at his younger brothers. Then he turned to Katsuyori and his wife. "Your misfortune this time is due entirely to the defection of your kinsmen. It must be fearful and unsettling for both you, my lord, and your wife to go through this without knowing what was in people's hearts. But the world is not filled only with people like those who betrayed you. Here at your final moment, at least, everyone with you is of one heart and one body. You can now believe in both man and the world, and walk through the portals of death with grace and an easy mind." Sozo stood straight up and walked over to his wife, who was with her ladies.

Suddenly there was the heartrending shriek of a child, and Katsuyori yelled out frantically, "Sozo! What have you done?"

Sozo had stabbed his own four-year-old son to death right before his wife's eyes, and now she was sobbing. Without even putting away his bloody sword, Sozo prostrated himself toward Katsuyori from a distance.

"As proof of what I have just declared to you, I have sent my own son ahead on the road of death. Certainly he would have been an encumbrance otherwise. My lord, I am going to accompany you; and whether I be first or last, it will take only an instant."

> How sad to see the flowers
> I knew would fall
> Departing before me,
> Not one to remain
> Until the end of spring.

Covering her face with her sleeves, Katsuyori's wife chanted these lines and cried pathetically. One of her ladies-in-waiting choked back her tears and continued:

> When they bloomed,
> Their numbers were beyond measure;
> But with the end of spring
> They fell without one blossom left behind.

As her voice trailed off, a number of women unsheathed their daggers and cut through their own breasts or stabbed their own throats, the flowing blood soaking their black hair. Suddenly the hum of an arrow sounded close by, and soon arrows were thudding into the ground all around them. The echo of guns could be heard in the distance.

"They've come!"

"Prepare yourself, my lord!" The warriors stood up together. Katsuyori looked at his son, ascertaining Taro's resolution.

"Are you ready?" Taro bowed and stood up. "I am ready to die right here at your side," he answered.

"This is good-bye, then." As father and son seemed ready to dash into the enemy, Katsuyori's wife shouted to her husband from behind, "I will depart before you."

Katsuyori stood stock-still and fixed his eyes on his wife. Holding a short sword, his wife looked up and closed her eyes. Her face was as pure and white as the moon rising over the edge of the mountain. She calmly intoned a verse from the Lotus Sutra, which she had loved to recite in former times.

"Tsuchiya! Tsuchiya!" Katsuyori called out.

"My lord?"

"Assist her."

But Katsuyori's wife did not wait for the man's blade, and pressed her own dagger straight into her mouth as she recited the sutra.

The instant the figure of his wife fell forward, one of her attendants began to encourage those left behind. "Her Ladyship departed ahead of us. None of us should be late in accompanying her on the road of death." With these words, she bared her throat to her own dagger and fell.

"It's time." Crying and calling to each other, the fifty remaining women were soon scattered like flowers in a garden blown by a winter storm. They lay either sideways or face down, or stabbed themselves while embracing one another. In the midst of this pathetic scene, one could hear the crying of infants not yet weaned or too small to leave their mothers' laps.

Sozo desperately put four women and the infants on horseback and lashed them to the saddles.

"It will not be counted as disloyalty if you do not die here. If you can get away with your lives, bring up your children and see that they hold memorial services for their pitiful former master's clan." Thus reprimanding those mothers who were crying so loudly with their children, Sozo ruthlessly beat the three horses he had set them on with the shaft of his spear. The horses galloped away as the mothers and their children sobbed and wailed.

Sozo then turned to his younger brothers. "Well, then, let's go." By that time they could see the faces of the Oda soldiers coming up the mountain. Katsuyori and his son were surrounded by the enemy. As Sozo ran to their side to assist them, he saw one of his lord's retainers running in the opposite direction in flight.

"You traitor!" Sozo shouted, chasing after the man. "Where are you going?" And he stabbed the man in the back. Then, wiping the blood from his sword, he ran straight into the midst of the enemy.

"Give me another bow! Sozo, give me another bow!" Katsuyori had broken the string of his bow twice already, and now took hold of a new one. Sozo stood close to his lord's side, shielding him as well as he could. When Katsuyori had loosed all his arrows, he threw down the bow and picked up a halberd, and then brandished a long sword. By this time the enemy was right in front of him, and a battle of naked cutting blades would last no more than a moment.

"This is the end!"

"Lord Katsuyori! Lord Taro! I'm going to precede you!"

Calling back and forth to one another, the remaining Takeda men were struck down. Katsuyori's armor was stained in red.

"Taro!" He called for his son, but his vision was blurred by his own blood. All the men around him looked like the enemy.

"My lord! I'm still here! Sozo is still at your side!"

"Sozo, quickly…I'm going to commit *seppuku*."

Leaning on the man's shoulder, Katsuyori retreated about a hundred paces. He knelt, but having received so many spear and arrow wounds, he could not use his hands at all. The more he hurried, the less his hands were able to function.

"Forgive me!" Unable to watch any more, Sozo quickly acted as second and cut off his lord's head. As Katsuyori fell forward, Sozo snatched up his head and held it, wailing in grief.

Handing Katsuyori's head to his eighteen-year-old brother, Sozo told him to take it and flee. But in tears, the younger man declared that he would die with his brother no matter what.

"Fool! Go now!" Sozo thrust him away, but it was too late. The enemy soldiers were now like an iron ring around them. Covered with wounds from numberless swords and spears, the Tsuchiya brothers died gloriously.

The middle brother had stayed with Katsuyori's son from beginning to end. The young lord and retainer were also struck down and killed at the same time. Taro was regarded as a beautiful youth, and even the writer of *The Chronicles of Nobunaga*, who showed no sympathy in describing the death of the Takeda clan, praised his wholehearted and beautiful death.

As he was but fifteen and from an illustrious family, Taro's face was quite refined and his skin was as white as snow. He had excelled others in manliness, had been reluctant to stain the family name, and had kept this spirit right up to the death of his father. There was no one who felt that his actions could be matched.

The entire affair was finished by the Hour of the Serpent. It was thus that the Takeda clan met its end.

* * *

The Oda soldiers who had attacked Kiso and Ina assembled at Suwa, eventually filling the city. Nobunaga's quarters were located at the Hoyo Temple, which had now become the headquarters for the entire campaign. On the twenty-ninth day of the month, the distribution of awards for the entire army was posted at the temple gate, and on the next day Nobunaga met with all his generals and held a congratulatory banquet in honor of their victories.

"It seems that you've done some heavy drinking today, Lord Mitsuhide. Quite rare for you, I think," Takigawa Kazumasu said to his neighbor.

"I'm drunk, but what am I going to do?" Mitsuhide looked completely inebriated, a condition he was never in. His face, which Nobunaga liked to compare to a kumquat, was bright red all the way up to his slightly receding hairline.

"How about another cup?" Pressing Kazumasu for more, Mitsuhide continued to talk in an excessively cheerful manner. "We don't often experience happy occasions like the one today, even if we live a long time. Look at that. We've gotten results from all our years of taking pains—not just on the other side of these walls or even just in all of Suwa—but now both Kai and Shinano are buried in the flags and banners of our allies. The desire we've cherished for so many years is being realized right before our eyes." His voice, as usual, was not very loud, but his words were heard quite distinctly by every person there. All those who had been talking noisily had fallen silent and were looking back and forth between Nobunaga and Mitsuhide.

Nobunaga was staring fixedly at Mitsuhide's bald head. There are times when the eye that is too perceptive discovers an unfortunate state of affairs that would have been better left unnoticed; this creates unnecessary disasters. Nobunaga had been perceiving Mitsuhide in just such a fashion for two days now. Mitsuhide had been doing his best to affect a bright and loquacious manner that did not fit him at all, and in Nobunaga's view there was absolutely no good reason for him to be doing that. There was a reason, however, for Nobunaga's view, which was quite clearly that at the distribution of awards he had intentionally excluded Mitsuhide.

To be left out of the distribution of awards should cause a warrior an acute feeling of desolation, and his shame at being a man without merit was worse than the actual rebuff itself. Mitsuhide had not been displaying that sense of dejection at all. On the contrary, he mixed with the other generals, talking happily and exhibiting a smiling face.

That was not honest. Mitsuhide was a man who would never really open himself up, and there was not much that was lovable in him. Why couldn't he grumble just once? The more Nobunaga stared at him, the more severe his look became. His drunken state probably intensified his feeling, but his reaction had been unconscious. Hideyoshi was absent, but if Nobunaga had been looking at him instead of Mitsuhide, there would have been no danger of such emotions being provoked. Even when he looked at Ieyasu, he did not become so ill-tempered. But when his eyes lighted upon Mitsuhide's balding head, they underwent a sudden change. It had not always been like this, and he could not have said for certain when the change had occurred.

But it was not a matter of a sudden change at a particular time or on a specific occasion. Indeed, if one searched for such a time, one came upon the period when—out of an excess of gratitude—Nobunaga had presented Mitsuhide with Sakamoto Castle, awarded him the castle at Kameyama, arranged his daughter's wedding, and finally endowed him with a province of five hundred thousand bushels.

This was extremely kind treatment, but it was soon after that that Nobunaga's perception of Mitsuhide had begun to change. And there was one clear cause: the fact that in Mitsuhide's bearing and character there was no trace of a willingness to change. When Nobunaga looked at the clear luster on the hairline of that "kumquat head" that never made a mistake—ever—Nobunaga's emotions turned their attention toward what he perceived as the stink of Mitsuhide's character. Perverse, almost scorched feelings would arise within him.

So it was not simply Nobunaga aiming his ill-tempered eye at someone, but rather Mitsuhide himself instigating the situation. One could see that Nobunaga's perversity manifested itself in his words and expression to the same extent that Mitsuhide's wise reasoning power shone. To be fair, it would be like judging whether the right or left hand claps first. At any rate, Mitsuhide was presently chatting with Takigawa Kazumasu, and the eyes that were staring fixedly at him were clearly in no laughing mood.

Mitsuhide noticed—perhaps something startled him unconsciously—for Nobunaga suddenly got up from his seat.

"Hey, Kumquat Head!"

Mitsuhide restrained himself and prostrated himself at Nobunaga's feet. He could feel the cold ribs of a fan lightly strike the nape of his neck two or three times.

"Yes, my lord?" Mitsuhide's color, his drunkenness, and even the shine on his forehead suddenly faded and changed to the color of clay.

"Leave the room." Nobunaga's fan left the nape of his neck, but the fan that pointed to the corridor looked just like a sword.

"I don't know what I've done, but if I've been an affront to you, my lord, and the company, I'm not sure where I should go. Please be fully critical of whatever it is that I've done wrong. I don't mind if you rebuke me right here." Even as he humbly apologized, he remained prostrate, slipped his body around, and somehow crawled out onto the broad veranda.

Nobunaga followed him. Wondering what could be the matter, the men filling the room quickly sobered up and suddenly felt their mouths become dry. Hearing a thudding noise echo from the wooden-floored veranda, even the generals who had looked away from the pitiful figure of Mitsuhide now turned their eyes back outside the room with a start.

Nobunaga had thrown his fan behind him. The generals could see that Nobunaga had Mitsuhide by the scruff of the neck. Each time the poor man struggled to lift his head to say something, Nobunaga would jerk it down and strike it against the balustrade of the veranda.

"What was that you said? What did you say just now? Something about the results we've gotten after all our pains, and what a truly happy day it is, as we see the army of the Oda clan filling Kai? You were saying something like that, weren't you?"

"That's...that's correct."

"Fool! When did you take pains? What kind of meritorious deeds did you accomplish in the invasion of Kai?"

"I—"

"What?"

"Even though I was drunk, I shouldn't have said such arrogant words."

"That's exactly right. You have no reason to be arrogant. You were careless with what you were hiding in your mind. You thought that I was distracted by the drinking and listening to someone else, and that you could finally complain."

"Heaven forbid! Let the gods of heaven and earth be my witnesses! Why, I've received so many favors from you...you raised me up from a man who wore rags and a single sword...."

"Shut up."

"Please let me go."

"Most certainly!" Nobunaga thrust him away. "Ranmaru! Water!" he called out in a loud voice. Ranmaru filled a vessel with water and brought it to him. As Nobunaga took the water, his eyes appeared to be on fire. His shoulders heaved with every breath.

Mitsuhide, however, had at some point gotten away from his master's feet and was now seven or eight feet down the corridor, adjusting his collar and smoothing his hair. He was prostrating himself so low that his chest was touching the wooden floor. The figure of Mitsuhide trying to look unruffled even now was hardly going to be seen in a favorable light, and Nobunaga's foot was starting for the man again.

If Ranmaru had not actually restrained him by the sleeve, the floor of the veranda would most likely have rung out again. Ranmaru did not directly touch on the event right before his eyes, but said only, "Please go back to your seat, my lord. Lord Nobutada, Lord Nobusumi, Lord Niwa, and all the generals are waiting."

Nobunaga went tamely back to the crowded room, but he did not sit down. He stood and looked around.

"Forgive me. I suppose I've been a bit of a killjoy. Each of you eat and drink to your heart's content." With these words he walked hastily off and shut himself up in his private quarters.

* * *

A flock of swallows was chirping under the eaves of the block of storehouses. Even though the sun was setting, the adults still appeared to be bringing food to the little ones in the nest.

"It could be the subject of a painting, don't you think?" In a room of a building situated some distance from the large garden, Saito Toshimitsu, a senior Akechi retainer, was entertaining a guest. The guest was the painter Yusho, who was not a native of Suwa. He must have been about fifty years old, and his robust physique gave no hint that he might be a painter. He spoke very little. Twilight settled on the white walls of the line of bean-paste warehouses.

"You must forgive me for suddenly calling on you in wartime like this, and talking on about nothing but the tedious affairs of a man no longer involved with the world. I'm sure you have many campaign responsibilities." Yusho seemed to be announcing his leave and began to rise from the cushion.

"No, please." Saito Toshimitsu was a very composed man, and without even moving, he detained his guest.

"Since you've come all the way here, it would not be polite to let you leave before you had talked to Lord Mitsuhide. If, after you leave, I tell my lord that Yusho had visited during his absence, he'll scold me and ask me why I didn't keep you here." And he intentionally started off on a new subject, doing his best to keep the unexpected caller entertained. At that time, Yusho was keeping a house in Kyoto, but he was originally from Omi in Mitsuhide's province. Not only that, but at one time, Yusho had received a warrior's stipend from the Saito clan in Mino. At that same time Toshimitsu—long before he had become a retainer of the Akechi clan—was serving the Saito clan.

After living as a *ronin*, Yusho had become an artist, citing the fall of Gifu as the reason for his course of action. Toshimitsu, however, had abandoned his former allegiance to the Saito. The discord that grew between Toshimitsu and his former masters was displayed even in front of Nobunaga, and disputes had been carried on almost as if they were asking for judgment. But now everyone had forgotten the stories that had excited society so much at that time, and those who looked upon his pure white sidelocks considered him to be a retainer the Akechi clan could not do without. Everyone respected his character and his position as an elder.

The allotment of lodgings had not been sufficient within Nobunaga's main camp at the Hoyo Temple, so some of the generals were quartered in various houses in Suwa.

The Akechi were bivouacked in the ancient buildings of a beanpaste wholesaler, and both the soldiers and their officers were relaxing after many days of hard fighting.

A youth who appeared to be the son of the master of the house came up and spoke to Toshimitsu.

"Won't you come and take a bath, Your Honor? All the samurai and even the foot soldiers have finished their evening meal."

"No, I'll wait until His Lordship comes back."

"His Lordship is rather late tonight, isn't he?"

"There's been a victory banquet today at the main camp. My lord very rarely touches *sake*, but perhaps he drank a little and is getting a bit tipsy with all the toasts."

"May I serve you your evening meal?"

"No, no, I'll wait for my meal as well, until I see that he's come back. I do feel sorry for the guest I've detained, though. Why don't you show him to the bath?"

"Would that be the traveling artist who's been here all afternoon?"

"That's right. The man who's crouched over there by himself looking at the tree peonies in the garden. He looks a little bored. Why don't you call him over?"

The youth withdrew, and then looked around at the back of the building. In front of the dark, luxuriantly blooming tree peonies, Yusho was sitting holding his knees, staring vacantly. A little while later, when Toshimitsu came through the gate, both the youth and Yusho were already gone.

Toshimitsu was apprehensive. He thought that Mitsuhide was far too late in returning. Even though he was well aware that a victory banquet would last well into the night.

Leading out through the ancient thatch-roofed gate, the path quickly joined the lakeside road. The last heat of the day still glimmered in the western sky over Lake Suwa. Toshimitsu looked down the road for some time. Sure enough, he finally saw his lord coming toward him. Horses, spearmen, and attendants all followed in one group. But the concern on Toshimitsu's brow did not diminish as they came closer. Something was not as it should be. Nothing in Mitsuhide's appearance suggested that he was returning from a victory banquet. His lord should have been riding home in brilliant array, swaying gallantly on horseback, drunk along with his attendants on today's gift of *sake*. But Mitsuhide was walking along, looking crestfallen.

A retainer was leading his horse, which loped along cheerlessly, while the attendants walked silently behind in exactly the same manner.

"I came out here to meet you. You must be tired." When Toshimitsu bowed before him, Mitsuhide looked as though he had been taken by surprise.

"Toshimitsu? I've been inconsiderate. You were good enough to worry about my coming home late. Forgive me. I drank a little too much today, so I intentionally walked home by the lake trying to sober up. Don't be worried by my color. I feel a lot better now."

Toshimitsu could see that his master had met with some unhappy experience. He had been Mitsuhide's close attendant for many years, so such a thing was unlikely to escape his notice. He did not, however, presume to ask about the matter. The old retainer was quick to look after his master's needs, hoping to cheer him up.

"How about a bowl of tea, and then a bath?"

Toshimitsu's reputation was enough to strike fear in the enemy on the battlefield, but as he helped Mitsuhide out of his clothes, Mitsuhide could only think of him as a solicitous old relative.

"A bath? Yes. A bath might be very refreshing at a time like this." And he followed Toshimitsu to the bathhouse.

For a while Toshimitsu listened to the sound of Mitsuhide splashing in the hot water in the bath. "Shall I scrub your back, my lord?" Toshimitsu called in.

"Send in the page," Mitsuhide replied. "I don't feel right about having you put your old body to work."

"Not at all."

Toshimitsu entered the bathroom, scooped up some hot water in a small wooden bucket, and went around behind his master. Certainly he had never done this before, but at that moment he only wanted to raise his master's unusually low spirits.

"Is it proper to have a general scrub the dirt from one's back?" Mitsuhide asked. He was modest to the very end. He always exhibited reserve even with his retainers, and it was questionable whether this was one of his good or bad points. Toshimitsu's own opinion was that it was not particularly good.

"Now, now. When this old warrior fights under your honored banner, he's Saito Toshimitsu of the Akechi clan. But Toshimitsu himself is not an Akechi. That being so, it will be a good memory for me, while I'm alive and serving you, to have washed the dirt off your skin just once."

Toshimitsu had bound up his sleeves and began to wash his master's back. As his back was being scrubbed, Mitsuhide bowed his head contentedly in silence. He reflected deeply on Toshimitsu's concern for him, and then on the relationship between himself and Nobunaga.

Ah, I've been wrong, he thought. Deep in his own heart, Mitsuhide blamed himself. What was it that was displeasing Mitsuhide and making him so unhappy? Certainly Nobunaga was a good master, but was his own loyalty equal to that of the old retainer who was now scrubbing his back? How shameful. It was just as though Toshimitsu were washing his heart with the hot water he poured down his back.

When he left the bath, Mitsuhide had changed both in appearance and in the tone of his voice. His mind had become completely refreshed, and Toshimitsu felt the same way.

"It was good to take a bath, just as you said. I guess it was fatigue as well as the *sake*."

"Do you feel better?"

"I'm all right now, Toshimitsu. Don't worry."

"I was worried because of the extraordinary unease on your face. That was the worst of all. Well, let me tell you that while you were gone we had a guest, and he's been waiting for your return."

"A guest? At these battlefield quarters?"

"Yusho was just traveling through Kai, and he said that before going elsewhere he wanted to stop and see you, and ask how you are."

"Where is he?"

"I had him stay in my room."

"Really? Well, let's go over there."

"He'll probably feel shamed if the lord actually walks over to see the guest. I'll bring him to you in a little while."

"No, no. Our guest is a man of taste. It won't be necessary to be overly formal."

An elegant dinner had been prepared for Mitsuhide in the hall of the main house, but he sat in Toshimitsu's room and ate a simple meal with his guest.

His face became even brighter after talking with Yusho for a while. He asked about the painting styles of the Southern and Northern Sung dynasties in China, discussed the artistic tastes of Shogun Ashikaga Yoshimasa and the merits of the Tosa school of painting, and talked about everything from the Kano style to the influence of Dutch painting. Throughout the conversation, it was clear that Mitsuhide's education had not been shallow.

"I've thought that when I grow old, I might return to more tranquil pursuits and my youthful studies, and even try to paint. Perhaps, before then, you could draw me an illustrated copybook."

"Of course, my lord."

Yusho had emulated the style of the ancient Chinese artist, Liang K'ai. He had recently developed his own school independent of the Kano or Tosa traditions and finally had become established in the art world. When Nobunaga had asked him to illustrate the sliding partitions at Azuchi, he had pretended to be sick and had refused. He had, after all, been a retainer of the Saito clan, which had been destroyed by Nobunaga. One could understand how Yusho might have felt too proud to decorate Nobunaga's living quarters with his own brush.

The phrase "soft on the outside, strong on the inside" might very well have applied to Yusho's character. Yusho was unable to trust the logic that Mitsuhide lived by. If Mitsuhide were to slip, even once, he would burst the dam holding his emotions in check and slide toward a fatal course.

Mitsuhide slept happily that night. Perhaps it was due to the bath. Or to the unexpected and pleasing guest.

The soldiers had gotten up before the sun, fed the horses, put on their armor, prepared their provisions, and were now waiting for their lord's appearance. That morning they were to assemble at the Hoyo Temple, depart from Suwa, and head out for Kofu. They would then pass down the coast road and make a triumphal return to Azuchi.

"You should prepare yourself quickly, my lord," Toshimitsu said to Mitsuhide.

"Toshimitsu, I slept well last night!"

"I'm glad to hear that."

"When Yusho leaves, you should give him my very best wishes and some money for the road."

"But you know, when I got up this morning and looked in on him, I discovered he had already gone. He got up and went out with the soldiers before the sun came up."

His is an enviable life, Mitsuhide said to himself as he looked at the morning sky.

Saito Toshimitsu unfolded a scroll. "He left this behind. I thought it might be something he had forgotten, but when I looked at it closely, I saw that the ink hadn't yet dried, and then I remembered that you had requested him to make an illustrated copybook. I think he stayed up until dawn working on it."

"What? He didn't sleep?"

Mitsuhide cast his eye over the scroll. The paper was all the more white in the morning sun, and on it a single branch of tree peonies had been freshly painted. An inscription in a corner of the painting read: *Tranquillity, this is nobility.*

Tranquillity, this is nobility, Mitsuhide recited silently as he rolled out the scroll, now coming upon the illustration of a large turnip. Next to the turnip was written, *Having a visitor is a taste.*

The turnip had been drawn in India ink without even a trace of effort; and if you looked at it closely, you could smell the fragrance of the earth. This turnip served as the root for a single leaf, and it seemed to be bursting with life. Its wild nature appeared to be laughing at Mitsuhide's rationalism with a marvelous artlessness and lack of concern.

He continued unfolding the scroll, but there was nothing else. The greater part of it was nothing but blank paper.

"It looks like it took him all night to do these two illustrations."

Toshimitsu was also impressed by the scroll, and bent over it in appreciation with Mitsuhide.

Mitsuhide was hesitant to look at it any longer, and asked Toshimitsu to roll it up.

At that point, the sound of the conch shell was heard in the distant sky. It was a call from the headquarters at the Hoyo Temple, signaling the troops throughout the town to get ready. Heard in the arena of the bloody war, the conch shell was a thing of indescribable dread, booming out sorrowful reverberations. But heard on a morning like this its sound was mild and almost quietly comforting.

Mitsuhide was soon on horseback himself. His brow this morning, much like the mountains of Kai, was completely unclouded and without even a hint of shade.

BOOK SEVEN

TENTH YEAR OF TENSHO
1582
SPRING

CHARACTERS AND PLACES

SHIMIZU MUNEHARU, commander
of Takamatsu Castle
AKECHI MITSUHARU, Mitsuhide's cousin
AKECHI MITSUTADA, Mitsuhide's cousin
FUJITA DENGO, senior Akechi retainer
AMANO GENEMON, senior Akechi retainer
YOMODA MASATAKA, senior Akechi retainer
MANASE, Kyoto physician
SHOHA AND SHOSITSU, poets
ODA NOBUTADA, Nobunaga's eldest son
SOTAN AND SOSHITSU, merchants from Kyushu
MURAI NAGATO, governor of Kyoto

TAKAMATSU, Shimizu Muneharu's castle
SAKAMOTO, Akechi Mitsuharu's castle
TAMBA, province of the Akechi clan
KAMEYAMA, Akechi Mitsuhide's castle
HONNO TEMPLE, Nobunaga's
temporary residence in Kyoto
MYOKAKU TEMPLE, Nobutada's
temporary residence in Kyoto

Fortress in a Lake

Two samurai galloped through the wicket gates of Okayama, their horses raising a cloud of dust as they hurried toward the castle. No one paid much attention to the riders. When they reached the gates, they announced that they carried an urgent dispatch from Lord Nobunaga in Kai.

Hideyoshi was in the citadel when a retainer came in to announce the arrival of the messengers.

"Have them wait in the Heron Room," he ordered.

This room was reserved for conversations of the most secret nature. Almost as soon as the two messengers had entered, Hideyoshi came in and sat down. One of the men took the letter from the folds of his kimono and laid it respectfully in front of Hideyoshi. It was wrapped in two or three sheets of oiled paper. Hideyoshi removed the outer wrapping and cut through the envelope.

"Ah, it's been a long time since I've looked at His Lordship's handwriting," he said. Before opening the letter, he held it reverently to his forehead: it was, after all, written by his lord's own hand.

When he finished reading, Hideyoshi placed the letter into his kimono and asked, "Did our troops in Kai achieve brilliant victories?"

"His Lordship's army was an irresistible force. About the time we left Kai, Lord Nobutada's army had already reached Suwa."

"That's just what you'd expect of Lord Nobunaga. He must have gone out into battle himself. Was he in good spirits?"

"I heard from one of the men on the campaign that going through the mountains was just like a spring flower-viewing outing. It seems that Lord Nobunaga will return by the coast road and view Mount Fuji on the way."

The messengers withdrew. Hideyoshi remained where he was, gazing at the painting of the white herons on the sliding doors. Yellow pigment had been applied to the eyes of the birds, and they looked as if they were staring back at him.

It will have to be Kanbei, Hideyoshi said to himself. He's the only one I can send. He summoned a page and said, "Kuroda Kanbei should be in the outer citadel. Have him and Hachisuka Hikoemon come here."

Hideyoshi took the letter out and read it once more. It was not really a letter, but the pledge he had requested from Nobunaga. Hideyoshi could have easily mobilized sixty thousand soldiers right here in Okayama. However, he had not crossed the border into the enemy province of Bitchu, which he had to conquer first if he was to defeat the Mori clan. There remained one obstacle in Hideyoshi's path into Bitchu that he was determined to remove—bloodlessly, if he could. This obstacle was the main castle of the seven fortresses that formed the enemy line of defense on the borders of the province: Takamatsu Castle.

Kanbei and Hikoemon came into the small room, and Hideyoshi immediately felt more at ease.

"His Lordship's pledge has just arrived," Hideyoshi began. "I'm afraid I'm going to ask you to go through more hardships. I'd like you to go to Takamatsu Castle."

"Would you mind if I read the pledge?" Kanbei asked.

Kanbei read it with the same respect he would have shown had he been addressing Nobunaga in person.

The pledge was addressed to the commander of Takamatsu Castle, Shimizu Muneharu. Nobunaga promised that if Muneharu capitulated, he would be rewarded with a domain consisting of the provinces of Bitchu and Bingo. He had taken an oath before the gods, Nobunaga continued, and nothing could induce him to go back on his word.

"I'd like you and Hikoemon to go to Takamatsu Castle as soon as possible," he told Kanbei. "I doubt there will be any problems when you meet General Muneharu and talk to him, but if there are, I don't imagine he'll remain unmoved after he sees this seal."

Hideyoshi looked optimistic, but the two other men were unable to share his confidence. Did he really believe that Shimizu Muneharu would betray his masters, the Mori, just because of this pledge, or did Hideyoshi have something else in mind?

The journey from Okayama to Takamatsu Castle took less than a day, and the messengers arrived all the quicker because they were on horseback. Passing through their own front lines, they looked up in the direction of the Kibi Mountains at the red setting sun.

From this point on, whoever they encountered would be the enemy. This was not the spring they had left behind in Okayama. The fields and villages were deserted.

A rider galloped from the front line to the palisade around Takamatsu Castle and waited for instructions. Finally, Kanbei and Hikoemon were ushered in through the palisade and led to the castle gate. Takamatsu was a typical example of a castle built on a plain. There were rice paddies and fields on either side of the road leading up to the main gate. The embankments and the outer stone walls stood in the middle of paddies. With each step up the stone stairs, the battlements and sharp, pointed walls of the main citadel loomed ever closer overhead.

Once inside the main citadel, it was clear to the envoys that this was the strongest of the seven fortresses on the border. The area inside the castle was broad, and although more than two thousand soldiers were stationed here, it was quiet. Because of Muneharu's decision to fight, the castle was accommodating an additional three thousand civilian refugees. Muneharu had decided to make his stand against the billowing waves of the eastern army in this one castle.

Kanbei and Hikoemon were shown into an empty room. Without his staff Kanbei limped inside with difficulty.

"Lord Muneharu will be here momentarily," the page said. He seemed to be less than twenty years old, and as he withdrew, his behavior was no different from what it would have been in peacetime.

The general came in, sat down unpretentiously, and said, "I am Shimizu Muneharu. I understand that you are envoys from Lord Hideyoshi. Welcome." He seemed to be about fifty, unassuming and plainly dressed. He had no retainers on either side of him, only a page of eleven or twelve kneeling behind him. The man was so lacking in ostentation that if it hadn't been for his sword and the one page, he would have looked like a village headman.

Kanbei, for his part, was extremely courteous with this unassuming general. "It's a pleasure to meet you. I am Kuroda Kanbei."

As the two men introduced themselves, Muneharu bowed affably. The envoys rejoiced, thinking that they would have no trouble in winning him over.

"Hikoemon," Kanbei said, "would you please tell General Muneharu the purport of His Lordship's message?" Although it would have been more proper for the senior of the two envoys to make the opening remarks, Kanbei thought that the older and mellower Hikoemon would more efficaciously present the merits of their case.

"Allow me to explain our mission, General. Lord Hideyoshi has ordered us to talk to you frankly, and I can do nothing less than that. Lord Hideyoshi would like to avoid a pointless battle if it is at all possible. I think you fully understand how things are going in the west. In terms of numbers, we can easily raise one hundred fifty thousand men, while the Mori have only forty-five thousand men, perhaps fifty at the very most. In addition, the Mori's allies—the Uesugi of Echigo, the Takeda of Kai, the warrior-monks of Mount Hiei and the Honganji, and the shogun—have all crumbled. What kind of moral justice can the Mori claim today by fighting and turning the west into scorched earth?

"On the other hand," Hikoemon went on, "Lord Nobunaga has won the favor of the Emperor and the love and respect of the people. The nation is finally emerging from the darkness of civil war and is greeting a new dawn. Lord Hideyoshi is pained by the thought that you and the many fine men who serve you will die. He wonders if there is not some means to avoid that sacrifice and asks you to reconsider one last time."

Taking out Nobunaga's pledge and a letter from Hideyoshi, Kanbei spoke next. "I will not talk of advantages and disadvantages. Instead, I would like to show you something that demonstrates the intentions of both Lord Hideyoshi and Lord Nobunaga. They both value good warriors. This, therefore, is a signed pledge promising you the provinces of Bitchu and Bingo."

Muneharu bowed respectfully to the document but did not pick it up. He said to Kanbei, "These are quite truly excessive words and this is a document granting me an unmerited reward. I have no idea what to say or what the proper etiquette might be. The stipend that I have received from the Mori clan is no more than seven thousand bushels, and surely I am nothing more than a country samurai approaching old age."

Muneharu said nothing about an agreement. Then there was silence. The two envoys sat in suspense. No matter what they said to him, he would only repeat, warmly and with great respect, "This is more than fair."

Neither all of Hikoemon's experience nor Kanbei's genius seemed to be of any use against this man. As envoys, however, they were determined to break through the wall, and they made their last effort.

"We have really said all that we can say," Kanbei said, "but if you have any particular desires or conditions you would like to add, we will be happy to listen to them and transmit them to Their Lordships. Please speak frankly."

"You're asking me to be frank?" Muneharu asked, almost as though he were talking to himself. He then looked at the two men. "Well, I wonder if you will listen. My hope is that, having reached the end of my life, I do not stray from the right path. That is my first principle. The Mori clan is neither better nor worse than your master in terms of loyalty to the Emperor. Unworthy as I am, I am a retainer of the Mori clan, and even though I've spent an idle life, I've received a stipend from the Mori for many years. My entire clan has received favors from them, and now, during these times of change, I have been ordered to guard the border. Even if I were aiming to make some small profit, and I accepted Lord Hideyoshi's kind offer and became the lord of two provinces, I would not be as happy as I am now. If I turned my back on my lord's clan, what kind of face would I be able to show to the world? At the very least, I would appear to be a complete hypocrite to my family and retainers, and I myself would be breaking every precept I have taught them all along." He laughed. "So, while I appreciate the kindness you've shown, please ask Lord Hideyoshi to forget about all this."

Shaking his head as though he were deeply sorry, Kanbei spoke quickly and distinctly. "I'm not going to be able to persuade you. Hikoemon, we should go."

Hikoemon was unhappy that they had failed, but he had feared from the first that that might happen. Both of them had predicted that Muneharu could not be bribed.

"The road will be dangerous during the night. Why don't you stay in the castle tonight, and then leave early tomorrow morning?" Muneharu insisted. It was not simply formality on his part, and the envoys knew he was a truly warm human being. He was their enemy, but he was an honest man.

"No, Lord Hideyoshi will be waiting anxiously for your reply," Hikoemon said.

The envoys asked only for torches and then set out on their way. Concerned that something might happen to them, Muneharu sent three of his retainers to take them as far as the front lines.

Kanbei and Hikoemon had ridden all the way to and from Takamatsu Castle without breaking their journey for rest or sleep. As soon as they arrived in Okayama, they went straight to Hideyoshi. Their report was short and factual: "General Muneharu refuses to capitulate. His resolve is firm, so another attempt at negotiation would be futile."

Hideyoshi did not appear to be surprised. He told the two men to come back after they had rested. Later that day, Hideyoshi summoned the envoys and several of his generals for a conference.

Referring to a map of the area, Kanbei reviewed the position of the defensive line of seven fortresses. Hideyoshi looked up from the map and stretched out as though he were tired. Earlier he had received news of Nobunaga's victory in Kai. Comparing the ease of his lord's successes with his own difficulties, Hideyoshi hoped that his prospects would improve from then on. He had at once addressed a letter to Nobunaga, to express his congratulations and explain the prospects for his own campaign, and to inform him that he had dropped the idea of trying to persuade Shimizu Muneharu to surrender.

Around the middle of the Third Month, the twenty thousand troops who had been standing by at Himeji entered Okayama, and the Ukita clan sent another ten thousand men. Thus, with a combined force of thirty thousand, Hideyoshi cautiously advanced into Bitchu. After marching only one league, he stopped and waited for reconnaissance reports; after another two leagues, he halted to reconnoiter again. Every soldier had heard the reports of the brilliant victories in Kai, so many found this prudent advance frustrating. Some hastily declared that Takamatsu Castle and the other smaller fortresses could be captured in a single swift advance.

When they understood actual battlefield conditions and the enemy's positions, however, they had to admit that winning a quick victory would be difficult.

Hideyoshi made his first camp on Mount Ryuo, a high plateau well to the north of Takamatsu Castle. From there he could look directly into the castle itself. At a glance he could see the lay of the land and appreciate the interdependence of the fortresses and main castle. He could also survey troop movements from the Mori clan's headquarters and be forewarned if they sent reinforcements.

Hideyoshi began the campaign by taking the small border fortresses one by one, until only Takamatsu remained. Concerned about this negative turn of events, Muneharu sent repeated messages to his overlords, the Mori, begging for reinforcements. One after another, couriers departed with ever more desperate appeals, but conditions did not permit the Mori to counterattack. And it would take them several weeks before they could assemble an army of forty thousand men and march to Takamatsu Castle. The only thing the Mori could do was encourage Muneharu to hold on and assure him that reinforcements were on their way. Then all communications between the castle and its allies were cut.

On the twenty-seventh day of the Fourth Month, Hideyoshi laid siege to Takamatsu Castle. But the fifteen thousand men at his headquarters on Mount Ryuo did not move. Hideyoshi positioned five thousand men on the high ground at Hirayama and the ten thousand men of the Ukita clan on Mount Hachiman.

Hideyoshi's generals positioned themselves at the rear of the Ukita contingent. It looked like the first arrangement of counters on a *go* board, and the positioning of his own retainers to the rear of the Ukita, who until recently had been allies of the Mori, was a matter of prudence.

There were skirmishes between the vanguards of the two armies from the first day of the siege. Kuroda Kanbei, who had just returned from inspecting the front lines, went to see Hideyoshi and described the first day's bloody engagement.

"During this morning's battle," Kanbei began, "Lord Ukita's warriors suffered more than five hundred casualties, while the enemy lost no more than a hundred men. Eighty of the enemy were killed, and twenty others were taken prisoner, but only because they were seriously wounded."

"It was to be expected," Hideyoshi said. "This castle will not fall without bloodshed. But it seems that the Ukita fought well."

The loyalty of the Ukita vanguard had indeed been tested.

* * *

With the Fifth Month the weather turned sunny and dry. The Ukita, who had suffered heavy casualties in the initial fighting, dug a trench across the front of the castle walls for five nights under cover of darkness. Once the trench was completed, they launched an attack on the castle.

When the defenders saw that the Ukita had advanced as far as the castle gate and outer walls, they hurled insults at them. It was easy to imagine the anger they felt toward these men who had once been their allies but who were now fighting as Hideyoshi's vanguard. As soon as they saw their opportunity, the defenders threw open the main gate and charged out.

"Attack these maggots!" they shouted.

"Kill them all!"

Samurai to samurai, soldier to soldier, they grappled and struck at each other. Heads were taken and raised, and they fought with a ferocity rarely seen even on a battlefield.

"Fall back! Fall back!" the Ukita general suddenly shouted in the middle of clouds of dust and smoke.

Glaring at the retreating Ukita, the defenders were carried away with the desire to crush them underfoot. They started to pursue them with cries of "Strike them down!" and "All the way to their banners!"

Too late, the mounted commander of the castle vanguard spotted the Ukita trench ahead. Seeing the trap, he tried to stop his men, but they stumbled forward, unable to see the danger. A volley of gunfire and thick gunpowder smoke instantly rose from the trench. The attackers staggered and fell.

"It's a trap! Don't fall into the enemy's trap! Lie down! Lie down!" the commander shouted. "Let them fire! Wait for them to reload, then jump on them!"

With fearful war cries, several men sacrificed themselves; they leaped up to draw enemy fire and were bathed in bullets. Judging the interval before the next round, others ran toward the trench and jumped in, filling the earth with fighting and blood.

That night it began to rain. The banners and the curtained enclosures of Mount Ryuo were drenched. Hideyoshi took cover in a hut and watched the melancholy clouds of the rainy season. He did not look very cheerful.

He looked around and called to a retainer, "Toranosuke, is that the sound of rain or someone's footsteps? Go see what it is."

Toranosuke went out but quickly returned and reported, "Lord Kanbei has just now returned from the battlefield. On the way back, one of the men carrying his litter slipped on the steep path, and Lord Kanbei took a hard fall. Lord Kanbei just laughed as though he were amused."

Why was Kanbei out at the front lines in this rain? As usual, Hideyoshi was impressed with Kanbei's untiring spirit.

Toranosuke withdrew to the next room and put firewood on the hearth. With the rain, the mosquitoes had begun to hatch, and they were especially troublesome that evening. The fire heated up the already muggy atmosphere, but at least it also smoked out the mosquitoes.

"It's smoky in here," Kanbei said, coughing. He limped past the pages and entered Hideyoshi's room unannounced.

He and Hideyoshi were soon talking happily. Their voices almost seemed to compete with each other.

"I think it's going to be difficult," Hideyoshi said.

Hideyoshi and Kanbei fell silent for a moment and listened to the dreary sound of the early summer rain pouring off the eaves of the makeshift hut.

"It's just a question of time," Kanbei began. "A second all-out offensive would be a gamble. On the other hand, we could resign ourselves to a long campaign and besiege the castle at our leisure, but there are great dangers in that, too. The forty thousand troops from the Mori's home province might arrive and attack us from the rear, and then we would be caught between them and the men in Takamatsu Castle."

"That's why I'm so depressed this rainy season. Don't you have any good ideas, Kanbei?"

"I've been walking around the front lines for the last two days, looking carefully at the position of the enemy castle and the surrounding geographical features. At this point I have only one plan on which we could stake everything."

"Takamatsu's fall is not just a question of taking a single enemy castle," Hideyoshi said. "If it falls, Yoshida Castle will soon be ours. But if we stumble here, that one defeat will cost us five years of work. We need a plan, Kanbei. I've asked the people in the next room to withdraw so you can speak without reserve. I want to know what you're thinking."

"It's rude of me to say so, but I suspect you have a plan too, my lord."

"I won't deny it."

"May I ask what yours is first?"

"Let's both write our ideas down," Hideyoshi suggested, bringing out paper, brush, and ink.

When they had finished writing, the two men exchanged sheets of paper. Hideyoshi had written one word, "water," and Kanbei had written two: "water attack."

Laughing out loud, the two men crumpled the sheets of paper and put them in their sleeves.

"Man's wisdom obviously doesn't exceed certain limits," Hideyoshi said.

"That's true," Kanbei agreed. "Takamatsu Castle stands on a plain conveniently surrounded by mountains. Not only that, but the Ashimori and seven other rivers run through the plain. It should not be difficult to divert the water of these rivers and flood the castle. It's a bold plan that most generals would not even think of. I can't help but admire how quickly you grasped the situation, my lord. But why do you hesitate to put it into action?"

"Well, since ancient times, there have been plenty of examples of successful attacks on castles using fire, but almost none with water."

"I think I've seen it mentioned in the military chronicles of the Later Han Dynasty and the period of the Three Kingdoms. In one of the chronicles I read something about our own country during the reign of Emperor Tenchi. When the Chinese invaded, our soldiers built dikes to store water. When the Chinese attacked, the Japanese soldiers were going to cut through the dikes and wash them all away."

"Yes, but they didn't actually have to put the plan into operation because the Chinese withdrew. If this plan is carried out, I'll be using a strategy that has no precedent. So I'm going to have to order some officials who have detailed knowledge of geography to determine what will be necessary in terms of time, expenses, and men for the engineering work."

What Hideyoshi wanted was not just a rough estimate, but concrete figures and a flawless plan.

"Absolutely. One of my retainers is very clever with such things, and if you order him to come here now, I think he'll have a clear answer for you right away. In fact, the strategy I had in mind is based on this man's ideas."

"Who is he?" Hideyoshi asked.

"Yoshida Rokuro," Kanbei replied.

"Well, call him right away." Then Hideyoshi added, "I also have someone at hand who is conversant with construction and land conditions. What would you think about calling him here at the same time and having him talk with Rokuro?"

"That would be good. Who is he?"

"He's not one of my retainers but a samurai from Bitchu. He's called Senbara Kyuemon. He's here in camp right now, and I have him working exclusively on making charts of the area."

Hideyoshi clapped his hands to summon a page, but all of his personal attendants and pages had withdrawn to some distance, and the sound of his clapping did not reach them. The din of the rain compounded the problem. Hideyoshi got up and stepped into the next room himself, and yelled out in a voice that would have been more proper on a battlefield, "Hey! Isn't anybody here?"

Once the decision had been taken to proceed with the water attack, the main camp on Mount Ryuo was found to be inconvenient. On the seventh day of the Fifth Month, Hideyoshi moved to Mount Ishii, which had been chosen because it overlooked Takamatsu Castle.

On the following day Hideyoshi said, "Let's start to measure the distances."

Hideyoshi, accompanied by half-a-dozen generals, rode to the west of Takamatsu Castle, to Monzen, on the banks of the Ashimori River. All the while he kept an eye on the castle to his right. Wiping the sweat from his face, Hideyoshi summoned Kyuemon. "What's the distance from the ridge of Mount Ishii to Monzen?" he asked.

"Under a league, my lord," Kyuemon answered.

"Lend me your map."

Taking the map from Kyuemon, Hideyoshi compared the construction of the proposed dike to the lay of the land. There were mountains on three sides, creating a natural baylike formation, extending in the west from Kibi to the mountainous area of the upper reaches of the Ashimori River; in the north from Mount Ryuo to the mountains along the border of Okayama; in the east to the edge of Mount Ishii and Kawazugahana. Takamatsu Castle was situated right in the middle of this open plain.

In Hideyoshi's eyes the fields, rice paddies, riding grounds, and villages on this flat plain were already submerged. The way he saw it, the mountainous banks on three sides could be viewed as a winding line of capes and beaches and Takamatsu Castle itself as a solitary man-made island.

Hideyoshi gave the map back to Kyuemon, reassured about the feasibility of the project, and once again mounted his horse. "Let's go!" he called out to his attendants, then said to Rokuro and Kyuemon, "I'm going to ride from here to Mount Ishii. Take the measurements for the dike by following the hoofmarks of my horse."

Hideyoshi turned his horse due east and galloped off, riding straight from Monzen to Harakozai, and then describing an arc from there to Mount Ishii. Kyuemon and Rokuro chased behind him, leaving a trail of powdered rice meal. After them followed laborers who drove in stakes to mark the line of the dike.

When the line that had been drawn became an embankment and the waters of the seven rivers were diverted to flow inside it, the entire area would become a huge lake shaped like a half-open lotus leaf. When the men looked carefully at the lay of the land that formed the border between Bizen and Bitchu, they realized that it must have been part of the sea in the distant past. The battle had commenced. It was not to be a battle of blood, but a war waged against the earth.

The length of the dike was to be one league; its width was to be thirty feet at the top and sixty feet at the base. The problem was its height, which had to be proportional to the height of the walls of Takamatsu Castle.

In fact, the primary factor assuring the success of the water attack was the fact that the castle's outer stone walls were only twelve feet high. Thus the height of the dike of twenty-four feet was figured from a base of twelve feet. It was calculated that if the water level rose to that height, it would not only submerge the castle's outer stone walls but also flood the castle itself under six feet of water.

It is only rarely, however, that a project is completed ahead of schedule. And the problem that so troubled Kanbei was one of human resources. For the most part, he would have to rely on the local farmers. The population of the neighboring villages, however, was rather sparse, because Muneharu had taken more than five hundred farming families into the castle before the siege, and many others had fled to the mountains.

The farmers who had taken refuge in the castle were ready to live or die with their lord. They were good, simple folk who had served Muneharu for years. Many of those who remained in the villages were people of bad character, or opportunists who were willing to work on a battlefield.

Hideyoshi could count on the cooperation of Ukita Naoie, and Kanbei was able to muster several thousand men from Okayama. But what troubled him was not getting this number of men together; his problem was how to use those human resources with the greatest efficiency.

On a tour of inspection, he called over Rokuro and asked for a progress report.

"I'm sorry to say that we may not meet His Lordship's schedule," Rokuro replied sadly.

Even the mathematical brain of this man could not figure out how to extract hard work from the mixed group of laborers and ruffians. For this reason a series of guard-houses had been set up every ninety yards along the dike, and soldiers were stationed at each of these surveillance points to encourage the laborers. Because the soldiers were simply there as passive observers, however, the thousands of men who swung their mattocks and shouldered dirt like ants were hardly spurred on at all.

Moreover, the timetable that Hideyoshi had imposed was extremely tight. Urgent messages reached him night and day. The forty thousand troops of the Mori had split into three armies under Kikkawa, Kobayakawa, and Terumoto, and they were getting closer to the provincial border by the hour.

Kanbei watched the laborers. Exhausted by working all hours of the day and night, some hardly moved at all. They had only two weeks to complete the project.

Two days. Three days. Five days passed.

Kanbei thought, Progress is so slow that we won't be able to complete the dike in fifty or even in a hundred days, much less in two weeks.

Rokuro and Kyuemon were going without sleep, supervising the workers. But no matter what they did, the men were disgruntled and insolent. To make matters worse, some laborers intentionally sabotaged the schedule by persuading even the comparatively submissive workers to hinder the project with deliberate slowness.

Kanbei was unable to watch passively. He finally began to visit the construction site himself, staff in hand. Standing on a hill of fresh earth at a section of the dike that had finally been completed, he looked down, with eyes aflame, at the thousands of workers. When he discovered someone showing the least bit of sloth, he would dash up to the laborer with a speed hardly befitting a cripple, and beat him with his staff.

"Get to work! Why are you being lazy?"

The laborers would tremble and work frantically, but only while Kanbei was watching them.

"The crippled demon warrior is looking!"

Kanbei finally made a report to Hideyoshi: "It's going to be impossible to finish on time. Just to make sure we are prepared, I'd like to request that you decide on some strategy beforehand in case the Mori reinforcements arrive while the construction is only half done. By the gods, it's more difficult getting these laborers to work than it is getting troops to maneuver."

Uncharacteristically nervous, Hideyoshi counted silently on his fingers. He was being informed hourly of the approach of a large Mori army, and he received the dispatches just as he might watch the clouds of an evening squall approach the mountains.

"Don't be discouraged, Kanbei. We still have another seven days."

"The construction is less than a third finished. How are we going to complete the dike in the few days we have left?"

"We can do it." This was the first time Hideyoshi had contradicted Kanbei so strongly. "We can finish it. But it won't be done if we only get the strength of three thousand men from our three thousand workers. Now if one man works like three or even five men, our three thousand workers will have the strength of ten thousand. If the samurai supervising them act in the same way, one man will be able to muster the spirit of ten men, and we should be able to accomplish anything we want. Kanbei, I'm coming to the construction site myself."

The following morning, a yellow-robed messenger ran around the construction site, ordering the laborers to stop their work and gather around a banner set up on the dike.

The workers from the night shift who were on their way home, and the men just now coming on, all followed their bosses. When the three thousand workers were assembled, it was difficult to differentiate the color of the earth from the color of the men themselves.

Prompted partly by uneasiness, the wave of blackened men moved forward. They had not lost their false show of courage, however, and continued to joke and banter. Suddenly the crowd became hushed as Hideyoshi moved toward the stool set up next to the banner. His pages and retainers were to his right and left, and stood back solemnly. The demon warrior, Kuroda Kanbei, who was the target of their daily malice, stood off to the side, resting on his staff. He addressed them from the top of the dike.

"Today it is Lord Hideyoshi's wish that you tell him your thoughts. As you all know, the time allotted for building the dike is more than halfway through, but the construction is going slowly. Lord Hideyoshi says that one of the reasons for this is that you have not been making a real effort. He has commanded you to gather here so that you can frankly explain why you are dissatisfied or unhappy, and what it is that you want."

Kanbei stopped for a moment and looked at the laborers. Here and there, men were whispering.

"The bosses of the various groups must understand the feelings of their men well. Don't miss this opportunity to tell His Lordship exactly what you want. Five or six men should come up here as representatives and speak out about your dissatisfactions and desires. If they are legitimate, they will be addressed."

With that, a tall man, stripped to the waist and with an insubordinate expression, came forward. Looking as if he were trying to gain favor with the herd of men, he climbed aggressively to the top of the dike. When they saw this, three or four more laborers swaggered up after him.

"Are these the only representatives?" Kanbei asked.

As they approached Hideyoshi's camp stool, each of them knelt down on the earth.

"It's not necessary to kneel," Kanbei told them. "Today His Lordship has cordially asked you to explain your discontent. You've come up here before him representing all of the laborers, so speak your minds freely. Whether or not we finish this construction on

time depends on you. We want you to tell us the reasons for the resentment and dissatisfaction you have hidden inside yourselves until now. Let's start with the man who came
up here first, on the right. Speak up now." Kanbei's tone was conciliatory.

When Kanbei urged them to speak a second time, one of the five men representing
the laborers spoke up.

"Well then, I'll take you at your word and speak, but don't get mad, all right? For one
thing…well, all right…please listen to this…."

"Speak."

"Well, you're paying us one *sho* of rice and a hundred *mon* for every sandbag we haul,
and the fact is that all of us—a couple of thousand poor folks—are real happy to be employed. But, well, we all think—and me, too—you might go back on your word because
we're all just laborers, anyway."

"Well now," Kanbei said, "why should a man with Lord Hideyoshi's reputation go
back on his word? Every time you carry a sandbag, you receive a branded strip of bamboo that you can exchange for pay in the evening, don't you?"

"Yes, Your Honor, we get the bamboo strips, but we only get paid one *sho* of brown
rice and a hundred *mon* even if we've carried ten or twenty sacks in one day. The rest is
military stubs and rice tickets to cash in later."

"That's right."

"So it troubles us, Your Honor. What we've earned would be fine in either rice or
money, but without the real thing, a poor day-laborer like me can't feed his wife and
children."

"Isn't one *sho* of rice and a hundred *mon* a living far better than what you usually
earn?"

"You shouldn't joke, Your Honor. We're not horses or cows, and if we worked like this
all year, we'd be done for. But, well, we've agreed to it, following His Lordship's orders,
and we've been working day and night. Now, we can do unreasonable work if we get our
wants filled along the way, and thinking that afterward we can drink *sake*, pay back our
debts, and buy some new clothes for the wife. But if we get paid in promises, we just can't
continue putting our hearts into the work."

"Well, you're pretty hard to understand. Lord Hideyoshi's army has made it a principle to rule benevolently and has done nothing despotic at all so far. What, really, do you
have to complain about?"

The five laborers laughed coldly. One of them said, "Your Honor, we're not complaining. Just pay us what we've earned. We can't fill our stomachs with waste paper and
rice tickets. And, more important than that, who is going to give us real money for that
waste paper on the day Lord Hideyoshi loses?"

"If that's what it is, you have nothing to worry about!"

"Ah, but wait. You say that you're going to win, and you and all these generals have
staked your lives on this gamble, but I wouldn't put a half share on a bet like that. Hey,
everybody! Isn't that right?"

As he waved his arms from the top of the dike, asking for the thousands of workers'
agreement, a shout arose instantaneously in response, and a wave of human heads undulated back and forth as far as the eye could see.

"Is that your only complaint?" Kanbei asked.

"Yeah. That's what we'd like to settle first," the man replied, looking to the crowd for support but not showing the least bit of fear.

"Absolutely not!" Kanbei spoke in his true voice for the first time. That instant, he threw down his staff, unsheathed his sword, and sliced the man in two. Turning quickly to another who had started to run away, he cut him down too. At the same time, Rokuro and Kyuemon—who were standing behind Kanbei—wielded their swords and finished off the other three men in a shower of gushing blood.

In this way Kanbei, Kyuemon, and Rokuro divided up their work and cut down five men in the instant it takes lightning to strike.

Struck by the speed and unexpectedness of the action, the laborers were as hushed as grass in a graveyard. The dissatisfied voices had been hushed in an instant. The faces that had been so impudent up until then—the defiant looks—were gone. Nothing was left but countless faces the color of earth, cowering in fear.

Standing over the five corpses, the three samurai glared ominously at the laborers, their blood-soaked swords still in their hands.

Kanbei finally shouted with all his ferocity, "These five men who represented you— we called them up here, listened to what they had to say, and gave them a very clear answer. Someone else may have something to say, too, however." He paused, waiting for someone to speak up. "Surely there's someone down there who wants to come up. Who's next? If there's anyone who thinks he wants to say something for everyone, now's the time to speak up!"

Kanbei was quiet for a moment, giving the men time to reflect on the matter. Among those numberless heads, there were very clearly men whose expressions were changing from fear to regret. Kanbei wiped the blood off his sword and returned it to its scabbard. Softening his expression, he lectured the laborers in a dignified manner.

"I see that no one is going to come up after these five men, so I imagine that means your intentions are different from theirs. If I'm right, then I'm going to have my say. Are there any objections?"

The several thousand laborers answered in the voices of men who had been saved from death. Not one of them had an objection. Nobody had any intention of complaining. The men who had spoken were clearly the ringleaders who had instigated the slowdowns. The rest were going to follow orders and work. Would Hideyoshi forgive them?

The three thousand men were speaking noisily back and forth, some in whispers, some yelling, so that one could hardly understand who was saying what. The feeling of the entire crowd, however, was united.

"Quiet now!" Kanbei waved his hand to control them. "All right. This is the way I think it should be. I'm not going to say anything complicated, but essentially it would be best if you all worked happily and quickly with your wives and children under His Lordship's administration. If you're indolent or greedy, you will only delay the arrival of the day you are looking forward to. The expeditionary army sent by Lord Nobunaga will not be defeated by the Mori. No matter how large a province the Mori control, it is a province that is doomed to fall. This is not because the Mori are weak, but because of the great movement of the times. Do you understand?"

"Yes," the laborers replied.

"Well then, are you going to work?"

"We're going to work. We're really going to work!"

"All right!" Kanbei nodded strongly and turned toward Hideyoshi. "My lord, you can hear how the workers have spoken, so won't you be generous with them this time?" He almost seemed to be pleading for the crowd.

Hideyoshi stood up. He gave a command to Kanbei and the two officials who were kneeling before him. Almost immediately, foot soldiers walked over, shouldering what appeared to be heavy money bags—a mountain of straw money bags.

Facing the laborers, who were caught up in their fears and regrets, Kanbei said, "You're really not to blame. All of you are in a pitiful situation. You've been led astray by two or three bad elements. That is what Lord Hideyoshi has declared; and so that you'll work with no other thoughts in mind, he has commanded that we give you a bonus to urge you on a little. Receive, express your thanks, and get quickly back to work."

When the command was given to the foot soldiers, every straw bag there was broken open and the mountain of coins poured out, almost covering the top of the dike.

"Grab however much you can and go. But only one fistful for each man."

He said this quite clearly, but the laborers still hesitated to make a move forward. They whispered among themselves and looked back and forth at each other, but the mountain of coins stayed right where it was.

"The fastest man will be the winner! Don't complain after it's all gone. Each man should take a fistful, so the men born with big hands can account themselves lucky, and the men with little hands shouldn't let anything slip between their fingers. Don't get excited and fail. Then go back to work."

The laborers no longer had any doubts. They could see that Kanbei meant what he said with his smiling face and jocular words. The laborers in the front of the crowd rushed up to the mountain of coins. They wavered a little, as though frightened by the sight of so much money, but as soon as the first man had grabbed a fistful and retreated, a chorus of happy voices suddenly arose. It sounded almost like a victory song.

Almost immediately such confusion took over that coins, men, and clods of earth were hardly distinguishable. No man, however, tried to cheat—somewhere along the line they had all thrown off their craftiness and dissatisfaction. Holding on to their handfuls of coins, they seemed to have been transformed, and each man ran off to his own work station.

The echoes of hoes and spades being used with real force filled the air. With spirited yells, men dumped earth, inserted poles through the straw carrying-baskets, and shouldered sandbags away. Real spirit was being mustered for the first time. The sweat the men were now wringing out of themselves increasingly gladdened and refreshed them, and they began to shout with enthusiasm among themselves.

"Who says we can't finish this dike in five days? Hey, everybody—remember the big flood?"

"That's right. This is nothing like trying to keep the flood waters out."

"Let's do it! Let's give it all we've got!"

"I'm not going to give up!"

In just half a day, more work was accomplished than in the previous five.

The overseers' whips and Kanbei's staff were no longer needed. Bonfires were lit at night, the dust from the earth darkened the day, and finally the work was almost finished.

As the landlocked dike neared completion, the related work of diverting the seven rivers around Takamatsu Castle also advanced. Nearly twenty thousand men had been put to work on that project. Damming up and drawing off the waters of the Ashimori and Naruya rivers were the construction projects considered to be the most difficult.

The official in charge of damming the Ashimori often complained to Hideyoshi, "The level of water is rising every day with the heavy rains in the mountains. There just doesn't seem to be any way of damming it."

Kanbei had gone to inspect the site with Rokuro the day before, and he understood the extreme difficulty of the situation.

"The current is so strong that even when we pushed in boulders that took twenty or thirty men to move, they were washed away immediately."

When even Kanbei could only bring back excuses, Hideyoshi went to the river himself to see the actual situation. But when he stood there and looked at the power of the rushing current, his own human knowledge was overwhelmed.

Rokuro came up and offered a suggestion: "If we cut down trees at the upper reaches of the river and push them in with the foliage still attached, it may slow the current a little."

This plan was put into operation, and for half a day, more than a thousand workers felled trees and tossed them whole into the river. But this, too, failed to slow the current.

Rokuro's next suggestion was to sink thirty large boats loaded with huge boulders at the site of the proposed dam.

Pulling the huge boats up against the current, however, proved to be impossible, so wooden planks were set out on the land, oil was poured over them, and, with great effort, the boats were pulled overland and sunk with their loads of boulders at the mouth of the river.

In the meantime the great dike, stretching an entire league, had been completed, and the rushing current of the Ashimori was transformed into foam and spray and diverted toward the plain around Takamatsu Castle.

At about the same time, the waters of the other six rivers were channeled into the area. Only the channeling of the Naruya River had proved too difficult for the workers to complete on time.

Fourteen days had passed since the seventh day of the Fifth Month, the day the work began. It had been completed in two weeks.

On the twenty-first day of the Fifth Month, the forty thousand Mori troops under Kikkawa and Kobayakawa arrived at the border—one day after the surroundings of Takamatsu Castle had been transformed into a muddy lake.

On the morning of the twenty-first, Hideyoshi stood with his generals at the headquarters on Mount Ishii and looked over his handiwork.

Whether one thought of it a grand spectacle or a wretched one, the swollen waters—aided by the rain during the night—had left Takamatsu Castle standing completely isolated in the middle of a lake. The outer stone walls, the forest, the drawbridge, the roofs of

595

the houses, the villages, the fields, the rice paddies, and the roads were all submerged, and the level was rising hourly.

"Where's the Ashimori?"

In response to Hideyoshi's question, Kanbei pointed to a stand of pines that could dimly be seen in the west.

"As you can see, there's an opening in the dike of about four hundred fifty yards in that area, and we're running the dammed-up waters of the Ashimori through that break."

Hideyoshi followed the line of the faraway mountains from west to south. Beneath the sky directly to the south, he could see Mount Hizashi on the border. With the dawn, the countless banners of the Mori's vanguard had appeared on the mountain.

"They're the enemy, but you can't help but sympathize with what Kikkawa and Kobayakawa must have felt this morning when they arrived and saw the lake. They must have stamped on the ground in vexation," Kanbei said.

Just at that moment, the son of the official in charge of the work at the Naruya River site prostrated himself in front of Hideyoshi. He was crying.

"What's the matter?" Hideyoshi asked.

"This morning," the young man replied, "my father declared that he was guilty of inexcusable negligence. He wrote you this letter of apology and committed *seppuku.*"

The official had been in charge of the difficult project of cutting five hundred yards through a mountain. Ninety yards remained that morning, thus he had not met his deadline. Taking responsibility for the failure, the man had taken his own life.

Hideyoshi gazed down at the man's son, whose hands, feet, and hair were still covered with mud. He gently beckoned him to his side.

"You are not to commit *seppuku* yourself. Pray for your father's soul by your action on the battlefield. All right?" And he lightly patted the youth's back.

The young man cried openly. The rain began to fall. Stripes of white rain began to pour into the muddy lake from the thick clouds that were quietly descending.

It was now the night of the twenty-second day of the Fifth Month, the evening after the arrival of the Mori troops at the border.

In the dark, two men swam like strange fish across the muddy lake and crawled up onto the dike. They triggered an array of clappers and bells that had been attached to a rope stretched along the water's edge, tied to the dwarf bamboo and brushwood, and made to look just like the brambles of a wild rose.

A bonfire burned brightly at each guardhouse along the dike. The guards came running quickly and captured one man, while the other was able to make good his escape.

"It doesn't make any difference whether he's one of the soldiers from the castle or on an errand from the Mori. Lord Hideyoshi should question this man carefully."

The commander of the guards sent the captive to Mount Ishii.

"Who is this man?" Hideyoshi asked as he went out to the veranda.

Retainers held lamps at either side of him, and he stared down at the enemy soldier, who was kneeling beneath the rain-covered eaves. The man knelt proudly, both arms bound with rope.

"This man's no soldier from the castle. I'll bet he's a messenger from the Mori. Wasn't he carrying anything?" he asked the retainer in charge of the prisoner.

In his preliminary investigation, the retainer had found in the man's clothing a *sake* bottle containing a letter, which he now placed before Hideyoshi.

"Hm...it seems to be a reply from Muneharu, addressed to Kikkawa and Kobaya-kawa. Bring the lamp a little closer."

The Mori reinforcements had been discouraged when they saw the lake that stretched as far as the eye could see. They had rushed to the castle, but had no idea how to aid it now that it was surrounded by water. They advised Muneharu to surrender to Hideyoshi and save the thousands of lives inside the castle.

The letter that Hideyoshi now held in his hand was Muneharu's response to that suggestion.

You have thought sympathetically of those of us here, and your words are filled with benevolence. But Takamatsu Castle is now the pivot of the western provinces, and its fall would surely signal the demise of the Mori clan. We have all received favors from the Mori clan since the time of Lord Motonari, and there is not one person here who would extend his life even by a day by selling the victory song to the enemy. We are firmly prepared for a siege, and are resolved to die with the castle.

In his letter, Muneharu was actually encouraging the reinforcements. The captured Mori messenger answered Hideyoshi's questions with unexpected frankness. Since Muneharu's letter had already been read by the enemy, he seemed resigned to the fact that it would be futile to hide anything. But Hideyoshi did not make a complete investigation. It was a matter of not humiliating a samurai. What was useless was simply appraised as such, and Hideyoshi turned his thoughts in another direction.

"I think that's enough. Untie this warrior's bonds and turn him loose."

"Turn him loose?"

"He swam across that muddy lake, and he looks cold. Feed him and send him off with a pass so he won't be arrested again on the way."

"Yes, my lord."

The retainer untied the messenger. The man had naturally been resolved to die, and was now confused. He bowed silently toward Hideyoshi and started to get up.

"I trust Lord Kikkawa is in good health," Hideyoshi said. "Please send him my warmest greetings."

The Mori messenger knelt down in the proper fashion. Feeling the depth of Hideyoshi's kindness, he bowed with the deepest respect.

"Also, I think there is a monk by the name of Ekei on Lord Terumoto's field staff. Ekei of Ankokuji."

"There is, my lord."

"I haven't seen him for a long time. Please send him my regards as well."

As soon as the messenger had gone, Hideyoshi turned and asked a retainer, "Do you have the letter I gave you earlier?"

"Quite securely, my lord."

"It contains a secret message of great importance. Take it directly to Lord Nobunaga."

"I shall deliver it to him without fail."

"Undoubtedly, that Mori retainer left on his errand with no less resolution than your own. But he was captured, and a letter containing the intentions of both Muneharu and Kikkawa fell into my hands. Be extremely careful."

Hideyoshi sat facing the lamp. The letter he had entrusted to the messenger to take to Azuchi requested Nobunaga to lead an army into the west.

The fate of the solitary Takamatsu Castle was like that of a fish already in the net. The combined armies of Mori Terumoto, Kobayakawa Takakage, and Kikkawa Motoharu had come. The hour was now! The conquest of the west could be completed with a single blow. Hideyoshi wanted to show this grand spectacle to Nobunaga, and he believed his lord's personal attendance would guarantee a momentous victory.

"KUMQUAT HEAD!"

The castle town of Azuchi had become the bustling center of a new culture. Lively, color-fully dressed citizens thronged its streets, and above, the brilliant golds and blues of the castle donjon looked as though they had been embroidered with the green of the new spring leaves.

Conditions could not have been more different from those in the west. In the Fifth Month, while Hideyoshi and his men had been toiling day and night in the mud to ac-complish their attack on Takamatsu Castle, the streets of Azuchi were hung with decora-tions, and the town was so animated that it looked as though its citizens were celebrating the New Year and the Midsummer Festival at the same time.

Nobunaga was preparing to welcome a guest of some importance. But who, people wondered, could be that important? The man who arrived at Azuchi on the fifteenth day of the Fifth Month was none other than Lord Tokugawa Ieyasu of Mikawa.

Less than one month before, Nobunaga had made his triumphal return from Kai through Ieyasu's province of Mikawa, so he might have been doing nothing more than re-turning the courtesy. But the visit was clearly in Ieyasu's interest; it was an era of sweeping change, and no time to neglect the future. Thus, though it was rare for Ieyasu to make formal visits to other provinces, he was coming to Azuchi, attended by a brilliant retinue of retainers.

The best lodgings in the town were set aside for him, and Akechi Mitsuhide was given responsibility for his reception. In addition, Nobunaga had ordered his son Nobutada, who was about to leave for the western provinces, to help with the preparations for an extravagant three-day banquet.

Some wondered aloud why Nobunaga was giving such a lavish welcome to Ieyasu, who was eight years his junior and the lord of a province that until recently had been small and weak. Others countered that there was nothing strange about it at all. The alliance between the Oda and the Tokugawa had endured for more than twenty years without suspicion, broken agreements, or fighting, which was a miracle in those days of betrayals and feudal power struggles.

A third group were of the opinion that the reason for the event was not something as trivial as repaying Ieyasu for his hospitality. They argued that in the future the lord of the Oda was going to accomplish great things. The west was a springboard to Japan's southernmost island of Kyushu, and from there to the rich lands of the Southern Seas. If Nobunaga was to succeed in their conquest, he would have to entrust the north of Japan to an ally he could trust.

For some time now, Nobunaga had planned to go to the western provinces himself to establish his own rule, just as he had done in Kai. Even now he was in the middle of busy preparations to leave for the front. Nevertheless, he put aside that important work to welcome Ieyasu.

Quite naturally, Ieyasu was given the best of what Azuchi could provide in terms of lodgings, furniture, and utensils, *sake* and food. But what Nobunaga wanted to give Ieyasu most of all were things that could be found in the humble tenements of the people and around the hearths of country folk—his friendship and trust.

It was these two things that had ensured the survival of their alliance. And, for his part, Ieyasu had proved himself a reliable ally time and time again. Ieyasu knew very well that his own interests were strongly tied to those of Nobunaga, despite the latter's occasional selfishness and willfulness. So even if he had drunk from a very bitter cup at times, he supported Nobunaga and had sworn to follow him to the very end.

If a disinterested third party were to look at the twenty-year alliance between the two men and to judge who had gained and who had lost, he would most likely have to say that both men had benefited. Without Ieyasu's friendship when he was young and beginning to set the direction of his life, Nobunaga would not have been in Azuchi. And if Ieyasu had never received Nobunaga's assistance, the weak and small province of Mikawa very likely would not have been able to withstand the pressures from its neighbors.

Aside from having bonds of friendship and self-interest, the two men had characters that were clearly complementary. Nobunaga had ambitions—and the will to realize them —the likes of which a prudent man like Ieyasu could not even imagine. Ieyasu, Nobunaga was the first to admit, had virtues that he himself lacked: patience, modesty, and frugality. Nor did Ieyasu seem to be ambitious for himself. He looked after the interests of his own province but never gave his ally cause for concern. He always stood his ground against their common enemies, a silent fortress at Nobunaga's rear.

In other words, Mikawa was an ideal ally, and Ieyasu a reliable friend. In looking back over the hardships and dangers they had faced over the past twenty years, Nobunaga was moved to call Ieyasu his "good old comrade," and praised him as the man who had done the most to make Azuchi a reality.

During the feast, Ieyasu expressed his heartfelt gratitude for Nobunaga's treatment, but periodically he felt that someone was missing, and finally he asked Nobunaga, "Wasn't Lord Mitsuhide in charge of the banquet? What's happened to him? I haven't seen him at all today, and I didn't see him at the Noh performance yesterday."

"Ah, Mitsuhide," Nobunaga answered. "He returned to Sakamoto Castle. He had to leave so quickly that he had no time to pay his respects." Nobunaga's answer was delivered in a voice that was refreshing and clear, and he showed no particular emotion as he spoke.

But Ieyasu was a little concerned. There were disturbing rumors spreading in the town. Nobunaga's brief and untroubled answer, however, seemed to belie the rumors, and Ieyasu let the matter drop.

Nevertheless, that night Ieyasu returned to his lodgings and listened to the stories that his retainers had heard about Mitsuhide's departure. And he could see that the situation was complicated enough not to be ignored. Listening to the different versions of the story, he pieced together what seemed to be the reason behind Mitsuhide's sudden departure.

It had happened on the day of Ieyasu's arrival. Without previous notice, Nobunaga had made an official inspection of the kitchens. It was the rainy season; Azuchi was hot and muggy. The smell of raw fish and preserved vegetables offended the senses. Not only that, but the foodstuffs that had been collected in great quantities from Sakai and Kyoto had been unpacked and piled up in terrible disarray. Flies swarmed over the food and on Nobunaga's face.

"This place stinks!" he growled angrily. Then, as he walked into the preparation room he continued, speaking to no one in particular, "What is this? All this dirt! All this waste! Are you going to cook for our honored guest in this stinking place? Are you going to serve him rotten fish? Throw all this stuff away!"

Nobunaga's anger was completely unexpected, and the kitchen officials flung themselves at his feet. It was a pitiful scene. Mitsuhide had done his best to purchase the finest ingredients and to have exquisite dishes prepared, going almost without sleep for several days, supervising his retainers and the kitchen workers. Now he could hardly believe his ears. He ran out in surprise and prostrated himself before his lord, explaining that the offensive smell was most certainly not caused by rotten fish.

"Don't give me any excuses!" Nobunaga interrupted. "Throw everything away! Get something else for tonight's banquet!"

Turning a deaf ear, Nobunaga walked away.

Mitsuhide sat silently for a while, almost as though he had lost the power to move his legs. At that point a messenger arrived and handed him a letter ordering him to collect his forces and leave immediately for the western provinces.

The Akechi retainers carried the many delicacies they had prepared for Ieyasu through the back gate and dumped them into the moat, exactly as they might have thrown out trash or a dead dog or cat. Silently, suppressing their tears, they poured their feelings into the black waters.

At night the frogs croaked loudly outside Mitsuhide's lodgings. What are you brooding over? the frogs seemed to ask. Were they crying in sympathy for him, or laughing at his stupidity? It depended on how one listened to them.

Mitsuhide had ordered that no one be let in, and now he sat alone in a large, empty room.

Though it was only the beginning of summer, a cooling, delicate breeze blew silently into the gloom. Mitsuhide was terribly pale. It seemed that the hair of his sidelocks stood straight up each time the candle flickered. His anguish could be seen in the disarray of his hair and in the dreadful color of his face.

Finally he slowly raised what Nobunaga had dubbed his "kumquat head" and looked out into the darkened garden. In the distance he saw a great number of lamps shining between the trees. It was the first night of the banquet in the castle.

Should I go like this, just as I was ordered? Mitsuhide asked himself. Or would it be better to go and pay my respects at the castle once before leaving? Mitsuhide had always been confused by such things. His ordinarily clear head was so tired at that point that he had to think hard in order not to make a mistake.

Having made this question into such a great issue, no matter how he long he considered the matter, he was at a complete loss about what to do. Most of the pain of confronting his difficulties welled up in an unconscious sigh of grief and he wondered: Are there other men in this world so difficult to understand? he wondered. What can a person do to suit my lord's temperament? He's so hard to please.

If he had been able to put aside the absolute nature of the lord-and-retainer relationship and speak honestly, he would have criticized Nobunaga. Mitsuhide had been endowed with critical faculties far beyond the common man's, and it was only because Nobunaga was his lord that he was cautious and, in fact, afraid of his own criticism.

"Tsumaki! Tsumaki!" Mitsuhide called, suddenly looking at the sliding doors on either side of him. "Dengo? Dengo, are you there?"

But the man who finally opened the door and bowed in front of him was neither Dengo nor Tsumaki. It was one of his personal attendants, Yomoda Masataka.

"Both men are busy with the disposal of the material we were going to use for the banquet and with the sudden preparations for our departure."

"Come with me to the castle."

"The castle? You're going to the castle?"

"I think it's proper to pay my respects to Lord Nobunaga once before we depart. Make the preparations."

Mitsuhide quickly got up to dress himself. He seemed to be spurring himself on before his resolution faded.

Masataka looked flustered. "This evening when I asked what you wanted to do, I thought you might want to go up to the castle, for just that reason. But we had no time, with His Lordship's sudden command. And you said then that we would leave without paying our respects to either Lord Nobunaga or Lord Ieyasu. Now, all the attendants and servants are engaged in cleaning up. May I ask you to wait for a little while?"

"No, no. I don't need many attendants. You'll be enough. Bring my horse."

Mitsuhide went out toward the entrance. There was not one retainer in the rooms he passed on his way. Only two or three pages followed behind him. But once he stepped outside, he could see small groups of retainers with their heads together, talking in the shadows of the trees and in the stables. Quite naturally, all the Akechi retainers were concerned about suddenly being dismissed as officials of the banquet and being ordered on the very same day to set out for the west.

Back and forth they expressed their resentment, their eyes filled with tears of grief. Their antagonism and anger toward Nobunaga, which had been intensifying since the Kai campaign, like oil poured on firewood, had been ignited by this latest incident.

At the camp in Suwa during the Kai campaign, Mitsuhide had already met with an unbearable public humiliation, an event that had not been hidden from his retainers. Why had Nobunaga been tormenting their master so much recently?

But today's shock was by far the worst, because the incident would be known to all the guests: Lord Ieyasu and his retainers, the nobility from Kyoto, and Mitsuhide's fellow Oda generals. To have suffered an insult here was the same as having one's shame exposed to the entire nation.

Such public humiliation was unbearable to anyone born a samurai.

"Your horse, my lord," Masataka said.

The retainers had still not noticed the attendant leading Mitsuhide's horse. Distracted by the events of the day, they still stood in small groups, discussing the matter.

Just as Mitsuhide was about to leave, someone dismounted in front of the gate. It was a messenger from Nobunaga.

"Lord Mitsuhide, are you leaving?" the man inquired.

"Not yet. I thought I would go to the castle once more, pay my respects to His Lordship and Lord Ieyasu, and leave."

"Lord Nobunaga was worried that you might consider doing that, and sent me here so that you wouldn't have to go to the castle in the middle of your haste to depart."

"What? Yet another message?" Mitsuhide said. He immediately went back inside, sat down, and listened respectfully to his lord's wishes.

The order for you to be dismissed from today's function and take your leave still stands as before, but there are further instructions concerning your departure as the vanguard to the western provinces. The Akechi forces are to march from Tajima into Inaba. You may enter Mori Terumoto's provinces at will. Do not be careless, and do not allow time to pass. You should return to Tamba at once, prepare your troops, and protect Hideyoshi's flank along the Sanin Road. I myself will soon head westward as a rear guard. Do not waste time and possibly cause us to miss this strategic opportunity.

Mitsuhide prostrated himself and responded that he would follow the instructions to the letter. Then, perhaps feeling that he had shown too much servility, he sat up, looked directly at the messenger, and said, "Please speak to His Lordship as you see fit."

Mitsuhide walked to the entrance to see the man off. With each step, his senses were set on edge by the wind that wafted through the almost empty building.

Until a few years ago, when I was given leave to return home, he always wanted me to see him once before I left, even if it was the middle of the night. How many times had

603

Nobunaga said, Come by for a bowl of tea, or If you're leaving in the morning, come by before dawn. Why has he come to despise me like this? He's even sent a messenger so he won't have to see me in person.

Don't even think. Don't even consider it. The more he made an effort not to, the more he grumbled and the more his heart was flooded by a silent monologue. The words were like bubbles rising up through fetid water.

"Does anyone see these flowers? They're useless too!"

Mitsuhide reached out for the large vase in the alcove and shook the flowers that had been beautifully arranged. As he carried the vase to the veranda, the water spilled noisily onto the floor. "Let's get out of here! It's time to leave! Are you ready?" he shouted to his retainers. Mitsuhide raised the vase over his head, aimed at a wide stepping stone, and threw it with all his might. It exploded amid a spray of water with a comforting sound, and water flew back onto Mitsuhide's face and chest. Mitsuhide turned his soaked face up toward the empty sky and laughed out loud. He laughed completely alone.

It was late at night, and as the fog settled in, the air became hot and humid. His retainers had finished packing and stood in ranks in front of the gate. The horses neighed under the low rain clouds in the sky.

"Has rain gear been prepared?" a retainer asked, looking inside the gate again.

"There's not a bit of starlight tonight, and if it starts to rain, the roads are going to become difficult. We'd better prepare a few extra torches," another yelled.

Every samurai's face was as gloomy as the night sky. Eyes were filled with anger, tears, bitterness, or sullen discontent. Very soon, Mitsuhide's voice could be heard as he rode away from the entrance with a group of mounted men.

"Sakamoto is almost within view," he said. "We should arrive there soon, even if it does rain."

Hearing the unusually cheerful voice of their lord, his retainers felt surprise more than anything else.

Earlier that evening, Mitsuhide had complained of a slight fever and had taken medicine, and now his attendants were anxious about the possibility of rain. He had responded to their concern in a voice purposefully loud enough for the men standing both inside and outside the gate to hear.

When Mitsuhide was announced, fire was passed from torch to torch until the number of lights seemed almost to multiply infinitely. Then, with flames held aloft, the retainers walked out one after another, following the vanguard.

After they had traveled about half a league, rain began to fall, the drops splashing the flames of the torches.

"It seems the guests in the castle still haven't gone to bed. Perhaps they're going to stay up all night."

Mitsuhide did not notice the rain. As he turned in his saddle and looked back toward the lake, the huge donjon of Azuchi Castle seemed to soar into a sky that was as black as ink. He imagined that the golden dolphins that adorned the roof sparkled brighter on this rainy night, glaring out into the darkness. Reflected in the lake, the sea of lights in the many-storied building seemed to shiver with cold.

"My lord, my lord! You shouldn't catch cold!" Fujita Dengo said with concern as he drew his horse up to Mitsuhide's and put a straw raincoat across his shoulders.

That morning the shore of Lake Biwa was once again lost in the mist, perhaps because the sky had not yet settled from the early summer rains. With the lapping waves and the mist that was indistinguishable from rain, the world appeared to be pure white.

The road was extraordinarily muddy, and the horses were spattered all the way up to their ears. Silently defying the previous night's rain and the condition of the road, the entire army tramped desolately toward Sakamoto. To the right was the lakeshore, to the left, Mount Hiei. As the wind blew down the mountain, it stiffened the straw raincoats the men were wearing and made them look like bristling hedgehogs.

"Ah, look over there, my lord. Lord Mitsuharu has come to greet you," Masataka said to Mitsuhide.

The castle on the lakeshore—Sakamoto Castle—was directly ahead. Mitsuhide nodded slightly, as though he had already noticed. Although Sakamoto was almost close enough to Azuchi for him to be able to turn around and see it, Mitsuhide looked as if he had walked a thousand leagues. As he stood in front of the castle commanded by his cousin, Akechi Mitsuharu, he felt exactly as though he had escaped from the tiger's den.

His attendants, however, were far more worried about Mitsuhide's periodic coughing than they were about what might have been on his mind, and they expressed their concern.

"You've been traveling all night in the rain with this cold, and you must be exhausted. Once you've gone inside the castle, you should waste no time in getting yourself warm and going to bed."

"Yes, I probably should."

Mitsuhide was truly a gentle lord. He listened intently to his retainers' advice and understood their anxiety. When they arrived at the pine grove in front of the gate, Dengo took the reins of Mitsuhide's horse and stood next to the saddle, ready to help his master dismount.

On the bridge across the moat, a line of Mitsuharu's retainers had drawn up. One of the retainers opened an umbrella and offered it deferentially. Masataka took the umbrella and held it over Mitsuhide's head.

Mitsuhide walked across the bridge. Looking down through the railing, he could see white water birds swimming around the pilings like scattered flowers over the blue-green water.

Mitsuharu, who had come out to welcome his cousin, now stepped out a few paces from the line of soldiers and bowed respectfully.

"We've been waiting for you since dawn," he said, leading Mitsuhide through the entrance. The ten or so principal retainers attached to Mitsuhide washed their muddy hands and feet, stacked their wet straw raincoats in a pile, and went into the citadel.

The other retainers stayed outside the moat, washing the horses and taking care of the baggage, while waiting to be told where their lodgings would be. The neighing of horses and the din of human voices could be heard far off in the distance.

Mitsuhide had changed out of his traveling clothes. He felt so relaxed in Mitsuharu's quarters that they could have been his own. He had a view of the lake and Mount Hiei from every room. The inner citadel was situated in an area that had once had the most picturesque scenery, but no one could appreciate that scenery now. Since Nobunaga had given the command for Mount Hiei to be destroyed by fire, the monasteries and temples had become mounds of ashes. The village houses at the foot of the mountain had only recently begun to be rebuilt.

The ruins of the castle at Mount Usa, where Mori Ranmaru's father had met his end, were also close by, as was the battlefield where the soldiers of the Asai and Asakura clans had grappled with the Oda, only to have their corpses piled high. When one thought about these ruins and past battles, one realized that the beauty of the scenery echoed with the wailing of ghosts. Mitsuhide sat listening to the sound of the early summer rains and remembering.

Meanwhile, Mitsuharu was in a small tearoom, watching the fire in the hearth and listening to the genial sound of the water boiling in a teakettle made by the master caster Yojiro. At that moment he was completely immersed in the art of tea.

From the time of Mitsuharu's adolescence, he and Mitsuhide had been brought up as brothers, sharing the suffering of the battlefield and the happiness of home life. And, rather than becoming estranged, as brothers tend to do after they grow up, their relationship continued to be a close one.

Their characters, however, would never be the same. So on this morning the two men quickly went to separate quarters in the castle, each assuming the lifestyle that his own heart dictated.

Well, I imagine he's already changed his clothes, Mitsuharu said to himself. He stood up from his place before the teakettle. Crossing the wet veranda, he went over the bridged corridor into the suite of rooms assigned to his cousin. He could hear Mitsuhide's close attendants in another room, but Mitsuhide was alone, sitting bolt upright and staring out over the lake.

"I'd like to offer you some tea," Mitsuharu said.

Mitsuhide turned toward his cousin and murmured, "Tea…," as though he were waking from a dream.

"A piece I had ordered from Yojiro in Kyoto has recently been delivered. It doesn't have the elegant patterns of an Ashiya kettle, but it has a rustic charm that pleases the eye. They say that new teakettles are no good, but as you'd expect of Yojiro, the water that comes from his kettles tastes just as good as the water that comes from the old ones. I had intended to serve you tea with it the next time you were here, and when I was informed this morning that you were suddenly returning from Azuchi, I immediately lit a fire in the hearth."

"That was kind of you, Mitsuharu, but I don't want any tea."

"Well, what about after your bath?"

"You won't need to prepare a bath either. Please just let me sleep a little. That's all I want."

Mitsuharu had heard a great many stories recently, so he was not completely blind to Mitsuhide's thoughts. Nevertheless, he did have some particular doubts about why his cousin had returned to Sakamoto so suddenly. It was hardly a secret that Mitsuhide had been given the responsibility of organizing the banquet Nobunaga was holding to welcome Ieyasu. Why had Mitsuhide been so suddenly dismissed just before the banquet? Ieyasu was certainly in Azuchi. Nevertheless, Mitsuhide's post had been given to someone else, and Mitsuhide himself had been ordered to leave.

Mitsuharu had not yet heard any details, but from the time he had been told of the events in Azuchi to the moment he saw Mitsuhide's face, he had come to understand that something had happened to upset Lord Nobunaga. Mitsuharu secretly grieved for his cousin.

And just as Mitsuharu had feared, ever since he had welcomed him at the castle that morning, Mitsuhide's appearance had not been encouraging. Seeing a grave shadow on his cousin's brow, however, was not such a surprise for Mitsuharu. He believed that there was no one who understood Mitsuhide's character as well as he did, because of their shared past.

"Yes, that makes sense. You spent the entire night coming from Azuchi on horseback. We're now in our fifties, and can't treat our bodies the way we could when we were young. Well, you should sleep for a while. Everything is prepared."

Mitsuharu did not force the issue or try to oppose his cousin's will. Mitsuhide got up and went inside the mosquito netting while the morning light still played across its threads.

* * *

Amano Genemon, Fujita Dengo, and Yomoda Masataka were waiting for Mitsuharu as he left Mitsuhide's room. The three men bowed.

"Excuse me, my lord," Dengo said. "We're very sorry to disturb you, but we wondered if we might have a word with you. It's a matter of some importance." Dengo was not speaking in his ordinary tone of voice.

Mitsuharu himself responded as though he had been expecting them. "Why don't we all go to the teahouse? Lord Mitsuhide has gone to sleep, and I was just thinking it would be a shame to waste the fire under the kettle."

"If we go to the teahouse, we won't have to keep people at a distance. That's an excellent idea."

"Let me show you the way."

"I'm afraid the three of us are provincials, so we don't understand much about tea, and we certainly weren't prepared to receive such an honor from you today."

"Don't think of it that way. I understand a little of what you are worried about, and for that reason alone the teahouse should be a good place to talk."

They sat down in the thin light coming through the translucent paper doors of the small teahouse. The water in the kettle had been boiling for some time, and now it bubbled with an even more congenial sound than before. Mitsuharu had shown his martial spirit on the battlefield many times, but here, in front of the hearth, he seemed to be a completely different person.

"Well, let's not bother with tea. What's on your minds?"

Thus encouraged, the three men looked resolutely back and forth at each other.

Finally Dengo, the man among them who seemed to have the most courage, said, "Lord Mitsuharu, this is mortifying....I can hardly bring myself to speak of it...." He raised his right sleeve to hide his tears.

The other two didn't cry, but they could not hide their swollen eyelids.

"Has something happened?" Mitsuharu was completely calm, and the three men quickly recovered. It was as though they had expected to be confronting fire but were seeing only water. Mitsuharu noticed their swollen eyes, but he himself was unmoved.

"The fact is," Mitsuharu continued, "I, too, am worried that this unexpected return means that Lord Nobunaga has been somehow offended. Why was Lord Mitsuhide dismissed from his duties at the banquet?"

The first to answer was Dengo. "Lord Mitsuhide is our master, but we are not blind to crime and our reasoning is not prejudiced, so we are not just going to rattle on with resentment about Lord Nobunaga without cause. We took great care to try to understand Lord Nobunaga's motives this time, both in terms of the circumstances of Lord Mitsuhide's dismissal, and why he was blamed. The case is exceedingly strange."

Dengo's throat was so dry that he could not go on. Yomoda Masataka came to his rescue and continued the story.

"We even tried to find relief by speculating there was some political motive, but no matter how we look at it, there is nothing we can really put together. The overall plan should have been clear in Lord Nobunaga's mind for some time now. So why would he dismiss the man to whom he had given the responsibility of organizing the banquet and grant the honor to someone else on the very day of the banquet? It almost seems to be a display of disunity intentionally put on for his guest, Lord Ieyasu."

Genemon went on, "When I look at the situation as my companions have already described it, I can only think of one reason for it, which is really no reason at all. For the last several years Lord Nobunaga's persistent enmity has caused him to view with hostility everything that Lord Mitsuhide does. His dislike has finally become frank and undisguised, and things have come to this point."

The three men stopped talking. There was a mountain of incidents they would have yet liked to describe. For example, at the camp in Suwa during the invasion of Kai, Nobunaga had pushed Mitsuhide's face down on the wooden floor of the corridor, calling him "Kumquat Head," and ordering him to leave. Thus he had been insulted in front of everyone, and there had been numerous times that he had been embarrassed in the same way at Azuchi. These incidents, each of which would take forever to recount, demonstrated Nobunaga's hostility toward Mitsuhide and had become the subject of gossip among the retainers of other clans. Mitsuharu was of the same flesh and blood as Mitsuhide, and because of his close kinship, he was naturally aware that those events that had occurred.

Mitsuharu had listened to everything without the least change of expression. "Well then, Lord Mitsuhide was dismissed for no particular reason? I'm relieved to hear that. Other clans have earned Lord Nobunaga's favor or disfavor, depending on his mood."

The expressions on the three men's faces suddenly changed. The muscles around Dengo's lips twitched, and he abruptly drew up closer to Mitsuharu.

"What do you mean, you're relieved?"

"Do I have to repeat myself? The blame is not with Lord Mitsuhide, so if this has happened because Lord Nobunaga was out of sorts, Lord Mitsuhide should be able to repair the unhappy situation when Lord Nobunaga is in a better mood."

Dengo was speaking more and more excitedly. "Aren't you viewing Lord Mitsuhide as an entertainer who has to ingratiate himself for the sake of his lord's mood? Is this the way one should think of Lord Akechi Mitsuhide? Don't you think he's been humiliated, insulted, and pressed to the brink of self-destruction?"

"Dengo, the veins in your temples are getting a little swollen. Calm down."

"I haven't been able to sleep for two nights. I can't just remain calm like you, my lord. My master and his retainers have been scorched in a boiling pot of injustice, ridicule, insults, and every kind of vexation."

"That's why I've asked you to calm yourself and try to get some sleep for two or three nights."

"That's absurd!" Dengo exclaimed. "It's said of samurai that the shame of once being covered with mud is difficult to wipe away. How many times have my lord and his retainers endured such shame on account of this vicious lord in Azuchi? And yesterday it wasn't just a matter of Lord Mitsuhide's role in the banquet being taken away. The order that came right after that made the entire Akechi clan look like dogs chasing wild boar or deer. Perhaps you've heard that we are to mobilize immediately for a departure to the west. We're supposed to attack the Mori's provinces in the Sanin to protect Lord Hideyoshi's flank. How can we go to the battlefield feeling the way we do? This situation is another example of the scheming of that vicious dog of a lord!"

"Restrain yourself! Whom are you referring to as a vicious dog?"

"Lord Nobunaga, the same man who constantly calls our lord 'Kumquat Head' in front of others. Look at men like Hayashi Sado, or Sakuma Nobumori and his son. For years they helped make Nobunaga as great as he is today. Then, almost immediately after they were rewarded with status and a castle, they were arrested for some trivial crime and either condemned to death or driven into exile. The final act of that vicious lord is always to chase someone away."

"Silence! You are not to speak so disrespectfully of Lord Nobunaga! Get out! Now!"

As Mitsuharu finally became angry and reprimanded the man, something could be faintly heard in the garden. It was difficult to tell whether it was a man approaching, or only the falling of autumn leaves.

Extreme care was taken day and night against the possibility of espionage, even in places where the enemy's presence was highly improbable. Thus even in the teahouse garden, there were samurai standing guard. Now one of the guards had come up to the teahouse and was bowing in front of the door. After handing a letter to Mitsuharu, he drew back a little and waited as motionless as a stone.

Soon Mitsuharu's voice could be heard from inside. "This will require an answer, and I will write one later. Have the monk wait."

The guard bowed politely toward the entrance and walked back to his post. His straw sandals made almost no sound on the path in the manner of someone slinking away.

For a while, Mitsuharu and the other three men sat in complete silence, enveloped in an excruciatingly icy atmosphere. From time to time, a ripe plum fell to the ground with a sound like a wooden hammer striking the earth. That sound was the only thing that relieved the silence. Suddenly a bright ray of sunlight struck the paper panels of the sliding door.

"Well, we should take our leave. You have some urgent business to attend to," Masataka said, taking the opportunity to withdraw, but Mitsuharu, who had unrolled the letter and read it in front of the three men, now rolled the letter up.

"Why don't you stay awhile?" he asked, smiling.

"No, we'll take our leave. We don't want to intrude any further."

After the three men had shut the sliding door tightly behind them, their footsteps disappeared in the direction of the bridged corridor, and they sounded as if they were walking across thin ice.

A few moments later Mitsuharu left as well. He called into the samurai quarters as he walked down the corridor. Mitsuharu immediately asked for writing paper and a brush, and fluidly set the brush to the paper as though he already had in mind what he was going to write.

"Take this to the Abbot of Yokawa's messenger and send him back."

He handed the letter to one of his attendants and, appearing to have no further interest in the matter, asked a page, "Is Lord Mitsuhide still sleeping?"

"When I checked, his room was very quiet," the page replied.

When he heard this, Mitsuharu's eyes brightened as though he too were really at peace for the first time that day.

The days passed. Mitsuhide spent the time in Sakamoto Castle, doing nothing. He had already received Nobunaga's command to depart for the western provinces, and should have returned as quickly as possible to his own castle to mobilize his retainers. Mitsuharu would have liked to tell him that spending such a long time in idleness was not going to be good for his reputation in Azuchi. When he thought about Mitsuhide's feelings, however, he was unable to speak out. The discontent that Dengo and Masataka had expressed so bitterly would naturally be in Mitsuhide's heart as well.

If that was so, Mitsuharu thought, a few days of peace and quiet would be the best preparation for the forthcoming campaign. Mitsuharu had complete faith in his cousin's intelligence and common sense. Wondering how Mitsuhide was passing the time, Mitsuharu visited his room. Mitsuhide was painting, copying from an open book.

"Well, what are you doing?" Mitsuharu stood at his side and watched, pleased at Mitsuhide's composure and happy that they could share something.

"Mitsuharu? Don't look. I still can't paint in front of others."

Mitsuhide put down the brush and displayed a bashfulness not often seen in men over fifty. He was so embarrassed that he hid the sketches he had discarded.

"Am I disturbing you?" Mitsuharu laughed. "Who painted the book you're using as a model?"

"It's one of Yusho's."

"Yusho? What's that fellow doing these days? We don't hear anything at all about him around here."

"He unexpectedly visited my camp one evening in Kai. He left the following morning before dawn."

"He's a strange fellow."

"No, I don't think he can be summed up simply as strange. He's a loyal man, and his heart is as upright as bamboo. He may have given up being a samurai, but he still seems like a warrior to me."

"I've heard he was a retainer of Saito Tatsuoki. Are you praising him because he remains faithful to his former lord even today?"

"During the construction of Azuchi, he was the only one who refused to participate, even though he was invited to do so by Lord Nobunaga himself. He won't bend for either fame or power. It seems that he had more self-respect than to paint for the enemy of his former lord."

Just then, one of Mitsuharu's retainers came in and knelt behind them, and the two men stopped talking. Mitsuharu turned and asked the man what his business was.

The samurai looked embarrassed. In his hand was a letter and what seemed to be a petition written on thick paper. As he spoke, he was obviously worried about Mitsuharu's reaction. "Another messenger from the Abbot of Yokawa has come to the castle gate, and he pressed me to deliver this letter once more to the lord of the castle. I refused, but he said he had come on orders and would not go away. What should I do?"

"What? Again?" Mitsuharu lightly clicked his tongue. "I sent a letter to the Abbot of Yokawa some time ago, carefully explaining to him that I could not possibly agree to the contents of his petition, so that it was useless for him to ask. Still he persisted, sending me letters two or three times after that. He's certainly headstrong. Just refuse to take it and sent him off."

"Yes, my lord."

With that, the messenger hurried off with the petition still in his hand. He looked as though he himself had been reprimanded.

As soon as the man had left, Mitsuhide spoke to his cousin.

"Would that be the Abbot of Yokawa from Mount Hiei?"

"That's right."

"Years ago, I was ordered to take part in the burning of Mount Hiei. We then made war not only on the warrior-monks, but also on the holy men, and on women and children—without distinction—cutting them down and tossing their bodies into the flames. We so utterly destroyed that mountain that trees could not have been expected to thrive there again, much less men. And now it seems that the priests who survived the massacre have gone back and are trying to make the place live again."

"That's right. From what I've heard, the mountaintop is just as desolate and ruined as it was before, but men of profound learning are calling together the scattered remnants of the believers and using every means possible to restore the mountain."

"That will be difficult while Lord Nobunaga is alive."

"And they're well aware of that. They've turned a great deal of their energy toward the Court, trying to get an edict from the Emperor to persuade Lord Nobunaga, but the prospects are dim, so recently they've looked for support from the common people. They're roaming every province, seeking contributions, knocking on every door, and I've heard that they're even constructing temporary shrines on the sites of the old temples."

"Well then, the errand of the messenger who was sent to you two or three times by the Abbot of Yokawa had something to do with that petition?"

"No." Mitsuharu quickly shifted his eyes and gazed peacefully into Mitsuhide's face. "The fact is that I thought it was something I needn't trouble you with, so I turned him down myself. Since you're asking me about it now, however, perhaps I should go over it with you. The Abbot of Yokawa knew that you would be staying here, and he wanted to have an audience with you at least once."

"The abbot said that he wanted to meet me?"

"Yes, and he also requested in his petition to have the respected name of Lord Mitsuhide on the subscription list for the restoration of Mount Hiei. I told him that both requests were absolutely out of the question."

"And even though you told him it was out of the question, and refused and then refused again, he still sent messengers to the castle three or four more times? Mitsuharu, I would be apprehensive about signing my name to the subscription list out of deference to Lord Nobunaga, but I wonder if I need to hesitate just to meet him."

"I think it's totally unnecessary for you to meet him," Mitsuharu said. "What purpose today would there be for you—who acted as a general at the destruction of Mount Hiei—to meet with a priest who survived that destruction?"

"He was an enemy at that time," Mitsuhide replied. "But now Mount Hiei has been made completely impotent, and the people there have prostrated themselves and pledged their allegiance to Azuchi."

"Certainly, in form. But how are the fellow priests and relatives of those who were massacred, and the monks whose ancient temples and monasteries were burned, going to forget the resentment that has lived in their hearts for so many years? The dead must have numbered ten thousand, and the buildings had been there since the time of Saint Dengyo."

Mitsuhide let out a long sigh. "There was no way I could avoid Nobunaga's orders, and I too became one of those insane arsonists on Mount Hiei that year. I stabbed to death both the warrior-monks and numberless unfortunate monks and laymen, young and old. When I think of that today, my breast is tortured just as though it were the burning mountain itself."

"But you've always said that we should take the broad view, and it doesn't sound as though you're doing that now. You destroy one to save many. If we burn one mountain but make the Buddhist Law shine brightly on another five mountains and a hundred peaks, then I think that the killings we samurai commit cannot be called murders."

"Of course that's right. But out of sympathy, I can't restrain a tear for Mount Hiei. Mitsuharu! In public I must hold back, but as an ordinary man I feel that there could be no harm in saying a prayer for the mountain, could there? I'm going to go to the mountain incognito tomorrow. I'll come back right after meeting the abbot."

That night, Mitsuharu stayed awake worrying even after he had gone to bed. Why was Mitsuhide so taken by the idea of going to Mount Hiei? Should he, Mitsuharu, try to stop him, or would it be better to let him do what he wanted? Considering the position

Mitsuhide was in now, it would be better for him to have no connection whatsoever with the restoration of Mount Hiei. And it would not be advisable for him to meet with the abbot, either.

This much Mitsuharu could think through clearly, but why had Mitsuhide looked displeased at his arbitrary rejection of the abbot's messenger and his refusal of the petition? Fundamentally, he did not seem very happy with Mitsuharu's handling of the situation.

What sort of plan was Mitsuhide conceiving, with Mount Hiei as its center? Obviously Mitsuhide's visit would provide good material for slanderous assertions that he was plotting against Nobunaga. And it was certainly a waste of time, just before his departure for a campaign in the western provinces.

"I'm going to stop him. I'm going to stop him no matter what he says." Having made this decision, Mitsuharu finally closed his eyes. In a head-on confrontation he would most likely receive an unpleasant tongue-lashing from Mitsuhide or make him very angry, but he was going to do his best to stop his cousin. So resolved, he went to sleep.

The next morning he got up earlier than usual, but as he was washing, he heard the rhythm of running feet hurrying down the main corridor to the entranceway. Mitsuharu called out and stopped one of the samurai.

"Who's leaving?"

"Lord Mitsuhide."

"What!"

"Yes, my lord. He's attired in light dress for the mountain and is accompanied only by Amano Genemon. They're planning to take their horses as far as Hiyoshi. Or that's what Lord Mitsuhide said as he was putting on his straw sandals at the entrance just now."

Mitsuharu never missed his morning prayers in front of the castle shrine and at the family altar, but this morning he neglected both. He dressed with both long and short swords and hurried toward the entrance. But Mitsuhide and his retainer had already gone, and only the attendants who had seen them off remained, looking toward the white clouds on Shimeigatake.

* * *

"It looks like the rainy season is ending here too."

The morning mist in the pine grove beyond the castle still had not cleared, and it made the surrounding area look almost like a scene at the bottom of the sea. The two mounted men hurried through the grove at a light gait. A large bird flew over them, flapping its wings majestically.

"The weather is fine, isn't it, Genemon?"

"If it stays like this, the mountain will be clear."

"I haven't felt this good in a long time," Mitsuhide said.

"That fact alone makes this trip worthwhile."

"I want to meet the Abbot of Yokawa more than anything else. That's my only business here."

"I daresay he will be surprised to see you."

"People would have been suspicious if I had invited him to Sakamoto Castle. I have to meet him in private. Make the arrangements, Genemon."

"People are more likely to see you at the foot of the mountain than on the mountain itself. It would be highly unpleasant if word got around to the villagers that Lord Mitsuhide was out on an excursion. You should wear your hood down over your face, at least as far as Hiyoshi."

Mitsuhide pulled his hood down, until only his mouth was visible.

"Your clothes are plain, and your saddle is just that of a common warrior's. No one will be likely to think that you are Lord Akechi Mitsuhide."

"If you treat me with that much courtesy, people will be suspicious immediately."

"I hadn't thought of that," Genemon said with a laugh. "I'll be a little more careful from now on, but don't blame me for being rude."

At the foot of Mount Hiei, rebuilding had been going on for two or three years, and the streets of Sakamoto were slowly taking on their former appearance. As the two riders passed through the village and turned off on the path going up to the Enryaku Temple, the morning sun finally began to sparkle on the waters of the lake.

"What shall we do with the horses once we dismount on the way up?" Genemon asked.

"A new shrine has been built on the site of the old one. There must be farmhouses nearby. If not, it should be all right to leave them with a workman at the shrine itself."

A lone rider was whipping his horse to catch up with them.

"Isn't that someone calling us from behind?" Genemon asked with some concern.

"If there's someone chasing us, I'm sure it's Mitsuharu. Yesterday he looked as though he wanted to stop me from making this trip."

"He possesses a gentility and sincerity you rarely see in men these days. He's almost too gentle to be a samurai."

"It is Mitsuharu, just as I thought."

"He certainly seems determined to stop you, my lord."

"Well, I won't turn back, no matter what he says. Maybe he's not going to try to stop me. If he wanted to do that, he'd have grabbed my horse's bridle at the castle gate. Look, he's dressed for a mountain excursion, too."

In the end, Mitsuharu had rethought his position before starting out. He felt that it would be best not to oppose Mitsuhide, but rather to come along with him for the day to make sure he made no mistakes.

As he brought up his horse alongside of his cousin, he smiled brightly. "You're too fast for me, my lord. I was taken by surprise this morning, and not a little shaken up. I didn't think you would leave at such an early hour."

"I didn't think you were planning to come with me. You wouldn't have had to chase us like that if we'd made arrangements last night."

"I was negligent. Even if you are traveling in disguise, I thought that you would be accompanied by at least ten mounted men carrying along a picnic, and that you would be traveling at a more leisurely pace."

"I would have liked that if this had been a normal excursion," Mitsuhide said. "But the only purpose of today's trip is to pray for those who went through hellfire years ago and to hold at least one memorial service for their bones. I hadn't thought about carrying up fine *sake* and delicacies."

"I may have said something that offended you yesterday, but I'm just prudent by nature. It was really nothing more than my not wanting you to do something that might be taken the wrong way in Azuchi. Given the way you're dressed, and that your intention is to say a mass for the dead, I'm sure Lord Nobunaga couldn't blame you even if he were to hear about it. The fact is that even though I reside in a castle close to Sakamoto, I haven't made one trip to the mountain. So I thought that today would be a good opportunity to visit the place. Well, lead on, Genemon."

Spurring his horse, Mitsuharu rode up next to Mitsuhide and began to make conversation as though he were afraid Mitsuhide might become bored. He discussed the plants and flowers they saw along the roadside, explained the habits of the different birds as he distinguished them by their calls, and generally carried on with the solicitude of a kind woman trying to cheer up an sick person.

Mitsuhide could not reject such a display of true feelings, but Mitsuharu talked almost exclusively about nature, while Mitsuhide's mind was immersed in human concerns whether he was asleep or awake or even holding a brush over a painting. He lived in human society, in the midst of contending demons and within the flames of wrath and malice. Even though the song of the cuckoo filled the mountain air, the hot blood that had risen to his temples during his retreat from Azuchi had not yet been calmed.

As Mitsuhide climbed Mount Hiei, his heart was not at peace even for a moment. How desolate the place looked, when contrasted with its former prosperity. Following the Gongen River up toward the Eastern Pagoda, the party saw no signs of human life. Only the birdsong hadn't changed. The mountain had been famous as a sanctuary for rare birds since ancient times.

"I don't see a single monk," Mitsuhide said as he stood in front of a ruined temple. He appeared to be surprised at Nobunaga's thoroughness. "Isn't there a single living soul on this mountain? Let's try the main temple."

He looked more than a little disappointed. Perhaps he had thought he would see the latent power of the warrior-monks come back to life on the mountain, in spite of Nobunaga's supremacy.

But when they finally arrived at the former location of the main temple and lecture hall, nothing remained but mounds of ashes. Only in the area of the monastery had a number of huts been erected. The scent of incense drifted from that direction, so Genemon went to investigate. He found four or five mountain hermits, sitting around a pot of rice gruel that was cooking over a fire.

"They say the Abbot of Yokawa isn't here," Genemon said.

"If the abbot is not there, is there not perhaps a scholar or elder from former times?"

Genemon inquired a second time, but his answer was not encouraging. "It seems there's no such person on the mountain. They're not allowed to come here without the permission of either Azuchi or the governor of Kyoto. Moreover, even now the law does not recognize any permanent residences on the mountain other than for a limited number of monks."

"The law is the law," Mitsuhide said, "but religious zeal is not like a fire that can be doused with water and disappear forever. Come to think of it, the elders probably thought that we're warriors from Azuchi, and they probably hid. The abbot and the elders who survived are probably somewhere on the mountain right now. Genemon, explain to those men that they should have no such worries, and ask them once again."

As Genemon started to walk off, Mitsuharu said to Mitsuhide, "I'll go. They are not likely to tell us anything, with Genemon's stern way of asking questions."

While he was waiting for Mitsuharu, however, Mitsuhide unexpectedly encountered someone he hadn't planned on meeting at all.

The man was dressed in a greenish brown hood and a monk's robe of the same color and wore white leggings and straw sandals. He was over seventy years of age, but his lips were a youthful red. His eyebrows were pure white, and he looked like a crane dressed in a monk's robe. He was accompanied by two servants and a child.

"Lord Mitsuhide? Well, well, I never thought I'd meet you here, my lord. I heard that you were in Azuchi. What brings you to this deserted mountain today?"

He hardly spoke like an old man; his voice was exceptionally resonant, and his lips formed a constant, untroubled smile.

On the contrary, it was Mitsuhide who appeared to be confused. Distracted by the sharp eyes beneath the old man's clear brow, his response was hesitant.

"It's Doctor Manase, isn't it? I've been staying at Sakamoto Castle for a few days, and I thought a little walk through the mountains might cheer me up from the gloom of the rainy season."

"There's no better medicine for the body or the mind than an occasional cleansing of the *ch'i* by walking through the hills and getting in touch with nature. At a a glance, I'd say you've been tired for some time. Are you returning to your home province on sick leave?" the doctor asked, narrowing his eyes to the size of needles. For some reason Mitsuhide found it impossible to deceive a man who had eyes like that. Manase had been practicing medicine at the time Yoshiaki's father, Yoshiteru, was shogun. The two men had not met for quite a while, but Mitsuhide had sat in the company of the great doctor a number of times at Azuchi Castle. Nobunaga had often invited Manase to be his guest at tea ceremonies, and whenever he was sick, he would call him immediately. He had more confidence in this man than in his own physicians.

By nature, however, Manase did not enjoy being employed by the powerful and, as he lived in Kyoto, traveling to Azuchi was a chore, despite his robust health.

At that point Mitsuharu returned without having gone to the hut, as Genemon had quickly run to call him back.

"We've bumped into someone, and it's an awkward situation," Genemon whispered to him as they walked back. But when Mitsuharu saw that it was Manase, he happily joined the conversation, indicating clearly that he had long been on friendly terms with the doctor.

"What a treat! It's Doctor Manase. You always look healthier than a man in his prime. Did you climb up from Kyoto today? Off on a mountain excursion?"

Manase enjoyed conversation and was happy to run into friends on the mountain.

"I climb Mount Hiei every year in the spring or early summer and again in the fall. But you know, there must be a lot of herbs that we haven't discovered yet right here."

As Manase talked, he did not seem to be paying particular attention to Mitsuhide, though he had been casting his doctor's eye over the man from time to time. Eventually he turned the subject to Mitsuhide's health.

"I've heard from Lord Mitsuharu that you'll soon be leaving to take part in the campaign in the west. Be sure to take good care of your health. When a man passes fifty, it's difficult to deny his age, no matter how strong he may be."

There was a concern in his advice that went beyond the words.

"Is that so?" Mitsuhide smiled and responded to Manase's advice as though they were discussing someone else's health. "Recently I've felt as though I've had a bit of a cold, but I've got a strong constitution and haven't really considered myself to be ill."

"Well, I wouldn't be so sure. It's all very fine when a sick man is conscious of his own illness and takes the proper precautions. But when a man is overconfident, as you are, he can fall quite gravely into error."

"Well then, do you think I am suffering from some chronic condition?"

"I can see, just by looking at your complexion and listening to your voice, that you're not in your usual state of health. Rather than saying that you are suffering from a chronic disease, I would suggest that your internal organs may have become fatigued, and that the subtle energies associated with them are out of balance."

"If you're just saying I'm fatigued, I'll certainly agree to that. From taking part in various battles over the past few years and from serving my lord, I've pushed my body beyond its limits time and again."

"Speaking about something like this to someone as knowledgeable as you is probably like teaching the Dharma to the Buddha, but you really should take care of your health. The five internal organs—the liver, heart, spleen, lungs, and kidneys—are manifested in the five aspirations, the five energies, and the five sounds. For example, if the liver is ill, you'll have copious tears; if the heart is injured, you'll be beset by fears, no matter how brave you are ordinarily; if the spleen is distressed, you'll be easily angered; if the lungs are not functioning properly, you'll go through mental agony and not have the psychological strength to understand why. And if your kidneys are weak, you'll have strong swings of mood."

Manase gazed steadily at Mitsuhide's complexion. For his part, Mitsuhide was confident of his own health and did not intend to listen to what Manase was going to say. He did his best to conceal what he felt behind a forced smile but was beginning to feel ill-humored and uneasy. Finally, his patience worn thin, he appeared to be waiting for an opportunity to get away from the old man.

Manase, however, was not going to stop what he had to say halfway through. Understanding exactly what the look in Mitsuhide's eyes meant, he continued to lecture him.

"What I noticed from the moment I met you was the color of your skin. You seem to be either very afraid or worried about something. You repress the anger in your eyes, but I can see that they are filled not only with the anger of a man but also with the tears of a woman. Haven't you recently felt a chill at night that goes all the way to the tips of your fingers and toes? What about a ringing in your ears? Or dried-up saliva and a taste in your mouth as though you've been chewing thorns? Do you have any of those symptoms?"

"There have been nights when I could not sleep, but last night I slept fine. Well, I certainly appreciate your concern, doctor, and during the campaign I'll take extra care about medicine and food." Taking this opportunity, Mitsuhide signaled to Genemon and Mitsuharu that it was time to go.

* * *

That day the Akechi retainer Shinshi Sakuzaemon belatedly left Azuchi for Sakamoto Castle, accompanied by a small party of men. His lord, Mitsuhide, had left in such haste that Shinshi had stayed behind to take care of unfinished business.

As soon as he had taken off his travel clothes, several men crowded around him in his room and questioned him.

"What was the situation like afterward?"

"What kind of rumors spread around Azuchi after His Lordship left?"

Shinshi spoke, gritting his teeth. "It's only been eight days since His Lordship left Azuchi, but for the men who receive their stipends from the Akechi clan, it's been like sitting on a bed of nails for three years. Every servant and commoner in Azuchi has walked by the empty banquet hall and yelled insults. 'Is this Lord Mitsuhide's empty mansion? No wonder it smells like rotten fish. With this kind of bad luck and disgrace, the light shining on that Kumquat Head is going to fade right away.'"

"No one criticized Lord Nobunaga's actions as unreasonable or unfair?"

"There must be some retainers who understand. What are they saying?"

"During the days after His Lordship's departure, the banquet was being held for Lord Ieyasu, so Azuchi Castle was involved in that and nothing else. Perhaps Lord Ieyasu thought it strange that the official in charge of the banquet had suddenly been changed, and I've heard that he asked Lord Nobunaga why Lord Mitsuhide had suddenly disappeared. Lord Nobunaga only replied nonchalantly that he had had him return to his home province."

Everyone who heard this report bit his lip. Shinshi went on to tell them that most of the senior Oda retainers seemed to think that Mitsuhide's adversity was their good luck. Furthermore, it was possible that Nobunaga was considering moving the Akechi clan to some out-of-the-way place. That was nothing more than a rumor, but there is rarely smoke without fire. Ranmaru, Nobunaga's favorite page, was the son of Mori Yoshinari, the Oda retainer who had died in battle years before at Sakamoto. For this reason Ranmaru secretly coveted Sakamoto Castle. There was even a rumor that he had already received a tacit promise from Nobunaga.

And there was more. Many were of the view that the order for Mitsuhide to advance toward the Sanin Road had more than likely been calculated so that when he occupied the area, he would be made its governor on the spot. Sakamoto Castle, so close to Azuchi, would then be presented to Mori Ranmaru.

As proof, Shinshi cited the military command given to Mitsuhide by Nobunaga on the nineteenth day of the month, and then he turned away in a fury. He need not have explained. The order had angered Mitsuhide and every one of his retainers. It read as follows:

In order for you to act as rear guard in Bitchu, you should set out from your own province in the next few days and thereby precede me to the battlefield. There you should wait for Hideyoshi's instructions.

This letter, circulated to all the generals and retainers of the Oda clan, was clearly written under Nobunaga's direction, so when it was brought to the warriors of the Akechi clan, their anger moved them to tears of rage. It had been customary to consider the Akechi clan superior to the Ikeda and the Hori, and as on the same level as Hideyoshi's Hashiba and the Shibata. Nevertheless, their lord's name had been recorded beneath those commanders' names in addition to his being put under Hideyoshi's command.

A lack of respect for one's rank was the greatest insult to a samurai. The shame of the banquet incident had been compounded in a military order. The men were outraged once again. By that time it was twilight, and the setting sun played over the walls. No one spoke, but tears stained the men's cheeks. Just then, the footsteps of several samurai could be heard in the corridor. Guessing that their lord was now returning, the men all scrambled out to meet him.

Only Shinshi, still in his travel clothes, held back waiting to be summoned. Mitsuhide, who had just returned from Mount Hiei, did not call Shinshi until after he had taken a bath and eaten.

No one was with him at that time but Mitsuharu, and Shinshi delivered a report that he had not given to the other retainers, which was that Nobunaga had made his decision and was preparing to set out from Azuchi on the twenty-ninth of the month. He would spend one night in Kyoto and then immediately go west.

Mitsuhide listened attentively. His eyes reflected his clear and observant intellect. He nodded at Shinshi's every word.

"How many will be accompanying him?" he asked.

"He will be accompanied by a few retainers and thirty or forty pages."

"What! He'll be going to Kyoto with so small an entourage?"

Mitsuharu had remained quietly in the background, but now that Mitsuhide, too, had sunk into silence, he dismissed Shinshi.

After Shinshi left, Mitsuharu and Mitsuhide were alone. Mitsuhide looked as though he wanted to open his heart to his cousin, but in the end, Mitsuharu did not give him the chance. Instead, Mitsuharu spoke of loyalty to Nobunaga and urged Mitsuhide to hasten to the western provinces so as not to offend his lord.

The upright character his cousin displayed was characterized by a strong and loving quality upon which Mitsuhide had relied for the last forty years, and he had faith in him now as the most dependable man in his clan. Therefore, even though Mitsuharu's attitude was not in tune with Mitsuhide's own innermost feelings, he was unable to be angry with him or try to pressure him.

After some moments of utter silence Mitsuhide suddenly said, "Let's send an advance party tonight to my retainers at Kameyama and have them prepare for the campaign as quickly as possible. Would you arrange that, Mitsuharu?"

Mitsuharu stood up happily.

That night, a small party of men hurried toward Kameyama Castle.

At about the fourth watch, Mitsuhide suddenly sat up. Had he been dreaming? Or had he been considering something and had decided against it? A little while later he pulled the coverlet over himself again, buried his face in the pillow, and tried to get back to sleep.

Was it mist or rain? The sound of the waves in the lake, or the wind blowing down Mount Hiei? The wind from the mountain did not stop playing through the eaves of the mansion all night. Although it did not find its way inside, the candle at Mitsuhide's pillow flickered as though it were being shaken by an evil spirit.

Mitsuhide turned over. Although it was the season of short nights, to him it seemed that the morning was long in coming. Finally, just as his breathing had become deep and even, once again he suddenly pushed away his covers and sat up with a start.

"Is anyone there?" he called toward the pages' quarters.

Sliding doors were opened far away. The page on night watch silently entered and prostrated himself.

"Tell Matabei to come right away," Mitsuhide ordered.

Everyone in the samurai quarters was asleep, but as several of Mitsuhide's retainers had left for Kameyama the previous evening, those who had stayed behind were tense, not knowing when their lord, Mitsuhide, might himself depart. Each man had gone to bed that evening with his traveling clothes next to his pillow.

"Did you summon me, my lord?"

Yomoda Matabei had quickly appeared. He was a robust young man who had caught Mitsuhide's eye. Mitsuhide motioned him closer and whispered an order to him.

Upon receiving secret orders from Mitsuhide, the young man's face registered strong emotion.

"I'll go at once!" he answered, responding to his lord's trust with his entire being.

"You'll be recognized as an Akechi samurai, so go quickly—before dawn breaks. Have your wits about you, and don't blunder."

After Matabei had withdrawn, there was still some time before it would begin to grow light and it was only now that Mitsuhide was able to sleep soundly. Contrary to his usual practice, he did not leave his room until broad daylight. Many of his retainers had guessed that the departure for Kameyama would take place that day and had expected an early announcement to that effect. They were quite surprised when they discovered that their lord was sleeping so uncommonly late.

At about noon, Mitsuhide's relaxed voice could be heard in the hall.

"I spent the entire day walking around the mountain yesterday and slept better last night than I have for a long time. Maybe that's why I feel so good today. I seem to have completely recovered from my cold."

A look of congratulations that might as well have reflected on their own improved health circulated among his retainers. Soon after that Mitsuhide issued a command to his attendants.

"This evening in the second half of the Hour of the Rooster, we will depart Sakamoto, cross the Shirakawa River, pass through northern Kyoto, and return to Kameyama. Make sure that all of the preparations are complete."

More than three thousand warriors were to accompany him to Kameyama. Evening was approaching, Mitsuhide dressed in his traveling clothes and then went to find Mitsuharu.

"Since I will be going to the western provinces, I have no idea when I will be back. This evening I'd like to sit down and eat dinner with you and your family."

And so they were once again altogether as a family circle until Mitsuhide departed.

The eldest person at the banquet was Mitsuhide's eccentric uncle, Chokansai, a man who had taken holy orders. Sixty-six years old that year and free from any illness, he was given to telling jokes. He sat next to Mitsuharu's seven-year-old son, teasing him good-naturedly.

But the sociable old man was the only one who smiled from beginning to end. Ignorant of the hidden reefs now threatening the Akechi clan, he simply entrusted his remaining years to the ship that passed over the spring sea, and looked as peaceful as ever.

"It's so lively here, I feel as though I've returned home again. Old man, give this cup to Mitsutada."

Mitsuhide had already drunk two or three cups and now passed the cup on to Chokansai, who in turn handed it to Mitsutada.

Mitsutada was the commander of Hachijo Castle and so had just arrived today. He was the youngest of the three cousins.

Mitsutada drank the *sake* and, moving over in front of Mitsuhide, returned the cup to him. Mitsuharu's wife held the *sake* bottle and poured, and just at that moment Mitsuhide's hand began to tremble in alarm. Ordinarily he was not the kind of man to be surprised by a sound, but now, as a warrior started to beat a drum in front of the castle, the color seemed to recede slightly from his face.

Chokansai turned to Mitsuhide and said, "It will soon be the Hour of the Rooster, so that must be the drum summoning your troops to the assembly ground."

Mitsuhide's mood seemed to sink even more. "I know," he said in what sounded like a bitter tone of voice, and he drained the last cup.

He was mounted within the hour. Beneath a sky of pale stars, three thousand men carrying torches left the lakeside castle in a meandering line and disappeared into the foothills of Shimeigatake. It was the evening of the twenty-sixth.

From the top of the castle Mitsuharu watched them go. He would form a regiment made up only of retainers from Sakamoto, and go on to join the main army at Kameyama later.

The army under Mitsuhide walked on without stopping. It was exactly midnight when the men looked from just south of Shimeigatake and saw the sleeping city of Kyoto.

To cross the Shirakawa River, they would descend the ridge of Mount Uriyu and come out on the road south of the Ichijo Temple. They had been climbing steadily, but from that point on the path would be all downhill.

"Take a rest!"

Mitsutada passed Mitsuhide's command on to the troops.

Mitsuhide dismounted as well and rested for a short while. If it had been daytime, he would have been able to look out over the various streets of the capital. But now the contours of the city were sunk in darkness, and only the distinctive features of the temple roofs and pagodas and the large river could be distinguished.

"Hasn't Yomoda Matabei overtaken us?"

"I haven't seen him since last night. Did you send him off on some mission, my lord?"

"That's right."

"Where did he go?"

"You'll know soon enough. If he comes back, send him to me. Even if we're en route."

"Yes, my lord."

In the second he fell silent, Mitsuhide's eyes were again looking eagerly out over the black roofs of the capital. Perhaps because the night mist would keep thickening and then thinning out, or because his eyes were becoming used to the night, he was gradually able to distinguish the buildings in the capital. The white walls of the Nijo Palace were brighter than anything else.

Naturally, Mitsuhide's gaze was captured by this one white point. It was there that Nobunaga's son, Nobutada, was staying. There also was Tokugawa Ieyasu, who had left Azuchi some days before and gone to the capital.

Lord Ieyasu has probably left the capital already, Mitsuhide thought.

Finally he quickly stood up, making all his generals jump.

"Let's go. My horse."

The dismay of his subordinates was like a wave that rippled out from the fitful actions of his isolated mind. For the last few days he had periodically secluded himself from his retainers, and he had behaved more like an orphan than like the leader of a samurai clan.

Although the soldiers who followed Mitsuhide had difficulty finding their way in the dark—surrounding him and yelling warnings back and forth—they gradually descended and approached the outskirts of the capital.

When the line of three thousand men and horses arrived at the Kamo River and paused momentarily, the soldiers all turned and looked to the rear, and Mitsuhide did the same: having observed the red waves on the river, they knew that the morning sun was rising over the ridges behind them.

The officer in charge of the army's provisions came up to Mitsutada and asked him about breakfast. "Shall we make the morning's preparations here or go on to Nishijin?"

Mitsutada was going to ask Mitsuhide what his intentions were, but at that moment Yomoda Masataka had pulled his horse alongside of Mitsuhide's, and the two men seemed to be gazing steadily at the Shirakawa, which they had crossed. Mitsutada held back for a moment.

"Masataka, is that Matabei?"

"I believe it is."

Mitsuhide and Masataka were watching a horseman hurriedly approaching through the morning mist.

"Matabei." While Mitsuhide waited right where he was for the man he had been expecting, he turned and spoke to the commanders around him. "Go ahead and cross the river. I'll follow you momentarily."

The advance guard had already waded across the shallows of the Kamo to the far bank. As the other commanders left Mitsuhide's side, their horses kicked up a white foam in the middle of the clear water. One by one they crossed the stream.

Mitsutada took this opportunity to ask, "Where shall we have our meal? Would it be convenient to have it at Nishijin?"

"Everyone's stomach must be empty, but we shouldn't stop in the city limits. Let's go as far as Kitano," Mitsuhide replied.

At a distance of about twenty yards, the approaching Yomoda Matabei dismounted and wound his horse's reins around a piling in the riverbed.

"Mitsutada and Masataka, the two of you cross the river as well, and wait for me on the other side. I'll follow soon."

After these last two men had gone some distance, Mitsuhide turned in the direction of Matabei for the first time and beckoned him over with a look.

"Yes, my lord!"

"What's going on in Azuchi?"

"The report you heard previously from Amano Genemon seems to be without error."

"The reason I sent you a second time was to get positive information on Lord Nobunaga's departure for the capital on the twenty-ninth, and on what kind of force he was taking with him. To give me some vague response about there being no mistakes in a former report is worthless. Make a clear report: was it reliable information or not?"

"It is certain that he will leave Azuchi on the twenty-ninth. I couldn't get the names of the main generals who will accompany him, and it was announced that forty or fifty pages and close attendants will be with him."

"What about his lodgings in the capital?"

"He'll be at the Honno Temple."

"What! The Honno Temple?"

"Yes, my lord."

"Not Nijo Palace?"

"All of the reports said that he would be staying at the Honno Temple," Matabei answered quite clearly, careful to avoid being scolded again.

THE SHRINE OF THE FIRE GOD

There was a huge gate at the very center of the compound's mud wall, and each of the sub-temples had its own enclosure and gate. The pine forest seemed to have been swept clean, and itself looked like a Zen garden. Birdsong, and the sunlight streaming through the treetops, added to the peace of the scene.

After tethering their horses, Mitsuhide and his retainers ate the meals they had packed for both breakfast and lunch. Although they had planned on having breakfast near the Kamo River, they had waited to eat until they had arrived at Kitano.

The soldiers carried a day's worth of provisions: a simple meal of uncooked bean paste, pickled plums, and brown rice. They had not eaten since the night before, and they now breakfasted happily.

Three or four monks from the nearby Myoshin Temple, who had recognized the men as members of the Akechi clan, had invited them into the temple compound.

Mitsuhide was sitting on a camp stool in the shadow of the curtain his attendants had set up. He had finished his meal and was dictating a letter to his secretary.

"The priests of the Myoshin Temple…they'd make perfect messengers! Call them back!" he ordered a page. When the priests had returned, Mitsuhide entrusted them with the letter his secretary had just written. "Would you please take this letter quickly to the residence of the poet Shoha?"

Immediately afterward he got up and walked back to his horse, telling the monks, "I'm afraid that we have no spare time on this trip. I'll have to forgo meeting the abbot. Please give him my regards."

The afternoon grew hot. The road to Saga was extraordinarily dry, and the horses' hooves kicked clouds of dust into the air. Mitsuhide rode in silence, thinking through a plan in his characteristically careful way, weighing its feasibility, the likely public reaction, and the possibility of failure. Like a horsefly that always comes back no matter how often it is brushed away, the scheme had become an obsession that Mitsuhide could not drive from his mind. A nightmare had sneaked into him and filled his entire body with poison. He had already lost his power to reason.

In all of his fifty-four years, Mitsuhide had never relied on his own wisdom the way he was doing now. Although objectively he would have had every reason to doubt his own judgment, subjectively he felt exactly the opposite. I haven't made the smallest mistake, Mitsuhide said to himself. No one could suspect what's on my mind.

While he had been in Sakamoto, he had wavered: Should he go ahead with the plan or scrap it? But this morning, when he heard the second report, his hair had suddenly stood on end. In his heart he had resolved that the time was now, and that heaven had sent him this opportunity. Nobunaga, accompanied by only forty or fifty lightly armed men, was staying at the Honno Temple in Kyoto. The demon that possessed Mitsuhide whispered to him that it was a unique opportunity.

His decision was not a positive act of his own will, but rather a reaction to external circumstances. Men like to believe that they live and act according to their own wills, but the grim truth is that outside events actually stir them to action. So while Mitsuhide believed that heaven was his ally in the present opportunity, part of him was beset by the fear as he rode along the road to Saga that heaven really was judging his every action.

Mitsuhide crossed the Katsura River and arrived at Kameyama Castle in the evening, just as the sun dropped below the horizon. Having been informed of their lord's return, the townspeople of Kameyama welcomed him home with bonfires that lit up the night sky. He was a popular ruler who had won the affection of the people as a result of his wise administration.

The number of days in a year that Mitsuhide spent with his family could be counted on the fingers of one hand. During long campaigns, he might not come home for two or three years. For that reason, those rare days he could be at home were animated by the delight of seeing his wife and children, and being a husband and father.

Mitsuhide had been blessed with an exceptionally large family of seven daughters and twelve sons. Two-thirds of them were married or had been adopted by other families, but several of the younger ones, as well as children of his kinsmen and their grandchildren, were still living at the castle.

His wife, Teruko, always said, "How old will I be when I no longer have to look after children?" She took in the children of clan members who had died in battle and even raised the children her husband had fathered with other women. This gentle, wise woman was contented with her lot, and although she was already fifty, she put up with the children and their mischief.

Since leaving Azuchi, Mitsuhide had not found a comfort equal to being at home, and he slept peacefully that night. Even on the next day, his children's cheerfulness and his faithful wife's smile soothed his heart.

It might be supposed that spending such a night would cause him to change his mind. But he did not waver in the least. On the contrary, he now had the courage to realize an even more secret ambition that lodged in his heart.

Teruko had been with him from the time he had had no lord to serve. Happy with her present estate, she had no other thoughts than to be a mother to her children. Look-ing at her now, Mitsuhide formed silent words in his breast. Your husband is not going to be like this forever. Everyone will soon be looking up to you as the wife of the next shogun. And as he gazed at the children and other members of his large household, for a moment he was caught up in his own fantasy. I'm going to move you all from this provincial castle to a palace even more elevated than Azuchi. How much happier you will be then!

Later that day, Mitsuhide left the castle, accompanied by a few attendants. He was lightly dressed and was not being waited upon by his usual retainers. Though there had been no official announcement, even the soldiers at the castle gate knew that their lord was going to spend the night at Atago Shrine.

Before departing for the west, Mitsuhide was going to the shrine to pray for good luck in battle. Accompanied by a few of his closest friends, he would stay in the shrine to hold a poetry party and would return the following day.

When he said that he was going to a shrine to pray for victory in battle, and that he was inviting some friends from the capital for a party, nobody suspected what was really in Mitsuhide's mind.

The twenty servants and half a dozen mounted retainers were dressed more lightly than they would have been had they been going hawking. On the day before, the monks of Itokuin Temple and the priests of Atago Shrine had been informed of the visit, so they were waiting to welcome their lord. As soon as he had dismounted, Mitsuhide asked for a monk by the name of Gyoyu.

"Is Shoha coming?" Mitsuhide asked the monk. When Gyoyu replied that the famous poet was already there waiting for him, Mitsuhide exclaimed, "What? Here already? Well, that's perfect. Has he brought other poets from the capital?"

"It seems that Master Shoha had very little time to prepare himself. He received your invitation yesterday evening, and found that whoever he tried to invite was unable to at-tend at such short notice. Along with his son, Shinzen, he was only able to bring two oth-ers: a disciple by the name of Kennyo, and a relative called Shoshitsu."

"Is that so?" Mitsuhide laughed. "Did he complain? I knew it was an unreasonable re-quest, but after honoring him time and time again by sending palanquins and escorts, this time I thought it would be much more elegant—and more enjoyable—if he was the one who went to some trouble to meet me. That's why I invited him to this place so sud-denly. But just as you might expect, Shoha didn't even feign illness. He scurried up the mountain at once."

With the two monks walking ahead and his attendants behind, Mitsuhide climbed a flight of high stone stairs. Just when it seemed as though there would be flat ground to walk on for a while, the stairs would begin again. As they climbed, the dark green of the cypress trees deepened even more, and the dark violet of the summer sky edged into evening. They felt the night approaching quickly. With every step, their skin could feel the sudden drop in temperature; it was considerably colder at the summit than it had been at the foot of the mountain.

"Master Shoha sends his apologies," Gyoyu told Mitsuhide when they had reached
the guest room of the temple. "He would have come to meet you, but since he thought

you would probably pray first at the temples and shrines on the way, he said he would greet you after your devotions."

Mitsuhide nodded silently. Then, after drinking a cup of water, he asked for a guide. "Before anything else, I'd like to offer a prayer to the patron deity, and then I'll visit the Atago Shrine while there's still some light."

The shrine priest led the way along a neatly swept path. He climbed the stairs of the outer shrine and lit the sacred candles. Mitsuhide bowed low, and stood in prayer for some time. Three times the priest whisked a branch of the sacred tree over Mitsuhide's head, and then offered him an earthen cup of sacred *sake*.

"I've heard that this shrine is dedicated to the fire god. Is that true?" Mitsuhide asked afterward.

"That is true, my lord," the priest replied.

"And I've heard that if you pray to this god and abstain from using fire, your prayers will be answered."

"That has been said since ancient times." The priest avoided giving a clear answer to the question, and turned it back on Mitsuhide. "I wonder how that tradition originated?" Then, changing the subject, he began to talk about the history of the shrine.

Bored by the priest's monologue, Mitsuhide gazed at the holy lamps in the outer shrine. Finally he stood up silently and descended the stairs. It was already dark when he walked to the Atago Shrine. Leaving the monks, he went alone to the nearby Temple of the Shogun Jizo. There he drew his fortune, but the first lot he pulled predicted bad luck. He drew again, and that one too read "Bad luck." For a moment, Mitsuhide stood as silent as stone. Picking up the box that held the fortunes, he lifted it reverently to his forehead, closed his eyes, and drew for the third time. This time the answer was "Great good fortune."

Mitsuhide turned and walked toward his waiting attendants. They had watched him from afar as he drew his fortune, imagining that he was only indulging a fancy. Mitsuhide was, after all, a man who prided himself on his intellect and who was, above all else, rational. He was hardly the kind of man who would use fortune-telling to reach a decision.

The flickering lamps of the guest room shone through the young leaves. For Shoha and his fellow poets, it would be a night of grinding ink on the inkstones as they recorded their own verses.

The night's entertainment began with a banquet at which Mitsuhide was the guest of honor. The guests bantered and laughed and drank many rounds of *sake*, and they were so engrossed in their conversation that they seemed to have forgotten all about poetry.

"The summer nights are short," their host, the abbot, announced. "It's getting late, and I'm afraid it's going to be light before we finish our hundred linked verses."

In another room, poetry mats had been arranged. Paper and an inkstone had been set in front of each cushion as though to encourage the participants to write elegant verses.

Shoha and Shoshitsu were both accomplished poets. Shoha was regarded affectionately by Nobunaga and was on familiar terms with Hideyoshi and the leading tea master of the day. He was a man who had a large circle of acquaintances.

"Well, my lord, would you give us the first verse," Shoha requested.

Mitsuhide, however, did not touch the paper in front of him. His elbow was still on the armrest, and he seemed to be looking out into the darkness of the garden where the leaves were stirring.

"It seems that you're racking your brains for your verse, my lord," Shoha teased Mitsuhide.

Mitsuhide picked up his brush and wrote:

The whole country knows
The time is now,
In the Fifth Month.

At a party like this, once the first verse was composed, the participants added verses in turn until anywhere from fifty to a hundred linked stanzas had been added. The party had begun with a verse by Mitsuhide. The closing verse that tied the work together was also composed by Mitsuhide:

Time for the provinces
To be at peace.

After the monks had extinguished the lamps and withdrawn, Mitsuhide appeared to fall asleep immediately. As he finally lay his head on the pillow, the mountain wind outside shook the trees and howled through the eaves of the roof as strangely as if that mythical, long-nosed monster, Tengu, were raising a fearful cry. Mitsuhide suddenly recalled the story he had heard from the priest at the shrine of the fire god. In his head he imagined Tengu rampaging through the jet black sky.

Tengu gnaws on fire and then flies up into the sky. A huge Tengu, and smaller Tengus without number, turned into fire and mounted the black wind. As the fires fell to earth, the shrine of the fire god immediately became a mass of firebrands.

He wanted to sleep. He wanted terribly to sleep. But Mitsuhide was not dreaming; he was thinking. And his brain could not stop the illusion in his mind. He turned over and started to think about the coming day. He knew that on the morrow Nobunaga would leave Azuchi for Kyoto.

And then the borderline between wakefulness and dream began to blur. And in this state, the difference between himself and Tengu disappeared. Tengu stood on the clouds and looked over the nation. Everything he saw was to his own advantage. In the west, Hideyoshi was nailed down at Takamatsu Castle, grappling with the armies of the Mori. If he could collude with the Mori and take the advantage, the army under Hideyoshi, which had spent so many wearisome years on the campaign, would be buried in the west and would never again see the capital.

Tokugawa Ieyasu, who was in Osaka, was a clever survivor. Once he saw that Nobunaga was dead, his attitude would depend entirely on what Mitsuhide offered. Hosokawa

Fujitaka would no doubt be momentarily indignant, but his son had married Mitsuhide's daughter, and he had been a devoted friend for many years. He would not be unwilling to cooperate.

Mitsuhide's muscles and blood were tingling. In fact, his ears burned with such intensity that he felt young again. Tengu turned over. Mitsuhide let out a groan.

"My lord?" In the next room, Shoha rose a little and called out, "What's the matter, my lord?"

Mitsuhide was dimly aware of Shoha's question but intentionally gave no answer. Shoha quickly went back to sleep.

The short night was soon over. Upon arising, Mitsuhide bade farewell to the others and descended the mountain while it was still shrouded in a thick morning mist.

* * *

On the thirtieth day of the month Mitsuharu arrived at Kameyama and joined forces with Mitsuhide. Members of the Akechi clan had been coming in from the entire province, swelling the already significant army from Sakamoto. Thus the castle town was crowded with horses and men; carts of military supplies jammed every intersection, and the streets had become nearly impassable. The sun shone down brightly, and it was suddenly almost like midsummer: porters filled the shops and argued with their mouths full of food; outside, the foot soldiers squeezing between the oxcarts yelled back and forth. Along the streets, flies buzzed and swarmed over the droppings left by the horses and oxen.

"Has your health held up?" Mitsuharu asked Mitsuhide.

"Just as you see." Mitsuhide smiled. He was much more amiable than he had been at Sakamoto, and the color had returned to his face.

"When do you plan to leave?"

"I've decided to wait it just a little, until the first day of Sixth Month."

"Well, what about Azuchi?"

"I've informed them, but I think Lord Nobunaga is already in Kyoto."

"The report is that he arrived there without incident last night. Lord Nobutada is staying at the Myokaku Temple, while Lord Nobunaga is at the Honno Temple."

"Yes, I've heard that." Mitsuhide's words trailed off into silence.

Mitsuharu suddenly got up. "I haven't seen your wife and children for a long time. Perhaps I'll go pay my respects."

Mitsuhide watched his cousin walk away. A moment later he looked as though his chest were so congested that he could neither spit nor swallow.

Two rooms away, Mitsuhide's retainer Saito Toshimitsu was conferring with other generals, studying military charts and discussing tactics. He left the room to talk with Mitsuhide.

"Are you going to send the supply train to the Sanin ahead of us?"

"The supply train? Hm...well, we don't need to send it ahead."

Suddenly Mitsuhide's uncle, Chokansai, who had just now arrived with Mitsuharu, looked in.

"Hey, he's not here. Where did the lord of Sakamoto go? Anybody here know?"

He looked around, goggle-eyed. Although he was an old man, he was so sunny and cheerful that he drove others to distraction. Even if the generals were about to leave on a campaign, Chokansai seemed as cheerful as usual. He turned in another direction. When he casually showed up at the ladies' apartments in the citadel, however, the women and their many children ran up to him.

"Oh, Lord Jester has come!" the children cried.

"Lord Jester! When did you get here?"

Whether he stood or sat, the happy voices around him did not cease.

"Are you staying overnight, Lord Jester?"

"Lord Jester, have you eaten yet?"

"Lift me up, Lord Jester!"

"Sing us a song!"

"Show us a dance!"

They jumped up on his lap. They played with him. They clung to him. They looked into his ears.

"Lord Jester! There's hair growing out of your ears!"

"One, two."

"Three, four." Singing out the numbers, little girls pulled out the hairs while a little boy sat astride his back, pushing down his old head.

"Play horsy! Play horsy and whinny!"

Chokansai crawled around submissively, and when he suddenly sneezed, the little boy fell off his back. The ladies-in-waiting and attendants laughed so hard they held their sides.

Even as night fell, the laughter and hubbub did not stop. The atmosphere of the ladies' apartments was as different from that of Mitsuhide's room in the main citadel as a meadow in spring might be from a snow-covered moor.

"Uncle, now that you're getting on in years," Mitsuharu said, "I'd be grateful if you'd stay here and take care of the family rather than coming with us on the campaign. I think I should tell our lord that."

Chokansai looked at his nephew and laughed. "My final role may have to be something like that. These little ones just won't leave me alone." Night had fallen, and they were badgering him to tell them one of his famous stories.

This was the last day left before the departure for the campaign. Mitsuharu had expected that there would be a general conference that evening, but as the main citadel was quiet, he went over to the second citadel and slept.

The next day Mitsuharu waited in anticipation all day, but no orders were forthcoming. Even when night fell, there was no movement in the main citadel. When he sent one of his retainers to ask about the situation, the answer came back that Mitsuhide had already gone to bed and was asleep. Mitsuharu was suspicious, but there was nothing he could do except go to sleep himself.

At about midnight Mitsuharu was awakened by the sound of whispering coming from the guardroom two doors down the hallway. Footsteps approached, and the door of his room slid open noiselessly.

"What is it?" Mitsuharu asked.

The guard, who must have thought Mitsuharu would be asleep, hesitated for a moment. Then he hurriedly prostrated himself and said, "Lord Mitsuhide is waiting for you in the main citadel."

Mitsuharu got up and began to dress; he asked what time it was.

"The first half of the Hour of the Rat," the guard replied.

Mitsuharu went out into the ink-black corridor. When he saw that Saito Toshimitsu was kneeling by the doorway, waiting for him, Mitsuharu wondered what the reason was for this unexpected summons in the middle of the night.

Toshimitsu walked ahead, holding a candle. They met no one during their long walk down the winding corridor. Almost everyone was peacefully asleep in the main citadel, but an unusual atmosphere permeated this one part of the building, and it seemed that men were up and about in two or three rooms.

"Where is His Lordship?"

"In his sleeping quarters."

Toshimitsu put out the candle at the entrance to the corridor leading to Mitsuhide's bedroom. With a look, he invited Mitsuharu to enter, and opened the heavy door. As soon as Mitsuharu had gone in, Toshimitsu shut the door behind him. It was only from the farthest room in the corridor—Mitsuhide's bedroom—that the faint light of a lamp leaked out.

When Mitsuharu looked into the room, he could see neither attendants nor pages. Mitsuhide was alone, dressed in a summer kimono of white gauze, his long sword beside him, his hand on an armrest at his side.

The light of the lamp was particularly pale because it was filtered through the green gossamer mosquito netting that hung around Mitsuhide. When he slept, the netting surrounded him on all four sides, but now the front was held up by a strip of bamboo.

"Come in, Mitsuharu," Mitsuhide said.

"What is this all about?" his cousin asked, after kneeling in front of Mitsuhide.

"Mitsuharu, would you risk your life for me?"

Mitsuharu knelt in silence, looking as though he had forgotten how to speak. Mitsuhide's eyes were ablaze with a strange light. His question had been simple and direct—the very words Mitsuharu had been afraid of hearing since Sakamoto. Now Mitsuhide had finally spoken, and though Mitsuharu was not surprised, the blood in his veins felt as though it had turned into ice.

"Are you against me, Mitsuharu?"

Still he did not answer. Mitsuhide, too, fell silent. His face displayed a certain paleness that was not due to the green netting or the guttering of the lamp, but to the reflection of some emotion in his heart.

Mitsuharu knew, almost by intuition, that Mitsuhide had prepared a contingency plan to use if he opposed him. Built into the wall beyond the mosquito netting, in the corner of a large alcove, was a secret chamber that could conceal an armed man. The flecks of gold on the surface of the hidden door shone ominously, as if glinting with the

631

bloodthirsty intent of the hidden assassin.

To Mitsuharu's right was a large sliding door. He could hear nothing from behind it, but he could sense the presence of Saito Toshimitsu and several other men who had their weapons drawn, just waiting for Mitsuhide's word. Mitsuharu could not resent Mitsuhide's heartless and underhanded behavior; pity came before that. Had the intelligent man he had known since his youth disappeared? He felt as though he were looking at nothing but the wreck of that man now.

"Mitsuharu, what is your answer?" Mitsuhide asked, edging closer.

Mitsuharu felt his cousin's hot breath burning like the fever of a sick man. "Why do you want me to risk my life?" he finally asked in reply. He knew very well what Mitsuhide was planning to do, so he was now deliberately feigning ignorance. He held on to the hope that somehow he could pull his cousin back from the brink.

At Mitsuharu's words, the veins on Mitsuhide's temples stood out even more. His voice became unusually husky as he said, "Mitsuharu, don't you know that something has been gnawing at me since I left Azuchi?"

"It's obvious."

"If that's so, then why are all these words necessary? A yes or a no will suffice."

"My lord, why are you the one who is refusing to speak? It is not only the fate of the Akechi clan that depends on what you say now but the future of the nation."

"What are you saying, Mitsuharu?"

"To think that you, of all people, should consider committing this outrage." Tears falling down his cheeks, Mitsuharu drew closer to Mitsuhide and dropped both hands to the floor in supplication. "I have never understood human character less than I have tonight. When we were both young and studied together in my father's house, what was it that we read? Was there a single word in the books of the ancient sages that approved of killing one's own lord?"

"Speak more quietly, Mitsuharu."

"Who's going to hear me? All you have here is assassins behind secret doors, waiting for your command. My lord...I have never once doubted your wisdom. But you seem to have changed so much from the man I used to know."

"It's too late, Mitsuharu."

"I must speak."

"It's useless."

"I must, even if it's useless." Bitter tears fell on Mitsuharu's hands.

Just then something moved behind the hidden door. Perhaps the assassin had sensed that the situation had become tense and was eager to act. But there was still no signal from Mitsuhide. He turned away from his cousin's weeping figure.

"You have studied so much more than others, your intellectual powers are much greater than most people's, and you have reached the age of mature judgment. Is there anything you don't understand?" Mitsuharu pleaded. "I am so ignorant that I lack the words. But even someone like me can read the word 'loyalty' and meditate on it until it has become a part of me. Although you've read ten thousand books, it will all come to naught if you lose sight of that word now. My lord, are you listening? Our blood has been drawn from a line of ancient warriors. Would you stain the honor of our ancestors? And what of your own children and their descendants? Think of the shame you'll heap on endless generations."

"You could enumerate those kinds of things without end," Mitsuhide replied. "What I intend to do transcends them all. Forget about changing my mind. I've considered the good sense you've just spoken about night after night, turning them over again and again in my brain. When I look back over the road I've traveled for the past fifty-five years, I know I would not be this distraught if I had not been born a samurai. Nor would I be intent on such a thing."

"And it's precisely because you were born a samurai that you should not act against your lord, no matter how much you've had to bear."

"Nobunaga rose against the shogun. And everyone knows how much bad karma he accumulated from burning down Mount Hiei. Look what befell his senior retainers— Hayashi, Sakuma, Araki. I cannot think of their tragic fates as other people's affairs."

"My lord, you've received a province. The clan lacks for nothing. Think of the favors he has bestowed upon us."

At this point Mitsuhide lost control, and his words burst forth like a river in flood. "What is the favor of an insignificant province like this? I would probably have this, even if I weren't talented. Once he has everything he needs from me, I'll be nothing more than a lapdog to be fed at Azuchi. Or maybe he'll consider me a useless luxury. He's even put me under Hideyoshi's command and ordered me to the Sanin. If that isn't a pronouncement of the Akechi clan's fate, I don't know what is. I was raised a samurai; I have inherited the blood of generations of warriors. Do you think I'm going to finish my days kowtowing while he orders me around? Can't you see through Nobunaga's black heart, Mitsuharu?"

Mitsuharu sat in stunned silence for a while, then asked, "To whom have you disclosed your intentions?"

"Besides you, a dozen of my most trusted retainers." Mitsuhide took a deep breath and listed the men's names.

Mitsuharu looked up to the ceiling and let out a long sigh. "What can I say now that you've told them?"

Mitsuhide suddenly moved forward and grabbed his cousin's collar with his left hand. "Is it no?" he asked. His right hand gripped the haft of his dagger, while his left shook Mitsuharu with terrifying strength. "Or is it yes?"

Every time Mitsuhide shook Mitsuharu, his head moved back and forth as though his neck contained no bones. Tears were streaming down his face.

"At this point it's no longer a matter of yes or no. But I don't know what it would have been if you had told me before you informed the others, my lord."

"Then you agree? You'll act with me?"

"You and I, my lord, are two men, but we are the same as one. If you were to die, I wouldn't want to live. Technically, we are lord and retainer, but we have the same roots and the same birth. We have lived our lives together until now, and I am naturally resolved to share whatever fate lies ahead."

"Don't worry, Mitsuharu. It's going to be all or nothing, but I feel our victory is certain. If we are successful, you won't be in charge of a minor castle like Sakamoto. I promise you that. At the very least, you'll have the title next to mine and will be the lord of a great number of provinces!"

"What! That is not the issue." Casting off the hand that held his collar, Mitsuharu pushed Mitsuhide back. "I'd like to cry…my lord, please allow me to cry."

"What are you sad about, you fool?"

"You're the fool!"

"Fool!"

The two called each other names back and forth and then embraced, tears rolling down their cheeks.

* * *

It certainly felt like summer; the first day of the Sixth Month was hotter than it had been for many years. In the afternoon, columns of cloud covered a section of the sky in the north, but the slowly setting sun continued to scorch the mountains and rivers of Tamba until dusk.

The town of Kameyama was now totally deserted. The soldiers and wagons that had packed its streets were gone. Soldiers, carrying firearms, banners, and spears, were marching out of the town in a long line, their heads baking in iron helmets. The townspeople crowded by the roadside to watch the army depart. Searching out the benefactors who had patronized their shops in the past, they wished them luck as loudly as they could and urged them on to great deeds.

But neither the marching soldiers nor the cheering crowds knew that this setting out was not the beginning of a campaign in the west, but the first step toward Kyoto. Except for Mitsuhide and a dozen men on his field staff, not one single person knew.

It would soon be the Hour of the Monkey. Booming through the blood-red western sun, conch shells resounded high and low, one after another. The soldiers, who had been doing little more than crowding around various encampments, got up immediately to get into their proper columns. Dividing into three lines, they formed ranks, banners aloft.

The greenery of the surrounding mountains and the pale green foliage nearby rustled with fragrance as the slight evening breeze wafted across the innumerable faces. Once again the conch sounded—this time from the distant forest.

From the grounds of the shrine of the war god Hachiman, Mitsuhide and his generals moved forward in brilliant array through the slanting rays of the western sun. Mitsuhide reviewed his troops, who massed together resembled a wall of iron. Every soldier looked up as Mitsuhide passed by, and even the rank and file felt proud to be under the command of such a great general.

Mitsuhide wore black armor with light green threading under a white and silver brocade coat. His long sword and saddle were of exceptional workmanship. Today he appeared much younger than usual, but this was not true of Mitsuhide alone. When a man put on his armor, he was ageless. Even alongside a warrior of sixteen on his first campaign, an old man did not show or feel his age.

Today, Mitsuhide's prayers had been more beseeching than those of any other man in his army. And for that reason, as he passed each soldier, his eyes looked strained by his resolve. The countenance of the commander-in-chief did not go unreflected in the martial spirit of his men. The Akechi had gone to war twenty-seven times. Today, however, the men were feverish with tension, as if they had intuited that the battle they were heading for was out of the ordinary.

Every man felt that he was setting out never to return. That mass intuition filled the place like a bleak mist, so that the nine banners emblazoned with blue bellflowers fluttering above each division seemed to be beating against a bank of cloud.

Mitsuhide reigned in his horse, turned to Saito Toshimitsu who was riding by his side, and asked, "How many men do we have altogether?"

"Ten thousand. If we include the various carriers and packers, there must be more than thirteen thousand men."

Mitsuhide nodded then said after a pause, "Ask the corps commanders to come here."

When the commanders had assembled in front of Mitsuhide's horse, he pulled back momentarily, and in his place his cousin Mitsutada came forward, flanked by generals to his left and right.

"This is a letter that arrived last night from Mori Ranmaru, who is now in Kyoto. I am going to read it to you so that it will be understood by everyone."

He opened the letter and read: "'By command of Lord Oda Nobunaga you are to come to the capital, so that His Lordship may review the troops before their departure for the west.'"

"We will leave at the Hour of the Rooster. Until then have your soldiers prepare their provisions, feed their horses, and rest."

If the sight of thirteen thousand men preparing their provisions in the field was quite a spectacle, it was a congenial one. In the meantime, the corps commanders who had been summoned were called once again—this time into the forest of the Hachiman shrine. There, enhanced by the shadows of dusk and the cries of the cicadas, the cool air felt almost like water.

A moment before, the sound of hands clapping in prayer could be heard from the shrine. It seemed as though Mitsuhide and his generals had been praying before the gods. Mitsuhide had persuaded himself that he was not acting purely out of the enmity and resentment he felt toward Nobunaga. The fear that he might end up like Araki or Sakuma had allowed him the rationalization that it was a matter of self-defense; he was like a cornered animal forced to strike first in order to stay alive.

From the shrine it was only five leagues to the Honno Temple, where his lightly protected enemy was staying. It was a once-in-a-lifetime opportunity. Conscious that his treachery looked like opportunism, he could not concentrate on his prayer. But he had no trouble in justifying his actions: he enumerated Nobunaga's crimes over the past two decades. In the end, although he had served Nobunaga for many years, Mitsuhide was nostalgic for the old shogunate, with all of its stagnation.

The commanders waited, crowding together. Mitsuhide's stool was still unoccupied. His pages said that he was still praying at the shrine and would soon return. Not long thereafter, the curtain parted. Greeting the men who had gathered there, Mitsuhide's close retainers entered one by one. Mitsuhide, Toshimitsu, Mitsuharu, Mitsutada, and Mitsuaki were the last to appear.

"Are these all of the corps commanders?" Mitsuhide asked.

With alarming speed, the immediate area was completely surrounded by soldiers. Caution could be read on Mitsuhide's face, and a wordless warning was very clearly concentrated in the eyes of the generals.

Mitsuhide said, "You may think it rather cold of me to take these kinds of precautions when talking to my retainers, and especially to retainers on whom I rely. Don't take this measure in the wrong way; it's only in order to disclose to you a great, long-awaited event—an event that will affect the entire nation and that will mean either our rise or our fall."

Thus he began the disclosure of his intentions. Mitsuhide enumerated his grievances against Nobunaga: the humiliations at Suwa and Azuchi and, the final indignity, an order to join the campaign in the west that implied he was subordinate to Hideyoshi. He went on to list the names of the men who had served Nobunaga for years, only to be driven to self-destruction. It was Nobunaga who was the enemy of righteousness, the destroyer of culture, and the conspirator who had overthrown institutions and brought the nation to chaos. He ended his speech by reciting a poem he had written.

> Let a person with no understanding
> Say what he will;
> I will have no regrets for either
> Position or fame.

While reciting the poem, Mitsuhide began to feel the pathos of his own situation, and tears began to run down his cheeks. His senior retainers, too, began to weep. Some among them even bit the sleeves of their armor or fell face down on the earth. There was only one man who did not weep—the veteran Saito Toshimitsu.

In order to bind their tears in a pledge of blood, Saito Toshimitsu broke in and said, "I think His Lordship has opened his heart to us because he considers us men he can trust. If a lord is shamed, his retainers die. Is it our lord alone who is being pained? These old bones of mine have little time left, but if I can witness the downfall of Lord Nobunaga and see my lord become the ruler of the nation, I will be able to die without any regrets."

Mitsuharu spoke next. "Each of us thinks of himself as His Lordship's right-hand man, so once he has spoken, there is only one road to take. We should not be late for our own deaths."

The corps commanders all answered in unison. The glint of emotion in every eye and open mouth seemed to say they knew no other word than *yes*. When Mitsuhide stood up, the men shook with their strong feeling. They congratulated him loudly, as was the time-honored custom when leaving for the front.

Yomoda Masataka looked up at the sky and then urged the men to prepare themselves mentally. "It will soon be the Hour of the Rooster. It's about five leagues to the capital. If we travel across country, we should be able to surround the Honno Temple by dawn. If we can take care of the Honno Temple before the Hour of the Dragon and then destroy the Myokaku Temple, everything should be settled before breakfast."

He had turned to Mitsuhide and Mitsuharu and had spoken with complete conviction. This speech, of course, was neither a recommendation nor counsel. It was to let the main commanders know that the country was already in their hands, and to exhort them to fire up their blood.

It was the second half of the Hour of the Rooster. The road was already dark in the shade of the mountain. The armor-clad men flowed in a black line through the village of Oji and finally reached the hill of Oinosaka. The night sky was full of stars, and the capital below looked like its reflection.

"FIFTY YEARS UNDER HEAVEN"

The reddish rays of the western sun fell into the empty moat of the Honno Temple. It was the first day of the Sixth Month. The sun had beat down relentlessly on the capital for the entire day, and now spots of dry mud were appearing even in the comparatively deep moat.

The tile-roofed mud walls ran for more than one hundred yards to the east and west, and for two hundred yards from north to south. The moat was over twelve feet wide, and deeper than usual for a temple. Passersby might look up at the roofs of the main temple and the ten or so monastery buildings, but nothing could really be seen from the outside. Only the famous honey locust tree in a corner of the compound was visible from quite some distance away. It was so large that people called it the Honno Forest, or the Locust Tree Grove.

The tree was as famous a landmark as the pagoda of the Eastern Temple. When the late afternoon sun filled its high branches, a multitude of crows raised a racket all at once. And no matter how fastidious and elegant the citizens of Kyoto tried to be, there were three things they could not avoid: stray dogs at night, cow dung in the streets in the morning, and crows in the afternoon.

Within the grounds of the temple there were still a number of vacant areas. Much construction was needed to complete the reconstruction of the twenty or so buildings that had been destroyed by fire during the civil wars in the capital. If a visitor walked in the direction of Fourth Street from the temple's main gate, he would see the mansion of the governor of Kyoto, the samurai quarter, and the streets of a well-regulated town. But in the northern part of the city, the slums remained like islands, just as they had been during the shogunate, and one narrow alleyway still richly deserved its old name, Sewer Street.

The children of the neighborhood almost burst from the alleys between the rough walls that wound beneath the twisted eaves of the single-roofed houses. With their boils, rashes, and sniveling noses, they flew through the streets like giant winged insects.

"The missionaries have come!" the children shouted.

"The priests from the Namban Temple are walking by with a pretty birdcage!"

The three missionaries laughed when they heard the children's voices, and slackened their steps as though waiting for friends.

The Namban Temple, as the missionaries' church was popularly known, was on nearby Fourth Street. The chanting of the religious services at the Honno Temple could be heard in the morning in the slums, and in the evening the church bell echoed through the alleyways. The gate of the Honno Temple was very imposing, and the monks who lived there walked through the streets with haughty expressions, but when the missionaries came through, they were humble and friendly toward the locals. Seeing a child with a boil on his face, they would pat his head and show him how to treat it; if they heard that someone was sick, they would visit that person. It was said that no one should interfere in a quarrel between husband and wife, but if the missionaries passed by on such an occasion, they would step in and try to settle it. Thus they earned a reputation for being kind and understanding. "They're really working for the sake of society," people said. "Maybe they are messengers from the gods."

The people had been struck with admiration for the missionaries for some time. Their good works extended to the poor, the sick, and the homeless. The church even had something like a charity hospital and a home for the aged. And if that wasn't enough, the missionaries liked children.

But when these selfsame missionaries ran into Buddhist priests on the streets, they did not treat them with the same humility as they did the children. Indeed, they looked at the priests as if they were bitter enemies. For this reason they would take the long way around through Sewer Street, avoiding the Honno Temple as much as possible. Today and the day before, however, they had had to make daily visits to the temple itself, because it had become the headquarters of Lord Nobunaga. This meant that the most powerful man in Japan was now their neighbor.

Carrying a small tropical bird in a gilded cage and some pastries made by the cook they had brought from their own country, the three missionaries now seemed to be on their way to offer presents to Lord Nobunaga.

"Missionaries! Hey, missionaries!"

"What kind of bird is that?"

"What's in the box?"

"If it's cake, give us some!"

"Give us some, missionary!"

The children of Sewer Street came up and blocked their way. The three missionaries did not look annoyed at all, but smilingly admonished them in broken Japanese as they walked along.

"These are for Lord Nobunaga. Don't be disrespectful. We'll give you all cakes when you come to the church with your mothers," one of the priests said.

The children tagged along behind, and ran around ahead of them. While the priests were thus surrounded, one of the children ran to the edge of the moat and fell in, making a sound just like a frog. The moat was empty, so there was no danger of the boy drowning, but the bottom of the moat was as muddy as a swamp. The child squirmed in it like a mudfish. The sides of the moat were made of stone, so even an adult would have had trouble climbing out. Indeed, sometimes a poor drunk would fall in and drown on a night when rainwater had filled it to overflowing.

Someone immediately notified the boy's family. The curious neighbors of Sewer Street clamored out of their houses like water boiling out of a pot, and the parents came running out barefoot. It was a calamity. But by the time they had arrived, the little boy had already been rescued. He looked like a lotus root plucked from the mud, and he was sobbing loudly.

He and two of the missionaries had mud splattered all over their hands and clothes. The third missionary had jumped into the moat after the boy, and he was completely covered in mud.

When the children looked at the missionaries, they ran around happily, hooting, clapping their hands, and shouting, "The missionary has turned into a catfish! His red beard is all muddy!"

But the parents of the boy thanked them and praised their god, even though they were not Christians. They bowed at the priests' feet and shed tears of thankfulness with their hands folded in prayer. In the black mountain of people that had formed behind them, words of praise for the missionaries went from mouth to mouth.

The missionaries showed no regret at having come this far only to have to turn back the way they had come, carrying their now useless presents. In their eyes, Nobunaga and the boy from the slums were exactly the same. Moreover, this incident had become talk that would spread from house to house, and the missionaries knew very well what a large and inspiring wave it might grow into.

"Sotan, did you see that?"

"Yes, I was impressed."

"That religion is frightening."

"Yes, it is. It really makes you think."

One of the speakers was a man of about thirty, while the other was much older. They looked like father and son. There was something about them that set them apart from the important merchants of Sakai—a part of their character, perhaps, that spoke of a liberal breadth and depth of upbringing. Nevertheless, looking at them, one knew at once they were merchants.

With Nobunaga in residence, the Honno Temple was no longer a simple temple. From the night of the twenty-ninth on, at the main gate of the temple there was a tumult of carts and palanquins, and the din of people going in and out. The audiences Nobunaga was now granting seemed matters of grave concern to the entire nation. Thus, a man might withdraw after having obtained at least a word or smile from Nobunaga and go home with the happy feeling that he had gained something worth a hundred or a thousand times the value of the rare utensils, fine wines, delicacies, or other gifts he had presented.

"Let's wait here for a moment. It looks as though a courtier is going through the gate."

"It must be the governor. Those look like his attendants."

The governor, Murai Nagato, and his attendants had stopped at the main gate and seemed to be waiting discreetly as the palanquin of an aristocrat was brought out. Very soon afterward, a few samurai led two or three bay and dappled horses behind a small procession of palanquins and litters. When the samurai recognized Nagato, they bowed as they went by, taking the horses' reins in one hand.

As soon as the crush was over, Nagato entered the gate. And when the two merchants had assured themselves that he was inside, they turned their steps in the same direction.

Naturally, the guards at the front gate were exceptionally severe. The people who passed in and out were not used to seeing the wartime glitter that shone from the spears, halberds, and even the eyes of the warriors stationed there. The guards all wore armor, and if anyone looked suspicious, they stopped that person with loud shouts and yells.

"Wait a minute! Where are you going?" the guard asked the two merchants.

"I am Soshitsu of Hakata," the older man said courteously. When he bowed his head, the younger man did the same

"I am Sotan, also of Hakata."

The guards looked as though they couldn't understand anything from that introduction alone, but their captain, who was standing in front of the guardhouse inside, motioned them through with a smile.

"Please, come in."

The Omotemido Hall was the main building of the temple compound, but the real center was Nobunaga's quarters. Outside of the room from which Nobunaga's voice could be heard, a brook murmured from a spring in the garden, and from the buildings a little farther beyond, the bright laughter of women occasionally wafted over on the breeze.

Nobunaga was speaking to a messenger from his third son, Nobutaka, and Niwa Nagahide: "That will be of some help to my old hand, Nagahide. Have him informed that everything is secure. I'll be going to the western provinces in a few days myself, so we'll be meeting there soon."

Nobutaka and Niwa's army was to sail for Awa the next morning. The messenger had come to give that report along with the information that Tokugawa Ieyasu had traveled from Osaka to Sakai.

Nobunaga looked around at the color of the sky as though he had just noticed it, and said to a page, "It's dusk. Roll up the blinds on the western side." Then he asked Nobutada, "Is it hot where you're staying too?"

Nobutada had come to the capital a little before his father and had taken lodgings at the nearby Myokaku Temple. He had been stationed there the evening his father had entered the capital, which was yesterday, and today as well, and he seemed a little tired. He had thought he would announce his leave, but his father said, "Why don't we have tea tonight in private? For the last two nights we've had guests, and it saddens me when there's not enough leisure. I'll invite some interesting people for you." Nobunaga was going to entertain his son, and he was not about to take no for an answer.

If he had been allowed to express what was really on his mind, Nobutada might have said that he was only twenty-five years old and did not understand tea as his father did. He had an especially strong aversion to those tea masters who wasted their leisure hours during wartime. If he was going to have the pleasure of being with his father, a tea master was not welcome. To be honest, in his heart he wanted to leave for the campaign right away. He did not want to be behind his younger brother, Nobutaka, by even an hour.

It seemed that Nobunaga had also invited Murai Nagato, not in his official capacity of governor of Kyoto, but as a friend. But Nagato was unable to forget the stiff formality that was usual between lord and retainer, and the conversation remained awkward. Awkwardness was one of the things Nobunaga detested. With daily events, the pressures of administering the government, guests coming in and out, and lack of sleep—when he was able to get away from public duties for a moment, he could not stand to be confronted with such formality. These situations always made him think fondly of Hideyoshi.

"Nagato?" Nobunaga said.

"Yes, my lord?"

"Isn't your son here?"

"He came with me, but he's a bit of an ignoramus, so I had him wait outside."

"That kind of reserve is really boring," Nobunaga muttered. When he had asked the man to bring along his son, obviously it was in order to talk lightheartedly, not in order to have a formal interview between lord and retainer. He did not order Nagato to call his son in, however.

"I wonder what happened to our guests from Hakata," Nobunaga said. He stood up and walked into the temple, leaving Nobutada and Nagato where they were.

Bomaru's voice could be heard in the pages' room. His older brother, Ranmaru, seemed to be scolding him for something or other. By this time, all of Mori Yoshinari's children were adults. It had been rumored recently that Ranmaru hoped to receive Sakamoto—presently an Akechi castle—which had been his father's domain. The report was circulating widely, and even Nobunaga was outraged by the thought of it. So to dissipate the public rumor, he now rethought his own rather unseemly policy of keeping Ranmaru dressed as a page and having him constantly at his side. To amend this would be for his own sake as well.

"Will you be going out into the garden?" Ranmaru asked.

Nobunaga had been standing on the veranda, and Ranmaru quickly ran out from the pages' room to place some sandals on the steppingstone. It was good to have someone so quick-witted and gentle in his service, Nobunaga thought; he had grown used to that kind of solicitude over ten or so years.

"No, I'm not going into the garden. It's been hot today, hasn't it?"

"Yes, the sun really burned down on us."

"Are the horses in the stable all healthy?"

"They seem to be a little low-spirited."

Nobunaga looked up and strained his eyes at the evening star, perhaps having sudden thoughts of the faraway western provinces. Ranmaru stared up blankly at Nobunaga's profile. Nobutada had also come in and was standing behind the two men, but Ranmaru's gaze showed that he had forgotten about the younger man's very existence. It was almost as though he were looking at his master for the last time. If his spirit had had the power of self-consciousness, he might have been even more aware of his strange intuition of that moment, and of the goose bumps that were even now appearing on his skin. It was just about the time Akechi Mitsuhide was arriving at Oinosaka.

The smoke from the stoves in the huge kitchen began to envelop the inside of the temple. Firewood was alight not only in the stoves but also in the baths. And not just at the Honno Temple: in the hour just before nightfall, smoke from cooking fires trailed off into the sky both inside and outside of the capital.

Nobunaga poured water over himself in the bath. A single white flower on a vine showed itself through the bamboo lattice of a high window cut out of the wall. After his hair was arranged and he had donned fresh clothes, Nobunaga walked back along the bridged corridor.

Ranmaru came up and announced that Sotan and Soshitsu of Hakata were waiting for him in the tearoom.

"They've been here since before dark, and the two of them swept the path from the tearoom to the entrance and polished the veranda themselves. Then Master Soshitsu watered the path and made a flower arrangement, while Master Sotan went to the kitchen and gave instructions for the dishes they would present to you."

"Why wasn't I informed earlier?"

"Well, they said that since they were the hosts, we should wait until everything was ready."

"It appears they have some sort of plan. Was Nobutada told about this? And Nagato?"

"I'll invite them right away."

When Ranmaru left, Nobunaga went to his quarters but very quickly redirected his steps toward the tearoom.

The building did not have the appearance of a tearoom. The building had been designed as a drawing room, and a smaller space had been created for the tea ceremony by the placement of folding screens.

The guests were Nobunaga, Nobutada, and Nagato and his son. The lamps added a refreshing atmosphere to the room. After the tea ceremony had been concluded, the hosts and their guests moved to a larger room, where they talked late into the night.

Nobunaga was still very hungry. He devoured the dishes placed before him, drank wine—which appeared as if it had been made of melted rubies—and occasionally took a European cake from the well-stocked plate, all the while conversing nonstop.

"I'd like to take a tour of the southern lands, with you and Sotan as my guides. Surely you've traveled to those places a number of times."

"I think about it all the time but haven't been able to go," Soshitsu answered.

"Sotan, you're young and healthy. Have you been there?"

"Not yet, my lord."

"Neither of you have been there?"

"No, even though our employees are constantly going back and forth."

"Well, I would think that would be a disadvantage for your trade. Even if someone like me had such hopes, there would never be a good time to leave Japan, so there's really nothing to be done. But you own ships and branch stores and are always free to travel. Why haven't you gone yet?"

"The rush of work you have with the affairs of the country is of a different nature than ours, but somehow we've been prevented in one way or another by our household affairs and will be unable to leave for one year or so. Nevertheless, on the day Your Lordship settles all of the many affairs you attend to, I'd like to go with you and Sotan and give you a grand tour."

"Let's do that! That's been one of my desires for such a long time. But Soshitsu, are you going to live that long?"

As the page poured out the wine, Nobunaga joked with the old man, but Soshitsu was not to be bested.

"Well now, rather than worrying about that, can you assure me that you're going to put everything in order of before I die? If you're the one that's too slow, I may not be able to wait."

"It should be soon," Nobunaga said, smiling, delighted by the old man's banter.

Soshitsu was able to speak his mind in a way that Nobunaga's generals could not. From time to time during the conversation, Nobutada and Nagato would feel uneasy about that, wondering if it was truly all right for these merchants to be speaking as frankly as they were. At the same time they wondered why these commoners had Nobunaga's favor. It was highly unlikely that Nobunaga tolerated them as friends just because they were tea masters.

Nobutada was bored by the conversation. Only when the talk between his father and the two merchants turned to the subject of the southern lands was Nobutada's interest engaged. Those things were all new to his ears, and inspired him to youthful dreams and ambitions.

Regardless of whether their understanding of the southern lands was deep or not, the intellectuals at that time had an interest in them. The very essence of Japanese culture was being rocked by a tidal wave of innovations from overseas, foremost among which was the gun.

Much of what was known about the south was brought by missionaries from Spain and Portugal; but men like Soshitsu and Sotan had started their trade without waiting for the missionaries. Their ships crossed to Korea and traded with China, Amoy, and Cambodia. The men who had told them of the wealth beyond the sea were not the missionaries, but Japanese pirates who made their lair near Hakata, in Kyushu.

Sotan had inherited his business from his father and had established branches in Luzon, Siam, and Cambodia. It is said that he is the man who imported waxtree nuts from south China and who developed a method of manufacturing wax, thereby making the lamp fuel that caused the nights in Japan to shine so much brighter. Improving the metallurgical techniques brought in from overseas, he is also credited with bringing about the refinement of iron smelting.

Soshitsu was also involved in overseas trade and was related to Sotan. There was not a lord on the island of Kyushu who had not borrowed money from him. He owned ten or more large ocean-going ships and a hundred smaller vessels.

It would not be an exaggeration to say that Nobunaga had picked up almost all of his knowledge about the world beyond Japan while drinking tea with these two men. Even now Nobunaga was absorbed in conversation, reaching out for one European cake after another. Soshitsu observed how many he was eating and remarked, "Those are made with something called sugar, so you should be careful about eating too many of them before you go to bed."

"Is sugar poisonous?" Nobunaga asked.

"If it isn't a poison, it certainly isn't healthful, either," Soshitsu answered. "Foods from the barbarian lands are thick and rich, while our Japanese foods have a blander taste. These cakes are much sweeter than our dried persimmons or rice cakes. Once you get a taste for sugar, you won't be satisfied with our own sweets anymore."

"Has a lot of this sugar already been imported to Kyushu?"

"Not so much. With an exchange rate of one weight of sugar to one weight of gold, we don't get much of a percentage. I'm thinking of shipping in some sugar plants and trying to transplant them to a warm region, but, like tobacco, I'm wondering if sugar would be a good thing to popularize in Japan."

"That's not like you," Nobunaga laughed. "Don't be so narrow-minded. It doesn't make any difference whether they're good or bad. Just lump them together and ship them in, and they'll bring a special quality to the culture. All sorts of things are finally being brought in from the western and southern seas right now. Their penetration to the east is unstoppable."

"I applaud your tolerance, my lord, and adopting that way of thinking would certainly be a great help to our business, of course. But I wonder if we should leave it at that."

"We should, without a doubt. Bring in everything new as fast as you can."

"As you wish, my lord."

"Or failing that, chew it up well and then spit it out," Nobunaga added.

"Spit it out?"

"Chew it well, take what's of good quality into your stomach, and spit out the dregs. If the warriors, farmers, artisans, and merchants of Japan understand that principle, there'll be no problems in importing anything."

"No, that's no good." Soshitsu waved his hand emphatically. He was against this altogether, and was quick to give his opinions about the direction of the government. "You, my lord, the ruler of this country, may feel that way, but recently I've seen some worrisome signs, and I, for one, cannot agree with you."

"What do you mean?"

"The spread of false religions."

"You mean the missionaries? Have the Buddhists been making demands on you, too, Soshitsu?"

"You're being a bit too disdainful. This problem is truly distressing the nation."

Soshitsu went on to tell the story of the child who had fallen into the moat a few hours before, and how the self-sacrifice of the missionaries had impressed the people.

"In less than ten years, thousands have abandoned the altars of their ancestors and converted to Christianity. And this has occurred not only in Omura and Nagasaki but also throughout Kyushu, in remote areas of Shikoku, and even in Osaka, Kyoto, and Sakai. Your Lordship has just said that it would be all right if whatever we brought into Japan were chewed up and spit out, but religion is unique and probably cannot be treated in that way. No matter how much the people chew, their souls are going to be drawn into

645

this heresy, and they won't give it up, even if you crucify them or cut off their heads."

Nobunaga was completely silent. His expression indicated that this was a problem of such gravity that it could not be discussed in a few words. He had burned Mount Hiei and, using a violence that had been beyond the reach of former rulers, had brought Buddhism to its knees. He had dealt with the clergy with a rain of hellfire and swords, but he himself knew better than anyone else that, wherever he went, the resentment toward him was unlikely to dissipate.

On the other hand, he had permitted the missionaries to build a church, he had publicly recognized their work, and from time to time he had even invited them to banquets. The Buddhist monks raised a hue and cry about which of them Nobunaga considered to be the foreigners—the Christians or themselves.

Nobunaga loathed explanations. He hated to hear something spelled out, but he respected a direct intuition between people. In fact, he was elated by it.

"Sotan." He now turned to converse with the other man. "What do you think about this? You're young, so I imagine that you naturally see things differently from Soshitsu."

Sotan looked cautiously at the lamp for a moment, but then answered quite clearly.

"I agree with you, my lord, that it would be all right to chew this matter of foreign religion well and then spit it out."

Nobunaga turned and looked at Soshitsu like someone who had just had his opinions confirmed. "Don't worry. You have to grasp the larger scheme of things. Centuries ago, Lord Michizane advocated the combination of the Japanese soul and Chinese know-how. Whether we import the customs of China or artifacts from the West, the colors of fall and the cherry blossoms of spring do not change. Rather, when rain falls on a pond, the water is renewed. You're making the mistake of gauging the ocean by the moat of the Honno Temple. Isn't that true, Soshitsu?"

"Yes, my lord, one must measure a moat by a moat's standards."

"And the same with culture from overseas."

"As I get old, even I have become like a frog in a well," Soshitsu said.

"I think you're more like a whale."

"Yes," Soshitsu agreed, "but a whale with narrow vision."

"Hey, bring some water," Nobunaga ordered the page sleeping behind him. He was not yet finished with the evening. Though they had not eaten or drunk for a while, the excitement of the conversation had continued on its own.

"Father," Nobutada said, sliding over to Nobunaga. "It's gotten awfully late. I'm going to take my leave."

"Stay a little longer," Nobunaga said, restraining him more than he would have ordinarily. "You're just over at Nijo, aren't you? Even if it's late, you're almost right next door. Nagato lives right in front of the gate, and our guests from Hakata are hardly going back there tonight."

"No, just me . . ." Soshitsu looked as though he were getting ready to leave. "I have an appointment tomorrow morning."

"Then the only person staying is Sotan?"

"I'll be on night duty. There's work left for me, tidying up the tearoom."

"I see. You won't stay for my sake. You're carrying that expensive tea equipment with you, and you must stay here to guard it tonight."

"I won't contradict you, my lord."

"Speak frankly," Nobunaga laughed. Suddenly looking behind him, he stared at the hanging scroll on the wall. "Mu Ch'i is very good, isn't he? You rarely see such skill nowadays. I've heard that Sotan owns a painting by Mu Ch'i called *Ships Returning from Far-away Ports*. I wonder if anyone is worthy of owning such a famous painting?"

Sotan suddenly laughed out loud, as though Nobunaga were not there.

"What are you laughing about, Sotan?"

Sotan looked at the people around him. "Lord Nobunaga would like to take my Mu Ch'i scroll with one of his sly stratagems: 'Is anyone worthy of owning such a painting?' This is like sending agent-provocateurs into an enemy province. You'd better look out for your precious oak tea caddy!" And he could not stop laughing.

He had hit dead center. For some time, Nobunaga had been after the painting. Both the tea caddy and the painting were family heirlooms, however, and for that reason even Nobunaga had not been able to speak his own mind freely.

But now the owner had been kind enough to bring up the matter, and Nobunaga thought that that was the same as promising to give him the object. Certainly, after laughing at him so audaciously, Sotan would not have the heart not to give him what he wanted.

So Nobunaga laughed too. "Well, you don't miss anything, Sotan. When you get to my age, a man can become a true disciple of tea." He was revealing the truth in a jest.

Soshitsu rejoined, "In a few days I'll be meeting Master Sokyu from Sakai. Let's deliberate together then about where the painting belongs. Of course, it would have been best to ask Mu Ch'i himself."

Nobunaga's mood was improving. And, although the attendants came to trim the wicks of the lamps a number of times, he simply sipped water and went on, oblivious of the passage of time.

It was a summer night, and the temple's shutters and doors were all open. Perhaps for that reason, the flames in the lamps were continually flickering and were capped by halos of evening mist.

If one had been able to read the future in the light of the lamps that evening, one might have divined an evil omen in the halos of mist or in the shades of light passing through the wicks of the lamps.

Someone knocked at the front gate of the temple. After a while an attendant announced that a dispatch had arrived from the western provinces. Taking advantage of the moment, Nobutada stood up and Soshitsu also begged to take his leave. Nobunaga then stood up also, to accompany them as far as the bridged corridor.

"Sleep well," Nobutada said, turning once more and looking at the figure of his father from the corridor.

Nagato and his son were standing next to Nobutada, holding lanterns. The halls of the Honno Temple compound sank back into a darkness as black as ink. It was the second half of the Hour of the Rat.

* * *

Mitsuhide was standing at a crossroads: a right turn would take him westward; a left turn would lead him through the village of Kutsukake and across the Katsura River, and on to the capital. He had reached the crest of the hill he had been climbing all his life. The two roads before him represented a turning point and a finality. But the view that presented itself to his eye that night did not compel him to reflection of any sort. Instead, the broad sky showing him the twinkling of peaceful stars seemed to promise a great change in the world, one that would begin with the new dawn.

No order had been given to rest, but Mitsuhide's horse had stopped, and he sat in the saddle, silhouetted against the starry sky. Perceiving that he was not going to move for the moment, the generals around him, clad in glittering armor—and the long lines of armored men, banners, and horses behind him—waited restlessly in the dark.

"There's a spring bubbling up over there. I can hear water murmuring, I think."

"There it is. Water!"

Groping along in the undergrowth of the precipice bordering the road, one of the men finally discovered a little stream in the rocks. One after another, the soldiers pushed forward to fill their canteens with the clear water.

"This will us get as far as Tenjin."

"Maybe we'll eat at Yamazaki."

"No, the night's so short, it'll probably get light when we get to the Kaiin Temple."

"The horses will get tired if we march during the daytime, so His Lordship is probably thinking that we should make as much progress as we can through the night and morning hours."

"That would be best until we get to the western provinces."

The foot soldiers, quite naturally, and even the samurai above them—with the exception of their commanders—still knew nothing at all. The whispers and laughing voices that did not quite reach the ears of the commanders manifested their assumption that the battlefield was still far away.

The line began to move. From that point, the commanders carried spears and advanced alongside of their troops with watchful eyes and a quickened pace.

To the left. To the left. The men began to descend the divide of Oinosaka to the east. Not one soldier turned off on the road to the west. Doubt reflected from eye to eye. But even those who were suspicious hurried on. The men behind simply looked up to the banners that fluttered in front of them; there was no mistake that this was the road on which their banners proceeded. The horses' hooves clattered on the steep slopes. From time to time the sound of the falling rocks became almost deafening. The army resembled a waterfall that would allow nothing to stand in its way.

Both men and horses were soaked with sweat, and their breath came in fiery gasps. Meandering through the deep mountain gorges, they once again descended. Quickly turning toward the babbling mountain stream, they pressed on toward the sheer slopes of Mount Matsuo.

"Take a rest."

"Break out the provisions."

"No fires are to be lit."

Orders were passed down, one after another. They were still only at Kutsukake, a village on the mountainside that was made up of no more than ten or so woodcutters' houses. Nevertheless, the warning of the central command had been strict, and patrols were quickly set in the area of the road that went down to the foothills.

"Where are you going?"

"Down to the valley to get some water."

"You're not allowed to separate from the ranks. Borrow some water from somebody else."

The soldiers opened up their provisions and silently started to eat. A good bit of whispering was heard as they chewed their food. A number of the men wondered why they were fortifying themselves with a meal at this apparently inopportune time, halfway down the mountain. They had already eaten a meal before they had left the Hachiman Shrine that night.

Why weren't they to eat when the sun came up, at Yamazaki or Hashimoto where they could tether their horses? Though they were puzzled, they still assumed that they were on their way to the western provinces. The road to Bitchu was not the only way that led to their destination. If they turned to the right at Kutsukake, they could pass through Oharano and come out in the direction of Yamazaki and Takatsuki.

But when they started off once again, the entire army descended straight ahead to Tsukahara without turning to either side, and went on to the village of Kawashima. By the fourth watch, the greater part of the army looked down at the unexpected sight of the Katsura River under the night sky.

The soldiers suddenly became agitated. As soon as they felt the cool breeze of the river, the entire army stopped in its tracks in fear.

"Settle down!" the officers ordered the men.

"Don't make so much noise! And don't talk to each other unnecessarily!"

The clear water of the river shimmered, and in the breeze from the river the nine standards with their blue bellflowers swayed like long poles bent into bows.

Amano Genemon, whose command was on the edge of the army's right wing as, was summoned by Mitsuhide. He jumped off his horse and ran toward his commander.

Mitsuhide was standing on a dry part of the riverbed. The penetrating eyes of the generals all turned in Genemon's direction. There were Saito Toshimitsu, his face rimmed with frost-white hair, and Mitsuharu, whose tragic face now appeared like a mask. Along with these two men, the many armored members of his field staff surrounded Mitsuhide like an iron barrel.

"Gengo," Mitsuhide said, "it will soon be light. You take a company and cross the river first. On the way you are to cut down anyone who might be able to run through our lines to warn the enemy. Also, there may be merchants and other travelers who are passing through the capital in the early dawn, and it will be necessary to take care of these people. This is extremely important."

"I understand."

"Wait." Mitsuhide called the man back. "As a precaution, I've sent some men to guard the road through the mountains from Hozu, down from northern Saga, and along the Nishijin Road from the Jizoin. Don't attack our own men by mistake." Mitsuhide's voice was cuttingly sharp; it was easy to see that his mind was now working at full speed and

649

that his blood vessels were so filled with tension they were close to bursting.

Watching Genemon's troops splash across the Katsura River, the remaining men felt increasingly uneasy. Mitsuhide remounted and, one after another, the men under his command followed his example.

"Give out the orders. Make sure no one misses a word."

One of the commanders at Mitsuhide's side cupped his hands around his mouth and shouted, "Take off your horses' shoes and throw them away!" The shrill command from the first ranks could be heard clearly. "The foot soldiers should all put on new straw sandals. Don't wear sandals with cords that are loose from walking on the mountain roads. If the cords have loosened, tie them firmly enough so that if they get wet, they won't chew up your feet. Gunners, cut your fuse cords to lengths of one foot and tie them in bundles of five. Unnecessary things, like the wrapping for provisions and personal effects, or anything that will be a burden to the free movement of your arms and legs, should be thrown into the river. Don't take anything but your weapons."

The army was dumbfounded. At the same time, something of a groundswell began to bubble up from the men. It was connected with neither the sound of voices nor the appearance of motion. The men looked to the left and right, but having been forbidden to talk among themselves, it simply went from face to face—a voiceless voice. Nevertheless, almost instantaneously, action was kindled wherever one looked. And it was so exceedingly swift that, superficially at least, any doubt, uneasiness, or alarm was nowhere apparent.

When everything was ready and the men had re-formed their ranks, the old warrior, Saito Toshimitsu, raised a voice that had been tempered in a hundred battles, and spoke to the troops almost as if he were reading.

"Rejoice. Today our master, Lord Akechi Mitsuhide, will become the ruler of the country. Do not entertain the least bit of doubt."

His voice carried all the way to the faraway foot soldiers and sandal bearers. Everyone gasped as though they were all breathing their last. But this gasp contained no trace of either joy or acclamation. It was more like a shudder. Toshimitsu closed his eyes and raised his voice almost as though he were scolding the men. Was he trying to reassure himself, too?

"No day will ever shine as brightly as today. We will rely especially on the samurai to achieve meritorious deeds. Even if you fall in battle today, your relatives will be rewarded in accordance with your actions." Toshimitsu's voice did not change much, right up to the time he finished speaking. He had been told what to say by Mitsuhide, and it was probably not in accord with his own thinking. "Let's cross the river!"

The sky was still dark. The current of the Katsura River momentarily checked the warhorses as they attempted to ford the stream. Curls of white waves surged and rolled back on themselves. The entire army shivered as the men sloshed through the water in soaked straw sandals. Although they were drenched, not one gunner let his fuse cords get wet. The clear water went up past their knees, and it was colder than ice. No doubt every soldier and officer was consumed by his own thoughts as he crossed the current. Each man considered the words that were spoken by Toshimitsu and the corps commanders before he began to ford the stream.

Well, we must be attacking Lord Ieyasu. Except for Tokugawa Ieyasu, there's no one nearby enough to attack. But what did Toshimitsu mean when he said our lord would become the ruler of the country from this day on?

That was as far as the soldiers' thoughts took them. In large part, the Akechi clan's warriors were men steeped in morality and justice, and it had still not occurred to them that the enemy was Nobunaga. The earnest, stubborn Akechi spirit, devoted to a sense of justice, had been passed from the company commanders down through the ranks, right to the lowest foot soldier and sandal bearer.

"Hey, it's getting light."

"Daybreak will be here soon."

They were in the area between Nyoigadake and the mountain range that delimitated the eastern edge of Kyoto. The edge of a mass of clouds was glittering a bright red.

When the men strained their eyes, they could see the city of Kyoto just barely visible in the dark of dawn. Behind them, toward Oinosaka or the border of the grassy province of Tamba, however, the stars were so clear and bright they might have been counted.

"A corpse!"

"There's another one over there too."

"Hey, and over here!"

The army was now approaching the eastern outskirts of Kyoto. With the exception of groves and thatched huts, there was only dew-covered farmland until one reached the pagoda of the Eastern Temple.

Dead bodies were strewn at the foot of the pines along the side of the road, in the middle of the road, and almost everywhere the soldiers looked. The dead all seemed to have been farmers from the area. Lying face down as though asleep in a field of eggplant flowers, a young girl lay dead, still clutching her basket, cut down by the single stroke of a sword.

It was apparent that the blood was still flowing, for it was fresher than the morning dew. Undoubtedly the troops of Amano Genemon that had set out before the main army saw these early-rising farmers in their fields, chased them down, and killed them. They may have felt pity for their innocence, but their orders were not to risk the success of the greater action to come.

Looking down at the fresh blood on the earth and up at the red clouds in the sky, Mitsuhide stood up in his stirrups, abruptly raised his whip into the air, and shouted, "On to the Honno Temple! Overrun it completely! My enemies are at the Honno Temple. Go! Go! I'll cut down anyone who lags behind!"

Now was the time for battle, and the nine banners emblazoned with the blue bellflowers split into three companies of three banners each. Striking into the entrance to Seventh Street, they trampled through city gate after city gate, swarming into the capital all at once. The Akechi army burst in through the gates at Fifth, Fourth, and Third streets, and poured into the city.

The mist was still thick, but a bright red dawn had begun to permeate the sky over the mountains, and as usual, the wicket gates were being opened for the people going to and fro.

The men crowded through the gates, and spears and guns swarmed in confusion.

Only the banners were kept down as the soldiers crowded through.

"Don't push! Don't be flustered! The rear corps should wait outside the gate for a moment."

Seeing the confusion, one of the commanders did what he could to restrain the men. Slipping the bar out of the large door, he opened the gate wide.

"All right! Go through!" he yelled, goading them on.

The order had been to rush in silently, without raising a battle cry, to keep the banners down, and even to keep the horses from neighing. But as soon as they crashed through the gates and stormed into the city, the Akechi troops had already worked themselves into a near frenzy.

"On to the Honno Temple!"

Through the general turmoil, the sound of opening doors could be heard coming from houses here and there, but as soon as the residents looked outside, they pulled their heads in again and slammed the doors tight.

Among the many units that pushed in on the Honno Temple, the forces that approached it the quickest were those led by Akechi Mitsuharu and Saito Toshimitsu, who could be seen in the vanguard.

"It's difficult to see in these narrow streets filled with mist. Don't get lost trying to get there before the others. The honey locust tree of the Honno Temple grove should be your landmark! Aim for the big bamboo stand between the clouds of mist. There it is! That's the honey locust tree of the Honno Temple!"

Galloping ahead on horseback and waving his hands furiously as he gave out instructions, Toshimitsu seemed to have pledged his warrior's voice to that one morning of his life.

The second army, led by Akechi Mitsutada, was also in motion. Those forces inundated the district around Third Street, passed through the inner section like smoke, and made a drive to encircle the Myokaku Temple in Nijo. This action was naturally coordinated with the forces attacking the Honno Temple and was calculated to finish off Nobunaga's son Nobutada.

It was no distance from this place to the Honno Temple. The armies were separated by the dark of predawn, but already at this point an indescribable noise was beginning to rise from the direction of the Honno Temple. The ringing sound of the conch shell and the booming of the gongs and drums could be heard. It would not be an exaggeration to say that the sound shook heaven and earth and was not like anything ordinarily heard in this world. There was no one in the capital that morning who did not either jump up in surprise or leap out of bed in response to the screams of his family.

Clamorous noises and voices quickly arose even in the ordinarily peaceful area of the nobles' mansions that surrounded the Imperial Palace. With all of this uproar and the echoing of the drumming horses' hooves, the sky of Kyoto itself seemed to be ringing.

The confusion of the city people, however, was only momentary, and as soon as the nobility and common people understood the situation, their homes were as quiet as they had been a while before, when they had been sleeping peacefully. No one ventured to go out into the streets.

It was still so dark the soldiers could not determine whose face was in front of them, and on their way to the Myokaku Temple, the second army mistook some of its own men, who had taken a roundabout way through another narrow street, for the enemy. Even though their commander had strictly warned them not to fire until the order was given, when they came to the corner of the intersection, the excited soldiers suddenly began to fire blindly through the mist.

When they smelled the gunpowder smoke, their spirits became all the more excited in spite of themselves. Even soldiers who had been in battles before might go through a situation like this before they achieved complete self-control.

"Hey! You can hear conch-shell horns and gongs over there. It's started over at the Honno Temple."

"They're fighting!"

"The attack is on!"

They couldn't tell if their feet were hitting the ground or not. Running forward, they still could not determine whose voices they heard, though there was no resistance in front of them. Still, the pores all over their bodies began to swell, and they were even unaware of the cold mist striking their goose-fleshed faces and hands. They shook with such feeling that all they could do was yell.

And so they raised their battle cry even before they saw the roofed walls of the Myokaku Temple. Unexpectedly, a cry rose up in the direction of the front of the unit, and the gongs and drums began to ring out impatiently as well.

Mitsuhide was with the third army. It would be proper to say that headquarters were located wherever he happened to be, and this time he had stopped at Horikawa. He was surrounded by members of his clan, and a camp stool had been set up for him, but he did not sit down even for a moment. His entire being was focused on the voices of the clouds and the shrieks of the mist, and he looked uninterruptedly into the sky in the direction of Nijo. From time to time his eyes overflowed with the red of the morning clouds, but still no flames or smoke reached skyward.

Nobunaga woke up with a start, but not for any particular reason. After a good night's sleep, he naturally woke up in the morning on his own. Since his youth he had always risen at dawn, no matter how late he had gone to bed. He awoke, or rather—while he was not yet fully conscious and his head was still on the pillow—he experienced a particular phenomenon. It was a transition from dreaming to wakefulness that lasted only a fraction of a second, but in that infinitesimal space, a number of thoughts would pass through his head with the speed of a flash of lightning.

They were memories of experiences that had occurred between the time of his youth and the present, or reflections on his present life, or goals for the future. Whatever they were, these thoughts would pass through his brain in that moment between dream and reality.

This experience was, perhaps, less a habit than an innate ability. As a child, he had already been an extraordinary dreamer. The brambles and thorns of reality, however—especially given his birth and breeding—would not permit him to live only in a world of dreams. The real world had added difficulties on top of difficulties and had taught him

653

the pleasure of cutting his way through them.

During this period of growth, when he was tested and returned victorious, and was tested again, he ultimately learned that he was not satisfied with the difficulties given to him. The highest pleasure of life, he found, lay in seeking out difficulties, plunging right into them, and then turning back to see them behind him. His convictions had been strengthened by the self-confidence he had gained from such experiences and had put him into a frame of mind far beyond the common sense one of ordinary men. After Azuchi, the idea of the impossible did not exist within his boundaries or in the world of his conceptions. That was because the works he had accomplished up to that point had not been done by following the path of ordinary men's common sense; rather, he had taken the path of making possible the impossible.

And that morning, on the border between the world of dreams and his mortal body, where the intoxication of the night before was perhaps still running fragrantly through his veins, pictures were being drawn in his brain: convoys of huge ships going to the southern islands, to the coast of Korea, and even to the great country of the Ming. He himself stood in the tower of a ship along with Sotan and Soshitsu. One more person would have to accompany him, he thought—Hideyoshi. He felt that the day he could make this into a reality was not far off.

In his mind, a small accomplishment like the domination of the western provinces and Kyushu was not enough to fill an entire lifetime.

It's dawn, he muttered to himself, and he rose and left his bedroom.

The heavy cedar door that opened to the corridor had been exquisitely fashioned so that when it was pulled open or closed, the sill naturally made a noise almost as if it were calling out. When the pages heard this sound in their faraway room, they jumped up with a start. The flickering light of the paper lantern was reflected by the thick pillars and planks of the veranda, which gleamed as if they had been polished with oil.

Aware that their lord had awakened, the pages quickened their steps toward the bathroom next to the kitchen. On their way, they heard a noise in the direction of the north corridor. It sounded like a window shutter being opened quickly.

Thinking that it might be Nobunaga, they stopped and peered back toward the blind corridor. The only person visible, however, was a woman wearing a cool, large-patterned kimono and a long outer coat patterned with pines and cherry blossoms. Her long black hair trailed behind her.

As the shutters were open, a morning sky the color of bellflowers appeared through the window, looking almost like a paper cutout. The breeze that wafted in rustled the woman's black hair and sent the fragrance of aloeswood all the way to the place where the pages were lingering.

"Ah, over there." The pages heard the sound of running water and ran off in the direction of the kitchen. The priests of the temple had not yet left their living quarters, so the windows and the huge main gate had not yet been opened. In the wide earthen-floored kitchen and on the elevated wooden platform, the humming of mosquitoes and the darkness of the night remained, but the steaminess of the summer morning could already be felt.

Nobunaga felt a unique dislike for that particular time of day. By the time the pages realized that he had left his sleeping quarters and had come running up, he had already finished rinsing his mouth and washing his hands. Walking over to the huge jar into which water flowed from a bamboo water pipe, he took a small pail and dipped it into a lacquered tub. Splattering water everywhere, just like a wagtail, he hastily washed his face.

"Ah, you're getting your sleeve wet, my lord."

"Let me change the water."

The pages were in dread. One of them fearfully lifted up Nobunaga's white sleeve from behind, while another dipped out fresh water. Still another held up a towel while kneeling at his feet. At the same time, the men in the samurai quarters left the night guardroom and began to open up the paneled doors in the court. Just at that moment, however, they became aware of an extraordinary noise coming from the direction of the outer main temple, and then of the reverberation of furious footsteps running toward the inner court.

Nobunaga turned around, his hair still dripping wet, and said impatiently, "Go see what it is, Bomaru." After giving the order, he continued vigorously rubbing his face with a cloth.

One of the pages said, "Maybe the guards at the outer temple have gotten into a fight or something."

Nobunaga did not acknowledge the remark. For a moment his eyes resembled the waters of an abyss, and sparkled as though he were searching for something, not in the outer world but within himself.

But only for a moment. It was not just outside the main temple. Here at the guest mansion, and from ridgepole to ridgepole of the ten or so monastery buildings, something as strong as an earthquake shaking the entire crust of the earth was being conveyed by an indefinable noise and a terrifying current of energy.

Any man, no matter how strong, is likely to feel confusion at such a moment. The blood retreated even from Nobunaga's face, and the pages attending him all turned pale. But they probably stood still for no more than a couple of breaths. Almost immediately, someone came running down the nearby corridor at great speed.

A man yelled, "My lord! My lord!"

The pages chorused, "Master Ranmaru! Master Ranmaru! Over here!" Nobunaga himself came out and called the man.

"Ranmaru! Where are you going?"

"Ah, you're here, my lord," Ranmaru said, almost falling down as he knelt. At a glance, Nobunaga could feel on the very surface of his flesh that what was happening was not just a simple matter of some samurai getting into a fight, or a row between the men at the stables.

"What's happened, Ranmaru? What's all the commotion?" he asked quickly, and Ranmaru was just as quick with his answer.

"The Akechi have committed an outrage. There are warriors outside, rioting and waving banners that are unmistakably emblazoned with the Akechi crest."

"What! The Akechi?" The words left his mouth in astonishment. His surprise demonstrated thoroughly that he had never expected—never even dreamed—that this would happen. But the singular physical shock and the emotional excitement he felt were halted

655

at his lips. Speaking with nearly the same calm he always possessed, his next words sounded almost like a growl.

"The Akechi…it was inevitable."

Turning quickly aside, Nobunaga dashed back into his room. Ranmaru started to follow him, but after five or six steps he turned back and scolded the trembling pages. "Each one of you get to work quickly. I've just ordered Bomaru to tell everyone to shut all of the gates and doors. Block all of the doorways, and don't let the enemy even get close to His Lordship." Before he was able to finish his words, bullets and arrows began to strike the kitchen door and the nearby windows like a downpour of rain. Countless arrows pierced deeply through the wooden doors, and the bright steel of their sharp points clearly proclaimed the battle to the people inside.

From south of Rokkaku, north of Nishikikoji, west of Toin, and east of Aburakoji, the four sides of the Honno Temple were engulfed in the armor of the Akechi forces and their battle cries. The tile-roofed walls could be easily seen, but, protected by the deep moat, they could not be so easily scaled.

The forest of spears, banners, guns, and halberds did nothing more than sway back and forth.

Some of the men leaped rashly to the base of the roofed wall; others could not jump so far. Many of those who tried fell to the bottom of the moat. And because of their heavy armor, those who fell in were buried up to their waists in the foul-smelling, muddy swamp water, the color of black ink. Even if they had been able to get up and call, their companions above never looked down.

The Akechi troops at Nishikikoji demolished the tenements of the neighborhood, while women with infants, old people, and children fled from underneath the wreckage, like hermit crabs scuttling away from empty shells. In this way the soldiers filled the moat with doors and roof planking.

Immediately, everyone scrambled to swarm over the wall. The gunners lined up their firearms and, aiming from the top of the wall down into the compound, fired off the first volley.

By then the buildings inside the temple compound were uncannily still. All of the doors in the front main temple were closed, and it was difficult to tell whether or not there was an enemy inside to shoot at. Flames and smoke began to rise from Sewer Street. The heat of the fire beneath the ruined houses immediately began to smolder and easily ignited one structure after the next. Soon all the poor people on the block stampeded out as though they would trample each other to death. Crying and screaming, they spilled onto the dry riverbed of the Kamo River and into the center of town, carrying nothing with them at all.

Viewed from the area of the main gate on the opposite side of the temple, it must have seemed as though the men who had already broken through the rear gate had begun to set fire to the kitchen. The main force that thronged at the front gate was in no mood to be bested by their comrades. In a rage, the rank and file yelled out to a wavering group of officers who seemed to be doing nothing more than wasting time in the area of the drawbridge.

"Smash on in!"

"Push on through! What are you doing?"

One of the officers faced the guard inside the gate.

"We are the Akechi forces on our way to the western provinces. We have come here in full array in order to respectfully salute Lord Oda Nobunaga."

It was a poor attempt to trick the defenders into opening the main gate, and it only delayed matters even more. The guard was naturally suspicious, and he had no reason to open the gate on his own, without asking for Nobunaga's orders.

He told them to wait. The ensuing silence inside the gate meant that the emergency was being reported to the main temple and that there would be an instantaneous rush to man defenses.

The warriors jostling behind were becoming impatient at having to use a stratagem to cross this little bit of moat and they began to push the lines in front of them.

"Attack! Attack! What are we waiting for?"

"Take the walls!"

Recklessly competing to take the entrance first, they pushed those who were wavering to the side and even knocked them down.

A number of men in the front were pushed into the moat, and battle cries were raised both by those on top and by those who had fallen in. Then, apparently on purpose, groups even farther behind began to push. More men fell into the moat. In an instant, one section of the moat was filled with mud-covered warriors.

One young warrior stepped over the mass of human beings and leaped for the base of the roofed wall. Another man followed his example.

"We're going over!"

Screaming and thrusting with their spears, the men crossed over and quickly clung to the top of the roofed wall. The jumble of warriors in the moat jostled and shoved like mudfish trying to jump out of a pond. The warriors above them trampled the backs, shoulders, and heads of their own comrades. One man after another was sacrificed wretchedly to the horrific, muddy rush. Because of their unseen distinguished service, however, voices soon yelled with pride from the top of the walls of the Honno Temple.

"I'm the first!"

So quickly did the others reach the wall that it was difficult to distinguish who was first and who second.

Inside the walls, the Oda samurai who were already running from the guard station inside the gate and the area around the stables seized any weapon they could and tried to stem the flood of this rushing river. It was, however, the same as trying to support a broken dam with nothing more than one's hands. Ignoring the swords and spears of the defenders, the Akechi vanguard quickly bounded through, stepping over the corpses of men who had engaged in the battle and were dyed in the flowing blood of their enemies.

As if to say that all they wanted was to visit the residence of Lord Nobunaga, they ran straight toward the main temple and the guest house. They were met, however by a hum of arrows like a roaring wind from the wide veranda of the main temple and from the balustrade of the guest house. The distance was advantageous for bowshot, but many of the arrows did not hit the advancing warriors, and instead dug harmlessly into the earth. Many others skipped along the ground or rebounded from the faraway walls.

Among the defenders, a number of brave men dressed only in sleeping attire, half-naked or even unarmed, grappled with the armored enemy. The guards who had received time off from duty had slept comfortably through the heat of the summer night. Now, perhaps ashamed to enter the fight late, they ran out to restrain the Akechi warriors—if only a little—with nothing more than the fierceness of their bodies and their own desperate efforts.

But the billowing waves of armor were not to be stopped and were already surging under the eaves of the temple. Darting back inside his room, Nobunaga had put on breeches over a garment of white silk and was fastening the cords as he gnashed his teeth.

"A bow! Bring me a bow!" he shouted.

After he'd yelled this order two or three times, someone finally knelt down and held a bow in front of him. Snatching it away, he bounded outside through the paneled doors, shouting back, "Let the women escape. Nothing is wrong with their getting away. Just don't let them become an encumbrance."

The noise of doors and screens being kicked in could be heard everywhere, and the screams of the women intensified the unnerving atmosphere under the shaking roof tiles. The women fled in confusion from room to room, running down the corridors and jumping over the handrails. Their ruffled trains and sleeves cut through the gloom like flying flames of white, red, and purple. But the bullets and arrows flew everywhere—into the shutters, the pillars, and the handrails. Nobunaga had already stepped out onto a corner of the veranda and was firing his arrows at the enemy. Around him were stuck the arrows that had been concentrated on his own figure.

Watching the fearful way he fought, even the women, who had lost all control of themselves, were unable to leave his side. All they could do was scream.

"Fifty years a human being under heaven." That line was from the play Nobunaga had loved so much, and it had characterized his view of life during his youth. He did not think of what was happening as a world-shaking event. He was certainly not dispirited by the thought that it might be the end.

Rather, he fought with a fierce, burning spirit that would not simply give up and die. The ideal that he held in his breast as the great work of his life had not yet been even half-finished. It would be too mortifying to be defeated in the middle of the journey. There was just too much to be regretted if he died this morning. So he took another arrow and notched it to the string. He listened to the string hum again and again, seeming to loose his anger with each arrow. Finally the string became frayed and the bow was ready to break.

"Arrows! I don't have any arrows! Bring me more!"

Continuing to call out behind him, he even picked up and shot the enemy's arrows that had missed him and fallen to the corridor. Just then, a woman wearing a red silk headband and gallantly trussing up one sleeve of her kimono carried in an armful of arrows and raised one to his hand. Nobunaga looked down at the woman.

"Ano? What you've done here is enough. Now try to escape."

He motioned her off emphatically with his chin, but the court lady, Ano, kept passing arrow after arrow to Nobunaga's right hand and would not leave, no matter how he upbraided her.

He shot with nobility and grace more than with skill, more with spirit than with great strength. The magnificent hum of his arrows seemed to say that the arrows themselves were too good for these menials, that the arrowheads were gifts from the man who would rule the nation. The arrows that Ano brought, however, were quickly spent.

Here and there in the temple garden the enemy lay, felled by his arrows. But, braving his fire, a number of the armored soldiers yelled out and pressed desperately in under the balustrade, and finally began to climb onto the bridged corridor.

"We can see you, Lord Nobunaga! You can't escape now! Give up your head like a man!"

The enemy were as thick as the crows on the honey locust tree in the morning and evening. Personal attendants and pages positioned themselves around Nobunaga in the rear and side corridors in a protective stance, their swords shining with a fire born of desperation. They were not going to let the enemy get close. The Mori brothers were among them. A number of these men who had refused to leave their lord at the very end and had fought to protect him now lay on top of their enemies exactly as they had grappled with them, both seeming to have died by the other's hands.

The guard corps at the outer temple had made the main temple their battleground and now fought a fierce and bloody fight to keep the enemy from approaching the court. But because the enemy forces seemed about to take the entrance to the bridged corridor that led to the court, the entire corps, which consisted of less than twenty men, formed a single unit and dashed together toward the interior.

Thus the Akechi warriors who had scrambled up to the bridged corridor were caught on both sides. Stabbed and cut, their corpses fell on top of one another. When the men from the outer temple saw that Nobunaga was still safe, they cried out in elation, "Now there's time! Now! Retreat as quickly as possible!"

"Idiots!" Nobunaga spat, tossing his bow away. It had broken and he was out of arrows. "This is no time to retreat! Lend me your spear!"

Upbraiding them, he grabbed a retainer's weapon and ran down the corridor like a lion. Finding an enemy warrior with his hand on the balustrade and about to climb over, he drove his spear straight down into the man.

Just then, an Akechi warrior drew back his small bow from the shade of a Chinese black pine. The arrow struck Nobunaga's elbow. Staggering back, Nobunaga leaned heavily against the shutter behind him.

At that very moment, some minor action was occurring outside the western wall. A force of retainers and foot soldiers under the command of Murai Nagato and his son had sallied out from the governor's mansion, which was located in the neighborhood of the Honno Temple. Striking at the encircling Akechi forces from behind, they attempted to enter the compound from the main gate.

The night before, Nagato and his son had stayed up late into the night talking with Nobunaga and Nobutada, returning to their mansion to sleep at about the time of the third watch. That, one could say, was the reason Nagato had been sleeping so soundly and had been caught off guard. As part of his duties, he should have known—at the very least—about the situation the moment the Akechi forces stepped inside the capital precincts. And then he should have immediately sent a warning to the nearby Honno

Temple, even if it had been just moments before the arrival of the hostile troops.

His negligence had been total and absolute. But the fault lay not with Nagato alone. Certainly, negligence could be attributed to all of those who were staying in the capital or who had mansions there.

"It seems there's some trouble outside," Nagato was told when he was first awakened. He had no idea of the magnitude of the trouble.

"Maybe it's a brawl or something. Go take a look," he told a retainer. Then, while he leisurely got out of bed, he heard one of his attendants calling out from the roof of the mud-walled gate.

"Smoke's coming up from Nishikikoji!"

Nagato clicked his tongue and muttered, "Probably some fire on Sewer Street again."

He was that mistaken about how much at peace the world was, and had completely forgotten that this was truly just one more day in the civil war.

"What! Akechi forces?" His astonishment lasted no more than a moment. "Damn!" and he leaped out of the mansion with almost nothing more than the clothes on his back. As soon as he saw the dense crowds of armored, mounted men, bristling with swords and spears in the dark morning mist, he hurried back inside the mansion, put on his armor, and grabbed his sword.

With a force of only thirty or forty men, he hastened off to fight at Nobunaga's side. The various Akechi corps had blocked off all the streets leading to the Honno Temple. The encounter with Nagato's force started at a corner of the compound's western wall and developed into fierce hand-to-hand fighting. Breaking through one small patrol, Nagato's little party pressed fairly close to the main gate; but once a detachment of the Akechi forces turned and witnessed this impertinent action, they readied their spears and charged. Nagato's tiny force was hardly a match for them, and both he and his son were wounded. With their numbers reduced by half, they were forced to retreat.

"Try to get to the Myokaku Temple! We will join Lord Nobutada!"

Above the huge roof of the Honno Temple, jet black smoke could be seen billowing up like thunderclouds. Was it the attacking Akechi forces, Nobunaga's retainers, or Nobunaga himself who had set fire inside the temple? The situation was so chaotic that no one could tell.

The smoke began to billow out from the outer temple, from a room in the court, and from the kitchen almost all at the same time.

A page and two other men were fighting in the kitchen like demons. It seemed that the monks from the temple kitchen had risen early—though not one of them was to be seen—because beneath the huge cauldrons the firewood had been kindled.

The page stood in the door of the kitchen and stabbed at least two of the Akechi men who had broken in. His spear finally taken from him and facing too many of the enemy, he jumped up to the wooden floor and kept the men at bay by throwing kitchen implements and anything else he could lay his hands on.

A tea master and another man who were also there brandished their swords and fought bravely alongside the page. And though the enemy felt scorn for these three lightly armed opponents, a group of samurai was unable to step up onto the wooden floor because of them.

"What's taking so long?"

A warrior who seemed to be the commander looked in, grabbed a firebrand from an oven, and threw it into the faces of the three men. He then threw a firebrand into the store room and one up toward the ceiling.

"Inside!"

"He must be inside!"

Their objective was Nobunaga.

In that instant they pushed their way inside, kicking the burning firewood around with their warriors' straw sandals as they split up inside the building. Flames quickly crawled up the sliding doors and pillars like red-leafed ivy. The figures of the page and the tea master were motionless as the flames enveloped them, too.

The stables were in a complete uproar. Ten or more horses had panicked and were kicking the walls of their stalls, knocking out the boards. Two of them finally broke the crossbars and bucked violently outside. Running wild, they galloped into the center of the Akechi forces while the other horses whinnied more and more violently as they saw the flames. The samurai at the stables left their post and went to defend the steps of the court where Nobunaga had last been seen. Making this their last stand, they were all struck down and fell together.

Even the stableboys, who could have escaped, stayed behind and fought until they were all killed. These men were ordinarily completely inconspicuous, but on this day they silently demonstrated with the sacrifice of their lives that they were not inferior to men who had large stipends or a high rank.

Carrying his blood-soaked spear, an Akechi warrior running from room to room stopped when he saw a comrade through the smoke.

"Minoura?"

"Hey!"

"Have you accomplished anything yet?"

"No, not yet."

Together they searched for Nobunaga—or, more accurately, they competed in finding him. Soon they separated, making their way through the smoke.

The fire seemed to have spread beneath the roof, and the inside of the temple was crackling. Even the leather and metal fittings on the warriors' armor felt hot to the touch. In an instant, the only human forms to be seen were either corpses or the warriors of the Akechi, and even a number of the Akechi ran outside as the fire crept along the roofs.

Of the men inside who still stood their ground, some were choking from the smoke, while others were covered with ashes. The doors and sliding panels had been kicked out in the hall, and now the flaming gold brocade and pieces of ignited wood swirled thick and fast, burning as brightly as a field on fire. But inside the small rooms and recesses it was dark, and forms were indistinct. Thick with smoke, the various corridors could not even be distinguished.

Ranmaru leaned heavily against the cedar door leading to the room he was guarding, and then quietly stood up. With a bloodied spear in hand, he looked to the right and then to the left. Hearing footsteps, he readied his spear.

Focusing his entire being on his sense of hearing, he listened for some sign from the room. The white figure that had rushed inside just now had been that of the General of the Right, Oda Nobunaga. He had fought until the very end, when he saw that flames were engulfing the temple and that all of the men around him had been struck down and killed. He had fought hand-to-hand with the common soldiers as if he had been one himself. Yet he had made the decision to commit *seppuku* not simply because he had considered his reputation and found it regrettable to leave his head to a nonentity. A man's death was predetermined, so he did not even regret the loss of his life. What he did regret losing was the great work of his life.

The Myokaku Temple was nearby. The mansion of the governor was also in the neighborhood. And there were samurai who were lodged inside the city. If by some chance contact was made with the outside, escape might be possible, Nobunaga thought. On the other hand, this inspiration, or rather this conspiracy, had been planned by that kumquat head, Mitsuhide. Mitsuhide's character was such that if he decided to take an action like this, he would carry it out with such care that not even water might leak through. Well then, it was time to be resolved.

Those two thoughts struggled with each other in Nobunaga's mind.

Looking on the corpses of the attendants who had died together in battle, he knew that his final moments were at hand. Quitting the battle, he withdrew into a room and placed Ranmaru outside to guard the door, saying, "If you hear my voice inside, you can take it that I am committing suicide. Put my body under some sliding panels and set them on fire. Until then, do not let the enemy make their way in." As Nobunaga gave these instructions, he looked steadily into Ranmaru's eyes.

The wooden door was secure. Nobunaga gazed for a moment at the yet unmarred gilded paintings on the walls. A thin wisp of smoke began to flow through from somewhere, but it seemed that it would be a little while before the flames would spread inside.

This is a matter of departure. I don't have to hurry.

He felt as though someone were speaking to him. As soon as he had entered the room, he had felt—even more than the heat that surrounded him on four sides—a burning thirst. He almost collapsed as he sat down in the center of the room, but quickly reconsidered and moved to the slightly elevated alcove. The area beneath him was ordinarily reserved for his retainers, after all. He imagined a cupful of water running down his throat, and for a moment he made an effort to settle his spirit securely just below his navel. To this purpose, he knelt formally with his legs tucked underneath him, straightened his posture and his clothes, and tried to behave as though his retainers were sitting before him just as they did in ordinary times.

It was a moment before his heavy breathing became peaceful.

Is this what it is to die?

He felt so peaceful that he doubted it himself. He was even aware of a desire to laugh.

So I slipped up too.

Even when he imagined Mitsuhide's shiny bald head, he felt no resentment at all. He was human, too, and had done this out of anger, Nobunaga supposed. His own negligence was the blunder of a lifetime, and he felt sorry that Mitsuhide's anger had been transformed into nothing more than foolish violence. Ah, Mitsuhide, will you not be following me in a few days? he asked.

His left hand held the scabbard of his short sword. His right hand extricated the blade.

There is no need to hurry.

Thus Nobunaga instructed himself. The flames had started to spread to this room. He closed his eyes. As he did so, everything he could recall from his earliest youth right up to the present day flashed through his mind as though he were riding a galloping horse. When he opened his eyes, the gold dust and illustrations on the four walls radiated a bright red. The paintings of the peonies on the coffered ceiling proliferated in flames. It truly took no longer than a single breath for him to die. At the moment of death, some extraordinary function inside his body seemed to be saying farewell to the ordinary reminiscences of the life he had led.

"No regrets!" Nobunaga said out loud.

Ranmaru heard Nobunaga's shout, and ran in. His master, wearing a white silk kimono, already lay facedown on the floor, embracing a flow of fresh blood. Ranmaru pulled the doors from the low closet and placed them over Nobunaga's corpse as though he were making a coffin. Closing the door peacefully once again, he stood back from the alcove. He grasped the short sword with which he, too, might commit *seppuku*, but his shining eyes settled on Nobunaga's corpse until the room was consumed in flames.

* * *

On the first three days of the Sixth Month, the sky over Kyoto was clear and the sun beat down. The weather in the mountainous western provinces, however, alternated between clear skies and clouds. Heavy rainfall had continued until the end of the Fifth Month. Then, for two or three days at the beginning of the Sixth Month, a violent southwest wind blew the ragged clouds from south to north, and the sky continued to change back and forth from bright and clear to cloudy.

Most people, tired of the rain and mildew, hoped for an early end to the rainy season, but Hideyoshi's army, which was conducting the long siege of Takamatsu Castle, prayed to the Eight Dragon Kings to send rain and more rain, which was their main weapon on that battlefield. The solitary castle was still completely isolated in the middle of the marshy lake. Sticking out here and there, like hair on someone with a scalp disease, were the trees of a few submerged forests and groves.

In the castle town, only the roofs of the common people's homes remained above the water; the farmhouses in the low-lying areas had already disappeared. Innumerable pieces of decomposing lumber swirled through the muddy current, or floated on the edges of the lake.

At a glance, the ripples of the muddy yellow water appeared to be standing still, but as the soldiers watched the edge of the shore, they could see that the water was invading the dry land inch by inch.

"There are some carefree fellows today! Look over there. They're as happy-go-lucky as you are."

Hideyoshi sat mounted on his horse, speaking to the pages behind him.

"Where?"

The pages all looked with inquisitive faces in the direction in which their master was pointing. Sure enough, playing on top of the driftwood, a number of snowy herons could be seen. The pages, still adolescents, shrugged their shoulders and chuckled. Listening to their childish talk, Hideyoshi lightly whipped his horse and returned to camp.

That was during the evening of the third day of the Sixth Month. There was still no way Hideyoshi could know about what had happened in Kyoto.

Hideyoshi rarely missed his daily rounds of the camp with a retinue of fifty to one hundred attendants. Occasionally pages accompanied the entourage. They carried a large, long-handled umbrella and paraded around with the brilliantly colored commander's standard. The soldiers who witnessed this "royal passage" looked up and thought, That's our Master going by. On the days they didn't see him, they somehow felt that something was missing.

As he rode by, Hideyoshi looked at the soldiers to the right and left, the sweaty and mud-caked troops who found great flavor in food that was barely edible, the soldiers who always had a laugh and hardly knew what boredom was.

Hideyoshi missed the days when he had been part of that exuberant cluster of youth. He had been given the command of the campaign a long five years ago. The battles and bitter fighting that had occurred at Kozuki Castle, Miki Castle, and other places had been gruelling beyond words. But beyond the hardship of battle, as a general he had also met with spiritual crises any number of times.

Nobunaga was a hard man to please, and it had not been easy to serve him at a distance and to keep his mind at ease. And of course, the generals surrounding Nobunaga were not exactly pleased with Hideyoshi's rise. Still, Hideyoshi was grateful, and in the mornings, when he prayed to the sun goddess, he gave thanks with an open heart for all the trials he had gone through in those five years.

A man would not have gone out in search of such ordeals. He himself thought that, no matter what heaven's intentions for him actually were, it had continued to send him difficulty after difficulty. There were days when he felt thankful for the hardships and reversals of his youth, because they had given him the will to survive his own physical weakness.

By this time the strategy for the water attack on Takamatsu Castle had been carried out, and Hideyoshi only waited for Nobunaga to come from the east. On Mount Hizashi, the thirty thousand Mori troops under the commands of Kikkawa and Kobayakawa waited to rescue the isolated castle. During periods of clear weather, Hideyoshi's umbrella and commanders' standard could be clearly seen by the enemy.

Just as Hideyoshi was returning to his quarters that evening, a messenger arrived by the Okayama Road and was immediately surrounded by guards. The road led to Hideyoshi's camp on Mount Ishii, but the traveler could also cross through Hibata and go on to Kobayakawa Takakage's camp at Mount Hizashi by the same route. Naturally, the road was heavily guarded.

The messenger, whipping his horse all the way, had been riding since the day before without stopping to eat or drink. By the time the guards got him back to the camp, he had lost consciousness.

It was the Hour of the Boar. Hideyoshi was still up. When Hikoemon returned, he,

Hideyoshi, and Hori Kyutaro went to the building that served as Hideyoshi's private quarters. There the three men sat together for a long time.

This conference was so secret even the pages had withdrawn. Only the poet Yuko was allowed to remain, and he sat behind the paper screen doors, whisking tea.

Just then, footsteps could be heard hurrying toward the buildings. A strict order had been given to keep the area clear of people, so when the footsteps approached the cedar door, they were met and intercepted with a quick reproach from the pages standing guard.

The pages sounded extremely excited, while the person they had challenged seemed to be impertinent and hot-blooded.

"Yuko, what's going on?" Hideyoshi asked.

"I'm not sure. Maybe it's a page and one of the men on guard duty."

"Take a look."

"Of course."

Yuko stood up and went out, leaving the tea utensils exactly as they were.

Looking outside, he found that—rather than the guard he expected—it was Asano Nagamasa who had been challenged by the pages.

The young pages, however, were not going to announce anyone while their orders were to keep everyone out. It didn't make any difference who it was—Asano or anyone else. Asano had responded that if they would not carry the message, he was going to push his way through. The pages replied that if he wanted to go through, he was welcome to try. They may have been nothing more than pages, but they had been given a post, and they were going to demonstrate that they were not there just for decoration.

Yuko first calmed the stubborn young guards, then asked, "Lord Asano, what's the matter?"

Asano showed him the letter case he held in his hand and told him about the messenger who had just arrived from Kyoto. He had heard that the meeting was private, but thought the message was not some trivial matter and so he wanted to talk to his lord for a moment.

"Wait just a moment, please." Yuko went back inside but quickly returned and invited Asano to come in.

Asano stepped in with a sidelong glance at the next room. The pages inside were silent. Looking the other way, they completely ignored him.

Moving aside a short standing lamp, Hideyoshi turned toward Asano, who had entered the room.

"I'm sorry to disturb you during a conference."

"That's all right. There's been a dispatch, it seems. Who is it from?"

"I've been told it's from Hasegawa Sojin, my lord."

Asano held out the message case. The red lacquer on the leather shone brightly in the lamplight.

"A dispatch from Sojin?" Hideyoshi said, taking the case.

Hasegawa Sojin was Nobunaga's companion in tea. He was not on particularly intimate terms with Hideyoshi, so it was strange that the tea master would suddenly be sending an urgent message to his camp. Moreover, according to Nagamasa, the messenger had left Kyoto at noon the previous day and had arrived just now, at the Hour of the Boar.

That meant it had taken him one full day and half a night to travel the seventy leagues from the capital to the camp. That was not an easy pace, even for a courier. There was no doubt that he had neither eaten nor drunk on the way and that he had ridden through the night.

"Hikoemon, bring the lamp a little closer."

Hideyoshi bent down and unrolled Sojin's letter. It was short and had obviously been written in a hurry. But with a single reading, the hair on the back of Hideyoshi's neck stood up in the lamplight.

The other men had been sitting behind Hideyoshi, a little way off, but when his color changed from the nape of his neck to his ears, Kyutaro, Asano, and Hikoemon all leaned forward in spite of themselves.

Asano asked, "My lord...what has happened?"

In the instant he was questioned, Hideyoshi came back to himself. Almost as though he doubted the words contained in the letter, he forced himself to read them once more. Then his tears began to fall onto the letter about whose contents there now could be no doubt.

"My lord, why these tears?" Hikoemon asked.

"This is not like you at all, my lord."

"Is it bad news?"

All three men imagined that the message had something to do with Hideyoshi's mother, whom he had left in Nagahama.

During the campaign, the men seldom spoke about their home provinces; but when they did, Hideyoshi always talked about his mother, so now they imagined that she was either seriously ill or had died.

Hideyoshi finally wiped away his tears and sat a little straighter. As he did so, he assumed a grave look, and his intense grief appeared to be pierced with an acute anger. Such intense rage was not usually felt at the death of a parent.

"I haven't the strength to tell you in words. The three of you come and look at this." He handed them the letter and looked the other way, hiding his tears with his arm.

Upon reading the letter, the three men looked as though they had been hit with a thunderbolt. Nobunaga and Nobutada were dead. Could it be true? Was the world so mysterious? Kyutaro, in particular, had met with Nobunaga just before coming to Mount Ishii. He had come here, after all, on Nobunaga's orders, and now he looked at the letter over and over again, unable to believe what it said. Both Kyutaro and Hikoemon shed tears, and the lamp, submerged in the gloom, could have been extinguished by those tears alone. Hideyoshi flinched impatiently, shifting his weight as he sat. He had come to grips with himself, and his lips were tightly shut.

"Hey! Somebody come here!" he shouted toward the pages' room. It was a shout loud enough to pierce the ceiling, and both Hikoemon and Asano—who were men of great courage—were so surprised that they nearly jumped up from their cushions. After all, Hideyoshi had been so sunk in tears that his spirit seemed to have been completely crushed.

"Yes, my lord!" a page replied. Vigorous footsteps accompanied the response. Hearing those footsteps and Hideyoshi's voice, Kyutaro and Hikoemon's grief was suddenly blown away.

"My lord?"

"Who is that?" Hideyoshi asked.

"Ishida Sakichi, my lord."

The short-statured Sakichi advanced from the shadow of the sliding door to the next room. Coming out to the middle of the tatami, he turned toward the lamp in the conference room and bowed with his hands pressed to the floor.

"Sakichi, run over to Kanbei's camp. Tell him that I need to talk with him right away. Hurry!"

If the situation had permitted, Hideyoshi would have liked to weep out loud. He had served Nobunaga from the age of seventeen. His head had been patted by the man's hands, and his own hands had carried his master's straw sandals. And now that master was no longer in the world. The relationship between Nobunaga and himself had been in no sense ordinary. It had been a relationship of one blood, one faith, and one life and death. Unexpectedly, the master had departed first, and Hideyoshi was aware that, from this time forth, he was in charge of his own life.

No one knew me as he did, Hideyoshi thought. In his last moments in the flames of the Honno Temple, he must have called out to me in his heart and left me with a trust. Insignificant as I am, I am not going to turn my back on my lord and his trust in me. Thus Hideyoshi made a pledge to himself. It was not a vain lamentation. His belief was simple: just before Nobunaga had died, he had left Hideyoshi with his dying instructions.

He was able to understand how deep his lord's resentment must have been. Judging by Nobunaga's attitude, Hideyoshi was able to imagine the regret in Nobunaga's breast as he left the world with his work half done. When he considered the matter from this point of view, Hideyoshi was no longer able to grieve. Nor was there time to think about plans for the future. His body was in the west, but his mind was already facing the enemy, Akechi Mitsuhide.

But there was also the question of how to deal with the enemy in front of him in Takamatsu Castle. And how was he to handle the thirty-thousand-man army of the Mori? How could he shift his position to Kyoto as quickly as possible from a battlefield in the western provinces? How to crush Mitsuhide; the problems that lay before him stretched out like a range of mountains.

He seemed to have reached a decision. He had one chance in a thousand, and his resolution to stake his life on a single possibility showed on his determined brow.

"Where is the messenger now?" Hideyoshi asked Asano, almost as soon as the page had left.

"I ordered the samurai to have him wait by the main temple," Asano answered.

Hideyoshi signaled at Hikoemon.

"Take him to the kitchen and give him something to eat. But keep him locked up in a room and don't let anyone talk to him," he ordered.

Seeing Hikoemon stand up to go with a knowing nod, Asano asked if he should go as well.

Hideyoshi shook his head. "No, I have another order for you, so wait just a moment," he said. "Asano, I want you to select some of the samurai under your command who have good ears and quick feet, and station them on all the roads from Kyoto to the Mori domain. I don't want even water to leak through. Arrest everyone who looks suspicious. Even if they don't look suspicious, investigate their identities and examine what they're carrying with them. This is extremely important. Go quickly, and be careful."

Asano left immediately. Now the only ones who remained were Kyutaro and Yuko.

"What time is it now, Yuko?"

"It's the second half of the Hour of the Boar."

"Today was the third of the month, right?"

"That's correct."

"Tomorrow's the fourth," he mumbled to himself. "Then the fifth." His eyes closed halfway, and he moved his fingers on his knee as though he were counting.

"It's difficult for me to just sit here. Won't you give me some orders?" Kyutaro begged.

"No, I want you to stay here a little longer," Hideyoshi said, trying to soothe the man's impatience. "Kanbei should be here soon. I know that Hikoemon went to take care of the courier, but while we have some free moments, why don't you go double-check?"

Kyutaro immediately got up and went off to the temple kitchen. The courier was in a small room next to the kitchen, hungrily eating some food that had been given to him. The man had not drunk or eaten anything since noon the day before, and when he finally finished filling himself, he sat back with a bulging stomach.

When Hikoemon saw that the man had finished, he beckoned him over and accompanied him to a room in the priests' quarters, the storeroom for the sutras. Telling him to sleep well, Hikoemon showed the courier into the room and locked the door securely from the outside. Just then, Kyutaro stepped quietly to Hikoemon's side and whispered in his ear.

"His Lordship is worried that news of the incident in Kyoto might leak out to the men."

Kyutaro's eyes revealed his intention to kill the messenger, but Hikoemon shook his head. After they had walked a few steps, Hikoemon said, "He'll probably die right where he is from overeating. Let's let him die innocently."

Looking toward the sutra room, Hikoemon held an extended palm out from his chest in prayer.

BOOK EIGHT

TENTH YEAR OF TENSHO
1582
SUMMER

Characters and Places

Hori Kyutaro, senior Oda retainer
Oda Nobutaka, Nobunaga's third son
Oda Nobuo, Nobunaga's second son
Niwa Nagahide, senior Oda retainer
Tsutsui Junkei, senior Oda retainer
Matsuda Tarozaemon, senior Akechi retainer
Ishida Sakichi, Hideyoshi's retainer
Samboshi, Nobunaga's grandson and heir
Takigawa Kazumasu, senior Oda retainer
Maeda Geni, senior Oda retainer
Sakuma Genba, Shibata Katsuie's nephew
Shibata Katsutoyo, Katsuie's adopted son

AN ILL-FATED MESSENGER

Hideyoshi had not moved. Fine pieces of ash were falling around the base of the lamp—probably the remains of Hasegawa's letter.

Kanbei came limping in, and Hideyoshi greeted him with a nod. Kanbei bent his crippled leg and lowered himself to the floor. During his captivity at Itami Castle, he had developed a chronic scalp condition that had never fully cleared up. When he sat close to the lamp, his thinning hair seemed almost transparent, giving him a grotesque appearance.

"I received your summons, my lord. What could be so urgent at this time of night?" Kanbei asked.

Hideyoshi replied, "Hikoemon will tell you." Then he folded his arms and hung his head with a long sigh.

"This will come as a shock, Kanbei," Hikoemon began.

Kanbei was known for his courage, but as he listened, he blanched. Saying nothing, he sighed deeply, folded his arms, and stared at Hideyoshi.

Kyutaro now edged forward on his knees, and said, "This is no time to be thinking of what is past. The wind of change is blowing through the world, and it's a fair wind for you. Time to raise your sails and depart."

Kanbei slapped his knee and said, "Well spoken! Heaven and earth are eternal, but life only progresses because all things change with the seasons. From a broader perspective, this is an auspicious event."

The two men's opinions made Hideyoshi smile with satisfaction, because they mirrored his own thoughts. Yet he could not admit to those feelings in public without running the risk of being misunderstood. For a retainer, the death of his lord was a tragedy, and one that must be avenged.

"Kanbei, Kyutaro, you've given me great encouragement. There's only one thing we can do now," Hideyoshi said with conviction. "Make peace with the Mori as quickly and secretly as possible."

The monk Ekei had come to Hideyoshi's camp as the Mori's envoy to negotiate a peace treaty. Ekei had contacted Hikoemon first, because of their long acquaintance; then he had met with Kanbei. Hideyoshi had so far refused to come to terms with the Mori, regardless of what they offered. When Ekei and Hikoemon had met earlier that day, they had parted without reaching an agreement.

Turning to Hikoemon, Hideyoshi said, "You met Ekei today. What are the Mori planning to do?"

"We could conclude a treaty quickly, if we agreed to their terms," Hikoemon replied.

"Absolutely not!" Hideyoshi said flatly. "As they stand, there is no way I can agree. And what did he offer you, Kanbei?"

"The five provinces of Bitchu, Bingo, Mimasaka, Inaba, and Hoki if we lift the siege of Takamatsu Castle and spare the lives of General Muneharu and his men."

"A handsome offer, superficially. But apart from Bingo, the four other provinces the Mori are offering are no longer under their control. We cannot accept those terms now without arousing their suspicions," Hideyoshi said. "But if the Mori have found out what has happened in Kyoto, they'll never agree to peace. With luck, they still know nothing. Heaven has given me a few hours' grace, but it will be tight."

"It's still only the third. If we requested a formal peace conference tomorrow, one could be held in two or three days," Hikoemon suggested.

"No, that's too slow," Hideyoshi countered. "We have to start immediately, and not even wait until dawn. Hikoemon, get Ekei to come here again."

"Should I send a messenger right now?" Hikoemon asked.

"No, wait a little. A messenger arriving in the middle of the night would make him suspicious. We should put a good deal of thought into what we're going to say."

Following Hideyoshi's orders, Asano Yahei's men began a close inspection of all travelers going in and out of the area. At about midnight, the guards stopped a blind man who was walking along with a heavy bamboo staff and asked him where he was going.

Surrounded by the soldiers, the man rested on his staff. "I'm going to a relative's house in the village of Niwase," he said with extreme humility.

"If you're going to Niwase, why are you on this mountain track in the middle of the night?" the officer in charge asked.

"I couldn't find an inn, so I just kept on walking," the blind man replied, lowering his head in an appeal for sympathy. "Perhaps you'd be so kind as to tell me where I might find a village with an inn."

The officer suddenly yelled out, "He's a fake! Tie him up."

The man protested, "I'm no fake! I'm a licensed blind musician from Kyoto, where I've lived for many years. But now my elderly aunt in Niwase is dying." He pressed his palms together in supplication.

"You're lying!" the officer said. "Your eyes may be closed, but I doubt if you need this!"

The officer abruptly grabbed the man's bamboo staff and cut it in half with his sword. A tightly rolled letter fell from the hollow interior.

The man's eyes now blazed like mirrors at the soldiers. Looking for the weakest point in the circle of men, he tried to make a run for it. But with more than twenty soldiers around him, even this fox of a man could not escape. The soldiers grappled him to the ground, trussed him up so that he could hardly move, and hoisted him over a horse like a piece of baggage.

The man heaped insults and curses on his captors. The officer stuffed some dirt in his mouth. Whipping the horse's belly, the soldiers hurried off to Hideyoshi's camp with their prisoner.

That same night a mountain ascetic was challenged by another patrol. In contrast to the cringing manner of the fake blind musician, the monk was haughty.

"I'm a disciple of the Shogo Temple," he announced arrogantly. "We mountain ascetics often walk the whole night through without taking a rest. I walk where I will, path or no path. What do you mean by asking me a trivial question like where am I going? Someone with a body like traveling clouds and flowing streams has no need of a destination."

The ascetic continued in this vein for a while, and then tried to run away. A soldier caught him in the shins with the shaft of his spear, and the man fell down with a scream.

Stripping the monk half-naked, the soldiers found that he was not a mountain ascetic at all. He was a warrior-monk of the Honganji, who was carrying a secret report to the Mori about the events at the Honno Temple. He too was immediately sent like a piece of baggage to Hideyoshi's camp.

There were only two captives that night, but if either of them had slipped through the cordon and accomplished his mission, the Mori would have known by the next morning about Nobunaga's death.

The fake ascetic had not been sent by Mitsuhide, but the man posing as a blind musician was an Akechi samurai with a letter from Mitsuhide for Mori Terumoto. He had left Kyoto on the morning of the second. Mitsuhide had sent another messenger that same morning—by sea from Osaka—but storms delayed him, and he reached the Mori too late.

"I thought we would be meeting in the morning," Ekei said after he greeted Hikoemon, "but your letter said to come as quickly as possible, so I came immediately."

"I'm sorry to get you out of bed," Hikoemon replied nonchalantly. "Tomorrow would have been fine, and I'm sorry my ineptly worded letter has deprived you of your sleep."

Kanbei led Ekei to an isolated spot vulgarly known as the Nose of the Frog, and from there to the empty farmhouse where they had held their previous meetings.

Sitting squarely in front of Ekei, Hikoemon said with deep feeling, "When you think about it, the two of us must be bound by a common karma."

Ekei nodded solemnly. The two men silently recalled their meeting in Hachisuka some twenty years before, when Hikoemon was still the leader of a band of *ronin*, and went by the name of Koroku. It was during his stay at Hikoemon's mansion that Ekei first heard about an extraordinary young samurai by the name of Kinoshita Tokichiro, who had lately been taken into Nobunaga's service at Kiyosu Castle. In those early years, when Hideyoshi still ranked far below Nobunaga's generals, Ekei had written to Kikkawa Motoharu: "Nobunaga's rule will last for a little while longer. When he falls, Kinoshita Tokichiro will be the next man with whom to reckon."

Ekei's predictions were astoundingly accurate: twenty years ago, he had perceived Hideyoshi's ability; ten years ago he had guessed Nobunaga's fall. That night, however, there was no way he could have known how right he was going to be.

Ekei was not an ordinary monk. When he was still a young acolyte studying in a temple, Motonari, the former lord of the Mori, had ordered him to enter his service. During Motonari's lifetime, his "little monk," as he affectionately called Ekei, had accompanied him on all his military campaigns.

After Motonari's death, Ekei had left the Mori and wandered throughout the empire. When he returned, he was made abbot of Ankokuji Temple, and served Terumoto, the new lord of the Mori, as a trusted adviser.

Throughout the war with Hideyoshi, Ekei had consistently argued for peace. He knew Hideyoshi well and did not think that the west would be able to endure his onslaught. Another factor influencing him was his long friendship with Hikoemon.

Ekei and Hikoemon had met any number of times before, but each time they had parted ways at the same impasse: Muneharu's fate. Hikoemon thus addressed Ekei:

"When I spoke to Lord Kanbei earlier, he told me that Lord Hideyoshi was far more generous than he has been perceived to be. He suggested that if just one more concession were made by the Mori, peace would surely ensue. Lord Kanbei said that if we were to lift the siege and spare Lord Muneharu's life, it would seem to the world as if the Oda army had been forced to conclude a peace treaty. Lord Hideyoshi could not present those terms to Lord Nobunaga. Our only condition is Muneharu's head. You should have no trouble in bringing the matter to a conclusion."

Hikoemon's terms had not changed, but he himself seemed a different man since their last meeting.

"I can only restate my position," Ekei replied. "If the Mori clan cedes five of its ten provinces, and Muneharu's life is not spared, they will have failed to abide by the Way of the Samurai."

"Nevertheless, did you verify their intentions after our last meeting?"

"There was no need to. The Mori will never agree to Muneharu's death. They prize loyalty above all else, and no one, from Lord Terumoto to his most lowly retainer, would begrudge the sacrifice, even if it means the loss of the whole of the western provinces."

The sky was beginning to grow paler; a rooster was heard in the distance. Night was turning to the dawn of the fourth day of the month.

Ekei would not agree, and Hikoemon would not give in. They were deadlocked.

"Well, there's nothing more to be said," Ekei concluded fatalistically.

"With my limited abilities," Hikoemon apologized, "I haven't been able to find common ground with you. With your permission, I'd like to ask Lord Kanbei to take my place."

"I'll be happy to speak with anyone," Ekei replied.

Hikoemon sent his son to get Kanbei, who soon arrived on his litter. He alighted and sat down clumsily with the other two men.

"I was the one who encouraged Hikoemon to trouble you once more for a final discussion," Kanbei said. "So, what is the outcome? Haven't the two of you worked out a compromise? You've talked half the night."

Kanbei's frankness had the effect of raising their spirits. Ekei's face brightened in the morning light. "We tried," he said, laughing. With the excuse that he had to prepare for Nobunaga's arrival, Hikoemon took his leave.

"Lord Nobunaga will stay for two or three days," Kanbei said. "Except for the time we have now, it's going to be difficult to meet again for peace talks."

Kanbei's diplomacy was simple and straightforward. It was also extremely high-handed: if the Mori wanted to argue about terms, no outcome but war was possible.

"If you can help the Oda clan today, surely you will be guaranteed a great future," Kanbei said.

With this change of adversary, Ekei lost his former eloquence. His expression, however, appeared to be far more buoyant than it had been when he was negotiating with Hikoemon.

"If there is a definite promise that Muneharu will commit *seppuku*, I will ask His Lordship about the condition of ceding the five provinces, and I'm sure he'll agree to a compromise. At any rate, won't you ask Lord Kikkawa and Lord Kobayakawa to reconsider the matter once more this morning? I suspect it will make the difference between peace and war."

When Kanbei put the matter in this way, Ekei felt compelled to act. Kikkawa's camp at Mount Iwasaki was only one league away. Kobayakawa's camp at Mount Hizashi was a little less than two leagues. Soon after, Ekei whipped his horse into a gallop.

After seeing the monk off, Kanbei went to Jihoin Temple. He looked into Hideyoshi's room and found him asleep. The lamp had gone out, the oil having burned dry. Kanbei shook Hideyoshi awake and said, "My lord, the day is breaking."

"Dawn?" Hideyoshi asked, rising groggily. Kanbei immediately told him of the meeting with Ekei. Hideyoshi scowled but got up quickly.

The pages were waiting at the entrance to the bathroom with water for his morning wash.

"As soon as I've eaten, I'll make a round of the camp. Bring my horse out as usual, and have my attendants stand by," he ordered as he dried his face.

Hideyoshi rode under a large red umbrella, preceded by his standard. Swaying slightly in the saddle, he rode under the new leaves of the flowering cherry trees that grew along the road from the temple gate to the foot of the mountain.

Hideyoshi's daily round of the camp was never at a set time, but it was rarely so early in the morning. Today he seemed in better humor, and from time to time he would joke with his attendants as if everything were perfectly normal. There were no indications that morning that news of the incident in Kyoto had leaked out even among his own men. After confirming this for himself, Hideyoshi returned to his headquarters at a leisurely pace.

Kanbei was waiting for him in front of the temple gate. His eyes told Hideyoshi that

Ekei's mission had ended in failure. The monk had ridden back from the Mori camp a little before Hideyoshi's return, but the response he brought had not changed:

> If we allow Muneharu to die, we are not living up to the Way of the Samurai. We will
> not agree to a peace that does not spare Muneharu's life.

"Have Ekei come here anyway," Hideyoshi ordered. He did not look in the least discouraged; in fact, he actually seemed to be growing more optimistic by the minute.

He invited the monk into a sunny room and made him comfortable. After talking
over old times and relating gossip from the capital, Hideyoshi moved the conversation on.
"Well now," he said, broaching the main subject, "it seems as though peace talks have
stalled because both sides cannot agree on Muneharu's fate. Couldn't you go privately to
General Muneharu, explain the circumstances to him, and recommend that he resign
himself? The Mori will never order a loyal retainer to commit *seppuku*, but if you explained the Mori clan's distress to him, Muneharu would gladly give his life. His death,
after all, will save the lives of the men in the castle and save the Mori from destruction."
With these words, Hideyoshi abruptly got up and left.

Inside Takamatsu Castle, the fates of more than five thousand soldiers and civilians
hung in the balance.

Hideyoshi's generals had brought three large ships, equipped with cannons, over the
mountains, and had begun to shell the castle. One of the towers had almost collapsed,
and there were many dead and wounded as a result of the bombardment. Added to that,
it was still the rainy season, and more and more people were falling sick and food supplies
were spoiling in the damp.

The defenders had collected doors and planking and built light boats with which to
attack Hideyoshi's warships. Two or three of the small craft had been sunk, but the sur-
vivors had swum back to the castle to lead a second attack.

When the Mori army arrived and their banners and flags were sighted from the castle, the defenders thought they had been saved. But soon after, they understood the impossibility of their situation. The distance between their rescuers and themselves, and the
consequent operational difficulties, would not allow for rescue. Although they were discouraged, they never lost the will to fight. On the contrary, after their realization they
were clearly resolved to die.

When a secret message came to the castle from the Mori giving Muneharu permission to capitulate in order to save the lives of the men inside, he sent back an indignant
response: "We have not yet learned what it is to surrender. At a time like this, we are
ready to die."

On the morning of the fourth day of the Sixth Month, the guards on the castle walls
spotted a small boat sculling toward them from the enemy shore. A samurai was handling
the oar, and his only passenger was a monk.

Ekei had come to ask Muneharu to commit *seppuku*. Muneharu listened in silence to
the monk's arguments. When Ekei had finished, and his entire body was soaked in sweat,

Muneharu spoke for the first time. "Well, today is truly my lucky day. When I look at your face, I know that your words are not fraudulent."

He did not say whether he agreed or disagreed. Muneharu's mind was already far beyond consent and refusal. "For some time, Lord Kobayakawa and Lord Kikkawa have been worried about me, worthless as I am, and have even advised me to capitulate. But I have not considered surrender just to save my own life, and so I refused. Now, if I can believe what you've told me, the Mori clan will be assured of security, and the people in the castle will be safe. If that's the case, there is no reason to refuse. On the contrary, it would be a great joy to me. A great joy!" he repeated emphatically.

Ekei was trembling. He had not thought that it would be so easy, that Muneharu would welcome death so gladly. At the same time, he felt ashamed. He himself was a monk, yet would he have the courage to transcend life and death in this way when his own time came?

"Then you agree?"

"Yes."

"Don't you need to discuss the matter with your family?"

"I'll inform them of my decision later. They should all rejoice with me."

"And—well, this is difficult to say, but it is a matter of some urgency—it is said that Lord Nobunaga will be arriving soon."

"It's the same to me whether it's done sooner or later. When is it to be?"

"Today. Lord Hideyoshi said by the Hour of the Horse, and that's only five hours away."

"If that's all the time there is," Muneharu said, "I should be able to prepare for death with ease."

* * *

Ekei first reported Muneharu's agreement to Hideyoshi, then rode at full gallop to the Mori camp at Mount Iwasaki.

Both Kikkawa and Kobayakawa were worried about the reason for his sudden return.

"Have they broken off talks?" Kobayakawa asked.

"No," Ekei replied. "There are prospects of success."

"Well then, Hideyoshi has yielded?" Kobayakawa asked, looking a little surprised. Ekei, however, shook his head.

"The person who has prayed more than anyone for a peaceful reconciliation has offered to sacrifice himself for the sake of peace."

"Who are you talking about?"

"General Muneharu. He said that he would repay with his life Lord Terumoto's protection for all these years."

"Ekei, did you talk to him at Hideyoshi's request?"

"You know I could not have gone out to the castle without his permission."

"Then you explained the situation to Muneharu, and he offered to commit *seppuku* of his own free will?"

"Yes. He will kill himself at the Hour of the Horse, on board a boat in full view of

677

both armies. At that moment the peace treaty will be concluded, the lives of the defenders will be saved, and the safety of the Mori clan will be assured forever."

Full of emotion, Kobayakawa asked, "What are Hideyoshi's intentions?"

"When he heard General Muneharu's offer, Lord Hideyoshi was deeply moved. He said that it would be heartless not to reward such matchless loyalty. Therefore, while your promise had been to cede five provinces, he would take only three and leave the remaining two, out of regard for Muneharu's sacrifice. If there is no disagreement, he will send a written pledge immediately after witnessing Muneharu's *seppuku*."

Soon after Ekei had left, Muneharu announced his decision. One after another, the samurai of Takamatsu Castle came before their lord to beg him to allow them to follow him in death. Muneharu argued, cajoled, and scolded, but they would not be mollified. He was at a loss what to do. But in the end he did not grant anyone's request.

He ordered an attendant to prepare a boat. Bitter wailing filled the castle. When the requests of all his retainers had been withdrawn, and Muneharu seemed to have a little breathing space, Gessho, his elder brother, came to speak with him.

"I heard everything you said," Gessho said. "But there's no need for you to die. Let me take your place."

"Brother, you are a monk, while I am a general. I appreciate your offer, but I cannot let anyone take my place."

"I was the eldest son, and I should have carried on the family name. Instead I chose to enter holy orders, putting you in the position that I should have taken. So today, when you have to commit *seppuku*, there is no reason why I should prolong what's left of my own life."

"No matter what you say," Muneharu replied, "I will not let you or anyone else commit *seppuku* in my place."

Muneharu refused Gessho's offer but allowed him to accompany him in the boat. Muneharu felt at peace. Calling his pages, he ordered them to put out a light blue ceremonial kimono for him to die in.

"And bring me a brush and ink," he ordered, remembering to write a letter to his wife and son.

The Hour of the Horse was fast approaching. Every single drop of drinking water had been regarded as essential to the lives of the people in the castle, but that day he ordered a bucketfull of water to be brought in, to clean off the dirt that had accumulated on his body during the forty days of the siege.

How peaceful was this lull in the fighting. The sun seemed to climb innocently to the middle of the sky. There was no wind at all, and the color of the muddy water on all sides of the castle was as murky as ever.

The small waves that lapped gently at the castle walls glinted in the sun, and from time to time the cry of the snowy egret could be heard in the silence.

A small red banner was raised at the Nose of the Frog on the opposite shore, indicating that the time had come. Muneharu stood up abruptly. An involuntary sob came from the midst of his attendants. Muneharu walked quickly in the direction of the castle walls, as though he had suddenly become deaf.

The oar made a loose pattern in the water. The boat carried five men: Muneharu,

Gessho, and three retainers. Every single man, woman, and child in the castle was perched on the walls and rooftops. They did not cry out when they watched Muneharu go but either folded their hands in prayer or wiped the tears from their eyes.

The boat sculled peacefully over the surface of the lake. When he turned around, Gessho could see that Takamatsu Castle was a good way behind them, and that the boat was halfway between the castle and the Nose of the Frog.

"This will do," Muneharu instructed the oarsman.

The man pulled up the oar without a word. They did not have to wait for long.

When the boat had set out from the castle, another had left the Nose of the Frog. That one carried Hideyoshi's witness, Horio Mosuke. A small red banner had been fixed to the prow and a red carpet spread over the wooden floor.

The little boat bearing Muneharu in his death robe floated gently as it waited for the Mosuke's boat with its fluttering red banner to pull alongside. The water was at peace. The surrounding mountains were at peace. The only sound to be heard was the oar of the approaching boat.

Muneharu faced the Mori camp on Mount Iwasaki and bowed. In his heart he gave thanks for the many years of patronage he had received. Gazing at his lord's banners, his eyes filled with tears.

"Is this boat carrying the defending general of Takamatsu Castle, Shimizu Muneharu?" Mosuke asked.

"You are correct," Muneharu answered politely. "I am Shimizu Muneharu. I have come to commit *seppuku* as a condition of the peace treaty."

"I have something else to say, so please wait a moment," Mosuke said. "Bring your boat a little closer," he instructed the retainer at the oar of Muneharu's boat.

The gunwales of the two boats lightly brushed each other.

Mosuke then said in a dignified manner, "I have a message from Lord Hideyoshi. Peace would have been impossible without your consent in this matter. The long siege must have been trying for you, and he would like you to accept this offering as a small token of his feelings. You should not be concerned if the sun climbs too high. Please finish your leave-taking at your leisure."

A cask of the best *sake* and a number of delicacies were transferred from one boat to the other.

Muneharu's face was filled with joy. "This is unexpected. And, if it is Lord Hideyoshi's wish, I will gladly sample them." Muneharu helped himself, and ladled cups for his companions. "Maybe it's because I haven't had such fine *sake* for a long time, but I'm feeling a little drunk. Please excuse my clumsiness, General Horio, but I would like to perform a final dance." Then turning to his companions, he asked, "We don't have a drum, but would you clap and beat the rhythm and sing?"

Muneharu stood up in the small boat and flicked open a white fan. As he moved to the rhythm of the clapping, the boat swayed slightly, making small waves. Mosuke could nor bear to look at him and hung his head.

As soon as the chanting stopped, Muneharu spoke distinctly once again. "General Mosuke, please witness this carefully."

Mosuke looked up and saw that Muneharu had knelt down and cut straight across

679

his stomach with his sword. As he spoke, his blood turned the inside of the boat red.

"Brother, I'm coming too!" Gessho cried out, slashing his own belly.

After Muneharu's retainers had handed the box containing Muneharu's severed head to Mosuke and returned to the castle, they followed their master in death.

When Mosuke arrived at the Jihoin Temple, he reported Muneharu's *seppuku* and displayed his head in front of Hideyoshi's camp stool.

"Such a pity," Hideyoshi lamented. "Muneharu was an excellent samurai." He had never appeared more moved. But soon thereafter, he summoned Ekei. When the monk arrived, Hideyoshi immediately showed him a document.

"The only thing that remains now is to exchange pledges. Look at what I've written, and then I'll send a messenger for the Mori's pledge."

Ekei looked over the pledge and then respectfully returned it to Hideyoshi. Hideyoshi asked for a brush and signed. He then cut his little finger and affixed a seal of blood next to his signature. The peace treaty was signed.

A few hours later, shock and a sense of loss swept over the Mori camp like a whirlwind with the report of Nobunaga's death. In Terumoto's field headquarters, the faction that had opposed peace all along now spoke up loudly, clamoring for an immediate attack on Hideyoshi.

"We were fooled!"

"That bastard completely took us in!"

"The peace treaty should be torn up!"

"We have not been deceived," Kobayakawa said firmly. "The talks were initiated by us, not by Hideyoshi. And there was no way he could have foreseen the disaster in Kyoto."

His brother Kikkawa, who spoke for those who favored the resumption of hostilities, urged Terumoto, "Nobunaga's death means the disintegration of the Oda forces; they will be no match for us now. Hideyoshi is the first one you'd name as a successor to Nobunaga, and it should be an easy matter to attack him here and now, especially considering the weakness at his rear. If we were to do that, we would become the rulers of the Empire."

"No, no. I disagree," Kobayakawa said. "Hideyoshi is the only man who can restore peace and order. And it's an old samurai saying that one does not strike an enemy in mourning. Even if we were to tear up the treaty and attack, if he survived, he would come back to take his revenge."

"We cannot let this opportunity slip by," Kikkawa insisted.

As a last resort, Kobayakawa brought up their former lord's dying instructions: "The clan must defend its own borders. No matter how strong or wealthy we become, we must never expand beyond the western provinces."

It was time for the lord of the Mori to give his decision. "I agree with my uncle Kobayakawa. We will not break the treaty and make Hideyoshi into an enemy for a second time."

By the time the secret conference ended, it was the evening of the fourth. As the two generals walked back to their camp, they met a party of their own scouts. The officer in charge pointed excitedly into the darkness and said, "The Ukita have started to withdraw their troops."

Listening to the report, Kikkawa clicked his tongue. The opportunity had already passed. Kobayakawa read his older brother's thoughts. "Are you still feeling some regrets?" he asked.

"Of course I am."

"Well, suppose we did take over the country," Kobayakawa continued, "do you think you'd be the man to rule?" There was a pause. "Judging from your silence, I suspect you don't think so. When someone without the proper ability rules the country, it leads to certain chaos. It would not stop at the fall of the Mori clan."

"You don't have to say any more, I understand," Kikkawa said, turning away. Looking up sadly at the night sky over the western provinces, he fought to hold back the tears that were rolling down his cheeks.

REQUIEM OF BLOOD

The need for the Oda troops' immediate withdrawal had been the reason behind the peace treaty, and Hideyoshi's allies, the Ukita, began to retreat that very night. Not one soldier, however, was withdrawn from Hideyoshi's main camp. On the morning of the fifth, Hideyoshi had still not made a move. Although his mind was racing toward the capital, he gave no indication that he was planning to break camp.

"Hikoemon, how much has the water level gone down?"

"About three feet."

"Don't let it fall too quickly."

Hideyoshi went out into the temple garden. Although the dike had been cut and the water was beginning to go down little by little, Takamatsu Castle was still stranded in the middle of the water. One of Hideyoshi's retainers had already gone to the castle the night before to accept its capitulation. And now the defenders were being ferried out.

When evening came, Hideyoshi sent a man to spy on the Mori. He then consulted with Kanbei and his other generals and quickly made preparations to strike camp. "Have them breach the dike right away," he ordered Kanbei.

The dike was now breached in ten places. Almost at once, the water began to stir. Innumerable whirlpools appeared as the waters rushed through the openings with a roar that sounded like a tidal wave.

Which would be faster, the water or Hideyoshi, who now whipped his horse toward the east? The high ground surrounding the castle had been transformed almost instantly into a dry plain, while the lowlands were marshes crisscrossed with rivers; so even if the Mori had considered giving chase, they would not have been able to cross over for another two or three days.

On the seventh, Hideyoshi arrived at the Fukuoka River crossing and found the river in flood. The soldiers made protective padding for the horses by lashing their packs together and then crossed over, forming a human chain by either linking hands or grasping the shaft of the spear carried by the man in front.

Hideyoshi had crossed first, and sat on his camp stool on the bank. "Don't panic! Take your time!" he shouted. He appeared to be completely untroubled by the wind and the rain. "If one man drowns, the enemy will say we lost five hundred; if you lose one piece of baggage, they'll say it was a hundred. Don't lose your life or your weapons here in vain."

The rear guard now caught up with the main army, and with the units trailing in one after another, both banks of the river were filled with soldiers. The commander of the rear guard came before Hideyoshi to report on the situation at Takamatsu. The retreat had been completed, and there was still no sign of the Mori. A look of relief spread over Hideyoshi's face. He looked as though he finally felt safe; now he could channel all his strength in one direction.

The army returned to Himeji on the morning of the eighth. Covered in mud, then drenched by the storm, the soldiers had covered twenty leagues in one day.

"The first thing I want to do," Hideyoshi said to his attendants, "is take a bath."

The governor of the castle prostrated himself before Hideyoshi. After congratulating him on his return, he informed him that two messengers had arrived, one from Nagahama with urgent news.

"I'll take care of it after having a bath. I'd like plenty of hot water. The rain soaked right through my armor and all the way to my underwear."

Hideyoshi sank into the hot water up to his shoulders. The morning sun was framed by the bathroom window; it poured down through the high latticework onto his face, suspended in the steam. As he sat there, the skin on his face seemed to boil to a darkish red, while large drops of sweat beaded on his forehead. Hundreds of tiny rainbows appeared in the steam.

Hideyoshi jumped out of the tub, making a noise like a waterfall. "Hey! Somebody come wash my back!" he called.

The two pages who were waiting outside ran in. Putting all of their strength into the task, they scrubbed him down from the back of his neck to his fingertips.

Hideyoshi suddenly laughed and said, "It comes off in a strange way!" Looking down around his feet, he saw that the dirt the pages had scraped off his body resembled bird droppings.

How could this man be possessed of such a dignified appearance on the battlefield? His naked body seemed a truly poor and meager thing. It was true that he had overworked himself during the five years of the western campaign, but there was altogether too little fat on his forty-six-year-old frame. Even now, traces of the poor, skinny farmboy from Nakamura lingered on. His body seemed like a withered pine growing out of the rock, or a dwarfed plum tree worn out by the wind and snow—strong, but showing signs of age.

It was not appropriate, however, to compare his age and physique with those of an ordinary man. Both his skin and his frame were filled with vitality. When he was happy or angry, there were even times when he looked like a young man.

As Hideyoshi relaxed after his bath, wiping himself dry, he called a page and said, "This is to be posted immediately: At the first call of the conch, the entire army is to eat its rations; at the second, the supply corps is to start out; at the third, the whole army is to assemble in front of the castle."

Hideyoshi then summoned Hikoemon and the officials in charge of the treasury and the granary.

"How much do we have in the treasury?" Hideyoshi asked.

"About seven hundred fifty weights of silver, and more than eight hundred pieces of gold," an official replied.

Hideyoshi turned to Hikoemon and ordered, "Take it and distribute it to the men, each according to his pay." He then asked how much rice was left in the storehouses, observing, "We won't be besieged here, so we don't need to keep any rice. Pay the retainers five times their rice stipend."

He left the bathroom and went directly to where the messenger from Nagahama was waiting. He had left his mother and his wife at Nagahama, and he had been constantly anxious about them.

As soon as Hideyoshi saw the messenger kneeling before him, he asked, "Are they all right? Has something happened?"

"Both your honored mother and wife are quite well."

"Really? Well then, is the castle at Nagahama under attack?"

"I was dispatched from Nagahama on the morning of the fourth, when a small enemy force had started to attack."

"The Akechi?"

"No, they were Asai *ronin* allied to the Akechi. But according to a rumor I heard on the road, a large Akechi force is now heading for Nagahama."

"What were the men at Nagahama going to do?"

"There are not enough men to withstand a siege, so in case of an emergency, they plan to move your family to a hiding place in the mountains."

The messenger placed a letter in front of Hideyoshi. It was from Nene. As the lord's wife, it was her duty to take care of everything while her husband was away. Although she must have written the letter in the midst of a storm of confusion and doubt, her handwriting was composed. The contents, however, clearly indicated that this letter might be her very last:

If worst comes to worst, I assure you, my lord, that your wife will do nothing to disgrace your name. Your mother's and my only concern is that you overcome your own difficulties in these important times.

The first call of the conch shell echoed through the castle and the town.

Hideyoshi gave his final instructions to his retainers in Himeji Castle: "Victory and defeat are in the hands of fate, but if I should be struck down by Mitsuhide, set fire to the castle and make sure nothing remains. We have to act bravely, following the example of the man who died at the Honno Temple."

The second call sounded, and the supply train started off. As the sun began to set in the west, Hideyoshi had his camp stool moved outside the castle and had the third conch shell call blown. Night had fallen on the wide fields and on the pine trees lining the coastal road. From evening until well past midnight, the ground shook as ten thousand men formed into their divisions outside Himeji Castle.

Dawn broke and, one by one, the silhouettes of the pines along the road became visible. In the east, a perfectly red morning sun rose over the horizon of the Harima Sea between the clouds of dawn, as though urging the men forward.

"Look!" Hideyoshi called out. "We have a fair wind. Our banners and pennants are blowing east. I know that a man's fate is uncertain. We do not know whether we will live to see tomorrow's dawn, but heaven shows us the way forward. Let us raise a mighty war cry and inform heaven of our departure."

* * *

In the ten days since the death of Nobunaga, the national situation had changed dramatically. In Kyoto, the people had been uneasy since the Honno Temple incident. Nobunaga's two senior generals, Shibata Katsuie and Takigawa Kazumasu, were far away; Tokugawa Ieyasu had withdrawn to his own home province; Hosokawa Fujitaka's and Tsutsui Junkei's commitments were unclear; and Niwa Nagahide was in Osaka.

The rumor that Hideyoshi's army had arrived in Amagasaki, near Kyoto, spread like the wind on the morning of the eleventh. Many could not believe it. There were other rumors—that Lord Ieyasu was moving westward; that Nobunaga's eldest surviving son, Nobuo, was mounting a counterattack; that the Akechi were fighting here or there. The most believable rumor was that Hideyoshi's army was pinned down by the Mori at Takamatsu. Only those who knew Hideyoshi well did not fall into that error.

The skills Hideyoshi had shown in the invasion of the western provinces over the last five years had taught many of Nobunaga's other generals his true value. Among those men were Niwa Nagahide, Nakagawa Sebei, Takayama Ukon, and Ikeda Shonyu. They perceived Hideyoshi's loyalty under such long adversity as unswerving devotion to their former lord. When they heard that Hideyoshi had made peace with the Mori and was marching at full speed toward the capital, they were pleased that their expectations had not been disappointed. As Hideyoshi made his way eastward, they sent him urgent messages, pressing him to hurry and informing him of the latest movements of the Akechi troops.

When Hideyoshi arrived at Amagasaki, Nakagawa Sebei and Takayama Ukon each took part of their forces and visited Hideyoshi's camp.

When the two generals arrived, the samurai on guard duty at the gate did not seem overjoyed at their presence, nor did he hurry to announce their arrival. "His Lordship is resting just now," he informed them.

The two men were taken aback. Sebei and Ukon knew well their own value as allies. The military strength of the man they sided with would be doubled. In addition, their nearby castles controlled the entrance to Kyoto. Certainly, securing those two key castles, which were almost in the middle of enemy territory, would give Hideyoshi tremendous strategic and logistic advantages.

Thus, when they came to Hideyoshi's camp, they took it for granted that Hideyoshi himself would come out to welcome them. All that the two generals could do was wait. During that time, they watched the arrival of stragglers. All the while, messengers were coming and going in all directions. Among them was a samurai whom Nakagawa Sebei recognized.

"Isn't that a Hosokawa samurai?" he muttered.

It was well known that the relationship between Mitsuhide and Hosokawa Fujitaka was very close. The two men had been close friends for many years, and their families were linked by marriage.

What is a messenger from the Hosokawa doing here? Sebei asked himself. This was a matter that concerned not only the two generals waiting to see Hideyoshi but the entire nation.

"He said Lord Hideyoshi was sleeping, but I think he's wide awake. He's being rather rude, no matter what he's doing," Ukon complained.

They were about to leave when one of Hideyoshi's pages ran up to them and invited them into the temple that served as Hideyoshi's headquarters. Hideyoshi was not in the room they were led into, but it was certain that he had been awake for some time. Loud laughter was coming from the abbot's quarters. This was not the kind of reception the two generals had anticipated. They had hurried here to ally themselves with Hideyoshi and strike at Mitsuhide. Ukon seemed vexed, a vaguely bitter look on his face; Sebei's expression was sullen.

The oppressive summer heat aggravated their dissatisfaction. The rainy season should have begun to clear by then, but the air refused to dry. In the sky, the clouds moved back and forth in an unsettled way, as if reflecting the state of the nation. From time to time the sun shone through the clouds with an intense brilliance that was enough to make a man feverish.

"It's hot, Sebei," Ukon commented.

"Yes, and there's no wind at all."

Naturally, the two men wore full armor. Even though modern armor had become lighter and more flexible, there was no doubt that beneath the leather breastplates, their sweat ran in rivulets.

Sebei opened his fan and cooled himself. Then, to show that they did not rank lower than Hideyoshi, Sebei and Ukon made a point of moving to the seats reserved for men of the highest rank.

Just then, a shout of greeting came in with the breeze. It was Hideyoshi, and as soon as he sat down in front of the men, he apologized profusely. "I'm really sorry to have been so rude. When I got up, I went over to the main temple; and while I was having my head shaved," he said, patting his bald head, "a messenger from Hosokawa Fujitaka arrived with an urgent dispatch. So I had to talk with him first and make you wait."

He sat in his usual way, oblivious to distinctions of rank. The two men forgot their formal greetings and simply stared at Hideyoshi's freshly shaved head, which reflected the green of the trees of the neighboring garden.

"At least my head is cool in this heat," Hideyoshi added with a grin. "Taking the tonsure is very refreshing."

Looking a little self-conscious, Hideyoshi vigorously rubbed his scalp. When Sebei and Ukon saw that Hideyoshi had gone so far as to shave his head for the sake of their former lord they forgot their earlier displeasure and instead felt ashamed of their own pettiness.

The only trouble was that each time they looked at Hideyoshi they wanted to laugh. Although no one called him Monkey to his face anymore, his former nickname and his present appearance provoked a certain feeling of amusement.

"Your speed surprised us," Sebei started. "You must not have slept at all between here and Takamatsu. We're relieved to see that you're in good health," he went on, fighting to stifle his laughter.

"You know," Hideyoshi said ingratiatingly, "I very much appreciated the reports you sent me. Because of them I was able to know the movements of the Akechi, and, more important, that the two of you were my allies."

Neither Sebei nor Ukon was so soft-headed that flattery could take him in. Almost ignoring Hideyoshi's last remark, they quickly began to give him advice.

"When will you be setting out for Osaka? Lord Nobutaka is there with Lord Niwa."

"I haven't got time to go to Osaka now; that's not where the enemy is. I sent a messenger to Osaka this morning."

"Lord Nobutaka is the third son of Lord Nobunaga. Shouldn't you meet him first?"

"I'm not asking him to come here. I have asked him to take part in the forthcoming battle, which will be the memorial service for Lord Nobunaga. He is with Niwa, so I thought it wouldn't be necessary to stick to formalities. He'll be joining our camp tomorrow for sure."

"What about Ikeda Shonyu?"

"We'll be meeting him as well. I haven't seen him yet, but he sent a messenger with a pledge of his support."

Hideyoshi was confident about his allies. Even Hosokawa Fujitaka had refused Mitsuhide's invitation. Instead, he had just sent a retainer to Hideyoshi telling him that he would not join forces with a rebel. Hideyoshi triumphantly stressed to the two generals that this loyalty was not only the natural trend of the world but also a great moral principle of the warrior class.

Finally, after talking over various subjects, both Sebei and Ukon formally delivered to Hideyoshi the hostages they had brought along with them as pledges of their good faith.

Hideyoshi declined with a laugh.

"That won't be necessary. I know you both so well. Send these children back to your castles right away."

That very day Ikeda Shonyu, who had known Hideyoshi since their early days together in Kiyosu Castle, joined Hideyoshi's army. Just before setting out that morning, Shonyu had also taken the tonsure.

"What! You had your head shaved too?" Hideyoshi said when he saw his friend.

"We did the same thing by chance."

"We think the same way."

Neither Hideyoshi nor Shonyu needed to say anything more. Shonyu now added his four thousand men to Hideyoshi's army. Hideyoshi had started with an army of about ten thousand men, but with the addition of Ukon's two thousand men, Sebei's two thousand five hundred men, Hachiya's one thousand, and the Ikeda corps of four thousand, the army now numbered more than twenty thousand troops.

At the first war conference, Sebei and Ukon unexpectedly began to argue with each other, neither man giving any ground.

"It has been a matter of samurai etiquette since ancient times that the lord of the castle closest to the enemy leads the vanguard," Ukon said. "So there is no reason at all why my troops should follow Sebei's."

Sebei refused to give in. "The division between rear and vanguard should have nothing to do with how close to or how far away from the battlefield a man's castle is. The caliber of the troops and the commander are what matter."

"Well then, are you saying that I am unworthy of leading the vanguard against the enemy?"

"I don't know about you. I am certain in my belief, however, that I am not going to yield to anyone. And I'm not going to hesitate in front of anyone in my desire to lead the vanguard in this battle. The order should be given to me, Nakagawa Sebei."

Sebei pressed Hideyoshi for the honor, but Ukon also bowed and looked up to him in the expectation of receiving the command. Hideyoshi, seated on his camp stool, made his decision with the demeanor of a commander-in-chief.

"Both of you have spoken well, so it stands to reason that Sebei should take up one line of the first battle formation and Ukon should take up the other. I expect you both to accomplish deeds worthy of your words."

Throughout the council, scouts came in to make their reports.

"Lord Mitsuhide has withdrawn from Horagamine and has concentrated his strength in the area around Yamazaki and Enmyoji. He also seemed to be falling back toward Sakamoto Castle, but suddenly this morning he began to demonstrate a clearly offensive disposition, and a division of his army is marching toward Shoryuji Castle."

With the receipt of this report, a strained expression abruptly appeared on the faces of the generals. The distance between their camp at Amagasaki and Yamazaki was less than a lightning strike away. They could already sense the enemy in that area.

Sebei and Ukon had been given the responsibility for leading the vanguard, and they stood up and asked, "Shouldn't we advance on Yamazaki at once?"

Hideyoshi, unmoved by the men's agitation and the pressure of the moment, answered with extreme deliberation.

"I think we should wait here one more day for Lord Nobutaka's arrival. It's obvious that during the one night and half a day that we wait, this great opportunity will slip away moment by moment, but I would like one of our late lord's sons to participate in the battle. I don't want to put Lord Nobutaka in a situation that he would regret for the rest of his life, one which would make him unable to face the world."

"But what if the enemy is able to take advantageous ground in the meantime?"

"Well, there are naturally limits even to waiting for Lord Nobutaka. We'll have to start out for Yamazaki by tomorrow, no matter what happens. Once the entire army has gathered at Yamazaki, we'll be in contact again, so both of you should go ahead and advance immediately."

Sebei and Ukon made their way out. The order of the vanguard's departure was to be as follows: first, the Takayama corps; second, the Nakagawa corps; and third, the Ikeda corps.

As soon as they left Tonda, the two-thousand-man Takayama corps dashed out as though they had already seen the enemy army. Watching the dust from their horses, Sebei and everyone in the second corps wondered if the Akechi forces hadn't already got to Yamazaki.

"They're going too fast even for that," some thought suspiciously.

Immediately after entering the village of Yamazaki, Ukon's men closed off all the gates on the roads that led to the town and even intercepted travelers on the backroads in the area.

The Nakagawa corps that came up later naturally encountered these roadblocks and suddenly understood the reason for Ukon's hurry: he could not bear to be in the second attacking line. Sebei abandoned this strategic position and immediately started off for a hill called Tennozan.

In the end Hideyoshi quartered his troops at Tonda that night, but the next day he finally received the report that Nobutaka and Niwa had reached the Yodo River.

As soon as he heard the news, Hideyoshi nearly knocked over his camp stool as he jumped up for joy. "A horse! Bring me a horse!" he ordered.

As he mounted, he turned to the men at the gate and yelled, "I'm going off to greet Lord Nobutaka!" and whipped his horse toward the Yodo River.

The wide river was almost overflowing. On the bank, Nobutaka's forces were divided into two corps of four and three thousand men respectively.

"Where is Lord Nobutaka?" Hideyoshi yelled as he dismounted among the sweaty soldiers who watched him go by. Nobody realized that it was Hideyoshi.

"It's me, Hideyoshi," he announced.

The soldiers gaped in surprise.

Hideyoshi did not wait for a formal welcome. Pushing his way through the throng of men, he headed for the tree beneath which Nobutaka had set up his standard.

Surrounded by his field staff, Nobutaka was resting on his camp stool, shading his eyes from the glare of the water. Suddenly he turned and saw Hideyoshi running toward him, yelling as he came. As soon as he saw Hideyoshi, Nobutaka was overcome by a feeling of gratitude. Here was a retainer whom his father had trained for many years, and what he was doing now went far beyond the normal ties that bound a lord and retainer. His eyes shone with a light that showed he was feeling an emotion usually reserved for blood relations.

"Hideyoshi!" Nobutaka called out.

Without waiting for Nobutaka to extend his hand, Hideyoshi suddenly walked up to him and grasped it firmly.

"Lord Nobutaka!" was all Hideyoshi said. Neither man said anything further, but their eyes spoke at length. Tears flowed down their cheeks. Through those tears Nobutaka was able to express all his feelings for his dead father to a retainer of his clan. And Hideyoshi understood what was in the young man's heart. He finally released the hand he had held so tightly and at the same time knelt to the ground.

"It's so good that you have come. There is no time to say anything more, and there's really nothing else in my heart. I'm just grateful to be with you now, and firmly believe that in heaven your father's soul will be pleased by this action. I feel as though I've finally been able to pay my respects to you here and have fulfilled my duty as a retainer. I'm happy for the first time since Takamatsu Castle."

Later that day Hideyoshi invited Nobutaka to accompany him back to his camp in Tonda, and together they turned toward Yamazaki.

They arrived at Yamazaki at the Hour of the Monkey, the ten thousand men of their reserve army adding to the eight thousand five hundred men of the three vanguard corps. Now there was no place in the mountains or village where horses and soldiers could not be seen.

"We've just received a report that an Akechi army has attacked the Nakagawa corps in the foothills east of Tennozan."

Now was the time to strike. Hideyoshi gave the command for the entire army to attack.

On the morning of the ninth, when Hideyoshi was leaving Himeji, Mitsuhide returned to Kyoto. Less than a week had gone by since Nobunaga's murder.

On the second, at the Hour of the Ram, while the ruins of the Honno Temple were still smoldering, Mitsuhide had left Kyoto to attack Azuchi. But on his very first step outside the capital, Mitsuhide ran into an obstacle at the river crossing at Seta. That morning he had sent a letter demanding the surrender of Seta Castle, but its governor had killed the messenger and set fire to the castle and the Seta Bridge.

Thus the Akechi troops were unable to cross the river. Mitsuhide's eyes burned with indignation. The fire-gutted bridge seemed almost to be mocking him. The world does not see you as you see the world.

Forced to return to Sakamoto Castle, Mitsuhide spent two or three fruitless days waiting until the bridge was repaired. By the time he rode into Azuchi, however, the town was deserted, and its huge castle housed neither master nor men. In the town, there were no goods or even a shop sign left to be seen. Nobunaga's family had fled, but in their haste they had been forced to leave behind Nobunaga's hoard of gold and silver, and his collection of works of art.

Mitsuhide was shown these things after his troops secured the castle, but he did not feel wealthier for it. Somehow he felt beggared.

This is not what I was looking for, he thought, and it's mortifying if people think it was.

He had all the gold and silver in the treasury distributed as rewards to his men. Common soldiers received several hundred gold pieces, while the highest-ranking generals received three to five thousand gold pieces.

What do I want? Mitsuhide asked himself time and again. To rule the nation! came the answer, but it had a hollow ring to it. He had to admit to himself that he had never embraced such lofty hopes, having neither the ambition nor the ability. All along, he had had only one motive: to kill Nobunaga. Mitsuhide's desires had been sated by the fires of the Honno Temple, and now all that was left was a passion so devoid of conviction that it seemed nothing more than frenzy.

According to a story circulating at the time, Mitsuhide had tried to kill himself as soon as he heard that Nobunaga was dead. His retainers had forcibly stopped him. In the instant that Nobunaga had been turned to ashes, the hatred that had frozen Mitsuhide's heart had dissolved like melting snow. The ten thousand soldiers who served him, however, did not share his attitude. On the contrary, they hoped that their real reward was yet to come.

"From this day on, Lord Mitsuhide is the ruler of the country," the Akechi generals announced with a conviction Mitsuhide lacked.

But the lord they looked up to was no more than a hollow simulacrum of his former self. He differed in appearance and disposition—even in intellect.

Mitsuhide remained in Azuchi from the fifth until the morning of the eighth, and during that time he took Hideyoshi's castle at Nagahama as well as Niwa Nagahide's at Sawayama. Once he had completely occupied the province of Omi, Mitsuhide re-outfitted his army and once again set off for the capital.

It was then that Mitsuhide received the news that the Hosokawa clan had refused to join him. He had been convinced that Hosokawa Tadaoki, his son-in-law, would be quick to follow him once Nobunaga had been overthrown. But the response carried back from the Hosokawa clan had been an angry refusal. So far Mitsuhide had been absorbed by the question of who would be his allies; he had given little thought to who would be his strongest enemy.

It was only then that Hideyoshi's existence struck Mitsuhide like a blow to the chest. He had not overlooked Hideyoshi's abilities and his military strength in the west. On the contrary, he knew that Hideyoshi was an immense threat. What gave Mitsuhide a little peace of mind was his belief that Hideyoshi was pinned down by the Mori and would be unable to return quickly. He thought that at least one of the two messengers he had sent to the Mori had accomplished his mission. And, no doubt, the Mori's response would arrive soon, informing him that they had attacked Hideyoshi and destroyed him. But nothing was heard from the Mori, nor was there any response from Nakagawa Sebei, Ikeda Shonyu, and Takayama Ukon. The news that reached Mitsuhide instead each morning sounded like a judgment from heaven.

For Mitsuhide, Sakamoto Castle held vivid memories of recent events: his humiliation by Nobunaga; his departure from Azuchi in a rage; his stay at Sakamoto where he had stood at the crossroads of doubt. Now there was no more doubt, no more resentment. And at the same time, he had lost all of his powers of self-examination. He had exchanged his true intelligence for the empty title of ruler of the nation.

On the night of the ninth, Mitsuhide still had no idea where Hideyoshi was, but the attitudes of the local lords made him feel uneasy. On the following morning he left his camp at Shimo Toba and climbed up to Horagamine Pass in Yamashiro, at which place he had arranged to join with Tsutsui Junkei's army.

"Has Tsutsui Junkei been sighted yet?" Mitsuhide asked his lookouts at regular intervals during the day.

Because Mitsuhide had been in collusion with Tsutsui Junkei before the attack on the

Honno Temple, he had never had cause to doubt his ally's loyalty—until now. At nightfall, there was still no sign of the Tsutsui forces. Not only that, but the three Oda retainers he had hoped to win over to his side—Nakagawa Sebei, Takayama Ukon, and Ikeda Shonyu—had not responded to his urgent summonses, even though they were nominally all under his command.

Mitsuhide's uneasiness was not unjustified. He consulted with Saito Toshimitsu. "Do you think something's wrong, Toshimitsu?"

Mitsuhide wanted to believe that something had happened to the messengers he had sent, or that Junkei and the others were merely delayed, but Saito Toshimitsu had already faced up to the truth.

"No, my lord," the old man replied. "I suspect Lord Tsutsui has no intention of coming. There's no reason for him to be so late traveling the level roads from Koriyama."

"No, there must be some reason," Mitsuhide insisted. He summoned Fujita Dengo, quickly wrote up a letter, and sent him to Koriyama. "Take the best horses. If you ride at top speed, you should be able to come back by morning."

"If Lord Tsutsui will talk with me, I'll be back at dawn," Dengo said.

"There's no reason why he shouldn't talk with you. Get an answer from him even if it's late at night."

"Yes, my lord."

Dengo immediately set off for Koriyama. Before he was able to return, however, scouts arrived with reports that Hideyoshi's forces were moving eastward and that the vanguard had already come as far as the neighboring province of Hyogo.

"Impossible! It must be a mistake!" Mitsuhide burst out when he heard the news. He could not believe that Hideyoshi had been able to make peace with the Mori, and, even if he had, that he could have moved his large army so quickly.

"I don't think this is a false report, my lord," Toshimitsu said, once again intuiting the truth. "In any event, I think we should determine a counterstrategy at once."

Perceiving that Mitsuhide was wavering, Toshimitsu rejoined with a concrete proposal. "If I were to wait for Lord Tsutsui here, you, my lord, could hasten to stop Hideyoshi from entering the capital."

"There isn't much hope that Tsutsui will come, is there?" Mitsuhide finally admitted.

"I think there are only one or two chances in ten of his joining your side, my lord."

"What strategy do you suggest for stopping Hideyoshi?"

"The only view we can take is that Ukon, Sebei, and Shonyu are already in league with Hideyoshi. If Tsutsui Junkei has joined him as well, our military strength will be insufficient to take the initiative and attack him. In my estimation, however, it will take Hideyoshi another five or six days to get his whole army here. During that time, if we reinforced the two castles at Yodo and Shoryuji, built forts along the north-south road to Kyoto, and mustered all the forces in Omi and the other areas, we might be able to hold him off temporarily."

"What? All of that would only stop him temporarily?"

"After that, we'll need a far grander strategy—going far beyond small local battles. But right now we're in a critical situation. You should leave immediately."

Toshimitsu waited for Fujita Dengo to return from his mission in Koriyama.

He arrived with anger stamped all over his brow. "It's no good," he said to Toshimitsu. "That bastard Junkei has also betrayed us. He made up some excuse for not coming here, but on the way back I discovered that he's been in contact with Hideyoshi. To think that a man who was so close to the Akechi clan would be capable of this!"

Dengo's abuse was unending, but Toshimitsu's lined face showed no emotion at all.

Mitsuhide left at about noon, having accomplished nothing. He arrived back at Shimo Toba about the same time that Hideyoshi was enjoying a short nap in Amagasaki. The heat on this day was the same at both the Zen temple in Amagasaki and the camp at Shimo Toba. As soon as Mitsuhide arrived back in camp, he met with his generals at headquarters and discussed battle strategy. He still did not realize that Hideyoshi was already within shouting distance at Amagasaki. Although Hideyoshi's vanguard was already moving into position, Mitsuhide judged that it would take several more days for Hideyoshi himself to arrive. It would not be right to attribute this mistake to his intellect. He had simply made a judgment based on common sense, using his own uncommon intelligence. Moreover, this particular judgment was in harmony with what everyone else deemed logical as well.

The conference had been completed without any waste of time, and Akechi Shigetomo was the first to leave. He immediately rode to Yodo to begin emergency construction work to strengthen the castle. The narrow mountain road to the capital would surely be a focus for the enemy assault. Yodo Castle was on its right, Shoryuji Castle on its left.

Mitsuhide issued an order to the divisions that had been deployed along the banks of the Yodo River: "Pull back to Shoryuji and take up defensive positions. Prepare for an enemy attack."

Mitsuhide made his preparations, but when he calculated the size of the enemy army, he could not completely relinquish his perception of his own weakness. A considerable number of soldiers had been gathering here from the capital and the surrounding area, putting themselves under his command throughout the day. But they were all low-ranking samurai or *ronin*—little better than mercenaries looking for a quick way to rise in the world. Not one of them had any military ability or the resources to lead.

"How many men have we got in all?" Mitsuhide asked his generals.

Counting the troops at Azuchi, Sakamoto, Shoryuji, Horagamine, and Yodo, Mitsuhide's forces numbered about sixteen thousand men.

"If only Hosokawa and Tsutsui would join me," Mitsuhide mumbled, "no one could dislodge me from the capital." Even after he had decided his strategy, he was troubled by the sizeable difference in the numbers of troops. Mitsuhide's brain worked in terms of calculations, and now there was not even a flicker of hope that he would have the advantage. Moreover, somewhere a tiny wisp of fear was finding its way into his consciousness. That in itself could make the difference between victory and defeat. He was beginning to sink beneath the waves that he himself had created.

Mitsuhide stood on the hill outside of camp, staring up at the clouds.

"Looks like rain," he muttered this into a wind that showed little sign of rain at all. It was essential for a general who was soon to engage in a battle to be aware of the weather. Mitsuhide stood and worried about the movement of the clouds and the direction of the wind for a long while.

693

Finally he looked down at the Yodo River. The small lights that swayed in the wind must have been those of his own patrol boats. The undulating line of the large river appeared to be white, while the mountains beyond were pitch black.

The broad sky stretched over the river, and to the faraway estuary of the sea at Amagasaki. As Mitsuhide's eyes stared in that direction, almost as though they were sending out shafts of light, he asked himself, What is Hideyoshi capable of? Then he called out in a harsh tone that he rarely employed, "Sakuza! Sakuza! Where is Sakuzaemon?"

He turned quickly and walked back to camp with long strides. A dark and violent wind was shaking the barracks like a huge wave.

"Yes, my lord! Yojiro is here!" an attendant answered, running out to meet him.

"Yojiro, the call to arms. We're marching out right away."

While the army was striking camp, Mitsuhide sent urgent dispatches to all his commanders, including his cousin Mitsuharu in Sakamoto Castle, informing them of his decision. He was not going to retreat and fight a defensive campaign. He had resolved to attack Hideyoshi with all his strength.

It was the second watch of the night. Not a single star was visible. A combat unit was the first to descend the hill; it was to stand guard at the upper and lower reaches of the Katsura River. The supply corps, the main units, and the rear guard came down behind them. A sudden shower began to fall. By the time the entire army was halfway across the river, pure white rain was beating down on it.

The wind came up as well—a cold wind from the northwest. The foot soldiers muttered to themselves as they stared at the dark surface of the river.

"Both the river and the wind are coming at us from the mountains of Tamba."

During the day, they might have been able to see. Oinosaka was not far away, and it was only ten days before that they had crossed Oinosaka and left the Akechi base at Kameyama Castle. To the men, however, it felt like something that had happened several years ago.

"Don't fall! Don't let your fuses get wet!" the officers yelled. The force of the current in the Katsura River was far more violent than usual, due probably to a heavy rainfall in the mountains.

The spear corps crossed, each man holding on to the spear of the man in front of him, followed by the gunners, who grasped each other's stocks and muzzles. The horsemen surrounding Mitsuhide galloped up the opposite bank, leaving a trail of froth and bubbles. From somewhere in front of them, the dull sound of sporadic gunfire could be heard, while in the distance sparks leaped into the sky, probably from burning farmhouses. As soon as the gunfire stopped, however, the fires also disappeared and everything returned to darkness.

A runner soon arrived with a report. "Our men have driven back an enemy reconnaissance party. They set several farmhouses alight as they retreated."

Taking no notice of this report, Mitsuhide advanced through Kuga Nawate, passed by Shoryuji Castle, which was held by his own men, and purposefully made his camp at Onbozuka, some five or six hundred yards farther to the southwest. The rain that had plagued them for the last two or three days now ceased, and stars began to glitter in a sky that had previously displayed nothing but different shades of ink.

The enemy is quiet too, Mitsuhide thought as he stood at Onbozuka, staring into the dark in the direction of Yamazaki. He felt deep emotion and tension at the thought that Hideyoshi's army was facing him from a distance of barely half a league. Making On-bozuka the focal point of his entire force, and using the Shoryuji Castle as his supply base, he deployed his troops in a line from the Yodo River in the southwest to the Enmyoji River, as though opening up a fan. By the time each corps of the advance guard had got-ten into position, it was almost dawn and the outline of the long, flowing Yodo River was beginning to become visible.

Suddenly the echo of violent gunfire could be heard in the direction of Tennozan. The sun had not yet risen, and the clouds were dark with thick mist. It was the thirteenth day of the Sixth Month, and so early that not even the whinnying of a single horse could be heard on the road to Yamazaki.

Looking out from Mitsuhide's main camp at Onbozuka, the soldiers could see Ten-nozan about half a league to the southwest. Hugging its left side was the road to Yamazaki and a large river—the Yodo.

Tennozan was steep, about nine hundred feet at its highest point. On the day before, when Hideyoshi's main army had advanced as far as Tonda, his officers had all looked straight ahead and stared at the mountain. Several of them had questioned the local guide. "What mountain is that?"

"Is that Yamazaki in the eastern foothills?"

"The enemy is at Shoryuji. Where is that in relation to Tennozan?"

Every corps had to be accompanied by someone who was familiar with the lay of the land. Everyone who understood strategy knew that the side that controlled the high ground would win the day.

And every general was also aware that the first man who planted his banner on Tennozan would win more glory than the one who took the first head on the plain. Each general had sworn that he would be that man. On the eve of the thirteenth, several of Hideyoshi's generals had asked him to adopt their plan of attack, and hoped they would be given the order to storm the mountain.

"Tomorrow will be the decisive battle," Hideyoshi said. "Yodo, Yamazaki, and Ten-nozan will be the main battlefields. Prove yourselves worthy of being called men. Don't compete with one another, or think only of your own glory. Remember that Lord Nobu-naga and the god of war will be looking down on you from heaven."

But as soon as they received Hideyoshi's permission, the gunners raced toward Ten-nozan in high spirits and in a disorganized melee in the dead of night. This strategic place that had attracted the eyes of all of Hideyoshi's generals had not been overlooked by Mitsuhide. He had decided to march at full speed, cross the Katsura River, and come out quickly at Onbozuka to take Tennozan.

Mitsuhide knew the topography of the area as well as did the generals of the enemy vanguard, Nakagawa Sebei and Takayama Ukon. And, although they were looking at the mountains and rivers of the same area, Mitsuhide's mind naturally went beyond the thoughts of the other men.

After Mitsuhide had crossed the Katsura River and marched through Kuga Nawate, he detached one division from his army and sent them on another route, saying, "Climb up the northern side of Tennozan and take the mountaintop. If the enemy attacks, make a stand and don't give up that strategic point."

It must be said that he was quick. Mitsuhide's commands and his actions were always timely; he never missed an opportunity to strike. Nevertheless, by this time Hideyoshi's forces, which had already reached Hirose on the southern slope, were also on the mountain.

It had been pitch black, however, and many of the soldiers were not at all familiar with the terrain.

"Here's a path going up."

"No, you can't go through that way."

"Yes, I think we can."

"This is the wrong way. There's a crag right above us."

Winding their way around the foot of the mountain, they all made haste to find a path to the top.

The path was steep, and it was still dark. Because they knew they were among allies, the men filed up without knowing whose unit or corps they were with. They simply hurried, huffing and puffing, to the summit. Then, just as they thought they were nearing the top, they were struck by a volley of gunfire.

The attack had come from the Akechi gunners under Matsuda Tarozaemon. It was clear afterward that the seven hundred men in the Matsuda corps had been divided into two units. The soldiers of Horio Mosuke, Nakagawa Sebei, Takayama Ukon, and Ikeda Shonyu had all scrambled to be first to climb up Tennozan, but it was only Hori Kyutaro who commanded his troops to take the crossroad up to the north side of the foothills. Quickly skirting the base of the mountain, they attempted a completely different action: to cut off the retreat of the enemy.

As expected, that lateral attack intercepted the Matsuda corps and placed its general, Matsuda Tarozaemon, right before their eyes. The collision was far more violent than the clash at the top of the mountain. Fighting was hand to hand amidst the pines and boulders strewn along the mountain slope. Firearms were too cumbersome, so the battle was fought mainly with spears, long swords, and halberds.

Some fell from the cliffs grappling with the enemy. Some who held down enemy soldiers were stabbed from behind. There were corps of archers as well and the singing of arrows and reports of the guns were incessant. But far louder were the war cries of the five or six hundred men. Those cries did not seem to be coming from the throats of individual men but from their entire beings, even from their hair and pores.

The men advanced and were pushed back, and at last the sun began to rise. A blue sky and white clouds were visible for the first time in a long while. With the rare sunshine, the cicadas seemed to have been struck dumb. In their place were the war cries of the soldiers shaking the mountain. Very quickly, bloodied corpses lay strewn over the slopes, piled atop one another. One body might be lying pathetically alone in one spot, while two or three might have fallen on top of each other in another place. The warriors were spurred by the sight of the corpses, and the soldiers who stepped over the dead bodies of their comrades entered a space beyond life and death. This was true for the soldiers of the Hori corps as well as for the men of the Akechi.

The situation at the top of the mountain was unclear, but here too a victory might be followed quickly by a defeat. During the fighting, the cries that issued from the Matsuda corps suddenly changed and became like the sounds a crying child makes between sobs. Optimism had changed to despair.

"What's the matter?"

"Why are we falling back? Don't retreat!"

Questioning their comrades' confusion, some of the men of the Matsuda corps yelled out in anger. But those men, too, quickly ran toward the foot of the mountain as though carried by an avalanche. Their commanding general, Matsuda Tarozaemon, had been struck by a bullet and carried away on the shoulders of his attendants in full view of his troops.

"Attack! Cut them down!"

The greater part of the Hori corps had already started out in pursuit, but Kyutaro yelled at the top of his voice, trying to stop his men.

"Don't pursue them!"

In the impetus of the moment, however, the command for restraint had little effect. As might have been expected, the vanguard of the Matsuda corps now came cascading down the mountain like a muddy stream. Reinforcements had not come, and their general had been shot. They had no choice but to flee.

The Hori corps had been no match for the Akechi in terms of numbers. Now, without a real battle and with nothing to check them, they were thrust down the mountain and crushed underfoot by a corps of the enemy that came running down the steep slope from above. The section of the Hori corps that had pursued the enemy down the mountain first was now caught in a pincer movement just as Kyutaro had feared, and an appalling battle ensued.

At that point, the combined forces of the Horio, Nakagawa, Takayama, and Ikeda corps reached the top of the mountain.

"We've won!"

"Tennozan is ours!"

The battle's first victory cheer was raised. Hideyoshi had been waiting for Nobutaka's arrival at the Yodo River, and so he had not yet arrived at the front line. It was late in the afternoon, about the Hour of the Ram, by the time he had added the forces of Nobutaka and Niwa Nagahide to his own army and advanced to the central camp. The morning rain had dried up under the hot sky, both men and horses were covered with sweat and dust, and the colorful armor and coats had all turned white. The only article that penetrated the hot day with any brilliance was Hideyoshi's standard of the golden gourds.

While there were still echoes of gunfire on Tennozan, every house in the village had seemed empty. When the Akechi forces retreated and the new tide of armor flooded the streets, however, pails of water, piles of melons, and kettles of barley tea suddenly appeared on every doorstep. As Hideyoshi's forces crowded through the streets, even women appeared among the crowd of villagers, wishing them well.

"Not a single enemy soldier's left over there?"

Hideyoshi did not dismount, but simply gazed steadily at the banners of his soldiers, now visible on the nearby mountain.

"Not one," Hikoemon replied. He had coordinated all the reports on battle conditions from the various corps, judged the general situation, and now reported to Hideyoshi. "The Matsuda corps lost its commander at the very outset of the attack. Some of his men fled toward the northern foothills, while the others joined their allies in the neighborhood of Tomooka."

"I wonder why someone like Mitsuhide would abandon this high ground so quickly."

"He probably didn't think we would arrive so soon. He was mistaken in his timing."

"What about his main force?"

"They seem to have camped in the area from the Yodo River to Shimoueno, with Shoryuji at their rear and the Enmyoji River in front of them."

At that moment war cries and gunfire could be heard in the direction of the Enmyoji River. It was the Hour of the Monkey.

The Enmyoji River, east of the village of Yamazaki, was a confluent of the Yodo River. The area where the two rivers met was a swamp covered with reeds and rushes, usually filled with the songs of bush warblers, but on this day no birdsong could be heard.

During the morning the enemy armies—the left wing of Mitsuhide's army and Hideyoshi's right wing—had lined the riverbanks on either side. From time to time the reeds would rustle in the wind. While the tips of the banner poles were visible, no men or horses could be seen on either bank. On the northern bank, however, the five thousand men under Saito Toshimitsu, Abe Sadaaki, and Akechi Shigetomo were ready to advance. On the southern bank, eight thousand five hundred men under Takayama Ukon, Nakagawa Sebei, and Ikeda Shonyu were arranged in one line after another. Steaming with sweat in that hot, damp place, they waited for the time to strike.

They were waiting for Hideyoshi to arrive and give his command.

"What is the main army doing?"

They cursed Hideyoshi's army for its late arrival, but they could only grit their teeth.

Akechi Mitsuhide, who was still at his main camp in Onbozuka, had heard early on about Matsuda Tarozaemon's death on Tennozan and the complete rout of his troops. He blamed himself for misjudging the timing of his own command. He knew quite well that, strategically, there was a great difference between fighting with Tennozan under the control of his own men and facing a decisive battle after having abandoned the high ground to the enemy.

Prior to advancing toward Tennozan, however, Mitsuhide had been distracted by three things: Tsutsui Junkei's betrayal; his order to strengthen Yodo Castle—misjudging the speed of Hideyoshi's attack; and a flaw in his character—he was indecisive. Should he take the offensive or the defensive? He had not decided which until his advance on Onbozuka.

The battle began almost by accident. Both armies had spent the morning among the reeds and rushes, being eaten by gnats and mosquitoes. Throughout this time, they faced each other squarely and waited for their generals' commands. At one point, however, a beautifully saddled horse suddenly sprang from Hideyoshi's side toward the bank of the Enmyoji River, possibly to slake its thirst.

Four or five soldiers—probably retainers of the horse's owner—chased after it. Gunfire rang out abruptly from the opposite bank, followed by one volley after another.

In response, Hideyoshi's troops fired their own volley toward the northern bank in order to help the soldiers, who had taken cover in the reeds. Now there was no time to wait for orders.

"Attack!"

Hideyoshi's order for a general assault actually came after the exchange of gunfire. The Akechi troops naturally reacted to the movement of the enemy, and, they, too, waded into the river.

The place where the Enmyoji River met the Yodo River was fairly wide, but not far from the convergence the Enmyoji was little more than a stream.

The current, however, was strong after several days of rain. While the Akechi gunners' corps appeared through the reeds on the northern bank and fired into the ranks of Hideyoshi's forces standing on the southern bank, corps of armored men—the soldiers of the spear corps, the picked troops of the Akechi—kicked up sprays of water as they pushed their way across to the other side.

"Send out the spear corps!" an officer of the Takayama corps yelled, jumping up on the bank.

Because the river was so narrow, the effectiveness of the gunners was limited. As the rear ranks moved up in order to let the front ranks reload, there was the possibility that the enemy would suddenly overrun the bank and leap into the midst of the gunners.

"Gunners, open up to the side! Don't obstruct the men in the front ranks!"

The Nakagawa corps had their spear points aligned and ready. Most of them now brandished those spears and struck downward from the bank and into the water.

They were, of course, aiming at the enemy, but rather than pulling back their spears and thrusting, it was speedier to simply hold them aloft and strike in an effort to prevent the enemy from even starting up the bank. The fierce clash occurred in the middle of the river, spear to spear, spear to long sword, and even spear to spear shaft. Men thrust into others and were stabbed in turn.

The soldiers yelled and grappled with each other, some falling dead into the water and raising a spray. The muddy current whirled around. Blood and gore floated to the surface of the water and then was washed away.

By that time the first corps under Nakagawa Sebei had relinquished the fight downstream to the soldiers under Takayama Ukon's command. Like the lines of young men shouldering a sacred palanquin during a festival, yelling in unison, they forced their way into the front line of battle.

Quickly stepping over the reeds on the eastern bank of the river, they dashed furiously into the midst of the enemy. The sun began to set. Burnt red clouds showing the approach of evening reflected their colors on the black clumps of men yelling beneath the desolate sky.

The violent battle continued for yet another hour. The tenacity of the Saito corps was surprising. Just as it seemed they might crumble, they rallied once more. Making their stand in a swamp, they fought back attack after attack. And they were not the only ones —almost all of the Akechi forces fought with uncanny resignation, and the desperate voice of the defeated army resounded with a bitterness that each man could imagine in Mitsuhide's breast.

"Retreat before we're surrounded! Fall back! Fall back!"

That pathetic chorus was raised by troops in rapid succession, and the sad news spread like the wind to the other two Akechi corps.

At the heart of the central army, which acted as a reserve corps, were the five thousand men directly under Mitsuhide at Onbozuka. At their right were four thousand more men, including two thousand under Fujita Dengo.

Dengo sounded the large drum and the men fanned out into a line of battle. The men of the archers' corps in front released their ghastly rain of arrows in whining unison, and immediately the enemy returned the action with a hail of bullets.

As a command from Dengo cut through the air, the archers dispersed and the gunners took their place. Without waiting an instant for the shroud of gunpowder smoke to clear, armored warriors with iron spears appeared before the enemy and began to cut their way through. Dengo and his hand-picked troops routed the Hachiya corps.

Taking that corps' place, the soldiers under Nobutaka resumed the attack and struck against the Akechi forces. But Dengo defeated them as well, chasing them back. For the time being, Dengo's troops seemed to have no worthy opponent.

The drum of the Fujita corps boomed. It seemed to express the clan's pride in being without rival, and it menaced the mounted samurai who had crowded in a protective ring around Nobutaka, causing them to mill about in confusion.

Just then, a corps of five hundred soldiers attacked the Fujita corps' flank, yelling war cries as though they made up a large army.

The clouds were still vaguely red, but on the ground it was already dark. Dengo was reflecting that he had gone too far, and changed his instructions.

"Shift to the right!" he commanded. "Turn! Turn as far as you can toward the right!" His intention was to have the entire force make a circle to rejoin the central army and then fight on firmly.

Suddenly, however, a unit under the command of Hori Kyutaro attacked fiercely from the left. To Dengo, it was as though enemy soldiers had suddenly bubbled up from the earth.

There was no way to retreat, Dengo realized at once, but there was also no time to correct his formation. The Hori warriors cut off his men with the speed of the wind and began to encircle them.

Nobutaka's standard seemed to flutter closer and closer to Dengo.

Just at that point, a band of five hundred men, including Dengo's son and his younger brother, promptly rode out in a black cluster and galloped fearlessly into the enemy. The night had grown dark. The wind carried the cries of the life-and-death struggles and filled the sky with the smell of blood.

Nobutaka's corps was respected as being the strongest among the divisions of Hideyoshi's army, and now it was reinforced with the three thousand men under the command of Niwa Nagahide. Brave and spirited as Dengo and his men were, they could not break through the enemy line.

Dengo was wounded in six places. Finally, after fighting and whirling about on his horse for so long, he began to lose consciousness. Suddenly a voice came from the darkness behind him.

Thinking it to be the voice of his son, he raised his head from the horse's mane. Just at that moment something struck him above the right eye. It felt like a star falling from heaven, hitting him on the forehead.

"Stay in the saddle! Hang on tight to the saddle! An arrow has glanced off you, and you have a light wound on your forehead." "Who is it? Who's holding me up?"

"It's me, Tozo."

"Ah, brother. What's happened to Ise Yosaburo?"

"He's already been cut down in battle."

"What about Suwa?"

"Suwa is dead too."

"And Denbei?"

"He's still surrounded by the enemy. Now let me accompany you. Lie against the front ring of your saddle."

Without talking further about Denbei's being either dead or alive, Tozo took the muzzle of his brother's horse and fled at top speed through the chaos.

THE TWO GATES

A lonely wind blew through the pines that grew around Mitsuhide's camp at Onbozuka. The curtain of the enclosure swelled in the wind like a large white living thing. It flapped incessantly, singing an eerie, uneasy dirge.

"Yoji, Yoji!" Mitsuhide called.

"Yes, my lord!"

"Was that a messenger?"

"Yes, my lord."

"Why didn't he report directly to me?"

"The report has not yet been confirmed."

"Is there a rule about what can and cannot reach my ears?" Mitsuhide asked, annoyed.

"I'm sorry, my lord."

"Take courage! Are you losing your nerve over bad omens?"

"No, my lord. But I fully expect to die."

"Really?"

Mitsuhide was suddenly aware of his shrill tone, and lowered his voice. He then considered that perhaps he himself should listen to the words with which he had just reproved Yojiro. The wind made a much more lonely sound than in the day. Vegetable gardens and fields lay beyond the gentle slope. To the east was Kuga Nawate; to the north, mountains; to the west, the Enmyoji River. But in the darkness, only the pale twinkling of stars shone over the battlefield.

Only three hours had passed between the Hour of the Monkey and the second half of the Hour of the Rooster. Mitsuhide's banners had filled the field. Where were they now? All had been struck down. He had listened to the names of dead men until he was no longer able to keep count.

It had only taken three hours. There was no doubt that Yojiro had just now received one more piece of bad news. And he had lost the courage to relay the matter to Mitsuhide. Reprimanded by his lord, Yojiro once again descended the hill. Looking around, he feebly leaned against the trunk of a pine and stared up at the stars.

A horseman rode up to Yojiro and halted in front of him.

"Friend or foe!" Yojiro shouted, challenging the stranger with the spear he had been using as a staff.

"Friend," the rider replied as he dismounted.

Just by looking at the shambling gait of the man, Yojiro could see that he was seriously wounded. Yojiro walked toward him and offered him his arm.

"Gyobu!" Yojiro said, recognizing his comrade. "Hold fast! Lean on me."

"Is that Yojiro? Where is Lord Mitsuhide?"

"On top of the hill."

"He's still here? This is a dangerous place for him now. He must leave right away."

Gyobu went up to Mitsuhide and prostrated himself in front of him, almost falling on his face. "The entire army has been routed. The dying fell on top of the dead; so many achieved glorious deaths in battle that I cannot remember their names."

Looking up, he could only see Mitsuhide's white face. It seemed as though it were floating beneath the dark shape of the pines. Mitsuhide said nothing, as though he had not been listening.

Gyobu went on, "At one point, we pressed close on Hideyoshi's center, but when darkness fell our retreat was cut off, and we could no longer find Lord Dengo. General Sanzaemon's division was surrounded by the enemy, and extremely bitter fighting ensued. He was able to escape with only two hundred men. His last words were, 'Go immediately to Onbozuka and tell His Lordship to withdraw to Shoryuji Castle as fast as he can, and then either prepare to hold the castle or retreat toward Omi during the night. I will act as his rear guard until then. After we receive news that His Lordship has withdrawn, we will gallop straight into Hideyoshi's camp and fight to the death.'"

Mitsuhide was still silent. When Gyobu had finished giving his report, he collapsed and breathed his last.

Mitsuhide stared at him from his seat and then looked vacantly at Yojiro. He asked, "Were Gyobu's wounds deep?"

"Yes, my lord," Yojiro answered, tears filling his eyes.

"He seems to be dead."

"Yes, my lord."

"Yojiro," Mitsuhide suddenly said in an entirely different tone. "What did the previous messenger report?"

"I will not conceal anything from you, my lord. Tsutsui Junkei's army appeared on the field and attacked our left wing. Saito Toshimitsu and his entire corps did not have the strength to hold them off, and they were completely routed."

"What! Was that it?"

"I knew that if I told you that now, it would be hard to accept. I had truly hoped to tell you when it wouldn't add to your unhappiness."

"This is the world of men." Then he added, "It makes no difference."

Mitsuhide laughed. At least it was something like a laugh. Then he abruptly waved toward the rear of the camp and impatiently called out for his horse.

Mitsuhide had sent most of his troops to the front, but there should have been at least two thousand men in the camp with his senior retainers. Leading this force, Mitsuhide was ready to join up with what was left of Sanzaemon's corps and attempt one last battle. Mounting his horse, he yelled out the orders for the attack in a voice that resounded through Onbozuka. Then, without waiting for the soldiers to assemble, he turned his horse around and started to gallop down the hill, accompanied by a few mounted samurai.

"Who are you?" Mitsuhide asked, bringing his horse to a stop. Someone had suddenly rushed out of the camp, run down the slope, and stood blocking the way, his arms stretched out wide.

"Tatewaki, why are you stopping me?" Mitsuhide asked sharply. It was one of Mitsuhide's senior retainers, Hida Tatewaki, and he quickly grabbed the bridle of Mitsuhide's horse. The unruly animal stamped the ground, unable to control itself.

"Yojiro! Sanjuro! Why didn't you stop him? Get off your horses, my lord," Hida Tatewaki said, scolding Mitsuhide's attendants. Then bowing in Mitsuhide's direction, he said, "The man before me is not the Lord Mitsuhide I serve. The war is not lost after one defeat. It is not like you to think about throwing away your life right after one battle. The enemy is going to ridicule us for having lost self-control. Even though you've been defeated here, you have a family in Sakamoto and several generals dispersed in the provinces just waiting for word from you. Surely you must not be without a plan for the future. First withdraw to Shoryuji Castle."

"What are you talking about, Tatewaki?" Mitsuhide shook his head almost in time with his horse's mane. "Are all the men we've lost going to rise up once again and regain their high spirits? I cannot abandon my men to the enemy and let them be killed. I'm going to deal one good blow to Hideyoshi and punish Tsutsui Junkei's treachery. I'm not looking for a place to die in vain. I'm going to show them who Mitsuhide is. Now let me pass!"

"Why are my wise lord's eyes so wild? Our army received a blow today, and at least three thousand men died while countless others were wounded. Our generals were struck down, and our new recruits have been scattered. How many soldiers do you think are left in this camp now?"

"Let me go! I can do exactly as I please! Let me go!"

"It's exactly that kind of irresponsible talk that proves you're only rushing off toward death, and I'm going to do my best to stop you. It would be one thing if there were still three or four thousand obstinate men here, but I suspect there are only four or five hundred who will be trailing behind you. All the others have slipped out of camp since evening and fled," Tatewaki said, his voice filled with tears.

Is a man's intellect so frail? And once that intellect fails, does he simply become a madman? Tatewaki gazed at Mitsuhide's frenzy and wondered how the man could have changed so much. Shedding bitter tears, he could not help remembering how prudent and intelligent Mitsuhide had once been.

Other generals now stood in front of Mitsuhide's horse. Two of them had already been on the front lines, but, concerned for their lord's safety, they had come back to the camp. One of them said, "We all agree with Lord Hida. Shoryuji is nearby, and it's certainly not too late to go there first and work out a strategy for our next step."

"As long as we're here, the enemy forces will be drawing closer and closer, and everything could come to an end right in this spot. We should whip our horses and move on to Shoryuji as fast as we can."

Tatewaki no longer asked what his lord's intentions were. He had the conch shell blown and quickly ordered a retreat to the north. Yojiro and another retainer abandoned their own horses and walked, each grasping the bridle of their master's horse and leading it to the north. The other soldiers and commanders on the hill followed them. But, just as Tatewaki had said, they numbered no more than five hundred men.

Miyake Tobei was the commander of Shoryuji Castle. Here, too, there were nothing but omens of defeat, and a desolate mood of doom filled the castle. Surrounded by faintly flickering lanterns, all present deliberated over how to save themselves. As they searched for some rational conclusion, even Mitsuhide realized that there was nothing to be done.

The sentries outside the castle had repeatedly reported the approach of the enemy, and the castle itself was not strong enough to resist the crushing force of Hideyoshi's army. Even Yodo Castle had been in this condition when he had ordered its repair some days ago. It was not unlike beginning to build a dike only after hearing the sounds of the billowing waves.

Perhaps the only thing Mitsuhide did not regret at this point was that a number of his generals and soldiers had remained loyal and fought a furious battle, poignantly demonstrating their loyalty. It was, in one sense, paradoxical that there were men within the Akechi clan—the clan that had struck down their own lord—who would still not break the bond between lord and retainer. Clearly Mitsuhide was a virtuous man, and those men were manifesting the ironclad law of the samurai.

For that reason, the number of dead and wounded was unusually high, even though the battle had lasted no more than three hours. It was later estimated that the Akechi had suffered more than three thousand casualties, while Hideyoshi's forces had lost more than three thousand three hundred. The number of wounded was incalculable. Thus one might understand the great spirit of the Akechi forces, which was in no way inferior to that of their general. Considering the small size of Mitsuhide's force—nearly half the size of his enemy's—and the disadvantageous ground on which it fought, his defeat was not one that could be ridiculed by the world.

* * *

The moon of the thirteenth day of the Sixth Month was blurred by thin clouds. One or two mounted warriors rode separately on ahead, while others followed a little behind. Thirteen mounted men rode in scattered groups from north of the Yodo River toward Fushimi.

When they had finally entered a dark trail in the depths of the mountain, Mitsuhide turned and asked Tatewaki, "Where are we?"

"This is Okame Valley, my lord."

Speckles of moonlight spilling through the branches fell on Tatewaki and the men who followed behind.

"Do you plan on crossing to the north of Momoyama and then coming out to the Kanshu Temple Road from Ogurusu?" Mitsuhide asked.

"That's right. If we pursue this course and get close to Yamashina and Otsu before it gets light, we won't have to worry."

Shinshi Sakuzaemon suddenly stopped his horse a little in front of Mitsuhide's and signaled them to be quiet. Mitsuhide and the horsemen following him also stopped. Without so much as a whisper, they watched Akechi Shigetomo and Murakoshi Sanjuro as they walked ahead as scouts. The two riders had stopped their horses next to a stream and signaled for the men behind them to wait. They stood there for some time, listening.

Was it an enemy ambush?

Finally, a look of relief appeared on their faces. Following the signals of the two men motioning ahead of them, they once again quietly moved forward. Both the moon and the clouds appeared to be hanging in the middle of the midnight sky. But no matter how stealthily they advanced, when the horses started up the slope, they kicked up stones or stepped on rotten wood, and even the echoes of such little sounds awakened the sleeping birds. Each time it happened, Mitsuhide and his followers quickly restrained their horses.

After their horrible defeat, they had fled to Shoryuji Castle and rested. Later they had discussed what was to be done, but in the end, the only possible plan was to retreat to Sakamoto. All of his retainers had prevailed on Mitsuhide to be patient. Leaving Miyake Tobei in charge of the castle, Mitsuhide slipped out at dusk.

The force that followed him right up to the time he left Shoryuji still numbered about four or five hundred men. But by the time they entered the village of Fushimi, most of them had deserted. The few who remained were his most trusted retainers, and they numbered only thirteen men.

"A great number of us would only stand out to the enemy, and anyone who hasn't re-solved to accompany our lord in either life or death would only be a hindrance. Lord Mitsuharu is in Sakamoto along with three thousand troops. All I care about is getting there safely. I pray to the gods to help our poor lord."

The loyal retainers who remained comforted each other in this way.

Although the area was hilly, it had no really steep places. The moon was visible, but because of the rain, the ground beneath the trees was muddy, and the road was dotted with puddles.

In addition, Mitsuhide and his retainers were exhausted. They were already close to Yamashina, and if they could only get to Otsu, they would be safe. That was how they en-couraged each other, but to the tired men themselves it seemed more like a hundred leagues.

"We've entered a village."

"This must be Ogurusu. Go quietly."

Thickly thatched mountain huts could be seen here and there. Mitsuhide's followers would have liked to avoid such human habitations as much as possible, but the road led between the houses. Fortunately, not a light was showing. The houses were surrounded by large bamboo thickets under a white moon, and all indications were that everyone was deeply asleep, completely unaware of the world's confusion.

With narrowed eyes that pierced the darkness, Akechi Shigetomo and Murakoshi Sanjuro scouted far ahead, riding along the narrow village road without mishap. Stopping where the road wound around a bamboo thicket, they waited for Mitsuhide and his group.

The figures of the two men, and the reflection of their spears, could be clearly seen from the shadows of the trees that stood fifty yards ahead.

The sound of bamboo being trampled and the grunt of a wild animal suddenly exploded from the darkness.

Tatewaki, who was leading his horse ahead of Mitsuhide, instinctively looked behind. Darkness lined the brushwood hedge of a hut covered by the gloom of the bamboo thicket. Some twenty yards behind, Mitsuhide's silhouette stood out as if he had been nailed to the spot.

"My lord," Tatewaki called.

There was no answer. The clumps of young bamboo swayed in a windless sky.

Tatewaki was about to turn back, when Mitsuhide suddenly spurred his horse forward and passed in front of him without a word. He was slumped over the horse's neck. Tatewaki thought it strange, but nevertheless followed along behind, as did the others.

They galloped along the road in this manner without incident for about three hundred yards. After joining up again with the two scouts, the thirteen men continued to advance, with Mitsuhide riding sixth from the front.

Suddenly, Murakoshi's horse reared up. In that instant, his drawn sword swept by the left of his saddle.

A loud clanging sound rang out as the sword cut the sharpened tip of a bamboo spear. The hands that held the spear quickly disappeared into the bamboo thicket, but the others had clearly seen what had happened.

"What was that? Bandits?"

"It must be. Watch out, they seem to be somewhere inside this big bamboo thicket."

"Murakoshi, are you all right?"

"What, you think I'm going to be hurt by the bamboo spear of some wandering thief?"

"Don't be distracted! Just hurry along. Distractions will be nothing but trouble."

"What about His Lordship?"

All of them turned around.

"Look, over there!

Suddenly they all turned pale. About a hundred paces in front of them, Mitsuhide had fallen from his horse. Worse, he was writhing on the ground, groaning in agony, and looked as though he was unable to stand up again.

"My lord!"

Shigetomo and Tatewaki dismounted, ran up to him, and tried to lift him back into the saddle. Mitsuhide no longer seemed to have the will to ride. He simply shook his head.

"What's happened to you, my lord?" Completely forgetting themselves, the other men crowded around in the dark. The groans of the suffering Mitsuhide and the sighs of the men filled the air. Just at that moment, the moon shone with special clarity.

Suddenly the undisguised footsteps and screams of the bandits came clamoring noisily out of the darkness of the bamboo thicket.

"It looks like the accomplices of the man with the bamboo spear are coming up at us from behind. It's the nature of these marauders to try to take advantage of any show of weakness. Sanjuro and Yojiro, take care of them."

At Shigetomo's words, the men split up. A spear was quickly positioned and swords drawn.

"Damn you!" With a thunderous yell, someone leaped into the bamboo thicket. A sound like a rain of leaves, or perhaps a pack of monkeys, split the silence of the night.

"Shigetomo... Shigetomo..." Mitsuhide whispered.

"I'm here, my lord."

"Ah...Shigetomo," Mitsuhide said again. He then groped around as though searching for the arms that were supporting him.

Blood was spurting from the side of his chest, his vision was fading, and he was finding it difficult to speak.

"I'm going to bind your wound and give you some medicine, so be patient for just a little while."

Mitsuhide shook his head to show that binding the wound would be unnecessary. Then his hands moved as though they were searching for something.

"What is it, my lord?"

"A brush..."

Shigetomo hurriedly took out paper and ink and a brush. Mitsuhide took the brush with shaking fingers and looked at the white paper. Shigetomo knew that he would be writing his death poem and began to feel a choking sensation in his chest. He could hardly stand to see Mitsuhide writing such a thing now and in this place, and in his attachment to what he felt was his lord's greater destiny, he said, "Don't take up your brush now, my lord. Otsu is hardly a breath away, and if we can just find our way there, you'll be welcomed by Lord Mitsuharu. Let me bandage up this wound."

As Shigetomo put the paper on the ground and began to untie his own sash, Mitsuhide suddenly waved his hand with surprising strength. Then, with his left hand, he lifted himself off the ground. Stretching out his right hand, he grasped the brush with almost crushing strength and started to write:

There are not two gates: loyalty and treason.

But his hand shook so much that he seemed to be unable to write the next line. Mitsuhide passed the brush to Shigetomo. "You write the rest."

Leaning on Shigetomo's lap, Mitsuhide turned his head toward the sky and gazed at the moon for a little while. When the color of death even paler than the moon had filled his face, he spoke with a voice surprisingly free of confusion and finished the verse.

The Great Way penetrates the font of the heart.

Waking from the dream of fifty-five years,
I return to the One.

Shigetomo put down the brush and began to weep. Just at that moment, Mitsuhide drew his short sword and cut his own throat. Sakuzaemon and Tatewaki ran back in shock and saw what had happened. Approaching the dead body of their lord, each man fell on his own blade. Another four men, then six, then eight surrounded Mitsuhide's body in the same way and followed him in death. In no time at all, their lifeless bodies formed the petals and heart of a flower of blood on the ground.

Yojiro had dashed into the bamboo thicket to fight with the bandits. Murakoshi called out into the darkness, worried that he might already have been cut down.

"Yojiro, come back! Yojiro! Yojiro!"

But regardless of the number of times he called, Yojiro did not come back again. Murakoshi had also received a number of wounds. When he was somehow able to crawl out through the bamboo stand, he saw the silhouette of a man passing right by him.

"Ah! Lord Shigetomo."

"Sanjuro?"

"How is His Lordship?"

"He has breathed his last."

"No!" Sanjuro was surprised. "Where?"

"He is right here, Sanjuro." Shigetomo indicated Mitsuhide's head, which he had wrapped in a cloth and attached to his saddle. He looked away sadly.

Sanjuro leaped with a violent force toward the horse. As he seized Mitsuhide's head, he raised a long, wailing cry. At length he asked, "What were his last words?"

"He recited a verse that began 'There are not two gates: loyalty and treason.'"

"He said that?"

"Even though he attacked Nobunaga, his action could not be questioned as a matter of loyalty or treason. Both he and Nobunaga were samurai, and they served the same Emperor. When he finally woke from fifty-five years of a dream, he found that even he was not someone who could escape from the world's blame and praise. After saying these words, he killed himself."

"I understand." Murakoshi was sobbing convulsively, wiping the tears from his face with his fist. "He neither listened to Lord Toshimitsu's admonishments nor refused to fight a decisive battle at Yamazaki on disadvantageous ground with a small army, because he depended on that Great Way. In that light, retreating from Yamazaki would have amounted to abandoning Kyoto. When I realize what was in his heart, I can't stop crying."

"No, even though he was defeated, he never abandoned the Way, and doubtless died with that long-cherished ambition. He showed his last verse to heaven. But you know, if we waste time here, those brigands will probably come back and attack again."

"Right."

"I was unable to take care of everything here by myself. I have left our lord's corpse without the head. Would you bury it so no one will find it?"

"What about the others?"

709

"They all gathered around his body and died bravely."

"After I've carried out your orders, I'll find some place to die too."

"I'm taking his head to give to Lord Mitsutada at the Chionin Temple. I'll think about disposing of myself after that. Well, good-bye then."

"Good-bye."

The two men went separate ways on the narrow path through the bamboo grove. The speckles of light scattered by the moon were lovely to behold.

* * *

Shoryuji Castle fell that night. It happened just as Mitsuhide was dying in Ogurusu. The generals Nakagawa Sebei, Takayama Ukon, Ikeda Shonyu, and Hori Kyutaro all moved their command posts there. Lighting a huge bonfire, they lined their camp stools outside the castle gate and waited for Nobutaka and Hideyoshi to arrive. Nobutaka soon stood before them.

To have taken the castle was a resplendent victory. Both soldiers and officers straightened their banners and looked up at Nobutaka with great reverence. As Nobutaka dismounted and passed through the ranks of the army, he nodded to the men with a friendly expression. He was almost overly polite to the generals, greeting them respectfully and showing his gratitude.

Taking Sebei's hand, he said with special affection, "It is due to your loyalty and courage that the Akechi were crushed in a single day's battle. My father's soul has been appeased, and I will not forget this."

He gave the same praise to Takayama Ukon and Ikeda Shonyu. Arriving a little later, however, Hideyoshi said nothing at all to those men. As he rode by them in his palanquin, he even appeared to be looking down on them.

Sebei was a man of unequaled ferocity, even in the midst of rough warriors, and it is likely that he felt offended by Hideyoshi's behavior. He cleared his throat loud enough to be heard. Hideyoshi glanced out from inside the palanquin and passed on with a parting remark.

"Good work, Sebei."

Sebei stamped his feet in anger. "Even Lord Nobutaka was civil enough to dismount for us, but this man is so arrogant that he goes right by in his palanquin. Maybe Monkey thinks he's already running the country," he said, loudly enough so that everyone around him could hear, but beyond that he could do nothing.

Ikeda Shonyu, Takayama Ukon, and the others held the same rank as Hideyoshi, but at some point Hideyoshi had started treating them as though they were his subordinates. They, too, had steadily come to feel that they were somehow under Hideyoshi's command. To be sure, that was not a pleasant feeling for any of them, but no one had protested.

Even on entering the castle, Hideyoshi simply gave a quick glance to the burned-out ruins of the building and gave no thought to resting. Ordering that a curtained enclosure be set up in the garden, he placed his camp stool next to Nobutaka's, quickly summoned the generals, and began giving out orders.

"Kyutaro, lead an army to the village of Yamashina and push on toward Awadaguchi.

Your objective is to come out at Otsu and cut off the road passage between Azuchi and Sakamoto." Then he turned to Sebei and Ukon. "You should hurry down the Tamba Road as quickly as possible. It appears that many of the enemy have fled toward Tamba, and we don't want to give them time to get to Kameyama Castle and make preparations. If we're slow here, we're likely to lose even more time. If you can reach Kameyama by midday tomorrow, it should fall without much trouble."

Some, then, were sent hurrying to Toba and the area of Shichijo, while others were to advance to the vicinities of Yoshida and Shirakawa. The instructions were highly explicit, and Nobutaka only sat to the side as they were being given. In the eyes of all the generals, Hideyoshi's attitude was nothing less than presumptuous.

Nevertheless, even Sebei, who had at first opened his mouth in anger, meekly accepted his orders like the others. Finally they distributed provisions to the soldiers for the first time since morning, ladled out some *sake*, filled their stomachs, and once again started off for the next battlefield.

Hideyoshi understood that there was a time and place for making people yield to his control, and his ploy this time had been to wait for the time when each of the generals had just won a victory. But Hideyoshi knew that his colleagues were men of matchless valor and unmanageable courage, and he was not so imprudent as to risk addressing them as subordinates by use of this ploy alone.

An army must have a leader. While Nobutaka should have been the commander-in-chief in terms of rank, he had only recently joined the campaign, and all of the generals recognized the fact that he was lacking in both authority and resolve. That being so, there was absolutely no one left to assume leadership other than Hideyoshi.

Although not one of the generals felt disposed to submit to Hideyoshi, each one knew that no one else was acceptable to the whole group. Hideyoshi had planned this battle to be the requiem for Nobunaga, and he had rallied them together. So if they now complained about his handling of them as subordinates, they would only have exposed themselves to the accusation of self-interest.

The generals had no time for rest but were to set off at once for the new battlefields to which they had been ordered. As they stood up together to depart, Hideyoshi remained in the commander's seat and gestured to each man with his chin.

Hideyoshi stayed at the Mii Temple, and on the night of the fourteenth there was another huge thunderstorm. The smoldering embers of Sakamoto Castle were extinguished, and all night long, pale white lightning flashed over the ink-colored lake and Shimeigatake.

With the dawn, however, the heavens were wiped clean and the hot summer sky appeared once again. From the main camp at the Mii Temple, a thick yellow smoke could be seen rising from the eastern bank of the lake in the direction of Azuchi.

"Azuchi is burning!"

At the report of the guards, the generals went out onto the veranda. Hideyoshi and the rest of them shaded their eyes with their hands.

A messenger reported, "Lord Nobuo, who was camped at Tsuchiyama in Omi, and Lord Gamo joined forces and have been attacking Azuchi since morning. They set fire to both the town and the castle, and the wind from the lake has engulfed all of Azuchi in flames. But there were no enemy soldiers left in Azuchi, so there was no battle."

Hideyoshi could imagine what was occurring far away.

"There was no reason to set that fire," he muttered sullenly. "No matter who he is, Lord Nobuo and even Gamo acted hastily."

But he soon calmed down. The culture that Nobunaga had spent the blood and resources of half a lifetime constructing was to be mourned in every way, but Hideyoshi had faith that very soon—and with his own strength—he would build an even greater castle and culture.

Just at that moment, another patrol of soldiers came from the main temple gate. They were gathered around a single man and were bringing him to Hideyoshi. "A farmer from Ogurusu by the name of Chobei says that he found Lord Mitsuhide's head."

It was the custom to inspect the head of an enemy general with grave decorum and etiquette, and Hideyoshi gave orders for his camp stool to be set up in front of the main temple. Soon thereafter, he sat down with the other generals and looked at Mitsuhide's head in silence.

Afterward, the head was exposed at the ruins of the Honno Temple. Only half a month had passed since the morning the standard of the bellflower had been set up amid the Akechi army's war cries.

Mitsuhide's head had been displayed for the benefit of the citizens of the capital, and they swarmed together at the site from morning till night. Even those who had denounced Mitsuhide's treason now said a prayer, while others threw flowers beneath the rotting skull.

Hideyoshi's military commands were simple and clear. He had only three laws: Be diligent in your work. Commit no wrongs. Troublemakers will be executed.

Hideyoshi had not yet conducted a formal funeral service for Nobunaga; the grand ceremony he had in mind could not be accomplished with military power alone, and it would not be right for it to be under only his patronage. The fire in the capital had finally died down, but the sparks had spread to all the provinces.

Nobunaga was dead, Mitsuhide was dead, and there was the possibility that the country would once again be divided into three spheres of influence, as it had been before Nobunaga. Worse, family feuds and rival warlords defending their own local interests might plunge the country into the chaos of the last years of the shogunate.

From the Mii Temple, Hideyoshi moved his entire army onto a fleet of warships, boarding everything from horses to gilded screens. That was on the eighteenth of the month, and the objective was to move to Azuchi. Another military force also snaked its way east along the land route. The line of ships moving over the lake was driven by the breeze that filled the banners, and it reflected the marching land army advancing along the coast.

But Azuchi was already nothing more than scorched earth, and as soon as the troops arrived, they found themselves disheartened. The gold-and-blue walls of Azuchi no longer existed. All the gates of the outer wall and the towering eaves of the Soken Temple had been burned to the ground. The castle town was even worse. There was nothing for which even the stray dogs could hunt, and the priests from the Christian church walked around with empty eyes.

Nobuo should have been there, but he was fighting rebels in Ise and Iga. It became clear that the burning of Azuchi had not been ordered by Nobuo. Certainly the fires had been started by his men, but it seemed plausible that that had been the result of a misunderstanding or perhaps of false rumors spread by the enemy.

Hideyoshi and Nobutaka had traveled to Azuchi together and lamented the destruction with deep feeling. Nevertheless, after they realized that the fires had not been set at Nobuo's command, their indignation seemed to abate somewhat. They stayed in Azuchi for only two days. The convoy of ships once again set sail, this time for the north. Hideyoshi was advancing his main army to his home castle at Nagahama.

The castle was safe. There was no sign of the enemy, and allied troops were already entering the castle grounds. When the commander's standard with the golden gourds was raised, the people of the castle town were overjoyed. They filled the streets through which Hideyoshi passed en route from his boat to the castle. Women, children, and the elderly prostrated themselves in the dirt to greet him. Some people cried, and some could not even lift their faces. There were some who cheered and waved their hands, while others even forgot themselves as they danced with joy. He purposefully passed by on horseback to respond to the enthusiastic welcome of his people.

For Hideyoshi, however, there remained a very serious anxiety, and it grew even more intense after he entered Nagahama Castle. He burned with such impatience and longing that he could not stand idle even for a moment. Were his mother and wife safe?

After sitting down in the inner citadel, he asked the question over and over to each one of the generals who came and went. He was suddenly very worried about the condition of his family.

"We've looked everywhere for them, but no clear report has come in yet," the generals said.

"Wasn't there anyone who knew anything about their whereabouts?" Hideyoshi asked.

"Well, we thought so," one general answered. "But none of the people seem to have seen them. When they fled the castle, their destination was kept an absolute secret."

"I see. It must be true. If their whereabouts had leaked out to the common people, the enemy would have given chase, and they would have been in danger."

Hideyoshi met another general and discussed an entirely different subject. That day the enemy troops at Sawayama Castle had abandoned the fortress and fled in the direction of Wakasa. The general reported that the castle had been returned to the control of its former commander, Niwa Nagahide.

Ishida Sakichi and four or five other members of the pages' group suddenly returned hurriedly from an unknown destination. Before they got to Hideyoshi's room, happy voices could be heard bubbling up in the corridor and the pages' room, and Hideyoshi asked those around him, "Has Sakichi come back? Why is he so slow in coming here?" He sent a man to rebuke him.

Ishida Sakichi had been born in Nagahama, and he knew the geography of the area better than anyone. He had thought, therefore, that now was the time to use his knowledge. He had been out on his own since noon, looking for the place where his lord's mother and his wife might be hiding.

Sakichi knelt respectfully in front of Hideyoshi. According to his report, Hideyoshi's mother, his wife, and the rest of the household were hiding in the mountains a little more than ten leagues from Nagahama. It seemed that they were barely keeping body and soul together.

"Well, let's get ready to leave right away. If we go now, we should be able to get there by tomorrow night," Hideyoshi said, standing. He was nearly unable to restrain himself, so great was his impatience.

"Take care of things while I'm gone," he ordered Kyutaro. "Hikoemon is stationed at Otsu, and Lord Nobutaka is still at Azuchi."

As Hideyoshi left the castle gate, he saw six or seven hundred men lined up and waiting for him. They had fought successive battles at Yamazaki and Sakamoto, and had had no time to rest even at Azuchi. The warriors had arrived only that morning, and their faces were still tired and muddy. Hideyoshi said, "It will be enough if fifty horsemen come with me."

Hideyoshi only said this after the mounted men carrying torches had started to lead the procession. Almost all of the soldiers, then, were to stay behind.

"That's dangerous," Kyutaro said. "Fifty horsemen are too few. The road you'll take tonight passes close by Mount Ibuki, and enemy forces may still be hiding there."

Both Kyutaro and Shonyu were especially vociferous in cautioning him, but Hideyoshi seemed convinced that there was no need for such concern. Answering that it was not worth worrying about, he ordered the men with the torches to lead the way. Leaving the castle gate, they went along the tree-lined road toward the northeast.

Riding through the night until about the fourth watch, Hideyoshi progressed five leagues down the road without too much haste.

The group arrived at Sanjuin Temple at midnight. Hideyoshi had thought the monks would be taken completely by surprise, but to his amazement, when they opened the main gate, he saw that the inside of the temple was brilliantly lit with lanterns, water had been splashed over the grounds, and the entire area had been swept clean.

"Somebody must have come ahead and announced that I was coming."

"It was me," Sakichi announced.

"You?"

"Yes. I thought that you would probably be stopping here to rest, my lord, so I had a young man who is a fast runner come ahead and order meals prepared for fifty men."

Sakichi had been an acolyte at Sanjuin Temple, but at twelve years of age he had been accepted by Hideyoshi as a page at Nagahama Castle. That had been eight years ago, and he had since become a twenty-year-old samurai. Sakichi had excellent good sense and was more quick-witted than most people.

At dawn, the outline of Mount Ibuki could be seen against the rose and pale blue hues of the sky, while nothing could be heard but the chirping of tiny birds. The dew was deep on the road, and darkness hung beneath the trees.

Hideyoshi looked happy. He knew that with every step he was getting closer to his mother and wife, and he seemed to mind neither the steep slope of the road nor his own fatigue. Now, the closer he approached Nishitani as the light increased on Mount Ibuki, the more he had the feeling of being held to his mother's breast.

No matter how long they climbed upstream along the Azusa River, they never seemed to come to its source. On the contrary, it opened up and they came out into a valley so wide that they might have forgotten they were in the middle of the mountains.

"That's Mount Kanakuso," announced the monk who was acting as guide, and he pointed to a steep peak directly in front of them. He wiped the sweat from his forehead. The sun had climbed to the center of the sky, and the heat of midsummer was rising.

The monk walked on ahead again on the narrow path. After a while the path became so narrow that Hideyoshi and his attendants had to dismount. Just at that moment the men around Hideyoshi stopped.

"It looks like the enemy," they said with alarm.

Hideyoshi and his small force had just climbed around the peak. There appeared to be a group of soldiers stationed on the mountainside in the distance. Those soldiers, too, seemed surprised, and they all stood up together. One of them seemed to be giving out commands while soldiers scattered in disorder.

"They could be remaining enemy soldiers," someone said. "I've heard that they've fled as far as Ibuki."

That was, indeed, a possibility, and the gunners immediately ran forward. The order was quickly given to get ready for battle, but the two monks who were acting as guides called them back.

"It's not the enemy. They're the lookouts from the temple. Don't shoot!"

They then turned toward the mountain in the distance and made themselves understood by gesturing and yelling at the top of their voices.

With that, the soldiers began to descend the mountain like stones tumbling down a cliff. Very soon, an officer with a small banner affixed to his back ran down to them. Hideyoshi recognized him as a retainer from Nagahama.

The Daikichi Temple was nothing more than a small mountain temple. When it rained, water leaked through the roof. When the wind blew, the walls and beams shook. Nene lived and waited upon her mother-in-law in the main temple, while the ladies-in-waiting lived in the priests' quarters. The retainers who came later from Nagahama built small huts in the area or lodged in farmhouses in the village. So in those wretched conditions, a large family of over two hundred had lived for over two weeks.

By the time news of Nobunaga's murder reached them, the advance guard of the Akechi army was already in sight of the castle, and there was hardly time to think of what to do. Nene had written a letter to her husband in the far-off western provinces, but it was truly at the last moment. Taking her mother-in-law, she had abandoned the castle and fled, leaving everything behind. All she was able to do was load a packhorse with a change of clothes for her mother-in-law and the presents her husband had received from Nobunaga.

In that situation Nene felt the tragic resolve and the great responsibility of a woman's lot. She was in charge of the castle in Hideyoshi's absence, and she had to serve his aged mother and run the large castle household. She must have wanted with all her heart the happiness of hearing her husband tell her that she had done well. He, however, was far away on the battlefield. Until recently she had lived in the safety of a castle while her husband was on the battlefield, but now, suddenly, there was no distinction between them.

During a war, this situation was no cause for despair, but Nene was pained by the question of where to move Hideyoshi's mother. Even if the castle was abandoned to the enemy, she was certain that Hideyoshi would quickly retake it. But as his wife, if she had allowed her mother-in-law to be injured, she would never have been able to face him again.

"Please just worry about protecting my mother-in-law. Don't think about me. And no matter how much you may regret leaving something behind, don't let yourselves be distracted by possessions." Thus Nene encouraged the women servants and everyone in the household as they moved desperately along the road to the east.

Nagahama was bordered on the west by Lake Biwa, the north was checked by hostile clans, and activity in the direction of the Mino Road was unclear. There was no recourse, then, but to flee toward Mount Ibuki.

When her clan was victorious, the warrior's wife would be filled with happiness. But once her husband had become the loser—or they were driven from his castle as fugitives —the pathetic wife must feel a wretchedness that could not be imagined by a man who worked in the fields or sold his wares in town.

From that day on the members of Hideyoshi's household went hungry, lay down to sleep in the open, and were frightened by the enemy patrols. During the night it was difficult to avoid the dew; during the day their white, bloodied feet pressed on in flight.

Through these difficulties there was one thing they kept in mind: when we're captured by the enemy, we'll show them. That was almost everyone's secret promise. The women were of one mind. The feeling among them was that if the fragrance that drifted from their rouge and the loveliness of their black hair did not project from their hearts on that day, they should be disdained and condemned as nothing but shams to hide their ugliness.

The village was an excellent refuge. Sentries had been posted at a distance, so there was no fear of a surprise attack. As it was midsummer, the bedding and provisions were made to last. Their greatest discomfort was only a matter of isolation. Being so far from human habitation, they had no idea of what was going on.

The messenger should return soon. Nene let her thoughts run toward the western sky. The night before she fled Nagahama she had hastily written a letter to her husband. She had heard nothing from the messenger since then. Perhaps he had fallen into the hands of the Akechi on the way, or had been unable to find their hiding place. She had thought about those possibilities day and night.

More recently she had heard that there had been a battle at Yamazaki. When told about the event, her blood raced to the surface of her skin, flushing her complexion.

"That's very likely. It's just like that boy," Hideyoshi's mother said.

The old lady's hair had turned completely white, and now she sat in the main hall of the Daikichi Temple from the time she rose in the morning to the time she went to bed, hardly moving at all and praying devoutly for her son's victory. No matter how chaotic the world became, she believed absolutely that the child to whom she had given birth would not turn from the Great Way. Even now when she gossiped with Nene, she still fell into her old habit of referring to Hideyoshi as "that boy."

"Let him return victorious, even if it's in exchange for this old body." That was her single day-long prayer. From time to time she would look up with a sigh of relief at the statue of the goddess Kannon.

"Mother, I have a feeling we're going to be receiving good news soon," Nene said one day.

"I've been feeling that myself, but I don't know why," Hideyoshi's mother said.

"I felt it all of a sudden when I looked up at the face of Kannon," Nene said. "Yesterday more than the day before, today more than yesterday, she seems to be smiling at us."

It was on the morning of Hideyoshi's arrival that the two women had been talking in this way.

The setting sun was bringing the shadow of the valley across the village, and the walls of the temple were already colored by twilight. Nene was striking the flint to light the lamps in the dark of the inner sanctuary, while the old lady sat in prayer in front of the statue of Kannon.

Suddenly they heard warriors hurrying outside. Hideyoshi's mother turned around in surprise and Nene went out to the veranda.

"His Lordship is coming!"

The shouts of the sentinels echoed throughout the compound. Every day sentinels went downstream about two leagues to stand watch. They all looked as if they had fallen on their faces after running up to the main gate, but when they saw Nene on the veranda, they started yelling at her from where they were, as though there wasn't enough time to come closer.

"Mother!" Nene shouted out.

"Nene!"

The old lady and her daughter-in-law embraced in tears, hardly aware that their happy voices had become one. The old lady prostrated herself before the image of Kannon. Nene knelt next to her and bowed with all her heart.

"The boy hasn't seen you for a long time. You look a little tired. Go brush your hair."

"Yes, Mother."

Nene quickly retired to her room. She brushed her hair, cupped some water from the bamboo conduit to wash her face, and quickly applied some makeup.

All of the members of the household and the samurai were in front of the gate, lined up according to age and rank to greet Hideyoshi. The faces of both old and young, many of whom were villagers, peeked from between the trees. Their eyes were wide with curiosity about what would happen next. After a short while two warriors running ahead of the others came up to the gate and announced that their lord and his company would arrive soon. When they finished their report to Nene, they joined the line of men at the very end, and everyone became hushed. Every man waited for Hideyoshi to appear in the distance. As she stood in the shadow of the expectant men, Nene's eyes looked strangely opaque.

Very soon thereafter a group of men and horses arrived, and the air was filled with the smell of sweat and dust and the din and bustle of those who had come out to greet their lord. The front gate of the temple was temporarily hidden by the whinnying line of horses and people congratulating the men on their safe arrival.

Hideyoshi was among them. He had ridden the short distance from the village, but dismounted in front of the temple gate. Handing the reins of his horse to an attendant, he looked over at a group of children standing at the end of the line of people at his right.

"There must be a lot of places to play in the mountains," he said. Then he patted the shoulders of the little boys and girls standing nearby. They were all children of his retainers, and their mothers, grandmothers, and grandfathers were there too. Hideyoshi smiled at each one of them as he walked toward the stone steps of the gate.

"Well, well. I see that everyone's safe. I'm relieved." Then he turned to the people on his left, where the warriors of his clan stood silently. Hideyoshi raised his voice a little. "I've come back. I understand the hardships you've suffered in my absence. You had to work very hard."

The warriors standing in line bowed low. Beneath the temple gate at the top of the steps, his main retainers and both young and old members of his immediate family waited to greet him. Hideyoshi merely looked to the right and left, demonstrating his own health with a smile. To his wife, Nene, he gave only a glance, and passed through the temple gate without speaking.

But from that point, the husband was accompanied by the figure of his modest wife. The pages that followed in a crowd and the members of his family either went off to rest as Nene had instructed them or simply saluted him from the veranda, each then disappearing into his own quarters.

In the high-ceilinged main temple, a solitary lamp flickered on a low stand. Next to it sat a single woman with hair as white as a silkworm cocoon, wearing a russet-colored kimono.

She could hear her son's voice as he was led up to the veranda by his wife. Without making a sound, his mother stood up and moved to the edge of the room. Hideyoshi paused beneath the shutter and brushed the dust from his coat. His head, which he had shaved at Amagasaki, was still wrapped in a hood.

Nene came around from behind her husband and spoke in a quiet voice. "Your mother has come out to greet you."

Hideyoshi quickly went up to his mother and prostrated himself. "I've given you so much trouble, Mother. Please forgive me," was all he could say.

The old lady retreated a little on her knees, then repeated her greeting, prostrating herself in front of her son. The etiquette of the occasion required that a greeting be made to the lord of the clan upon his triumphal return; it was the tradition of the warrior class, not a simple, everyday matter between parent and child. But as soon as Hideyoshi saw his mother safe and sound, he was unable to feel anything but affection for his own flesh and blood. Silently he approached his old mother. With modest manners, however, she resisted him.

"You've returned safely. But before you ask about my hardships or well-being, why don't you tell me about Lord Nobunaga's death? And tell me if you've destroyed our hateful enemy, Mitsuhide?"

Hideyoshi unconsciously straightened his collar. His mother continued, "I wonder if you know that what your old mother worried about day after day was not whether you were alive or dead. I worried about whether you would act like the great General Hideyoshi, a retainer of Lord Nobunaga. Even as I wondered about how you would manage after the death of our lord, I heard about your march on Amagasaki and Yamazaki. But after that, we heard nothing."

"I was slow in letting you know."

Her words seemed reserved and spoken without love, but Hideyoshi trembled with happiness, as though his blood were rushing through his entire body. Rather than being soothed by a natural motherly love, he felt that his mother's present admonishment showed a far greater love, and it gave him encouragement for the future.

He then told them in detail of the events that had happened since Nobunaga's death, and of the great deeds he wished to accomplish. He spoke about these things plainly so that his old mother would understand them well.

His mother now shed tears for the first time, and then praised her son. "You did well by destroying the Akechi in only a few days. Lord Nobunaga's soul must feel satisfied, and he should have no regrets about having given you his affection. To tell the truth, I was determined not to let you spend a single night here if you had come before seeing Mitsuhide's head."

"No, and I wouldn't have been able to see you before finishing that matter, so there was nothing I could do but fight on doggedly until two or three days ago."

"Being able to meet you here safely like this must mean that the road you've taken is in harmony with the intentions of the gods and Buddhas. Well…Nene, come over here, too. We should give thanks together."

With that, the old lady turned once again to the statue of Kannon. Until that time, Nene had sat modestly apart from Hideyoshi and his mother. When her mother-in-law requested her presence, however, she quickly got up to walk into the main sanctuary.

After lighting the lantern in the Buddhist shrine, she returned and, for the first time, sat next to her husband. The three of them bowed together in the direction of the faint light. After Hideyoshi raised his head and gazed at the image, the three bowed again. A mortuary tablet bearing Lord Nobunaga's name had been placed in the shrine.

When they had finished, Hideyoshi's mother looked as though a heavy weight had been lifted from their hearts.

"Nene," the old lady called softly. "That boy is fond of a bath. Has it been prepared?"

"Yes. I thought it would be more relaxing for him than anything else, so I'm having one prepared right now."

"It would be good if he could at least wash off the sweat and dirt. In the meantime, I'll go to the kitchen and have them prepare something he likes to eat."

The old lady left the two of them alone.

"Nene."

"Yes?"

"I suspect you went through a lot of hardships this time, too. But even with managing everything else, you kept my mother safe. That was really my only concern as well."

"The wife of a warrior is always ready for difficulties like these, so it didn't seem so bad."

"Really? Then you've understood that there is nothing more satisfying than to look around and see your difficulties behind you."

"When I see that my husband has come home safely, I know just what you mean."

They returned to Nagahama the following day. The morning sun reflected on the white mist. Following the Azusa River, the road grew progressively narrower, and the warriors dismounted and led their horses.

Halfway through the journey, they encountered one of the staff officers from Nagahama who had come to report on the war situation.

"Your letter concerning the punishment of the Akechi was sent to the other clans, and, perhaps due to the speed with which it was notified, the army of Lord Ieyasu has returned to Hamamatsu from Narumi. On the other hand, Lord Katsuie's army, which had come as far as the Omi border, seems now to have halted its advance."

Hideyoshi smiled silently and then almost muttered to himself. "It seems that Lord Ieyasu also felt a little confused this time. Of course it was only an indirect result, but it seems that checking Ieyasu dispersed Mitsuhide's military strength. How chagrined the Tokugawa warriors must be to have gone back without a fight."

Thus, on the twenty-fifth of the month, the day after he safely returned his mother to Nagahama, he departed for Mino.

There had been agitation in Mino, but as soon as his army advanced, the area was subdued. First presenting Nobutaka with the castle at Inabayama, he demonstrated his loyalty toward the clan of his former lord. Then he waited calmly for the conference at Kiyosu, which was to begin on the twenty-seventh of that month.

War of Words

Shibata Katsuie was fifty-two years old that year. As a military commander, he was the veteran of many battles; as a man, he had experienced many vicissitudes on the road of life. He was of a good lineage and had a distinguished career; he commanded a powerful army, and he was blessed with a robust physique. No one doubted that he had been chosen by the times. He himself assumed that this was unquestionably the case. On the fourth day of the Sixth Month, he was encamped at Uozaki in Etchu. The moment he heard the news of the Honno Temple incident, he told himself, What I do now is of the utmost importance, and I must do it well.

For this reason, his actions were delayed. He was that circumspect. His mind, however, hurried to Kyoto like a squall.

He was the most senior Oda retainer and the military governor of the northern provinces. Now, equipped with a lifetime of wisdom and strength, he was gambling his entire career on one move. Abandoning the battlefield in the north, he hastened toward the capital. Though one might say he hastened, in fact it took him several days to leave Etchu, and he spent several days more in his home castle at Kitanosho in Echizen. He himself did not consider his progress to be slow. Once a man like Katsuie moved on such an important mission, everything had to be done according to the rules, and that necessitated a proper prudence and correct timing.

The speed with which he moved his troops seemed remarkable to Katsuie, but by the time his main force reached the border of Echizen and Omi, it was already the fifteenth of the month. It was not until noon on the following day that the rear guard from Kitanosho caught up with him, and the entire army rested their horses at the mountain pass. Looking down onto the plain, they could see that the summer clouds were already high in the sky.

It had been twelve days since Katsuie had heard of Nobunaga's death. It is true that Hideyoshi—who was fighting the Mori in the western provinces—had heard the report from Kyoto one day ahead of Katsuie. But on the fourth of the month Hideyoshi had made peace with the Mori, on the fifth he had departed, on the seventh he had arrived at Himeji, on the ninth he had turned toward Amagasaki, on the thirteenth he had struck down Mitsuhide in the battle at Yamazaki, and by the time Katsuie had reached the borders of Omi, he had already swept the capital clear of the remaining enemy troops.

Certainly the road leading to the capital from Echizen was longer and more difficult than the one leading from Takamatsu, but the difficulties that faced Hideyoshi and those that Katsuie confronted were not of the same order. Katsuie had the clear advantage. In managing his troop movements and in disengaging himself from the battlefield, his circumstances were far easier than Hideyoshi's. Why, then, was he so late? It was simply that Katsuie put prudence and abiding by the rules ahead of speed.

The experience that he had gained by participating in so many battles, and the self-confidence that had come about as a result, had created a shell around his thinking and power of discrimination. Those qualities were actually a hindrance to swift action when national affairs were at a turning point, and they contributed to Katsuie's inability to go beyond conventional tactics and strategies.

The mountain village of Yanagase was full of horses and men. West of it was the direction of the capital. Going east, the army would pass Lake Yogo and enter the road to Nagahama Castle. Katsuie had set up his temporary headquarters in the compound of a small mountain shrine.

Katsuie was extremely sensitive to the temperature, and appeared to be suffering from the intense heat and the climb on that day in particular. When he had had his camp stool set up in the shade of the trees, he had a curtain stretched from tree to tree, and he took off his armor behind it. He then turned his back to his foster son, Katsutoshi, and said, "Wipe off my back, Katsutoshi."

Two pages held large fans and cooled Katsuie's sides. When the sweat dried, his body began to itch.

"Katsutoshi, rub harder. Much harder," he fretted.

The boy was still only fifteen years old. It was rather touching to see him acting with such filial piety in the middle of a march.

Something like a rash covered Katsuie's skin. And Katsuie was not the only one to suffer that summer. Many of the soldiers who were wearing leather and metal armor developed a skin condition that might be called an armor rash, but Katsuie's case was particularly severe.

He told himself that his weakness during the summers was the result of having spent the greater part of the past three years at his post in the northern provinces. But the undeniable truth was that the older he got, the weaker he seemed to become. Katsutoshi rubbed harder, as he had been told, until he drew fatty red blood from Katsuie's skin.

Two messengers arrived. One was Hideyoshi's retainer, the other a retainer of Nobutaka. Each carried a letter from his lord, and together they presented their letters to Katsuie.

Hideyoshi and Nobutaka, both whom were encamped at the Mii Temple in Otsu, had written their letters personally. Both were dated from the fourteenth of the month. Hideyoshi's letter said:

I have today inspected the head of the rebel general, Akechi Mitsuhide. With this, the requiem for our late lord has ended with appropriate results. We wished to announce this quickly to all the Oda retainers residing in the northern provinces and to send a summary immediately. Needless to say, while His Lordship's passing was the cause of unbearable grief for all of us, the rebel general's head has been exposed and the rebel troops exterminated to the last man, all within eleven days of his death. We do not take pride in this, but believe that it will placate our lord's soul in the underworld, if only a little.

Hideyoshi had concluded in his letter that the outcome of the tragedy should be a matter for great rejoicing, but Katsuie did not rejoice in the least. On the contrary, the very opposite emotion appeared on his face even before he had finished reading. In his answer, however, he naturally wrote that nothing could have made him happier than Hideyoshi's news. He also emphasized the fact that his own army had gotten as far as Yanagase.

Contemplating what he knew now from both the reports of the messengers and the contents of the letters, Katsuie felt unsure about what to do next. When the messengers left, he selected a number of young men with stout legs and sent them from Otsu to Kyoto to investigate the real conditions of the area. He seemed to be resolved to stay camped where he was until he knew the full story.

"Is there any reason to think this might be a false report?" Katsuie asked. He was even more surprised than he had been when he received the tragic report about Nobunaga some days before.

If someone were to have faced Mitsuhide's army in a "requiem battle" ahead of Katsuie himself, it should surely have been Nobutaka or Niwa Nagahide, or even one of the Oda retainers in the capital who might have joined forces with Tokugawa Ieyasu, who was, after all, in Sakai at the time. And, in that case, the victory would not have been won in one day and one night. No one in the Oda clan was of a higher rank than Katsuie, and he knew quite well that if he had been there, everyone would have had to look up to him as commander-in-chief in the battle against the Akechi. That would have been a matter of course.

Katsuie never considered Hideyoshi to be as insignificant as he appeared. On the contrary, he knew Hideyoshi quite well and had never made light of his abilities. Nevertheless, it was a mystery to Katsuie how Hideyoshi had been able to leave the western provinces so quickly.

Katsuie's camp was fortified the following day. Roadblocks were set up, and travelers from the capital were stopped by sentries and questioned thoroughly.

Any information was immediately relayed from the various officers to headquarters in the main camp. From the talk that was gathered from the streets, one could no longer doubt both the complete destruction of the Akechi and the fall of Sakamoto Castle. Moreover, according to some travelers, flames and black smoke had been rising in the area of Azuchi that day and the day before, and someone reported that Lord Hideyoshi had led a section of his army toward Nagahama.

The next day Katsuie's mind was no more at peace than before. He was still having trouble deciding what he should do next. He was distraught by shame. He had brought his army from the north this far, and he could not bear to stand aside while Hideyoshi leaped into action.

What was to be done? The natural responsibility of the senior retainer of the Oda clan would have been to attack the Akechi, but that work had been finished by Hideyoshi. Under the present conditions, then, what would be his greatest and most urgent business? And what strategy would he use in the face of Hideyoshi's present upper hand?

Katsuie was obsessed by Hideyoshi. Moreover, his thoughts were strongly dominated by a dislike that bordered on outright hatred. Summoning his senior advisers, he deliberated on the subject until the late hours of the night. On the following day, couriers and secret messengers hurried out in all directions from the staff headquarters. At the same time Katsuie himself addressed a particularly friendly letter directly to Takigawa Kazumasu.

Although he had already sent the messenger from Nobutaka back to his master carrying a special response, he now wrote and sent yet another letter to Nobunaga's son. He selected a senior retainer as the envoy and sent two more clever retainers along with him, indicating the importance of their mission.

As for contacting the other close retainers, two scribes took down Katsuie's words and then spent half a day writing out more than twenty letters. The gist of the letters was that on the first day of the Seventh Month they were to meet in Kiyosu to discuss such important problems as who would be the successor to Nobunaga, and how the former domain of the Akechi was to be divided.

As the initiator of the conference, Katsuie would recover some of his dignity as senior retainer. Certainly it was fully acknowledged that without him such important problems could not be resolved. With this leverage as his "key," Katsuie changed direction and turned toward Kiyosu Castle in Owari.

On the way, from what he heard and from the reports of his scouts, he discovered that many of the surviving Oda retainers had been heading toward Kiyosu before his letters had even been delivered. Samboshi, the son of Nobunaga's heir, Nobutada, was already there, and naturally the common view was that the center of the Oda clan would be moved there too. Katsuie, however, suspected that Hideyoshi had taken a presumptuous lead and had orchestrated this as well.

* * *

Every day Kiyosu Castle presented the extraordinary spectacle of magnificent processions of mounted men going up the hill to the castle gate.

The land from which Nobunaga had begun his life's work was now regarded as the conference ground where the settlement of the clan's affairs would be discussed.

On the surface, the surviving Oda retainers who had gathered claimed that they had come to pay their respects to Samboshi. No one mentioned that he had received Shibata

Katsuie's letters or that he had come at Hideyoshi's invitation.

But everyone knew that a conference would soon begin in the castle. The subject of the conference was also common knowledge. Only the public notice of the day and time needed to be posted. Once the retainers had payed their respects to Samboshi, not one of them would be returning to his home province. Each had a good number of soldiers waiting at their lodgings in the castle town.

The population of the castle town had swollen tremendously, and that, combined with the midsummer heat and the town's small size, created an atmosphere of extraordinary confusion and noise. With horses running furiously through the streets, fights among servants, and frequent outbreaks of fire, there was no time for boredom.

Toward the end of the month Nobunaga's two surviving sons, Nobutaka and Nobuo, and his former generals, including Katsuie and Hideyoshi, arrived.

Only Takigawa Kazumasu had not yet made an appearance. Because of his absence, he was the object of frank and unfavorable criticism in the streets.

"Takigawa was happy enough to accept posts when Lord Nobunaga was alive and was even appointed to the important position of governor-general of eastern Japan, so why is he so late in arriving in this present crisis? It's a shameful display on his part."

There were others even more unabashed in their criticism.

"He's a clever politician, and he is not a man of unshakable loyalty. That's probably why he hasn't stirred yet."

That sort of talk made the rounds of the taverns.

Soon thereafter, criticism concerning Katsuie's lateness in attacking Mitsuhide was also heard here and there. Of course, the various clans residing in Kiyosu heard it as well, and Hideyoshi's retainers quickly brought it to his attention.

"Really? So that's started too? It's criticism of Katsuie, so no one is going to think that the rumors are being spread by Katsuie himself, but to me it looks like an attempt on his part to cause dissension among us—a battle of scheming before the big conference. Well, let them have their little tricks. Takigawa has been won over by Katsuie anyway, so let it be."

Before the conference, each man conjectured about his own future and groped for what was in the others' minds. In the meantime there were the usual unspoken understandings and antagonisms, spreading false rumors, winning over others, splitting the opposition, and every other stratagem.

The communication between Shibata Katsuie and Nobutaka was particularly conspicuous; the one man was of the highest rank among the clan's elders, while the other was the third son of Nobunaga. The intimacy between these two went beyond official business and could not be kept secret.

The general opinion was that Katsuie planned to ignore Nobunaga's second son, Nobuo, and establish Nobutaka as the next heir. They all took it for granted, however, that Nobuo would oppose Nobutaka.

There was little reason to doubt that Nobunaga's successor would naturally be either Nobutaka or Nobuo, the younger brothers of Nobutada, who had died at Nijo Castle at the time of his father's death. Everyone, however, was confused over which one of these two should be supported.

Nobuo and Nobutaka: both were born in the First Month of the first year of Eiroku and were now twenty-four years old. Though it seems strange that they could be born in the same year and still be called older and younger brothers, the explanation is that they had different mothers. Although Nobuo was considered the elder brother and Nobutaka the younger, Nobutaka had actually been born twenty days earlier than Nobuo. It would have been natural, then, for Nobutaka to be called the elder brother, except for the fact that his mother was a woman from a small, obscure clan, and so he was designated Nobunaga's third son while Nobuo was established as the second.

Therefore, while these men were called brothers, the intimacy between true flesh-and-blood relatives was absent. Nobuo's disposition was lethargic and negative, and the only positive feeling he displayed was his constant opposition to Nobutaka, whom he looked down upon as his subordinate "younger brother."

When these two were fairly compared, everyone recognized that Nobutaka had far more the disposition to be Nobunaga's successor. On the battlefield he was much more like a general than was Nobuo; he displayed an ambitious spirit in his everyday words and actions, and, more than anything else, he was not retiring like his brother.

So it was natural that he began to show an aggressive attitude quite suddenly after going to Yamazaki and displaying a dominating presence in Hideyoshi's camp. His willingness to bear the responsibilities of the Oda heir were manifested clearly in his recent words and behavior, and as striking proof of the ambition he was entertaining, after the battle of Yamazaki he began to detest Hideyoshi.

For Nobuo, who had panicked when the Akechi had attacked and whose own army had set fire to Azuchi Castle, Nobutaka had some harsh words.

"If punishments are going to be clearly imposed, they will have to ask him about his responsibility. Nobuo is a fool." Although those sentiments were not spoken publicly, the atmosphere in Kiyosu was tense, and it was certain that someone must have repeated the words to Nobuo. It was a situation in which covert schemes brought out the most repugnant aspects of human nature.

The conference was supposed to begin on the twenty-seventh of the month, but because Takigawa Kazumasu was late in arriving, it was postponed one day after another until finally, on the first day of the Seventh Month, an announcement was circulated to all of the important retainers staying in Kiyosu: "Tomorrow, at the second half of the Hour of the Dragon, everyone should proceed to the castle, there to determine who will be the ruler of the nation. The chairman of this great conference will be Shibata Katsuie."

Nobutaka lent prestige to Katsuie, while Katsuie provided influence for Nobutaka, and they boasted that they would have their own way at this conference. Moreover, when the conference finally opened, it appeared that a great number of men were already leaning in their direction.

All of the many partitions in Kiyosu Castle had been opened that day, no doubt because the sun continued to shine and the heat and stuffiness would otherwise have been unbearable. That action, however, also implied that a certain amount of care was being taken not to allow private conversations. Almost all the guards inside the castle were retainers of Shibata Katsuie.

By the Hour of the Snake, all of the lords were seated in the great hall.

Their seating arrangements were as follows:

Katsuie and Takigawa sat on the right, facing Hideyoshi and Niwa on the left. Lesser retainers, such as Shonyu, Hosokawa, Tsutsui, Gamo, and Hachiya, were seated behind them. At the very front in the seats of highest rank were Nobutaka and Nobuo. But from the side, Hasegawa Tamba could be seen holding a small boy.

That was, of course, Samboshi.

Waiting modestly beside them was Maeda Geni, the retainer who had received Nobutada's last order when the latter was about to die in the battle at Nijo Castle. Apparently he did not feel it an honor to be the only survivor present.

Samboshi was only two years old, and as his guardian held him on his lap directly in front of the assembled lords, he could barely keep still. He stretched out his hand and pushed Tamba's chin and then stood up in his lap.

To help the perplexed Tamba, Geni tried to humor the child by whispering something from behind; at that, Samboshi reached over Tamba's shoulder and pulled Geni's ear. Bewildered, Geni did not protest, and once again the wet nurse who had been kneeling behind them placed a folded paper crane into Samboshi's hand. Geni's ear was saved.

The eyes of all the assembled generals fixed on the innocent child. Some showed a faint smile, while others shed silent tears. Only Katsuie looked out over the great hall with a sullen face. He appeared as though he would have liked to mutter something about a "nuisance."

As the chairman of the conference and as the dignified and solemn spokesman, he should have begun the proceedings by speaking first. Nevertheless, now everyone was distracted and he had lost the opportunity to speak. He seemed to be almost unbearably distraught at his own vain efforts.

At length Katsuie opened his mouth and said, "Lord Hideyoshi."

Hideyoshi looked straight at him.

Katsuie forced a smile. "What shall we do?" he asked, exactly as though he were opening negotiations. "Lord Samboshi is an innocent child. Being confined to his guardian's knee must be trying for him."

"That could be so," Hideyoshi said in a noncommittal tone.

Katsuie must have thought that Hideyoshi was becoming conciliatory, and he quickly mustered a confrontational attitude. Antipathy mixed with dignity stiffened his entire frame, and he now displayed an expression that showed his extreme displeasure.

"Well, Lord Hideyoshi. Are you not the person who requested Lord Samboshi's presence? I really have no idea, but—"

"You're not mistaken. I'm the one who advocated it of necessity."

"Of necessity?"

Katsuie smoothed the wrinkles from his kimono. It was still before noon so the heat was not too oppressive, but because of the thickness of his garments and his skin condition, he seemed to be very uncomfortable. Such a thing might seem trivial, but it influenced the tone of his voice and gave him a grim expression.

Katsuie's view of Hideyoshi underwent a change after Yanagase. Until that time, he had thought of Hideyoshi as his junior, and was of the opinion that their relationship had not been a particularly good one. But the battle of Yamazaki had been a turning point.

727

Hideyoshi's name was now being mentioned every day with rising authority in connection with the work left undone after the death of Nobunaga. It was unbearable for Katsuie to observe this phenomenon passively. And his feelings were compounded by his reaction to Hideyoshi's having fought the requiem battle for Nobunaga.

That Hideyoshi was viewed on equal terms with him caused Katsuie the greatest unhappiness. He could not bear to have his many years as an elder of the Oda clan overlooked because of this man's few meritorious deeds. Why should Shibata Katsuie be put into a lower position than someone who was now wearing a kimono and headdress so proudly, but who in the old days in Kiyosu was nothing more than a menial risen up from moat cleaner and dung sweeper? Today, Katsuie's breast was like a tightly strung bow, pulled taut by innumerable emotions and strategies.

"I don't know how you're thinking about today's conference, Lord Hideyoshi, but generally the lords seated here are all bearing firmly in mind that it is the first time the Oda clan has met like this to discuss such important matters. Why *must* we have a two-year-old child here?" Katsuie asked bluntly.

Both his speech and his conduct seemed to be asking for a sympathetic response not only from Hideyoshi but from all the great lords there. When he realized that he was not going to get a clear answer from Hideyoshi, he continued in the same tone of voice.

"We have no time to dally. Why don't we ask the young lord to retire before we begin this conference? Do you agree, Lord Hideyoshi?"

Hideyoshi looked undistinguished, even in a formal kimono. There was no mistaking his humble origins when he appeared among the others.

As for his rank, he had been given a number of important titles when Nobunaga was alive. He had fully demonstrated his real strength both during the western campaign and in his victory at Yamazaki.

But meeting Hideyoshi face to face, you might doubt whether you would side with him in those dangerous times and risk your life for him.

There were men who, at a glance, seemed to be quite impressive. Takigawa Kazumasu, for example, had a stately bearing that no one would deny belonged to a first-rate general. Niwa Nagahide possessed an elegant simplicity and, with his receding hair, he appeared to be a stalwart warrior. Gamo Ujisato was the youngest, but with the respectability of his family line and the nobility of his character, he seemed to possess a strong moral sense. In composure and dignity, Ikeda Shonyu was even less imposing than Hideyoshi, but there was a certain light that shone from his eyes. And there was Hosokawa Fujitaka, who appeared so upright and gentle, but whose maturity made him inscrutable.

So although Hideyoshi's appearance was ordinary, he looked downright shabby when he sat with those men. The men who gathered for the conference that day in Kiyosu were of the foremost rank among their contemporaries. Maeda Inuchiyo and Sassa Narimasa had not attended because they were still fighting in the northern campaign. And, although he was a special case, if Tokugawa Ieyasu's name were added, it might be said that the men in Kiyosu that day were the leaders of the country. And Hideyoshi was among them, regardless of his appearance.

Hideyoshi himself realized the greatness of his colleagues' rank, and he was discreet and humble. His arrogance after the victory at the battle of Yamazaki was nowhere to be seen. From the beginning he was extremely serious. Even in response to Katsuie's words, he was respectfully reserved. But now it seemed that he could no longer avoid a response to Katsuie's persistent request.

"No, what you're saying is quite reasonable. There is a reason for Lord Samboshi to attend this conference, but because he's still of such an innocent age, and the conference promises to be a long one, he's certain to feel cramped. If it is your wish, lord, let's ask him to withdraw right away." Answering Katsuie with such moderate language, Hideyoshi turned a little and asked the guardian to withdraw.

The man nodded and, taking Samboshi up from his lap, put him into the hands of the wet nurse behind him. Samboshi appeared to be very pleased with the great crowd of fully attired men and strongly rejected the wet nurse's hand. When she held on to him anyway and stood up to go, he suddenly swung his arms and legs and broke out crying. He then threw the folded paper crane into the midst of the seated lords.

Tears suddenly came to every man's eyes.

The clock struck noon. The tension in the great hall was tangible.

Katsuie made the opening address. "The tragic death of Lord Nobunaga has caused us great sadness, but we must now choose a worthy successor to continue his work. We must serve him in death as we did in life. This is the Way of the Samurai."

Katsuie questioned the men about the succession. He sought proposals from those present again and again, but no one would be the first to come forward and express his private opinion. Even if anyone had been rash enough to express his own thoughts on that occasion, if by any chance the man he supported as the Oda successor was not chosen in the final selection, his life would have been in certain danger.

No one was going to open his mouth indiscreetly, and they all sat in complete silence. Katsuie patiently let the group's silent modesty pass for exactly that. Perhaps he had foreseen this course of events. Deliberately he took on a dignified tone and spoke. "If none of you has any particular opinion, for the present I will offer my own humble opinion as senior retainer."

At that moment, a sudden change of complexion appeared on the face of Nobutaka, who was seated in the place of honor. Katsuie looked at Hideyoshi, who in turn was looking back and forth from Takigawa to Nobutaka.

Those subtle movements set up unseen waves from mind to mind for just an instant. Kiyosu Castle was filled with a silent tension, almost as though it were devoid of human beings.

Finally Katsuie spoke. "It is my view that Lord Nobutaka is of the appropriate age, and has the natural ability and lineage to be the successor to our lord. Lord Nobutaka is my choice."

It was a very well-put statement that came close to being a proclamation. Katsuie thought that he had already taken control.

But then someone spoke up. "No, that's not right." It was Hideyoshi. "In terms of lineage," he went on, "the correct succession is from Nobunaga's eldest son, Lord Nobutada, to his son, Lord Samboshi. The province has its laws and the clan has its household regulations."

Katsuie's face flushed darkly. "Ah, wait a moment, Lord Hideyoshi."

729

"No," Hideyoshi continued, "you're going to say that Lord Samboshi is still an infant. But if the entire clan—beginning with you yourself, my lord, and all the other retainers and generals—is here to protect him, there should be no discontent. Our devotion should have nothing to do with age. As for me, I believe that if the succession is to be correctly followed, Lord Samboshi must be the heir."

Taken aback, Katsuie took a handkerchief from his kimono and wiped the sweat from his neck. What Hideyoshi was asserting was indeed the law of the Oda clan. It could not be taken as opposition simply for opposition's sake.

The other man who had great consternation written on his face was Nobuo. As Nobutaka's main rival, he had formally been proclaimed elder brother, and his mother had been of excellent lineage. There was no doubt that he, too, had secret expectations of being named successor to his father.

As his anticipation had been implicitly denied, his mean-spiritedness quickly became manifest, and he looked as though he could not stand to be there any longer.

Nobutaka, on the other hand, glared at Hideyoshi.

Katsuie could say nothing either positive or negative, but only mumbled to himself. No one else expressed an opinion of either approval or disapproval.

Katsuie had exposed his true colors, and Hideyoshi had spoken just as frankly. The opinions of the two men were completely opposed and, having been so clearly stated to be so, siding with either one was going to be a serious matter. Utter silence encased everyone like a thick crust.

"As for the succession...well, yes. But this is different from what it might be in times of peace. Lord Nobunaga's work is still only half done, with many difficulties remaining. Even more than when he was in this world."

Katsuie repeatedly called for his colleagues to speak, and every time he opened his mouth—almost groaning—Takigawa would nod. But it appeared that it was still difficult to see through the minds of the others.

Hideyoshi spoke up once again. "If Lord Nobutada's wife were only just pregnant now, and we were waiting for the umbilical cord to be cut to verify whether the child was a boy or girl, a conference like this would be necessary. But we have a suitable heir, so where is the need for dissent or discussion? I think we should immediately decide upon Lord Samboshi."

He persisted in this position, not even glancing at the faces of the other men. It was primarily an objection aimed at Katsuie.

Although the positions of the other generals were not voiced outright, they seemed to be moved by Hideyoshi's opinions and to agree with him in their hearts. Just before the conference, the generals had seen the helpless figure of Nobutada's orphaned son, and every one of them had children in his own household. They were samurai, a calling in which a man might be alive today but could never know about tomorrow. As each one of them looked at the pitiful figure of Samboshi, he could not help but be deeply touched.

That sentiment was backed by a noble and sound argument. Even though the generals held their own silence, it was natural that they were moved by Hideyoshi's assertion.

In contrast, while Katsuie's argument sounded reasonable to a certain degree, it was weak at its foundation. It was really based on expediency, and it stripped Nobuo of his status. It was far more likely that Nobuo would stand aside to support Samboshi than that he would do so to back the succession of Nobutaka.

Katsuie struggled to find an argument to use against Hideyoshi. He had not thought that Hideyoshi would easily agree with his own proposal at today's conference, but he had not estimated how vigorously the man would insist on backing Samboshi. Nor had he foreseen that so many of the other generals would lean toward supporting the child.

"Hm, well now, let me see. Your words may seem logical by the force of argument, but there is a great difference between taking charge of a two-year-old lord and looking up to a man who has both proper age and military ability. Remember that we remaining retainers must shoulder the responsibility both for the morale of the administration and for the long-range policies for the future. There are also a number of difficulties with the Mori and the Uesugi. What's going to happen if we have an infant lord? Our former lord's work could be stopped halfway, and left as it is, the Oda clan's domain could actually diminish. No, if we choose a defensive attitude, our enemies on all four sides will think that their opportunity has come and will invade. Then the country will sink into chaos once again. No, I think your idea is dangerous. What do you think, all of you?"

Looking around at the men seated in the hall, his eyes searched out supporters. Not only was there no clear response from anywhere, but suddenly another eye caught his own.

"Katsuie."

A voice called his name, exhibiting an opposing force that might as well be cutting him from the side.

"Well, Nagahide, what is it?" Katsuie shot back a reply filled with disgust, almost as a reflex action.

"I've listened to your prudent thoughtfulness for some time now, but I can't help being persuaded by Hideyoshi's argument. I'm fully in agreement with what Hideyoshi says."

Niwa had the rank of elder. With Niwa breaking the silence and clearly placing his banner in Hideyoshi's camp, Katsuie and everyone attending the conference suddenly became agitated.

"Why do you say that, Niwa?"

Niwa had known Katsuie for years, and knew him well. Thus, he spoke soothingly. "Don't be angry, Katsuie." Looking at Katsuie with a kindly expression, he went on, "Regardless of what might be said, wasn't it Hideyoshi who most pleased our lord? And when Lord Nobunaga met his untimely death, it was Hideyoshi who returned from the west to attack the immoral Mitsuhide."

Katsuie's face was smeared with his own wretchedness. But he would not be broken, and his obstinacy was manifest right in his physical body.

Niwa Nagahide went on, "At that time you were involved in the campaign in the north. Even if the troops under your command had not been ready but you had whipped your horses to the capital as soon as you heard of Lord Nobunaga's death, you might have crushed the Akechi on the spot—your status is so much higher than Hideyoshi's, after all. Because of your negligence, however, you were simply late, and that was certainly regrettable."

That opinion was in the breast of every man there, and Niwa's words expressed their innermost feelings. That negligence was Katsuie's weakest point. The single factor of having arrived late and not participated in the battle for their late lord could not be excused in any way. After Niwa had brought it out into the open, he unreservedly gave his own approval to Hideyoshi's proposal, saying that it was both just and proper.

When Niwa finished speaking, the atmosphere in the great hall had changed. It was now filled with gloom.

As if to help Katsuie in his crisis, Takigawa quickly took the opportunity to whisper to the man next to him, and soon sighs and low voices filled the room.

A resolution was going to be difficult. It could be a turning point for the Oda clan. On the surface, it was never anything more than the noise of individual voices, but beneath the uproar there was great anxiety concerning the outcome of the confrontation between Katsuie and Hideyoshi.

In the midst of the oppressive atmosphere, a tea master came in and quietly informed Katsuie that it was now past noon. Nodding to the man, Katsuie ordered him to bring him something to wipe the sweat from his body. When one of the attendants gave him a damp white cloth, he grabbed it in his large hand and wiped the sweat from his neck.

Just at that time, Hideyoshi put his left hand to his side. Grimacing with knitted brows, he turned to Katsuie and said, "You'll have to excuse me for a moment, Lord Katsuie. I seem to have a sudden case of indigestion."

Suddenly he stood up and retired several rooms away from the conference hall.

"It hurts," he complained loudly, disconcerting the men around him.

Looking very ill, he lay down. Apparently in full control of himself, however, he placed the cushion to face the cool breeze wafting in from the garden, turned his back to the others, and loosened his sweat-soaked collar by himself.

But the doctor and the attendants were alarmed. His retainers also came in anxiously, one after another, to look in on him.

But Hideyoshi never even looked around. With his back still turned to them, he waved them away as he might a fly.

"This happens all the time. Just leave me in peace, and I'll be better soon."

The attendants quickly prepared a sweet-smelling decoction for him, which Hideyoshi drank in one gulp. Then he lay down again and seemed to fall asleep, so his attendants and samurai withdrew to the next room.

The conference hall was some distance away, so Hideyoshi did not know what happened after he had excused himself. He had left just as the attendants were repeatedly announcing the noon hour, however, so his departure had most likely given the generals the opportunity to adjourn for lunch.

About two hours passed. During that time, the afternoon sun of the Seventh Month shone relentlessly. The castle was as peaceful as though nothing were happening at all.

Niwa came into the room and asked, "How are you feeling, Hideyoshi? Has your stomach settled down?"

Hideyoshi turned and propped himself up on one elbow. Seeing Niwa's face, he seemed to quickly regain consciousness and sat up straight. "My goodness, excuse me!"

"Katsuie asked me to come and fetch you."

"What about the conference?"

"It cannot resume without you. Katsuie said we would continue after you came back."

"I have said all I had to say."

"After an hour's rest in their rooms, the retainers' mood seems to have changed. Even Katsuie has had second thoughts."

"Let's go."

Hideyoshi stood up. Niwa smiled, but an unsmiling Hideyoshi was already leaving the room.

Katsuie greeted him with a direct look in the eye, while the men gathered there seemed somehow relieved. The atmosphere of the conference hall had changed. Katsuie stated positively that he had given in and accepted Hideyoshi's proposal. A measure had been agreed upon establishing Samboshi as Nobunaga's heir.

With Katsuie's conciliation, the entire conference hall was swept clean of the ominous clouds in an instant. A blending spirit of peace was beginning to arise.

"Everyone agreed that Lord Samboshi should be regarded as the head of the Oda clan, and I have no objection." Katsuie repeated. Seeing that his own view had been rejected by everyone, Katsuie had quickly withdrawn his previous remarks but had barely survived his disappointment.

There was, however, one hope he still held.

It had to do with the next item to be discussed by the conference: the fate of the former Akechi domain—or, in other words, the problem of how the domain would be divided up between the surviving Oda retainers.

Because it was a substantial problem directly affecting the interests of all the generals, it was a difficulty—even more so than the problem of succession—that no one expected to be able to avoid.

"This matter should be decided upon by the senior retainers." Hideyoshi, who had obtained the first victory, expressed his modest opinion, and it greatly smoothed the progress of the conference.

"Well, what are the thoughts of our most senior retainer?"

Niwa, Takigawa, and the others now saved the crushed Katsuie from disgrace, giving him the central position in the conference.

The presence of Hideyoshi, however, was difficult to deny, and the draft proposal was eventually sent to him as well. Apparently it could not be finished without first asking his opinion.

"Bring me a brush," he ordered. Dipping the brush in the ink, he artlessly drew a line through three or four clauses and wrote in his own opinions. With this revision, he sent it back.

Once again it was sent to Katsuie, and Katsuie looked displeased. He thought silently for some time; the clause containing his own hopes was still wet with the ink that had been drawn across it. Hideyoshi, however, had also inked a line through the section allotting himself Sakamoto Castle, which he had replaced by the province of Tamba.

Exhibiting a lack of selfishness, he was proposing that Katsuie exhibit the same quality. Finally, a good portion of the Akechi domain was allotted to Nobuo and Nobutaka, and the rest was assigned as allotments to men according to their merits at the battle of Yamazaki.

"There will be more business tomorrow," Katsuie began. "And with this long conference taking place in such heat, I'm sure you're all tired. I certainly am. Shall we adjourn, my lords?"

Katsuie finally refused to make a quick reply to Hideyoshi's new proposals. There was no objection to that. The afternoon sun was shining brightly, and the heat was becoming more and more severe. The first day was finished.

On the following day Katsuie presented the senior retainers with a compromise. The night before he had gathered his own retainers, and they had put their heads together in a discussion at their lodgings. Hideyoshi, however, turned down the new proposal as well.

On that day again the clause containing the allotments came between the two men and opposition between them seemed to be intensifying. The general trend, however, was already supporting Hideyoshi. No matter how Katsuie persevered, Hideyoshi's conditions were followed in the end.

At noon there was a break, and at the Hour of the Ram the decisions were presented to all the generals.

The territory being distributed was the Akechi's confiscated land as well as Nobunaga's personal domain.

The first on the list for the division of the Oda provinces was Lord Nobuo, who received the entire province of Owari, followed by Lord Nobutaka, who was given Mino. One was the cradle of the Oda clan; the other, Nobunaga's second home.

There were two clauses, however, that added a good bit more to the original proposal: Ikeda Shonyu was given Osaka, Amagasaki, and Hyogo, which were worth one hundred twenty thousand bushels; Niwa Nagahide received Wakasa and two districts of Omi. Hideyoshi received the province of Tamba.

Katsuie's only grant was Hideyoshi's own castle of Nagahama. It was the strategic bottleneck on the road leading from Katsuie's home province of Echizen to Kyoto. Katsuie had requested the province forcibly and had hoped for three or four other districts, but Hideyoshi had scratched out all other grants. Hideyoshi's only condition was that Nagahama would be given to Katsutoyo, Katsuie's adopted son.

The night before, the retainers of the Shibata clan had surrounded Katsuie and advocated a protest against such a humiliating share. They even encouraged him to reject the conditions and leave, and Katsuie was of the same mind right up to the time of his arrival on the second day of the conference. When he faced the men seated there, however, it was evident that the general trend was not to accept what he alone was demanding.

"It wouldn't be right to humble myself, but I shouldn't be viewed as selfish, either. A majority are going to approve of these articles anyway, so if I don't show sympathy for them, it might get worse later on."

In view of the opinions of those seated at the conference, he could naturally do nothing more than restrain himself.

If I can only take the strategic area of Nagahama from Hideyoshi, he thought. In the end, he hoped to realize his secret intentions on another day, and accepted the conditions as they were.

In contrast to Katsuie's vacillation, Hideyoshi's attitude seemed to be one of unconcern. From the time of the campaign in the western provinces to the victory at Yamazaki, Hideyoshi had taken the leadership in both military and administrative policies, and people naturally thought he would expect to receive more than the others. Despite those notions, however, what he did receive was nothing more than the province of Tamba. He gave up his domain of Nagahama and granted Sakamoto—which everyone would have thought it proper for him to take—to Niwa.

And Sakamoto was the key to Kyoto. Did he purposely not take Sakamoto, hoping to indicate that he had no desire to take the reins of the government? Or did he simply feel that he should leave such small matters up to the opinions of the group, because it would fall into the right person's hands? Nobody understood yet what was in his heart.

MIDNIGHT WARNING

The conference had finally agreed that the province for Nobunaga's heir, Samboshi, would be three hundred thousand bushels in Omi. The protectors of the young lord were to be Hasegawa Tamba and Maeda Geni, but they were to be assisted by Hideyoshi. Azuchi had been lost to the flames, and until a new castle could be built, Samboshi's residence would be Gifu Castle.

Samboshi's two uncles, Nobuo and Nobutaka, were to act as his guardians. In addition to these articles, there was the matter of the structure of the administration. It would be the responsibility of Katsuie, Hideyoshi, Niwa, and Shonyu to send generals to Kyoto as representatives of the Oda.

The proposals were quickly decided upon. At a closing ceremony, pledges of loyalty to the new lord were signed and sworn to in front of the altar to Nobunaga.

It was the third day of the Seventh Month. The ceremony marking the first anniversary of Nobunaga's death should have been held the day before. If the conference had gone smoothly, the ceremony might have been conducted on the day itself, but because of Katsuie's reservations, the night had passed by and the memorial service had been postponed until the following day.

Wiping the sweat from their bodies and changing into mourning dress, the generals waited for the appointed hour for the memorial service in the castle's chapel.

The hum of mosquitoes was thick around the eaves, and a thin new moon hung in the sky. Quietly the generals crossed over to the secondary citadel. Red and white lotuses were depicted on the sliding doors of the chapel. One by one the men came in and sat down.

Only Hideyoshi did not appear. Eyes were strained in doubt. But as the generals looked in the direction of the faraway altar, among the austere articles such as the shrine, the mortuary tablet, the golden screen, the offertory flowers, and the incense burner, they could see Hideyoshi sitting coolly and smugly beneath the altar, holding the young Samboshi on his lap.

Each one of them wondered what he was doing. When they thought it over, however, they remembered that it had been the judgment of the majority at the conference that afternoon that Hideyoshi would be recognized as an aide to the young lord, along with his two guardians. On those grounds he could not be accused of being presumptuous.

And, simply because he could not find any reason to censure Hideyoshi, Katsuie looked extremely displeased.

"Please go up to the altar in the proper order," Katsuie growled at Nobuo and Nobutaka, twisting his chin. His voice was low, but it was boiling over with vexation.

"Pardon me, please," Nobuo said to Nobutaka, and stood up first.

Now it was Nobutaka's turn to look displeased. He seemed to feel that being placed behind Nobuo in front of the assembled generals would place him in a subordinate position in the future.

Nobuo faced his father's mortuary tablet, closed his eyes, and put his hands together in prayer. Offering incense, he prayed once again in front of the shrine and then withdrew.

Seeing that the man was about to return directly to his own seat, Hideyoshi cleared his throat once as if to bring attention to the child, Samboshi, who was sitting on his lap. Without actually saying "Your new lord is over here!" he attracted Nobuo's attention.

Nobuo seemed almost startled at Hideyoshi's deliberate gesture, and hurriedly turned in their direction on his knees. He was by nature a weak man, and his alarm seemed almost pitiful.

Looking up at Samboshi, Nobuo bowed reverently. In fact, he was too polite.

It was not the young lord who nodded his approval; it was Hideyoshi. Samboshi was a fretful, spoiled child, but for some reason, seated on Hideyoshi's lap, he was as quiescent as a little doll.

When Nobutaka stood up, he likewise prayed in front of the soul of his father. But having witnessed Nobuo's precedent and apparently not wanting to be laughed at by the other generals, he bowed reverently toward Samboshi with a truly correct demeanor. He then went back to his seat.

The next was Shibata Katsuie. When his large frame knelt before the shrine, almost hiding it from view, both the red and white lotuses on the partitions and the flickering lamps tinted his figure in what seemed like red flames of wrath. Perhaps he was giving Nobunaga's soul a lengthy report on the conference and pledging his support for his new lord. But with the offering of incense, Katsuie remained a long time in silent prayer with his palms pressed solemnly together. Then, withdrawing about seven paces, he straightened his back and turned in the direction of Samboshi.

Since Nobuo and Nobutaka had already bowed reverently to Samboshi, Katsuie could not very well be negligent in that regard. Very likely feeling that it was unavoidable, he swallowed his pride and bowed.

Hideyoshi looked as though he were nodding in approval of Katsuie as well. Katsuie jerked his short, thick neck to the side and returned with a rustle to his own seat.

After that, he looked angry enough to spit.

Niwa, Takigawa, Shonyu, Hachiya, Hosokawa, Gamo, Tsutsui, and the other generals paid their respects. Then they moved to the banquet room used for such affairs and, at the invitation of Nobutada's widow, settled down to a meal. The tables were set for more than forty guests. The cups were passed around, and the lamps flickered in the cool night breeze. As the men made themselves comfortable with pleasant words for the first time in two days, each was feeling a little drunk.

The banquet that evening was a bit unusual in that it was given after a memorial service, and so no one got very drunk. Nevertheless, as the *sake* began to be felt, the generals left their seats to talk to others, and laughter and animated conversations could be heard here and there.

A particularly large number of cups and men gathered in front of Hideyoshi. And then one more man stepped into the crowd.

"How about a cup?" asked Sakuma Genba.

Genba's matchless valor in the battles in the north had been highly praised, and it was said that no enemy ever encountered him twice. Katsuie's love for the man was extraordinary. He was fond of describing him as "my Genba," or "*my* nephew." In his pride he spoke publicly and freely about Genba's martial virtues.

Katsuie had a great number of nephews, but when he said "my nephew," he meant Genba alone.

Even though Genba was only twenty-eight years old, he held Oyama Castle as a general of the Shibata clan and had received a province and rank hardly inferior to the great generals gathered in the banquet room.

"Say, Hideyoshi," Katsuie said. "Give a cup to that nephew of mine, too."

Hideyoshi looked around as though he had just noticed Genba.

"Nephew?" Hideyoshi said, studying the younger man. "Ah, you." Certainly, he did appear to be the hero everyone talked about, and his sturdy frame overshadowed the short-statured, frail-looking Hideyoshi.

Genba did not, however, have his uncle's pockmarked face. He was fair-skinned but robust, and at a glance seemed to have the brows of a tiger and the body of a leopard.

Hideyoshi presented the man with a cup. "It's understandable that Lord Katsuie has such fine young men in his clan. Here, have a cup."

But Genba shook his head. "If I'm going to receive a cup, I'd like that big one."

The cup in question still contained some *sake.*

Hideyoshi artlessly emptied it out and called, "Somebody come serve him."

The mouth of the gold-lacquered flask touched the edge of the vermilion cup, and even though the bottle was quickly emptied, the cup itself was not yet full. Someone brought in another flask, and the cup was finally filled to the brim.

The handsome young hero narrowed his eyes, raised the cup to his lips, and drank it dry in one gulp.

"Well then. What about you?"

"I haven't got that kind of talent," Hideyoshi said, smiling.

At Hideyoshi's refusal to drink, Genba pressed harder.

"Why won't you drink?"

"I'm not a strong drinker."

"What! Just this little bit."

"I drink, but not a lot."

Genba roared with laughter. Then he said, loudly enough so that everyone would hear, "The rumors that you hear are certainly true. Lord Hideyoshi is good at making excuses, and he's certainly modest. A long time ago—over twenty years—he was an underling sweeping up horse droppings and carrying Lord Nobunaga's sandals. It's admirable of him not to have forgotten those days."

He laughed at his own effrontery. The others must have been startled. The chattering stopped suddenly, and everyone looked back and forth from Hideyoshi, who was still sitting across from Genba, to Katsuie.

In an instant, everyone forgot about his cup and suddenly sobered up. Hideyoshi only smiled as he looked at Genba. His forty-five-year-old eyes simply gazed at the youth of twenty-eight. Their dissimilarity was not just a matter of a difference of age. The life Hideyoshi had lived the first twenty-eight years after his birth and the path Genba had followed for his twenty-eight years were extremely different in terms of both environment and experience. Genba might have been considered as just a little boy who knew nothing of hardships in the real world. For this reason he had a reputation for arrogance as well as for bravery. And apparently he was a man who did not employ caution in a place that was more dangerous than any battlefield—a room in which the leading men of the day were gathered.

"But, Hideyoshi, there is just one thing I can't stand. No, listen, Hideyoshi. Do you have ears to hear?" At that point he was yelling at Hideyoshi disrespectfully. It appeared to be less a matter of being drunk than of something eating at him from inside. Hideyoshi, however, looked at his drunken state and spoke to him almost with affection.

"You're drunk," he said.

"What!" Genba shook his head violently and straightened his posture. "This is no small problem to be written off to drunkenness. Listen. Just a little while ago in the chapel, when Lord Nobuo and Lord Nobutaka and all the other generals came to do reverence to the soul of Lord Nobunaga, didn't you sit in the seat of honor with Lord Samboshi on your lap and make them bow in your direction, one after another?"

"Well, well," Hideyoshi said, laughing.

"What are you laughing about? Is something funny, Hideyoshi? I don't doubt that your shrewd design was to hold up Lord Samboshi as an ornament for your own insignificant self so that you could receive the bows of the Oda family and its generals. Yes, that's it. And if I had been present, I would have had the pleasure of pulling your head right off. Lord Katsuie and the distinguished men sitting here are so good-natured that I get impatient, and—"

At that moment Katsuie, who was sitting about two seats away from Hideyoshi, drained his cup and looked around at the other men. "Genba, what do you mean by talking in such a way about another man? No, Lord Hideyoshi, my nephew is not speaking out of malice. So just ignore him," he said, laughing.

Hideyoshi was unable to show his anger and unable to laugh. He had been placed in a predicament in which he could only force a subtle smile, but his own particular appearance was well fitted for such situations.

"Lord Katsuie, don't let this upset you. It's all right," Hideyoshi said ambiguously. He was clearly pretending to be drunk.

"Don't pretend, Monkey. Hey, Monkey!" Tonight Genba was acting even more arrogantly than usual. "'Monkey!' Now that was a slip, but it's not so easy to change a name that was commonly used for twenty years. That's right, it's that 'Monkey' that comes to mind. A long time ago, he was the monkeylike underling being chased around and around from job to job in Kiyosu Castle. At that time, my uncle occasionally served on night duty. I heard that one night when he was bored, he invited Monkey over and gave him *sake,* and when my uncle got tired from drink he lay down. Then, when he asked Monkey to come over and massage his legs, the tactful Monkey happily did so."

All the men present had lost their pleasant feelings of intoxication. Each man's face turned pale while his mouth went sour. This was not a simple situation. It was very likely that beyond the walls not so far removed from the banquet, in the shadows of the trees and under the floors, were swords, spears, and bows hidden by the Shibata. Were they not persistently trying to provoke Hideyoshi? A weird sensation, shared by everyone, began to grow out of the feelings of distrust, and that sensation rode the inklike evening breeze and the shadows of the lamps that flickered throughout the hall. It was the middle of the summer, but every man felt a chill along his spine.

Hideyoshi waited until Genba had finished and then laughed out loud.

"No, Lord Nephew, I wonder from whom you heard that. You've reminded me of a pleasant memory. Twenty years ago, this old monkey had the reputation of being good at massage, and the entire Oda clan had me rub them down. Lord Katsuie's legs were not the only ones to get massaged. And then, when I was given some sweets in reward, how good they tasted! That makes me nostalgic now, nostalgic for the taste of those sweets." Hideyoshi laughed again.

"Did you hear that, Uncle?" Genba asked grandiosely. "Give something nice to Hideyoshi. If you ask him to massage your legs now, he might even do it."

"Don't go too far in this game, Nephew. Listen, Lord Hideyoshi, he's just being playful."

"That's all right. Why, even now I still occasionally massage a certain person's legs."

"And who would that be?" Genba asked with a sneer.

"My mother. She's seventy years old this year, and massaging her legs is a unique pleasure for me. Since I've been on the battlefield for so many years, however, I haven't had that pleasure at all recently. Well, I'll take my leave now, but the rest of you stay as long as you like."

Hideyoshi was the first to leave the banquet. As he left and walked down the main corridor, no one got up to stop him. On the contrary, the other lords thought it wise of him to have left, and were all relieved of the sensation of intense danger they had felt.

Two pages suddenly came out of the room near the entrance where they had been stationed, and followed after him. They had been able to perceive the atmosphere that had pervaded the castle for two days, even from their room. But Hideyoshi had not permitted a large number of his retainers to enter the castle, so when the two pages saw that their lord was safe, their minds were set at ease.

They had already stepped outside and were summoning the attendants and horses when a voice called out from behind.

"Lord Hideyoshi! Lord Hideyoshi!"

Someone was looking for him in the dark, open field. A crescent moon floated in the sky.

"I'm over here."

Hideyoshi was already mounted. Recognizing the sound of a slap against the seat of a saddle, Takigawa Kazumasu ran over to him.

"What is it?" Hideyoshi asked with a glance of the same sort that a lord might give to his retainer.

Takigawa said, "You must have gotten very angry this evening. But it was only because of the *sake*. And Lord Katsuie's nephew is still young, as you can see. I hope you'll forgive him." Then he added, "This is something that was arranged beforehand, and you may have forgotten about it, but on the fourth—tomorrow—the celebration announcing Lord Samboshi's succession will be held, and you should be sure not to miss it. Lord Katsuie was very concerned about this after you left just now."

"Is that so? Well…"

"Be sure to be there."

"I understand."

"And again, about tonight. Please forget about it. I told Lord Katsuie that you were a big-hearted person and not likely to be offended by the jests of a drunken young man on one occasion."

Hideyoshi's horse had started to move. "Let's go!" he shouted to the pages, almost knocking Takigawa to the ground.

Hideyoshi's lodgings were in the western section of town. They consisted of a small Zen temple and a wealthy family's house that he was renting. Quartering his men and horses at the temple, he himself occupied a floor of the house.

It had been easy for the family to accommodate him, but he had been accompanied by seven or eight hundred retainers. That was actually not very many men, however, as the Shibata clan, it was rumored, had quartered approximately ten thousand of its soldiers in Kiyosu.

As soon as Hideyoshi returned to his lodgings, he complained that it was smoky inside. Ordering the windows to be opened, he almost kicked off his ceremonial robes with the paulownia crest. Then he quickly stripped naked and requested a bath.

Thinking that his lord was in a bad mood, the page warily poured a pail of hot water over Hideyoshi's back. Hideyoshi, however, yawned as he sank into the tub. Then, as if he were stretching his arms and legs, he let out a grunt. "I'm loosening up a little," he observed, then grumbled about the stiffness of the last two days. "Has the mosquito netting been put up?"

"We've already put it up, my lord," responded the pages who were holding his sleeping kimono.

"Fine, fine. All of you should turn in early too. And tell that to the men on guard as well," Hideyoshi said from inside the mosquito netting.

The door was closed, but the windows were open to let in the breeze, and the light from the moon seemed almost to be quivering. Hideyoshi began to feel drowsy.

"My lord?" called a voice from outside.

"What is it? Is that Mosuke?"

"Yes, my lord. The Abbot Arima is here. He says he'd like to see you in private."

"What, Arima?"

"I told him that you had gone to sleep early, but he insisted."

For a moment no answer came from inside the mosquito netting. Finally Hideyoshi said, "Show him in. But give him my apologies for not getting up, and tell him that I was indisposed at the castle and took some medicine."

Mosuke's footsteps quietly descended the steps from the mezzanine. Then someone could be heard climbing the steps, and very soon a man was kneeling in front of Hideyoshi on the wooden floor.

"Your attendants told me you were asleep, but..."

"Your Reverence?"

"I have something of great urgency to tell you, so I ventured to come over in the middle of the night."

"With two days of conferences, I've become both mentally and physically exhausted. But what brings you here in the middle of the night?"

The abbot spoke softly. "Are you planning to attend the banquet for Lord Samboshi at the castle tomorrow?"

"Well, I might be able to if I take some medicine. My malady could just be heatstroke, and people will be annoyed if I'm not there."

"Perhaps your being indisposed is a premonition."

"Well now, why do you say that?"

"Some hours ago, you withdrew about halfway through the banquet. Soon after that, only the Shibata and their allies remained, and they were very intently discussing something in secret. I didn't understand what was going on, but Maeda Geni was anxious about the situation too, and we secretly listened in on them."

Suddenly becoming silent, the abbot peeped inside the mosquito netting as if to make sure that Hideyoshi was listening.

A pale blue bug was chirping at the corner of the netting, and Hideyoshi was lying down as before, looking up at the ceiling.

"Go ahead."

"We don't know in detail what they plan to do, but what we're sure of is that they are not going to let you live. Tomorrow when you go up to the castle, they want to take you into a room, confront you with a list of your crimes, and force you to commit *seppuku*. If you refuse, they plan to kill you in cold blood. Furthermore, they are planning to station soldiers in the castle and even take control of the castle town."

"Well now, that's rather intimidating."

"In fact, Geni was anxious to come here and inform you himself, but we were afraid that his leaving the castle would be noticed, so I came here instead. If you are sick just at this moment, it must be heaven's protection. Perhaps you should reconsider attending tomorrow's ceremony."

"I wonder what I should do."

"I hope you won't be attending. By any means!"

"It's a celebration for the accession of the young lord, and all are supposed to attend. I'm grateful for your good intentions, Your Reverence. Thank you very much."

Inside the mosquito netting, Hideyoshi pressed his palms together in prayer toward the retreating footsteps of the abbot.

Hideyoshi was very good at sleeping. To fall asleep immediately, wherever the thought occurs to one, may seem like an easy ability to acquire, but it is, in fact, quite difficult.

He had acquired this mysterious skill—so close to enlightenment—out of of necessity, and he had formulated it into as a sort of motto to follow, both to alleviate the pressure of the battlefield and to preserve his own health.

Detachment. For Hideyoshi, that simple word was a talisman.

Detachment might not seem to be a very impressive quality, but it was at the heart of his skill at sleeping. Impatience, delusion, attachment, doubt, urgency—every kind of bond was cut through in an instant with his two eyelids, and he slept with a mind as blank as a virgin sheet of paper. And conversely, he would wake up in a moment, completely alert.

But detachment was not only for when he fought cleverly and his plans went as he intended. Over the years he had made many blunders, but during those times he never brooded over his failures and lost battles. On such occasions he recalled that one word: detachment.

The kind of earnestness people often spoke of—sustained determination and perseverance, or singleminded concentration—was not a special quality for him, but rather a natural part of daily life. Thus for him, it was far more essential to aim toward that detachment that would allow him to remove himself from those qualities—even if just for a moment—and allow his soul to breathe. In turn, he naturally left the problems of life and death up to that one concept: detachment.

He had been lying down just a short time. Had he slept an hour?

Hideyoshi got up and went down the stairs to the toilet. Immediately, a man on duty was kneeling on the floored veranda, holding up a paper lantern. Very soon thereafter, when he stepped from the toilet, another man was holding a small dipper filled with water, and, drawing near, he poured the water over Hideyoshi's hands.

As Hideyoshi wiped his hands, he gazed at the position of the moon over the eaves, then turned to his two pages and asked, "Is Gonbei there?"

When the man he had asked for appeared, Hideyoshi started back toward the stairs to the second floor, looking back at Gonbei as he walked.

"Go to the temple and tell the men we're leaving. The division of soldiers and the streets by which to advance were all written down this evening when we left the castle and given to Asano Yahei, so get instructions from him."

"Yes, my lord."

"Wait a moment. I forgot about something. Tell Kumohachi to come see me."

Gonbei's footsteps went from the stand of trees behind the house off in the direction of the temple. After he had left, Hideyoshi quickly dressed in his armor and went out.

Hideyoshi's lodgings stood near the crossroads of the Ise and Mino roads. He passed by the corner of the store house and walked off in the direction of that crossroads.

At that moment Kumohachi, who had just received Hideyoshi's summons, ran tottering up from behind. "I'm here and at your service!" He came around and knelt in front of Hideyoshi.

Kumohachi was an old warrior of seventy-five years, but he was not easily bested even by younger men, and Hideyoshi saw that he had come with his armor already on.

"Well now, this is not a matter that necessitates armor. I'd like you to do something in the morning. I want you to stay behind."

"In the morning? You mean at the castle?"

"That's right. You've understood well, typical of your years of service. I want you to go with a message to the castle that I fell ill during the night and suddenly had to return to Nagahama. Also say that I deeply regret not being able to attend the ceremony, but that I hope everything will be well. I imagine that Katsuie and Takigawa will dwell on that for a while, so I want you to wait there, appearing to be senile and hard of hearing. Don't react to anything you hear, and then leave as though nothing had happened."

"I understand, my lord."

The old warrior was bent at the waist like a shrimp, but his spear never left his hand. Bowing once before standing up, he turned his body as though his armor weighed heavily upon him, and shuffled off.

Almost all of the men at the temple had already lined up on the road in front of the gate. Each corps, which was identified by its banner, was in turn divided into companies. The commanders readied their horses at the head of each unit.

The fires on the fuse cords flickered back and forth, but not a single torch was lit.

The moon in the sky was only a slender crescent. Along the row of trees, the seven hundred troops swayed silently in the dark, like waves on a shore.

"Hey! Yahei!" Hideyoshi called out as he walked along next to the line of officers and men. The men were not easily distinguishable in the shadows of the trees, and here was a short man beating a bamboo staff on the ground as he walked along with six or seven men following behind. Most of the soldiers probably thought he was the head of a group of packers, but when they realized it was Hideyoshi, they became even more hushed, pulling their horses back so they would not get in the way.

"Here I am! Over here!"

Asano Yahei had been at the base of the stone steps giving instructions to a group of men. When he heard Hideyoshi's voice, he finished up quickly and ran over to him.

"Are you ready?" Hideyoshi spoke to him impatiently, hardly giving him time to kneel. "If you're all set, move out."

"Yes, my lord, we're ready."

Taking charge of the commander's standard with the golden gourds that had been propped up in a corner of the gate, he carried it out into the middle of the ranks and quickly mounted his own horse to join the troops.

Hideyoshi rode out, accompanied by his pages and about thirty mounted men. The conch shell might have been blown at that moment, but circumstances prohibited the use of the conch or of torches. Yahei had received the golden fan of command from Hideyoshi and, in his stead, waved it once, twice, and then a third time. With that signal, the seven-hundred-man army began gradually to advance.

The head of the procession then changed direction and, turning on the road, passed by Hideyoshi. The position of corps commander was filled exclusively by trusted retainers. That one saw almost none of the faces of the old and experienced veterans was most likely because many of them had been left at Hideyoshi's castles in Nagahama and Himeji, and at his other estates.

At midnight, Hideyoshi's soldiers left the castle at Kiyosu, looking as though they were the main force accompanying their lord. Taking the Mino road, they started out for Nagahama.

Hideyoshi himself departed immediately afterward with no more than thirty or forty men. He took a completely different route and hurried along the back roads where no one would notice him. He finally arrived in Nagahama the following day at dawn.

* * *

"We slipped up, Genba," Katsuie said.

"No, it was a plan that really had no room for mistakes."

"Do you really think there is such a plan? Somewhere there was an oversight, and that's why the fish slipped out of the net so easily."

"Well, it's not that I didn't say anything about it. If you're going to strike, strike! If we had attacked that scum's quarters, we'd have been able to look at Hideyoshi's head by now. But all you could talk about was doing it in secret. Now all our efforts have come to nothing because you wouldn't listen to me."

"Ah, you're still young. You were asking me to use a flawed plan, and the plan I had devised was superior. The best strategy was to wait until Hideyoshi came up to the castle and force him to disembowel himself. Nothing could have been better than that. But according to the reports last night, Hideyoshi was suddenly striking camp. Now, at first, I thought that was unfortunate, but then I reconsidered. If that bastard was leaving Kiyosu at night, it was a gift from heaven—because he was leaving unannounced, I could have denounced his crimes. I instructed you to lie in ambush and strike him down on the way so that justice might be served."

"That was a careless mistake on your part, Uncle, from the very beginning."

"My mistake? Why?"

"Your first mistake was in thinking Monkey would play into our hands by coming to today's celebration. Then, although you instructed me to go with some soldiers to ambush him, your second mistake was in forgetting to take the precaution of ordering men to guard the backroads."

"Fool! I gave you the orders and had the other generals follow your instructions solely because I had faith that you would not overlook things like that. And you have the impudence to say that hiding soldiers only on the main road and letting Hideyoshi slip through is my fault! You should reflect a little on your own inexperience!"

"Well, I apologize for my error this time, but hereafter, Uncle, please refrain from rattling on with too much artifice. A person who gets carried away with his own clever schemes is going to drown in them someday."

"What are you saying? You think I use too much cunning?"

"It's your constant habit."

"You...you fool!"

"It's not just me, Uncle. Everybody says so. 'Lord Katsuie makes people cautious, because no one can never tell what he is plotting.'"

Katsuie was silent, knitting his thick black eyebrows.

For a long time, the relationship of uncle and nephew had been far warmer than that between lord and retainer. But too much familiarity had eroded authority and respect in the relationship, and those qualities were now missing. That morning Katsuie could hardly restrain the sullen look on his face.

It was a complicated sense of displeasure. He had not slept at all the night before. Having ordered Genba to strike down the fleeing Hideyoshi, Katsuie had waited until dawn for the report that would clear the gloom that filled his heart.

When Genba returned, however, he did not make the report Katsuie had been waiting for so tensely.

"The only people who passed by were Hideyoshi's retainers. Hideyoshi himself was nowhere to be seen. I thought it would be disadvantageous to attack them, so I came back with nothing to show for my efforts."

That report, added to Katsuie's fatigue from the night before, put him in a state of true despondency.

Then, when even Genba found fault with him, there was little wonder that he was feeling depressed that morning.

He could not remain in such a mood, however. Today was the celebration of the announcement of Samboshi's succession. After his breakfast Katsuie took a nap and had a bath, then he once again arrayed himself in his sweltering ceremonial robes and headgear.

Katsuie was not the kind of man who, once depressed, remained visibly so. Today the sky was filled with clouds and it was even more humid than the day before, but his demeanor on the road to Kiyosu Castle was far more majestic than that of anyone else in the castle town, and his face sparkled with sweat.

The fierce men who only the night before had fastened the cords of their helmets, crawled through the grass and bushes with their spears and firearms, and looked to take Hideyoshi's life on the road were now arrayed in court hats and ceremonial kimonos. Their bows were in their cases and their spears and halberds sheathed, and they now meandered in innocent-looking attire up to the castle.

The men who climbed to the castle were not from the Shibata clan alone, of course, but were also from the Niwa, the Takigawa, and other clans. The only men who had been there the day before but who were no longer present were those under the command of Hideyoshi.

Takigawa Kazumasu informed Katsuie that Kumohachi had been waiting in the castle since early morning, as a representative of Hideyoshi.

"He said Hideyoshi would not be able to attend today because of illness and was sending his apologies to Lord Samboshi. He also mentioned that he had hoped for an audience with you, my lord. He's been waiting for a little while."

Katsuie nodded bitterly. While it angered him that Hideyoshi was scrupulously feigning ignorance of the whole affair, he too had to pretend to know nothing, and now granted an audience to Kumohachi. Katsuie then cantankerously asked one question after another. What kind of illness did Hideyoshi have? If he had decided to return home so suddenly the night before, why hadn't he informed Katsuie? If he had, Katsuie himself would have come to visit and taken care of all the arrangements. But it seemed that old Kumohachi had grown extremely deaf and was only able to hear about half of what Katsuie was saying.

And no matter what was being said, the old man appeared not understand, but repeated the same answer over and over. Feeling that the interview was as useless as beating the air, Katsuie could not help but be vexed at Hideyoshi's ulterior motives in sending such a senile old warrior as a formal envoy. No matter how much he rebuked the old man, nothing came of it. With pent-up anger from his irritation, he asked Kumohachi one more question to finish the conversation.

"Envoy, how old are you, anyway?"

"Exactly...yes, indeed."

"I'm asking you about your age....How old are you?"

"Yes, it's just as you say."

"What?"

Katsuie felt as though he were being made a fool of. Thrusting his angry face next to Kumohachi's ear, he yelled out in a voice loud enough to crack a mirror.

"How old are you this year?"

Thereupon Kumohachi nodded vigorously and answered with exceeding calm.

"Ah, I see. You're asking me my age. I'm ashamed to say that I've done nothing of merit that the world might have heard of, but this year I'll be seventy-five."

Katsuie was dumbfounded.

How ridiculous it was for him to be losing his temper with this old man, with today's pressure of work in front of him and the probability that he would be unable to relax all day. Along with an awareness of self-scorn, Katsuie felt his hostility toward Hideyoshi moving him to make a pledge that the two of them would shortly not exist under the same sky.

"Go on home. That's enough."

Gesturing with his chin, he ordered the old man to leave, but Kumohachi's buttocks seemed to be stuck to the floor with rice paste.

"What? What if there's a reply?" he asked, gazing sedately at Katsuie.

"There is none! No reply at all! Just tell Hideyoshi that we'll meet wherever we chance to meet."

With this parting remark, Katsuie turned and walked away down the narrow corridor toward the inner citadel. Kumohachi also ambled down the corridor. With one hand on his hip, he turned toward Katsuie's retreating image. Chuckling to himself, he finally walked on toward the castle gate.

The celebration for Samboshi's accession was completed that day, and a feast was given that surpassed the one of the evening before. Three halls were opened up inside the castle for the announcement of the new lord's installation, and people attended in far greater numbers than the day before. The main topic of conversation among the guests was Hideyoshi's insulting behavior. To feign illness and be absent on the day of this important event was outrageous, and there were some who said that Hideyoshi's disloyalty and insincerity could clearly be seen.

Katsuie knew quite well that the criticism of Hideyoshi was being artificially generated by the followers of Takigawa Kazumasu and Sakuma Genba, but he indulged in the comfort of gloating secretly over the knowledge that the advantage was going to him.

After the conference, the observance of the anniversary of Nobunaga's death, and the day of celebration, Kiyosu was inundated by heavy rains every day.

Some of the lords left for their provinces the day after the celebration. A number of the others, however, were held back by the rising waters of the Kiso River. Those who remained behind waited for the weather to clear, thinking it might happen the next day or the day after that, but they could really do nothing more than pass the days in inactivity in their lodgings.

To Katsuie, however, the time was not necessarily wasted.

The comings and goings of Katsuie and Nobutaka between their respective lodgings were quite noticeable. It must be remembered that Oichi, Katsuie's wife, was Nobunaga's younger sister and therefore Nobutaka's aunt. Moreover, it was Nobutaka who had persuaded Oichi to remarry and become Katsuie's wife. It was really from the time of the marriage that the relationship between Nobutaka and Katsuie had become intimate. Certainly they were more than simple in-laws.

Takigawa Kazumasu was at those meetings as well, and his presence seemed to have some significance.

On the tenth day of the month Takigawa sent out an invitation for a morning tea ceremony to all the remaining lords.

The gist of the invitation was as follows:

The recent rains are clearing, and each of you is thinking of returning to his home province. It is a maxim among warriors, however, that uncertainty governs the time of their next meeting. As we remember our former lord, I would like to offer you a bowl of plain tea in the morning dew. I know you must be in a hurry to leave for home after this long stay, but I do anticipate your presence.

That was all it said, and it was nothing more than what might be expected. But the people of Kiyosu gaped at the men going in and out that morning.

What was it? A secret council of war? Men like Hachiya, Tsutsui, Kanamori, and Kawajiri attended the tea ceremony that morning, while Nobutaka and Katsuie were probably the guests of honor. But whether the meeting was the tea ceremony it purported to be, or some secret affair, could not have been known by anyone other than the host and his guests that day.

Later that afternoon the generals finally returned to their home provinces. On the night of the fourteenth Katsuie announced that he would leave for Echizen, and on the fifteenth he left Kiyosu.

As soon as he had crossed the Kiso River and entered Mino, however, Katsuie was troubled by rumors that Hideyoshi's army had closed all the passes in the mountains between Tarui and Fuwa and was barring his way home.

Katsuie had only just decided that he would attack Hideyoshi, but now the situation had been reversed, and he found the path home as dangerous as thin ice. To get to Echizen Katsuie had to pass Nagahama, and his antagonist had already returned there. Would Hideyoshi let him pass through without challenging him?

When Katsuie had left Kiyosu, his generals had advised him to take a more roundabout route, through Takigawa Kazumasu's province in Ise. But if he had done so, the world would certainly have believed he was afraid of Hideyoshi—a loss of face that Katsuie would have been unable to bear. As they entered Mino, however, the central question persisted with every step.

Reports of troop movements in the mountains ahead forced Katsuie to halt his army's advance and arrange its units into battle formation until the reports could be verified.

A rumor was then reported that units under Hideyoshi's command had been sighted in the area of Fuwa, and as Katsuie and his field staff sat on their horses, their hair stood on end. Trying to imagine the numbers and strategy of the enemy waiting in their path, they were overcome by feelings as black as ink.

The troops were brought to a sudden halt in front of the Ibi River, while Katsuie and his staff quickly discussed the matter in the wood of the local village shrine. Should they strike on ahead, or retreat? One possible strategy would be to retreat for the present and take possession of Kiyosu and Samboshi. They could then denounce Hideyoshi's crimes, unite the other lords, and set out in a more imposing manner. On the other hand, they had a large force, and it would give them joy as a samurai to fight their way through, routing the enemy with a quick victory.

As they thought over the possible results of each alternative, they realized that the former plan would mean a protracted war, while the latter would bring a prompt decision. As for that, however, instead of crushing Hideyoshi with one quick blow, their own defeat was not entirely out of the question.

Certainly the mountainous terrain north of Sekigahara was very advantageous for men lying in ambush. In addition, the troops that Hideyoshi had withdrawn to Nagahama would no longer be the small force of the recent past. From southern Omi to the areas of Fuwa and Yoro, a large number of men from small castles, powerful provincial families, and scattered samurai residences had connections with Hideyoshi. Those with connections to the Shibata were few.

"No matter how I think this through, there just doesn't seem to be a good strategy for confronting Hideyoshi here. His quick return home must have been planned exactly to take this kind of advantage. I think we should not risk the battle he wants under these conditions," Katsuie said, echoing the advice of his generals.

Genba, however, laughed scornfully. "That's probably the right course of action if you're resolved to become a laughingstock for being so afraid of Hideyoshi." In any war council, the suggestion to retreat is the weak one, while the counsel to advance is considered more forceful. Genba's opinion in particular exerted a strong influence on the members of the field staff. His matchless courage, his rank within the clan, and the affection with which he was regarded by Katsuie were all factors to be taken into consideration.

"To flee at the sight of the enemy, without exchanging a single arrow, would ruin the reputation of the Shibata clan," one general said.

"It would be a different matter if we had made such a decision before leaving Kiyosu."

"It's just as Lord Genba says. If people hear that we came this far and then retreated, we'll become a laughingstock for generations to come."

"How about retreating after fighting an engagement?"

"They're only Monkey's soldiers, anyway."

The younger warriors all shouted out their support of Genba.

The only man who remained silent was Menju Shosuke.

"What do you think, Shosuke?"

Katsuie rarely asked Shosuke for his opinion. Recently, Shosuke had been out of favor with Katsuie, and he usually refrained from speaking. He answered docilely, "I think Genba's opinion is absolutely correct."

Among the others, who were all hot-blooded and ready to fight, Shosuke had appeared to be as cold as water and lacking in courage in spite of his youth. But he had responded as if there were no alternative.

"If even Shosuke can speak like this, we'll follow Genba's advice and push straight on through, just as we are. But we should send out scouts as soon as we've crossed the river, and not hurry down the road carelessly. Move out plenty of foot soldiers first, and have a spear corps follow them immediately. Place the gunners ahead of the rear guard. When soldiers are lying in ambush, firearms are not apt to be of much use up front. If the enemy is there and the scouts give us the signal, sound the drum immediately, but don't show them a hair's-breadth of confusion. The unit commanders should all wait for my orders."

Its direction settled, the army crossed the Ibi River. Nothing happened. As it began to advance toward Akasaka, there was no sign of the enemy.

The reconnaissance units were far ahead and approaching the neighborhood of the village of Tarui. Nothing unusual could be discerned there, either.

A lone traveler approached. He looked suspicious, and one of the soldiers from the reconnaissance unit ran up ahead and took him into custody. Threatened and questioned by the scouts, the man was quick to talk, but it was those who did the threatening who were dismayed.

"If you're asking me if I saw Lord Hideyoshi's men on the road, well, yes, I most certainly did. Early this morning, in the area of Fuwa, and just now passing through Tarui."

"About how many men were there?"

"I'm not sure, but certainly it was a force of several hundred."

"Several hundred?"

The scouts looked back and forth at each other. Dismissing the man, they immediately reported back to Katsuie.

The news was rather unexpected. The enemy was such a small force that Katsuie and his generals now had even more misgivings. However, the order to push ahead was given, and the army marched on. Just at that moment it was reported that an envoy from Hideyoshi was riding in their direction. When the man finally came in sight, they could see that he was not an armored warrior but was, instead, a striking youth wearing a printed gossamer silk coat and a wisteria-colored kimono. Even the reins of his horse were ornately decorated.

"My name is Iki Hanshichiro," the youth announced, "Lord Hidekatsu's page. I am here to offer my services as a guide to Lord Katsuie."

Hanshichiro trotted right past the scouts, who were completely taken aback. Yelling in a confused voice, their commander chased after him, nearly falling off his horse in pursuit.

Katsuie and his field staff looked with suspicion at the young man. They had anticipated a battle, and their excitement and anticipation of a fight had soared. Then, in the midst of their spears and burning fuse cords, this elegant young man gracefully dismounted and bowed politely.

"Lord Hidekatsu's page? I have no idea what that means, but bring him here. Let's talk with him," Katsuie ordered.

Katsuie had stamped down the grass by the roadside and was standing in the shade of some trees. Having his camp stool set down, he managed to conceal the rigid tension of his subordinates, as well as his own. He invited the envoy to sit down.

"You have a message?"

"You must be exhausted from the long trip home in this heat," Hanshichiro said formally.

Oddly, his words sounded exactly like those of a peacetime greeting. Taking a letter box that was hanging from his shoulder by a red cord, he continued, "Lord Hideyoshi sends his greetings." Then he handed the missive to Katsuie.

Katsuie received the letter suspiciously and did not open it right away. Blinking, he looked at Hanshichiro.

"You say you're Lord Hidekatsu's page?"

"Yes, my lord."

"Is Lord Hidekatsu in good health?"

"Yes, my lord."

"I imagine he's grown up."

"He'll be seventeen years old this year, my lord."

"Well, he's that old already? Time passes quickly, doesn't it. It's been a long time since I've seen him."

"Today he was ordered by his father to come as far as Tarui to extend a welcome."

"What?" Katsuie stammered. A pebble beneath one leg of his camp stool was crushed by the weight of his heavy body, which equaled the surprise in his heart. Hidekatsu, who was Nobunaga's son, had been adopted by Hideyoshi.

"Welcome? Welcome who?" Katsuie asked this time.

"Why, Your Lordship, of course."

Hanshichiro covered his face with his fan and laughed. His adversary's eyelids and mouth were twitching uncontrollably, so he could hardly suppress a smile.

"Me? He's come to welcome *me*?" Katsuie continued to mumble to himself.

"First take a look at the letter, my lord," Hanshichiro requested.

Katsuie had been in such a daze that he had completely forgotten about the letter in his hand. Katsuie nodded repeatedly for no particular reason. As his eyes followed the written words, a range of emotions swept across his face. The letter was not from Hidekatsu at all, but was unmistakably from Hideyoshi's brush. It was quite openhearted.

The road between northern Omi and Echizen is one you've traveled many times before, so I assume you know the way. Nevertheless, I am sending my foster son, Hidekatsu, to guide you. There is a baseless rumor abroad, unworthy of our notice, that Nagahama would be an advantageous place from which to hinder your return home. In order to contradict such mean-spirited reports, I have sent my foster son to greet you, and you may take him as a hostage until you have passed through with peace of mind. I would have liked to entertain you at Nagahama, but I have been sick since leaving Kiyosu....

Reassured by the words of the envoy and the letter, Katsuie could not help reflecting on his own timidity. He had been cowering before what might have been in Hideyoshi's heart, and now he was relieved. For some time he had been regarded as a clever strategist, and was acknowledged to be so full of intrigue that whenever he did anything, people were quick to say that Katsuie was up to his old tricks again. At moments like these, however, he was not even going to bother to cover up his emotions with a feigned nonchalance. It was that part of his character that the late Nobunaga had understood well. He had considered Katsuie's courage, conspiratorial mind, and honesty to be distinctive features that could be put to good use. Thus he had given Katsuie the heavy responsibility of being commander-in-chief of the northern campaign, had put numerous warriors and a large province into his charge, and had relied upon him fully. Now, when Katsuie thought about the lord who had known him better than anyone else and contemplated the fact that he was no longer in the world, he felt that there was no one in whom he could put his trust.

But now he was suddenly touched by Hideyoshi's letter, and the emotions he had harbored toward his rival were completely reversed in an instant. He now frankly reflected on the fact that their enmity had been based entirely on his own suspicions and timidity.

So Katsuie rethought the situation.

"Now that our lord is gone, Hideyoshi will be the man in whom to put our trust."

That night he talked warmly with Hidekatsu. The following day he crossed Fuwa with the young man and entered Nagahama, still holding on to his new warm impressions.

But in Nagahama, after he and his senior retainers had accompanied Hidekatsu as far as the castle gate, he was shaken once again, when he found out that Hideyoshi had not been in Nagahama for some time. He had gone on to Kyoto, where he had been involved in important state affairs.

"I've been taken in by Hideyoshi again!" Katsuie said, his irritation quickly returning, and he hurried to start out again on the road home.

* * *

It was the end of the Seventh Month. Fulfilling the promise he had made, Hideyoshi surrendered the castle and lands of Nagahama to Katsuie, who gave it to his foster son, Katsutoyo.

Katsuie still did not know why Hideyoshi had insisted at the conference of Kiyosu that the castle be given to Katsutoyo. And neither the men at the conference nor the public at large were suspicious about the condition or even stopped to consider what Hideyoshi had in mind.

Katsuie had another foster son, Katsutoshi, a boy who would be fifteen years old that year. Those members of the Shibata clan who had any feelings about it at all lamented that if the relationship between Katsuie and Katsutoyo was that cold, they could only fear for the future of the clan.

"Katsutoyo is so irresolute," Katsuie complained. "He never does anything with real clarity and decision. He doesn't even have the proper disposition to be my son. Katsutoshi, on the other hand, has no trace of malice in him at all. He's really taken to me as his father."

But if Katsuie preferred Katsutoshi to Katsutoyo, he favored his nephew, Genba, even more. His love for Genba went beyond that felt naturally for a nephew or son, and he had an inclination to indulge the emotion. Thus Katsuie kept a watchful eye on Genba's younger brothers, Yasumasa and Katsumasa, installing each of them in strategic castles while they were still only in their twenties.

In the midst of all that deep affection between family members and retainers, only Katsutoyo felt dissatisfied with his foster father and the Sakuma brothers.

Once, during the New Year's celebrations, for example, when Katsuie's family and retainers had come to congratulate him on the New Year, the first toast was offered by Katsuie. Katsutoyo had naturally assumed that it would be offered to him, and had advanced respectfully on his knees.

"It's not for you, Katsutoyo, it's for Genba," Katsuie said, holding the cup back.

It became known in other quarters that this slight was a matter of discontent for Katsutoyo, and the story was doubtless heard by spies from other provinces. Certainly such information reached Hideyoshi's ears.

Before surrendering Nagahama to Katsutoyo, it was necessary for Hideyoshi to move his own family to a new home.

"We'll be moving to Himeji in just a little while. It's mild in winter, and there's fish from the Inland Sea."

With these orders, Hideyoshi's mother, wife, and the entire household moved to his castle in Harima. But Hideyoshi himself did not go.

There was no time to waste. He had the castle at Takaradera near Kyoto completely renovated. It had been Mitsuhide's stronghold at the time of the battle of Yamazaki, and there was a reason Hideyoshi did not send his mother and wife to live there. He went from Takaradera Castle to the capital on alternate days. When he returned, he supervised construction; when he was absent, he was seeing to the government of the nation.

He was now taking the responsibility upon himself for safeguarding the Imperial Palace, for the administration of the city, and for overseeing the various provinces. According to the original decision of the Kiyosu conference, all phases of the government of Kyoto were to be managed equally by the four regents—Katsuie, Niwa, Shonyu, and Hideyoshi—and were never supposed to be Hideyoshi's responsibility alone. But Katsuie was far away in Echizen, carrying on some secret maneuvers with Nobutaka and others in Gifu and Ise; Niwa, though close by in Sakamoto, seemed already to have given over his responsibility entirely to Hideyoshi; and Shonyu had quite gallantly declared that, although he had been given a title, the problems of dealing with the administration and the nobility were beyond his abilities, and he would have nothing more to do with either.

It was in just these areas that Hideyoshi had true ability. His talents were far more administrative than anything else. Hideyoshi knew that battle was not his main talent. But he understood clearly that if a man held high ideals but was defeated on the battlefield, great administrative works would not go forward. Thus he risked everything on a battle, and once he had started a campaign, he fought to the bitter end.

In rewarding his martial accomplishments, the Imperial Court informed Hideyoshi that he would be given the rank of Lieutenant-General of the Imperial Guard. Hideyoshi declined, protesting that his merits did not deserve such an honor, but the Court graciously insisted, and he finally accepted a lesser title.

How many there are who are quick to find fault when they witness those who do good in the world! How many of the mean-spirited ones talk against those who work with upright hearts!

This is always true, and whenever great changes occur, the flood of gossip is liable to be especially violent.

"Hideyoshi is exposing his arrogance quickly. Even his subordinates are grasping authority."

"They're ignoring Lord Katsuie. It's as though there were no one else to serve."

"When you look at the influence he's gained recently, it's as though they're proclaiming that Lord Hideyoshi is Lord Nobunaga's successor."

The criticism aimed at him was noisy indeed. But, as always in such cases, the identities of the accusers remained unknown.

Whether or not he heard the rumors, Hideyoshi was unconcerned. He had no leisure to listen to gossip. In the Sixth Month, Nobunaga had died; in the middle of that month, the battle had been fought at Yamazaki; in the Seventh Month, the conference at Kiyosu had been held; at the end of that month, Hideyoshi had withdrawn from Nagahama, moving his family to Himeji; and in the Eighth Month, he had begun construction on Takaradera Castle. Now he continued to go back and forth between Kyoto and Yamazaki. If he was in Kyoto, in the morning he would be bowing at the Imperial Palace; in the afternoon he would be inspecting the city, in the evening he would look over governmental matters, send out replies to letters, and greet guests; at midnight he would review letters from distant provinces; and at dawn he would make decisions concerning the petitions of his subordinates. Every day he would whip his horse off somewhere while still chewing the food from his last meal.

He frequently had a number of destinations—the mansion of a court noble, meetings, inspections—and recently he had been heading off repeatedly toward the northern part of Kyoto. It was there that he had ordered an enormous construction project to be started. Within the grounds of the Daitoku Temple, he had begun to build yet another temple, the Sokenin.

"It must be completed by the seventh day of the Tenth Month. Finish clearing the area by the eighth day, and complete preparations for all the ceremonies by the ninth day. There should be nothing left to be done by the tenth day."

This he said very firmly to Hikoemon and to his brother-in-law, Hidenaga. No matter what construction project Hideyoshi undertook, he would not change the time limit.

The memorial service was held within a lamplit shrine that was one hundred eighty-four yards wide. The brightly colored canopy sparkled, the thousands of lanterns looked like stars, and the smoke from the incense drifted among the fluttering banners, creating purple clouds above the heads of the crowds of mourners.

Among the priests alone, venerable scholars from the five major Zen temples and priests from the eight Buddhist sects attended. People of the time who observed the service described it as though the five hundred *arhats* and the three thousand disciples of the Buddha were all before their very eyes.

After the ceremonies of reading from the sutras and scattering flowers before the Buddha had taken place, the Zen abbots paid their respects. Finally, Abbot Soken recited the parting *gatha* and, with all of his strength, yelled "*Kwatz!*" For an instant all was hushed. Then, as the solemn music was played once again, the lotus flowers fell, and one by one the participants offered incense at the altar.

Among the mourners, however, about half of the Oda relatives who undoubtedly should have attended were absent. Samboshi had not appeared, neither had Nobutaka, Katsuie, or Takigawa.

But perhaps most unfathomable of all were the intentions of Tokugawa Ieyasu. After the Honno Temple incident, he was in a unique position. What his thoughts were, or how his cold eyes regarded present events, no one was able to judge.

BOOK NINE

TENTH YEAR OF TENSHO
1582
WINTER

CHARACTERS AND PLACES

FUWA HIKOZO, senior Shibata retainer
KANAMORI GOROHACHI, senior Shibata retainer
SASSA NARIMASA, senior Oda retainer
and ally of Shibata Katsuie
SAKUMA YASUMASA, Genba's brother
MENJU SHOSUKE, Shibata Katsuie's page
YAMAJI SHOGEN, retainer of Shibata Katsutoyo
MAEDA TOSHINAGA, Inuchiyo's son

ECHIZEN, province of the Shibata clan
KITANOSHO, main castle of the Shibata clan
FUCHU, Maeda Toshinaga's castle

THE SNOWS OF ECHIZEN

Day and night, the snow fell on wintry Echizen, leaving no opening through which a man could free his heart. But within the castle walls of Kitanosho, it was warmer than usual that year. That uncommon state of affairs was due to the presence of Lady Oichi and her three daughters. The lady herself was rarely seen, but her daughters could not bear to be confined to their apartments. The eldest, Chacha, was fifteen, the middle sister eleven, and the youngest only nine. To these girls, even falling leaves were a cause for wonder, and their laughter rang through the corridors of the citadel.

Katsuie was drawn by their voices to the women's quarters, where he hoped to forget his many cares amid their gay laughter, but whenever he appeared, the expressions on the faces of the girls darkened, and they neither laughed nor smiled. Even Lady Oichi was solemn and quiet, beautiful and cold.

"Please come in, my lord," she would say, inviting him to sit by the small silver fretwork brazier.

Even after their marriage, they spoke to each other with the formality of a retainer addressing a member of his lord's family.

"Your loneliness must be all the greater when you see the snow and feel the cold of this place for the first time, my lady," Katsuie said sympathetically.

"Not so much, my lord," Oichi replied, but it was clear that she longed for a warmer land. "When do the snows of Echizen begin to melt?" she asked.

"This is not Gifu or Kiyosu. When the rape flowers are blooming and the cherry blossoms are beginning to fall there, these mountains are still patched with melting snow."

"And until then?"

"It's like this every day."

"You mean it never melts?"

"Just snow a thousand feet deep!" Katsuie replied sharply. Upon being reminded of the length of time the snow would cover Echizen, his heart was filled with bitter resentment. Thus he was unable to spend even a moment's leisure with his family.

Katsuie returned to the citadel as quickly as he had left. Accompanied by his pages, he walked off in great strides along the roofed corridor through which the snowy wind was blowing. As soon as he had gone, the three girls went out to the veranda to sing songs, not of Echizen but of their native Owari.

Katsuie did not look back. Before entering the main citadel, he ordered one of his pages, "Tell Gozaemon and Gohei to come to my room at once."

Both men were important retainers of the Shibata clan, and elders upon whom Katsuie relied.

"Did you send a messenger to Maeda Inuchiyo?" Katsuie asked Gozaemon.

"Yes, my lord. He left a little while ago," the man replied. "Did you want to add something to it, my lord?"

Katsuie nodded silently; he seemed to be lost in thought. The previous evening a council of the entire clan had discussed a weighty matter: Hideyoshi. And their decision had not been a passive one. They had the whole winter to carry out a plan: Takigawa Kazumasu was to rally Ise; Nobutaka was to persuade Gamo Ujisato to join them, and to request assistance from Niwa Nagahide; Katsuie himself would write to Tokugawa Ieyasu to sound out his intentions; and a messenger had already been sent to the scheming old shogun, Yoshiaki. Finally, it was hoped that when the moment came, the Mori would attack Hideyoshi from the rear.

That was the plan, but Ieyasu's attitude was totally unclear. And although it was easy to tempt Yoshiaki's inconstancy, there seemed to be little hope of persuading the Mori to unite with their cause. Not only that, but Gamo Ujisato, the man to be drawn in by Nobutaka, was already allied to Hideyoshi, while Niwa stood tactfully in the center, declaring that he could not take sides with any of his former lord's retainers, and that he would only stand in the defense of the rightful heir, Lord Samboshi.

During this time, Hideyoshi was holding in Kyoto the magnificent memorial service for Nobunaga that had attracted the attention of the entire nation. Hideyoshi's increasing fame was making the proud Katsuie think about whether he should act and how fast. But the mountains of Echizen responded to Katsuie's scheming with snow. He planned great campaigns, but he could not move his army to fight them.

During the conference, a letter had arrived from Kazumasu, advising Katsuie that the best strategy was to wait until spring and complete their great undertaking in one campaign. Until then, Kazumasu said, Katsuie was to make peace with Hideyoshi. Katsuie had considered his advice and decided it was the correct way to handle the situation.

"If there is something else you would like to say to Lord Inuchiyo, I will send another messenger," Gozaemon repeated, observing Katsuie's worried expression.

Katsuie confided his doubts to these men. "At the conference I agreed to send two trusted retainers along with Inuchiyo to negotiate peace with Hideyoshi, but now I don't know."

"What do you mean, my lord?" one of the retainers asked.

"I don't know about Inuchiyo."

"Are you worried about his abilities as an envoy?"

"I'm well acquainted with his abilities. But when Hideyoshi was still a foot soldier, they were close friends."

"I don't think you have anything to worry about."

"You don't?"

"Not in the least," Gozaemon declared. "Both Inuchiyo's province in Noto and his son's in Fuchu are surrounded by your own estates and the castles of your retainers. So not only is he geographically isolated from Hideyoshi, but he will have to leave his wife and children as hostages."

Gohei was of the same opinion. "There has never been any discord between the two of you, my lord, and Lord Inuchiyo has served you faithfully throughout the long northern campaign. Many years ago, when he was a young samurai in Kiyosu, Lord Inuchiyo had a reputation for being wild. But he has changed. These days his name is associated with integrity and honesty, and people are quick to acknowledge their faith in him. So, rather than worry, I wonder if he isn't the most suitable man we could send."

Katsuie began to believe that they were right. Now he could laugh, knowing that his own suspicions was nothing more than that. But if the plan did somehow go wrong, the entire situation could quickly turn against Katsuie. Moreover, he was uneasy because his army would be unable to move until the spring. Nobutaka's isolation in Gifu and Takigawa's in Ise troubled him even more. Therefore the envoy's mission was crucial to the success of the entire strategy.

A few days later Inuchiyo arrived at Kitanosho. He would be forty-four that year—a year younger than Hideyoshi. He had been tempered by his years on the battlefield, and even with the loss of one eye, he looked cool and self-possessed.

When he received Katsuie's warm reception, he smiled at its excess. Lady Oichi was also there to greet him, but Inuchiyo said gallantly, "It must be unpleasant for you to be in this cold room with a group of coarse samurai, my lady."

Urged to withdraw, Lady Oichi left for her own apartments. Katsuie mistook this for deference, but Inuchiyo had intended it as a gesture of sympathy for Oichi, in whom he saw Nobunaga, her dead brother.

"You're living up to your old reputation. I've heard you were an old hand at this," Katsuie said.

"You mean *sake*?"

"I mean a *lot* of *sake*."

Inuchiyo laughed heartily, his one eye blinking in the light of the candles. He was still the handsome man Hideyoshi had known in his youth.

"Hideyoshi was never much of a drinker," Katsuie said.

"That's true. His face turned red right away."

"But I recall that when you were young, the two of you often spent the whole night drinking together."

"Yes, as far as debauchery went, that young Monkey never got tired. He was an expert. Whenever I drank too much, I would just fall down and sleep anywhere."

"I imagine you're still close friends."

"Not really. No one is less reliable than a former drinking partner."

"Is that so?"

"Surely you must remember, Lord Katsuie, those days of eating, drinking, and singing until dawn. Friends will put their arms around each other's shoulders, revealing things they wouldn't even talk to their own brothers about. At the time, you think that person is the best friend you ever had, but later you both get involved in the real world and you have a lord or a wife and children. When you both look back at the feelings you had when you were living together in the barracks, you find that they've changed quite a bit. The way you see the world, the eyes with which you look at others—you've grown up. Your friend is not the same, and neither are you. The really true, pure, and devoted friends are the men we meet in the midst of adversity."

"Well then, I've been under the wrong impression."

"What do you mean, my lord?"

"I thought that you and Hideyoshi had a deeper relationship, and I was about to ask you to do me a favor."

"If you're going to fight with Hideyoshi," Inuchiyo said, "I will not raise my spear against him, but if you're going to hold peace talks, I'd like to take it upon myself to be in the vanguard. Or is it something different?"

Inuchiyo had hit the mark. Without saying anything further, he smiled and raised his cup.

How had the plan leaked out to him? Katsuie's eyes showed his confusion. After thinking it over for a moment, however, he realized it had been he himself who had been testing out Inuchiyo on the subject of Hideyoshi from the very beginning.

Even though he was living in the provinces, Inuchiyo was not the kind of man who lived in a corner. Certainly he would know what was going on in Kyoto, and he would have a clear understanding of the trouble between Hideyoshi and Katsuie. Furthermore, Inuchiyo had received Katsuie's urgent summons and come quickly, despite the snow.

As Katsuie reflected on the matter, he had to rethink his view of Inuchiyo, in order to know how to control him. Inuchiyo was a man whose power would grow with the years. Like Sassa Narimasa, he was under Katsuie's command on Nobunaga's orders. During the five years of the northern campaign, Katsuie had treated Inuchiyo like one of his own retainers, and Inuchiyo had obeyed Katsuie. But now that Nobunaga was dead, Katsuie wondered if the relationship would continue unchanged. It came down to this: Katsuie's authority had depended on Nobunaga. With Nobunaga dead, Katsuie was only one general among many.

"I have no desire to fight with Hideyoshi, but I fear that rumor may have it otherwise," Katsuie said with a laugh.

As a man matures, he becomes practiced in a in way of laughing that draws a veil over his true feelings. "It seems strange," Katsuie continued, "to send an envoy to Hideyoshi when we are not at war, but I've received a number of letters from both Lord Nobutaka and Takigawa urging me to send someone. It's been less than six months since Lord Nobunaga died, and already there are rumors that his surviving retainers are fighting among themselves. This is a disgraceful state of affairs. Besides, I don't think we should give the Uesugi, the Hojo, and the Mori the chance they're looking for."

"I understand, my lord," Inuchiyo said.

Katsuie had never been very good at explanations, and Inuchiyo summarily accepted his assignment, as though it were unnecessary to listen to the tedious details. Inuchiyo left Kitanosho on the following day. He was accompanied by two men, Fuwa Hikozo and Kanamori Gorohachi. Both were trusted retainers of the Shibata clan, and while they went along as envoys, they were really there to keep an eye on Inuchiyo.

On the twenty-seventh of the Tenth Month, the three men arrived at Nagahama to collect Katsutoyo. Unfortunately, the young man was ill. The envoys counseled him to stay behind, but Katsutoyo insisted on coming, and the party traveled from Nagahama to Otsu by boat. Spending one night in the capital, they arrived at Takaradera Castle the following day.

This was the battlefield where Mitsuhide had been defeated that past summer. Where before there had been nothing more than a poor village with a decaying post station, now a prosperous castle town was springing up. After the envoys had crossed the Yodo River, they could see scaffolding covering the castle. The road was deeply rutted with the tracks of oxen and horses, and everything they saw spoke of Hideyoshi's energetic plans.

Even Inuchiyo was beginning to question Hideyoshi's intentions. Katsuie, Takigawa, and Nobutaka accused Hideyoshi of neglecting Lord Samboshi and of working for his own advantage. In Kyoto he was building up his power base, while outside of the capital he was expending huge amounts on castle construction. These projects had nothing to do with enemy clans in the west or north, so against whom was he preparing his army in the very heart of the nation?

What had Hideyoshi said in his defense? He, too, had several complaints: There was the unfulfilled promise made at the Kiyosu conference to move Samboshi to Azuchi, and there was the memorial service for Nobunaga that Nobutaka and Katsuie had failed to attend.

The meeting between Hideyoshi and the envoys took place in the partially reconstructed main citadel. A meal and tea were served before the negotiations began. It was the first time Hideyoshi and Inuchiyo had met since the death of Nobunaga.

"Inuchiyo, how old are you now?" Hideyoshi asked.

"I'll be forty-five soon."

"We're both becoming old men."

"What do you mean? I'm still a year younger than you, aren't I?"

"Ah, that's right. Like a little brother—a year younger. But looking at the two of us now, you look the more mature."

"You're the one who looks old for your age."

Hideyoshi shrugged. "I've looked old since my youth. But frankly speaking, no matter how old I get, I still don't feel like much of an adult, and that worries me."

"Someone said that a man should be unwavering after the age of forty."

"It's a lie."

"You think so?"

"A *gentleman* is unwavering—that's how the saying goes. It would be more true in our case that forty is the age of our first wavering. Isn't that pretty much true for you, Inuchiyo?"

763

"You're still playing the fool, Lord Monkey. Don't you agree, gentlemen?"

Inuchiyo smiled at his companions, who had not failed to notice that he was familiar enough with Hideyoshi to call him "Lord Monkey" to his face.

"Somehow I can't agree with either Lord Inuchiyo's opinion or yours, my lord," said Kanamori, who was the oldest of the group.

"How is that?" asked Hideyoshi, who was clearly enjoying the conversation.

"As far as my ancient self goes, I would say that a man is unwavering from the age of fifteen."

"That's a little early, isn't it?"

"Well, look at young men on their first campaign."

"You have a point. Unwavering at the age of fifteen, even more so at nineteen or twenty, but at forty you slowly start to come undone. Well then, what happens at about the time of one's respected old age?"

"When you get to fifty or sixty, you're really confused."

"And at seventy or eighty?"

"Then you start forgetting that you're confused."

They all laughed.

It seemed as though the feasting would last until evening, but Katsutoyo's condition was deteriorating. The conversation changed, and Hideyoshi suggested that they move to another room. A physician was summoned. He immediately gave Katsutoyo some medicine, and everything was done to warm the room in which the talks would be held.

Once the four men were settled, Inuchiyo opened the proceedings. "I believe you have received a letter from Lord Nobutaka, who also counsels peace with Lord Katsuie," Inuchiyo began.

Hideyoshi nodded, apparently eager to listen. Inuchiyo reminded him of their common duty as retainers of Nobunaga, then frankly admitted that it was Hideyoshi who had truly discharged that duty completely. But after that, it appeared that he was out of harmony with the senior retainers, neglecting Lord Samboshi and working for his own advantage. Even if this were untrue, Inuchiyo felt that it was regrettable that Hideyoshi's actions were open to such an interpretation.

He suggested to Hideyoshi that he should look at the situation from the standpoints of Nobutaka and Katsuie. One of them had met with disappointment, while the other now felt ill at ease. Katsuie, who had been called "Jar-Bursting" and "the Demon," had been slow in moving and was a step behind Hideyoshi. Even at the conference in Kiyosu, had not Katsuie deferred to him?

"So won't you end this quarrel?" Inuchiyo asked finally. "It's not really a problem for someone like me, but Lord Nobunaga's family is still embroiled in it. It's unbecoming that his surviving retainers should share the same bed and have different dreams."

The look in Hideyoshi's eyes seemed to change with Inuchiyo's words. Inuchiyo had laid the blame for the quarrel at Hideyoshi's door, and he steeled himself for a violent refutation.

Unexpectedly, Hideyoshi nodded vigorously. "You're absolutely right," he said with a sigh. "I'm really not to blame, and if I were to list my excuses, there would be a mountain of them. But when I look at the situation the way you've explained it, it would appear that

I've gone too far. And in that sense, I've been wrong. Inuchiyo, I leave it in your hands."

The negotiations were concluded on the spot. Hideyoshi had spoken so frankly that the envoys felt somewhat bemused, but Inuchiyo knew Hideyoshi well.

"I'm very grateful to you. Just hearing that has made it worth coming all the way here from the north," he said with great satisfaction.

Fuwa and Kanamori, however, did not show their joy unguardedly. Understanding the reason for their reticence, Inuchiyo went a step further.

"But Lord Hideyoshi, if you have some dissatisfaction you'd like to express about Lord Katsuie, I hope you'll express it frankly. I'm afraid these peace accords won't last long if you're concealing something. I will spare no effort to settle any problem, no matter what it might be."

"That's unnecessary," Hideyoshi said, laughing. "Am I the kind of person who keeps something bottled up inside and remains silent? I've said everything I want to say, to both Lord Nobutaka and Lord Katsuie. I've already sent a long letter that explains everything in detail."

"Yes, the letter was shown to us before we left Kitanosho. Lord Katsuie felt that everything you had written was reasonable and would not have to be brought up again during these peace talks."

"I understand that Lord Nobutaka suggested holding peace talks after reading my letter. Inuchiyo, I was being particularly careful not to upset Lord Katsuie before you came here."

"Well, you know, an elder statesman should be accorded respect in any situation. But I know I've rattled the horns of Demon Shibata from time to time."

"It's difficult to do anything without rattling those horns. Even when we were both young, those horns were strangely scary—especially for me. In fact, the Demon's horns were even scarier than Nobunaga's moods."

"Did you hear that?" Inuchiyo laughed. "Did you hear that, gentlemen?" Both men were drawn into the laughter. To say such things in front of them was hardly speaking ill of their lord behind his back. Rather, they felt it was a shared sentiment they could not deny.

The human mind is a subtle thing. After that moment, Kanamori and Fuwa felt more at ease with Hideyoshi and relaxed their watchfulness of Inuchiyo.

"I think this is indeed a happy event," Kanamori said.

"We really couldn't be happier," Fuwa added. "More than that, I have to thank you for your generosity; we have completed our mission and saved our honor."

The next day, however, Kanamori still had misgivings and said to Fuwa, "If we go back to Echizen and report to our lord without Lord Hideyoshi's having put anything in writing, won't this agreement seem a bit unreliable?"

Before departing that day, the envoys once again went to the castle to meet with Hideyoshi, to pay their respects.

Several attendants and horses were waiting outside the main entrance, and the envoys thought that Hideyoshi must have been receiving guests. But in fact it was Hideyoshi himself who was going out. At that moment he stepped from the main citadel.

"I'm glad you came," he said. "Well, let's go inside." Turning around, Hideyoshi led

765

his guests to a room. "I had a really good laugh last night. Thanks to you, I slept late this morning."

And sure enough, he looked as though he had just gotten up and washed his face. That morning, however, each of the envoys looked somehow different—as though he had woken up inside a different shell.

"You've been much too hospitable in the midst of all your work, but we are returning home today," Kanamori said.

Hideyoshi nodded. "Is that so? Well, please give my regards to Lord Katsuie on your return."

"I'm sure Lord Katsuie will be delighted by the outcome of the peace talks."

"My heart has been lifted just by your coming here as envoys. Now all those people who would like to make us fight will be disappointed."

"But won't you please take your brush and sign a solemn pledge, just to stop up the mouths of such people?" Kanamori entreated.

That was it. That was what had suddenly become essential for the envoys that morning. The peace talks had gone too smoothly, and they had become uneasy with words alone. Even if they reported to Katsuie what had transpired, without some sort of document it was nothing more than a verbal promise.

"All right." The look on Hideyoshi's face showed full agreement. "I'll give one to you, and I'll expect one from Lord Katsuie. But this pledge isn't limited to Lord Katsuie and me. If the names of the other veteran generals are not attached as well, the document will be meaningless. I'll speak to Niwa and Ikeda immediately. That should be all right, shouldn't it?"

Hideyoshi's eyes met Inuchiyo's.

"That should be fine," Inuchiyo answered clearly. His eyes read everything in Hideyoshi's heart—he had seen the future even before leaving Kitanosho. If Inuchiyo could be called a rogue, he was a likable one.

Hideyoshi stood up. "I was just about to leave myself. I'll go with you as far as the castle town."

They left the citadel together.

"I haven't seen Lord Katsutoyo today. Has he already left?" Hideyoshi asked.

"He is still unwell," Fuwa said. "We left him at his lodgings."

They mounted their horses and rode as far as the crossroads in the castle town.

"Where are you off to today, Hideyoshi?" Inuchiyo asked.

"I'm going to Kyoto, as usual."

"Well, we'll separate here then. We still have to return to our lodgings and make our preparations for the journey."

"I'd like to look in on Lord Katsutoyo," Hideyoshi said, "to see if he's improved."

Inuchiyo, Kanamori, and Fuwa returned to Kitanosho on the tenth day of the same month, and immediately reported to Katsuie. Katsuie was overjoyed that his plan to establish a pretense of peace had been carried out more smoothly than he had anticipated.

Soon thereafter Katsuie held a secret meeting with his most trusted retainers and told them, "We'll keep the peace through the winter. As soon as the snows melt, we'll butcher our old enemy with a single blow."

As soon as Katsuie had completed the first stage of his strategy by making peace with Hideyoshi, he dispatched another envoy, this time to Tokugawa Ieyasu. That was at the end of the Eleventh Month.

For the last half year—since the Sixth Month—Ieyasu had been absent from the center of activity. After the Honno Temple incident, the entire nation's attention had been focused on filling the void that had been created when the center had so suddenly collapsed. During that time, when no one had had a moment to look anywhere else, Ieyasu had taken his own independent road.

At the time of Nobunaga's murder, he had been on a sightseeing tour of Sakai and had barely been able to return to his own province with his life. Immediately ordering military preparations, he pushed as far as Narumi. But the motive behind that action was quite different from the one Katsuie had had for crossing over Yanagase from Echizen.

When Ieyasu heard that Hideyoshi had reached Yamazaki, he said, "Our province is entirely at peace." Then he withdrew his army to Hamamatsu.

Ieyasu had never considered himself to be in the same category as Nobunaga's surviving retainers. He was an ally of the Oda clan, while Katsuie and Hideyoshi were Nobunaga's generals. He wondered why he should take part in the struggle among the surviving retainers, why he should fight to pick over the ashes. And there was something far more substantial for him now. For some time he had watched eagerly for a chance at territorial expansion into Kai and Shinano, the two provinces that bordered his own. He had been unable to play his hand while Nobunaga was alive, and there would likely be no better opportunity than now.

The man who foolishly opened up a path toward that goal and who gave Ieyasu a splendid opportunity was Hojo Ujinao, the lord of Sagami, another of the men who took advantage of the Honno Temple incident. Thinking that the time was ripe, a huge Hojo army of fifty thousand men crossed into the former Takeda domain of Kai. It was a large-scale invasion, executed almost as though Ujinao had simply taken a brush and drawn a line across a map, taking possession of what he thought he could.

That action gave Ieyasu a splendid reason to dispatch troops. The force he raised, however, consisted of only eight thousand men. The three-thousand-man vanguard checked a Hojo force of well over ten thousand men before it joined Ieyasu's main force. The war lasted more than ten days. Finally, the Hojo army could do nothing more than make a last stand or—as Ieyasu had hoped for and as it finally did—sue for peace.

"Joshu will be handed to the Hojo, while the two provinces of Kai and Shinano will be awarded to the Tokugawa clan."

That was the agreement to which they came, and it was just as Ieyasu had intended.

* * *

Their packhorses and traveling attire covered with the snow of the northern provinces, Shibata Katsuie's envoys to Kai arrived on the eleventh day of the Twelfth Month. They were first asked to rest in the guest quarters in Kofu. Their party was a large one and was led by two senior Shibata retainers, Shukuya Shichizaemon and Asami Dosei.

For two days they were more or less entertained. Otherwise, however, it seemed that they were being put off.

Ishikawa Kazumasa apologized profusely, telling the party that Ieyasu was still busy with military affairs.

The envoys grumbled at the coolness of their reception. In response to the many gifts of friendship from the Shibata clan, the Tokugawa retainers had simply received a list of the gifts and had given no other recognition at all. On their third day, they were granted an audience with Ieyasu.

It was the middle of a severe winter. Nevertheless, Ieyasu was sitting in a large room without even a hint of a warming fire. He did not look to be a man who had been afflicted by hardships and reverses since his youth. The flesh of his cheeks was plump. His large earlobes gave a certain weight to his entire body, like the rings of an iron teakettle, and caused the visitors to wonder if the man could really be a great general still only forty years old.

If Kanamori had come as an envoy, he would have quickly seen that the phrase "unwavering at the age of forty" applied absolutely to this man.

"Thank you for coming all this way with so many gifts of friendship. Is Lord Katsuie in good health?"

He spoke in an extremely dignified manner, and his voice overwhelmed the others, even though it was soft. His retainers stared at the two envoys, both of whom felt like the representatives of a dependent clan bringing tribute. To relate the message from their lord now would be mortifying. But there was nothing else they could do.

"Lord Katsuie congratulates you on your conquest of the provinces of Kai and Shinano. As a token of his congratulations, he sends these gifts to you."

"Lord Katsuie has sent you here to give me his congratulations at a time when we've been out of contact for so long? My goodness, how polite."

So the envoys set out on the road home with a truly bad aftertaste in their mouths. Ieyasu had not given them any message for Katsuie. It was going to be difficult reporting to Katsuie that Ieyasu had not said a kind word about him, quite apart from reporting the cold treatment they themselves had received.

Particularly galling was the fact that Ieyasu had written no reply to the warm letter Katsuie had sent. In short, it was not simply that their mission had ended in complete failure, but Katsuie seemed to have humbled himself in front of Ieyasu far more than was necessary for his own ends.

The two envoys discussed the situation with some anxiety. Naturally their enemy, Hideyoshi, featured in their somber thoughts, but so did their long-standing foes, the Uesugi. If, added to those dangers, there were the threat of discord between the Shibata and Tokugawa clans... They could only pray that that would not come to pass.

But the speed of change always outruns the imaginary fears of such timid people. At about the time the envoys returned to Kitanosho, the promises made the month before were broken, and just before the year's end, Hideyoshi began to move against northern Omi. At the same time, for unknown reasons Ieyasu suddenly withdrew to Hamamatsu.

It had been about ten days since Inuchiyo had returned to Kitanosho. Katsuie's step-son, Katsutoyo, who had been forced to stay at Takaradera Castle because of illness, had finally recovered and went to take his leave of his host.

"I shall never forget your kindness," Katsutoyo said to Hideyoshi.

Hideyoshi accompanied Katsutoyo as far as Kyoto and took pains to ensure that his return journey to Nagahama Castle was comfortable.

Katsutoyo ranked with the highest in the Shibata clan, but he was shunned by Katsuie and looked down upon by the rest of the clan. Hideyoshi's kind treatment had worked a change in Katsutoyo's attitude to his stepfather's enemy.

For nearly half a month after Hideyoshi had seen off Inuchiyo and then Katsutoyo, he did not seem to be occupying himself with castle construction or events in Kyoto. Rather, he turned his attention to some unseen arena.

At the beginning of the Twelfth Month, Hikoemon—who had been sent to Kiyosu—returned to Hideyoshi's headquarters. With that one move, Hideyoshi departed from the passive and patient period of rest he had gone through since the Kiyosu conference, and for the first time slapped down the stone on the *go* board of national politics, signaling a return to the active mode.

Hikoemon had gone to Kiyosu to persuade Nobuo that his brother Nobutaka's secret maneuvers were more and more threatening and that Katsuie's military preparations were at present quite clear. Nobutaka had not moved Lord Samboshi to Azuchi, in breach of the treaty signed after the Kiyosu conference, but had interned him at his own castle in Gifu. That amounted to kidnapping the legitimate Oda heir.

Hideyoshi's petition went on to explain that in order to bring the affair to an end it would be necessary to strike at Katsuie—the ringleader of the plot and the cause of the instability—while the Shibata were unable to move because of the snow.

Nobuo had been disaffected from the very beginning, and it was obvious that he disliked Katsuie. Certainly he did not believe he could rely on Hideyoshi for his future, but the latter was a far better choice than Katsuie. So there was no reason for him to deny Hideyoshi's petition.

"Lord Nobuo was really quite enthusiastic," Hikoemon reported. "He said that if you, my lord, would personally take part in a campaign against Gifu, he himself would join you. Rather than granting us the petition, he seemed to be actively encouraging us."

"He was enthusiastic? Really, I can almost see him."

Hideyoshi pictured the pitiful scene to himself. Here was the noble sire of an illustrious house but also a man whose character made him difficult to save.

Nevertheless, it was a piece of good luck. Before Nobunaga's death, Hideyoshi had never been the kind of man to proclaim his own aspirations or grand ideas, but after Nobunaga died—and especially after the battle at Yamazaki—he had become aware of the real possibility that he was destined to rule the nation. He no longer concealed either his self-confidence or his pride.

And there was another remarkable change. A man who aims at becoming the ruler of the nation is usually accused of wanting to expand his own power, but recently people were beginning to treat Hideyoshi as Nobunaga's natural successor.

Suddenly, very suddenly, a small army seemed to come together at the front gate of the Sokoku Temple. The soldiers arrived from the west, south, and north to gather under the standard of the golden gourds, until a fair-sized force had assembled in the center of Kyoto.

It was the seventh day of the Twelfth Month. The morning sun shone down through a dry, sweeping wind.

The people had no idea what was going on. The great funeral service held during the Tenth Month had been conducted with magnificence and pomp. It was easy for the people to be caught up in their own petty judgments. Their expressions showed that they had fooled themselves into believing that there would not be another war for the present.

"Lord Hideyoshi himself is riding at the very front. The Tsutsui forces are here, and so is Lord Niwa's army."

But the voices at the side of the road were puzzled about the destination of this expedition. The meandering line of armor and helmets passed very quickly through Keage and joined the forces waiting at Yabase. The warships ferrying troops split the white waves in close formation, heading northeast, while the army taking the land route camped for three nights at Azuchi, arriving at Sawayama Castle on the tenth.

On the thirteenth Hosokawa Fujitaka and his son, Tadaoki, arrived from Tamba and immediately requested an audience with Hideyoshi.

"I'm glad you've come," Hideyoshi said warmly. "I imagine you were troubled a good bit by the snow."

Considering the situation they were in, Fujitaka and his son must have spent the last six months feeling as though they were walking on thin ice. Mitsuhide and Fujitaka had been steadfast friends long before either had served Nobunaga. Tadaoki's wife was Mitsuhide's daughter. Beyond that, there were many other bonds between the retainers of the two clans. For those reasons alone, Mitsuhide had been sure that Fujitaka and his son would side with him in his rebellion.

But Fujitaka had not joined him. If he had allowed himself to be swayed by his own personal feelings, his clan would probably have been destroyed with the Akechi. Certainly he must have felt as though he had been balancing eggs one on top of another. To have acted with prudence outwardly and avoided danger within must have been painful beyond words. He had saved Tadaoki's wife, but his clemency had created internal strife within his clan.

By now Hideyoshi had absolved him and recognized the loyalty shown by the Hosokawa. Thus they were receiving Hideyoshi's hospitality. As Hideyoshi looked at Fujitaka, he saw that his sidelocks had turned the color of frost over the last half year. Ah, this man is a master, Hideyoshi thought, and at the same time recognized that for a man to take a stand in the general trend of things and make no mistakes, he would have to whittle away at his flesh and the blackness of his hair. In spite of himself, he felt sorry for Fujitaka every time he looked at him.

"The drum is being beaten from over the lake and from the castle town as well, and you appear to be ready to attack. I hope you will honor us by placing my son in the vanguard," Fujitaka began.

"Do you mean the siege of Nagahama?" replied Hideyoshi. He seemed to be speaking off the point, but then responded in a different vein. "We're attacking from both land and sea. But you know, the real focus of the attack is inside the castle, not outside. I'm sure Katsutoyo's retainers will come here this evening."

As Fujitaka considered Hideyoshi's words, he meditated once again on the old saying "He who rests his men well will be able to employ them to desperate efforts."

As Fujitaka's son looked at Hideyoshi, he also remembered something. When the Hosokawa clan's fate had stood at a great crossroads, and its retainers had all met to deliberate a course of action, Fujitaka had spoken and directly indicated the position to take: "In this generation, I have seen only two truly uncommon men: one of them is Lord Tokugawa Ieyasu, the other is unmistakably Lord Hideyoshi."

Recalling those words now, the young man could only wonder if they were true. Was this what his father called an uncommon man? Was Hideyoshi really one of the two truly great generals of his generation?

When they had withdrawn to their quarters, Tadaoki expressed his doubts.

"I guess you don't understand," Fujitaka mumbled in response. "You're still lacking in experience." Aware of Tadaoki's dissatisfied look, he guessed what was on his son's mind and said, "The closer you get to a large mountain, the less its great size can be perceived. When you start to climb, you will not understand its size at all. When you listen and then compare everyone's comments, you can understand that most men will speak without having seen the entire mountain and, having seen only one peak or valley, will imagine they have seen everything. But they'll really be doing nothing more than making judgments on the whole while having seen only one part."

Tadaoki's mind was left with its former doubts, despite the lesson he had received. He knew, however, that his father had experienced far more of the world than he had, and so he could do nothing more than accept what his father was saying.

Surprisingly enough, two days after their arrival, Nagahama Castle passed into Hideyoshi's hands without injury to a single soldier. It had been exactly as Hideyoshi had predicted to Fujitaka and his son: "The castle will be captured from within."

The envoys were three of Shibata Katsutoyo's senior retainers. They brought a written pledge in which Katsutoyo and all of his retainers swore to obey and serve Hideyoshi.

"They have acted with discrimination," Hideyoshi said with apparent satisfaction. According to the terms of the pledge, the castle's territory would remain the same as before, and Katsutoyo would be allowed to continue as its possessor.

When Hideyoshi gave up the castle, people commented on how quickly he had resigned himself to the loss of such a strategic location. Retaking the castle had been executed as easily as passing something from the left hand to the right.

But even if Katsutoyo had asked for reinforcements from Echizen, they could not have come because of the heavy snows. In addition, Katsuie would only have treated him harshly, just as he had done before. When Katsutoyo had fallen ill on his mission to Hideyoshi, Katsuie had made his anger plain to the whole clan.

"To take advantage of Hideyoshi's hospitality under the pretense of illness, and then to return after spending several days as his guest—that man is a fool beyond words."

Reports of Katsuie's harsh words eventually reached Katsutoyo.

Now, surrounded by Hideyoshi's army, Nagahama Castle was isolated, and Katsutoyo had nowhere to turn.

His senior retainers, who had already guessed his intentions, announced, "Those retainers who have family in Echizen should go back. Those who feel like staying here with Lord Katsutoyo and aligning themselves with Lord Hideyoshi may stay. His Lordship understands, however, that many of you may feel it would be difficult to remain true to the Way of the Samurai by leaving the Shibata clan and turning your back on Lord Katsuie. Those who feel that way may withdraw without hesitation."

For a moment the atmosphere was filled with tension. The men simply hung their heads in bitterness, and there were few objections. That night *sake* cups were raised in an honorable separation of lord and retainers, but fewer than one out of ten returned to Echizen.

In this way Katsutoyo cut his ties with his stepfather and allied himself with Hideyoshi. From that time on he was officially under Hideyoshi's command, but it had only been a matter of form. Long before these events, Katsutoyo's heart had already been like a little bird being fed in Hideyoshi's cage.

At any rate, the seizure of Nagahama was now complete. To Hideyoshi, however, it had been nothing more than a passing event on the way to Gifu—Nobutaka's main castle.

The pass over Fuwa was famous as a place that was difficult to cross in winter, and conditions on the plain of Sekigahara were especially severe.

From the eighteenth to the twenty-eighth day of the Twelfth Month, Hideyoshi's army marched across Sekigahara. The army was divided into corps, and those corps were further broken down into divisions: packhorses, gunners, spearmen, mounted warriors, and foot soldiers. Defying the snow and mud, they pushed on. It took Hideyoshi's force of about thirty thousand soldiers two days to cross into Mino.

The main camp was set up at Ogaki. From there, Hideyoshi attacked and took all of the smaller castles in the area. This was immediately reported to Nobutaka, who spent several days in complete confusion. He hardly knew what strategy to take, much less how to fight a defensive battle.

Nobutaka had thought only of grandiose schemes but had had no idea how to accomplish them. Until then he had allied himself to men like Katsuie and Takigawa and submitted schemes for attacking Hideyoshi, but he had never expected to be attacked by him.

At his wits' end, Nobutaka left his fate to the discretion of his senior retainers. But after arriving at the current pass, they had nothing left that could be called "discretion."

There was nothing the senior retainers could do but kowtow at Hideyoshi's camp just as Katsutoyo's retainers had done. Nobutaka's mother was sent as a hostage, and his senior retainers had to send their own mothers as well.

Niwa begged Hideyoshi to spare Nobutaka's life. Hideyoshi, as might be expected, pardoned him. Granting them peace for the time, he smiled at Nobutaka's senior retainers and asked, "Has Lord Nobutaka come to his senses? It will be a blessing if he has."

The hostages were immediately sent to Azuchi. Immediately thereafter Samboshi, who had been kept at Gifu, was turned over to Hideyoshi and moved to Azuchi as well.

After that, Nobuo was put in charge of the young lord. Having delivered that trust, Hideyoshi made a triumphal return to Takaradera Castle. New Year's Eve was celebrated two days after his return. Then came the first day of the eleventh year of Tensho. From morning on, sunshine glittered on the snow that had recently fallen on the trees just planted on the grounds of the renovated castle.

The fragrance of the New Year's rice cakes drifted through the grounds, and the sound of the drum reverberated through the corridors for more than half a day. But at noon an announcement rang out from the main citadel: "Lord Hideyoshi is going to Himeji!"

Hideyoshi arrived at Himeji around midnight on New Year's Day. Greeted by the flames of bonfires, he quickly entered the castle. The greatest joy, however, was not Hideyoshi's, but his people's, as they watched the flourish of the grand spectacle: all his retainers and their families were assembled at the main gate of the castle to welcome him.

Dismounting, he handed the reins to an attendant and, for a moment, looked up at the keep. In the Sixth Month of the previous summer, just before his forced march to Yamazaki and his great victory to avenge Nobunaga, he had stood at the same gate and wondered whether he would come back alive.

His last orders to his retainers had been clear: "If you hear that I have been defeated, kill my entire family and burn the castle to the ground."

Now he was back in Himeji Castle, having arrived exactly at midnight on New Year's Day. If he had faltered for a moment and wasted time by thinking about his wife and mother in Nagahama, he would have been unable to fight with the desperation of a man who expects to meet his death in battle. He would have been pressed by the power of the Mori in the west and watched the Akechi grow stronger in the east.

In the case of both the individual and the entire country, the border between rising and falling is always a wager based on life or death—life in the midst of death, death in the midst of life.

Hideyoshi, however, had not returned to rest. As soon as he entered the main citadel, and even before changing from his traveling clothes, he met with the officials of the castle. He listened attentively to the report on subsequent events in the west and the situation in his various estates.

It was the second half of the Hour of the Rat—midnight. Although unconcerned about their own exhaustion, Hideyoshi's retainers were worried that perhaps the strain might begin to affect their lord's health.

"Your honored mother and Lady Nene have been waiting for you since this evening. Why don't you go inside and show them how well you are?" Hideyoshi's brother-in-law Miyoshi suggested. As he walked on inside, he found his mother, wife, nieces, and sisters-in-law waiting for him. Though they had not slept at all, they greeted him in a line, kneeling with their hands to the floor. Hideyoshi passed by each of their bowed heads with sparkling eyes and a smile. Finally he stood before his old mother and said, "I have a moment of leisure this New Year's and have returned to be with you for a little while."

While he was paying his respects to his mother, Hideyoshi looked the image of what she so often called him—"that boy."

From within a large white silk hood, his mother's face beamed with a joy beyond words. "The road you have chosen was filled with extraordinary hardships," she said.

"And last year in particular was not an easy one. But you endured everything."

"It's been colder this winter than any other year I can remember," Hideyoshi said, "but you look very well, Mother."

"They say that age is something that slips up on you, and somehow I've already gone past my seventieth year. I've lived a long life—much longer than I expected. Never did I think I would live this long."

"No, no. You have to live until you're a hundred. As you can see, I'm still a boy."

"You're going to be forty-six this New Year's," the old lady said with a laugh. "How can you say you're still a boy?"

"But, Mother, aren't you the one who's always calling me 'that boy' from morning to night?"

"That's just a habit, you know."

"Well, I hope you'll always call me that. To confess the truth, even though I keep getting older, the development of my mind just can't keep up with the years. More than that, Mother, if you weren't here I'd lose my greatest motivation and might stop growing altogether."

Miyoshi, who had appeared behind him, saw that Hideyoshi was still there, engrossed in conversation with his mother. Surprised, he said, "Haven't you taken off your traveling clothes yet, my lord?"

"Ah, Miyoshi. Why don't you sit down?"

"I'd like to, but why don't you take a bath first?"

"Yes, you're right. Lead on, Nene."

Hideyoshi was surprised at the cock's crow. He had spent most of the night talking and had only slept for a short while. At dawn, Hideyoshi put on a ceremonial hat and kimono and went to pray at the castle shrine. He then ate rice cakes and soup in Nene's room. After that he went to the main citadel. Today, the second day of the new year, the line of people who had come up to the castle to wish him New Year's greetings seemed endless.

Hideyoshi greeted each one of them, offering each a cup of *sake*. The well-wishers then walked by any number of groups of preceding visitors, their faces bright and cheerful. Passing through the main and west citadels, one could see that every room was filled with guests—here was a group chanting Noh verses, there was a group reciting poetry. Even after noon, more well-wishers came before Hideyoshi.

Hideyoshi took care of all business in Himeji until the fifth, and that evening he startled his retainers by announcing that he would be leaving for Kyoto on the following day. They rushed to get things ready in time. They had thought that he would be staying in Himeji until the middle of the month, and indeed until noon Hideyoshi had showed no inclination to leave at all.

It was only much later that people understood the motives behind his actions. Hideyoshi moved quickly and never lost an opportunity.

Seki Morinobu commanded Kameyama Castle in Ise. Although nominally one of Nobutaka's retainers, he was now on friendly terms with Hideyoshi. During the holidays,

Seki came to Himeji in secret to offer his congratulations for the New Year.

As he was congratulating Hideyoshi, a messenger arrived from Ise. Seki's castle had been seized by Nobutaka's leading supporter, Takigawa Kazumasu.

Hideyoshi left Himeji without a moment's delay. He reached Takaradera Castle that evening, entered Kyoto on the seventh, arrived at Azuchi on the following day, and had an audience with the three-year-old Samboshi on the ninth.

"I have just now asked Lord Samboshi for permission to subdue Takigawa Kazumasu," Hideyoshi said to Seki and the other lords as he walked into the hall, almost as if he had kicked a ball into their midst. "Katsuie is behind this. So what we have to do is conquer Ise before Katsuie's soldiers are able to move."

Hideyoshi issued a proclamation from Azuchi. It was circulated widely in his domains, as well as to the generals in those areas friendly to him, and called for all just warriors to gather at Azuchi. How pitiful for the creator of the blind strategy that inspired that proclamation. There in Kitanosho, married to the beautiful Lady Oichi and surrounded by deep snow, Shibata Katsuie waited vainly for nature to take its course.

If only the spring sun would come and melt the snow. But the snow walls that had seemed to him an impenetrable defense were crumbling even before the advent of spring.

Katsuie was shaken by blow after blow: the fall of Gifu Castle, the revolt in Nagahama, Nobutaka's surrender. And now Hideyoshi was going to attack Ise. Katsuie felt he could neither leave nor sit still. But the snow on his borders was as deep as on the mountain passes of Szechuan. Neither soldiers nor military supplies would be able to cross them.

He had no need to worry about an attack from Hideyoshi. He would march forward the day that the snow melted, but who could tell when that would be? The snow seemed to have become a protective wall for the enemy.

Kazumasu is a veteran, too, Katsuie thought, but taking the little castles at Kameyama and Mine was a careless movement of soldiers without much regard for timing. That was stupid. Katsuie was furious.

Although his own strategy was riddled with faults, he criticized the actions of Takigawa Kazumasu, who had attacked too early.

But even if Kazumasu had abided by Katsuie's plans and waited for the snows to melt, Hideyoshi—who had already seen through the enemy's intentions—would not have spared them the time. In a word, Hideyoshi had outwitted Katsuie. He had seen what was in Katsuie's heart from the time the man had sent envoys for peace talks.

Katsuie was not simply going to take all that sitting down. Twice he sent out messengers: first to the ex-shogun Yoshiaki, asking him to encourage the Mori to attack from the western provinces; then to Tokugawa Ieyasu.

But on the eighteenth day of the First Month, Ieyasu, for reasons unknown, met secretly with Nobunaga's eldest son, Nobuo. Ieyasu had been professing strict neutrality, so what was his plan now? And why was a man of such cunning meeting with one entirely lacking in that quality?

Ieyasu had invited Nobuo, who was timidly being swept along in the violent tide of the times, to his own private quarters. There he favored that frail man with entertainment and secret conversations. Ieyasu treated Nobuo exactly as an adult would treat a child, and whatever conclusions the two reached remained secret. At any rate, Nobuo returned to Kiyosu delighted. His appearance was that of a commoner very pleased with himself, and there was also something of a guilty conscience about him. He seemed extremely hesitant to look Hideyoshi in the eye.

And where was Hideyoshi on the eighteenth day of the First Month? What was he doing? Accompanied by only a few trusted retainers, he had wound around the northern part of Lake Biwa, stealthily traversing the mountainous area on the border of Omi and Echizen.

As Hideyoshi toured the mountain villages and high ground, which were still under deep snow, he pointed out strategic places with his bamboo staff and gave out orders as he walked.

"Is that Mount Tenjin? Build some ramparts there, too. And construct some right away on that mountain over there as well."

On the seventh day of the Second Month, Hideyoshi sent a letter from Kyoto addressed to the Uesugi, proposing an alliance.

The reason was not complicated. The Shibata and the Uesugi had continually fought bloody battles over a number of years, now taking land from one another, now losing it. It was likely that Katsuie would now be thinking about mending those old grudges so that he could concentrate all of his strength on the confrontation with Hideyoshi. But his stubbornness and pride made it unlikely that he would succeed in carrying off so subtle a strategy.

Two days after sending the letter to the Uesugi in the north, Hideyoshi announced his army's departure for Ise. He divided his forces into three corps, which advanced along three different routes.

With war cries, under clouds of banners and drums, their march shook the mountains and ridges. All three armies crossed the central mountain range of Omi and Ise and regrouped in the areas of Kuwana and Nagashima. That was where Takigawa Kazumasu was to be found.

"First let's see what battle formation Hideyoshi chooses," Kazumasu said when he heard that the enemy was approaching. He was fully confident of his own ability.

It was a matter of timing, and he had misjudged the moment to begin hostilities. The treaty between Katsuie, Nobutaka, and Kazumasu had been kept secret even from their own advisers, but now the fuse had been blindly ignited because Kazumasu had been so eager for an opportunity. Dispatches were sent to Gifu and Echizen. Leaving two thousand soldiers in Nagashima Castle, Kazumasu himself went to Kuwana Castle.

The castle was protected on one side by the sea and on the other by the hills around the castle town, and it was easier to defend than Nagashima. Even so, Kazumasu's strategy was not simply to retreat to this narrow strip of land. Hideyoshi would have to divide his sixty-thousand-man army to attack Gifu, Nagashima, and Kuwana, as well as the various other castles in the area, so even if his main army attacked, it would not be with overwhelming strength.

On the one hand, he had heard that the enemy army was impressive in its numbers, but on the other, he knew that its soldiers would be taking the roads over the peaks of the

Owari-Kai mountain range. It was obvious that the supply train carrying the munitions and provisions would be very long.

With that in mind, Kazumasu believed that destroying Hideyoshi would be no difficult task at all. Draw him in, attack mercilessly, watch for the opportunity to get Nobutaka on his feet again, unite with the soldiers in Gifu, and destroy Nagahama.

Contrary to Kazumasu's expectations, Hideyoshi had not bothered to take the small castles, but had decided to attack the enemy's main stronghold. At that moment, urgent messages began to come to Hideyoshi from Nagahama, Sawayama, and Azuchi. The situation was not an easy one; the clouds and surging tides that covered the world changed with every passing day.

The first dispatch read: "The vanguard of Echizen has passed through Yanagase. A part of it will soon be invading northern Omi."

The next courier bore a similar message: "Katsuie's patience has finally broken. Instead of waiting for the thaw, he has engaged twenty or thirty thousand coolies to clear the snow from the road."

Yet a third messenger reported how critical the situation was: "It is probable that the Shibata forces left Kitanosho around the second day of the Third Month. By the fifth, the vanguard had advanced as far as Yanagase in Omi. By the seventh, one division was threatening our positions on Mount Tenjin, while other divisions set fire to the villages of Imaichi, Yogo, and Sakaguchi. The main army of twenty thousand men under the command of Shibata Katsuie and Maeda Inuchiyo is steadily advancing southward."

"Strike camp immediately," Hideyoshi ordered. And then, "On to northern Omi."

Leaving the Ise campaign to Nobuo and Ujisato, Hideyoshi turned his army toward Omi. On the sixteenth he reached Nagahama, and on the seventeenth his troops were snaking their way along the lakeside road that led to northern Omi. He himself rode on horseback. The spring breeze played on his face as he rode beneath the commander's standard of the golden gourds.

At the border of Omi in the mountainous area of Yanagase, the fresh snow lay in pleats and folds. The wind blowing over the area and swooping down on the lake from the north was still cold enough to redden the noses of the warriors. At dusk the army divided to take up positions. The soldiers could almost smell the enemy. And yet not a single column of smoke from an enemy campfire, or a single enemy soldier, could be seen.

But the officers pointed out the enemy positions to their men. "There are Shibata units along the base of Mount Tenjin and in the area of Tsubakizaka. There is also a large division of the enemy stationed in the areas of Kinomoto, Imaichi, and Sakaguchi, so stay on your guard, even when you sleep."

But the white mist trailed into camp, ushering in an evening so peaceful it could hardly be imagined that the world was at war.

Suddenly, sporadic gunfire was heard in the distance—all from Hideyoshi's side. Not a single shot was returned throughout the night. Was the enemy asleep?

At dawn the gunners who had been sent to test out the enemy's front line pulled back. Hideyoshi ordered the commanders of the musket corps to report to his headquarters, where he listened carefully to their reports of the enemy positions.

"Have you seen any trace of Sassa Narimasa's troops?" Hideyoshi asked.

Hideyoshi wanted to be sure, but all three commanders answered in the same way. "The banners of Sassa Narimasa are nowhere to be seen."

Hideyoshi nodded, acknowledging that it might be true. Even if Katsuie had come, he would be unable to do so without anxiety because of the Uesugi at his rear. Hideyoshi could imagine that Sassa had been left behind for precisely that reason.

The order to eat breakfast was issued. The rations carried during a campaign were unpolished rice balls packed with bean paste and wrapped in oak leaves. Hideyoshi talked with his pages while chewing his rice noisily. Before he had eaten half of it, the others had finished.

"Don't you chew your food?" he asked.

"Aren't you just a slow eater, my lord?" the pages answered. "It's our custom to eat quickly and shit quickly."

"That's a good way to be," Hideyoshi replied. "Shitting quickly is good, I guess, but you all should try to eat like Sakichi."

The pages looked at Sakichi. Like Hideyoshi, Sakichi had eaten only half of his rice and was chewing it as carefully as an old lady.

"I'll tell you why," Hideyoshi continued. "It's all right to eat quickly on days when there's going to be a fight, but it's different when you're besieged in a castle and there are limited provisions that you have to stretch out for the day. At that time you'll be able to see the wisdom of eating slowly both in the well-being of the castle and in your own health. Also, when you're deep in the mountains and plan to hold out for a long time without provisions, you may have to chew on anything—roots or leaves—just to satisfy your stomach. Chewing well is an everyday matter, and if you don't get into the habit you won't be able to do it voluntarily when the time comes." Suddenly getting up from his camp stool, he waved them along. "Come on. Let's go climb Mount Fumuro."

Mount Fumuro is one of a cluster of mountains at the northern edge of two lakes—the smaller Lake Yogo and the larger Lake Biwa. From the village of Fumuro at its foot to its summit is a height of almost eight hundred meters and a walking distance of over two leagues. If the traveler wanted to climb its steep slope, he would have to plan on taking at least half a day.

"He's leaving!"

"Where's he going so suddenly?"

The warriors guarding Hideyoshi noticed the retreating figures of the pages and ran after them. They could see Hideyoshi happily walking on ahead, grasping a bamboo staff, and looking for all the world as if he were off on a hawking expedition.

"Are you going to climb the mountain, my lord?"

Hideyoshi pointed halfway up the slope with his staff.

"Right. Up to about there."

When they had climbed about a third of the way up the mountain, they came to a small area of level ground. Hideyoshi stood looking around, as the wind cooled the sweat on his forehead. From his position he had a bird's-eye view of the area from Yanagase to the lower Yogo. The road to the northern provinces, which wound its way through the mountains and connected several villages, looked like a single ribbon.

"Which one is Mount Nakao?"

"That's it over there."

Hideyoshi looked in the direction in which the warrior was pointing. That was the enemy's main camp. A large number of banners followed the lines of the mountain and continued down to its base. There a single army corps could be recognized. But if one looked further, one could see that the banners belonging to the forces of the north filled the mountains in the distance and occupied the strategic areas on peaks closer at hand and all along the road. It was just as though some military expert had made that piece of heaven and earth his base and was trying his hand at a tremendous expansion of his formation. There were no cracks or spaces in the subtlety of the arrangement or in the strategy of the positioning of troops. The grandeur with which they showed themselves ready to swallow the enemy was beyond words.

Hideyoshi silently looked out over the scene. He then looked back toward Katsuie's main camp on Mount Nakao and gazed fixedly at it for a long time.

Looking closely, he could see a group of men working like ants on the southern face of the main camp area on Mount Nakao. And not in just one or two places. He could detect activity in all of the slightly elevated locations.

"Well, it looks like Katsuie intends to make this a long campaign."

Hideyoshi had the answer. The enemy was building fortifications at the southern end of the main camp. The entire battle array, which spread out like a fan from the central army, had been positioned with great care. It would make a steady, carefully controlled advance. There was no sign of preparations for a surprise attack.

Hideyoshi could read the enemy's plan. In a word, Katsuie intended to keep him pinned down here to give his allies in Ise and Mino the time to prepare for a combined offensive from the front and rear.

"Let's go back," Hideyoshi said, and started off. "Isn't there another way down?"

"Yes, my lord," a page answered proudly.

They came to an allied camp just between Mount Tenjin and Ikenohara. From the banners, they knew it was Hosokawa Tadaoki's post.

"I'm thirsty," Hideyoshi said after presenting himself at the gate.

Tadaoki and his retainers thought that Hideyoshi was conducting a surprise inspection.

"No," Hideyoshi explained, "I'm just on my way back from Mount Fumuro. But since I'm here..." As Hideyoshi stood before Tadaoki, he drank some water and gave orders: "Strike camp immediately and go home. Then take all of the warships docked at Miyazu in Tango and attack the enemy coast."

Hideyoshi had conceived of the idea of a navy when he was climbing the mountain. The plan did not seem to have anything to do with what he was involved with at the time, but that kind of discrepancy was, perhaps, peculiar to his way of thinking. His thought processes were not limited by what he saw in front of him.

After half a day of military observations, Hideyoshi had almost completely determined his strategy. That night he summoned all of the generals to his headquarters and told them what he was going to do: because the enemy was preparing for extended hostilities, Hideyoshi's forces would also construct a number of ramparts and prepare for protracted hostilities.

The construction of a chain of fortresses was begun. The engineering was on a grand scale—geared to encourage morale. Hideyoshi's decision to begin building right in front of the enemy, at a time when a decisive battle seemed imminent, could be called either reckless or courageous. It could easily have lost him the war. But he was willing to take that chance in order to connect himself to the people of the province.

The fighting style of Nobunaga had been characterized by an irresistible force; it was said that "where Nobunaga advances, the grasses and trees wither." But Hideyoshi's fighting style was different. Where he advanced, where he made his camp, he naturally drew people to him. Winning over the local people was an important matter to attend to before ever trying to defeat the enemy.

Strict military discipline is vital, but even on days when blood seemed to flow, there was something of a spring breeze wherever Hideyoshi set up his camp stool. Someone even wrote: "Where Hideyoshi lives, the spring wind blows."

The lines of fortresses were to run through two areas. The first ran from Kitayama in Nakanogo, along the route to the northern provinces through Mount Higashino, Mount Dangi, and Mount Shinmei; the second went along Mount Iwasaki, Mount Okami, Shizugatake, Mount Tagami, and Kinomoto. Such a huge undertaking would require tens of thousands of laborers.

Hideyoshi recruited the men from the province of Nagahama. He had signposts advertising the work raised in the areas especially devastated by war. The mountains were filled with refugees. Lumber was cut, roads were opened, fortifications were constructed everywhere, and it was easy to believe that a line of fortresses would spring up overnight. But the construction work was not so easy. A single fort required a watchtower and barracks, and also moats and ramparts. Three wooden palisades were set up, while huge rocks and trees were stockpiled directly above the road that the enemy would most likely take to attack.

Both a trench and a palisade connected the area between Mount Higashino and Mount Dangi, which was the zone most likely to be used as the battlefield. The excavation for this alone was daunting, but the necessary work was completed in only twenty days. Women and children participated in the effort.

The Shibata conducted night raids and played petty tricks and were able to impede progress, but seeming to realize that they were having no real success against men who were constantly prepared, they became as quiet as the mountain itself.

It was almost uncanny. Why didn't they just make their move? But Hideyoshi understood. His constant thought—that his adversary was a strong old veteran and not an easy mark—was reflected in Katsuie's mind as well. But there were other important reasons.

Katsuie's military preparations were already complete, but he felt that the time was not yet ripe to mobilize the allies he held in reserve.

Those allies were, of course, the forces of Nobutaka in Gifu. Once Nobutaka was able to move, Takigawa Kazumasu would also be able to attack from Kuwana Castle. Then, for the first time, Katsuie's plans could be transformed into an effective strategy.

Katsuie knew that if it were not done in that way, victory would not easily be achieved. That was how he had secretly and quite anxiously calculated the situation from the very beginning. The calculation itself was based on the comparative strengths of Hideyoshi's provinces and his own.

At that time, given Hideyoshi's sudden popularity and power after the Battle of Yamazaki, the allies he could count on were the provinces of Harima, Tajima, Settsu, Tango, Yamato, and a few others, for a total a military strength of sixty-seven thousand soldiers. If the soldiers of Owari, Ise, Iga, and Bizen were added to that, the total would be about one hundred thousand.

Katsuie could bring together the main strength of Echizen, Noto, Oyama, Ono, Matsuto, and Toyama. That would mean a force of perhaps no more than forty-five thousand men. If, however, he added Nobutaka's Mino and Ise and Kazumasu's provincial strength, he would have a military force of close to sixty-two thousand men, a number with which he could almost compete with the enemy.

A Bowl of Tea

The man appeared to be a traveling monk, but walked with the gait of a fighting man. Right now he was climbing the Shufukuji road.

"Where are you going!" the Shibata guard challenged.

"It's me," the priest replied, pushing back his monk's hood.

The sentries signaled to the palisade behind them. At the wooden gate was huddled yet another party of men. The monk approached the officer and said a few words. There appeared to be some confusion for a few moments, but then the officer himself led out a horse and handed the priest the reins.

Mount Yukiichi was the encampment of Sakuma Genba and his younger brother, Yasumasa. The man dressed as a priest was Mizuno Shinroku, a retainer of Yasumasa. He had been entrusted with a secret message, and was now kneeling in front of his lord, inside his headquarters.

"How did it go? Good or bad news?" Yasumasa asked impatiently.

"Everything is arranged," Shinroku replied.

"Were you able to meet him? Did everything go well?"

"The enemy already has strict lookouts, but I was able to meet with Lord Shogen."

"What are his intentions?"

"I have them written down in a letter."

He looked inside his wickerwork hat and tore off the joint of the hat's cord. A letter that had been pasted underneath fell onto his lap. Shinroku straightened out the creases and put the letter into his lord's hand.

Yasumasa studied the envelope for some time.

"Yes, this is definitely Shogen's handwriting, but it's addressed to my brother. Come with me. We'll go see my brother right now and notify the main camp at Mount Nakao."

Lord and retainer went out through the palisade and climbed to the peak of Mount Yukiichi. The arrangement of men and horses, the palisade gates and the barracks became progressively tighter and more controlled as they reached the top. Finally the main citadel, which looked like a castle, came into view, and they could see innumerable curtained enclosures spread over the peak.

"Tell my brother that I am here." As Yasumasa spoke to the guard, one of Genba's retainers came running up.

"I'm afraid Lord Genba is not in his quarters, my lord."

"Has he gone to Mount Nakao?"

"No, he's over there."

Looking in the direction in which the retainer was pointing, he saw his brother, Genba, sitting with five or six warriors and pages on the grass beyond the main citadel. It was difficult to see what they were doing.

When he came closer, he could see that Genba was having one of the pages hold a mirror while another held a basin. There, under a blue sky, he was shaving as though he had no other care in the world.

It was the twelfth day of the Fourth Month.

Summer had already come, and in the castle towns on the plains, the heat could be felt. But in the mountains, spring was now at its height.

Yasumasa walked over and knelt on the grass.

"Well, brother?" Genba looked at him out of the corner of his eye, but continued to thrust out his chin in front of the mirror until he was finally finished shaving. Only after the razor was put away and the shaved hair was washed from his face with the water in the basin did he turn completely to face his little brother. "What is it, Yasumasa?"

"Would you have all the pages withdraw, please?"

"Why don't we go back to my quarters?"

"No, no. This is really the best place for a secret discussion."

"You think so? All right." Turning to his pages, Genba ordered them to withdraw some distance.

The pages took the mirror and basin and left. The samurai also withdrew. The Sakuma brothers remained facing each other on the top of the mountain. One other man was there—Mizuno Shinroku, who had come along with Yasumasa.

In accordance with his position, Shinroku was still at a distance, prostrating himself toward his two superiors.

At that point Genba noticed him. "Shinroku has returned, has he?"

"He has and he reports that everything went smoothly. His errand seems to have been successful."

"I'm sure it wasn't easy. Well, what about Shogen's reply?"

"Here is Shogen's letter."

Genba opened the letter as soon as he held it in his hand. An open pleasure filled his eyes and hung on the corners of his mouth. What kind of secret success could have made him so happy? His shoulders shook almost uncontrollably.

"Shinroku, come a little closer. You're too far away over there."

"Yes, my lord."

"According to Shogen's letter, it appears that the real details were entrusted to you. Tell me everything Shogen had to say."

"Lord Shogen said that both he and Lord Ogane had had differences of opinion with their lord, Katsutoyo, even before Nagahama changed sides. Hideyoshi knew that and though they have been put in charge of the fortresses at Mount Dangi and Mount Shinmei, they are under the watchful eye of Hideyoshi's trusted retainer, Kimura Hayato. They can hardly make a move."

"But both Shogen and Ogane intend to escape and come here."

"They plan to kill Kimura Hayato tomorrow morning, and then bring their men over to our side."

"If this is going to happen tomorrow morning, there's no time to lose. Send out a force to them," Genba ordered Yasumasa. He then interrogated Shinroku once again. "Some reports say that Hideyoshi is in his main camp, while others claim that he is in Nagahama. Do you know where he is?"

Shinroku admitted that he did not.

For the Shibata side, the question of whether Hideyoshi was at the front or at Nagahama was an extremely important one.

Without knowing where he was, the Shibata were uncertain how to proceed. Katsuie's strategy was not for a single frontal attack. He had been waiting quite some time for the opportunity to have Nobutaka's Gifu army spring into action. Takigawa Kazumasu's forces could then initiate their attack, and together the two armies of Mino and Ise would threaten Hideyoshi's rear. At that point Katsuie's main force of twenty thousand men could rush in and drive Hideyoshi into a corner at Nagahama.

Katsuie had already received a letter from Nobutaka to that effect. If Hideyoshi was at Nagahama, he would quickly catch wind of such operations and see to it that both Gifu and Yanagase were ready. If Hideyoshi was now on the front lines, Katsuie would have to be fully ready, for the time for Nobutaka's uprising was now.

But before any of those plans could be carried out, the Shibata had to pin down Hideyoshi to create the right circumstances for Nobutaka to move.

"That one point remains unclear," Genba said again. There was no doubt that during the long period of waiting, which had lasted for more than a month, he was becoming more and more depressed. "Well, we succeeded in luring Shogen, and we should rejoice in that alone. Lord Katsuie must be informed immediately. We will wait for Shogen's signal tomorrow."

Yasumasa and Shinroku left first and returned to their own camp. Genba called over a page to bring him his favorite horse. Accompanied by ten warriors, he left immediately for the main camp on Mount Nakao.

The newly built road between Mount Yukiichi and the main camp at Nakao was about four yards wide and meandered along for over two leagues, along the ridgeline of the mountains. The spring greenery of the mountains filled the warriors' eyes, and as Genba whipped his horse along, even he was overcome by a poetic sentiment.

The main camp at Mount Nakao was surrounded by several palisades. Each time Genba approached a gate, he would simply give his name and ride through, looking down at the guards from his saddle.

But just as he was about to ride through the gate to the main citadel, the commander of the guards called out abruptly and challenged him. "Wait! Where are you going?"

Genba turned around and stared at the man.

"Ah, is that you, Menju? I've come to see my uncle. Is he in his quarters or at staff headquarters?"

Menju frowned, walked around in front of Genba, and said angrily, "Dismount first, please."

"What?"

"This gate is very close to Lord Katsuie's headquarters. It doesn't make any difference who you are or how much of a hurry you're in, it is not permitted to ride in on horseback."

"You dare say that to me, Menju?" Genba said angrily, but according to military discipline he could not really refuse. Instead he dismounted as Menju had required him to do and barked, "Where's my uncle?"

"He's in the middle of a military conference."

"Who's attending?"

"Lord Haigo, Lord Osa, Lord Hara, Lord Asami, and Lord Katsutoshi."

"If that's so, it'll be all right if I join them."

"No, I'll announce you."

"That won't be necessary."

Genba pushed his way through. Menju watched him as he walked off. A look of misery clouded his face. The challenge he had thrown out just now, at the risk of his own reputation, was not simply for the sake of military law. He had been secretly trying to get Genba to reflect on his attitude for some time.

The attitude shown in the proud manner Genba usually displayed was connected with his uncle's favoritism. When he observed how the lord of Kitanosho acted with biased blind love toward his nephew, Menju could not help feeling uneasy about the future. At the very least, he felt that it was not right for Genba to be calling the commander-in-chief "uncle."

But Genba paid no attention to such matters as Menju's unhappy thoughts. He now walked directly into his uncle's headquarters, ignoring the other retainers there, and whispered to his uncle, "When you're finished, I have a private matter to discuss with you."

Katsuie quickly ended the conference. After the generals had all withdrawn, he leaned from his camp stool and spoke excitedly with his nephew. After giving a self-satisfied laugh, Genba silently showed Shogen's answer as though he knew it would give Katsuie great pleasure.

Katsuie was immensely pleased. The plot that he had conceived and asked Genba to put into effect was working. On that account alone, the happiness of having seen everything go according to plan was greater for him than for anyone. He, in particular, had the reputation for loving intrigue, and as he read Shogen's reply he was so happy that he was almost drooling.

The aim of the plot was to weaken the enemy from within. From Katsuie's point of view, the presence of men like Shogen and Ogane in Hideyoshi's army provided opportunities for hatching plot after plot.

As for Shogen, he believed that the victory would go to the Shibata. That belief was surprisingly blind. It is true that at a later date he, too, would be anguished and undoubtedly questioned by his own conscience. But the letter of consent had already been sent, and it was no longer a matter for deliberation. For better or worse, Shogen's betrayal was definitely set for the following morning, and he waited to invite the Shibata army into his fortress.

* * *

The twelfth day of the month, midnight. The bonfires were smoldering, and the only sound to be heard in the mist-shrouded mountain camp was the soughing of the pine trees.

"Open the gate!" someone called out in a hushed voice, knocking repeatedly on the wooden gate of the palisade.

The small fort on Motoyama had formerly been Shogen's headquarters, but Hideyoshi had replaced him with Kimura Hayato.

"Who is it?" the sentry asked, peering through the palisade.

A solitary figure was standing outside in the dark. "Call Commander Osaki," the figure said.

"First tell me who you are and where you've come from."

The man outside did not reply for a moment. A misty rain was falling, and the sky was the color of India ink. "That's something I can't tell you. I must speak with Osaki Uemon, here at the palisade. Just tell him that."

"Friend or foe?"

"Friend, of course! Do you think an enemy could have come up this far so easily? Are your guards that careless? If this were some enemy plot, would I be knocking at the gate?"

The man's explanation seemed reasonable. The guard nodded and went to fetch Osaki.

"What is it?" Osaki asked.

"Are you Commander Osaki?"

"Yes, I am. What do you want?"

"My name is Nomura Shojiro, and I am a retainer of Lord Katsutoyo, presently in the service of Lord Shogen."

"What business do you have here in the middle of the night?"

"I have to speak to Lord Hayato at once. I know this must sound suspicious, but I have something of great importance that I must tell him immediately."

"Can't you tell me and let me relay the message?"

"No, I must speak with him in person. As a sign of my good faith, I'll entrust these to you," Nomura said, removing his swords and handing them through the palisade to Osaki.

Osaki realized Nomura was genuine and opened the gate, then led him to Hayato's quarters. It was a wartime camp, and there was really no difference in the security measures, night or day.

The place Nomura was led to was called the main citadel, but it was really just a hut, and Hayato's living quarters were little more than a board fence.

Hayato came in and quietly sat down. "What do you have to say?" he asked, looking directly at Nomura. Possibly because of the lamplight shining from the side, Hayato's face looked extremely pale.

"I believe you have been invited to attend a tea ceremony tomorrow morning at Lord Shogen's camp on Mount Shinmei."

A questioning look burned in Nomura's eyes, and the weird quiet of the night gave a faint shiver to the man's voice. Both Hayato and Osaki experienced an uncanny sensation.

"That's right," Hayato answered.

"Have you already agreed to attend, my lord?"

"Yes. Since he went to the trouble of sending me an invitation, I sent a messenger back with my acceptance."

"When did you send the messenger, my lord?"

"About noon today."

"Then that must be exactly the trick I thought it was!"

"Trick?"

"You must on no account go tomorrow morning. The tea ceremony is a ploy. Shogen is planning to murder you. He has already met with a secret messenger from the Shibata and sent a written pledge to them. Make no mistake, his plan is first to kill you and then to raise the banner of rebellion."

"How did you find this out?"

"The day before yesterday, Shogen summoned three Buddhist priests from the nearby Shufuku Temple to perform a memorial service for his ancestors. I had seen one of those men before, and he was without doubt a Shibata samurai. I was surprised, and sure enough, after the service, he complained of stomach pains and remained at the camp after the other two had left. He left the next morning, saying that he was returning to the Shufuku Temple, but just to make sure I had one of my retainers follow him. Just as I had thought, he did not return to the Shufuku Temple at all, but instead ran straight to Sakuma Genba's camp."

Hayato nodded as though he did not need to hear any more. "I appreciate your warning. Lord Hideyoshi did not trust Shogen nor Ogane, and said that we should be wary of them. Their treachery has become clear. What do you think we should do, Osaki?"

Osaki drew closer and offered his thoughts. Nomura's ideas were considered as well, and a plan was conceived on the spot. Osaki sent messengers to Nagahama.

In the meantime, Hayato wrote a letter and entrusted it to Osaki. It was a short note to Shogen, explaining that he could not attend the tea ceremony because of ill health.

As the day dawned, Osaki took the letter and went to call on Shogen at Mount Shinmei.

The custom of that time was to hold frequent tea ceremonies in camp. Everything, of course, was prepared with simplicity—the tea room was only a temporary shelter with rough plaster walls, reed mats, and a vase containing wild flowers. The purpose of the tea ceremony was to cultivate the inner strength needed to endure the fatigue of a long campaign.

787

Early that morning Shogen had swept the dewy ground and set the coals in the hearth. Soon Ogane and Kinoshita arrived. Both of them were retainers of Shibata Katsutoyo. Shogen had taken them into his confidence, and they had taken a solemn oath to act with him.

"Hayato's late, isn't he?" Ogane commented.

Somewhere a rooster crowed, and the guests both looked nervous. Shogen, however, acted as a host should and stayed perfectly calm. "He'll be here soon enough," he said confidently.

Of course, the man they were waiting for never came; instead a page appeared with the letter Hayato had entrusted to Osaki.

The three men looked at one another.

"What about the messenger?" Shogen asked.

The page replied that the man had left immediately upon delivering the letter.

The same anxious look darkened the faces of the three men. No matter how brave they were, they could not feel at ease, knowing that their treachery might have been exposed.

"How could it have leaked out?" Ogane asked.

Even their mumbling sounded like complaints. Now that the plot had been exposed, the tea ceremony was forgotten, and their thoughts turned to making good their own escape. Both Ogane and Kinoshita appeared as though they could hardly bear to stay there a moment longer.

"There's nothing we can do after this." As that lament escaped Shogen's lips, the other two men felt as though they had been struck in the chest. Shogen, however, glared at them as if he were telling them to keep their heads.

"The two of you should take your men and go as quickly as possible to Ikenohara. Wait there near the big pine tree. I'm going to send a letter to Nagahama. Then I'll follow you right away."

"To Nagahama? What sort of letter?"

"My mother, wife, and children are still in the castle. I can escape, but my mother and the others will certainly be held hostage if we wait too long."

"I suspect you're too late. Do you really think there's still time?"

"What am I going to do? Just abandon them there? Ogane, pass me that inkstone over there."

Shogen began to run his brush rapidly over the sheet of paper. Just then, one of his retainers came in to report that Nomura Shojiro had disappeared.

Shogen threw down his brush in disgust. "It was him, then. I've been negligent about that fool for some time. He'll pay for this."

He glared as though he were giving someone the evil eye, and the hand that held the letter addressed to his wife began to shake.

"Ippeita!" he shrieked.

The man quickly appeared.

"Take a horse and hurry to Nagahama. Find my family and put them on a boat. Don't even think about saving their possessions; just scull across the lake to Lord Katsuie's camp. I'm relying on you. Go immediately, and don't waste a single moment," he ordered.

Almost before he finished speaking, Shogen had fastened the bindings on his armor. Holding a long spear, he ran out of the building. Ogane and Kinoshita both quickly gathered their men and went down the mountain.

At about that time the dawn was turning white, and Hayato had sent out his forces. When the men led by Ogane and Kinoshita reached the foot of the mountain, they were ambushed by Osaki. Those who survived the attack tried to flee to the big pine tree in Ikenohara where they would wait for Shogen. But Hayato's men had gone around the northern end of Mount Dangi and cut off their escape by that road. Encircled this time, almost all of them were annihilated.

Shogen was only one step behind them. He, too, fled in that direction with a few men. He wore his helmet with deer antlers and his black leather armor and carried his long spear under his arm as he rode. He truly looked like a warrior ready to cut through the wind and the bravest of Katsutoyo's retainers, but he had already strayed from the Way of the Samurai, and the sounds of righteousness and lofty ideals were lacking in the galloping of his horse's hooves.

Suddenly he was surrounded by Hayato's troops.

"Don't let the traitor get away!"

They heaped abuse on Shogen, but he fought as though he was not afraid to die. Carving out a road of blood as he passed, he finally escaped from the iron cage. Whipping his horse at full speed for about two leagues, he soon joined up with Yasumasa's army, which had been waiting since the night before. Had the assassination of Hayato been a success, the two fortresses on Motoyama would have been attacked and taken at the appearance of Shogen's signal fires. But the plan had not gone as expected, and Shogen had barely escaped with his life.

As he listened to the way events had turned out from his brother Yasumasa, Genba looked disgusted. "What? You mean that Hayato got the first move on them because the plot was exposed this morning?" he said. "Well, Shogen's plan must have been poorly conceived. Tell all three men to come here."

Until then Genba had done everything to induce Shogen to betray his lord, but now that the scheme had fallen short of his expectations, he talked about him as though he were nothing but trouble.

Shogen and the two others were expecting to be well received, but they were to be greatly disappointed by Genba's attitude. Shogen asked to meet Katsuie and report some highly secret information to him in order to make up for his failure.

"That sounds hopeful, doesn't it?" Genba's mood showed a little improvement, but to Ogane and Kinoshita he was just as brusque as before. "The two of you stay here. Only Shogen will be going with me to the main camp."

With that, they left immediately for Mount Nakao.

The incident that morning, with all of its complications, had been reported in detail to Katsuie.

When, not long thereafter, Genba accompanied Shogen to Katsuie's camp, the latter sat waiting for them on his general's stool with a haughty look. Katsuie always looked dignified no matter what the situation. Shogen was quickly granted an audience.

"You failed this time, Shogen," Katsuie said.

The expression on his face as he spat out his real feelings was a complex one. It was commonly said that the Shibata uncle and nephew both had calculating, self-interested natures, and now both Katsuie and Genba waited with cold expressions for Shogen to speak.

"The oversight was mine," Shogen said, aware that he could do nothing more than apologize. At that point he must have repented his decision bitterly, but now there was no way of going back. Bearing shame on top of shame and stifling his anger, he could only bow his head to the ground in front of that arrogant and selfish lord.

All he could do was beg for Katsuie's mercy. He did, however, have another plan with which he might curry favor with Katsuie, and it had to do with the question of Hideyoshi's whereabouts. Both Katsuie and Genba had a deep interest in that question, and when Shogen mentioned the subject, they listened eagerly.

"Where is Hideyoshi now?"

"Hideyoshi's whereabouts are kept secret even from his own men," Shogen explained. "Though he was seen during the construction of the fortresses, he hasn't been in camp here for some time. But he's probably in Nagahama, and he might make preparations for attacking from Gifu, while watching the situation here at the same time. He may be putting himself in a position to react to conditions in either place."

Katsuie nodded gravely, exchanging glances with Genba. "That's it. That must be it. He must be in Nagahama."

"But what kind of proof do you have?"

"I have no real proof," Shogen replied. "But if you'll give me a few days I'll verify the details of Hideyoshi's whereabouts. There were several men in Nagahama who took a kind interest in me, and I'm sure that when they know that I'm supporting you, my lord, they'll slip out of Nagahama and inquire about me here. Also, the reports from the spies I sent out should be coming in soon. Beyond that, I would like to offer a strategy that will defeat Hideyoshi," he concluded, with a look that hinted at the extent of his faith in his scheme.

"You should be very, very careful, don't you think? But let's hear what you have to say."

At dawn on the nineteenth day of the month, Shogen and Genba visited Katsuie's headquarters a second time. What Shogen carried with him that morning was certainly valuable. Genba had already heard Shogen's information, but as Katsuie now heard it for the first time, his eyes widened like saucers, and the hairs all over his body stood on end.

Shogen spoke with great excitement. "For the past few days Hideyoshi has been at Nagahama. Two days ago, on the seventeenth, he suddenly led a force of twenty thousand men out of the castle there and force-marched to Ogaki, where he set up camp. It goes without saying that by crushing Lord Nobutaka in Gifu with a single blow, he would cut off any anxiety about being attacked from the rear. We can surmise, then, that he is resolved to raise his entire force, turn in that direction, and make a move for a decisive, all-or-nothing battle. It is said that before leaving Nagahama," Shogen continued, "Hideyoshi had all the hostages from Lord Nobutaka's family killed, so you can understand the resolve with which the bastard moved on Gifu. And there's more. Yesterday his vanguard set fires in various places and is preparing for a siege of Gifu Castle."

The day we've been waiting for is coming, Katsuie thought, almost licking his lips.

Genba was of the same mind. He burned with the same thoughts, but even more so. Here was an opportunity—a matchless opportunity. But how could they make full use of it?

Little opportunities here, little opportunities there during hostilities came in waves of tens of thousands, but a truly great opportunity on which hung a man's rise or fall in a single blow came only once. Now Katsuie was at the point of grasping or of failing to grasp that kind of opportunity. Katsuie nearly drooled as he thought the possibilities through, and Genba's face was flushed.

"Shogen," Katsuie finally began, "if you have some sort of strategy to offer, please speak frankly."

"My own humble opinion is that we should not miss this opportunity, but should attack the two enemy fortresses at Mount Iwasaki and Mount Oiwa. We could act in concert with Lord Nobutaka, even though Gifu is far away, and act just as quickly as Hideyoshi. Your allies could, at the same time, attack and destroy Hideyoshi's fortresses."

"Ah, that is exactly what I'd like to do, but such things are more easily said than done, Shogen. The enemy is also not without men, and they're building fortresses too, aren't they?"

"When you look at Hideyoshi's battle formation from within, there is one very large opening," Shogen replied. "Consider this. The two enemy fortresses at Iwasaki and Oiwa are far from your camp, but you still consider them to be central strongholds. The fact is, however, that the construction of both of those fortresses is much flimsier and rougher than that of any of the others. Add to this that both the commanders and the soldiers protecting these places are under the impression that the enemy would never attack them. To all appearances, they have been extremely negligent in their preparations. If we mount a surprise attack, it must be there. Moreover, once we destroy the enemy's very core, how much more easily the other castles would fall!"

Katsuie and Genba both agreed heartily with Shogen's plan.

"Shogen has seen through the enemy's ruse," Katsuie said. "This is the best plan we could have made for confounding Hideyoshi."

It was the first time Shogen had been so highly praised by Katsuie. For some days he had been despondent and deflated, but now his expression suddenly changed.

"Take a look at this," he said, spreading out a map. The fortresses at Dangi, Shinmei, Mount Iwasaki, and Mount Oiwa stood on the eastern shore of Lake Yogo. There were also a number of fortresses from the southern area of Shizugatake to Mount Tagami, the chain of camps stretching along the road to the northern provinces, and several other military positions. All were clearly shown, and the topography of the area—with its lakes, mountains, fields, and valleys—was delineated in detail.

The impossible had become possible. Clearly it was a great disadvantage for Hideyoshi, Katsuie gloated, that a secret map like this had been spread out in his enemy's headquarters before the battle.

It could be said that Katsuie derived great joy from that fact alone. Examining the map closely, he praised Shogen once again.

"This is a wonderful gift, Shogen."

Standing at one side, Genba was also scrutinizing the map, but looking up, he suddenly said with conviction, "Uncle, this plan of Shogen's—to penetrate deep behind the enemy lines and take the two fortresses of Iwasaki and Oiwa—I'd like you to send me as the vanguard! I am confident that a surprise attack with the necessary resolution and speed could be handled by no one other than myself."

"Well, now, wait a moment...."

Katsuie shut his eyes in quiet deliberation, as though apprehensive of the younger man's ardor. Genba's self-confidence and zeal quickly resisted that hesitation.

"What other plans are you entertaining for this opportunity? Surely there's no room in your thoughts for something else?"

"What? I don't think so."

"Heaven's opportunities don't wait, you know. While we stand here like this, our chance may be slipping away moment by moment."

"Don't be so hasty, Genba."

"No. The more you deliberate, the more time slips away. Are you unable to make a decision when a victory of such magnitude is right before your eyes? Ah, it makes me think Demon Shibata is getting old."

"You're talking foolishness. It's just that you're still young. You've got the courage for battle, but you're still inexperienced when it comes to strategy."

"Why do you say that?" Genba's face began to flush, but Katsuie would not be agitated. He was a veteran of innumerable battles, and was not about to lose his composure.

"Think for a moment, Genba. There is nothing more dangerous than going deep behind enemy lines. Is it worth the risk? Aren't we at a point where we must think this through over and over so there will be no regrets?"

Genba laughed out loud. But behind the hint that his uncle's anxiety was of no value, Genba's youthful iron will was also laughing at age's discrimination and vacillation.

Katsuie, however, did not reproach his nephew's open derisive laughter. He seemed to show affection for the young man's lack of inhibition. He actually seemed to love Genba's high spirits.

Genba had been accustomed to his uncle's favor for some time. He could quickly read through the man's emotions and come to terms with them easily. Now he insisted further. "It's true that I'm young, but I fully understand the danger of penetrating the enemy lines. In this situation I would be relying solely on strategy, and not be impatient for merit. I'll dare to do it just because there's danger involved."

Katsuie was still unable to give his approval freely. As before, he was lost in deliberation. Genba gave up badgering his uncle, and suddenly turned to Shogen.

"Let me see the map."

Without moving from the camp stool Genba unrolled the map, stroked his cheek with one hand, and remained silent.

Nearly an hour passed.

Katsuie had been concerned at the time his nephew had spoken with such zeal, but when he observed Genba silently contemplating the map, he suddenly felt sure of the younger man's reliability.

"All right." Finally putting an end to his own deliberations, he turned and spoke to his nephew. "Don't make any mistakes, Genba. I'm giving you the order to go deep behind the enemy lines tonight."

Genba looked up, and at the same time stood straight up from the camp stool. He was almost insanely happy and bowed with great civility. But while Katsuie admired this nephew who was so happy at being put in command of the vanguard, he knew it was a position that might easily mean a man's death if he made a mistake.

"I'm telling you again—once you've accomplished your goal of destroying Iwasaki and Oiwa, retreat with the speed of the wind."

"Yes, Uncle."

"This hardly needs to be said, but a safe retreat is extremely important in war—especially in a fight involving the penetration of enemy territory. If you fail to withdraw safely, it's like forgetting the last basketful of earth when digging a well a hundred fathoms deep. Go with the speed of the wind, and come back in the same way."

"I've understood your warning well."

His hope having now been realized, Genba was perfectly docile. Katsuie immediately assembled his generals. By evening the orders had gone out to each of the camps, and the preparations for every corps seemed to be complete.

It was the night of the nineteenth day of the Fourth Month. The eighteen-thousand-man army left the camp in secret exactly at the second half of the Hour of the Rat. The attacking force was divided into two corps of four thousand men each. They moved down the mountain toward Shiotsudani, crossed over Tarumi Pass, and pressed eastward along the western bank of Lake Yogo.

In a diversionary maneuver, the twelve thousand men of Katsuie's main army took a different route. Advancing along the road to the northern provinces, they gradually turned southeast. Their action was intended to assist the success of the surprise attack corps led by Sakuma Genba, and at the same time it would police any movements from the enemy fortresses.

Among the main forces of the diversionary army, Shibata Katsumasa's single corps of three thousand men went southeast of the slope at Iiura, hid their banners and armor, and stealthily observed the enemy movements in the direction of Shizugatake.

Maeda Inuchiyo had been charged with guarding a line that stretched from Shiotsu to Mount Dangi and Mount Shinmei.

Shibata Katsuie departed from the main camp at Mount Nakao with an army of seven thousand men, and he advanced as far as Kitsunezaka on the road to the northern provinces. It was in order to draw in and incapacitate Hidemasa's five thousand men stationed on Mount Higashino that Katsuie's army now proudly displayed its banners and marched on.

The night sky slowly began to brighten with the approach of dawn. It was the twentieth day of the Fourth Month of the lunar calendar—very close to the summer solstice—and the nights were short.

It was just about at that time that the generals of the vanguard began to gather on the white shore of Lake Yogo. Following the vanguard of four thousand men, a second corps came quickly up behind them. That was the force that would penetrate deep behind the enemy lines, and Sakuma Genba was in its midst.

The mist was thick.

Suddenly a rainbow-colored light appeared in the middle of the lake. That in itself might have made the men think that it would shortly be dawn. But they could hardly see the tails on the horses in front of them, and the path through the grassy plain was still dark.

As the mist swirled by the banners, armor, and spears, the men all appeared as though they were walking through water.

They were oppressed by thoughts that tightened their chests. The cold mist gathered on their eyebrows and on the hairs of their nostrils.

A splashing noise and laughter and animated voices could be heard from the lake shore. Scouts from the attacking troops quickly got down on all fours and crept forward to investigate who might be out in the middle of the mist. It turned out to be two samurai and maybe ten grooms from the fortress at Mount Iwasaki; they had just walked into the shallows of the lake and were washing horses.

The scouts waited for troops from the vanguard to move up and signaled to them silently with waves of the hand. Then, when they were sure the enemy was trapped, they suddenly yelled, "Take them alive!"

Caught unawares, the warriors and grooms splashed through the water in surprise and ran along the shore.

"The enemy! It's the enemy!"

Five or six men escaped, but the rest were captured.

"Well, well, the season's first game."

The Shibata warriors grabbed the prisoners by their collars and took them to their commander, Fuwa Hikozo, who questioned them from horseback.

A message was sent to Sakuma Genba, asking what should be done with the prisoners. The response spurred them to quick action: "Do not be delayed by these men. Kill them at once and continue immediately to Mount Oiwa."

Fuwa Hikozo dismounted, drew his sword, and personally decapitated one man. He then shouted out a command to all the members of the vanguard. "Here! have a festival of blood! Hack off the heads of the others and present them as an offering to the god of war. Then raise your war cries and move on to attack the fortress at Oiwa!"

The soldiers around Hikozo almost fought over the chance to cut off the heads of the grooms. Raising their bloody swords high in the morning sky, they offered the lifeblood of their prisoners and yelled to the demons. The entire army raised war cries in response.

Billowing waves of armor shook and trembled through the morning mist as each man competed to be first. Sweating horse brushed past sweating horse in the struggle to take the lead, and one spear corps after another rushed forward in the confusion of glittering spearheads.

Gunfire could already be heard, spears and long swords flashed in the morning light, and a strange sound was coming from the area of Mount Oiwa's first palisade.

How deep the lingering dreams of the short summer night! The slopes of Mount Oiwa, defended by Nakagawa Sebei, and Mount Iwasaki, held by Takayama Ukon—the center of Hideyoshi's fortifications—were bound by the mist and as quiet, as if no one knew yet of the oncoming flood of men.

The construction of the fortress at Mount Oiwa had been quick and simple. Naka-gawa Sebei slept in a rest hut along the ramparts halfway up the mountain.

Not yet fully conscious, he suddenly raised his head and muttered. "What's going on?"

On the border between dream and reality, and without knowing why, he got up abruptly and put on the armor that had been placed near his bed.

As he was finishing, someone knocked at the door of the rest hut and then seemed to be pushing against it with his body as well.

The door fell inward, and three or four retainers tumbled in.

"The Shibata!" they cried.

"Calm down!" Sebei reprimanded them.

From the incoherent reports of the surviving grooms, Sebei was unable to find out where the enemy had broken through or who was leading them.

"It would be an extraordinary feat for even a daring enemy to break this far through the lines. These men will not be easy to deal with. I don't know who's leading them, but I suspect that of all the commanders of the Shibata forces it's most likely to be Sakuma Genba."

Sebei had quickly grasped the situation, and a shudder ran through his entire frame. It would be difficult to deny that the man is a powerful enemy, he thought. But opposed to that overwhelming feeling, a different kind of strength bubbled up from within, and he rebounded.

Grabbing his long spear, he yelled, "Let's go fight!"

Sporadic gunfire could be heard in the distance, from the foot of the mountain. Then suddenly it was heard unexpectedly close, from a wooded area on the southwest slope.

"They've taken the shortcuts too."

Because of the thickness of the mist, the enemy banners could not be seen clearly, and that had the effect of making the Nakagawa forces even more fretful.

Sebei called out once again. His voice echoed in the heart of the mountain.

The thousand-man Nakagawa corps defending the mountain was now awakened by the attack coming in right before its eyes. It had been taken completely by surprise. As far as the men knew, the main Shibata position was a great distance away—a belief that had put them off their guard. The enemy would surely not attack such a safe place! But before they even realized that their belief had been mistaken, the enemy had already descended like a gale.

Sebei stamped the earth and upbraided his men for their complacency and negligence. One by one his officers sought him out and, either sighting his commander's standard or recognizing his voice, they and their soldiers hurriedly gathered around him and formed a real army.

"Is Genba in command?"

"Yes, my lord," a retainer replied.

"How many men does he have?" Sebei continued.

"Fewer than ten thousand."

"One line of attack or two?"

"There appear to be two armies. Genba is attacking from Niwatonohama, and Fuwa Hikozo has taken the path from Mount Onoji."

Even with all of its men assembled, the fortress was defended by no more than a thousand men. The attacking forces of the enemy were reported to be close to ten thousand.

Both shortcuts and the barrier gates at the foot of the mountain were inadequate. It was easy to see that it would only be a matter of time before they were annihilated.

"Confront the enemy at the shortcut!" Sebei sent his right-hand man off first with three hundred soldiers, and then encouraged his own men. "The rest of you come with me. The Nakagawa forces have never been bested since coming out of Ibaraki in Settsu. Don't step back a single pace from the enemy in front of us now!"

At the head of the commander's standard and the banners, Nakagawa Sebei took the lead and whipped his horse toward the foot of the mountain at full speed.

* * *

On the morning of the same day, six or seven warships moved north across Lake Biwa like a flock of water birds. On the curtain enfolding the bridge of one of the ships, a large iris crest fluttered in the wind.

Niwa Nagahide was standing on the bridge of the ship when he suddenly saw black smoke rising from a mountain on the north side of the lake and yelled out to the men around him. "Is that near Oiwa or Shizugatake?" he asked.

"It looks like Shizugatake," one of the members of his staff replied.

In fact, as one looked out in that direction, the mountains appeared to be piled one on top of another, so that the flames from Mount Oiwa looked quite convincingly as though they were rising from Shizugatake.

"It's hard to understand." Niwa knitted his brow and continued to gaze steadily out into the distance.

It was surprising how overly accurate his premonition was. At dawn that day—the twentieth of the month—he had received a message from his son, Nabemaru:

There have been suspicious movements in both Katsuie's and Genba's camps during the night.

At that time he had guessed that what he must be seeing was an enemy attack. Hideyoshi was busy attacking Gifu. And if their enemies were aware of it, they would know that it was the moment to strike at Hideyoshi's unguarded position.

Niwa felt apprehensive as soon as he heard his son's report. Boarding his meager force of a thousand men aboard five or six ships, he had them cross the lake to the vicinity of Kuzuo.

Just as he had feared, there were flames from the direction of Shizugatake, and when they finally approached the shore at Kuzuo, he could hear gunfire.

"The enemy seems to have overrun the fortress at Motoyama. Shizugatake is also in danger, and I doubt if Mount Iwasaki will be able to hold out."

Niwa asked two of the staff officers for their opinions.

"The situation certainly doesn't look good," one of the men answered. "The enemy has sent in a large force, and it would appear that our numbers are not going to be sufficient to help our allies in this emergency. The best plan would be to return to Sakamoto and entrench ourselves in the castle there."

"You're talking nonsense," Niwa said, dismissing the suggestion. "Disembark the entire army immediately. Then take the ships to Kaitsu and bring a third of Nagamaru's forces."

"Will there be time, my lord?"

"Everyday calculations have absolutely no value when it comes to war. Our mere presence will have an effect. It will take them some time to realize how few of us there are. And that will delay them. Get the troops landed, and hurry back to Kaitsu."

The army landed at Ozaki, and the ships set sail immediately. Niwa brought his horse to a stop in a village to question the locals.

The villagers told him that the battle had begun at dawn and was completely unexpected. Just as they had seen the flames from Mount Oiwa, they had heard war cries like the sound of tidal waves. Then, warriors from the Sakuma forces, perhaps a reconnoitering party, had whipped their horses through the village from the direction of Yogo. Rumor had it that Nakagawa Sebei's forces defended the fortress but were cut down to the last man.

When asked if they knew anything about Kuwayama's men in the area of Shizugatake, the villagers answered that just moments ago, Lord Kuwayama Shigeharu had led all of his forces from the fortress at Shizugatake and was now hurrying along the mountain road in the direction of Kinomoto.

This information left Niwa in openmouthed surprise. He had come with reinforcements, ready to entrench himself here with his allies, but the Nakagawa forces had been annihilated and the Kuwayama forces had abandoned their posts and were fleeing as fast as they could. What disgraceful conduct! What had they been thinking? Niwa pitied Kuwayama's confusion.

"And this happened just now?" he asked the villagers.

"They couldn't be much farther than half a league away," the farmer replied.

"Inosuke!" he called out to a retainer. "Run after the Kuwayama corps and talk with Lord Shigeharu. Tell him that I've come and that we'll defend Shizugatake together. Tell him to turn back immediately!"

"Yes, my lord!"

The man whipped his horse and hurried off in the direction of Kinomoto.

Kuwayama had tried two or three times that morning to persuade Nakagawa to retreat, but had offered him no help at all and had completely lost his head at the onslaught of the Sakuma forces. As soon as he heard of the destruction of the Nakagawa corps, he wavered all the more. Then, in the face of the rout of the central camp of his allies, he abandoned Shizugatake without firing a single bullet or wielding a spear in resistance, fleeing with a pace that left every man for himself.

His intentions were to join up with their allies at Kinomoto and then wait for Hidenaga's orders. But now, en route, here was a man from the Niwa clan informing him of

Niwa's reinforcements. Suddenly gaining courage, he reorganized his troops, made a quick turnaround, and went back to Shizugatake.

In the meantime Niwa had reassured the villagers. Ascending Shizugatake, he was finally united with Kuwayama Shigeharu.

He wrote a letter at once, sending it by dispatch to Hideyoshi's camp in Mino, informing him of the urgency of the situation.

The Sakuma forces at Mount Oiwa made a provisional camp there and, secure in their feeling of triumph, rested quietly for more than two hours from about the Hour of the Horse. The warriors were weary after the intense battle and the long march that had started the night before. After eating their provisions, however, they took pride in their blood-soaked hands and feet; lighthearted talk arose here and there, and their fatigue was forgotten.

Orders were given, and the officers were told to relay them from corps to corps.

"Sleep! Sleep! Close your eyes for a while. No one knows what's going to happen tonight!"

The clouds overhead looked like the clouds of summer, and the cries of the season's first cicadas could be heard in the trees. The wind wafted pleasantly over the mountains from lake to lake, and the soldiers—who had now satisfied their empty stomachs—finally felt themselves becoming drowsy. Still holding their firearms and spears, they sat down.

In the shade of the trees, the horses closed their eyes as well, and even the group commanders leaned against the trunks and fell asleep.

Everything was quiet, but it was the kind of silence that comes after an intense fight. The camp of their enemies—who had been wrapped in dreams until just before dawn—had been turned to ashes, and all of its soldiers become corpses left to the clusters of grass. It was now fully day, but death was in the air. Except for the alertness of the sentries everything was subdued, even the atmosphere in the staff headquarters was hushed.

The loud snores of the commander-in-chief, Genba, leaked happily through the curtains. Suddenly, five or six horses came to a halt somewhere, and a group of men in helmets and armor ran in the direction of the field staff headquarters. The members of the staff, who had sat sleeping around Genba, quickly looked outside.

"What's up?" they yelled.

"It's Matsumura Tomojuro, Kobayashi Zusho, and the other scouts."

"Come on in."

The man who invited them in was Genba. Awakened unexpectedly, his eyes were wide with surprise and still red from a lack of sleep. It appeared that just before taking a nap, he had gulped down a good deal of *sake*. A large red *sake* cup lay empty next to his seat.

Matsumura knelt in a corner of the curtained enclosure and then reported what they had observed.

"There's no longer even a single enemy soldier at Mount Iwasaki. We thought there was a chance that they had hidden their banners and were planning to lie in wait for us, so we looked around to make sure. But the commanding general, Takayama Ukon, and everyone under his command have gone to Mount Tagami."

Genba clapped his hands.

"They ran away?" He laughed out loud and looked around at his staff officers. "He says Ukon ran away! He's a fast one, isn't he!" He laughed again, sending his entire body into convulsions of glee.

It seemed he had not yet sobered up from the drunken state he had fallen into after the victory *sake*. Genba could not stop laughing.

Just then, the messenger who had been sent to Katsuie's main camp to report on the war situation returned with Katsuie's instructions.

"Are there no enemy movements in the area of Kitsunezaka?" Genba asked.

"Nothing in particular. Lord Katsuie seems to be in very fine spirits."

"I imagine he was quite pleased."

"Yes, he was." The messenger continued to answer Genba's repeated questions without even the chance to wipe the sweat from his brow. "When I described the details of this morning's battle to him, he said, 'Is that so? Well, that's just like that nephew of mine.'"

"Well, what about Sebei's head?"

"He examined it immediately and said that it was definitely Sebei's. Looking around at the men who were with him, he declared it to be a good omen, and his mood seemed to improve even more."

Genba was in a very good mood himself. Hearing of Katsuie's happiness, he exulted in his own triumph and burned with the desire to surprise his uncle with even greater joy.

"I suppose that the lord of Kitanosho still doesn't know that the fortress at Mount Iwasaki has also fallen into my hands," he laughed. "He gets satisfied just a little too quickly."

"No, the capture of Iwasaki was reported to him at about the time I was taking my leave."

"Well then, there's no need to send another dispatch, is there?"

"If that were the only thing."

"At any rate, by tomorrow morning Shizugatake is going to be mine."

"Well, as for that..."

"What do you mean?"

"Lord Katsuie said you might get carried away with this victory and start viewing the enemy as being too easy to deal with, and this might begin to put you off guard."

"You're talking foolishness," Genba said, laughing. "I'm not going to get drunk on this one victory."

"But just before you left, Lord Katsuie gave you that one warning in particular, telling you to make a clean retreat when you've entered deep into the enemy's territory. It's dangerous to stay here very long. Today again, he told me to tell you to return right away."

"He said to withdraw immediately?"

"His words were that you should withdraw quickly and unite forces with our allies to the rear."

"How weak-willed!" Genba grunted, showing a thin derisive smile. "Well, all right."

At that point, several scouts entered with their reports. Niwa's three thousand men had joined forces with the Kuwayama corps, and together they were reinforcing the defenses at Shizugatake.

That simply threw oil on the fire of Genba's eagerness to attack. Such news will make a truly brave general want to fight all the more.

"This will be interesting."

Genba brushed aside the camp curtain and went outside. Looking out over the new greenery of the mountains, he could see Shizugatake at a distance of about two leagues to the south. Closer and below where he stood, a general was climbing up from the foot of the mountain, accompanied by a number of attendants. The defending commander of the wooden barrier gate was hurrying ahead to show him the way.

Genba clicked his tongue and muttered, "That must be Dosei."

As soon as he recognized a general always at his uncle's side, he guessed the man's errand before meeting him.

"Ah, here you are."

Dosei wiped the sweat from his brow. Genba simply stood there without inviting the man inside the curtained enclosure. "Lord Dosei, what are you doing here?" he asked flatly.

Dosei looked as though he did not wish to say anything there and then, but Genba spoke out first.

"We'll camp here tonight and withdraw tomorrow. This was reported to my uncle already." He looked like he did not want to hear anything else about it.

"I've been informed." Dosei politely introduced his remarks with a greeting. He then congratulated Genba at length on his great victory at Mount Oiwa, but Genba was not able to bear his roundaboutness.

"Did my uncle send you here because he's still anticipating trouble?"

"As you've conjectured, he's extremely anxious about your plan to camp here. His wishes are for you to withdraw from enemy territory by tonight at the latest and return to his main camp."

"Don't worry, Dosei. When my picked troops advance, they have explosive power; when they stand to defend a place, they're like steel walls. We have not been shamed yet."

"Lord Katsuie has had faith in you from the very beginning, but when you look at this from a military standpoint, to be delayed when you've penetrated deep inside enemy territory is not really the accomplishment of your strategy."

"Wait a moment, Dosei. Are you saying that I don't understand the art of war? And are those your words or my uncle's?"

At that point even Dosei was getting nervous, and there was really nothing he could do but stay silent. He began to feel that his role as a messenger was putting him in danger.

"If you say so, my lord. I shall report the extent of your conviction to Lord Katsuie."

Dosei hurriedly took his leave, and when Genba returned to his seat he quickly sent out orders. Dispatching one corps of men to Mount Iwasaki, he also directed a number of small reconnaissance parties to Minegamine and the vicinity of Kannonzaka, between Shizugatake and Mount Oiwa.

Soon thereafter, another voice was heard making an announcement.

"Lord Joemon has just arrived on orders from the main camp at Kitsune."

The messenger this time had not come for simple conversation or to relay Katsuie's thoughts. Rather, he delivered formal military orders, the content of which was yet another request to retreat. Genba listened tamely, but his answer, as before, firmly up-held his own view and he showed no indication of submitting.

"He has already given me the responsibility of supervising an incursion deep into enemy territory. To comply with what he asks now would be to omit the finishing touch to a military operation that has been successful so far. I would like him to trust me with the baton of command for just one more step."

So Genba neither bowed to what the envoy had been sent to say nor submitted to his commander-in-chief's very explicit orders. He had used his ego as a shield. Standing be-fore him now, even Joemon—who had been chosen to come here by Katsuie himself—was unable to prevail upon the man's rigidity.

"There's nothing more I can do," Joemon said, washing his hands of the whole affair. His final words were accompanied by a slightly indignant look. "I cannot imagine what Lord Katsuie will think, but I will pass your answer on to him."

Joemon quickly returned without further conversation. He naturally whipped his horse to quicken his return, just as he had in coming.

Thus the third messenger returned, and by the time the fourth arrived, the sun was growing dim in the west. The old warrior, Ota Kuranosuke, a veteran retainer and per-sonal attendant to Katsuie, talked at length. He spoke, however, more about the relation-ship between uncle and nephew than about the order itself, and did his best to soften the youthful Genba's rigid stance.

"Now, now. I understand your resolve, but of all the members of your family, Lord Katsuie holds you in the highest esteem, and that's why he's so worried now. Particularly, now that you've destroyed one section of the enemy, we will be able to consolidate our position, continue to make one victory after another, and break down the enemy's weak points step by step. That is our larger strategy, and it's the one that has been decided upon in order to take control of the country. Listen, Lord Genba, you should stop here."

"The road is going to be dangerous when the sun goes down, old man. Go back."

"You won't do it, will you?"

"What are you talking about?"

"What is your decision?"

"I wasn't thinking of making that decision from the very beginning."

Fatigued, the old retainer left.

The fifth messenger arrived.

Genba had become even more rigid. He had come so far, and he was not going to turn back. He refused to see the messenger, but the man was not some minor retainer. The messengers who had come that day had all been distinguished men, but the fifth one was a particularly powerful member of Katsuie's entourage.

"I know that our envoys to you may not have been satisfactory, but now Lord Katsuie has talked about coming here himself. We, his close attendants, have urged him to stay in camp and I, as unworthy as I am, have come in his place. I implore you to think about this clearly and then strike camp and leave Mount Oiwa as quickly as possible."

He made his plea while prostrating himself outside the curtained enclosure.

Genba, however, had judged the situation thus: Even if Hideyoshi had been informed of the incident and had hurried from Ogaki, it was still a distance of thirteen leagues from there to here, and it would have taken until nightfall for the warning to arrive. It would also not be an easy matter to get away quickly from Gifu. Therefore, the soonest imaginable time for the completion of that shift in field positions would be tomorrow night or the day after.

"That nephew of mine is not going to listen, no matter who I send," Katsuie complained. "I'll have to go there myself and make him withdraw by nightfall."

The main camp at Kitsune had received word that day of the raiding army's happy success and was temporarily overjoyed. But the order for a swift retreat had not been carried out. In fact, Genba had dismissed all of the distinguished envoys with a refusal to obey and a derisive sneer.

"Ah, that nephew of mine is going to be the end of me," Katsuie lamented, barely able to contain himself. When word leaked out about the internal discord within the field staff—that Genba's willfulness was being criticized by Katsuie—the martial spirit within the camp somehow lost its cheerfulness.

"Another envoy has left camp."

"What! Another?"

The repeated comings and goings between the main camp and Mount Oiwa pained the hearts of the warriors.

For half a day, Katsuie felt his life would be shortened. During the time he waited for the return of his fifth envoy, he could hardly stay seated on his camp stool. The camp was located at a temple in Kitsunezaka, and it was along the corridors of that building that Katsuie now wandered silently, looking in the direction of the temple gate.

"Shichiza hasn't returned yet?" he asked his close attendants innumerable times. "It's already evening, isn't it?"

As dusk pressed in, he became irritated. The evening sun was now casting its light on the bell tower.

"Lord Yadoya has returned!" That was the message relayed by the warrior at the temple gate.

"What happened?" Katsuie asked anxiously.

The man delivered his report frankly. Genba had at first refused to meet him, but Yadoya had persisted. He had related his lord's view in detail, but in vain. Genba insisted that even if Hideyoshi rushed to Mount Oiwa from Ogaki, it would take him at least one or two days. Thus Genba would be able to destroy Hideyoshi's troops quite easily because they would be so fatigued from the long journey. For that reason, he had declared his resolution to remain on Mount Oiwa and in no way appeared ready to change his mind.

Katsuie's eyes glistened with anger. "That fool!" he yelled, almost as if he were spitting blood. Then, beneath a heavy groan that shook his entire frame, he muttered, "Genba's behavior is outrageous."

"Yaso! Yaso!" Looking all around him and into the warriors' waiting area in the next room, Katsuie yelled out in a high-pitched voice.

"Are you looking for Yoshida Yaso?" Menju Shosuke asked in return.

"Of course!" Katsuie shrieked, venting his anger on Shosuke. "Call him here right now! Tell him to come here right away!"

Running footsteps echoed through the temple. Yoshida Yaso received Katsuie's orders and immediately whipped his horse toward Mount Oiwa.

The long day finally darkened and the flames of the bonfires began to flicker in the shadows of the young leaves. They reflected what was now deep within Katsuie's breast.

The return trip of two leagues could be completed in the twinkling of an eye by a fast horse, and Yaso returned in no time at all.

"I told him that this was the last you had to say and admonished him thoroughly, but Lord Genba would not consent to a retreat."

The sixth report was the same. Katsuie no longer had the energy to be angry and would have shed tears had he not been on the battlefield. Instead, he simply sank into grief and blamed himself, regretting the blind love he had held for Genba until now.

"I'm the one who was wrong," he lamented.

On the battlefield—where a man must act strictly according to military discipline— Genba had taken advantage of his close ties to his uncle. He had made a decision that could affect the rise or fall of the entire clan, and had insisted on his own selfish way without the least bit of reflection.

But who was it who had allowed the young man to become accustomed to that kind of action? Wasn't this morass the result of his own heedless love for his nephew? Through it he had first lost his foster son, Katsutoyo, and Nagahama Castle. Now he was about to lose an enormous and irretrievable opportunity upon which rested the fate of the entire Shibata clan.

When these thoughts came to him, Katsuie sank deep into a remorse for which there was absolutely no one else to blame.

Yaso had more to report: the words that Genba had actually spoken. In response to Yaso's advice, Genba had laughed and even ridiculed his uncle:

"Long ago, when people mentioned the name of Lord Katsuie, they called him the Demon Shibata, and said he was a general of devilish contrivances and mysterious schemes—at least from what I've heard. Today, however, his tactics come from an old head out of touch with the times. You can't wage war today with old-fashioned strategies. Look at our penetration into the enemy territory this time. At the beginning, my uncle wouldn't even give his permission for the plan. He should leave the whole thing to me and watch for the next day or two."

Katsuie's gloom and wretchedness were unbearable to watch. He, more than anyone, knew Hideyoshi's true value as a general. The comments he had made to Genba and his other retainers had never been anything more than strategic remarks aimed at taking away their fear of the enemy. In his very bowels, Katsuie knew that Hideyoshi was a formidable adversary, especially after his withdrawal from the western provinces and his performance at the Battle of Yamazaki and the conference at Kiyosu. Now this powerful enemy was before him, and at the very opening of these all-or-nothing hostilities, he saw that his own ally was a stumbling block.

"Genba's behavior is outrageous. Never once have I suffered a defeat or shown my back to the enemy. Ahh, this was inevitable."

The night darkened, and Katsuie's anguish turned to resignation.

Messengers were not sent out again.

GENBA'S STRATAGEM

That very same day—the twentieth of the month, at the Hour of the Horse—Hidenaga sent his first report to Hideyoshi's camp at Ogaki.

> This morning a Sakuma force of eight thousand men took to the mountain trails and entered deep into our territory.

It was thirteen leagues from Kinomoto to Ogaki, and even for a mounted messenger, the courier had been amazingly fast.

Hideyoshi had just come back from the bank of the Roku River, where he had gone to observe the level of the rising water. There had been violent rains in Mino for the past few days, and the Goto and Roku rivers, both of which flowed between Ogaki and Gifu, were flooding.

The original plan had called for a general attack on Gifu Castle on the nineteenth, but the heavy rains and the floodwaters of the Roku River had obstructed Hideyoshi, and there were no prospects of crossing the river again that day. He had been waiting two days now for a chance to move on.

Hideyoshi received the urgent letter from the messenger outside camp and read the note while still in the saddle. After thanking the messenger, he went back to his quarters without any visible show of emotion.

"How about making me a bowl of tea, Yuko?" he asked. At about the time he was finishing his bowl of tea, a second messenger arrived:

> The twelve thousand-man main army under Lord Katsuie has taken up its positions. It is moving out of Kitsunezaka in the direction of Mount Higashino.

Hideyoshi had moved to his camp stool in the curtained headquarters, and now he called in various members of his staff and told them, "An urgent message has just come from Hidenaga."

Coolly, he read the letter aloud. The generals looked alarmed as they listened. The third dispatch was from Hori Kyutaro, who clearly detailed the brave fight and death of Nakagawa and the loss of Mount Iwasaki because of Takayama's retreat. Hideyoshi closed his eyes for a moment when he learned of Nakagawa's death in battle. For a moment, a desolate look came over the faces of the generals, and they blurted out pathetic questions. Every one of them stared at Hideyoshi, as if trying to read from his face how they would handle this dangerous situation.

"Sebei's death is a great loss," Hideyoshi said, "but he did not die in vain." He spoke a little louder. "Be of good spirits, and thereby, you'll pay tribute to Sebei's spirit. More and more, heaven is prophesying that a great victory will be ours. Katsuie was entrenched in his mountain castle, withdrawn from the world and unable to find his way. Now he has left the fortress that was a prison for him and arrogantly drawn his formation out far and wide. That shows that his luck has run out. We should be able to destroy the bastard completely before he even quarters his troops. The time has come for us to realize our great desire and fight this decisive battle for the nation! The time has come, and not one of you should fall behind!"

The dire news was suddenly transformed by Hideyoshi's few words into a reason for cheer.

"The victory is ours!" Hideyoshi declared. Then, without losing any time, he began to give out orders. The generals receiving his commands took their leave at once and each man almost flew back to his camp.

These men, who had been pressed by the alarming feeling that they were in critical danger, now felt impatient and strained, waiting for their own names to be called as Hideyoshi gave out his commands.

Except for Hideyoshi's pages and attendants, practically all the generals had withdrawn to make their preparations. But two local men, Ujiie Hiroyuki and Inaba Ittetsu, as well as Horio Mosuke, who was under Hideyoshi's direct command, had not received any orders.

Looking as though he could hardly contain himself, Ujiie came forward on his own and said, "My lord, I have a favor to ask: I would also like to prepare my own forces to go with you."

"No, I want you to stay at Ogaki. I'll need you to keep Gifu under control." He then turned to Mosuke. "I want you to stay here too."

With those last orders, Hideyoshi left the enclosure. He called for his page and asked him, "What about the couriers I ordered before? Are they ready?"

"Yes, my lord! They're waiting for your instructions."

The page ran off quickly and returned with fifty runners.

Hideyoshi turned to the runners and addressed them directly. "Today is a day like no other in our lives. It is a great blessing for you to have been chosen to be the heralds of this day."

He continued with individual orders. "Twenty of you will announce to the villages on the road between Tarui and Nagahama that torches should be set along the roads at nightfall. Also, no obstructions like handcarts, stock, or lumber should be left in the way. Children should be kept indoors and bridges should be strengthened."

The twenty men on his right nodded simultaneously. To the remaining thirty men he gave the following instructions: "The rest of you go to Nagahama at top speed. Have the garrison prepare itself, and tell the elders of the towns and villages that military provisions should be placed along the roads that we'll be traveling."

The fifty men ran off right away.

Hideyoshi immediately issued a command to the retainers around him and then mounted his black horse.

Just then Ujiie ran up unexpectedly. "My lord! Wait a moment!" Clinging to Hideyoshi's saddle, the warrior was weeping silently.

Leaving Ujiie alone in Gifu, with the possibility that he might communicate with Nobutaka and rebel, had been a source of anxiety for Hideyoshi. To forestall betrayal, he had ordered Horio Mosuke to stay with Ujiie.

Ujiie was mortified not only by the thought that he had been doubted but also by the realization that Mosuke would be left out of the most important battle of his life just because of him.

It was in response to those deep emotions that Ujiie now clung to the bridle of Hideyoshi's horse. "Even if it's not right for me to accompany you, I beg you to allow General Mosuke at least to be at your side. I'll be happy to disembowel myself right here to remove your anxiety!"

And he put his hand on his dagger.

"Keep your head, Ujiie!" Hideyoshi shouted, striking the man's hand with his whip. "Mosuke can follow me if he wants to come with me that much. But he should come after the army has left. And for that matter, we can't just leave you. You should come along too."

Almost insane with joy, Ujiie turned toward the staff headquarters and called out in a loud voice, "Lord Mosuke! Lord Mosuke! We've received permission to go! Come out and show your gratitude."

The two men prostrated themselves on the ground, but all that remained was the sound of a whip in the wind. Hideyoshi's horse was already galloping off in the distance.

Even his attendants were caught off guard and had to scramble to catch up.

The men on foot, as well as those who quickly mounted their horses, chased after their master all at once without any formation or order.

It was the Hour of the Ram. Not even two hours had passed between the arrival of the first courier and Hideyoshi's departure. During that time, Hideyoshi had turned a defeat in northern Omi into an opportunity for victory. He had created a new strategy for his entire army on the spot. He had instructed couriers and sent them out with orders along the thirteen-league road to Kinomoto—the road that would be his path to all or nothing.

He had been resolved in both body and mind.

With the impetus of that resolve, he himself and a force of fifteen thousand men sped straight ahead, while five thousand men remained behind.

Hideyoshi and his advance guard entered Nagahama that afternoon at the Hour of the Monkey. One corps followed another, and the last men and horses to leave Ogaki must have been departing just about the same time the advance guard was entering Nagahama.

Hideyoshi was not negligent when he arrived at Nagahama, but immediately made preparations for taking the initiative against the enemy. In fact, he never even dismounted. After eating rice balls and slaking his thirst with a ladle of water, he quickly departed from Nagahama and hurried on through Sone and Hayami. He arrived at Kinomoto at the Hour of the Dog.

It had taken them only five hours to travel from Ogaki, because they had come the entire way without stopping.

Hidenaga's fifteen thousand men were at Mount Tagami. Kinomoto was actually a post station on the road that skirted the eastern slope of the mountain. A division of the army on the peak was stationed there. Just outside the village of Jizo, the men had constructed an observation tower.

"Where are we? What's the name of this place?" Hideyoshi asked, pulling his galloping horse to an abrupt halt and holding on tightly.

"This is Jizo."

"We're close to the camp at Kinomoto."

The answers came from some of the retainers around him. Hideyoshi remained in the saddle.

"Give me some water," he ordered. Taking the ladle offered him, he swallowed down the water in one gulp and stretched for the first time since he had left Ogaki, then dismounted and quickly walked to the base of the watchtower and looked up to the sky. The tower was unroofed and had no stairway. The soldiers simply climbed up by stepping on roughly spaced wooden footholds.

Suddenly Hideyoshi seemed to recall his days as a young foot soldier. Tying the cord of his commander's fan to the sword he was wearing, he began to climb to the top of the tower. His pages pushed him up by his hindquarters, and a sort of human ladder was formed.

"This is dangerous, my lord."

"Don't you need a ladder?"

The men below called to him, but Hideyoshi was already well over twenty feet from the ground.

The violent storm that had passed over the plains of Mino and Owari had abated. The sky was clear and full of stars, and Lake Biwa and Lake Yogo were like two mirrors thrown onto the plain.

When Hideyoshi, who had seemed weary from the journey, stood on the tower—his resolute figure outlined against the night sky—he was far more happy than tired. The more dangerous the situation and the deeper his hardships, the happier he became. It was the happiness that arose from surmounting adversities and being able to turn and see them behind him, and he had experienced it to greater and lesser degrees since the time of his youth. He himself claimed that the greatest happiness of life was to stand at the difficult border between success and failure.

But now, as he gazed out over nearby Shizugatake and Mount Oiwa, he looked like a man who was confident of victory.

Hideyoshi, however, was far more cautious than most men. Now, as was his habit, he peacefully closed his eyes and placed himself in a position where the world was neither enemy nor ally. Extricating himself from earthly inconsistencies, he himself became the heart of the universe and listened for the declaration of heaven's will.

"It's just about finished up already," he muttered, finally displaying a smile. "That Sakuma Genba came out looking so fresh and green. What could he have been dreaming of?"

Descending the tower, he immediately climbed halfway up Mount Tagami, where, he was greeted by Hidenaga. As soon as he finished giving Hidenaga his orders, Hideyoshi once again descended the mountain, passed through Kuroda, crossed over Kannonzaka, went along the east of Yogo, and arrived at Mount Chausu, where he rested for the first time since departing Ogaki.

He was accompanied by two thousand soldiers. His persimmon-colored silk armor coat was covered with the sweat and dust of the day. But it was in that dirty coat, and with the steady movements of his military fan, that he gave out the instructions for the battle.

It was already late at night, somewhere between the second half of the Hour of the Boar and the first half of the Hour of the Rat.

Hachigamine lay to the east of Shizugatake. Genba had brought up a single corps there during the evening. His plan for the attack on Shizugatake the following morning was to act in concert with the vanguard at Iiurazaka and Shimizudani to the northwest and to isolate the enemy fortress.

Stars filled the entire sky. The mountains, however, covered with trees and shrubs, were as black as ink, and the path that wound through them was nothing more than a narrow woodcutters' trail.

One of the sentries grunted.

"What's going on?" another man asked.

"Come here and take a look," yet another man called from a little farther off. The sound of men rustling through the undergrowth could be heard, and then the figures of sentries appeared on the ridge.

"There seems to be a sort of glow in the sky," one of them said, pointing toward the southeast.

"Where?"

"From the right of that big cypress all the way to the south."

"What do you think it is?"

They all laughed.

"It must be the farmers near Otsu or Kuroda burning something."

"There shouldn't be any farmers left in the villages. They've all run away to the mountains."

"Well then, maybe it's the bonfires of the enemy stationed at Kinomoto."

"I don't think so. On a night when the clouds are low it would be different, but it's strange to see the sky colored like this on a clear night. There are too many trees blocking our view here, but we should be able to see if we climb up to the edge of that cliff."

"Hold up! That's dangerous!"

"If you slip, you'll fall all the way into the valley!"

They tried to stop him, but he climbed out onto the rock face, clinging to the vines. His silhouette looked like that of a monkey on top of the rocky mountain.

"Oh no! This is horrible!" he suddenly called out.

His exclamation startled everyone below.

"What is it? What do you see?"

The man on the ridge stood silently, almost as though he were in a daze. One after another, the men below climbed up to where he was. When they reached the top, they all trembled. Standing on the rocky clifftop, they could see not only Lake Yogo and Lake Biwa but also the road to the northern provinces that wound its way south along the lake. Even the base of Mount Ibuki was visible.

Night had fallen, so it was difficult to see clearly, but there appeared to be a single line of flames flowing like a river all the way from Nagahama to Kinomoto near the foot of the mountain they were on. The flames stretched from point to point as far as the eye could see—a steady stream of fire with circles of light.

"What's that?"

Dazzled for a moment, they suddenly came to their senses.

"Let's go! Quick!"

The sentries scrambled down the cliff face almost as if they'd lost their grip, and ran off to inform the main camp.

With glorious expectations for the next day, Genba had gone to sleep early. His soldiers too were already asleep.

It was close to the Hour of the Boar when Genba sat up, aroused from his light sleep.

"Tsushima!" he called out.

Osaki Tsushima was sleeping nearby, and by the time he got up, Genba was already standing before him, grasping a spear he had taken from the hand of a page.

"I just heard a horse whinny. Go out and check."

"Right!"

As Tsushima lifted the curtain he ran headlong into a man yelling for his life.

"This is an emergency!" the man said, panicked.

Genba raised his voice and asked, "What do you have to report?"

In his agitated state the man was unable to report on the urgent situation with conciseness.

"There are a great number of torches and bonfires along the road between Mino and Kinomoto, and they're moving along in an alarming red line. Lord Katsumasa thinks it's got to be an enemy movement."

"What! A line of fire on the Mino road?"

Genba looked as though he still did not understand. But one step behind that urgent report from Shimizudani came a similar dispatch from Hara Fusachika, who was camped at Hachigamine.

The soldiers in camp began to wake up in the dark commotion. Ripples spread out immediately.

Curiously, Hideyoshi was coming back from Mino. But Genba could not quite believe it; he still wore the unwavering look of someone who persists in his own convictions. "Tsushima! Go verify this!"

With that order he demanded his camp stool and consciously put on an air of composure. Certainly he understood the subtle feelings of his retainers as they looked to see what was written on his face.

Osaki returned quickly. He had ridden to Shimizudani, then to Hachigamine, and then continued from Mount Chausu to Kannonzaka in order to ascertain the facts. And the facts were these:

"Not only can you see the torches and bonfires, but if you listen carefully you can hear the whinnying of the horses and the clattering of their hooves. It's nothing to joke about. You'll need to plan a counter strategy as quickly as possible."

"Well, what about Hideyoshi?"

"It's thought that Hideyoshi is in the van."

Genba was now so taken aback that he could hardly find the words to speak. Biting his lip, he looked up silently, his face pale.

After a while he said, "We'll retreat. There's nothing else we can do, is there? A large army is on its way, and our troops are isolated here."

Genba had stubbornly refused to obey Katsuie's orders the night before. Now he himself ordered his panicked troops to make preparations to strike camp, and hastened his retainers and pages.

"Is the messenger from Hachigamine still here?" Genba asked the retainers around him as he mounted his horse. Told that the messenger was still in camp, he summoned him.

"Go back immediately and tell Hikojiro that our main corps is now beginning a retreat, pulling back through Shimizudani, Iiurazaka, Kawanami, and Moyama. Hikojiro's forces should follow us as a rear guard."

As soon as he had finished giving the order, Genba joined his retainers and started down the pitch-dark mountain path.

Thus, Sakuma's main army began its general retreat during the second half of the Hour of the Boar. The moon was not out when they set off. For about half an hour they burned no torches, to prevent the enemy from discovering their whereabouts. Instead, they stumbled down the narrow paths by the light of their fuse cords and the stars.

Comparing their movements in terms of time, Genba must have started to strike camp just as Hideyoshi had climbed up Mount Chausu from Kuroda village and was taking a rest.

It was there that Hideyoshi talked with Niwa Nagahide, who had come in haste from Shizugatake to have an audience with him. Nagahide was an honored guest, and Hideyoshi's treatment of him was polite indeed.

"I hardly know what to say at present," he said. "You've gone to great trouble since this morning."

With those few words, he shared the commander's seat with Nagahide, later asking about matters like the enemy's situation and the lay of the land. From time to time the laughing voices of the two men could be heard on the night wind blowing across the mountaintop.

During that time, the soldiers following Hideyoshi continued coming into camp in groups of two and three hundred.

"Genba's forces have already started to retreat toward Shimizudani and have left a rear guard in the area of Hachigamine," a scout reported.

Hideyoshi then issued an order to Nagahide to relay the following information and commands to all the fortresses of their allies:

At the Hour of the Ox, I will begin a surprise attack on Genba. Gather the local people and have them yell battle cries from the mountaintops at dawn. Just as dawn breaks, you will hear gunfire, which will signal that the opportunity has come for getting the enemy in our grasp. You should know without being told that the firing before dawn will be coming from the muskets of the enemy. The conch shell will be the signal for the general attack. The chance should not be missed.

As soon as Nagahide departed, Hideyoshi had the camp stool taken away. "They say Genba's running away. Follow his path of retreat and pursue him furiously," he said, telling the warriors around him to relay that order to the entire army. "And be sure not to fire your muskets until the sky begins to turn light."

It was not a level road they were on, but really just a mountain path with a good many dangerous spots. The attack began with one corps after another starting out, but they could not advance as fast as they would have liked.

Along the way, men dismounted and led their horses through swamps or along cliff faces where there was no road at all.

After midnight the moon rose to the middle of the sky and helped the Sakuma forces along their path of retreat. Its light, however, was also a blessing for Hideyoshi's pursuit of them.

The two armies were no more than three hours apart. Hideyoshi had sent an overwhelmingly large army into this one battle, and his warriors' morale was high. The probable outcome was clear before the fighting began.

The sun was high. It was almost the Hour of the Dragon. There had been fighting on the shore of Lake Yogo, but the Shibata had fled once again, collecting themselves in the area of Moyama and the Sokkai Pass.

Here, Maeda Inuchiyo and his son were camped, their banners flying peacefully. Very peacefully. Seated on his camp stool, Inuchiyo no doubt had coolly observed the gunfire and sparks that had been spreading over Shizugatake, Oiwa, and Shimizudani since dawn.

He commanded a wing of Katsuie's army, which put him in a truly delicate position, for his personal feelings and his duty to Katsuie were in conflict. One mistake and his province and entire family would perish. The situation was very clear. If he opposed Katsuie, he would be destroyed. If he abandoned his long friendship with Hideyoshi, however, he would be betraying his emotions.

Katsuie...Hideyoshi...

Comparing the two men, Inuchiyo very likely would not make a mistake in choosing between them. When he had left his castle at Fuchu for the battlefield, his wife had been worried about her husband's intentions and had questioned him closely.

"If you don't fight Lord Hideyoshi, you won't be fulfilling your duty as a warrior," she had said.

"Do you think so?"

"But I don't think that you need to honor your word to Lord Katsuie."

"Don't be foolish. Do you think I'm capable of betraying my word as a warrior once I've given it?"

"Well then, which one are you going to support?"

"I'm leaving it up to heaven. I don't know what else I can do. Man's wisdom is too limited for something like this."

The bloody, screaming Sakuma forces were fleeing toward the Maeda positions.

"Don't panic! Don't act disgracefully!" Genba, who was also fleeing in that direction accompanied by a group of mounted men, leapt from his crimson saddle and rebuked his troops with hoarse shrieks. "What's the matter with you? Are you going to run, after so little fighting?"

Reproaching his warriors, Genba was trying to encourage himself at the same time. As he sat down heavily on one of the rocks, his shoulders heaved and he seemed almost to be breathing fire. A bitter taste filled his mouth. The effort he had made not to lose his dignity as a general in the middle of this confusion and disaster was extraordinary, considering his youth.

It was only now that he was told that his younger brother had been killed. With open disbelief he listened to the reports informing him that many of his commanders had died.

"What about my other brothers?"

In response to that abrupt question, a retainer pointed them out behind him. "Two of your brothers are over there, my lord."

Genba, with bloodshot eyes, spotted the two men. Yasumasa had stretched out on the ground and was staring absentmindedly up to the sky. The youngest brother slept with his head dangling off to the side, while blood from a wound filled his lap.

Genba felt affection for his brothers and was relived that they were still alive, but the sight of those same brothers—his own flesh and blood—also seemed to enrage him.

"Stand up, Yasumasa!" he yelled. "And pull yourself together, Shichiroemon! It's too early for you to be lying on the ground. What are you doing!"

Mustering his courage, Genba stood up with some difficulty. He, too, seemed to have sustained a wound.

"Where's Lord Inuchiyo's camp? On the top of that hill?" He started to walk away, dragging one of his feet, but turned back and looked at his younger brothers, who seemed to be coming behind him. "You don't have to come. You two should collect some men and prepare for the enemy. Hideyoshi is not going to waste time."

Genba sat on the commander's stool within the enclosure and waited. Inuchiyo soon appeared.

"I was sorry to hear what happened," he sympathized.

"Don't be." Genba managed to force a bitter smile. "With such mediocre thinking, I was bound to lose."

It was such an unexpectedly tame answer that Inuchiyo looked again at Genba. It seemed that Genba was taking the blame for his defeat entirely upon himself. Genba did not complain about Inuchiyo not sending his troops into battle.

"For the present, would you give us your assistance by holding off the attacking Hideyoshi forces with your fresh troops?"

"Of course. But do you want the spear corps or the firearm corps?"

"I would like the gunners' corps to lie in wait a good bit out in front. They could shoot into the confusion of the advancing enemy, and we could then act as a second force, brandishing our own bloody spears and fighting like we're ready to die. Go quickly! I beg of you!"

On any other day, Genba would not have begged Inuchiyo for anything. Even Inuchiyo could not help feeling pity for the man. He understood that Genba's humility was most likely due to the weakness he felt because of his defeat. But it also might have been because Genba already understood Inuchiyo's real intentions.

"The enemy seems to be approaching," Genba said, not relaxing even for a moment. As he muttered these words, he stood up. "Well then," he said, "I'll see you later." He lifted the curtain and went out, but then turned to Inuchiyo, who was coming out from behind to see him off. "We may not meet again on this earth, but I do not plan on dying ignominiously."

Inuchiyo escorted him as far as the place where he had been lingering a little while before. Genba bade him good-bye and descended the slope with quick steps. The scene below that filled his field of vision had changed completely from what it had been only minutes before.

The Sakuma forces had numbered eight thousand men, but it appeared that only about one-third of them remained. The others were either dead or wounded or had deserted. Those who did remain were either routed soldiers or distracted commanders, and their yells of confusion made the situation seem even worse than it was.

It was clear that Genba's younger brothers were incapable of organizing the chaos. Most of the senior officers were dead. The various corps had no leaders, and the soldiers were unsure of who would be next in command, while Hideyoshi's army was already visible in the distance. Even if the Sakuma brothers had been able to stop the rout at that point, little could have been done about the army's wavering.

But the gunners of the Maeda army ran as quietly as water through all the screaming and, quickly spreading out at some distance outside the camp, lay down. Observing that action, Genba yelled out a command in a penetrating voice, and finally the confusion abated a little.

The knowledge that fresh troops from the Maeda had entered the field became an extraordinary source of strength for Genba's soldiers, as well as for Genba and his remaining officers.

"Don't retreat a step until we see that damned monkey's head at the end of one of our spears! Don't let the Maeda laugh at us! Don't shame yourselves!"

Spurring them on, Genba moved around through his officers and men. As might be expected, the soldiers who had followed him that far were alive to the feeling of honor. Blood and gore, dried by a sun that had been shining brightly since the early hours of the day, stained the armor and spears of many. Dirt and bits of grass were mixed in with the filth.

Every man's face showed that he craved a drink of water, even if just a mouthful. But there was no time for that. Great clouds of yellow dust and the sounds of the enemy's horses were already approaching from the distance.

But Hideyoshi, who had advanced thus far from Shizugatake with a force that had swept over everything, pulled back just before Moyama.

"This camp is under the command of Maeda Inuchiyo and his son, Toshinaga," Hideyoshi announced.

With that observation, he suddenly brought the rushing advance of his vanguard to a halt. He then reorganized his his battle array and brought his men into formation.

At that point the two armies were out of firing range. Genba continued to command the Maeda gunners to take up a position in the path of the enemy's advance, but the dust covered Hideyoshi's army, which refused to advance into firing range.

After he had parted from Genba, Inuchiyo lingered at the edge of the mountain and watched the situation from afar. His intentions were a puzzle even to the generals around him. Two of his samurai, however, led out his horse.

Well, now he's determined to go out and fight. In their hearts, that is what his soldiers seemed to hope. But as Inuchiyo was stepping into the stirrups, he was whispering with a messenger who had just returned with an answer from Toshinaga's encampment. Inuchiyo mounted his horse but did not seem ready to move.

There was a noisy outburst in the direction of the foot of the mountain. When Inuchiyo and everyone else looked down that way, they could see that a frightened horse from the rear of their formation had broken its tether and was running wild through the camp.

That would not have been a difficult situation in normal times, but at that juncture, confusion created more confusion and resulted in an uproar.

Inuchiyo looked back at the two samurai and signaled to them with his eyes.

"Carry on, everyone," he said to the retainers around him, and hastened his horse forward.

At the same moment, rattling musket fire echoed across the plain. That would have come from their own gunners' corps, and Hideyoshi's forces must have opened their assault simultaneously. With those thoughts, Inuchiyo charged down the slope, looking at the clouds of dust and gunpowder smoke off to the side.

"Now! Now!" he muttered, and struck his saddle incessantly.

Gongs and large war drums were being beaten in one section of the encampment at Moyama, adding to the confusion. It seemed that Hideyoshi's irresistible forces had stepped over their own casualties on the gunners' line of defense and were already breaking deeply into the heart of the Sakuma and Maeda corps. And, as easily as they had thrown the central army into confusion, they were now coming with such fury that nothing could stop them.

Observing the violent fighting, Inuchiyo avoided the road, joined forces with his son, Toshinaga, and quickly started to withdraw.

Some of his officers were both angry and suspicious, but for Inuchiyo it was nothing more than the action he had decided upon earlier. In his heart of hearts, Inuchiyo had always been independent, and his wish had been for neutrality. Because of the position of his province, he had been sought after by Katsuie and had been compelled to join that man's side. But now, because of his friendship with Hideyoshi, he quietly retreated.

But Hideyoshi's advancing troops tore relentlessly into the Maeda army, and some of the rear guard were cut down.

In the meantime, Inuchiyo and his son led their almost completely uninjured troops out of camp; from Shiotsu they took a roundabout route through Hikida and Imajo and finally withdrew into Fuchu Castle. During the violent battle, which lasted two days, the Maeda encampment was like a solitary forest standing peacefully in the midst of the clouds of chaos.

* * *

What had conditions been in Katsuie's camp since the night before?

Katsuie had sent six different messengers to Genba, and each messenger had returned in complete failure. Katsuie then lamented that nothing more could be done and went to sleep with bitter resignation. In fact, he should not have been able to sleep at all: he was reaping what he himself had sown—his favoritism toward Genba had yielded the poison of blind love. He had made a grave mistake in being led by his emotions into confounding the flesh-and-blood bond of an uncle and his nephew with the solemn ties between a commander and his subordinate.

Now Katsuie fully understood. Genba had also been the cause of the rebellion of Katsuie's foster son, Katsutoyo, at Nagahama. And he had heard of Genba's unpleasant haughty behavior toward Maeda Inuchiyo, of all people, on the battlefield in Noto.

Even recognizing such flaws in the man, Katsuie was still sure that Genba's fiber was far above the average.

"Ah, but now those very qualities may prove to have been fatal," he mumbled, turning over in his sleep.

At the moment when the lamps were beginning to flicker, a number of warriors came running down the corridor. In the next room and the room next to that, Menju Shosuke and others started up from their sleep.

Hearing voices in response to those footsteps, the men who had been guarding Katsuie's quarters quickly ran out into the corridor.

"What's happened?"

The bearing of the warrior who had rushed in as a spokesman was not normal. He spoke so quickly that his words jumbled together.

"The sky over Kinomoto has been red for some time. Our scouts have just returned from Mount Higashino—"

"Don't be so long-winded! Just give us the essentials!" Menju abruptly admonished the man.

"Hideyoshi has arrived from Ogaki. His army is making a great uproar in the vicinity of Kinomoto," the warrior said in one breath.

"What? Hideyoshi?"

The agitated men had come as quickly as they could to report the situation at Katsuie's sleeping quarters, but Katsuie had already heard what had been said and came out to the corridor himself.

"Did you hear what they were saying just now, my lord?"

"I heard," Katsuie replied. His face looked even more ashen than it had earlier in the evening. "As for that, Hideyoshi did the same thing during the campaign in the western provinces."

As might be expected, Katsuie remained calm and tried to quiet those around him, but he could not conceal his own residual emotions. He had warned Genba, and from the way he was speaking now, it seemed almost as though he were proud that that warning had hit the mark. But this was also the voice of that brave general who had once been called Jar-Bursting Shibata or Demon Shibata. Those who heard it now could only feel pity.

"I can no longer rely on Genba. From here on I'll have to take my own stand, so we can fight to our hearts' content. Don't waver and don't be alarmed. We should be happy that Hideyoshi has finally come."

Gathering his generals, Katsuie sat down on his camp stool and issued the orders for troop dispositions. He behaved with the vigor of a young man. He had anticipated Hideyoshi's coming as only a slight possibility; as soon as the possibility became a real threat, his camp was thrown into confusion. Not a few men left their posts of duty with the excuse of illness, others disobeyed orders, and many soldiers deserted in confusion and panic. It was a sad state of affairs: of seven thousand soldiers, not even three thousand now remained.

This was the army that had departed from Echizen with a will firmly set to fight Hideyoshi. Those men should not have been ready to run away at the first actual threat from him.

What had led them to that point—an army of over seven thousand men? It had been one thing only: the lack of an authoritative command. Also, Hideyoshi's actions had been unexpectedly swift, and that only dumbfounded them all the more. Rumors and false reports ran rampant, and thus cowardice was encouraged.

When Katsuie observed his troops' ugly confusion, he was not merely disheartened, but enraged. Gnashing his teeth, he seemed unable to keep from spitting out his indignation to the officers around him. First sitting, then standing, then walking around, the warriors around Katsuie had been unable to calm themselves down at all. His orders had been relayed two or three times, but the answers had been unclear.

"Why are you all so flustered?" he asked, rebuking those around him. "Calm down! Leaving posts of duty and spreading rumors and gossip only causes our men to become more confused. Anyone committing such acts will be severely punished," he said, adding one rebuke to another.

A number of his subordinates dashed out a second time, announcing his strict orders. But even after that, Katsuie could be heard shouting in a high-pitched voice, "Don't get excited! Don't get confused!" But his intentions to suppress the turmoil only resulted in adding one more voice to the wild commotion.

Dawn had almost come.

The war cries and musket fire that had moved from the area of Shizugatake to the western bank of Lake Yogo echoed across the water.

"The way things are going, Hideyoshi should be getting here soon!"

"At least by noon."

"What! You think they're going to wait until then?"

Cowardice engendered more cowardice, and finally fear enveloped the entire camp.

"There must be ten thousand of the enemy!"

"No, I think there must be twenty thousand!"

"What? With that kind of power, there must be thirty thousand of them!"

The soldiers were caught up in their own fears, and no one felt comfortable without the agreement of his companions. Then a rumor that sounded like the truth started to circulate.

"Maeda Inuchiyo has gone over to Hideyoshi!"

At that point, the Shibata officers were no longer able to control their troops. Katsuie finally mounted his horse. Riding around the area of Kitsunezaka, he personally berated the soldiers in the separate encampments. Apparently he had come to the conclusion that it would be ineffective to let his own generals pass on the strict orders coming from headquarters.

"Anyone leaving camp for no reason will be cut down immediately," he screamed. Chase down and shoot any cowardly deserters! Anyone spreading rumors or dampening the martial spirit of the men is to be killed on the spot!"

But the situation had advanced too far, and the revival of Katsuie's severe martial spirit was in vain. Over half of his seven thousand troops had already deserted, and the remaining men hardly had their feet on the ground. In addition, they had already lost confidence in their own commander-in-chief. Reduced as he was to a position lacking in respect, even Demon Shibata's orders sounded hollow.

He rode back into his main camp, which was already under attack.

Ah, he thought, the end has come for me, too.... Seeing his dispirited army, Katsuie realized the futility of the situation. His fierce spirit, however, pushed him on relentlessly toward his own desperate death. As dawn began to break, horses and men were scattered thinly over his sparse camp.

"My lord, this way. Over here for just a moment." Two warriors held on to either side of Katsuie's armor as though they were supporting his large body. "It's not like you to be this quick-tempered." Leading him forcibly through the maelstrom of horses and men and out of the temple gate, they shouted desperately at the others, "Hurry up and bring his horse! Where is our lord's horse!"

In the meantime Katsuie himself was shouting. "I will not retreat! Who do you think I am! I'm not running away from this place!" His fierce words came with increasing vehemence. Once again he glared and yelled at the staff officers who would not leave his side. "Why are you doing this? Why are you keeping me from going out to attack? While you hold me down, why aren't you attacking the enemy?"

A mount was brought up. A soldier carrying the beautiful commander's standard emblazoned with the golden emblem came and stood next to it.

"We can't stem the tide here, my lord. If you die in this place, it will be in vain. Why don't you fall back to Kitanosho and put your thoughts into a plan for another attempt?"

Katsuie shook his head and yelled, but the men around him hastily forced his body into the saddle. The situation was urgent. Suddenly the captain of the pages, Menju Shosuke, a man who had never distinguished himself in battle, ran forward and prostrated himself in front of Katsuie's horse.

"Please, my lord! Allow me to take your commander's standard."

To ask one's lord for permission to carry the commander's standard meant that one was volunteering to make a stand in his place.

Shosuke said nothing more but remained kneeling in front of Katsuie. He displayed no particular preparedness for death, desperation, or ferocity; he looked as he usually did when he appeared before Katsuie as the captain of the pages.

"What? You want me to give you the commander's standard?"

Mounted on his horse, Katsuie stared down at Shosuke's back in amazement. The generals around him, struck with surprise, also fixed their eyes on Shosuke. Among Katsuie's many personal attendants, few had been treated more coldly than Shosuke had been.

Katsuie, who held that kind of prejudice against Shosuke, must have known what effect it had been having better than anyone else. And yet, wasn't that very Shosuke now before Katsuie, offering to put himself in Katsuie's place?

The wind of defeat blew desolately across the camp, and it had been unbearable for Katsuie to watch his men wavering since dawn. The cowards who had quickly thrown down their weapons and deserted had not been few in number; Katsuie had looked warmly upon many of those men and had given them his favors for many years. As those thoughts came to him, Katsuie was unable to hold back his tears.

But whatever Katsuie was thinking, he now kicked his horse's flanks with the heels of his stirrups, and chased away the pained look in his face with a thundering roar.

"What are you talking about, Shosuke? Once you die, that's the time for me to die! Now move away!"

Shosuke scurried away from the rearing horse but grabbed its reins.

"Then let me accompany you."

Against Katsuie's will, Menju put the battlefield behind him and hurried off in the direction of Yanagase. Both the man who guarded the commander's standard and Katsuie's retainers surrounded his horse and hurried him off in the middle of their group.

But Hideyoshi's vanguard had already broken through Kitsunezaka and, ignoring the Shibata warriors standing in its defense, put their sights on the golden standard fleeing into the distance.

"That's Katsuie! Don't let him get away!" A crowd of swift-running spearmen gathered together and ran in Katsuie's direction.

"We'll take our leave here, my lord!" Tossing off those words of farewell, the generals fleeing with Katsuie suddenly left his side, wheeled around, and dashed into the midst of the fierce spears of the pursuing troops. Their corpses soon fell to the ground.

Menju Shosuke had also turned and faced the enemy's onslaught, but now he once again chased after his lord's horse and yelled at Katsuie from behind.

"The commander's standard...please...let me carry it!"

They were just outside of Yanagase.

Katsuie brought his horse to a halt and took the gold commander's standard from the man next to him. It held so many memories—he had raised it in his camps together with his reputation as the "Demon Shibata."

"Here, Shosuke. Take it among my warriors!"

With those words, he suddenly tossed the standard to Shosuke.

Shosuke bent forward and agilely caught it by the shaft.

He was overjoyed. Waving the standard for a moment or two, he sent his final words in the direction of Katsuie's back.

"Good-bye, my lord!"

Katsuie turned, but his horse continued galloping toward the mountainous area of Yanagase. Only ten mounted men were accompanying him.

The commander's standard had been tossed into Shosuke's hands just as he had begged, but at that moment Katsuie had also left him with the words, "Take it among my warriors!"

That had been his request and it no doubt had been made in consideration of the men who were being left to their deaths along with Shosuke.

Some thirty men instantly gathered beneath the standard. Those were the only men who truly respected their own honor and who were willing to die for their lord.

Ah, there are some honorable Shibata men left, Shosuke thought, looking happily at the faces around him. "Come on! Let's show them how to die happily!"

Putting the standard into the hands of one of the warriors, he dashed out in front, hurrying west from Yanagase village toward the northern ridge of Mount Tochinoki. When the small force of not even forty men made the resolve to go forward, they manifested a spirit far more intense than that of the thousands of men on Kitsunezaka that morning.

"Katsuie has fallen back to the mountains!"

"It appears that he's made his final resolve and is prepared to die."

As might be expected, the pursuing Hideyoshi troops exhorted each other to go on.

"We'll have Katsuie's head!"

Each one fought to take the lead as they started to climb Mount Tochinoki. Flashing the golden standard on the mountaintop, the Shibata warriors watched breathlessly as the numbers of enemy warriors—who were scrambling up even in places where there was no path—increased moment by moment.

"There's still time to pass around a farewell cup of water," Shosuke said.

In those few moments, Shosuke and his comrades scooped up and shared the water that trickled from between the crags on the mountaintop and calmly prepared themselves for death. Shosuke suddenly turned to his brothers Mozaemon and Shobei.

"Brothers, you should escape and return to our village. If all three of us achieve death in battle at once, no one will be able to carry on the family name or take care of our mother. Mozaemon, the elder brother is supposed to carry on the family name, so why don't you go now?"

"If the younger brothers are cut down by the enemy," Mozaemon replied, "can the elder brother face his mother with the words 'I'm home now?' No, I'll stay here. Shobei, you should go."

"That would be horrible!"

"Why?"

"For me to be sent home alive at a time like this would hardly be a pleasure for our mother. And our dead father must be looking at his sons from the other world today as well. It will not be my feet that walk back to Echizen today."

" Well then, we'll die together!"

Their souls united in a pledge of death, the three brothers stood unwavering beneath the commander's standard.

Shosuke made no further mention to his brothers about wanting them to return home.

The three brothers took their farewell drink from a scoop of clear spring water and, as a refreshing spirit passed through their breasts, all turned in the direction of their mother's home.

One can imagine the prayers that were in their hearts. The enemy was approaching from all sides, close enough now that the individual voices of enemy soldiers could be heard.

"Guard the commander's standard, Shobei," Shosuke said to his younger brother as he put on his face guard. He was pretending to be Katsuie, and did not want the enemy to recognize him.

Five or six musket balls snapped past his head. Taking that as their cue, the thirty men invoked Hachiman, the god of war, and struck out for the enemy.

They divided into three units and attacked the advancing enemy. The men coming up from below were breathing hard and could not stand up to the desperate figures running down at them. Long swords poured down on the helmets of Hideyoshi's men, spears pierced their breasts, and their wretched corpses fell everywhere.

"Let no one be too eager to die!" Shosuke shouted suddenly as he withdrew inside a palisade.

As the commander's standard followed him, so too did his remaining men.

"It's said that the slap of five fingers is not as strong as the blow of a single fist. If our little force scatters, its effects will be weakened. Stay beneath the standard whether we advance or retreat."

Given that caution, they leaped out once again. Whirling one way, they cut furiously into the enemy; whirling another, they pierced him with spears. Then, like the wind, they withdrew to their ramparts.

Thus, they sallied forward six or seven times to fight.

The attackers had already lost more than two hundred men. It was close to noon, and an intense sun shone high overhead. The fresh blood on the armor and helmets dried quickly, giving off a black luster like that of lacquer.

There were fewer than ten men remaining beneath the commander's standard, and their fiery eyes hardly seemed to see each other. Not one man was uninjured.

An arrow pierced Shosuke's shoulder. As he looked at the fresh blood flowing over his sleeve, he pulled the arrow from his body with his own hand. Then he turned in the direction from which the arrow had come. The tops of a great number of helmets could be seen approaching, rustling through the bamboo grass like wild pigs.

Shosuke used the time he had left to speak quietly to his comrades. "We have fought every way we could, and we have nothing to regret. Everyone choose a respectable enemy and make a splendid name for yourself. Let me be the first, dying in our lord's stead. Do not let the commander's standard fall. Carry it high, one man after another!"

Those blood-smeared warriors so prepared to die raised the standard toward the enemy coming through the bamboo grass. The warriors moving in their direction must have been uncommonly fierce men. They came on unflinchingly, demonstrating the oaths they had made with their spears. Shosuke faced them and yelled out to dampen their spirits.

"How discourteous of you! Low-class nobodies! Are you thinking of putting your spears into the body of Shibata Katsuie?"

Shosuke looked like a demon, and in fact no one was able to stand in front of him. A number of men were speared down almost at his feet.

Observing the man's ferocity and fighting desperately with men who were willing to defend their commander's standard to the death, even the most violent braggarts of the attacking troops broke their encirclement and opened up a path to the foot of the mountain.

"Here I am! Katsuie himself is coming! If Hideyoshi is here, have him meet me mounted and alone! Come on out, monkey-face!" Shosuke yelled out as he went down the slope road.

Right there he pierced an armored warrior with a mortal wound. His elder brother, Mozaemon, had already been struck down; his little brother, Shobei, had crossed long swords with an enemy warrior, and each had struck the other dead. Shobei had fallen to the base of a nearby crag.

Beside him, the gold commander's standard lay abandoned, now completely red.

From both the top and the bottom of the slope, innumerable spears now pressed in on Shosuke's body, every warrior wanting to take the commander's standard and the head they believed to be Katsuie's.

Each man vied with the others for the prize. Beneath the confusion of spears, Menju Shosuke achieved death in battle.

A handsome young warrior of only twenty-five years, he had been held in low esteem by men like Katsuie and Genba because of his reticence, gentility, grace, and love of learning—Shosuke's innocent features were still concealed by his face guard.

"I killed Shibata Katsuie!" a samurai yelled.

"His commander's standard was taken by these hands!" shouted another.

Then every voice was raised, one man claiming this, another claiming that, until the entire mountain shook.

And still Hideyoshi's men had no idea that the head belonged not to Shibata Katsuie, but to Menju Shosuke, the captain of his pages.

"We've killed Katsuie!"

"I've held the head of the lord of Kitanosho!"

Pushing and shoving, their cries reverberated through the air. "The standard! The gold standard! And his head! We took his head!"

A TRUE FRIEND

Katsuie had barely escaped with his life, but his army had been annihilated. Until that morning, the Shibata standard with its golden emblem had flown in the vicinity of Yanagase, but now only Hideyoshi's standard could be seen. It shone brilliantly in the bright sunshine, impressing all who saw it, symbolizing a reality that transcended ordinary wisdom and strength.

The flags and banners of Hideyoshi's army—which stretched out along the roads, and covered the fields presented a grand spectacle of victory. They were packed so closely together that they resembled a thick golden haze.

The army started eating its provisions. Hostilities had begun early that morning and had lasted for about eight hours. When the meal was finished, the entire army was given orders to advance north immediately.

As the men approached Tochinoki Pass, they could see the Tsuruga Sea to the west, while the mountains of Echizen opened up to the north seemingly right under their horses' hooves.

The sun was already beginning to sink, and heaven and earth burned with an evening glow encompassing all the colors of a rainbow.

Hideyoshi's face was burnt a deep red. He did not, however, appear to be a man who had not slept for days. He seemed to have forgotten that men need to sleep. Constantly advancing, he had not yet ordered a halt. At that time of year the nights were at their shortest. While it was still light, the main army bivouacked at Imajo in Echizen. The vanguard went on, however, having been ordered to advance as far as Wakimoto—more than two leagues away—while the rear guard stopped at Itadori, about the same distance behind the central army. Thus, the camp that night stretched for four leagues from van to rear.

That night Hideyoshi fell into contented slumber—one that even the song of the mountain cuckoo could not disturb.

Tomorrow we'll get to Fuchu Castle, Hideyoshi thought just before going to sleep. But how will Inuchiyo receive us?

What was Inuchiyo doing at that time? He had passed through the area at noon that same day and, while the sun was still high in the sky, had withdrawn his army into Fuchu, his son's castle.

"Thank the gods you're safe," his wife said as she came out to greet him.

"Take care of the wounded. You can look to me later on."

Inuchiyo did not even take off his sandals or untie his armor; he just stood in front of the castle. His pages were also there, lined up behind him, solemnly waiting.

Finally, corps after corps of warriors marched smartly through the gate, carrying the corpses of their fallen comrades, on top of which they had laid their banners. Next, those wounded in battle were either carried in or walked in, leaning on their comrades' shoulders.

The thirty-odd casualties the Maeda had suffered in the retreat did not compare with the losses of the Shibata and Sakuma. The bell was rung at the temple, and as the sun dipped in the sky, the smoke from cooking fires began to rise from all parts of the castle. The order was given for the soldiers to eat their rations. The troops, however, did not disperse, but stayed in their units, as if they were still on the battlefield.

A guard at the main gate yelled, "The lord of Kitanosho has arrived at the castle gate."

"What! Lord Katsuie here!" Inuchiyo muttered in astonishment. This was an unexpected development, and Inuchiyo seemed unable to bear to meet the man—now a fugitive. For a moment he was sunk in thought, but then he said, "Let's go out to greet him."

Inuchiyo followed his son out of the keep. Descending the last set of stairs, he walked to the darkened connecting corridor. One of his attendants, Murai Nagayori, followed after him.

"My lord," Murai whispered.

Inuchiyo looked at Murai questioningly.

The retainer whispered in his lord's ear, "Lord Katsuie's arrival here is an incomparable and happy opportunity. If you kill him and send his head to Lord Hideyoshi, your and Lord Hideyoshi's relationship will be patched up without difficulty."

Without warning Inuchiyo struck the man in the chest. "Shut up!" he thundered.

Murai staggered back to the wooden wall behind him and just barely avoided falling over. Turning pale, he had the presence of mind neither to stand up nor to sit completely down.

Glaring at him, Inuchiyo spoke with undisguised anger. "It is an outrageous act to whisper into a lord's ear an immoral, cowardly plan that a man should be ashamed to utter. You consider yourself a samurai, but you know nothing of the Way of the Samurai! What kind of man would sell the head of a general who had come knocking at his gate, just to profit his own clan? Much less when he's spent as many years campaigning with that general as I have!"

Leaving the trembling Murai behind, Inuchiyo went out toward the main entrance to greet Katsuie. Katsuie had come up to the castle gate still on horseback. He held the shaft of a broken spear in one hand and did not appear to be wounded, but his entire face—his entire being—was suffused with desolation.

The reins of his horse were held by Toshinaga, who had run out to greet him. The eight men who accompanied him had stayed outside the main gate. So Katsuie was alone.

"I'm greatly obliged to you." With those courteous words to Toshinaga, Katsuie dismounted. He looked Inuchiyo in the face and spoke in a loud voice full of self-scorn. "We lost! We lost!"

He was in surprisingly good spirits. It may have been that he was just pretending, but he seemed far more relaxed than Inuchiyo had imagined he would be. Inuchiyo was kinder than usual in greeting the defeated general. Toshinaga was no less concerned than his father and helped the fugitive take off his blood-soaked sandals.

"I feel as though I've come home to my own house."

Kindness makes a deep impression on a man in the abyss of destruction and causes him to abandon any suspicions and bitterness. It is the only thing that will make him think that there is still light in the world.

Apparently now quite happy, Katsuie continued to congratulate father and son on their escape. "This defeat was entirely due to my own oversights. I brought troubles onto you, too, and I hope you'll forgive me," he apologized. "I'll retreat as far as Kitanosho and put my affairs in order and without any regrets. I wonder if you wouldn't give me a bowl of rice and tea."

Demon Shibata seemed to have become the Buddha Shibata. Even Inuchiyo was unable to hold back his tears.

"Bring some tea and rice quickly. And *sake*," Inuchiyo ordered. He could think of few words of comfort for the man. Nevertheless, he felt that he had to say something. "It's often said that victory and defeat are the stuff of a warrior's life. If you consider today's disaster in terms of human destiny, you know that to be proud of victory is the first step toward the day of destruction, and to be completely defeated is the first step toward the day of victory. The eternal cycle of man's rise and fall is not just a matter of temporary joy and sorrow."

"Therefore, what I regret is neither my own personal destruction nor the perpetual cycle of change," Katsuie said. "I only regret the loss of my reputation. But rest assured, Inuchiyo. It is all predestined."

For him to say such a thing was a complete departure from the Katsuie of olden days. But he seemed to be neither tormented nor confused.

When the *sake* arrived, Katsuie happily took a cup and, supposing that it would be his farewell, poured one for father and son as well. He heartily ate the simple meal Inuchiyo had ordered.

"I've never tasted anything like the rice I've eaten today. I'll never forget your kindness." That said, he took his leave.

Inuchiyo, who accompanied him outside, immediately noticed that his mount was exhausted. Ordering a page to bring out his own beloved dapple-gray horse, he offered it to Katsuie. "Put your mind at ease," Inuchiyo said. "We will hold this place until you get to Kitanosho."

Katsuie started to leave but then turned the horse around and came up to Inuchiyo as though he had suddenly remembered something. "Inuchiyo, you and Hideyoshi have been close friends since your youth. The battle having turned out this way, I release you from your duty to me as a retainer."

Those were to be his last words to Inuchiyo. As he mounted his horse, his expression was devoid of any falsehood. Confronted with such feeling, Inuchiyo bowed with heartfelt emotion. The figure of Katsuie leaving the castle gate was black against the red of the evening sun. The tiny remaining army of eight mounted men and ten or so foot soldiers now took flight to Kitanosho.

Two or three mounted men galloped into Fuchu Castle. Their news was soon common knowledge throughout the stronghold. "The enemy is camped at Wakimoto. Lord Hideyoshi has set up camp at Imajo, so there is little prospect of an attack tonight."

Hideyoshi slept happily through the night—really more like half the night—at Imajo, and on the following day he left camp early and rode to Wakimoto.

Kyutaro came out to greet him. He erected the commander's standard, indicating the presence of the commander-in-chief.

"What went on in Fuchu Castle last night?" Hideyoshi asked.

"There appeared to be a great deal of activity."

"Are they fortifying the place? Maybe the Maeda want to fight." Answering his own question, he looked toward Fuchu. Suddenly he turned to Kyutaro and ordered him to prepare his troops.

"Are you going into battle in person?" Kyutaro asked.

"Of course." Hideyoshi nodded as though he were looking out over a large level road. Kyutaro quickly communicated Hideyoshi's words to the various generals and blew the conch shell to assemble the vanguard. Very soon the men had fallen into ranks, ready to march.

It was less than two hours to Fuchu. Kyutaro rode in front while Hideyoshi himself rode in the middle of the vanguard. They were soon in sight of the castle walls. Inside the castle, the men were naturally feeling extremely tense. Viewed from the top of the keep, the columns of men and Hideyoshi's standard of the golden gourds looked close enough to touch.

The order to halt had not yet been given. And, as Hideyoshi was in their midst, the soldiers of the vanguard were sure that he would surround the castle immediately.

Moving toward the main gate of Fuchu Castle, Hideyoshi's men—now like a rushing river—displayed the "crane wing" formation. For a moment, only the commander's standard did not move.

Just then, the entire structure of the castle spat out gunpowder smoke.

"Move back a little, Kyutaro. Move back!" Hideyoshi ordered. "Don't have the soldiers spread out or take up battle array. Order them to regroup and stand out of formation."

The soldiers in the vanguard retreated, and the muskets within the castle were silenced. The fighting spirits of both sides, however, could have exploded in an instant.

"Somebody take the commander's standard and advance twenty yards ahead of me," Hideyoshi ordered. "I won't need anyone to lead my horse; I'll be going into the castle by myself."

He had not informed anyone of his intentions beforehand, and spoke quite suddenly from the saddle. Ignoring the shocked expressions of his generals, he immediately went forward with his horse at a canter toward the main gate of the castle.

"Just a moment! Wait just a moment so I can go ahead of you!"

A samurai went stumbling quickly after him, but when he had gotten barely ten yards in front of Hideyoshi, bearing the commander's standard as he had been ordered, several shots rang out, their fire directed toward the golden gourds.

"Hold your fire! Hold your fire!"

Yelling in a loud voice, Hideyoshi galloped in the direction of the musket fire like an arrow shot from a bow.

"It's me! Hideyoshi! Don't you recognize me?" As he approached the castle, he took the golden baton of command from his waist and waved it at the soldiers in the castle. "It's me! Hideyoshi! Hold your fire!"

Astonished, two men leaped from the armory next to the main gate and pushed the gate open.

"Lord Hideyoshi?"

This turn of events seemed to be totally unexpected, and they greeted him with some embarrassment. Hideyoshi recognized both of the men. He had already dismounted and was walking toward them.

"Has Lord Inuchiyo returned?" he asked, then added, "Are both he and his son all right?"

"Yes, my lord" one of the men replied. "They both returned without mishap."

"Good, good. I'm relieved to hear that. Take my horse, will you?"

Handing his horse's bridle over to the two men, Hideyoshi went in through the castle gate exactly as if he were walking into his own house, accompanied by his own attendants.

The warriors filling the castle like a forest were overawed as—almost in a daze—they observed the behavior of the man. At that moment Inuchiyo and his son ran out in Hideyoshi's direction. As they approached each other, the two men spoke out at once, like the old friends they were.

"Well, well now!"

"Inuchiyo! What are you up to?" Hideyoshi asked.

"Nothing at all," Inuchiyo replied with a laugh. "Come in and sit down."

Accompanied by his son, Inuchiyo led the way in to the main citadel. Expressly avoiding the formal entrance, they opened up the gate to the gardened area and led their guest directly toward the inner apartments, stopping to look at the purple irises and the white azaleas in the garden along the way.

It was the same treatment one would give a close family friend, and Inuchiyo was acting the way he had acted when he and Hideyoshi had lived in houses separated by a hedge.

Finally, Inuchiyo invited Hideyoshi inside.

Hideyoshi, however, stood looking around without even moving to untie his straw sandals. "That building over there—is that the kitchen?" he asked. When Inuchiyo answered affirmatively, Hideyoshi started walking toward it. "I want to see your wife. Is she here?"

Inuchiyo was completely taken aback. He was about to tell Hideyoshi that if he wanted to meet his wife, he would call her right away, but there was not enough time for that. Instead, he hurriedly told Toshinaga to take their guest to the kitchen.

Having sent his son to chase after Hideyoshi, he himself hurried down the corridor to warn his wife.

The most surprised of all were the cooks and the maidservants. Here was a short samurai—clearly a general—in a persimmon-colored armor coat, walking nonchalantly into the kitchen and calling out as if he were a member of the lord's family.

"Hey! Is Lady Maeda here? Where is she?"

No one knew who he was. Everyone looked puzzled, but upon seeing his golden baton of command and formal sword, they all quickly knelt and bowed. He had to be a general of high rank, but no one had seen him among the Maeda before.

"Hey, Lady Maeda, where are you? It's me, Hideyoshi. Come on, show your face!"

Inuchiyo's wife was preparing food with some of the servants when she heard all the commotion. She came out wearing an apron and with her sleeves tied back. For a moment she simply stood and stared. "I must be dreaming," she murmured.

"It's been a long time, my lady. I'm glad to see you're well as always."

When Hideyoshi started to step forward, she roused herself and, quickly loosening the cord at her sleeves, prostrated herself on the wooden floor.

Hideyoshi artlessly sat down. "The first thing I want to tell you, my lady, is that your daughter and the ladies in Himeji have become good friends. Please set your mind at ease about that. Also, although your husband saw some trying moments in this last campaign, he showed no confusion about whether to advance or retreat, and you could say that the Maeda camp came away from the battle undefeated."

Inuchiyo's wife placed the palms of her hands together beneath her bowed forehead.

At that point Inuchiyo came in looking for his wife and saw Hideyoshi.

"This is no place to receive you properly. Before anything else, at least please remove your sandals and come up off the dirt floor."

Husband and wife did everything they could to persuade him to step up onto the wooden floor, but Hideyoshi declined, speaking to them as informally as before. "I'm in a hurry to get to Kitanosho and really can't spare the time right now. But may I take advantage of your kindness and ask for a bowl of rice?"

"That's an easy request to fill. But won't you come in just for a moment?"

Hideyoshi made no move to untie his straw sandals and relax. "We'll do that on another day. Today I have to move fast."

Both husband and wife knew the good and bad points of Hideyoshi's character. Theirs had never been a friendship that placed great value on obligations or pretense. Inuchiyo's wife retied the cord holding up her sleeves, and she herself stood in front of the cutting board in the kitchen.

It was the kitchen for the entire castle, and a great number of maidservants, cooks, and even officials were working there. But Lady Maeda was not a woman who did not know how to prepare a savory meal on short notice.

Both on that day and the day before, she herself had looked after the wounded and helped with the preparation of their food. But even on uneventful days, she would come to the kitchen to prepare something for her husband. Now the Maeda clan governed a large province. But in the poverty of their days in Kiyosu, when their neighbor Tokichiro was no better off than they, the two families would often go to each other to borrow a measure of rice, a handful of salt, or even an evening's worth of oil for the lamp. In those days they could see how well off the neighbors were by the light shining in their windows at night.

This woman is no less a good wife than my own Nene, Hideyoshi thought. In that short interlude of reflection, however, Inuchiyo's wife had finished preparing two or three dishes. She led the way from the kitchen, carrying the tray herself.

In the hilly area that stretched toward the western citadel, a small pavilion stood in a copse of pines. The attendants spread a rug out over the grass next to it and set down two trays of food and flasks of *sake*.

"Can't I at least serve you something better, even if you're in a hurry?" Inuchiyo's wife asked.

"No, no. Won't your husband and son join me?"

Inuchiyo sat down facing Hideyoshi, and Toshinaga held up the *sake* flask. There was a building here, but the guest and his hosts did not use it. A wind blew through the pines, but they hardly heard it.

Hideyoshi did not drink more than one cup of *sake* but hurriedly ate up the two bowls of rice that Inuchiyo's wife had prepared for him.

"Ah, I'm full. I'm sorry to impose, but might I ask for a bowl of tea?"

Preparations had already been made in the pavilion. Inuchiyo's wife quickly went inside and served Hideyoshi a bowl of tea.

"Well, my lady," Hideyoshi said as he drank, looking at her as though he were about to ask her advice. "I've given you a lot of trouble, but now, on top of that, I'd like to borrow your husband for a little while."

Inuchiyo's wife laughed cheerfully. "'To borrow my husband?' It's been a long time since you've used that phrase."

Hideyoshi and Inuchiyo both laughed, and Hideyoshi said, "Listen to that, Inuchiyo. It appears that women don't easily forget old grudges. She's still talking today about how I used to 'borrow' you to go drinking." Returning the tea bowl, he laughed again. "But today it's just a little different from the past, and if my lady doesn't disagree, I'm sure your husband won't either. I would definitely like him to go with me to Kitanosho. It would be fine if your son stays here to take care of you."

Seeing that the question had already been settled between the talking and the laughing, Hideyoshi quickly made the decision on his own. "What I would like, then, is for your son to stay here and your husband to ride with me. Inuchiyo has no equal as a man skilled in battle. Then, on the happy day when we return from the campaign, I'd like to stop here again and impose on you for a few days. We'll depart tomorrow morning. I'll take my leave for today."

The entire family saw him as far as the entrance to the kitchen. On the way Inuchiyo's wife said, "Lord Hideyoshi, you said that Toshinaga should stay here to take care of his mother, but I don't think I'm that old or that lonely yet. There will be enough warriors left guarding the castle, and no one will need to feel anxious about its defense."

Inuchiyo was of the same mind. As they walked hurriedly toward the entrance, Hideyoshi and the Maeda family finalized the hour of departure for the following day and settled other details.

"I'll be waiting for the next time you drop by," Inuchiyo's wife said as she bade him farewell at the entrance to the kitchen; her husband and son took him as far as the front gate of the castle.

The very night Hideyoshi took leave of the Maeda family and returned to his own camp, two very important men from the Shibata side were brought in as prisoners. One of them was Sakuma Genba. The other was Katsuie's foster son, Katsutoshi. Both had been captured during their flight through the mountains to Kitanosho. Genba had been wounded. With the heat of the summer, the wound had become infected and quickly began to fester. The emergency treatment often used by warriors was moxibustion, and Genba had stopped at a farmhouse in the mountains, asked for moxa, and applied it around the opening of the wound.

While Genba was busy applying the moxa, the farmers held a secret conclave in which they decided that they would probably receive a handsome reward for turning Katsutoshi and Genba over to Hideyoshi. That night they surrounded the hut where the two were sleeping, trussed them up like pigs, and carried them to Hideyoshi's camp.

When Hideyoshi heard about that, he did not look very happy. Contrary to the farmers' expectations, he punished them severely.

The following day Hideyoshi, accompanied by Inuchiyo and his son, spurred his horse toward Katsuie's castle at Kitanosho. By afternoon, Echizen's capital was filled with Hideyoshi's troops.

Along the way, the Tokuyama and Fuwa clans had already seen what was in the wind, and many men surrendered at the gate of Hideyoshi's camp.

Hideyoshi camped on Mount Ashiba and had the castle at Kitanosho surrounded so tightly that a drop of water could not have trickled through. As soon as that was done, Kyutaro's corps was given the work of breaking through a section of the palisade. Then Genba and Katsutoshi were led up close to the castle walls.

Beating the attack drum, the soldiers assailed the ears of Katsuie, who was inside the castle. "If you have any last words for your foster son and Genba, you'd better come out and say them now!"

That message was given two or three times, but the castle remained silent. Katsuie did not appear, perhaps thinking that to see the two men would be unbearable. And of course it was clear that Hideyoshi's strategy was to destroy the morale of the men in the castle.

Stragglers from Katsuie's army had arrived during the night, and now the castle was sheltering about three thousand souls, including noncombatants.

In addition, Genba and Katsutoshi had been taken alive by the enemy, and even Katsuie could not help thinking that his end had come. The attack drums of the enemy were unceasing. By nightfall, the surrounding palisades had all been broken through, and the entire area was filled with Hideyoshi's forces to within thirty or forty yards of the castle walls themselves.

Nevertheless, inside the castle the situation remained peaceful. After a while the enemy's drums ceased; night was approaching, and generals who seemed to be envoys were going back and forth from the castle to the outside. Maybe there was a move afoot to spare Katsuie's life, or perhaps the generals were envoys for capitulation. Such rumors spread, but the atmosphere inside the castle did not seem to corroborate those theories.

As the evening passed, the main citadel—which had been as black as ink—was cheerfully lit with lanterns. The northern enclosure and the western citadel were also lit up. Bright lamps shone at intervals even in the keep, where desperate soldiers were on watch, waiting to do battle.

The attacking troops wondered what was going on. But the mystery was soon solved. They could hear the beating of drums now along with the flowing sound of flutes. Folk songs heavy with the accent of the northern provinces drifted to within earshot.

"The people in the castle know this is their last night and are probably enjoying a farewell banquet. How sad."

The attacking troops outside the castle felt sympathy for its inhabitants. Both the men inside the castle and those outside had been soldiers under the command of the Oda, and there was not a person there who did not know Katsuie's past. For that reason alone, the situation was a deeply emotional one.

A final banquet was held in the castle of Kitanosho. It was attended by more than eighty people—the entire clan and the senior retainers. Katsuie's wife and her daughters sat under the bright lamps in the middle of the group while the enemy army waited outside, only a short distance away.

"We didn't even get together like this to celebrate the first day of the new year!" someone said, and the entire family laughed. "With the dawn, the first day of our life in the next world will begin. Tonight will be our New Year's Eve in this world."

With the numerous lamps and the many laughing voices, the gathering seemed no different from an ordinary banquet. Only the presence of armed warriors caused a bleak cloud to float through the hall.

The makeup and dress of Oichi and her three daughters lent an unbelievably fresh and even elegant air to the event. The youngest of the three sisters was only ten years old, and when they saw the child making merry among the trays of food and the noisy people, gulping her food and playing pranks on her older sisters, even the old warriors who thought nothing of their imminent deaths had to look off in another direction.

Katsuie had drunk too much. Any number of times, as he offered a cup to someone, he would let his loneliness slip, saying, "If only Genba were here." When he heard someone expressing chagrin at Genba's failure, he would protest: "Stop blaming Genba. This disaster is fully on account of my own mistakes. When I hear you blaming Genba, I feel worse than if I were being attacked."

He took care that everyone around him was drinking and distributed the best *sake* in the storehouse to the warriors in the towers. With the *sake* came his message:

"Express your farewells to your hearts' content. Reciting poems wouldn't be at all amiss."

Songs were heard coming from the towers, and laughing voices filled the room. Even in front of Katsuie drums were sounded, and the silver fans of the dancers drew elegant lines in the air.

"Long ago, Lord Nobunaga would get up and dance at the slightest provocation and try to force me to do the same, but I was always ashamed of my inability." Katsuie reminisced. "How regrettable! I should have learned at least one dance just for tonight."

In his heart he must have truly missed his former lord. And there was something else. Even though he had been driven to his present predicament—which was truly nothing less than hopeless—by a single monkey-faced soldier, it is certain that he secretly hoped at least to die a glorious death.

He was only fifty-three years old. As a general, his future should have been ahead of him, but now his only hope was for a noble death.

The *sake* made the rounds. Cup after cup was consumed, and the many barrels dried up with the night. There was singing accompanied by drums, dances with silver fans, and cheerful shouts and laughing voices, but nothing that they did could completely sweep away the atmosphere of sorrow.

From time to time, an icy silence and the black smoke coughed into the night by the flickering of the lamps exposed on the eighty drunken faces a pale color that had nothing to do with drinking *sake*. The lamps showed it was midnight, but still the banquet went on. Oichi's daughters leaned against her lap and began to sleep. To them, this banquet had become too boring to bear, it seemed.

At some point the youngest daughter had taken over her mother's lap as a pillow and was now sleeping silently. As Oichi touched her daughter's hair, she struggled to hold back her tears. The middle daughter also eventually began to doze. Only the eldest, Chacha, seemed to understand what her mother was thinking. She knew what the evening's banquet was about and yet, she still managed to look serene.

The girls were beautiful, and all three resembled their mother, but Chacha was especially endowed with the aristocratic bearing that ran through the blood of the Oda. The combination of her youth and natural beauty could not help but make the beholder sad.

"She's so innocent," Katsuie said suddenly, looking at the sleeping face of the youngest child. He then spoke with Lady Oichi about the fate of the girls. "Your own status is that of Lord Nobunaga's sister, and it has not yet been even a year since you became my wife. It would be better if you took the children and left the castle before dawn. I'll have Tominaga accompany you to Hideyoshi's camp."

Oichi answered with tears in her eyes. "No!" she said through her tears. "When a woman marries into a warrior family, she is resolved to accept her own karma. To tell me to leave the castle now is truly cold-hearted, and it's unthinkable that I should go begging at Hideyoshi's camp gate, asking him to spare my life."

She looked at Katsuie, shaking her head behind her sleeve. But Katsuie tried once again. "No, no. It gives me pleasure to think that you would be so faithful to me when our relationship is still so shallow, but your three daughters are the children of Lord Asai. More than that, Hideyoshi would certainly not be heartless to the sister of Lord Nobunaga or to her children. So you should go ahead and leave, and leave quickly. Go prepare yourself."

Calling over one of his retainers, Katsuie gave the man instructions and told them to get started. But Oichi only shook her head and refused to move.

"But even though you are so determined, may these innocent children at least leave the castle as my lord wishes?"

She gave the appearance of agreeing with him. Then she shook awake the youngest child, who was sleeping on her lap, and told the children they were to be sent outside the castle.

Chacha clung to her mother. "I don't want to go. I don't want to go. I want to be with you, Mother!"

Katsuie spoke to her and her mother tried to persuade her, but they were unable to stop her desperate tears. Finally she was led away and forced out of the castle against her will. The sobs of the three girls could be heard as they moved far into the distance. It was already close to the fourth watch of the night, and the joyless party was over. The warriors quickly retied the leather straps of their armor, picked up their weapons, and began to disperse to their final posts, the posts that would be the places of their deaths.

Katsuie, his wife, and the several members of the clan moved together into the interior of the main citadel.

Oichi had a small desk brought to her and began to grind the ink for her death poem. Katsuie also left a poem.

While the night was the same everywhere, it was not the same for everyone. The dawn was quite different for the vanquished and the victor.

"Make sure we have taken the surrounding walls by the time the sky turns white," Hideyoshi ordered, and then waited peacefully for the dawn.

The town was also relatively calm. Fires broke out in two or three places. They had not been set by Hideyoshi's soldiers but more likely had been started accidentally by the confused townspeople. Because they could serve as bonfires that would illuminate surprise attacks from the soldiers in the castle, they were allowed to burn all night.

Various generals had gone in and out of Hideyoshi's quarters from evening until midnight. Because of that, there was talk that either a movement was afoot to spare Katsuie's life or that the castle would soon capitulate. Nevertheless, even after midnight, no change was made in the original battle strategy.

The quick activity in every camp meant that dawn was close. Soon the conch shell was sounded. The beating of the drum began splitting the mist. It reverberated with a boom throughout the entire camp.

The assault began precisely at the Hour of the Tiger as had been planned. The attack commenced as the troops facing the castle wall opened a barrage of gunfire.

The popping of the guns reverberated uncannily through the mist, but then suddenly both the gunfire and the war cries of the vanguard stopped.

Just then a lone rider broke through the mist, whipping his horse from Kyutaro's position to Hideyoshi's camp stool. Behind him ran a single enemy samurai and three young girls.

"Hold your fire! Stop the attack!" the rider shouted.

The fugitives were, of course, Nobunaga's nieces. Ignorant of the wearers, the soldiers watched as six elegant sleeves went by, soaked in the mist. The eldest sister held her middle sister's hand, while she in turn took care of the youngest. They tiptoed over the stony road. It was considered the proper etiquette for fugitives to go with very little to protect their feet, and the little princesses were no exception, walking on the earth in nothing but heavy silk socks.

The youngest stopped walking and said she wanted to return to the castle. The samurai who had accompanied them from the castle calmed her down by putting her on his back.

"Where are we going?" the little girl asked with a shudder.

"We're going to a nice man's place," Shinroku answered.

"No! I don't want to go!" the girl cried.

The older girls did their best to calm her down.

"Mother should be coming later on. Right, Shinroku?"

"Yes. Of course she is."

Pattering on like that, they finally approached the stand of pines where Hideyoshi had made his camp.

Hideyoshi came out from behind the curtain and stood beneath a pine tree, watching them approach. He walked up to meet the girls.

"They all have the family resemblance," he said when he saw them up close.

Was it the figure of Nobunaga or that of Oichi that was conjured up within his breast? Whichever it was, he was completely charmed and could only mutter that they were good children. A tassel hung elegantly from Chacha's plum-colored sleeve. Against the middle sister's sleeve, which was embroidered with a bold pattern, was a red sash. The youngest girl was dressed no less elegantly than her sisters. Each had a tiny satchel scented with aloeswood and a tiny golden bell.

"How old are you?" Hideyoshi asked. But none of the three would answer. On the contrary, their lips turned so white they gave the impression that if you touched them they would burst into tears.

Hideyoshi laughed lightly and displayed a smile. "There is nothing to fear, my little princesses. From now on you can play with me." And he pointed to his own nose.

The middle sister laughed a little, perhaps because she was the only one who was reminded of a monkey.

But suddenly the gunfire and war cries shook the area even more strongly than before, sweeping over the entire area of the castle. Overhead, the morning sky began to appear.

The little princesses saw the smoke rising from the castle walls and started to scream and cry in confusion.

Hideyoshi put the girls in the care of a retainer, then called vehemently for a horse and rode off in the direction of the castle.

The two moats along the outer walls that drew in the waters of the Kuzuryu River did not allow the attacking troops an easy approach.

When at last, however, they were able to cross the outer moat, the soldiers in the castle had set fire to the bridge at the front gate. The flames leaped to the tower over the gate and spread to the area of the barracks. The resistance of the defenders was furious beyond the attackers' anticipation.

At noon the outer castle fell. The attackers flowed into the main citadel from every one of the gates.

Katsuie and his senior retainers had gone to the keep to make their final stand. The mighty keep was a nine-story building with iron doors and stone pillars.

After two hours of fighting in the keep, the attacking soldiers had sustained many more casualties than they had suffered during the whole morning. The courtyard and the tower were a sea of flames. Hideyoshi ordered a temporary retreat. Perhaps because he saw that they were making little headway, he pulled back every corps.

During that time he selected several hundred stalwart warriors. No one was to carry firearms; only spears and swords.

"Now I'm going to see it done! Cut your way into the tower!" he ordered.

The specially picked spear corps immediately enveloped the tower like a swarm of wasps and soon penetrated into the interior.

Jet black smoke poured from the third floor, from the fourth, then from the fifth.

"Good!" Hideyoshi yelled when a huge umbrella of flames shot out from the tower's multifaceted eaves.

That was the flash that signaled Katsuie's end. Katsuie and the eighty members of his household held the attackers back on the third and fourth floors of the keep and fought hard until the very end, slipping in the spilled blood. But now three members of his family called to him.

"Prepare yourself quickly, my lord!"

Running up to the fifth floor, he joined Lady Oichi. After witnessing her death, Shibata Katsuie ended his life by cutting open his stomach.

It was the Hour of the Monkey. The keep burned all night. The magnificent buildings that had stood on the banks of the Kuzuryu River since the time of Nobunaga burned like a funeral pyre for innumerable past dreams and a thousand souls. Nothing, however, could be found in the ashes that in any way resembled Katsuie.

It was said that he had packed dry grass into the tower with meticulous care so that he would be burned up completely. And for that reason, Katsuie's head could never be offered as sure proof of his death. For a while some said that Katsuie had escaped, but Hideyoshi reacted with almost complete indifference to those rumors. By the following day he had already turned toward Kaga.

Oyama Castle in Kaga had been until the day before the headquarters of Sakuma Genba. When the fall of Kitanosho was reported, the people in that area could see what was in the wind and surrendered to Hideyoshi. He entered Oyama Castle without a fight. But the more victories his armies won, the more he warned them about the gravity of the situation and cautioned them against the slackening of military discipline. His aim was to overawe the solid warriors of the Shibata and their allies once and for all.

Sassa Narimasa in Toyama Castle was one of those warriors. Indeed, he was a strong supporter of the Shibata and held Hideyoshi in complete contempt. In terms of lineage, Sassa was far above Hideyoshi. He had been Katsuie's second in command during the northern campaign, and during the campaign against Hideyoshi, he had been asked to stay behind, not only to check the Uesugi clan but also to manage internal matters in the north.

Sassa is here. That is the stance he took as he glared out of the castle, standing firm in his guardianship of the northern provinces. Even though Katsuie had already perished and Kitanosho had fallen, there was a good possibility that—with his natural ferocity and professed dislike of Hideyoshi—Sassa might make a desperate effort to step into Katsuie's shoes and do his best to prolong the war. And he was indeed thinking of doing that by combining his own fresh troops with the remaining Shibata.

Hideyoshi purposely did not confront the man. The numbers of Hideyoshi's army demonstrated his power, and he decided to let their presence persuade Sassa to reconsider his position. In the meantime he approached the Uesugi clan with an invitation to form an alliance. Uesugi Kagekatsu sent a retainer to congratulate Hideyoshi on his victory and to respond affirmatively to Hideyoshi's offer.

Considering the apparently friendly relationship between Hideyoshi and the Uesugi clan, Sassa Narimasa found it impossible to plan a battle of resistance. He therefore disguised his intentions and finally declared his submission to Hideyoshi. He then married his daughter to Inuchiyo's second son, Toshimasa, and settled down with relief in his own province. Thus the area north of Kitanosho was pacified by momentum, and virtually no fighting had been required.

Having secured the north, Hideyoshi's victorious army returned to Nagahama Castle on the Boys' Festival, the fifth day of the Fifth Month.

At Nagahama Hideyoshi listened to reports of the situation in Gifu. After Kitanosho, it was chiefly Gifu Castle that continued its attacks on Hideyoshi, but after the great defeat of the Shibata, the martial spirit of Nobutaka and his soldiers was considerably dampened. To make matters worse, there were in Nagahama Castle many retainers from Gifu who had deserted Nobutaka and joined Hideyoshi. In the end, the situation had become so extreme that a mere twenty-seven men remained with Nobutaka.

Because Nobutaka had relied particularly upon the Shibata, for him their destruction was akin to cutting the roots of a plant. His men all deserted him, except for his favorites. Nobuo assembled his forces and surrounded Nobutaka's castle. He sent a message saying that his brother should go to Owari.

Nobutaka left Gifu Castle, took a boat, and landed at Utsumi in Owari. One of Nobuo's attendants went to Nobutaka with an order for him to commit *seppuku*, and, feeling that his time had come, Nobutaka calmly wrote out his last words and then took his own life. Thus Nobutaka's end was caused by his own brother. But the man who was behind his death was Hideyoshi. It is hardly necessary to say that Hideyoshi was unwilling to attack Nobutaka—who was so closely related to Nobunaga—with his own army, and so resorted to using Nobuo.

At any rate, the mediocrity of Nobuo and Nobutaka cannot be doubted. If they had made their minds one as brothers—or if either one had been distinguished in bravery and blessed with an eye that could perceive the tide of the times—they would not have experienced such a collapse in the end. Compared with Nobuo, who showed a good-natured stupidity, Nobutaka was a bit more courageous. But he was really not much more than an incompetent bluffer.

On that seventh day Hideyoshi left for Azuchi, stopping at Sakamoto Castle on the eleventh. In Ise, Takigawa Kazumasu also surrendered. Hideyoshi gave him a province in Omi worth five thousand bushels. He did not venture to question Kazumasu about his past crimes.

BOOK TEN

ELEVENTH YEAR OF TENSHO
1583

CHARACTERS AND PLACES

GAMO UJISATO, senior Oda retainer
NAKAGAWA KANEMON, commander of Inuyama Castle
IKEDA YUKISUKE, Shonyu's son
BITO JINEMON, retainer to Hideyoshi
MORI NAGAYOSHI, Ikeda Shonyu's son-in-law
SAKAI TADATSUGU, senior Tokugawa retainer
HONDA HEIHACHIRO, senior Tokugawa retainer
II HYOBU, senior Tokugawa retainer
MIYOSHI HIDETSUGU, Hideyoshi's nephew
ODA NOBUTERU, Nobuo's uncle

ISE, Oda Nobuo's province
NAGASHIMA, Oda Nobuo's main castle
OGAKI, Ikeda Shonyu's castle
MOUNT KOMAKI, fortified position held by Ieyasu
GAKUDEN, Hideyoshi's main camp
OKAZAKI, Tokugawa Ieyasu's castle
OSAKA, Hideyoshi's new castle

THE SINS OF THE FATHER

In just one short year, Hideyoshi had risen so rapidly to prominence that even he was surprised. He had struck down the Akechi and the Shibata; Takigawa and Sassa knelt before him; Niwa held him in special confidence; and Inuchiyo had demonstrated his loyalty to their old friendship.

Hideyoshi now controlled almost all the provinces that Nobunaga had conquered. Even his relationship with provinces outside Nobunaga's sphere of influence had undergone a complete change. The Mori, who for years had obstinately resisted Nobunaga's plans for hegemony, had signed a treaty of alliance and sent hostages.

There was, however, one man who remained an open question: Tokugawa Ieyasu. There had been no communication between the two for some time. They were silent, like poor chess players waiting for the other side to make a good move.

The silence was finally broken by a diplomatic overture from Ieyasu, soon after Hideyoshi's return to Kyoto on the twenty-first day of the Fifth Month. Ieyasu's most senior general, Ishikawa Kazumasa, called on Hideyoshi at Takaradera Castle.

"I have come to convey Lord Ieyasu's congratulations. Your great victory has brought peace to the nation." With that solemn announcement, Kazumasa presented Hideyoshi with a valuable antique tea container called *Hatsuhana*.

Hideyoshi had become a devotee of the tea ceremony, and he was delighted to receive the precious gift. But it was also clear that he derived even greater satisfaction from having received the courtesy from Ieyasu first. Kazumasa had planned on returning to Hamamatsu that very day, but Hideyoshi detained him.

"You don't have to hurry," Hideyoshi said. "Stay for two or three days. I'll tell Lord Ieyasu that I insisted. Especially since we're having a little family celebration tomorrow."

What Hideyoshi called "a little family celebration" was the banquet to mark his investiture with a new court title, which was the seal of imperial approval on his domestic policies and military successes. He was also to announce the construction of a major new castle in Osaka.

The banquet lasted three days. A seemingly endless line of guests made its way up to the castle, and the narrow streets of the town were clogged with the carriages of courtiers, and their servants and horses.

Kazumasa was forced to admit that Nobunaga's mantle had come to rest on Hideyoshi's shoulders. Until that day he had firmly believed that it would be his lord, Ieyasu, who would succeed Nobunaga, but the time he spent with Hideyoshi changed his mind. When he compared Hideyoshi's and Ieyasu's provinces and reflected on the differences between their troops, he concluded sadly that the Tokugawa domain was still a small provincial outpost in eastern Japan.

A few days later, Kazumasa announced his intention to leave, and Hideyoshi accompanied him as far as Kyoto. As they were riding along, Hideyoshi turned in the saddle and looked back. He beckoned to Kazumasa, who was riding some way behind, to join him. As a retainer of another clan, Kazumasa had been received with the courtesy due to a guest, but he quite naturally rode behind Hideyoshi.

Hideyoshi said warmly, "We decided to travel together, and that doesn't mean that we should ride separately. The road to Kyoto is particularly boring, so let's talk as we ride."

Kazumasa hesitated for a moment but then rode up to Hideyoshi's side.

"It's inconvenient going back and forth to Kyoto," Hideyoshi went on. "So within the year I'm going to move to Osaka, which is close to the capital." He then described his plans to build a castle.

"You've chosen a good location in Osaka," Kazumasa remarked. "It's said that Lord Nobunaga had his eye on Osaka for a number of years."

"Yes, but the warrior-monks of the Honganji were entrenched in their temple-fortress there, so he was forced to settle for Azuchi."

Before long they entered the city of Kyoto, but just as Kazumasa was about to take his leave, Hideyoshi stopped him once again and said, "It wouldn't be advisable to take the land route in this heat. You'd better take a boat across the lake from Otsu. Let's have some lunch with Maeda Geni while the boat's being prepared."

He was referring to the man he had recently appointed to the governorship of Kyoto. Giving Kazumasa no chance to refuse, Hideyoshi led him to the governor's mansion. The courtyard had been swept clean, as though the visitor had been expected, and Geni's reception of Kazumasa was extremely courteous.

Hideyoshi continuously urged Kazumasa to relax, and during lunch they talked of nothing else but the castle he was going to build.

Geni brought in a large sheet of paper and spread it out on the floor. A plan for a castle was being shown to an envoy from another province, and both the man showing it and the man being shown it looked apprehensive of the reason for Hideyoshi's openness; the only apparent explanation was that Hideyoshi had forgotten that Kazumasa was a retainer of the Tokugawa clan, as well as the status of his own relationship with that clan.

"I've heard that you're quite an expert on castles," Hideyoshi told Kazumasa, "so if you have any suggestions, please don't hesitate."

Just as Hideyoshi had said, Kazumasa was quite well versed in castle construction. Normally such plans would be top secret—hardly something to show to a retainer from a rival province—but Kazumasa put away his doubts about Hideyoshi's intentions and studied the plans.

Kazumasa knew Hideyoshi was unlikely to do anything small, but he was overawed by the scale of the project. When Osaka had been the headquarters of the warrior-monks of the Honganji, their fortress had occupied an area of one thousand square yards. In Hideyoshi's plan, that became the foundation for the main citadel. The area's topography —rivers, mountains, and seacoast—had been taken into consideration; their advantages and disadvantages had been considered, and the comparative difficulties of attack and defense and other logistical problems had all been thought out. The main citadel, and the second and third, were all surrounded by earthen walls. The circuit of the outer walls was more than six leagues. The tallest building within the walls was a five-story keep, which would be pierced with openings from which to shoot arrows. The tiles of the roof were to be gold-leafed.

In his amazement Kazumasa could only marvel in silent awe at what he saw before him. But what he had been staring at was still nothing more than a part of the project. The moat surrounding the castle took its water from the Yodo River. With the prosperous mercantile city of Sakai close by, Osaka was connected with numerous trade routes to China, Korea, and Southeast Asia. The nearby Yamato and Kawachi mountain chains formed a natural defensive wall. The Sanin and Sanyo roads connected Osaka with sea and land routes to Shikoku and Kyushu, and made it a gateway with access to all outlying areas. As the location of the country's most important castle and a place from which to rule the nation, Osaka was many times superior to Nobunaga's Azuchi. Kazumasa could discover nothing lacking here.

"What do you think?" Hideyoshi asked.

"Absolutely perfect. It's a plan on a grand scale," Kazumasa replied. There was nothing more he could honestly say.

"It will be sufficient, don't you think?"

"On the day it's completed, it will be the largest castle town in the whole country," Kazumasa said.

"That's what I intend."

"When do you anticipate its completion?"

"I'd like to move in before the year is through."

Kazumasa blinked disbelievingly. "What! By the end of the year?"

"Well, about then."

"It could take ten years for an engineering project of that size."

"In ten years the world will have changed, and I'll be an old man," Hideyoshi said, laughing. "I've ordered the overseers to complete the castle's interior, including its decorations, within three years."

"I can't imagine it's going to be easy to make the craftsmen and laborers work at such a pace. And the amounts of stone and lumber you will need are going to be immense."

"I'm bringing in lumber from twenty-eight provinces."

"How many laborers will you need?"

"I'm not sure about that. I suppose I'll need well over a hundred thousand. My officials say that it will require about sixty thousand men working every day for three months just to dig the inner and outer moats."

Kazumasa fell silent. He was depressed as he reflected on the great difference between this project and the castles of Okazaki and Hamamatsu in his own province. But would Hideyoshi really be able to bring the huge stones he needed to Osaka, an area totally lacking in quarries? And where, in these difficult times, did he think he could find the huge sums to pay for the project? He wondered whether Hideyoshi's great plans were really anything more than bragging.

Just then something urgent seemed to have occurred to Hideyoshi, and he called for his secretary and began dictating a letter. Completely forgetting that Kazumasa was there, he looked over what had been written down, nodded, and started to dictate another letter. Even if Kazumasa had not wanted to listen to what was being said, Hideyoshi was right in front of him and he could not help but hear. Hideyoshi seemed to be dictating an extremely important letter to the Mori clan.

Once again Kazumasa was embarrassed and hardly knew what to do with himself. He said, "Your official business seems to be rather urgent. Shall I withdraw?"

"No, no, that won't be necessary. I'll be done in a moment."

Hideyoshi continued with his dictation. He had received a letter from a member of the Mori clan congratulating him on his victory against the Shibata. Now, under the pretext of giving an account of the battle of Yanagase, he was demanding that his correspondent define his own attitude concerning the future of his clan. It was a personal letter, and an extremely important one.

Kazumasa sat next to him, silently looking at the stands of bamboo groves, while Hideyoshi dictated:

"If I had given Katsuie a moment's rest, it would have taken much longer to defeat him. But the fate of Japan hung in the balance, so I had to resign myself to the loss of my men. I attacked Katsuie's main castle at the second half of the Hour of the Tiger, and by the Hour of the Horse I took the citadel."

When he dictated the words, "the fate of Japan," his eyes were ablaze just as they had been when the castle fell. The letter then took a turn that would rivet the Mori clan's attention on his words.

"It would be futile to mobilize our troops, but if necessary I will visit your province in person to determine the matter of boundaries. Therefore, it is important that you use discretion and be resolved not to provoke me."

Kazumasa unconsciously stole a look at Hideyoshi and marveled at the man's boldness. Here was Hideyoshi lightheartedly dictating some very frank words, almost as if he were sitting cross-legged in front of his correspondent, having a friendly chat. Was he being arrogant or just naïve?

"Both the Hojo in the east and the Uesugi in the north have entrusted matters to my resolve. If you are also prepared to let me work freely, the government of Japan will be better than it has been since ancient times. Give this deep thought and your own personal care. If you have any objections, please let me know before the Seventh Month. It is essential that you relay all of this in detail to Lord Mori Terumoto."

Kazumasa's eyes watched the play of the wind in the bamboo, but his ears were absolutely fascinated with what Hideyoshi was saying. His heart quivered like the bamboo leaves in the wind. It appeared that, for this man, even the titanic task of building Osaka Castle was something he did in his spare time. And he asserted, even to the Mori clan, that if they objected they should let him know before the Seventh Month—before he went to war again.

Kazumasa was beyond admiration; he felt exhausted.

At that moment an attendant announced that Kazumasa's ship was ready to sail. Hideyoshi took one of the swords from his waist and presented it to Kazumasa. "It may be a little old, but people say it's a good blade. Please take it as a small token of my appreciation."

Kazumasa took it and reverently lifted it to his forehead.

When they went outside, Hideyoshi's personal guards were waiting to escort Kazumasa to the port of Otsu.

* * *

There was a mountain of problems awaiting Hideyoshi both inside Kyoto and out. After Yanagase, the fighting had come to an end; but even though Takigawa had submitted, there were still a few rebels who obstinately refused to surrender. Remnants of the Ise army had entrenched themselves in Nagashima and Kobe, and Oda Nobuo was in charge of mopping up the last pockets of resistance.

When he heard that Hideyoshi had returned from Echizen, Nobuo left the front for Kyoto and met Hideyoshi on that very day.

"When Ise submits, you may occupy Nagashima Castle," Hideyoshi told him.

That very mediocre prince left Kyoto for Ise in high spirits.

It was the time of day when the lamps were lit. The courtiers who had come calling had departed and all the other guests had gone. Hideyoshi took a bath and then, as he joined Hidekatsu and Maeda Geni for dinner, an attendant informed him that Hikoemon had just arrived.

The wind rustled the rattan blinds, and the loud laughter of young women drifted in on the air. Hikoemon did not go inside immediately, but first rinsed his mouth and smoothed his hair. He had returned on horseback from Uji and was covered with dust.

His mission had been to meet Sakuma Genba, who was a prisoner at Uji. It had appeared to be an easy mission but was in fact rather difficult, as Hideyoshi knew quite well. That was the reason he had chosen Hikoemon.

Genba had been captured but not executed. Instead, he had been imprisoned at Uji. Hideyoshi had ordered that he not be treated harshly or humiliated. He knew that Genba was a man of matchless courage, who, if released, would become a raging tiger. Thus, a strict guard was kept on him at all times.

Even though Genba was a captive enemy general, Hideyoshi felt sorry for him. He loved Genba's natural talents just as Katsuie had, and felt that it would be a shame to put him to death. So, soon after Hideyoshi returned to Kyoto, he sent a messenger to express his feelings and try to reason with Genba.

"Katsuie is gone now," the messenger began, "and you should hereafter think of Hideyoshi as taking his place. If you do, you will be free to return to your home province and castle."

Genba laughed. "Katsuie was Katsuie. It is impossible for Hideyoshi to replace him. Katsuie has already committed suicide, and I have no thoughts of remaining in this world. I will never serve Hideyoshi, even if he gives me control of the entire nation."

Hikoemon had been the second messenger. He had left with the knowledge that it would be difficult. And sure enough, he had failed to change Genba's mind.

"How did it go?" Hideyoshi asked. He sat enveloped in the mosquito smudge rising from a silver censer.

"He wasn't interested," Hikoemon replied. "He only implored me to cut his head off."

"If that was his only response, it would not be sympathetic to push the matter any further." Hideyoshi seemed to be giving up the idea of persuading Genba, and the lines on his face suddenly disappeared.

"I know what you were hoping for, my lord, but I'm afraid I wasn't a very competent messenger."

"There's no need to apologize," Hideyoshi consoled him. "Even though Genba is a prisoner, he will not bow to me to save his life. His sense of honor is outstanding. I regret losing a man with that kind of fortitude and determination. If he had been persuaded by you and had come to change his loyalty, that alone might have made me lose my respect for him." He added, "You're a samurai, and you knew that in the bottom of your heart, so it makes sense that you were unable to change his mind."

"Forgive me."

"I'm sorry to have troubled you with this. But didn't Genba say anything else?"

"I asked why he had not chosen to die on the battlefield, but had run away into the mountains and been captured by farmers instead. I also asked why he spent his days as a captive, waiting to be beheaded, rather than killing himself."

"What did he say?"

"He asked me if I thought *seppuku* or being killed on the battlefield are the greatest acts of courage for a samurai, then he said he was of a different opinion: he thought a warrior must try his best to survive."

"What else?"

"When he escaped from the battle at Yanagase, he did not know whether Katsuie was alive or dead, so he was trying to get back to Kitanosho to help plan a counterattack. On the way, however, the pain from his wounds became unbearable, and he stopped at a farmhouse and asked for *moxa*."

"Sad...very sad."

"He also very calmly said that he had borne the shame of being taken alive and sent to prison so that if the guards had presented him with an opening he might have escaped, stalked you, and taken your life. Thus he might have been able to appease Katsuie's anger and been able to beg forgiveness for the mistake he had made when he penetrated the enemy lines at Shizugatake."

"Ah, what a shame." Tears of sympathy welled up in Hideyoshi's eyes. "To have mis-used a man like that and sent him to his death—that was Katsuie's fault. Well, we'll let him have what he wants, and allow him to die with grace. See to it, Hikoemon."

"I understand, my lord. Tomorrow, then?"

"The sooner the better."

"And the place?"

"Uji."

"Should he be led around and exhibited?"

Hideyoshi thought for a moment. "I suppose that would be Genba's wish. Execute him in a field at Uji after you've led him through the capital."

The next day Hideyoshi gave two silk kimonos to Hikoemon just before he left for Uji.

"I expect Genba's clothes are dirty. Give him these for his death clothes."

That day Hikoemon rode to Uji once more to meet with Genba, who was now in solitary confinement.

"Lord Hideyoshi has commanded that you be led through Kyoto and then beheaded on a field in Uji, as you have wished," he said.

Genba did not look the least bit unhappy. "I'm grateful," he replied politely.

"Lord Hideyoshi has also provided these clothes."

Genba looked at the kimonos and said, "I am truly grateful for Lord Hideyoshi's kindness. But I don't think the crest and tailoring would suit me. Please return them."

"Not suit you?"

"These are clothes that a foot soldier would wear. For me, Lord Katsuie's nephew, to be seen wearing them by the people of the capital would only shame my late uncle. The clothes I am wearing may be rags, but even though they are still grimy from battle, I would rather be led around in them. But if Lord Hideyoshi will allow me to wear one new kimono, I would like something a little more suitable."

"I'll ask him. What is your wish?"

"A red wide-sleeved coat with a bold pattern. Beneath that, a red silk kimono with silver embroidery." Genba did not mince his words. "It is no secret that I was captured by farmers, tied up, and sent here. I bore the shame of being captured alive. My aim was still to take Lord Hideyoshi's head, but that, too, was unfulfilled. When I am taken to my place of execution, I imagine that it will cause some excitement in the capital. I regret wearing a miserable silk garment like this, but if I am to wear a better one, I want it to be like the gaudy clothes I wore on the battlefield, with a banner flying from my back. Beyond that, and as proof that I have no bad feelings about being tied up, I would like to be tied up in front of everyone when I get into the cart."

Genba's frankness was truly one of his most likable traits. When Hikoemon related Genba's wishes to Hideyoshi, he immediately ordered the clothes to be sent.

The day of Genba's execution arrived. The prisoner took a bath and tied up his hair. He then put on the red kimono and, over that, the broad-sleeved coat with the large patterns. He held out his hands to be bound and then got up into the cart. That year he was a robust thirty years old, such a handsome man that everyone lamented his death.

The cart was taken along the streets of Kyoto, and then back to Uji, where an animal skin was spread out on the ground.

"You may cut your own stomach," Genba's executioner offered.

A short sword was presented to him, but Genba only laughed. "You don't need to make allowances for me."

The ropes were not untied, and he was beheaded.

* * *

The end of the Sixth Month approached.

"The construction of Osaka Castle should be moving right along," Hideyoshi said. "Let's go take a look."

When he arrived, the men in charge of the project explained what had been achieved up to that point. The marsh at Naniwa was being filled, and canals had already been dug through its length and breadth. The makeshift shops of merchants were beginning to appear on the site of the castle town. Looking out toward the sea at the harbor of Sakai and the mouth of the Yasuji River, one could see hundreds of boats carrying stones, their full sails almost touching. Hideyoshi stood on the spot where the main citadel would be constructed and, looking landward, saw the tens of thousands of laborers and artisans of all trades. These men were working day and night in shifts so that the construction would never stop.

Workers were levied from every clan; when a lord was negligent in sending his quota, he was severely punished, regardless of his status. There was a line of command of subcontractors, foremen, and sub-foremen for every trade at each work station. Responsibilities were clearly defined for those in charge. If anyone was found lacking, he was immediately beheaded. The samurai from each clan who served as inspectors did not wait for punishment but committed *seppuku* on the spot.

But what concerned Hideyoshi most right now was Ieyasu. Throughout Hideyoshi's life, he had secretly thought that the most formidable man of the times—other than Lord Nobunaga—was Ieyasu. Given his own conspicuous rise to power, he imagined that it would be almost impossible to avoid a confrontation with him.

During the Eighth Month, he ordered Tsuda Nobukatsu to take a famous sword made by Fudo Kuniyuki and present it to Ieyasu.

"Tell Lord Ieyasu that I was immensely pleased with the famous and matchless piece of pottery he presented to me when he sent Ishikawa Kazumasa."

Nobukatsu left for Hamamatsu toward the beginning of the month and returned on about the tenth day.

"The Tokugawa clan's hospitality was so gracious that I almost felt embarrassed. They were truly attentive," he reported.

"Did Lord Ieyasu appear to be in good health?"

"He seemed to be extremely well."

"What about the discipline of his retainers?"

"It had a quality you don't see in other clans—an appearance of indomitability."

"I've heard that he employs a great number of newcomers as well."

"It would seem that many are former retainers of the Takeda."

During his conversation with Nobukatsu, Hideyoshi was suddenly struck by the contrast between his own age and Ieyasu's. Certainly he was Ieyasu's elder. Ieyasu was forty-one and he was forty-six—a difference of five years. But far more than Shibata Katsuie—who was his senior by a number of years—had done, the younger Ieyasu was giving him cause for a good deal of thought.

Nevertheless, all of that was hidden in his heart. Outwardly it was not in the least bit apparent that, soon after the hostilities with the Shibata, he anticipated yet another battle. Which is to say that the relationship between the two men seemed to be totally satisfactory. In the Tenth Month Hideyoshi petitioned the emperor on Ieyasu's behalf to give him a higher court rank.

* * *

In Azuchi, Lord Samboshi was just four years old. Several provincial lords came to greet the New Year and to pay their respects and pray for his continued health.

"Excuse me, Lord Shonyu?"

"Well, Lord Gamo, how fortuitous."

The two men had met by chance in front of the great hall of the main citadel. One of them was Ikeda Shonyu, who had been moved from Osaka to Ogaki Castle to make room for Hideyoshi. The other was Gamo Ujisato.

"You look healthier all the time," Gamo said. "That's the best you could ask for."

"No, my health goes along with the years, but we've been busy anyway. For a number of nights I haven't been able to sleep, even in Ogaki."

"You have the additional burden of being in charge of the construction of Osaka Castle, Lord Shonyu."

"That kind of work is appropriate for men like Matsuda and Ishida, but it's not fitting for us soldiers."

"I disagree. It's not like Lord Hideyoshi to put men in unsuitable places. You can be sure he has a need for you somewhere among the officials."

"I'm really annoyed that you can see that kind of resource in me," Shonyu replied, laughing. "By the way, what about your New Year's greetings to the young lord?"

"I just now took my leave."

"I was just leaving myself, so it's good timing, and there's a private matter I'd very much like to talk over with you."

"To tell the truth, as soon as I saw you, I realized there was also a matter I would like to ask you about."

"We must be having the same thoughts. Where shall we talk?"

Shonyu gestured toward a small room off the great hall.

The two men sat down in the empty room. There was no brazier, but the New Year's sun coming through the sliding paper doors was warm.

"Have you heard the rumors?" Shonyu began.

"I have. It's being said that Lord Nobuo has been killed. And it sounds like the truth."

Shonyu frowned and sighed. "We're already seeing the signs that there will be some kind of disturbance this year. How bad it will get depends on who the antagonists are, but the recent omens are troubling. You're younger than I am, Lord Gamo, but it appears to me that your judgment is better than mine. Don't you have the wit to come up with a good idea before something regrettable happens?"

He looked deeply anxious.

Gamo answered with another question. "Where can these rumors be coming from?"

"I can't tell you that. But where there's smoke, there's fire."

"Do you think there's something we don't know?"

"No, not at all. The facts are just in the wrong order. To begin with, Lord Nobuo went to Takaradera Castle to call on Lord Hideyoshi in the Eleventh Month of last year. It's said that Lord Hideyoshi himself took charge of the reception held for thanking Lord Nobuo for subjugating Ise, and his hospitality was so great that Lord Nobuo stayed for four days."

"Indeed?"

"Lord Nobuo's retainers had expected him to leave the castle on the following day, but on the second day there was no word from him, nor on the third day, nor even on the fourth. Well, it seems that they imagined the worst, and even his servants outside of the castle started blurting out a number of wild suppositions."

"So that's it," Gamo laughed. "When you expose the roots of these stories, most of them are fabrications, aren't they?"

But Shonyu continued to look worried, and went on quickly, "After that, there was more public discussion of the matter, and various competing rumors ran back and forth between Ise, Nagashima, Osaka, and the capital. The first one claims that the origin of the false report of Nobuo's death came not from among Lord Nobuo's attendants but from the mouths of Hideyoshi's servants. The men at Takaradera Castle refute this. They claim that the rumor was born from the suspicions and dark spirits of Lord Nobuo's retainers. While each side is loudly denouncing the other, the rumor of Lord Nobuo's murder is spreading like the wind."

"Do people believe it?"

"It's hard to fathom the mind of the common man, but after witnessing Lord Nobutaka's end directly after the fall of the Shibata, it's certain that a number of Lord Nobuo's relatives and retainers must be having bad dreams and asking themselves who's going to be next."

Then Gamo spoke openly about his own fears. He inched closer to where Shonyu knelt and said, "There should be a firm understanding between Hideyoshi and Nobuo regardless of the kind of rumors that are making the rounds. But there just may be considerable discord between them, too."

Gamo stared at Shonyu, who nodded vigorously.

"Look at the situation since the death of Lord Nobunaga," Gamo said. "Most people think that after peace returned Lord Hideyoshi should have passed all authority to his former lord's heir. But no matter how you reason it through, it's clear that Lord Samboshi is far too young and that the successor should be Lord Nobuo. If Hideyoshi does not submit to Lord Nobuo, he could be accused of being disloyal and of forgetting the many favors the Oda clan bestowed upon him."

"It's all a little unsavory, isn't it? Nobuo's intentions are transparent, and yet he doesn't seem to understand that what is about to happen is just the opposite of what he would like."

"But do you think it's really possible that he's holding such optimistic thoughts?"

"He may be. What kind of calculations will be going on in the mind of a pampered fool, after all?"

"It's certain that they're hearing these rumors in Osaka and that misunderstandings are just going to increase."

"This is awkward, to be sure," Shonyu sighed.

As Hideyoshi's generals, both Shonyu and Gamo were bound to him by the absolute bond that existed between lord and retainer. But they were also bound to a set of conditions that now might not be so easily resolved.

First of all, at the time Gamo had been receiving Nobunaga's favors, he had married Nobunaga's youngest daughter. Moreover, Shonyu and Nobunaga had had the same wet nurse, and Shonyu's relationship with his former lord as a foster brother had been particularly close. Therefore, even at the conference in Kiyosu, the two men ranked as relatives. Quite naturally, they could not be indifferent to the problems facing the Oda clan, and except for the young Samboshi, the only person of Nobunaga's direct bloodline was Nobuo.

The two men would not have been so perplexed if they could have found anything of merit in Nobuo's character, but it was clear that he was nothing more than a mediocrity. Both before and after the conference at Kiyosu, it was clear to everyone that he was not the man to grasp the reins that had fallen from Nobunaga's hands.

But unfortunately no one would tell Nobuo the truth. The good-natured young aristocrat—who had always leaned on the strength of his retainers, who had bowed and nodded approval at flatterers on every occasion, and who had been taken in by others who had manipulated him to their own advantage—had let a great moment in history pass by without even being aware of it.

Nobuo had secretly met with Ieyasu the year before and after the battle of Yanagase, had forced his brother to commit suicide on Hideyoshi's advice. More recently he had been rewarded with the provinces of Ise, Iga, and Owari for his victory in Ise and, perhaps thinking that his day was at hand, expected that Hideyoshi would next transfer the authority of the central government to him.

"But we can't just let the situation continue like this and look on like spectators. Don't you have some good ideas, Lord Shonyu?"

"No, I hoped to get some from you. You've got to think of something, Lord Gamo."

"I think the best thing would be to have Lord Nobuo meet with Lord Hideyoshi. Then he could speak frankly."

"That's an excellent idea. Well, he's been assuming an air of importance recently, so how will we go about this?"

"I'll invent some pretext."

For Nobuo, something that might have been interesting yesterday today was not. In his heart he was always discontented. Moreover, he was not the kind of man who would reflect on why that was so. The previous autumn he had moved to Nagashima Castle in his new province of Ise, and he had been granted a new court rank. When he went out the crowds bowed to him, and when he returned he was greeted by flutes and stringed instruments. There was nothing he wished for that he could not have, and that spring he was still only twenty-six years old. The tragedy of Nobuo was that living in such enviable conditions, he was all the less satisfied.

"Ise is too provincial," he would complain. "Why is Hideyoshi building that absurdly big castle in Osaka? Is he planning on living there himself, or is he going to invite the rightful heir to do so?"

When he spoke that way, it was Nobunaga speaking in his head. It was as though he had received his father's form but not his substance. "That Hideyoshi is immodest. He's forgotten that he was my father's retainer, and now he not only taxes my father's remaining retainers and hurries to build a gigantic castle, but he treats me as though I were an encumbrance. Lately he doesn't consult with me about anything."

The silence between the two men dated from the Eleventh Month of the previous year. Recent rumors that Hideyoshi was making plans and leaving him out of them were quite enough to raise his suspicions.

At the same time, Nobuo let out certain unguarded statements among his retainers, and those became public, so that his innermost thoughts became a further irritation to Hideyoshi. As a result, the New Year passed by without their exchanging greetings.

At New Year's, when Nobuo was playing kickball in the rear garden with his ladies-in-waiting and pages, a samurai announced a visitor. It was Gamo. He was two years older than Nobuo and was married to Nobuo's sister.

"Gamo? He's here just at the right time," Nobuo said, gracefully kicking the ball. "He'll be a good opponent. Bring him to the garden immediately."

The messenger left but quickly returned, saying, "Lord Gamo says he's in a hurry and is waiting for you in the guest room."

"What about kickball?"

"He said to tell you that he has no skill at the game."

"What a peasant!" Nobuo laughed, showing a line of elegantly blackened teeth.

A number of days after Gamo's visit, a letter arrived from Gamo and Shonyu. Nobuo had been in a very good mood, and he quickly summoned four of his elder retainers and passed on the information.

"We're going to Otsu tomorrow. They say that Hideyoshi is waiting for me at the Onjo Temple."

"Will that be safe, my lord?" one of the four elders asked.

Nobuo smiled, clearly displaying his blackened teeth.

"Hideyoshi must be troubled by the public rumors about our falling out. I'm sure that's it. He hasn't been dutiful to the person closest to my father."

"But what sort of arrangements have been made for this meeting?"

In his answer Nobuo sounded quite self-assured. "It's like this. A while ago, Gamo came and said that there was gossip of something unseemly between Hideyoshi and me, but Gamo assured me Hideyoshi harbors no grudge at all. He asked me to go to the Onjo Temple in Otsu and have a New Year's meeting with him. I felt there was no reason to have any animosity toward Hideyoshi and agreed to go. Both Lord Shonyu and Lord Gamo assured me that I would be quite safe."

It could be said that Nobuo's tendency to accept at face value whatever was written or spoken was the result of his upbringing. So his elder retainers were all the more inclined to be prudent, and they could not hide their misgivings.

Crowding together, they looked over Gamo's letter.

"There's no mistake," one said, "it seems to be in his handwriting."

"Nothing else can be done," another replied. "If Lord Shonyu and Lord Gamo have gone to the trouble to handle the matter this far, we should not be remiss."

And so it was decided that the four senior retainers would accompany Nobuo to Otsu.

On the following day Nobuo set out for Otsu. When he arrived at the Onjo Temple, Gamo called on him immediately, and Ikeda appeared a little later.

"Lord Hideyoshi arrived yesterday," Shonyu said. "He's waiting for you."

The place for the meeting had been prepared at Hideyoshi's lodgings, the main temple, but upon being asked politely when it would be convenient for him to meet Hideyoshi, Nobuo replied with a little display of willfulness, "I'm tired from the trip, so I'd like to rest all day tomorrow."

"Well then, we'll make arrangements for the day after tomorrow." And the two men returned to inform Hideyoshi.

No one had the leisure to spend an entire day doing nothing, but since Nobuo had said he wanted to rest, everyone spent the day in useless tedium.

Upon his arrival, Nobuo had been annoyed to find that Hideyoshi and his retainers had occupied the main buildings, while the smaller ones had been allotted to his party. In arranging the day of the meeting Nobuo had tried to be a little self-assertive and had acted on whim, but the next day he himself seemed to be greatly troubled by his own boredom, and he started to complain.

"Even my senior retainers aren't here."

Nobuo spent the day being shown the temple's treasured books of poetry and being bored to tears by the endless talk of the old priests. When evening finally came, his four senior retainers appeared in his room. "Did you have a good rest, my lord?" one of the four asked.

The fools! Nobuo was angry. He wanted to scream that he was bored and had nothing to do, but instead he replied, "Yes, thank you. Did each of you make yourself comfortable in your own lodgings?"

"There was no time to make ourselves comfortable."

"Why is that?"

"The messengers from the other clans were unending."

"There were that many visitors? Why didn't you come and tell me?"

"You said that you wanted to rest for the day, and we did not want to disturb you, my lord."

Drawing circles with his fingers and tapping his kneecaps, Nobuo looked at them with haughty disinterest.

"Well, fine. But the four of you should eat your evening meal with me. We'll have a little *sake* too." The senior retainers looked at each other and seemed to be embarrassed. "Is there something else that will prevent you from doing that?" Nobuo asked.

One of the retainers said, as though he were apologizing, "The fact is that a while ago a messenger came with an invitation from Lord Hideyoshi, and we came here to ask your permission."

"What! Hideyoshi invited you! What's this? Another tea ceremony?" A frown appeared on Nobuo's face.

"No, I don't think it's anything like that. I doubt that he would invite retainers like us, especially for tea, and leave our lord out, when there are other lords here he could have invited instead. He said there was something he wanted to talk over with us."

"How strange," Nobuo said, but then shrugged his shoulders. "Well, if he's invited you, I wonder if he's going to talk about finally having me fully take over the Oda clan. That might be it. It would be improper for Hideyoshi to lord it over the rightful heir. The people would never stand for it."

The main temple hall was deserted. Only the lamps waited for the night. The guests arrived. It was the middle of the First Month and bitterly cold. Then someone else approached, clearing his throat. Because the person was accompanied by an attendant, Nobuo's four retainers immediately realized that it must be Hideyoshi. He seemed to be giving orders in a loud voice as he walked along.

"Sorry to keep you waiting," he said as he entered the room, and then coughed into his hand.

When they looked up, they could see that he was now alone—not even a page was behind him.

The four men were ill at ease. As each one greeted him, Hideyoshi blew his nose.

"You appear to have a cold, my lord," one of Nobuo's retainers said affably.

"I just can't seem to get over it," Hideyoshi replied in no less a friendly manner.

It was a rather plain setting for a discussion. Neither food nor drink were offered, nor did Hideyoshi begin with any small talk. "Aren't you troubled by Lord Nobuo's recent behavior?" he began.

The four men were filled with apprehension. They were shocked by what seemed to be a reprimand, and thought he was laying the blame on them as Nobuo's senior advisers. "You're doing your best, I suppose," he said then, and the color returned to their faces. "All of you are intelligent men, but I suspect you can't do much under Lord Nobuo. I understand. I've taxed my own ingenuity for his sake, but regrettably, it seems like I'm always meeting with reverses."

He said these last words emphatically, and the four men felt extremely cramped. Hideyoshi continued to expose his innermost feelings, making his dissatisfaction with Nobuo very plain. "I have made my decision," Hideyoshi said. "I feel sorry that you four have spent many years serving this man. To be brief, we can end the matter without fuss if you can persuade Lord Nobuo either to commit *seppuku* or to become a priest. As a reward, I will give you lands in Ise and Iga."

It was not just the cold that chilled the four men to the bone. The four walls felt like silent swords and spears. Hideyoshi's eyes shone fixedly, tiny pinpoints of light. Those eyes required the retainers to say either yes or no.

He would not give them time to consider his offer or allow them to leave without hearing their answer. They were in a desperate situation. The four men hung their heads in grief. Finally, however, they agreed and quickly wrote and signed pledges.

"My retainers are drinking *sake* in the Willow Room," Hideyoshi said. "Go and join them. I'd like to go with you, but I'm going to bed early because of this cold."

Picking up the pledges, he retired to his quarters in the temple.

Nobuo was unable to settle down that night. At dinner he had sat with his retainers and attendants, the priests, and even the virgin priestesses from the neighboring shrine. He had been cheerful and talked in a loud voice, but when everyone had left and he was once again alone, he constantly asked his pages and the samurai on guard, "What time is it now? Haven't the senior retainers come back from the main temple yet?"

After a while only one of the men returned.

"Are you alone, Saburobei?" Nobuo asked at the retainer suspiciously.

The expression on the man's face was not normal, and even Nobuo felt apprehensive. Prostrating himself with both hands to the floor, the old man could not even look up. Nobuo could hear him sobbing.

"What is it, Saburobei? Did something happen while you were talking with Hideyoshi?"

"It was a painful meeting."

"What! Did he call you over to scold you?"

"If that had been it, it would not have been painful at all. What happened was totally unexpected. We were forced to sign pledges. You, too, must be resolved, my lord." He went on to reveal Hideyoshi's order in its entirety, then said, "We knew that if we said no, he would kill us on the spot, so there was nothing we could do but sign. Later I saw my chance during a drinking party with his retainers and ran back here alone. There'll be an uproar when they discover I'm gone. You are not safe here, my lord. You must leave immediately."

Nobuo's lips had lost their color. The movements of his eyes seemed to show that he had heard only half of what the man had said. His heart beat as fearfully as a fire bell, and he could hardly sit still. "But…then…what about the others?"

"I came back here on my own. I don't know about the others."

"The others, they signed the pledge too?"

"They did."

"So they're still drinking with Hideyoshi's retainers? I misjudged them. They're lower than beasts!"

He stood up as he continued this abuse and snatched the long sword from the hands of the page behind him. As he walked hastily out of the room, the flustered Saburobei chased after him, pleading to know where his lord was going. Nobuo turned around and, lowering his voice, asked for a horse to be brought immediately.

"Wait for a moment, my lord." Understanding his lord's intentions, Saburobei dashed off to the stables.

The horse was a fine one, a bay called Sledgehammer. As soon as Nobuo was in the saddle, he galloped through the rear gate into the cover of night. No one knew he was gone until the following day. Naturally, the meeting with Hideyoshi was canceled on the excuse that Nobuo had fallen ill, and Hideyoshi calmly returned to Osaka as though that was exactly what he had expected.

Nobuo returned to Nagashima, shut himself up inside his castle, and, still on the pretext of illness, would not show his face even to his own retainers. But his seclusion was not entirely on account of a feigned malady. He had really become quite ill. Only the doctor went in and out of the inner apartments, and although the plum blossoms behind the castle bloomed, the music ceased, and the garden was quiet and deserted.

In the castle town, on the other hand, and all over Ise and Iga, rumors spread and multiplied by the day. Nobuo's flight from the Onjo Temple had fueled everyone's suspicions.

Nobuo's senior retainers confined themselves to their castles—almost as if by prearrangement—and never came to Nagashima. That only encouraged the rumors and worsened the unease throughout the province.

The truth was always difficult to discover, but it was certain that the discord between Nobuo and Hideyoshi had once again ignited. Naturally, Nobuo's status was the center of the storm, and there did appear to be someone he could rely upon. Nobuo was conservative by nature, and believed in the efficacy of secret plots and stratagems. Although he always seemed to be in agreement with his allies, he was also quick to hint that he had other friends who would cover him from behind if the situation did not turn out the way he wanted. Unless he had a secret ally in reserve, he could never be at ease.

Nobuo now remembered the one great player who had stood in the shadows. That man, of course, was the sleeping dragon of Hamamatsu, Lord Tokugawa Ieyasu.

But the results of playing with strategy depend on the other players. The fact that Nobuo would consider using Ieyasu as his means to check Hideyoshi only demonstrated his lack of understanding of the other parties involved. The man with a devious mind never truly knows his opponent. He is like the hunter who chases after the deer and fails to see the mountains.

Beyond that, it was the natural conclusion to his kind of thinking that Nobuo would push Ieyasu to the fore and attempt to prevent Hideyoshi's rise to power. One night, after the beginning of the Second Month, Nobuo sent a messenger to Ieyasu. The two men bound themselves in a secret military alliance based on the mutual understanding that they were both waiting for the time when they could strike at Hideyoshi.

Then, on the sixth day of the Third Month, the three senior retainers who had not been seen in the castle since that night at the Onjo Temple suddenly appeared. They had been specially invited by Nobuo to a banquet. Ever since the incident at the Onjo Temple, Nobuo had been convinced that the men were traitors, plotting with Hideyoshi. Just seeing them made him sick with rancor.

Nobuo nonchalantly entertained the three men, and after they had eaten, he said suddenly, "Ah, Nagato, I'd like you to see a new firearm that has just arrived from a blacksmith in Sakai."

They went to another room, and as Nagato looked at the musket, Nobuo's retainer suddenly yelled, "By my lord's command!" and grabbed him from behind.

"This is despicable!" Nagato gasped, tying to draw his sword from its sheath. But he was knocked to the ground by his more powerful assailant and could only struggle helplessly in his grip.

Nobuo stood up and ran around the room, yelling, "Let him go! Let him go!" But the violent scuffle continued. Holding his unsheathed sword over his head, Nobuo screamed once again, "If you don't let him go, I won't be able to cut the bastard down! Let him go!"

The assassin was holding Nagato by the throat, but seeing his chance, he thrust the man away. In the same instant, and without waiting for Nobuo to strike, he stabbed Nagato with his short sword.

A group of samurai, now kneeling outside of the room, announced that they had killed the other two retainers. Nobuo nodded his approval. But then he heaved a great sigh. Regardless of their crimes, to have executed three senior advisers who had been at his side for many years was a merciless act. Such brutality, of course, had also been in Nobunaga's blood. But in Nobunaga's case it was born of passion and imbued with great significance. Nobunaga's evil and violence were seen as drastic but necessary remedies for the ills of the times; Nobuo's actions, however, arose from nothing more than his own petty emotions.

The killings in Nagashima Castle could have churned up raging waves that might have led to disturbances on all sides beginning that very night. But the murder of the three senior retainers had been carried out in secret, and on the very next day, soldiers from Nagashima were dispatched to attack each of the retainers' castles.

It was not unreasonable for people to imagine that the next great battle was imminent. Something had been smoldering since the year before, but the flame that leaped out here might be the one that would finally scorch all the world. That was no longer just idle speculation, but seemed a certainty.

THE HOODED WARRIOR

Ikeda Shonyu was famous for three things: his short stature, his courage, and his skill at the spear dance. He was forty-eight, the same age as Hideyoshi.

Hideyoshi had no son; Shonyu, however, had three in whom he could take pride, and all three of them had grown to manhood. The eldest, Yukisuke, was twenty-five and the commander of Gifu Castle; the second, Terumasa, was twenty and the commander of Ikejiri Castle; and the youngest would be fourteen this year and was still at his father's side.

Shonyu's relationship with Hideyoshi went back to the time when Hideyoshi was still called Tokichiro. By this time, however, a large gulf had opened up between the two. But Shonyu had not been left behind by the times. After Nobunaga's death, he was one of the four men—along with Katsuie, Niwa, and Hideyoshi—who had been appointed to administer the government of Kyoto, and even if the position was a temporary one, it was prestigious. Moreover, right here in Mino, father and sons possessed three castles, while his son-in-law, Nagayoshi, was the commander of Kaneyama Castle.

It could not be said that he had fared badly. Nor was there any reason for him to feel uneasy. Hideyoshi was always tactful and often paid attention to his old friend. He even had his nephew, Hidetsugu, engaged to Shonyu's daughter.

Thus in peacetime Hideyoshi shrewdly strengthened the ties between them against the day of emergency, but this year—as the decisive battle became more and more inevitable—he leaned more heavily on Shonyu as his main ally. Now he suddenly sent a messenger to Ogaki offering to adopt his son-in-law, Nagayoshi, and to give him the provinces of Owari, Mino, and Mikawa.

Twice Hideyoshi sent letters written by his own hand. The fact that Shonyu did not send a quick response did not mean he was envious or mean-hearted. He knew well that serving Hideyoshi would be more advantageous than serving anyone else. And he understood that, while Hideyoshi had great ambitions, he himself would also receive great advantages.

What made it difficult for Shonyu to rouse himself to a response was simply the problem of the widely discussed moral justification for war between the eastern and western armies. The Tokugawa accused Hideyoshi of being a traitor who had already eliminated one of the sons of his former lord and was now ready to strike down his heir, Nobuo.

If I ally myself to Hideyoshi, Shonyu thought, I will have taken a poor step in terms of moral duty; if I help Nobuo, I'll be standing on moral duty, but my hopes for the future will be dim.

And Shonyu had yet another worry. Shonyu had close ties with Nobunaga, and because of that deep relationship he could not easily sever his relationship with Nobuo, even after Nobunaga's death. To make matters worse, his eldest son was a hostage in Ise, and Shonyu did not feel he could just abandon him to be killed. So, every time he received one of Hideyoshi's letters, Shonyu was confused. When he discussed the matter with his retainers, he listened to advice from two factions, one stressing the importance of justice and counseling against abandoning moral duty; and the other arguing that now was the time when a great advantage might be gained for the prosperity of the clan.

What was he going to do? Just as his confusion was growing more and more acute, his eldest son was unexpectedly sent home from Nagashima. Nobuo thought that Shonyu would be grateful to him and never betray him. Such an obvious ruse might have had the desired effect on someone else, but Shonyu was a man of some insight. He understood the act to be nothing more than a childish, high-pressure goodwill sales tactic and a transparent political calculation.

"I've made my decision. In a dream the Buddha told me to join the western army," he announced to his retainers. On the same day he sent a letter to Hideyoshi, declaring himself his ally.

He was, of course, lying about the dream from the Buddha, but immediately after Shonyu had made his decision, the general's innate ambition was suddenly set aflame by a casual conversation with his eldest son.

What Yukisuke mentioned was that the commander of Inuyama Castle, Nakagawa Kanemon, had received his orders to return to Inuyama soon after he himself had been released from Nagashima.

Until that day, Shonyu had been unable to decide whether Inuyama Castle would be his ally or enemy, but now that he had sent word of his support for Hideyoshi, Inuyama Castle would be an enemy right in front of him. Moreover, the castle was in a strategic area with natural defenses, and it was certain that Ieyasu and Nobuo considered Nakagawa Kanemon able enough to entrust with the first-line defenses of their provinces. If that were so, he had no doubt been suddenly detached from the Ise army for that purpose and ordered to return to his own castle.

"Summon the leader of the Blue Herons," Shonyu ordered an attendant.

In a valley beyond the rear entrance of the castle was a collection of huts belonging to the men employed from outside of the clan. They were called the Blue Heron Corps.

From that encampment, Shonyu's attendant called out a short, solidly built young man of about twenty-five years of age. It was Sanzo, the captain of the Blue Herons. Receiving his instructions from the attendant, he went through the rear castle gate and into the inner garden.

Shonyu was standing in the shade of a tree, and beckoned him forward with a thrust of his chin. Then, as Sanzo prostrated himself at his lord's feet, Shonyu gave him his orders in person.

The name of the Blue Heron Corps was derived from the color of their blue cotton uniforms. Whenever an incident occurred, they would fly off to unknown destinations, like a flock of blue herons taking flight.

Three days later, Sanzo returned from some undisclosed location. He quickly went through the rear gate of the castle and, just as before, bowed before Shonyu in the inner garden. Shonyu then received the freshly bloodstained sword that Sanzo took from an oil-paper wrapping and inspected it carefully.

"This is it, certainly," Shonyu said, nodding, and then added in praise, "You did well." He gave several gold coins to Sanzo as a reward.

There was little doubt that the sword was the one carried by Nakagawa Kanemon, the commander of Inuyama Castle. His family crest was lacquered onto the scabbard.

"Thank you for your generosity, my lord," Sanzo said, and started to withdraw, but Shonyu told him to wait. Once again summoning an attendant, he had so much money set in front of Sanzo that it would have to be carried out on the back of a horse. An official and the personal attendant wrapped the coins in a number of reed-mat bales as Sanzo stood there in openmouthed surprise.

"I want you to do another job, Sanzo."

"Yes, my lord."

"I've given the details very carefully to three of my most trusted men. I want you to disguise yourself as a packhorse driver, load this money on a horse, and ride along behind those three men."

"And what is our destination?"

"Don't ask."

"Yes, my lord."

"If everything goes as planned, I'll promote you to the rank of samurai."

"Thank you, my lord."

Sanzo was a bold and fearless man, but he was more unnerved by the sight of the great amount of money than he would have been by a pool of blood. He prostrated himself again, putting his head to the ground almost excessively. When he raised it, he saw an old man, who looked like a country samurai, and two stout youths who were loading the bales of money onto a horse's saddle.

Shonyu and Yukisuke shared a bowl of morning tea in the tearoom. Appearing to be simply the long-separated father and son privately eating breakfast together, they were actually totally engrossed in a secret discussion.

"I'll set out for Gifu immediately," Yukisuke said finally.

When he left the tearoom, Yukisuke quickly ordered his retainers to prepare his horse.

He had planned to return immediately to his own castle at Gifu, but now those plans were postponed for two or three days.

"Don't make any mistakes tomorrow night," Shonyu cautioned him in a low voice.

Yukisuke nodded with a knowing expression, but in the eyes of his father this ardent young man still looked like a mere child.

But on the evening of the following day—the thirteenth of the month—what Shonyu's thoughts had been and why he had sent Yukisuke to Gifu the day before were known by everyone inside Ogaki Castle.

Suddenly there came a notice to mobilize. The notice was a great surprise, even to Shonyu's retainers.

In the midst of all the confusion, a commander stepped into the attendant warriors' room, where a number of young samurai were in an uproar of excitement. Making a show of tying up the leather strings to his gloves, he looked at the warriors with an ashen face and said, "We're going to take Inuyama Castle before the night is through."

As might be expected, the one calm spot in the midst of all that commotion was the private room of the commanding general, Shonyu.

With his second son, Terumasa, at his side, he was now exchanging toasts of *sake*. Both father and son sat on their camp stools, waiting for the hour of departure.

Normally, when the departure of troops was announced, the conch shells were blown, drums and banners flourished, and the troops wound their way majestically through the castle town. But on this occasion mounted men were left in small groups of two or three; foot soldiers were placed both in front and in back; the banners were folded and the firearms concealed. On that hazy spring night in the Third Month, the townspeople might have turned to look and wondered what was happening, but no one would have thought that it was a departure for the front.

Just three leagues from Ogaki, as the troops gathered together once more, Shonyu addressed them: "Let's finish up this battle by dawn, and return home before the day is through. You should travel as lightly as you can."

The town of Inuyama and its castle were directly on the other bank. The river in that spot was the upper reaches of the Kiso. Echoes of the water beating against the boulders or splashing through the shallows reverberated through the air, but wrapped in the deep vapors, the moon, the mountain, and the water appeared to be encased in mica. All that was visible from the shore was the dim light of the lamps on the other shore.

"Dismount."

Shonyu himself got off his horse and set up his camp stool on the riverbank.

"Lord Yukisuke is on time. There are his troops over there," one of Shonyu's retainers pointed out.

Shonyu stood up and peered upstream.

"Scout! Scout!" he called immediately.

One of the scouts ran up to confirm the report. Very soon thereafter, a force of four or five hundred men joined the nearly six hundred troops led by Ikeda Shonyu, and the silhouettes of a thousand men moved together like merging schools of fish.

Sanzo finally trailed in after Yukisuke's men. The sentries on guard looking back towards the rear surrounded him with spears and brought him before Shonyu's camp stool.

Shonyu did not give Sanzo the opportunity to say anything unnecessary as he questioned him on the essential points of his mission.

By that time a number of flat-bottomed fishing boats that had been scattered along the bank began making their way across the water. Dozens of lightly armored soldiers leaned forward and leaped out, one after another, onto the opposite bank. The poles were then quickly set to bring the boats back to transport yet another group across.

In the twinkling of an eye, the only man left on the bank was Sanzo. Finally the shouts of the warriors shook the damp night sky, from the opposite bank to the area just below the castle. In that instant one corner of the sky turned red, and sparks danced and glittered above the castle town.

Shonyu's clever plan had worked perfectly. Inuyama Castle fell in only an hour, its defenders taken by a surprise that was made more complete by treachery inside the castle and the town. Treachery was certainly one reason why a castle with such good natural defenses fell in such a short time. But there was yet another reason: Shonyu had once been the commander of Inuyama Castle, and the townspeople, the headmen in the surrounding villages, and even the farmers still remembered their former master. Although Shonyu had sent retainers to buy off those men with money just before the attack, the success of the plan owed far more to his former position than to bribery.

* * *

A man belonging to an illustrious family in decline tends to attract a complicated set of characters. The farsighted, the frivolous, the men who deplore the present evils but are unable to speak their own words or offer loyal advice—all of those quickly leave the scene. And those who are sensitive to the trends but have neither the strength nor the talent to check the decline also move on at some point.

The only men remaining are of two kinds: those who have no outstanding talents that would support their lives elsewhere if they did leave, and those truly faithful men who are retainers to the very end, through poverty and decline, life and death, happiness and grief.

But who are the true samurai? Those who live expediently or those who remain simply for the sake of opportunism? This is not easily understood, because all of them use every bit of their ingenuity to deceive their lords into overevaluating their talents.

Although he was an opportunist, Ieyasu was a player of an entirely different cast from the infantile Nobuo, who knew absolutely nothing about the world. Ieyasu held Nobuo in the palm of his hand like a chessman-in-reserve.

"Well now, you've gone to extraordinary lengths, Lord Nobuo," Ieyasu said. "Really, I'll just have a little more rice. I was brought up in a modest household, so both my palate and my stomach are overwhelmed by the luxury of tonight's meal."

It was the night of the thirteenth. When Ieyasu arrived in Kiyosu that afternoon, Nobuo took him to a temple where the two of them held secret talks for several hours. A banquet was held that evening in the guest rooms in the castle.

Ieyasu had not moved to the center even during the Honno Temple incident. Now, however, he was gambling the Tokugawa clan's entire strength—a strength he had spent many years in building up—and had ridden to Kiyosu himself. Nobuo looked to Ieyasu as his savior. He was going to do his best to entertain him, and now he put delicacies in front of him.

But to Ieyasu's eyes, Nobuo's hospitality was really nothing but immature child's play, and he could only feel sorry for the man. At a former time, Ieyasu had feasted and entertained Nobunaga for seven days when the latter was making a triumphal return from Kai on the pretext of sightseeing at Mount Fuji. When he recalled the scale of that event, Ieyasu could only pity the poverty of this evening.

A human being could only view the situation with pity, and Ieyasu felt his share. He was, however, a man who knew that the nature of the universe was change. So, even though he felt pity and sympathy in the middle of such a banquet, he did not suffer any pangs of conscience about his ulterior motive, which was simply to use this fragile and aristocratic fop as his own puppet. The reason was clear: there is no one more likely to kindle disaster than the foolish heir of an illustrious family who has been bequeathed both an inheritance and a reputation. And the more he is capable of being used, the more dangerous he becomes.

Hideyoshi most likely thought the same as Ieyasu. But while Hideyoshi considered Nobuo a hindrance to his own goals and thought of ways to dispose of him, Ieyasu was finding ways to use him. Those opposing viewpoints were based on the same fundamental goal for both Hideyoshi and Ieyasu. And no matter which man won, Nobuo's fate would be the same because he was simply unable to abandon the idea that he was Nobunaga's heir.

"What do you mean?" Nobuo said. "The real feast is just starting. It's a fine spring night, and it would be a shame to go to bed so soon."

Nobuo was trying his best to entertain Ieyasu, but the truth was that Ieyasu had work to do.

"No, Lord Nobuo. His Lordship shouldn't have any more *sake*. At least judging from the color of his face. Send the cup in our direction."

But Nobuo had not noticed the guest of honor's embarrassing boredom. His efforts were now guided by his misinterpretation of the sleepy look in his guest's eyes. He whispered to his retainers, and the sliding paper doors at the end of the room were quickly removed, revealing an orchestra and dancers. To Ieyasu it was the usual contrivance, but with a patient look he displayed interest at moments, laughed from time to time, and clapped his hands when the performance ended.

Taking this opportunity, his retainers tugged at Ieyasu's sleeve and quietly signaled him that it was time for bed, but in that very instant a comedian appeared with a flourish of musical instruments.

"For the honored guest this evening, we are now going to present a performance of Kabuki, recently received in the capital...."

The man's loquacity was incredible. He then sang an introduction to the play. Then another actor introduced a stanza from a chorus and some chants from the Christian mass, which had recently been gaining favor among the lords of the western provinces.

He played an instrument that resembled the viola used in church services, and his clothes were embroidered with a Western-style design and trimmed with lace, dazzlingly harmonized with a traditional Japanese kimono.

The audience was impressed and fascinated. There was no doubt that what pleased the common man also gave pleasure to the great lords and samurai.

"Lord Nobuo, Lord Ieyasu says that he's getting sleepy," Okudaira said to Nobuo, who had been completely taken by the play.

Nobuo quickly got up to see Ieyasu off, walking him to his apartments himself. The Kabuki performance had not yet finished, and the viola, flutes, and drums could still be heard.

The following morning Nobuo arose at what was for him an exceptionally early hour and went off to Ieyasu's apartments. There he found Ieyasu ready with the fresh face of dawn, discussing some matter with his retainers.

"What about Lord Ieyasu's breakfast?" Nobuo inquired.

When a retainer told him that breakfast had already been served, Nobuo looked a little embarrassed.

At that point a samurai on guard in the garden and a soldier up in the reconnaissance tower yelled back and forth about something going on in the distance. That caught the attention of both Ieyasu and Nobuo, and as they sat silently for a moment, a samurai came up to make a report.

"Black smoke has been visible for a while now in the sky far off to the northwest. At first we thought it was a forest fire, but the smoke gradually changed its location, and then a number of other smoke clouds started rising into the sky."

Nobuo shrugged. If it had been the southeast, he might have thought of the battlefields in Ise or other places, but his expression indicated that he didn't understand at all.

Ieyasu, who had heard reports of Nakagawa's death two days earlier, said, "Isn't that the direction of Inuyama?" Without waiting for an answer, he gave orders to the men around him. "Okudaira, go take a look."

Okudaira ran down the corridor with Nobuo's retainers and climbed the reconnaissance tower.

The footsteps of the men hurriedly descending the tower clearly indicated that a disaster had already occurred.

"It could be Haguro, Gakuden, or Inuyama, but whichever it is, it's in that area for sure," Okudaira reported.

The castle had become as agitated as a boiling teakettle. The conch shell could be heard outside, but most of the warriors who immediately rushed around collecting their weapons did not notice that Ieyasu was already there.

When Ieyasu was informed for certain that the flames were coming from the direction of Inuyama, he yelled, "We've bungled it!" and hurried off in a way that was not typical of him.

He whipped his horse to a gallop and rode off toward the smoke in the northwest. His retainers rode at his right and left, not wishing to be left behind. It was no great distance from Kiyosu to Komaki, or from Komaki to Gakuden. From Gakuden to Haguro was another league; and finally, from Haguro to Inuyama, the same distance. By the time they arrived at Komaki, they knew the entire story. Sometime in the early hours of the morning, the castle at Inuyama had fallen. Ieyasu reined in his horse and gazed steadily at the smoke rising from a number of places between Haguro and the neighborhood of Inuyama.

"I'm too late," he muttered bitterly. "I shouldn't be making mistakes like this."

Ieyasu could almost see the face of Shonyu in the rising black smoke. When he had heard the rumor that Nobuo had sent Shonyu's son back to his father, he had had misgivings about the consequences of Nobuo's good-natured act. Nevertheless, he did not think that Shonyu could have hidden his true posture and committed such an underhanded act with such cynicism and speed.

It's not that I didn't know Shonyu is such a crafty old fox, Ieyasu thought. There was no need to consider once again the strategic importance of the stronghold of Inuyama. Close as it was to Kiyosu, its importance in the war against Hideyoshi's army would only increase. Inuyama controlled the upper reaches of the Kiso River, the border between Mino and Owari, and the all-important crossing to Unuma. It was in a position worth a hundred ramparts, and now it had been lost to the enemy.

"Let's go back," Ieyasu said. "The way those flames are rising, there's no doubt that Shonyu and his son have already withdrawn to Gifu."

Ieyasu suddenly turned his horse around, and at that moment the expression on his face returned to normal. The feeling that he imparted to the retainers around him was one of confidence; he was certain he would more than make up for this loss. As they talked vehemently about Shonyu's ingratitude, deplored the cowardice of his surprise attack, and threatened to teach him a lesson on the next battlefield, Ieyasu seemed not to hear them. Grinning silently, he turned his horse back toward Kiyosu.

On the way back they ran into Nobuo, who had left Kiyosu a good bit later at the head of his army. Nobuo stared at Ieyasu as though his return were something completely unexpected.

"Was everything all right at Inuyama?" he asked.

Before Ieyasu could respond, laughing voices were heard among the retainers behind him. As he explained the situation to Nobuo, Ieyasu was truly kind and courteous. Nobuo was crestfallen. Ieyasu brought his horse alongside Nobuo's and comforted him.

"Don't worry. If we have had one defeat here, Hideyoshi will have an even bigger one. Look over there."

With his eyes he indicated the hill at Komaki.

Long before, Hideyoshi had made the acutely strategic observation that Nobunaga should move from Kiyosu to Komaki. It was really nothing more than a round hill only two hundred and eighty feet high, but it dominated the plain on which it stood and would be a convenient base from which to mount an attack in any direction. In a battle on the Owari-Mino plain, if Komaki was fortified, the western army would be impeded in its advance, and thus it would make an excellent location for strategies of both attack and defense.

There was really no time to explain all that to Nobuo, and Ieyasu turned around and pointed, this time speaking to his own retainers. "Start building fortifications on Mount Komaki right away."

As soon as he had given the orders, he began to trot alongside Nobuo, exchanging pleasant conversation with him as they rode back to Kiyosu.

At the time everyone thought Hideyoshi was in Osaka Castle, but he had been in Sakamoto Castle since the thirteenth day of the Third Month, the day Ieyasu was talking with Nobuo in Kiyosu. That kind of tardiness was not typical of him.

Ieyasu had already roused himself to action, completing his plans and making steady progress in his anticipated push from Hamamatsu to Okazaki and then Kiyosu; but Hideyoshi, who had often shocked the world with his lightning speed, was slow to start this time. Or so it seemed.

"Somebody come here! Aren't my pages here?"

It was the master's voice. And, as usual, it was loud.

The young pages, who had intentionally withdrawn to the faraway pages' room, hurriedly put away the game of *suguroku* they had been surreptitiously playing. From among them, the thirteen-year-old Nabemaru went running off as fast as he could to the room where his lord was repeatedly clapping his hands.

By now Hideyoshi had gone out onto the veranda. Through the front castle gate he could see the tiny figure of Sakichi hastening up the slope from the castle town, and, without looking around toward the footsteps behind him, he shouted out an order to admit him.

Sakichi entered and knelt in front of Hideyoshi.

After he listened to Sakichi's report of the situation at Osaka Castle, Hideyoshi asked, "And Chacha? Are Chacha and her sisters well, too?"

For a moment Sakichi displayed an expression that seemed to indicate that he couldn't remember. To answer as though he had been waiting for that question would only make Hideyoshi suspicious (That damned Sakichi has found out), and would undoubtedly make him feel uncomfortable later on. The proof was that in the instant he had asked awkwardly about Chacha, Hideyoshi's lordly expression had crumbled and a blush filled what seemed to be his prevaricating face. He looked extremely self-conscious.

Sakichi alertly saw through his discomfort and could not help feeling amused.

After the fall of Kitanosho, Hideyoshi had cared for Oichi's three daughters as though they were his own. When he had built Osaka Castle, he had had a small, bright enclosure constructed just for them. From time to time he would visit and play with them as though he were taking care of some rare birds in a golden cage.

"What are you laughing about, Sakichi?" Hideyoshi challenged him. But he himself felt slightly amused. Obviously, Sakichi had already understood.

"No, it's nothing at all. I was distracted by my other responsibilities and returned without visiting the three princesses' quarters."

"Is that so? Well, fine." With that, Hideyoshi quickly changed the subject to other gossip. "What rumors did you hear around the Yodo River and Kyoto while you were on the road?"

Hideyoshi inevitably asked a question like that whenever he sent a messenger to a far-off place.

"Wherever I went, war was the only topic of conversation."

When he questioned Sakichi further about conditions in Kyoto and Osaka, he found out that everyone thought that the battle provoked by Nobuo would not actually be fought between Hideyoshi and the Oda heir, but that it would be between Hideyoshi and Ieyasu. After Nobunaga's death, it was thought that peace would finally be established by Hideyoshi, but once again the nation had been divided in half, and the people's hearts were steeped in anxiety at the specter of a great conflict that would probably extend into every province.

Sakichi withdrew, and as he left, two of Niwa Nagahide's generals, Kanamori Kingo and Hachiya Yoritaka, appeared. Hideyoshi had been going to great lengths to make Niwa his ally because he knew that he would be at a serious disadvantage if he drove him into the enemy camp. Apart from the loss of military strength, Niwa's defection would convince the world that Nobuo and Ieyasu had right on their side. Niwa had been second only to Katsuie among Nobunaga's retainers, and he was held in great respect as a man of rare gentility and sincerity.

It was certain that Ieyasu and Nobuo were also offering Niwa every enticement to join them. Perhaps finally moved by Hideyoshi's enthusiasm, however, Niwa had sent Kanamori and Hachiya as the first reinforcements from the north. Hideyoshi was pleased but was nevertheless not completely reassured.

Before nightfall messengers arrived three times with reports on the situation in Ise. Hideyoshi read the dispatches and questioned the messengers in person, entrusted them with verbal replies, and had letters of response written as he ate his evening meal.

A large folding screen stood in the corner of the room. A map of Japan on its two panels had been painted in gold leaf. Hideyoshi looked at the map and asked, "Haven't we heard from Echizen? What about the messenger I sent to the Uesugi?"

While his retainers made some excuse about the distances involved, Hideyoshi counted on his fingers. He had sent messages to the Kiso and to the Satake. The net of his diplomacy had been carefully thrown over the length and breadth of the country shown on the screen. By his very nature, Hideyoshi considered war to be the last resort. It was an article of faith with him that diplomacy itself was a battle. But it was not diplomacy for its own sake. Nor did it have its source in military weakness. His diplomacy was always backed up by military strength and was employed after his military authority and troops had been completely provided for. But diplomacy had not worked with Ieyasu. He had said nothing about it to anyone, but long before the situation had reached this pass, Hideyoshi had sent a man to Hamamatsu with the following message:

If you will take into consideration my petition to the Emperor last year for your promotion, you will understand my warm feelings toward you. Is there any reason we should fight? It is generally accepted throughout the nation that Lord Nobuo is weakminded. No matter how much you wave the flag of moral duty and embrace the remnants of the Oda clan, the world is not going to admire your efforts as those of a man of virtue commanding a righteous army. In the end, there is no value in the two of us fighting. You are an intelligent man, and if you come to terms with me, I will add the provinces of Owari and Mino to your domain.

The outcome of such proposals depends on the other party, however, and the answer that was returned to Hideyoshi had been clearly negative. But even after he had cut off relations with Nobuo, Hideyoshi still sent messengers with even better conditions than before, trying to persuade Ieyasu. The envoys only incurred Ieyasu's indignation, however, and returned utterly discomfited.

"Lord Ieyasu replies that it is Lord Hideyoshi who does not understand him," the envoy reported.

Hideyoshi forced a smile and retorted, "Ieyasu doesn't understand my genuine feelings, either."

No matter what else he did, however, the time he spent in Sakamoto was consumed entirely by work. Sakamoto was both his military headquarters for Ise and southern Owari and the center of a diplomatic and intelligence network that stretched from the north to the western provinces. As the center for secret operations, Sakamoto was much more convenient than Osaka. Also, messengers could come and go to and from Sakamoto without attracting undue attention.

On the surface, the two spheres of influence seemed to be distinctly drawn: Ieyasu from the east to the northeast, and Hideyoshi from the capital to the west. But even in Hideyoshi's stronghold of Osaka, there were innumerable people in collusion with the Tokugawa. Nor could it be said that there was no one at court who supported Ieyasu and waited for Hideyoshi to stumble.

Even among the samurai clans, there were fathers and mothers in the service of provincial lords in Osaka and Kyoto whose children served generals of the eastern army. Brothers fought on separate sides. Thus the tragic stage was set for bloody conflicts to erupt within families.

Hideyoshi knew the bitter hardships that war brought. The world had been at war from the time he was growing up in his mother's dilapidated house in Nakamura. It had been the same throughout the many years of his wanderings. With Nobunaga's appearance on the stage, society's suffering had become even more severe for a while, but it had been accompanied by a brightness and joy in the lives of the common people. People believed that Nobunaga was going to usher in an era of lasting peace. But he had been cut down halfway through his work.

Hideyoshi had vowed to overcome the setback of Nobunaga's death, and the effort he had made—almost without sleep or rest—had brought him within one step of his goal. Now that final step he needed to take to achieve his ambition was near. It could be said that he had traveled nine hundred leagues of a thousand-league journey. But those last hundred leagues were the hardest. He had presumed that at some point, as a matter of course, he would have to confront the last obstacle—Ieyasu—and either remove it from his path or destroy it. But when he approached, he discovered it was going to be more unyielding than he had imagined.

During the ten days Hideyoshi spent in Sakamoto, Ieyasu moved his army as far as Kiyosu. It was clear that Ieyasu planned to stir up war like a hornet's nest in Iga, Ise, and Kishu and advance westward, entering Kyoto and pressing in on Osaka in one blow, like the path of a typhoon.

But Ieyasu did not think the road was going to be an easy one. He was anticipating one huge engagement on his advance toward Osaka, and Hideyoshi was expecting that as well. But where would it be? The only place of sufficient size to be the site of this all-or-nothing battle between east and west was the broad Nobi Plain that bordered the Kiso River.

A man of initiative would gain the advantage by constructing fortifications and holding the high ground. While Ieyasu had already attended to that and was fully prepared, Hideyoshi could be said to have made a belated start. Even on the evening of the thirteenth day of the month, he still had not moved from Sakamoto.

Despite appearances, however, his seeming tardiness was not the result of negligence. Hideyoshi knew Ieyasu could not be compared with either Mitsuhide or Katsuie. He had to delay in order to complete his own preparations. He waited to win over Niwa Nagahide; he waited to make sure the Mori could do nothing in the western provinces; he waited to destroy the dangerous remnants of the warrior-monks in Shikoku and Kishu; finally, he waited to split the opposition of the generals in nearby Mino and Owari.

The stream of messengers was unending, and Hideyoshi received them even while he ate. He had just finished his meal and put down his chopsticks when a dispatch arrived. He reached out to take the letter box.

It was something he had been waiting for: the answer from Bito Jinemon, whom he had sent as the second messenger to Ikeda Shonyu's castle at Ogaki. Would it be good or bad news? There had been no news at all from the envoys he had sent to win over other castles. Hideyoshi opened the letter, feeling as though he was cutting open the envelope of an oracle, and read it.

"Fine," was all he said.

Late that night after he had gone to sleep, he suddenly got up as though he had just thought of something and called for the samurai on night watch.

"Is Bito's messenger returning tomorrow morning?"

"No," the guard replied, "he was pressed for time, and after a short rest he returned to Mino, taking to the road at night." Sitting on top of his bedding, Hideyoshi took up his brush and wrote a letter to Bito.

Thanks to your great efforts, Shonyu and his son have pledged their solidarity with me, and nothing could give me greater joy. But there is something I must say right away: If Nobuo and Ieyasu know that Shonyu is going to support me, they will surely become threatening in every manner conceivable. Do not react. Do nothing rash. Ikeda Shonyu and Mori Nagayoshi have always been brave and proud men with great contempt for the enemy.

As soon as he put down his pen, he sent the note to Ogaki.

Two days later, however, on the evening of the fifteenth, another message was delivered from Ogaki.

Inuyama Castle had fallen. At the same time Shonyu and his son had made their decision, they had captured the most strategic stronghold on the Kiso River and presented it as a gift of their support for Hideyoshi. It was good news.

Hideyoshi was pleased. But he was troubled as well.

On the following day Hideyoshi was in Osaka Castle. During the next few days omens of failure multiplied. After the happy victory at Inuyama, Hideyoshi learned that Shonyu's son-in-law, Nagayoshi, wanting to achieve a great military exploit of his own, had planned to make a surprise attack on the Tokugawa fortifications at Mount Komaki. His army had been intercepted by the enemy near Haguro, and it was rumored that he had perished with many of his troops.

"We lost this man because of his fighting spirit. Such foolishness is unpardonable!" Hideyoshi's bitter lament was aimed at himself.

Just as Hideyoshi was ready to leave Osaka on the nineteenth, another piece of bad news arrived from Kishu. Hatakeyama Sadamasa had rebelled and was pressing in on Osaka from both land and sea. Nobuo and Ieyasu were most likely behind this. Even if they were not, the discontented remnants of the warrior-monks of the Honganji were always watching for an opportunity to attack. Hideyoshi was obliged to postpone the day of his departure, in order to complete the defenses of Osaka.

It was early in the morning of the twenty-first day of the Third Month. The wrens sang their high-pitched songs in the reeds of Osaka. Cherry blossoms fell, and in the streets, the fallen blooms swirled around the long procession of armored men and horses, making it appear as though nature itself were sending them off. The townspeople who had come to watch formed an endless fence along the roadside.

The army following Hideyoshi that day numbered more than thirty thousand men. Everyone strained to catch a glimpse of Hideyoshi in their midst, but he was so small and ordinary-looking that, surrounded by his mounted generals, he easily escaped notice.

But Hideyoshi looked at the crowd and secretly smiled with assurance. Osaka is going to prosper, he thought. It seems to be flourishing already, and that's the best omen of all. The crowd wore bright colors and bold patterns, and there were no indications of a town in decline. Was it because they had faith in the new castle at its very center?

We'll win. This time we can win. That is how Hideyoshi divined the future.

That night the army camped at Hirakata, and early on the following morning, the thirty-thousand-man army continued east, following a serpentine path along the Yodo River.

When they arrived in Fushimi, about four hundred men came forward to meet them at the river crossing.

"Whose banners are those?" Hideyoshi asked.

The generals narrowed their eyes suspiciously. Nobody could identify the huge banners of black Chinese characters on a field of red. There were also five golden pendants and a commander's standard with insignias of eight smaller circles around a large central one on a golden fan. Beneath those banners thirty mounted warriors, thirty spearmen, thirty gunners, twenty archers, and a corps of foot soldiers waited in full formation, their clothing rustling brilliantly in the river breeze.

"Go find out who they are," Hideyoshi ordered a retainer.

The man quickly returned and said, "It's Ishida Sakichi."

Hideyoshi lightly struck his saddle.

"Sakichi? Well, well, that's who it had to be," he said in a happy voice, as though something had just occurred to him.

Approaching Hideyoshi's horse, Ishida Sakichi greeted his lord. "I made a promise to you before, and today I have prepared for your use a force financed with the money I earned from clearing the unused land in this area."

"Well, come along, Sakichi. Get in with the supply train at the rear."

More than ten thousand bushels' worth of men and horses—Hideyoshi was impressed with Sakichi's ingenuity.

That day the majority of the troops passed through Kyoto and took the Omi Road. For Hideyoshi, there were memories of the reverses of his youth in every tree and blade of grass.

"There's Mount Bodai," Hideyoshi muttered. Looking up at the mountain, he remembered its lord, Takenaka Hanbei, the hermit of Mount Kurihara. When he reflected on it now, he was thankful that he had not spent a single day in idleness during that short springtime of life. The reverses of his youth and the struggles of that time had made him what he was today, and he felt that he had actually been blessed by that dark world and the muddy currents of its streets.

Hanbei, who called Hideyoshi his lord, had been a true friend whom he had been unable to forget. Even after Hanbei's death, whenever Hideyoshi encountered troubles he would think to himself, If only Hanbei were here. Yet he had allowed the man to die without any reward whatsoever. Suddenly Hideyoshi's eyelids were warm with tears of sadness, blurring his view of the peak of Mount Bodai.

And he thought of Hanbei's sister, Oyu....

Just at that moment he saw the white hood of a Buddhist nun in the shadow of the pines at the side of the road. The nun's eyes momentarily met Hideyoshi's. He reined in his horse and seemed about to give out an order, but the woman beneath the pines had already vanished.

That night in camp Hideyoshi received a plate of rice cakes. The man who delivered it said that it had been brought by a nun who had not given her name.

"These are delicious," Hideyoshi said, eating a couple of the cakes even though he had already taken his evening meal. As he commented on the cakes, there were tears in his eyes.

Later on, the quick-eyed page mentioned Hideyoshi's strange mood to the generals who were attending him. All of them looked surprised and appeared as though they couldn't even guess the reason for their lord's behavior. They worried about his grief, but as soon as his head was on the pillow, Hideyoshi's high-pitched snore was the same as usual. He slept happily for just four hours. In the morning, when the sky was still dark, he got up and departed. During that day, the first and second detachments arrived at Gifu. Hideyoshi was greeted by Shonyu and his son, and soon the castle was overflowing with the huge army, both inside and out.

Torches and bonfires lit the night sky over the Nagara River. Far away, the third and fourth units could be seen flowing continually east all night long.

"It's been a long time!"

Their voices broke out in unison the moment Hideyoshi and Shonyu met.

"It really pleases me that both you and your son are united with me at this time. And I can't even express what you've done for me with the gift of Inuyama Castle. No, even I was impressed with your speed and how alert you were to that opportunity."

Hideyoshi was outspoken in his praise of Shonyu's achievements, but said nothing about the great defeat of his son-in-law after the victory at Inuyama.

But even if Hideyoshi was saying nothing about it, Shonyu was ashamed. He seemed to be deeply embarrassed that his victory at Inuyama could not atone for the defeat and loss that Nagayoshi had incurred. The letter from Hideyoshi delivered to him by Bito Jinemon had particularly warned against being drawn into a challenge from Ieyasu, but it had come too late.

Shonyu now spoke about that event. "I hardly know how to apologize for our defeat, because of my son-in-law's foolishness."

"You're too concerned about that," Hideyoshi said, laughing. "That's not like the Ikeda Shonyu I know."

Should I blame Shonyu or just let it alone? Hideyoshi wondered when he awoke the following morning. Regardless of anything else, however, the advantage of having Inuyama Castle in his hands before the coming great battle was extraordinary. Hideyoshi praised Shonyu for his meritorious deed over and over again, and not just to console him.

On the twenty-fifth Hideyoshi rested and assembled his army, which numbered more than eighty thousand men.

Leaving Gifu the next morning, he arrived at Unuma at noon and immediately had a bridge of boats constructed across the Kiso River. The army then camped for the night. On the morning of the twenty-seventh it broke camp and headed toward Inuyama. Hideyoshi entered Inuyama Castle exactly at noon.

"Bring me a horse with strong legs," he ordered, and immediately after finishing his lunch, he galloped from the castle gate, accompanied by only a few mounted men in light armor.

"Where will you be going, my lord?" a general asked, chasing after him at full gallop.

"Just a few of you should come along," Hideyoshi replied. "If there are too many of us, we'll be spotted by the enemy."

Hurrying through the village of Haguro, where Nagayoshi had reportedly been killed, they climbed Mount Ninomiya. From there Hideyoshi could look down into the enemy's main camp at Mount Komaki.

The combined forces of Nobuo and Ieyasu were said to number about sixty-one thousand men. Hideyoshi narrowed his eyes and looked far into the distance. The sun at midday was glaringly bright. Silently put his hand over his eyes, he quietly gazed out over Mount Komaki, which was covered with the enemy forces.

On that day Ieyasu was still in Kiyosu. He had gone to Mount Komaki, given his instructions for the battle lineup, and quickly returned. It was as though a *go* master were moving a single stone on the board with extreme care.

On the evening of the twenty-sixth, Ieyasu received a confirmed report that Hideyoshi was in Gifu. Ieyasu, Sakakibara, Honda, and other retainers were seated in a room. They were just being told that the construction of the fortifications at Mount Komaki had been completed.

"So Hideyoshi's come?" Ieyasu muttered. As he and the other men looked around at each other, he smiled, the skin under his eyes wrinkling like a turtle's. It was happening just as he had foreseen.

Hideyoshi had always been quick to start, and the fact that he was not displaying his usual speed this time caused Ieyasu substantial concern. Would he make his stand in Ise, or would he come east to the Nobi Plain? As Hideyoshi was still at Gifu he could go in either direction. Ieyasu waited for the next report, which when it came told him that Hideyoshi had built a bridge across the Kiso River and was at Inuyama Castle.

Ieyasu received this information at dusk on the twenty-seventh day of the month, and the look on his face announced that the time had come. Preparations for the battle were completed during the night. On the twenty-eighth, Ieyasu's army advanced toward Mount Komaki to the thunder of drums and the fluttering of banners.

Nobuo had returned to Nagashima, but upon receiving a report of the situation, he immediately hurried to Mount Komaki where he joined forces with Ieyasu.

"I've heard that Hideyoshi's forces here alone number more than eighty thousand men and his entire forces combined are well beyond a hundred and fifty thousand," Nobuo said, as if he had never thought that he was the cause of this great battle. His trembling eyes revealed what could be not concealed within his breast.

* * *

Shonyu grimaced in the smoke of the evening kitchen fires as he rode out through the castle gate.

The Ikeda warriors were apprehensive of his frame of mind just from glancing at his face. They all knew that Shonyu's bad mood was due to Nagayoshi's defeat. Owing to his misjudgment, he had burdened his allies with a severe blow at the very outset of the war, even before Hideyoshi, the commander-in-chief, had arrived on the battlefield.

Ikeda Shonyu had always been confident that no one had ever pointed a finger of scorn at him, and for a man who had lived a warrior's life for forty-eight years, this disgrace must have been unexpected, at the very least.

"Yukisuke, come over here. Terumasa, you come, too. The senior retainers should come up close, too."

Sitting cross-legged in the hall of the main citadel, he had called together his sons Yukisuke and Terumasa and his senior retainers.

"I want to hear your unreserved opinions. First, take a look at this," he said, producing a map from his kimono.

As the men passed the map around, they realized what Shonyu was suggesting.

On the map a line had been drawn in red ink from Inuyama through the mountains and over the rivers to Okazaki in Mikawa. After looking at the map, the men silently waited to see what Shonyu would say next.

"If we put Komaki and Kiyosu aside and advance our men along one road to the Tokugawa main castle at Okazaki, there's no doubt that even Ieyasu will be thrown into confusion. The only thing we need to be concerned about is how to keep our army from being seen by the enemy at Mount Komaki."

No one was quick to speak. It was an unusual plan. If a single mistake was made, it might result in a disaster that could be fatal to all of their allies.

"I'm thinking of offering this plan to Lord Hideyoshi. If it works, both Ieyasu and Nobuo will be able to do nothing as we take them captive."

Shonyu wanted to perform some meritorious deed to make up for his son-in-law's defeat. He wanted to stare back in triumph at the people who were gossiping maliciously about him. Although they understood that those were his intentions, no one was ready to criticize what he had in mind. No one was ready to say, "No, clever plans rarely invite merit. This is dangerous."

At the end of the conference the plan had won unanimous support. All the commanders begged to be put in the vanguard that would go deep into enemy territory and destroy Ieyasu in the very bosom of his own province.

A similar plan had been tried at Shizugatake by Shibata Katsuie's nephew, Genba. Nevertheless, Shonyu was ready to advocate the plan to Hideyoshi and said, "We'll go to the main camp at Gakuden tomorrow."

He spent the night sleeping on the idea. At dawn, however, a messenger came from Gakuden and told him, "As he makes the inspection rounds today, Lord Hideyoshi is likely to stop at Inuyama Castle around noon."

As Hideyoshi felt the mild breeze of the beginning of the Fourth Month wafting over him, he rode out of Gakuden and, after carefully observing Ieyasu's camp at Mount Komaki and the enemy fortifications in the area, took the road to Inuyama accompanied by ten pages and close attendants.

Whenever Hideyoshi met with Shonyu, he treated him like an old friend. When they were young samurai in Kiyosu, Shonyu, Hideyoshi, and Inuchiyo had often gone out drinking together.

"By the way, how's Nagayoshi?" he asked.

It had been reported that Nagayoshi had been killed, but he had only been badly injured.

"He made a mess of things with his hotheadedness, but his recovery has been extraordinarily quick. All he can talk about is getting to the front as quickly as possible and clearing his name."

Hideyoshi turned to one of his retainers and asked, "Ichimatsu, of all the enemy fortifications we saw at Mount Komaki today, which looked to be the strongest?"

That was the sort of question he liked to ask, calling the men around him and listening happily to the frank words of the young warriors.

At such times, the crowd of young personal retainers that surrounded him never minced their words. When they became heated, Hideyoshi became heated too, and such an atmosphere made it difficult for an outsider to tell whether the arguers were lord and retainers or just friends. Once Hideyoshi became a little serious, however, everyone immediately straightened up.

Shonyu was seated next to him and finally broke in on the conversation. "I have something I would earnestly like to talk to you about, too."

Hideyoshi leaned over to listen to him and nodded. He then commanded everyone to withdraw.

The room was empty of everyone but Shonyu and Hideyoshi. They were in the hall of the main citadel, and as there was a clear field of vision, it was not necessary for him to be on his guard.

"What is it about, Shonyu?"

"You've been making the inspection tour today, and I imagine you've made some decisions. Don't you think Ieyasu's preparations at Mount Komaki are perfect?"

"Well, they're splendid. I don't think anyone but Ieyasu could have put up such fortifications and positions in such a short time."

"I've ridden out and looked around a number of times too, and I don't see how we can make an attack," Shonyu said.

"The way it's set up, we're just going to be facing each other," Hideyoshi replied.

"Ieyasu's aware that his opponent is a true opponent," Shonyu went on, "so he's acting with prudence. At the same time, our allies know that this is the first time we'll be confronting the famous Tokugawa forces in a decisive battle. So it's naturally turned into a situation like this—staring each other down."

"It's interesting. For a number of days there hasn't even been the sound of gunfire. It's a quiet battle with no fighting."

"Well, if I may…" Shonyu advanced on his knees, spread out a map, and enthusiastically explained his plan.

Hideyoshi listened just as enthusiastically, nodding a number of times. But the expression on his face did not indicate that he was going to be drawn easily into a quick agreement.

"If you'll give me your permission, I'll raise my entire clan and attack Okazaki. Once we strike the Tokugawa's home province at Okazaki, and Ieyasu hears that it's being trampled beneath our horses' hooves, it won't make any difference how well prepared his ramparts at Mount Komaki are, or how great a military genius he may be. He'll crumble from within even without our attacking him."

"I'll think about it," Hideyoshi said, avoiding a quick answer. "But you think about it one more night too—not as something of your own, but objectively. It's a clever plan and a heroic undertaking, so it's dangerous on that account alone."

Shonyu's strategy was indeed an original idea, and it was clear that even the prudent Hideyoshi was impressed, but Hideyoshi's thoughts were quite different.

By nature, Hideyoshi did not care for clever strategies or surprise attacks. Rather than military strategies, he preferred diplomacy; rather than easy, short-term victories, he preferred mastery over the total situation, even if it took a long time.

"Well, let's not be in a hurry," he said. Then he relaxed a little. "I'll make my mind up by tomorrow. Come to the main camp tomorrow morning."

Hideyoshi's personal retainers had been waiting in the corridor and now came to his side. When they got as far as the entrance of the main citadel, a strangely dressed samurai was crouched in obeisance next to the place where the horses were tethered. His head and one arm were bandaged, and the coat over his armor was of gold brocade against a white background.

"Who's that?"

The man raised his bound head a little.

"I'm ashamed to say that it's me, Nagayoshi, my lord."

"Well, Nagayoshi? I heard you were confined to your bed. How are your wounds?"

"I was determined to be up by today."

"Don't push yourself so hard. If you'll only let your body recover, you will be able to wipe away your disgrace at any time."

At the mention of the word "disgrace," Nagayoshi began to cry.

Taking a letter from his coat and reverently handing it to Hideyoshi, he prostrated himself once again.

"I would be honored if you would read this, my lord."

Hideyoshi nodded, perhaps feeling compassion for the man's misery.

After finishing the day's inspection rounds of the battlefield, Hideyoshi returned to Gakuden at dusk. His camp was not on high ground like the enemy's on Mount Komaki, but Hideyoshi had used the forests, fields, and streams in the vicinity to their fullest advantage, and his army's position was surrounded by two square leagues of trenches and palisades.

As a further precaution, the compound of the village shrine was disguised to look as though it was the place where Hideyoshi was staying.

From Ieyasu's point of view, Hideyoshi whereabouts were unclear. He could have been at either the camp at Gakuden or Inuyama Castle. Security at the front lines was so tight that not even water could seep through, so surveillance by one side or the other was certainly impossible.

"I haven't been able to take a bath since leaving Osaka. Today I want to wash the sweat off for once."

An outdoor bath was immediately prepared for Hideyoshi. After digging a hole in the earth, his attendants lined it with huge sheets of oiled paper. Filling the hole with water, they next heated a piece of scrap iron in a fire and threw it in to warm the water. Then they lined up planks around the hole and erected a curtain around the area.

"Ah, the water's great." In that simple open-air bath, the master of a less-than-splendid body soaked in hot water and looked up at the stars of the evening sky. This is the greatest luxury in the world, he thought as he rubbed the dirt from his body.

Since the year before, he had been clearing away the land around Osaka and setting in motion the construction of a castle of unprecedented majesty. His own greatest human pleasures were in places like this, however, rather than in the golden rooms and jeweled towers of the castle. He felt a sudden nostalgia for his home in Nakamura, where his mother would wash his back when he was small.

It had been a long time since Hideyoshi had felt so relaxed, and it was in that state that he walked into his quarters.

"Ah, you're all here already!" Hideyoshi exclaimed when he saw that the generals he had summoned that evening were waiting for him.

"Take a look at this," he said, taking a map and a letter from his coat and handing them over to his generals. The letter was a petition written in blood by Nagayoshi. The map was Shonyu's.

"What do you think of this plan?" Hideyoshi asked. "I want to hear everyone's frank opinions."

For a while no one said a word. Everyone appeared to be sunk in thought.

Finally one of the generals said, "I think it's an exquisite plan."

Half of the men were in favor, but the other half were opposed, saying, "A clever plan is a risky gamble."

The conference was deadlocked.

Hideyoshi simply listened with a smile. The subject was so momentous that a council resolution was not going to be settled upon easily.

"We'll have to leave it to your own wise decision, my lord."

The generals returned to their own camps at nightfall.

The truth was that Hideyoshi had already made up his mind on the return trip from Inuyama. He had called a conference not because he could not make up his own mind. In fact, he had invited his generals to a brief conference because he had already made his decision. Again it was a matter of psychological leadership. His generals returned to their camps with the impression that he would probably not put the plan into use.

But in his own mind Hideyoshi had already settled on action. If he did not accept Shonyu's suggestion, his and Nagayoshi's positions as warriors would become onerous. Moreover, it was certain that if their obstinate temperaments were repressed, they would somehow be manifested at a later time.

It was a dangerous situation in terms of military command. More than that, Hideyoshi feared that if Shonyu became discontented, Ieyasu would certainly try to tempt him to change sides.

Ikeda Shonyu is my subordinate now. If he imagines himself to be the butt of dishonorable rumors, his haste is not unreasonable, Hideyoshi thought.

The present situation was deadlocked, and a positive move to invite some sort of change would have to be played.

"That's it," Hideyoshi said aloud. "Rather than wait for Shonyu to come here tomorrow morning, I'll send a messenger to him tonight."

Upon receiving the urgent letter, Shonyu flew off toward Hideyoshi's camp. It was the fourth watch, and the night was still dark.

"I have decided, Shonyu."

"Good! Are you going to favor me with the command to make a surprise attack on Okazaki?"

The two men finished all the preliminaries before dawn. Shonyu joined Hideyoshi for breakfast and then returned to Inuyama.

On the following day, the battlefield outwardly appeared to be in the doldrums, but there were subtle signs of delicate movement.

Resounding in the thinly clouded afternoon sky, both enemy and ally gunfire could be heard coming from the direction of Onawate. From the Udatsu Road, sand and dust could be seen far off, at the place where two or three thousand soldiers of the western army were beginning to attack enemy fortifications.

"The general attack is starting!"

As they looked out into the distance, the generals felt a wild surging excitement. This was, indeed, a turning point in history. Whichever man won, the age would belong to him.

Ieyasu knew that Hideyoshi had feared and respected Nobunaga more than anyone else. Now there was no one he feared or respected more than Ieyasu. Not a single banner in the entire camp on Mount Komaki moved that morning. It was almost as though strict orders had been given not to react to the small attacking sorties from the western army that would be testing the eastern army's resolve.

Evening arrived. A corps of the western army that had withdrawn from the fighting delivered a sheaf of propaganda handbills they had picked up along the road to Hideyoshi's main camp.

When Hideyoshi read one of them, he became enraged.

Hideyoshi caused the suicide of Lord Nobutaka, the son of his former lord, Nobunaga, to whom he owed so much. He has now rebelled against Lord Nobuo. He has constantly caused turmoil within the warrior class, has brought disasters to the common people, and has been the chief instigator of the present conflict, using every means to achieve his own ambitions.

The flyer went on to claim that Ieyasu had risen up with a true justification for war and that he led the army of moral duty.

An expression of rage—rare for Hideyoshi—contorted his face. "Which one of the enemy wrote this tract?" he demanded.

"Ishikawa Kazumasa," a retainer replied.

"Secretary!" Hideyoshi yelled, looking over his shoulder. "Have placards raised everywhere with the same message: The man who takes Ishikawa Kazumasa's head will receive a reward of ten thousand bushels."

Even with that command, Hideyoshi's anger did not subside, and calling for the generals who happened to be present, he gave the order for a sortie himself.

"So this is how that damned Kazumasa behaves!" he fumed. "I want you to take a reserve corps and help our men in front of Kazumasa's lines. Attack him throughout the night. Attack him tomorrow morning. Attack him tomorrow night. Follow one attack with another, and don't give Kazumasa the chance to take a breath."

Finally he called out for rice and pressed for his evening meal to be brought in right away. Hideyoshi never forgot to eat. Even as he was eating, however, messengers continued to go back and forth between Gakuden and Inuyama.

Then the final messenger arrived with a report from Shonyu. Mumbling to himself, Hideyoshi leisurely drank the soup from the bottom of his bowl. That evening, the sound of musket fire could be heard far behind the main camp. The firing had been echoing here and there on the front lines since dawn and continued until the following day. Even now this was considered to be the opening action of a general attack by Hideyoshi's western army.

The first blow of the day before, however, had been a feint by Hideyoshi, while the real movement had been the preparations at Inuyama for Shonyu's surprise attack on Okazaki.

The strategy was to divert Ieyasu's attention, while Shonyu's troops took back roads and struck at Ieyasu's main castle.

Shonyu's army consisted of four corps:

First Corps: Ikeda Shonyu's six thousand men.

Second Corps: Mori Nagayoshi's three thousand men.

Third Corps: Hori Kyutaro's three thousand men.

Fourth Corps: Miyoshi Hidetsugu's eight thousand men.

The vanguard First and Second Corps naturally constituted the main strength of these forces—warriors who were ready for victory or death.

It was now the sixth day of the Fourth Month. Waiting until the dead of night, Shonyu's twenty thousand troops finally departed Inuyama in the utmost secrecy. The banners were lowered, the horses' hooves muted. Riding through the night, they met the dawn at Monoguruizaka.

The soldiers ate their provisions and had a short rest, then went on and made camp at the village of Kamijo, from which a reconnaissance party was sent out to Oteme Castle.

Earlier, the commander of the Blue Herons, Sanzo, had been sent by Shonyu to Morikawa Gonemon, the commander of castle, who had promised to betray Ieyasu. But now, just to make sure, Sanzo was sent out again.

Shonyu was now deep inside enemy territory. The army advanced, step by step, hourly approaching Ieyasu's main castle. Ieyasu, of course, was absent, as were all of his generals and soldiers, who had gone to the front lines at Mount Komaki. It was toward this vacant house, the empty cocoon that the core of the Tokugawa clan's home province had become, that Shonyu would aim his lethal blow.

The commander of Oteme Castle, who had been aligned with the Tokugawa, but tempted by Shonyu, had already accepted his pledge from Hideyoshi for a domain of fifty thousand bushels.

The castle gate was open, and its commander came out to greet the invaders himself, showing them the way. The samurai class under the old shogunate did not have a monopoly of immorality and degradation. Under Ieyasu's rule, both lord and retainer had eaten cold rice and gruel; they had fought battles; they had taken up the hoe, worked in the fields, and done piecework to survive. Finally they had overcome every hardship and had become strong enough to stand against Hideyoshi. Still, even here, there existed such samurai as Morikawa Gonemon.

"Well, General Gonemon," Shonyu said, his face aglow with happiness. "I'm grateful that you haven't gone back on your promise and have come out to greet us today. If everything turns out as planned, I'll send that proposal for fifty thousand bushels directly to Lord Hideyoshi."

"No, I already received Lord Hideyoshi's pledge last night."

With Gonemon's reply, Shonyu was once again surprised at Hideyoshi's vigilance and reliability.

The army now divided into three columns and started out for the plain of Nagakute. It passed another fortress, Iwasaki Castle, which was defended by only two hundred thirty soldiers.

"Leave it alone. A little castle like that hardly merits taking. Let's not play along the way."

Looking askance at the castle, both Shonyu and Nagayoshi rode by as though it was not even dust in their eyes. But just as they were passing by, they were showered with gunfire from inside the castle, and one of the bullets grazed the flank of Shonyu's horse. The horse reared, nearly throwing Shonyu from the saddle.

"What impudence!" Raising his whip, Shonyu shouted at the soldiers of the First Corps. "Finish off that little castle now!"

The troops' first fighting action had been approved. All of their pent-up energy was released. Two commanders each led about a thousand men and charged the castle. Even a much stronger fortress would not have been able to withstand warriors with their kind of spirit, and this castle was defended by a small force of men.

In the twinkling of an eye, its stone walls were scaled, its moat was filled, fires were set, and the sun was blotted out with black smoke. At that point, the castle's commanding general came out fighting and was killed in battle. The castle's soldiers were all killed with the exception of one man, who escaped and raced to Mount Komaki to inform Ieyasu of the emergency. During the short battle, Nagayoshi's Second Corps had put a good distance between itself and the First Corps. The men now rested and ate their provisions.

As the soldiers ate their meal, they looked up and wondered what the reason for the rising smoke might be. Very soon, however, a runner from the front lines informed them of the fall of Iwasaki Castle. The horses nipped at the grass while laughter reverberated across the plain.

Upon learning the same information, the Third Corps naturally stopped and rested both men and horses at Kanahagiwara. At the very rear, the Fourth Corps also reined in the horses and waited for the corps in front to start advancing again.

Spring was departing in the mountains and summer was near. The azure of the sky was beautifully clear, deeper even than the sea. Shortly after stopping, the horses became drowsy, and the high-pitched songs of the skylark and bulbul could be heard in the barley fields and forests.

Two days before this, during the evening of the sixth day of the Fourth Month, two farmers from the village of Shinoki had crawled through the fields and run from tree to tree, avoiding the lookouts of the western army.

"We have something to tell Lord Ieyasu! It's very important!" the two men yelled as they ran into the main camp at Mount Komaki.

Ii Hyobu led them to Ieyasu's headquarters. A few moments before Ieyasu had been talking with Nobuo, but after Nobuo had left, Ieyasu had taken the copy of the *Analects* of Confucius from the top of his armor chest and began to read silently, ignoring the sounds of distant gunfire.

Five years younger than Hideyoshi, he was forty-two years old this year, a general in his prime. His appearance was so mild and good-natured—and he had such such soft flesh and pale skin—that an observer might have doubted that he had been through every extremity, and had fought battles in which he had rallied his troops with nothing more than the look in his eye.

"Who is it? Naomasa? Come in, come in."

Closing the *Analects*, Ieyasu pulled his stool around.

The two farmers reported that on that very evening, some units of Hideyoshi's army had left Inuyama and were heading in the direction of Mikawa.

"You've done well," Ieyasu said. "You'll be rewarded!"

Ieyasu's brow tightened. If Okazaki was attacked, nothing could be done. Even he hadn't thought that the enemy would leave Mount Komaki and strike out for his home province of Mikawa.

"Summon Sakai, Honda, and Ishikawa immediately," he said calmly.

He ordered the three generals to guard Mount Komaki in his absence. He would lead the bulk of his forces himself and go in pursuit of Shonyu's army.

At about that time, a country samurai had come to report to Nobuo's camp. By the time Nobuo brought the man to speak with Ieyasu, Ieyasu had already summoned a conference of his field staff.

"You come too, Lord Nobuo! I think we can say that this pursuit is going to finish with an impressive battle, and if you're not present, it's going to lack significance."

Ieyasu's forces were to be divided into two corps, and would total fifteen thousand nine hundred men. Mizuno Tadashige's four thousand troops would act as the army's vanguard.

By the night of the eighth day of the month, the main corps under Ieyasu and Nobuo had left Mount Komaki. Finally they crossed over the Shonai River. The units under Nagayoshi and Kyutaro were bivouacking only two leagues away in the village of Kamijo.

The dim white light on the water-covered rice fields and little streams showed that the dawn was near, but black shadows lay all around, and dark clouds hung low to the earth.

"Hey! There they are!"

"Get down! Lie down!"

In the rice paddies, in the clumps of bushes, in the shadows of the trees, in the hollows of the ground, the figures of the men in the pursuing army all bent down quickly. Straining their ears, they could hear the western army moving in a long black line along the single road that disappeared into a forest in the distance.

The pursuing troops divided into two corps and secretly trailed behind the tail end of the enemy, which was composed of the Fourth Corps of the western army led by Mikoshi Hidetsugu.

That was the shape of the fate of both armies on the morning of the ninth day of the month. Moreover, the commander selected by Hideyoshi for this important undertaking—his own nephew Hidetsugu—was still unaware of the situation as dawn began to break.

While Hideyoshi had appointed the steady Hori Kyutaro as the leader of the invasion of Mikawa, it was Hidetsugu whom he designated as commander-in-chief. Hidetsugu, however, was still only a sixteen-year-old boy, so Hideyoshi had selected two senior generals and ordered them to watch over the young commander.

The troops were still tired as the sun peacefully announced the dawn of the ninth day of the month. Knowing that the men must be hungry, Hidetsugu gave the order to stop. At the command to eat their provisions, the generals and soldiers sat down and ate their morning meal.

The place was Hakusan Woods, so-called because Hakusan Shrine stood at the top of a small hill there. Hidetsugu set up his stool on the hill.

"Don't you have any water?" the young man asked a retainer. "There's none left in my canteen, and my throat is really dry."

Taking the canteen, he gulped down every last drop of water.

"It's not good to drink too much when we're on the move. Be a little patient, my lord," a retainer reproved him.

But Hidetsugu did not even turn to look at him. The men whom Hideyoshi had sent to watch him were eyesores to the young man. He was sixteen years old, a commanding general, and naturally in a fighting mood.

"Who's that running in this direction?"

"It's Hotomi."

"What's Hotomi doing here?" Hidetsugu narrowed his eyes and stretched up to see. The commander of the spear corps, Hotomi, approached him and knelt. He was out of breath.

"Lord Hidetsugu, we have an emergency!"

"Really."

"Please climb a little farther up to the top of the hill."

"There." Hotomi pointed out a cloud of dust. "It's still far away, but it's moving from the shelter of those mountains toward the plain."

"It's not a whirlwind, is it? It's bunched up in front, with a crowd following to the rear. It's an army, that's for sure."

"You have to make a decision, my lord."

"Is it the enemy?"

"I don't think it could be anyone else."

"Wait, I wonder if it really is the enemy."

Hidetsugu was still acting with indifference. He seemed to think that it just could not be true.

But as soon as his retainers reached the top of the hill, they all shouted together.

"Damn!"

"I thought the enemy might have a plan to follow us. Prepare yourselves!"

Unable to wait for Hidetsugu's orders, all of them moved to take action, kicking up bits of grass and dust in their haste. The ground shook, the horses whinnied, officers and men shouted back and forth. In the moment it took to transform the rest period for a meal into readiness for battle, the commanders of the Tokugawa army had given the orders for a wild fusillade of bullets and arrows directly into Hidetsugu's troops.

"Fire! Loose your arrows!"

"Strike into them!"

Observing the confusion of the enemy, the mounted men and spear corps suddenly charged.

"Don't let them get close to His Lordship!"

The shouts surrounding Hidetsugu were now only wild voices calling to protect his life.

Here, there, from among the trees and shrubs, from everywhere along the road, came swarms of enemy soldiers. The only force that was unable to open up an escape route was a small one made up of Hidetsugu and his retainers.

Hidetsugu had been slightly wounded in two or three places and labored furiously with his spear.

"Are you still here, my lord?"

"Hurry! Retreat! Move back!"

When his retainers saw him, they spoke almost as if they were scolding him. Every one of them died fighting. Kinoshita Kageyu saw that Hidetsugu had lost sight of his horse and was now on foot.

"Here! Take this one! Use the whip and get out of this place without looking back!"

Giving Hidetsugu his own horse, Kageyu planted his banner in the ground and cut his way through as many of the enemy soldiers as he could before he was finally killed as well. Hidetsugu put his hand on the horse, but before he could mount it, the animal was hit by a bullet.

"Lend me your horse!"

Fleeing desperately through the midst of the fighting, Hidetsugu had spied a mounted warrior hurrying by close to him and had yelled out. Abruptly pulling the reins and turning around, the man looked down at Hidetsugu.

"What is it, my young lord?"

"Give me your horse."

"That's like asking for someone's umbrella on a rainy day, isn't it? No, I won't lend it to you, even if it is my lord's command."

"Why not?"

"Because you're retreating and I'm one of the soldiers still charging ahead."

Flatly refusing, the man dashed off. From his back, a single strand of bamboo grass whistled in the wind.

"Damn!" Hidetsugu swore as he watched him go. It seemed that in that man's eyes, he had been less than a leaf of bamboo grass along the roadside. Looking behind him, Hidetsugu could see a cloud of dust being raised by the enemy. But a group of routed soldiers from different corps carrying spears, firearms, and long swords saw Hidetsugu and shouted for him to stop.

"My lord! If you run that way, you'll meet up with yet another enemy unit!"

As they approached, they surrounded him and then pulled him away to escape toward the Kanare River.

On their way they picked up a runaway horse, and Hidetsugu was finally mounted. But when they took a short rest at a place called Hosogane, they were again attacked by the enemy and, suffering another defeat, fled in the direction of Inaba.

Thus the Fourth Corps was routed. The Third Corps, which was led by Hori Kyutaro, consisted of about three thousand men. A distance of one to one and a half leagues was maintained between the corps, and messengers had constantly kept communications open between the forces, so that if the First Corps took a rest, the advance of the other corps was naturally halted as well, one after another.

Kyutaro suddenly cupped his ear and listened. "That was gunfire, wasn't it?"

Just at that moment, one of Hidetsugu's retainers whipped his horse into the resting camp and tumbled forward.

"Our men have been completely routed. The main army has been annihilated by the

Tokugawa forces, and even Lord Hidetsugu's safety is uncertain. Turn back immediately!" he wailed.

Kyutaro was taken by surprise, but his composed brow checked the impulse of the moment.

"Are you in the messenger corps?"

"Why are you asking me that now?"

"If you're not one of the messengers, why have you come running up so upset? Did you run away?"

"No! I came here to inform you of the situation. I don't know if it was cowardly or not, but this is an emergency, and I came as fast as I could to inform Lord Nagayoshi and Lord Shonyu."

With that parting remark, the man whipped his horse and disappeared, continuing on to the next corps up ahead.

"Since a retainer came instead of a messenger, we can only surmise that our men at the rear have suffered a total defeat."

Suppressing the restlessness in his heart, Kyutaro remained seated on his camp stool for another moment.

"Everyone come here!" Already aware of the situation, his retainers and officers gathered around, their faces pale. "The Tokugawa forces are about to attack us. Don't waste your bullets. Wait until the enemy has come to within sixty feet before firing." After instructing them in the disposition of troops, he made one concluding remark. "I will give one hundred bushels for every dead enemy warrior."

What he anticipated was not off the mark. The Tokugawa force that had struck Hidetsugu's corps with an obliterating blow was now descending on his own corps fiercely. The Tokugawa commanders were themselves frightened by the unrelenting force of their troops' spirit.

Froth covered the horses' mouths, the men's faces were tense with determination, and the armor that was coming in waves was covered with blood and dust. As the Tokugawa forces pressed closer and closer into firing range, Kyutaro watched carefully and then gave the command.

"Fire!"

At that instant, gunfire created a dreadful roar and a wall of smoke. With matchlock firearms, the time it took to load and fire was a period of perhaps five or six breaths, even for well-practiced men. Because of that, a system of alternating volleys was used. Thus, after each fusillade, another fell upon the enemy in rapid succession. The assaulting army fell helter-skelter before this defense. Their vast numbers could be seen on the ground between the clouds of gunpowder smoke.

"They're prepared!"

"Stop! Fall back!"

The Tokugawa commanders yelled orders to fall back, but their charging soldiers could not be so easily stopped.

Kyutaro saw that the moment had come and shouted to the troops to counterattack. The victory was now clear, both psychologically and physically, without anyone having to wait for the actual result. The corps of warriors that had been so brilliantly victorious now received themselves what they had given to Hidetsugu only moments before.

Throughout Hideyoshi's army Hori Kyutaro's spear corps was famed for its great efficiency. The corpses of men who had been pierced by the points of those spears now deterred the horses carrying the commanders who were trying to flee. The Tokugawa generals escaped, swinging their long swords behind them as they fled the pursuing points of the spears.

MASTER STROKE

The plain of Nagakute was covered with a thin veil of gunpowder smoke and filled with the stink of corpses and blood. With the morning sun, it smoldered with all the colors of the rainbow.

Peace had already returned there, but the soldiers who had brought carnage with them were now heading for Yazako, like the clouds of an evening shower. Flight simply provoked more flight, endless flight and destruction.

Kyutaro did not lose his head as he pursued the Tokugawa troops. "The rear guard should not follow us. Take the roundabout way toward Inokoishi and pursue them along two roads."

One unit broke away and followed a different road, while Kyutaro led six hundred men against the retreating enemy. The dead and wounded abandoned along the road by the Tokugawa could not have numbered less than five hundred men, but Kyutaro's soldiers also grew fewer and fewer as they continued.

Although the main corps had advanced far ahead, two men still breathing among the corpses now crossed spears, then abandoned them as too cumbersome and drew their swords. Grappling, then breaking loose, they fell down, stood up again, and fought interminably in their own private battle. Finally one took the other's head. Yelling almost insanely, the victor chased after his companions in the main corps, disappeared once again into the miasma of smoke and blood, and, struck by a stray bullet, fell dead before he could catch up with his comrades.

Kyutaro was yelling himself hoarse. "It's useless to chase after them for too long. Genza! Momoemon! Stop the troops! Tell them to fall back!"

Several of his retainers rode forward and, with difficulty, restrained their troops.

"Fall back!"

"Draw up beneath the commander's standard!"

Hori Kyutaro dismounted and walked from the road onto the promontory of a bluff. From where he stood, his field of vision was unobstructed. He stared steadily out into the distance.

"Ah, he has come so quickly," he muttered.

The expression on his face showed that he had become completely sobered. Turning to his attendants, he invited them to take a look.

In the west, in an elevated area just opposite the morning sun, something was glittering on Mount Fujigane.

Was it not Ieyasu's emblem—the commander's standard with the golden fan? Kyutaro raised his voice in grief. "It's a sad thing to say, but we have no strategy for dealing with such a great foe. Our work here is finished."

Collecting his troops, Kyutaro quickly began to retreat. But at that point, four messengers from the First and Second Corps came together from the direction of Nagakute looking for him.

"The order is for you to turn back and join forces with the vanguard. This comes directly from Lord Shonyu."

Kyutaro flatly refused. "Absolutely not. We're retreating."

The messengers could hardly believe their ears. "The battle is starting now! Please turn back and join our lords' forces immediately!" they repeated, raising their voices.

Kyutaro raised his voice as well. "If I said I'm retreating, I'm retreating! We have to make sure that Lord Hidetsugu is safe. Besides, more than half of this section of the army has sustained wounds, and if our men come up against a fresh enemy, it will be a disaster. I, for one, am not going to fight a battle that I know I'll lose. You can tell that to Lord Shonyu and to Lord Nagayoshi as well!"

With those parting words, he rode off at a gallop.

Hori Kyutaro's corps ran into Hidetsugu and his surviving troops in the vicinity of Inaba. Then, setting fire to the farmhouses along the way, they defended themselves time and again from the pursuing Tokugawa troops and finally returned to Hideyoshi's main camp at Gakuden before sunset.

The messengers who had come seeking Kyutaro's aid were outraged.

"What kind of cowardice is it to run away to the main camp without even looking back at your allies' desperate situation?"

"He's clearly lost his nerve."

"Today Hori Kyutaro showed us his true character. We'll despise him if we return alive."

They now turned toward their own isolated corps, led by Shonyu, and whipped their horses' flanks in fits of rage.

Indeed, the two corps under the command of Shonyu and Nagayoshi were now only fodder for Ieyasu. The two men were as different as their abilities. The battle between Hideyoshi and Ieyasu at this time was like a grand championship match in sumo, and each man understood his opponent well. Both Hideyoshi and Ieyasu had realized early on that the situation would reach the present pass, and each knew through his own circumspection that his enemy was not a man who could be brought down by a cheap trick or showmanship. But pity the brave and ferocious soldier who acts with a warrior's pride alone. Burning with nothing but his own will, he knows neither the enemy nor his own capacities.

Having had his camp stool set up on Mount Rokubo, Shonyu inspected the more than two hundred enemy heads that had been taken at Iwasaki Castle.

It was morning, just about the first half of the Hour of the Dragon. Shonyu still had not the slightest idea of the disaster that had occurred at his rear. Looking only at the smoking ruins of the enemy castle in front of him, he was drunk on the small pleasure that the warrior falls into so easily.

After the inspection of the heads and the recording of the meritorious deeds of the troops, breakfast was eaten. As the soldiers chewed their food, they occasionally looked toward the northwest. Suddenly something in that direction caught Shonyu's attention as well.

"Tango, what's that in the sky over there?" Shonyu asked.

The generals around Shonyu all turned to the northwest.

"Could it be an insurrection?" one suggested.

But as they continued to eat what was left of their rations, they suddenly heard some confused shouting at the foot of the hill.

As they were wondering what it was about, a messenger from Nagayoshi ran up to them. "We've been taken off guard! They've come up behind us!" the man shouted as he prostrated himself in front of Shonyu's camp stool.

The generals felt as if a chill wind had blown clear through their armor.

"What do you mean, they've come up behind us?" Shonyu asked.

"An enemy force followed Lord Hidetsugu's rear guard."

"The rear guard?"

"They made a sudden attack from both flanks."

Shonyu stood up abruptly, just as a second messenger arrived from Nagayoshi.

"There's no time to lose, my lord. Lord Hidetsugu's rear guard has been completely routed."

There was a sudden stir of motion on the hill, and following that, the noise of short-tempered commands and the sounds of soldiers flowing down the road to the bottom of the hill.

From the shady side of Mount Fujigane, the commander's standard of the golden fan shone brilliantly above the Tokugawa army. There was something almost bewitching about the symbol, and it sent a shiver through the soul of every warrior of the western army on the plain.

There is a great psychological difference between the spirit of an advancing army and that of an army that has turned back. Nagayoshi, who was now encouraging his men from horseback, looked like a man who was anticipating his own death. His armor was made of black leather with dark blue threading, and his coat was gold brocade on a white background. Deer horns adorned his helmet, which he wore thrown back on his shoulders. His head was still wrapped down to his cheeks in the white bandage that covered his wounds.

The Second Corps had been resting at Oushigahara, but as soon as he heard about the Tokugawa forces' pursuit, Nagayoshi roused his men and glared at the golden fan on Mount Fujigane.

"This man is a worthy opponent," he said. "The failure at Haguro that I wash away today won't be just for me. I'll show them that I'll wipe away my father-in-law's disgrace as well."

Today he intended to vindicate his honor. Nagayoshi was a handsome man, and the death attire that he wore today seemed all too desolate for him.

"Did you deliver the report to the vanguard?"

The messenger, who had returned, brought his horse up next to his lord's, adjusted himself to his lord's pace, and made his report.

Nagayoshi, looking straight ahead, held the reins loosely as he listened. "What about the men at Mount Rokubo?" he asked.

"The men were quickly put in order, and they're now coming along behind us."

"Well then, tell Lord Kyutaro of the Third Corps that we have combined our forces and are advancing to confront Ieyasu at Mount Fujigane, so he should pull back in this direction to support us."

Just as the man galloped off, two mounted messengers hurried up with the same instructions for Kyutaro from Shonyu.

But, as has already been related, Kyutaro refused that request and the messengers returned in outrage. By the time Nagayoshi received their reports, his army had already marched through a swampy area between the mountains and was starting to climb to the top of Gifugadake in search of a good position. Before them waved Ieyasu's standard of the golden fan.

The lay of the land was complicated. In the distance, an approach to one section of the open plain of Higashi Kasugai wound and bent its way along, now scissored between the mountains, now embracing smaller plains. The Mikawa road that connected with Okazaki could be seen in the distant south.

But mountains covered more than half of the field of vision. There were no steep precipices or high crags but only undulating waves of hills. As spring departed, the trees were covered with faintly red buds.

Messengers were exchanged in rapid succession, but the thoughts of Nagayoshi and Shonyu were communicated without words. Shonyu's six thousand troops were immediately divided into two units. About four thousand men headed toward the north, and then made their formation to the southeast on high ground. The commander's standard and banners clearly announced that the generals here were Shonyu's eldest son, Yukisuke, and his second son, Terumasa.

That was the right wing. The left wing was made up of Nagayoshi's three thousand soldiers on Gifugadake. Leading the remaining two thousand soldiers, Shonyu stayed with them as a reserve corps. Shonyu set up his commander's standard at the very center of this crane-wing formation.

"I wonder how Ieyasu is going to attack," he said.

Looking up at the sun, the men could see that it was still only the second half of the Hour of the Dragon. Had the hours been long or short? It was not a day for measuring time in the ordinary way. Their throats were dry, but they did not want water.

The uncanny silence made their flesh crawl. A bird cried wildly as it flew across the valley. But that was all. The birds had all flown to some other more peaceful mountain leaving the place to men.

Ieyasu appeared to be too stoop-shouldered. After passing forty he had become somewhat fleshy, and even when he put on his armor, his back was rounded, his shoulders plump; his head seemed to be almost stuffed into his shoulders by his heavy decorated helmet. His right hand, which held the baton of command, and his left were both on his knees. Seated on the edge of his camp stool with his thighs apart, he slouched forward in a way that affected his dignity.

And yes, that was his ordinary posture, even when seated before a guest or walking around. He was not one to stick out his chest. His senior retainers had once advised him to correct his posture, and Ieyasu had nodded vaguely in assent. But as he was talking with his retainers one night, he told them a little about his past.

"I was brought up in poverty. More than that, I was a hostage in another clan from the time I was six, and everyone I saw around me had more rights than I did. So I naturally got into the habit of not going around with my chest stuck out, even when I was with other children. Another reason for my bad posture is that when I studied in the cold room at the Rinzai Temple, I read my books at a desk so low I had to hold on to them like a hunchback. I became almost obsessed by the thought that someday I would be released as a hostage from the Imagawa clan and my body would become my own again. I couldn't play like a child."

It seemed that Ieyasu could never forget the time he had spent with the Imagawa clan. There was no one among his attendant retainers who had not heard the stories of his days as a hostage.

"But you know," he continued, "according to what I was told by Sessai, priests have more respect for what a man's shoulders say about him than what his face does. It seems that he could tell if a man had reached enlightenment just by looking at his shoulders. So, when I looked to see what the abbot's shoulders were like, I found that they were always as round and soft as a halo. If a man wanted to put the entire universe in his breast, he couldn't do it with his chest stuck out. So I started to think that my own posture was not so bad."

Having set up his headquarters in Fujigane, Ieyasu looked around calmly.

"Is that Gifugadake? The men there must be Nagayoshi's. Well, I suppose Shonyu's forces will very soon be getting themselves ready at some mountain or another. One of you scouts hurry and take a look."

The scouts quickly returned and made their reports to Ieyasu. Of course, the information about the enemy positions came in piecemeal. As Ieyasu listened to the reports, he formulated his strategy.

By that time it was already the Hour of the Serpent. Nearly two hours had passed since the enemy's banners had appeared on the mountain before them.

But Ieyasu was composed. "Shiroza. Hanjuro. Come over here." Still seated, he looked around with a serene expression.

"Yes, my lord?" The two samurai approached him, their armor clattering.

Ieyasu asked for the two men's opinions as he compared the map in front of him with the immediate scene.

"When I think about it, it seems that Shonyu's forces at Kobehazama must consist of the real veterans. Depending on how they move, we may be at a real disadvantage here at Fujigane."

One of the men pointed to the peaks in the southeast and answered, "If you're resolved to a decisive battle of close fighting, I think that the foothills over there could be much better places to plant your banners."

"Good! Let's move."

His decision was that quick. The change in the army's position was made immediately. From the foothills, the elevated land held by the enemy was close enough to touch.

Separated only by a marsh and the low area of Karasuhazama, the soldiers could see their enemies' faces and even hear their voices carried on the wind.

Ieyasu ordered the placement of each unit, while he himself had his camp stool set up in a place with an unobstructed view.

"Well, I see that Ii is leading the vanguard today," Ieyasu said.

"The Red Guard has come out to the front!"

"They look good, but I wonder how well they'll fight."

Ii Hyobu was twenty-three years old. Everyone knew that the young man was highly regarded by Ieyasu, and until that morning he had been among the retainers at Ieyasu's side. For his part, Ieyasu viewed Ii as a man that could be put to good use, and he had given him the command of three thousand men and the responsibility for leading the vanguard. That position held the possibility of yielding both the greatest fame and the bitterest hardship.

"Show your spirit just as you please today," Ieyasu counseled.

Ii was so young, however, that Ieyasu took the precaution of attaching two of his experienced retainers to his unit. He added, "Listen to the words of these veterans."

The brothers Yukisuke and Terumasa looked out at the Red Guard from their elevated position at Tanojiri, to the south.

"Strike at that ostentatious Red Corps that's making such a show!" Yukisuke ordered.

With that, the brothers sent a unit of two or three hundred men out from the side of a ravine and a attack corps of one thousand men from the front lines, first opening up with their firearms. At the same time, the foothills erupted in thunderous gunfire, and white smoke spread out like a cloud. As the smoke turned into a light haze and drifted toward the marsh, Ii's red-clad warriors quickly ran toward the low ground. A group of black-armored warriors and foot soldiers ran out to meet them. The distance between the two groups was quickly breached, and the two spear corps engaged in hand-to-hand fighting.

The real heroics of a warrior's battle were usually seen in the fight of spear against spear. More than that, the outcome of battle was often decided by the actions of the spearmen.

It was here that the Ii corps killed several hundred of the enemy. The Red Guard, however, did not escape without casualties, and a good number of Ii's retainers met their deaths.

Ikeda Shonyu had been thinking about the plan of battle for some time. He saw that the troops under his sons were engaged in hand-to-hand fighting with the Red Guards, and that the battle was gradually becoming intensified. "Now's your chance!" he yelled behind him.

A corps of about two hundred men who were ready to win or die had readied their spears beforehand and were waiting for the moment. As soon as they were given the command to advance, they were to rush out into the direction of Nagakute. It was in Shonyu's character to choose unusual battle tactics even at a time like this. The unit of attack troops received the command, circled around Nagakute, and aimed at the troops that remained after the Tokugawa's left wing had pushed forward. The plan was to swiftly attack the enemy's center and, when the enemy's battle array was in confusion, to capture the commander-in-chief, Tokugawa Ieyasu.

The plan, however, did not succeed. Discovered by the Tokugawa before reaching their objective, they received a heavy fusillade of musket fire and were brought to a standstill in a swampy area where it was difficult to move. Unable to advance or retreat, they sustained pitiful losses.

Nagayoshi looked out at the battle situation from Gifugadake and clicked his tongue. "Ah, they were sent too early," he cried out. "It's not like my father-in-law to be so impatient." Today it was the young man who, in every situation, was far more composed than his father-in-law. In fact, Nagayoshi was resolved in his heart that that day was to be the day of his death. With no other thoughts or distractions, he simply looked straight ahead at the commander's stool under the golden fan in the foothills in front of him.

If only I can kill Ieyasu, he thought. Ieyasu, for his part, kept his eye on Gifugadake more than on any other area, aware that the spirit in Nagayoshi's ranks was high. When a scout informed him about the way Nagayoshi was dressed that day, he issued a warning to the men around him.

"Nagayoshi appears to be dressed in his death outfit today, and there's nothing more intimidating than an enemy determined to die. Don't make light of him and be taken in by the god of death."

Thus, the confrontation was not going to be easily initiated by either side. Nagayoshi watched his opponent's movements, feeling in his heart that if the battle at Tanojiri intensified, Ieyasu would not be able to look on simply as a spectator. Surely he would detach a division of soldiers and send them as reinforcements. And with that opportunity Nagayoshi would strike.

But Ieyasu was not going to be taken in easily.

"Nagayoshi is fiercer than most men. If he's this quiet, it's certain that he's up to something."

But the situation at Tanojiri betrayed Nagayoshi's expectations, and the signs of the Ikeda brothers' defeat were coming thick and fast. Finally he resolved that he could wait no longer. But just at that moment, the commander's standard with the golden fan that had remained invisible until now was suddenly raised in the foothills where Ieyasu waited.

Half of Ieyasu's army dashed toward Tanojiri, while the remaining men raised their voices and attacked Gifugadake.

Nagayoshi's troops charged out to meet them, and with the collision of the two armies, the lowland area of Karasuhazama was turned into a whirlpool of blood.

The gunfire was unceasing. It was a desperate battle in a place hemmed in by hills, and the whinnying of horses and the clanging of long swords and spears echoed back and forth. The voices of the warriors calling out their names to their opponents shook heaven and earth.

Soon there was not a single position unengaged throughout the narrow confines of the area, not a single commander or soldier who was not fighting for his life. Just as some troops appeared to be victorious, they crumbled; and just as others seemed to be defeated, they struck through. No one knew who had won, and for a while it was a battle in the dark.

Some men were struck down and killed, while others were victorious and called out their own names. Of those who received wounds, some were called cowards, while others were praised as brave men. If an observer looked carefully, however, he could see that each individual was hurrying along toward eternity, creating his own unique fate.

Shame was the one thing that would not let Nagayoshi think about returning alive to the everyday world. It was the reason he had put on his death robes today.

"I will meet Ieyasu!" Nagayoshi vowed.

As the battle became more and more chaotic, Nagayoshi called together forty or fifty warriors and started out for the commander's standard of the golden fan.

"I'm going to meet Ieyasu. Now!" and he started to whip his horse toward the opposite hill.

"Stop! You're not going anywhere!" a Tokugawa soldier shouted.

"Get Nagayoshi!"

"He's the man with the white hood, riding at a gallop!"

The waves of armored men that tried to stop him ran up to his side and were trampled or, approaching him, were wrapped in sprays of blood.

But then, one bullet from the driving rain of musket fire, shot from a gun that was aimed at the warrior in the white brocade coat, hit him directly between the eyes.

The white hood around Nagayoshi's head suddenly turned red. Falling back on his horse, he had one last glimpse of the sky in the Fourth Month, and in that valley, the heroic young man of twenty-six years fell to the ground, still holding the reins. Hyakudan, Nagayoshi's favorite horse, reared up and whinnied in grief.

A shout like a great sob rose up from his men as they quickly rushed to his side. Carrying his corpse on their shoulders, they withdrew to the top of Gifugadake. Men from the Tokugawa forces ran after them, fighting for the symbol of their deed, shouting, "Take his head!"

The warriors who had lost their leader were close to tears. Wheeling around with frightening expressions, they turned their spears back on their pursuers. Somehow they were able to hide Nagayoshi's body. But the news that Nagayoshi had been struck down blew like a chill wind across the entire battlefield. Along with the other tides of war that had been turning against their position, yet another disaster had befallen Shonyu's forces.

It was as though boiling water had been poured onto a hill of ants: everywhere warriors were fleeing in confusion.

"They're hardly worth calling allies!" Shonyu shouted as he climbed toward higher ground and, in contrast to the peaceful surroundings, sputtered in rage at the few soldiers he encountered. "I'm right here! Don't make a disgraceful retreat! Have you forgotten what you learned every day? Go back! Go back and fight!"

But the group of black-hooded men around him did not stop their own flight in the general collapse. On the contrary, only a pitiful young page of fifteen or sixteen approached him falteringly.

Leading up a stray horse, he offered it to his lord.

In the battle at the bottom of the hill, Shonyu's horse had been shot and he had fallen to the ground. He had been surrounded by the enemy, but had desperately cut open a path and climbed up.

"I don't need a horse anymore. Set up my camp stool here."

The page set up the camp stool behind him, and Shonyu sat down.

"Forty-eight years end here," he muttered to himself. Still looking at the page, he talked on. "You're Shirai Tango's son, aren't you? I imagine your father and mother are waiting. Run as quickly as you can to Inuyama. Look, the bullets are coming! Get out of here fast! Now!"

Having chased the teary-eyed page away, he was alone and felt free from care. Calmly he took his last look at the world.

Very soon he could hear a noise like the fighting of wild animals, and the trees shook in the crags directly beneath him. It appeared that some of his black-hooded warriors still remained and were brandishing their weapons in mortal combat.

Shonyu felt numb. It was no longer a matter of victory or defeat. The sorrow of parting from the world made him reflect on the faraway past, tinged with the scent of his mother's milk.

Suddenly the shrubs directly in front of him began to shake.

"Who is it!" Shonyu's eyes shone with rage. "Is it the enemy?" he called out. His voice was so calm that the approaching Tokugawa warrior unconsciously stepped back in shock.

Shonyu called out again, pressing the man further. "Are you one of the enemy? If you are, take my head and you'll achieve a great deed. The man who is speaking now is Ikeda Shonyu."

The warrior crouching down in the thick undergrowth raised his head and looked at Shonyu sitting there. He shuddered for a moment and then spoke in an arrogant voice as he stood up.

"Well, I've encountered a good one here. I am Nagai Denpachiro of the Tokugawa clan. Prepare yourself!" he shouted, and thrust out his spear.

In response to his shout, quick resistance from the sword of the famous fierce general would have been expected, but Denpachiro's spear slid deeply into his opponent's side without any trouble at all. Rather than Shonyu, whose side had been pierced through, it was Denpachiro who tumbled forward from the momentum of his excessive force.

Shonyu fell over, the spearpoint protruding from his back.

"Take my head!" he yelled again.

He did not have his long sword in his hand even now. On his own he had invited his death, on his own he was offering his head. Denpachiro had been in an arrogant trance, but when he was suddenly aware of the feelings of this enemy general and the way he was meeting his final moments, he was struck with a violent emotion that made him want to weep.

"Ah!" he cried out, but then was so beside himself with joy at his unexpected great achievement that he forgot what to do next.

Just then he heard the rustling sounds of his allies fighting to be the first to climb up from beneath the crags.

"I'm Ando Hikobei! Prepare yourself!"

"My name is Uemura Denemon!"

"I'm Hachiya Shichibei of the Tokugawa clan!"

Each announced his name as they competed to be the one to take Shonyu's head.

By whose sword had the head been taken? Their bloody hands grabbed the topknot and swung it around.

"I took the head of Ikeda Shonyu!" yelled Nagai Denpachiro.

"No, I took it!" cried Ando Hikobei.

"Shonyu's head is mine!" Uemura Denemon shouted.

A storm of blood, a storm of violent voices, a storm of selfish desire for fame. Four men, five men—a growing cluster of warriors, with the single head at its center, set off the direction of Ieyasu's campstool.

"Shonyu has been killed!"

That shout became a wave that went from the peaks to the marsh and caused the Tokugawa forces all over the battlefield to bellow with joy.

The men of the Ikeda forces who had managed to escape did not shout at all. In a moment, those men had lost both heaven and earth, and like dry leaves they now searched for a place to go where their lives might be spared.

"Don't let one of them return alive!"

"Chase after them! Run them down!"

The victors, driven by an insatiable bloodlust, slaughtered the Ikeda wherever they found them.

For men who had already forgotten about their own lives, violently taking other lives very likely felt like nothing more than playing with fallen flowers. Shonyu had been finished off, Nagayoshi had been killed in battle, and now the remaining Ikeda formations at Tanojiri were scattered by the Tokugawa.

One after another, the generals brought the stories of their exploits into the camp that spread out under Ieyasu's golden fan.

"There are so few of them."

Ieyasu was troubled.

This great general rarely displayed his emotions, but he worried about the warriors who had gone out in pursuit of the defeated enemy. Many had not returned, even though the conch had been blown several times. Perhaps they had been carried away with their victory.

Ieyasu repeated himself two or three times.

"This is not a matter of adding victory on top of victory," he said. "It's not good to want to win still more after you've already won."

He did not mention Hideyoshi's name, but no doubt he had intuited that that natural-born strategist had already pointed a finger in this direction in reaction to the great defeat suffered by his army.

"A long pursuit is dangerous. Has Shiroza gone?"

"Yes. He hurried off some time ago with your orders."

Hearing Ii's answer, Ieyasu gave out another order. "You go too, Ii. Reprimand those who have gotten carried away and order them to abandon the chase."

When the pursuing Tokugawa forces reached the Yada River, they found Naito Shirozaemon's squad lined up along the bank, each man holding out the shaft of his spear horizontally.

"Stop!"

"Halt!"

"The order has come from our lord's main camp not to make a long pursuit!"

With those words from the men along the bank, the pursuers were halted.

Ii galloped up and nearly made himself hoarse, yelling at the men as he rode back and forth.

"Our lord has said that those men who become so proud of their victory that they get carried away and go after the enemy will be asking for a court-martial when they return to camp. Go back! Go on back!"

Finally their blind enthusiasm ebbed away, and the men all withdrew from the bank of the river.

It was just about the second half of the Hour of the Horse, and the sun was in the middle of the sky. It was the Fourth Month, and the shape of the clouds indicated that summer was near. Every soldier's face was smeared with earth, blood, and sweat, and appeared to be on fire.

At the Hour of the Ram, Ieyasu went down from the encampment on Fujigane, crossed the Kanare River, and formally inspected the heads at the foot of Mount Gondoji.

The fight had lasted half a day, and all across the battlefield, the dead were counted. Hideyoshi's side had lost more than two thousand five hundred men, while the casualties from the Ieyasu's and Nobuo's armies amounted to five hundred ninety dead and several hundred wounded.

"This great victory is nothing we should be too proud of," a general cautioned. "The Ikeda were only a branch of Hideyoshi's army, but we took our entire force from Mount Komaki and used them here. At the same time, it would be fatal to our allies if we were to suffer a collapse here for some reason. I think the best measure would be for us to withdraw to Obata Castle as quickly as possible."

Another general immediately countered, saying, "No, no. Once victory is in your grasp, you should take the initiative with daring. That's what war is all about. It's certain that when Hideyoshi hears about his great defeat, it's going to provoke him to anger. He'll probably assemble his forces and rush here. Shouldn't we wait for him, prepare ourselves as warriors, and then take Lord Monkey's head?"

In response to those two arguments Ieyasu said again, "We shouldn't try to add victory to victory." And then, "Our men are all tired. Hideyoshi is most likely raising the dust on his way here even now, but we shouldn't meet him today. It's too soon. Let's retire to Obata."

With that quick decision, they passed south of Hakusan Woods and entered Obata Castle while the sun was still high.

After bringing the entire army inside Obata Castle and closing the castle gates, Ieyasu savored the day's great victory for the first time. As he looked back on it, he felt satisfied that the half-day battle had been fought faultlessly. The soldiers' and officers' satisfaction was in such exploits as taking the first head or having the first spear out to the enemy, but the commander-in-chief's secret satisfaction lay in only one thing: the feeling that his own clear-sightedness had hit the mark.

But it takes a master to know one. Ieyasu's only concern now was Hideyoshi's subsequent movements. He strove to be flexible as he pondered this problem, and rested for a while in the main citadel at Obata, relaxing both body and mind.

After Shonyu and his son had departed on the morning of the ninth, Hideyoshi summoned Hosokawa Tadaoki to his camp at Gakuden and gave him, as well as several other generals, the command for an immediate attack on Mount Komaki. After they attacked he climbed the observation tower and watched the progress of the battle. Masuda Jinemon waited at his side, looking out into the distance.

"You know, as hot-blooded as Lord Tadaoki is, won't it be a problem if he penetrates too deeply into the enemy?"

Worrying about how close the Hosokawa forces had come to the enemy ramparts, Jinemon looked at the expression on Hideyoshi's brow.

"It'll be all right. Tadaoki may be young, but Takayama Ukon is a man of good sense. If he's there with him, it will be fine."

Hideyoshi's mind was far away. How had Shonyu fared? All he could think about was the good news that he hoped would come from that quarter.

At about noon, a number of mounted men rode up, having withdrawn from Nagakute. With wretched looks on their faces, they related the tragic news: the main army of Hidetsugu had been completely crushed, and it was unclear whether Hidetsugu was alive or dead.

"What! Hidetsugu?" Hideyoshi was plainly surprised. He was not someone who could look unperturbed at hearing something shocking. "Well, what an oversight!" He said this not so much to criticize the shortcomings of Hidetsugu and Shonyu as to admit his own failure and praise the insight of his enemy, Ieyasu.

"Jinemon," he called, "blow the conch shell for the men to assemble."

Hideyoshi immediately sent out yellow-hooded messengers to each of his divisions with emergency orders, and within an hour, twenty thousand soldiers had departed from Gakuden and hurried toward Nagakute.

That rapid shift did not go unnoticed at the Tokugawa headquarters on Mount Komaki. Ieyasu was already gone, and a small number of men had been left for its defense.

"It appears that Hideyoshi himself is at the head of his army."

When Sakai Tadatsugu, one of the generals left in charge of Mount Komaki, heard that news, he clapped his hands and said, "This is turning out just as we expected! While Hideyoshi is gone, we can burn his headquarters at Gakuden and the fortress at Kurose. Now is the time to make the kill. Everyone follow me for a grand attack!"

But Ishikawa Kazumasa, another of the generals left in charge, opposed him directly.

"Why are you being so hasty, Lord Tadatsugu? Hideyoshi is almost divinely inspired in his military strategies. Do you think a man like that would leave an incapable general in charge of defending his headquarters, no matter how much of a hurry he was in to depart?"

"Any human being may not be up to his usual capacities when he's acting in haste. Hideyoshi had the conch blown to assemble, and he departed in such a hurry one may suppose even he was confused at the news of the defeat at Nagakute. We shouldn't miss the chance now to set fire to Lord Monkey's tail."

"That's superficial thinking!" Ishikawa Kazumasa laughed out loud and resisted Tadatsugu all the more. "It would be Hideyoshi's style to leave behind a considerable military force to take advantage of the situation that would exist if we left our own fortifications. And it would be ridiculous for a small force like ours to sally out now."

Disgusted with all the confusion, Honda Heihachiro stood up indignantly. "Is this a discussion? People who like discussions are just prattlers. Personally, I can't just sit here idly. Pardon me for leaving first."

Honda was both a poor talker and a man of strong character. Both Tadatsugu and Kazumasa had been insisting on the validity of their own arguments and engendering a controversy. They now looked in shock at Honda's indignant departure.

"Honda, where are you going?" they asked hurriedly.

Honda turned around and spoke as though he had come to some deep conclusion. "I have been my lord's retainer ever since I was an infant. Considering the situation he's in, I can do nothing but go to his side."

"Wait!" Kazumasa appeared to think that Honda was simply being hotheaded, and raised his hand to restrain him. "We were commanded by our lord to defend Mount Komaki in his absence, but we were not commanded to do just as we pleased. Calm down a little."

Tadatsugu also tried to calm him down. "Honda, will it achieve anything if you go out alone right now, of all times? The defense of Mount Komaki is more important."

Honda's mouth curled up in a thin smile, as though he pitied their narrow thinking, but he spoke politely, as the two other men were superior to him in both rank and age.

"I'm not going with the other generals. Each of you can do as he pleases. But Hideyoshi is leading a fresh army toward Lord Ieyasu, and as for me, I can't just stand here without doing anything. Think about it. Our lord's forces must be exhausted from fighting last night and this morning, and if the twenty thousand men Hideyoshi is leading join the rest of the enemy in an attack from both the front and the rear, how do you suppose Lord Ieyasu will get away safely? The way I see it is, even if I am wrong in rushing off to Nagakute alone, if my lord is killed in battle, I am resolved to die with him. That should not trouble you."

At those words, all murmuring stopped. Honda led out his own small force of three hundred men and dashed away from Mount Komaki. Infected with the man's spirit, Kazumasa also collected his two hundred men and joined the determined party.

Their joint forces numbered fewer than six hundred men, but Honda's spirit enveloped them from the time they left Mount Komaki. What was an army of twenty thousand men, after all? And who was this Lord Monkey, anyway?

The foot soldiers were lightly armored, the banners were rolled up, and as the horses were whipped, the dust from their little force flew up like a tornado hurrying toward the east.

As they came out to the southern bank of the Ryusenji River, they found Hideyoshi's army moving along the northern bank, troop after troop.

"Well, there they are!"

"The commander's standard with the golden gourds."

"Hideyoshi must be surrounded by his retainers."

Honda and his men had ridden up without stopping, and were looking over at the opposite bank, noisily pointing and holding their hands over their eyes. All of them shook with excitement.

It was such a short distance that if Honda's men had yelled out, the enemy's shouts would have reached right back to them. The faces of the enemy soldiers were visible, and the footsteps of twenty thousand men mixed with the clatter of innumerable horses' hooves crossed the river and reverberated against the chests of the men who were watching.

"Kazumasa!" Honda yelled behind him.

"What is it?"

"Do you see that on the opposite bank?"

"Yes, it's an immense army. Their line looks longer than the river itself."

"That's just like Hideyoshi," Honda laughed. "It's his skill to take an army of that size and then move it as though the men were his own hands and feet. He may be the enemy, but you have to give him credit."

"I've been looking at them for a while. Do you suppose Hideyoshi is over there, where you see the commander's standard with the golden gourds?"

"No, no. I'm sure he's hidden somewhere in the middle of another group of men. He's not going to ride out in the open where he'd be the target for someone's gun."

"The enemy soldiers are moving quickly, but they're all looking over here with suspicion."

"What we must do here is delay Hideyoshi on the road along the Ryusenji River, even if just for a few moments."

"Should we attack?"

"No, the enemy has twenty thousand men, and our own forces only number five hundred, so if we attacked them it would take only an instant for the surface of the river to be dyed red with our blood. I'm resolved to die, but not pointlessly."

"Ah, so you want to give our lord's army in Nagakute enough time to be fully prepared and waiting for Hideyoshi."

"That's right," Honda nodded, striking his horse's saddle. "To buy time for our allies in Nagakute, we should do our best to get a firm grip on Hideyoshi's feet and slow down his attack—even if just a little—with our own deaths. Act with that in mind, Tadatsugu."

"Good. I understand."

Kazumasa and Honda turned their horses' heads to the side.

"Divide your gunners into three groups. As they hurry along the road, each group can alternately kneel and fire at the enemy on the opposite bank."

The enemy moved quickly along the opposite bank, seeming almost to keep pace with the quick-running current. Honda's men had to do everything with the same rhythm but in double-time and constantly on the run—whether it was an attack or the reorganization of their units.

Because they were close to the water, the musket fire echoed far more loudly than it ordinarily would have, and the gunpowder smoke spread over the river like a vast curtain. As one unit leaped in front and fired, the next unit readied its muskets. Then that unit jumped forward, taking the place of the first unit, and immediately fired toward the opposite bank.

A number of Hideyoshi's troops were seen to tumble over in rapid succession. Very quickly, the line of marching men started to waver.

"Who in the world can that be, challenging us with such a tiny force?"

Hideyoshi was surprised. With a look of shock on his face, he unconsciously stopped his horse.

The generals riding around him and the men close by all shaded their eyes with their hands and looked at the opposite bank, but no one could give a quick answer to Hideyoshi's question.

"To act so bravely toward an army of this size with a little force of less than a thousand men, that must be a daring commander! Does anybody recognize him?"

Hideyoshi asked the question repeatedly, looking around at the men in front and behind him.

Then someone at the head of the line said, "I know who that is."

The man who spoke was Inaba Ittetsu, the commander of Sone Castle in Mino. In spite of his venerable age, he had joined this great battle for Hideyoshi's sake and had been at his side as a guide from the very beginning of the campaign.

"Ah, Ittetsu. Do you recognize the enemy general on the other side of the river?"

"Well, from the antlers on his helmet and the white braid on his armor, I'm sure it must be Ieyasu's right-hand man, Honda Heihachiro. I remember him clearly from the battle at Ane River years ago."

When Hideyoshi heard this, he looked as though he were about to shed tears. "Ah, what a brave man! With one small force he strikes at twenty thousand. If that is Honda, he must be a stalwart fellow. How touching that he would try to help Ieyasu escape by momentarily obstructing us here and by dying himself," he muttered. And then, "He's to be sympathized with. Our men are not to shoot a single arrow or bullet in his direction, no matter how much of an attack the man might make. If there is some karmic relation between us, I'll make him one of my own retainers one day. He's a man to be loved. Don't shoot; just let him go."

During that time, of course, the three groups of gunners on the other bank busily continued to load their muskets and shoot relentlessly. One or two bullets even came close to Hideyoshi. Just then, the armored warrior upon whom Hideyoshi had been straining his eyes—Honda, the man wearing the helmet adorned with deer antlers—went down to the water's edge, dismounted, and washed his horse's muzzle with water from the river.

Separated from him by the width of the river, Hideyoshi looked at the man, while Honda gazed steadily at the group of generals—one of whom was clearly Hideyoshi—who had stopped their horses.

Hideyoshi's gunners' corps began to open fire in response, but Hideyoshi once again reproved his entire army. "Don't shoot! Just hurry on! Hurry on ahead!" With that, he urged his horse on with all the more speed.

When Honda observed that action on the other bank, he yelled out, "Don't let them go!" and doubled his speed. Moving ahead on the road, he once again made a fierce musket attack on Hideyoshi's troops, but Hideyoshi would not take up the challenge and soon took up a position on a hill close to the plain of Nagakute.

As soon as they arrived at their destination, Hideyoshi gave orders to three of his generals to take the same number of light cavalry units and ride out quickly. "Do what you can with the Tokugawa forces that are withdrawing from Nagakute to Obata."

He made his headquarters on the hill, while his twenty thousand fresh troops spread out beneath the red evening sun, demonstrating their intention to take revenge upon Ieyasu.

Hideyoshi assigned two men as chiefs of a scouting unit, and they went off secretly toward Obata Castle. After that, Hideyoshi quickly worked out the military operations for his entire army. But before the orders could be sent out, an urgent report arrived:

"Ieyasu is no longer on the battlefield."

"That can't be!" the generals all said together. As Hideyoshi sat silently, the three commanders he had previously sent out toward Nagakute came hurrying back.

"Ieyasu and his main force have already withdrawn to Obata. We encountered a few scattered groups of the enemy that were late in retreating toward the castle, but the others seem to have been about an hour ahead of us," they reported.

Of the three hundred Tokugawa soldiers they had killed, not one had been a general of note.

"We were too late." Hideyoshi had no way to dispel his anger, and it clearly burned in the color of his face.

The scouts' reports were all the same: the castle at Obata had closed its gates and appeared to be quiet, proof that Ieyasu had already withdrawn into the castle and was calmly savoring today's military victory as he rested.

In the midst of his complicated emotions, Hideyoshi unconsciously clapped his hands and congratulated Ieyasu. "That's Ieyasu for you! He has remarkable speed. He retreats into a castle and closes up the gates without any boasting. This is one bird we're not going to catch with either birdlime or a net. But you watch, I'll make Ieyasu behave a little more properly after a few years and have him bow in front of me."

It was already twilight, and a night attack on a castle was considered something to avoid. Moreover, the army had come from Gakuden without rest, so further action tonight was temporarily postponed. The orders were changed. The men were to eat their provisions. Clouds of campfire smoke climbed into the evening sky.

The scouts who had gone from Obata quickly returned. Ieyasu had been sleeping but got up to hear the report. Apprised of the situation, he announced that everyone would immediately be returning to Mount Komaki. His generals argued emphatically for a midnight attack on Hideyoshi, but Ieyasu just laughed and left for Mount Komaki by a circuitous route.

TAIKO

Having no other recourse, Hideyoshi turned his army around and withdrew to the forti-fied camp at Gakuden. He could not deny that the defeat at Nagakute had been a serious blow, even though it had been caused by the overzealousness of Shonyu. But it was also a fact that, on this particular occasion, Hideyoshi had been slow in starting.

It was not because Hideyoshi was measuring himself against Ieyasu on the battlefield for the first time. He had know Ieyasu long before engaging him in battle. Rather, because it was a standoff of master against master—a match between two champions—Hideyoshi was being especially circumspect.

"Don't pay any attention to small castles on the way. Don't waste time," Hideyoshi had warned, but Shonyu had been challenged by the garrison of Iwasaki and had stopped to crush it.

The abilities of Ieyasu and Hideyoshi would determine the outcome of the battle. When Hideyoshi heard of the defeat at Nagakute, he was convinced that his opportunity had come. The deaths of Shonyu and Nagayoshi would surely be the bait for taking Ieyasu alive.

But the enemy had appeared like fire and disappeared like the wind, and after he had gone, it was as silent as the woods. When Ieyasu withdrew to Mount Komaki, Hideyoshi felt he had just missed bagging a scared rabbit, but told himself that he had suffered only a little wound to the finger. Certainly there had been no great damage to his military strength. Psychologically, however, he had given Ieyasu's side a victory.

At any rate, after the violent half-day battle at Nagakute, both men were extremely prudent and watched the other's movements closely. And while each waited to seize a fa-vorable opportunity, neither man would have even considered making a careless attack. Provocations, however, were made repeatedly.

For example, when Hideyoshi sent his entire sixty-two-thousand-man army out to Mount Komatsuji on the eleventh day of the Fourth Month, the reaction at Mount Komaki was nothing more than a peaceful, wry smile.

After that, on the twenty-second day of the same month, a provocation was set up by Ieyasu's side. A combined force of eighteen thousand men was divided into sixteen units and emerged heading toward the east.

Beating drums and raising war cries, a vanguard led by Sakai Tadatsugu and Ii Hyobu made repeated challenges, almost as if to say, "Come out, Hideyoshi!"

The moated palisades were defended by Hori Kyutaro and Gamo Ujisato. Gazing out at the raucous enemy forces, Kyutaro ground his teeth.

After Nagakute, the enemy had been spreading rumors that Hideyoshi's soldiers were frightened of the Tokugawa warriors. But Hideyoshi had made it clear that the soldiers were to make no sorties without his express order, so they could do nothing more than send runners flying off to the main camp.

When the messenger arrived, Hideyoshi was playing *go*.

"A large Tokugawa force is approaching our men at the double moats," the man announced.

Hideyoshi raised his eyes from the *go* board for a moment and asked the messenger, "Has Ieyasu himself appeared?"

"Lord Ieyasu has not come out himself," the man replied.

Hideyoshi picked up a black stone, placed it on the board and said, without looking up, "Tell me if Ieyasu makes an appearance. Unless he comes out at the head of his army, Kyutaro and Ujisato can fight or not, as they please."

At about the same time, Ii Hyobu and Sakai Tadatsugu at the front lines sent messengers twice with pleas to Ieyasu at Mount Komaki.

"Now is the time for you to make a personal appearance. If you do it immediately, we will undoubtedly be able to strike a fatal blow to the main body of Hideyoshi's troops."

To that Ieyasu responded, "Has Hideyoshi himself made a move? If he's still at Mount Komatsuji, there's no need for me to go out, either."

In the end, Ieyasu did not leave Mount Komaki.

During that time, Hideyoshi clearly meted out the praise and blame for the battle at Nagakute. He was particularly careful about the presentation of increases in stipends and rewards, but did not say a word to his nephew Hidetsugu. And, after having fled from Nagakute, Hidetsugu seemed to feel awkward in front of his uncle. On his return to camp he simply reported that he had come back and later tried to explain the reason for his defeat. But Hideyoshi only talked to the other generals seated around him and did not look Hidetsugu in the face.

"It was my own blunder that sent Shonyu to his death," Hideyoshi said. "From the time of his youth, we shared our poverty, our nighttime amusements, and our whoring around. I'll never be able to forget him."

Every time he talked with others about his old friend, his eyes filled with tears.

Then one day, without letting anyone know what he was thinking, Hideyoshi suddenly ordered the construction of fortifications at Oura. Two days later, on the last day of the Fourth Month, he gave out more instructions: "I plan on taking a chance tomorrow on the battle of a lifetime. We're going to see who falls, Ieyasu or Hideyoshi. Sleep well, prepare yourselves, and don't be caught off guard."

The following day was the first of the Fifth Month. Expecting that it would be the day on which the great decisive battle would be fought, the entire army had been preparing itself since the night before. Now, finally seeing Hideyoshi in front of them, the soldiers listened to his words in blank amazement.

"We're going back to Osaka! All of the troops should withdraw." Then came his next orders. "The corps under Kuroda Kanbei and Akashi Yoshiro should coordinate with the troops at the double moats. The position of rear guard is to be taken by Hosokawa Tadaoki and Gamo Ujisato."

Sixty thousand troops moved out. Heading west, they began their retreat just as the morning sun appeared over the horizon. Hori Kyutaro was left at Gakuden and Kato Mitsuyasu at Inuyama Castle. Except for them, all the troops crossed the Kiso River and entered Oura.

This sudden withdrawal caused Hideyoshi's generals to wonder about his true intentions. Hideyoshi gave orders in a carefree way, but withdrawing such a large army was even more difficult than leading it to attack. The responsibility of taking up the rear guard was considered to be the most difficult of all, and it was claimed that only the bravest warriors were suitable for the work.

When the men at Ieyasu's headquarters saw Hideyoshi's army suddenly withdraw to the west that morning, they were all seized with doubt and reported the event to Ieyasu.

The generals there were in complete agreement.

"There's no doubt about it. We've crushed the enemy's will to fight."

"If we give chase and attack, the western forces will be totally routed and a great victory will surely be ours!"

Each of them spoke enthusiastically for an attack and asked for the command, but Ieyasu did not look the least bit happy. He strictly refused permission for a pursuit.

He knew that a man like Hideyoshi would not withdraw a large army without reason. He also knew that while he had sufficient strength for defense, he did not have the forces to fight with Hideyoshi in an unobstructed battle on an open plain.

"Warfare is not a gamble. Are we going to stake our lives on an event when we have no idea of the outcome? Put out your hand to grasp something only when destiny has come to bless you."

Ieyasu hated taking risks. He also knew himself very well. In that regard, the absolute opposite of Ieyasu was Nobuo. Nobuo was constantly under the illusion that he himself had the same great popularity and genius as Nobunaga. He could not keep quiet at this time, even though the other generals were sitting in silence after Ieyasu had told them that there would be no pursuit.

"It is said that a soldier respects the opportunity given him. How can we sit here and let this heaven-sent opportunity pass us by? Please leave the pursuit to me." Nobuo argued with increasing vehemence.

Ieyasu admonished him with two or three words, but Nobuo was parading his courage more than he ever had before. Arguing with Ieyasu, he acted like a spoiled child who would listen to nobody.

"Well then, there's nothing to be done. Do as you please."

Ieyasu gave his permission, knowing full well that disaster would follow. Nobuo immediately led out his own army and chased after Hideyoshi.

After Nobuo left, Ieyasu put Honda in charge of a group of soldiers and sent him along behind. Just as Ieyasu had thought he would do, Nobuo fought Hideyoshi's rear guard as it withdrew and, while he looked superior for a moment, was quickly defeated. In this way he caused the death in battle of a great number of his retainers.

If Honda's reinforcements had not come from the rear, Nobuo himself might have become one of the greatest prizes of Hideyoshi's rear guard. Retreating to Mount Komaki, Nobuo did not appear before Ieyasu right away. But Ieyasu heard the details of the situation from Honda. With no change of expression, he nodded and said, "It was only to be expected."

When Hideyoshi retreated, it was not just a simple withdrawal. As his army moved along the road he said to his retainers, "Shouldn't we take some nice souvenir?"

Kaganoi Castle stood on the left bank of the Kiso River, in an area to the northeast of Kiyosu Castle. Two of Nobuo's retainers had entrenched themselves there, prepared to act as one of Nobuo's wings in case of an emergency.

"Take it." Hideyoshi gave the command to his generals as though he were pointing at a persimmon on a branch.

The army crossed the Kiso River and took up a position at the Seitoku Temple. At the center of the reserve army, Hideyoshi opened the attack on the morning of the fourth day of the month. From time to time he went out on his horse and watched the battle from a hill in the vicinity of Tonda.

During the fighting on the following day, the commander of the castle was killed. The castle itself, however, did not fall until the evening of the sixth.

Hideyoshi had fortifications built for a later day at a strategic point in Taki, and returned as far as Ogaki on the thirteenth. At Ogaki Castle he met with Shonyu's surviving family, and comforted his wife and mother.

"I can imagine that you feel lonely. But keep the promising futures of your children in mind. You should try to live the rest of your lives in harmony, rejoicing in the growth of young trees and watching the flowers of the season."

Hideyoshi also called over Shonyu's two surviving sons and encouraged them to be strong. That night he became like one of the family and talked for hours about his memories of Shonyu.

"I'm a short man, and Shonyu was too. When that short little man entertained the other generals, he'd often do the spear dance when he got drunk. I don't suppose he ever showed it to the members of his family, but it went something like this." Doing an imitation, he made them all laugh. He stayed in the castle for a number of days, but finally, on the twenty-first of the month, he took the Omi Road back to Osaka Castle.

Osaka was now a large city, radically changed from the little port of Naniwa, and when Hideyoshi's army arrived, the people jostled together along the streets and in the vicinity of the castle, cheering them on until nightfall.

The external construction work for Osaka Castle had already been completed. When night fell, an otherworldly scene unfolded. Bright lamps shone from the innumerable windows of the five-story keep of the main citadel, as well as from the second and third citadels, adorning the night sky and illuminating the boundaries of the castle on all four sides: to the east, the Yamato River; to the north, the Yodo River; to the west, the Yokobori River; and to the south, the great dry moat.

Hideyoshi had left his camp at Gakuden, changing his mind and taking up the strategy of a "fresh start." But how had Ieyasu reacted to that change? He had sat and watched as Hideyoshi's retreating troops marched away. And even though he had heard about the distress of his allies at Kaganoi Castle, he had not sent reinforcements.

"What's the matter?" Voices of indignation rose among Nobuo's subordinates. Nobuo, however, had already ignored Ieyasu's advice, attacked Hideyoshi's rear guard, and met with an ignominious defeat. Saved by Honda, he had finally returned to camp. Thus Nobuo now felt that he had lost his right to say anything at all.

Thus, festering discord had become the weak point of the allied army. More than that, the main advocate of this great battle had been Nobuo, not Ieyasu. Nobuo had preached the cause of duty to Ieyasu, and the lord of Mikawa had risen up to help him. His standpoint, therefore, was one of an ally, and so it was all the more difficult to control Nobuo. Finally he made a suggestion. "While Hideyoshi is in Osaka, sooner or later he will move on Ise. Indeed, for our allies, some worrisome signs have already appeared. I think you should return to your main castle at Nagashima as soon as possible."

Taking this opportunity, Nobuo quickly returned to Ise. Ieyasu remained at Mount Komaki for a little while, but he too finally departed for Kiyosu, leaving Sakai Tadatsugu in command. The people of Kiyosu came out to greet Ieyasu with cheers of victory, but not in the same numbers as the people of Osaka had for Hideyoshi.

The citizens and soldiers hailed the battle of Nagakute as a great victory for the Tokugawa clan, but Ieyasu cautioned his retainers against frivolous pride and sent the following message to his troops:

Militarily, Nagakute was a victory, but in terms of castles and land, Hideyoshi has taken the real advantage. Do not be so happily dull-headed as to get drunk on a false reputation.

During the stalemate at Mount Komaki, the fact was that in Ise, where there had been no battles for a while, Hideyoshi's allies had taken the castles at Mine, Kanbe, Kokufu, and Hamada, and attacked and destroyed the castle at Nanokaichi. Before anyone was aware of it, most of Ise had fallen into Hideyoshi's hands.

Hideyoshi was at Osaka Castle for about one month, looking to the affairs of its internal administration, making plans for regulating the areas around the capital, and enjoying his own private life. For the present, he regarded the Mount Komaki crisis as someone else's concern.

During the Seventh Month he traveled to Mino and back. Then, in about the middle of the Eighth Month he said, "It's boring to drag this out for too long. This autumn I'll have to finish the matter up once and for all."

Once again, he announced that a great army would depart for the front. For two days before the departure, the flutes and drums of Noh plays resounded through the depths of the main citadel. From time to time the boisterous laughter of a large crowd of people could be heard.

Engaging a troupe of Noh actors, Hideyoshi invited his mother, his wife, and his kinsmen in the castle to share one day of enjoyment together.

Among the guests were the three princesses who were being raised in seclusion in the third citadel. Chacha was seventeen that year; the middle sister was thirteen; and the youngest of the three was going to be eleven.

Just one year before, on the day Kitanosho Castle fell, the girls had looked behind them at the smoke enshrouding the death of their foster father, Shibata Katsuie, and their mother. They had been moved from the camp in the northern provinces and had seen no one but strangers, no matter where they looked. For a while their eyes were swollen with tears day and night, and not a single smile appeared on the youthful faces that ordinarily would have been full of mirth. But the three princesses finally got used to the people in the castle and, humored by Hideyoshi's easygoing style, became fond of him as "our interesting uncle."

That day, after a number of performances, that "interesting uncle" went into the dressing room enclosure, changed into costume, and came out on the stage himself.

"Look! It's uncle!" one of the girls called out.

"My, he looks so funny!"

Ignoring the presence of the others, the two younger princesses clapped their hands and pointed, unable to stop laughing. As might be expected, the eldest sister, Chacha, reprimanded them. "You shouldn't point. Just watch quietly," she said. She did her best to sit modestly, but Hideyoshi's antics were so funny that, in the end, Chacha hid her mouth behind her sleeve and laughed as though her sides would burst.

"What's this? When we laugh, we get scolded. But you're laughing now."

With her two sisters poking fun at her, Chacha could only laugh more and more.

Hideyoshi's mother also laughed from time to time as she watched her son's comic dance, but Nene, used to her husband's antics and his constant joking inside the family circle, did not look particularly amused.

What interested Nene today was the peaceful observation of her husband's concubines, who were sitting here and there, surrounded by maids.

While they were still in Nagahama, he had had only two mistresses, but after they had moved to Osaka Castle, before she knew it there was a concubine in the second citadel, and another in the third.

It was hard to believe, but in his triumphal return from the siege of the north, he had brought back Asai Nagamasa's three orphaned daughters and was lovingly raising them in the second citadel.

It pained the ladies who served Nene—Hideyoshi's true wife, after all—that the eldest sister, Chacha, was even more beautiful than her mother.

"Lady Chacha is already seventeen years old. Why does His Lordship gaze at her the way he'd look at a flower in a vase?"

They only added fuel to the fire with comments like that, but Nene simply laughed. "There's nothing to be done; it's like a scratch on a pearl," she'd say.

Formerly, she, too, had been as jealous as any other wife might be, and when she was living in Nagahama she had gone as far as to complain to Nobunaga, who had sent her a written reply:

You were born a woman, and have chanced to meet an extremely unusual man. I imagine that there must be faults in such a man, but his good points are numerous. When you are looking out from the midst of a large mountain, you can't understand how big that mountain truly is. Be at peace, and enjoy living with this man in the way he wants to live. I am not saying that jealousy is a bad thing. To a certain extent, jealousy adds depth to the life of a married couple.

So in the end, it was she who had been reprimanded. Having learned by that experience, Nene had set her mind on self-control and had planned on becoming a woman who could overlook her husband's affairs. Recently, however, there were days when she felt threatened, wondering if her husband wasn't beginning to indulge himself too much.

At any rate, he was now approaching the age of forty-seven, the most prosperous time for a man. While he had his hands full with external problems like the battle at Mount Komaki, he was also very busy with internal affairs like the administration of his bedroom. And so he lived insatiably, day by day, with the vitality of a healthy man—so much so that an observer might have wondered how he was able to sort out the common from the uncommon, the magnanimous gesture from the discreet, and grand public actions from the ones that should be totally hidden away.

"Watching the dance is amusing, but when I go out and perform on stage, it's not so much fun at all. In fact, it's hard."

Hideyoshi had come up behind his mother and Nene. He had just a moment ago left the stage at the applause of the spectators and appeared not to have sobered up from the excitement of the act.

"Nene," he said, "let's spend a quiet evening in your room tonight. Would you prepare a banquet?"

As the performance ended, the bright light of the lamps flooded the area, and the guests made their way back to the third and second citadels.

Hideyoshi now dropped in at Nene's room, accompanied by a large crowd of actors and musicians. His mother had retired to her quarters, so husband and wife were alone with their guests.

It was customary for Nene to pay attention to such people and their servants, and to all her subordinates. Especially after today's gathering, she enjoyed thanking them for their services and seeing them frivolously exchanging *sake* cups, and making conversation with their audience.

Hideyoshi had been sitting by himself from the very beginning, and since everyone seemed to be ignoring him, he looked a little morose.

"Nene, I suppose it would be all right if I had a cup too," he said.

"Do you think you should?"

"Do *you* think I'm not going to drink? Why do you think I came to your room?"

"Well, your mother said, 'That boy will be heading for Mount Komaki again the day after tomorrow,' and she strictly ordered me to apply the usual *moxa* to your shins and hips before you leave for the front."

"What! She said to apply *moxa*?"

"She worries that the lingering heat of autumn will still be over the battlefield, and if you drink bad water, your liable to fall ill. I'll apply the *moxa* and give you a cup of *sake* after that."

"That's ridiculous. I don't like *moxa*."

"Whether you like it or not, those are your mother's orders."

"Well, just for that I'm staying away from your room. Of all the people watching my performance this afternoon, you were the only one who didn't laugh. You looked so serious."

"That's my nature. Even if you tell me to behave like the pretty girls, I can't." Nene showed a little anger. Then, suddenly, tears welled up in her eyes as she recalled the old days when she herself was Chacha's age and Hideyoshi was the twenty-five-year-old Tokichiro.

Hideyoshi looked curiously at his wife and asked, "Why are you crying?"

"I don't know," Nene said, looking away, and Hideyoshi turned to face her directly.

"Are you saying that it's going to be lonely when I go to the front again?"

"Since the beginning of our married life, how many days have you spent at home?"

"There's nothing to be done until we put the world at peace, even if you don't like war," Hideyoshi replied. "And if the unforeseen hadn't happened to Lord Nobunaga, I'd probably be in charge of some countryside castle, sitting out my life and forced to be at your side exactly the way you like it."

"People are going to hear the nasty things you're saying. I understand exactly what's in a man's heart."

"And I understand a woman's heart too!"

"You always make fun of me. I'm not speaking out of jealousy, like some ordinary woman."

"Any wife would say that."

"Will you listen to me without making this into a joke?"

"All right. I'm listening with great respect."

"I resigned myself a long time ago. So I'm hardly going to tell you that I'm lonely taking care of your castle when you're on a campaign."

"A virtuous woman, a faithful wife! This is why the Tokichiro of so long ago put his mark on you."

"Don't carry your joking too far! That is why your mother spoke to me."

"What did my mother say?"

"She said I was so submissive that you were going to get carried away and become dissipated. She told me I should speak up to you from time to time."

"Is that the reason for the *moxa*?" Hideyoshi laughed.

"You don't have a thought about her worries. Your self-indulgent intemperance has led you to be unfilial."

"When was I intemperate?"

"Weren't you making a lot of noise about something in Lady Sanjo's room right up until dawn two nights ago?"

The attendants and actors drinking in the next room pretended not to listen to the rare—well, perhaps not so rare—argument between husband and wife. Just at that point, however, Hideyoshi raised his voice and yelled, "Hey, now! What does the audience think of this couple's performance?"

One of the actors answered, "Yes indeed, it looks to me like a game of kickball between blind people."

"Even a dog wouldn't nibble at that," Hideyoshi laughed.

"Come on. There's no end to such winning and losing."

"You there, the flutist, what did you think?"

"Well, I was watching it as I might my own business. Who's to blame, who's to fault? Blame! Fault! Blam! Foom! Blam! Foom!"

Hideyoshi suddenly snatched Nene's over-kimono and threw it out as a prize.

On the following day Hideyoshi's family was unable to get even a glimpse of him, even though they were in the same castle. Throughout the day Hideyoshi was pressed with the work of giving instructions to his retainers and generals.

On the twenty-sixth day of the Eighth Month, Ieyasu received an urgent report that Hideyoshi was coming. He hastened from Kiyosu to Iwakura with Nobuo, and set up a position opposing Hideyoshi. Ieyasu again took up a totally defensive position and warned his men not to initiate any movement or challenge on their own.

"This is a man who doesn't know the meaning of enough."

Hideyoshi had already found Ieyasu's patience difficult to deal with, but he was not completely without such resources himself. He knew that it was impossible to open the wreath shell's cap, even with a hammer, but if the tail end of its shell was roasted, however, the meat could be taken out easily. It was this sort of ordinary reasoning that now occupied his thinking. Quietly sending Niwa Nagahide to see about concluding a peace agreement was like heating the wreath shell's tail.

Niwa was the most senior among the Oda clan's retainers and was a dependable and popular character. Now that Katsuie was dead and Takigawa Kazumasu was in reduced circumstances, Hideyoshi did not forget the necessity of winning over that warm, good man as his own "chessman in reserve" before the hostilities at Mount Komaki began.

Niwa was in the north with Inuchiyo, but Niwa's generals, Kanamori Kingo and Hachiya Yoritaka, were participating in the war on Hideyoshi's side. Before anyone even knew it, those two generals had gone back and forth a number of times between Hideyoshi and their home province of Echizen.

The content of the letters that were being sent was unknown even to the envoys, but finally Niwa himself made a secret journey to Kiyosu and had an interview with Ieyasu.

Such talks, however, were conducted in extreme secrecy. The only men who knew about them on Hideyoshi's side were Niwa and his two generals. At Hideyoshi's suggestion, Ishikawa Kazumasa became his go-between.

Eventually, however, someone within the Tokugawa clan leaked a rumor that secret peace talks had been initiated. That set off great agitation in Ieyasu's defenses centered at Mount Komaki.

When rumors leak out, they are always accompanied by malicious gossip. In this case the name that surfaced was one that was already held in suspicion by his fellow retainers—that of Ishikawa Kazumasa.

"It's being said that Kazumasa is the mediator. Somehow there's always something that smells funny between Hideyoshi and Kazumasa."

There were some people who spoke about it directly to Ieyasu, but he rebuked whoever spoke to him and never doubted Kazumasa in the least.

But once that kind of doubt had arisen among the retainers, the morale of the whole clan began to suffer.

Ieyasu, of course, was in favor of holding peace talks, but when he saw the internal condition of his forces, he suddenly rejected Niwa's messenger.

"I have no desire for peace," Ieyasu said. "I have no hopes for a settlement with Hideyoshi, no matter what conditions he offers. We're going to fight a decisive battle here, I'm going to take Hideyoshi's head, and we'll let the nation know what true duty is."

When this was announced officially throughout Ieyasu's camp, the soldiers were pleased, and the dark rumors about Kazumasa were swept away.

"Hideyoshi's started to break down!"

Their spirits revitalized, they became all the more aggressive.

Hideyoshi received the bitter cup with resignation. To him, the result seemed not altogether bad. So he did not venture to use military strength that time either, but ordered his forces to occupy strategic areas. Toward the middle of the Ninth Month, he sent his soldiers back once more and entered the castle at Ogaki.

How many times was it now that the citizens of Osaka had watched Hideyoshi and his army leave for the front and then return, going back and forth between the castle and Mino?

It was now the twentieth day of the Tenth Month—already late autumn. Hideyoshi's army, which usually passed through Osaka, Yodo, and Kyoto, suddenly changed its route at Sakamoto and this time passed through Koga in Iga and went on toward Ise. There it left the Mino Road and took the one that led to Owari.

Dispatch after urgent dispatch was sent out from Nobuo's branch castles and spies in Ise, almost as though a dike had unexpectedly opened in a number of places and the muddy waters of a turbulent river were rushing that way.

"It's Hideyoshi's main force!"

"These are not soldiers under the command of a single general, as we've seen until now."

On the twenty-third of the month Hideyoshi's army camped at Hanetsu and built fortifications at Nawabu.

With Hideyoshi's army closing in on his castle, Nobuo was unable to keep his composure. For about a month now he had had forebodings that the storm was approaching. Which is to say that Ishikawa Kazumasa's actions—which had been kept an absolute secret by the Tokugawa clan—had been mysteriously exaggerated and discussed by someone, though nobody could quite say who.

The rumor went that the inner circle of the Tokugawa clan was not really united. It appeared that a number of Ieyasu's retainers were hostile to Kazumasa and were just waiting for the right moment.

It was also being widely rumored that the Tokugawa had been negotiating with Hideyoshi, that Ieyasu was trying to make peace quickly, before news of the rupture of his inner circle leaked out, but that negotiations had been broken off because the conditions set by Hideyoshi were too severe.

Nobuo was frankly pained. What, after all, would happen to him if Ieyasu made peace with Hideyoshi?

"If Hideyoshi changes direction and heads out on the Ise Road, you had better be resigned to the fact that there is already a secret understanding between Hideyoshi and Ieyasu to sacrifice your clan, my lord."

And, just as Nobuo had feared, Hideyoshi's army suddenly confirmed his worse nightmares. There was no plan he could follow other than to report the emergency to Ieyasu and call for his help.

Sakai Tadatsugu was in charge of Kiyosu Castle during Ieyasu's absence. When he received the urgent report from Nobuo, he immediately had a runner relay it to Ieyasu, who raised all his forces on the same day and marched to Kiyosu. He then quickly sent reinforcements under Sakai Tadatsugu to Kuwana.

Kuwana is the geographical neck of Nagashima. Nobuo also took soldiers there and placed them facing Hideyoshi, who had set up his headquarters in the village of Nawabu.

Nawabu was on the bank of the Machiya River, about one league to the southwest of Kuwana, but the mouths of the Kiso and Ibi rivers were close by, and it was an excellent place from which to threaten Nobuo's headquarters.

Late autumn. The numerous reeds in the area concealed several hundred thousand soldiers, and the smoke of the campfires spread out thickly over the riverbank, morning and night. The order for battle had still not been given. The relaxed soldiers even went fishing for gobies. At such times, when the lightly armored Hideyoshi made a tour of the encampments and suddenly appeared on horseback, the flustered rank-and-file would quickly throw away their fishing rods. But even if Hideyoshi noticed this, he would just pass by smiling.

The fact is that if it hadn't been this particular place, he too would have wanted to fish for gobies and walk barefoot. He was still, in some ways, a boy at heart, and such scenes called forth the pleasures of his childhood.

Across this river was the earth of Owari. Under the autumn sun, the smell of the earth of his birthplace tantalized his senses.

Tomita Tomonobu and Tsuda Nobukatsu had returned from a mission and were waiting impatiently for his return.

Leaving his horse at the gate, Hideyoshi hurried along at a pace unusual for him. He himself led the two men who had come out to greet him to a hut in the middle of a heavily guarded stand of trees.

"What was Lord Nobuo's answer?" he asked. His voice was low, but there was an extraordinary expectant light in his eyes.

Tsuda spoke first. "Lord Nobuo says that he understands your feelings very well and gives his consent for a meeting."

"What! He's agreed?"

"Not only that, but he was extremely pleased."

"Really?" Hideyoshi expanded his chest and let out a tremendous sigh. "Really? That's really what happened?" he repeated.

Hideyoshi's intentions in advancing along the Ise Road at this time had been based on a gamble from the very beginning. He had hoped for a diplomatic solution, but if that had failed, he would strike at Kuwana, Nagashima, and Kiyosu. That would open Mount Komaki to attack from the rear.

Tsuda was related to the Oda clan and was a second cousin to Nobuo, to whom he explained the advantages and disadvantages of the situation, and from whom he finally elicited an answer.

"I'm not the kind of person who likes war at all," Nobuo replied. "If Hideyoshi thinks that much of me and wants to hold a peace conference, I would not be indisposed toward meeting him."

From the very first battle at Mount Komaki, Hideyoshi had seen that Ieyasu would be difficult to deal with. After that, he had studied the inner workings of the human heart and had manipulated the men around him from the shadows.

In the inner circles of the Tokugawa clan, Ishikawa Kazumasa was regarded with some suspicion, due to Hideyoshi's influence. Thus, when Niwa Nagahide moved toward arbitration, the men in Nobuo's inner circle who had former connections with him were quickly ostracized as a peace faction. Nobuo himself was uneasy about Ieyasu's true intentions, and the Tokugawa eyed Nobuo's army with vigilance. This state of affairs had evolved under specific orders from faraway Osaka.

It was an article of faith with Hideyoshi that no matter what kind of diplomatic scheme he used, the sacrifices involved were far preferable to those made in war. More than that, after having tried the alternatives—facing Ieyasu directly at Mount Komaki, engaging in some clever military plan, and even making a menacing bluff—Hideyoshi felt that making war on Ieyasu was having absolutely no effect and that he would have to try some other tack.

The meeting the following day with Nobuo was exactly the realization of such deliberation and forethought.

Hideyoshi got up early and, looking up at the sky, said, "The weather's just right."

In the sky the night before, the cloud movements of late autumn had given him some anxiety; and he feared that if by any chance it became windy and rainy, Nobuo's side might say it wanted to postpone the time or change the place, and it might then be suspected by the Tokugawa. Hideyoshi had gone to sleep concerned about how unsavory that might be, but this morning the clouds had blown away and the sky was bluer than usual for the time of year. Hideyoshi took it as a good omen and, wishing himself luck, mounted his horse and left the camp at Nawabu.

His attendants were only a few senior retainers and pages and the two former envoys, Tomita and Tsuda. When the group finally crossed the Machiya River, however, Hideyoshi had taken the precaution to hide a number of his soldiers among the reeds and farmhouses during the night before. Hideyoshi chatted amiably on horseback as though he didn't see them, and finally dismounted at the bank of the Yada River close to the western outskirts of Kuwana.

"Shall we wait here for Lord Nobuo to come?" he asked, and, sitting down on his camp stool, he looked out at the local scenery.

Not long thereafter, Nobuo, accompanied by a group of mounted retainers, arrived on time. Nobuo must have spotted the men waiting on the riverbank as well, and he immediately began conferring with the generals to his right and left as he focused his eyes on Hideyoshi. He brought his horse to a halt in the distance and dismounted, apparently still quite apprehensive.

The crowd of warriors that accompanied him opened up to the right and left. Placing himself at their center, Nobuo started toward Hideyoshi, his armor displaying all of his martial prestige.

Hideyoshi. Here was the man who, until just the other day, had been vilified to the nation as the worst kind of assassin and inhuman ingrate. Here was the enemy whose crimes had been enumerated by both himself and Ieyasu. Even though he had agreed to Hideyoshi's proposal and was meeting him here, Nobuo was unable to feel at ease. What were the man's true intentions?

As Hideyoshi caught sight of Nobuo standing in all his dignity, he left his stool behind him and, completely alone, went hurrying toward him.

"Ah, Lord Nobuo!" He was waving both hands, just as though this were some unplanned and unexpected meeting.

Nobuo was bewildered, but the retainers around him, who looked so imposing with their spears and armor, gaped in openmouthed surprise.

But this was not their only shock. Hideyoshi was now kneeling at Nobuo's feet, prostrating himself so that his face nearly touched Nobuo's straw sandals.

Then, taking the hand of the stunned Nobuo, he said, "My lord, there hasn't been a day this year that I haven't thought about wanting to meet you. Before anything else, I'm extremely pleased to see that you're in good health. What kind of evil spirit could have confused you, my lord, and brought us to fight one another? From this day forth you will be my lord, just as before."

"Hideyoshi, please get up. I'm speechless at your repentance. We were both at fault. But first please get up."

Nobuo pulled Hideyoshi up with the hand the latter had grasped.

The meeting of the two men on the eleventh day of the Eleventh Month went smoothly, and the peace accord was agreed upon. It goes without saying that the proper order of things would have been for Nobuo to have discussed the matter with Ieyasu and to have gotten his agreement before the fact. But he responded totally to this opportune blessing, and an independent peace was established.

The simple fact was that the beanbag that Ieyasu had thrown around and used for his own purposes was being snatched from the side by Hideyoshi. Essentially, Nobuo had been taken in.

One can only imagine the sweet words Hideyoshi used to gain Nobuo's favor. In fact, in all his years of service, Hideyoshi had rarely moved Nobuo's father, Nobunaga, to

915

anger, so appeasing Nobuo must have been easy for him. But the conditions of the peace accords that had first been communicated by the two envoys were neither sweet nor easy:

Item: Hideyoshi would adopt Nobuo's daughter.
Item: The four districts in northern Ise that Hideyoshi had occupied would be returned to Nobuo.
Item: Nobuo would send women and children from his clan as hostages.
Item: Three districts in Iga, seven districts in southern Ise, Inuyama Castle in Owari, and the fortress at Kawada would be given to Hideyoshi.
Item: All of the temporary fortifications belonging to both sides in the two provinces of Ise and Owari were to be destroyed.

Nobuo affixed his seal to the document. As gifts from Hideyoshi that day, Nobuo received twenty pieces of gold and a sword made by Fudo Kuniyuki. He was also presented with thirty-five thousand bales of rice as spoils of war from the Ise area.

Hideyoshi had bowed to Nobuo and shown him respect, and had given him gifts as proof of his goodwill. Treated in that way, Nobuo could not help but smile with satisfaction. It is certain, however, that Nobuo had not considered how his scheming was going to come back at him. In terms of the ebb and flow of the violent tides of the times, Nobuo could only be called an unpardonable fool. There would be no blame if Nobuo had remained on the sidelines. But he had come out at the very center, had been made a tool of war, and had caused a great number of men to die under his banners.

* * *

The one who was most surprised when the facts were out was Ieyasu, who had already moved from Okazaki to Kiyosu to gain a war footing and confront Hideyoshi. It was the morning of the twelfth.

Sakai Tadatsugu suddenly whipped his horse to the castle, having traveled overnight from Kuwana.

It was unusual for a commander at the front lines to leave his battle position and come to Kiyosu unannounced. Moreover, Tadatsugu was a sixty-year-old veteran. Why had this old man traveled all night with only a few attendants?

It was before breakfast, but Ieyasu came out of his bedroom, sat down in the audience chamber, and asked, "What is it, Tadatsugu?"

"Lord Nobuo met with Hideyoshi yesterday. The rumor is that they made peace without consulting you, my lord."

Tadatsugu could see the repressed emotion on Ieyasu's face, and, unexpectedly, it made Tadatsugu's own lips twitch. He could hardly hold his feelings back. He wanted to shout that Nobuo was a great fool. Perhaps that is what Ieyasu was holding down in his heart. Should he be angry? Should he laugh? No doubt he was repressing all those things inside of himself at once, almost as though he could not accept the violent emotions raging inside him.

Ieyasu appeared to be dazed. He was dumbfounded. That was all his expression said.

The two men sat in that way for some time. Finally, Ieyasu blinked two or three times. Then he pinched his large earlobe with his left hand and rubbed the side of his face. He was puzzled. His round back began to move a little from side to side. His left hand dropped back to his knee.

"Tadatsugu, are you sure?" he asked.

"I wouldn't come to report such a thing lightly. But dispatches will arrive later with more detailed information."

"You still haven't heard anything from Lord Nobuo?"

"We heard the report that he had left Nagashima, passed through Kuwana, and stopped at Yadagawara, but I thought he was just looking over the defenses and the disposition of his troops. Even when he returned to his castle, we had no idea of what his intentions had been."

Subsequent reports confirmed the rumors of Nobuo's separate peace agreement, but no word came from Nobuo himself throughout the entire day. The truth was soon known generally among the Tokugawa clan's retainers. Each time they met, their excited voices rose as they confirmed together what they could hardly believe. Gathering at Kiyosu, they accused Nobuo of lacking integrity and wondered aloud how the Tokugawa could face the nation with dignity after the predicament in which they had been placed.

"If this is the truth, we're not going to let him be, even if he is Lord Nobuo," the hot-blooded Honda said.

"First we should take Lord Nobuo out of Nagashima and investigate this crime," Ii added with a furious glare. "After that we should fight a decisive battle with Hideyoshi."

"I agree!"

"Isn't it because of Lord Nobuo that we mobilized in the first place?"

"We advocated the upholding of duty and rose up only because Lord Nobuo came begging for Lord Ieyasu's help and crying that Lord Nobunaga's descendants would perish because of Hideyoshi's ambitions! Now the banner of that war of duty—the embodiment of justice—has tumbled over to the enemy's side. The stupidity of that man is beyond words!"

"As the situation is now, it's an affront to His Lordship's dignity, and we've become a laughingstock. It's also an insult to the spirits of our comrades who died at Mount Komaki and Nagakute."

"They were made to die tragically meaningless deaths, and there's no reason why the living should have to bear such painful thoughts. What kind of decision can our lord have made by now?"

"He stayed in his living quarters all morning. He called a meeting of the senior retainers, and it seems that they've been deliberating all day."

"How about someone here delivering our opinion to the senior retainers?"

"That's right. Who would be good?"

They all looked around at one another.

"What about you, Ii? And Honda, you should go too." Honda and Ii were just about to leave the room as representatives for the others when a messenger came in with specific information.

"Two envoys from Lord Nobuo have just arrived."

"What! Envoys from Nagashima?"

The news made the men's indignation boil up again.

As the envoys had already been taken into the large audience chamber, however, it was very likely that they were already face to face with Ieyasu. Calmly reassuring each other that their lord's intentions would now be made clear, the men decided to wait for the result of the meeting.

Nobuo's envoys were his uncle, Oda Nobuteru, and Ikoma Hachiemon. As might be imagined, it was extremely awkward for those men to face Ieyasu, let alone try to explain Nobuo's thoughts, and they waited in the room, withering at the mere thought of the meeting.

Soon enough, Ieyasu appeared with a page. He was dressed in a kimono, without armor, and seemed to be in a good mood.

He sat down on a cushion and said, "I've heard that Lord Nobuo has made peace with Hideyoshi."

The two messengers responded in the affirmative as they prostrated themselves, unable even to raise their heads.

Nobuteru said, "The sudden peace talks with Lord Hideyoshi were surely both unexpected and mortifying to your clan, and we can only respectfully appreciate what your thoughts must be, but in fact, His Lordship put much deep thought into the situation before him, and—"

"I understand," Ieyasu replied. "You don't need to give me some long explanation."

"The details are fully explained in this letter, so, ah, if you would read it—"

"I'll take a look at it later on."

"The only thing that pains His Lordship is the thought that you may be angry," Hachiemon said.

"Now, now. That's not worth his consideration. From the very beginning, these hostilities had nothing to do with my own desires or plans."

"We understand completely."

"That being so, the hope I entertain for Lord Nobuo's well-being is unchanged."

"His Lordship will be relieved to hear it."

"I've had a meal prepared for you in another room. That this war has been terminated so quickly is the greatest blessing of all. Have a leisurely lunch before you go."

Ieyasu went back into the interior of the castle. The messengers from Nagashima were entertained with food and drink in another room, but they ate hurriedly and soon left.

When Ieyasu's retainers heard about this, they were outraged.

"His Lordship must have some deeper thoughts. Otherwise, how could he so easily approve of this monstrous alliance of Lord Nobuo and Hideyoshi?"

During this time, Ii and Honda went off to the senior retainers to inform them of the young retainers' opinion.

"Secretary!" Ieyasu called out.

After meeting with Nobuo's envoys in the audience chamber he had returned to his own quarters and sat quietly alone for a while. Now his voice rang out.

The secretary brought out an inkstone and waited for his lord's dictation.

"I want to sent congratulatory letters to both Lord Nobuo and Lord Hideyoshi."

As he dictated the letters, Ieyasu looked off obliquely and closed his eyes. Indeed, as he polished the sentences to be written down, he seemed first to absorb thoughts in his breast that must have been like draughts of molten iron.

When the two letters were finished, Ieyasu gave an order to a page to summon Ishikawa Kazumasa.

The secretary left the two letters in front of Ieyasu, bowed, and withdrew. As he left, a personal attendant came in carrying a candle and quietly lit two lamps.

At some point the sun had set. Looking at the lamps, Ieyasu felt that somehow the day had been a short one. He wondered if that was why—even with all the pressure of work—he was still feeling an emptiness in his heart.

As though from far away, he could hear the sound of the sliding door opening softly.

Kazumasa, dressed in civilian clothes like his lord, was bowing in the doorway. Almost none of the warriors of the clan had yet untied their armor. Nevertheless, Kazumasa realized that Ieyasu had been dressed in plain clothes since the morning and had quickly changed into a kimono.

"Ah, Kazumasa? You're too far away over there. Come a little closer."

The man who had not changed at all here was Ieyasu. As Kazumasa came before him, however, he seemed almost to have been disarmed.

"Kazumasa, I'd like you to be my envoy tomorrow morning to Lord Hideyoshi's camp and Lord Nobuo's headquarters at Kuwana."

"Certainly."

"Letters of congratulation are right here."

"Congratulations for the peace accords?"

"That's right."

"I think I understand what's in your mind, my lord. You won't be showing your dissatisfaction, but when he sees such magnanimity, even Lord Nobuo will probably be embarrassed."

"What are you saying, Kazumasa? It would be cowardly of me to embarrass Lord Nobuo, and a declaration to continue fighting from a sense of duty would look a little strange. Whether it's a false peace or whatever it is, I have no reason to voice dissatisfaction about peace. You are to explain earnestly and even happily that I think it is splendid from the bottom of my heart, and that I rejoice together with all the subjects of the Empire."

Kazumasa was someone who knew his lord's heart well, and now Ieyasu had given him careful instructions concerning his mission. But for Kazumasa, there was yet one more pain he had to bear. That was the misunderstanding the other retainers had had about him from the very beginning—that he and Hideyoshi had some intimate connection. The year before, after Hideyoshi's victory at Yanagase, Kazumasa had been selected as Ieyasu's envoy to Hideyoshi.

At that time Hideyoshi's joy had been extraordinary. He had invited the various lords to a tea ceremony at Osaka Castle, which was still under construction.

After that, whenever there was occasion for some communication with the Tokugawa clan, Hideyoshi would inevitably ask for news of Kazumasa, and would always talk about Kazumasa to the lords who had friendly relations with the Tokugawa clan.

That Kazumasa was quite popular with Lord Hideyoshi was deeply carved into the minds of the Tokugawa warriors. During the standoff at Mount Komaki, and again during Niwa's attempt at reconciliation, the eyes of his allies would be scrutinizing Kazumasa's actions, regardless of the situation.

As might be expected, Ieyasu was not affected by that at all.

"Well, it's pretty noisy out there, isn't it?"

Animated voices were coming from the hall, which was a number of rooms away from where Ieyasu and Kazumasa were sitting. It seemed that the retainers who were dissatisfied with the peace accords were expressing their doubts and indignation at Kazumasa's being called before their lord.

Ii and Honda, who were acting as representatives, and some of the others had surrounded Tadatsugu a while before.

"Didn't you lead the vanguard and stay in the castle town of Kuwana? Aren't you abashed at not having known that Lord Nobuo and Hideyoshi were able to meet at Yadagawara? And what about the fact that Hideyoshi's messengers came right into Kuwana Castle? What's happened now that you've found out about their illicit peace treaty and have come running here?"

They grilled Tadatsugu. First of all, it was Hideyoshi, a man who was little likely to make a plan that would leak out ahead of time. For Tadatsugu, that was justification enough. In the face of the concentrated dissatisfaction, however, he could only receive their indignation and abuse with resignation and apologize to them with the forbearance becoming an old general.

But it was the purpose of neither Ii nor Honda to persecute the old man. Rather, they wanted to deliver their own opinions to their lord and to repudiate the peace accords. And they wanted to tell the world that the Tokugawa clan had nothing to do with Nobuo's peace talks.

"Would you please intercede for us? You're a respected elder."

"No, that would be a serious breach of etiquette," Tadatsugu answered.

But Honda insisted. "These men have not loosened their armor and are dressed for the battlefield. Everyday etiquette does not apply in this situation."

"There's no time for that," Ii said. "We're burning up with the fear that something may happen before he talks to us. If you won't be our intermediary, then it can't be helped. We'll have to appeal directly through his personal attendants and meet him in his quarters."

"No! He's in the middle of a conversation with Lord Kazumasa right now. You must not intrude on him."

"What! Kazumasa?"

The fact that Kazumasa was alone with their lord at this time only added to their uneasiness and discomfort. From the beginning of the campaign at Mount Komaki, they had viewed Kazumasa as a man playing a double game. And when Niwa Nagahide initiated a reconciliation, it was Kazumasa who had been involved in the negotiations. They suspected that Kazumasa was somehow in the shadows of the most recent maneuvers, too.

When those feelings suddenly broke into a noisy commotion, it reached Ieyasu's ears, even though he was some distance away. A page now hurried down the corridor toward the retainers.

"You're being summoned!" the page announced.

Taken by surprise, they looked around at each other in awe. But the expression on the faces of the obstinate Honda and Ii revealed that a summons was just what they wanted. Urging on Sakai Tadatsugu and the others, they filed into the audience chamber.

Ieyasu's room was soon filled to overflowing with samurai in full armor.

Everyone's attention was focused on Ieyasu. Next to him sat Kazumasa. Sakai Tadatsugu was next, and behind them the very backbone of the Tokugawa clan was represented.

Ieyasu started to speak but, suddenly turning toward the lowest seats, he said, "The men in the lowest seats are a little too far away. My voice isn't very loud, so come up a little closer."

The men all packed in more closely together, and those in the lowest seats all gathered around Ieyasu as he began to speak.

"Yesterday Lord Nobuo made peace with Hideyoshi. I am thinking of sending out an official notice of this to the entire clan tomorrow morning, but apparently you've all heard the news and it's worried you considerably. Please forgive me. I was not trying to keep the facts from you."

All of them hung their heads.

"It was my mistake to mobilize in response to Lord Nobuo's plea. It was also my fault that so many good retainers were killed in the battles at Mount Komaki and Nagakute. Once again, the fact that Lord Nobuo secretly joined hands with Hideyoshi and rendered your righteous indignation and loyal anger meaningless is by no means his fault. Rather, it is due to my own oversights and lack of wisdom. You have all been completely and unselfishly sincere, and as your lord, I cannot find the words to apologize properly. Please forgive me."

At some point, everyone there had lowered his head. No one looked at Ieyasu's face. Shivers of unmanly weeping undulated from shoulder to shoulder like waves.

"There's nothing we can do, so please endure this. Strengthen your resolve and wait for another day."

After they had sat down, neither Ii nor Honda had said a word. Indeed, both men had taken out handkerchiefs and, looking aside, wiped their faces.

"This is a blessing. The war is over, and tomorrow I'll return to Okazaki. All of you should soon be on the road home, too, to see the faces of your wives and children," Ieyasu said, as he too blew his nose.

On the following day, the thirteenth of the month, Ieyasu and the greater part of the Tokugawa army withdrew from Kiyosu Castle and returned to Okazaki in Mikawa. On the morning of the same day, Ishikawa Kazumasa went to Kuwana with Sakai Tadatsugu. After meeting with Nobuo, he went on to visit Hideyoshi at Nawabu. Relaying Ieyasu's formal greetings, he presented the letter of congratulations and left. After Kazumasa had gone, Hideyoshi looked at the men around him.

"Look at that," he said. "That's just like Ieyasu. No one else would have been able to swallow this painful blow as though it were simply hot tea."

As the man who had made Ieyasu drink molten iron, Hideyoshi appreciated his feelings very well. Putting himself in Ieyasu's place, he asked himself if he would have been able to react in the same way.

As these days passed, one man who felt quite happy with himself was Nobuo. After the meeting at Yadagawara, he became Hideyoshi's perfect puppet. Regardless of the situation, he would ask himself, "I wonder what Hideyoshi would think about this."

Just as he had formerly relied on Ieyasu, he now worried about how Hideyoshi would react to whatever he did.

He therefore was inclined to go along with exactly what Hideyoshi had desired in fulfilling the conditions laid down in the peace treaty. Portions of his lands, the hostages, and the written pledges were all presented without exception.

At that point Hideyoshi relaxed a little. Nevertheless, thinking that the army should remain at Nawabu until the following year, he sent a messenger to the men in charge at Osaka and made preparations to spend the winter in the field.

It goes without saying that from the very beginning Hideyoshi's object of concern had been Ieyasu, not Nobuo. Since he had not yet concluded matters with Ieyasu, he could not say that the situation was under control, and his aims were only half-fulfilled. One day Hideyoshi visited Kuwana Castle, and after talking with Nobuo about various subjects, he asked, "How have you been feeling recently?"

"I'm in great health! And I'm sure it's because I have no unpleasant thoughts. I've recovered from the exhaustion of the battlefield, and my mind is completely at ease."

Nobuo displayed a bright and cheerful laughter, and Hideyoshi nodded a number of times, as though he were holding a child on his knee.

"Yes, yes. I imagine that that meaningless war wore you out, my lord. But you know, there a still are few remaining difficulties."

"What do you mean, Hideyoshi?"

"If Lord Ieyasu is left just as he is, he may cause you some trouble."

"Really? But he sent a retainer here with a message of congratulations."

"Well, he certainly wouldn't have wanted to go against your will."

"To be sure."

"So you'll have to say something first. In his heart, Lord Tokugawa would clearly like to make peace with me, but if he gave in on his own, he would lose face. Since there's no reason to confront me, he's probably perplexed. Why don't you help him out?"

There are many men among the sons of famous families who are extremely selfish, quite probably because of the illusion that everyone around them exits for their sake. Never would they think about serving someone else. But, being spoken to in that way by Hideyoshi, even Nobuo was able to conceive of something greater than his own interest.

So, several days later, he suggested that he himself act as a mediator between Hideyoshi and Ieyasu. That was his natural responsibility, but he hadn't thought of taking it on until Hideyoshi had suggested it.

"If he'll agree to our conditions, we'll forgive his armed action in deference to your handling the situation."

Hideyoshi was taking the position of a victor but wanted to convey the terms for peace through Nobuo's mouth.

The conditions were that Ieyasu's son, Ogimaru, was to be adopted by Hideyoshi, and that Kazumasa's son, Katsuchiyo, and Honda's son, Senchiyo, were to be delivered as hostages.

Other than the destruction of the fortifications, the division of lands formerly agreed upon by Nobuo, and the confirmation of the status-quo by the Tokugawa clan, Hideyoshi did not seek any further changes.

"There is some resentment in my heart concerning Lord Ieyasu that will not easily be cleared away, but I can endure it for the sake of your honor. And since you've decided to take on this task, it would be distressing to delay it too long. Why don't you send a messenger to Okazaki right away?"

Thus instructed, Nobuo sent two of his senior retainers as representatives to Okazaki that very day.

The conditions could not really be called severe, but when he heard them, even Ieyasu had to call on his reserves patience.

Even though Ogimaru was said to be adopted, he was truly a hostage. And sending the sons of senior retainers to Osaka was clearly a pledge of the defeated. Though his retainers were upset, Ieyasu remained calm so that Okazaki would remain calm as well.

"I agree to the conditions, and I'll ask you to take care of the matter," he replied to the envoys.

Back and forth they went, a number of times. Then, on the twenty-first day of the Eleventh Month, Tomita Tomonobu and Tsuda Nobukatsu came to Okazaki to sign a peace treaty.

On the twelfth day of the Twelfth Month, Ieyasu's son was sent to Osaka. Kazumasa's and Honda's sons went with him. The warriors who saw off the hostages lined up along the streets and wept. Their action at Mount Komaki—an action that had temporarily shaken the entire nation—had ended in this.

Nobuo came to Okazaki on the fourteenth, toward the year's end, and stayed until the twenty-fifth. Ieyasu did not say one unpleasant word. For ten days he entertained that good-natured man whose future was so obvious, and then sent him home again.

The eleventh year of Tensho came to a close. People had an inordinate number of feelings about the passing year. Among the things they felt keenly was the certainty that the world had changed. It had been only a year and a half since Nobunaga's death in the tenth year of Tensho. Everyone was surprised that such sweeping changes had come so quickly.

The exalted position, the popularity, and the mission that had formerly been Nobunaga's had quickly become Hideyoshi's. Indeed, the liberality of Hideyoshi's character was in accord with the times, and helped create subtle revolutions and advances in society and government.

Watching the trends of the day, even Ieyasu could not help scolding himself for the stupidity of rowing against them. Of the men who had gone against the tide of fortune, not one had escaped with his life since time immemorial, as he knew very well. At the foundation of his thinking was the cardinal rule that the observer should distinguish between the smallness of man and the vastness of time, and not resist the man who had grasped the moment. Thus he deferred at each step to Hideyoshi.

At any rate, the man who saw in the New Year while he was at the very height of prosperity was Hideyoshi. He was now in his forty-ninth year. At the age of fifty, in one more year, he would be in the prime of manhood.

The New Year's guests numbered many times more than they had the year before, and, dressed in their finery, they filled Osaka Castle, bringing with them the feeling of the springtime that was close at hand.

Ieyasu, of course, did not come, and a small number of provincial lords who paid deference to Ieyasu followed suit. Moreover, there were certain forces that even now decried Hideyoshi and rushed around making military preparations and gathering secret intelligence. Those men also refrained from tying up their horses at the gate of Osaka Castle.

Hideyoshi observed all that as he continued to greet guest after guest.

As the year entered the Second Month, Nobuo visited from Ise. If he had come at New Year's with all the other provincial lords, it would have been as though he were making a New Year's call on Hideyoshi, and that would have been beneath his dignity. Or so he reasoned.

There was nothing easier than satisfying Nobuo's conceit. Using the same courtesy he had shown when he knelt in front of Nobuo at Yadagawara, Hideyoshi demonstrated a perfect sincerity in his hearty welcome. What Hideyoshi had said at Yadagawara was not a lie, Nobuo thought. When rumors surfaced about Ieyasu, Nobuo criticized the man's calculating nature because he thought it would please Hideyoshi. But Hideyoshi simply nodded silently.

On the second day of the Third Month, Nobuo returned to Ise in great joy. During his stay in Osaka, he had been told that he had been invested with a court title, thanks to Hideyoshi's good offices. Nobuo had remained in Kyoto for about five days, receiving the congratulations of many callers. It seemed to him that the sun would hardly rise if it were not for Hideyoshi.

The traffic of provincial lords to and from Osaka during the New Year, and the activities of Nobuo in particular, were reported in detail to Hamamatsu. Ieyasu, however, could now do nothing more than observe Hideyoshi's appeasement of Nobuo from the sidelines.

Epilogue

Between the spring and fall of that year Hideyoshi sent ships to the south and horses to the north in his campaigns to subdue the country. He returned to Osaka Castle in the Ninth Month and began overseeing the internal administration and foreign affairs of the Empire.

From time to time he would look back on the mountains he had climbed to get thus far, and at such moments he could not help congratulating himself on the first half of his life. In the coming year he would be fifty years old, the season in which a man reflects on his past and is made to think about his next step.

Then, because he was human and indeed was subject to carnal passions more than the common run of men, it was natural that at night he would reflect on those passions that had governed his life in the past and continued to do so in the present, and would wonder where they might lead in the future.

It is the autumn of my life. Not many more months remain of my forty-ninth year.

As he compared his life to climbing mountains, he felt as if he were looking down toward the foothills after having climbed almost to the summit.

The summit is believed to be the object of the climb. But its true object—the joy of living—is not in the peak itself, but in the adversities encountered on the way up. There are valleys, cliffs, streams, precipices, and slides, and as he walks these steep paths, the climber may think he cannot go any farther, or even that dying would be better than going on. But then he resumes fighting the difficulties directly in front of him, and when he is finally able to turn and look back at what he has overcome, he finds he has truly experienced the joy of living while on life's very road.

How boring would be a life lacking the confusions of many digressions or the difficult struggles! How soon would a man grow tired of living if he only walked peacefully along a level path. In the end, a man's life lies in a continuous series of hardships and struggles, and the pleasure of living is not in the short spaces of rest. Thus Hideyoshi, who was born in adversity, grew to manhood as he played in its midst.

In the Tenth Month of the fourteenth year of Tensho, Hideyoshi and Ieyasu met in Osaka Castle for a historic peace conference. Undefeated in the field, Ieyasu nevertheless ceded the political victory to Hideyoshi. Two years before, Ieyasu had sent his son as a hostage to Osaka, and now he took Hideyoshi's sister as his bride. The patient Ieyasu would wait for his chance—perhaps the bird would yet sing for him.

After a great banquet to celebrate making peace with his strongest rival, Hideyoshi retired to the inner apartments of the castle, where he and his most trusted retainers hailed his victory over many cups of *sake*. Hours later, Hideyoshi rose shakily to his feet and bid the company good night. Slowly he stumbled down the hall, a short, monkeyfaced man surrounded by his ladies-in-waiting, almost hidden by the colorful, rustling silks of their many-layered kimonos. The laughter of the women could be heard all along the gilded corridors as the tiny figure of Japan's supreme ruler was led to his bed.

In the dozen years left to him, Hideyoshi solidified his grip on the nation, breaking the power of the samurai clans forever. His patronage of the arts created an opulence and beauty still celebrated as Japan's Renaissance. Titles were heaped upon him by the Emperor: Kampaku. Taiko. But Hideyoshi's dreams did not end at the water's edge; his ambitions reached beyond, to the lands he had dreamed of as a child—the realm of the Ming emperors. But there the armies of the Taiko would fail to conquer. The man who never doubted that he could turn every setback to his own purpose, that he could persuade his enemies to be his friends, that he could even make the silent bird wish to sing a song of his own choosing—in the end he had to yield to a greater force, and a more patient man. But he left a legacy whose brilliance yet remains as the memory of a Golden Age.